THE
HUNT
FOR
RED
OCTOBER

THE
HUNT
FOR
RED
OCTOBER

TOM CLANCY

BERKLEY BOOKS, NEW YORK

This Berkley book contains the complete
text of the original hardcover edition.
It has been completely reset in a typeface
designed for easy reading, and was printed
from new film.

THE HUNT FOR RED OCTOBER

A Berkley Book/published by arrangement with
Naval Institute Press

PRINTING HISTORY
Naval Institute Press edition published 1984
Berkley edition/October 1985

ISBN: 0-425-08383-7

A BERKLEY BOOK ® TM 757,375
Berkley Books are published by The Berkley Publishing Group,
200 Madison Avenue, New York, New York 10016.
The name "BERKLEY" and the stylized "B" with design are
trademarks belonging to Berkley Publishing Corporation.
PRINTED IN THE UNITED STATES OF AMERICA

Acknowledgments

For technical information and advice I am especially indebted to Michael Shelton, former naval aviator; Larry Bond, whose naval wargame, "Harpoon," was adopted for the training of NROTC cadets; Drs. Gerry Sterner and Craig Jeschke; and Lieutenant Commander Gregory Young, USN.

For Ralph Chatham,
a sub driver who spoke the truth,
and for all the men who wear dolphins

THE FIRST DAY

FRIDAY, 3 DECEMBER

The Red October

Captain First Rank Marko Ramius of the Soviet Navy was dressed for the Arctic conditions normal to the Northern Fleet submarine base at Polyarnyy. Five layers of wool and oilskin enclosed him. A dirty harbor tug pushed his submarine's bow around to the north, facing down the channel. The dock that had held his *Red October* for two interminable months was now a water-filled concrete box, one of the many specially built to shelter strategic missile submarines from the harsh elements. On its edge a collection of sailors and dockyard workers watched his ship sail in stolid Russian fashion, without a wave or a cheer.

"Engines ahead slow, Kamarov," he ordered. The tug slid out of the way, and Ramius glanced aft to see the water stirring from the force of the twin bronze propellers. The tug's commander waved. Ramius returned the gesture. The tug had done a simple job, but done it quickly and well. The *Red October,* a *Typhoon*-class sub, moved under her own power towards the main ship channel of the Kola Fjord.

"There's *Purga,* Captain." Gregoriy Kamarov pointed to the icebreaker that would escort them to sea. Ramius nodded. The two hours required to transit the channel would tax not his seamanship but his endurance. There was a cold north wind blowing, the only sort of north wind in this part of the world. Late autumn had been surprisingly mild, and scarcely any snow had fallen in an area that measures it in meters; then a week before a major winter storm had savaged the Murmansk coast, breaking pieces off the Arctic icepack. The icebreaker was no formality. The *Purga* would butt aside any ice that might have drifted overnight into the channel. It would not do at all for the Soviet Navy's newest missile submarine to be damaged by an errant chunk of frozen water.

The water in the fjord was choppy, driven by the brisk wind. It began to lap over the *October*'s spherical bow, rolling back down the flat missile deck which lay before the towering black sail. The water was coated with the bilge oil of numberless ships, filth that would not evaporate in the low temperatures and that left a black ring on the rocky walls of the fjord as though from the bath of a slovenly giant. An altogether apt simile, Ramius thought. The Soviet giant cared little for the dirt it left on the face of the earth, he grumbled to himself. He had learned his seamanship as a boy on inshore fishing boats, and knew what it was to be in harmony with nature.

"Increase speed to one-third," he said. Kamarov repeated his captain's order over the bridge telephone. The water stirred more as the *October* moved astern of the *Purga.* Captain Lieutenant Kamarov was the ship's navigator, his last duty station having been harbor pilot for the large combatant vessels based on both sides of the wide inlet. The two officers kept a weather eye on the armed icebreaker three hundred meters ahead. The *Purga*'s after deck had a handful of crewmen stomping about in the cold, one wearing the white apron of a ship's cook. They wanted to witness the *Red October*'s first operational cruise, and besides, sailors will do almost anything to break the monotony of their duties.

Ordinarily it would have irritated Ramius to have his ship escorted out—the channel here was wide and deep—but not today. The ice was something to worry about. And so, for Ramius, was a great deal else.

"So, my Captain, again we go to sea to serve and protect the *Rodina!*" Captain Second Rank Ivan Yurievich Putin poked his head through the hatch—without permission, as usual—and clambered up the ladder with the awkwardness of a landsman. The tiny control station was already crowded enough with the captain, the navigator, and a mute lookout. Putin was the ship's *zampolit* (political officer). Everything he did was to serve the *Rodina* (Motherland), a word that had mystical connotations to a Russian and, along with V. I. Lenin, was the Communist party's substitute for a godhead.

"Indeed, Ivan," Ramius replied with more good cheer than he felt. "Two weeks at sea. It is good to leave the dock. A seaman belongs at sea, not tied alongside, overrun with bureaucrats and workmen with dirty boots. And we will be warm."

"You find this cold?" Putin asked incredulously.

For the hundredth time Ramius told himself that Putin was the perfect political officer. His voice was always too loud, his humor too affected. He never allowed a person to forget what he was. The perfect political officer, Putin was an easy man to fear.

"I have been in submarines too long, my friend. I grow accustomed to moderate temperatures and a stable deck under my feet." Putin did not notice the veiled insult. He'd been assigned to submarines after his first tour on destroyers had been cut short by chronic seasickness—and perhaps because he did not resent the close confinement aboard submarines, something that many men cannot tolerate.

"Ah, Marko Aleksandrovich, in Gorkiy on a day like this, flowers bloom!"

"And what sort of flowers might those be, Comrade Political Officer?" Ramius surveyed the fjord through his binoculars. At noon the sun was barely over the southeast horizon, casting orange light and purple shadows along the rocky walls.

"Why, snow flowers, of course," Putin said, laughing loudly. "On a day like this the faces of the children and the women glow pink, your breath trails behind you like a cloud, and the vodka tastes especially fine. Ah, to be in Gorkiy on a day like this!"

The bastard ought to work for Intourist, Ramius told himself, except that Gorkiy is a city closed to foreigners. He had been there twice. It had struck him as a typical Soviet city, full of ramshackle buildings, dirty streets, and ill-clad citizens. As it was in most Russian cities, winter was Gorkiy's best season. The snow hid all the dirt. Ramius, half Lithuanian, had childhood memories of a better place, a coastal village whose Hanseatic origin had left rows of presentable buildings.

It was unusual for anyone other than a Great Russian to be aboard—much less command—a Soviet naval vessel. Marko's father, Aleksandr Ramius, had been a hero of the Party, a dedicated, believing Communist who had served Stalin faithfully and well. When the Soviets first occupied Lithuania in 1940, the elder Ramius was instrumental in rounding up political dissidents, shop owners, priests, and anyone else who might have been troublesome to the new regime. All were shipped off to fates that now even Moscow could only guess at. When the Germans invaded a year later, Aleksandr fought heroically as a political commissar, and was later to distinguish himself in the Battle of Leningrad. In 1944 he returned to his native land with the spearhead of the Eleventh Guards Army to wreak bloody vengeance on those who had collaborated with the Germans or been suspected of such. Marko's father had been a true Soviet hero—and Marko was deeply ashamed to be his son. His mother's health had been broken during the endless siege of Leningrad. She died giving birth to him, and he was raised by his paternal grandmother in Lithuania while his father strutted through the Party Central Committee in Vilnius, awaiting his promotion to Moscow. He got that, too, and was a candidate member of the Politburo when his life was cut short by a heart attack.

Marko's shame was not total. His father's prominence had made his current goal a possibility, and Marko planned to wreak his own vengeance on the Soviet Union, enough, perhaps, to satisfy the thousands of his countrymen who had died before he was even born.

"Where we are going, Ivan Yurievich, it will be colder still."

Putin clapped his captain's shoulder. Was his affection feigned or real? Marko wondered. Probably real. Ramius was an honest man, and he recognized that this short, loud oaf did have some human feelings.

"Why is it, Comrade Captain, that you always seem glad to leave the *Rodina* and go to sea?"

Ramius smiled behind his binoculars. "A seaman has one country, Ivan Yurievich, but two wives. You never understand that. Now I go to my other wife, the cold, heartless one that owns my soul." Ramius paused. The smile vanished. "My only wife, now."

Putin was quiet for once, Marko noted. The political officer had been there, had cried real tears as the coffin of polished pine rolled into the cremation chamber. For Putin the death of Natalia Bogdanova Ramius had been a cause of grief, but beyond that the act of an uncaring God whose existence he regularly denied. For Ramius it had been a crime committed not by God but the State. An unnecessary, monstrous crime, one that demanded punishment.

"Ice." The lookout pointed.

"Loose-pack ice, starboard side of the channel, or perhaps something calved off the east-side glacier. We'll pass well clear," Kamarov said.

"Captain!" The bridge speaker had a metallic voice. "Message from fleet headquarters."

"Read it."

"'Exercise area clear. No enemy vessels in vicinity. Proceed as per orders. Signed, Korov, Fleet Commander.'"

"Acknowledged," Ramius said. The speaker clicked off. "So, no *Amerikantsi* about?"

"You doubt the fleet commander?" Putin inquired.

"I hope he is correct," Ramius replied, more sincerely than his political officer would appreciate. "But you remember our briefings."

Putin shifted on his feet. Perhaps he was feeling the cold.

"Those American 688-class submarines, Ivan, the *Los Angeles*es. Remember what one of their officers told our spy? That they could sneak up on a whale and bugger it before it knew they were there? I wonder how the KGB got that bit of information. A beautiful Soviet agent, trained in the ways of the decadent West, too skinny, the way the imperialists like their women, blond hair . . ." The captain grunted amusement. "Probably the American officer was a boastful boy, trying to find a way to do something similar to our agent, no? And feeling his liquor, like most sailors. Still. The American *Los*

Angeles class, and the new British *Trafalgar*s, those we must guard against. They are a threat to us."

"The Americans are good technicians, Comrade Captain," Putin said, "but they are not giants. Their technology is not so awesome. *Nasha lutcha,*" he concluded. Ours is better.

Ramius nodded thoughtfully, thinking to himself that *zampoliti* really ought to know something about the ships they supervised, as mandated by Party doctrine.

"Ivan, didn't the farmers around Gorkiy tell you it is the wolf you do not see that you must fear? But don't be overly concerned. With this ship we will teach them a lesson, I think."

"As I told the Main Political Administration," Putin clapped Ramius' shoulder again, *"Red October* is in the best of hands!"

Ramius and Kamarov both smiled at that. You son of a bitch! the captain thought, saying in front of my men that *you* must pass on my fitness to command! A man who could not command a rubber raft on a calm day! A pity you will not live to eat those words, Comrade Political Officer, and spend the rest of your life in the gulag for that misjudgment. It would almost be worth leaving you alive.

A few minutes later the chop began to pick up, making the submarine roll. The movement was accentuated by their height above the deck, and Putin made excuses to go below. Still a weak-legged sailor. Ramius shared the observation silently with Kamarov, who smiled agreement. Their unspoken contempt for the *zampolit* was a most un-Soviet thought.

The next hour passed quickly. The water grew rougher as they approached the open sea, and their icebreaker escort began to wallow on the swells. Ramius watched her with interest. He had never been on an icebreaker, his entire career having been in submarines. They were more comfortable, but also more dangerous. He was accustomed to the danger, though, and the years of experience would stand him in good stead now.

"Sea buoy in sight, Captain." Kamarov pointed. The red lighted buoy was riding actively on the waves.

"Control room, what is the sounding?" Ramius asked over the bridge telephone.

"One hundred meters below the keel, Comrade Captain."

"Increase speed to two-thirds, come left ten degrees." Ramius looked at Kamarov. "Signal our course change to *Purga,* and hope he doesn't turn the wrong way."

Kamarov reached for the small blinker light stowed under the bridge coaming. The *Red October* began to accelerate slowly, her 30,000-ton bulk resisting the power of her engines. Presently the bow wave grew to a three-meter standing arc of water; man-made combers rolled down the missile deck, splitting against the front of the sail. The *Purga* altered course to starboard, allowing the submarine to pass well clear.

Ramius looked aft at the bluffs of the Kola Fjord. They had been carved to this shape millennia before by the remorseless pressure of towering glaciers. How many times in his twenty years of service with the Red Banner Northern Fleet had he looked at the wide, flat U-shape? This would be the last. One way or another, he'd never go back. Which way would it turn out? Ramius admitted to himself that he didn't much care. Perhaps the stories his grandmother had taught him were true, about God and the reward for a good life. He hoped so—it would be good if Natalia were not truly dead. In any case, there was no turning back. He had left a letter in the last mailbag taken off before sailing. There was no going back after that.

"Kamarov, signal to *Purga:* 'Diving at—,'" he checked his watch, "'—1320 hours. Exercise OCTOBER FROST begins as scheduled. You are released to other assigned duties. We will return as scheduled.'"

Kamarov worked the trigger on the blinker light to transmit the message. The *Purga* responded at once, and Ramius read the flashing signal unaided: "IF THE WHALES DON'T EAT YOU. GOOD LUCK TO *RED OCTOBER!*"

Ramius lifted the phone again, pushing the button for the sub's radio room. He had the same message transmitted to fleet headquarters, Severomorsk. Next he addressed the control room.

"Depth under the keel?"

"One hundred forty meters, Comrade Captain."

"Prepare to dive." He turned to the lookout and ordered him below. The boy moved towards the hatch. He was probably glad to return to the warmth below, but took the time for one last look at the cloudy sky and receding cliffs. Going to sea on a submarine was always exciting, and always a little sad.

"Clear the bridge. Take the conn when you get below, Gregoriy." Kamarov nodded and dropped down the hatch, leaving the captain alone.

Ramius made one last careful scan of the horizon. The sun

was barely visible aft, the sky leaden, the sea black except for the splash of whitecaps. He wondered if he were saying good-bye to the world. If so, he would have preferred a more cheerful view of it.

Before sliding down he inspected the hatch seat, pulling it shut with a chain and making sure the automatic mechanism functioned properly. Next he dropped eight meters down the inside of the sail to the pressure hull, then two more into the control room. A *michman* (warrant officer) shut the second hatch and with a powerful spin turned the locking wheel as far as it would go.

"Gregoriy?" Ramius asked.

"Straight board shut," the navigator said crisply, pointing to the diving board. All hull-opening indicator lights showed green, safe. "All systems aligned and checked for dive. The compensation is entered. We are rigged for dive."

The captain made his own visual inspection of mechanical, electrical, and hydraulic indicators. He nodded, and the *michman* of the watch unlocked the vent controls.

"Dive," Ramius ordered, moving to the periscope to relieve Vasily Borodin, his *starpom* (executive officer). Kamarov pulled the diving alarm, and the hull reverberated with the racket of a loud buzzer.

"Flood the main ballast tanks. Rig out the diving planes. Ten degrees down-angle on the planes," Kamarov ordered, his eyes alert to see that every crewman did his job exactly. Ramius listened carefully but did not look. Kamarov was the best young seaman he had ever commanded, and had long since earned his captain's trust.

The *Red October*'s hull was filled with the noise of rushing air as vents at the top of the ballast tanks were opened and water entering from the tank floods at the bottom chased the buoying air out. It was a lengthy process, for the submarine had many such tanks, each carefully subdivided by numerous cellular baffles. Ramius adjusted the periscope lens to look down and saw the black water change briefly to foam.

The *Red October* was the largest and finest command Ramius had ever had, but the sub had one major flaw. She had plenty of engine power and a new drive system that he hoped would befuddle American and Soviet submarines alike, but she was so big that she changed depth like a crippled whale. Slow going up, even slower going down.

"Scope under." Ramius stepped away from the instrument after what seemed a long wait. "Down periscope."

"Passing forty meters," Kamarov said.

"Level off at one hundred meters." Ramius watched his crewmen now. The first dive could make experienced men shudder, and half his crew were farmboys straight from training camp. The hull popped and creaked under the pressure of the surrounding water, something that took getting used to. A few of the younger men went pale but stood rigidly upright.

Kamarov began the procedure for leveling off at the proper depth. Ramius watched with a pride he might have felt for his own son as the lieutenant gave the necessary orders with precision. He was the first officer Ramius had recruited. The control room crew snapped to his command. Five minutes later the submarine slowed her descent at ninety meters and settled the next ten to a perfect stop at one hundred.

"Well done, Comrade Lieutenant. You have the conn. Slow to one-third speed. Have the sonarmen listen on all passive systems." Ramius turned to leave the control room, motioning Putin to follow him.

And so it began.

Ramius and Putin went aft to the submarine's wardroom. The captain held the door open for the political officer, then closed and locked it behind himself. The *Red October*'s wardroom was a spacious affair for a submarine, located immediately forward of the galley, aft of the officer accommodations. Its walls were soundproofed, and the door had a lock because her designers had known that not everything the officers had to say was necessarily for the ears of the enlisted men. It was large enough for all of the *October*'s officers to eat as a group— though at least three of them would always be on duty. The safe containing the ship's orders was here, not in the captain's stateroom where a man might use his solitude to try opening it by himself. It had two dials. Ramius had one combination, Putin the other. Which was hardly necessary, since Putin undoubtedly knew their mission orders already. So did Ramius, but not all the particulars.

Putin poured tea as the captain checked his watch against

the chronometer mounted on the bulkhead. Fifteen minutes until he could open the safe. Putin's courtesy made him uneasy.

"Two more weeks of confinement," the *zampolit* said, stirring his tea.

"The Americans do this for two *months,* Ivan. Of course, their submarines are far more comfortable." Despite her huge bulk, the *October*'s crew accommodations would have shamed a gulag jailer. The crew consisted of fifteen officers, housed in fairly decent cabins aft, and a hundred enlisted men whose bunks were stuffed into corners and racks throughout the bow, forward of the missile room. The *October*'s size was deceptive. The interior of her double hull was crammed with missiles, torpedoes, a nuclear reactor and its support equipment, a huge backup diesel power plant, and bank of nickle-cadmium batteries outside the pressure hull, which was ten times the size of its American counterparts. Running and maintaining the ship was a huge job for so small a crew, even though extensive use of automation made her the most modern of Soviet naval vessels. Perhaps the men didn't need proper bunks. They would only have four or six hours a day to make use of them. This would work to Ramius' advantage. Half of his crew were draftees on their first operational cruise, and even the more experienced men knew little enough. The strength of his enlisted crew, unlike that of Western crews, resided much more in his eleven *michmanyy* (warrant officers) than in his *glavnyy starshini* (senior petty officers). All of them were men who would do—were specifically trained to do—exactly what their officers told them. And Ramius had picked the officers.

"You want to cruise for two months?" Putin asked.

"I have done it on diesel submarines. A submarine belongs at sea, Ivan. Our mission is to strike fear into the hearts of the imperialists. We do not accomplish this tied up in our barn at Polyarnyy most of the time, but we cannot stay at sea any longer because any period over two weeks and the crew loses efficiency. In two weeks this collection of children will be a mob of numbed robots." Ramius was counting on that.

"And we could solve this by having capitalist luxuries?" Putin sneered.

"A true Marxist is objective, Comrade Political Officer," Ramius chided, savoring this last argument with Putin. "Objectively, that which aids us in carrying out our mission is good, that which hinders us is bad. Adversity is supposed to hone one's spirit and skill, not dull them. Just being aboard a submarine is hardship enough, is it not?"

"Not for you, Marko." Putin grinned over his tea.

"I am a seaman. Our crewmen are not, most never will be. They are a mob of farmers' sons and boys who yearn to be factory workers. We must adjust to the times, Ivan. These youngsters are not the same as we were."

"That is true enough," Putin agreed. "You are never satisfied, Comrade Captain. I suppose it is men like you who force progress upon us all."

Both men knew exactly why Soviet missile submarines spent so little of their time—barely fifteen percent of it—at sea, and it had nothing to do with creature comforts. The *Red October* carried twenty-six SS-N-20 Seahawk missiles, each with eight 500-kiloton multiple independently targetable reentry vehicles—MIRVs—enough to destroy two hundred cities. Land-based bombers could only fly a few hours at a time, then had to return to their bases. Land-based missiles arrayed along the main East-West Soviet rail network were always where paramilitary troops of the KGB could get at them lest some missile regiment commander suddenly came to realize the power at his fingertips. But missile submarines were by definition beyond any control from land. Their entire mission was to disappear.

Given that fact, Marko was surprised that his government had them at all. The crew of such vessels had to be trusted. And so they sailed less often than their Western counterparts, and when they did it was with a political officer aboard to stand next to the commanding officer, a second captain always ready to pass approval on every action.

"Do you think you could do it, Marko, cruise for two months with these farmboys?"

"I prefer half-trained boys, as you know. They have less to unlearn. Then I can train them to be seamen the right way, my way. My personality cult?"

Putin laughed as he lit a cigarette. "That observation has been made in the past, Marko. But you are our best teacher and your reliability is well known." This was very true. Ramius had sent hundreds of officers and seamen on to other submarines whose commanders were glad to have them. It was another paradox that a man could engender trust within a society that scarcely recognized the concept. Of course, Ramius was a loyal Party member, the son of a Party hero who had been carried to his grave by three Politburo members. Putin waggled his finger. "You should be commanding one of our higher naval schools, Comrade Captain. Your talents would better serve the state there."

"It is a seaman I am, Ivan Yurievich. Only a seaman, not a schoolmaster—despite what they say about me. A wise man knows his limitations." And a bold one seizes opportunities. Every officer aboard had served with Ramius before, except for three junior lieutenants, who would obey their orders as readily as any wet-nosed *matros* (seaman), and the doctor, who was useless.

The chronometer chimed four bells.

Ramius stood and dialed in his three-element combination. Putin did the same, and the captain flipped the lever to open the safe's circular door. Inside was a manila envelope plus four books of cipher keys and missile-targeting coordinates. Ramius removed the envelope, then closed the door, spinning both dials before sitting down again."

"So, Ivan, what do you suppose our orders tell us to do?" Ramius asked theatrically.

"Our duty, Comrade Captain." Putin smiled.

"Indeed." Ramius broke the wax seal on the envelope and extracted the four-page operation order. He read it quickly. It was not complicated.

"So, we are to proceed to grid square 54-90 and rendezvous with our attack submarine *V. K. Konovalov*—that's Captain Tupolev's new command. You know Viktor Tupolev? No? Viktor will guard us from imperialist intruders, and we will conduct a four-day acquisition and tracking drill, with him hunting us— if he can." Ramius chuckled. "The boys in the attack submarine directorate still have not figured how to track our new drive system. Well, neither will the Americans. We are to confine our operations to grid square 54-90 and the immediately surrounding squares. That ought to make Viktor's task a bit easier."

"But you will not let him find us?"

"Certainly not," Ramius snorted. "Let? Viktor was once my pupil. You give nothing to an enemy, Ivan, even in a drill. The imperialists certainly won't! In trying to find us, he also practices finding their missile submarines. He will have a fair chance of locating us, I think. The exercise is confined to nine squares, forty thousand square kilometers. We shall see what he has learned since he served with us—oh, that's right, you weren't with me then. That's when I had the *Suslov*."

"Do I see disappointment?"

"No, not really. The four-day drill with *Konovalov* will be interesting diversion." Bastard, he said to himself, you knew beforehand exactly what our orders were—and you do know Viktor Tupolev, liar. It was time.

Putin finished his cigarette and his tea before standing. "So, again I am permitted to watch the master captain at work—befuddling a poor boy." He turned towards the door. "I think—"

Ramius kicked Putin's feet out from under him just as he was stepping away from the table. Putin fell backwards while Ramius sprang to his feet and grasped the political officer's head in his strong fisherman's hands. The captain drove his neck downward to the sharp, metal-edged corner of the wardroom table. It struck the point. In the same instant Ramius pushed down on the man's chest. An unnecessary gesture—with the sickening crackle of bones Ivan Putin's neck broke, his spine severed at the level of the second cervical vertebra, a perfect hangman's fracture.

The political officer had no time to react. The nerves to his body below the neck were instantly cut off from the organs and muscles they controlled. Putin tried to shout, to say something, but his mouth flapped open and shut without a sound except for the exhalation of his last lungful of air. He tried to gulp air down like a landed fish, and this did not work. Then his eyes went up to Ramius, wide in shock—there was no pain, and no emotion but surprise. The captain laid him gently on the tile deck.

Ramius saw the face flash with recognition, then darken. He reached down to take Putin's pulse. It was nearly two minutes before the heart stopped completely. When Ramius was sure that his political officer was dead, he took the teapot from the table and poured two cups' worth on the deck, careful to drip some on the man's shoes. Next he lifted the body to the wardroom table and threw open the door.

"Dr. Petrov to the wardroom at once!"

The ship's medical office was only a few steps aft. Petrov was there in seconds, along with Vasily Borodin, who had hurried aft from the control room.

"He slipped on the deck where I spilled my tea," Ramius gasped, performing closed heart massage on Putin's chest. "I tried to keep him from falling, but he hit his head on the table.

Petrov shoved the captain aside, moved the body around, and leapt on the table to kneel astride it. He tore the shirt open, then checked Putin's eyes. Both pupils were wide and fixed. The doctor felt around the man's head, his hands working downward to the neck. They stopped there, probing. The doctor shook his head slowly.

"Comrade Putin is dead. His neck is broken." The doctor's hands came loose, and he closed the *zampolit*'s eyes.

"No!" Ramius shouted. "He was alive only a minute ago!" The commanding officer was sobbing. "It's my fault. I tried to catch him, but I failed. My fault!" He collapsed into a chair and buried his face in his hands. "My fault," he cried, shaking his head in rage, struggling visibly to regain his composure. An altogether excellent performance.

Petrov placed his hand on the captain's shoulder. "It was an accident, Comrade Captain. These things happen, even to experienced men. It was not your fault. Truly, Comrade."

Ramius swore under his breath, regaining control of himself. "There is nothing you can do?"

Petrov shook his head. "Even in the finest clinic in the Soviet Union nothing could be done. Once the spinal cord is severed, there is no hope. Death is virtually instantaneous—but also it is quite painless," the doctor added consolingly.

Ramius drew himself up as he took a long breath, his face set. "Comrade Putin was a good shipmate, a loyal Party member, and a fine officer." Out the corner of his eye he noticed Borodin's mouth twitch. "Comrades, we will continue our mission! Dr. Petrov, you will carry our comrade's body to the freezer. This is—gruesome, I know, but he deserves and will get an honorable military funeral, with his shipmates in attendance, as it should be, when we return to port."

"Will this be reported to fleet headquarters?" Petrov asked.

"We cannot. Our orders are to maintain strict radio silence." Ramius handed the doctor a set of operations orders from his pocket. Not those taken from the safe. "Page three, Comrade Doctor."

Petrov's eyes went wide reading the operational directive.

"I would prefer to report this, but our orders are explicit: Once we dive, no transmissions of any kind, for any reason."

Petrov handed the papers back. "Too bad, our comrade would have looked forward to this. But orders are orders."

"And we shall carry them out."

"Putin would have it no other way," Petrov agreed.

"Borodin, observe: I take the comrade political officer's missile control key from his neck, as per regulations," Ramius said, pocketing the key and chain.

"I note this, and will so enter it in the log," the executive officer said gravely.

Petrov brought in his medical corpsman. Together they took the body aft to the medical office, where it was zippered into a body bag. The corpsman and a pair of sailors then took it forward, through the control room, into the missile compartment. The entrance to the freezer was on the lower missile deck, and the men carried the body through the door. While two cooks removed food to make room for it, the body was set reverently down in the corner. Aft, the doctor and the executive officer made the necessary inventory of personal effects, one copy for the ship's medical file, another for the ship's log, and a third for a box that was sealed and locked up in the medical office.

Forward, Ramius took the conn in a subdued control room. He ordered the submarine to a course of two-nine-zero degrees, west-northwest. Grid square 54-90 was to the east.

THE SECOND DAY

SATURDAY, 4 DECEMBER

The Red October

It was the custom in the Soviet Navy for the commanding officer to announce his ship's operational orders and to exhort the crew to carry them out in true Soviet fashion. The orders were then posted for all to see—and be inspired by—outside the ship's Lenin Room. In large surface ships this was a classroom where political awareness classes were held. In *Red October* it was a closet-sized library near the wardroom where Party books and other ideological material were kept for the men to read. Ramius disclosed their orders the day after sailing to give his men the chance to settle into the ship's routine. At the same time he gave a pep talk. Ramius always gave a good one. He'd had a lot of practice. At 0800 hours, when the forenoon watch was set, he entered the control room and took some file cards from an inside jacket pocket.

"Comrades!" he began, talking into the microphone, "this is the captain speaking. You all know that our beloved friend and comrade, Captain Ivan Yurievich Putin, died yesterday in a tragic accident. Our orders do not permit us to inform fleet headquarters of this. Comrades, we will dedicate our efforts and our work to the memory of our comrade, Ivan Yurievich Putin—a fine shipmate, an honorable Party member, and a courageous officer.

"Comrades! Officer and men of *Red October!* We have orders from the Red Banner Northern Fleet High Command, and they are orders worthy of this ship and this crew!

"Comrades! Our orders are to make the ultimate test of our new silent propulsion system. We are to head *west,* past the North Cape of America's imperialist puppet state, Norway, then to turn southwest towards the Atlantic Ocean. We will pass all of the imperialist sonar nets, and we will *not* be detected! This will be a true test of our submarine and his capabilities. Our own ships will engage in a major exercise too locate us and at the same time to befuddle the arrogant imperialist navies. Our mission, first of all, is to evade detection by anyone. We will teach the Americans a lesson about Soviet technology that they will not soon forget! Our orders are to continue southwest, skirting the American coast to challenge and defeat their newest and best hunter submarines. We will proceed all the way to our socialist brothers in Cuba, and we will be the *first ship* to make use of a new and supersecret nuclear submarine base that we have been building for two years right under their imperialist noses on the south coast of Cuba. A fleet replenishment vessel is already en route to rendezvous with us there.

"Comrades! If we succeed in reaching Cuba undetected by the imperialists—and we will!—the officers and men of *Red October* will have a week—*a week*—of shore leave to visit our fraternal socialist comrades on the beautiful island of Cuba. I have been there, comrades, and you will find it to be exactly what you have read, a paradise of warm breezes, palm trees, and comradely good fellowship." By which Ramius meant women. "After this we will return to the Motherland by the same route. By this time, of course, the imperialists will know who and what we are, from their slinking spies and cowardly reconnaissance aircraft. It is intended that they should know this, because we will again evade detection on the trip home. This will let the imperialists know that they may not trifle with the men of the Soviet Navy, that we can approach their coast at the time of our choosing, and that they must respect the Soviet Union!

"Comrades! We will make the first cruise of *Red October* a memorable one!"

Ramius looked up from his prepared speech. The men on watch in the control room were exchanging grins. It was not often that a Soviet sailor was allowed to visit another country, and a visit by a nuclear submarine to a foreign country, even an ally, was nearly unprecedented. Moreover, for Russians the island of Cuba was as exotic as Tahiti, a promised land of white sand beaches and dusky girls. Ramius knew differently. He had read articles in *Red Star* and other state journals about the joys of duty in Cuba. He had also been there.

Ramius changed cards in his hands. He had given them the good news.

"Comrades! Officers and men of *Red October!*" Now for the bad news that everyone was waiting for. "This mission will not be an easy one. It demands our best efforts. We must maintain absolute radio silence, and our operating routines must be *perfect!* Rewards only come to those who truly earn them. Every officer and every man aboard, from your commanding officer to the newest *matros*, must do his socialist duty and do it well! If we work together as comrades, as the New Soviet Men we are, we shall succeed. You young comrades new to the sea: Listen to your officers, to your *michmanyy*, and to your *starshini*. Learn your duties well, and carry them out exactly. There are no small jobs on this ship, no small responsibilities. Every comrade depends for his life upon every other. Do your duty, follow your orders, and when we have completed this voyage, you will be true Soviet sailors! That is all." Ramius released his thumb from the mike switch and set it back in the cradle. Not a bad speech, he decided—a large carrot and a small stick.

In the galley aft a petty officer was standing still, holding a warm loaf of bread and looking curiously at the bulkhead-mounted speaker. That wasn't what their orders were supposed to be, was it? Had there been a change in plans? The *michman* pointed him back to his duties, grinning and chuckling at the prospect of a week in Cuba. He had heard a lot of stories about Cuba and Cuban women and was looking forward to seeing if they were true.

In the control room Ramius mused. "I wonder if any American submarines are about?"

"Indeed, Comrade Captain," nodded Captain Second Rank Borodin, who had the watch. "Shall we engage the caterpillar?"

"Proceed, Comrade."

"Engines all stop," Borodin ordered.

"All stop." The quartermaster, a *starshina* (petty officer), dialed the annunciator to the STOP position. An instant later the order was confirmed by the inner dial, and a few seconds after that the dull rumble of the engines died away.

Borodin picked up the phone and punched the button for engineering. "Comrade Chief Engineer, prepare to engage the caterpillar."

It wasn't the official name for the new drive system. It had no name as such, just a project number. The nickname *caterpillar* had been given it by a young engineer who had been involved in the sub's development. Neither Ramius nor Borodin knew why, but as often happens with such names, it had stuck.

"Ready, Comrade Borodin," the chief engineer reported back in a moment.

"Open doors fore and aft," Borodin ordered next.

The *michman* of the watch reached up the control board and threw four switches. The status light over each changed from red to green. "Doors show open, Comrade."

"Engage caterpillar. Build speed slowly to thirteen knots."

"Build slowly to one-three knots, Comrade," the engineer acknowledged.

The hull, which had gone momentarily silent, now had a new sound. The engine noises were lower and very different from what they had been. The reactor plant noises, mainly from pumps that circulated the cooling water, were almost imperceptible. The caterpillar did not use a great deal of power for what it did. At the *michman*'s station the speed gauge, which had dropped to five knots, began to creep upward again. Forward of the missile room, in a space shoehorned into the crew's accommodations, the handful of sleeping men stirred briefly in their bunks as they noted an intermittent rumble aft and the hum of electric motors a few feet away, separated from them by the pressure hull. They were tired enough even on their first day at sea to ignore the noise, fighting back to their precious allotment of sleep.

"Caterpillar functioning normally, Comrade Captain," Borodin reported.

"Excellent. Steer two-six-zero, helm," Ramius ordered.

"Two-six-zero, Comrade." The helmsman turned his wheel to the left.

The USS Bremerton

Thirty miles to the northeast, the USS *Bremerton* was on a heading of two-two-five, just emerging from under the icepack. A 688-class attack submarine, she had been on an ELINT—electronic intelligence gathering—mission in the Kara Sea when she was ordered west to the Kola Peninsula. The Russian missile boat wasn't supposed to have sailed for another week, and the *Bremerton*'s skipper was annoyed at this latest intelligence screw-up. He would have been in place to track the *Red October* if she had sailed as scheduled. Even so, the American sonarmen had picked up on the Soviet sub a few minutes earlier, despite the fact that they were traveling at fourteen knots.

"Conn, sonar."

Commander Wilson lifted the phone. "Conn, aye."

"Contact lost, sir. His screws stopped a few minutes ago and have not restarted. There's some other activity to the east, but the missile sub has gone dead."

"Very well. He's probably settling down to a slow drift. We'll be creeping up on him. Stay awake, Chief." Commander Wilson thought this over as he took two steps to the chart table. The two officers of the fire control tracking party who had just been establishing the track for the contact looked up to learn their commander's opinion.

"If it was me, I'd go down near the bottom and circle slowly right about here." Wilson traced a rough circle on the chart that enclosed the *Red October*'s position. "So let's creep up on him. We'll reduce speed to five knots and see if we can move in and reacquire him from his reactor plant noise." Wilson turned to the officer of the deck. "Reduce speed to five knots."

"Aye, Skipper."

Severomorsk, USSR

In the Central Post Office building in Severomorsk a mail sorter watched sourly as a truck driver dumped a large canvas sack on his work table and went back out the door. He was late—well, not really late, the clerk corrected himself, since the idiot had not been on time once in five years. It was a Saturday, and he resented being at work. Only a few years before, the forty-hour week had been started in the Soviet Union. Unfortunately this change had never affected such vital public services as mail delivery. So, here he was, still working a six-day week—and without extra pay! A disgrace, he thought, and had said often enough in his apartment, playing cards with his workmates over vodka and cucumbers.

He untied the drawstring and turned the sack over. Several smaller bags tumbled out. There was no sense in hurrying. It was only the beginning of the month, and they still had weeks to move their quota of letters and parcels from one side of the building to the other. In the Soviet Union every worker is a government worker, and they have a saying: As long as the bosses pretend to pay us, we will pretend to work.

Opening a small mailbag, he pulled out an official-looking envelope addressed to the Main Political Administration of the Navy in Moscow. The clerk paused, fingering the envelope. It probably came from one of the submarines based at Polyarnyy, on the other side of the fjord. What did the letter say? the sorter wondered, playing the mental game that amused mailmen all over the world. Was it an announcement that all was ready for the final attack on the imperialist West? A list of Party members who were late paying their dues, or a requisition for more toilet paper? There was no telling. Submariners! They were all prima donnas—even the farmboy conscripts still picking shit from between their toes paraded around like members of the Party elite.

The clerk was sixty-two. In the Great Patriotic War he had been a tankrider serving in a guards tank corps attached to Konev's First Ukrainian Front. That, he told himself, was a man's job, riding into action on the back of the great battle tanks, leaping off to hunt for the German infantrymen as they cowered in their holes. When something needed doing against those slugs, it was *done!* Now what had become of Soviet fighting men? Living aboard luxury liners with plenty of good food and warm beds. The only warm bed he had ever known was over the exhaust vent of his tank's diesel—and he'd had to fight for that! It was crazy what the world had become. Now sailors acted like czarist princes and wrote tons of letters back and forth and called it work. These pampered boys didn't know what hardship was. And their privileges! Every word they committed to paper was priority mail. Whimpering letters to their sweethearts, most of it, and here he was sorting through it all on a Saturday to see that it got to their womenfolk—even though they couldn't possibly have a reply for two weeks. It just wasn't like the old days.

The sorter tossed the envelope with a negligent flick of the wrist towards the surface mailbag for Moscow on the far side of his work table. It missed, dropping to the concrete floor. The letter would be placed aboard the train a day late. The sorter didn't care. There was a hockey game that night, the biggest game of the young season, Central Army against Wings. He had a liter of vodka bet on Wings.

Morrow, England

"Halsey's greatest popular success was his greatest error. In establishing himself as a popular hero with legendary aggressiveness, the admiral would blind later generations to his impressive intellectual abilities and a shrewd gambler's instinct to—" Jack Ryan frowned at his computer. It sounded too much like a doctoral dissertation, and he had already done one of those. He thought of dumping the whole passage from the memory disk but decided against it. He had to follow this line of reasoning for his introduction. Bad as it was, it did serve as a guide for what he wanted to say. Why was it that introductions always seemed to be the hardest part of a history book? For three years now he had been working on *Fighting Sailor,* an authorized biography of Fleet Admiral William Halsey. Nearly all of it was contained on a half-dozen floppy disks lying next to his Apple computer.

"Daddy?" Ryan's daughter was staring up at him.

"And how's my little Sally today?"

"Fine."

Ryan picked her up and set her on his lap, careful to slide his chair away from the keyboard. Sally was all checked out on games and educational programs, and occasionally thought that this meant she was able to handle Wordstar also. Once that had resulted in the loss of twenty thousand words of electronically recorded manuscript. And a spanking.

She leaned her head against her father's shoulder.

"You don't look fine. What's bothering my little girl?"

"Well, Daddy, y'see, it's almost Chris'mas, an . . . I'm not sure that Santa knows where we are. We're not where we were last year."

"Oh, I see. And you're afraid he doesn't come here?"

"Uh huh."

"Why didn't you ask me before? Of course he comes here. Promise."

"Promise?"

"Promise."

"Okay." She kissed her father and ran out of the room, back to watching cartoons on the telly, as they called it in England. Ryan was glad she had interrupted him. He didn't want to forget to pick up a few things when he flew over to Washington. Where was—oh, yeah. He pulled a disk from his desk drawer and inserted it in the spare disk drive. After clearing the screen, he scrolled up the Christmas list, things he still had to get. With a simple command a copy of the list was made on the adjacent printer. Ryan tore the page off and tucked it in his wallet. Work didn't appeal to him this Saturday morning. He decided to play with his kids. After all, he'd be stuck in Washington for much of the coming week.

The V. K. Konovalov

The Soviet submarine *V. K. Konovalov* crept above the hard sand bottom of the Barents Sea at three knots. She was at the southwest corner of grid square 54-90 and for the past ten hours had been drifting back and forth on a north-south line, waiting for the *Red October* to arrive for the beginning of Exercise OCTOBER FROST. Captain Second Rank Viktor Alexievich Tupolev paced slowly around the periscope pedestal in the control room of his small, fast attack sub. He was waiting for his old mentor to show up, hoping to play a few tricks on him. He had served with the Schoolmaster for two years. They had been good years, and while he found his former commander to be something of a cynic, especially about the Party, he would unhesitatingly testify to Ramius' skill and craftiness.

And his own. Tupolev, now in his third year of command, had been one of the Schoolmaster's star pupils. His current vessel was a brand-new *Alfa*, the fastest submarine ever made. A month earlier, while Ramius had been fitting out the *Red*

October after her initial shakedown, Tupolev and three of his officers had flown down to see the model sub that had been the test-bed for the prototype drive system. Thirty-two meters long and diesel-electric powered, it was based in the Caspian Sea, far from the eyes of imperialist spies, and kept in a covered dock, hidden from their photographic satellites. Ramius had had a hand in the development of the caterpillar, and Tupolev recognized the mark of the master. It would be a bastard to detect. Not quite impossible, though. After a week of following the model around the north end of the Caspian Sea in an electrically powered launch, trailing the best passive sonar array his country had yet made, he thought he had found a flaw. Not a big one, just big enough to exploit.

Of course there was no guarantee of success. He was not only in competition with a machine, but also with the captain commanding her. Tupolev knew this area intimately. The water was almost perfectly isothermal; there was no thermal layer for a submarine to hide under. They were far enough from the freshwater rivers on the north coast of Russia not to have to worry about pools and walls of variable salinity interfering with their sonar searches. The *Konovalov* had been built with the best sonar systems the Soviet Union had yet produced, copied closely from the French DUUV-23 and a bit improved, the factory technicians said.

Tupolev planned to mimic the American tactic of drifting slowly, with just enough speed to maintain steerage, perfectly quiet and waiting for the *Red October* to cross his path. He would then trail his quarry closely and log each change in course and speed, so that when they compared logs in a few weeks the Schoolmaster would see that his erstwhile student had played his own winning game. It was about time someone did.

"Anything new on sonar?" Tupolev was getting tense. Patience came hard to him.

"Nothing new, Comrade Captain." The *starpom* tapped the X on the chart that marked the position of the *Rokossovskiy*, a *Delta*-class missile sub they had ben tracking for several hours in the same exercise area. "Our friend is still cruising in a slow circle. Do you think that *Rokossovskiy* might be trying to confuse us? Would Captain Ramius have arranged for him to be here, to complicate our task?"

The thought had occurred to Tupolev. "Perhaps, but probably not. This exercise was arranged by Korov himself. Our mission orders were sealed, and Marko's orders should have been also. But then, Admiral Korov is an old friend of our Marko." Tupolev paused for a moment and shook his head. "No. Korov is an honorable man. I think Ramius is proceeding this way as slowly as he can. To make us nervous, to make us question ourselves. He will know we are to hunt him and will adjust his plans accordingly. He might try to enter the square from an unexpected direction—or to make us think that he is. You have never served under Ramius, Comrade Lieutenant. He is a fox, that one, an old gray-whiskered fox. I think we will continue to patrol as we are for another four hours. If we have not yet acquired him then, we will cross over to the southeast corner of the square and work our way in to the center. Yes."

Tupolev had never expected that this would be easy. No attack submarine commander had ever embarrassed Ramius. He was determined to be the first, and the difficulty of the task would only confirm his own prowess. In one or two more years, Tupolev planned to be the new master.

THE THIRD DAY

SUNDAY, 5 DECEMBER

The Red October

The *Red October* had no time of her own. For her the sun neither rose nor set, and the days of the week had little significance. Unlike surface ships, which changed their clocks to conform with the local time wherever they were, submarines generally adhered to a single time reference. For American subs this was Zulu, or Greenwich mean time. For the *Red October* it was Moscow standard time, which by normal reckoning was actually one hour ahead of standard time to save on utility expenses.

Ramius entered the control room in mid-morning. Their course was now two-five-zero, speed thirteen knots, and the submarine was running thirty meters above the bottom at the west edge of the Barents Sea. In a few more hours the bottom would drop away to an abyssal plain, allowing them to go much deeper. Ramius examined the chart first, then the numerous banks of instruments covering both side bulkheads in the compartment. Last he made some notations in the order book.

"Lieutenant Ivanov!" he said sharply to the junior officer of the watch.

"Yes, Comrade Captain!" Ivanov was the greenest officer aboard, fresh from Lenin's Komsomol School in Leningrad, pale, skinny, and eager.

"I will be calling a meeting of the senior officers in the wardroom. You will now be the officer of the watch. This is your first cruise, Ivanov. How do you like it?"

"It is better than I had hoped, Comrade Captain," Ivanov replied with greater confidence than he could possibly have felt.

"That is good, Comrade Lieutenant. It is my practice to give junior officers as much responsibility as they can handle. While we senior officers are having our weekly political discussion, *you* are in command of this vessel! The safety of this ship and all his crew is *your* responsibility! You have been taught all you need to know, and my instructions are in the order book. If we detect another submarine or surface ship you will inform me at once and instantly initiate evasion drill. Any questions?"

"No, Comrade Captain." Ivanov was standing at rigid attention.

"Good." Ramius smiled. "Pavel Ilych, you will forever remember this as one of the great moments of your life. I know, I can still remember my first watch. Do not forget your orders or your responsibilities!"

Pride sparkled in the boy's eyes. It was too bad what would happen to him, Ramius thought, still the teacher. On first inspection, Ivanov looked to have the makings of a good officer.

Ramius walked briskly aft to the ship's medical office.

"Good morning, Doctor."

"Good morning to you, Comrade Captain. It is time for our political meeting?" Petrov had been reading the manual for the sub's new X-ray machine.

"Yes, it is, Comrade Doctor, but I do not wish you to attend. There is something else I want you to do. While the senior officers are at the meeting, I have the three youngsters standing watch in control and the engineering spaces."

"Oh?" Petrov's eyes went wide. It was his first time on a submarine in several years.

Ramius smiled. "Be at ease, Comrade. I can get from the wardroom to control in twenty seconds, as you know, and Comrade Melekhin can get to his precious reactor just as fast. Sooner or later our young officers must learn to function on their own. I prefer that they learn sooner. I want you to keep an eye on them. I know that they all have the knowledge to do their duties. I want to know if they have the temperament. If Borodin or I watch over them, they will not act normally. And in any case, this is a medical judgment, no?"

"Ah, you wish me to observe how they react to their responsibilities."

"Without the pressure of being observed by a senior line officer," Ramius confirmed. "One must give young officers room to grow—but not too much. If you observe something that you question, you will inform me at once. There should be no problems. We are in open sea, there is no traffic about, and the reactor is running at a fraction of its total power. The first test for young officers ought to be an easy one. Find some excuse for traveling back and forth, and keep an eye on the children. Ask questions about what they are doing."

Petrov laughed at that. "Ah, and also you would have me learn a few things, Comrade Captain? They told me about you at Severomorsk. Fine, it will be as you say. But this will be the first political meeting I have missed in years."

"From what your file says, you could teach Party doctrine to the Politburo, Yevgeni Konstantinovich." Which said little about his medical ability, Ramius thought.

The captain moved forward to the wardroom to join his brother officers, who were waiting for him. A steward had left several pots of tea along with black bread and butter to snack on. Ramius looked at the corner of the table. The bloodstains had long since been wiped away, but he could remember exactly what it looked like. This, he reflected, was one difference between himself and the man he had murdered. Ramius had a conscience. Before taking his seat, he turned to lock the door behind him. His officers were all sitting at attention, since the compartment was not large enough for them to stand once the bench seats were folded down.

Sunday was the normal day for the political awareness session at sea. Ordinarily Putin would have officiated, reading some *Pravda* editorials, followed by selected quotations from the works of Lenin and a discussion of the lessons to be learned from the readings. It was very much like a church service.

With the demise of the *zampolit* this duty developed upon the commanding officer, but Ramius doubted that regulations anticipated the sort of discussion on today's agenda. Each officer in this room was a member of his conspiracy. Ramius outlined their plans—there had been some minor changes which he had not mentioned to anyone. Then he told them about the letter.

"So, there is no going back," Borodin observed.

"We have all agreed upon our course of action. Now we are committed to it." Their reactions to his words were just what he expected them to be—sober. As well they might be. All were single; no one left behind a wife or children. All were Party members in good standing, their dues paid up to the end of the year, their Party cards right where they were supposed to be, "next to their hearts." And each one shared with his comrades a deep-seated dissatisfaction with, in some cases a hatred of, the Soviet government.

The planning had begun soon after the death of his Natalia. The rage he had almost unknowingly suppressed throughout his life had burst forth with a violence and passion that he had struggled to contain. A lifetime of self-control had enabled him to conceal it, and a lifetime of naval training had enabled him to choose a purpose worthy of it.

Ramius had not yet begun school when he first heard tales from other children about what his father Aleksandr had done in Lithuania in 1940 and after that country's dubious liberation from the Germans in 1944. These were the repeated whisperings of their parents. One little girl told Marko a story that he recounted to Aleksandr, and to the boy's uncomprehending horror her father vanished. For his unwitting mistake Marko was branded an informer. Stung by the name he was given for committing a crime—which the State taught was not a crime at all—whose enormity never stopped pulling at his conscience, he never informed again.

In the formative years of his life, while the elder Ramius ruled the Lithuanian Party Central Committee in Vilnius, the motherless boy was raised by his paternal grandmother, common practice in a country savaged by four years of brutal war. Her only son left home at an early age to join Lenin's Red Guards, and while he was away she kept to the old ways, going to mass every day until 1940 and never forgetting the religious education that had been passed on to her. Ramius remembered her as a silver-haired old woman who told wonderful bedtime stories. Religious stories. It would have been far too dangerous for her to bring Marko to the religious ceremonies that had never been entirely stamped out, but she did manage to have him baptized a Roman Catholic soon after his father had deposited him with her. She never told Marko about this. The risk would have been too great. Roman Catholicism had been brutally suppressed in the Baltic states. It was a religion, and as he grew older Marko learned that Marxism-Leninism was a jealous god, tolerating no competing loyalties.

Grandmother Hilda told him nighttime stories from the Bible, each with a lesson of right and wrong, virtue and reward. As a child he found them merely entertaining, but he never told his father about them because even then he knew that Aleksandr would object. After the elder Ramius again resumed control of his son's life, this religious education faded into Marko's memory, neither fully remembered nor fully forgotten.

As a boy, Ramius sensed more than thought that Soviet Communism ignored a basic human need. In his teens, his misgivings began to take a coherent shape. The Good of the People was a laudable enough goal, but in denying a man's soul, an enduring part of his being, Marxism stripped away the foundation of human dignity and individual value. It also cast aside the objective measure of justice and ethics which, he decided, was the principal legacy of religion to civilized life. From earliest adulthood on, Marko had his own idea about right and wrong, an idea he did not share with the State. It gave him a means of gauging his actions and those of others. It was something he was careful to conceal. It served as an anchor for his soul and, like an anchor, it was hidden far below the visible surface.

Even as the boy was grappling with his first doubts about his country, no one could have suspected it. Like all Soviet children, Ramius joined the Little Octobrists, then the Young Pioneers. He paraded at the requisite battle shrines in polished

boots and blood-red scarf, and gravely stood watch over the
remains of some unknown soldier while clasping to his chest
a deactivated PPSh submachinegun, his back ramrod straight
before the eternal flame. The solemnity of such duty was no
accident. As a boy Marko was certain that the brave men whose
graves he guarded so intensely had met their fates with the
same sort of selfless heroism that he saw portrayed in endless
war movies at the local cinema. They had fought the hated
Germans to protect the women and children and old people
behind the lines. And like a nobleman's son of an earlier Russia,
he took special pride in being the son of a Party chieftain. The
Party, he heard a hundred times before he was five, was the
Soul of the People; the unity of Party, People, and Nation was
the holy trinity of the Soviet Union, albeit with one segment
more important than the others. His father fit easily into the
cinematic image of a Party apparatchik. Stern but fair, to Marko
he was a frequently absent, gruffly kind man who brought his
son what presents he could and saw to it that he had all the
advantages the son of a Party secretary was entitled to.

Although outwardly he was the model Soviet child, inwardly
he wondered why what he learned from his father and in school
conflicted with the other lessons of his youth. Why did some
parents refuse to let their children play with him? Why when
he passed them did his classmates whisper *"stukach,"* the cruel
and bitter epithet of informer? His father and the Party taught
that informing was an act of patriotism, but for having done it
once he was shunned. He resented the taunts of his boyhood
peers, but he never once complained to his father, knowing
that this would be an evil thing to do.

Something was very wrong—but what? He decided that he
had to find the answers for himself. By choice Marko became
individual in his thinking, and so unknowingly committed the
gravest sin in the Communist pantheon. Outwardly the model
of a Party member's son, he played the game carefully and
according to all the rules. He did his duty for all Party organ-
izations, and was always the first to volunteer for the menial
tasks allotted to children aspiring to Party membership, which
he knew was the only path to success or even comfort in the
Soviet Union. He became good at sports. Not team sports—
he worked at track and field events in which he could compete
as an individual and measure the performance of others. Over

the years he learned to do the same in all of his endeavors, to watch and judge the actions of his fellow citizens and officers with cool detachment, behind a blank face that concealed his conclusions.

In the summer of his eighth year the course of his life was forever changed. When no one would play with "the little *stukach,*" he would wander down to the fishing docks of the small village where his grandmother had made her home. A ragtag collection of old wooden boats sailed each morning, always behind a screen of patrol boats manned by MGB—as the KGB was then known—border guards, to reap a modest harvest from the Gulf of Finland. Their catch supplemented the local diet with needed protein and provided a minuscule income for the fishermen. One boat captain was old Sasha. An officer in the czar's navy, he had revolted with the crew of the cruiser *Avrora,* helping to spark the chain of events that changed the face of the world. Marko did not learn until many years later that the crewmen of the *Avrora* had broken with Lenin— and been savagely put down by Red Guards. Sasha had spent twenty years in labor camps for his part in that collective in- discretion and only been released at the beginning of the Great Patriotic War. The *Rodina* had found herself in need of expe- rienced seamen to pilot ships into the ports of Murmansk and Archangel, to which the Allies were bringing weapons, food, and the sundries that allow a modern army to function. Sasha had learned his lesson in the gulag: he did his duty efficiently and well, asking for nothing in return. After the war he'd been given a kind of freedom for his services, the right to perform back-breaking work under perpetual suspicion.

By the time Marko met him, Sasha was over sixty, a nearly bald man with ropy old muscles, a seaman's eye, and a talent for stories that left the youngster wide-eyed. He'd been a mid- shipman under the famous Admiral Marakov at Port Arthur in 1906. Probably the finest seaman in Russian history, Marakov's reputation as a patriot and an innovative fighting sailor was sufficiently unblemished that a Communist government would eventually see fit to name a missile cruiser in his memory. At first wary of the boy's reputation, Sasha saw something in him that others missed. The boy without friends and the sailor without a family became comrades. Sasha spent hours telling and retelling the tale of how he had been on the admiral's flagship, the *Petropavlovsk,* and participated in the one Russian victory over the hated Japanese—only to have his battleship sunk and his admiral killed by a mine while returning to port. After this Sasha had led his seamen as naval infantry, winning three decorations for courage under fire. This experience—he waggled his finger seriously at the boy—taught him of the mindless corruption of the czarist regime and convinced him to join one of the first naval soviets when such action meant certain death at the hands of the czar's secret police, the *okhrana.* He told his own version of the October Revolution from the thrilling perspective of an eyewitness. But Sasha was very careful to leave the later parts out.

He allowed Marko to sail with him and taught him the fundamentals of seamanship that decided a boy not yet nine that his destiny lay on the sea. There was a freedom at sea he could never have on land. There was a romance about it that touched the man growing within the boy. There were also dangers, but in a summer-long series of simple, effective lessons, Sasha taught the boy that preparation, knowledge, and discipline can deal with any form of danger; that danger confronted properly is not something a man must fear. In later years Marko would reflect often on the value this summer had held for him, and wonder just how far Sasha's career might have led if other events had not cut it short.

Marko told his father about Sasha towards the end of that long Baltic summer and even took him to meet the old seadog. The elder Ramius was sufficiently impressed with him and what he had done for his son that he arranged for Sasha to have command of a newer, larger boat and moved him up on the list for a new apartment. Marko almost believed that the Party could do a good deed—that he himself had done his first manly good deed. But old Sasha died the following winter, and the good deed came to nothing. Many years later Marko realized that he hadn't known his friend's last name. Even after years of faithful service to the *Rodina,* Sasha had been an unperson.

At thirteen Marko traveled to Leningrad to attend the Nakhimov School. There he decided that he, too, would become a professional naval officer. Marko would follow the quest for adventure that had for centuries called young men to the sea. The Nakhimov School was a special three-year prep school for youngsters aspiring to a career at sea. The Soviet Navy at that time was little more than a coastal defense force, but Marko wanted very much to be a part of it. His father urged him to a life of Party work, promising rapid promotion, a life of comfort and privilege. But Marko wanted to earn whatever he received on his own merits, not to be remembered as an appendage of the "liberator" of Lithuania. And a life at sea offered romance and excitement that even made serving the State something he could tolerate. The navy had little tradition to build on. Marko sensed that in it there was room to grow, and saw that many aspiring naval cadets were like himself, if not mavericks then as close to mavericks as was possible in a society so closely controlled as his own. The teenager thrived with his first experience of fellowship.

Nearing graduation, his class was exposed to the various components of the Russian fleet. Ramius at once fell in love with submarines. The boats at that time were small, dirty, and smelled from the open bilges that the crews used as a convenient latrine. At the same time submarines were the only offensive arm that the navy had, and from the first Marko wanted to be on the cutting edge. He'd had enough lectures on naval history to know that submarines had twice nearly strangled England's maritime empire and had successfully emasculated the economy of Japan. This had greatly pleased him; he was glad the Americans had crushed the Japanese navy that had so nearly killed his mentor.

He graduated from the Nakhimov School first in his class, winner of the gold-plated sextant for his mastery of theoretical navigation. As leader of his class, Marko was allowed the school of his choice. He selected the Higher Naval School for Underwater Navigation, named for Lenin's Komsomol, VVMUPP, still the principal submarine school of the Soviet Union.

His five years at VVMUPP were the most demanding of his life, the more so since he was determined not to succeed but to excel. He was first in his class in every subject, in every year. His essay on the political significance of Soviet naval power was forwarded to Sergey Georgiyevich Gorshkov, then commander in chief of the Baltic Fleet and clearly the coming man in the Soviet Navy. Gorshkov had seen the essay published in *Morskoi Sbornik (Naval Collections)*, the leading Soviet naval journal. It was a model of progressive Party thought, quoting Lenin six different times.

By this time Marko's father was a candidate member of the Presidium, as the Politburo was then called, and very proud of his son. The elder Ramius was no one's fool. He finally recognized that the Red Fleet was a growing flower and that his son would someday have a position of importance in it. His influence moved his son's career rapidly along.

By thirty, Marko had his first command and a new wife. Natalia Bogdanova was the daughter of another Presidium member whose diplomatic duties had taken him and his family all over the world. Natalia had never been a healthy girl. They had no children, their three attempts each ending in miscarriage, the last of which had nearly killed her. She was a pretty, delicate woman, sophisticated by Russian standards, who polished her husband's passable English with American and British books— politically approved ones to be sure, mainly the thoughts of Western leftists, but also a smattering of genuine literature, including Hemingway, Twain, and Upton Sinclair. Along with his naval career, Natalia had been the center of his life. Their marriage, punctuated by prolonged absences and joyous returns, made their love even more precious than it might have been.

When construction began on the first class of Soviet nuclear-powered submarines, Marko found himself in the yards learning how the steel sharks were designed and built. He was soon known as a very hard man to please as a junior quality control inspector. His own life, he was aware, would ride on the workmanship of these often drunk welders and fitters. He became an expert in nuclear engineering, spent two years as a *starpom*, and then received his first nuclear command. She was a *November*-class attack submarine, the first crude attempt by the Soviets to make a battleworthy long-range attack boat to threaten Western navies and lines of communication. Not a month later a sister ship suffered a major reactor casualty off the Norwegian coast, and Marko was first to arrive on the scene. As ordered, he successfully rescued the crew, then sank the disabled sub lest Western navies learn her secrets. Both tasks he performed expertly and well, a noteworthy tour de force for a young commander. Good performance was something he had always felt it was important to reward in his subordinates, and the fleet commander at that time felt the same way. Marko soon moved on to a new *Charlie I*–class sub.

It was men like Ramius who went out to challenge the Americans and the British. Marko took few illusions with him. The Americans, he knew, had long experience in naval warfare—their own greatest fighter, Jones, had once served the Russian navy for the Czaritza Catherine. Their submariners were legendary for their craftiness, and Ramius found himself pitted against the last of the war-trained Americans, men who had endured the sweaty fear of underwater combat and utterly defeated a modern navy. The deadly serious game of hide-and-seek he played with them was not an easy one, the less so because they had submarines years ahead of Soviet design. But it was not a time without a few victories.

Ramius gradually learned to play the game by American rules, training his officers and men with care. His crews were rarely as prepared as he wished—still the Soviet Navy's greatest problem—but where other commanders cursed their men for their failings, Marko corrected the failings of his men. His first *Charlie*-class submarine was called the Vilnius Academy. This was partially a slur against his half-Lithuanian blood—though since he had been born in Leningrad of a Great Russian, his internal passport designated him as that—but mainly recognition that officers came to him half-trained and left him ready for advancement and eventual command. The same was true of his conscripted crewmen. Ramius did not permit the hazing and low-level terrorism normal throughout the Soviet military. He saw his task as the building of seamen, and he produced a greater percentage of reenlistments than any other submarine commander. A full ninth of the *michmanyy* in the Northern Fleet submarine force were Ramius-trained professionals. His brother submarine commanders were delighted to take aboard his *starshini*, and more than one advanced to officer's school.

After eighteen months of hard work and diligent training, Marko and his Vilnius Academy were ready to play their game of fox and hounds. He happened upon the USS *Triton* in the Norwegian Sea and hounded her mercilessly for twelve hours. Later he would note with no small satisfaction that the *Triton* was soon thereafter retired, because, it was said, the oversized vessel had proven unable to deal with the newer Soviet designs. The diesel-powered submarines of the British and the Norwegians that he occasionally happened across while snorkling he dogged ruthlessly, often subjecting them to vicious sonar lashing. Once he even acquired an American missile submarine, managing to maintain contact with her for nearly two hours before she vanished like a ghost into the black waters.

The rapid growth of the Soviet Navy and the need for qualified officers during his early career prevented Ramius from attending the Frunze Academy. This was normally a *sine qua non* of career advancement in all of the Soviet armed services. Frunze, in Moscow near the old Novodevichiy Monastery, was named for a hero of the Revolution. It was the premiere school for those who aspired to high command, and though Ramius had not attended it as a student, his prowess as an operational commander won him an appointment as an instructor. It was something earned solely on merit, for which his highly placed father was not responsible. That was important to Ramius.

The head of the naval section at Frunze liked to introduce Marko as "our test pilot of submarines." His classes became a prime attraction not only for the naval officers in the academy but also for the many others who came to hear his lectures on naval history and maritime strategy. On weekends spent at his father's official dacha in the village of Zhukova-1, he wrote manuals for submarine operations and the training of crews, and specifications for the ideal attack submarine. Some of his ideas had been controversial enough to upset his erstwhile sponsor, Gorshkov, by this time commander in chief of the entire Soviet Navy—but the old admiral was not entirely displeased.

Ramius proposed that officers in the submarine service should work in a single class of ship—better yet, the same ship—for years, the better to learn their profession and the capabilities of their vessels. Skilled captains, he suggested, should not be forced to leave their commands for desk-bound promotions. Here he lauded the Red Army's practice of leaving a field commander in his post so long as the man wanted it, and deliberately contrasted his view on this matter with the practice of imperialist navies. He stressed the need for extended training in the fleet, for longer-service enlisted men, and for better living conditions on submarines. For some of his ideas he found a sympathetic ear in the high command. For others he did not, and thus Ramius found himself destined never to have his own admiral's flag. By this time he did not care. He loved his submarines too much ever to leave them for a squadron or even a fleet command.

After finishing at Frunze, he did indeed become a test pilot of submarines. Marko Ramius, now a captain first rank, would take out the first ship of every submarine class to "write the book" on its strengths and weaknesses, to develop operational routines and training guidelines. The first of the *Alfa*s was his, the first of the *Delta*s and *Typhoon*s. Aside from one extraordinary mishap on an *Alfa,* his career had been one uninterrupted story of achievement.

Along the way he became the mentor of many young officers. He often wondered what Sasha would have thought as he taught the demanding art of submarine operations to scores of eager young men. Many of them had already become commanding officers themselves; more had failed. Ramius was a commander who took good care of those who pleased him— and took good care of those who did not. Another reason why he had never made admiral was his unwillingness to promote officers whose fathers were as powerful as his own but whose abilities were unsatisfactory. He never played favorites where duty was concerned, and the sons of a half-dozen high Party officials received unsatisfactory fitness reports despite their active performance in weekly Party discussions. Most had become *zampoliti*. It was this sort of integrity that earned him trust in fleet command. When a really tough job was at hand, Ramius' name was usually the first to be considered for it.

Also along the way he had gathered to himself a number of young officers whom he and Natalia virtually adopted. They were surrogates for the family Marko and his wife never had. Ramius found himself shepherding men much like himself, with long-suppressed doubts about their country's leadership. He was an easy man to talk to, once a man had proven himself. To those with political doubts, those with just grievances, he gave the same advice: "Join the Party." Nearly all were already Komsomol members, of course, and Marko urged them to take the next step. This was the price of a career at sea, and guided by their own craving for adventure most officers paid that price. Ramius himself had been allowed to join the Party at eighteen, the earliest possible age, because of his father's influence. His occasional talks at weekly Party meetings were perfect recitations of the Party line. It wasn't hard, he'd tell his officers patiently. All you had to do was repeat what the Party said—just change the words around slightly. This was much easier than navigation—one had only to look at the political officer to see that! Ramius became known as a captain whose officers were both proficient and models of political conformity. He was one of the best Party recruiters in the navy.

Then his wife died. Ramius was in port at the time, not unusual for a missile sub commander. He had his own dacha in the woods west of Polyarnyy, his own Zhiguli automobile, the official car and driver those which his command station enjoyed, and numerous other creature comforts that came with his rank and his parentage. He was a member of the Party elite, so when Natalie had complained of abdominal pain, going to the Fourth Department clinic which served only the privileged had been a natural mistake—there was a saying in the Soviet Union: Floors parquet, docs okay. He'd last seen his wife alive lying on a gurney, smiling as she was wheeled towards the operating room.

The surgeon on call had arrived at the hospital late, and drunk, and allowed himself too much time breathing pure oxygen to sober up before starting the simple procedure of removing an inflamed appendix. The swollen organ burst just as he was retracting tissue to get at it. A case of peritonitis immediately followed, complicated by the perforated bowel the surgeon caused by his clumsy haste to repair the damage.

Natalia was placed on antibiotic therapy, but there was a shortage of medicine. The foreign—usually French—pharmaceuticals used in Fourth Department clinics had run out. Soviet antibiotics, "plan" medications, were substituted. It was a common practice in Soviet industry for workers to earn bonuses by manufacturing goods over the usual quota, goods that bypassed what quality control existed in Soviet industry. This particular batch of medication had never been inspected or tested. *And the vials had probably been filled with distilled water instead of antibiotics,* Marko learned the next day. Natalia had lapsed into deep shock and coma, dying before the series of errors could be corrected.

The funeral was appropriately solemn, Ramius remembered

bitterly. Brother officers from his own command and over a hundred other navy men whom he had befriended over the years were there, along with members of Natalia's family and representatives of the Local Party Central Committee. Marko had been at sea when his father died, and because he had known the extent of Aleksandr's crimes, the loss had had little effect. His wife's death, however, was nothing less than a personal catastrophe. Soon after they had married Natalia had joked that every sailor needs someone to return to, that every woman needs someone to wait for. It had been as simple as that—and infinitely more complex, the marriage of two intelligent people who had over fifteen years learned each other's foibles and strengths and grown ever closer.

Marko Ramius watched the coffin roll into the cremation chamber to the somber strain of a classical requiem, wishing that he could pray for Natalia's soul, hoping that Grandmother Hilda had been right, that there was something beyond the steel door and mass of flame. Only then did the full weight of the event strike him: *the State had robbed him of more than his wife, it had robbed him of a means to assuage his grief with prayer, it had robbed him of the hope—if only an illusion— of ever seeing her again.* Natalia, gentle and kind, had been his only happiness since that Baltic summer long ago. Now that happiness was gone forever. As the weeks and months wore on he was tormented by her memory; a certain hairstyle, a certain walk, a certain laugh encountered on the streets or in the shops of Murmansk was all it took to thrust Natalia back to the forefront of his consciousness, and when he was thinking of his loss, he was not a professional naval officer.

The life of Natalia Bogdanova Ramius had been lost at the hands of a surgeon who had been drinking while on call—a court-martial offense in the Soviet Navy—but Marko could not have the doctor punished. The surgeon was himself the son of a Party chieftain, his status secured by his own sponsors. Her life might have been saved by proper medication, but there had not been enough foreign drugs, and Soviet pharmaceuticals were untrustworthy. The doctor could not be made to pay, the pharmaceutical workers could not be made to pay—the thought echoed back and forth across his mind, feeding his fury until he decided that the State would be made to pay.

The idea had taken weeks to form and was the product of

a career of training and contingency planning. When the construction of the *Red October* was restarted after a two-year hiatus, Ramius knew that he would command her. He had helped with the designing of her revolutionary drive system and had inspected the model, which had been running on the Caspian Sea for some years in absolute secrecy. He asked for relief from his command so that he could concentrate on the construction and outfitting of the *October* and select and train his officers beforehand, the earlier to get the missile sub into full operation. The request was granted by the commander of the Red Banner Northern Fleet, a sentimental man who had also wept at Natalia's funeral.

Ramius had already known who his officers would be. All graduates of the Vilnius Academy, many the "sons" of Marko and Natalia, they were men who owed their place and their rank to Ramius; men who cursed the inability of their country to build submarines worthy of their skills; men who had joined the Party as told and then become even more dissatisfied with the Motherland as they learned that the price of advancement was to prostitute one's mind and soul, to become a highly paid parrot in a blue jacket whose every Party recitation was a grating exercise in self-control. For the most part they were men for whom this degrading step had not borne fruit. In the Soviet Navy there were three routes to advancement. A man could become a *zampolit* and be a pariah among his peers. Or he could be a navigation officer and advance to his own command. Or he could be shunted into a specialty in which he would gain rank and pay—but never command. Thus a chief engineer on a Soviet naval vessel could outrank his commanding officer and still be his subordinate.

Ramius looked around the table at his officers. Most had not been allowed to pursue their own career goals despite their proficiency and despite their party membership. The minor infractions of youth—in one case an act committed at age eight—prevented two from ever being trusted again. With the missile officer, it was because he was a Jew; though his parents had always been committed, believing Communists, neither they nor their son was ever trusted. Another officer's elder brother had demonstrated against the invasion of Czechoslovakia in 1968 and disgraced his whole family. Melekhin, the chief engineer and Ramius' equal in rank, had never been allowed the route to command simply because his superiors wanted him to be an engineer. Borodin, who was ready for his own command, had once accused a *zampolit* of homosexuality; the man he had informed on was the son of the chief *zampolit* of the Northern Fleet. There are many paths to treason.

"And what if they locate us?" Kamarov speculated.

"I doubt that even the Americans can find us when the caterpillar is operating. I am certain that our own submarines cannot. Comrades, I helped design this ship," Ramius said.

"What will become of us?" the missile officer muttered.

"First we must accomplish the task at hand. An officer who looks too far ahead stumbles over his own boots."

"They will be looking for us," Borodin said.

"Of course," Ramius smiled, "but they will not know where to look until it is too late. Our mission, comrades, is to avoid detection. And so we shall."

THE FOURTH DAY

MONDAY, 6 DECEMBER

CIA Headquarters

Ryan walked down the corridor on the top floor of the Langley, Virginia, headquarters of the Central Intelligence Agency. He had already passed through three separate security checks, none of which had required him to open his locked briefcase, now draped under the folds of his buff-colored toggle coat, a gift from an officer in the Royal Navy.

What he had on was mostly his wife's fault, an expensive suit bought on Savile Row. It was English cut, neither conservative nor on the leading edge of contemporary fashion. He had a number of suits like this arranged neatly in his closet by colors, which he wore with white shirts and striped ties. His only jewelry was a wedding band and a university ring, plus an expensive but accurate digital watch on a more expensive gold band. Ryan was not a man who placed a great deal of value in appearances. Indeed, his job was to see through these in the search for hard truth.

He was physically unremarkable, an inch over six feet, and his average build suffered a little at the waist from a lack of exercise enforced by the miserable English weather. His blue eyes had a deceptively vacant look; he was often lost in thought, his face on autopilot as his mind puzzled through data or research material for his current book. The only people Ryan needed to impress were those who knew him; he cared little for the rest. He had no ambition to celebrity. His life, he judged, was already as complicated as it needed to be—quite a bit more complicated than most would guess. It included a wife he loved and two children he doted on, a job that tested his intellect, and sufficient financial independence to choose his own path. The path Jack Ryan had chosen was in the CIA. The agency's official motto was, The truth shall make you free. The trick, he told himself at least once a day, was finding that truth, and while he doubted that he would ever reach this sublime state of grace, he took quiet pride in his ability to pick at it, one small fragment at a time.

The office of the deputy director for intelligence occupied a whole corner of the top floor, overlooking the tree-covered Potomac Valley. Ryan had one more security check to pass.

"Good morning, Dr. Ryan."

"Hi, Nancy." Ryan smiled at her. Nancy Cummings had held her secretarial job for twenty years, had served eight DDIs, and if the truth were known she probably had as good a feel for the intelligence business as the political appointees in the adjacent office. It was the same as with any large business—the bosses came and went, but the good executive secretaries lasted forever.

"How's the family, Doctor? Looking forward to Christmas?"

"You bet—except my Sally's a little worried. She's not sure Santa knows that we've moved, and she's afraid he won't make it to England for her. He will," Ryan confided.

"It's so nice when they're that little." She pressed a hidden button. "You can go right in, Dr. Ryan."

"Thanks, Nancy." Ryan twisted the electronically protected knob and walked into the DDI's office.

Vice Admiral James Greer was reclining in his high-backed judge's chair reading through a folder. His oversized mahogany desk was covered with neat piles of folders whose edges were bordered with red tape and whose covers bore various code words.

"Hiya, Jack!" he called across the room. "Coffee?"

"Yes, thank you, sir."

James Greer was sixty-six, a naval officer past retirement age who kept working through brute competence, much as Hyman Rickover had, though Greer was a far easier man to work for. He was a "mustang," a man who had entered the naval service as an enlisted man, earned his way into the Naval Academy, and spent forty years working his way to a three-star flag, first commanding submarines, then as a full-time intelligence specialist. Greer was a demanding boss, but one who took care of those who pleased him. Ryan was one of these.

Somewhat to Nancy's chagrin, Greer liked to make his own coffee with a West Bend drip machine on the credenza behind his desk, where he could just turn around to reach it. Ryan poured himself a cup—actually a navy-style handleless mug. It was traditional navy coffee, brewed strong, with a pinch of salt.

"You hungry, Jack?" Greer pulled a pastry box from a desk drawer. "I got some sticky buns here."

"Why, thanks, sir. I didn't eat much on the plane." Ryan took one, along with a paper napkin.

"Still don't like to fly?" Greer was amused.

Ryan sat down in the chair opposite his boss. "I suppose I ought to be getting used to it. I like the Concorde better than the wide-bodies. You only have to be terrified half as long."

"How's the family?"

"Fine, thank you, sir. Sally's in first grade—loves it. And little Jack is toddling around the house. These buns are pretty good."

"New bakery just opened up a few blocks from my place. I pass it on the way in every morning." The admiral sat upright in his chair. "So, what brings you over today?"

"Photographs of the new Soviet missile boat, *Red October*," Ryan said casually between sips.

"Oh, and what do our British cousins want in return?" Greer asked suspiciously.

"They want a peek at Barry Somers' new enhancement gadgets. Not the machines themselves—at first—just the finished product. I think it's a fair bargain, sir." Ryan knew the CIA didn't have any shots of the new sub. The operations directorate did not have a man at the building yard at

Severodvinsk or a reliable man at the Polyarnyy submarine base. Worse, the rows of "boat barns" built to shelter the missile submarines, modeled on World War II German submarine pens, made satellite photography impossible. "We have ten frames, low obliques, five each bow and stern, and one from each perspective is undeveloped so that Somers can work on them fresh. We are not committed, sir, but I told Sir Basil that you'd think it over."

The admiral grunted. Sir Basil Charleston, chief of the British Secret Intelligence Service, was a master of the quid pro quo, occasionally offering to share sources with his wealthier cousins and a month later asking for something in return. The intelligence game was often like a primitive marketplace. "To use the new system, Jack, we need the camera used to take the shots."

"I know." Ryan pulled the camera from his coat pocket. "It's a modified Kodak disk camera. Sir Basil says it's the coming thing in spy cameras, nice and flat. This one, he says, was hidden in a tobacco pouch."

"How did you know that—that we need the camera?"

"You mean how Somers uses lasers to—"

"Ryan!" Greer snapped. "How much do you know?"

"Relax, sir. Remember back in February, I was over to discuss those new SS-20 sites on the Chinese border? Somers was here, and you asked me to drive him out to the airport. On the way out he started babbling about this great new idea he was heading west to work on. He talked about it all the way to Dulles. From what little I understood, I gather that he shoots laser beams through the camera lenses to make a mathematical model of the lens. From that, I suppose, he can take the exposed negative, break down the image into the—original incoming light beams, I guess, then use a computer to run *that* through a computer-generated theoretical lens to make a perfect picture. I probably have it wrong." Ryan could tell from Greer's face that he didn't.

"Somers talks too goddamned much."

"I told him that, sir. But once the guy gets started, how the hell do you shut him up?"

"And what do the Brits know?" Greer asked.

"Your guess is as good as mine, sir. Sir Basil asked me about it, and I told him that he was asking the wrong guy—I mean, my degrees are in economics and history, not physics. I told him we needed the camera—but he already knew that. Took it right out of his desk and tossed it to me. I did not reveal a thing about this, sir."

"I wonder how many other people he spilled to. Geniuses! They operate in their own crazy little worlds. Somers is like a little kid sometimes. And you know the First Rule of Security: The likelihood of a secret's being blown is proportional to the *square* of the number of people who're in on it." It was Greer's favorite dictum.

His phone buzzed. "Greer . . . Right." He hung up. "Charlie Davenport's on the way up, per your suggestion, Jack. Supposed to be here half an hour ago. Must be the snow." The admiral jerked a hand towards the window. There were two inches on the ground, with another inch expected by nightfall. "One flake hits this town and everything goes to hell."

Ryan laughed. That was something Greer, a down-easter from Maine, never could seem to understand.

"So, Jack, you say this is worth the price?"

"Sir, we've wanted these pictures for some time, what with all the contradictory data we've been getting on the sub. It's your decision and the judge's but, yes, I think they're worth the price. These shots are very interesting."

"We ought to have our own men in that damned yard," Greer grumped. Ryan didn't know how Operations had screwed that one up. He had little interest in field operations. Ryan was an analyst. How the data came to his desk was not his concern, and he was careful to avoid finding out. "I don't suppose Basil told you anything about their man?"

Ryan smiled, shaking his head. "No, sir, and I did not ask." Greer nodded his approval.

"Morning, James!"

Ryan turned to see Rear Admiral Charles Davenport, director of naval intelligence, with a captain trailing in his wake.

"Hi, Charlie. You know Jack Ryan, don't you?"

"Hello, Ryan."

"We've met," Ryan said.

"This is Captain Casimir."

Ryan shook hands with both men. He'd met Davenport a few years before while delivering a paper at the Naval War College in Newport, Rhode Island. Davenport had given him a hard time in the question-and-answer session. He was supposed to be a bastard to work for, a former aviator who had lost flight status after a barrier crash and, some said, still bore a grudge. Against whom? Nobody really knew.

"Weather in England must be as bad as here, Ryan." Davenport dropped his bridge coat on top of Ryan's. "I see you stole a Royal Navy overcoat."

Ryan was fond of his toggle coat. "A gift, sir, and quite warm."

"Christ, you even talk like a Brit. James, we gotta bring this boy home."

"Be nice to him, Charlie. He's got a present for you. Grab yourself some coffee."

Casimir scurried over to fill a mug for his boss, then sat down at his right hand. Ryan let them wait a moment before opening his briefcase. He took out four folders, keeping one and handing the others around.

"They say you've been doing some fairly good work, Ryan," Davenport said. Jack knew him to be a mercurial man, affable one moment, brittle the next. Probably to keep his subordinates off balance. "And—Jesus Christ!" Davenport had opened his folder.

"Gentlemen, I give you *Red October,* courtesy of the British Secret Intelligence Service," Ryan said formally.

The folders had the photographs arranged in pairs, four each of four-by-four prints. In the back were ten-by-ten blowups of each. The photos had been taken from a low-oblique angle, probably from the rim of the graving dock that had held the boat during her post-shakedown refit. The shots were paired, fore and aft, fore and aft.

"Gentlemen, as you can see, the lighting wasn't all that great. Nothing fancy here. It was a pocket camera loaded with 400-speed color film. The first pair was processed normally to establish high levels. The second was pushed for greater brightness using normal procedures. The third pair was digitally enhanced for color resolution, and the fourth was digitally enhanced for line resolution. I have undeveloped frames of each view for Barry Somers to play with."

"Oh?" Davenport looked up briefly. "That's right neighborly of the Brits. What's the price?" Greer told him. "Pay up. It's worth it."

"That's what Jack says."

"Figures," Davenport chuckled. "You know he really is working for them."

Ryan bristled at that. He liked the English, liked working with their intelligence community, but he knew what country he came from. Jack took a deep breath. Davenport liked to goad people, and if he reacted Davenport would win.

"I gather that Sir John Ryan is still well connected on the other side of the ocean?" Davenport said, extending the prod.

Ryan's knighthood was an honorary one. It was his reward for having broken up a terrorist incident that had erupted around him in St. James's Park, London. He'd been a tourist at the time, the innocent American abroad, long before he'd been asked to join the CIA. The fact that he had unknowingly prevented the assassination of two very prominent figures had gotten him more publicity than he'd ever wanted, but it had also brought him in contact with a lot of people in England, most of them worth the time. Those connections had made him valuable enough that the CIA asked him to be part of a joint American-British liaison group. That was how he had established a good working relationship with Sir Basil Charleston.

"We'd have lots of friends over there, sir, and some of them were kind enough to give you these," Ryan said coolly.

Davenport softened. "Okay, Jack, then you do me a favor. You see whoever gave us these gets something nice in his stocking. They're worth plenty. So, exactly what do we have here?"

To the unschooled observer, the photographs showed the standard nuclear missile submarine. The steel hull was blunt at one end, tapered at the other. The workmen standing on the floor of the dock provided scale—she was huge. There were twin bronze propellers at the stern, on either side of a flat appendage which the Russians called a beaver tail, or so the intelligence reports said. With the twin screws the stern was unremarkable except in one detail.

"What are these doors for?" Casimir asked.

"Hmm. She's a big bastard." Davenport evidently hadn't heard. "Forty feet longer than we expected, by the look of her."

"Forty-four, roughly." Ryan didn't much like Davenport, but the man did know his stuff. "Somers can calibrate that for us. And more beam, two meters more than the other *Typhoon*s.

She's an obvious development of the *Typhoon* class, but—"

"You're right, Captain," Davenport interrupted. "What are those doors?"

"That's why I came over." Ryan had wondered how long this would take. He'd caught onto them in the first five seconds. "I don't know, and neither do the Brits."

The *Red October* had two doors at the bow and stern, each about two meters in diameter, though they were not quite circular. They had been closed when the photos were shot and only showed up well on the number four pair.

"Torpedo tubes? No—four of them are inboard." Greer reached into his drawer and came out with a magnifying glass. In an age of computer-enhanced imagery it struck Ryan as charmingly anachronistic.

"You're the sub driver, James," Davenport observed.

"Twenty years ago, Charlie." He'd made the switch from line officer to professional spook in the early sixties. Captain Casimir, Ryan noted, wore the wings of a naval aviator and had the good sense to remain quiet. He wasn't a "nuc."

"Well, they can't be torpedo tubes. They have the normal four of them at the bow, inboard of these openings . . . must be six or seven feet across. How about launch tubes for the new cruise missile they're developing?"

"That's what the Royal Navy thinks. I had a chance to talk it over with their intelligence chaps. But I don't buy it. Why put an anti-surface-ship weapon on a strategic platform? We don't, and we deploy our boomers a lot further forward than they do. The doors are symmetrical through the boat's axis. You can't launch a missile out of the stern, sir. The openings barely clear the screws."

"Toward sonar array," Davenport said.

"Granted they could do that, if they trail one screw. But why two of them?" Ryan asked.

Davenport gave him a nasty look. "They love redundancies."

"Two doors forward, to aft. I can buy cruise missile tubes. I can buy a towed array. But both sets of doors exactly the same size?" Ryan shook his head. "Too much of a coincidence. I think it's something new. That's what interrupted her construction for so long. They figured something new for her and spent the last two years rebuilding the *Typhoon* configuration to accommodate it. Note also that they added six more missiles for good measure."

"Opinion," Davenport observed.

"That's what I'm paid for."

"Okay, Jack, what do you think it is?" Greer asked.

"Beats me, sir. I'm no engineer."

Admiral Greer looked his guests over for a few seconds. He smiled and leaned back in his chair. "Gentlemen, we have what? Ninety years of naval experience in this room, plus this young amateur." He gestured at Ryan. "Okay, Jack, you've set us up for something. Why did you bring this over personally?"

"I want to show these to somebody."

"Who?" Greer's head cocked suspiciously to one side.

"Skip Tyler. Any of you fellows know him?"

"I do," Casimir nodded. "He was a year behind me at Annapolis. Didn't he get hurt or something?"

"Yeah," Ryan said. "Lost his leg in an auto accident four years ago. He was up for command of the *Los Angeles* and a drunk driver clipped him. Now he teached engineering at the Academy and does a lot of consulting work with Sea Systems Command—technical analysis, looking at their ship designs. He has a doctorate in engineering from MIT, and he knows how to think unconventionally."

"How about his security clearance?" Greer asked.

"Top secret or better, sir, because of his Crystal City work."

"Objections, Charlie?"

Davenport frowned. Tyler was not part of the intelligence community. "Is this the guy who did the evaluation of the new *Kirov?*"

Yes, sir, now that I think about it," Casimir said. "Him and Saunders over at Sea Systems."

"That was a nice piece of work. It's okay with me."

"When do you want to see him?" Greer asked Ryan.

"Today, if it's all right with you, sir. I have to run over to Annapolis anyway, to get something from the house, and— well, do some quick Christmas shopping."

"Oh? A few dolls?" Davenport asked.

Ryan turned to look the admiral in the eye. "Yes, sir, as a matter of fact. My little girl wants a Skiing Barbie doll and some Jordache doll outfits. Didn't you ever play Santa, Admiral?"

Davenport saw that Ryan wasn't going to back off anymore. He wasn't a subordinate to be browbeaten. Ryan could always walk away. He tried a new tack. "Did they tell you over there that *October* sailed last Friday?"

"Oh?" They hadn't. Ryan was caught off guard. "I thought she wasn't scheduled to sail until this Friday."

"So did we. Her skipper is Marko Ramius. You heard about him?"

"Only secondhand stuff. The Brits say he's pretty good."

"Better than that," Greer noted. "He's about the best sub driver they have, a real charger. We had a considerable file on him when I was at DIA. Who's bird-diggin' him for you, Charlie?"

"Bremerton" was assigned to it. She was out of position doing some ELINT work when Ramius sailed, but she was ordered over. Her skipper's Bud Wilson. Remember his dad?"

Greer laughed out loud. "Red Wilson? Now there was one spirited submarine driver! His boy any good?"

"So they say. Ramius is about the best the Soviets have, but Wilson's got a 688 boat. By the end of the week, we'll be able to start a new book on *Red October*." Davenport stood. "We gotta head back, James." Casimir hurried to get the coats. "I can keep these?"

"I suppose, Charlie. Just don't go hanging them on the wall, even to throw darts at. And I guess you want to get moving, too, Jack?"

"Yes, sir."

Greer lifted his phone. "Nancy, Dr. Ryan will need a car and a driver in fifteen minutes. Right." He set the receiver down and waited for Davenport to leave. "No sense getting you killed out there in the snow. Besides, you'd probably drive on the wrong side of the road after a year in England. Skiing Barbie, Jack?"

"You had all boys, didn't you, sir? Girls are different." Ryan grinned. "You've never met my little Sally."

"Daddy's girl?"

"Yep. God help whoever marries her. Can I leave these photographs with Tyler?"

"I hope you're right about him, son. Yes, he can hold onto them—if and only if he has a good place to keep them."

"Understood, sir."

"When you get back—probably be late, the way the roads are. You're staying at the Marriott?"

"Yes, sir."

Greer thought that over. "I'll probably be working late. Stop by here before you bed down. I may want to go over a few things with you."

"Will do, sir. Thanks for the car." Ryan stood.

"Go buy your dolls, son."

Greer watched him leave. He liked Ryan. The boy was not afraid to speak his mind. Part of that came from having money and being married to more money. It was a sort of independence that had advantages. Ryan could not be bought, bribed, or bullied. He could always go back to writing history books full time. Ryan had made money on his own in four years as a stockbroker, betting his own money on high-risk issues and scoring big before leaving it all behind—because, he said, he hadn't wanted to press his luck. Greer didn't believe that. He thought Jack had been bored—bored with making money. He shook his head. The talent that had enabled him to pick winning stocks Ryan now applied to the CIA. He was rapidly becoming one of Greer's star analysts, and his British connections made him doubly valuable. Ryan had the ability to sort through a pile of data and come out with the three or four facts that meant something. This was too rare a thing at the CIA. The agency still spent too much of its money collecting data, Greer thought, and not enough collating it. Analysts had none of the supposed glamour—a Hollywood-generated illusion—of a secret agent in a foreign land. But Jack knew how to analyze reports from such men and data from technical sources. He knew how to make a decision and was not afraid to say what he thought, whether his bosses liked it or not. This sometimes grated the old admiral, but on the whole he liked having subordinates whom he could respect. The CIA had too many people whose only skill was kissing ass.

The U.S. Naval Academy

The loss of his left leg above the knee had not taken away Oliver Wendell Tyler's roguish good looks or his zest for life. His wife could testify to this. Since leaving the active service four years before, they had added three children to the two they already had and were working on a sixth. Ryan found him sitting at a desk in an empty classroom in Rickover Hall, the U.S. Naval Academy's science and engineering building. He was grading papers.

"How's it goin', Skip?" Ryan leaned against the door frame. His CIA driver was in the hall.

"Hey, Jack! I thought you were in England." Tyler jumped to his foot—his own phrase—and hobbled over to grab Ryan's hand. His prosthetic leg ended in a square, rubber-coated band instead of a pseudo-foot. It flexed at the knee, but not by much. Tyler had been a second-squad All American offensive tackle sixteen years before, and the rest of his body was as hard as the aluminum and fiberglass in his left leg. His handshake could make a gorilla wince. "So, what are you doing here?"

"I had to fly over to get some work done and do a little shopping. How's Jean and your . . . five?"

"Five and two-thirds."

"Again? Jean ought to have you fixed."

"That's what she said, but I've had enough things disconnected." Tyler laughed. "I guess I'm making up for all those monastic years as a nuc. Come on over and grab a chair."

Ryan sat on the corner of the desk and opened his briefcase. He handed Tyler a folder.

"Got some pictures I want you to look at."

"Okay." Tyler flipped it open. "Whose—a Russian! Big bastard. That's the basic *Typhoon* configuration. Lots of modifications, though. Twenty-six missiles instead of twenty. Looks longer. Hull's flattened out some, too. More beam?"

"Two or three meters' worth."

"I heard you were working with the CIA. Can't talk about that, right?"

"Something like that. And you never saw these pictures, Skip. Understood?"

"Right." Tyler's eyes twinkled. "What do you want me not to look at them for?"

Ryan pulled the blowups from the back of the folder. "These doors, bow and stern."

"Uh-huh." Tyler set them down side by side. "Pretty big. They're two meters or so, paired fore and aft. They look symmetrical through the long axis. Not cruise missile tubes, eh?"

"On a boomer? You put something like that on a strategic missile sub?"

"The Russkies are a funny bunch, Jack, and they design things their own way. This is the same bunch that built the *Kirov* class with a nuclear reactor *and* an oil-fired steam plant. Hmm . . . twin screws. The aft doors can't be for a sonar array. They'd foul the screws."

"How 'bout if they trail one screw?"

"They do that with surface ships to conserve fuel, and sometimes with their attack boats. Operating a twin-screw missile boat on one wheel would probably be tricky on this baby. The *Typhoon*'s supposed to have handling problems, and boats that handle funny tend to be sensitive to power settings. You end up jinking around so much that you have trouble holding course. You notice how the doors converge at the stern?"

"No, I didn't."

Tyler looked up. "Damn! I should have realized it right off the bat. It's a propulsion system. You shouldn't have caught me marking papers, Jack. It turns your brain to Jell-O."

"Propulsion system?"

"We looked at this—oh, must have been twenty some years ago—when I was going to school here. We didn't do anything with it, though. It's too inefficient."

"Okay, tell me about it."

"They called it a tunnel drive. You know how out West they have lots of hydroelectric power plants? Mostly dams. The water spills onto wheels that turn generators. Now there's a few new ones that kind of turn that around. They tap into underground rivers, and the water turns impellers, and they turn the generators instead of a modified mill wheel. An impeller is like a propeller, except the water drives it instead of the other way around. There's some minor technical differences, too, but nothing major. Okay so far?

"With this design, you turn that around. You suck water in the bow and your impellers eject it out the stern, and that moves the ship." Tyler paused, frowning. "As I recall you have to have more than one per tunnel. They looked at this back in the early sixties and got to the model stage before dropping it. One of the things they discovered is that one impeller doesn't work as well as several. Some sort of back pressure thing. It was a new principle, something unexpected that cropped up. They ended up using four, I think, and it was supposed to look something like the compressor sets in a jet engine."

"Why did we drop it?" Ryan was taking rapid notes.

"Mostly efficiency. You can only get so much water down the pipes no matter how powerfully your motors are. And the drive system took up a lot of room. They partially beat that with a new kind of electric induction motor, I think, but even then you'd end up with a lot of extraneous machinery inside the hull. Subs don't have that much room to spare, even this monster. The top speed limit was supposed to be about ten knots, and that just wasn't good enough, even though it did virtually eliminate cavitation sounds."

"Cavitation?"

"When you have a propeller turning in the water at high speed, you develop an area of low pressure behind the trailing edge of the blade. This can cause water to vaporize. That creates a bunch of little bubbles. They can't last long under the water pressure, and when they collapse the water rushes forward to pound against the blades. That does three things. First, it makes noise, and us sub drivers hate noise. Second, it can cause vibration, something else we don't like. The old passenger liners, for example, used to flutter several inches at the stern, all from cavitation and slippage. It takes a hell of a lot of force to vibrate a 50,000-ton ship; that kind of force breaks things. Third, it tears up the screws. The big wheels only used to last a few years. That's why back in the old days the blades were bolted onto the hub instead of being cast in one piece. The vibration is mainly a surface ship problem, and the screw degradation was eventually conquered by improved metallurgical technology.

"Now, this tunnel drive system avoids the cavitation problem. You still have cavitation, but the noise from it is mainly lost in the tunnels. That makes good sense. The problem is that you can't generate much speed without making the tunnels too wide to be practical. While one team was working on this, another was working on improved screw designs. Your typical sub screw today is pretty large, so it can turn more slowly for a given speed. The slower the turning speed, the less cavitation you get. The problem is also mitigated by depth. A few hundred feet down, the higher water pressure retards bubble formation."

"Then why don't the Soviets copy our screw designs?"

"Several reasons, probably. You design a screw for a specific hull and engine combination, so copying ours wouldn't automatically work for them. A lot of this work is still empirical, too. There's a lot of trial and error in this. It's a lot harder, say, then designing an airfoil, because the blade cross-section changes radically from one point to another. I suppose another reason is that their metallurgical technology isn't as good as ours—same reason that their jet and rocket engines are less efficient. These new designs place great value on high-strength alloys. It's a narrow specialty, and I only know the generalities."

"Okay, you say that this is a silent propulsion system, and it has a top speed limit of ten knots?" Ryan wanted to be clear on this.

"Ballpark figure. I'd have to do some computer modeling to tighten that up. We probably still have the data laying around at the Taylor Laboratory." Tyler referred to the Sea Systems Command design facility on the north side of the Severn River. "Probably still classified, and I'd have to take it with a big grain of salt."

"How come?"

"All this work was done twenty years ago. They only got up to fifteen-foot models—pretty small for this sort of thing. Remember that they had already stumbled across one new principle, that back-pressure thing. There might have been more out there. I expect they tried some computer models, but even if they did, mathematical modeling techniques back then were dirt-simple. To duplicate this today I'd have to have the old data and programs from Taylor, check it all over, then draft a new program based on this configuration." He tapped the photographs. "Once that was done, I'd need access to a big league mainframe computer to run it."

"But you could do it?"

"Sure. I'd need exact dimensions on this baby, but I've done this before for the bunch over at Crystal City. The hard part's getting the computer time. I need a big machine."

"I can probably arrange access to ours."

Tyler laughed. "Probably not good enough, Jack. This is specialized stuff. I'm talking about a Cray-2, one of the biggies. To do this you have to mathematically simulate the behavior of millions of little parcels of water, the water flow over—and through, in this case—the whole hull. Same sort of thing NASA has to do with the Space Shuttle. The actual work is easy enough—it's the *scale* that's tough. They're simple calculations, but you have to make millions of them per second. That means a big Cray, and there's only a few of them around. NASA has one in Houston, I think. The navy has a few in Norfolk for ASW work—you can forget about those. The air force has one in the Pentagon, I think, and all the rest are in California."

"But you could do it?"

"Sure."

"Okay, get to work on it, Skip, and I'll see if we can get you the computer time. How long?"

"Depending on how good the stuff at Taylor is, maybe a week. Maybe less."

"How much do you want for it?"

"Aw, come on, Jack!" Tyler waved him off.

"Skip, it's Monday. You get us this data by Friday and there's twenty thousand dollars in it. You're worth it, and we want this data. Agreed?"

"Sold." They shook hands. "Can I keep the pictures?"

"I can leave them if you have a secure place to keep them. Nobody gets to see them, Skip. Nobody."

"There's a nice safe in the superintendent's office."

"Fine, but he doesn't see them." The superintendent was a former submariner.

"He won't like it," Tyler said. "But okay."

"Have him call Admiral Greer if he objects. This number." Ryan handed him a card. "You can reach me here if you need me. If I'm not in, ask for the admiral."

"Just how important is this?"

"Important enough. You're the first guy who's come up with a sensible explanation for these hatches. That's why I came here. If you can model this for us, it'll be damned useful. Skip, one more time: This is highly sensitive. If you let anybody see these, it's my ass."

"Aye aye, Jack. Well, you've laid a deadline on me, I better get down to it. See you." After shaking hands, Tyler took out a lined pad and started listing the things he had to do. Ryan left the building with his driver. He remembered a Toys-R-Us right up Route 2 from Annapolis, and he wanted to get that doll for Sally.

CIA Headquarters

Ryan was back at the CIA by eight that evening. It was a quick trip past the security guards to Greer's office.

"Well, did you get your Surfing Barbie?" Greer looked up.

"Skiing Barbie," Ryan corrected. "Yes, sir. Come on, didn't you ever play Santa?"

"They grew up too fast, Jack. Even my grandchildren are all past that stage." He turned to get some coffee. Ryan wondered if he ever slept. "We have something more on *Red October*. The Russians seem to have a major ASW exercise running in the northeast Barents Sea. Half a dozen ASW search aircraft, a bunch of frigates, and an *Alfa*-class attack boat, all running around in circles."

"Probably an acquisition exercise. Skip Tyler says those doors are for a new drive system."

"Indeed." Greer sat back. "Tell me about it."

Ryan took out his notes and summarized his education in submarine technology. "Skip says he can generate a computer simulation of its effectiveness," he concluded.

Greer's eyebrows went up. "How soon?"

"End of week, maybe. I told him if he had it done by Friday we'd pay him for it. Twenty thousand sound reasonable?"

"Will it mean anything?"

"If he gets the background data he needs, it ought to, sir. Skip's a very sharp cookie. I mean, they don't give doctorates away at MIT, and he was in the top five of his Academy class."

"Worth twenty thousand dollars of our money?" Greer was notoriously tight with a buck.

Ryan knew how to answer this. "Sir, if we followed normal procedure on this, we'd contract one of the Beltway Bandits—," Ryan referred to the consulting firms that dotted the beltway around Washington, D.C., "—they'd charge us five or ten times as much, and we'd be lucky to have the data by Easter. This way we might just have it while the boat's still at sea. If worse comes to worst, sir, I'll foot the bill. I figured you'd want this data fast, and it's right up his alley."

"You're right." It wasn't the first time Ryan had short-circuited normal procedure. The other times had worked out fairly well. Greer was a man who looked for results. "Okay, the Soviets have a new missile boat with a silent drive system. What does it all mean?"

"Nothing good. We depend on our ability to track their boomers with our attack boats. Hell, that's why they agreed a few years back to our proposal about keeping them five hundred miles from each other's coasts, and why they keep their missile subs in port most of the time. This could change the game a bit. By the way, *October*'s hull, I haven't seen what it's made of."

"Steel. She's too big for a titanium hull, at least for what it would cost. You know what they have to spend on their *Alfa*s."

"Too much for what they got. You spend that much money for a superstrong hull, then put a noisy power plant in it. Dumb."

"Maybe. I wouldn't mind having that speed, though. Anyway, if this silent drive system really works, they might be able to creep up onto the continental shelf."

"Depressed-trajectory shot," Ryan said. This was one of the nastier nuclear war scenarios in which a sea-based missile was fired within a few hundred miles of its target. Washington is a bare hundred air miles from the Atlantic Ocean. Though a missile on a low, fast flight path loses much of its accuracy, a few of them can be launched to explode over Washington in less than a few minutes' time, too little for a president to react. If the Soviets were able to kill the president that quickly, the resulting disruption of the chain of command would give them ample time to take out the land-based missiles—there would be no one with authority to fire. This scenario is a grand-strategic version of a simple mugging, Ryan thought. A mugger doesn't attack his victim's arms—he goes for the head. "You think *October* was built with that in mind?"

"I'm sure the thought occurred to them," Greer observed. "It would have occurred to us. Well, we have *Bremerton* up there to keep an eye on her, and if this data turns out to be useful we'll see if we can come up with an answer. How are you feeling?"

"I've been on the go since five-thirty London time. Long day, sir."

"I expect so. Okay, we'll go over the Afghanistan business tomorrow morning. Get some sleep, son."

"Aye, aye, sir." Ryan got his coat. "Good night."

It was a fifteen-minute drive to the Marriott. Ryan made the mistake of turning the TV on to the beginning of Monday Night Football. Cincinnati was playing San Francisco, the two best quarterbacks in the league pitted against one another. Football was something he missed living in England, and he managed to stay awake nearly three hours before fading out with the television on.

SOSUS Control

Except for the fact that everyone was in uniform, a visitor might easily have mistaken the room for a NASA control center. There were six wide rows of consoles, each with its own TV screen and typewriter keyboard supplemented by lighted plastic buttons, dials, headphone jacks, and analog and digital controls. Senior Chief Oceanographic Technician Deke Franklin was seated at console fifteen.

The room was SOSUS (sonar surveillance system) Atlantic Control. It was in a fairly nondescript building, uninspired government layer cake, with windowless concrete walls, a large air-conditioning system on a flat roof, and an acronym-coded blue sign on a well-tended but now yellowed lawn. There were armed marines inconspicuously on guard inside the three entrances. In the basement were a pair of Cray-2 supercomputers tended by twenty acolytes, and behind the building was a trio of satellite ground stations, all up- and down-links. The men at the consoles and the computers were linked electronically by satellite and landline to the SOSUS system.

Throughout the oceans of the world, and especially astride the passages that Soviet submarines had to cross to reach the open sea, the United States and other NATO countries had deployed gangs of highly sensitive sonar receptors. The hundreds of SOSUS sensors received and forwarded an unimaginably vast amount of information, and to help the system operators classify and analyze it a whole new family of computers had to be designed, the supercomputers. SOSUS served its purpose admirably well. Very little could cross a barrier without being detected. Even the ultraquiet American and British attack submarines were generally picked up. The sensors, lying on the bottom of the sea, were periodically updated; many now had their own signal processors to presort the data they forwarded, lightening the load on the central computers and enabling more rapid and accurate classification of targets.

Chief Franklin's console received data from a string of sensors planted off the coast of Iceland. He was responsible for an area forty nautical miles across, and his sector overlapped the ones east and west so that, theoretically, three operators were constantly monitoring any segment of the barrier. If he got a contact, he would first notify his brother operators, then type a contact report into his computer terminal, which would in turn be displayed on the master control board in the control room at the back of the floor. The senior duty officer had the frequently exercised authority to prosecute a contact with a wide range of assets, from surface ships to antisubmarine aircraft. Two world wars had taught American and British officers the necessity of keeping their sea lines of communication— SLOCs—open.

Although this quiet, tomblike facility had never been shown to the public, and though it had none of the drama associated with military life, the men on duty here were among the most important in the service of their country. In a war, without them, whole nations might starve.

Franklin was leaning back in his swivel chair, puffing contemplatively on an old briar pipe. Around him the room was dead quiet. Even had it not been, his five-hundred-dollar headphones would have effectively sealed him off from the outside world. A twenty-six year chief, Franklin had served his entire career on destroyers and frigates. To him, submarines and submariners were the enemy, regardless of what flag they might fly or what uniform they might wear.

An eyebrow went up, and his nearly bald head cocked to one side. The pulls on the pipe grew irregular. His right hand reached forward to the control panel and switched off the signal processors so that he could get the sound without computerized interference. But it was no good. There was too much background noise. He switched the filters back on. Next he tried some changes in his azimuth controls. The SOSUS sensors were designed to give bearing checks through the selective use of individual receptors, which he could manipulate electronically, first getting one bearing, then using a neighboring gang to triangulate for a fix. The contract was very faint, but not too far from the line, he judged. Franklin queried his computer terminal. The USS *Dallas* was up there. *Gotcha!* he said with a thin smile. Another noise came through, a low-frequency rumble that only lasted a few seconds before fading out. Not all that quiet, though. Why hadn't he heard it before switching the reception azimuth? He set his pipe down and began making adjustments on his control board.

"Chief?" A voice came over his headphones. It was the senior duty officer.

"Yes, Commander?"

"Can you come back to control? I have something I want you to hear."

"On the way, sir." Franklin rose quietly. Commander Quentin was a former destroyer skipper on a limited duty after a winning battle with cancer. Almost a winning battle, Franklin corrected himself. Chemotherapy had killed the cancer—at the cost of nearly all his hair, and turning his skin into a sort of transparent parchment. Too bad, he thought, Quentin was a pretty good man.

The control room was elevated a few feet from the rest of the floor so that its occupants could see over the whole crew of duty operators and the main tactical display on the far wall. It was separated from the floor by glass, which allowed them to speak to one another without disturbing the operators. Franklin found Quentin at his command station, where he could tap into any console on the floor.

"Howdy, Commander." Franklin noted that the officer was gaining some weight back. It was about time. "What do you have for me, sir?"

"On the Barents Sea net." Quentin handed him a pair of phones. Franklin listened for several minutes, but he didn't sit down. Like many people he had a gut suspicion that cancer was contagious.

"Damned if they ain't pretty busy up there. I read a pair of *Alfa*s, a *Charlie*, a *Tango*, and a few surface ships. What gives, sir?"

"There's a *Delta* there, too, but she just surfaced and killed her engines."

"Surfaced, Skipper?"

"Yep. They were lashing her pretty hard with active sonar, then a 'can queried her on a gertrude."

"Uh-huh. Acquisition game, and the sub lost."

"Maybe. Quentin rubbed his eyes. The man looked tired. He was pushing himself too hard, and his stamina wasn't half what it should have been. "But the *Alfa*s are still pinging, and now they're headed west, as you heard."

"Oh." Franklin pondered that for a moment. "They're looking for another boat, then. The *Typhoon* that was supposed to have sailed the other day, maybe?"

"That's what I thought—except she headed west, and the exercise area is northeast of the fjord. We lost her the other day on SOSUS. *Bremerton*'s up sniffing around for her now."

"Cagey skipper," Franklin decided. "Cut his plant all the way back and just drifting."

"Yeah," Quentin agreed. "I want you to move down to the North Cape barrier supervisory board and see if you can find her, Chief. She'll still have her reactor working, and she'll be making some noise. The operators we have on that sector are a little young. I'll take one and switch him to your board for a while."

"Right, Skipper," Franklin nodded. That part of the team was still green, used to working on ships. SOSUS required more finesse. Quentin didn't have to say that he expected Franklin to check in on the whole North Cape team's boards and maybe drop a few small lessons as he listened in on their channels.

"Did you pick up on *Dallas?*"

"Yes, sir. Real faint, but I think I got her crossing my sector, headed northwest for Toll Booth. If we get an Orion down there, we might just get her locked in. Can we rattle their cage a little?"

Quentin chuckled. He didn't much care for submarines either. "No, NIFTY DOLPHIN is over. Chief. We'll just log it and let the skipper know when he comes back home. Nice work, though. You know her reputation. We're not supposed to hear her at all."

"That'll be the day!" Franklin snorted.

"Let me know what you find, Deke."

"Aye aye, Skipper. You take care of yourself, hear?"

THE FIFTH DAY

TUESDAY, 7 DECEMBER

Moscow

It was not the grandest office in the Kremlin, but it suited his needs. Admiral Yuri Ilych Padorin showed up for work at his customary seven o'clock after the drive from his six-room apartment in the Kutuzovskiy Prospekt. The large office windows overlooked the Kremlin walls; except for those he would have had a view of the Mosow River, now frozen solid. Padorin did not miss the view, though he had won his spurs commanding river gunboats forty years before, running supplies across the Volga into Stalingrad. Padorin was now the chief political officer of the Soviet Navy. His job was men, not ships.

On the way in he nodded curtly to his secretary, a man of forty. The yeoman leaped to his feet and allowed his admiral into the inner office to help him off with his greatcoat. Padorin's navy-blue jacket was ablaze with ribbons and the gold star medal of the most coveted award in the Soviet Military, Hero of the Soviet Union. He had won that in combat as a freckled boy of twenty, shuttling back and forth on the Volga. Those were good days, he told himself, dodging bombs from the

German Stukas and the more random artillery fire with which the Fascists had tried to interdict his squadron . . . Like most men he was unable to remember the stark terror of combat.

It was a Tuesday morning, and Padorin had a pile of mail waiting on his desk. His yeoman got him a pot of tea and a cup—the usual Russian glass cup set in a metal holder, sterling silver in this case. Padorin had worked long and hard for the perqs that came with this office. He settled in his chair and read first through the intelligence dispatches, information copies of data sent each morning and evening to the operational commands of the Soviet Navy. A political officer had to keep current, to know what the imperialists were up to so that he could brief his men on the threat.

Next came the official mail from within the People's Commissariat of the Navy and the Ministry of Defense. He had access to all of the correspondence from the former, while that from the latter had been carefully vetted since the Soviet armed services share as little information as possible. There wasn't too much mail from either place today. The usual Monday afternoon meeting had covered most of what had to be done that week, and nearly everything Padorin was concerned with was now in the hands of his staff for disposition. He poured a second cup of tea and opened a new pack of unfiltered cigarettes, a habit he'd been unable to break despite a mild heart attack three years earlier. He checked his desk calendar— good, no appointments until ten.

Near the bottom of the pile was an official-looking envelope from the Northern Fleet. The code number at the upper left corner showed that it came from the *Red October*. Hadn't he just read something about that?

Padorin rechecked his ops dispatches. So, Ramius hadn't turned up in his exercise area? He shrugged. Missile submarines were supposed to be elusive, and it would not have surprised the old admiral at all if Ramius were twisting a few tails. The son of Aleksandr Ramius was a prima donna who had the troubling habit of seeming to build his own personality cult: he kept some of the men he trained and discarded others. Padorin reflected that those rejected for line service had made excellent *zampoliti*, and appeared to have more line knowledge than was the norm. Even so, Ramius was a captain who needed watching. Sometimes Padorin suspected that he was too much a sailor and not enough a Communist. On the other hand, his father had been a model Party member and a hero of the Great Patriotic War. Certainly he had been well thought of, Lithuanian or not. And the son? Years of letter-perfect performance, as many years of stalwart Party membership. He was known for his spirited participation at meetings and occasionally brilliant essays. The people in the naval branch of the GRU, the Soviet military intelligence agency, reported that the imperialists regarded him as a dangerous and skilled enemy. Good, Padorin thought, the bastards ought to fear our men. He turned his attention back to the envelope.

Red October, now there was a fitting name for a Soviet warship! Named not only for the revolution that had forever changed the history of the world but also for the Red October Tractor Plant. Many was the dawn when Padorin had looked west to Stalingrad to see if the factory still stood, a symbol of the Soviet fighting men struggling against the Hitlerite bandits. The envelope was marked Confidential, and his yeomen had not opened it as he had the other routine mail. The admiral took his letter opener from the desk drawer. It was a sentimental object, having been his service knife years before. When his first gunboat had been sunk under him, one hot August night in 1942, he had swum to shore and been pounced on by a German infantryman who hadn't expected resistance from a half-drowned sailor. Padorin had surprised him, sinking the knife in his chest and braking off half the blade as he stole his enemy's life. Later a machinist had trimmed the blade down. It was no longer a proper knife, but Padorin wasn't about to throw this sort of souvenir away.

"Comrade Admiral," the letter began—but the type had been scratched out and replaced with a hand-written "Uncle Yuri." Ramius had jokingly called him that years back when Padorin was chief political officer of the Northern Fleet. "Thank you for your confidence, and for the opportunity you have given me with command of this magnificent ship!" Ramius ought to be grateful, Padorin thought. Performance or not, you don't give this sort of command to—

What? Padorin stopped reading and started over. He forgot the cigarette smoldering in his ashtray as he reached the bottom

of the first page. A joke. Ramius was known for his jokes—
but he'd pay for this one. This was going too fucking far! He
turned the page.

"This is no joke, Uncle Yuri—Marko."

Padorin stopped and looked out the window. The Kremlin
wall at this point was a beehive of niches for the ashes of the
Party faithful. He couldn't have read the letter correctly. He
started to read it again. His hands began to shake.

He had a direct line to Admiral Gorshkov, with no yeomen
or secretaries to bar the way.

"Comrade Admiral, this is Padorin."

"Good morning, Yuri," Gorshkov said pleasantly.

"I must see you immediately. I have a situation here."

"What sort of situation?" Gorshkov asked warily.

"We must discuss it in person. I am coming over now."
There was no way he'd discuss this over the phone; he knew
it was tapped.

The USS Dallas

Sonarman Second Class Ronald Jones, his division officer noted,
was in his usual trance. The young college dropout was hunched
over his instrument table, body limp, eyes closed, face locked
into the same neutral expression he wore when listening to one
of the many Bach tapes on his expensive personal cassette player.
Jones was the sort who categorized his tapes by their flaws, a
ragged piano tempo, a botched flute, a wavering French horn.
He listened to sea sounds with the same discriminating intensity. In all the navies of the world, submariners were regarded
as a curious breed, and submariners themselves looked upon
sonar operators as odd. Their eccentricities, however, were
among the most tolerated in the military service. The executive
officer liked to tell a story about a sonar chief he'd served with
for two years, a man who had patrolled the same areas in missile submarines for virtually his whole career. He became so
familiar with the humpback whales that summered in the area
that he took to calling them by name. On retiring, he went to
work for the Woods Hole Oceanographic Institute, where his
talent was regarded not so much with amusement as awe.

Three years earlier, Jones had been asked to leave the
California Institute of Technology in the middle of his junior

year. He had pulled one of the ingenious pranks for which Cal Tech students were justly famous, only it hadn't worked. Now he was serving his time in the navy to finance his return. It was his announced intention to get a doctorate in cybernetics and signal processing. In return for an early out, after receiving his degree he would go to work for the Naval Research Laboratory. Lieutenant Thompson believed it. On joined the *Dallas* six months earlier, he had read the files of all his men. Jones' IQ was 158, the highest on the boat by a fair margin. He had a placid face and sad brown eyes that women found irresistible. On the beach Jones had enough action to wear down a squad of marines. It didn't make much sense to the lieutenant. He'd been the football hero at Annapolis. Jones was a skinny kid who listened to Bach. It didn't figure.

The USS *Dallas*, a 688-class attack submarine, was forty miles from the coast of Iceland, approaching her patrol station, code-named Toll Booth. She was two days late getting there. A week earlier, she had participated in the NATO war game NIFTY DOLPHIN, which had been postponed several days because the worst North Atlantic weather in twenty years had delayed other ships detailed to it. In that exercise the *Dallas*, teamed with HMS *Swiftsure*, had used the foul weather to penetrate and ravage the simulated enemy formation. It was yet another four-oh performance for the *Dallas* and her skipper, Commander Bart Mancuso, one of the youngest submarine commanders in the U.S. Navy. The mission had been followed by a courtesy call at the *Swiftsure*'s Royal Navy base in Scotland, and the American sailors were still shaking off hangovers from the celebration . . . Now they had a different mission, a new development in the Atlantic submarine game. For three weeks, the *Dallas* was to report on traffic in and out of Red Route One.

Over the past fourteen months, newer Soviet submarines had been using a strange, effective tactic for shedding their American and British shadowers. Southwest of Iceland the Russian boats would race down the Reykjanes Ridge, a finger of underwater highlands pointing to the deep Atlantic basin. Spaced at intervals from five miles to half a mile, these mountains with their knife-edged ridges of brittle igneous rock rivaled the Alps in size. Their peaks were about a thousand feet beneath the stormy surface of the North Atlantic. Before the late sixties submarines could barely approach the peaks, much less probe their myriad valleys. Throughout the seventies Soviet naval survey vessels had been seen patrolling the ridge—in all seasons, in all weather, quartering and requartering the area in thousands of cruises. Then, fourteen months before the *Dallas'* present patrol, the USS *Los Angeles* had been tracking a Soviet *Victor II*–class attack submarine. The *Victor* had skirted the Icelandic coast and gone deep as she approached the ridge. The *Los Angeles* had followed. The *Victor* proceeded at eight knots until she passed between the first pair of seamounts, informally known as Thor's Twins. All at once she went to full speed and moved southwest. The skipper of the *Los Angeles* made a determined effort to track the *Victor* and came away from it badly shaken. Although the 688-class submarines were faster than the older *Victors,* the Russian submarine had simply not slowed down—for fifteen hours, it was later determined.

At first it had not been all that dangerous. Submarines had highly accurate inertial navigation systems able to fix their positions to within a few hundred yards from one second to another. But the *Victor* was skirting cliffs as though her skipper could see them, like a fighter dodging down a canyon to avoid surface-to-air missile fire. The *Los Angeles* could not keep track of the cliffs. At any speed over twenty knots both her passive and active sonar, including the echofathometer, became almost useless. The *Los Angeles* thus found herself navigating completely blind. It was, the skipper later reported, like driving a car with the windows painted over, steering with a map and a stopwatch. This was theoretically possible, but the captain quickly realized that the inertial navigation system had a built-in error factor of several hundred yards; this was aggravated by gravitational disturbances, which affected the "local vertical," which in turn affected the inertial fix. Worst of all, his charts were made for surface ships. Objects below a few hundred feet had been known to be misplaced by miles—something that mattered to no one until recently. The interval between mountains had quickly become less than his cumulative navigational error—sooner or later his submarine would drive into a mountainside at over thirty knots. The captain backed off. The *Victor* got away.

Initially it was theorized that the Soviets had somehow staked out one particular route, that their submarines were able to follow it at high speed. Russian skippers were known to pull some crazy stunts, and perhaps they were trusting to a combination of inertial systems, magnetic and gyro compasses attuned to a specific track. This theory had never developed much of a following, and in a few weeks it was known for certain that the Soviet submarines speeding through the ridge were following a multiplicity of tracks. The only thing American and British subs could do was stop periodically to get a sonar fix of their positions, then race to catch up. But the Soviet subs never slowed, and the 688s and *Trafalgar*s kept falling behind.

The *Dallas* was on Toll Booth station to monitor passing Russian subs, to watch the entrance to the passage the U.S. Navy was now calling Red Route One, and to listen for any external evidence of a new gadget that might enable the Soviets to run the ridge so boldly. Until the Americans could copy it, there were three unsavory alternatives: they could continue losing contact with the Russians; they could station valuable attack subs at the known exits from the route; or they could set up a whole new SOSUS line.

Jones' trance lasted ten minutes—longer than usual. He ordinarily had a contact figured out in far less time. The sailor leaned back and lit a cigarette.

"Got something, Mr. Thompson."

"What is it?" Thompson leaned against the bulkhead.

"I don't know." Jones picked up a spare set of phones and handed them to his officer. "Listen up, sir."

Thompson himself was a masters candidate in electrical engineering, an expert in sonar system design. His eyes screwed shut as he concentrated on the sound. It was a very faint low-frequency rumble—or swish. He couldn't decide. He listened for several minutes before setting the headphones down, then shook his head.

"I got it a half hour ago on the lateral array," Jones said. He referred to a subsystem of the BQQ-5 multifunction submarine sonar. Its main component was an eighteen-foot-diameter dome located in the bow. The dome was used for both active and passive operations. A new part of the system was a gang of passive sensors which extended two hundred feet down both sides of the hull. This was a mechanical analog to the sensory organs on the body of a shark. "Lost it, got it back, lost it, got it back," Jones went on. "It's now screw sounds, not whales or fish. More like water going through a pipe, except for that funny rumble that comes and goes. Anyway, the bearing is about two-five-zero. That puts it between us and Iceland, so it can't be too far away."

"Let's see what it looks like. Maybe that'll tell us something."

Jones took a double-plugged wire from a hook. One plug went into a socket on his sonar panel, the other into the jack on a nearby oscilloscope. The two men spent several minutes working with the sonar controls to isolate the signal. They ended up with an irregular sine wave which they were only able to hold a few seconds at a time.

"Irregular," Thompson said.

"Yeah, it's funny. It sounds regular, but it doesn't look regular. Know what I mean, Mr. Thompson?"

"No, you've got better ears."

"That's cause I listen to better music, sir. That rock stuff'll kill your ears."

Thompson knew he was right, but an Annapolis graduate doesn't need to hear that from an enlisted man. His vintage Janis Joplin tapes were his own business. "Next step."

"Yessir." Jones took the plug from the oscilloscope and moved it into a panel to the left of the sonar board, next to a computer terminal.

During her last overhaul, the *Dallas* had received a very special toy to go along with her BQQ-5 sonar system. Called the BC-10, it was the most powerful computer yet installed aboard a submarine. Though only about the size of a business desk, it cost over five million dollars and ran at eighty million operations per second. It used newly developed sixty-four-bit chips and made use of the latest processing architecture. Its bubble memory could easily accommodate the computing needs of a whole squadron of submarines. In five years every attack sub in the fleet would have one. Its purpose, much like that of the far larger SOSUS system, was to process and analyze sonar signals; the BC-10 stripped away ambient noise and other naturally produced sea sounds to classify and identify man-made noise. It could identify ships by name from their individual acoustical signatures, much as one could identify the finger or voice prints of a human.

As important as the computer was its programming software. Four years before, a PhD candidate in geophysics who was working at Cal Tech's geophysical laboratory had completed a program of six hundred thousand steps designed to predict earthquakes. The problem the program addressed was one of signal versus noise. It overcame the difficulty seismologists and genuinely unusual signals that foretell a seismic event.

The first Defense Department use of the program was in the Air Force Technical Applications Command (AFTAC), which found it entirely satisfactory for its mission of monitoring nuclear events throughout the world in accordance with arms control treaties. The Navy Research Laboratory also redrafted it for its own purposes. Though inadequate for seismic predictions, it worked very well indeed in analyzing sonar signals. The program was known in the navy as the signal algorythmic processing system (SAPS).

"SAPS SIGNAL INPUT," Jones typed into the video display terminal (VDT).

"READY," the BC-10 responded at once.

"RUN."

"WORKING."

For all the fantastic speed of the BC-10, the six hundred thousand steps of the program, punctuated by numerous GOTO loops, took time to run as the machine eliminated natural sounds with its random profile criteria and then locked into the anomalous signal. It took twenty seconds, an eternity in computer time. The answer came up on the VDT. Jones pressed a key to generate a copy on the adjacent matrix printer.

"Hmph." Jones tore off the page. "'ANOMALOUS SIGNAL EVALUATED AS MAGMA DISPLACEMENT.' That's SAPS' way of saying take two aspirin and call me at end of the watch."

Thompson chuckled. For all the ballyhoo that had accompanied the new system, it was not all that popular in the fleet. "Remember what the papers said when we were in England? Something about seismic activity around Iceland, like when that island poked up back in the sixties."

Jones lit another cigarette. He knew the student who had originally drafted this abortion they called SAPS. One problem

was that it had a nasty habit of analyzing the wrong signal—
and you couldn't tell it was wrong from the results. Besides,
since it had been originally designed to look for seismic events,
Jones suspected it of a tendency to interpret anomalies as seismic events. He didn't like the built-in bias, which he felt the
research laboratory had not entirely removed. It was one thing
to use computers as a tool, quite another to let them do your
thinking for you. Besides, they were always discovering new
sea sounds that nobody had ever heard before, much less classified.

"Sir, the frequency is all wrong for one thing—nowhere
near low enough. How 'bout I try an' track in on this signal
with the R-15?" Jones referred to the towed array of passive
sensors the *Dallas* was trailing behind her at low speed.

Commander Mancuso came in just then, the usual mug of
coffee in his hand. If there was one frightening thing about the
captain, Thompson thought, it was his talent for showing up
when something was going on. Did he have the whole boat
wired?

"Just wandering by," he said casually. "What's happening
this fine day?" The captain leaned against the bulkhead. He
was a small man, only five eight, who had fought a battle
against his waistline all his life and was now losing because
of the good food and lack of exercise on a submarine. His dark
eyes were surrounded by laugh lines that were always deeper
when he was playing a trick on another ship.

Was it day, Thompson wondered? The six-hour one-in-three
rotating watch cycle made for a convenient work schedule, but
after a few changes you had to press the button on your watch
to figure out what day it was, else you couldn't make the proper
entry in the log.

"Skipper, Jones picked up a funny signal on the lateral. The
computer says it's magma displacement."

"And Jonesy doesn't agree with that." Mancuso didn't have
to make it a question.

"No, sir, Captain, I don't. I don't know what it is, but for
sure it ain't that."

"You against the machine again?"

"Skipper, SAPS works pretty well most of the time, but
sometimes it's a real *kludge*." Jones' epithet was the most

perjorative curse of electronics people. "For one thing the frequency is all wrong."

"Okay, what do you think?"

"I don't know, Captain. It isn't screw sounds, and it isn't any naturally produced sound that I've heard. Beyond that . . ." Jones was struck by the informality of the discussion with his commanding officer, even after three years on nuclear subs. The crew of the *Dallas* was like one big family, albeit one of the old frontier families, since everybody worked pretty damned hard. The captain was the father. The executive officer, everyone would readily agree, was the mother. The officers were the older kids, and the enlisted men were the younger kids. The important thing was, if you had something to say, the captain would listen to you. To Jones, this counted for a lot.

Mancuso nodded thoughtfully. "Well, keep at it. No sense letting all this expensive gear go to waste."

Jones grinned. Once he had told the captain in precise detail how he could convert this equipment into the world's finest stereo rig. Mancuso had pointed out that it would not be a major feat, since the sonar gear in this room alone cost over twenty million dollars.

"Christ!" The junior technician bolted upright in his chair. "Somebody just stomped on the gas."

Jones was the sonar watch supervisor. The other two watch-standers noted the new signal, and Jones switched his phones to the towed array jack while the two officers kept out of the way. He took a scratch pad and noted the time before working on his individual controls. The BQR-15 was the most sensitive sonar rig on the boat, but its sensitivity was not needed for this contact.

"Damn," Jones muttered quietly.

"*Charlie,*" said the junior technician.

Jones shook his head. "*Victor. Victor* class for sure. Doing turns for thirty knots—big burst of cavitation noise, he's digging big holes in the water, and he doesn't care who knows it. Bearing zero-five-zero. Skipper, we got good water around us, and the signal is real faint. He's not close." It was the closest thing to a range estimate Jones could come up with. Not close meant anything over ten miles. He went back to working his controls. "I think we know this guy. This is the one with a bent blade on his screw, sounds like he's got a chain wrapped around it."

"Put it on speaker," Mancuso told Thompson. He didn't want to disturb the operators. The lieutenant was already keying the signal into the BC-10.

The bulkhead-mounted speaker would have commanded a four-figure price in any stereo shop for its clarity and dynamic perfection; like everything else on the 688-class sub, it was the very best that money could buy. As Jones worked on the sound controls they heard the whining chirp of propeller cavitation, the thin screech associated with a bent propeller blade, and the deeper rumble of a _Victor_'s reactor plant at full power. The next thing Mancuso heard was the printer.

"_Victor I_–class, number six," Thompson announced.

"Right," Jones nodded. "_Vic_-six, bearing still zero-five-zero." He plugged the mouthpiece into his headphones. "Conn, sonar, we have a contact. A _Victor_ class, bearing zero-five-zero, estimated target speed thirty knots."

Mancuso leaned out into the passageway to address Lieutenant Pat Mannion, office of the deck. "Pat, man the fire-control tracking party."

"Aye, Cap'n."

"Wait a minute!" Jones' hand went up. "Got another one!" He twiddled some knobs. "This one's a _Charlie_ class. Damned if he ain't digging holes, too. More easterly, bearing zero-seven-three, doing turns for about twenty-eight knots. We know this guy, too. Yeah, _Charlie II_, number eleven." Jones slipped a phone off one ear and looked at Mancuso. "Skipper, the Russkies have sub races scheduled for today?"

"Not that they told me about. Of course, we don't get the sports page out here," Mancuso chuckled, swirling the coffee around in his cup and hiding his real thoughts. What the hell was going on? "I suppose I'll go forward and take a look at this. Good work, guys."

He went a few steps forward into the attack center. The normal steaming watch was set. Mannion had the conn, with a junior officer of the deck and seven enlisted men. A first-class firecontrolman was entering data from the target motion analyzer into the Mark 117 fire control computer. Another officer was entering control to take charge of the tracking exercise. There was nothing unusual about this. The whole watch went about its work alertly but with the relaxed demeanor that came with years of training and experience. While the other armed services routinely had their components run exercises against allies or themselves in emulation of Eastern Bloc tactics, the navy had its attack submarines play their games against the real thing—and constantly. Submariners typically operated on what was effectively an at-war footing.

"So we have company," Mannion observed.

"Not that close," Lieutenant Charles Goodman noted. "These bearings haven't changed a whisker."

"Conn, sonar." It was Jones' voice. Mancuso took it.

"Conn, aye. What is it, Jonesy?"

"We got another one, sir. *Alfa 3*, bearing zero-five-five. Running flat out. Sounds like an earthquake, but faint, sir."

"*Alfa 3?* Our old friend, the *Politovskiy*. Haven't run across her in a while. Anything else you can tell me?"

"A guess, sir. The sound on this one warbled, then settled down, like she was making a turn. I think she's heading this way—that's a little shaky. And we have some more noise to the northeast. Too confused to make any sense of just now. We're working on it."

"Okay, nice work, Jonesy. Keep at it."

"Sure thing, Captain."

Mancuso smiled as he set the phone down, looking over at Mannion. "You know, Pat, sometimes I wonder if Jonesy isn't part witch."

Mannion looked at the paper tracks that Goodman was drawing to back up the computerized targeting process. "He's pretty good. Problem is, he thinks we work for him."

"Right now we are working for him." Jones was their eyes and ears, and Mancuso was damned glad to have him.

"Chuck?" Mancuso asked Lieutenant Goodman.

"Bearing still constant on all three contacts, sir." Which probably meant they were heading for the *Dallas*. It also meant that they could not develop the range data necessary for a fire control solution. Not that anyone wanted to shoot, but this was the point of the exercise.

"Pat, let's get some sea room. Move us about ten miles east," Mancuso ordered casually. There were two reasons for this. First, it would establish a base line from which to compute probable target range. Second, the deeper water would make for better acoustical conditions, opening up to them the distant sonar convergence zone. The captain studied the chart as his navigator gave the necessary orders, evaluating the tactical situation.

Bartolomeo Mancuso was the son of a barber who closed his shop in Cicero, Illinois, every fall to hunt deer on Michigan's Upper Peninsula. Bart had accompanied his father on these hunts, shot his first deer at the age of twelve and every year thereafter until entering the Naval Academy. He had never bothered about that. Since becoming an officer on nuclear submarines he had learned a much more diverting game. Now he hunted people.

Two hours later an alarm bell went off on the ELF radio in the sub's communications room. Like all nuclear submarines, the *Dallas* was trailing a lengthy wire antenna attuned to the extremely low-frequency transmitter in the central United States. The channel had a frustratingly narrow data band width. Unlike a TV channel, which transmitted thousands of bits of data per frame, thirty frames per second, the ELF radio passed on data slowly, about one character every thirty seconds. The duty radioman waited patiently while the information was recorded on tape. When the message was finished, he ran the tape at high speed and transcribed the message, handing it to the communications officer who was waiting with his code book.

The signal was actually not a code but a "one-time-pad" cipher. A book, published every six months and distributed to every nuclear submarine, was filled with randomly generated transpositions for each letter of the signal. Each scrambled three-letter group in this book corresponded to a preselected word or phrase in another book. Deciphering the message by hand took under three minutes, and when that was completed it was carried to the captain in the attack center.

NHG	JPR	YTR
FROM COMSUBLANT	TO LANTSUBS AT SEA	STANDBY
OPY　　TBD	QEQ	GER
POSSIBLE　MAJOR	REDEPLOYMENT ORDER	LARGE-SCALE
MAL	ASF	NME
UNEXPECTED	REDFLEET OPERATION	IN PROGRESS
TYQ	ORV	
NATURE UNKNOWN	NEXT ELF MESSAGE	
HWZ		
COMMUNICATE SSIX		

COMSUBLANT—commander of the Submarine Force in the Atlantic—was Mancuso's big boss, Vice Admiral Vincent Gallery. The old man was evidently contemplating a reshuffling of his entire force, no minor affair. The next wake-up signal, AAA—encrypted, of course—would alert them to go to periscope-antenna depth to get more detailed instructions from SSIX, the submarine satellite information exchange, a geosynchronous communications satellite used exclusively by submarines.

The tactical situation was becoming clearer, though its strategic implications were beyond his ability to judge. The ten-mile move eastward had given them adequate range information for their initial three contacts and another *Alfa* which had turned up a few minutes later. The first of the contacts, *Vic 6*, was now within torpedo range. A Mark 48 was locked in on her, and there was no way that her skipper could know the *Dallas* was here. *Vic 6* was a deer in his sights—but it wasn't hunting season.

Though not much faster than the *Victor*s and *Charlie*s, and ten knots slower than the smaller *Alfa*s, the *Dallas* and her sisters could move almost silently at nearly twenty knots. This was a triumph of engineering and design, the product of decades of work. But moving without being detected was useful only if the hunter could at the same time detect his quarry. Sonars lost effectiveness as their carrier platform increased speed. The *Dallas'* BQQ-5 retained twenty percent effectiveness at twenty knots, nothing to cheer about. Submarines running at high speed from one point to another were blind and unable to harm anyone. As a result, the operating pattern of an attack submarine was much like that of a combat infantryman. With a rifleman it was called dash-and-cover; with a sub, sprint-and-drift. After detecting a target, a sub would race to a more advantageous position, stop to reacquire her prey, then dash again until a firing position had been achieved. The sub's quarry would be moving too, and if the submarine could gain position in front of it, she had then only to lie in wait like a great hunting cat to strike.

The submariner's trade required more than skill. It required instinct, and an artist's touch; monomaniacal confidence, and the aggressiveness of a professional boxer. Mancuso had all of these things. He had spent fifteen years learning his craft, watching a generation of commanders as a junior officer, listening carefully at the frequent round-table discussions which made submarining a very human profession, its lessons passed on by verbal tradition. Time on shore had been spent training in a variety of computerized simulators, attending seminars, comparing notes and ideas with his peers. Aboard surface ships and ASW aircraft he learned how the "enemy"—the surface sailors—played his own hunting game.

Submariners lived by a simple motto: There are two kinds of ships, submarines . . . and targets. What would *Dallas* be hunting? Mancuso wondered. Russian subs? Well, if that was the game and the Russians kept racing around like this, it ought to be easy enough. He and the *Swiftsure* had just bested a team of NATO ASW experts, men whose countries depended on their ability to keep the sea-lanes open. His boat and his crew were performing as well as any man could ask. In Jones he had one of the ten best sonar operators in the fleet. Mancuso was ready, whatever the game might be. As on the opening day of hunting season, outside considerations were dwindling away. He was becoming a weapon.

CIA Headquarters

It was 4:45 in the morning, and Ryan was dozing fitfully in the back of a CIA Chevy taking him from the Marriott to Langley. He'd been over for what? twenty hours? About that, enough time to see his boss, see Skip, get the presents for Sally, and check the house. The house looked to be in good shape. He had rented it to an instructor at the Naval Academy. He could have gotten five times the rent from someone else, but he didn't want any wild parties in his home. The officer was a Bible-thumper from Kansas, and made an acceptable custodian.

Five and a half hours of sleep in the past—thirty? Something like that; he was too tired to look at his watch. It wasn't fair. Sleeplessness murders judgment. But it made little sense telling himself that, and telling the admiral would make less.

He was in Greer's office five minutes later.

"Sorry to have to wake you up, Jack."

"Oh, that's all right, sir," Ryan returned the lie. "What's up?"

"Come on over and grab some coffee. It's going to be a long day."

Ryan dropped his topcoat on the sofa and walked over to pour a mug of navy brew. He decided against Coffee Mate or sugar. Better to endure it naked and get the caffeine full force.

"Any place I can shave around here, sir?"

"Head's behind the door, over in the corner." Greer handed him a yellow sheet torn from a telex machine. "Look at this."

TOP SECRET
102200Z*****38976

NSA SIGINT BULLETIN

REDNAV OPS

MESSAGE FOLLOWS

AT 083145Z NSA MONITOR STATIONS [DELETED] [DELETED] AND [DELETED] RECORDED AN ELF BROADCAST FROM REDFLEET ELF FACILITY SEMIPOLIPINSK XX MESSAGE DURATION 10 MINUTES XX 6 ELEMENTS XX

ELF SIGNAL IS EVALUATED AS "PREP" BROADCAST TO REDFLEET SUBMARINES AT SEA XX

AT 090000Z AN "ALL SHIPS" BROADCAST WAS MADE BY REDFLEET HEADQUARTERS CENTRAL COMMO STATION TULA AND SATELLITES THREE AND FIVE XX BANDS USED: HF VHF UHF XX MESSAGE DURATION 39 SECONDS WITH 2 REPEATS IDENTICAL CONTENT MADE AT 091000Z AND 092000Z XX 475 5-ELEMENT CIPHER GROUPS XX

SIGNAL COVERAGE AS FOLLOWS: NORTHERN FLEET AREA BALTIC FLEET AREA AND MED SQUADRON AREA XX NOTE FAR EAST FLEET NOT REPEAT NOT AFFECTED BY THIS BROADCAST XX

NUMEROUS ACKNOWLEDGMENT SIGNALS EMANATED FROM ADDRESSES IN AREAS CITED ABOVE XX ORIGIN AND TRAFFIC ANALYSIS TO

FOLLOW XX NOT COMPLETED AT THIS TIME XX
BEGINNING AT 100000Z NSA MONITOR STATIONS
[DELETED] [DELETED] AND [DELETED] RE-
CORDED INCREASED HF AND VHF TRAFFIC AT
REDFLEET BASES POLYARNYY SEVEROMORSK
PECHENGA TALLINN KRONSTADT AND EAST-
ERN MED AREA XX ADDITIONAL HF AND VHF
TRAFFIC FROM REDFLEET ASSETS AT SEA XX
AMPLIFICATION TO FOLLOW XX

EVALUATION: A MAJOR UNPLANNED REDFLEET
OPERATION HAS BEEN ORDERED WITH FLEET
ASSETS REPORTING AVAILABILITY AND STATUS
XX

END BULLETIN

NSA SENDS

102215Z

BREAKBREAK

Ryan looked at his watch. "Fast work by the boys at NSA,
and fast work by our duty watch officers, getting everybody
up." He drained his mug and went over for a refill. "What's
the word on signal traffic analysis?"

"Here." Greer handed him a second telex sheet.

Ryan scanned it. "That's a lot of ships. Must be nearly
everything they have at sea. Not much on the ones in port,
though."

"Landline," Greer observed. "The ones in port can phone
fleet ops, Moscow. By the way, that *is* every ship they have
at sea in the Western Hemisphere. Every damned one. Any
ideas?"

"Let's see, we have that increased activity in the Barents
Sea. Looks like a medium-sized ASW exercise. Maybe they're
expanding it. Doesn't explain the increased activity in the Baltic
and Med, though. Do they have a war game laid on?"

"Nope. They just finished CRIMSON STORM a month
ago."

Ryan nodded. "Yeah, they usually take a couple of months
to evaluate that much data—and who'd want to play games
up there at this time of the year? The weather's supposed to

be a bitch. Have they ever run a major game in December?"

"Not a big one, but most of these acknowledgments are from submarines, son, and subs don't care a whole lot about the weather."

"Well, given some other preconditions, you might call this ominous. No idea what the signal said, eh?"

"No. They're using computer-based ciphers, same as us. If the spooks at the NSA can read them, they're not telling me about it." In theory the National Security Agency came under the titular control of the director of Central Intelligence. In fact it was a law unto itself. "That's what traffic analysis is all about, Jack. You try to guess intentions by who's talking to whom."

"Yes, sir, but when everybody's talking to everybody—"

"Yeah."

"Anything else on alert? Their army? Voyska PVO?" Ryan referred to the Soviet air defense network.

"Nope, just the fleet. Subs, ships, and naval aviation."

Ryan stretched. "That makes it sound like an exercise, sir. We'll want a little more data on what they're doing, though. Have you talked to Admiral Davenport?"

"That's the next step. Haven't had time. I've only been in long enough to shave myself and turn the coffee on." Greer sat down and set his phone receiver in the desk speaker before punching in the numbers.

"Vice Admiral Davenport." The voice was curt.

"Morning, Charlie, James here. Did you get that NSA -976?"

"Sure did, but that's not what got me up. Our SOSUS net went berserk a few hours ago."

"Oh?" Greer looked at the phone, then at Ryan.

"Yeah, nearly every sub they have at sea just put the pedal to the metal, and all at about the same time."

"Doing what exactly, Charlie?" Greer prompted.

"We're still figuring that out. It looks like a lot of boats are heading into the North Atlantic. Their units in the Norwegian Sea are racing southwest. Three from the western Med are heading that way, too, but we haven't got a clear picture yet. We need a few more hours."

"What do they have operating off our coast, sir?" Ryan asked.

"They woke you up, Ryan? Good. Two old *November*s.

One's a raven conversion doing an ELINT job off the cape. The other one's sitting off King's Bay making a damned nuisance of itself."

Ryan smiled to himself. An American or allied ship was a *she;* the Russians used the male pronoun for a ship; and the intelligence community usually referred to a Soviet ship as *it*.

"There's a *Yankee* boat," Davenport went on, "a thousand miles south of Iceland, and the initial report is that it's heading north. Probably wrong. Reciprocal bearing, transcription error, something like that. We're checking. Must be a goof, because it was heading south earlier."

Ryan looked up. "What about their other missile boats?"

"Their *Delta*s and *Typhoon*s are in the Barents Sea and the Sea of Okhotsk, as usual. No news on them. Oh, we have attack boats up there, of course, but Gallery doesn't want them to break radio silence, and he's right. So all we have at the moment is the report on the stray *Yankee*."

"What are we doing, Charlie?" Greer asked.

"Gallery has a general alert out to his boats. They're standing by in case we need to redeploy. NORAD has gone to a slightly increased alert status, they tell me." Davenport referred to the North American Aerospace Defense Command. "CINCLANT and CINCPAC fleet staffs are up and running around in circles, like you'd expect. Some extra P-3s are working out of Iceland. Nothing much else at the moment. First we have to figure out what they're up to."

"Okay, keep me posted."

"Roger, if we hear anything, I'll let you know, and I trust—"

"We will." Greer killed the phone. He shook a finger at Ryan. "Don't you go to sleep on me, Jack."

"On top of this stuff?" Ryan waved his mug.

"You're not concerned, I see."

"Sir, there's nothing to be concerned about yet. It's what, one in the afternoon over there now? Probably some admiral, maybe old Sergey himself, decided to toss a drill at his boys. He wasn't supposed to be all that pleased with how CRIMSON STORM worked out, and maybe he decided to rattle a few cages—ours included, of course. Hell, their army and air force aren't involved, and it's for damned sure that if they were planning anything nasty the other services would know about it. We'll have to keep an eye on this, but so far I don't see anything to—" Ryan almost said lose sleep over "—sweat about."

"How old were you at Pearl Harbor?"

"My father was nineteen, sir. He didn't marry until after the war, and I wasn't the first little Ryan." Jack smiled. Greer knew all this. "As I recall you weren't all that old yourself."

"I was a seaman second on the old *Texas.*" Greer had never made it into that war. Soon after it started he'd been accepted by the Naval Academy. By the time he had graduated from there and finished training at submarine school, the war was almost over. He reached the Japanese coast on his first cruise the day after the war ended. "But you know what I mean."

"Indeed I do, sir, and that's why we have the CIA, DIA, NSA, and NRO, among others. If the Russkies can fool all of us, maybe we ought to read up on our Marx."

"All those subs heading into the Atlantic . . ."

"I feel better with word that the *Yankee* is heading north. They've had enough time to make that a hard piece of data. Davenport probably doesn't want to believe it without confirmation. If Ivan was looking to play hardball, that *Yankee*'d be heading south. The missiles on those old boats can't reach very far. Sooo—we stay up and watch. Fortunately, sir, you make a decent cup of coffee."

"How does breakfast grab you?"

"Might as well. If we can finish up on the Afghanistan stuff, maybe I can fly back tomorr—tonight."

"You still might. Maybe this way you'll learn to sleep on the plane."

Breakfast was sent up twenty minutes later. Both men were accustomed to big ones, and the food was surprisingly good. Ordinarily CIA cafeteria food was government-undistinguished, and Ryan wondered if the night crew, with fewer people to serve, might take the time to do their job right. Or maybe they had sent out for it. The two men sat around until Davenport phoned at quarter to seven.

"It's definite. All the boomers are heading towards port. We have good tracks on two *Yankee*s, three *Delta*s, and a *Typhoon*. *Memphis* reported when her *Delta* took off for home at twenty knots after being on station for five days, and then Gallery queried *Queenfish*. Same story—looks like they're all headed for the barn. Also we just got some photos from a Big Bird pass over the fjord—for once it wasn't covered with clouds—

and we have a bunch of surface ships with bright infrared signatures, like they're getting steam up."

"How about *Red October?*" Ryan asked.

"Nothing. Maybe our information was bad, and she didn't sail. Wouldn't be the first time."

"You don't suppose they've lost her?" Ryan wondered aloud.

Davenport had already thought of that. "That would explain the activity up north, but what about the Baltic and Med business?"

"Two years ago we had that scare with *Tullibee*," Ryan pointed out. "And the CNO was so pissed he threw an all-hands rescue drill on both oceans."

"Maybe," Davenport conceded. The blood in Norfolk was supposed to have been ankle deep after that fiasco. The USS *Tullibee*, a small one-of-a-kind attack sub, had long carried a reputation for bad luck. In this case it had spilled over onto a lot of others.

"Anyway, it looks a whole lot less scary than it did two hours back. They wouldn't be recalling their boomers if they were planning anything against us, would they?" Ryan said.

"I see that Ryan still has your crystal ball, James."

"That's what I pay him for, Charlie."

"Still, it is odd," Ryan commented. "Why recall all of the missile boats? Have they ever done this before? What about the ones in the Pacific?"

"Haven't heard about those yet," Davenport replied. "I've asked CINCPAC for data, but they haven't gotten back to me yet. On the other question, no, they've never recalled all their boomers at once, but they do occasionally reshuffle all their positions at once. That's probably what this is. I said they're heading towards port, not into it. We won't know that for a couple of days."

"What if they're afraid they've lost one?" Ryan ventured.

"No such luck," Davenport scoffed. "They haven't lost a boomer since that *Golf* we lifted off Hawaii, back when you were in high school, Ryan. Ramius is too good a skipper to let that happen."

So was Captain Smith of the *Titanic*, Ryan thought.

"Thanks for the info, Charlie." Greer hung up. "Looks like you were right, Jack. Nothing to worry about yet. Let's get that data on Afghanistan in here—and just for the hell of it, we'll look at Charlie's pictures of their Northern Fleet when we're finished."

Ten minutes later a messenger arrived with a cart from central files. Greer was the sort who liked to see the raw data himself. This suited Ryan. He'd known of a few analysts who had based their reports on selective data and been cut off at the knees for it by this man. The information on the cart was from a variety of sources, but to Ryan the most significant were tactical radio intercepts from listening posts on the Pakistani border, and, he gathered, from inside Afghanistan itself. The nature and tempo of Soviet operations did not indicate a backing off, as seemed to be suggested by a pair of recent articles in *Red Star* and some intelligence sources inside the Soviet Union. They spent three hours reviewing the data.

"I think Sir Basil is placing too much stock in political intelligence and too little in what our listening posts are getting in the field. It would not be unprecedented for the Soviets not to let their field commanders know what's going on in Moscow, of course, but on the whole I do not see a clear picture," Ryan concluded.

The admiral looked at him. "I pay you for answers, Jack."

"Sir, the truth is that Moscow moved in there by mistake. We know that from both military and political intelligence reports. The tenor of the data is pretty clear. From where I sit, I don't see that *they* know what they want to do. In a case like this the bureaucratic mind finds it most easy to do nothing. So, their field commanders are told to continue the mission, while the senior party bosses fumble around looking for a solution and covering their asses for getting into the mess in the first place."

"Okay, so we know that we don't know."

"Yes, sir. I don't like it either, but saying anything else would be a lie."

The admiral snorted. There was a lot of that at Langley, intelligence types giving answers when they didn't even know the questions. Ryan was still new enough to the game that when he didn't know, he said so. Greer wondered if that would change in time. He hoped not.

After lunch a package arrived by messenger from the National Reconnaissance Office. It contained the photographs taken earlier in the day on two successive passes by a KH-11 satellite.

They'd be the last such photos for a while because of the restrictions imposed by orbital mechanics and the generally miserable weather on the Kola Peninsula. The first set of visible light shots taken an hour after the FLASH signal had gone out from Moscow showed the fleet at anchor or tied to the docks. On infrared a number of them were glowing brightly from internal heat, indicating that their boilers or gas-turbine engine plants were operating. The second set of photos had been taken on the next orbital pass at a very low angle.

Ryan scrutinized the blowups. "Wow! *Kirov, Moskva, Kiev,* three *Kara*s, five *Kresta*s, four *Krivak*s, eight *Udaloy*s, and five *Sovremenny*s."

"Search and rescue exercise, eh?" Greer gave Ryan a hard look. "Look at the bottom here. Every fast oiler they have is following them out. That's most of the striking force of the Northern Fleet right there, and if they need oilers, they figure to be out for a while."

"Davenport could have been more specific. But we still have their boomers heading back in. No amphibious ships in this photo, just combatants. Only the new ones, too, the ones with range and speed."

"And the best weapons."

"Yeah," Ryan nodded. "And all scrambled in a few hours. Sir, if they had this planned in advance, we'd have known about it. This must have been laid on today. Interesting."

"You've picked up the English habit of understatement, Jack." Greer stood up to stretch. "I want you to stay over an extra day."

"Okay, sir." He looked at his watch. "Mind if I phone the wife? I don't want her to drive out to the airport for a plane I'm not on."

"Sure, and after you're finished that, I want you to go down and see someone at DIA who used to work for me. See how much operational data they're getting on this sortie. If this is a drill, we'll know soon enough, and you can still take your Surfing Barbie home tomorrow."

It was a Skiing Barbie, but Ryan didn't say so.

THE SIXTH DAY

WEDNESDAY, 8 DECEMBER

CIA Headquarters

Ryan had been to the office of the director of central intelligence several times before to deliver briefings and occasional personal messages from Sir Basil Charleston to his highness, the DCI. It was larger than Greer's, with a better view of the Potomac Valley, and appeared to have been decorated by a professional in a style compatible with the DCI's origins. Arthur Moore was a former judge of the Texas State Supreme Court, and the room reflected his southwestern heritage. He and Admiral Greer were sitting on a sofa near the picture window. Greer waved Ryan over and passed him a folder.

The folder was made of red plastic and had a snap closure. Its edges were bordered with white tape and the cover had a simple white paper label bearing the legends EYES ONLY Δ and WILLOW. Neither notation was unusual. A computer in the basement of the Langley headquarters selected random names at the touch of a key; this prevented a foreign agent from inferring anything from the name of the operation. Ryan opened the folder and looked first at the index sheet. Evidently there were only three copies of the WILLOW document, each initialed by its owner. This one was initialed by the DCI himself. A CIA document with only three copies was unusual enough that Ryan, whose highest clearance was NEBULA, had never encountered one. From the grave looks of Moore and Greer, he guessed that these were two of the Δ-cleared officers; the other, he assumed, was the deputy director of operations (DDO), another Texan named Robert Ritter.

Ryan turned the index sheet. The report was a xeroxed copy of something that had been typed on a manual machine, and it had too many strikeovers to have been done by a real secretary. If Nancy Cummings and the other elite executive secretaries had not been allowed to see this . . . Ryan looked up.

"It's all right, Jack," Greer said. "You've just been cleared for WILLOW."

Ryan sat back, and despite his excitement began to read the document slowly and carefully.

The agent's code name was actually CARDINAL. The highest ranking agent-in-place the CIA had ever had, he was the stuff that legends are made of. CARDINAL had been recruited more than twenty years earlier by Oleg Penkovskiy. Another legend—a dead one—Penkovskiy had at the time been a colonel in the GRU, the Soviet military intelligence agency, a larger and more active counterpart to America's Defense Intelligence Agency (DIA). His position had given him access to daily information on all facets of the Soviet military, from the Red Army's command structure to the operational status of intercontinental missiles. The information he smuggled out through his British contact, Greville Wynne, was supremely valuable, and Western countries had come to depend on it—too much. Penkovskiy was discovered during the Cuban Missile Crisis in 1962. It was his data, ordered and delivered under great pressure and haste, that told President Kennedy that Soviet strategic systems were not ready for war. This information enabled the president to back Khrushchev into a corner from which there was no easy exit. The famous blink ascribed to Kennedy's steady nerves was, as in many such events throughout history, facilitated by his ability to see the other man's cards. This advantage was given him by a courageous agent whom he would never meet. Penkovskiy's response to the FLASH request from Washington was too rash. Already under suspicion, this finished him. He paid for his treason with his life. It was CARDINAL who first learned that he was being watched more closely than was the norm for a society where everyone is watched. He warned Penkovskiy—too late. When it became clear that the colonel could not be extracted from the Soviet Union, he himself urged CARDINAL to betray him. It was the final ironic joke of a brave man that his own death would advance the career of an agent whom he had recruited.

CARDINAL's job was necessarily as secret as his name. A senior adviser and confidant of a Politburo member, CARDINAL often acted as his representative within the Soviet military establishment. He thus had access to political and military intelligence of the highest order. This made his information extraordinarily valuable—and, paradoxically, highly suspect. Those few experienced CIA case officers who knew of him found it impossible to believe that he had not been "turned" somewhere along the line by one of the thousands of KGB counterintelligence officers whose sole duty it is to watch everyone and everything. For this reason CARDINAL-coded material was generally cross-checked against the reports of other spies and sources. But he had outlived many small-fry agents.

The name CARDINAL was known in Washington only to the top three CIA executives. On the first day of each month a new code name was chosen for his data, a name made known only to the highest echelon of CIA officers and analysts. This month it was WILLOW. Before being passed on, grudgingly, to outsiders, CARDINAL data was laundered as carefully as Mafia income to disguise its source. There were also a number of security measures that protected the agent and were unique to him. For fear of cryptographic exposure of his identity, CARDINAL material was hand delivered, never transmitted by radio or landline. CARDINAL himself was a very careful man—Penkovskiy's fate had taught him that. His information was conveyed through a series of intermediaries to the chief of the CIA's Moscow station. He had outlived twelve station chiefs; one of these, a retired field officer, had a brother who was a Jesuit. Every morning the priest, an instructor in philosophy and theology at Fordham University in New York, said mass for the safety and the soul of a man whose name he would never know. It was as good an explanation as any for CARDINAL's continued survival.

Four separate times he had been offered extraction from the Soviet Union. Each time he had refused. To some this was proof that he'd been turned, but to others it was proof that like most successful agents CARDINAL was a man driven by something he alone knew—and therefore, like most successful agents, he was probably a little crazy.

The document Ryan was reading had been in transit for twenty hours. It had taken five for the film to reach the American embassy in Moscow, where it was delivered at once to the station chief. An experienced field officer and former reporter for the *New York Times,* he worked under the cover of press attaché. He developed the film himself in his private darkroom. Thirty minutes after its arrival, he inspected the five exposed frames through a magnifying glass and sent a FLASH-priority dispatch to Washington saying that a CARDINAL signal was en route. Next he transcribed the message from the film to flash paper on his own portable typewriter, translating from the Russian as he went. This security measure erased both the agent's handwriting and, by the paraphrasing automatic to translation, any personal peculiarities of his language. The film was then burned to ashes, the report folded into a metal container much like a cigarette case. This held a small pyrotechnic charge that would go off if the case were improperly opened or suddenly shaken; two CARDINAL signals had been lost when their cases were accidentally dropped. Next the station chief took the case to the embassy's courier-in-residence, who had already been booked on a three-hour Aeroflot flight to London. At Heathrow Airport the courier sprinted to make connections with a Pan Am 747 to New York's Kennedy International, where he connected with the Eastern shuttle to Washington's National Airport. By eight that morning the diplomatic bag was in the State Department. There a CIA officer removed the case, drove it immediately to Langley, and handed it to the DCI. It was opened by an instructor from the CIA's technical services branch. The DCI made three copies on his personal Xerox machine and burned the flash paper in his ashtray. These security measures had struck a few of the men who had succeeded to the office of the DCI as laughable. The laughs had never outlasted the first CARDINAL report.

When Ryan finished the report he referred back to the second page and read it through again, shaking his head slowly. The

WILLOW document was the strongest reinforcement yet of his desire not to know how intelligence information reached him. He closed the folder and handed it back to Admiral Greer.

"Christ, sir."

"Jack, I know I don't have to say this—but what you have just read, nobody, not the president, not Sir Basil, not God if He asks, *nobody* learns of it without the authorization of the director. Is that understood?" Greer had not lost his command voice.

"Yes, sir." Ryan bobbed his head like a schoolboy.

Judge Moore pulled a cigar from his jacket pocket and lit it, looking past the flame into Ryan's eyes. The judge, everyone said, had been a hell of a field officer in his day. He'd worked with Hans Tofte during the Korean War and had been instrumental in bringing off one of the CIA's legendary missions, the disappearance of a Norwegian ship that had been carrying a cargo of medical personnel and supplies for the Chinese. The loss had delayed a Chinese offensive for several months, saving thousands of American and allied lives. But it had been a bloody operation. All of the Chinese personnel and all of the Norwegian crewmen had vanished. It was a bargain in the simple mathematics of war, but the morality of the mission was another matter. For this reason, or perhaps another, Moore had soon thereafter left government service to become a trial lawyer in his native Texas. His career had been spectacularly successful, and he'd advanced from wealthy courtroom lawyer to distinguished appellate judge. He had been recalled to the CIA three years earlier because of his unique combination of absolute personal integrity and experience in black operations. Judge Moore hid a Harvard law degree and a highly ordered mind behind the facade of a West Texas cowboy, something he had never been but simulated with ease.

"So, Dr. Ryan, what do you think of this?" Moore said as the deputy director of operations came in. "Hi, Bob, come on over here. We just showed Ryan here the WILLOW file."

"Oh?" Ritter slid a chair over, neatly trapping Ryan in the corner. "And what does the admiral's fair-haired boy think of that?"

"Gentlemen, I assume that you all regard this information as genuine," Ryan said cautiously, getting nods. "Sir, if this information was hand delivered by the Archangel Michael, I'd have trouble believing it—but since you gentlemen say it's reliable..." They wanted his opinion. The problem was, his conclusion was too incredible. Well, he decided, I've gotten this far by giving my honest opinions...

Ryan took a deep breath and gave them his evaluation.

"Very well, Dr. Ryan," Judge Moore nodded sagaciously. "First I want to hear what else it might be, then I want to defend your analysis."

"Sir, the most obvious alternative doesn't bear much thinking about. Besides, they've been able to do it since Friday and they haven't done it," Ryan said, keeping his voice low and reasonable. Ryan had trained himself to be objective. He ran through the four alternatives he had considered, careful to examine each in detail. This was no time to allow personal views to intrude on his thinking. He spoke for ten minutes.

"I suppose there's one more possibility, Judge," he concluded. "This could be disinformation aimed at blowing this source. I cannot evaluate that possibility."

"The thought has occurred to us. All right, now that you've gone this far, you might as well give your operational recommendation."

"Sir, the admiral can tell you what the navy'll say."

"I sorta figured that one out, boy," Moore laughed. "What do you think?"

"Judge, setting up the decision tree on this will not be easy—there are too many variables, too many possible contingencies. But I'd say yes. If it's possible, if we can work out the details, we ought to try. The biggest question is the availability of our own assets. Do we have the pieces in place?"

Greer answered. "Our assets are slim. One carrier, *Kennedy*. I checked. *Saratoga*'s in Norfolk with an engineering casualty. On the other hand, HMS *Invincible* was just over here for the NATO exercise, sailed from Norfolk Monday night. Admiral White, I believe, commanding a small battle group."

"Lord White, sir?" Ryan asked. "The earl of Weston?"

"You know him?" Moore asked.

"Yes, sir. Our wives are friendly. I hunted with him last September, a grouse shoot inn Scotland. He makes noises like a good operator, and I hear he has a good reputation."

"You're thinking we might want to borrow their ships, James?" Moore asked. "If so, we'll have to tell them about this. But we have to tell our side first. There's a meeting of the National Security Council at one this afternoon. Ryan, you will prepare the briefing papers and deliver the briefing yourself."

Ryan blinked. "That's not much time, sir."

"James here says you work well under pressure. Prove it." He looked at Greer. "Get a copy of his briefing papers and be ready to fly to London. That's the president's decision. If we want their boats, we'll have to tell them why. That means briefing the prime minister, and that's your job. Bob, I want you to confirm this report. Do what you have to do, but do not get WILLOW involved."

"Right," Ritter replied.

Moore looked at his watch. "We'll meet back here at 3:30, depending on how the meeting goes. Ryan, you have ninety minutes. Get cracking."

What am I being measured for? Ryan wondered. There was talk in the CIA that Judge Moore would be leaving soon for a comfortable ambassadorship, perhaps to the Court of St. James's, a fitting reward for a man who had worked long and hard to reestablish a close relationship with the British. If the judge left, Admiral Greer would probably move into his office. He had the virtues of age—he wouldn't be around that long—and of friends on Capitol Hill. Ritter had neither. He had complained too long and too openly about congressmen who leaked information on his operations and his field agents, getting men killed in the process of demonstrating their importance on the local cocktail circuit. He also had an ongoing feud with the chairman of the Select Intelligence Committee.

With that sort of reshuffling at the top and this sudden access to new and fantastic information . . . What does it mean for me? Ryan asked himself. They couldn't want him to be the next DDI. He knew he didn't have anything like the experience required for that job—though maybe in another five or six years . . .

Reykjanes Ridge

Ramius inspected his status board. The *Red October* was heading southwest on track eight, the westernmost surveyed route on what Northern Fleet submariners called Gorshkov's Railroad. His speed was thirteen knots. It never occurred to him that this was an unlucky number, an Anglo-Saxon superstition. They would hold this course and speed for another twenty hours. Immediately behind him, Kamarov was seated at the submarine's gravitometer board, a large rolled chart behind him. The young lieutenant was chain-smoking, and looked tense as he ticked off their position on the chart. Ramius did not disturb him. Kamarov knew this job, and Borodin would relieve him in another two hours.

Installed in the *Red October*'s keel was a highly sensitive device called a gradiometer, essentially two large lead weights separated by a space of one hundred yards. A laser-computer system measured the space between the weights down to a fraction of an angstrom. Distortions of that distance or lateral movement of the weights indicated variations in the local gravitational field. The navigator compared these highly precise local values to the values on his chart. With careful use of gravitometers in the ship's inertial navigation system, he could plot the vessel's location to within a hundred meters, half the length of the ship.

The mass-sensing system was being added to all the submarines that could accommodate it. Younger attack boat commanders, Ramius knew, had used it to run the Railroad at high speed. Good for the commander's ego, Ramius judged, but a little hard on the navigator. He felt no need for recklessness. Perhaps the letter had been a mistake . . . No, it prevented second thoughts. And the sensor suites on attack submarines simply were not good enough to detect the *Red October* so long as he maintained his silent routine. Ramius was certain of this; he had used them all. He would get where he wanted to go, do what he wanted to do, and nobody, not his own countrymen, not even the Americans, would be able to do a thing about it. That's why earlier he had listened to the passage of an *Alfa* thirty miles to his east and smiled.

The White House

Judge Moore's CIA car was a Cadillac limousine that came with a driver and a security man who kept an Uzi submachinegun under the dashboard. The driver turned right off Pennsylvania Avenue onto Executive Drive. More a parking lot than a street, this served the needs of senior officials and reporters who worked at the White House and the Executive

Office Building. "Old State," that shining example of Institutional Grotesque that towered over the executive mansion. The driver pulled smoothly into a vacant VIP slot and jumped out to open the doors after the security man had swept the area with his eyes. The judge got out first and went ahead, and as Ryan caught up he found himself walking on the man's left, half a step behind. It took a moment to remember that this instinctive action was exactly what the marine corps had taught him at Quantico was the proper way for a junior officer to accompany his betters. It forced Ryan to consider just how junior he was.

"Ever been in here before, Jack?"

"No, sir, I haven't."

Moore was amused. "That's right, you come from around here. Now, if you came from farther away, you'd have made the trip a few times." A marine guard held the door open for them. Inside a Secret Service agent signed them in. Moore nodded and walked on.

"Is this to be in the Cabinet Room, sir?"

"Uh-uh. Situation Room, downstairs. It's more comfortable and better equipped for this sort of thing. The slides you need are already down there, all set up. Nervous?"

"Yes, sir, I sure am."

Moore chuckled. "Settle down, boy. The president has wanted to meet you for some time now. He liked that report on terrorism you did a few years back, and I've shown him some more of your work, the one on Russian missile submarine operations, and the one you just did on management practices in their arms industries. All in all, I think you'll find he's a pretty regular guy. Just be ready when he asks questions. He'll hear every word you say, and he has a way of hitting you with good ones when he wants." Moore turned to descend a staircase. Ryan followed him down three flights, then they came to a door which led to a corridor. The judge turned left and walked to yet another door, this one guarded by another Secret Service agent.

"Afternoon, Judge. The president will be down shortly."

"Thank you. This is Dr. Ryan. I'll vouch for him."

"Right." The agent waved them in.

It was not nearly as spectacular as Ryan had expected. The Situation Room was probably no larger than the Oval Office upstairs. There was expensive-looking wood paneling over what were probably concrete walls. This part of the White House dated back to the complete rebuilding job done under Truman. Ryan's lectern was to his left as he went in. It stood in front and slightly to the right of a roughly diamond-shaped table, and behind it was the projection screen. A note on the lectern said the slide projector in the middle of the table was already loaded and focused, and gave the order of the slides, which had been delivered from the National Reconnaissance Office.

Most of the people were already here, all of the Joint Chiefs of Staff and the secretary of defense. The secretary of state, he remembered, was still shuttling back and forth between Athens and Ankara trying to settle the latest Cyprus situation. This perennial thorn in NATO's southern flank had flared up a few weeks earlier when a Greek student had run over a Turkish child with his car and been killed by a gang minutes later. By the end of the day fifty people had been injured, and the putatively allied countries were once more at each other's throats. Now two American aircraft carriers were cruising the Aegean as the secretary of state labored to calm both sides. It was bad enough that two young people had died, Ryan thought, but not something to get a country's army mobilized for.

Also at the table were General Thomas Hilton, chairman of the Joint Chiefs of Staff, and Jeffrey Pelt, the president's national security adviser, a pompous man Ryan had met years before at Georgetown University's Center for Strategic and International Studies. Pelt was going through some papers and dispatches. The chiefs were chatting amicably among themselves when the commandant of the marine corps looked up and spotted Ryan. He got up and walked over.

"You Jack Ryan?" General David Maxwell asked.

"Yes, sir." Maxwell was a short, tough fireplug of a man whose stubbly haircut seemed to spark with aggressive energy. He looked Ryan over before shaking hands.

"Pleased to meet you, son. I liked what you did over in London. Good for the corps." He referred to the terrorist incident in which Ryan had very nearly been killed. "That was good, quick action you took, Lieutenant."

"Thank you, sir. I was lucky."

"Good officer's supposed to be lucky. I hear you got some interesting news for us."

"Yes sir. I think you will find it worth your time."

"Nervous?" The general saw the answer and smiled thinly. "Relax, son. Everybody in this damned cellar puts his pants on the same way as you." He backhanded Ryan to the stomach and went back to his seat. The general whispered something to Admiral Daniel Foster, chief of naval operations. The CNO looked Ryan over for a moment before going back to what he was doing.

The president arrived a minute later. Everyone in the room stood as he walked to his chair, on Ryan's right. He said a few quick things to Dr. Pelt, then looked pointedly at the DCI.

"Gentlemen, if we can bring this meeting to order, I think Judge Moore has some news for us."

"Thank you, Mr. President. Gentlemen, we've had an interesting development today with respect to the Soviet naval operation that started yesterday. I have asked Dr. Ryan here to deliver the briefing."

The president turned to Ryan. The younger man could feel himself being appraised. "You may proceed."

Ryan took a sip of ice water from a glass hidden in the lectern. He had a wireless control for the slide projector and a choice of pointers. A separate high-intensity light illuminated his notes. The pages were full of errors and scribbled corrections. There had not been time to edit the copy.

"Thank you, Mr. President. Gentlemen, my name is Jack Ryan, and the subject of this briefing is recent Soviet naval activity in the North Atlantic. Before I get to that it will be necessary for me to lay a little groundwork. I trust you will bear with me for a few minutes, and please feel free to interrupt with questions at any time." Ryan clicked on the slide projector. The overhead lights near the screen dimmed automatically.

"These photographs come to us courtesy of the British," Ryan said. He now had everyone's attention. "The ship you see here is the Soviet fleet ballistic missile submarine *Red October,* photographed by a British agent in her dock at their submarine base at Polyarnyy, near Murmansk in northern Russia. As you can see, she is a very large vessel, about 650 feet long, a beam of roughly 85 feet, and an estimated submerged displacement of 32,000 tons. These figures are roughly comparable to those of a World War I battleship."

Ryan lifted a pointer. "In addition to being considerably larger than our own *Ohio*-class Trident submarines, *Red October* has a number of technical differences. She carries twenty-six missiles instead of our twenty-four. The earlier *Typhoon*-class vessels, from which she was developed, only have twenty.

October carries the new SS-N-20 sea-launched ballistic missile, the Seahawk. It's a solid-fuel missile with a range of about six thousand nautical miles, and it carries eight multiple independently targetable reentry vehicles, MIRVs, each with an estimated yield of five hundred kilotons. It's the same RV carried by their SS-18s, but there are less of them per launcher.

"As you can see, the missile tubes are located forward of the sail instead of aft, as in our subs. The forward diving planes fold into slots in the hull here; ours go on the sail. She has twin screws; ours have one propeller. And finally, her hull is oblate. Instead of being cylindrical like ours, it is flattened out markedly top and bottom."

Ryan clicked to the next slide. It showed two views superimposed, bow over stern. "These frames were delivered to us undeveloped. They were processed by the National Reconnaissance Office. Please note the doors here at the bow and here at the stern. The British were a little puzzled by these, and that's why I was permitted to bring the shots over earlier this week. We weren't able to figure out this function at the CIA either, and it was decided to seek the opinion of an outside consultant."

"Who decided?" the secretary of defense demanded angrily. "Hell, I haven't even seen them yet!"

"We only got them Monday, Bert," Judge Moore replied soothingly. "These two on the screen are only four hours old. Ryan suggested an outside expert, and James Greer approved it. I concurred."

"His name is Oliver W. Tyler. Dr. Tyler is a former naval officer who is now associate professor of engineering at the Naval Academy and a paid consultant to Sea Systems Command. He's an expert in the analysis of Soviet naval technology. Skip— Dr. Tyler—concluded that these doors are the intake and exhaust vents for a new silent propulsion system. He is currently developing a computer model of the system, and we hope to have this information by the end of the week. The system itself is rather interesting." Ryan explained Tyler's analysis briefly.

"Okay, Dr. Ryan." The president leaned forward. "You've just told us that the Soviets have built a missile submarine that's supposed to be hard for our men to locate. I don't suppose that's news. Go on."

"Red October's captain is a man named Marko Ramius. That is a Lithuanian name, although we believe his internal

passport designates his nationality as Great Russian. He is the son of a high Party official, and as good a submarine commander as they have. He's taken out the lead ship of every Soviet submarine class for the past ten years.

"*Red October* sailed last Friday. We do not know exactly what her orders were, but ordinarily their missile subs—that is, those with the newer long-range missiles—confine their activities to the Barents Sea and adjacent areas in which they can be protected from our attack boats by land-based ASW aircraft, their own surface ships, and attack submarines. About noon local time on Sunday, we noted increased search activity in the Barents Sea. At the time we took this to be a local ASW exercise, and by late Monday it looked to be a test of *October*'s new drive system.

"As you all know, early yesterday saw a vast increase in Soviet naval activity. Nearly all of the blue-water ships assigned to their Northern Fleet are now at sea, accompanied by all of their fast fleet-replenishment vessels. Additional fleet auxiliaries sailed from the Baltic Fleet bases and the western Mediterranean. Even more disquieting is the fact that nearly every nuclear submarine assigned to the Northern Fleet—their largest—appears to be heading into the North Atlantic. This includes three from the Med, since submarines there come from the Northern Fleet, not the Black Sea Fleet. Now we think we know why all this happened." Ryan clicked to the next slide. This one showed the North Atlantic, from Florida to the Pole, with Soviet ships marked in red.

"The day *Red October* sailed, Captain Ramius evidently posted a letter to Admiral Yuri Ilych Padorin. Padorin is chief of the Main Political Administration of their navy. We do not know what that letter said, but here we can see its results. This began to happen not four hours after that letter was opened. Fifty-eight nuclear-powered submarines and twenty-eight major surface combatants all headed our way. This is a remarkable reaction in four hours. This morning we learned what their orders are.

"Gentlemen, these ships have been ordered to locate *Red October,* and if necessary, to sink her." Ryan paused for effect. "As you can see, the Soviet surface force is here, about halfway between the European mainland and Iceland. Their submarines, these in particular, are all heading southwest towards the U.S. coast. Please note, there is no unusual activity on the Pacific side of either country—except we have information that Soviet fleet ballistic missile submarines in *both* oceans are being recalled to port.

"Therefore, while we do not know exactly what Captain Ramius said, we can draw some conclusions from these patterns of activity. It would appear that they think he's heading in our direction. Given his estimated speed as something between ten and thirty knots, he could be anywhere from here, below Iceland, to here, just off our coast. You will note that in either case he has successfully avoided detection by all four of these SOSUS barriers—"

"Wait a minute. You say they have issued orders to their ships to sink one of their submarines?"

"Yes, Mr. President."

The president looked at the DCI. "This is reliable information, Judge?"

"Yes, Mr. President, we believe it to be solid."

"Okay, Dr. Ryan, we're all waiting. What's this Ramius fellow up to?"

"Mr. President, our evaluation of this intelligence data is that *Red October* is attempting to defect to the United States."

The room went very quiet for a moment. Ryan could hear the whirring of the fan in the slide projector as the National Security Council pondered that. He held his hands on the lectern to keep them from shaking under the stare of the ten men in front of him.

"That's a very interesting conclusion, Doctor." The president smiled. "Defend it."

"Mr. President, no other conclusion fits the data. The really crucial thing, of course, is the recall of their other missile boats. They've never done that before. Add to that the fact that they have issued orders to sink their newest and most powerful missile sub, and that they are chasing in this direction, and one is left with the conclusion that they think she has left the reservation and is heading this way."

"Very well. What else could it be?"

"Sir, he could have told them that he's going to fire his missiles. At us, at them, the Chinese, or just about anyone else."

"And you don't think so?"

"No, Mr. President. The SS-N-20 has a range of six thousand miles. That means he could have hit any target in the

Northern Hemisphere from the moment he left the dock. He's had six days to do that, but he has not fired. Moreover, if he had threatened to launch his birds, he would have to consider the possibility that the Soviets would enlist our assistance to locate and sink him. After all, if our surveillance systems detect the launch of nuclear-armed missiles in any direction, things could get very tense, very quickly."

"You know he could fire his birds in both directions and start World War III," the secretary of defense observed.

"Yes, Mr. Secretary. In that case we'd be dealing with a total madman—more than one, in fact. On our missile boats there are five officers, who must all agree and act in unison to fire their missiles. The Soviets have the same number. For political reasons their nuclear warhead security procedures are even more elaborate than ours. Five or more people, all of whom wish to end the world?" Ryan shook his head. "That seems most unlikely, sir, and again, the Soviets would be well advised to inform us and enlist our aid."

"Do you really think they would inform us?" Dr. Pelt asked. His tone indicated what he thought.

"Sir, that's more a psychological question than a technical one, and I deal principally with technical intelligence. Some of the men in this room have met their Soviet counterparts and are better equipped to answer that than I am. My answer to your question, however, is yes. That would be the only rational thing for them to do, and while I do not regard the Soviets as entirely rational by our standards, they are rational by their own. They are not given to this sort of high-stakes gambling."

"Who is?" the president observed. "What else might it be?"

"Several things, sir. It could simply be a major naval exercise aimed at testing their ability to close our sea lines of communication and our ability to respond, both on short notice. We reject this possibility for several reasons. It's too soon after their autumn naval exercise, CRIMSON STORM, and they are only using nuclear submarines; no diesel-powered boats seem to be involved. Clearly speed is at a premium in their operation. And as a practical matter, they do not run major exercises at this time of year."

"And why is that?" the president asked.

Admiral Foster answered for Ryan. "Mr. President, the weather up there at this time of the year is extremely bad. Even we don't schedule exercises under these conditions."

"I seem to recall we just ran a NATO exercise, Admiral," Pelt noted.

"Yes, sir, south of Bermuda, where the weather's a lot nicer. Except for an antisub exercise off the British Isles, all of NIFTY DOLPHIN was held on our side of the lake."

"Okay, let's get back to what else their fleet might be up to," the president ordered.

"Well, sir, it might not be an exercise at all. It could be the real thing. This could be the beginning of a conventional war against NATO, its first step being interdiction of the sea lines of communication. If so, they've achieved complete strategic surprise and are now throwing it away by operating so overtly that we cannot fail to notice or react forcefully. Moreover, there is no corresponding activity whatever in their other armed services. Their army and air force—except for maritime surveillance aircraft—and their Pacific Fleet are engaged in routine training operations.

"Finally, this could be an attempt to provoke or divert us, drawing our attention to this while they are preparing to spring a surprise somewhere else. If so, they're going about it in a strange way. If you try to provoke somebody, you don't do it in his front yard. The Atlantic, Mr. President, is still our ocean. As you can see from this chart, we have bases here in Iceland, the Azores, all up and down our coast. We have allies on both sides of the ocean, and we can establish air superiority over the entire Atlantic if we so choose. Their navy is numerically large, larger than ours in some critical areas, but they cannot project force as well as we can—not yet, anyway—and certainly not right off our coast." Ryan took a sip of water.

"So, gentlemen, we have a Soviet missile submarine at sea when all the others, in both oceans, are being recalled. We have their fleet at sea with orders to sink that sub, and evidently they are chasing it in our direction. As I said, this is the only conclusion that fits the data."

"How many men on the sub, Doctor?" the president asked.

"We believe 110 or so, sir."

"So, 110 men all decide to defect to the United States at one time. Not an altogether bad idea," the president observed wryly, "but hardly a likely one."

Ryan was ready for that. "There is precedent for this, sir. On November 8, 1975, the *Storozhevoy,* a Soviet *Krivak*-class missile frigate, attempted to run from Riga, Latvia, to the Swedish island of Gotland. The political officer aboard, Valery Sablin, led a mutiny of the enlisted personnel. They locked their officers in their cabins and raced away from the dock. They came close to making it. Air and fleet units attacked them and forced them to halt within fifty miles of Swedish territorial waters. Two more hours and they would have made it. Sablin and twenty-six others were court-martialed and shot. More recently we have had reports of mutinous episodes on several Soviet vessels—especially submarines. In 1980 an *Echo*-class Soviet attack submarine surfaced off Japan. The captain claimed to have had a fire aboard, but photographs taken by naval reconnaissance aircraft—ours and Japanese—did not show smoke or fire-damaged debris being jettisoned from the submarine. However, the crewmen on deck did show sufficient evidence of trauma to support the conclusion that a riot had taken place aboard. We have had similar, sketchier reports for some years now. While I admit this is an extreme example, our conclusion is decidedly not without precedent."

Admiral Foster reached inside his jacket and came out with a plastic-tipped cigar. His eyes sparkled behind the match. "You know, I could almost believe this."

"Then I wish you'd tell us all why, Admiral," the president said, "because I still don't."

"Mr. President, most mutinies are led by officers, not enlisted men. The reason for this is simply that the enlisted men do not know how to navigate the ship. Moreover, officers have the advantages and educational background to know that successful rebellion is a possibility. Both of these factors would be even more true in the Soviet Navy. What if just the officers are doing this?"

"And the rest of the crew is going along with them?" Pelt asked. "Knowing what would happen to them and their families?"

Foster puffed a few times on his cigar. "Ever been to sea, Dr. Pelt? No? Let's imagine for the moment that you're taking a world cruise, on the *Queen Elizabeth 2*, say. One fine day you're in the middle of the Pacific Ocean—but how do you know exactly where you are? You don't know. You know what the officers tell you. Oh, sure, if you know a little astronomy, you might be able to estimate your latitude to within a few hundred miles. With a good watch and some knowledge of spherical trigonometry you might even guess your longitude to within a few hundred. Okay? That's on a ship that you can see from.

"These guys are on a submarine. You can't see a whole lot. Now, what if the officers—not even all the officers—are doing this? How will the crew know what's going on?" Foster shook his head. "They won't. They can't. Even our guys might not, and our men are trained a lot better than theirs. Their seamen are nearly all conscripts, remember. On a nuclear submarine you are absolutely cut off from the outside world. No radios except for ELF and VLF—and that's all encrypted; messages have to come through the communications officer. So, he has to be in on it. Same thing with the boat's navigator. They use inertial navigation systems, same as us. We have one of theirs, from that *Golf* we lifted off Hawaii. In their machine the data is also encrypted. The quartermaster reads the numbers off the machine, and the navigator gets their position from a book. In the Red Army, on *land,* maps are classified documents. Same thing in their navy. The enlisted men don't get to see charts and are not encouraged to know where they are. This would be especially true on missile submarines, right?

"On top of all that, these guys are working sailors, nucs. When you're at sea, you have a job to do, and you do it. On their ships, that means from fourteen to eighteen hours a day. These kids are all draftees with very simple training. They're taught to perform one or two tasks—and to follow their orders exactly. The Soviets train people to do their jobs by rote, with as little thinking as possible. That's why on major repair jobs you see officers holding tools. Their men will have neither the time nor the inclination to question their officers about what's going on. You do your job, and depend on everybody else to do his. That's what discipline at sea is all about." Foster tapped his cigar ash into an ashtray. "Yes, sir, you get the officers together, maybe not even all of them, and this would work. Getting ten or twelve dissidents together is a whole lot easier than assembling a hundred."

"Eas*ier,* but hardly easy, Dan," General Hilton objected. "For Christ's sake, they have at least one political officer aboard, plus moles from their intelligence outfits. You really think a Party hack would go along with this?"

"Why not? You heard Ryan—that frigate's mutiny was led by the political officer."

"Yeah, and since then they have shaken up that whole directorate," Hilton responded.

"We have defecting KGB types all the time, all good Party members," Foster said. Clearly he liked the idea of a defecting Russian sub.

The president took all this in, then turned to Ryan. "Dr. Ryan, you have managed to persuade me that your scenario is a theoretical possibility. Now, what does the CIA think we ought to do about it?"

"Mr. President, I'm an intelligence analyst, not—"

"I know very well what you are, Dr. Ryan. I've read enough of your work. I can see you have an opinion. I want to hear it."

Ryan didn't even look at Judge Moore. "We grab her, sir."

"Just like that?"

"No, Mr. President, probably not. However, Ramius could surface off the Virginia Capes in a day or two and request political asylum. We ought to be prepared for that contingency, sir, and my opinion is that we should welcome him with open arms." Ryan saw nods from all the chiefs. Finally somebody was on his side.

"You've stuck your neck out on this one," the president observed kindly.

"Sir, you asked me for an opinion. It will probably not be that easy. These *Alfa*s and *Victor*s appear to be racing for our coast, almost certainly with the intention of establishing an interdiction force—effectively a blockade of our Atlantic coast."

"Blockade," the president said, "an ugly word."

"Judge," General Hilton said, "I suppose it's occurred to you that this is a piece of disinformation aimed at blowing whatever highly placed source generated this report?"

Judge Moore affected a sleepy smile. "It has, Gener'l. If this is a sham, it's a damned elaborate one. Dr. Ryan was directed to prepare this briefing on the assumption that this data is genuine. If it is not, the responsibility is mine." God bless you, Judge, Ryan said to himself, wondering just how gold-plated the WILLOW source was. The judge went on, "In any case, gentlemen, we will have to respond to this Soviet activity whether our analysis is accurate or not."

"Are you getting confirmation on this, Judge?" the president asked.

"Yes, sir, we are working on that."

"Good." The president was sitting straight, and Ryan noted his voice become crisper. "The judge is correct. We have to react to this, whatever they're really up to. Gentlemen, the Soviet Navy is heading for our coast. What are we doing about it?"

Admiral Foster answered first. "Mr. President, our fleet is pulling to sea at this moment. Everything that'll steam is out already, or will be by tomorrow night. We've recalled our carriers from the South Atlantic, and we are redeploying our nuclear submarines to deal with this threat. We began this morning to saturate the air over their surface force with P-3C Orion patrol aircraft, assisted by British Nimrods operating out of Scotland. General?" Foster turned to Hilton.

"At this moment we have E-3A Sentry AWACS-type aircraft circling them along with Dan's Orions, both accompanied by F-15 Eagle fighters out of Iceland. By this time Friday we'll have a squadron of B-52s operating from Loring Air Base in Maine. These will be armed with Harpoon air-to-surface missiles, and they'll be orbiting the Soviets in relays. Nothing aggressive, you understand," Hilton smiled. "Just to let them know we're interested. If they continue to come this way, we will redeploy some tactical air assets to the East Coast, and, subject to your approval, we can activate some national guard and reserve squadrons quietly."

"Just how will you do that quietly?" Pelt asked.

"Dr. Pelt, we have a number of guard outfits scheduled to run through our Red Flag facility at Nellis in Nevada starting this Sunday, a routine training rotation. They go to Maine instead of Nevada. The bases are pretty big, and they belong to SAC." Hilton referred to the Strategic Air Command. "They have good security."

"How many carriers do we have handy?" the president asked.

"Only one at the moment, sir, *Kennedy*. *Saratoga* stripped a main turbine last week, and it'll take a month to replace. *Nimitz* and *America* are both in the South Atlantic right now, *America* coming back from the Indian Ocean, *Nimitz* heading out to the Pacific. Bad luck. Can we recall a carrier from the eastern Med?"

"No." The president shook his head. "This Cyprus thing is

still too sensitive. Do we really need to? If anything ... untoward happens, can we handle their surface force with what we have at hand?"

"Yes, sir!" General Hilton said at once. "Dr. Ryan said it: the Atlantic is our ocean. The air force alone will have over five hundred aircraft designated for this operation, and another three or four hundred from the navy. If any sort of shooting match develops, that Soviet fleet will have an exciting and short life."

"We will try to avoid that, of course," the president said quietly. "The first press reports surfaced this morning. We had a call from Bud Wilkins of the *Times* right before lunch. If the American people find out too soon what the scope of this is ... Jeff?"

"Mr. President, let's assume for the moment that Dr. Ryan's analysis is correct. I don't see what we can do about it," Pelt said.

"What?" Ryan blurted. "I, ah, beg your pardon, sir."

"We can't exactly steal a Russian missile sub."

"Why not!" Foster demanded. "Hell, we have enough of their tanks and aircraft." The other chiefs agreed.

"An aircraft with a crew of one or two is one thing, Admiral. A nuclear-powered submarine with twenty-six rockets and a crew of over a hundred is something else. Naturally, we can give asylum to the defecting officers."

"So, you're saying that if the thing does come sailing into Norfolk," Hilton joined in, "we give it back! Christ, man, it carries two hundred warheads! They just might use those goddamned things against us someday, you know. Are you *sure* you want to give them back?"

"That's a billion-dollar asset, General," Pelt said diffidently.

Ryan saw the president smile. He was said to like lively discussions. "Judge, what are the legal ramifications?"

"That's admiralty law, Mr. President." Moore looked uneasy for once. "I've never had an admiralty practice, takes me all the way back to law school. Admiralty is *jus gentium*—the same legal codes theoretically apply to all countries. American and British admiralty courts routinely cite each other's rulings. But as for the rights that attach to a mutinous crew—I have no idea."

"Judge, we are not dealing with mutiny or piracy," Foster noted. "The correct term is *barratry,* I believe. Mutiny is when

the crew rebels against lawful authority. Gross misconduct of
the officers is called barratry. Anyway, I hardly think we need
to attack legal folderol to a situation involving nuclear weapons."

"We might, Admiral," the president mused. "As Jeff said,
this is a highly valuable asset, legally their property, and they
will know we have her. I think we are agreed that not all the
crew is likely to be in on this. If so, those not party to the
mutiny—barratry, whatever—will want to return home after
it's all over. And we'll have to let them go, won't we?"

"Have to?" General Maxwell was doodling on a pad. "Have
to?"

"General," the president said firmly, "we will not, repeat
not, be party to the imprisonment or murder of men whose
only desire is to return to home and family. Is that understood?"
He looked around the table. "If they know we have her, they'll
want her back. And they will know we have her from the
crewmen who want to return home. In any case, big as this
thing is, how could we hide her?"

"We might be able to," Foster said neutrally, "but as you
say, the crew is a complication. I presume we'll have the chance
to look her over?"

"You mean conduct a quarantine inspection, check her for
seaworthiness, maybe make sure they're not smuggling drugs
into the country?" The president grinned. "I think we might
arrange that. But we are getting ahead of ourselves. There's a
lot of ground to cover before we get to that point. What about
or allies?"

"The English just had one of their carriers over here. Could
you use her, Dan?" General Hilton asked.

"If they let us borrow her, yes. We just finished that ASW
exercise south of Bermuda, and the Brits acquitted themselves
well. We could use *Invincible,* the four escorts, and the three
attack boats. The force is being recalled at high speed because
of this."

"Do they know of this development, Judge?" the president
asked.

"Not unless they've developed it themselves. This information is only a few hours old." Moore did not reveal that Sir
Basil had his own ear in the Kremlin. Ryan didn't know much
about it himself, had only heard some disconnected rumblings.

"With your permission, I have asked Admiral Greer to be ready to fly to England to brief the prime minister."

"Why not just send—"

Judge Moore was shaking his head. "Mr. President, this information—let's say it's only delivered by hand." Eyebrows went up all around the table.

"When is he leaving?"

"This evening, if you wish. There are a couple of VIP flights leaving Andrews tonight. Congressional flights." It was the usual end-of-session junket season. Christmas in Europe, on fact-finding missions.

"General, do we have anything quicker?" the president asked Hilton.

"We can scratch up a VC-141. Lockheed JetStar, almost as fast as a -135, and we can have it up in half an hour."

"Do it."

"Yes, sir, I'll call them in right now." Hilton rose and walked to a phone in the corner.

"Judge, tell Greer to pack his bags. I'll have a cover letter waiting for him on the plane to give to the prime minister. Admiral, you want the *Invincible?*"

"Yes, sir."

"I'll get her for you. Next, what do we tell our people at sea?"

"If *October* just sails in, it won't be necessary, but if we have to communicate with her—"

"Excuse me, Judge," Ryan said, "that is rather likely—that we'll have to. They'll probably have these attack boats on the coast before she gets here. If so, we'll have to warn her off if only to save the defecting officers. They are out to locate and sink her."

"We haven't detected her. What makes you think they can?" Foster asked, miffed at the suggestion.

"They did build her, Admiral. So they might know things about her that will enable them to locate her more easily than us."

"Makes sense," the president said. "That means somebody goes out to brief the fleet commanders. We can't broadcast this, can we, Judge?"

"Mr. President, this source is too valuable to compromise in any way. That's all I can say here, sir."

"Very well, somebody flies out. Next thing is, we'll have to talk to the Soviets about this. For the moment they can say that they're operating in home waters. When will they pass Iceland?"

"Tomorrow night, unless they change course," Foster answered.

"Okay, we give it a day, for them to call this off and for us to confirm this report. Judge, I want something to back up this fairy tale in twenty-four hours. If they haven't turned back by midnight tomorrow, I'll call Ambassador Arbatov into my office Friday morning." He turned to the chiefs. "Gentlemen, I want to see contingency plans for dealing with this situation by tomorrow afternoon. We will meet here tomorrow at two. One more thing: *no leaks!* This information does not go beyond this room without my personal approval. If this story breaks to the press, I'll have heads on my desk. Yes, General?"

"Mr. President, in order to develop those plans," Hilton said after sitting back down, "we have to work through our field commanders and some of our own operations people. Certainly we'll need Admiral Blackburn." Blackburn was CINCLANT, commander in chief of the Atlantic.

"Let me think that one over. I'll be back to you in an hour. How many people at the CIA know about this?"

"Four, sir. Ritter, Greer, Ryan, and myself, sir. That's all."

"Keep it that way." The president had been bedeviled by security leaks for months.

"Yes, Mr. President."

"Meeting is adjourned."

The president stood. Moore walked around the table to keep him from leaving at once. Dr. Pelt stayed also as the rest filed out of the room. Ryan stood outside the door.

"That was all right." General Maxwell grabbed his hand. He waited until everyone else was a few yards down the hall before going on. "I think you're crazy, son, but you sure put a burr under Dan Foster's saddle. No, even better: I think he got a hard-on." The little general chuckled. "And if we get the sub, maybe we can change the president's mind and arrange for the crew to disappear. The judge did that once, you know." It was a thought that chilled Ryan as he watched Maxwell swagger down the hall.

"Jack, you want to come back in here a minute?" Moore's voice called.

"You're an historian, right?" the president asked, reviewing his notes. Ryan hadn't even noticed him holding a pen.

"Yes, Mr. President. That's what my graduate degree's in." Ryan shook his hand.

"You have a fine sense of the dramatic, Jack. You would have made a decent trial lawyer." The president had made his reputation as a hard-driving state's attorney. He had survived an unsuccessful Mafia assassination attempt early in his career which hadn't hurt his political ambitions one bit. "Damned nice briefing."

"Thank you, Mr. President." Ryan beamed.

"The judge tells me you know the commander of that British task force."

It was like a sandbag hitting his head. "Yes, sir. Admiral White. I've hunted with him, and our wives are good friends. They're close to the Royal Family."

"Good. Somebody has to fly out to brief our fleet commander, then go on to talk to the Brits, if we get their carrier, as I expect we will. The judge says we ought to let Admiral Davenport go out with you. So, you fly out to *Kennedy* tonight, then on to *Invincible*."

"Mr. President, I—"

"Come now, Dr. Ryan," Pelt smiled thinly. "You are uniquely suited to this. You already have access to the intelligence, you know the British commander, and you're a naval intelligence specialist. You fit. Tell me, how eager do you think the navy is about getting this *Red October*?"

"Of course they're interested in it, sir. To get a chance to look at it, better yet to run it, take it apart, and run it some more. It would be the intelligence coup of all time."

"That's true. But maybe they're a little too eager."

"I don't understand what you mean, sir," Ryan said, though he understood it just fine. Pelt was the president's favorite. He was not the Pentagon's favorite.

"They might take a chance that we might not want them to take."

"Dr. Pelt, if you're saying that a uniformed officer would—"

"He's not saying that. At least not exactly. What he's saying is that it might be useful for me to have somebody out there who can give me an independent, civilian point of view."

"Sir, you don't know me."

"I've read a lot of your reports." The chief executive was smiling. It was said he could turn dazzling charm on and off like a spotlight. Ryan was being blinded, knew it, and couldn't do a thing about it. "I like your work. You have a good feel for things, for facts. Good judgment. Now, one reason I got to where I am is good judgment, too, and I think you can handle what I have in mind. The question is, will you do it, or won't you?"

"Do what, exactly, sir?"

"After you get out there, you stay put for a few days, and report directly to me. Not through channels, directly to me. You'll get the cooperation you need. I'll see to that."

Ryan didn't say anything. He'd just become a spy, a field officer, by presidential fiat. Worse, he'd be spying on his own side.

"You don't like the idea of reporting on your own people, right? You won't be, not really. Like I said, I want an independent, civilian opinion. We'd prefer to send an experienced case officer out, but we want to minimize the number of people involved in this. Sending Ritter or Greer out would be far too obvious, whereas you, on the other hand, are a relative—"

"Nobody?" Jack asked.

"As far as they're concerned, yes," Judge Moore replied. "The Soviets have a file on you. I've seen parts of it. They think you're an upper-class drone, Jack."

I am a drone, Ryan thought, unmoved by the implicit challenge. In this company I sure as hell am.

"Agreed, Mr. President. Please forgive me for hesitating. I've never been a field officer before."

"I understand." The president was magnanimous in victory. "One more thing. If I understand how submarines operate, Ramius could just have taken off, not saying anything. Why tip them off? Why the letter? The way I read this, it's counterproductive."

It was Ryan's turn to smile. "Ever meet a sub driver, sir? No? How about an astronaut?"

"Sure, I've met a bunch of the Shuttle pilots."

"They're the same breed of cat, Mr. President. As to why he left the letter, there's two parts to that. First, he's probably mad about something, exactly what we'll find out when we see him. Second, he figures he can pull this off regardless of what they try to stop him with—and he wants them to know that. Mr. President, the men who drive subs for a living are aggressive, confident, and very, very smart. They like nothing better than making somebody else, a surface ship operator for example, look like an idiot."

"You just scored another point, Jack. The astronauts I've met, on most things they're downright humble, but they think they're gods when it comes to flying. I'll keep that in mind. Jeff, let's get back to work. Jack, keep me posted."

Ryan shook his hand again. After the president and his senior adviser left, he turned to Judge Moore. "Judge, what the hell did you tell him about me?"

"Only the truth, Jack." Actually, the judge had wanted this operation to be run by one of the CIA's senior case officers. Ryan had not been part of this scheme, but presidents have been known to spoil many carefully laid plans. The judge took this philosophically. "This is a big move up in the world for you, if you do your job right. Hell, you might even like it."

Ryan was sure he wouldn't, and he was right.

CIA Headquarters

He didn't speak the whole way back to Langley. The director's car pulled into the basement parking garage, where they got out and entered a private elevator that took them directly to Moore's office. The elevator door was disguised as a wall panel, which was convenient but melodramatic, Ryan thought. The DCI went right to his desk and lifted a phone.

"Bob, I need you in here right now." He glanced at Ryan, standing in the middle of the room. "Looking forward to this, Jack?"

"Sure, Judge," Ryan said without enthusiasm.

"I can see how you feel about this spying business, but the whole thing could develop into an extremely sensitive situation. You ought to be damned flattered you're being trusted with it."

Ryan caught the between-the-line message just as Ritter breezed in.

"What's up, Judge?"

"We're laying an operation on. Ryan is flying out to the

Kennedy with Charlie Davenport to brief the fleet commanders on this *October* business. The president bought it."

"Guess so. Greer left for Andrews just before you pulled in. Ryan gets to fly out, eh?"

"Yes. Jack, the rules is this: you can brief the fleet commander and Davenport, that's all. Same for the Brits, just the boss-sailor. If Bob can confirm WILLOW, the data can be spread out, but only as much as is absolutely necessary. Clear?"

"Yes, sir. I suppose somebody has told the president that it's hard to accomplish anything if nobody knows what the hell is going on. Especially the guys who're doing the work."

"I know what you're saying, Jack. We have to change the president's mind on that. We will, but until we do, remember— he is the boss. Bob, we'll need to rustle something up so he'll fit in."

"Naval officer's uniform? Let's make him a commander, three stripes, usual ribbons." Ritter looked Ryan over. "Say a forty-two long. We can have him outfitted in an hour, I expect. This operation have a name?"

"That's next." Moore lifted his phone again and tapped in five numbers. "I need two words . . . Uh-huh, thank you." He wrote a few things down. "Okay, gentlemen, you're calling this Operation MANDOLIN. You, Ryan, are Magi. Ought to be easy to remember, given the time of year. We'll work up a series of code words based on those while you're being fitted. Bob, take him down there yourself. I'll call Davenport and have him arrange the flight."

Ryan followed Ritter to the elevator. It was going too fast, everyone was being too clever, he thought. This Operation MANDOLIN was racing forward before they knew what the hell they were going to do, much less how. And the choice of his code name struck Ryan as singularly inappropriate. He wasn't anyone's wise man. The name should have been something more like "Halloween."

THE SEVENTH DAY

THURSDAY, 9 DECEMBER

The North Atlantic

When Samuel Johnson compared sailing in a ship to "being in jail, with the chance of being drowned," at least he had the consolation of travelling to his ship in a safe carriage, Ryan thought. Now he was going to sea, and before he got to his ship Ryan stood the chance of being smashed to red pulp in a plane crash. Jack sat hunched in a bucket seat on the port side of a Grumman Greyhound, known to the fleet without affection as a COD (for carrier onboard delivery), a flying delivery truck. The seats, facing aft, were too close together, and his knees jutted up against his chin. The cabin was far more amenable to cargo than to people. There were three tons of engine and electronics parts stowed in crates aft—there, no doubt, so that the impact of a plane crash on the valuable equipment would be softened by the four bodies in the passenger section. The cabin was not heated. There were no windows. A thin aluminum skin separated him from a two-hundred-knot wind that shrieked in time with the twin turbine engines. Worst of all, they were flying through a storm at five thousand feet, and the

COD was jerking up and down in hundred-foot gulps like a berserk roller coaster. The only good thing was the lack of lighting, Ryan thought—at least nobody can see how green my face is. Right behind him were two pilots, talking away loudly so they could be heard over the engine noise. The bastards were enjoying themselves!

The noise lessened somewhat, or so it seemed. It was hard to tell. He'd been issued foam-rubber ear protectors along with a yellow, inflatable life preserver and a lecture on what to do in the event of a crash. The lecture had been perfunctory enough that it took no great intellect to estimate their chances of survival if they did crash on a night like this. Ryan hated flying. He had once been a marine second lieutenant, and his active career had ended after only three months when his platoon's helicopter had crashed on Crete during a NATO exercise. He had injured his back, nearly been crippled for life, and ever since regarded flying as something to be avoided. The COD, he thought, was bouncing more down than up. It probably meant they were close to the *Kennedy*. The alternative did not bear thinking about. They were only ninety minutes out of Oceana Naval Air Station at Virginia Beach. It felt like a month, and Ryan swore to himself that he'd never be afraid on a civilian airliner again.

The nose dropped about twenty degrees, and the aircraft seemed to be flying right at something. They were landing, the most dangerous part of carrier flight operations. He remembered a study conducted during the Vietnam War in which carrier pilots had been fitted with portable electrocardiographs to monitor stress, and it had surprised a lot of people that the most stressful time for carrier pilots wasn't while they were being shot at—it was while they were landing, particularly at night.

Christ, you're full of happy thoughts! Ryan told himself. He closed his eyes. One way or another, it would be over in a few seconds.

The deck was slick with rain and heaving up and down, a black hole surrounded by perimeter lights. The carrier landing was a controlled crash. Massive landing gear struts and shock absorbers were needed to lessen the bone-crushing impact. The aircraft surged forward only to be jerked to a halt by the arresting wire. They were down. They were safe. Probably. After a moment's pause, the COD began moving forward again. Ryan heard some odd noises as the plane taxied and realized that they came from the wings folding up. The one danger he had not considered was flying on an aircraft whose wings were supposed to collapse. It was, he decided, just as well. The plane finally stopped moving, and the rear hatch opened.

Ryan flipped off his seatbelts and stood rapidly, banging his head on the low ceiling. He didn't wait for Davenport. With his canvas bag clutched to his chest he darted out of the rear of the aircraft. He looked around, and was pointed to the *Kennedy*'s island structure by a yellow-shirted deck crewman. The rain was falling heavily, and he felt rather than saw that the carrier was indeed moving on the fifteen-foot seas. He ran towards an open, lighted hatch fifty feet away. He had to wait for Davenport to catch up. The admiral didn't run. He walked with a precise thirty-inch step, dignified as a flag officer should be, and Ryan decided that he was probably annoyed that his semisecret arrival prohibited the usual ceremony of bosun's pipes and side boys. There was a marine standing inside the hatch, a corporal, resplendent in striped blue trousers, khaki shirt and tie, and snow-white pistol belt. He saluted, welcoming both aboard.

"Corporal, I want to see Admiral Painter."

"The admiral's in flag quarters, sir. Do you require escort?"

"No, son. I used to command this ship. Come along, Jack." Ryan got to carry both bags.

"Gawd, sir, you actually used to do this for a living?" Ryan asked.

"Night carrier landings? Sure, I've done a couple of hundred. What's the big deal?" Davenport seemed surprised at Ryan's awe. Jack was sure it was an act.

The inside of the *Kennedy* was much like the interior of the USS *Guam,* the helicopter assault ship Ryan had been assigned to during his brief military career. It was the usual navy maze of steel bulkheads and pipes, everything painted the same shade of cave-gray. The pipes had some colored bands and stenciled acronyms which probably meant something to the men who ran the ship. To Ryan they might as well have been neolithic cave paintings. Davenport led him through a corridor, around a corner, down a "ladder" made entirely of steel and so steep he almost lost his balance, down another passageway, and around another corner. By this time Ryan was thoroughly lost. They came to a door with a marine stationed in front. The sergeant saluted perfectly, and opened the door for them.

Ryan followed Davenport in—and was amazed. Flag quarters on the USS *Kennedy* might have been transported as a block from a Beacon Hill mansion. To his right was a wall-sized mural large enough to dominate a big living room. A half-dozen oils, one of them a portrait of the ship's namesake, President John Fitzgerald Kennedy, dotted the other walls, themselves covered with expensive-looking paneling. The deck was covered in thick crimson wool, and the furniture was pure civilian, French provincial, oak and brocade. One could almost imagine they were not aboard a ship at all, except that the ceiling—"overhead"—had the usual collection of pipes, all painted gray. It was a decidedly odd contrast to the rest of the room.

"Hi ya, Charlie!" Rear Admiral Joshua Painter emerged from the next room, drying his hands with a towel. "How was it coming in?"

"Little rocky," Davenport allowed, shaking hands. "This is Jack Ryan."

Ryan had never met Painter but knew him by reputation. A Phantom pilot during the Vietnam War, he had written a book, *Paddystrikes,* on the conduct of the air campaigns. It had been a truthful book, not the sort of thing that wins friends. He was a small, feisty man who could not have weighed more than a hundred thirty pounds. He was also a gifted tactician and a man of puritanical integrity.

"One of yours, Charlie?"

"No, Admiral, I work for James Greer. I am not a naval officer. Please accept my apologies. I don't like pretending to be what I'm not. The uniform was the CIA's idea." This drew a frown.

"Oh? Well, I suppose that means you're going to tell me what Ivan's up to. Good, I hope to hell somebody knows. First time on a carrier? How did you like the flight in?"

"It might be a good way to interrogate prisoners of war," Ryan said as offhandedly as he could. The two flag officers had a good laugh at his expense, and Painter called for some food to be sent in.

The double doors to the passageway opened serveral minutes

later and a pair of stewards—"mess management specialists"—came in, one bearing a tray of food, the other two pots of coffee. The three men were served in a style appropriate to their rank. The food, served on silver-trimmed plates, was simple but appetizing to Ryan, who hadn't eaten in twelve hours. He dished cole slaw and potato salad onto his plate and selected a pair of corned-beef-on-ryes.

"Thank you. That's all for now," Painter said. The stewards came to attention before leaving. "Okay, let's get down to business."

Ryan gulped down half a sandwich. "Admiral, this information is only twenty hours old." He took the briefing folders from his bag and handed them around. His delivery took twenty minutes, during which he managed to consume the two sandwiches and a goodly portion of his cole slaw and spill coffee on his hand-written notes. The two flag officers were a perfect audience, not interrupting once, only darting a few disbelieving looks at him.

"God Almighty," Painter said when Ryan finished. Davenport just stared poker-faced as he contemplated the possibility of examining a Soviet missile sub from the inside. Jack decided he'd be a formidable opponent over cards. Painter went on, "Do you really believe this?"

"Yes, sir, I do." Ryan poured himself another cup of coffee. He would have preferred a beer to go with his corned beef. It hadn't been bad at all, and good kosher corned beef was something he'd been unable to find in London.

Painter leaned back and looked at Davenport. "Charlie, you tell Greer to teach this lad a few lessons—like how a bureaucrat ain't supposed to stick his neck this far out on the block. Don't *you* think this is a little far-fetched?"

"Josh, Ryan here's the guy who did the report last June on Soviet missile-sub patrol patterns."

"Oh? That was a nice piece of work. It confirmed something I've been saying for two or three years." Painter rose and walked to the corner to look out at the stormy sea. "So, what are we supposed to do about all this?"

"The exact details of the operation have not been determined. What I expect is that you will be directed to locate *Red October* and attempt to establish communications with her skipper. After that? We'll have to figure a way to get her to a safe place. You see, the president doesn't think we'll be able to hold onto her once we get her—if we get her."

"What?" Painter spun around and spoke a tenth of a second before Davenport did. Ryan explained for several minutes.

"Dear God above! You give me one impossible task, then you tell me that if we succeed in it, we gotta give the goddamned thing back to them!"

"Admiral, my recommendation—the president asked me for one—was that we keep the submarine. For what it's worth, the Joint Chiefs are on your side, too, along with the CIA. As it is, though, if the crewmen want to go back home, we have to send them back, and then the Soviets will know we have the boat for sure. As a practical matter, I can see the other side's point. The vessel is worth a pile of money, and it is their property. And how would we hide a 30,000-ton submarine?"

"You hide a submarine by sinking it," Painter said angrily. "They're designed to do that, you know. 'Their property!' We're not talking about a damned passenger liner. That's something designed to kill people—our people!"

"Admiral, I am on your side," Ryan said quietly. "Sir, you said we've given you an impossible task, Why?"

"Ryan, finding a boomer that does not want to be found is not the easiest thing in the world. We practice against our own. We damned near always fail, and you say this one's already passed all the northeast SOSUS lines. The Atlantic's a rather large ocean, and a missile sub's noise footprint is very small."

"Yes, sir." Ryan noted to himself that he might have been overly optimistic about their chances for success.

"What sort of shape are you in, Josh?" Davenport asked.

"Pretty good, really. The exercise we just ran, NIFTY DOLPHIN, worked out all right. Our part of it," Painter corrected himself. *"Dallas* raised some hell on the other side. My ASW crews are functioning very well. What sort of help are we getting?"

"When I left the Pentagon, the CNO was checking the availability of P-3s out on the Pacific, so you'll probably be seeing more of those. Everything that'll move is putting to sea. You're the only carrier, so you've got overall tactical command, right? Come on, Josh, you're our best ASW operator."

Painter poured some coffee for himself. "Okay, we have one carrier deck. *America* and *Nimitz* are still a good week away. Ryan, you said you're flying out to *Invincible*. We get her, too, right?"

"The president was working on that. Want her?"

"Sure. Admiral White has a good nose for ASW, and his boys really lucked out during DOLPHIN. They killed two of our attack boats, and Vince Gallery was some kind of pissed about that. Luck's a big part of this game. That would give us two decks instead of one. I wonder if we can get some more S-3s?" Painter referred to the Lockheed Vikings, carrier-borne antisubmarine aircraft.

"Why?" Davenport asked.

"I can transfer my F-18s to shore, and that'll give us room for twenty more Vikings. I don't like losing the striking power, but what we're going to need is more ASW muscle. That means more S-3s. Jack, you know that if you're wrong, that Russkie surface force is going to be a handful to deal with. You know how many surface-to-surface missiles they're packing?"

"No, sir." Ryan was certain it was too many.

"We're one carrier, and that makes us their primary target. If they start shooting at us, it'll get awful lonesome—then it'll get awful exciting." The phone rang. "Painter here . . . Yes. Thank you. Well, *Invincible* just turned around. Good, they're giving her to us along with two tin cans. The rest of the escorts and the three attack subs are still heading home." He frowned. "I can't really fault them for that. That means we have to give them some escorts, but it's a good trade. I want that flight deck."

"Can we chopper Jack out to her?" Ryan wondered if Davenport knew what the president had ordered him to do. The admiral seemed interested in getting him off the *Kennedy*.

Painter shook his head. "Too far for a chopper. Maybe they can send a Harrier back for him."

"The Harrier's a fighter, sir," Ryan commented.

"They have an experimental two-seat version set up for ASW patrolling. It's supposed to work reasonably well outside their helo perimeter. That's how they bagged one of our attack boats, caught her napping." Painter finished off the last of his coffee.

"Okay, gentlemen, let's get ourselves down to ASW control and try and figure a way to run this circus act. CINCLANT will want to hear what I have in mind. I suppose I'd better decide for myself. We'll also call *Invincible* and have them send a bird back to ferry you out, Ryan."

Ryan followed the two admirals out of the room. He spent two hours watching Painter move ships around the ocean like a chess master with his pieces.

The USS Dallas

Bart Mancuso had been on duty in the attack center for more than twenty hours. Only a few hours of sleep separated his stretch from the previous one. He had been eating sandwiches and drinking coffee, and two cups of soup had been thrown in by his cooks for variety's sake. He examined his latest cup of freeze-dried without affection.

"Cap'n?" He turned. It was Roger Thompson, his sonar officer.

"Yes, what is it?" Mancuso pulled himself away from the tactical display that had occupied his attention for several days. Thompson was standing at the rear of the compartment. Jones was standing beside him holding a clipboard and what looked like a tape machine.

"Sir, Jonesy has something I think you ought to look at."

Mancuso didn't want to be bothered—extended time on duty always taxed his patience. But Jones looked eager and excited. "Okay, come on over to the chart table."

The *Dallas'* chart table was a new gadget wired into the BC-10 and projected onto a TV-type glass screen four feet square. The display moved as the *Dallas* moved. This made paper charts obsolete, though they were kept anyway. Charts can't break.

"Thanks, Skipper," Jones said, more humbly than usual. "I know you're kinda busy, but I think I got something here. That anomalous contact we had the other day's been bothering me. I had to leave it after the ruckus the other Russkie subs kicked up, but I was able to come back to it three times to make sure it was still there. The fourth time it was gone, faded out. I want to show you what I worked up. Can you punch up our course track for back then on this baby, sir?"

The chart table was interfaced through the BC-10 into the ship's inertial navigation system, SINS. Mancuso punched the command in himself. It was getting so that they couldn't flush the head without a computer command . . . The *Dallas'* course track showed up as a convoluted red line, with tick marks displayed at fifteen-minute intervals.

"Great!" Jones commented. "I've never seen it do that before. That's all right. Okay." Jones pulled a handful of pencils from his back pocket. "Now, I got the contact first at 0915 or so, and the bearing was about two-six-nine." He set a pencil down, eraser at *Dallas'* position, point directed west towards the target. "Then at 0930 it was bearing a two-six-zero. At 0948, it was two-five-zero. There's some error built into these, Cap'n. It was a tough signal to lock in on, but the errors should average out. Right about then we got all this other activity, and I had to go after them, but I came back to it about 1000, and the bearing was two-four-two." Jones set down another pencil on the due-east line traced when the *Dallas* had moved away from the Icelandic coast. "At 1015 it was two-three-four, and at 1030 it was two-two-seven. These last two are shaky, sir. The signal was real faint, and I didn't have a very good lock on it." Jones looked up. He appeared nervous.

"So far, so good. Relax, Jonesy. Light up if you want."

"Thanks, Cap'n." Jones fished out a cigarette and lit it with a butane lighter. He had never approached the captain quite this way. He knew Mancuso to be a tolerant, easygoing commander—if you had something to say. He was not a man who liked his time wasted, and it was sure as hell he wouldn't want it wasted now. "Okay, sir, we gotta figure he couldn't be too far away from us, right? I mean, he had to be between us and Iceland. So let's say he was about halfway between. That gives him a course about like this." Jones set down some more pencils.

"Hold it, Jonesy. Where does the course come from?"

"Oh, yeah." Jones flipped open his clipboard. "Yesterday morning, night, whatever it was, after I got off watch, it started bothering me, so I used the move we made offshore as a baseline to do a little course track for him. I know how, Skipper. I read the manual. It's easy, just like we used to do at Cal Tech to chart star motion. I took an astronomy course in my freshman year."

Mancuso stifled a groan. It was the first time he had ever heard this called easy, but on looking at Jones' figures and diagrams, it appeared that he had done it right. "Go on."

Jones pulled a Hewlitt Packard scientific calculator from his pocket and what looked like a National Geographic map liberally coated with pencil marks and scribblings. "You want to check my figures, sir?"

"We will, but I'll trust you for now. What's the map?"

"Skipper, I know it's against the rules an' all, but I keep this as a personal record of the tracks the bad guys use. It doesn't leave the boat, sir, honest. I may be a little off, but all this translates to a course of about two-two-zero and a speed of ten knots. And *that* aims him right at the entrance of Route One. Okay?"

"Go on." Mancuso had already figured that one. Jonesy was on to something.

"Well, I couldn't sleep after that, so I skipped back to sonar and pulled the tape on the contact. I had to run it through the computer a few times to filter out all the crap—sea sounds, the other subs, you know—then I rerecorded it at ten times normal speed." He set his cassette recorder on the chart table. "Listen to this, Skipper."

The tape was scratchy, but every few seconds there was a *thrum*. Two minutes of listening seemed to indicate a regular interval of about five seconds. By this time Lieutenant Mannion was looking over Thompson's shoulder, listening, and nodding speculatively.

"Skipper, that's gotta be a man-made sound. It's just too regular for anything else. At normal speed it didn't make much sense, but once I speeded it up, I had the sucker."

"Okay, Jonesy, finish it," Mancuso said.

"Captain, what you just heard was the acoustical signature of a Russian submarine. He was heading for Route One, taking the inshore track off the Icelandic coast. You can bet money on that, Skipper."

"Roger?"

"He sold me, Captain," Thompson replied.

Mancuso took another look at the course track, trying to figure an alternative. There wasn't any. "Me, too. Roger, Jonesy makes sonarman first class today. I want to see the paper work done by the turn of the next watch, along with a nice letter of commendation for my signature. Ron," he poked the sonarman in the shoulder, "that's all right. Damned well done!"

"Thanks, Skipper." Jones' smile stretched from ear to ear.

"Pat, please call Lieutenant Butler to the attack center."

Mannion went to the phones to call the boat's chief engineer.

"Any idea what it is, Jonesy?" Mancuso turned back.

The sonarman shook his head. "It isn't screw sounds. I've never heard anything like it." He ran the tape back and played it again.

Two minutes later, Lieutenant Earl Butler came into the attack center. "You rang, Skipper?"

"Listen to this, Earl." Mancuso rewound the tape and played it a third time.

Butler was a graduate of the University of Texas and every school the navy had for submarines and their engine systems. "What's that supposed to be?"

"Jonesy says it's a Russian sub. I think he's right."

"Tell me about the tape," Butler said to Jones.

"Sir, it's speeded up ten times, and I washed it through the BC-10 five times. At normal speed it doesn't sound like much of anything." With uncharacteristic modesty, Jones did not point out that it had sounded like something to him.

"Some sort of harmonic? I mean, if it was a propeller, it'd have to be a hundred feet across, and we'd be hearing one blade at a time. The regular interval suggests some sort of harmonic." Butler's face screwed up. "But a harmonic what?"

"Whatever it was, it was headed right here." Mancuso tapped Thor's Twins with his pencil.

"That makes him a Russian, all right," Butler agreed. "Then they're using something new. Again."

"Mr. Butler's right," Jones said. "It does sound like a harmonic rumble. The other funny thing is, well, there was this background noise, kinda like water going through a pipe. I don't know, it didn't pick up on this. I guess the computer filtered it off. It was real faint to start with—anyway, that's outside my field."

"That's all right. You've done enough for one day. How do you feel?" Mancuso asked.

"A little tired, Skipper. I've been working on this for a while."

"If we get close to this guy again, you think you can track him down?" Mancuso knew the answer.

"You bet, Cap'n! Now that we know what to listen for, you bet I'll bag the sucker!"

Mancuso looked at the chart table. "Okay, if he was heading

for the Twins, and then ran the route at, say twenty-eight or thirty knots, and then settled down to his base course and speed of about ten or so . . . that puts him about here now. Long ways off. Now, if we run at top speed . . . forty-eight hours will put us here, and that'll put us in front of him. Pat?"

"That's about right, sir," Lieutenant Mannion concurred. "You're figuring he ran the route at full speed, then settled down—makes sense. He wouldn't need the quiet drive in that damned maze. It gives him a free shot for four or five hundred miles, so why not uncrank his engines? That's what I'd do."

"That's what we'll try and do, then. We'll radio in for permission to leave Toll Booth station and track this character down. Jonesy, running at max speed means you sonarmen will be out of work for a while. Set up the contact tape on the simulator and make sure the operators all know what this guy sounds like, but get some rest. All of you. I want you at a hundred percent when we try to reacquire this guy. Have yourself a shower. Make that a Hollywood shower—you've earned it—and rack out. When we do go after this character, it'll be a long, tough hunt."

"No sweat, Captain. We'll get him for you. Bet on it. You want to keep my tape, sir?"

"Yeah." Mancuso ejected the tape and looked up in surprise. "You sacrificed a Bach for this?"

"Not a good one, sir. I have a Christopher Hogwood of this piece that's much better."

Mancuso pocketed the tape. "Dismissed, Jonesy. Nice work."

"A pleasure, Cap'n." Jones left the attack center counting the extra money for jumping a rate.

"Roger, make sure your people are well rested over the next two days. When we do go after this guy, it's going to be a bastard."

"Aye, Captain."

"Pat, get us up to periscope depth. We're going to call this one into Norfolk right now. Earl, I want you thinking about what's making that noise."

"Right, Captain."

While Mancuso drafted his message, Lieutenant Mannion brought the *Dallas* to periscope-antenna depth with an upward angle on the diving planes. It took five minutes to get from five hundred feet to just below the stormy surface. The submarine was subject to wave action, and while it was very gentle by surface ship standards, the crew noted her rocking. Mannion raised the periscope and ESM (electronic support measures) antenna, the latter used for the broad-band receiver designed to detect possible radar emissions. There was nothing in view—he could see about five miles—and the ESM instruments showed nothing except for aircraft sets, which were too far away to matter. Next Mannion raised two more masts. One was a reed-like UHF (ultrahigh frequency) receiving antenna. The other was new, a laser transmitter. This rotated and locked onto the carrier wave signal of the Atlantic SSIX, the communications satellite used exclusively by submarines. With the laser, they could send high-density transmissions without giving away the sub's position.

"All ready, sir," the duty radioman reported.

"Transmit."

The radioman pressed a button. The signal, sent in a fraction of a second, was received by photovoltaic cells, read over to a UHF transmitter, and shot back down by a parabolic dish antenna towards Atlantic Fleet Communications headquarters. At Norfolk another radioman noted the reception and pressed a button that transmitted the same signal up to the satellite and back to the *Dallas*. It was a simple way to identify garbles.

The *Dallas* operator compared the received signal with the one he'd just sent. "Good copy, sir."

Mancuso ordered Mannion to lower everything but the ESM and UHF antennae.

Atlantic Fleet Communications

In Norfolk the first line of the dispatch revealed the page and line of the one-time-pad cipher sequence, which was recorded on computer tape in the maximum security section of the communications complex. An officer typed the proper numbers into his computer terminal, and an instant later the machine generated a clear text. The officer checked it again for garbles. Satisfied there were none, he took the printout to the other side of the room where a yeoman was seated at a telex. The officer handed him the dispatch.

The yeoman keyed up the proper addressee and transmitted the message by dedicated landline to COMSUBLANT Operations, half a mile away. The landline was fiber optic, located in a steel conduit under a paved street. It was checked three times a week for security purposes. Not even the secrets of nuclear weapons performance were as closely guarded as day-to-day tactical communications.

COMSUBLANT *Operations*

A bell went off in the operations room as the message came up on the "hot" printer. It bore a Z prefix, which indicated FLASH-priority status.

Z090414ZDEC

T O P S E C R E T T H E O

FM: USS DALLAS

TO: COMSUBLANT

INFO: CINCLANTFLT

//NOOOOO//

REDFLEET SUBOPS
1. REPORT ANOMALOUS SONAR CONTACT ABOUT 0900Z 7DEC AND LOST AFTER INCREASE IN REDFLEET SUB ACTIVITY. CONTACT SUBSE-QUENTLY EVALUATED AS REDFLEET SSN/SSBN TRANSITING ICELAND INSHORE TRACK TO-WARDS ROUTE ONE. COURSE SOUTHWEST SPEED TEN DEPTH UNKNOWN.
2. CONTACT EVIDENCED UNUSUAL REPEAT UN-USUAL ACOUSTICAL CHARACTERISTICS. SIG-NATURE UNLIKE ANY KNOWN REDFLEET SUBMARINE.
3. REQUEST PERMISSION TO LEAVE TOLL BOOTH TO PURSUE AND INVESTIGATE. BELIEVE A NEW DRIVE SYSTEM WITH UNUSUAL SOUND CHAR-ACTERISTICS BEING USED THIS SUB. BELIEVE GOOD PROBABILITY CAN LOCATE AND IDEN-TIFY.

A lieutenant junior grade took the dispatch to the office of Vice Admiral Vincent Gallery. COMSUBLANT had been on duty since the Soviet subs had started moving. He was in an evil mood.

"A FLASH priority from *Dallas,* sir."

"Uh-huh." Gallery took the yellow form and read it twice. "What do you suppose this means?"

"No telling, sir. Looks like he heard something, took his time figuring it out, and wants another crack at it. He seems to think he's onto something unusual."

"Okay, what do I tell him? Come on, mister. You might be an admiral yourself someday and have to make decisions." An unlikely prospect, Gallery thought.

"Sir, *Dallas* is in an ideal position to shadow their surface force when it gets to Iceland. We need her where she is."

"Good textbook answer." Gallery smiled up at the youngster, preparing to cut him off at the knees. "On the other hand, *Dallas* is commanded by a fairly competent man who wouldn't be bothering us unless he really thought he had something. He doesn't go into specifics, probably because it's too complicated for a tactical FLASH dispatch, and also because he thinks that we know his judgment is good enough to take his word on something. 'New drive system with unusual sound characteristics.' That may be a crock, but he's the man on the scene, and he wants an answer. We tell him yes."

"Aye aye, sir," the lieutenant said, wondering if the skinny old bastard made decisions by flipping a coin when his back was turned.

The Dallas

Z090432ZDEC

TOP SECRET

FM: COMSUBLANT

TO: USS DALLAS

A. USS DALLAS Z090414ZDEC

B. COMSUBLANT INST 2000.5

OPAREA ASSIGNMENT //N04220//

1. REQUEST REF A GRANTED.
2. AREAS BRAVO ECHO GOLF REF B ASSIGNED FOR UNRESTRICTED OPS 090500Z TO 140001Z. REPORT AS NECESSARY. VADM GALLERY SENDS.

"Hot damn!" Mancuso chuckled. That was one nice thing about Gallery. When you asked him a question, by God, you got an answer, yes or no, before you could rig your antenna in. Of course, he reflected, if it turned out that Jonesy was wrong and this was a wild-goose chase, he'd have some explaining to do. Gallery had handed more than one sub skipper his head in a bag and set him on the beach.

Which was where he was headed regardless, Mancuso knew. Since his first year at Annapolis all he had ever wanted was command of his own attack boat. He had that now, and he knew that the rest of his career would be downhill. In the rest of the navy your first command was just that, a first command. You could move up the ladder and command a fleet at sea eventually, if you were lucky and had the right stuff. Not submariners, though. Whether he did well with the *Dallas* or poorly, he'd lose her soon enough. He had this one and only chance. And afterwards, what? The best he could hope for was command of a missile boat. He'd served on those before and was sure that commanding one, even a new *Ohio*, was about as exciting as watching paint dry. The boomer's job was to stay hidden. Mancuso wanted to be the hunter, that was the exciting end of the business. And after commanding a missile boat? He could get a "major surface command," perhaps a nice oiler— it would be like switching mounts from Secretariat to Elsie the Cow. Or he could get a squadron command and sit in an office onboard a tender, pushing paper. At best in that position he'd go to sea once a month, his main purpose being to bother sub skippers who didn't want him there. Or he could get a desk job in the Pentagon—what fun! Mancuso understood why some of the astronauts had cracked up after coming back from the moon. He, too, had worked many years for this command, and in another year his boat would be gone. He'd have to give the *Dallas* to someone else. But he did have her now.

"Pat, let's lower all masts and take her down to twelve hundred feet."

"Aye aye, sir. Lower the masts," Mannion ordered. A petty officer pulled on the hydraulic control levers.

"ESM and UHF masts lowered, sir," the duty electrician reported.

"Very well. Diving officer, make your depth twelve hundred feet."

"Twelve hundred feet, aye," the diving officer responded. "Fifteen degrees down-angle on the planes."

"Fifteen degrees down, aye."

"Let's move her, Pat."

"Aye, Skipper. All ahead full."

"All ahead full, aye." The helmsman reached up to turn the annunciator.

Mancuso watched his crew at work. They did their jobs with mechanistic precision. But they were not machines. They were men. His.

In the reactor spaces aft, Lieutenant Butler had his enginemen acknowledge the command and gave the necessary orders. The reactor coolant pumps went to fast speed. An increased amount of hot, pressurized water entered the exchanger, where its heat was transferred to the steam on the outside loop. When the coolant returned to the reactor it was cooler than it had been and therefore denser. Being denser, it trapped more neutrons in the reactor pile, increasing the ferocity of the fission reactic and giving off yet more power. Farther aft, saturated steam in the "outside" or nonradioactive loop of the heat exchange system emerged through clusters of control valves to strike the blades of the high-pressure turbine. The *Dallas'* huge bronze screw began to turn more quickly, driving her forward and down.

The engineers went about their duties calmly. The noise in the engine spaces rose noticeably as the systems began to put out more power, and the technicians kept track of this by continuously monitoring the banks of instruments under their hands. The routine was quiet and exact. There was no extraneous conversation, no distraction. Compared to a submarine's reactor spaces, a hospital operating room was a den of libertines.

Forward, Mannion watched the depth gauge go below six hundred feet. The diving officer would wait until they got to nine hundred feet before starting to level off, the object being to zero the dive out exactly at the ordered depth. Commander Mancuso wanted the *Dallas* below the thermocline. This was the border between different temperatures. Water settled in isothermal layers of uniform stratification. The relatively flat boundary where warmer surface water met colder depth water was a semipermeable barrier which tended to reflect sound waves. Those waves that did manage to penetrate the thermocline were mostly trapped below it. Thus, though the *Dallas* was now running below the thermocline at over thirty knots and making as much noise as she was capable of, she would still be difficult to detect with surface sonar. She would also be largely blind, but then, there was not much down there to run into.

Mancuso lifted the microphone for the PA system. "This is the captain speaking. We have just started a speed run that will last forty-eight hours. We are heading towards a point where we hope to locate a Russian sub that went past us two days ago. This Russkie is evidently using a new and rather quiet propulsion system that nobody's run across before. We're going to try and get ahead of him and track on him as he passes us again. This time we know what to listen for, and we'll get a nice clear picture of him. Okay, I want everyone on this boat to be well rested. When we get there, it'll be a long, tough hunt. I want everybody at a hundred percent. This one will probably be interesting." He switched off the microphone. "What's the movie tonight?"

The diving officer watched the depth gauge stop moving before answering. As chief of the boat, he was also manager of the *Dallas'* cable TV system, three video-cassette recorders in the mess room which led to televisions in the wardroom, and various other crew accommodations. "Skipper, you got a choice. *Return of the Jedi* or two football tapes: Oklahoma-Nebraska and Miami-Dallas. Both those games were played while we were on the exercise, sir. It'll be like watching them live." He laughed. "Commercials and all. The cooks are already making the popcorn."

"Good. I want everybody nice and loose." Why couldn't they ever get Navy tapes, Mancuso wondered. Of course, Army had creamed them this year . . .

"Morning, Skipper." Wally Chambers, the executive officer, came into the attack center. "What gives?"

"Come on back to the wardroom, Wally. I want you to listen

to something." Mancuso took the cassette from his shirt pocket and led Chambers aft.

The V. K. Konovalov

Two hundred miles northeast of the *Dallas*, in the Norwegian Sea, the *Konovalov* was racing southwest at forty-one knots. Captain Tupolev sat alone in the wardroom rereading the dispatch he'd received two days before. His emotions alternated between rage and grief. The Schoolmaster had done *that!* He was dumbfounded.

But what was there to do? Tupolev's orders were explicit, the more so since, as his *zampolit* had pointed out, he was a former pupil of the traitor Ramius. He, too, could find himself in a very bad position. If the slug succeeded.

So, Marko had pulled a trick on everyone, not just the *Konovalov*. Tupolev had been slinking about the Barents Sea like a fool while Marko had been heading the other way. Laughing at everyone, Tupolev was sure. Such treachery, such a hellish threat against the *Rodina*. It was inconceivable—and all too conceivable. All the advantages Marko had. A four-room apartment, a dacha, his own Zhiguli. Tupolev did not yet have his own automobile. He had earned his way to a command, and now it was all threatened by—this! He'd be lucky to keep what he had.

I have to kill a friend, he thought. Friend? Yes, he admitted to himself, Marko had been a good friend and a fine teacher. Where had he gone wrong?

Natalia Bogdanova.

Yes, that had to be it. A big stink, the way that had happened. How many times had he had dinner with them, how many times had Natalia laughed about her fine, strong, big sons? He shook his head. A fine woman killed by a damned incompetent fool of a surgeon. Nothing could be done about it, he was the son of a Central Committee member. It was an outrage the way things like that still happened, even after three generations of building socialism. But nothing was sufficient to justify this madness.

Tupolev bent over the chart he'd brought back. He'd be on his station in five days, in less time if the engine plant held together and Marko wasn't in too much of a hurry—and he wouldn't be. Marko was a fox, not a bull. The other *Alfa*s would get there ahead of his, Tupolev knew, but it didn't matter. He had to do this himself. He'd get ahead of Marko and wait. Marko would try to slink past, and the *Konovalov* would be there. And the *Red October* would die.

The North Atlantic

The British Sea Harrier FRS.4 appeared a minute early. It hovered briefly off the *Kennedy*'s port beam as the pilot sized up his landing target, the wind, and sea conditions. Maintaining a steady thirty-knot forward speed to compensate for the carrier's forward speed, he side-slipped his fighter neatly to the right, then dropped it gently amidships, slightly forward of the *Kennedy*'s island structure, exactly in the center of the flight deck. Instantly a gang of deck crewmen raced for the aircraft, three carrying heavy metal chocks, another a metal ladder which he set up by the cockpit, whose canopy was already coming open. A team of four snaked a fueling hose towards the aircraft, eager to demonstrate the speed with which the U.S. Navy services aircraft. The pilot was dressed in an orange coverall and yellow life jacket. He set his helmet on the back of the front seat and came down the ladder. He watched briefly to be sure his fighter was in capable hands before sprinting to the island. He met Ryan at the hatch.

"You Ryan? I'm Tony Parker. Where's the loo?" Jack gave him the proper directions and the pilot darted off, leaving Ryan standing there in a flight suit, holding his bag and feeling stupid. A white plastic flight helmet dangled from his other hand as they watched the crewmen fueling the Harrier. He wondered if they knew what they were doing.

Parker was back in three minutes. "Commander," he said, "there's one thing they've never put in a fighter, and that's a bloody toilet. They fill you up with coffee and tea and send you off, and you've no place to go."

"I know the feeling. Anything else you have to do?"

"No, sir. Your admiral chatted with me on the radio when I was flying in. Looks like your chaps have finished fueling my bird. Shall we be off?"

"What do I do with this?" Ryan held up his bag, expecting to have to hold it in his lap. His briefing papers were inside the flight suit, tucked against his chest.

"We put it in the boot, of course. Come along, sir."

Parker walked out to the fighter jauntily. The dawn was a feeble one. There was a solid overcast at one or two thousand feet. It wasn't raining, but looked as though it might. The sea, still rolling at about eight feet, was a gray, crinkled surface dotted with whitecaps. Ryan could feel the *Kennedy* moving, surprised that something so huge could be made to move at all. When they got to the Harrier, Parker took the duffle in one hand and reached for a recessed handle on the underside of the fighter. Twisting and pulling the lever, he revealed a cramped space about the size of a small refrigerator. Parker stuffed the bag into it, slamming the door shut behind it, making sure the locking lever was fully engaged. A deck crewman in a yellow shirt conferred with the pilot. Aft a helicopter was revving its engines, and a Tomcat fighter was taxiing towards a midships catapult. On top of this a thirty-knot wind was blowing. The carrier was a noisy place.

Parker waved Ryan up the ladder. Jack, who liked ladders about as much as he liked flying, nearly fell into his seat. He struggled to get situated properly, while a deck crewman strapped him into the four-point restraint system. The man put the helmet on Ryan's head and pointed to the jack for its intercom system. Maybe American crews really did know something about Harriers. Next to the plug was a switch. Ryan flipped it.

"Can you hear me, Parker?"

"Yes, Commander. All settled in?"

"I suppose."

"Right." Parker's head swiveled to check the engine intakes. "Starting the engine."

The canopies stayed up. Three crewmen stood close by with large carbon dioxide extinguishers, presumably in case the engine exploded. A dozen others were standing by the island, watching the strange aircraft as the Pegasus engine screamed to life. Then the canopy came down.

"Ready, Commander?"

"If you are."

The Harrier was not a large fighter, but it was certainly the loudest. Ryan could feel the engine noise ripple through his body as Parker adjusted his thrust-vector controls. The aircraft wobbled, dipped at the nose, then rose shakily into the air.

Ryan saw a man by the island point and gesture to them. The Harrier slid to port, moving away from the island as it gained in height.

"That wasn't too bad," Parker said. He adjusted the thrust controls, and the Harrier began true forward flight. There was little feeling of acceleration, but Ryan saw that the *Kennedy* was rapidly falling behind. A few seconds later they were beyond the inner ring of escorts.

"Let's get on top of this muck," Parker said. He pulled back on the stick and headed for the clouds. In seconds they were in them, and Ryan's field of view was reduced from five miles to five feet in an instant.

Jack looked around his cockpit, which had flight controls and instruments. Their airspeed showed one hundred fifty knots and rising, altitude four hundred feet. This Harrier had evidently been a trainer, but the instrument panel had been altered to include the read-out instruments for a sensor pod that could be attached to the belly. A poor man's way of doing things, but from what Admiral Painter said it had evidently worked well enough. He figured the TV-type screen was the FLIR readout, which monitored a forward-looking infrared heat sensor. The airspeed gauge now said three hundred knots, and the climb indicator showed a twenty-degree angle of attack. It felt like more than that.

"Should be hitting the top of this soon," Parker said. "Now!"

The altimeter showed twenty-six thousand feet when Ryan was blasted by pure sunlight. One thing about flying that he never got used to was that no matter how awful the weather was on the ground, if you flew high enough you could always find the sun. The light was intense, but the sky's color was noticeably deeper than the soft blue seen from the ground. The ride became airliner smooth as they escaped the lower turbulence. Ryan fumbled with his visor to shield his eyes.

"That better, sir?"

"Fine, Lieutenant. It's better than I expected."

"What do you mean, sir?" Parker inquired.

"I guess it beats flying on a commercial bird. You can see more. That helps."

"Sorry we don't have any extra fuel, or I'd show you some aerobatics. The Harrier will do almost anything you ask of her."

"That's all right."

"And your admiral," Parker went on conversationally, "said that you don't fancy flying."

Ryan's hands grabbed the armrests as the Harrier went through three complete revolutions before snapping back to level flight. He surprised himself by laughing. "Ah, the British sense of humor."

"Orders from your admiral, sir," Parker semi-apologized. "We wouldn't want you to think the Harrier's another bloody bus."

"Which admiral, Ryan wondered, Painter or Davenport? Probably both. The top of the clouds was like a rolling field of cotton. He'd never appreciated that before, looking through a foot-square window on an airliner. In the back seat he almost felt as if he were sitting outside.

"May I ask a question, sir?"

"Sure."

"What's the flap?"

"What do you mean?"

"I mean, sir, that they turned my ship around. Then I get orders to ferry a VIP from *Kennedy* to *Invincible*."

"Oh, okay. Can't say, Parker. I'm delivering some messages to your boss. I'm just the mailman," Ryan lied. Roll that one three times.

"Excuse me, Commander, but you see, my wife is expecting a child, our first, soon after Christmas. I hope to be there, sir."

"Where do you live?"

"Chatham, that's—"

"I know. I live in England myself at the moment. Our place is in Marlow, upriver from London. My second kid got started over there."

"Born there?"

"Started there. My wife says it's those strange hotel beds, do it to her every time. If I were a betting man, I'd give you good odds, Parker. First babies are always late anyway."

"You say you live in Marlow?"

"That's right, we built a house there earlier this year."

"Jack Ryan—John Ryan? The same chap who—"

"Correct. You don't have to tell anybody that, Lieutenant."

"Understood, sir. I didn't know you were a naval officer."

"That's why you don't have to tell anyone."

"Yes, sir. Sorry for the stunt earlier."

"That's all right. Admirals must have their little laughs. I understand you guys just ran an exercise with our guys."

"Indeed we did, Commander. I sank one of your submarines, the *Tullibee*. My systems operator and I, that is. We caught her near the surface at night with our FLIR and dropped noise-makers all round her. You see, we didn't let anyone know about our new equipment. All's fair, as you know. I understand her commander was bloody furious. I'd hoped to meet him in Norfolk, but he didn't arrive until the day we sailed."

"You guys have a good time in Norfolk?"

"Yes, Commander. We were able to get in a day's shooting on your Chesapeake Bay, the Eastern Shore, I believe you call it."

"Oh yeah? I used to hunt there. How was it?"

"Not bad. I got my three geese in half an hour. Bag limit was three—stupid."

"You called in and blasted three geese in a half hour this late in the season?"

"That is how I earn my modest living, Commander, shooting," Parker commented.

"I was up for a grouse shoot with your admiral last September. They made me use a double. If you show up with my kind of gun—I use a Remington automatic—they look at you like you're some kind of terrorist. I got stuck with a pair of Purdeys that didn't fit. Got fifteen birds. Seemed an awful lazy way to hunt, though, with one guy loading my gun for me, and another platoon of ghillies driving the game. We just about annihilated the bird population, too."

"We have more game per acre than you do."

"That's what the admiral said. How far to *Invincible?*"

"Forty minutes."

Ryan looked at the fuel gauges. They were half empty already. In a car he'd be thinking about a fill-up. All that fuel gone in half an hour. Well, Parker didn't seem excited.

The landing on HMS *Invincible* was different from the COD's arrival on the *Kennedy*. The ride became rocky as Parker descended through the clouds, and it occurred to Ryan that they were on the leading edge of the same storm he'd endured the night before. The canopy was coated with rain, and he heard the impact of thousands of raindrops on the airframe—or was it hail? Watching the instruments, he saw that Parker leveled out at a thousand feet, while they were still in clouds, then descended more slowly, breaking into the clear at a hundred feet. The *Invincible* was scarcely a half the *Kennedy*'s size. He watched her bobbing actively on the fifteen-foot seas. Parker used the same technique as before. He hovered briefly on the carrier's port side, then slid to the right, dropping the fighter twenty feet onto a painted circle. The landing was hard, but Ryan was able to see it coming. The canopy came up at once.

"You can get out here," Parker said. "I have to taxi to the elevator."

A ladder was already in place. He unbuckled and got out. A crewman had already retrieved his bag. Ryan followed him to the island and was met by an ensign—a sublieutenant, the British call the rank.

"Welcome aboard, sir." The youngster couldn't be more than twenty, Ryan thought. "Let me help you out of the flight suit."

The sublieutenant stood by as Ryan unzipped and took off his helmet, Mae West, and coverall. He retrieved his cap from the bag. In the process he bounced off the bulkhead a few times. The *Invincible* seemed to be corkscrewing in a following sea. A bow wind and a following sea? In the North Atlantic in winter, nothing was too crazy. The officer took his bag, and Ryan held onto the briefing material.

"Lead on, *lef*tenant," Ryan gestured. The youngster shot up a series of three ladders, leaving Jack painting behind, thinking about the jogging he wasn't getting in. The combination of the ship's motion and an inner ear badly scrambled from the day's flying made him dizzy, and he found himself bumping into things. How did professional pilots do it?

"Here's the flag bridge, sir." The sublieutenant held the door open.

"Hello, Jack!" boomed the voice of Vice Admiral John White, eighth earl of Weston. He was a tall, well-built man of fifty with a florid complexion set off by a white scarf at his neck. Jack had first met him earlier in the year, and since then his wife Cathy and the countess, Antonia, had become close friends, members of the same circle of amateur musicians. Cathy Ryan played classical piano. Toni White, an attractive woman of forty-four, owned a Guarnieri del Jesu violin. Her husband was a man whose peerage was treated as the convenient afterthought. His career in the Royal Navy had been built entirely on merit. Jack walked over to take his hand.

"Good day, Admiral."

"How was your flight?"

"Different. I've never been in a fighter before, much less one with ambitions to mate with a hummingbird," Ryan smiled. The bridge was overheated, and it felt good.

"Jolly good. Let's go aft to my sea cabin." White dismissed the sublieutenant, who handed Jack his bag before withdrawing. The admiral led him aft through a short passageway and left into a small compartment.

It was surprisingly austere, considering that the English liked their comforts and that White was a peer. There were two curtained portholes, a desk, and a couple of chairs. The only human touch was a color photograph of his wife. The entire port wall was covered with a chart of the North Atlantic.

"You look tired, Jack." White waved him to the upholstered chair.

"I am tired. I've been on the go since—hell, since 6:00 A.M. yesterday. I don't know about time changes, I think my watch is still on European time."

"I have a message for you." White pulled a slip of paper from his pocket and handed it over.

"Greer to Ryan. WILLOW confirmed," Ryan read. "Basil sends regards. Ends." Somebody had confirmed WILLOW. Who? Maybe Sir Basil, maybe Ritter. Ryan would not quote odds on that one.

Jack tucked it in his pocket. "This is good news, sir."

"Why the uniform?"

"Not my idea, Admiral. You know who I work for, right? They figured I'd be less conspicuous this way."

"At least it fits." The admiral lifted a phone and ordered refreshments sent to them. "How's the family, Jack?"

"Fine, thank you, sir. The day before I came over Cathy and Toni were playing over at Nigel Ford's place. I missed it. You know, if they get much better, we ought to have a record cut. There aren't too many violin players better than your wife."

A steward arrived with a plateful of sandwiches. Jack had never figured out the British taste for cucumbers on bread.

"So, what's the flap?"

"Admiral, the significance of the message you just gave me is that I can tell this to you and three other officers. This is very hot stuff, sir. You'll want to make your choices accordingly."

"Hot enough to turn my little fleet around." White thought it over before lifting the phone and ordering three of his officers to the cabin. He hung up. "Captain Carstairs, Captain Hunter, and Commander Barclay—they are, respectively, *Invincible*'s commanding officer, my fleet operations officer, and my fleet intelligence officer."

"No chief of staff?"

"Flew home, death in the family. Something for your coffee?" White extracted what looked like a brandy bottle from a desk drawer.

"Thank you, Admiral." He was grateful for the brandy. The coffee needed the help. He watched the admiral pour a generous amount, perhaps with the ulterior motive of making him speak more freely. White had been a British sailor longer than he'd been Ryan's friend.

The three officers arrived together, two carrying folding metal chairs.

"Admiral," Ryan began, "you might want to leave that bottle out. After you hear this story, we might all need a drink." He passed out his two remaining briefing folders and talked from memory. His delivery took fifteen minutes.

"Gentlemen," he concluded, "I must insist that this information be kept strictly confidential. For the moment no one outside this room may learn it."

"That is too bad," Carstairs said. "This makes for a bloody good sea story."

"And our mission?" White was holding the photographs. He poured Ryan another shot of brandy, gave the bottle a brief look, then stowed it back in the desk.

"Thank you, Admiral. For the moment our mission is to locate *Red October*. After that we're not sure. I imagine just locating her will be hard enough."

"An astute observation, Commander Ryan," Hunter said.

"The good news is that Admiral Painter has requested that CINCLANT assign you control of several U.S. Navy vessels, probably three 1052-class frigates, and a pair of FFG *Perry*s. They all carry a chopper or two."

"Well, Geoffrey?" White asked.

"It's a start," Hunter agreed.

"They'll be arriving in a day or two. Admiral Painter asked me to express his confidence in your group and its personnel."

"A whole fucking Russian missile submarine . . ." Barclay said almost to himself. Ryan laughed.

"Like the idea, Commander?" At least he had one convert.

"What if the sub is heading for the U.K.? Does it then become a British operation?" Barclay asked pointedly.

"I suppose it would, but from the way I read the map, if Ramius was heading for England, he'd already be there. I saw a copy of the president's letter to the prime minister. In return for your assistance, the Royal Navy gets the same access to the data we develop as our guys get. We're on the same side, gentlemen. The question is, can we do it?"

"Hunter?" the admiral asked.

"If this intelligence is correct . . . I'd say we have a good chance, perhaps as good as fifty percent. On one hand, we have a missile submarine attempting to evade detection. On the other, we have a great deal of ASW arrayed to locate her, and she will be heading towards one of only a few discrete locations. Norfolk, of course, Newport, Groton, King's Bay, Port Everglades, Charleston. A civilian port such as New York is less likely, I think. The problem is, what with Ivan sending all his *Alfa*s racing to your coast, they will get there ahead of *October*. They may have a specific port target in mind. We'll know that in another day. So, I'd say they have an equal chance. They'll be able to operate far enough off your coast that your government will have no viable legal reason to object to whatever they do. If anything, I'd say the Soviets have the advantage. They have both a clearer idea of the submarine's capabilities and a simpler overall mission. That more than balances their less capable sensors."

"Why isn't Ramius coming on faster?" Ryan asked. "That's the one thing I can't figure. Once he clears the SOSUS lines off Iceland, he's clear into the deep basin—so why not crack his throttles wide open and race for our coast?"

"At least two reasons," Barclay answered. "How much operational intelligence data do you see?"

"I handle individual assignments. That means I hop around a lot from one thing to another. I know a good deal about their boomers, for example, but not as much about their attack boats." Ryan didn't have to explain he was CIA.

"Well, you know how compartmentalized the Sovs are. Ramius probably doesn't know where their attack submarines are, not all of them. So, if he were to race about, he'd run the off chance of blundering into a stray *Victor* and being sunk without ever knowing what was happening. Second, what if the Soviets did enlist American assistance, saying perhaps that a missile sub had been taken over by a mutinous crew of Maoist counterrevolutionaries—and then your navy detects a missile submarine racing down the North Atlantic towards the American coast. What would your president do?"

"Yeah," Ryan nodded. "We'd blow it the hell out of the water."

"There you have it. Ramius is in the trade of stealth, and he'll likely stick to what he knows," Barclay concluded. "Fortunately or unfortunately, he's jolly good at it."

"How soon will we have performance data on this quiet drive system?" Carstairs wanted to know.

"Next couple of days, we hope."

"Where does Admiral Painter want us?" White asked.

"The plan he submitted to Norfolk puts you on the right flank. He wants *Kennedy* inshore to handle the threat from their surface force. He wants your force farther out. You see, Painter thinks there's the chance that Ramius will come straight south from the G-I-U.K. gap into the Atlantic basin and just sit for a while. The odds favor his not being detected there, and if the Soviets send the fleet after him, he's got the time and supplies to sit out there longer than they can maintain a force off our coast—both for technical and political reasons. Additionally, he wants your striking power out here to threaten their flank. It has to be approved by the commander in chief of the Atlantic Fleet, and a lot of details remain to be worked out. For example, Painter requested some E-3 Sentries to support you out here."

"A month in the middle of the North Atlantic in winter?" Carstairs winced. He had been the *Invincible*'s executive officer during the war around the Falklands and had ridden in the violent South Atlantic for endless weeks.

"Be happy for the E-3s." The admiral smiled. "Hunter, I want to see plans for using all these ships the Yanks are giving us, and how we can cover a maximum area. Barclay, I want to see your evaluation of what our friend Ramius will do. Assume he's still the clever bastard we've come to know and love."

"Aye aye, sir." Barclay stood with the others.

"Jack, how long will you be with us?"

"I don't know, Admiral. Until they recall me to the *Kennedy*, I guess. From where I sit, this operation was laid on too fast. Nobody really knows what the hell we're supposed to do."

"Well, why don't you let us see to this for a while? You look exhausted. Get some sleep."

"True enough, Admiral." Ryan was beginning to feel the brandy.

"There's a cot in the locker over there. I'll have someone set it up for you, and you can sleep in here for the time being. If anything comes in for you, we'll get you up."

"That's kind of you, sir." Admiral White was a good guy, Jack thought, and his wife was something very special. In ten minutes, Ryan was on the cot and asleep.

The Red October

Every two days the *starpom* collected the radiation badges. This was part of a semiformal inspection. After seeing to it that every crewman's shoes were spit-shined, every bunk was properly made, and every footlocker was arranged according to the book, the executive officer would take the two-day-old badges and hand the sailors new ones, usually along with some terse advice to square themselves away as New Soviet Men ought. Borodin had this procedure down to a science. Today, as always, the trip from one compartment to another took two hours. When he was finished, the bag on his left hip was full of old badges, and the one on his right depleted of new ones. He took the badges to the ship's medical officer.

"Comrade Petrov, I have a gift for you." Borodin set the leather bag on the physician's desk.

"Good." The doctor smiled up at the executive officer. "With all the healthy young men I have little to do but read my journals."

Borodin left Petrov to his task. First the doctor set the badges out in order. Each bore a three-digit number. The first digit identified the badge series, so that if any radiation were detected there would be a time reference. The second digit showed where the sailor worked, the third where he slept. This system was easier to work with than the old one, which had used individual numbers for each man.

The developing process was cookbook-simple. Petrov could do it without a thought. First he switched off the white overhead light and replaced it with a red one. Then he locked his office door. Next he took the development rack from its holder on the bulkhead, broke open the plastic holders, and transferred the film strips to spring clips on the rack.

Petrov took the rack into the adjacent laboratory and hung it on the handle of the single filing cabinet. He filled three large square basins with chemicals. Though a qualified physician, he had forgotten most of his inorganic chemistry and didn't remember exactly what the developing chemicals were. Basin number one was filled from bottle number one. Basin two was filled from bottle two, and basin three, he remembered, was filled with water. Petrov was in no hurry. The midday meal was not for two more hours, and his duties were truly boring. The last two days he had been reading his medical texts on tropical diseases. The doctor was looking forward to visiting Cuba as much as anyone aboard. With luck a crewman would come down with some obscure malady, and he'd have something interesting to work on for once.

Petrov set the lab timer for seventy-five seconds and submerged the film strips in the first basin as he pressed the start button. He watched the timer under the red light, wondering if the Cubans still made rum. He had been there, too, years before, and acquired a taste for the exotic liquor. Like any good Soviet citizen, he loved his vodka but had the occasional hankering for something different.

The timer went off and he lifted the rack, shaking it carefully over the tank. No sense getting the chemical—silver nitrate? something like that—on his uniform. The rack went into the second tank, and he set the timer again. Pity the orders had been so damned secret—he could have brought his tropical uniform. He'd sweat like a pig in the Cuban heat. Of course, none of those savages ever bothered to wash. Maybe they had learned something in the past fifteen years? He'd see.

The timer *ding*ed again, and Petrov lifted the rack a second time, shaking it and setting it in the water-filled basin. Another boring job completed. Why couldn't a sailor fall down a ladder and break something? He wanted to use his East German X-ray machine on a live patient. He didn't trust the Germans, Marxists or not, but they did make good medical equipment, including his X-ray, autoclave, and most of his pharmaceuticals. Time. Petrov lifted the rack and held it up against the X-ray reading plate, which he switched on.

"Nichevo!" Petrov breathed. He had to think. His badge was fogged. Its number was 3-4-8: third badge series, frame fifty-four (the medical office, galley section), aft (officers') accommodations.

Though only two centimeters across, the badges were made with variable sensitivity. Ten vertically segmented columns were used to quantify the exposure level. Petrov saw that his was fogged all the way to segment four. The engine room crewmen's were fogged to segment five, and the torpedomen, who spent all their time forward, showed contamination only in segment one.

"Son of a bitch." He knew the sensitivity levels by heart. He took the manual down to check them anyway. Fortunately, the segments were logarithmic. His exposure was twelve rads. Fifteen to twenty-five for the engineers. Twelve to twenty-five rads in two days, not enough to be dangerous. Not really life threatening, but . . . Petrov went back into his office, careful to leave the films in the labs. He picked up the phone.

"Captain Ramius? Petrov here. Could you come aft to my office, please?"

"On the way, Comrade Doctor."

Ramius took his time. He knew what the call was about. The day before they sailed, while Petrov had been ashore procuring drugs for his cupboard, Borodin had contaminated the badges with the X-ray machine.

"Yes, Petrov?" Ramius closed the door behind him.

"Comrade Captain, we have a radiation leak."

"Nonsense. Our instruments would have detected it at once."

Petrov got the films from the lab and handed them to the captain. "Look here."

Ramius held them up to the light, scanning the film strips

top to bottom. He frowned. "Who knows of this?"

"You and I, Comrade Captain."

"You will tell no one—no one." Ramius paused. "Any chance that the films were—that they have something wrong, that you made an error in the developing process?"

Petrov shook his head emphatically. "No, Comrade Captain. Only you, Comrade Borodin, and I have access to these. As you know, I tested random samples from each batch three days before we sailed." Petrov wouldn't admit that, like everyone, he had taken the samples from the top of the box they were stored in. They weren't really random.

"The maximum exposure I see here is . . . ten to twenty?" Ramius understated it. "Whose numbers?"

"Bulganin and Surzpoi. The torpedomen forward are all under three rads."

"Very well. What we have here, Comrade Doctor, is a possible minor—minor, Petrov—leak in the reactor spaces. At worst a gas leak of some sort. This has happened before, and no one has ever died from it. The leak will be found and fixed. We will keep this little secret. There is no reason to get the men excited over nothing."

Petrov nodded agreement, knowing that men had died in 1970 in an accident on the submarine *Voroshilov,* more in the icebreaker *Lenin.* Both accidents were a long time ago, though, and he was sure Ramius could handle things. Wasn't he?

The Pentagon

The E ring was the outermost and largest of the Pentagon's rings, and since its outside windows offered something other than a view of sunless courtyards, this was where the most senior defense officials had their offices. One of these was the office of the director of operations for the Joint Chiefs of Staff, the J-3. He wasn't there. He was down in a subbasement room known colloquially as the Tank because its metal walls were dotted with electronic noisemakers to foil other electronic devices.

He had been there for twenty-four hours, though one would not have known this from his appearance. His green trousers were still creased, his khaki shirt still showed the folds made by the laundry, its collar starched plywood-stiff, and his tie was held neatly in place by a gold marine corps tiepin. Lieutenant General Edwin Harris was neither a diplomat nor a service academy graduate, but he was playing peacemaker. An odd position for a marine.

"God damn it!" It was the voice of Admiral Blackburn, CINCLANT. Also present was his own operations officer, Rear Admiral Pete Stanford. "Is this any way to run an operation?"

The Joint Chiefs were all there, and none of them thought so.

"Look, Blackie, I told you where the orders come from." General Hilton, chairman of the Joint Chiefs of Staff, sounded tired.

"I understand that, General, but this is largely a submarine operation, right? I gotta get Vince Gallery in on this, and you should have Sam Dodge working up at this end. Dan and I are both fighter jocks, Pete's an ASW expert. We need a sub driver in on this."

"Gentlemen," Harris said calmly, "for the moment the plan we have to take to the president need only deal with the Soviet threat. Let's hold this story about the defecting boomer in abeyance for the moment, shall we?"

"I agree," Stanford nodded. "We have enough to worry about right here."

The attention of the eight flag officers turned to the map table. Fifty-eight Soviet submarines and twenty-eight surface warships, plus a gaggle of oilers and replenishment ships, were unmistakably heading for the American coast. To face this, the U.S. Navy had one available carrier. The *Invincible* did not rate as such. The threat was considerable. Among them the Soviet vessels carried over three hundred surface-to-surface cruise missiles. Though principally designed as antiship weapons, the third of them believed to carry nuclear warheads were sufficient to devastate the cities of the East Coast. From a position off New Jersey, these missiles could range from Norfolk to Boston.

"Josh Painter proposes that we keep *Kennedy* inshore," Admiral Blackburn said. "He wants to run the ASW operation from his carrier, transferring his light attack squadrons to shore and replacing them with S-3s. He wants *Invincible* out on their seaward flank."

"I don't like it," General Harris said. Neither did Pete Stanford, and they had agreed earlier that the J-3 would launch the counterplan. "Gentlemen, if we're only going to have one deck to use, we damned well ought to have a carrier and not an oversized ASW platform."

"We're listening, Eddie," Hilton said.

"Let's move *Kennedy* out here." He moved the counter to a position west of the Azores. "Josh keeps his attack squadrons. We move *Invincible* inshore to handle the ASW work. It's what the Brits designed her for, right? They're supposed to be good at it. *Kennedy* is an offensive weapon, her mission is to threaten them. Okay, if we deploy like this, she is the threat. From over here she can range against their surface force from outside their surface-to-surface missile perimeter—"

' "Better yet," Stanford interjected, pointing to some vessels on the map, "threaten this service force here. If they lose these oilers, they ain't going home. To meet that threat they'll have to redeploy themselves. For starters, they'll have to move *Kiev* offshore to give themselves some kind of air defense against *Kennedy*. We can use the spare S-3s from shore bases. They can still patrol the same areas." He traced a line about five hundred miles off the coast.

"Leaves *Invincible* kind of naked, though," the CNO, Admiral Foster, noted.

"Josh was asking about some E-3 coverage for the Brits." Blackburn looked at the air force chief of staff, General Claire Barnes.

"You want help, you get help," Barnes said. "We'll have a Sentry operating over *Invincible* at dawn tomorrow, and if you move her inshore we can maintain that round the clock. I'll throw in a wing of F-16s if you want."

"What do you want in return, Max?" Foster asked. Nobody called him Claire.

"The way I see this, you have *Saratoga*'s air wing sitting around doing nothing. Okay, by Saturday I'll have five hundred tactical fighters deployed from Dover to Loring. My boys don't know much about antiship stuff. They'll have to learn in a hurry. I want you to send your kids to work with mine, and I also want your Tomcats. I like the fighter-missile combination. Let one squadron work out of Iceland, the other out of New England to track the Bears Ivan's starting to send our way. I'll sweeten that. If you want, we'll send some tankers to Lajes to help keep *Kennedy*'s birds flying."

"Blackie?" Foster asked.

"Deal," Blackburn nodded. "The only thing that bothers me is that *Invincible* doesn't have all that much ASW capacity."

"So we get more," Stanford said. "Admiral, what say we take *Tarawa* out of Little Creek, team her with *New Jersey*'s group, with a dozen ASW choppers aboard and seven or eight Harriers?"

"I like it," Harris said quickly. "Then we have two baby carriers with a noteworthy striking force right in front of their groups, *Kennedy* playing stalking tiger to their east, and a few hundred tactical fighters to the west. They have to come into a three-way box. This actually gives us more ASW patrolling capacity than we'd have otherwise."

"Can *Kennedy* handle her mission alone out there?" Hilton asked.

"Depend on it," Blackburn replied. "We can kill any one, maybe any two of these four groups in an hour. The ones nearest shore will be your job, Max."

"How long did you two characters rehearse this?" General Maxwell, commandant of the marine corps, asked the operations officer. Everyone chuckled.

The Red October

Chief Engineer Melekhin cleared the reactor compartment before beginning the check for the leak. Ramius and Petrov were there also, plus the engineering duty officers and one of the young lieutenants, Svyadov. Three of the officers carried Geiger counters.

The reactor room was quite large. It had to be to accommodate the massive, barrel-shaped steel vessel. The object was warm to the touch despite being inactive. Automatic radiation detectors were in every corner of the room, each surrounded by a red circle. More were hanging on the fore and aft bulkheads. Of all the compartments on the submarine, this was the cleanest. The deck and bulkheads were spotless white-painted steel. The reason was obvious: the smallest leak of reactor coolant had to be instantly visible even if all the detectors failed.

Svyadov climbed an aluminum ladder affixed to the side of the reactor vessel to run the detachable probe from his counter

over every welded pipe joint. The speaker-annunciator on the
hand-held box was turned to maximum so that everyone in the
compartment could hear it, and Svyadov had an earpiece plugged
in for even greater sensitivity. A youngster of twenty-one, he
was nervous. Only a fool would feel entirely safe looking for
a radiation leak. There is a joke in the Soviet Navy: How do
you tell a sailor from the Northern Fleet? He glows in the dark.
It had been a good laugh on the beach, but not now. He knew
that he was conducting the search because he was the youngest,
least experienced, and most expendable officer. It was an effort
to keep his knees from wobbling as he strained to reach all
over and around the reactor piping.

The counter was not entirely silent, and Svyadov's stomach
cringed at each click generated by the passage of a random
particle through the tube of ionized gas. Every few seconds
his eyes flickered to the dial that measured intensity. It was
well inside the safe range, hardly registering at all. The reactor
vessel was a quadruple-layer design, each layer several centimeters of tough stainless steel. The three inner spaces were
filled with a barium-water mixture, then a barrier of lead, then
polyethylene, all designed to prevent the escape of neutrons
and gamma particles. The combination of steel, barium, lead,
and plastic successfully contained the dangerous elements of
the reaction, allowing only a few degrees of heat to escape,
and the dial showed, much to his relief, that the radiation level
was less than that on the beach at Sochi. The highest reading
was made next to a light bulb. This made the lieutenant smile.

"All readings in normal range, comrades," Svyadov reported.

"Start over," Melekhin ordered, "from the beginning."

Twenty minutes later Svyadov, now sweating from the warm
air that gathered at the top of the compartment, made an identical report. He came down awkwardly, his arms and legs tired.

"Have a cigarette," Ramius suggested. "You did well, Svyadov."

"Thank you, Comrade Captain. It's warm up there from the
lights and the coolant pipes." The lieutenant handed the counter
to Melekhin. The lower dial showed a cumulative count, well
within the safe range.

"Probably some contaminated badges," the chief engineer
commented sourly. "It would not be the first time. Some joker

in the factory or at the yard supply office—something for our friends in the GRU to check into. 'Wreckers!' A joke like this ought to earn somebody a bullet."

"Perhaps," Ramius chuckled. "Remember the incident on *Lenin?*" He referred to the nuclear-powered icebreaker that had spent two years tied to the dock, unusable because of a reactor mishap. "A ship's cook had some badly crusted pans, and a madman of an engineer suggested that he use live steam to get them cleaned. So the idiot walked down to the steam generator and opened an inspection valve, with his pots under it!"

Melekhin rolled his eyes. "I remember it! I was a staff engineering officer then. The captain had asked for a Kazakh cook—"

"He liked horsemeat with his kasha," Ramius said.

"—and the fool didn't know the first thing about a ship. Killed himself and three other men, contaminated the whole fucking compartment for twenty months. The captain only got out of the gulag last year."

"I bet the cook got his pans cleaned, though," Ramius observed.

"Indeed, Marko Aleksandrovich—they may even be safe to use in another fifty years." Melekhin laughed raucously.

That was a hell of a thing to say in front of a young officer, Petrov thought. There was nothing, nothing at all funny about a reactor leak. But Melekhin was known for his heavy sense of humor, and the doctor imagined that twenty years of working on reactors allowed him and the captain to view the potential dangers phlegmatically. Then, there was the implicit lesson in the story: never let someone who does not belong into the reactor spaces.

"Very well," Melekhin said, "now we check the pipes in the generator room. Come, Svyadov, we still need your young legs."

The next compartment aft contained the heat exchanger/ steam generator, turboalternators, and auxiliary equipment. The main turbines were in the next compartment, now inactive while the electrically driven caterpillar was operating. In any case, the steam that turned them was supposed to be clean. The only radioactivity was in the inside loop. The reactor coolant, which carried short-lived but dangerous radioactivity, never flashed to steam. This was in the outside loop and boiled from uncontaminated water. The two water supplies met but never mixed inside the heat exchanger, the most likely site for a coolant leak because of its more numerous fittings and valves.

The more complex piping required a full fifty minutes to check. These pipes were not as well insulated as those forward. Svyadov nearly burned himself twice, and his face was bathed in perspiration by the time he finished his first sweep.

"Readings all safe again, comrades."

"Good," Melekhin said. "Come down and rest a moment before you check it again."

Svyadov almost thanked his chief for that, but this would not have done at all. As a young, dedicated officer and member of the Komsomol, no exertion was too great. He came down carefully, and Melekhin handed him another cigarette. The chief engineer was a gray-haired perfectionist who took decent care of his men.

"Why, thank you, Comrade," Svyadov said.

Petrov got a folding chair. "Sit, Comrade Lieutenant, rest your legs."

The lieutenant sat down at once, stretching his legs to work out the knots. The officers at VVMUPP had told him how lucky he was to draw this assignment. Ramius and Melekhin were the two best teachers in the fleet, men whose crews appreciated their kindness along with their competence.

"They really should insulate those pipes," Ramius said. Melekhin shook his head.

"Then they'd be too hard to inspect." He handed the counter to his captain.

"Entirely safe," the captain read off the cumulative dial. "You get more exposure tending a garden."

"Indeed," Melekhin said. "Coal miners get more exposure than we do, from the release of radon gas in the mines. Bad badges, that's what it has to be. Why not take out a whole batch and check it?"

"I could, Comrade," Petrov answered. "But then, due to the extended nature of our cruise, we'd have to run for several days without any. Contrary to regulations. I'm afraid."

"You are correct. In any case the badges are only a backup to our instruments." Ramius gestured to the red-circled detectors all over the compartment.

"Do you really want to recheck the piping?" Melekhin asked.

"I think we should," Ramius said.

Svyadov swore to himself, looking down at the deck.

"There is no extravagance in the pursuit of safety," Petrov quoted doctrine. "Sorry, Lieutenant." The doctor was not a bit sorry. He had been genuinely worried, and was now feeling a lot better.

An hour later the second check had been completed. Petrov took Svyadov forward for salt tablets and tea to rehydrate himself. The senior officers left, and Melekhin ordered the reactor plant restarted.

The enlisted men filed back to their duty stations, looking at one another. Their officers had just checked the "hot" compartments with radiation instruments. The medical corpsman had looked pale a while earlier and refused to say anything. More than one engine attendant fingered his radiation badge and checked his wristwatch to see how long it would be before he went off duty.

THE EIGHTH DAY

FRIDAY, 10 DECEMBER

HMS Invincible

Ryan awoke in the dark. The curtains were drawn on the cabin's two small portholes. He shook his head a few times to clear it and began to assess what was going on around him. The *Invincible* was moving on the seas, but not as much as before. He got up to look out of a porthole and saw the last red glow of sunset aft under scudding clouds. He checked his watch and did some clumsy mental arithmetic, concluding that it was six in the evening, local time. That translated to about six hours of sleep. He felt pretty good, considering. A minor headache from the brandy—so much for the theory that good stuff doesn't give you a hangover—and his muscles were stiff. He did a few sit-ups to work out the knots.

There was a small bathroom—head, he corrected himself—adjoining the cabin. Ryan splashed some water on his face and washed his mouth out, not wanting to look in the mirror. He decided he had to. Counterfeit or not, he was wearing his country's uniform and he had to look presentable. It took a minute to get his hair in place and the uniform arranged properly. The CIA had done a nice job of tailoring, given such short notice. Finished, he went out the door towards the flag bridge.

"Feeling better, Jack?" Admiral White pointed him to a tray full of cups. It was only tea, but it was a start.

"Thank you, Admiral. Those few hours really helped. I guess I'm in time for dinner."

"Breakfast," White corrected him with a laugh.

"What—uh, pardon me, Admiral?" Ryan shook his head again. He was still a little groggy.

"That's a sun*rise*, Commander. Change in orders, we're heading west again. *Kennedy*'s moving east at high speed, and we're to take station inshore."

"Who said, sir?"

"CINCLANT. I gather Joshua was not at all pleased. You are to remain with us for the moment, and under the circumstances it seemed the reasonable thing to let you sleep. You did appear to need it."

Must have been eighteen hours, Ryan thought. No wonder he felt stiff.

"You do look much better," Admiral White noted from his leather swivel chair. He got up, took Ryan's arm, and guided him aft. "Now for breakfast. I've been waiting for you. Captain Hunter will brief you on your revised orders. Weather's clearing up for a few days, they tell me. Escort assignments are being reshuffled. We're to operate in conjunction with your *New Jersey* group. Our antisubmarine operations begin in earnest in another twelve hours. It's a good thing you got that extra sleep, lad. You'll bloody need it."

Ryan ran his hand over his face. "Can I shave, sir?"

"We still permit beards. Let it wait until after breakfast."

Flag quarters on HMS *Invincible* were not quite to the standard of those on the *Kennedy*—but close. White had a private dining area. A steward in a white livery served them expertly, setting a third place for Hunter, who appeared within a few minutes. When they started talking, the steward was excused.

"We rendezvous with a pair of young *Knox*-class frigates in two hours. We already have them on radar. Two more 1052s, plus an oiler and two *Perry*s will join us in another thirty-six hours. They were on their way home from the Med. With our own escorts, a total of nine warships. A noteworthy collection, I think. We'll be working five hundred miles offshore, with the *New Jersey–Tarawa* force two hundred miles to our west."

"*Tarawa?* What do we need a regiment of marines for?" Ryan asked.

Hunter explained briefly. "Not a bad idea, that. The funny thing is, with *Kennedy* racing for the Azores, that rather leaves us guarding the American coast." Hunter grinned. "This may be the first time the Royal Navy has ever done that—certainly since it belonged to us."

"What are we up against?"

"The first of the *Alfa*s will be on your coast tonight, four of them ahead of all the others. The Soviet surface force passed Iceland last night. It's divided into three groups. One is built around their carrier *Kiev*, two cruisers and four destroyers; the second, probably the force flag, is built around *Kirov*, with three additional cruisers and six destroyers; and the third is centered on *Moskva*, three more cruisers and seven destroyers. I gather that the Soviets will want to use the *Kiev* and *Moskva* groups inshore, with *Kirov* guarding them out to sea—but *Kennedy*'s relocation will make them rethink that. Regardless, the total force carries a considerable number of surface-to-surface missiles, and potentially, we are very exposed. To help out with that, your air force has an E-3 Sentry detailed to arrive here in an hour ɔ exercise with our Harriers, and when we get farther west, we ll have additional land-based air support. On the whole our position is hardly an enviable one, but Ivan's is rather less so. So far as the question of finding *Red October* is concerned?" Hunter shrugged. "How we conduct our search will depend on how Ivan deploys. At the moment we're conducting some tracking drills. The lead *Alfa* is eighty miles northwest of us, steaming at forty-plus knots, and we have a helicopter in pursuit—which is roughly what it amounts to," the fleet operations officer concluded. "Will you join us below?"

"Admiral?" Ryan wanted to see *Invincible*'s combat information center.

"Certainly."

Thirty minutes later Ryan was in a darkened, quiet room whose walls were a solid bank of electronic instruments and glass plotting panels. The Atlantic Ocean was full of Russian submarines.

The White House

The Soviet ambassador entered the Oval Office a minute early,
at 10:59 A.M. He was a short, overweight man with a broad
Slavic face and eyes that would have done a professional gambler proud. They revealed nothing. He was a career diplomat,
having served in a number of posts throughout the Western
world, and a thirty-year member of the Communist party's
Foreign Department.

"Good morning, Mr. President, Dr. Pelt," Alexei Arbatov
nodded politely to both men. The president, he noted at once,
was seated behind his desk. Every other time he'd been here
the president had come around the desk to shake hands, then
sat down beside him.

"Help yourself to some coffee, Mr. Ambassador," Pelt offered. The special assistant to the president for national security
affairs was well known to Arbatov. Jeffrey Pelt was an academic from the Georgetown University's Center for Strategic
and International Studies—an enemy, but a well-mannered,
kulturny enemy. Arbatov had a fondness for the niceties of
formal behavior. Today, Pelt was standing at his boss's side,
unwilling to come too close to the Russian bear. Arbatov did
not get himself any coffee.

"Mr. Ambassador," Pelt began, "we have noted a troubling
increase in Soviet naval activity in the North Atlantic."

"Oh?" Arbatov's eyebrows shot up in a display of surprise
that fooled no one, and he knew it. "I have no knowledge of
this. As you know, I have never been a sailor."

"Shall we dispense with the bullshit, Mr. Ambassador?" the
president said. Arbatov did not permit himself to be surprised
by the vulgarity. It made the American president seem very
Russian, and like Soviet officials he seemed to need a professional like Pelt around to smooth the edges. "You certainly
have nearly a hundred naval vessels operating in the North
Atlantic or heading in that direction. Chairman Narmonov and
my predecessor agreed years ago that no such operation would
take place without prior notification. The purpose of this agreement, as you know, was to prevent acts that might appear to
be unduly provocative to one side or the other. This agreement
has been kept—until now.

"Now, my military advisers tell me that what is going on looks very much like a war exercise, indeed, could be the precursor to a war. How are we to tell the difference? Your ships are now passing east of Iceland, and will soon be in a position from which they can threaten our trade routes to Europe. This situation is at the least unsettling, and at the most a grave and wholly unwarranted provocation. The scope of this action has not yet been made public. That will change, and when it does, Alex, the American people will demand action on my part." The president paused, expecting a response but getting only a nod.

Pelt went on for him. "Mr. Ambassador, your country has seen fit to cast aside an agreement which for years has been a model of East-West cooperation. How can you expect us to regard this as anything other than a provocation?"

"Mr. President, Dr. Pelt, truly I have no knowledge of this." Arbatov lied with the utmost sincerity. "I will contact Moscow at once to ascertain the facts. Is there any message you wish me to pass along?"

"Yes. As you and your superiors in Moscow will understand," the president said, "we will deploy our ships and aircraft to observe yours. Prudence requires this. We have no wish to interfere with whatever legitimate operations your forces may be engaged in. It is not our intention to make a provocation of our own, but under the terms of our agreement we have the right to know what is going on, Mr. Ambassador. Until we do, we are unable to issue the proper orders to our men. It would be well for your government to consider that having so many of your ships and our ships, your aircraft and our aircraft in close proximity is an inherently dangerous situation. Accidents can happen. An action by one side or the other which at another time would seem harmless might seem to be something else entirely. Wars have begun in this way, Mr. Ambassador." The president leaned back to let that thought hang in the air for a moment. When he went on, he spoke more gently. "Of course, I regard this possibility as remote, but is it not irresponsible to take such chances?"

"Mr. President, you make your point well, as always, but as you know, the sea is free for the passage of all, and—"

"Mr. Ambassador," Pelt interrupted, "consider a simple analogy. Your next-door neighbor begins to patrol his front yard with a loaded shotgun while your children are at play in your own front yard. In this country such action would be technically legal. Even so, would it not be a matter of concern?"

"So it would, Dr. Pelt, but the situation you describe is very different—"

Now the president interrupted. "Indeed it is. The situation at hand is far more dangerous. It is the breach of an agreement, and I find that especially disquieting. I had hoped that we were entering a new era of Soviet-American relations. We have settled our trade differences. We have just concluded a new grain agreement. You had a major part in that. We have been moving forward, Mr. Ambassador—is this at an end?" The president shook his head emphatically. "I hope not, but the choice is yours. The relationship between our countries can only be based on trust.

"Mr. Ambassador, I trust that I have not alarmed you. As you know, it is my habit to speak plainly. I personally dislike the greasy dissimulation of diplomacy. At times like this, we must communicate quickly and clearly. We have a dangerous situation before us, and we must work together, rapidly, to resolve it. My military commanders are greatly concerned, and I need to know—today—what your naval forces are up to. I expect a reply by seven this evening. Failing that I will be on the direct line to Moscow to demand one."

Arbatov stood. "Mr. President, I will transmit your message within the hour. Please keep in mind, however, the time differential between Washington and Moscow—"

"I know that a weekend has just begun, and that the Soviet Union is a worker's paradise, but I expect that some of your country's managers may still be at work. In any case, I will detain you no further. Good day."

Pelt led Arbatov out, then came back and sat down.

"Maybe I was just a little tough on him," the president said.

"Yes, sir." Pelt thought that he had been too damned tough. He had little affection for the Russian but he too liked the niceties of diplomatic exchange. "I think we can say that you succeeded in getting your message across."

"He knows."

"He knows. But he doesn't know we know."

"We think," the president grimaced. "What a crazy goddamned game this is! And to think I had a nice, safe career going for me putting mafiosi in jail . . . Do you think he'll snap at the bait I offered?"

"'Legitimate operations?' Did you see his hands twitch at that? He'll go after it like a marlin after a squid." Pelt walked over to pour himself half a cup of coffee. It pleased him that the china service was gold trimmed. "I wonder what they'll call it? Legitimate operations . . . probably a rescue mission. If they call it a fleet exercise they admit to violating the notification protocol. A rescue operation justifies the level of activity, the speed with which it was laid on, and the lack of publicity. Their press never reports this sort of thing. As a guess, I'd say they'll call it a rescue, say a submarine is missing, maybe even to the point of calling it a missile sub."

"No, they won't go that far. We also have that agreement about keeping our missile subs five hundred miles offshore. Arbatov probably has his instructions on what to tell us already, but he'll play for all the time he can. It's also vaguely possible that he's in the dark. We know how they compartmentalize information. You suppose we're reading too much into this talent for obfuscation?"

"I think not, sir. It is a principle of diplomacy," Pelt observed, "that one must know something of the truth in order to lie convincingly."

The president smiled. "Well, they've had enough time to play this game. I hope my belated reaction will not disappoint them."

"No, sir. Alex must have half expected you to kick him out the door."

"The thought's occurred to me more than once. His diplomatic charm has always been lost on me. That's the one thing about the Russians—they remind me so much of the mafia chieftains I used to prosecute. The same smattering of culture and good manners, and the same absence of morality." The president shook his head. He was talking like a hawk again. "Stay close, Jeff. I have George Farmer coming in here in a few minutes, but I want you around when our friend comes back."

Pelt walked back to his office pondering the president's remark. It was, he admitted to himself, crudely accurate. The most wounding insult to an educated Russian was to be called *nekulturny*, uncultured—the term didn't translate adequately—

yet the same men who sat in the gilt boxes at the Moscow State Opera weeping at the end of a performance of *Boris Gudunov* could immediately turn around and order the execution or imprisonment of a hundred men without blinking. A strange people, made more strange by their political philosophy. But the president had too many sharp edges, and Pelt wished he'd learn to soften them. A speech in front of the American Legion was one thing, a discussion with the ambassador of a foreign power was something else.

CIA Headquarters

"CARDINAL's in trouble, Judge." Ritter sat down.

"No surprise there." Moore removed his glasses and rubbed his eyes. Something Ryan had not seen was the cover note from the station chief in Moscow saying that to get his latest signal out, CARDINAL had bypassed half the courier chain that ran from the Kremlin to the U.S. embassy. The agent was getting bold in his old age. "What does the station chief say exactly?"

"CARDINAL's supposed to be in the hospital with pneumonia. Maybe it's true, but . . ."

"He's getting old, and it is winter over there, but who believes in coincidences?" Moore looked down at his desk. "What do you suppose they'd do if they've turned him?"

"He'd die quietly. Depends on who turned him. If it was the KGB, they might want to make something out of it, especially since our friend Andropov took a lot of their prestige with him when he left. But I don't think so. Given who his sponsor is, it would raise too much of a ruckus. Same thing if the GRU turns him. No, they'd grill him for a few weeks, then quietly do away with him. A public trial would be too counterproductive."

Judge Moore frowned. They sounded like doctors discussing a terminally ill patient. He didn't even know what CARDINAL looked like. There was a photograph somewhere in the file, but he had never seen it. It was easier that way. As an appellate court judge he had never had to look a defendant in the eye; he'd just reviewed the law in a detached way. He tried to keep his stewardship of the CIA the same way. Moore knew that this might be perceived as cowardly, and was very different from what people expect of a DCI—but even spies got old, and old men developed consciences and doubts that rarely troubled the young. It was time to leave the "Company." Nearly three years, it was enough. He'd accomplished what he was supposed to do.

"Tell the station chief to lay off. No inquiries of any kind directed at CARDINAL. If he's really sick, we'll be hearing from him again. If not, we'll know that soon enough, too."

"Right."

Ritter had succeeded in confirming CARDINAL's reports. One agent had reported that the fleet was sailing with additional political officers, another that the surface force was commanded by an academic sailor and crony of Gorshkov, who had flown the Severomorsk and boarded the *Kirov* minutes before the fleet had sailed. The naval architect who was believed to have designed the *Red October* was supposed to have gone with him. A British agent had reported that detonators for the various weapons carried by the surface ships had been hastily taken aboard from their usual storage depots ashore. Finally, there was an unconfirmed report that Admiral Korov, commander of the Northern Fleet, was not at his command post; his whereabouts were unknown. Together the information was enough to confirm the WILLOW report, and more was still coming in.

The U.S. Naval Academy

"Skip?"

"Oh, howdy, Admiral. Will you join me?" Tyler waved to a vacant chair across the table.

"I got a message from the Pentagon for you." The superintendent of the Naval Academy, a former submarine officer, sat down. "You have an appointment tonight at 1930 hours. That's all they said."

"Great!" Tyler was just finishing his lunch. He'd been working on the simulation program nearly around the clock since Monday. The appointment meant that he would have access to the air force's Cray-2 tonight. His program was just about ready.

"What's this all about anyway?"

"Sorry, sir, I can't say. You know how it is."

The White House

The Soviet ambassador was back at four in the afternoon. To avoid press notice he had been taken into the Treasury building across the street from the White House and brought through a connecting tunnel which few knew existed. The president hoped that he had found this unsettling. Pelt hustled in to be there when Arbatov arrived.

"Mr. President," Arbatov reported, standing at attention. The president had not known that he had any military experience. "I am instructed to convey to you the regrets of my government that there has not been time to inform you of this. One of our nuclear submarines is missing and presumed lost. We are conducting an emergency rescue operation."

The president nodded soberly, motioning the ambassador to a chair. Pelt sat next to him.

"This is somewhat embarrassing, Mr. President. You see, in our navy as in yours, duty on a nuclear submarine is a posting of the greatest importance, and consequently those selected for it are among our best educated and trusted men. In this particular case several members of the crew—the officers, that is—are sons of high Party officials. One is even the son of a Central Committee member—I cannot say which, of course. The Soviet Navy's great effort to find her sons is understandable, though I admit a bit undisciplined." Arbatov feigned embarrassment beautifully, speaking as though he were confiding a great family secret. "Therefore, this has developed into what your people call an 'all hands' operation. As you undoubtedly know, it was undertaken virtually overnight."

"I see," the president said sympathetically. "That makes me feel a little better, Alex. Jeff, I think it's late enough in the day. How about you fix us all a drink. Bourbon, Alex?"

"Yes, thank you, sir."

Pelt walked over to a rosewood cabinet against the wall. The ornate antique contained a small bar, complete with an ice bucket which was stocked every afternoon. The president often liked to have a drink or two before dinner, something else that reminded Arbatov of his countrymen. Dr. Pelt had had ample experience playing presidential bartender. In a few minutes he came back with three glasses in his hands.

"To tell you the truth, we rather suspected this was a rescue operation," Pelt said.

"I don't know how we get our young men to do this sort of work." The president sipped at his drink. Arbatov worked hard on his. He had said frequently at local cocktail parties that he preferred American bourbon to his native vodka. Maybe it was true. "We've lost a pair of nuclear boats, I believe. How many does this make for you, three, four?"

"I don't know, Mr. President. I expect your information on this is better than my own." The president noted that he had just told the truth for the first time today. "Certainly I can agree with you that such duty is both dangerous and demanding."

"How many men aboard, Alex?" the president asked.

"I have no idea. A hundred more or less, I suppose. I've never been aboard a naval vessel."

"Mostly kids, probably, just like our crews. It is indeed a sad commentary on both our countries that our mutual suspicions must condemn so many of our best young men to such hazards, when we know that some won't be coming back. But—how can it be otherwise?" The president paused, turning to look out the windows. The snow was melting on the South Lawn. It was time for his next line.

"Perhaps we can help," the president offered speculatively. "Yes, perhaps we can use this tragedy as an opportunity to reduce those suspicions by some small amount. Perhaps we can make something good come from this to demonstrate that our relations really have improved."

Pelt turned away, fumbling for his pipe. In their many years of friendship he could never understand how the president got away with so much. Pelt had met him at Washington University, when he was majoring in political science, the president in prelaw. Back then the chief executive had been president of the dramatics society. Certainly amateur theatrics had helped his legal career. It was said that at least one Mafia don had been sent up the river by sheer rhetoric. The president referred to it as his sincere act.

"Mr. Ambassador, I offer you the assistance and the resources of the United States in the search for your missing countrymen."

"That is most kind of you, Mr. President, but—"

The president held his hand up. "No buts, Alex. If we cannot cooperate in something like this, how can we hope to cooperate in more serious matters? If memory serves, last year when one of our navy patrol aircraft crashed off the Aleutians, one of your fishing vessels"—it had been an intelligence trawler—"picked up the crew, saved their lives. Alex, we owe you a debt for that, a debt of honor, and the United States will not be said to be ungrateful." He paused for effect. "They're probably all dead, you know. I don't suppose there's more chance of surviving a sub accident than of surviving a plane crash. But at least the crew's families will know. Jeff, don't we have some specialized submarine rescue equipment?"

"With all the money we give the navy? We damned well ought to. I'll call Foster about it."

"Good," the president said. "Alex, it is too much to expect that your mutual suspicions will be allayed by something so small as this. Your history and ours conspire against us. But let's make a small beginning with this. If we can shake hands in space or over a conference table in Vienna, maybe we can do it here also. I will give the necessary instructions to my commanders as soon as we're finished here."

"Thank you, Mr. President." Arbatov concealed his uneasiness.

"And please convey my respects to Chairman Narmonov and my sympathy for the families of your missing men. I appreciate his effort, and yours, in getting this information to us."

"Yes. Mr. President." Arbatov rose. He left after shaking hands. What were the Americans really up to? He'd warned Moscow: call it a rescue mission and they'd demand to help. It was their stupid Christmas season, and Americans were addicted to happy endings. It was madness not to call it something else—to hell with the protocol.

At the same time he was forced to admire the American president. A strange man, very open, yet full of guile. A friendly man most of the time, yet always ready to seize the advantage. He remembered stories his grandmother had told, about how the gypsies switched babies. The American president was very Russian.

"Well," the president said after the doors closed, "now we can keep a nice close eye on them, and they can't complain. They're lying and we know it—but they don't know we know.

And we're lying, and they certainly suspect it, but not why we're lying. Gawd! and I told him this morning that not knowing was dangerous! Jeff, I've been thinking about this. I do not like the fact that so much of their navy is operating off our coast. Ryan was right, the Atlantic is our ocean. I want the air force and the navy to cover them like a goddamned blanket! That's our ocean, and I damned well want them to know it." The president finished off his drink. "On the question of the sub, I want our people to have a good look at it, and whoever of the crew wants to defect, we take care of. Quietly, of course."

"Of course. As a practical matter, having the officers is as great a coup as having the submarine."

"But the navy still want to keep it."

"I just don't see how we can do that, not without eliminating the crewmen, and we can't do that."

"Agreed." The president buzzed his secretary. "Get me General Hilton."

The Pentagon

The air force's computer center was in a subbasement of the Pentagon. The room temperature was well below seventy degrees. It was enough to make Tyler's leg ache where it met the metal-plastic prosthesis. He was used to that.

Tyler was sitting at a control console. He had just finished a trial run of his program, named MORAY after the vicious eel that inhabited oceanic reefs. Skip Tyler was proud of his programming ability. He'd taken the old dinosaur program from the files of the Taylor Lab, adapted it to the common Defense Department computer language, ADA—named for Lady Ada Lovelace, daughter of Lord Byron—and then tightened it up. For most people this would have been a month's work. He'd done it in four days, working almost around the clock not only because the money was an attractive incentive but also because the project was a professional challenge. He ended the job quietly satisfied that he could still meet an impossible deadline with time to spare. It was eight in the evening. MORAY had just run through a one-variable-value test and not crashed. He was ready.

He'd never seen the Cray-2 before, except in photographs, and he was pleased to have a chance to use it. The -2 was five units of raw electrical power, each one roughly pentagonal in shape, about six feet high and four across. The largest unit was the main-frame processor bank; the other four were memory banks, arrayed around it in a cruciform configuration. Tyler typed in the command to load his variable sets. For each of the *Red October*'s main dimensions—length, beam, height— he input ten discrete numerical values. Then came six subtly different values for her hull form block and prismatic coeffi- cients. There were five sets of tunnel dimensions. This aggre- gated to over thirty thousand possible permutations. Next he keyed in eighteen power variables to cover the range of possible engine systems. The Cray-2 absorbed this information and placed each number in its proper slot. It was ready to run.

"Okay," he announced to the system operator, an air force master sergeant.

"Roge." The sergeant typed "XQT" into his terminal. The Cray-2 went to work.

Tyler walked over to the sergeant's console.

"That's a right lengthy program you've input, sir." The sergeant laid a ten-dollar bill on the top of the console. "Betcha my baby can run it in ten minutes."

"Not a chance." Tyler laid his own bill next to the sergeant's. "Fifteen minutes, easy."

"Split the difference?"

"Alright. Where's the head around here?"

"Out the door, sir, turn right, go down the hall and it's on the left."

Tyler moved towards the door. It annoyed him that he could not walk gracefully, but after four years the inconvenience was a minor one. He was alive—that's what counted. The accident had occurred on a cold, clear night in Groton, Connecticut, only a block from the shipyard's main gate. On Friday at three in the morning he was driving home after a twenty-hour day getting his new command ready for sea. The civilian yard worker had had a long day also, stopping off at a favorite watering hole for a few too many, as the police established afterwards. He got into his car, started it, and ran a red light, ramming Tyler's Pontiac broadside at fifty miles per hour. For him the accident was fatal. Skip was luckier. It was at an intersection, and he had the green light; when he saw the front end of the Ford not a foot from his left-side door, it was far too late. He did not remember going through a pawnshop window, and the next week, when he hovered near death at the Yale–New Haven hospital, was a complete blank. His most vivid memory was of waking up, eight days later he was to learn, to see his wife, Jean, holding his hand. His marriage up to that point had been a troubled one, not an uncommon problem for nuclear submarine officers. His first sight of her was not a complimentary one—her eyes were bloodshot, her hair was tousled—but she had never looked quite so good. He had never appreciated just how important she was. A lot more important than half a leg.

"Skip? Skip Tyler!"

The former submariner turned awkwardly to see a naval officer running towards him.

"Johnnie Coleman! How the hell are you!"

It was Captain Coleman now, Tyler noted. They had served together twice, a year on the *Tecumseh*, another on the *Shark*. Coleman, a weapons expert, had commanded a pair of nuclear subs.

"How's the family, Skip?"

"Jean's fine. Five kids now, and another on the way."

"Damn!" they shook hands with enthusiasm. "You always were a randy bugger. I hear you're teaching at Annapolis."

"Yeah, and a little engineering stuff on the side."

"What are you doing here?"

"I'm running a program on the air force computer. Checking a new ship configuration for Sea Systems Command." It was an accurate enough cover story. "What do they have you doing?"

"OP-02's office. I'm chief of staff for Admiral Dodge."

"Indeed?" Tyler was impressed. Vice Admiral Sam Dodge was the current OP-02. The office of the deputy chief of naval operations for submarine warfare had administrative control of all aspects of submarine operations. "Keeping you busy?"

"You know it! The crap's really hit the fan."

"What do you mean?" Tyler hadn't seen the news or read a paper since Monday.

"You kidding?"

"I've been working on this computer program twenty hours a day since Monday, and I don't get ops dispatches anymore." Tyler frowned. He had heard something the other day at the Academy but not paid any attention to it. He was the sort who could focus his whole mind on a single problem.

Coleman looked up and down the corridor. It was late on a Friday evening, and they had it entirely to themselves. "Guess I can tell you. Our Russian friends have some sort of major exercise laid on. Their whole Northern Fleet's at sea, or damned near. They have subs all over the place."

"Doing what?"

"We're not sure. Looks like they might have a major search and rescue operation. The question is, after what? They have four *Alfa*s doing a max speed run for our coast right now, with a gaggle of *Victor*s and *Charlie*s charging in behind them. At first we were worried that they wanted to block the trade routes, but they blitzed right past those. They're definitely heading for our coast, and whatever they're up to, we're getting tons of information."

"What do they have moving?" Tyler asked.

"Fifty-eight nuclear subs, and thirty or so surface ships."

"Gawd! CINCLANT must be going ape!"

"You know it, Skip. The fleet's at sea, all of it. Every nuke we have is scrambling for a redeployment. Every P-3 Lockheed ever made is either over the Atlantic or heading that way." Coleman paused. "You're still cleared, right?"

"Sure, for the work I do for the Crystal City gang. I had a piece of the evaluation of the new *Kirov*."

"I thought that sounded like your work. You always were a pretty good engineer. You know, the old man still talks about that job you did for him on the old *Tecumseh*. Maybe I can get you in to see what's happening. Yeah, I'll ask him."

Tyler's first cruise after graduating from nuc school in Idaho had been with Dodge. He'd done a tricky repair job on some ancillary reactor equipment two weeks earlier than estimated with a little creative effort and some back-channel procurement of spare parts. This had earned him and Dodge a flowery letter of commendation.

"I bet the old man would love to see you. When will you be finished down here?"

"Maybe half an hour."

"You know where to find me?"

"Have they moved OP-02?"

"Same place. Call me when you're finished. My extension is 78730. Okay? I gotta get back."

"Right." Tyler watched his old friend disappear down the

corridor, then proceeded on his way to the men's room, wondering what the Russians were up to. Whatever it was, it was enough to keep a three-star admiral and his four-striped captain working on a Friday night in Christmas season.

"Eleven minutes, 53.18 seconds, sir," the sergeant reported, pocketing both bills.

The computer printout was over two hundred pages of data. The cover sheet plotted a rough-looking bell curve of speed solutions, and below it was the noise prediction curve. The case-by-case solutions were printed individually on the remaining sheets. The curves were predictably messy. The speed curve showed the majority of solutions in the ten- to twelve-knot range, the total range going from seven to eighteen knots. The noise curve was surprisingly low.

"Sergeant, that's one hell of a machine you have here."

"Believe it, sir. And reliable. We haven't had an electronic fault all month."

"Can I use a phone?"

"Sure, take your pick, sir."

"Okay, Sarge." Tyler picked up the nearest phone. "Oh, and dump the program."

"Okay." He typed in some instructions. "MORAY is . . . gone. Hope you kept a copy, sir."

Tyler nodded and dialed the phone.

"OP-02A, Captain Coleman."

"Johnnie, this is Skip."

"Great! Hey, the old man wants to see you. Come right up."

Tyler placed the printout in his briefcase and locked it. He thanked the sergeant one more time before hobbling out the door, giving the Cray-2 one last look. He'd have to get in here again.

He could not find an operating elevator and had to struggle up a gently sloped ramp. Five minutes later he found a marine guarding the corridor.

"You Commander Tyler, sir?" the guard asked. "Can I see some ID, please?"

Tyler showed the corporal his Pentagon pass, wondering how many one-legged former submarine officers there might be.

"Thank you, Commander. Please go down the corridor. You know the room, sir?"

"Sure. Thanks, Corporal."

Vice Admiral Dodge was sitting on the corner of a desk reading over some message flimsies. Dodge was a small, combative man who'd made his mark commanding three separate boats, then pushing the *Los Angeles*–class attack submarines through their lengthy development program. Now he was "Grand Dolphin," the senior admiral who fought all the battles with Congress.

"Skip Tyler! You're looking good, laddy." Dodge gave Tyler's leg a furtive glance as he came over to take his hand. "I hear you're doing a great job at the Academy."

"It's all right, sir. They even let me scout the occasional ballgame."

"Hmph, shame they didn't let you scout Army."

Tyler hung his head theatrically. "I did scout Army, sir. They were just too tough this year. You heard about their middle linebacker, didn't you?"

"No, what about him?" Dodge asked.

"He picked armor as his duty assignment, and they gave him an early trip to Fort Knox—not to learn about tanks. To *be* a tank."

"Ha!" Dodge laughed. "Johnnie says you have a bunch of new kids."

"Number six is due the end of February," Tyler said proudly.

"Six? You're not a Catholic or a Mormon, are you? What's with all this bird hatching?"

Tyler gave his former boss a wry look. He'd never understood that prejudice in the nuclear navy. It came from Rickover, who had invented the disparaging term *bird hatching* for fathering more than one child. What the hell was wrong with having kids?

"Admiral, since I'm not a nuc anymore, I have to do *something* on nights and weekends." Tyler arched his eyebrows lecherously. "I hear the Russkies are playing games."

Dodge was instantly serious. "They sure are. Fifty-eight attack boats—every nuclear boat in the Northern Fleet—heading this way with a big surface group, and most of their service forces tagging along."

"Doing what?"

"Maybe you can tell me. Come on back to my inner sanctum." Dodge led Tyler into a room where he saw another new gadget, a projection screen that displayed the North Atlantic from the Tropic of Cancer to the polar ice pack. Hundreds of ships were represented. The merchantmen were white, with flags to identify their nationality; the Soviet ships were red, and their shapes depicted their ship type; the American and allied ships were blue. The ocean was getting crowded.

"Christ."

"You got that one right, lad," Tyler nodded grimly. "How are you cleared?"

"Top secret and some special things, sir. I see everything we have on their hardware, and I do a lot of work with Sea Systems on the side."

"Johnnie said you did the evaluation of the new *Kirov* they just sent out to the Pacific—not bad, by the way."

"These two *Alfas* heading for Norfolk?"

"Looks like it. And they're burning a lot of neutrons doing it." Dodge pointed. "That one's heading to Long Island Sound as though to block the entrance to New London and that one's heading to Boston, I think. These *Victors* are not far behind. They already have most of the British ports staked out. By Monday they'll have two or more subs off every major port we have."

"I don't like the looks of this, sir."

"Neither do I. As you see, we're nearly a hundred percent at sea ourselves. The interesting thing, though—what they're doing just doesn't figure. I—" Captain Coleman came in.

"I see you let the prodigal son in, sir," Coleman said.

"Be nice to him, Johnnie. I seem to remember when he was a right fair sub driver. Anyway, at first it looked like they were going to block the SLOCs, but they went right past. What with these *Alfas*, they might be trying to blockade our coast."

"What about out west?"

"Nothing. Nothing at all, just routine activity."

"That doesn't make any sense," Tyler objected. "You don't ignore half the fleet. Of course, if you're going to war you don't announce it by kicking every boat to max power either."

"The Russians are a funny bunch, Skip," Coleman pointed out.

"Admiral, if we start shooting at them—"

"We hurt 'em," Dodge said. "With all the noise they're

making we have good locations on near all of 'em. They have to know that, too. That's the one thing that makes me believe they're not up to anything really bad. They're smart enough not to be that obvious—unless that's what they want us to think."

"Have they said anything?" Tyler asked.

"Their ambassador says they've lost a boat, and since it has a bunch of big shots' kids aboard, they laid on an all-hands rescue mission. For what that's worth."

Tyler set his briefcase down and walked closer to the screen. "I can see the pattern for a search and rescue, but why blockade our ports?" He paused, thinking rapidly as his eyes scanned the top of the display. "Sir, I don't see any boomers up here."

"They're in port—all of 'em, on both oceans. The last *Delta* tied up a few hours ago. That's funny, too," Dodge said, looking at the screen again.

"All of them, sir?" Tyler asked as offhandedly as he could. Something had just occurred to him. The display screen showed the *Bremerton* in the Barents Sea but not her supposed quarry. He waited a few seconds for an answer. Getting none, he turned to see the two officers observing him closely.

"Why do you ask, son?" Dodge said quietly. In Sam Dodge, gentleness could be a real warning flag.

Tyler thought this one over for a few seconds. He'd given Ryan his word. Could he phrase his answer without compromising it and still find out what he wanted? Yes, he decided. There was an investigative side to Skip Tyler's character, and once he was onto something, his psyche compelled him to run it down.

"Admiral, do they have a missile sub at sea, a brand new one?"

Dodge stood very straight. Even so he still had to look up at the younger man. When he spoke, his voice was glacial. "Exactly where did you get that information, Commander?"

Tyler shook his head. "Admiral, I'm sorry, but I can't say. It's compartmented, sir. I think this is something you ought to know, and I'll try to get it to you."

Dodge backed off to try a different tack. "You used to work for me, Skip." The admiral was unhappy. He'd bent a rule to show something to his former subordinate because he knew him well and was sorry that he had not received the command he had worked so hard for. Tyler was technically a civilian, even though his suits were still navy blue. What made it really bad was that he knew something himself. Dodge had given him some information, and Tyler wasn't giving any back.

"Sir, I gave my word," Skip apologized. "I will try to get this to you. That's a promise, sir. May I use a phone?"

"Outer office," Dodge said flatly. There were four telephones within sight.

Tyler went out and sat at a secretary's desk. He took his notebook from a coat pocket and dialed the number on the card Ryan had left him.

"Acres," a female voice answered.

"Could I speak to Dr. Ryan, please?"

"Dr. Ryan is not here at the moment."

"Then . . . give me Admiral Greer, please."

"One moment, please."

"James Greer?" Dodge was behind him. "Is that who you're working for?"

"This is Greer. Your name Skip Tyler?"

"Yes, sir."

"You have that information for me?"

"Yes, sir, I do."

"Where are you?"

"In the Pentagon, sir."

"Okay, I want you to drive right up here. You know how to find the place? The guards at the main gate will be waiting for you. Get moving, son." Greer hung up.

"You're working for the CIA?" Dodge asked.

"Sir—I can't say. If you will excuse me, sir, I have some information to deliver."

"Mine?" the admiral demanded.

"No, sir. I already had it when I came in here. That's the truth, Admiral. And I will try to get this back to you."

"Call me," Dodge ordered. "We'll be here all night."

CIA Headquarters

The drive up the George Washington Parkway was easier than he expected. The decrepit old highway was crowded with shoppers but moved along at a steady crawl. He got off at the right exit and presently found himself at the guard post for the main highway entrance to the CIA. The barrier was down.

"Your name Tyler, Oliver W.?" the guard asked. "ID please." Tyler handed him his Pentagon pass.

"Okay, Commander. Pull your car right to the main entrance. Somebody will be there to meet you."

It was another two minutes to the main entrance through mostly empty parking lots glazed with ice from yesterday's melted snow. The armed guard who was waiting for him tried to help him out of the car. Tyler didn't like to be helped. He shrugged him off. Another man was waiting for him under the canopied main entrance. They were waved right through to the elevator.

He found Admiral Greer sitting in front of his office fireplace, seemingly half asleep. Skip didn't know that the DDI had only returned from England a few hours earlier. The admiral came to and ordered his plain-clothes security officer to withdraw. "You must be Skip Tyler. Come on over and sit down."

"That's quite a fire you have going there, sir."

"I shouldn't bother. Looking at a fire makes me go to sleep. Of course, I could use a little sleep right now. So, what do you have for me?"

"May I ask where Jack is?"

"You may ask. He's away."

"Oh." Tyler unlocked his briefcase and removed the printout. "Sir, I ran the performance model for this Russian sub. May I ask her name?"

Greer chuckled. "Okay, you've earned that much. Her name is *Red October*. You'll have to excuse me, son. I've had a busy couple of days, and being tired makes me forget my manners. Jack says you're pretty sharp. So does your personnel file. Now, you tell me. What'll she do?"

"Well, Admiral, we have a wide choice of data here, and—"

"The short version, Commander. I don't play with computers. I have people who do that for me."

"From seven to eighteen knots, the best bet is ten to twelve. With that speed range, you can figure a radiated noise level about the same as that of a *Yankee* doing six knots, but you'd have to factor reactor plant noise into that also. Moreover, the character of the noise will be different from what we're used to. These multiple impeller models don't put out normal propulsion noises. They seem to generate an irregular harmonic rumble. Did Jack tell you about this? It results from a backpressure wave in the tunnels. This fights the water flow, and that makes the rumble. Evidently there's no way around it. Our guys spent two years trying to find one. What they got was a new principle of hydrodynamics. The water almost acts like air in a jet engine at idle or low speed, except that water doesn't compress like air does. So, our guys will be able to detect something, but it will be different. They're going to have to get used to a wholly new acoustical signature. Add to that the lower signal intensity, and you have a boat that will be harder to detect than anything they have at this time."

"So that's what all this says." Greer riffled through the pages.

"Yes, sir. You'll want to have your own people look through it. The model—the program, that is—could stand a little improvement. I didn't have much time. Jack said you wanted this in a hurry. May I ask a question, sir?"

"You can try." Greer leaned back, rubbing his eyes.

"Is, ah, *Red October* at sea? That's it, isn't it? They're trying to locate her right now?" Tyler asked innocently.

"Uh huh, something like that. We couldn't figure what these doors meant. Ryan said you might be able to, and I suppose he was right. You've earned your money, Commander. This data might just enable us to find her."

"Admiral, I think *Red October* is up to something, maybe even trying to defect to the United States."

Greer's head came around. "Whatever makes you think that?"

"The Russkies have a major fleet operation in progress. They have subs all over the Atlantic, and it looks like they're trying to blockade our coast. The story is a rescue job for a lost boat. Okay, but Jack shows up Monday with pictures of a new missile boat—and today I hear that all of their other missile boats have been recalled to port." Tyler smiled. "That's kind of an odd set of coincidences, sir."

Greer turned and stared at the fire. He had just joined the DIA when the army and air force had pulled off the daring raid on the Song Tay prison camp twenty miles west of Hanoi. The raid had been a failure because the North Vietnamese had removed all of the captured pilots a few weeks before, something that aerial photographs could not determine. But everything else had gone perfectly. After penetrating hundreds of miles into hostile territory, the raiding force appeared entirely by surprise and caught many of the camp guards literally with their pants down. The Green Berets did a letter-perfect job of getting in and out. In the process they killed several hundred enemy troops, themselves sustaining a single casualty, a broken ankle. The most impressive part of the mission, however, was its secrecy. Operation KINGPIN had been rehearsed for months, and despite this its nature and objective had not been guessed by friend or enemy—until the day of the raid itself. On that day a young air force captain of intelligence went into his general's office to ask if a deep-penetration raid into North Vietnam had been laid on for the Song Tay prisoner-of-war camp. His astonished commander proceeded to grill the captain at length, only to learn that the bright young officer had seen enough disjointed bits and pieces to construct a clear picture of what was about to happen. Events like this gave security officers peptic ulcers.

"*Red October*'s going to defect, isn't she?" Tyler persisted.

If the admiral had had more sleep he might have bluffed it out. As it was, his response was a mistake. "Did Ryan tell you this?"

"Sir, I haven't spoken with Jack since Monday. That's the truth, sir."

"Then where did you get this other information?" Greer snapped.

"Admiral, I used to wear the blue suit. Most of my friends still do. I hear things," Tyler evaded. "The whole picture dropped into place an hour ago. The Russkies have never recalled all of their boomers at once. I know, I used to hunt them."

Greer sighed. "Jack thinks the same as you. He's out with the fleet right now. Commander, if you tell that to anyone, I'll have your other leg mounted overtop that fireplace. Do you understand me?"

"Aye aye, sir. What are we going to do with her?" Tyler smiled to himself, thinking that as a senior consultant to Sea Systems Command, he'd sure as hell get a chance to look at a for-real Russian submarine.

"Give her back. After we've had a chance to look her over,

of course. But there's a lot of things that could happen to prevent our ever seeing her."

It took Skip a moment to grasp what he'd just been told. "Give her back! Why, for Christ's sake?"

"Commander, just how likely do you think this scenario is? Do you think the whole crew of a submarine has decided to come over to us all at once?" Greer shook his head. "Smart money is that it's only the officers, maybe not all of them, and that they're trying to get over here without the crew's knowing what they're up to."

"Oh." Tyler considered that. "I suppose that does make sense—but why give her back? This isn't Japan. If somebody landed a MiG-25 here we wouldn't give it back."

"This is not like holding onto a stray fighter plane. The boat is worth a billion dollars, more if you throw in the missiles and warheads. And legally, the president says, it's their property. So if they find out we have her, they'll ask for her back, and we'll have to give her back. Okay, how will they know we have her? Those crew members who don't want to defect will ask to go home. Whoever asks, we send."

"You know, sir, that whoever does want to go back will be in a whole shitload of trouble—excuse me, sir."

"A shitload and a half." Tyler hadn't known that Greer was a mustang and could swear like a real sailor. "Some will want to stay, but most won't. They have families. Next you'll ask me if we might arrange for the crew to disappear."

"The thought has occurred to me," Tyler said.

"It's occurred to us, too. But we won't. Murder a hundred men? Even if we wanted to, there's no way we could conceal it in this day and age. Hell, I doubt even the Soviets could. Besides that, this simply is not the sort of thing you do in peacetime. That's one difference between us and them. You can take those reasons in any order you want."

"So, except for the crew, we'd keep her . . ."

"Yes, if we could hide her. And if a pig had wings, it could fly."

"Lots of places to hide her, Admiral. I can think of a few right here on the Chesapeake, and if we could get her round to Horn, there's a million little atolls we could use, and they all belong to us."

"But the crew will know, and when we send them home,

they'll tell their bosses," Greer explained patiently. "And Moscow will ask for her back. Oh, sure, we'll have a week or so to conduct, uh, safety and quarantine inspections, to make sure they weren't trying to smuggle cocaine into the country." The admiral laughed. "A British admiral suggested we invoke the old slave-trading treaty. Somebody did that back in World War II, to put the grab on a German blockade runner right before we got into it. So, we'll get a ton of intelligence regardless."

"Better to keep her, and run her, and take her apart..." Tyler said quietly, staring into the orange-white flames on the oak logs. How do we keep her? he wondered. An idea began to rattle around in his head. "Admiral, what if we could get the crew off without them knowing that we have the submarine?"

"Your full name is Oliver Wendell Tyler? Well, son, if you were named after Harry Houdini instead of a justice of the Supreme Court, I—" Greer looked into the engineer's face. "What do you have in mind?"

While Tyler explained Greer listened intently.

"To do this, sir, we'll have to get the navy in on it right quick. Specifically, we'll need the cooperation of Admiral Dodge, and if my speed figures for this boat are anything like accurate, we'll have to move smartly."

Greer rose and walked around the couch a few times to get his circulation going. "Interesting. The timing would be almost impossible, though."

"I didn't say it would be easy, sir, just that we *could* do it."

"Call home, Tyler. Tell your wife you won't be making it home. If I don't get any sleep tonight, neither do you. There's coffee behind my desk. First I have to call the judge, then we'll talk to Sam Dodge."

The USS Pogy

"Pogy, this is Black Gull 4. We're getting low on fuel. Have to return to the barn," the Orion's tactical coordinator reported, stretching after ten hours at his control console. "Anything you want us to get you? Over."

"Yeah, have a couple cases of beer sent out," Commander Wood replied. It was the current joke between P-3C and submarine crews. "Thanks for the data. We'll take it from here. Out."

Overhead, the Lockheed Orion increased power and turned southwest. The crewmen aboard would each hoist an extra beer or two at dinner, saying it was for their friends on the submarine.

"Mr. Dyson, take her two hundred feet. One-third speed."

The officer of the deck gave the proper orders as Commander Wood moved over to the plot.

The USS *Pogy* was three hundred miles northeast of Norfolk, awaiting the arrival of two Soviet *Alfa*-class submarines which several relays of antisubmarine patrol aircraft had tracked all the way from Iceland. The *Pogy* was named for a distinguished World War II fleet submarine, named in turn for an undistinguished game fish. She had been at sea for eighteen hours, and was fresh from an extended overhaul at the Newport News shipyard. Nearly everything aboard was either straight from manufacturers' crates or had been completely worked over by the skilled shipfitters on the James River. This was not to say that everything worked properly. Many items had failed in one way or another on the post-overhaul shakedown the previous week, a fact less unusual than lamentable, Commander Wood thought. The *Pogy*'s crew was new, too. Wood was on his first deployment as a commanding officer after a year of desk duty in Washington, and too many of the enlisted men were green, just out of sub school at New London, still getting accustomed to their first cruise on a submarine. It takes time for men used to blue skies and fresh air to learn the regime inside a thirty-two-foot-diameter steel pipe. Even the experienced men were making adjustments to their new boat and officers.

The *Pogy* had met her top speed of thirty-three knots on post-overhaul trials. This was fast for a ship but slower than the speed of the *Alfa*s she was listening to. Like all American submarines, her long suit was stealth. The *Alfa*s had no way of knowing she was there and that they would be easy targets for her weapons, the more so since the patrolling Orion had fed the *Pogy* exact range information, something that ordinarily takes time to deduce from a passive sonar plot.

Lieutenant Commander Tom Reynolds, the executive officer

and fire control coordinator, stood casually over the tactical plot. "Thirty-six miles to the near one, and forty on the far one." On the display they were labeled Pogy-Bait 1 and 2. Everyone found the use of this service epithet amusing.

"Speed forty-two?" Wood asked.

"Yes, Captain." Reynolds had handled the radio exchange until Black Gull 4 had announced its intention to return to base. "They're driving those boats for all they're worth. Right for us. We have hard solutions on both . . . zap! What do you suppose they're up to?"

"The word from CINCLANT is that their ambassador says they're on a SAR mission for a lost boat." His voice indicated what he thought of that.

"Search and rescue, eh?" Reynolds shrugged. "Well, maybe they think they lost a boat off Point Comfort, 'cause if they don't slow down real fast, that's where they'll end up. I've never heard of *Alfa*s operating this close to our coast. Have you, sir?"

"Nope." Wood frowned. The thing about the *Alfa*s was that they were fast and noisy. Soviet tactical doctrine seemed to call for them mainly in defensive roles: as "interceptor submarines" they could protect their own missile subs, and with their high speed they could engage American attack submarines, then evade counterattack. Wood didn't think the doctrine was sound, but that was all right with him.

"Maybe they want to blockade Norfolk," Reynolds suggested.

"You might have a point there," Wood said. "Well, in any case, we'll just sit tight and let them burn right past us. They'll have to slow as they cross the continental shelf line, and we'll tag along behind them, nice and quiet."

"Aye," Reynolds said.

If they had to shoot, both men reflected, they'd find out just how tough the *Alfa* really was. There had been much talk about the strength of the titanium used for her hull, whether it really would withstand the force of several hundred pounds of high explosive in direct contact. A new shaped-charge warhead for the Mark 48 torpedo had been developed for just this purpose and for handling the equally tough *Typhoon* hull. Both officers set this thought aside. Their assigned mission was to track and shadow.

The E. S. Politovskiy

Pogy-Bait 2 was known to the Soviet Navy as the *E. S. Politovskiy*. This *Alfa*-class attack sub was named for the chief engineering officer of the Russian fleet who had sailed all the way around the world to meet his appointment with destiny in the Tsushima Straits. Evgeni Sigismondavich Politovskiy had served the czar's navy with skill and a devotion to duty equal to that of any officer in history, but in his diary, which was discovered years later in Leningrad, the brilliant officer had decried in the most violent terms the corruption and excesses of the czarist regime, giving a grim counterpoint to the selfless patriotism he had shown as he sailed knowingly to his death. This made him a genuine hero for Soviet seamen to emulate, and the State had named its greatest engineering achievement in his memory. Unfortunately the *Politovskiy* had enjoyed no better luck than he had enjoyed in the face of Togo's guns.

The *Politovskiy*'s acoustical signature was labeled *Alfa 3* by the Americans. This was incorrect; she had been the first of the *Alfa*s. The small, spindle-shaped attack submarine had reached forty-three knots three hours into her initial builder's trials. Those trials had been cut short only a minute later by an incredible mishap: a fifty-ton right whale had somehow blundered in her path, and the *Politovskiy* had rammed the unfortunate creature broadside. The impact had smashed ten square meters of bow plating, annihilated the sonar dome, knocked a torpedo tube askew, and nearly flooded the torpedo room. This did not count shock damage to nearly every interior system from electronic equipment to the galley stove, and it was said that if anyone but the famous Vilnius headmaster had been in command, the submarine would surely have been lost. A two-meter segment of the whale's rib was now a permanent fixture at the officer's club in Severomorsk, dramatic testament to the strength of Soviet submarines; in fact the damage had taken over a year to repair, and by the time the *Politovskiy* sailed again there were already two other *Alfa*s in service. Two days after sailing on her next shakedown, she suffered another major casualty, the total failure of her high-pressure turbine. This had taken six months to replace. There had been three more minor incidents since, and the submarine was forever marked as a bad luck ship.

Chief Engineer Vladimir Petchukocov was a loyal Party member and a committed atheist, but he was also a sailor and therefore profoundly superstitious. In the old days, his ship would have been blessed on launching and thereafter every time she sailed. It would have been an impressive ceremony, with a bearded priest, clouds of incense, and evocative hymns. He had sailed without any of that and found himself wishing otherwise. He needed some luck. Petchukocov was having trouble with his reactor.

The *Alfa* reactor plant was small. It had to fit into a relatively small hull. It was also powerful for its size, and this one had been running at one hundred percent rated power for just over four days. They were racing for the American coast at 42.3 knots, as fast as the eight-year-old plant would permit. The *Politovskiy* was due for a comprehensive overhaul: new sonar, new computers, and a redesigned reactor control suite were all planned for the coming months. Petchukocov thought it irresponsible—reckless—to push his submarine so hard, even if everything were functioning properly. No *Alfa* plant on a submarine had ever been pushed this hard, not even a new one. And on this one, things were beginning to come apart.

The primary high-pressure reactor coolant pump was beginning to vibrate ominously. This was particularly worrying to the engineer. There was a backup, but the secondary pump had a lower rated power, and using it meant losing eight knots of speed. The *Alfa* plant achieved its high power not with a sodium-cooled system—as the Americans thought—but by running at a far higher pressure than any reactor system afloat and using a revolutionary heat exchange system that boosted the plant's overall thermal efficiency to forty-one percent, well in excess of that for any other submarine. But the price of this was a reactor that at full power was red-lined on every monitor gauge—and in this case the red lines were not mere symbolism. They signified genuine danger.

This fact, added to the vibrating pump, had Petchukocov seriously concerned; an hour earlier he had pleaded with the captain to reduce power for a few hours so that his skilled crew of engineers could make repairs. It was probably only a bad bearing, after all, and they had spares. The pump had been designed so that it would be easy to fix. The captain had wavered, wanting to grant the request, but the political officer had intervened, pointing out that their orders were both urgent and explicit: they had to be on station as quickly as possible; to do otherwise would be "politically unsound." And that was that.

Petchukocov bitterly remembered the look in his captain's eyes. What was the purpose of a commanding officer if his every order had to be approved by a political flunky? Petchukocov had been a faithful Communist since joining the Octobrists as a boy—but damn it! what was the point of having specialists and engineers? Did the Party really think that physical laws could be overturned by the whim of some apparatchik with a heavy desk and a dacha in the Moscow suburbs? The engineer swore to himself.

He stood alone at the master control board. This was located in the engine room, aft of the compartment that held the reactor and the heat exchanger/steam generator, the latter placed right at the submarine's center of gravity. The reactor was pressurized to twenty kilograms per square centimeter, about twenty-eight hundred pounds per square inch. Only a fraction of this pressure came from the pump. The higher pressure caused a higher boiling point for the coolant. In this case, the water was heated to over 900° Celsius, a temperature sufficient to generate steam, which gathered at the top of the reactor vessel; the steam bubble applied pressure to the water beneath, preventing the generation of more steam. The steam and water regulated one another in a delicate balance. The water was dangerously radioactive as a result of the fission reaction taking place within the uranium fuel rods. The function of the control rods was to regulate the reaction. Again, the control was delicate. At most the rods could absorb just less than one percent of the neutron flux, but this was enough either to permit the reaction or to prevent it.

Petchukocov could recite all this data in his sleep. He could draw a wholly accurate schematic diagram of the entire engine plant from memory and could instantly grasp the significance of the slightest change in his instrument readings. He stood perfectly straight over the control board, his eyes tracing the myriad dials and gauges in a regular pattern, one hand poised over the SCRAM switch, the other over the emergency cooling controls.

He could hear the vibration. It had to be a bad bearing getting worse as it wore more and more unevenly. If the crankshaft bearings went bad, the pump would seize, and they'd have to stop. This would be an emergency, though not really a dangerous one. It would mean that repairing the pump—if they could repair it at all—would take days instead of hours, eating up valuable time and spare parts. That was bad enough. What was worse, and what Petchukocov did not know, was that the vibration was generating pressure waves in the coolant.

To make use of the newly developed heat exchanger, the *Alfa* plant had to move water rapidly through its many loops and baffles. This required a high-pressure pump which accounted for one hundred fifty pounds of the total system pressure—almost ten times what was considered safe in Western reactors. With the pump so powerful, the whole engine room complex, normally very noisy at high speed, was like a boiler factory, and the pump's vibration was disturbing the performance of the monitor instruments. It was making the needles on his gauges waver, Petchukocov noted. He was right, and wrong. The pressure gauges were really wavering because of the thirty-pound overpressure waves pulsing through the system. The chief engineer did not recognize this for what it was. He had been on duty too many hours.

Within the reactor vessel, these pressure waves were approaching the frequency at which a piece of equipment resonated. Roughly halfway down the interior surface of the vessel was a titanium fitting, part of the backup cooling system. In the event of a coolant loss, and *after* a successful SCRAM, valves inside and outside the vessel would open, cooling the reactor either with a mixture of water and barium or, as a last measure, with seawater which could be vented in and out of the vessel—at the cost of ruining the entire reactor. This had been done once, and though it had been costly, the action of a junior engineer had prevented the loss of a *Victor*-class attack sub by catastrophic meltdown.

Today the inside valve was closed, along with the corresponding through-hull fitting. The valves were made of titanium because they had to function reliably after prolonged exposure to high temperature, and also because titanium was very corrosion-resistant—high-temperature water was murderously corrosive. What had not been fully considered was that the metal was also exposed to intense nuclear radiation, and this particular titanium alloy was not completely stable under extended neutron bombardment. The metal had become brittle over the years. The minute waves of hydraulic pressure were beating against the clapper in the valve. As the pump's frequency of vibration changed it began to approach the frequency at which the clapper vibrated. This caused the clapper to snap harder and harder against its retaining ring. The metal at its edges began to crack.

A *michman* at the forward end of the compartment heard it first, a low buzz coming through the bulkhead. At first he thought it was feedback noise from the PA speaker, and he waited too long to check it. The clapper broke free and dropped out of the valve nozzle. It was not very large, only ten centimeters in diameter and five millimeters thick. This type of fitting is called a butterfly valve, and the clapper looked just like a butterfly, suspended and twirling in the water flow. If it had been made of stainless steel it would have been heavy enough to fall to the bottom of the vessel. But it was made of titanium, which was both stronger than steel and very much lighter. The coolant flow moved it up, towards the exhaust pipe.

The outward-moving water carried the clapper into the pipe, which had a fifteen-centimeter inside diameter. The pipe was made of stainless steel, two-meter sections welded together for easy replacement in the cramped quarters. The clapper was borne along rapidly towards the heat exchanger. Here the pipe took a forty-five-degree downward turn and the clapper jammed momentarily. This blocked half of the pipe's channel, and before the surge of pressure could dislodge the clapper too many things happened. The moving water had its own momentum. On being blocked, it generated a back-pressure wave within the pipe. Total pressure jumped momentarily to thirty-four hundred pounds. This caused the pipe to flex a few millimeters. The increased pressure, lateral displacement of a weld joint, and cumulative effect of years of high-temperature erosion of the steel damaged the joint. A hole the size of a pencil point opened. The escaping water flashed instantly into steam, setting off alarms in the reactor compartment and neighboring spaces. It ate at the remainder of the weld, rapidly expanding the failure until reactor coolant was erupting as though from a horizontal fountain. One jet of steam demolished the adjacent reactor-control wiring conduits.

What had just begun was a catastrophic loss-of-coolant accident.

The reactor was fully depressurized within three seconds. Its many gallons of coolant exploded into steam, seeking release into the surrounding compartment. A dozen alarms sounded at once on the master control board, and in the blink of an eye Vladimir Petchukocov faced his ultimate nightmare. The engineer's automatic trained reaction was to jam his finger on the SCRAM switch, but the steam in the reactor vessel had disabled the rod control system, and there wasn't time to solve the problem. In an instant, Petchukocov knew that his ship was doomed. Next he opened the emergency coolant controls, admitting seawater into the reactor vessel. This automatically set off alarms throughout the hull.

In the control room forward, the captain grasped the nature of the emergency at once. The *Politovskiy* was running at one hundred fifty meters. He had to get her to the surface immediately, and he shouted orders to blow all ballast and make full rise on the diving planes.

The reactor emergency was regulated by physical laws. With no reactor coolant to absorb the heat of the uranium rods, the nuclear reaction actually stopped—there was no water to attenuate the neutron flux. This was no solution, however, since the residual decay heat was sufficient to melt everything in the compartment. The cold water admitted into the vessel drew off the heat but also slowed down too many neutrons, keeping them in the reactor core. This caused a runaway reaction that generated even more heat, more than any amount of coolant could control. What had started as a loss-of-coolant accident became something worse: a cold-water accident. It was now only a matter of minutes before the entire core melted, and the *Politovskiy* had that long to get to the surface.

Petchukocov stayed at his post in the engine room, doing what he could. His own life, he knew, was almost certainly lost. He had to give his captain time to surface the boat. There was a drill for this sort of emergency, and he barked orders to implement it. It only made things worse.

His duty electrician moved along the electrical control panels switching from main power to emergency, since residual steam power in the turboalternators would die in a few more seconds. In a moment the submarine's power completely depended on standby batteries.

In the control room power was lost to the electrically controlled trim tabs on the trailing edge of the diving planes, which automatically switched back to electrohydraulic control. This powered not just the small trim tabs but the diving planes as well. The control assemblies moved instantly to a fifteen-degree up-angle—and she was still moving at thirty-nine knots. With all her ballast tanks now blasted free of water by compressed air, the submarine was very light, and she rose like a climbing aircraft. In seconds the astonished control room crew felt their boat rise to an up-angle that was forty-five degrees and getting worse. A moment later they were too busy trying to stand to come to grips with the problem. Now the *Alfa* was climbing almost vertically at thirty miles per hour. Every man and unsecured item aboard fell sternward.

In the motor control room aft, a crewman crashed against the main electrical switchboard, short-circuiting it with his body, and all power aboard was lost. A cook who had been inventorying survival gear in the torpedo room forward struggled into the escape trunk as he fought his way into an exposure suit. Even with only a year's experience, he was quick to understand the meaning of the hooting alarms and unprecedented actions of his boat. He yanked the hatch shut and began to work the escape controls as he had been taught in submarine school.

The *Politovskiy* soared through the surface of the Atlantic like a broaching whale, coming three quarters of her length out of the water before crashing back.

The USS Pogy

"Conn, sonar."

"Conn, aye, Captain speaking."

"Skipper, you better hear this. Something just went crazy on Bait 2," *Pogy*'s chief reported. Wood was in the sonar room in seconds, putting on earphones plugged into a tape recorder which had a two-minute offset. Commander Wood heard a whooshing sound. The engine noises stopped. A few seconds later there was an explosion of compressed air, and a staccato of hull popping noises as a submarine changed depth rapidly.

"What's going on?" Wood asked quickly.

The E. S. Politovskiy

In the *Politovskiy*'s reactor, the runaway fission reaction had virtually annihilated both the incoming seawater and the uranium fuel rods. Their debris settled on the after wall of the reactor vessel. In a minute there was a meter-wide puddle of radioactive slag, enough to form its own critical mass. The reaction continued unabated, this time directly attacking the tough stainless steel of the vessel. Nothing man made could long withstand five thousand degrees of direct heat. In ten seconds the vessel wall failed. The uranium mass dropped free, against the aft bulkhead.

Petchukocov knew he was dead. He saw the paint on the forward bulkhead turn black, and his last impression was of a dark mass surrounded with the blue glow. The engineer's body vaporized an instant later, and the mass of slag dropped to the next bulkhead aft.

Forward, the submarine's nearly vertical angle in the water eased. The high-pressure air in the ballast tanks spilled out of the bottom floods and the tanks filled with water, dropping the angle of the boat and submerging her. In the forward part of the submarine men were screaming. The captain struggled to his feet, ignoring his broken leg, trying to get control, to get his men organized and out of the submarine before it was too late, but the luck of Evgeni Sigismondavich Politovskiy would plague his namesake one last time. Only one man escaped. The cook opened the escape trunk hatch and got out. Following what he had learned during the drill, he began to seal the hatch so that men behind him could use it, but a wave slapped him off the hull as the sub slid backwards.

In the engine room, the changing angle dropped the melted core to the deck. The hot mass attacked the steel deck first, burning through that, then the titanium of the hull. Five seconds later the engine room was vented to the sea. The *Politovskiy*'s largest compartment filled rapidly with water. This destroyed what little reserve buoyancy the ship had, and the acute down-angle returned. The *Alfa* began her last dive.

The stern dropped just as the captain began to get his control room crew to react to orders again. His head struck an instrument console. What slim hopes his crew had died with him. The *Politovskiy* was falling backwards, her propeller windmilling the wrong way as she slid to the bottom of the sea.

The Pogy

"Skipper, I was on the *Chopper* back in sixty-nine," the *Pogy*'s chief said, referring to a horrifying accident on a diesel-powered submarine.

"That's what it sounds like," his captain said. He was now listening to direct sonar input. There was no mistaking it. The submarine was flooding. They had heard the ballast tanks refill; this could only mean interior compartments were filling with water. If they had been closer, they might have heard the screams of men in that doomed hull. Wood was just as happy he couldn't. The continuing rush of water was dreadful enough. Men were dying. Russians, his enemy, but men not unlike himself, and there was not a thing that could be done about it.

Bait 1, he saw, was proceeding, unmindful of what had happened to her trailing sister.

The E. S. Politovskiy

It took nine minutes for the *Politovskiy* to fall the two thousand feet to the ocean floor. She impacted savagely on the hard sand bottom at the edge of the continental shelf. It was a tribute to her builders that her interior bulkheads held. All the compartments from the reactor room aft were flooded and half the crew killed in them, but the forward compartments were dry. Even this was more curse than blessing. With the aft air storage banks unusable and only emergency battery power to run the complex environmental control systems, the forty men had only a limited supply of air. They were spared a rapid death from the crushing North Atlantic only to face a slower one from asphyxiation.

THE NINTH DAY

SATURDAY, 11 DECEMBER

The Pentagon

A female yeoman first class held the door open for Tyler. He walked in to find General Harris standing alone over the large chart table pondering the placement of tiny ship models.

"You must be Skip Tyler." Harris looked up.

"Yes, sir." Tyler was standing as rigidly at attention as his prosthetic leg allowed. Harris came over quickly to shake hands.

"Greer says you used to play ball."

"Yes, General, I played right tackle at Annapolis. Those were good years." Tyler smiled, flexing his fingers. Harris looked like an iron-pumper.

"Okay, if you used to play ball, you can call me Ed." Harris poked him in the chest. "Your number was seventy-eight, and you made All American, right?"

"Second string, sir. Nice to know somebody remembers."

"I was on temporary duty at the Academy for a few months back then, and I caught a couple games. I never forget a good offensive lineman. I made All Conference at Montana—long time ago. What happened to the leg?"

"Drunk driver clipped me. I was the lucky one. The drunk didn't make it."

"Serves the bastard right."

Tyler nodded agreement, but remembered that the drunken shipfitter had had his own wife and family, according to the police. "Where is everybody?"

"The chiefs are at their normal—well, normal for a week-day, not a Saturday—intelligence briefing. They ought to be down in a few minutes. So, you're teaching engineering at Annapolis now, eh?"

"Yes, sir. I got a doctorate in that along the way."

"Name's Ed, Skip. And this morning you're going to tell us how we can hold onto that maverick Russian sub?"

"Yes, sir—Ed."

"Tell me about it, but let's get some coffee first." The two men went to a table in the corner with coffee and donuts. Harris listened to the younger man for five minutes, sipping his coffee and devouring a couple of jelly donuts. It took a lot of food to support his frame.

"Son of a gun," the J-3 observed when Tyler finished. He walked over to the chart. "That's interesting. Your idea depends a lot on sleight of hand. We'd have to keep them away from where we're pulling this off. About here, you say?" He tapped the chart.

"Yes, General. The thing is, the way they seem to be op-erating we can do this to seaward of them—"

"And do a double shuffle. I like it. Yeah, I like it, but Dan Foster won't like losing one of our own boats."

"I'd say it's worth the trade."

"So would I," Harris agreed. "But they're not my boats. After we do this, where do we hide her—if we get her?"

"General, there are some nice places right here on the Ches-apeake Bay. There's a deep spot on the York River and another on the Patuxent, both owned by the navy, both marked Keep Out on the charts. Nice thing about subs, they're supposed to be invisible. You just find a deep enough spot and flood your tanks. That's temporary, of course. For a more permanent spot, maybe Truk or Kwajalein in the Pacific. Nice and far from any place."

"And the Soviets would never notice the presence of a sub tender and three hundred submarine technicians there all of a sudden? Besides, those islands don't really belong to us anymore, remember?"

Tyler hadn't expected this man to be a dummy. "So, what if they do find out in a few months? What will they do, announce it to the whole world? I don't think so. By that time we'll have all the information we want, and we can always produce the defecting officers in a nice news conference. How would that look for them? Anyway, it figures that after we've had her for a while, we'll break her up. The reactor'll go to Idaho for tests. The missiles and warheads will get taken off. The electronics gear will be taken to California for testing, and the CIA, NSA, and navy will have gunfights over the crypto gear. The stripped hulk will be taken to a nice deep spot and scuttled. No evidence. We don't have to keep this a secret forever, just for a few months."

Harris set his cup down. "You'll have to forgive me for playing devil's advocate. I see you've thought this out. Fine, I think it's worth a hard look. It means coordinating a lot of hardware, but it doesn't really interfere with what we're already doing. Okay, you have my vote."

The Joint Chiefs arrived three minutes later. Tyler had never seen so many stars in one room.

"You wanted to see all of us, Eddie?" Hilton asked.

"Yes, General. This is Dr. Skip Tyler."

Admiral Foster came over first to take his hand. "You got us that performance data on *Red October* that we were just briefed on. Good work, Commander."

"Dr. Tyler thinks we should hold onto her if we get her," Harris said deadpan. "And he thinks he has a way we can do it."

"We already thought of killing the crew," Commandant Maxwell said. "The president won't let us."

"Gentlemen, what if I told you that there was a way to send the crewmen home without them knowing that we have her? That's the issue, right? We have to send the crewmen back to Mother Russia. I say there's a way to do that, and the remaining question is where to hide her."

"We're listening," Hilton said suspiciously.

"Well, sir, we'll have to move quickly to get everything in

place. We'll need *Avalon* from the West Coast. *Mystic* is already aboard the *Pigeon* in Charleston. We need both of them, and we need an old boomer of our own that we can afford to do without. That's the hardware. The real trick, however, is the timing—and we have to find her. That may be the hardest part."

"Maybe not," Foster said. "Admiral Gallery reported this morning that *Dallas* may be onto her. Her report dovetails nicely with your engineering model. We'll know more in a few days. Go on."

Tyler explained. It took ten minutes since he had to answer questions and use the chart to diagram time and space constraints. When he was finished, General Barnes was at the phone calling the commander of the Military Airlift Command. Foster left the room to call Norfolk, and Hilton was on his way to the White House.

The Red October

Except for those on watch, every officer was in the wardroom. Several pots of tea were on the table, all untouched, and again the door was locked.

"Comrades," Petrov reported, "the second set of badges was contaminated, worse than the first."

Ramius noted that Petrov was rattled. It wasn't the first set of badges, or the second. It was the third and fourth since sailing. He had chosen his ship's doctor well.

"Bad badges," Melekhin growled. "Some bastard of a trickster in Severomorsk—or perhaps an imperialist spy playing a typical enemy trick on us. When they catch the son of a bitch I will shoot him myself—whoever he is! This sort of thing is treasonous!"

"Regulations require that I report this," Petrov noted. "Even though the instruments show safe levels."

"Your adherence to the rules is noted, Comrade Doctor. You have acted correctly," Ramius said. "And now regulations stipulate that we make yet another check. Melekhin, I want you and Borodin to do it personally. First check the radiation instruments themselves. If they are working properly, we will be certain that the badges are defective—or have been tampered with. If so, my report on this incident will demand someone's head." It was not unknown for drunken shipyard workers to be sent to the gulag. "Comrades, in my opinion there is nothing at all to concern us. If there were a leak, Comrade Melekhin would have discovered it days ago. So. We all have work to do."

They were all back in the wardroom half an hour later. Passing crewmen noticed this, and already the whispering started.

"Comrades," Melekhin announced, "we have a major problem."

The officers, especially the younger ones, looked a little pale. On the table was a Geiger counter stripped into a score of small parts. Next to it was a radiation detector taken off the reactor room bulkhead, its inspection cover removed.

"Sabotage," Melekhin hissed. It was a word fearsome enough to make any Soviet citizen shudder. The room went deathly still, and Ramius noted that Svyadov was holding his face under rigid control.

"Comrades, mechanically speaking these instruments are quite simple. As you know, this counter has ten different settings. We can choose from ten sensitivity ranges, using the same instrument to detect a minor leak or to quantify a major one. We do that by dialing this selector, which engages one of ten electrical resistors of increasing value. A child could design this, or maintain and repair it." The chief enginer tapped the underside of the selector dial. "In this case the proper resistors have been clipped off, and new ones soldered on. Settings one to eight have the same impedance value. All of our counters were inspected by the same dockyard technician three days before we sailed. Here is his inspection sheet." Melekhin tossed it on the table contemptuously.

"Either he or another spy sabotaged this and all the other counters I've looked at. It would have taken a skilled man no more than an hour. In the case of this instrument." The engineer turned the fixed detector over. "You see that the electrical parts have been disconnected, except for the test circuit, which was rewired. Borodin and I removed this from the forward bulkhead. This is skilled work; whoever did this is no amateur. I believe that an imperialist agent has sabotaged our ship. First he disabled our radiation monitor instruments, then he probably arranged a low-level leak in our hot piping. It would appear, comrades, that Comrade Petrov was correct. We may have a leak. My apologies, Doctor."

Petrov nodded jerkily. Compliments like this he could easily forego.

"Total exposure, Comrade Petrov?" Ramius asked.

"The greatest is for the enginemen, of course. The maximum is fifty rads for Comrades Melekhin and Svyadov. The other engine crewmen run from twenty to forty-five rads, and the cumulative exposure drops rapidly as one moves forward. The torpedomen have only five rads or so, mostly less. The officers exclusive of engineers run from ten to twenty-five." Petrov paused, telling himself to be more positive. "Comrades, these are not lethal doses. In fact, one can tolerate a dose of up to a hundred rads without any near-term physiological effects, and one can survive several hundred. We do face a serious problem here, but it is not yet a life-threatening emergency."

"Melekhin?" the captain asked.

"It is my engine plant, and my responsibility. We do not yet *know* that we have a leak. The badges could still be defective or sabotaged. This could all be a vicious psychological trick played on us by the main enemy to damage our morale. Borodin will assist me. We will personally repair these and conduct a thorough inspection of all reactor systems. I am too old to have children. For the moment, I suggest that we deactivate the reactor and proceed on battery. The inspection will take us four hours at most. I also recommend that we reduce reactor watches to two hours. Agreed, Captain?"

"Certainly, Comrade. I know that there is nothing you cannot repair."

"Excuse me, Comrade Captain," Ivanov spoke up. "Should we report this to fleet headquarters?"

"Our orders are not to break radio silence," Ramius said.

"If the imperialists were able to sabotage our instruments . . . What if they knew our orders beforehand and are attempting to make us use the radio so they can locate us?" Borodin asked.

"A possibility," Ramius replied. "First we will determine if we have a problem, then its severity. Comrades, we have a fine crew and the best officers in the fleet. We will see to our own problems, conquer them, and continue our mission. We all have a date in Cuba that I intend to meet—to hell with imperialist plots!"

"Well said," Melekhin concurred.

"Comrades, we will keep this secret. There is no reason to excite the crew over what may be nothing, and at most is something we can handle on our own." Ramius ended the meeting.

Petrov was less sure, and Svyadov was trying very hard not to shake. He had a sweetheart at home and wanted one day to have children. The young lieutenant had been painstakingly trained to understand everything that went on in the reactor systems and to know what to do if things went awry. And it was some consolation to know that most of the solutions to reactor problems to be found in the book had been written by some of the men in this room. Even so, something that could neither be seen nor felt was invading his body, and no rational person would be happy with that.

The meeting adjourned. Melekhin and Borodin went aft to the engineering stores. A *michman* electrician came with them to get the proper parts. He noted that they were reading from the maintenance manual for a radiation detector. When he went off duty an hour later, the whole crew knew that the reactor had been shut down yet again. The electrician conferred with his bunkmate, a missile maintenance technician. Together they discussed the reason for working on a half dozen Geiger counters and other instruments, and their conclusion was an obvious one.

The submarine's bosun overheard the discussion and pondered the conclusion himself. He had been on nuclear submarines for ten years. Despite this he was not an educated man and regarded any activity in the reactor spaces as something to the left of witchcraft. It worked the ship, how he did not know, though he was certain that there was something unholy about it. Now he began to wonder if the devils he never saw inside that steel drum—were coming loose? Within two hours the entire crew knew that something was wrong and that their officers had not yet figured out a way to deal with it.

The cooks bringing food forward from the galley to the crew spaces were seen to linger in the bow as long as they could. Men standing watch in the control room shifted on their feet more than usual, Ramius noted, hurrying forward at the change of watch.

The USS New Jersey

It took some getting used to, Commodore Zachary Eaton reflected. When his flagship was built, he was sailing boats in a bathtub. Back then the Russians were allies, but allies of convenience, who shared a common enemy instead of a common goal. Like the Chinese today, he judged. The enemy then had been the Germans and the Japanese. In his twenty-six-year career, he had been to both countries many times, and his first command, a destroyer, had been home-ported at Yokoshuka. It was a strange world.

There were several nice things about his flagship. Big as she was, her movement on the ten-foot seas was just enough to remind him that he was at sea, not at a desk. Visibility was about ten miles, and somewhere out there, about eight hundred miles away, was the Russian fleet. His battleship was going to meet them just like in the old old days, as if the aircraft carrier had never come along. The destroyers *Caron* and *Stump* were in sight, five miles off either bow. Further forward, the cruisers *Biddle* and *Wainwright* were doing radar picket duty. The surface action group was marking time instead of proceeding forward as he would have preferred. Off the New Jersey coast, the helicopter assault ship *Tarawa* and two frigates were racing to join up, bringing ten AV-8B Harrier attack fighters and fourteen ASW helicopters to supplement his air strength. This was useful, but not of critical concern to Eaton. The *Saratoga*'s air wing was now operating out of Maine, along with a goodly collection of air force birds working hard to learn the maritime strike business. HMS *Invincible* was two hundred miles to his east, conducting aggressive ASW patrols, and eight hundred miles east of that force was the *Kennedy,* hiding under a weather front off the Azores. It slightly irked the commodore that the Brits were helping out. Since when did the U.S. Navy need help defending the American coast? Not that they didn't owe us the favor, though.

The Russians had split into three groups, with the carrier *Kiev* easternmost to face the *Kennedy*'s battle group. His expected responsibility was the *Moskva* group, with the *Invincible* handling the *Kirov*'s. Data on all three was being fed to him continuously and digested by his operations staff down in flag plot. What were the Soviets up to? he wondered.

He knew the story that they were searching for a lost sub, but Eaton believed that as much as if they'd explained that they had a bridge they wanted to sell. Probably, he thought, they want to demonstrate that they can trail their coats down our coast whenever they want, to show that they have a seagoing fleet and to establish a precedent for doing this again.

Eaton did not like that.

He did not much care for his assigned mission either. He had two tasks that were not fully compatible. Keeping an eye on their submarine activity would be difficult enough. The *Saratoga*'s Vikings were not working his area, despite his request, and most of the Orions were working farther out, closer to the *Invincible*. His own ASW assets were barely adequate for local defense, much less active sub hunting. The *Tarawa* would change that, but also change his screening requirements. His other mission was to establish and maintain sensor contact with the *Moskva* group and to report at once any unusual activity to CINCLANTFLT, the commander in chief of the Atlantic Fleet. This made sense, sort of. If their surface ships did anything untoward, Eaton had the means to deal with them. It was being decided now how closely he should shadow them.

The problem was whether he should be nearby or far away. Near meant twenty miles—gun range. The *Moskva* had ten escorts, none of which could possibly survive more than two of his sixteen-inch projectiles. At twenty miles he had the choice of using full-sized or subcaliber rounds, the latter guided to their targets by a laser designator installed atop the main director tower. Tests the previous year had determined that he could maintain a steady firing rate of one round every twenty seconds, with the laser shifting fire from one target to another until there were no more. But this would expose the *New Jersey* and her escorts to torpedo and missile fire from the Russian ships.

Backing farther off, he could still fire sabot rounds from fifty miles, and they could be directed to the target by a laser designator aboard the battlewagon's helicopter. This would expose the chopper to surface-to-air missile fire and to Soviet helicopters suspected of having air-to-air missile capability. To help out with this, the *Tarawa* was bringing a pair of Apache attack helicopters, which carried lasers, air-to-air missiles, and their own air-to-surface missiles; they were antitank weapons expected to work well against small warships.

His ships would be exposed to missile fire, but he didn't fear for his flagship. Unless the Russians were carrying nuclear warheads, their antiship missiles would not be able to damage his ship gravely—the *New Jersey* had upwards of a foot of class B armor plate. They would, however, play hell with his radar and communications gear, and worse, they would be lethal to his thin-hulled escorts. His ships carried their own antiship missiles, Harpoons and Tomahawks, though not as many as he would have liked.

And what about a Russian sub hunting them? Eaton had been told of none, but you never knew where one might be hiding. Oh well—he couldn't worry about everything. A submarine could sink the *New Jersey,* but she would have to work at it. If the Russians were really up to something nasty, they'd get the first shot, but Eaton would have enough warning to launch his own missiles and get off a few rounds of gunfire while calling for air support—none of which would happen, he was sure.

He decided that the Russians were on some sort of fishing expedition. His job was to show them that the fish in these waters were dangerous.

Naval Air Station, North Island, California

The oversized tractor-trailer crept at two miles per hour into the cargo bay of the C-5A Galaxy transport under the watchful eyes of the aircraft's loadmaster, two flight officers, and six naval officers. Oddly, only the latter, none of whom wore aviator's wings, were fully versed in the procedure. The vehicle's center of gravity was precisely marked, and they watched the mark approach a particular number engraved on the cargo bay floor. The work had to be done exactly. Any mistake could fatally impair the aircraft's trim and imperil the lives of the flight crew and passengers.

"Okay, freeze it right there," the senior officer called. The driver was only too glad to stop. He left the keys in the ignition, set all the brakes, and put the truck in gear before getting out. Someone else would drive it out of the aircraft on the other .

side of the country. The loadmaster and six airmen immediately went to work, snaking steel cables to eyebolts on the truck and trailer to secure the heavy load. Shifting cargo was something else an aircraft rarely survived, and the C-5A did not have ejection seats.

The loadmaster saw to it that his ground crewmen were properly at work before walking over to the pilot. He was a twenty-five-year sergeant who loved the C-5s despite their blemished history.

"Cap'n, what the hell is this thing?"

"It's called a DSRV, Sarge, deep submergence rescue vehicle."

"Says *Avalon* on the back, sir," the sergeant pointed out.

"Yeah, so it has a name. It's a sort of a lifeboat for submarines. Goes down to get the crew out if something screws up."

"Oh." The sergeant considered that. He'd flown tanks, helicopters, general cargo, once a whole battalion of troops on his—he thought of the aircraft as his—Galaxy before. This was the first time he had ever flown a ship. If it had a name, he reasoned, it was a ship. Damn, the Galaxy could do anything! "Where we takin' it, sir?"

"Norfolk Naval Air Station, and I've never been there either." The pilot watched the securing process closely. Already a dozen cables were attached. When a dozen more were in place, they'd put tension on the cables to prevent the minutest shift. "We figure a trip of five hours, forty minutes, all on internal fuel. We got the jet stream on our side today. Weather's supposed to be okay until we hit the coast. We lay over for a day, then come back Monday morning."

"Your boys work pretty fast," said the senior naval officer, Lieutenant Ames, coming over.

"Yes, Lieutenant, another twenty minutes." The pilot checked his watch. "We ought to be taking off on the hour."

"No hurry, Captain. If this thing shifts in flight, I guess it would ruin our whole day. Where do I send my people?"

"Upper deck forward. There's room for fifteen or so just aft of the flight deck." Lieutenant Ames knew this but didn't say so. He'd flown with his DSRV across the Atlantic several times and across the Pacific once, every time on a different C-5.

"May I ask what the big deal is?" the pilot inquired.

"I don't know," Ames said. "They want me and my baby in Norfolk."

"You really take that little bitty thing underwater, sir?" the loadmaster asked.

"That's what they pay me for. I've had her down to forty-eight hundred feet, almost a mile." Ames regarded his vessel with affection.

"A mile *under* water, sir? Jesus—uh, pardon me, sir, but I mean, isn't that a little hairy—the water pressure, I mean?"

"Not really. I've been down to twenty thousand aboard *Trieste*. It's really pretty interesting down there. You see all kinds of strange fish." Though a fully qualified submariner, Ames' first love was research. He had a degree in oceanography and had commanded or served in all of the navy's deep-submergence vehicles except the nuclear-powered *NR-1*. "Of course, the water pressure would do bad things to you if anything went wrong, but it would be so fast you'd never know it. If you fellows want a check ride, I could probably arrange it. It's a different world down there."

"That's okay, sir." The sergeant went back to swearing at his men.

"You weren't serious," the pilot observed.

"Why not? It's no big deal. We take civilians down all the time, and believe me, it's a lot less hairy than riding this damned white whale during a midair refueling."

"Uh-huh," the pilot noted dubiously. He'd done hundreds of those. It was entirely routine, and he was surprised that anyone would find it dangerous. You had to be careful, of course, but, hell, you had to be careful driving every morning. He was sure that an accident on this pocket submarine wouldn't leave enough of a man to make a decent meal for a shrimp. It takes all kinds, he decided. "You don't go to sea by yourself in that, do you?"

"No, ordinarily we work off a submarine rescue ship, *Pigeon* or *Ortolan*. We can also operate off a regular submarine. That gadget you see there on the trailer is our mating collar. We can nest on the back of a sub at the after escape trunk, and the sub takes us where we need to go."

"Does this have to do with the flap on the East Coast?"

"That's a good bet, but nobody's said anything official to us. The papers say the Russians have lost a sub. If so, we might go down to look at her, maybe rescue any survivors. We can take off twenty or twenty-five men at a time, and our mating collar is designed to fit Russian subs as well as our own."

"Same size?"

"Close enough." Ames cocked an eyebrow. "We plan for all kinds of contingencies."

"Interesting."

The North Atlantic

The YAK-36 Forger had left the *Kiev* half an hour before, guided first by gyro compass and now by the ESM pod on the fighter's stubby rudder fin. Senior Lieutenant Viktor Shavrov's mission was not an easy one. He was to approach the American E-3A Sentry radar surveillance aircraft, one of which had been shadowing his fleet for three days now. The AWACS (airborne warning and control system) aircraft had been careful to circle well beyond SAM range, but had stayed close enough to maintain constant coverage of the Soviet fleet, reporting every maneuver and radio transmission to their command base. It was like having a burglar watching one's apartment and being unable to do anything about it.

Shavrov's mission was to do something about it. He couldn't shoot, of course. His orders from Admiral Stralbo on the *Kirov* had been explicit about that. But he was carrying a pair of Atoll heat-seeking missiles which he would be sure to show the imperialists. He and his admiral expected that this would teach them a lesson: the Soviet Navy did not like having imperialist snoopers about, and accidents had been known to happen. It was a mission worthy of the effort it took.

This effort was considerable. To avoid detection by the airborne radar Shavrov had to fly as low and slow as his fighter could operate, a bare twenty meters above the rough Atlantic; this way he would get lost in the sea return. His speed was two hundred knots. This made for excellent fuel economy, though his mission was at the ragged edge of his fuel load. It also made for very rough flying as his fighter bounced through the roiled air at the wave tops. There was a low-hanging mist that cut visibility to a few kilometers. So much the better, he thought. The nature of the mission had chosen him, rather than the other way around. He was one of the few Soviet pilots experienced in low-level flying. Shavrov had not become a sailor-pilot by himself. He'd started flying attack helicopters for frontal aviation in Afghanistan, graduating to fixed-wing aircraft after a year's bloody apprenticeship. Shavrov was an expert in nap-of-the-earth flying, having learned it by necessity, hunting the bandits and counterrevolutionaries that hid in the towering mountains like hydrophobic rats. This skill had made him attractive to the fleet, which had transferred him to sea duty without his having had much say in the matter. After a few months he had no complaints, his perqs and extra pay being more attractive than his former frontal aviation base on the Chinese border. Being one of the few hundred carrier-qualified Soviet airmen had softened the blow of missing his chance to fly the new MiG-27, though with luck, if the new full-sized carrier were ever finished, he'd have the chance to fly the naval version of that wonderful bird. Shavrov could wait for that, and with a few successful missions like this one he might have his squadron command.

He stopped daydreaming—the mission was too demanding for that. This was real flying. He'd never flown against Americans, only against the weapons they gave to the Afghan bandits. He had lost friends to those weapons, some of whom had survived their crashes only to be done to death by the Afghan savages in ways that would have made even a German puke. It would be good to teach the imperialists a lesson personally.

The radar signal was growing stronger. Beneath his ejection seat a tape recorder was making a continuous record of the signal characteristics of the American aircraft so that the scientific people would be able to devise a means of jamming and foiling the vaunted American flying eye. The aircraft was only a converted 707, a glorified passenger plane, hardly a worthy opponent for a crack fighter pilot! Shavrov checked his chart. He'd have to find it soon. Next he checked his fuel. He'd dropped his last external tank a few minutes earlier, and all he had now was his internal fuel. The turbofan was guzzling fuel, something he had to keep an eye on. He planned to have only five or ten minutes of fuel left when he returned to his ship.

This did not trouble him. He already had over a hundred carrier landings.

There! His hawk's eyes caught the glint of sun off metal at one o'clock high. Shavrov eased back on his stick and increased power gently, bringing his Forger into a climb. A minute later he was at two thousand meters. He could see the Sentry now, its blue paint blending neatly into the darkening sky. He was coming up beneath its tail, and with luck the empennage would shield him from the rotating radar antenna. Perfect! He'd blaze by her a few times, letting the flight crew see his Atolls, and—

It took Shavrov a moment to realize that he had a wingman.

Two wingmen.

Fifty meters to his left and right, a pair of American F-15 Eagle fighters. The visored face of one pilot was staring at him.

"YAK-106, YAK-106, please acknowledge." The voice on the SSB (single side band) radio circuit spoke flawless Russian. Shavrov did not acknowledge. They had read the number off his engine intake housing before he had known they were there.

"106, 106, this is the Sentry aircraft you are now approaching. Please identify yourself and your intentions. We get a little anxious when a stray fighter comes our way, so we've had three following you for the past hundred kilometers."

Three? Shavrov turned his head around. A third Eagle with four sparrow missiles was hanging fifty meters from his tail, his "six."

"Our men compliment you on your ability to fly low and slow, 106."

Lieutenant Shavrov was shaking with rage as he passed four thousand meters, still eight thousand from the American AWACS. He had checked his six every thirty seconds on the way in. The Americans must have been riding back there, hidden in the mist, and vectored in on him by instructions from the Sentry. He swore to himself and held course. He'd teach that AWACS a lesson!

"Break off, 106." It was a cool voice, without emotion except perhaps a trace of irony. "106, if you do not break off, we will consider your mission to be hostile. Think about it, 106. You are beyond radar coverage of your own ships, and you are not yet within missile range of us."

Shavrov looked to his right. The Eagle was breaking off—
so was the one to the left. Was it a gesture, taking the heat off
of him and expecting some courtesy in return? Or were they
clearing the way for the one behind him—he checked, still
there—to shoot? There was no telling what these imperialist
criminals would do; he was at least a minute from the fringe
of their missile range. Shavrov was anything but a coward.
Neither was he a fool. He moved his stick, curving his fighter
a few degrees to the right.

"Thank you, 106," the voice acknowledged. "You see, we
have some trainee operators aboard. Two of them are women,
and we don't want them to get rattled their first time out."
Suddenly it was too much. Shavrov thumbed the radio switch
on his stick.

"Shall I tell you what you can do with your women, Yankee?"

"You are *nekulturny,* 106," the voice replied softly. "Perhaps
the long overwater flight has made you nervous. You must be
about at the limit of your internal fuel. Bastard of a day to fly,
what with all these crazy, shifting winds. Do you need a position
check, over?"

"Negative, Yankee!"

"Course back to *Kiev* is one-eight-five, true. Have to be
careful using a magnetic compass this far north, you know.
Distance to *Kiev* is 318.6 kilometers. Warning—there is a
rapidly moving cold front moving in from the southwest. That's
going to make flying a little rough in a few hours. Do you
require an escort back to *Kiev?*"

"Pig!" Shavrov swore to himself. He switched his radio off,
cursing himself for his lack of discipline. He had allowed the
Americans to wound his pride. Like most fighter pilots, he had
a surfeit of that.

"106, we did not copy your last transmission. Two of my
Eagles are heading that way. They will form up on you and
see that you get home safely. Have a happy day, Comrade.
Sentry-November, out."

The American lieutenant turned to his colonel. He couldn't
keep a straight face any longer. "God, I thought I'd strangle
talking like that!" He sipped some Coke from a plastic cup.
"He really thought he'd sneak up on us."

"In case you didn't notice, he did get within a mile of Atoll range, and we don't have authorization to shoot at him until he flips one at us—which might wreck our day," the colonel grumped. "Nice job of twisting his tail, Lieutenant."

"A pleasure, Colonel." The operator looked at his screen. "Well, he's heading back to momma, with Cobras 3 and 4 on his six. He's going to be one unhappy Russkie when he gets home. If he gets home. Even with those drop tanks, he must be near his range limit." He thought for a moment. "Colonel, if they do this again, how 'bout we offer to take the guy home with us?"

"Get a Forger—what for? I suppose the navy'd like to have one to play with, they don't get much of Ivan's hardware, but the Forger's a piece of junk."

Shavrov was tempted to firewall his engine but restrained himself. He'd already shown enough personal weakness for one day. Besides, his YAK could only break Mach 1 in a dive. Those Eagles could do it straight up, and they had plenty of fuel. He saw that they both carried FAST-pack comformal fuel cells. They could cross whole oceans with those. Damn the Americans and their arrogance! Damn his own intelligence officer for telling him he could sneak up on the Sentry! Let the air-to-air armed Backfires go after them. They could handle that famed overbred passenger bus, could get to it faster than its fighter guardians could react.

The Americans, he saw, were not lying about the weather front. A line of cold weather squawls racing northeast was just on the horizon as he approached the *Kiev*. The Eagles backed off as he approached the formation. One American pilot pulled alongside briefly to wave goodbye. His head bobbed at Shavrov's return gesture. The Eagles paired up and turned back north.

Five minutes later he was aboard the *Kiev*, still pale with rage. As soon as the wheels were choked he jumped to the carrier deck, stomping off to see his squadron commander.

The Kremlin

The city of Moscow was justly famous for its subway system. For a pittance, people could ride nearly anywhere they wanted on a modern, safe, garishly decorated electric railway system. In case of war, the underground tunnels could serve as a bomb shelter for the citizens of Moscow. This secondary use was the result of the efforts of Nikita Khrushchev, who when construction was begun in the mid-thirties had suggested to Stalin that the system be driven deep. Stalin had approved. The shelter consideration had been decades ahead of its time; nuclear fission had then only been a theory, fusion hardly thought of at all.

On a spur of the line running from Sverdlov Square to the old airport, which ran near the Kremlin, workers bored a tunnel that was later closed off with a ten-meter-thick steel and concrete plug. The hundred-meter-long space was connected to the Kremlin by a pair of elevator shafts, and over time it had been converted to an emergency command center from which the Politburo could control the entire Soviet empire. The tunnel was also a convenient means of going unseen from the city to a small airport from which Politburo members could be flown to their ultimate redoubt, beneath the granite monolith at Zhiguli. Neither command post was a secret to the West—both had existed far too long for that—but the KGB confidently reported that nothing in the Western arsenals could smash through the hundreds of feet of rock which in both places separated the Politburo from the surface.

This fact was of little comfort to Admiral Yuri Ilych Padorin. He found himself seated at the far end of a ten-meter-long conference table looking at the grim faces of the ten Politburo members, the inner circle that alone made the strategic decisions affecting the fate of his country. None of them were officers. Those in uniform reported to these men. Up the table to his left was Admiral Sergey Gorshkov, who had disassociated himself from this affair with consummate skill, even producing a letter in which he had opposed Ramius' appointment to command the *Red October*. Padorin, as chief of the Main Political Administration, had successfully blocked Ramius' transfer, pointing out that Gorshkov's candidate for command was occasionally late in paying his Party dues and did not speak up at the regular meetings often enough for an officer of his rank. The truth was that Gorshkov's candidate was not so proficient an officer as Ramius, whom Gorshkov had wanted for his own operations staff, a post that Ramius had successfully evaded for years.

Party General Secretary and President of the Union of Soviet Socialist Republics Andre Narmonov shifted his gaze to Padorin. His face gave nothing away. It never did, unless he wished it to—which was rare enough. Narmonov had succeeded Andropov when the latter had suffered a heart attack. There were rumors about that, but in the Soviet Union there are always rumors. Not since the days of Laventri Beria had the security chieftain come so close to power, and senior Party officials had allowed themselves to forget that. It would not be forgotten again. Bringing the KGB to heel had taken a year, a necessary measure to secure the privileges of the Party elite from the supposed reforms of the Andropov clique.

Narmonov was the apparatchik par excellence. He had first gained prominence as a factory manager, an engineer with a reputation for fulfilling his quota early, a man who produced results. He had risen steadily by using his own talents and those of others, rewarding those he had to, ignoring those he could. His position as general secretary of the Communist Party was not entirely secure. It was still early in his stewardship of the Party, and he depended on a loose coalition of colleagues— not friends, these men did not make friends. His succession to this chair had resulted more from ties within the Party structure than from personal ability, and his position would depend on consensus rule for years, until such time as his will could dictate policy.

Narmonov's dark eyes, Padorin could see, were red from tobacco smoke. The ventilation system down here had never worked properly. The general secretary squinted at Padorin from the other end of the table as he decided what to say, what would please the members of this cabal, these ten old, passionless men.

"Comrade Admiral," he began coldly, "we have heard from Comrade Gorshkov what the chances are of finding and destroying this rebellious submarine before it can complete its unimaginable crime. We are not pleased. Nor are we pleased with the fantastic error in judgment that gave command of our most valuable ship to this slug. What I want to know from you, Comrade, is what happened to the *zampolit* aboard, and what security measures were taken by your office to prevent this infamy from taking place!"

There was no fear in Narmonov's voice, but Padorin knew

it had to be there. This "fantastic error" could ultimately be laid at the chairman's feet by members who wanted another in that chair—unless he were able somehow to separate himself from it. If this meant Padorin's skin, that was the admiral's problem. Narmonov had had men flayed before.

Padorin had prepared himself for this over several days. He was a man who had lived through months of intensive combat operations and had several boats sunk from under him. If his body was softer now, his mind was not. Whatever his fate might be, Padorin was determined to meet it with dignity. If they remember me as a fool, he thought, it will be as a courageous fool. He had little left to live for in any case. "Comrade General Secretary," he began, "the political officer aboard *Red October* was Captain Ivan Yurievich Putin, a stalwart and faithful Party member. I cannot imagine—"

"Comrade Padorin," Defense Minister Ustinov interrupted, "we presume that you also could not imagine the unbelievable treachery of this Ramius. You now expect us to trust your judgment on this man also?"

"The most disturbing thing of all," added Mikhail Alexandrov, the Party theoretician who had replaced the dead Mikhail Suslov and was even more determined than the departed ideologue to be simon-pure on Party doctrine, "is how tolerant the Main Political Administration has been toward this renegade. It is amazing, particularly in view of his obvious efforts to construct his own personality cult throughout the submarine service, even in the political arm, it would seem. Your criminal willingness to overlook this—this *obvious* aberration from Party policy—does not make your judgment appear very sound."

"Comrades, you are correct in judging that I erred badly in approving Ramius for command, and also that we allowed him to select most of *Red October*'s senior officers. At the same time, we chose some years ago to do things in this way, to keep officers associated with a single ship for many years, and to give the captain great sway over their careers. This is an operational question, not a political one."

"We have already considered that," Narmonov replied. "It is true that in this case there is enough blame for more than one man." Gorshkov didn't move, but the message was explicit: his effort to separate himself from this scandal had failed.

Narmonov didn't care how many heads it took to prop up his chair.

"Comrade Chairman," Gorshkov objected, "the efficiency of the fleet—"

"Efficiency?" Alexandrov said. "Efficiency. This Lithuanian half-breed is *efficiently* making fools of our fleet with his chosen officers while our remaining ships blunder about like newly castrated cattle." Alexandrov alluded to his first job on a state farm. A fitting beginning, it was generally thought, for the man who held the position of chief ideologue was as popular in Moscow as the plague, but the Politburo had to have him or one like him. The ideological chieftain was always the kingmaker. Whose side was he on now—in addition to his own?"

"The most likely explanation is that Putin was murdered," Padorin continued. "He alone of the officers left behind a wife and family."

"That's another question, Comrade Admiral." Narmonov seized this issue. "Why is it that none of these men are married? Didn't that tell you something? Must we of the Politburo supervise everything? Can't you think for yourselves?"

As if you want us to, Padorin thought. "Comrade General Secretary, most of our submarine commanders prefer young, unmarried officers in their wardrooms. Duty at sea is demanding, and single men have fewer distractions. Moreover, each of the senior officers aboard is a Party member in good standing with a praiseworthy record. Ramius had been treacherous, there is no denying that, and I would gladly kill the son of a bitch with my own hands—but he has deceived more good men than there are in this room."

"Indeed," Alexandrov observed. "And now that we are in this mess, how do we get out of it?"

Padorin took a deep breath. He'd been waiting for this. "Comrades, we have another man aboard *Red October,* unknown to either Putin or Captain Ramius, an agent of the Main Political Administration."

"What?" Gorshkov said. "And why did I not know of this?"

Alexandrov smiled. "That's the first intelligent thing we've heard today. Go on."

"This individual is covered as an enlisted man. He reports

directly to our office, bypassing all operational and political channels. His name is Igor Loginov. He is twenty-four, a—"

"Twenty-four!" Narmonov shouted. "You trust a child with this responsibility?"

"Comrade, Loginov's mission is to blend in with the conscripted crewmen, to listen in on conversations, to identify likely traitors, spies, and saboteurs. In truth he looks younger still. He serves alongside young men, and he must be young himself. He is, in fact, a graduate of the higher naval school for political officers at Kiev and the GRU intelligence academy. He is the son of Arkady Ivanovich Loginov, chief of the Lenin Steel Plant at Kazan. Many of you here know his father." Narmonov was among those who nodded, a flickering of interest in his eyes. "Only an elite few are chosen for this duty. I have met and interviewed this boy myself. His record is clear, he is a Soviet patriot without question."

"I know his father," Narmonov confirmed. "Arkady Ivanovich is an honorable man who has raised several good sons. What are this boy's orders?"

"As I said, Comrade General Secretary, his ordinary duties are to observe the crewmen and report on what he sees. He's been doing this for two years, and he is good at it. He does not report to the *zampolit* aboard, but only to Moscow or to one of my representatives. In a genuine emergency, his orders are to report to the *zampolit*. If Putin is alive—and I do not believe this, comrades—he would be part of the conspiracy, and Loginov would know not to do this. In a true emergency, therefore, his orders are to destroy the ship and make his escape."

"This is possible?" Narmonov asked. "Gorshkov?"

"Comrades, all of our ships carry powerful scuttling charges, submarines especially."

"Unfortunately," Padorin said, "these are generally not armed, and only the captain can activate them. Ever since the incident on *Storozhevoy,* we in the Main Political Administration have had to consider that an incident such as this one was indeed a possibility, and that its most damaging manifestation would involve a missile-carrying submarine."

"Ah," Narmonov observed, "he is a missile mechanic."

"No, Comrade, he is a ship's cook," Padorin replied.

"Wonderful! He spends all his day boiling potatoes!" Narmonov's hands flew up in the air, his hopeful demeanor gone in an instant, replaced with palpable wrath. "You wish your bullet now, Padorin?"

"Comrade Chairman, this is a better cover assignment than you may imagine." Padorin did not flinch, wanting to show these men what he was made of. "On *Red October* the officers' accommodations and galley are aft. The crew's quarters are forward—the crew eat there since they do not have a separate messroom—with the missile room in between. As a cook he must travel back and forth many times each day, and his presence in any particular area will not be thought unusual. The food freezer is located adjacent to the lower missile deck forward. It is not our plan that he should activate the scuttling charges. We have allowed for the possibility that the captain could disarm them. Comrades, these measures have been carefully thought out."

"Go on," Narmonov grunted.

"As Comrade Gorshkov explained earlier, *Red October* carries twenty-six Seahawk missiles. These are solid-fuel rockets, and one has a range-safety package installed."

"Range safety?" Narmonov was puzzled.

Up to this point the other military officers at the meeting, none of them Politburo members, had kept their peace. Padorin was surprised when General V.M. Vishenkov, commander of the Strategic Rocket Forces, spoke up. "Comrades, these details were worked out through my office some years ago. As you know, when we test our missiles, we have safety packages aboard to explode them if they go off course. Otherwise they might land on one of our own cities. Our operational missiles do not ordinarily carry them—for the obvious reason, the imperialists might learn a way to explode them in flight."

"So, our young GRU comrade will blow up the missile. What of the warheads?" Narmonov asked. An engineer by training, he could always be distracted by technical discourse, always impressed by a clever one.

"Comrade," Vishenkov went on, "the missile warheads are armed by accelerometers. Thus they cannot be armed until the missile reaches its full programmed speed. The Americans use the same system, and for the same reason, to prevent sabotage. These safety systems are absolutely reliable. You could drop one of the reentry vehicles from the top of the Moscow television transmitter onto a steel plate and it would not fire." The general referred to the massive TV tower whose construction Narmonov had personally supervised while head of the Central Communications Directorate. Vishenkov was a skilled political operator.

"In the case of a solid-fuel rocket," Padorin continued, recognizing his debt to Vishenkov, wondering what he'd ask for in return, and hoping he'd live long enough to deliver, "a safety package ignites all of the missile's three stages simultaneously."

"So the missile just takes off?" Alexandrov asked.

"No, Comrade Academician. The upper stage might, if it could break through the missile tube hatch, and this would flood the missile room, sinking the submarine. But even if it did not, there is sufficient thermal energy in either of the first two stages to reduce the entire submarine to a puddle of molten iron, twenty times what is necessary to sink it. Loginov has been trained to bypass the alarm system on the missile tube hatch, to activate the safety package, set a timer, and escape."

"Not just to destroy the ship?" Narmonov asked.

"Comrade General Secretary," Padorin said, "it is too much to ask a young man to do his duty, knowing that it means certain death. We would be unrealistic to expect this. He must have at least the possibility of escape, otherwise human weakness might lead to failure."

"This is reasonable," Alexandrov said. "Young men are motivated by hope, not fear. In this case, young Loginov would hope for a considerable reward."

"And get it," Narmonov said. "We will make every effort to save this young man, Gorshkov."

"If he is truly reliable," Alexandrov noted.

"I know that my life depends on this, Comrade Academician," Padorin said, his back still straight. He did not get a verbal answer, only nods from half the heads at the table. He had faced death before and was at the age where it remains the last thing a man need face.

The White House

Arbatov came into the Oval Office at 4:50 P.M. He found the president and Dr. Pelt sitting in easy chairs across from the chief executive's desk.

"Come on over, Alex. Coffee?" The president pointed to a tray on the corner of his desk. He was not drinking today, Arbatov noted.

"No, thank you, Mr. President. May I ask—"

"We think we found your sub, Alex," Pelt answered. "They just brought these dispatches over, and we're checking them now." The adviser held up a ring binder of message forms.

"Where is it, may I ask?" The ambassador's face was dead-pan.

"Roughly three hundred miles northeast of Norfolk. We have not located it exactly. One of our ships noted an underwater explosion in the area—no, that's not right. It was recorded on a ship, and when the tapes were checked a few hours later, they thought they heard a submarine explode and sink. Sorry, Alex," Pelt said. "I should have known better than to read through all this stuff without an interpreter. Does your navy talk in its own language, too?"

"Officers do not like for civilians to understand them," Arbatov smiled. "This has doubtless been true since the first man picked up a stone."

"Anyway, we have ships and aircraft searching the area now."

The president looked up. "Alex, I talked to the chief of naval operations, Dan Foster, a few minutes ago. He said not to expect any survivors. The water there's over a thousand feet deep, and you know what the weather is like. They said it's right on the edge of the continental shelf."

"The Norfolk Canyon, sir," Pelt added.

"We are conducting a thorough search," the president continued. "The navy is bringing in some specialized rescue equipment, search gear, all that sort of thing. If the submarine is located, we'll get somebody down to them on the chance there might be survivors. From what the CNO tells me it is just possible that there might be if the interior partitions—bulkheads, I think he called them—are intact. The other question is their air supply, he said. Time is very much against us, I'm afraid. All this fantastically expensive equipment we buy them, and they can't locate one damned object right off our coast."

Arbatov made a mental record of these words. It would make a worthwhile intelligence report. The president occasionally let—

"By the way, Mr. Ambassador, what exactly was your submarine doing there?"

"I have no idea, Dr. Pelt."

"I trust it was not a missile sub," Pelt said. "We have an agreement to keep those five hundred miles offshore. The wreck will of course be inspected by our rescue craft. Were we to learn that it is indeed a missile sub..."

"Your point is noted. Still, those are international waters."

The president turned and spoke softly. "So is the Gulf of Finland, Alex, and, I believe, the Black Sea." He let this observation hang in the air for a moment. "I sincerely hope that we are not heading back to that kind of situation. Are we talking about a missile submarine, Alex?"

"Truly, Mr. President, I have no idea. Certainly I should hope not."

The president could see how carefully the lie was phrased. He wondered if the Russians would admit that there was a captain out there who had disregarded his orders. No, they would probably claim a navigation error.

"Very well. In any case, we will be conducting our own search and rescue operation. We'll know soon enough what sort of vessel we're talking about." The president looked suddenly uneasy. "One more thing Foster talked about. If we find bodies—pardon the crudity on a Saturday afternoon—I expect that you will want them returned to your country."

"I have had no instructions on this," the ambassador answered truthfully, caught off guard.

"It was explained to me in too much detail what a death like this does to a man. In simple terms, they're crushed by the water pressure, not a very pretty thing to see, they tell me. But they were men, and they deserve some dignity even in death."

Arbatov conceded the point. "If this is possible, then, I believe that the Soviet people would appreciate this humanitarian gesture."

"We'll do our best."

And the American best, Arbatov remembered, included a ship named the *Glomar Explorer*. This notorious exploration ship had been built by the CIA for the specific purpose of recovering a Soviet *Golf*-class missile submarine from the floor of the Pacific Ocean. She had been placed in storage, no doubt to await the next such opportunity. There would be nothing the Soviet Union could do to prevent the operation, a few hundred miles off the American coast, three hundred miles from the United States' largest naval base.

"I trust that the precepts of international law will be observed, gentlemen. That is, with respect to the vessel's remains and the crew's bodies."

"Of course, Alex." The president smiled, gesturing to a memorandum on his desk. Arbatov struggled for control. He'd been led down this path like a schoolboy, forgetting that the American president had been a skilled courtroom tactician—not something that life in the Soviet Union prepares a man for—and knew all about legal tricks. Why was this bastard so easy to underestimate?

The president was also struggling to control himself. It was not often that he saw Alex flustered. This was a clever opponent, not easily caught off balance. Laughing would spoil it.

The memorandum from the attorney general had arrived only that morning. It read:

Mr. President,

Pursuant to your request, I have asked the chief of our admiralty law department to review the question of international law regarding the ownership of sunken or derelict vessels, and the law of salvage pertaining to such vessels. There is a good deal of case law on the subject. One simple example is *Dalmas v Stathos* (84FSuff. 828, 1949 A.M.C. 770 [S.D.N.Y. 1949]):

No problem of foreign law is here involved, for it is well settled that "salvage is a question arising out of the *jus gentium* and does not ordinarily depend on the municipal law of particular countries."

The international basis for this is the Salvage Convention of 1910 (Brussels), which codified the transnational nature and admiralty and salvage law. This was ratified by the United States in the Salvage Act of

1912, 37 Stat. 242, (1912), 46 U.S.C.A. §§ 727-731; and also in 37 Stat. 1658 (1913).

"International law will be observed, Alex," the president promised. "In all particulars." And whatever we get, he thought, will be taken to the nearest port, Norfolk, where it will be turned over to the receiver of wrecks, an overworked federal official. If the Soviets want anything back, they can bring action in admiralty court, which means the federal district court sitting in Norfolk, where, if the suit were successful—*after* the value of the salvaged property was determined, and *after* the U.S. Navy was paid a proper fee for its salvage effort, also determined by the court—the wreck would be returned to its rightful owners. Of course, the federal district court in question had, at last check, an eleven-month backlog of cases.

Arbatov would cable Moscow on this. For what good it would do. He was certain the president would take perverse pleasure in manipulating the grotesque American legal system to his own advantage, all the time pointing out that, as president, he was constitutionally unable to interfere with the working of the courts.

Pelt looked at his watch. It was about time for the next surprise. He had to admire the president. For a man with only limited knowledge of international affairs only a few years earlier, he'd learned fast. This outwardly simple, quiet-talking man was at his best in face to face situations, and after a lifetime's experience as a prosecutor, he still loved to play the game of negotiation and tactical exchange. He seemed able to manipulate people with frighteningly casual skill. The phone rang and Pelt got it, right on cue.

"This is Dr. Pelt speaking. Yes, Admiral—where? When? Just one? I see . . . Norfolk? Thank you, Admiral, that is very good news. I will inform the president immediately. Please keep us advised." Pelt turned around. "We got one, alive, by God!"

"A survivor off the lost sub?" The president stood.

"Well, he's a Russian sailor. A helicopter picked him up an hour ago, and they're flying him to the Norfolk base hospital. They picked him up 290 miles northeast of Norfolk, so I guess that makes it fit. The men on the ship say he's in pretty bad shape, but the hospital is ready for him."

The president walked to his desk and lifted the phone. "Grace, ring me Dan Foster right now . . . Admiral, this is the president. The man they picked up, how soon to Norfolk? Another two hours?" He grimaced. "Admiral, you get on the phone to the naval hospital, and you tell them that *I* say they are to do everything they can for that man. I want him treated like he was my own son, is that clear? Good. I want hourly reports on his condition. I want the best people we have in on this, the very best. Thank you, Admiral." He hung up. "All right!"

"Maybe we were too pessimistic, Alex," Pelt chirped up.

"Certainly," the president answered. "You have a doctor at the embassy, don't you?"

"Yes, we do, Mr. President."

"Take him down, too. He'll be extended every courtesy. I'll see to that. Jeff, are they searching for other survivors?"

"Yes, Mr. President. There's a dozen aircraft in the area right now, and two more ships on the way."

"Good!" The president clapped his hands together, enthusiastic as a kid in a toystore. "Now, if we can find some more survivors, maybe we can give your country a meaningful Christmas present, Alex. We will do everything we can, you have my word on that."

"That is very kind of you, Mr. President. I will communicate this happy news to my country at once."

"Not so fast, Alex." The chief executive held his hand up. "I'd say this calls for a drink."

THE TENTH DAY

SUNDAY, 12 DECEMBER

SOSUS Control

At SOSUS Control in Norfolk, the picture was becoming increasingly difficult. The United States simply did not have the technology to keep track of submarines in the deep ocean basins. The SOSUS receptors were principally laid at shallow-water choke points, on the bottom of undersea ridges and highlands. The strategy of the NATO countries was a direct consequence of this technological limitation. In a major war with the Soviets, NATO would use the Greenland–Iceland–United Kingdom SOSUS barrier as a huge tripwire, a burglar alarm system. Allied submarines and ASW patrol aircraft would try to seek out, attack, and destroy Soviet submarines as they approached it, before they could cross the lines.

The barrier had never been expected to halt more than half of the attacking submarines, however, and those that succeeded in slipping through would have to be handled differently. The deep ocean basins were simply too wide and too deep—the average depth was over two miles—to be littered with sensors as the shallow choke points were. This was a fact that cut both ways. The NATO mission would be to maintain the Atlantic Bridge and continue transoceanic trade, and the obvious Soviet mission would be to interdict this trade. Submarines would have to spread out over the vast ocean to cover the many possible convoy routes. NATO strategy behind the SOSUS barriers, then, was to assemble large convoys, each ringed with destroyers, helicopters, and fixed-wing aircraft. The escorts would try to establish a protective bubble about a hundred miles across. Enemy submarines would not be able to exist within that bubble; if in it they would be hunted down and killed— or merely driven off long enough for the convoy to speed past. Thus while SOSUS was designed to neutralize a huge, fixed expanse of sea, deep-basin strategy was founded on mobility, a moving zone of protection for the vital North Atlantic shipping.

This was an altogether sensible strategy, but one that could not be tested under realistic conditions, and, unfortunately, one that was largely useless at the moment. With all of the Soviet *Alfa*s and *Victor*s already on the coast, and the last of the *Charlie*s, *Echoe*s, and *November*s just arriving on their stations, the master screen Commander Quentin was staring at was no longer filled with discrete little red dots but rather with large circles. Each dot or circle designated the position of a Soviet submarine. A circle respresented an estimated position, calculated from the speed with which a sub could move without giving off enough noise to be localized by the many sensors being employed. Some circles were ten miles across, some as much as fifty; an area anywhere from seventy-eight to two thousand square miles had to be searched if the submarine were again to be pinned down. And there were just too damned many of the boats.

Hunting the submarines was principally the job of the P-3C Orion. Each Orion carried sonobuoys, air-deployable active and passive sonar sets that were dropped from the belly of the aircraft. On detecting something, a sonobuoy reported to its mother aircraft and then automatically sank lest it fall into unfriendly hands. The sonobuoys had limited electrical power and thus limited range. Worse, their supply was finite. The sonobuoy inventory was already being depleted alarmingly, and soon they would have to cut back on expenditures. Additionally, each P-3C carried FLIRs, forward-looking infrared scanners, to identify the heat signature of a nuclear sub, and MADs, magnetic anomaly detectors that located the disturbance in the earth's magnetic field caused by a large chunk of ferrous metal like a submarine. MAD gear could only detect a magnetic disturbance six hundred yards to the left and right of an aircraft's course track, and to do this the aircraft had to fly low, consuming fuel and limiting the crew's visual search range. FLIR had roughly the same limitation.

Thus the technology used to localize a target first detected by SOSUS, or to "delouse" a discrete piece of ocean preparatory to the passage of a convoy, simply was not up to a random search of the deep ocean.

Quentin leaned forward. A circle had just changed to a dot. A P-3C had just dropped an explosive sounding charge and localized an *Echo*-class attack sub five hundred miles south of the Grand Banks. For an hour they had a near-certain shooting solution on that *Echo;* her name was written on the Orion's Mark 46 ASW torpedoes.

Quentin sipped at his coffee. His stomach rebelled at the additional caffeine, remembering the abuse of four months of hellish chemotherapy. If there were to be a war, this was one way it might start. All at once, their submarines would stop, perhaps just like this. Not sneaking to kill convoys in midocean but attacking them closer to shore, the way the Germans had done . . . and all the American sensors would be in the wrong place. Once stopped the dots would grow to circles, ever wider, making the task of finding the subs all the more difficult. Their engines quiet, the boats would be invisible traps for the passing merchant vessels and warships racing to bring life-saving supplies to the men in Europe. Submarines were like cancer. Just like the disease that he had only barely defeated. The invisible, malignant vessels would find a place, stop to infect it, and on his screen the malignancies would grow until they were attacked by the aircraft he controlled from this room. But he could not attack them now. Only watch.

"PK EST 1 HOUR—RUN," he typed into his computer console.

"23," the computer answered at once.

Quentin grunted. Twenty-four hours earlier the PK, probability of a kill, had been forty—forty probable kills in the first hour after getting a shooting authorization. Now it was barely half that, and this number had to be taken with a large grain of salt, since it assumed that everything would work, a happy state of affairs found only in fiction. Soon, he judged, the number would be under ten. This did not include kills from friendly submarines that were trailing the Russians under strict orders not to reveal their positions. His sometime allies in the *Sturgeons*, *Permits*, and *Los Angeles*es were playing their own ASW game by their own set of rules. A different breed. He tried to think of them as friends, but it never quite worked. In his twenty years of naval service submarines had always been the enemy. In war they would be useful enemies, but in a war it was widely recognized that there was no such thing as a friendly submarine.

A B-52

The bomber crew knew exactly where the Russians were. Navy Orions and air force Sentries had been shadowing them for days now, and the day before, he'd been told, the Soviets had sent an armed fighter from the *Kiev* to the nearest Sentry. Possibly an attack mission, probably not, it had in any case been a provocation.

Four hours earlier the squadron of fourteen had flown out of Plattsburg, New York, at 0330, leaving behind black trails of exhaust smoke hidden in the predawn gloom. Each aircraft carried a full load of fuel and twelve missiles whose total weight was far less than the -52's design bombload. This made for good, long range.

Which was exactly what they needed. Knowing where the Russians were was only half the battle. Hitting them was the other. The mission profile was simple in concept, rather more difficult in execution. As had been learned in missions over Hanoi—in which the B-52 had participated and sustained SAM (surface-to-air missile) damage—the best method of attacking a heavily defended target was to converge from all points of the compass at once, "like the enveloping arms of an angry bear," the squadron commander had put it at the briefing, indulging his poetic nature. This gave half the squadron relatively direct courses to their target; the other half had to curve around, careful to keep well beyond effective radar coverage; all had to turn exactly on cue.

The B-52s had turned ten minutes earlier, on command from the Sentry quarterbacking the mission. The pilot had added a twist. His course to the Soviet formation took his bomber right down a commercial air route. On making his turn, he had switched his IFF transponder from its normal setting to international. He was fifty miles behind a commercial 747, thirty miles ahead of another, and on Soviet radar all three Boeing products would look exactly alike—harmless.

It was still dark down on the surface. There was no indication that the Russians were alerted yet. Their fighters were only supposed to be VFR (visual flight rules) capable, and the pilot imagined that taking off and landing on a carrier in the dark was pretty risky business, doubly so in bad weather.

"Skipper," the electronic warfare officer called on the intercom, "we're getting L- and S-band emissions. They're right where they're supposed to be."

"Roger. Enough for a return off us?"

"That's affirm, but they probably think we're flying Pan Am. No fire control stuff yet, just routine air search."

"Range to target?"

"One-three-zero miles."

It was almost time. The mission profile was such that all would hit the 125-mile circle at the same moment.

"Everything ready?"

"That's a roge."

The pilot relaxed for another minute, waiting for the signal from the entry.

"FLASHLIGHT, FLASHLIGHT, FLASHLIGHT." The signal came over the digital radio channel.

"That's it! Let 'em know we're here," the aircraft commander ordered.

"Right." The electronic warfare officer flipped the clear plastic cover off his set of toggle switches and dials controlling the aircraft's jamming systems. First he powered up his systems. This took a few seconds. The -52's electronics were all old seventies-vintage equipment, else the squadron would not be part of the junior varsity. Good learning tools, though, and the lieutenant was hoping to move up to the new B-1Bs now beginning to come off the Rockwell assembly line in California. For the past ten minutes the ESM pods on the bomber's nose and wingtips had been recording the Soviet radar signals, classifying their exact frequencies, pulse repetition rates, power, and the individual signature characteristics of the transmitters. The lieutenant was brand new to this game. He was a recent graduate of electronic warfare school, first in his class. He considered what he should do first, then selected a jamming mode, not his best, from a range of memorized options.

The Nikolayev

One hundred twenty-five miles away on the *Kara*-class cruiser *Nikolayev,* a radar *michman* was examining some blips that seemed to be in a circle around his formation. In an instant his screen was covered with twenty ghostly splotches tracing crazily in various directions. He shouted the alarm, echoed a second later by a brother operator. The officer of the watch hurried over to check the screen.

By the time he got there the jamming mode had changed and six lines like the spokes of a wheel were rotating slowly around a central axis.

"Plot the strobes," the officer ordered.

Now there were blotches, lines, and sparkles.

"More than one aircraft, Comrade." The *michman* tried flipping through his frequency settings.

"Attack warning!" another *michman* shouted. His ESM receiver had just reported the signals of aircraft search-radar sets of the type used to acquire targets for air-to-surface missiles.

The B-52

"We got hard targets," the weapons officer on the -52 reported. "I got a lock on the first three birds."

"Roger that," the pilot acknowledged. "Hold for ten more seconds."

"Ten seconds," the officer replied. "Cutting switches . . . *now.*"

"Okay, kill the jamming."

"ECM systems off."

The Nikolayev

"Missile acquisition radars have ceased," the combat information center officer reported to the cruiser's captain, just now arrived from the bridge. Around them the *Nikolayev*'s crew was racing to battle stations. "Jamming has also ceased."

"What is out there?" the captain asked. Out of a clear sky his beautiful clipper-bowed cruiser had been threatened—and now all was well?

"At least eight enemy aircraft in a circle around us."

The captain examined the now normal S-band air search screen. There were numerous blips, mainly civilian aircraft. The half circle of others had to be hostile, though.

"Could they have fired missiles?"

"No, Comrade Captain, we would have detected it. They jammed our search radars for thirty seconds and illuminated us with their own search systems for twenty. Then everything stopped."

"So, they provoke us and now pretend nothing has happened?" the captain growled. "When will they be within SAM range?"

"This one and these two will be within range in four minutes if they do not change course."

"Illuminate them with our missile control systems. Teach the bastards a lesson."

The officer gave the necessary instructions, wondering who was being taught what. Two thousand feet above one of the B-52s was an EC-135 whose computerized electronic sensors were recording all signals form the Soviet cruiser and taking them apart, the better to know how to jam them. It was the first good look at the new SA-N-8 missile system.

Two F-14 Tomcats

The double-zero code number on its fuselage marked the Tomcat as the squadron commander's personal bird; the black ace of spades on the twin-rudder tail indicated his squadron, Fighting 41, "The Black Aces." The pilot was Commander Robby Jackson, and his radio call sign was Spade 1.

Jackson was leading a two-plane section under the direction

of one of the *Kennedy*'s E-2C Hawkeyes, the navy's more diminutive version of the air force's AWACS and close brother to the COD, a twin-prop aircraft whose radome makes it look like an airplane being terrorized by a UFO. The weather was bad—depressingly normal for the North Atlantic in December—but was supposed to improve as they headed west. Jackson and his wingman, Lieutenant (j.g.) Bud Sanchez, were flying through nearly solid clouds, and they had eased their formation out somewhat. In the limited visibility both remembered that each Tomcat had a crew of two and a price of over thirty million dollars.

They were doing what the Tomcat does best. An all-weather interceptor, the F-14 has transoceanic range, Mach 2 speed, and a radar computer fire control system that can lock onto and attack six separate targets with long-range Phoenix air-to-air missiles. Each fighter was now carrying two of those along with a pair each of AIM-9M Sidewinder heat-seekers. Their prey was a flight of YAK-36 Forgers, the bastard V/STOL fighters that operated from the carrier *Kiev*. After harassing the Sentry the previous day, Ivan had decided to close with the *Kennedy* force, no doubt guided in with data from a reconnaissance satellite. The Soviet aircraft had come up short, their range being fifty miles less than they needed to sight the *Kennedy*. Washington decided that Ivan was getting a little too obnoxious on this side of the ocean. Admiral Painter had been given permission to return the favor, in a friendly sort of way.

Jackson figured that he and Sanchez could handle this, even outnumbered. No Soviet aircraft, least of all the Forger, was equal to the Tomcat—certainly not while I'm flying it, Jackson thought.

"Spade 1, your target is at your twelve o'clock and level, distance now twenty miles," reported the voice of Hummer 1, the Hawkeye a hundred miles aft. Jackson did not acknowledge.

"Got anything, Chris?" he asked his radar intercept officer, Lieutenant Commander Christiansen.

"An occasional flash, but nothing I can use." They were tracking the Forgers with passive systems only, in this case an infrared sensor.

Jackson considered illuminating their targets with his powerful fire control radar. The Forgers' ESM pods would sense this at once, reporting to their pilots that their death warrant had been written but not yet signed. "How about *Kiev?*"

"Nothing. The *Kiev* group is under total EMCON."

"Cute," Jackson commented. He guessed that the SAC raid on the *Kirov-Nikolayev* group had taught them to be more careful. It was not generally known that warships often made no use whatever of their radar systems, a protective measure called EMCON, for emission control. The reason was that a radar beam could be detected at several times the distance at which it generated a return signal to its transmitter and could thus tell an enemy more than it told its operators. "You suppose these guys can find their way home without help?"

"If they don't, you know who's gonna get blamed." Christiansen chuckled.

"That's a roge," Jackson agreed.

"Okay, I got infrared acquisition. Clouds must be thinning out some." Christiansen was concentrating on his instruments, oblivious of the view out of the canopy.

"Spade 1, this is Hummer 1, your target is twelve o'clock, at your level, range now ten miles." The report came over the secure radio circuit.

Not bad, picking up the Forgers' heat signature through this slop, Jackson thought, especially since they had small, inefficient engines.

"Radar coming on, Skipper," Christiansen advised. *"Kiev* has an S-band air search just come on. They have us for sure."

"Right." Jackson thumbed his mike switch. "Spade 2, illuminate targets—now."

"Roger, lead," Sanchez acknowledged. No point hiding now.

Both fighters activated their powerful AN/AWG-9 radars. It was now two minutes to intercept.

The radar signals, received by the ESM threat-receivers on the Forgers' tail fins, set off a musical tone in the pilot headsets which had to be turned off manually, and lit up a red warning light on each control panel.

The Kingfisher Flight

"Kingfisher flight, this is *Kiev,*" called the carrier's air operations officer. "We show two American fighters closing you at high speed from the rear."

"Acknowledged." The Russian flight leader checked his mirror. He'd hoped to avoid this, though he hadn't expected to. His orders were to take no action unless fired upon. They had just broken into the clear. Too bad, he'd have felt safer in the clouds.

The pilot of Kingfisher 3, Lieutenant Shavrov, reached down to arm his four Atolls. Not this time, Yankee, he thought.

The Tomcats

"One minute, Spade 1, you ought to have visual any time," Hummer 1 called in.

"Roger . . . Tallyho!" Jackson and Sanchez broke into the clear. The Forgers were a few miles ahead, and the Tomcats' 250-knot speed advantage was eating that distance up rapidly. The Russian pilots are keeping a nice, tight formation, Jackson thought, but anybody can drive a bus.

"Spade 2, let's go to burners on my mark. Three, two, one— mark!"

Both pilots advanced their engine controls and engaged their afterburners, which dumped raw fuel into the tail pipes of their new F-110 engines. The fighters lept forward with a sudden double thrust and went quickly through Mach 1.

The Kingfisher Flight

"Kingfisher, warning, warning, the *Amerikantsi* have increased speed," *Kiev* cautioned.

Kingfisher 4 turned in his seat. He saw the Tomcats a mile aft, twin dart-like shapes racing before trails of black smoke. Sunlight glinted off one canopy, and it almost looked like the flashes of a—

"They're attacking!"

"What?" The flight leader checked his mirror again. "Negative, negative—hold formation!"

The Tomcats screeched fifty feet overhead, the sonic booms they trailed sounding just like explosions. Shavrov acted entirely on his combat-trained instincts. He jerked back on his stick and triggered his four missiles at the departing American fighters.

"Three, what did you do?" the Russian flight leader demanded.

"They were attacking us, didn't you hear?" Shavrov protested.

The Tomcats

"Oh shit! Spade Flight, you have four Atolls after you," the voice of the Hawkeye's controller said.

"Two, break right," Jackson ordered. "Chris, activate countermeasures." Jackson threw his fighter into a violent evasive turn to the left. Sanchez broke the other way.

In the seat behind Jackson's, the radar intercept officer flipped switches to activate the aircraft's defense systems. As the Tomcat twisted in midair, a series of flares and balloons was ejected from the tail section, each an infrared or radar lure for the pursuing missiles. All four were targeted on Jackson's fighter.

"Spade 2 is clear, Spade 2 is clear. Spade 1, you still have four birds in pursuit," the voice from the Hawkeye said.

"Roger." Jackson was surprised at how calmly he took it. The Tomcat was doing over eight hundred miles per hour and accelerating. He wondered how much range the Atoll had. His rearward-looking-radar warning light flicked on.

"Two, get after them!" Jackson ordered.

"Roger, lead." Sanchez swept into a climbing turn, fell off into a hammerhead, and dove at the retreating Soviet fighters.

When Jackson turned, two of the missiles lost lock and kept going straight into open air. A third, decoyed into hitting a flare, exploded harmlessly. The fourth kept its infrared seeker head on Spade 1's glowing tail pipes and bored right in. The missile struck the Spade 1 at the base of its starboard rudder fin.

The impact tossed the fighter completely out of control. Most of the explosive force was spent as the missile blasted through the boron surface into open air. The fin was blown completely off, along with the right-side stabilizer. The left fin was badly holed by fragments, which smashed through the back of the fighter's canopy, hitting Christiansen's helmet. The right engine's fire warning lights came on at once.

Jackson heard the *oomph* over his intercom. He killed every engine switch on the right side and activated the in-frame fire extinguisher. Next he chopped power to his port engine, still on afterburner. By this time the Tomcat was in an inverted spin. The variable-geometry wings angled out to low-speed configuration. This gave Jackson aeleron control, and he worked quickly to get back to normal attitude. His altitude was four thousand feet. There wasn't much time.

"Okay, baby," he coaxed. A quick burst of power gave him back aerodynamic control, and the former test pilot snapped his fighter over—too hard. It went through two complete rolls before he could catch it in level flight. "Gotcha! You with me, Chris?"

Nothing. There was no way he could look around, and there were still four hostile fighters behind him.

"Spade 2, this is lead."

"Roger, lead." Sanchez had the four Fighters bore-sighted. They had just fired at his commander.

Hummer 1

On Hummer 1, the controller was thinking fast. The Forgers were holding formation, and there was a lot of Russian chatter on the radio circuit.

"Spade 2, this is Hummer 1, break off, I say again, break off, do not, repeat do not fire. Acknowledge. Spade 2, Spade 1 is at your nine o'clock, two thousand feet below you." The officer swore and looked at one of the enlisted men he worked with.

"That was too fast, sir, just too fuckin' fast. We got tapes of the Russkies. I can't understand it, but it sounds like *Kiev* is right pissed."

"They're not the only ones," the controller said, wondering if he had done the right thing calling Spade 2 off. It sure as hell didn't feel that way.

The Tomcats

Sanchez' head jerked in surprise. "Roger, breaking off." His thumb came off the switch. "Goddammit!" He pulled his stick back, throwing the Tomcat into a savage loop. "Where are you, lead?"

Sanchez brought his fighter under Jackson's and did a slow circle to survey the visible damage.

"Fire's out, Skipper. Right side rudder and stabilizer are gone. Left side fin—shit, I can see through it, but it looks like it oughta hold together. Wait a minute. Chris is slumped over, Skipper. Can you talk to him?"

"Negative, I've tried. Let's go back home."

Nothing would have pleased Sanchez more than to blast the Forgers right out of the sky, and with his four missiles he could have done this easily. But like most pilots, he was highly disciplined.

"Roger, lead."

"Spade 1, this is Hummer 1, advise your condition, over."

"Hummer 1, we'll make it unless something else falls off. Tell them to have docs standing by. Chris is hurt. I don't know how bad."

It took an hour to get to the *Kennedy*. Jackson's fighter flew badly, would not hold course in any specific attitude. He had to adjust trim constantly. Sanchez reported some movement in the aft cockpit. Maybe it was just the intercom shot out, Jackson thought hopefully.

Sanchez was ordered to land first so that the deck would be cleared for Commander Jackson. On the final approach the Tomcat started to handle badly. The pilot struggled with his fighter, planting it hard on the deck and catching the number one wire. The right-side landing gear collapsed at once, and the thirty-million-dollar fighter slid sideways into the barrier that had been erected. A hundred men with fire-fighting gear raced toward it from all directions.

The canopy went up on emergency hydraulic power. After unbuckling himself Jackson fought his way around and tried to grab for his backseater. They had been friends for many years

Chris was alive. It looked like a quart of blood had poured down the front of his flight suit, and when the first corpsman took the helmet off, he saw that it was still pumping out. The second corpsman pushed Jackson out of the way and attached a cervical collar to the wounded airman. Christiansen was lifted gently and lowered onto a stretcher whose bearers ran towards the island. Jackson hesitated a moment before following it.

Norfolk Naval Medical Center

Captain Randall Tait of the Navy Medical Corps walked down the corridor to meet with the Russians. He looked younger than his forty-five years because his full head of black hair showed not the first sign of gray. Tait was a Mormon, educated at Brigham Young University and Stanford Medical School, who had joined the navy because he had wanted to see more of the world than one could from an office at the foot of the Wasatch Mountains. He had accomplished that much, and until today had also avoided anything resembling diplomatic duty. As the new chief of the Department of Medicine at Bethesda Naval Medical Center he knew that couldn't last. He had flown down to Norfolk only a few hours earlier to handle the case. The Russians had driven down, and taken their time doing it.

"Good morning, gentlemen. I'm Dr. Tait." They shook hands all around, and the lieutenant who had brought them up walked back to the elevator.

"Dr. Ivanov," the shortest one said. "I am physician to the embassy."

"Captain Smirnov." Tait knew him to be assistant naval attaché, a career intelligence officer. The doctor had been briefed on the helicopter trip down by a Pentagon intelligence officer who was now drinking coffee in the hospital commissary.

"Vasily Petchkin, Doctor. I am second secretary to the embassy." This one was a senior KGB officer, a "legal" spy with a diplomatic cover. "May we see our man?"

"Certainly. Will you follow me please?" Tait led them back down the corridor. He'd been on the go for twenty hours. This was part of the territory as chief of service at Bethesda. He got all the hard calls. One of the first things a doctor learns is how not to sleep.

The whole floor was set up for intensive care, Norfolk Naval Medical Center having been built with war casualties in mind. Intensive Care Unit Number Three was a room twenty-five feet square. The only windows were on the corridor wall, and the curtains had been drawn back. There were four beds, only one occupied. The young man in it was almost totally concealed. The only thing not hidden by the oxygen mask covering his face was an unruly clump of wheat-colored hair. The rest of his body was fully draped. An IV stand was next to the bed, its two bottles of fluid merging in a single line that led under the covers. A nurse dressed like Tait in surgical greens was standing at the foot of the bed, her green eyes locked on the electrocardiograph readout over the patient's head, dropping momentarily to make a notation on his chart. On the far side of the bed was a machine whose function was not immediately obvious. The patient was unconscious.

"His condition?" Ivanov asked.

"Critical," Tait replied. "It's a miracle he got here alive at all. He was in the water for at least twelve hours, probably more like twenty. Even accounting for the fact that he was wearing a rubber exposure suit, given the ambient air and water temperatures there's just no way he ought to have been alive. On admission his core temperature was 23.8°C." Tait shook his head. "I've read about worse hypothermia cases in the literature, but this is by far the worst I've ever seen."

"Prognosis?" Ivanov looked into the room.

Tait shrugged. "Hard to say. Maybe as good as fifty-fifty, maybe not. He's still extremely shocky. He's a fundamentally healthy person. You can't see it from here, but he's in superb physical shape, like a track and field man. He has a particularly strong heart; that's probably what kept him alive long enough to get here. We have the hypothermia pretty much under control now. The problem is, with hypothermia so many things go wrong at once. We have to fight a number of separate but connected battles against different systemic enemies to keep them from overwhelming his natural defenses. If anything's going to kill him, it'll be the shock. We're treating that with electrolytes, the normal routine, but he's going to be on the edge for several days at least I—"

Tait looked up. Another man was pacing down the hall. Younger than Tait, and taller, he had a white lab coat over his greens. He carried a metal chart.

"Gentlemen, this is Doctor—Lieutenant—Jameson. He's the physician of record on the case. He admitted your man. What do you have, Jamie?"

"The sputum sample showed pneumonia. Bad news. Worse, his blood chemistry isn't getting any better, and his white count is *dropping*."

"Great." Tait leaned against the window frame and swore to himself.

"Here's the printout from the blood analyzer." Jameson handed the chart over.

"May I see this, please?" Ivanov came around.

"Sure." Tait flipped the metal cloud chart open and held it so that everyone could see it. Ivanov had never worked with a computerized blood analyzer, and it took several seconds for him to orient himself.

"This is not good."

"Not at all," Tait agreed.

"We're going to have to jump on that pneumonia, hard," Jameson said. "This kid's got too many things going wrong. If the pneumonia really takes hold . . ." He shook his head.

"Keflin?" Tait asked.

"Yeah." Jameson pulled a vial from his pocket. "As much as he'll handle. I'm guessing that he had a mild case before he got dumped in the water, and I hear that some penicillin-resistant strains have been cropping up in Russia. You use mostly penicillin over there, right?" Jameson looked down at Ivanov.

"Correct. What is this keflin?"

"It's a big gun, a synthetic antibiotic, and it works well on resistant strains."

"Right now, Jamie," Tait ordered.

Jameson walked around the corner to enter the room. He injected the antibiotic into a 100cc piggyback IV bottle and hung it on a stand.

"He's so young," Ivanov noted. "He treated our man initially?"

"His name's Albert Jameson. We call him Jamie. He's twenty-nine, graduated Harvard third in his class, and he's been with us ever since. He's board-certified in internal medicine and virology. He's as good as they come." Tait suddenly realized how uncomfortable he was dealing with the Russians. His education and years of naval service taught him that these men were the enemy. That didn't matter. Years before he had sworn an oath to treat patients without regard to outside considerations. Would they believe or did they think he'd let their man die because he was a Russian? "Gentlemen, I want you to understand this: we're giving your man the very best care we can. We're not holding anything back. If there's a way to give him back to you alive, we'll find it. But I can't make any promises."

The Soviets could see that. While waiting for instructions from Moscow, Petchkin had checked up on Tait and found him to be, though a religious fanatic, an efficient and honorable physician, one of the best in government service.

"Has he said anything?" Petchkin asked, casually.

"Not since I've been here. Jamie said that right after they started warming him up he was semiconscious and babbled for a few minutes. We taped it, of course, and had a Russian-speaking officer listen to it. Something about a girl with brown eyes, didn't make any sense. Probably his sweetheart—he's a good-looking kid, he probably has a girl at home. It was totally incoherent, though. A patient in his condition has no idea what's going on."

"Can we listen to the tape?" Petchkin said.

"Certainly. I'll have it sent up."

Jameson came around the corner. "Done. A gram of keflin every six hours. Hope it works."

"How about his hands and feet?" Smirnov asked. The captain knew something about frostbite.

"We're not even bothering about that," Jameson answered. "We have cotton around the digits to prevent maceration. If he survives the next few days, we'll get blebs and maybe have some tissue loss, but that's the least of our problems. You guys know what his name is?" Petchkin's head snapped around. "He wasn't wearing any dogtags when he arrived. His clothes didn't have the ship's name. No wallet, no identification, not even any coins in the pockets. It doesn't matter very much for his initial treatment, but I'd feel better if you could pull his medical records. It would be good to know if he has any allergies or underlying medical conditions. We don't want him to go into shock from an allergic reaction to drug treatment."

"What was he wearing?" Smirnov asked.

"A rubber exposure suit," Jameson answered. "The guys

who found him left it on him, thank God. I cut it off him when he arrived. Under that, shirt, pants, handerchief. Don't you guys wear dogtags?"

"Yes," Smirnov responded. "How did you find him?"

"From what I hear, it was pure luck. A helicopter off a frigate was patrolling and spotted him in the water. They didn't have any rescue gear aboard, so they marked the spot with a dye marker and went back to their ship. A bosun volunteered to go in after him. They loaded him and a raft cannister into the chopper and flew him back, with the frigate hustling down south. The bosun kicked out the raft, jumped in after it—and landed on it. Bad luck. He broke both his legs, but he did get your sailor into the raft. The tin can picked them up an hour later and they were both flown directly here."

"How is your man?"

"He'll be all right. The left leg wasn't too bad, but the right tibia was badly splintered," Jameson went on. "He'll recover in a few months. Won't be doing much dancing for a while, though."

The Russians thought the Americans had deliberately removed their man's identification. Jameson and Tait suspected that the man had disposed of his tags, possibly hoping to defect. There was a red mark on the neck that indicated forcible removal.

"If it is permitted," Smirnov said, "I would like to see your man, to thank him."

"Permission granted, Captain," Tait nodded. "That would be kind of you."

"He must be a brave man."

"A sailor doing his job. Your people would do the same thing." Tait wondered if this were true. "We have our differences, gentlemen, but the sea doesn't care about that. The sea— well, she tries to kill us all regardless what flag we fly."

Petchkin was back looking through the window, trying to make out the patient's face.

"Could we see his clothing and personal effects?" he asked.

"Sure, but it won't tell you much. He's a cook. That's all we know," Jameson said.

"A cook?" Petchkin turned around.

"The officer who listened in on the tape—obviously he was

an intelligence officer, right? He looked at the number on his shirt and said it made him a cook." The three-digit number indicated that the patient had been a member of the port watch, and that his battle station was damage control. Jameson wondered why the Russians numbered all their enlisted men. To be sure they didn't trespass? Petchkin's head, he noticed, was almost touching the glass pane.

"Dr. Ivanov, do you wish to attend the case?" Tait asked.

"Is this permitted?"

"It is."

"When will he be released?" Petchkin inquired. "When may we speak with him?"

"Released?" Jameson snapped. "Sir, the only way he'll be out of here in less than a month will be in a box. So far as consciousness is concerned, that's anyone's guess. That's one very sick kid you have in there."

"But we must speak to him!" the KGB agent protested.

Tait had to look up at the man. "Mr. Petchkin, I understand your desire to communicate with your man—but he is my patient now. We will do nothing, repeat *nothing*, that might interfere with his treatment and recovery. I got orders to fly down here to handle this. They tell me those orders came from the White House. Fine. Doctors Jameson and Ivanov will assist me, but that patient is now my responsibility, and my job is to see to it that he walks out of this hospital alive and well. Everything else is secondary to that objective. You will be extended every courtesy. But I make the rules here." Tait paused. Diplomacy was not something he was good at. "Tell you what, you want to sit in there yourselves in relays, that's fine with me. But you have to follow the rules. That means you scrub, change into sterile clothing, and follow the instructions of the duty nurse. Fair enough?"

Petchkin nodded. American doctors think they are gods, he said to himself.

Jameson, busy reexamining the blood analyzer printout, had ignored the sermon. "Can you gentlemen tell us what kind of sub he was on?"

"No," Petchkin said at once.

"What are you thinking, Jamie?"

"The dropping white count and some of these other indi-

cators are consistent with radiation exposure. The gross symptoms would have been masked by the overlying hypothermia."
Suddenly Jameson looked at the Soviets. "Gentlemen, we have to know this, was he on a nuclear sub?"

"Yes," Smirnov answered, "he was on a nuclear-powered submarine."

"Jamie, take his clothing to radiology. Have them check the buttons, zipper, anything metal for evidence of contamination."

"Right." Jameson went to collect the patient's effects.

"May we be involved in this?" Smirnov asked.

"Yes, sir," Tait responded, wondering what sort of people these were. The guy had to come off a nuclear submarine, didn't he? Why hadn't they told him at once? Didn't they want him to recover?

Petchkin pondered the significance of this. Didn't they know he had come off a nuclear-powered sub? Of course—he was trying to get Smirnov to blurt out that the man was off a missile submarine. They were trying to cloud the issue with this story about contamination. Nothing that would harm the patient, but something to confuse their class enemies. Clever. He'd always thought the Americans were clever. And he was supposed to report to the embassy in an hour—report what? How was he supposed to know who the sailor was?

Norfolk Naval Shipyard

The USS *Ethan Allen* was about at the end of her string. Commissioned in 1961, she had served her crews and her country for over twenty years, carrying Polaris sea-launched ballistic missiles in endless patrols through sunless seas. Now she was old enough to vote, and this was very old for a submarine. Her missile tubes had been filled with ballast and sealed months before. She had only a token maintenance crew while the Pentagon bureaucrats debated her future. There had been talk of a complicated cruise missile system to make her into a SSGN like the new Russian *Oscar*s. This was judged too expensive. *Ethan Allen*'s was generation-old technology. Her S5W reactor was too dated for much more use. Nuclear radiation had bombarded the metal vessel and its internal fittings with many billions of neutrons. As recent examination of test strips had revealed, over time the character of the metal had changed, becoming dangerously brittle. The system had at most another three years of useful life. A new reactor would be too expensive. The *Ethan Allen* was doomed by her senescence.

The maintenance crew was made up of members of her last operational team, mainly old-timers looking forward to retirement, with a leavening of kids who needed education in repair skills. The *Ethan Allen* could still serve as a school, especially a repair school since so much of her equipment was worn out.

Admiral Gallery had come aboard early that morning. The chiefs had regarded that as particularly ominous. He had been her first skipper many years before, and admirals always seemed to visit their early commands—right before they were scrapped. He'd recognized some of the senior chiefs and asked them if the old girl had any life left in her. To a man, the chiefs said yes. A ship becomes more than a machine to her crew. Each of a hundred ships, built by the same men at the same yard to the same plans, will have her own special characteristics— most of them bad, really, but after her crew becomes accustomed to them they are spoken of affectionately, particularly in retrospect. The admiral had toured the entire length of the *Ethan Allen*'s hull, pausing to run his gnarled, arthritic hands over the periscope he had used to make certain that there really was a world outside the steel hull, to plan the rare "attack" against a ship hunting his sub—or a passing tanker, just for practice. He'd commanded the *Ethan Allen* for three years, alternating his gold crew with another officer's blue crew, working out of Holy Loch, Scotland. Those were good years, he told himself, a damned sight better than sitting at a desk with a lot of vapid aides running around. It was the old navy game, up or out: just when you got something that you were really good at, something you really liked, it was gone. It made good organizational sense. You had to make room for the youngsters coming up—but, God! to be young again, to command one of the new ones that now he only had the opportunity to ride a few hours at a time, a courtesy to the skinny old bastard in Norfolk.

She'd do it, Gallery knew. She'd do fine. It was not the end he would have preferred for *his* fighting ship, but when you came down to it, a decent end for a fighting ship was something rare. Nelson's *Victory*, the *Constitution* in Boston harbor, the odd battleship kept mummified by her namesake state—they'd had honorable treatment. Most warships were sunk as targets or broken up for razor blades. The *Ethan Allen* would die for a purpose. A crazy purpose, perhaps crazy enough to work, he said to himself as he returned to COMSUBLANT headquarters.

Two hours later a truck arrived at the dock where the *Ethan Allen* lay dormant. The chief quartermaster on deck at the time noted that the truck came from Oceana Naval Air Station. Curious, he thought. More curiously, the officer who got out was wearing neither dolphins nor wings. He saluted the quarterdeck first, then the chief who had the deck while *Ethan Allen*'s remaining two officers supervised a repair job on the engine spaces. The officer from the naval air station made arrangements for a work gang to load the sub with four bullet-shaped objects, which went through the deck hatches. They were large, barely able to fit through the torpedo and capsule loading hatches, and it took some handling to get them emplaced. Next came plastic pallets to set them on and metal straps to secure them. They look like bombs, the chief electrician thought as the younger men did the donkey work. But they couldn't be that; they were too light, obviously made of ordinary sheet metal. An hour later a truck with a pressurized tank on its loadbed arrived. The submarine was cleared of her personnel and carefully ventilated. Then three men snaked a hose to each of the four objects. Finished, they ventilated the hull again, leaving gas detectors near each object. By this time, the crew noted, their dock and the one next to it were being guarded by armed marines so that no one could come over and see what was happening to the *Ethan Allen*.

When the loading, or filling, or whatever, was finished, a chief went below to examine the metal shells more carefully. He wrote down the stenciled acronym PPB76A/J6713 on a pad. A chief yeoman looked the designation up in a catalog and did not like what he found—Pave Pat Blue 76. Pave Pat Blue 76 was a bomb, and the *Ethan Allen* had four of them aboard. Nothing nearly so powerful as the missile warheads she had once carried, but a lot more ominous, the crew agreed. The smoking lamp was out by mutual accord before anyone made an order of it.

Gallery came back soon thereafter and spoke with all of the senior men individually. The youngsters were sent ashore with their personal gear and an admonition that they had not seen, felt, heard, or otherwise noticed anything unusual on the *Ethan Allen*. She was going to be scuttled at sea. That was all. Some political decision in Washington—and if you tell *that* to anyone, start thinking about a twenty-year tour at McMurdo Sound, as one man put it.

It was a tribute to Vincent Gallery that each of the old chiefs stayed aboard. Partly it was a chance for one last cruise on the old girl, a chance to say goodbye to a friend. Mostly it was because Gallery said it was important, and the old-timers remembered that his word had been good once.

The officers showed up at sundown. The lowest-ranking among them was a lieutenant commander. Two four-striped captains would be working the reactor, along with three senior chiefs. Two more four-stripers would handle the navigation, a pair of commanders the electronics. The rest would be spread around to handle the plethora of specialized tasks necessary to the operation of a complex warship. The total complement, not even a quarter the size of a normal crew, might have caused some adverse comment on the part of the senior chiefs, who didn't consider just how much experience these officers had.

One officer would be working the diving planes, the chief quartermaster was scandalized to learn. The chief electrician he discussed this with took it in stride. After all, he noted, the real fun was driving the boats, and officers only got to do that at New London. After that all they got to do was walk around and look important. True, the quartermaster agreed, but could they handle it? If not, the electrician decided, they would take care of things—what else were chiefs for but to protect officers from their mistakes? After that they argued good-naturedly over who would be chief of the boat. Both men had nearly identical experience and time in rate.

The USS *Ethan Allen* sailed for the last time at 2345 hours. No tug helped her away from the dock. The skipper eased her deftly away from the dock with gentle engine commands and strains on his lines that his quartermaster could only admire. He'd served with the skipper before, on the *Skipjack* and the *Will Rogers*. "No tugs, no nothin'," he reported to his bunkmate later. "The old man knows his shit." In an hour they were past the Virginia Capes and ready to dive. Ten minutes later they were gone from sight. Below, on a course of one-one-zero, the small crew of officers and chiefs settled into the demanding routine of running their old boomer shorthanded. The *Ethan Allen* responded like a champ, steaming at twelve knots, her old machinery hardly making any noise at all.

THE ELEVENTH DAY

MONDAY, 13 DECEMBER

An A-10 Thunderbolt

It was a lot more fun than flying DC-9s. Major Andy Richardson had over ten thousand hours in those and only six hundred or so in his A-10 Thunderbolt II strike fighter, but he much preferred the smaller of the twin-engine aircraft. Richardson belonged to the 175th Tactical Fighter Group of the Maryland Air National Guard. Ordinarily his squadron flew out of a small military airfield east of Baltimore. But two days earlier, when his outfit had been activated, the 175th and six other national guard and reserve air groups had crowded the already active SAC base at Loring Air Force Base in Maine. They had taken off at midnight and had refueled in midair only half an hour earlier, a thousand miles out over the North Atlantic. Now Richardson and his flight of four were skimming a hundred feet over the black waters at four hundred knots.

A hundred miles behind the four fighters, ninety aircraft were following at thirty thousand feet in what would look very much to the Soviets like an alpha strike, a weighted attack mission of armed tactical fighters. It was exactly that—and also a feint. The real mission belonged to the low-level team of four.

Richardson loved the A-10. She was called with backhanded affection the Warthog or just plain Hog by the men who flew her. Nearly all tactical aircraft had pleasing lines conferred on them by the need in combat for speed and maneuverability. Not the Hog, which was perhaps the ugliest bird ever built for the U.S. Air Force. Her twin turbofan engines hung like afterthoughts at the twin-rudder tail, itself a throwback to the thirties. Her slablike wings had not a whit of sweepback and were bent in the middle to accommodate the clumsy landing gear. The undersides of the wings were studded with many hard points so ordance could be carried, and the fuselage was built around the aircraft's primary weapon, the GAU-8 thirty-millimeter rotary cannon designed specifically to smash Soviet tanks.

For tonight's mission, Richardson's flight had a full load of depleted uranium slugs for their Avenger cannons and a pair of Rockeye cluster bomb cannisters, additional antitank weapons. Directly beneath the fuselage was a LANTIRN (low-altitude navigation and targeting infrared for night) pod; all the other ordnance stations save one were occupied by fuel tanks.

The 175th had been the first national guard squadron to receive LANTIRN. It was a small collection of electronic and optical systems that enabled the Hog to see at night while flying at minimum altitude searching for targets. The systems projected a heads-up display (HUD) on the fighter's windshield, in effect turning night to day and making this mission profile marginally less hazardous. Beside each LANTIRN pod was a smaller object which, unlike the cannon shells and Rockeyes, was intended for use tonight.

Richardson didn't mind—indeed, he relished—the hazards of the mission. Two of his three comrades were, like him, airline pilots, the third a crop duster, all experienced men with plenty of practice in low-level tactics. And their mission was a good one.

The briefing, conducted by a naval officer, had taken over an hour. They were paying a visit to the Soviet Navy. Richardson had read in the papers that the Russians were up to something, and when he had heard at the briefing that they were sending their fleet to trail its coat this close to the American coast, he had been shocked by their boldness. It had angered him to learn that one of their crummy little day fighters had back-shot a navy Tomcat the day before, nearly killing one of its officers. He wondered why the navy was being cut out of the response. Most of the *Saratoga*'s air group was visible on the concrete pads at Loring, sitting alongside the B-52s, A-6E Intruders, and F-18 Hornets with their ordnance carts a few feet away. He guessed that his mission was only the first act, the delicate part. While Soviet eyes were locked on the alpha strike hovering at the edge of their SAM range, his flight of four would dash in under radar cover to the fleet flagship, the nuclear-powered battle cruiser *Kirov*. To deliver a message.

It was surprising that guardsmen had been selected for this mission. Nearly a thousand tactical aircraft were now mobilized on the East Coast, about a third of them reservists of one kind or another, and Richardson guessed that that was part of the message. A very difficult tactical operation was being run by second-line airmen, while the regular squadrons sat ready on the runways of Loring, and McGuire, and Dover, and Pease, and several other bases from Virginia to Maine, fueled, briefed, and ready. Nearly a thousand aircraft! Richardson smiled. There wouldn't be enough targets to go around.

"Linebacker Lead, this is Sentry-Delta. Target bearing zero-four-eight, range fifty miles. Course is one-eight-five, speed twenty."

Richardson did not acknowledge the transmission over the encrypted radio link. The flight was under EMCON. Any electronic noise might alert the Soviets. Even his targeting radar was switched off, and only passive infrared and low-light television sensors were operating. He looked quickly left and right. Second-line flyers, hell! he said to himself. Every man in the flight had at least four thousand miles, more than most regular pilots would ever have, more than most of the astronauts, and their birds were maintained by people who tinkered with airplanes because they liked to. The fact of the matter was that his squadron had better aircraft-availability rates than any regular squadron and had had fewer accidents than the wet-nosed hotdogs who flew the warthogs in England and Korea. They'd show the Russkies that.

He smiled to himself. This sure beat flying his DC-9 from Washington to Providence and Hartford and back every day for U.S. Air! Richardson, who had been an air force fighter pilot, had left the service eight years earlier because he craved the higher pay and flashy lifestyle of a commercial airline pilot. He'd missed Vietnam, and commercial flying did not require anything like this degree of skill; it lacked the *rush* of skimming at treetop level.

So far as he knew, the Hog had never been used for maritime strike missions—another part of the message. It was no surprise that she'd be good at it. Her antitank munitions would be effective against ships. Her cannon slugs and Rockeye clusters were designed to shred armored battle tanks, and he had no doubts what they would do to thin-hulled warships. Too bad this wasn't for real. It was about time somebody taught Ivan a lesson.

A radar sensor light blinked on his threat receiver; S-band radar, it was probably meant for surface search, and was not powerful enough for a return yet. The Soviets did not have any aerial radar platforms, and their ship-carried sets were limited by the earth's curvature. The beam was just over his head; he was getting the fuzzy edge of it. They would have avoided detection better still by flying at fifty feet instead of a hundred, but orders were not to.

"Linebacker flight, this is Sentry-Delta. Scatter and head in," the AWACS commanded.

The A-10s separated from their interval of only a few feet to an extended attack formation that left miles between aircraft. The orders were for them to scatter at thirty miles' distance. About four minutes. Richardson checked his digital clock; the Linebacker flight was right on time. Behind them, the Phantoms and Corsairs in the alpha strike would be turning toward the Soviets, just to get their attention. He ought to be seeing them soon . . .

The HUD showed small bumps on the projected horizon— the outer screen of destroyers, the *Udaloys* and *Sovremennys*. The briefing officer had shown them silhouettes and photos of the warships.

Beep! his threat receiver chirped. An X-band missile guidance radar had just swept over his aircraft and lost it, and was now trying to regain contact. Richardson flipped on his ECM (electronic countermeasures) jamming systems. The destroyers were only five miles away now. Forty seconds. Stay dumb, comrades, he thought.

He began to maneuver his aircraft radically, jinking up, down, left, right, in no particular pattern. It was only a game, but there was no sense in giving Ivan an easy time. If this had been for real, his Hogs would be blazing in behind a swarm of antiradar missiles and would be accompanied by Wild Weasel aircraft trying to scramble and kill Soviet missile control systems. Things were moving very fast now. A screening destroyer loomed in his path, and he nudged his rudder to pass clear of her by a quarter mile. Two miles to the *Kirov*—eighteen seconds.

The HUD system painted an intensified image. The *Kirov*'s pyramidal mast-stack-radar structure was filling his windshield. He could see blinking signal lights all around the battle cruiser. Richardson gave more right rudder. They were supposed to pass within three hundred yards of the ship, no more, no less. His Hog would blaze past the bow, the others past the stern and either beam. He didn't want to cut it too close. The major checked to be certain that his bomb and cannon controls were locked in the safe position. No sense getting carried away. About now in a real attack he'd trigger his cannon and a stream of solid slugs would lance the light armor of the *Kirov*'s forward missile magazines, exploding the SAM and cruise missiles in a huge fireball and slicing through the superstructure as if it were thin as newsprint.

At five hundred yards, the captain reached down to arm the flare pod, attached next to the LANTIRN.

Now! He flipped the switch, which deployed half a dozen high-intensity magnesium parachute flares. All four Linebacker aircraft acted within seconds. Suddenly the *Kirov* was inside a box of blue-white magnesium light. Richardson pulled back on his stick, banking into a climbing turn past the battle cruiser. The brilliant light dazzled him, but he could see the graceful lines of the Soviet warship as she was turning hard on the choppy seas, her men running along the deck like ants.

If we were serious, you'd all be dead now—get the message?

Richardson thumbed his radio switch. "Linebacker Lead to Sentry-Delta," he said in the clear. "Robin Hood, repeat, Robin Hood. Linebacker flight, this is lead, form up on me. Let's go home!"

"Linebacker flight, this is Sentry-Delta. Outstanding!" the controller responded. "Be advised that *Kiev* has a pair of Forgers in the air, thirty miles east, heading your way. They'll have to hustle to catch up. Will advise. Out."

Richardson did some fast arithmetic in his head. They probably could not catch up, and even if they did, twelve Phantoms from the 107th Fighter Interceptor Group were ready for it.

"Hot damn, lead!" Linebacker 4, the crop duster, moved gingerly into his slot. "Did you see those turkeys pointing up at us? God damn, did we rattle their cage!"

"Heads up for Forgers," Richardson cautioned, grinning ear to ear inside his oxygen mask. *Second-line flyers, hell!*

"Let 'em come," Linebacker 4 replied. "Any of those bastards closes me and my thirty, it'll be the last mistake he ever makes!" Four was a little too aggressive for Richardson's liking, but the man did not know how to drive his Hog.

"Linebacker flight, this is Sentry-Delta. The Forgers have turned back. You're in the clear. Out."

"Roger that, out. Okay, flight, let's settle down and head home. I guess we've earned our pay for the month." Richardson looked to make sure he was on an open frequency. "Ladies and gentlemen, this is Captain Barry Friendly," he said, using the in-house U.S. Air public relations joke that had become a tradition in the 175th. "I hope you have enjoyed your flight, and thank you for flying Warthog Air."

The *Kirov*

On the *Kirov,* Admiral Stralbo raced from the combat information center to the flag bridge, too late. They had acquired the low-level raiders only a minute from the outer screen. The box of flares was already behind the battle cruiser, several still burning in the water. The bridge crew, he saw, was rattled.

"Sixty to seventy seconds before they were on us, Comrade

Admiral," the flag captain reported, "we were tracking the orbiting attack force and these four—we think, four—racing in under our radar coverage. We had missile lock on two of them despite their jamming."

Stralbo frowned. That performance was not nearly good enough. If the strike had been real, the *Kirov* would have been badly damaged at least. The Americans would gladly trade a pair of fighters for a nuclear powered cruiser. If all American aircraft attacked like this . . .

"The arrogance of the Americans is fantastic!" The fleet *zampolit* swore.

"It was foolish to provoke them," Stralbo observed sourly. "I knew that something like that would happen, but I expected it from *Kennedy.*"

"That was a mistake, a pilot error," the political officer replied.

"Indeed, Vasily. And *this* was no mistake! They just sent us a message, telling us that we are fifteen hundred kilometers from their shore without useful air cover, and that they have over five hundred fighters waiting to pounce on us from the west. In the meantime *Kennedy* is stalking us to the east like a rabid wolf. We are not in an attractive position."

"The Americans would not be so brash."

"Are you sure of that, Comrade Political Officer? Sure? What if one of their aircraft commits a 'pilot error'? And sinks one of our destroyers? And what if the American president gets a direct link to Moscow to apologize before we can ever report it? They swear it was an accident and promise to punish the stupid pilot—then what? You think the imperialists are so predictable this close to their own coastline? I do not. I think they are praying for the smallest excuse to pounce on us. Come to my cabin. We must consider this."

The two men went aft. Stralbo's cabin was a spartan affair. The only decoration on the wall was a print of Lenin speaking to Red Guards.

"What is our mission, Vasily?" Stralbo asked.

"To support our submarines, help them to conduct the search—"

"Exactly. Our mission is to support, not to conduct offensive operations. The Americans do not want us here. Objectively,

I can understand this. With all our missiles we are a threat to them."

"But our orders are not to threaten them," the *zampolit* protested. "Why would we want to strike their home-land?"

"And, of course, the imperialists recognize that we are peaceful socialists! Come now, Vasily, these are our enemies! Of course they do not trust us. Of *course* they wish to attack us, given the smallest excuse. They are already interfering with our search, pretending to help. They do not want us here— and in allowing ourselves to be provoked by their aggressive actions, we fall into their trap." The admiral stared down at his desk. "Well, we shall change that. I will order the fleet to discontinue anything that may appear the least bit aggressive. We will end all air operations beyond normal local patrolling. We will not harass their nearby fleet units. We will use only normal navigational radars."

"And?"

"And we will swallow our pride and be as meek as mice. Whatever provocation they make, we will not react to it."

"Some will call this cowardice, Comrade Admiral," the *zampolit* warned.

Stralbo had expected that. "Vasily, don't you see? In pre-tending to attack us they have already victimized us. They force us to activate our newest and most secret defense systems so they can gather intelligence on our radars and fire control systems. They examine the performance of our fighters and helicopters, the maneuverability of our ships, and most of all, our command and control. We shall put an end to that. Our primary mission is too important. If they continue to provoke us, we will act as though our mission is indeed peaceful— which it is as far as they are concerned—and protest our in-nocence. And we make them the aggressors. If they continue to provoke us, we shall watch to see what their tactics are, and give them nothing in return. Or would you prefer that they prevent us from carrying out our mission?"

The *zampolit* mumbled his consent. If they failed in their mission, the charge of cowardice would be a small matter indeed. If they found the renegade submarine, they'd be heroes regardless of what else happened.

The Dallas

How long had he been on duty? Jones wondered. He could have checked easily enough by punching the button on his digital watch, but the sonarman didn't want to. It would be too depressing. Me and my big mouth—*you bet, Skipper, my ass!* he swore to himself. He'd detected the sub at a range of about twenty miles, maybe, had just barely gotten her—and the fuckin' Atlantic Ocean was three thousand miles across, at least sixty footprint diameters. He'd need more than luck now.

Well, he did get a Hollywood shower out of it. Ordinarily a shower on a freshwater-poor ship meant a few seconds of wetting down and a minute or so of lathering, followed by a few more seconds of rinsing the suds off. It got you clean but was not very satisfying. This was an improvement over the old days, the oldtimers liked to say. But back then, Jones often responded, the sailors had to pull oars—or run off diesel and batteries, which amounted to the same thing. A Hollywood shower is something a sailor starts thinking about after a few days at sea. You leave the water running, a long, continuous stream of wonderfully warm water. Commander Mancuso was given to awarding this sensuous pastime in return for above-average performance. It gave people something tangible to work for. You couldn't spend extra money on a sub, and there was no beer or women.

Old movies—they were making an effort on that score. The boat's library wasn't bad, when you had time to sort through the jumble. And the *Dallas* had a pair of Apple computers and a few dozen game programs for amusement. Jones was the boat champion at Choplifter and Zork. The computers were also used for training purposes, of course, for practice exams and programmed learning tests that ate up most of the use time.

The *Dallas* was quartering an area east of the Grand Banks. Any boat transiting Route One tended to come through here. They were moving at five knots, trailing out the BQR-15 towed-array sonar. They'd had all kinds of contacts. First, half the submarines in the Russian Navy had whipped by at high speed, many trailed by American boats. An *Alfa* had burned past them at over forty knots, not three thousand yards away. It would have been so easy, Jones had thought at the time. The *Alfa* had been making so much noise that one could have heard it with a glass against the hull, and he'd had to turn his amplifiers down to minimums to keep the noise from ruining his ears. A pity they couldn't have fired. The setup had been so simple, the firing solution so easy that a kid with an old-fashioned sliderule could have done it. That *Alfa* had been meat on the table. The *Victor*s came running next, and the *Charlie*s and *November*s last of all. Jones had been listening to surface ships a ways to the west, a lot of them doing twenty knots or so, making all kinds of noise as they pounded through the waves. They were way far off, and not his concern.

They had been trying to acquire this particular target for over two days, and Jones had had only an odd hour of sleep here and there. Well, that's what they pay me for, he reflected bleakly. This was not unprecedented, he'd done it before, but he'd be happy when the labor ended.

The large-aperture towed array was at the end of a thousand-foot cable. Jones referred to the use of it as trolling for whales. In addition to being their most sensitive sonar rig, it protected the *Dallas* against intruders shadowing her. Ordinarily a submarine's sonar will work in any direction except aft—an area called the cone of silence, or the baffles. The BQR-15 changed that. Jones had heard all sorts of things on it, subs and surface ships all the time, low-flying aircraft on occasion. Once, during an exercise off Florida, it had been the noise of diving pelicans that he could not figure out until the skipper had raised the periscope for a look. Then off Bermuda they had encountered mating humpbacks, and a very impressive noise that was. Jones had a personal copy of the tape of them for use on the beach; some women had found it interesting, in a kinky sort of way. He smiled to himself.

There was a considerable amount of surface noise. The signal processors filtered most of it out, and every few minutes Jones switched them off his channel, getting the sound unimpeded to make sure that they weren't filtering too much out. Machines were dumb; Jones wondered if SAPS might be letting some of that anomalous signal get lost inside the computer chips. That was a problem with computers, really a problem with programming: you'd tell the machine to do something, and it would go do it to the wrong thing. Jones often amused himself working up programs. He knew a few people from college who drew up game programs for personal computers; one of them was making good money with Sierra On-Line Systems...

Daydreaming again, Jonesy, he chided himself. It wasn't easy listening to nothing for hours on end. It would have been a good idea, he thought, to let sonarmen read on duty. He had better sense than to suggest it. Mr. Thompson might go along, but the skipper and all the senior officers were ex-reactor types with the usual rule of iron: You shall watch every instrument with absolute concentration all the time. Jones didn't think this was very smart. It was different with sonarmen. They burned out too easily. To combat this Jones had his music tapes and his games. He could lose himself in any sort of diversion, especially Choplifter. A man had to have something, he reasoned, to lose his mind in, at least once a day. And something on duty in some cases. Even truck drivers, hardly the most intellectual of people, had radios and tape players to keep from becoming mesmerized. But sailors on a nuclear sub costing the best part of a billion...

Jones leaned forward, pressing the headphones tight against his head. He tore a page of doodles from his scratch pad and noted the time on a fresh sheet. Next he made some adjustments on his gain controls, already near the top of the scale, and flipped off the processors again. The cacophony of surface noise nearly took his head off. Jones tolerated this for a minute, working the manual muting controls to filter out the worst of the high-frequency noise. Aha! Jones said to himself. Maybe SAPS is messing me up a little—too soon to tell for sure.

When Jones had first been checked out on this gear in sonar school he'd had a burning desire to show it to his brother, who had a masters in electrical engineering and worked as a consultant in the recording industry. He had eleven patents to his name. The stuff on the *Dallas* would have knocked his eyes out. The navy's systems for digitalizing sound were years ahead of any commercial technique. Too bad it was all classified right alongside nuclear stuff...

"Mr. Thompson," Jones said quietly, not looking around, "can you ask the skipper if maybe we can swing more easterly and drop down a knot or two?"

"Skipper," Thompson went out into the passageway to relay

the request. New course and engine orders were given in fifteen seconds. Mancuso was in sonar ten seconds after that.

The skipper had been sweating this. It had been obvious two days ago that their erstwhile contact had not acted as expected, had not run the route, or had never slowed down. Commander Mancuso had guessed wrong on something—had he also guessed wrong on their visitor's course? And what did it mean if their friend had not run the route? Jones had figured that one out long before. It made her a boomer. Boomer skippers never go fast.

Jones was sitting as usual, hunched over his table, his left hand up commanding quiet as the towed array came around to a precise east-west azimuth at the end of its cable. His cigarette burned away unnoticed in the ashtray. A reel-to-reel tape recorder was operating continuously in the sonar room, its tapes changed hourly and kept for later analysis on shore. Next to it was another whose recordings were used aboard the *Dallas* for reexamination of contacts. He reached up and switched it on, then turned to see his captain looking down at him. Jones' face broke into a thin, tired smile.

"Yeah," he whispered.

Mancuso pointed to the speaker. Jones shook his head. "Too faint, Cap'n. I just barely got it now. Roughly north, I think, but I need some time on that." Mancuso looked at the intensity needle Jones was tapping. It was down to zero—almost. Every fifty seconds or so it twitched, just a little. Jones was making furious notes. "The goddamned SAPS filters are blanking part of this out!!!!! We need smoother amplifiers and better manual filter controls!!" he wrote.

Mancuso told himself that this was faintly ridiculous. He was watching Jones as he had watched his wife when she'd had Dominic and he was timing the twitches on a needle as he had timed his wife's contractions. But there was no thrill to match this. The comparison he used to explain it to his father was the thrill you got on the first day of hunting season, when you hear the leaves rustle and you know it's not a man making the noise. But it was better than that. He was hunting men, men like himself in a vessel like his own . . .

"Getting louder, Skipper." Jones leaned back and lit a cigarette. "He's heading our way. I make him three-five-zero, maybe more like three-five-three. Still real faint, but that's our boy. We got him." Jones decided to risk an impertinence. He'd earned a little tolerance. "We wait or we chase, sir?"

"We wait. No sense spooking him. We let him come in nice and close while we do our famous imitation of a hole in the water, then we tag along behind him to wax his tail for a while. I want another tape of this set up, and I want the BC-10 to run a SAPS scan. Use the instruction to bypass the processing algorithms. I want this contact analyzed, not interpreted. Run it every two minutes. I want his signature recorded, digitalized, folded, spindled, and mutilated. I want to know everything there is about him, his propulsion noises, his plant signature, the works. I want to know exactly who he is."

"He's a Russkie, sir," Jones observed.

"But which Russkie?" Mancuso smiled.

"Aye, Cap'n." Jones understood. He'd be on duty another two hours, but the end was in sight. Almost. Mancuso sat down and lifted a spare set of headphones, stealing one of Jones' cigarettes. He'd been trying to break the habit for a month. He'd have a better chance on the beach.

HMS Invincible

Ryan was now wearing a Royal Naval uniform. This was temporary. Another mark of how fast this job had been laid on was that he had only the one uniform and two shirts. All of his wardrobe was now being cleaned and in the interim he had on a pair of English-made trousers and a sweater. Typical, he thought—nobody even knows I'm here. They had forgotten him. No messages from the president—not that he'd ever expected one—and Painter and Davenport were only too glad to forget that he was ever on the *Kennedy*. Greer and the judge were probably going over some damned fool thing or another, maybe chuckling to themselves about Jack Ryan having a pleasure cruise at government expense.

It was not a pleasure cruise. Jack had rediscovered his vulnerability to seasickness. The *Invincible* was off Massachusetts, waiting for the Russian surface force and hunting vigorously after the red subs in the area. They were steaming in circles on an ocean that would not settle down. Everyone was busy—

except him. The pilots were up twice a day or more, exercising
with their U.S. Air Force and Navy counterparts working from
shore bases. The ships were practicing surface warfare tactics.
As Admiral White had said at breakfast, it had developed into
a jolly good extension of NIFTY DOLPHIN. Ryan didn't like
being a supernumerary. Everyone was polite, of course. Indeed,
the hospitality was nearly overpowering. He had access to the
command center, and when he watched to see how the Brits
hunted subs down, everything was explained to him in sufficient detail that he actually understood about half of it.

At the moment he was reading alone in White's sea cabin,
which had become his permanent home aboard. Ritter had
thoughtfully tucked a CIA staff study into his duffle bag. Entitled "Lost Children: A Psychological Profile of East Bloc
Defectors," the three-hundred-page document had been drafted
by a committee of psychologists and psychiatrists who worked
with the CIA and other intelligence agencies helping defectors
settle into American life—and, he was sure, helping spot security risks in the CIA. Not that there were many of those, but
there were two sides to everything the Company did.

Ryan admitted to himself that this was pretty interesting
stuff. He had never really thought about what makes a defector,
figuring that there were enough things happening on the other
side of the Iron Curtain to make any rational person want to
take whatever chance he got to run west. But it was not that
simple, he read, not that simple at all. Everyone who came
over was a fairly unique individual. While one might recognize
the inequities of life under Communism and yearn for justice,
religious freedom, a chance to develop as an individual, another
might simply want to get rich, having read about how greedy
capitalists exploit the masses and decided that being an exploiter
has its good points. Ryan found this interesting if cynical.

Another defector type was the fake, the imposter, someone
planted on the CIA as a living piece of disinformation. But this
kind of character could cut both ways. He might ultimately
turn out to be a genuine defector. America, Ryan smiled, could
be pretty seductive to someone used to the gray life in the
Soviet Union. Most of the plants, however, were dangerous
enemies. For this reason a defector was never trusted. Never.
A man who had changed countries once could do it again. Even

the idealists had doubts, great pangs of conscience at having deserted their motherland. In a footnote a doctor commented that the most wounding punishment for Aleksander Solzhenitsyn was exile. As a patriot, being alive far from his home was more of a torment than living in a gulag. Ryan found that curious, but enough so to be true.

The rest of the document addressed the problem of getting them settled. Not a few Soviet defectors had committed suicide after a few years. Some had simply been unable to cope with freedom, the way that long-term prison inmates often fail to function without highly structured control over their lives and commit new crimes hoping to return to their safe environment. Over the years the CIA had developed a protocol for dealing with this problem, and a graph in an appendix showed that the severe maladjustment cases were trending dramatically down. Ryan took his time reading. While getting his doctorate in history at Georgetown University he had used a little free time to audit some psychology classes. He had come away with the gut suspicion that shrinks didn't really know much of anything, that they got together and agreed on random ideas they could all use . . . He shook his head. His wife occasionally said that, too. A clinical instructor in ophthalmic surgery on an exchange program at St. Guy's Hospital in London, Caroline Ryan regarded everything as cut and dried. If someone had eye trouble, she would either fix it or not fix it. A mind was different, Jack decided after reading through the document a second time, and each defector had to be treated as an individual, handled carefully by a sympathetic case officer who had both the time and inclination to look after him properly. He wondered if he'd be good at it.

Admiral White walked in. "Bored, Jack?"

"Not exactly, Admiral. When do we make contact with the Soviets?"

"This evening. Your chaps have given them a very rough time over that Tomcat incident."

"Good. Maybe people will wake up before something really bad happens."

"You think it will?" White sat down.

"Well, Admiral, if they really are hunting a missing sub, yes. If not, then they're here for another purpose entirely, and

I've guessed wrong. Worse than that, I'll have to live with that misjudgment—or die with it."

Norfolk Naval Medical Center

Tait was feeling better. Dr. Jameson had taken over for several hours, allowing him to curl up on a couch in the doctor's lounge for five hours. That was the most sleep he ever seemed to get in one shot, but it was sufficient to make him look indecently chipper to the rest of the floor staff. He made a quick phone call and some milk was sent up. As a Mormon, Tait avoided everything with caffeine—coffee, tea, even cola drinks—and though this type of self-discipline was unusual for a physician, to say nothing of a uniformed officer, he scarcely thought about it except on rare occasions when he pointed out its longevity benefits to his brother practitioners. Tait drank his milk and shaved in the restroom, emerging ready to face another day.

"Any word on the radiation exposure, Jamie?"

The radiology lab had struck out. "They brought a nucleonics officer over from a sub tender, and he scanned the clothes. There was a possible twenty-rad contamination, not enough for frank physiological effects. I think what it might have been was that the nurse took the sample from the back of his hand. The extremities might still have been suffering from the vascular shutdown. That could explain the depleted white count. Maybe."

"How is he otherwise?"

"Better. Not much, but better. I think maybe the keflin's taking hold." The doctor flipped open the chart. "White count is coming back. I put a unit of whole blood into him two hours ago. The blood chemistry is approaching normal limits. Blood pressure is one hundred over sixty-five, heart rate is ninety-four. Temperature ten minutes ago was 100.8—it's been fluctuating for several hours.

"His heart looks pretty good. In fact, I think he's going to make it, unless something unexpected crops up." Jameson reminded himself that in extreme hypothermia cases the unexpected can take a month or more to appear.

Tait examined the chart, remembering what he had been like years ago. A bright young doc, just like Jamie, certain that he could cure the world. It was a good feeling. A pity that experience—in his case, two years at Danang—beat that out of you. Jamie was right, though; there was enough improvement here to make the patient's chances appear measurably better.

"What are the Russians doing?" Tait asked.

"Petchkin has the watch at the moment. When it came his turn, and he changed into scrubs—you know he has that Captain Smirnov holding onto his clothes, like he expected us to steal them or something?"

Tait explained that Petchkin was a KGB agent.

"No kidding? Maybe he has a gun tucked away." Jameson chuckled. "If he does, he'd better watch it. We got three marines up here with us."

"Marines. What for?"

"Forgot to tell you. Some reporter found out we had a Russkie up here and tried to bluff his way onto the floor. A nurse stopped him. Admiral Blackburn found out and went ape. The whole floor's sealed off. What's the big secret, anyway?"

"Beats me, but that's the way it is. What do you think of this Petchkin guy?"

"I don't know. I've never met any Russians before. They don't smile a whole lot. The way they're taking turns watching the patient, you'd think they expect us to make off with him."

"Or maybe that he'll say something they don't want us to hear?" Tait wondered. "Did you get the feeling that they might not want him to make it? I mean, when they didn't want to tell us about what his sub was?"

Jameson thought about that. "No. The Russians are supposed to make a secret of everything, aren't they? Anyway, Smirnov did come through with it."

"Get some sleep, Jamie."

"Aye, Cap'n." Jameson walked off toward the lounge.

We asked them what kind of a sub, the captain thought, meaning whether it was a nuke or not. What if they thought we were asking if it was a missile sub? That makes sense, doesn't it? Yeah. A missile sub right off our coast, and all this activity in the North Atlantic. Christmas season. Dear God! If they were going to do it, they'd do it right now, wouldn't they? He walked down the hall. A nurse came out of the room with a blood sample to be taken down to the lab. This was being done hourly, and it left Petchkin alone with the patient for a few minutes.

Tait walked around the corner and saw Petchkin through the window, sitting in a chair at the corner of the bed and watching his countryman, who was still unconscious. He had on green scrubs. Made to put on in a hurry, these were reversible, with a pocket on both sides so a surgeon didn't have to waste a second to see if they were inside out. As Tait watched, Petchkin reached for something through the low collar.

"Oh, God!" Tait raced around the corner and shot through the swinging door. Petchkin's look of surprise changed to amazement as the doctor batted a cigarette and lighter from his hand, then to outrage as he was lifted from his chair and flung towards the door. Tait was the smaller of the two, but his sudden burst of energy was sufficient to eject the man from the room. "Security!" Tait screamed.

"What is the meaning of this?" Petchkin demanded. Tait was holding him in a bearhug. Immediately he heard feet racing down the hall from the lobby.

"What is it, sir?" A breathless marine lance corporal with a .45 Colt in his right hand skidded to a halt on the tile floor.

"This man just tried to kill my patient!"

"What!" Petchkin's face was crimson.

"Corporal, your post is now at that door. If this man tries to get into that room, you will stop him any way you have to. Understood?"

"Aye aye, sir!" the corporal looked at the Russian. "Sir, would you please step away from the door?"

"What is the meaning of this outrage!"

"Sir, you will step away from the door, right now." The marine holstered his pistol.

"What is going on here?" It was Ivanov, who had sense enough to ask this question in a quiet voice from ten feet away.

"Doctor, do you want your sailor to survive or not?" Tait asked, trying to calm himself.

"What—of course we wish him to survive. How can you ask this?"

"Then why did Comrade Petchkin just try to kill him?"

"I did not do such a thing!" Petchkin shouted.

"What did he do, exactly?" Ivanov asked.

Before Tait could answer, Petchkin spoke rapidly in Russian, then switched to English. "I was reaching for a smoke, that is all. I have no weapon. I wish to kill no one. I only wish to have a cigarette."

"We have No Smoking signs all over the floor, except in the lobby—you didn't see them? You were in a room in intensive care, with a patient on hundred-percent oxygen, the air and bedclothes saturated with oxygen, and you were going to flick your goddamned Bic!" The doctor rarely used profanity. "Oh sure, you'd get burned some, and it would look like an accident—and that kid would be dead! I know what you are, Petchkin, and I don't think you're that stupid. Get off my floor!"

The nurse, who had been watching this, went into the patient's room. She came back out with a pack of cigarettes, two loose ones, a plastic butane lighter, and a curious look on her face.

Petchkin was ashen. "Dr. Tait, I assure you that I had no such intention. What are you saying would happen?"

"Comrade Petchkin," Ivanov said slowly in English, "there would be an explosion and fire. You cannot have a flame near oxygen."

"Nichevo!" Petchkin finally realized what he had done. He had waited for the nurse to leave—medical people never let you smoke when you ask. He didn't know the first thing about hospitals, and as a KGB agent he was accustomed to doing whatever he wanted. He started speaking to Ivanov in Russian. The Soviet doctor looked like a parent listening to a child's explanation for a broken glass. His response was spirited.

For his part, Tait began to wonder if he hadn't overreacted—anyone who smoked was an idiot to begin with.

"Dr. Tait," Petchkin said finally, "I swear to you that I had no idea of this oxygen business. Perhaps I am a fool."

"Nurse," Tait turned, "we will not leave this patient unattended by our personnel at any time—never. Have a corpsman come to pick up the blood samples and anything else. If you have to go to the head, get relief first."

"Yes, Doctor."

"No more screwing around, Mr. Petchkin. Break the rules

again, sir, and you're off the floor again. Do you understand?"

"It will be as you say, Doctor, and allow me, please, to apologize."

"You stay put," Tait said to the marine. He walked away shaking his head angrily, mad at the Russians, embarrassed with himself, wishing he were back at Bethesda where he belonged, and wishing he knew how to swear coherently. He took the service elevator down to the first floor and spent five minutes looking for the intelligence officer who had flown down with him. Ultimately he found him in a game room playing Pac Man. They conferred in the hospital administrator's vacant office.

"You really thought he was trying to kill the guy?" the commander asked incredulously.

"What was I supposed to think?" Tait demanded. "What do you think?"

"I think he just screwed up. They want that kid alive—no, first they want him talking—more than you do."

"How do you know that?"

"Petchkin calls their embassy every hour. We have the phones tapped, of course. How do you think?"

"What if it's a trick?"

"If he's that good an actor he belongs in the movies. You keep that kid alive, Doctor, and leave the rest to us. Good idea to have the marine close, though. That'll rattle 'em a bit. Never pass up a chance to rattle 'em. So, when will he be conscious?"

"No telling. He's still feverish, and very weak. Why do they want him to talk?" Tait asked.

"To find out what sub he was on. Petchkin's KGB contact blurted that out on the phone—sloppy! *Very* sloppy! They must be real excited about this."

"Do we know what sub it was?"

"Sure," the intelligence officer said mischievously.

"Then what's going on, for Lord's sake!"

"Can't say, Doc." The commander smiled as if he knew, though he was as much in the dark as anyone.

Norfolk Naval Shipyard

The USS *Scamp* sat at the dock while a large overhead crane settled the *Avalon* in its support rack. The captain watched impatiently from atop the sail. He and his boat had been called in from hunting a pair of *Victor*s, and he did not like it one bit. The attack boat skipper had only run a DSRV exercise a few weeks before, and right now he had better things to do than play mother whale to this damned useless toy. Besides, having the minisub perched on his after escape trunk would knock ten knots off his top speed. And there'd be four more men to bunk and feed. The *Scamp* was not all that large.

At least they'd get good food out of this. The *Scamp* had been out five weeks when the recall order arrived. Their supply of fresh vegetables was exhausted, and they availed themselves of the opportunity to have fresh food trucked down to the dock. A man tires quickly of three-bean salad. Tonight they'd have real lettuce, tomatoes, fresh corn instead of canned. But that didn't make up for the fact that there were Russians out there to worry about.

"All secure?" the captain called down to the curved after deck.

"Yes, Captain. We're ready when you are," Lieutenant Ames answered.

"Engine room," the captain called down on intercom. "I want you ready to answer bells in ten minutes."

"Ready now, Skipper."

A harbor tug was standing by to help maneuver them from the dock. Ames had their orders, something else that the captain didn't like. Surely they would not be doing any more hunting, not with that damned *Avalon* strapped on.

The Red October

"Look here, Svyadov," Melekhin pointed, "I will show you how a saboteur thinks."

The lieutenant came over and looked. The chief engineer was pointing at an inspection valve on the heat exchanger. Before he got an explanation, Melekhin went to the bulkhead phone.

"Comrade Captain, this is Melekhin. I have found it. I require the reactor to be stopped for an hour. We can operate the caterpillar on batteries, no?"

"Of course, Comrade Chief Engineer," Ramius said, "proceed."

Melekhin turned to the assistant engineering officer. "You will shut the reactor down and connect the batteries to the caterpillar motors."

"At once, Comrade." The officer began to work the controls.

The time taken to find the leak had been a burden on everyone. Once they had discovered that the Geiger counters were sabotaged and Melekhin and Borodin had repaired them, they had begun a complete check of the reactor spaces, a devilishly tricky task. There had never been a question of a major steam leak, else Svyadov would have gone looking for it with a broomstick—even a tiny leak could easily shave off an arm. They reasoned that it had to be a small leak in the low-pressure part of the system. Didn't it? It was the not knowing that had troubled everyone.

The check made by the chief engineer and executive officer had lasted no less than eight hours, during which the reactor had again been shut down. This cut all electricity off throughout the ship except for emergency lights and the caterpillar motors. Even the air systems had been curtailed. That had set the crew muttering to themselves.

The problem was, Melekhin could still not find the leak, and when the badges had been developed a day earlier, there was nothing on them! How was this possible?

"Come, Svyadov, tell me what you see." Melekhin came back over and pointed.

"The water test valve." Opened only in port, when the reactor was cold, it was used to flush the cooling system and to check for unusual water contamination. The thing was grossly unremarkable, a heavy-duty valve with a large wheel. The spout underneath it, below the pressurized part of the pipe, was threaded rather than welded.

"A large wrench, if you please, Lieutenant. Melekhin was drawing the lesson out, Svyadov thought. He was the slowest of teachers when he was trying to communicate something important. Svyadov returned with a meter-long pipe wrench. The chief engineer waited until the plant was closed down, then double-checked a gauge to make sure the pipes were depressurized. He was a careful man. The wrench was set on the fitting, and he turned it. It came off easily.

"You see, Comrade Lieutenant, the threads on the pipe actually go up onto the valve casing. Why is this permitted?"

"The threads are on the outside of the pipe, Comrade. The valve itself bears the pressure. The fitting which is screwed on is merely a directional spigot. The nature of the union does not compromise the pressure loop."

"Correct. A screw fitting is not strong enough for the plant's total pressure." Melekhin worked the fitting all the way off with his hands. It was perfectly machined, the threads still bright from the original engine work. "And there is the sabotage."

"I don't understand."

"Someone thought this one over very carefully, Comrade Lieutenant." Melekhin's voice was half admiration, half rage. "At normal operating pressure, cruising speed, that is, the system is pressurized to eight kilograms per square centimeter, correct?"

"Yes, Comrade, and at full power the pressure is ninety percent higher." Svyadov knew all this by heart.

"But we rarely go to full power. What we have here is a dead-end section of the steam loop. Now, here a small hole has been drilled, not even a millimeter. Look." Melekhin bent over to examine it himself. Svyadov was happy to keep his distance. "Not even a millimeter. The saboteur took the fitting off, drilled the hole, and put it back. The tiny hole permits a minuscule amount of steam to escape, but only very slowly. The steam cannot go up, because the fitting sits against this flange. Look at this machine work! It is perfect, you see, perfect! The steam, therefore, cannot escape upward. It can only force its way down the threads around and around, ultimately escaping inside the spout. Just enough. Just enough to contaminate this compartment by a tiny amount." Melekhin looked up. "Someone was a very clever man. Clever enough to know exactly how this system works. When we reduced power to check for the leak before, there was not enough pressure remaining in the loop to force the steam down the threads, and we could not find the leak. There is only enough pressure at normal power levels—but if you suspect a leak, you power-down the system. And if we had gone to maximum power, who can say what might have happened?" Melekhin shook his head in admiration. "Someone was very, very clever.

I hope I meet him. Oh, I hope I meet this clever man. For when I do, I will take a pair of large steel pliers—," Melekhin's voice lowered to a whisper, "—and I will crush his balls! Get me the small electric welding set, Comrade. I can fix this myself in a few minutes."

Captain First Rank Melekhin was as good as his word. He wouldn't let anyone near the job. It was his plant, and his responsibility. Svyadov was just as happy for that. A tiny bead of stainless steel was worked into the fault, and Melekhin filed it down with jeweler's tools to protect the threads. Then he brushed rubber-based sealant onto the threads and worked the fitting back into place. The whole procedure took twenty-eight minutes by Svyadov's watch. As they had told him in Leningrad, Melekhin was the best engineer in submarines.

"A static pressure test, eight kilograms," he ordered the assistant engineer officer.

The reactor was reactivated. Five minutes later the pressure went all the way to normal power. Melekhin held a counter under the spout for ten minutes—and got nothing, even on the number two setting. He walked to the phone to tell the captain the leak was fixed.

Melekhin had the enlisted men let back into the compartment to return the tools to their places.

"You see how it is done, Lieutenant?"

"Yes, Comrade. Was that one leak sufficient to cause all of our contamination?"

"Obviously."

Svyadov wondered about this. The reactor spaces were nothing but a collection of pipes and fittings, and this bit of sabotage could not have taken long. What if other such time bombs were hidden in the system?

"Perhaps you worry too much, Comrade," Melekhin said. "Yes, I have considered this. When we get to Cuba, I will have a full-power static test made to check the whole system, but for the moment I do not think this is a good idea. We will continue the two-hour watch cycle. There is the possibility that one of our own crewmen is the saboteur. If so, I will not have people in these spaces long enough to commit more mischief. You will watch the crew closely."

THE TWELFTH DAY

TUESDAY, 14 DECEMBER

The Dallas

"Crazy Ivan!" Jones shouted loudly enough to be heard in the attack center. "Turning to starboard!"

"Skipper!" Thompson repeated the warning.

"All stop!" Mancuso ordered quickly. "Rig ship for ultra-quiet!"

A thousand yards ahead of the *Dallas*, her contact had just begun a radical turn to the right. She had been doing so about every two hours since they had regained contact, though not regularly enough for the *Dallas* to settle into a comfortable pattern. Whoever is driving that boomer knows his business, Mancuso thought. The Soviet missile submarine was making a complete circle so her bow-mounted sonar could check for anyone hiding in her baffles.

Countering this maneuver was more than just tricky—it was dangerous, especially the way Mancuso did it. When the *Red*

October changed course, her stern, like those of all ships, moved in the direction opposite the turn. She was a steel barrier directly in the *Dallas'* path for as long as it took her to move through the first part of the turn, and the 7,000-ton attack submarine took a lot of space to stop.

The exact number of collisions that had occurred between Soviet and American submarines was a closely guarded secret; that there had been such collisions was not. One characteristically Russian tactic for forcing Americans to keep their distance was a stylized turn called the Crazy Ivan in the U.S. Navy.

The first few hours they had trailed this contact, Mancuso had been careful to keep his distance. He had learned that the submarine was not turning quickly. She was, rather, maneuvering in a leisurely manner, and seemed to ascend fifty to eighty feet as she turned, banking almost like an aircraft. He suspected that the Russian skipper was not using his full maneuverability—an intelligent thing for a captain to do, keeping some of his performance in reserve as a surprise. These facts allowed the *Dallas* to traii very closely indeed and gave Mancuso a chance to chop his speed and drift forward so that he barely avoided the Russian's stern. He was getting good at it— a little too good, his officers were whispering. The last time they had not missed the Russian's screws by more than a hundred fifty yards. The contact's large turning circle was taking her completely around the *Dallas* as the latter sniffed at her prey's trail.

Avoiding collision was the most dangerous part of the maneuver, but not the only part. The *Dallas* also had to remain invisible to her quarry's passive sonar systems. For her to do so the engineers had to cut power in their S6G reactor to a tiny fraction of its total output. Fortunately the reactor was able to run on such low power without the use of a coolant pump, since coolant could be transferred by normal convection circulation. In addition, a strict silent ship routine was enforced. No activity on the *Dallas* that might generate noise was permitted, and the crew took it seriously enough that even ordinary conversations in the mess were muted.

"Speed coming down," Lieutenant Goodman reported. Mancuso decided that the *Dallas* would not be part of a ramming this time and went aft to sonar.

"Target is still turning right," Jones reported quietly. "Ought to be clear now. Distance to the stern, maybe two hundred yards, maybe a shade less . . . Yeah, we're clear now, bearing is changing more rapidly. Speed and engine noises are constant. A slow turn to the right." Jones caught the captain out of the corner of his eye and turned to hazard an observation. "Skipper, this guy is real confident in himself. I mean, *real* confident."

"Explain," Mancuso said, figuring he knew the answer.

"Cap'n, he's not chopping speed the way we do, and we turn a lot sharper than this. It's almost like—like he's doing this out of habit, y'know? Like he's in a hurry to get some-where, and really doesn't think anybody can track—wait . . . Yeah, okay, he's just about reversed course now, bearing off the starboard bow, say half a mile . . . Still doing the slow turn. He'll go right around us again. Sir, if he knows anybody's back here, he's playing it awful cool. What do you think, Frenchie?"

Chief Sonarman Laval shook his head. "He don't know we're here." The chief didn't want to say anything else. He thought Mancuso's close tailing was reckless. The man had balls, playing with a 688 like this, but one little screw-up and he'd find himself with a pail and shovel, on the beach.

"Passing down the starboard side. No pinging." Jones took out his calculator and punched in some numbers. "Sir, this angular turn rate at this speed makes the range about a thousand yards. You suppose his funny drive system goofs up his rudders any?"

"Maybe." Mancuso took a spare set of phones and plugged them in to listen.

The noise was the same. A swish, and every forty or fifty seconds an odd, low-frequency rumble. This close they could also hear the gurgling and throbbing of the reactor pump. There was a sharp sound, maybe a cook moving a pan on a metal grate. No silent ship drill on this boat. Mancuso smiled to himself. It was like being a cat burglar, hanging this close to an enemy submarine—no, not an enemy, not exactly—hearing everything. In better acoustical conditions they could have heard conversations. Not well enough to understand them, of course, but as if they were at a dinner party listening to the gabble of a dozen couples at once.

"Passing aft and still circling. His turning radius must be a good thousand yards," Mancuso observed.

"Yes, Cap'n, about that," Jones agreed.

"He just can't be using all his rudder, and you're right, Jonesy, he is very damned casual about this. Hmph, the Russians are all supposed to be paranoid—not this boy." So much the better, Mancuso thought.

If he were going to hear the *Dallas* it would be now, with the bow-mounted sonar pointed almost directly at them. Mancuso took off his headphones to listen to his boat. The *Dallas* was a tomb. The words *Crazy Ivan* had been passed, and within seconds his crew had responded. How do you reward a whole crew? Mancuso wondered. He knew he worked them hard, sometimes too hard—but damn! Did they deliver!

"Port beam," Jones said. "Exactly abeam now, speed unchanged, traveling a little straighter, maybe, distance about eleven hundred, I think." The sonarman took a handkerchief from his back pocket and used it to wipe his hands.

There's tension all right, but you'd never know it listening to the kid, the captain thought. Everyone in his crew was acting like a professional.

"He's passed us. On the port bow, and I think the turn has stopped. Betcha he's settled back down on one-nine-zero." Jones looked up with a grin. "We did it again, Skipper."

"Okay. Good work, you men." Mancuso went back to the attack center. Everyone was waiting expectantly. The *Dallas* was dead in the water, drifting slowly downward with her slight negative trim.

"Let's get the engines turned back on. Build her up slowly to thirteen knots." A few seconds later an almost imperceptible noise began as the reactor plant increased power. A moment after that the speed gauge twitched upward. The *Dallas* was moving again.

"Attention, this is the captain speaking," Mancuso said into the sound-powered communications system. The electrically powered speakers were turned off, and his word would be relayed by watchstanders in all compartments. "They circled us again without picking us up. Well done, everybody. We can all breathe again." He placed the handset back in its holder. "Mr. Goodman, let's get back on her tail."

"Aye, Skipper. Left five degrees rudder, helm."

"Left five degrees rudder, aye." The helmsman acknowledged the order, turning his wheel as he did so. Ten minutes later the *Dallas* was back astern of her contact.

A constant fire control solution was set up on the attack director. The Mark 48 torpedoes would barely have sufficient distance to arm themselves before striking the target in twenty-nine seconds.

Ministry of Defense, Moscow

"And how are you feeling, Misha?"

Mikhail Semyonovich Filitov looked up from a large pile of documents. He looked flushed and feverish still. Dmitri Ustinov, the defense minister, worried about his old friend. He should have stayed in the hospital another few days as the doctors had advised. But Misha had never been one to take advice, only orders.

"I feel good, Dmitri. Any time you walk out of a hospital you feel good—even if you are dead," Filitov smiled.

"You still look sick," Ustinov observed.

"Ah! At our age you always look sick. A drink, Comrade Defense Minister?" Filitov hoisted a bottle of Stolychnaya vodka from a desk drawer.

"You drink too much, my friend," Ustinov chided.

"I do not drink enough. A bit more antifreeze and I would not have caught cold last week." He poured two tumblers half full and held one out to his guest. "Here, Dmitri, it is cold outside."

Both men tipped their glasses, took a gulp of the clear liquid, and expelled their breath with an explosive *pah*.

"I feel better already." Filitov's laugh was hoarse. "Tell me, what became of that Lithuanian renegade?"

"We're not sure," Ustinov said.

"Still? Can you tell me now what his letter said?"

Ustinov took another swallow before explaining. When he finished the story Filitov was leaning forward at his desk, shocked.

"Mother of God! And he has still not been found? How many heads?"

"Admiral Korov is dead. He was arrested by the KGB, of

course, and died of a brain hemorrhage soon thereafter."

"A nine-millimeter hemorrhage, I trust," Filitov observed coldly. "How many times have I said it? What goddamned use is a navy? Can we use it against the Chinese? Or the NATO armies that threaten us—no! How many rubles does it cost to build and fuel those pretty barges for Gorshkov, and what do we get for it—nothing! Now he loses one submarine and the whole fucking fleet cannot find it. It is a good thing that Stalin is not alive."

Ustinov agreed. He was old enough to remember what happened then to anyone who reported results short of total success. "In any case, Padorin may have saved his skin. There is one extra element of control on the submarine."

"Padorin!" Filitov took another gulp of his drink. "That eunuch! I've only met him, what, three times. A cold fish, even for a commissar. He never laughs, even when he drinks. Some Russian he is. Why is it, Dmitri, that Gorshkov keeps so many old farts like that around?"

Ustinov smiled into his drink. "The same reason I do, Misha." Both men laughed.

"So, how will Comrade Padorin save our secrets and keep his skin? Invent a time machine?"

Ustinov explained to his old friend. There weren't many men whom the defense minister could speak to and feel comfortable with. Filitov drew the pension of a full colonel of tanks and still wore the uniform proudly. He had faced combat for the first time on the fourth day of the Great Patriotic War, as the Fascist invaders were driving east. Lieutenant Filitov had met them southeast of Brest Litovsk with a troop of T-34/76 tanks. A good officer, he had survived his first encounter with Guderian's panzers, retreated in good order, and fought a constant mobile action for days before being caught in the great encirclement at Minsk. He had fought his way out of that trap, and later another at Vyasma, and had commanded a battalion spearheading Zhukov's counterblow from the suburbs of Moscow. In 1942 Filitov had taken part in the disastrous counteroffensive toward Kharkov but again escaped, this time on foot, leading the battered remains of regiment from that dreadful cauldron on the Dnieper River. With another regiment later that year he had led the drive that shattered the Italian Army on the flank of Stalingrad and encircled the Germans. He'd been wounded twice in that campaign. Filitov had acquired the reputation of a commander who was both good and lucky. That luck had run out at Kursk, where he had battled the troopers of SS division *Das Reich*. Leading his men into a furious tank battle, Filitov and his vehicle had run straight into an ambush of eighty-eight-millimeter guns. That he had survived at all was a miracle. His chest still bore the scars from the burning tank, and his right arm was next to useless. This was enough to retire a charging tactical commander who had won the old star of the Hero of the Soviet Union no less than three times, and a dozen other decorations.

After months of being shuttled from one hospital to another, he had become a representative of the Red Army in the armament factories that had been moved to the Urals east of Moscow. The drive that made him a premiere combat soldier would come to serve the State even better behind the lines. A born organizer, Filitov learned to run roughshod over factory bosses to streamline production, and he cajoled design engineers to make the small but often crucial changes in their products that would save crews and win battles.

It was in these factories that Filitov and Ustinov first met, the scarred combat veteran and the gruff apparatchik detailed by Stalin to produce enough tools to drive the hated invaders back. After a few clashes, the young Ustinov came to recognize that Filitov was totally fearless and would not be bullied on a question involving quality control or fighting efficiency. In the midst of one disagreement, Filitov had practically dragged Ustinov into the turret of a tank and taken it through a combat training course to make his point. Ustinov was the sort who only had to be shown something once, and they soon became fast friends. He could not fail to admire the courage of a soldier who could say no to the people's commissar of armaments. By mid-1944 Filitov was a permanent part of his staff, a special inspector—in short, a hatchet man. When there was a problem at a factory, Filitov saw that it was settled, quickly. The three gold stars and the crippling injuries were usually enough to persuade the factory bosses to mend their ways—and if not, Misha had the booming voice and vocabulary to make a sergeant major wince.

Never a high Party official, Filitov gave his boss valuable input from people in the field. He still worked closely with the tank design and production teams, often taking a prototype or randomly chosen production model through a test course with a team of picked veterans to see for himself how well things worked. Crippled arm or not, it was said that Filitov was among the best gunners in the Soviet Union. And he was a humble man. In 1965 Ustinov thought to surprise his friend with general's stars and was somewhat angered by Filitov's reaction—he had not earned them on the field of battle, and that was the only way a man could earn stars. A rather impolitic remark, as Ustinov wore the uniform of a marshal of the Soviet Union, earned for his Party work and industrial management, it nevertheless demonstrated that Filitov was a true New Soviet Man, proud of what he was and mindful of his limitations.

It is unfortunate, Ustinov thought, that Misha has been so unlucky otherwise. He had been married to a lovely woman, Elena Filitov, who had been a minor dancer with the Kirov when the youthful officer had met her. Ustinov remembered her with a trace of envy; she had been the perfect soldier's wife. She had given the State two fine sons. Both were now dead. The elder had died in 1956, still a boy, an officer cadet sent to Hungary because of his political reliability and killed by counterrevolutionaries before his seventeenth birthday. He was a soldier who had taken a soldier's chance. But the younger had been killed in a training accident, blown to pieces by a faulty breech mechanism in a brand-new T-55 tank in 1959. That had been a disgrace. And Elena had died soon thereafter, of grief more than anything else. Too bad.

Filitov had not changed all that much. He drank too much, like many soldiers, but he was a quiet drunk. In 1961 or so, Ustinov remembered, he had taken to cross-country skiing. It made him healthier and tired him out, which was probably what he really wanted, along with the solitude. He was still a fine listener. When Ustinov had a new idea to float before the Politburo, he usually tried it out on Filitov first to get his reaction. Not a sophisticated man, Filitov was an uncommonly shrewd one who had a soldier's instinct for finding weaknesses and exploiting strengths. His value as a liaison officer was unsurpassed. Few men living had three gold stars won on the field of battle. That got him attention, and it still made officers far his senior listen to him.

"So, Dmitri Fedorovich, do you think this would work? Can one man destroy a submarine?" Filitov asked. "You know, rockets, I don't."

"Certainly. It's merely a question of mathematics. There is enough energy in a rocket to melt the submarine."

"And what of our man?" Filitov asked. Always the combat soldier, he would be the type to worry about a brave man alone in enemy territory.

"We will do our best, of course, but there is not much hope."

"He must be rescued, Dmitri! Must! You forget, young men like that have a value beyond their deeds, they are not mere machines who perform their duties. They are symbols for our other young officers, and alive they are worth a hundred new tanks or ships. Combat is like that, Comrade. We have forgotten this—and look what has happened in Afghanistan!"

"You are correct, my friend, but—only a few hundred kilometers from the American coast, if that much?"

"Gorshkov talks so much about what his navy can do, let him do this!" Filitov poured another glass. "One more, I think."

"You are not going skiing again, Misha." Ustinov noted that he often fortified himself before driving his car to the woods east of Moscow. "I will not permit it."

"Not today, Dmitri, I promise—though I think it would do me good. Today I will go to the *banya* to take steam and sweat the rest of the poisons from this old carcass. Will you join me?"

"I have to work late."

"The *banya* is good for you," Filitov persisted. It was a waste of time, and both knew it. Ustinov was a member of the "nobility" and would not mingle in the public steam baths. Misha had no such pretentions.

The Dallas

Exactly twenty-four hours after reacquiring the *Red October*, Mancuso called a conference of his senior officers in the wardroom. Things had settled down somewhat. Mancuso had even managed to squeeze in a couple of four-hour naps and was feeling vaguely human again. They now had time to build an accurate sonar picture of the quarry, and the computer was refining a signature classification that would be out to the other fleet attack boats in a matter of weeks. From trailing they had a very accurate model of the propulsion system's noise characteristics, and from the bihourly circling they had also built a picture of the boat's size and power plant specifications.

The executive officer, Wally Chambers, twirled a pencil in his fingers like a baton. "Jonesy's right. It's the same power plant that the *Oscar*s and *Typhoon*s have. They've quieted it down, but the gross signature characteristics are virtually identical. Question is, what's it turning? It sounds like the propellers are ducted somehow, or shrouded. A directional prop with a collar around it, maybe, or some sort of tunnel drive. Didn't we try that once?"

"Long time ago," Lieutenant Butler, the engineering officer, said. "I heard a story about it while I was at Arco. It didn't work out, but I don't remember why. Whatever it is, it's really knocked down on the propulsion noises. That rumble though . . . It's some sort of harmonic all right—but a harmonic what? You know, except for that we'd never have picked it up in the first place."

"Maybe," Mancuso said. "Jonesy says that the signal processors have tended to filter this noise out, almost as though the Soviets know what SAPS does and have tailored a system to beat it. But that's hard to believe." There was general agreement on this point. Everyone knew the principles on which SAPS operated, but there were probably not fifty men in the country who could really explain the nuts and bolts details.

"We're agreed she's a boomer?" Mancuso asked.

Butler nodded. "No way you could fit that power plant into an attack hull. More important, she acts like a boomer."

"Could be an *Oscar*," Chambers suggested.

"No. Why send an *Oscar* this far south? *Oscar*'s an antiship platform. Uh-uh, this guy's driving a boomer. He ran the route at the speed he's running now—and that's acting like a missile boat," Lieutenant Mannion noted. "What are they up to with all this other activity? That's the real question. Maybe trying to sneak up on our coast—just to see if they can do it. It's been done before, and all this other activity makes for a hell of a diversion."

They all considered that. The trick had been tried before by both sides. Most recently, in 1978, a Soviet *Yankee*-class missile sub had closed to the edge of the continental shelf off the coast of New England. The evident objective had been to see if the United States could detect it or not. The navy had succeeded, and then the question had been whether or not to react and let the Soviets know.

"Well, I think we can leave the grand strategy to the folks on the beach. Let's phone this one in. Lieutenant Mannion, tell the OOD to get us to periscope depth in twenty minutes. We'll try to slip away and back without his noticing." Mancuso frowned. This was never easy.

A half an hour later the *Dallas* radioed her message.

Z140925ZDEC

TOP SECRET THEO

FR: USS DALLAS

TO: COMSUBLANT

INFO: CINCLANTFLT

A. USS DALLAS Z090414ZDEC

1. ANOMALOUS CONTACT REACQUIRED 0538Z 13DEC. CURRENT POSITION LAT 42° 35′ LONG 49° 12′. COURSE 194 SPEED 13 DEPTH 600. HAVE TRACKED 24 HOURS WITHOUT COUNTERDETECTION. CONTACT EVALUATED AS REDFLEET SSBN GROSS SIZE, ENGINE CHARACTERISTICS INDICATIVE TYPHOON CLASS. HOWEVER CONTACT USING NEW DRIVE SYSTEM NOT REPEAT NOT PROPELLERS. HAVE ESTABLISHED DETAILED SIGNATURE PROFILE.
2. RETURNING TO TRACKING OPERATIONS. REQUEST ADDITIONAL OPAREA ASSIGNMENTS. AWAIT REPLY 1030Z.

COMSUBLANT Operations

"Bingo!" Gallery said to himself. He walked back to his office, careful to close the door before lifting the scrambled line to Washington.

"Sam, this is Vince. Listen up: *Dallas* reports she is tracking a Russian boomer with a new kind of quiet drive system, about six hundred miles southwest of the Grand Banks, course one-nine-four, speed thirteen knots."

"All right! That's Mancuso?" Dodge said.

"Bartolomeo Vito Mancuso, my favorite Guinea," Gallery confirmed. Getting him this command had not been easy because of his age. Gallery had gone the distance for him. "I told you the kid was good, Sam."

"Jesus, you see how close they are to the *Kiev* group?" Dodge was looking at his tactical display.

"They are cutting it close," Gallery agreed. *"Invincible's* not too far away, though, and I have *Pogy* out there, too. We moved her off the shelf when we called *Scamp* back in. I figure *Dallas* will need help. The question is how obvious do we want to be."

"Not very. Look, Vince, I have to talk to Dan Foster about this."

"Okay. I have to reply to *Dallas* in, hell, in fifty-five minutes. You know the score. He has to break contact to reach us, then sneak back. Hustle, Sam."

"Right, Vince." Dodge switched buttons on his phone. "This is Admiral Dodge. I need to talk to Admiral Foster right now."

The Pentagon

"Ouch. Between *Kiev* and *Kirov*. Nice." Lieutenant General Harris took a marker from his pocket to represent the *Red October*. It was a sub-shaped piece of wood with a Jolly Roger attached. Harris had an odd sense of humor. "The president says we can try and keep her?" he asked.

"If we can get her to the place we want at the time we want," General Hilton said. "Can *Dallas* signal her?"

"Good trick, General." Foster shook his head. "First things first. Let's get *Pogy* and *Invincible* there for starters, then we figure out how to warn him. From this course track, Christ, he's heading right for Norfolk. You believe the balls on this guy? If worse comes to worse, we can always try to escort him in."

"Then we'd have to give the boat back," Admiral Dodge objected.

"We have to have a fall-back position, Sam. If we can't warn him off, we can try and run a bunch of ships through with him to keep Ivan from shooting."

"The law of the sea is your bailiwick, not mine," General Barnes, the air force chief of staff, commented. "But from where I sit doing that could be called anything from piracy to an overt act of war. Isn't this exercise complicated enough already?"

"Good point, General," Foster said.

"Gentlemen, I think we need time to consider this. Okay, we still have time, but right now let's tell *Dallas* to sit tight and track the bugger," Harris said. "And report any changes in course or speed. I figure we have about fifteen minutes to do that. Next we can get *Pogy* and *Invincible* staked out on their path."

"Right, Eddie." Hilton turned to Admiral Foster. "If you agree, let's do that right now."

"Send the message, Sam," Foster ordered.

"Aye aye." Dodge went to the phone and ordered Admiral Gallery to send the reply.

Z141030ZDEC

TOP SECRET

FR: COMSUBLANT

TO: USS DALLAS

A. USS DALLAS Z140925ZDEC

1. CONTINUE TRACKING. REPORT ANY CHANGES IN COURSE OR SPEED. HELP ON THE WAY.
2. ELF TRANSMISSION "G" DESIGNATES FLASH OPS DIRECTIVE READY FOR YOU.
3. YOUR OPAREA UNRESTRICTED BRAVO ZULU DALLAS KEEP IT UP. VADM GALLERY SENDS.

"Okay, let's look at this," Harris said. "What the Russians are up to never has figured, has it?"

"What do you mean, Eddie?" Hilton asked.

"Their force composition for one thing. Half these surface platforms are antiair and antisurface, not primary ASW assets. And why bring *Kirov* along at all? Granted she makes a nice force flag, but they could do the same thing with *Kiev.*"

"We talked about that already," Foster observed. "They ran down the list of what they had that could travel this far at a high speed of advance and took everything that would steam. Same with the subs they sent, half of them are antisurface SSGNs with limited utility against submarines. The reason, Eddie, is that Gorshkov wants every platform here he can get. A half-capable ship is better than nothing. Even one of the old *Echo*es might get lucky, and Sergey is probably hitting the knees every night praying for luck."

"Even so, they've split their surface groups into three forces, each with antiair and antisurface elements, and they're kind of thin on ASW hulls. Nor have they sent their ASW aircraft to stage out of Cuba. Now that is curious," Harris pointed out.

"It would blow their cover story. You don't look for a dead sub with aircraft—well, they might, but if they started using a wing of Bears out of Cuba, the president would go ape," Foster said. "We'd harass them so much they'd never accomplish anything. For us this would be a technical operation, but they factor politics into everything they do."

"Fine, but that still doesn't explain it. What ASW ships and choppers they do have are pinging away like mad. You might look for a dead sub that way, but *October* ain't dead, is she?"

"I don't understand, Eddie," Hilton said.

"How would you look for a stray sub, given these circumstances?" Harris asked Foster.

"Not like this," Foster said after a moment. "Using surface, active sonar would warn the boat off long before they could get a hard contact. Boomers are fat on passive sonar. She'd hear them coming and skedaddle out of the way. You're right, Eddie. It's a sham."

"So what the hell are their surface ships up to?" Barnes asked, puzzled.

"Soviet naval doctrine is to use surface ships to support submarine operations," Harris explained. "Gorshkov is a decent tactical theoretician, and occasionally a very innovative gent.

He said years ago that for submarines to operate effectively they have to have outside help, air or surface assets in direct or proximate support. They can't use air this far from home without staging out of Cuba, and at best finding a boat in open ocean that doesn't want to be found would be a difficult assignment.

"On the other hand, they know where she's heading, a limited number of discrete areas, and those are staked out with fifty-eight submarines. The purpose of the surface forces, therefore, is not to participate in the hunt itself—though if they got lucky, they wouldn't mind. The purpose of the surface forces is to keep us from interfering with their submarines. They can do that by staking out the areas we're likely to be with their surface assets and watching what we're doing." Harris paused for a moment. "That's smart. We have to cover them, right? And since they're on a 'rescue' mission, we have to do more or less what they're doing, so we ping away also, and they can use our own ASW expertise against us for their own purposes. We play right into their hands."

"Why?" Barnes asked again.

"We're committed to helping in the search. If we find their boat, they're close enough to find out, acquire, localize, and shoot—and wh t can we do about it? Not a thing.

"Like I said, they figure to locate and shoot with their submarines. A surface acquisition would be pure luck, and you don't plan for luck. So, the primary objective of the surface fleet is to ride shotgun for, and draw out forces away from, their subs. Secondarily they can act as beaters, driving the game to the shooters—and again, since we're pinging, we're helping them. We're providing an additional stalking horse." Harris shook his head in grudging admiration. "Not too shabby, is it? If *Red October* hears them coming, she runs a little harder for whatever port the skipper wants, right into a nice, tight trap. Dan, what are the chances they can bag her coming into Norfolk, say?"

Foster looked down at the chart. Russian submarines were staked out on every port from Maine to Florida. "They have more subs than we have ports. Now we know that this guy can be picked up, and there's only so much area to cover off each port, even outside the territorial limit . . . You're right, Eddie.

They have too good a chance of making the kill. Our surface groups are too far away to do anything about it. Our subs don't know what's happening, we have orders not to tell them, and even if we could, how could they interfere? Fire at the Russian subs before they could shoot—and start a war?" Foster let out a long breath. "We gotta warn him off."

"How?" Hilton asked.

"Sonar, a gertrude message maybe," Harris suggested.

Admiral Dodge shook his head. "You can hear that through the hull. If we continue to assume that only the officers are in on this, well, the crew might figure out what's happening, and there's no predicting the consequences. Think we can use *Nimitz* and *America* to force them off the coast? They'll be close enough to enter the operation soon. Damn! I don't want this guy to get this close, then get blown away right off our coast."

"Not a chance," Harris said. "Ever since the raid on *Kirov* they've been acting too docile. That's pretty cute, too. I bet they had that figured out. They know that having so many of their ships operating off our coast is bound to provoke us, so they make the first move, we up the ante, and they just plain fold—so now if we keep leaning on them, we're the bad guys. They're just doing a rescue operation, not threatening anybody. The *Post* reported this morning that we have a Russian survivor in the Norfolk naval hospital. Anyway, the good news is that they've miscalculated *October*'s speed. These two groups will pass her left and right, and with their seven-knot speed advantage they'll just pass her by."

"Disregard the surface groups entirely?" Maxwell asked.

"No," Hilton said, "that tells them we are no longer buying the cover story. They'd wonder why—and we still have to cover their surface groups. They're a threat whether they're acting like honest merchants or not."

"What we can do is pretend to release *Invincible*. With *Nimitz* and *America* ready to enter the game, we can send her home. As they pass *October* we can use that to our advantage. We put *Invincible* to seaward of their surface groups as though she's heading home and interpose her on *October*'s course. We still have to figure out a way to communicate with her, though. I can see how to get the assets in place, but that hurdle remains, gentlemen. For the moment, are we agreed to position *Invincible* and *Pogy* for the intercept?"

The Invincible

"How far is she from us?" Ryan asked.

"Two hundred miles. We can be there in ten hours." Captain Hunter marked the position on the chart. "USS *Pogy* is coming east, and she ought to be able to rendezvous with *Dallas* an hour or so after we do. This will put us about a hundred miles east of this surface group when *October* arrives. Bloody hell, *Kiev* and *Kirov* are a hundred miles east and west of her."

"You suppose her captain knows it?" Ryan looked at the chart, measuring the distances with his eyes.

"Unlikely. He's deep, and their passive sonars are not as good as ours. Sea conditions are against it also. A twenty-knot surface wind can play havoc with sonar, even that deep."

"We have to warn him off." Admiral White looked at the ops dispatch. "'Without using acoustical devices.'"

"How the hell do you do that? You can't reach down that far with a radio," Ryan noted. "Even I know that. My God, this guy's come four thousand miles, and he's going to get killed within sight of his objective."

"How to communicate with a submarine?"

Commander Barclay straightened up. "Gentlemen, we are not trying to communicate with a submarine, we are trying to communicate with a man."

"What are you thinking?" Hunter asked.

"What do we know about Marko Ramius?" Barclay's eyes narrowed.

"He's a cowboy, typical submarine commander, thinks he can walk on water," Captain Carstairs said.

"Who spent most of his time in attack submarines," Barclay added. "Marko's bet his life that he could sneak into an American port undetected by anyone. We have to shake that confidence to warn him off."

"We have to talk to him first," Ryan said sharply.

"And so we shall," Barclay smiled, the thought now fully formed in his mind. "He's a former *attack* submarine commander. He'll still be thinking about how to attack his enemies, and how does a sub commander do that?"

"Well?" Ryan demanded.

Barclay's answer was the obvious one. They discussed his

idea for another hour, then Ryan transmitted it to Washington for approval. A rapid exchange of technical information followed. The *Invincible* would have to make the rendezvous in daylight, and there was not time for that. The operation was set back twelve hours. The *Pogy* joined formation with the *Invincible,* standing as sonar sentry twenty miles to her east. An hour before midnight, the ELF transmitter in northern Michigan transmitted a message: "G." Twenty minutes later, the *Dallas* approached the surface to get her orders.

THE THIRTEENTH DAY

WEDNESDAY, 15 DECEMBER

The Dallas

"Crazy Ivan," Jones called out again, "turning to port!"

"Okay, all stop," Mancuso ordered, holding a dispatch in his hand which he had been rereading for hours. He was not pleased with it.

"All stop, sir," the helmsman responded.

"All back full."

"All back full, sir." The helmsman dialed in the command and turned, his face a question.

Throughout the *Dallas* the crew heard noise, too much noise as poppet valves opened to vent steam onto the reverse turbine blades, trying to spin the propeller the wrong way. It made for instant vibration and caviation noises aft.

"Right full rudder."

"Right full rudder, aye."

"Conn, sonar, we are cavitating," Jones spoke over the intercom.

"Very well, sonar!" Mancuso answered sharply. He did not understand his new orders, and things he didn't understand made him angry.

"Speed down to four knots," Lieutenant Goodman reported.

"Rudder amidships, all stop."

"Rudder amidships aye, all stop aye," the helmsman responded at once. He didn't want the captain barking at him. "Sir, my rudder is amidships."

"Jesus!" Jones said in the sonar room. "What's the skipper doin'?"

Mancuso was in sonar a second later.

"Still doing the turn to port, Cap'n. He's astern of us 'cause of the turn we made," Jones observed as neutrally as he could. It was close to an accusation, Mancuso noticed.

"Flushing the game, Jonesy," Mancuso said coolly.

You're the boss, Jones thought, smart enough not to say anything else. The captain looked as though he was going to snap somebody's head off, and Jones had just used up a month's worth of tolerance. He switched his phones to the towed array plug.

"Engine noises diminishing, sir. He's slowing down." Jones paused. He had to report the next part. "Sir, it's a fair guess he heard us."

"He was supposed to," Mancuso said.

The Red October

"Captain, an enemy submarine," the *michman* said urgently.

"Enemy?" Ramius asked.

"American. He must have been trailing us, and he had to back down to avoid a collision when we turned. Definitely an American, broad on the port bow, range under a kilometer, I think." He handed Ramius his phones.

"688," Ramius said to Borodin. "Damn! He must have stumbled across us in the past two hours. Bad luck."

The Dallas

"Okay, Jonesy, yankee-search him." Mancuso gave the order for an active sonar search personally. The *Dallas* had slewed farther around before coming to a near halt.

Jones hesitated for a moment, still reading the reactor plant noise on his passive systems. Reaching, he powered up the active transducers in the BQQ-5's main sphere at the bow.

Ping! A wave front of sound energy was directed at the target.

Pong! The wave was reflected back off the hard steel hull and returned to the *Dallas.*

"Range to target 1,050 yards," Jones said. The returning pulse was processed through the BC-10 computer and showed some rough details. "Target configuration is consistent with a *Typhoon*-class boomer. Angle on the bow seventy or so. No doppler. He's stopped." Six more pings confirmed this.

"Secure pinging," Mancuso said. There was some small satisfaction in learning that he had elevated the contact correctly. But not much.

Jones killed power to the system. What the hell did I have to do that for? he wondered. He'd already done everything but read the number off her stern.

The Red October

Every man on the *October* knew now that they had been found. The lash of the sonar waves had resounded through the hull. It was not a sound a submariner liked to hear. Certainly not on top of a troublesome reactor, Ramius thought. Perhaps he could make use of this . . .

The Dallas

"Somebody on the surface," Jones said suddenly. "Where the hell did they come from? Skipper, there was nothing, *nothing,* a minute ago, and now I'm getting engine sounds. Two, maybe more—make that two 'cans . . . and something bigger. Like they were sitting up there waiting for us. A minute ago they were sitting still. Damn! I didn't hear a *thing.*"

The Invincible

"We timed that rather nicely," Admiral White said.

"Lucky," Ryan observed.

"Luck is part of the game, Jack."

HMS *Bristol* was the first to pick up the sound of the two

submarines and of the turn the *Red October* had made. Even at five miles the subs were barely readable. The Crazy Ivan maneuver had terminated three miles away, and the surface ships had been able to get good position fixes by reading off the *Dallas'* active sonar emissions.

"Two helicopters en route, sir," Captain Hunter reported. "They'll be on station in another minute."

"Signal *Bristol* and *Fife* to stay to windward of us. I want *Invincible* between them and the contact."

"Aye aye, sir." Hunter relayed the order to the communications room. The destroyermen on the escorts would find that order peculiar, using a carrier to screen destroyers.

A few seconds later a pair of Sea King helicopters stopped and hovered fifty feet over the surface, letting down dipping sonars at the end of a cable as they struggled to hold position. These sonars were far less powerful than ship-carried sonars and had distinctive characteristics. The data they developed was transmitted by digital link to the *Invincible*'s command center.

The Dallas

"Limeys," Jones said at once. "That's a helicopter set, the 195, I think. That means the big ship off to the south is one of their baby carriers, sir, with a two-can escort."

Mancuso nodded. "HMS *Invincible*. She was over our side of the lake for NIFTY DOLPHIN. That means the Brit varsity, their best ASW operators."

"The big one's moving this way, sir. Turns indicate ten knots. The choppers—two of them—have both of us. No other subs around that I hear."

The Invincible

"Positive sonar contact," said the metal speaker. "Two submarines, range two miles from *Invincible*, bearing zero-two-zero."

"Now for the hard part," Admiral White said.

Ryan and the four Royal Navy officers who were privy to the mission were on the flag bridge, with the fleet ASW officer in the command center below, as the *Invincible* steamed slowly north, slightly to the left of the direct course to the contacts.

All five swept the contact area with powerful binoculars.

"Come on, Captain Ramius," Ryan said quietly. "You're supposed to be a hotshot. Prove it."

The Red October

Ramius was back in his control room scowling at his chart. A stray American *Los Angeles* stumbling onto him was one thing, but he had run into a small task force. English ships, at that. Why? Probably an exercise. The Americans and the English often work together, and pure accident had walked *October* right into them. Well. He'd have to evade before he could get on with what he wanted to do. It was that simple. Or was it? A hunter submarine, a carrier, and two destroyers after him. What else? He would have to find out if he were going to lose them all. This would take the best part of a day. But now he'd have to see what he was up against. Besides, it would show them that he was confident, that he could hunt *them* if he wished.

"Borodin, bring the ship to periscope depth. Battle stations."

The Invincible

"Come up, Marko," Barclay urged. "We have a message for you, old boy."

"Helicopter three reports contact is coming up," the speaker said.

"All right!" Ryan pounded his hand on the rail.

White lifted a phone. "Recall one of the helicopters."

The distance to the *Red October* was down to a mile and a half. One of the Sea Kings lifted up and circled around, reeling in its sonar transducer.

"Contact depth is five hundred feet, coming up slowly."

The Red October

Borodin was pumping water slowly from the *October*'s trim tanks. The missile submarine increased speed to four knots, and most of the force required to change her depth came from the diving planes. The *starpom* was careful to bring her up slowly, and Ramius had her heading directly towards the *Invincible*.

The Invincible

"Hunter, are you up on your Morse?" Admiral White inquired.

"I believe so, Admiral," Hunter answered. Everyone was getting excited. What a chance this was!

Ryan swallowed hard. In the past few hours, while the *Invincible* had been lying still on the rolling sea, his stomach had really gone bad. The pills the ship's doctor had given him helped, but now the excitement was making it worse. There was an eighty-foot sheer drop from the flag bridge to the sea. Well, he thought, if I have to puke, there's nothing in the way. Screw it.

The Dallas

"Hull popping noises, sir," Jones said. "Think he's heading up."

"Up?" Mancuso wondered for a second. "Yeah, that fits. He's a cowboy. He wants to see what he's up against before he tries to evade. That fits. I bet he doesn't know where we've been the past few days." The captain went forward to the attack center.

"Looks like he's going up, Skipper," Mannion said, watching the attack director. "Dumb." Mannion had his own opinion of submarine captains depending on their periscopes. Too many of them spent too much time looking out at the world. He wondered how much of this was an implicit reaction to the enforced confinement of submarining, something just to make sure that there really was a world up there, to make sure the instruments were correct. Entirely human, Mannion thought, but it could make you vulnerable...

"We go up, too, Skipper?"

"Yeah, slow and easy."

The Invincible

The sky was half-filled with white, fleecy clouds, their undersides gray with the threat of rain. A twenty-knot wind was blowing from the southwest, and a six-foot sea was running, its dark waves streaked with whitecaps. Ryan saw the *Bristol* and *Fife* holding station to windward. Their captains, no doubt, were muttering a few choice words at this disposition. The American escorts, which had been detached the previous day, were now sailing to rendezvous with the USS *New Jersey.*

White was talking into the phone again. "Commander, I want to know the instant we get a radar return from the target area. Train every set aboard onto that patch of ocean. I also want to know of any, repeat any, sonar signals from the area ... That is correct. Depth of target? Very well. Recall the second helicopter, I want both on station to windward."

They had agreed that the best method of passing the message would be to use a blinker light. Only someone placed in the direct line of sight would be able to read the signal. Hunter moved to the light, holding a sheet of paper Ryan had given him. The yeomen and signalmen normally stationed here were gone.

The Red October

"Thirty meters, Comrade Captain," Borodin reported. The battle watch was set in the control center.

"Periscope," Ramius said calmly. The oiled metal tube hissed upward on hydraulic pressure. The captain handed his cap to the junior officer of the watch as he bent to look into the eyepiece. "So, we have here three imperialist ships. HMS *Invincible.* Such a name for a ship!" He scoffed for his audience. "Two escorts, *Bristol*, and a County-class cruiser."

The Invincible

"Periscope, starboard bow!" the speaker announced.

"I see it!" Barclay's hand shot out to point. "There it is!"

Ryan strained to find it. "I got it." It was like a small broomstick sitting vertically in the water, about a mile away. As the waves rolled past, the bottommost visible part of the periscope flared out.

"Hunter," White said quietly. To Ryan's left the captain began jerking his hand on the lever that controlled the light shutters.

The Red October

Ramius didn't see it at first. He was making a complete circle of the horizon, checking for any other ships or aircraft. When he finished the circuit, the flashing light caught his eye. Quickly he tried to interpret the signal. It took him a moment to realize it was pointed right at him.

AAA AAA AAA RED OCTOBER RED OCTOBER CAN YOU READ THIS CAN YOU READ THIS PLEASE PING US ONE TIME ON ACTIVE SONAR IF YOU CAN READ THIS PLEASE PING US ONE TIME ON ACTIVE SONAR IF YOU CAN READ THIS AAA AAA AAA RED OCTOBER RED OCTOBER CAN YOU READ THIS CAN YOU READ THIS

The message kept repeating. The signal was jerky and awkward. Ramius didn't notice this. He translated the English signal in his head, at first thinking it was a signal to the American submarine. His knuckles went white on the periscope hand grips as he translated the message in his mind.

"Borodin," he said finally, after reading the message a fourth time, "we set up a practice firing solution on *Invincible*. Damn, the periscope rangefinder is sticking. A single ping, Comrade. Just one, for range."

Ping!

The Invincible

"One ping from the contact area, sir, sounds Soviet," the speaker reported.

White lifted his phone. "Thank you. Keep us informed." He set it back down. "Well, gentlemen . . ."

"He did it!" Ryan sang out. "Send the rest, for Christ's sake!"

"At once." Hunter grinned like a madman.

RED OCTOBER RED OCTOBER YOUR WHOLE FLEET IS CHASING AFTER YOU YOUR WHOLE FLEET IS CHASING AFTER YOU YOUR PATH IS

BLOCKED BY NUMEROUS VESSELS NUMEROUS
ATTACK SUBMARINES ARE WAITING TO ATTACK
YOU REPEAT NUMEROUS ATTACK SUBMARINES
ARE WAITING TO ATTACK YOU PROCEED TO
RENDEZVOUS 33N 75W WE HAVE SHIPS THERE
WAITING FOR YOU REPEAT PROCEED TO REN-
DEZVOUS 33N 75W WE HAVE SHIPS THERE WAIT-
ING FOR YOU IF YOU UNDERSTAND AND AGREE
PLEASE PING US AGAIN ONE TIME

The Red October

"Distance to target, Borodin?" Ramius asked, wishing he had
more time as the message was repeated again and again.

"Two thousand meters, Comrade Captain. A nice, fat target
for us if we . . ." The *starpom*'s voice trailed off as he saw the
look on his commander's face.

They know our name, Ramius was thinking, *they know our
name! How can this be? They knew where to find us—exactly!
How? What can the Americans have? How long has the* Los
Angeles *been trailing us? Decide—you must decide!*

"Comrade, one more ping on the target, just one."

The Invincible

"One more ping, Admiral."

"Thank you." White looked at Ryan. "Well, Jack, it would
seem that your intelligence estimate was indeed correct. Jolly
good."

"Jolly good my ass, my Lord Earl! I was right. Son of a
bitch!" Ryan's hands flew up in the air, his seasickness forgotten. He calmed down. The occasion called for more decorum. "Excuse me, Admiral. We have some things to do."

The Dallas

Whole fleet is chasing after you . . . Proceed to 33N 75W. What
the hell was going on? Mancuso wondered, catching the end
of the second signal.

"Conn, sonar. Getting hull popping noises from the target.
His depth is changing. Engine noise increasing."

"Down scope." Mancuso lifted the phone. "Very well, sonar. Anything else, Jones?"

"No, sir. The helicopters are gone, and there aren't any emissions from the surface ships. What gives, sir?"

"Beats me." Mancuso shook his head as Mannion brought the *Dallas* back in pursuit of the *Red October*. What the hell was happening here? the captain wondered. Why was a Brit carrier signaling to a Russian submarine, and why were they sending her to a rendezvous off the Carolinas? *Whose* subs were blocking her path? It couldn't be. No way. It just couldn't be . . .

The Invincible

Ryan was in the *Invincible*'s communications room. "MAGI TO OLYMPUS," he typed into the special encoding device the CIA had sent out with him, "PLAYED MY MANDOLIN TODAY. SOUNDED PRETTY GOOD. I'M PLANNING A LITTLE CONCERT, AT THE USUAL PLACE. EXPECT GOOD CRITICAL REVIEWS. AWAITING INSTRUCTIONS." Ryan had laughed before at the code words he was supposed to use for this. He was laughing now, for a different reason.

The White House

"So," Pelt observed, "Ryan expects the mission will be successful. Everything's going according to plan, but he didn't use the code group for certain success."

The president leaned back comfortably. "He's honest. Things can always go wrong. You have to admit, though, things do look good."

"This plan the chiefs came up with is crazy, sir."

"Perhaps, but you've been trying to poke a hole in it for several days now, and you haven't succeeded. The pieces will all fall in place shortly."

The president was being clever, Pelt saw. The man liked being clever.

The Invincible

"OLYMPUS TO MAGI. I LIKE OLD-FASHIONED MANDOLIN MUSIC. CONCERT APPROVED," the message said.

Ryan sat back comfortably, sipping at his brandy. "Well, that's good. I wonder what the next part of the plan is."

"I expect that Washington will let us know. For the moment," Admiral White said, "we'll have to move back west to interpose ourselves between *October* and the Soviet fleet."

The Avalon

Lieutenant Ames surveyed the scene through the tiny port on the *Avalon*'s bow. The *Alfa* lay on her port side. She had obviously hit stern first, and hard. One blade was snapped off the propeller, and the lower rudder fin was smashed. The whole stern might have been knocked off true; it was hard to tell in the low visibility.

"Moving forward slowly," he said, adjusting the controls. Behind him an ensign and a senior petty officer were monitoring instruments and preparing to deploy the manipulator arm, attached before they sailed, which carried a television camera and floodlights. These gave them a slightly wider field of view than the navigation ports permitted. The DSRV crept forward at one knot. Visibility was under twenty yards, despite the million candles of illumination from the bow lights.

The sea floor at this point was a treacherous slope of alluvial silt dotted with boulders. It appeared that the only thing that had prevented the *Alfa* from sliding farther down was her sail, driven like a wedge into the bottom.

"Holy gawd!" The petty officer saw it first. There was a crack in the *Alfa*'s hull—or was there?

"Reactor accident," Ames said, his voice detached and clinical. "Something burned through the hull. Lord, and that's *titanium!* Burned right through, from the inside out. There's another one, two burn-throughs. This one's bigger, looks like a good yard across. No mystery what killed her, guys. That's two compartments open to the sea." Ames looked over to the depth gauge: 1,880 feet. "Getting all this on tape?"

"Aye, Skipper," the electrician first class answered. "Crummy way to die. Poor bastards."

"Yeah, depending on what they were up to." Ames maneuvered the *Avalon* around the *Alfa*'s bow, working the directional propeller carefully and adjusting trim to cruise down the other side, actually the top of the dead sub. "See any evidence of a hull fracture?"

"No," the ensign answered, "just the two burn-throughs. I wonder what went wrong?"

"A for-real China Syndrome. It finally happened to somebody." Ames shook his head. If there was anything the navy preached about reactors, it was safety. "Get the transducer against the hull. We'll see if anybody's alive in there."

"Aye." The electrician worked the waldo controls as Ames tried to keep the *Avalon* dead still. Neither task was easy. The DSRV was hovering, nearly resting on the sail. If there were survivors, they had to be in the control room or forward. There could be no life aft.

"Okay, I got contact."

All three men listened intently, hoping for something. Their job was search and rescue, and as submariners themselves they took it seriously.

"Maybe they're asleep." The ensign switched on the locater sonar. The high-frequency waves resonated through both vessels. It was a sound fit to wake the dead, but there was no response. The air supply in the *Politovskiy* had run out a day before.

"That's that," Ames said quietly. He maneuvered upward as the electrician rigged in the manipulator arm, looking for a spot to drop a sonar transponder. They would be back again when the topside weather was better. The navy would not pass up this chance to inspect an *Alfa*, and the *Glomar Explorer* was sitting unused somewhere on the West Coast. Would she be activated? Ames would not bet against that.

"*Avalon, Avalon,* this is *Scamp*—" the voice on the gertrude was distorted but readable, "—return at once. Acknowledge."

"*Scamp,* this is *Avalon.* On the way."

The *Scamp* had just received an ELF message and gone briefly to periscope depth for a FLASH operational order. "PROCEED AT BEST SPEED TO 33N 75W." The message didn't say why.

CIA Headquarters

"CARDINAL is still with is," Moore told Ritter.

"Thank God for that." Ritter sat down.

"There's a signal en route. This time he didn't try to kill himself getting it to us. Maybe being in the hospital scared him a little. I'm extending another offer to extract him."

"Again?"

"Bob, we have to make the offer."

"I know. I had one sent myself a few years back, you know. The old bastard just doesn't want to quit. You know how it goes, some people thrive on the action. Or maybe he hasn't worked out his rage yet . . . I just got a call from Senator Donaldson." Donaldson was the chairman of the Select Committee on Intelligence.

"Oh?"

"He wants to know what we know about what's going on. He doesn't buy the cover story about a rescue mission, and thinks we know something different."

Judge Moore leaned back. "I wonder who planted that idea in his head?"

"Yeah. I have a little idea we might try. I think it's time, and this is a dandy opportunity."

The two senior executives discussed this for an hour. Before Ritter left for the Hill, they cleared it with the president.

Washington, D.C.

Donaldson kept Ritter waiting in his outer office for fifteen minutes while he read the paper. He wanted Ritter to know his place. Some of the DDO's remarks about leaks from the Hill had touched a sore spot with the senator from Connecticut, and it was important for appointed and civil service officials to understand the difference between themselves and the elected representatives of the people.

"Sorry to keep you waiting, Mr. Ritter." Donaldson did not rise, nor did he offer to shake hands.

"Quite all right, sir. Took the chance to read a magazine. Don't get to do that much, what with the schedule I work." They fenced with each other from the first moment.

"So, what are the Soviets up to?"

"Senator, before I address that subject, I must say this: I had to clear this meeting with the president. This information is for you alone, no one else may hear it, sir. No one. That comes from the White House."

"There are other men on my committee, Mr. Ritter."

"Sir, if I do not have your word, as a gentleman," Ritter added with a smile, "I will not reveal this information. Those are my orders. I work for the executive branch, Senator. I take my orders from the president." Ritter hoped his recording device was getting all of this.

"Agreed," Donaldson said reluctantly. He was angry because of the foolish restrictions, but pleased that he was getting to hear this. "Go on."

"Frankly, sir, we're not sure exactly what's going on," Ritter said.

"Oh, so you've sworn me to secrecy so that I can't tell anyone that, again, the CIA doesn't know what the hell is going on?"

"I said we don't know exactly what's happening. We do know a few things. Our information comes mainly from the Israelis, and some from the French. From both channels we have learned that something has gone very wrong with the Soviet Navy."

"I gathered that. They've lost a sub."

"At least one, but that's not what's going on. Someone, we think, has played a trick on the operations directorate of the Soviet Northern Fleet. I can't say for sure, but I think it was the Poles."

"Why the Poles?"

"I don't know for sure that it is, but both the French and Israelis are well connected with the Poles, *and* the Poles have a long-standing beef with the Soviets. I do know—at least I think I know—that whatever this is did not come from a Western intelligence agency."

"So, what's happening?" Donaldson demanded.

"Our best guess is that someone has committed at least one forgery, possibly as many as three, all aimed at raising hell in the Soviet Navy—but whatever it was, it's gotten far out of hand. A lot of people are working hard to cover their asses, the Israelis say. As a guess, I think they managed to alter a submarine's operational orders, then forged a letter from her skipper threatening to fire his missiles. The amazing thing is that the Soviets went for it." Ritter frowned. "We may have it all backwards, though. All we really know for sure is that somebody, probably the Poles, has played a fantastic dirty trick on the Russians."

"Not us?" Donaldson asked pointedly.

"No, sir, absolutely not! If we tried something like that—even if we succeeded, which isn't likely—they might try the same thing with us. You could start a war that way, and you know the president would never authorize it."

"But someone at the CIA might not care what the president thinks."

"Not in my department! It would be my head. Do you really think we could run an operation like this and then successfully conceal it? Hell, Senator, I *wish* we could."

"Why the Poles, and why are they able to do it?"

"We've been hearing for some time about a dissident faction inside their intelligence community, one that does not especially love the Soviets. You can pick any number of reasons why. There's the fundamental historical enmity, and the Russians seem to forget that the Poles are Polish first, Communists second. My own guess is that it's this business with the pope, even more than the martial law thing. We know that our old friend Andropov initiated a replay of the Edward II/Becket business. The pope has given Poland a great deal of prestige, done things for the country that even Party members feel good about. Ivan went and spit on their whole country when he did that—you wonder that they're mad? As to their ability, people seem to overlook just what a class act their intelligence service always has been. They're the ones who made the Enigma break-through in 1939, not the Brits. They're damned effective, and for the same reason as the Israelis. They have enemies to the east and the west. That sort of thing breeds good agents. We know for certain that they have a lot of people inside Russia, guest workers paying Narmonov off for the economic supports given to their country. We also know that a lot of Polish engineers are working in Soviet shipyards. I admit it's funny, neither country has much of a maritime tradition, but the Poles build a lot of Soviet merchant hulls. Their yards are more efficient than the Russian ones, and lately they've been giving technical help, mainly in quality control, to the naval building yards."

"So, the Polish intelligence service has played a trick on

the Soviets," Donaldson summarized. "Gorshkov is one of the guys who took a hard line on intervention, wasn't he?"

"True, but he's probably just a target of opportunity. The real aim of this has to be to embarrass Moscow. The fact that this operation attacks the Soviet Navy has no significance in itself. The objective is to raise hell in their senior military channels, and they all come together in Moscow. God, I wish I knew what was really happening! From the five percent we do know, this operation has to be a real masterpiece, the sort of thing legends are made of. We're working on it, trying to find out. So are the Brits, and the French, and the Israelis— Benny Herzog of the Mossad is supposed to be going ape. The Israelis *do* pull this kind of trick on their neighbors, regularly. They say officially that they don't know anything beyond what they've told us. Maybe so. Or maybe they gave the Poles some technical help—hard to say. It's certain that the Soviet Navy is a strategic threat to Israel. But we need more time on that. The Israeli connection looks a little too pat at this point."

"But you don't know what's happening, just the how and why."

"Senator, it's not that easy. Give us some time. At the moment we may not even want to know. To summarize, somebody has laid a colossal piece of disinformation on the Soviet Navy. It was probably aimed at merely shaking them up, but it has clearly gotten out of hand. How or why it happened, we do not know. You can bet, however, that whoever initiated this operation is working very hard to cover his tracks." Ritter wanted the senator to get this right. "If the Soviets find out who did it, their reaction will be nasty—depend on it. In a few weeks we might know more. The Israelis owe us for a few things, and eventually they'll let us in on it."

"For a couple more F-15s and a company of tanks," Donaldson observed.

"Cheap at the price."

"But if we're not involved in this, why the secrecy?"

"You gave me your word, Senator," Ritter reminded him. "For one thing, if word leaked out, would the Soviets believe we're not involved? Not likely! We're trying to civilize the intelligence game. I mean, we're still enemies, but having the various intelligence services in conflict uses up too many assets, and it's dangerous to both sides. For another, well, if we ever do find out how all this happened, we just might want to make use of it ourselves."

"Those reasons are contraditory."

Ritter smiled. "The intelligence game is like that. If we find out who did this, we can use that information to our advantage. In any case, Senator, you gave me your word, and I will report that to the president on my return to Langley."

"Very well." Donaldson rose. The interview was at an end. "I trust you will keep us informed of future developments."

"That's what we have to do, sir." Ritter stood.

"Indeed. Thank you for coming down." They did not shake hands this time either.

Ritter walked into the hall without passing through the ante-room. He stopped to look down into the antrium of the Hart building. It reminded him of the local Hyatt. Uncharacteristically, he took the stairs instead of the elevator down to the first floor. With luck he had just settled a major score. His car was waiting for him outside, and he told the driver to head for the FBI building.

"Not a CIA operation?" Peter Henderson, the senator's chief aide, asked.

"No, I believe him," Donaldson said. "He's not smart enough to pull something like that."

"I don't know why the president doesn't get rid of him," Henderson commented. "Of course, the kind of person he is, maybe it's better that he's incompetent." The senator agreed.

When he returned to his office, Henderson adjusted the venetian blinds on his window, though the sun was on the other side of the building. An hour later the driver of a passing Black & White taxicab looked up at the window and made a mental note.

Henderson worked late that night. The Hart building was nearly empty with most of the senators out of town. Donaldson was there only because of personal business and to keep an eye on things. As chairman of the Select Committee on Intelligence, he had more duties than he would have liked at this time of year. Henderson took the elevator down to the main lobby, looking every inch the senior congressional aide—a three-piece gray suit, an expensive leather attaché case, his hair just so, and his stride jaunty as he left the building. A Black & White cab came around the corner and stopped to let out a fare. Henderson got in.

"Watergate," he said. Not until the taxi had driven a few blocks did he speak again.

Henderson had a modest one-bedroom condo in the Watergate complex, an irony that he himself had considered many times. When he got to his destination he did not tip the driver. A woman got in as he walked to the main entrance. Taxis in Washington are very busy in the early evening.

"Georgetown University, please," she said, a pretty young woman with auburn hair and an armload of books.

"Night school?" the driver asked, checking the mirror.

"Exams," the girl said, her voice a trace uneasy. "Psych."

"Best thing to do with exams is relax," the driver advised. Special Agent Hazel Loomis fumbled with her books. Her purse dropped to the floor. "Oh, damn." She bent over to pick it up, and while doing so retrieved a miniature tape recorder that another agent had left under the driver's seat.

It took fifteen minutes to get to the university. The fare was $3.85. Loomis gave the driver a five and told him to keep the change. She walked across the campus and entered a Ford which drove straight to the J. Edgar Hoover Building. A lot of work had gone into this—and it had been so easy!

"Always is, when the bear walks into your sight." The inspector who had been running the case turned left onto Pennsylvania Avenue. "The problem is finding the damned bear in the first place."

The Pentagon

"Gentlemen, you have been asked here because each of you is a career intelligence officer with a working knowledge of submarines and Russian," Davenport said to the four officers seated in his office. "I have need of officers with your qualifications. This is a volunteer assignment. It could involve a considerable element of danger—we cannot be sure at this point. The only other thing I can say is that this will be a dream job for an intelligence officer—but the sort of dream that you'll never be able to tell anyone about. We're all used to that, aren't we?"

Davenport ventured a rare smile. "As they say in the movies, if you want in, fine; if not, you may leave at this point, and nothing will ever be said. It is asking a lot to expect men to walk into a potentially dangerous assignment blindfolded."

Of course nobody left; the men who had been called here were not quitters. Besides, something would be said, and Davenport had a good memory. These were professional officers. One of the compensations for wearing a uniform and earning less money than an equally talented man can make in the real world is the off chance of being killed.

"Thank you, gentlemen. I think you will find this worth your while." Davenport stood and handed each man a manila envelope. "You will soon have the chance to examine a Soviet missile submarine—from the inside." Four pairs of eyes blinked in unison.

33N 75W

The USS *Ethan Allen* had been on station now for more than thirty hours. She was cruising in a five-mile circle at a depth of two hundred feet. There was no hurry. The submarine was making just enough speed to maintain steerage way, her reactor producing only ten percent of rated power. The chief quartermaster was assisting in the galley.

"First time I've ever done this in a sub," one of the *Allen*'s officers who was acting as ship's cook noted, stirring an omelette.

The quartermaster sighed imperceptibly. They ought to have sailed with a proper cook, but theirs had been a kid, and every enlisted man aboard now had over twenty years of service. The chiefs were all technicians, except the quartermaster, who could handle a toaster on a good day.

"You cook much at home, sir?"

"Some. My parents used to have a restaurant down at Pass Christian. This is my mama's special Cajun omelette. Shame we don't have any bass. I can do some nice things with bass and a little lemon. You fish much, Chief?"

"No, sir." The small complement of officers and senior chiefs was working in an informal atmosphere, and the quartermaster was a man accustomed to discipline and status boundaries. "Commander, can I ask what the hell we're doing?"

"Wish I knew, Chief. Mostly we're waiting for something."

"But what, sir?"

"Damned if I know. You want to hand me those ham cubes? And could you check the bread in the oven? Ought to be about done."

The New Jersey

Commander Eaton was perplexed. His battle group was holding twenty miles south of the Russians. If it hadn't been dark he could have seen the *Kirov's* towering superstructure on the horizon from his perch on the flat bridge. Her escorts were in a single broad line ahead of the battle cruiser, pinging away in the search for a submarine.

Since the air force had staged its mock attack the Soviets had been acting like sheep. This was out of character to say the least. The *New Jersey* and her escorts were keeping the Russian formation under constant observation, and a pair of Sentry aircraft were watching for good measure. The Russian redeployment had switched Eaton's responsibility to the *Kirov* group. This suited him. His main battery turrets were trained in, but the guns were loaded with eight-inch guided rounds and the fire control stations were fully manned. The *Tarawa* was thirty miles south, her armed strike force of Harriers sitting ready to move at five-minute notice. The Soviets had to know this, even though their ASW helicopters had not come within five miles of an American ship for two days. The Bear and Backfire bombers which were passing overhead in shuttle rounds to Cuba—only a few, and those returning to Russia as quickly as they could be turned around—could not fail to report what they saw. The American vessels were in extended attack formation, the missiles on the *New Jersey* and her escorts being fed continuous information from the ships' sensors. And the Russians were ignoring them. Their only electronic emissions were routine navigation radars. Strange.

The *Nimitz* was now within air range after a five-thousand-mile dash from the South Atlantic; the carrier and her nuclear-powered escorts, the *California, Bainbridge,* and *Truxton,* were now only four hundred miles to the south, with the *America* battle group half a day behind them. The *Kennedy* was five hundred miles to the east. The Soviets would have to consider the danger of three carrier air wings at their backs and hundreds of land-based air force birds gradually shifting south from one base to another. Perhaps this explained their docility.

The Backfire bombers were being escorted in relays all the way from Iceland, first by navy Tomcats from the *Saratoga*'s air wing, then by air force Phantoms operating in Maine, which handled the Soviet aircraft off to Eagles and Fighting Falcons as they worked down the coast almost as far south as Cuba. There was not much doubt how seriously the United States was taking this, though American units were no longer actively harassing the Russians. Eaton was glad they weren't. There was nothing more to be gained from harassment, and anyway, if it had to, his battle group could switch from a peace to a war footing in about two minutes.

The Watergate Apartments

"Excuse me. I just moved in down the hall, and my phone isn't hooked up yet. Would you mind if I made a call?"

Henderson arrived at that decision quickly enough. Five three or so, auburn hair, gray eyes, adequate figure, a dazzling smile, and fashionably dressed. "Sure, welcome to the Watergate. Come on in."

"Thank you. I'm Hazel Loomis. My friends call me Sissy." She held out her hand.

"Peter Henderson. The phone's in the kitchen. I'll show you." Things were looking up. He'd just ended a lengthy relationship with one of the senator's secretaries. It had been hard on both of them.

"I'm not disturbing anything, am I? You don't have anyone here, do you?"

"No, just me and the TV. Are you new to D.C.? The night life isn't all it's cracked up to be. At least, not when you have to go to work the next day. Who do you work for—I take it you're single?"

"That's right. I work for DARPA, as a computer programmer. I'm afraid I can't talk about it very much."

All sorts of good news, Henderson thought. "Here's the phone."

Loomis looked around quickly as though evaluating the job

the decorator had done. She reached into her purse and took
out a dime, handing it to Henderson. He laughed.

"The first call is free, and believe me, you can use my phone
whenever you want."

"I just knew," she said, punching the buttons, "that this
would be nicer than living in Laurel. Hello, Kathy? Sissy. I
just got moved in, haven't even got my phone hooked up yet
... Oh, a guy down the hall was kind enough to let me use his
phone ... Okay, see you tomorrow for lunch. Bye, Kathy."

Loomis looked around. "Who decorated for you?"

"Did it myself. I minored in art at Harvard, and I know
some nice shops in Georgetown. You can find some good
bargains if you know where to look."

"Oh, I'd just *love* to have my place look like this! Could
you show me around?"

"Sure, the bedroom first?" Henderson laughed to show that
he had no untoward intentions—which of course he did, though
he was a patient man in such matters. The tour, which lasted
several minutes, assured Loomis that the condo was indeed
empty. A minute later there was a knock at the door. Henderson
grumbled good-naturedly as he went to answer it.

"Pete Henderson?" The man asking the question was dressed
in a business suit. Henderson had on jeans and a sport shirt.

"Yes?" Henderson backed up, knowing what this had to be.
What came next, though, surprised him.

"You're under arrest, Mr. Henderson," Sissy Loomis said,
holding up her ID card. "The charge is espionage. You have
the right to remain silent, you have the right to speak with an
attorney. If you give up the right to remain silent, everything
you say will be recorded and may be used against you. If you
do not have an attorney or cannot afford one, we will see to
it that an attorney is appointed to represent you. Do you understand these rights, Mr. Henderson?" It was Sissy Loomis'
first espionage case. For five years she had specialized in bank
robbery stakeouts, often working as a teller with a .357 magnum
revolver in her cash drawer. "Do you wish to waive these
rights?"

"No, I do not." Henderson's voice was raspy.

"Oh, you will," the inspector observed. "You will." He
turned to the three agents who accompanied him. "Take this

place apart. Neatly, gentlemen, and quietly. We don't want to wake anyone. You, Mr. Henderson, will come with us. You can change first. We can do this the easy way or the hard way. If you promise to cooperate, no cuffs. But if you try to run— you don't want to do that, believe me." The inspector had been in the FBI for twenty years and had never even drawn his service revolver in anger, while Loomis had already shot and killed two men. He was old-time FBI, and couldn't help but wonder what Mr. Hoover would think of that, not to mention the new Jewish director.

The Red October

Ramius and Kamarov conferred over the chart for several minutes, tracing alternate course tracks before agreeing on one. The enlisted men ignored this. They had never been encouraged to know about charts. The captain walked to the aft bulkhead and lifted the phone.

"Comrade Melekhin," he ordered, waiting a few seconds. "Comrade, this is the captain. Any further difficulties with the reactor systems?"

"No, Comrade Captain."

"Excellent. Hold things together another two days." Ramius hung up. It was thirty minutes to the turn of the next watch.

Melekhin and Kirill Surzpoi, the assistant engineer, had the duty in the engine room. Melekhin monitored the turbines and Surzpoi handled the reactor systems. Each had a *michman* and three enlisted men in attendance. The engineers had had a very busy cruise. Every gauge and monitor in the engine spaces, it seemed, had been inspected, and many had been entirely rebuilt by the two senior officers, who had been helped by Valintin Bugayev, the electronics officer and on-board genius who was also handling the political awareness classes for the crewmen. The engine room crewmen were the most rattled on the vessel. The supposed contamination was common knowledge—there are no long-lived secrets on a submarine. To ease their loads ordinary seamen were supplementing the engine watches. The captain called this a good chance for the cross-training he believed in. The crew thought it was a good way to get poisoned. Discipline was being maintained, of course. This was owing partly to the trust the men had in their commanding officer, partly to their training, but mostly to their knowledge of what would happen if they failed to carry out their orders immediately and enthusiastically.

"Comrade Melekhin," Surzpoi called, "I am showing pressure fluctuation on the main loop, number six gauge."

"Coming." Melekhin hurried over and shoved the *michman* out of the way when he got to the master control panel. "More bad instruments! The others show normal. Nothing important," the chief engineer said blandly, making sure everyone could hear. The whole compartment watch saw the chief engineer whisper something to his assistant. The younger one shook his head slowly, while two sets of hands worked the controls.

A loud two-phase buzzer and a rotating red alarm light went off.

"SCRAM the pile!" Melekhin ordered.

"SCRAMing." Surzpoi stabbed his finger on the master shutdown button.

"You men, get forward!" Melekhin ordered next. There was no hesitation. "No, you, connect battery power to the caterpillar motors, quickly!"

The warrant officer raced back to throw the proper switches, cursing his change of orders. It took forty seconds.

"Done, Comrade!"

"Go!"

The warrant officer was the last man out of the compartment. He made certain that the hatches were dogged down tight before running to the control room.

"What is the problem?" Ramius asked calmly.

"Radiation alarm in the heat-exchange room!"

"Very well, go forward and shower with the rest of your watch. Get control of yourself." Ramius patted the *michman* on the arm. "We have had these problems before. You are a trained man. The crewmen look to you for leadership."

Ramius lifted the phone. It was a moment before the other end was picked up. "What has happened, Comrade?" The control room crew watched their captain listen to the answer. They could not help but admire his calm. Radiation alarms had sounded throughout the hull. "Very well. We do not have too many hours of battery power left, Comrade. We must go to snorkling depth. Stand by to activate the diesel. Yes." He hung up.

"Comrades, you will listen to me." Ramius' voice was under total control. "There has been a minor failure in the reactor control systems. The alarm you heard was not a major radiation leak, but rather a failure of the reactor rod control systems. Comrades Melekhin and Surzpoi successfully executed an emergency reactor shutdown, but we cannot operate the reactor properly without the primary controls. We will, therefore, complete our cruise on diesel power. To ensure against any *possible* radiation contamination, the reactor spaces have been isolated, and all compartments, engineering spaces first, will be vented with surface air when we snorkle. Kamarov, you will go aft to work the environmental controls. I will take the conn."

"Aye, Comrade Captain!" Kamarov went aft.

Ramius lifted the microphone to give this news to the crew. Everyone was waiting for something. Forward, some crewmen muttered among themselves that *minor* was a word suffering from overuse, that nuclear submarines did not run on diesel and ventilate with surface air for the hell of it.

Finished with his terse announcement, Ramius ordered the submarine to approach the surface.

The Dallas

"Beats me, Skipper." Jones shook his head. "Reactor noises have stopped, pumps are cut way back, but he's running at the same speed, just like before. On battery, I guess."

"Must be a hell of a battery system to drive something that big this fast," Mancuso observed.

"I did some computations on that a few hours ago." Jones held up his pad. "This is based on the *Typhoon* hull, with a nice slick hull coefficient, so it's probably conservative."

"Where did you learn to do this, Jonesy?"

"Mr. Thompson looked up the hydrodynamic stuff for me. The electrical end is fairly simple. He might have something exotic—fuel cells, maybe. If not, if he's running ordinary batteries, he has enough raw electrical power to crank every car in L.A."

Mancuso shook his head. "Can't last forever."

Jones held up his hand. "Hull creaking . . . Sounds like he's going up some."

The Red October

"Raise snorkle," Ramius said. Looking through the periscope he verified that the snorkle was up. "Well, no other ships in view. That is good news. I think we have lost our imperialist hunters. Raise the ESM antenna. Let's be sure no enemy aircraft are lurking about with their radars."

"Clear, Comrade Captain." Bugayev was manning the ESM board. "Nothing at all, not even airline sets."

"So, we have indeed lost our rat pack." Ramius lifted the phone again. "Melekhin, you may open the main induction and vent the engine spaces, then start the diesel." A minute later everyone aboard felt the vibration as the *October*'s massive diesel engine cranked on battery power. This sucked up all the air from the reactor spaces, replacing it with air drawn through the snorkle and ejecting the "contaminated" air into the sea.

The engine continued to crank two minutes, and throughout the hull men waited for the rumble that would mean the engine had caught and could generate power to run the electric motors. It didn't catch. After another thirty seconds the cranking stopped. The control room phone buzzed. Ramius lifted it.

"What is wrong with the diesel, Comrade Chief Engineer?" the captain asked sharply. "I see. I'll send men back—oh. Stand by." Ramius looked around, his mouth a thin, bloodless smile. The junior engineering officer, Svyadov, was standing at the back of the compartment. "I need a man who knows diesel engines to help Comrade Melekhin."

"I grew up on a State farm," Bugayev said. "I started playing with tractor engines as a boy."

"There is an additional problem . . ."

Bugayev nodded knowingly. "So I gather, Comrade Captain, but we need the diesel, do we not?"

"I will not forget this, Comrade," Ramius said quietly.

"Then you can buy me some rum in Cuba, Comrade." Bugayev smiled courageously. "I wish to meet a Cuban comrade, preferably one with long hair."

"May I accompany you, Comrade?" Svyadov asked anxiously. He had just been going on watch, approaching the reactor room hatch, when he'd been knocked aside by escaping crewmen.

"Let us assess the nature of the problem first," Bugayev said, looking at Ramius for confirmation.

"Yes, there is plenty of time. Bugayev, report to me yourself in ten minutes."

"Aye aye, Comrade Captain."

"Svyadov, take charge of the lieutenant's station." Ramius pointed to the ESM board. "Use the opportunity to learn some new skills."

The lieutenant did as he was ordered. The captain seemed very preoccupied. Svyadov had never seen him like this before.

THE FOURTEENTH DAY

THURSDAY, 16 DECEMBER

A Super Stallion

They were traveling at one hundred fifty knots, two thousand feet over the darkened sea. The Super Stallion helicopter was old. Built towards the end of the Vietnam War, she had first seen service clearing mines off Haiphong harbor. That had been her primary duty, pulling a sea sled and acting as a flying minesweeper. Now, the big Sikorski was used for other purposes, mainly long-range heavy-lift missions. The three turbine engines perched atop the fuselage packed a considerable amount of power and could carry a platoon of armed combat troops a great distance.

Tonight, in addition to her normal flight crew of three, she was carrying four passengers and a heavy load of fuel in the outrigger tanks. The passengers were clustered in the aft corner of the cargo area, chatting among themselves or trying to over the racket of the engines. Their conversation was animated. The intelligence officers had dismissed the danger implicit in their mission—no sense dwelling on that—and were speculating on what they might find aboard an honest-to-God Russian submarine. Each man considered the stories that would result, and decided it was a shame that they would never be able to tell them. None voiced this thought, however. At most a handful of people would ever know the entire story; the others would only see disjointed fragments that later might be thought parts of any number of other operations. Any Soviet agent trying to determine what this mission had been would find himself in a maze with dozens of blank walls.

The mission profile was a tight one. The helicopter was flying on a specific track to HMS *Invincible*, from which they would fly to the USS *Pigeon* aboard a Royal Navy Sea King. The Stallion's disappearance from Oceana Naval Air Station for only a few hours would be viewed merely as a matter of routine.

The helicopter's turboshaft engines, running at maximum cruising power, were gulping down fuel. The aircraft was now four hundred miles off the U.S. coast and had another eighty miles to go. Their flight to the *Invincible* was not direct; it was a dogleg course intended to fool whoever might have noticed their departure on radar. The pilots were tired. Four hours is a long time to sit in a cramped cockpit, and military aircraft are not known for their creature comforts. The flight instruments glowed a dull red. Both men were especially careful to watch their artificial horizon; a solid overcast denied them a fixed reference point aloft, and flying over water at night was mesmerizing. It was by no means an unusual mission, however. The pilots had done this many times, and their concern was not unlike that of an experienced driver on a slick road. The dangers were real, but routine.

"Juliet 6, your target is bearing zero-eight-zero, range seventy-five miles," the Sentry called in.

"Thinks we're lost?" Commander John Marcks wondered over the intercom.

"Air force," his copilot replied. "They don't know much about flying over water. They think you get lost without roads to follow."

"Uh-huh," Marcks chuckled. "Who do you like in the Eagles game tonight?"

"Oilers by three and a half."

"Six and a half. Philly's fullback is still hurt."

"Five."

"Okay, five bucks. I'll go easy on you." Marcks grinned. He loved to gamble. The day after Argentina had attacked the Falklands, he'd asked if anyone in the squadron wanted to take Argentina and seven points.

A few feet above their heads and a few feet aft, the engines were racing at thousands of RPM, turning gears to drive the seven-bladed main rotor. They had no way of knowing that a fracture was developing in the transmission casing, near the fluid test port.

"Juliet 6, your target has just launched a fighter to escort you in. Will rendezvous in eight minutes. Approaching you at eleven o'clock, angels three."

"Nice of them," Marcks said.

Harrier 2-0

Lieutenant Parker was flying the Harrier that would escort the Super Stallion. A sublieutenant sat in the back seat of the Royal Navy aircraft. Its purpose was not actually to escort the chopper to the *Invincible;* it was to make a last check for any Soviet submarines that might notice the Super Stallion in flight and wonder what it was doing.

"Any activity on the water?" Parker asked.

"Not a glimmer." The sublieutenant was working the FLIR package, which was sweeping left and right over their course track. Neither man knew what was going on, though both had speculated at length, incorrectly, on what it was that was chasing their carrier all over the bloody ocean.

"Try looking for the helicopter," Parker said.

"One moment . . . There. Just south of our track." The sublieutenant pressed a button and the display came up on the pilot's screen. The thermal image was mainly of the engines clustered atop the aircraft inside the fainter, dull-green glow of the hot rotor tips.

"Harrier 2-0, this is Sentry Echo. Your target is at your one o'clock, distance twenty miles, over."

"Roger, we have him on our IR box. Thank you, out,"

Parker said. "Bloody useful things, those Sentries."

"The Sikorski's running for all she's worth. Look at that engine signature."

The Super Stallion

At this moment the transmission casing fractured. Instantly the gallons of lubricating oil became a greasy cloud behind the rotor hub, and the delicate gears began to tear at one another. An alarm light flashed on the control panels. Marcks and the copilot instantly reached down to cut power to all three engines. There was not enough time. The transmission tried to freeze, but the power of the three engines tore it apart. What happened was the next thing to an explosion. Jagged pieces burst through the safety housing and ripped the forward part of the aircraft. The rotor's momentum twisted the Stallion savagely around, and it dropped rapidly. Two of the men in the back, who had loosened their seatbelts, jerked out of their seats and rolled forward.

"MAYDAY MAYDAY MAYDAY, this is Juliet 6," the copilot called. Commander Marcks' body slumped over the controls, a dark stain at the back of his neck. "We're goin' in, we're goin' in. MAYDAY MAYDAY MAYDAY."

The copilot was trying to do something. The main rotor was windmilling slowly—too slowly. The automatic decoupler that was supposed to allow it to autorotate and give him a vestige of control had failed. His controls were nearly useless, and he was riding the point of a blunt lance towards a black ocean. It was twenty seconds before they hit. He fought with his airfoil controls and tail rotor in order to jerk the aircraft around. He succeeded, but it was too late.

Harrier 2-0

It was not the first time Parker had seen men die. He had taken a life himself after sending a Sidewinder missile up the tailpipe of an Argentine Dagger fighter. That had not been pleasant. This was worse. As he watched, the Super Stallion's hump-backed engine cluster blew apart in a shower of sparks. There was no fire as such, for what good it did them. He watched and tried to will the nose to come up—and it did, but not enough. The Stallion hit the water hard. The fuselage snapped apart in the middle. The front end sank in an instant, but the after part wallowed for a few seconds like a bathtub before beginning to fill with water. According to the picture supplied by the FLIR package, no one got clear before it sank.

"Sentry, Sentry, did you see that, over?"

"Roger that, Harrier. We're calling a SAR mission right now. Can you orbit?"

"Roger, we can loiter here." Parker checked his fuel. "Nine-zero minutes. I—stand by." Parker nosed his fighter down and flicked on his landing lights. This lit up the low-light TV system. "Did you see that, Ian?" he asked his backseater.

"I think it moved."

"Sentry, Sentry, we have a possible survivor in the water. Tell *Invincible* to get a Sea King down here straightaway. I'm going down to investigate. Will advise."

"Roger that, Harrier 2-0. Your captain reports a helo spooling up right now. Out."

The Royal Navy Sea King was there in twenty-five minutes. A rubber-suited paramedic jumped in the water to get a collar on the one survivor. There were no others, and no wreckage, only a slick of jet fuel evaporating slowly into the cold air. A second helicopter continued the search as the first raced back to the carrier.

The Invincible

Ryan watched from the bridge as the medics carried the stretcher into the island. Another crewman appeared a moment later with a briefcase.

"He had this, sir. He's a lieutenant commander, name of Dwyer, one leg and several ribs broken. He's in a bad way, Admiral."

"Thank you." White took the case. "Any possibility of other survivors?"

The sailor shook his head. "Not a good one, sir. The Sikorski must have sunk like a stone." He looked at Ryan. "Sorry, sir."

Ryan nodded. "Thanks."

"Norfolk on the radio, Admiral," a communications officer said.

"Let's go, Jack." Admiral White handed him the briefcase and led him to the communications room.

"The chopper went in. We have one survivor being worked on right now," Ryan said over the radio. It was silent for a moment.

"Who is it?"

"Name's Dwyer. They took him right to sick bay, Admiral. He's out of action. Tell Washington. Whatever this operation is supposed to be, we have to rethink it."

"Roger. Out," Admiral Blackburn said.

"Whatever we decide to do," Admiral White observed, "it will have to be fast. We must get our helo off to the *Pigeon* in two hours to have her back before dawn."

Ryan knew exactly what that would mean. There were only four men at sea who both knew what was going on and were close enough to do anything. He was the only American among them. The *Kennedy* was too far away. The *Nimitz* was close enough, but using her would mean getting the data to her by radio, and Washington was not enthusiastic about that. The only other alternative was to assemble and dispatch another intelligence team. There just wasn't enough time.

"Let's get this case open, Admiral. I need to see what this plan is." They picked up a machinist's mate on the way to White's cabin. He proved to be an excellent locksmith.

"Dear God!" Ryan breathed, reading the contents of the case. "You better see this."

"Well," White said a few minutes later, "that is clever."

"It's cute, all right," Ryan said. "I wonder what genius thought it up. I know I'm going to be stuck with this. I'll ask Washington for permission to take a few officers along with me."

Ten minutes later they were back in communications. White had the compartment cleared. Then Jack spoke over the encrypted voice channel. Both hoped the scrambling device worked.

"I hear you fine, Mr. President. You know what happened to the helicopter."

"Yes, Jack, most unfortunate. I need you to pinch-hit for us."

"Yes, sir, I anticipated that."

"I can't order you, but you know what the stakes are. Will you do it?"

Ryan closed his eyes. "Affirmative."

"I appreciate it, Jack."

Sure you do. "Sir, I need your authorization to take some help with me, a few British officers."

"One," the president said.

"Sir, I need more than that."

"One."

"Understood, sir. We'll be moving in an hour."

"You know what's supposed to happen?"

"Yes, sir. The survivor had the ops orders with him. I've already read them over."

"Good luck, Jack."

"Thank you, sir. Out." Ryan flipped off the satellite channel and turned to Admiral White. "Volunteer once, just one time, and see what happens."

"Frightened?" White did not appear amused.

"Damned right I am. Can I borrow an officer? A guy who speaks Russian if possible. You know what this may involve."

"We'll see. Come on."

Five minutes later they were back in White's cabin awaiting the arrival of four officers. All turned out to be lieutenants, all under thirty.

"Gentlemen," the admiral began, "this is Commander Ryan. He needs an officer to accompany him on a voluntary basis for a mission of some importance. Its nature is secret and most unusual, and there may be some danger involved. You four have been asked here because of your knowledge of Russian. That is all I can say."

"Going to talk to a Sov submarine?" the oldest of them chirped up. "I'm your man. I have a degree in the language, and my first posting was aboard HMS *Dreadnought*."

Ryan weighed the ethics of accepting the man before telling him what was involved. He nodded, and White dismissed the others.

"I'm Jack Ryan." He extended his hand.

"Owen Williams. So, what are we up to?"

"The submarine is named *Red October—*"

"*Krazny Oktyabr.*" Williams smiled.

"And she's attempting to defect to the United States."

"Indeed? So that's what we've been mucking about for. Jolly decent of her CO. Just how certain are we of this?"

Ryan took several minutes to detail the intelligence information. "We blinkered instructions to him, and he seems to have played along. But we won't know for sure until we get aboard. Defectors have been known to change their minds, it happens a lot more often than you might imagine. Still want to come along?"

"Miss a chance like this? Exactly how do we get aboard, Commander?"

"The name's Jack. I'm CIA, not navy." He went on to explain the plan.

"Excellent. Do I have time to pack some things?"

"Be back here in ten minutes," White said.

"Aye aye, sir." Williams drew to attention and left.

White was on the phone. "Send Lieutenant Sinclair to see me." The admiral explained that he was the commander of the *Invincible*'s marine detachment. "Perhaps you might need another friend along."

The other friend was an FN nine-millimeter automatic pistol with a spare clip and a shoulder holster that disappeared nicely under his jacket. The mission orders were shredded and burned before they left.

Admiral White accompanied Ryan and Williams to the flight deck. They stood at the hatch, looking at the Sea King as its engines screeched into life.

"Good luck, Owen." White shook hands with the youngster, who saluted and moved off.

"My regards to your wife, Admiral." Ryan took his hand.

"Five and a half days to England. You'll probably see her before I do. Be careful, Jack."

Ryan smiled crookedly. "It's my intelligence estimate, isn't it? If I'm right, it'll just be a pleasure cruise—assuming the helicopter doesn't crash on me."

"The uniform looks good on you, Jack."

Ryan hadn't expected that. He drew himself to attention and saluted as he'd been taught at Quantico. "Thank you, Admiral. Be seeing you."

White watched him enter the chopper. The crew chief slid the door shut, and a moment later the Sea King's engines increased power. The helicopter lifted unevenly for a few feet before its nose dipped to port and began a climbing turn to the south. Without flying lights the dark shape was lost to sight in less than a minute.

33N 75W

The *Scamp* rendezvoused with the *Ethan Allen* a few minutes after midnight. The attack sub took up station a thousand yards astern of the old missile boat, and both cruised in an easy circle as their sonar operators listened to the approach of a diesel-powered vessel, the USS *Pigeon*. Three of the pieces were now in place. Three more were to come.

The *Red October*

"There is no choice," Melekhin said. "I must continue to work on the diesel."

"Let us help you," Svyadov said.

"And what do you know of diesel fuel pumps?" Melekhin asked in a tired but kind voice. "No, Comrade. Surzpoi, Bugayev, and I can handle it alone. There is no reason to expose you also. I will report back in an hour."

"Thank you, Comrade." Ramius clicked the speaker off. "This cruise has been a troublesome one. Sabotage. Never in my career has something like this happened! If we cannot fix the diesel . . . We have only a few hours more of battery power, and the reactor requires a total overhaul and safety inspection. I swear to you, Comrades, if we find the bastard who did this to us . . ."

"Shouldn't we call for help?" Ivanov asked.

"This close to the American coast, and perhaps an imperialist submarine still on our tail? What sort of 'help' might we get, eh? Comrades, perhaps our problem is no accident, have you considered that? Perhaps we have become pawns in a murderous game." He shook his head. "No, we cannot risk this. The Americans must not get their hands on this submarine!"

CIA Headquarters

"Thank you for coming on such short notice, Senator. I apologize for getting you up so early." Judge Moore met Donaldson at the door and led him into his capacious office. "You know Director Jacobs, don't you?"

"Of course, and what brings the heads of the FBI and CIA together at dawn?" Donaldson asked with a smile. This had to be good. Heading the Select Committee was more than a job, it was fun, real fun to be one of the few people who were really in the know.

The third person in the room, Ritter, helped a fourth person out of a high-backed chair that had blocked him from view. It was Peter Henderson, Donaldson saw to his surprise. His aide's suit was rumpled as though he'd been up all night. Suddenly it wasn't fun anymore.

Judge Moore waxed solicitous. "You know Mr. Henderson, of course."

"What is the meaning of this?" Donaldson asked, his voice more subdued than anyone expected.

"You lied to me, Senator," Ritter said. "You promised that you would not reveal what I told you yesterday, knowing all the time you'd tell this man—"

"I did no such thing."

"—who then told a fellow KGB agent," Ritter went on. "Emil?"

Jacobs set his coffee down. "We've been onto Mr. Henderson for some time. It was his contact that had us stumped. Some things are just too obvious. A lot of people in D.C. have regular cab pickup. Henderson's contact was a cab driver. We finally got it right."

"The way we found out about Henderson was through you, Senator." Moore explained: "We had a very good agent in Moscow a few years ago, a colonel in their Strategic Rocket Forces. He'd been giving us good information for five years, and we were about to get him and his family out. We try to do that, you know; you can't run agents forever, and we really owed this man. But I made the mistake of revealing his name to your committee. One week later, he was gone—vanished.

He was eventually shot, of course. His wife and three daughters were sent to Siberia. Our information is that they live in a lumber settlement east of the Urals. Typical sort of place, no plumbing, lousy food, no medical facilities available, and since they're the family of a convicted traitor, you can probably imagine what sort of hell they must endure. A good man dead, and a family destroyed. Try thinking about that, Senator. This is a true story, and these are real people.

"We didn't know at first who had leaked it. It had to be you, or one of two others, so we began to leak information to individual committee members. It took six months, but your name came up three times. After that we had Director Jacobs check out all of your staffers. Emil?"

"When Henderson was an assistant editor of the Harvard *Crimson*, in 1970, he was sent to Kent State to do a piece on the shooting. You remember, the 'Days of Rage' thing after the Cambodian incursion and that awful screw-up with the national guard. I was in on that, too, as luck would have it. Evidently it turned Henderson's stomach. Understandable. But not his reaction. When he graduated and joined your staff he started talking with his old activist friends about his job. This led to a contract from the Russians, and they asked for some information. That was during the Christmas bombing—he really didn't like that. He delivered. It was low-level stuff at first, nothing they couldn't have gotten a few days later from the *Post*. That's how it works. They offered the hook, and he nibbled at it. A few years later, of course, they struck the hook nice and hard and he couldn't get away. We all know how the game works.

"Yesterday we planted a tape recorder in his taxi. You'd be amazed how easy it was. Agents get lazy, too, just like the rest of us. To make a long story short, we have you on tape promising not to reveal the information to anyone, and we have Henderson here spilling that data not three hours later to a known KGB agent, also on tape. You have violated no laws, Senator, but Mr. Henderson has. He was arrested at nine last night. The charge is espionage, and we have the evidence to make it stick."

"I had no knowledge whatever of this," Donaldson said.

"We hadn't the slightest thought that you might," Ritter said.

Donaldson faced his aide. "What do you have to say for yourself?"

Henderson didn't say anything. He thought about saying how sorry he was, but how to explain his emotions? The dirty feeling of being an agent for a foreign power, juxtaposed with the thrill of fooling a whole legion of government spooks. When he was caught these emotions changed to fear at what would happen to him, and relief that it was all over.

"Mr. Henderson has agreed to work for us," Jacobs said helpfully. "As soon as you leave the Senate, that is."

"What does that mean?" Donaldson asked.

"You've been in the Senate, what? Thirteen years, isn't it? You were originally appointed to fill out an unexpired term, if memory serves," Moore said.

"You might try asking my reaction to blackmail," the senator observed.

"Blackmail?" Moore held his hands out. "Good Lord, Senator, Director Jacobs has already told you that you have broken no laws, and you have my word that the CIA will not leak a word of this. Now, whether or not the Justice Department decides to prosecute Mr. Henderson is not in our hands. 'Senate Aide Convicted of Treason: Senator Donaldson Professes No Knowledge of Aide's Action.'"

Jacobs went on, "Senator, the University of Connecticut has offered you the chair in their school of government for some years now. Why not take it?"

"Or Henderson goes to prison. You put that on my conscience?"

"Obviously he cannot go on working for you, and it should be equally obvious that if he is fired after so many years of exemplary service in your office, it will be noticed. If, on the other hand, you decide to leave public life, it would not be too surprising if he were not able to get a job of equivalent stature with another senator. So, he will get a nice job in the General Accounting Office, where he will still have access to all sorts of secrets. Only from now on," Ritter said, "we decide which secrets he passes along."

"No statute of limitations on espionage," Jacobs pointed out.

"If the Soviets find out," Donaldson said, and stopped. He

didn't really care, did he? Not about Henderson, not about the fictitious Russian. He had an image to save, losses to cut.

"You win, Judge."

"I thought you'd see it our way. I'll tell the president. Thanks for coming in, Senator. Mr. Henderson will be a little late to the office this morning. Don't feel too badly about him, Senator. If he plays ball with us, in a few years we might let him off the hook. It's happened before, but he'll have to earn it. Good morning, sir."

Henderson would play along. His alternative was life in a maximum security penitentiary. After listening to the tape of his conversation in the cab, he'd made his confession in front of a court stenographer and a television camera.

The Pigeon

The ride to the *Pigeon* had been mercifully uneventful. The catamaran-hull rescue ship had a small helicopter platform aft, and the Royal Navy helicopter had hovered two feet above it, allowing Ryan and Williams to jump down. They were taken immediately to the bridge as the helicopter buzzed back northeast to her home.

"Welcome aboard, gentlemen," the captain said agreeably. "Washington says you have orders for me. Coffee?"

"Do you have tea?" Williams asked.

"We can probably find some."

"Let's go someplace we can talk in private," Ryan said.

The Dallas

The *Dallas* was now in on the plan. Alerted by another ELF transmission, Mancuso had brought her to antenna depth briefly during the night. The lengthy EYES ONLY message had been decrypted by hand in his cabin. Decryption was not Mancuso's strong point. It took him an hour as Chambers conned the *Dallas* back to trail her contact. A crewman passing the captain's cabin heard a muted *damn* through the door. When Mancuso reappeared, his mouth couldn't keep from twitching into a smile. He was not a good card player either.

The Pigeon

The *Pigeon* was one of the navy's two modern submarine rescue ships designed to locate and reach a sunken nuclear sub quickly enough to save her crew. She was outfitted with a variety of sophisticated equipment, chief among them the DSRV. This vessel, the *Mystic*, was hanging on its rack between the *Pigeon*'s twin catamaran hulls. There was also a 3-d sonar operating at low power, mainly as a beacon, while the *Pigeon* cruised in slow circles a few miles south of the *Scamp* and *Ethan Allen*. Two *Perry*-class frigates were twenty miles north, operating in conjunction with three Orions to sanitize the area.

"*Pigeon*, this is *Dallas*, radio check, over."

"*Dallas*, this is *Pigeon*. Read you loud and clear, over," the rescue ship's captain replied on the secure radio channel.

"The package is here. Out."

"Captain, on *Invincible* we had an officer send the message with a blinker light. Can you handle the blinker light?" Ryan asked.

"To be part of this? Are you kidding?"

The plan was simple enough, just a little too cute. It was clear that the *Red October* wanted to defect. It was even possible that everyone aboard wanted to come over—but hardly likely. They were going to get everyone off the *Red October* who might want to return to Russia, then pretend to blow up the ship with one of the powerful scuttling charges Russian ships are known to carry. The remaining crewmen would then take their boat northwest into Pamlico Sound to wait for the Soviet fleet to return home, sure that the *Red October* had been sunk and with the crew to prove it. What could possibly go wrong? A thousand things.

The Red October

Ramius looked through his periscope. The only ship in view was the USS *Pigeon*, though his ESM antenna reported surface radar activity to the north, a pair of frigates standing guard over the horizon. So, this was the plan. He watched the blinker light, translating the message in his mind.

Norfolk Naval Medical Center

"Thanks for coming down, Doc." The intelligence officer had taken over the office of assistant hospital administrator. "I understand our patient woke up."

"About an hour ago," Tait confirmed. "He was conscious for about twenty minutes. He's asleep now."

"Does that mean he'll make it?"

"It's a positive sign. He was reasonably coherent, so there's no evident brain damage. I was a little worried about that. I'd have to say the odds are in his favor now, but these hypothermia cases have a way of souring on you in a hurry. He's a sick kid, that hasn't changed." Tait paused. "I have a question for you, Commander: Why aren't the Russians happy?"

"What makes you think that?"

"Kind of hard to miss. Besides, Jamie found a doctor on staff who understands Russian, and we have him attending the case."

"Why didn't you let me know about that?"

"The Russians don't know either. That was a medical judgment, Commander. Having a physician around who speaks the patient's language is simply good medical practice." Tait smiled, pleased with himself for having thought up his own intelligence ploy while at the same time adhering to proper medical ethics and naval regulations. He took a file card from his pocket. "Anyway, the patient's name is Andre Katyskin. He's a cook, like we thought, from Leningrad. The name of his ship was the *Politovskiy.*"

"My compliments, Doctor." The intelligence officer acknowledged Tait's maneuver, though he wondered why it was that amateurs had to be so damned clever when they butted into things that didn't concern them.

"So why are the Russians unhappy?" Tait did not get an answer. "And why don't *you* have a guy up there? You knew all along, didn't you? You knew what ship he escaped from, and you knew why she sank . . . So, if they wanted most of all to know what ship he came from, and if they don't like the news they got—does that mean they have *another* missing sub out there?"

CIA Headquarters

Moore lifted his phone. "James, you and Bob get in here right now!"

"What is it, Arthur?" Greer asked a minute later.

"The latest from CARDINAL." Moore handed xeroxed copies of a message to both men. "How quick can we get word out?"

"That far out? Means a helicopter, a couple of hours at least. We have to get this out quicker than that," Greer urged.

"We can't endanger CARDINAL, period. Draw up a message and get the navy or air force to relay it by hand." Moore didn't like it, but he had no choice.

"It'll take too long!" Greer objected loudly.

"I like the boy, too, James. Talking about it doesn't help. Get moving."

Greer left the room cursing like the fifty-year sailor he was.

The Red October

"Comrades. Officers and men of *Red October,* this is the captain speaking." Ramius' voice was subdued, the crewmen noticed. The incipient panic that had started a few hours earlier had driven them to the brittle edge of riot. "Efforts to repair our engines have failed. Our batteries are nearly flat. We are too far from Cuba for help, and we cannot expect help from the *Rodina.* We do not have enough electrical power even to operate our environmental control systems for more than a few hours. We have no choice, we must abandon ship.

"It is no accident that an American ship is now close to us, offering what they call assistance. I will tell you what has happened, comrades. An imperialist spy has sabotaged our ship, and somehow they knew what our orders were. They were waiting for us, comrades, waiting and hoping to get their dirty hands on our ship. They will not. The crew will be taken off. They will not get our *Red October!* The senior officers and I will remain behind to set off the scuttling charges. The water here is five thousand meters deep. They will not have our ship. All crewmen except those on duty will assemble in their quarters. That is all." Ramius looked around the control room. "We have lost, comrades. Bugayev, make the necessary signals to Moscow and to the American ship. We will then dive to a hundred meters. We will take no chance that they will seize our ship. I take full responsibility for this—disgrace! Mark this well, comrades. The fault is mine alone."

The Pigeon

"Signal received: 'SSS,'" the radioman reported.

"Ever been on a submarine before, Ryan?" Cook asked.

"Nope, I hope it's safer 'n flying." Ryan tried to make a joke of it. He was deeply frightened.

"Well, let's get you down to *Mystic*."

The Mystic

The DSRV was nothing more than three metal spheres welded together with a propeller on the back and some boiler plating all around to protect the pressure-bearing parts of the hull. Ryan was first through the hatch, then Williams. They found seats and waited. A crew of three was already at work.

The *Mystic* was ready for operation. On command, the *Pigeon*'s winches lowered her to the calm water below. She dived at once, her electric motors hardly making any noise. Her low-power sonar system immediately acquired the Russian submarine, half a mile away, at a depth of three hundred feet. The operating crew had been told that this was a straightforward rescue mission. They were experts. The *Mystic* was hovering over the missile sub's forward escape trunk within ten minutes.

The directional propellers worked them carefully into place and a petty officer made certain that the mating skirt was securely fastened. The water in the skirt between *Mystic* and *Red October* was explosively vented into a low-pressure chamber on the DSRV. This established a firm seal between the two vessels, and the residual water was pumped out.

"Your ball now, I guess." The lieutenant motioned Ryan to the hatch in the floor of the middle segment.

"I guess." Ryan knelt by the hatch and banged a few times with his hand. No response. Next he tried a wrench. A moment later three clangs echoed back, and Ryan turned the locking wheel in the center of the hatch. When he pulled the hatch up, he found another that had already been opened from below. The lower perpendicular hatch was shut. Ryan took a deep breath and climbed down the ladder of the white painted cylinder, followed by Williams. After reaching the bottom Ryan knocked on the lower hatch.

The Red October

It opened at once.

"Gentlemen, I am Commander Ryan, United States Navy. Can we be of assistance?"

The man he spoke to was shorter and heavier than himself. He wore three stars on his shoulder boards, an extensive set of ribbons on his breast, and a broad gold stripe on his sleeve. So, this was Marko Ramius...

"Do you speak Russian?"

"No sir, I do not. What is the nature of your emergency, sir?"

"We have a major leak in our reactor system. The ship is contaminated aft of the control room. We must evacuate."

At the words *leak* and *reactor* Ryan felt his skin crawl. He remembered how positive he had been that his scenario was correct. On land, nine hundred miles away, in a nice, warm office, surrounded by friends—well, not enemies. The looks he was getting from the twenty men in this compartment were lethal.

"Dear God! Okay, let's get moving then. We can take off twenty-five men at a time, sir."

"Not so fast, Commander Ryan. What will become of my men?" Ramius asked loudly.

"They will be treated as our guests, of course. If they need medical attention, they will get it. They will be returned to the Soviet Union as quickly as we can arrange it. Did you think we'd put them in prison?"

Ramius grunted and turned to speak with the others in Russian. On the flight from the *Invincible* Ryan and Williams had decided to keep the latter's knowledge of Russian secret for a while, and Williams was now dressed in an American uniform. Neither thought a Russian would notice the different accent.

"Dr. Petrov," Ramius said, "you will take the first group of twenty-five. Keep control of the men, Comrade Doctor! Do not let the Americans speak to them as individuals, and let no man wander off alone. You will behave correctly, no more, no less."

"Understood, Comrade Captain."

Ryan watched Petrov count the men off as they passed through the hatch and up the ladder. When they were finished, Williams secured first the *Mystic*'s hatch and then the one on the *October*'s escape truck. Ramius had a *michman* check it. They heard the DSRV disengage and motor off.

The silence that ensued was as long as it was awkward. Ryan and Williams stood in one corner of the compartment, Ramius and his men opposite them. It made Ryan think back to high school dances where boys and girls gathered in separate groups and there was a no-man's-land in the middle. When an officer fished out a cigarette, he tried breaking the ice.

"May I have a cigarette, sir?"

Borodin jerked the pack, and a cigarette came part way out. Ryan took it, and Borodin lit it with a paper match.

"Thanks. I gave it up, but underwater in a sub with a bad reactor, I don't think it's too dangerous, do you?" Ryan's first experience with a Russian cigarette was not a happy one. The black coarse tobacco made him dizzy, and it added an acrid smell to the air around them, which was already thick with the odor of sweat, machine oil, and cabbage.

"How did you come to be here?" Ramius asked.

"We were heading towards the coast of Virginia, Captain. A Soviet submarine sank there last week."

"Oh?" Ramius admired the cover story. "A Soviet submarine?"

"Yes, Captain. The boat was what we call an *Alfa*. That's all I know for sure. They picked up a survivor, and he's in the Norfolk naval hospital. May I ask your name, sir?"

"Marko Aleksandrovich Ramius."

"Jack Ryan."

"Owen Williams." They shook hands all around.

"You have a family, Commander Ryan?" Ramius asked.

"Yes, sir. A wife, a son, and a daughter. You, sir?"

"No, no family." He turned and addressed a junior officer in Russian. "Take the next group. You heard my instructions to the doctor?"

"Yes, Comrade Captain!" the young man said.

They heard the *Mystic's* electric motors overhead. A moment later came the metallic clang of the mating collar gripping the escape trunk. It had taken forty minutes, but it had seemed like a week. God, what if the reactor really was bad? Ryan thought.

The Scamp

Two miles away, the *Scamp* had halted a few hundred yards from the *Ethan Allen*. Both submarines were exchanging messages on their gertrudes. The *Scamp* sonarmen had noted the passage of the three submarines an hour earlier. The *Pogy* and *Dallas* were now between the *Red October* and the other two American subs, their sonar operators listening intently for any interference, any vessel that might come their way. The transfer area was far enough offshore to miss the coastal traffic of commercial freighters and tankers, but that might not keep them from meeting a stray vessel from another port.

The Red October

When the third set of crewmen left under the control of Lieutenant Svyadov, a cook at the end of the line broke away, explaining that he wanted to retrieve his cassette tape machine, something he had saved months for. No one noticed when he didn't return, not even Ramius. His crewmen, even the experienced *michmanyy,* jostled one another to get out of their submarine. There was only one more group to go.

The Pigeon

On the *Pigeon*, the Soviet crewmen were taken to the crew's mess. The American sailors were observing their Russian counterparts closely, but no words passed. The Russians found the tables set with a meal of coffee, bacon, eggs, and toast. Petrov was happy for that. It was no problem keeping control of the men when they ate like wolves. With a junior officer acting as interpreter, they asked for and got plenty of additional bacon. The cooks had orders to stuff the Russians with all the food they could eat. It kept everyone busy as a helicopter landed from shore with twenty new men, one of whom raced to the bridge.

The Red October

"Last group," Ryan murmured to himself. The *Mystic* mated again. The last round trip had taken an hour. When the pair of hatches was opened, the lieutenant from the DSRV came down.

"Next trip will be delayed, gentlemen. Our batteries have about had it. It'll take ninety minutes to recharge. Any problem?"

"It will be as you say," Ramius replied. He translated for his men and then ordered Ivanov to take the next group. "The senior officers will stay behind. We have work to do." Ramius took the young officer's hand. "If something happens, tell them in Moscow that we have done our duty."

"I will do that, Comrade Captain." Ivanov nearly choked on his answer.

Ryan watched the sailors leave. The *Red October*'s escape trunk hatch was closed, then the *Mystic*'s. One minute later there was a clanging sound as the minisub lifted free. He heard the electric motors whirring off, fading rapidly away, and felt the green-painted bulkheads closing in on him. Being on an airplane was frightening, but at least the air didn't threaten to crush you. Here he was, underwater, three hundred miles from shore in the world's largest submarine, with only ten men aboard who knew how to run her.

"Commander Ryan," Ramius said, drawing himself to attention, "my officers and I request political asylum in the United States—and we bring you this small present." Ramius gestured toward the steel bulkheads.

Ryan had already framed his reply. "Captain, on behalf of the president of the United States, it is my honor to grant your request. Welcome to freedom, gentlemen."

No one knew that the intercom system in the compartment had been switched on. The indicator light had been unplugged hours before. Two compartments forward the cook listened, telling himself that he had been right to stay behind, wishing he had been wrong. Now what will I do? he wondered. His duty. That sounded easy enough—but would he remember how to carry it out?

"I don't know what to say about you guys." Ryan shook

everyone's hand again. "You pulled it off. You really pulled it off!"

"Excuse me, Commander," Kamarov said. "Do you speak Russian?"

"Sorry, Lieutenant Williams here does, but I do not. A group of Russian-speaking officers was supposed to be here in my place, but their helicopter crashed at sea last night." Williams translated this. Four of the officers had no knowledge of English.

"And what happens now?"

"In a few minutes, a missile submarine will explode two miles from here. One of ours, an old one. I presume that you told your men you were going to scuttle—Jesus, I hope you didn't say what you were really doing?"

"And have a war aboard my ship?" Ramius laughed. "No, Ryan. Then what?"

"When everybody thinks *Red October* has sunk, we'll head northwest to the Ocracoke Inlet and wait. USS *Dallas* and *Pogy* will be escorting us. Can these few men operate the ship?"

"These men can operate any ship in the world!" Ramius said it in Russian first. His men grinned. "So, you think that our men will not know what has become of us?"

"Correct. *Pigeon* will see an underwater explosion. They have no way of knowing it's in the wrong place, do they? You know that your navy has many ships operating off our coast right now? When they leave, well, then we'll figure out where to keep this present permanently. I don't know where that will be. You men, of course, will be our guests. A lot of our people will want to talk with you. For the moment, you can be sure that you will be treated very well—better than you can imagine." Ryan was sure that the CIA would give each a considerable sum of money. He didn't say so, not wanting to insult this kind of bravery. It had surprised him to learn that defectors rarely expect to receive money, almost never ask for any.

"What about political education?" Kamarov asked.

Ryan laughed. "Lieutenant, somewhere along the line somebody will take you aside to explain how our country works. That will take about two hours. After that you can immediately start telling us what we do wrong—everybody else in the world does, why shouldn't you? But I can't do that now. Believe this, you will love it, probably more than I do. I have never lived in a country that was not free, and maybe I don't appreciate my home as much as I should. For the moment, I suppose you have work to do."

"Correct," Ramius said. "Come, my new comrades, we will put you to work also."

Ramius led Ryan aft through a series of watertight doors. In a few minutes he was in the missile room, a vast compartment with twenty-six dark-green tubes towering through two decks. The business end of a boomer, with two-hundred-plus thermonuclear warheads. The menace in this room was enough to make hair bristle at the back of Ryan's neck. These were not academic abstractions, these were real. The upper deck he walked on was a grating. The lower deck, he could see, was solid. After passing through this and another compartment they were in the control room. The interior of the submarine was ghostly quiet; Ryan sensed why sailors are superstitious.

"You will sit here." Ramius pointed Ryan to the helmsman's station on the port side of the compartment. There was an aircraft-style wheel and a gang of instruments.

"What do I do?" Ryan asked, sitting.

"You will steer the ship, Commander. Have you never done this before?"

"No, sir. I've never been on a submarine before."

"But you are a naval officer."

Ryan shook his head. "No, captain. I work for the CIA."

"CIA?" Ramius hissed the acronym as if it were poisonous.

"I know, I know." Ryan dropped his head on the wheel. "They call us the Dark Forces. Captain, this is one Dark Force who's probably going to wet his pants before we're finished here. I work at a desk, and believe me on this if nothing else—there's nothing I'd like better than to be home with my wife and kids right now. If I had half a brain, I would have stayed in Annapolis and kept writing my books."

"Books? What do you mean?"

"I'm an historian, Captain. I was asked to join the CIA a few years ago as an analyst. Do you know what that is? Agents bring in their data, and I figure out what it means. I got into this mess by mistake—shit, you don't believe me, but it's true. Anyway, I used to write books on naval history."

"Tell me your books," Ramius ordered.

"*Options and Decisions, Doomed Eagles*, and a new one coming out next year, *Fighting Sailor*, a biography of Admiral Halsey. My first one was about the Battle of Leyte Gulf. It was reviewed in *Morskoi Sbornik*, I understand. It dealt with the nature of tactical decisions made under combat conditions. There's supposed to be a dozen copies at the Frunze library."

Ramius was quiet for a moment. "Ah, I know this book. Yes, I read parts of it. You were wrong, Ryan. Halsey acted stupidly."

"You will do well in my country, Captain Ramius. You are already a book critic. Captain Borodin, can I trouble you for a cigarette?" Borodin tossed him a full pack and matches. Ryan lit one. It was terrible.

The Avalon

The *Mystic*'s fourth return was the signal for the *Ethan Allen* and *Scamp* to act. The *Avalon* lifted off her bed and motored the few hundred yards to the old missile boat. Her captain was already assembling his men in the torpedo room. Every hatch, door, manhole, and drawer had been opened all over the boat. One of the officers was coming forward to join the others. Behind him trailed a black wire that led to each of the bombs aboard. This he connected to a timing device.

"All ready, Captain."

The Red October

Ryan watched Ramius order his men to their posts. Most went aft to run the engines. Ramius had the good manners to speak in English, repeating himself in Russian for those who did not understand their new language.

"Kamarov and Williams, will you go forward and secure all hatches." Ramius explained for Ryan's benefit. "If something goes wrong—it won't, but if it does—we do not have enough men to make repairs. So, we seal the entire ship."

It made sense to Ryan. He set an empty cup on the control pedestal to serve as an ashtray. He and Ramius were alone in the control room.

"When are we to leave?" Ramius asked.

"Whenever you are ready, sir. We have to get to Ocracoke Inlet at high tide, about eight minutes after midnight. Can we make it?"

Ramius consulted his chart. "Easily."

Kamarov led Williams through the communications room forward of control. They left the watertight door there open, then went forward to the missile room. Here they climbed down a ladder and walked forward on the lower missile deck to the forward missile room bulkhead. They proceeded through the door into the stores compartments, checking each hatch as they went. Near the bow they went up another ladder into the torpedo room, dogging the hatch down behind them, and proceeded aft through the torpedo storage and crew spaces. Both men sensed how strange it was to be aboard a ship with no crew, and they took their time, Williams twisting his head to look at everything and asking Kamarov questions. The lieutenant was happy to answer them in his mother language. Both men were competent officers, sharing a romantic attachment to their profession. For his part, Williams was greatly impressed by the *Red October* and said as much several times. A great deal of attention had been paid to small details. The deck was tiled. The hatches were lined with thick rubber gaskets. They hardly made any noise at all as they moved about checking watertight integrity, and it was obvious that more than mere lip service had been paid to making this submarine a quiet one.

Williams was translating a favorite sea story into Russian as they opened the hatch to the missile room's upper deck. When he stepped through the hatch behind Kamarov, he remembered that the missile room's bright overhead lights had been left on. Hadn't they?

Ryan was trying to relax and failing at it. The seat was uncomfortable, and he recalled the Russian joke about how they were shaping the New Soviet Man—with airliner seats that contorted an individual into all kinds of impossible shapes. Aft, the engine room crew had begun powering up the reactor. Ramius was speaking over the intercom phone with his chief engineer, just before the sound of moving reactor coolant increased to generate steam for the turboalternators.

Ryan's head went up. It was as though he felt the sound before hearing it. A chill ran up the back of his neck before his brain told him what the sound had to be.

"What was that?" he said automatically, knowing already what it was.

"What?" Ramius was ten feet aft, and the caterpillar engines were now turning. A strange rumble reverberated through the hull.

"I heard a shot—no, several shots."

Ramius looked amused as he came a few steps forward. "I think you hear the sounds of the caterpillar engines, and I think it is your first time on a submarine boat, as you said. The first time is always difficult. It was so even for me."

Ryan stood up. "That may be, Captain, but I know a shot when I hear it." He unbottoned his jacket and pulled out the pistol.

"You will give me that." Ramius held out his hand. "You may not have a pistol on my submarine!"

"Where are Williams and Kamarov?" Ryan wavered.

Ramius shrugged. "They are late, yes, but this is a big ship."

"I'm going forward to check."

"You will stay at your post!" Ramius ordered. "You will do as I say!"

"Captain, I just heard something that sounded like gunshots, and I am going forward to check it out. Have you ever been shot at? I have. I have the scars on my shoulder to prove it. You'd better take the wheel, sir."

Ramius picked up a phone and punched a button. He spoke in Russian for a few seconds and hung up. "I will go to show you that my submarine has no souls—ghosts, yes? Ghosts, no ghosts." He gestured to the pistol. "And you are no spy, eh?"

"Captain, believe what you want to believe, okay? It's a long story, and I'll tell it to you someday." Ryan waited for the relief that Ramius had evidently called for. The rumble of the tunnel drive made the sub sound like the inside of a drum.

An officer whose name he did not remember came into the control room. Ramius said something that drew a laugh—which stopped when the officer saw Ryan's pistol. It was obvious that neither Russian was happy he had one.

"With your permission, Captain?" Ryan gestured forward.

"Go on, Ryan."

The watertight door between control and the next space had been left open. Ryan entered the radio room slowly, eyes tracing left and right. It was clear. He went forward to the missile room door, which was dogged tight. The door, four feet or so high and about two across, was locked in place with a central wheel. Ryan turned the wheel with one hand. It was well oiled. So were the hinges. He pulled the door open slowly and peered around the hatch coaming.

"Oh, shit," Ryan breathed, waving the captain forward. The missile compartment was a good two hundred feet long, lit only by six or eight small glow lights. Hadn't it been brightly lit before? At the far end was a splash of bright light, and the far hatch had two shapes sprawled on the gratings next to it. Neither moved. The light Ryan saw them by was flickering next to a missile tube.

"Ghosts, Captain?" he whispered.

"It is Kamarov." Ramius said something else under his breath in Russian.

Ryan pulled the slide back on his FN automatic to make sure a round was in the chamber. Then he stepped out of his shoes.

"Better let me handle this. Once upon a time I was a lieutenant in the marines." And my training at Quantico, he thought to himself, had damned little to do with this. Ryan entered the compartment.

The missile room was almost a third of the submarine's length and two decks high. The lower deck was solid metal. The upper one was made of metal grates. Sherwood Forest, this place was called on American missile boats. The term was apt enough. The missile tubes, a good nine feet in diameter and painted a darker green than the rest of the room, looked like the trunks of enormous trees. He pulled the hatch shut behind him and moved to his right.

The light seemed to be coming from the farthest missile tube on the starboard side of the upper missile deck. Ryan stopped to listen. Something was happening there. He could hear a low rustling sound, and the light was moving as though it came from a hand-held work lamp. The sound was traveling down the smooth sides of the interior hull plating.

"Why me?" he whispered to himself. He'd have to get past thirteen missile tubes to get to the source of that light, cross over two hundred feet of open deck.

He moved around the first one, pistol in his right hand at waist level, his left hand tracing the cold metal of the tube. Already he was sweating into the checkered hard-rubber pistol grips. That, he told himself, is why they're checkered. He got between the first and second tubes, looked to port to make sure nobody was there, and got ready to move forward. Twelve to go.

The deck grating was welded out of eighth-inch metal bars. Already his feet hurt from walking on it. Moving slowly and carefully around the next circular tube, he felt like an astronaut orbiting the moon and crossing a continuous horizon. Except on the moon there wasn't anybody waiting to shoot you.

A hand came down on his shoulder. Ryan jumped and whirled around. Ramius. He had something to say, but Ryan put his fingertips on the man's lips and shook his head. Ryan's heart was beating so loudly that he could have used it for sending Morse code, and he could hear his own breathing—so why the hell hadn't he heard Ramius?

Ryan gestured his intention to go around the outboard side of each missile. Ramius indicated that he would go around the inboard sides. Ryan nodded. He decided to button his jacket and turn the collar up. It would make him a harder target. Better a dark shape than one with a white triangle on it. Next tube.

Ryan saw that words were painted on the tubes, with other inscriptions forged onto the metal itself. The letters were in Cyrillic and probably said No Smoking or Lenin Lives or something similarly useless. He saw and heard everything with great acuity, as though someone had taken sandpaper to all his senses to make him fantastically alert. He edged around the next tube, his fingers flexing nervously on the pistol grip, wanting to wipe the sweat from his eyes. There was nothing here; the port side was okay. Next one . . .

It took five minutes to get halfway down the compartment, between the sixth and seventh tubes. The noise from the forward end of the compartment was more pronounced now. The light was definitely moving. Not by much, but the shadow of the number one tube was jittering ever so slightly. It had to be a work light plugged into a wall socket or whatever they called that on a ship. What was he doing? Working on a missile? Was there more than one man? Why didn't Ramius do a head count getting his crew into the DSRV?

Why didn't *I?* Ryan swore to himself. Six more to go.

As he went around the next tube he indicated to Ramius that there was probably one man all the way at the far end. Ramius nodded curtly, having already reached that conclusion. For the first time he noticed that Ryan's shoes were off, and, thinking that was a good idea, he lifted his left foot to take off a shoe. His fingers, which felt awkward and stiff, fumbled with the shoe. It fell on a loose piece of grating with a clatter. Ryan was caught in the open. He froze. The light at the far end shifted, then went dead still. Ryan darted to his left and peered around the edge of the tube. Five more to go. He saw part of a face—and a flash.

He heard the shot and cringed as the bullet hit the after bulkhead with a *clang.* Then he drew back for cover.

"I will cross to the other side," Ramius whispered.

"Wait till I say." Ryan grabbed Ramius' upper arm and went back to the starboard side of the tube, pistol in front. He saw the face and this time he fired first, knowing he'd miss. At the same moment he pushed Ramius left. The captain raced to the other side and crouched behind a missile tube.

"We have you," Ryan said aloud.

"You have nothing." It was a young voice, young and very scared.

"What are you doing?" Ryan asked.

"What do you think, Yankee?" This time the taunt was more effective.

Probably figuring a way to set off a warhead, Ryan decided. A happy thought.

"Then you will die too," Ryan said. Didn't the police try to reason with barricaded suspects? Didn't a New York cop say on TV once, "We try to bore them to death?" But those were criminals. What was Ryan dealing with? A sailor who stayed behind? One of Ramius' own officers who'd had second thoughts? A KGB agent? A GRU agent covered as a crewman?

"Then I will die," the voice agreed. The light moved. Whatever he was doing, he was trying to get back to it.

Ryan fired twice as he went around the tube. Four to go. His bullets clanged uselessly as they hit the forward bulkhead. There was a remote chance that a carom shot—no . . . He looked left and saw that Ramius was still with him, shading to the port side of the tubes. He had no gun. Why hadn't he gotten himself one?

Ryan took a deep breath and leaped around the next tube. The guy was waiting for this. Ryan dove to the deck, and the bullet missed him.

"Who are you?" Ryan asked, raising himself on his knees and leaning against the tube to catch his breath.

"A Soviet patriot! You are the enemy of my country, and you shall not have this ship!"

He was talking too much, Ryan thought. Good. Probably. "You have a name?"

"My name is of no account."

"How about a family?" Ryan asked.

"My parents will be proud of me."

A GRU agent. Ryan was certain. Not the political officer. His English was too good. Probably some kind of backup for the political officer. He was up against a trained field officer. Wonderful. A trained agent, and just like he said, a patriot. Not a fanatic, a man trying to do his duty. He was scared, but he'd do it.

And blow this whole fucking ship up, with me on it.

Still, Ryan knew he had an edge. The other guy had something he had to do. Ryan only had to stop him or delay him long enough. He went to the starboard side of the tube and looked around the edge with just his right eye There was no light at his end of the compartment—another edge. Ryan could see him more easily than he could see Ryan.

"You don't have to die, my friend. If you just set the gun down . . ." And *what?* End up in a federal prison? More likely just disappear. Moscow could not learn that the Americans had their sub.

"And CIA will not kill me, eh?" the voice sneered, quavering. "I am no fool. If I am to die, it will be to my purpose, my friend!"

Then the light clicked off. Ryan had wondered how long that would take. Did it mean that he was finished whatever the hell he was doing? If so, in an instant they'd be all gone. Or maybe the guy just realized how vulnerable the light made him. Trained field officer or not, he was a kid, a frightened kid, and probably had as much to lose as Ryan had. Like hell, Ryan thought, I have a wife and two kids, and if I don't get to him fast, I'll sure as hell lose them.

Merry Christmas, kids, your daddy just got blown up. Sorry there's no body to bury, but you see . . . It occurred to Ryan to pray briefly—but for what? For help in killing another man? *It's like this, Lord . . .*

"Still with me, Captain?" he called out.

"Da."

That would give the GRU agent something to worry about. Ryan hoped the captain's presence would force the man to shade more to the port side of his tube. Ryan ducked and rushed around the port side of his. Three to go. Ramius followed suit on his side. He drew a shot, but Ryan heard it miss.

He had to stop, to rest. He was hyperventilating. It was the wrong time for that. He had been a marine lieutenant—for three whole months before the chopper crashed—and he was supposed to know what to do! He had *led* men. But it was a whole lot easier to lead forty men with rifles than it was to fight all by himself.

Think!

"Maybe we can make a deal," Ryan suggested.

"Ah, yes, we can decide which ear the shot comes in."

"Maybe you'd like being an American."

"And my parents, Yankee, what of them?"

"Maybe we can get them out," Ryan said from the starboard side of his tube, moving left as he waited for a reply. He jumped again. Now there were two missile tubes separating him from his friend in the GRU, who was probably trying to crosswire the warheads and make half a cubic mile of ocean turn to plasma.

"Come, Yankee, we will die together. Now only one *puskatel* separates us."

Ryan thought quickly. He couldn't remember how many times he'd fired, but the pistol held thirteen rounds. He'd have enough. The extra clip was useless. He could toss it one way and move the other, creating a diversion. Would it work? Shit! It worked in the movies. It was for damned sure that doing nothing wasn't going to work.

Ryan took the gun in his left hand and fished in his coat pocket for the spare clip with his right. He put the clip in his mouth while he switched the gun back. A poor highwayman's shift . . . He took the clip in his left hand. Okay. He had to toss the clip right and move left. Would it work? Right or wrong, he didn't have a hell of a lot of time.

At Quantico he was taught to read maps, evaluate terrain, call in air and artillery strikes, maneuver his squads and fire teams with skill—and here he was, stuck in a goddamned steel pipe three hundred feet under water, shooting it out with pistols in a room with two hundred hydrogen bombs!

It was time to do something. He knew what that had to be—but Ramius moved first. Out the corner of his eye he caught the shape of the captain running toward the forward bulkhead. Ramius leaped at the bulkhead and flicked a light switch on as the enemy fired at him. Ryan tossed the clip to the right and ran forward. The agent turned to his left to see what the noise was, sure that a cooperative move had been planned.

As Ryan covered the distance between the last two missile tubes he saw Ramius go down. Ryan dove past the number one missile tube. He landed on his left side, ignoring the pain that set his arm on fire as he rolled to line up his target. The man was turning as Ryan jerked off six shots. Ryan didn't hear himself screaming. Two rounds connected. The agent was lifted off the deck and twisted halfway around from the impact. His pistol dropped from his hand as he fell limp to the deck.

Ryan was shaking too badly to get up at once. The pistol, still tight in his hand, was aimed at his victim's chest. He was breathing hard and his heart was racing. Ryan closed his mouth and tried to swallow a few times; his mouth was as dry as cotton. He got slowly to his knees. The agent was still alive, lying on his back, eyes open and still breathing. Ryan had to use his hand to stand up.

He'd been hit twice, Ryan saw, once in the upper left chest and once lower down, about where the liver and spleen are. The lower wound was a wet red circle which the man's hands clutched. He was in his early twenties, if that, and his clear blue eyes were staring at the overhead while he tried to say something. His face was rigid with pain as he mouthed words, but all that came out was an unintelligible gurgle.

"Captain," Ryan called, "you okay?"

"I am wounded, but I think I shall live, Ryan. Who is it?"

"How the hell should I know?"

The blue eyes fixed on Jack's face. Whoever he was, he knew death was coming to him. The pain on the face was replaced by something else. Sadness, an infinite sadness... He was still trying to speak. A pink froth gathered at the corners of his mouth. Lung shot. Ryan moved closer, kicking the gun clear and kneeling down beside him.

"We could have made a deal," he said quietly.

The agent tried to say something, but Ryan couldn't understand it. A curse, a call for his mother, something heroic? Jack would never know. The eyes went wide with pain one last time. The last breath hissed out through the bubbles and the hands on the belly went limp. Ryan checked for a pulse at the neck. There was none.

"I'm sorry." Ryan reached down to close his victim's eyes. He was sorry—why? Tiny beads of sweat broke out all over his forehead, and the strength he had drawn up in the shootout deserted him. A sudden wave of nausea overpowered him. "Oh, Jesus, I'm—" He dropped to all fours and threw up violently, his vomit spilling through the grates onto the lower deck ten feet below. For a whole minute his stomach heaved, well past the time he was dry. He had to spit several times to get the worst of the taste from his mouth before standing.

Dizzy from the stress and the quart of adrenalin that had been pumped into his system, he shook his head a few times, still looking at the dead man at his feet. It was time to come back to reality.

Ramius had been hit in the upper leg. It was bleeding. Both his hands, covered with blood, were placed on the wound, but it didn't look that bad. If the femoral artery had been cut, the captain would already have been dead.

Lieutenant Williams had been hit in the head and chest. He was still breathing but unconscious. The head wound was only a crease. The chest wound, close to the heart, made a sucking noise. Kamarov was not so lucky. A single shot had gone straight through the top of his nose, and the back of his head was a bloody wreckage.

"Jesus, why didn't somebody come and help us!" Ryan said when the thought hit him.

"The bulkhead doors are closed, Ryan. There is the—how do you say it?"

Ryan looked where the captain pointed. It was the intercom system. "Which button?" The captain held up two fingers. "Control room, this is Ryan. I need help here, your captain has been shot."

The reply came in excited Russian, and Ramius responded loudly to make himself heard. Ryan looked at the missile tube. The agent had been using a work light, just like an American one, a lightbulb in a metal holder with wire across the front. A door into the missile tube was open. Beyond it a smaller hatch, evidently leading into the missile itself, was also open.

"What was he doing, trying to explode the warheads?"

"Impossible," Ramius said, in obvious pain. "The rocket warheads—we call this special safe. The warheads cannot—not fire."

"So what was he doing?" Ryan went over to the missile tube. A sort of rubber bladder was lying on the deck. "What's this?" He hefted the gadget in his hand. It was made of rubber or rubberized fabric with a metal or plastic frame inside, a metal nipple on one corner, and a mouthpiece.

"He was doing something to the missile, but he had an escape device to get off the sub," Ryan said. "Oh, Christ! A timing device." He bent down to pick up the work light and switched it on, then stood back and peered into the missile compartment. "Captain, what's in here?"

"That is—the guidance compartment. It has a computer that tells the rocket how to fly. The door—," Ramius' breaths were coming hard, "—is a hatch for the officer."

Ryan peered into the hatch. He found a mass of multicolored wires and circuit boards connected in a way he'd never seen before. He poked through the wires half expecting to find a ticking alarm clock wired to some dynamite sticks. He didn't.

Now what should he do? The agent had been up to something—but what? Did he finish? How could Ryan tell? He couldn't. One part of his brain screamed at him to do something, the other part said that he'd be crazy to try.

Ryan put the rubber-coated handle to the light between his teeth and reached into the compartment with both hands. He grabbed a double handful of wires and yanked back. Only a few broke loose. He released one bunch and concentrated on the other. A clump of plastic and copper spaghetti came loose. He did it again for the other bunch. "Aaah!" he gasped, receiving an electric shock. An eternal moment followed while he waited to be blown up. It passed. There were more wires to pull. In under a minute he'd ripped out every wire he could see along with a half-dozen small breadboards. Next he smashed the light against everything he thought might break until the compartment looked like his son's toybox—full of useless fragments.

He heard people running into the compartment. Borodin was in front. Ramius motioned him over to Ryan and the dead agent.

"Sudets?" Borodin said. "Sudets?" He looked at Ryan. "This is cook."

Ryan took the pistol from the deck. "Here's his recipe file. I think he was a GRU agent. He was trying to blow us up. Captain Ramius, how about we launch this missile—just jettison the goddamned thing, okay?"

"A good idea, I think." Ramius' voice had become a hoarse whisper. "First close the inspection hatch, then we—can fire from the control room."

Ryan used his hand to sweep the fragments away from the missile hatch, and the door slid neatly back into place. The tube hatch was different. It was a pressure-bearing one and much heavier, held in place by two spring-loaded latches. Ryan slammed it three times. Twice it rebounded, but the third time it stuck.

Borodin and another officer were already carrying Williams aft. Someone had set a belt on Ramius' leg wound. Ryan got him to his feet and helped him walk. Ramius grunted in pain every time he had to move his left leg.

"You took a foolish chance, Captain," Ryan observed.

"This is my ship—and I do not like the dark. It was my fault! We should have made a careful counting as the crew left."

They arrived at the watertight door. "Okay, I'll go through first." Ryan stepped through and helped Ramius through backward. The belt had loosened, and the wound was bleeding again.

"Close the hatch and lock it," Ramius ordered.

It closed easily. Ryan turned the wheel three times, then got under the captain's arm again. Another twenty feet and they were in the control room. The lieutenant at the wheel was ashen.

Ryan sat the captain in a chair on the port side. "You have a knife, sir?"

Ramius reached in his pocket and came out with a folding knife and something else. "Here, take this. It's the key for the rocket warheads. They cannot fire unless this is used. You keep it." He tried to laugh. It had been Putin's, after all.

Ryan flipped it around his neck, opened the knife, and cut the captain's pants all the way up. The bullet had gone clean through the meaty part of the thigh. He took a clean handkerchief from his pocket and held it against the entrance wound. Ramius handed him another handkerchief. Ryan placed this against the half-inch exit wound. Next he set the belt across both, drawing it as tight as he could.

"My wife might not approve, but that will have to do."

"Your wife?" Ramius asked.

"She's a doc, an eye surgeon to be exact. The day I got shot she did this for me." Ramius' lower leg was growing pale. The belt was too tight, but Ryan didn't want to loosen it just yet. "Now, what about the missile?"

Ramius gave an order to the lieutenant at the wheel, who relayed it through the intercom. Two minutes later three officers entered the control room. Speed was cut to five knots, which took several minutes. Ryan worried about the missile and whether or not he had destroyed whatever boobytrap the agent had installed. Each of the three newly arrived officers took a key from around his neck. Ramius did the same, giving his second key to Ryan. He pointed to the starboard side of the compartment.

"Rocket control."

Ryan should have guessed as much. Arrayed throughout the control room were five panels, each with three rows of twenty-six lights and a key slot under each set.

"Put your key in number one, Ryan." Jack did, and the others inserted their keys. The red light came on and a buzzer sounded.

The missile officer's panel was the most elaborate. He turned a switch to flood the missile tube and open the number one hatch. The red panel lights began to blink.

"Turn your key, Ryan," Ramius said.

"Does this fire the missile?" Christ, what if that happens? Ryan wondered.

"No no. The rocket must be armed by the rocket officer. This key explodes the gas charge."

Could Ryan believe him? Sure he was a good guy and all that, but how could Ryan know he was telling the truth?

"Now!" Ramius ordered. Ryan turned his key at the same instant as the others. The amber light over the red light blinked on. The one under the green cover stayed off.

The *Red October* shuddered as the number one SS-N-20 was ejected upward by the gas charge. The sound was like a truck's air brake. The three officers withdrew their keys. Immediately the missile officer shut the tube hatch.

The Dallas

"What?" Jones said. "Conn, sonar, the target just flooded a tube—a missile tube? God almighty!" On his own, Jones powered up the under-ice sonar and began high-frequency pinging.

"What the hell are you doing?" Thompson demanded. Mancuso was there a second later.

"What's going on?" the captain snapped. Jones pointed at his display.

"The sub just launched a missile, sir. Look, Cap'n, two targets. But it's just hangin' there, no missile ignition. God!"

The Red October

Will it float? Ryan wondered.

It didn't. The Seahawk missile was pushed upward and to starboard by the gas charge. It stopped fifty feet over her deck as the *October* cruised past. The guidance hatch that Ryan had closed was not fully sealed. Water filled the compartment and flooded the warhead bus. The missile in any case had a sizable negative bouyancy, and the added mass in the nose tipped it over. The nose-heavy trim gave it an eccentric path, and it spiraled down like a seedpod from a tree. At ten thousand feet water pressure crushed the seal over the missile blast cones, but the Seahawk, otherwise undamaged, retained its shape all the way to the bottom.

The Ethan Allen

The only thing still operating was the timer. It had been set for thirty minutes, which had allowed the crew plenty of time to board the *Scamp,* now leaving the area at ten knots. The old reactor had been completely shut down. It was stone cold. Only a few emergency lights remained on from residual battery power. The timer had three redundant firing circuits, and all went off within a millisecond of one another, sending a signal down the detonator wires.

They had put four Pave Pat Blue bombs on the *Ethan Allen*. The Pave Pat Blue was a FAE (fuel-air explosive) bomb. Its blast efficiency was roughly five times that of an ordinary chemical explosive. Each bomb had a pair of gas-release valves, and only one of the eight valves failed. When they burst open, the pressurized propane in the bomb casings expanded violently outward. In an instant the atmospheric pressure in the old submarine tripled as her every part was saturated with an explosive air-gas mixture. The four bombs filled the *Ethan Allen* with the equivalent of twenty-five tons of TNT evenly distributed throughout the hull.

The squibs fired almost simultaneously, and the results were catastrophic: the *Ethan Allen*'s strong steel hull burst as if it were a balloon. The only item not totally destroyed was the reactor vessel, which fell free of the shredded wreckage and dropped rapidly to the ocean floor. The hull itself was blasted into a dozen pieces, all bent into surreal shapes by the explosion. Interior equipment formed a metallic cloud within the shattered hull, and everything fluttered downward, expanding over a wide area during the three-mile descent to the hard sand bottom.

The Dallas

"Holy shit!" Jones slapped the headphones off and yawned to clear his ears. Automatic relays within the sonar system protected his ears from the full force of the explosion, but what had been transmitted was enough to make him feel as though his head had been hammered flat. The explosion was heard through the hull by everyone aboard.

"Attention all hands, this is the captain speaking. What you just heard is nothing to worry about. That's all I can say."

"Gawd, Skipper!" Mannion said.

"Yeah, let's get back on the contact."

"Aye, Cap'n." Mannion gave his commander a curious look.

The White House

"Did you get the word to him in time?" the president asked.

"No, sir." Moore slumped into his chair. "The helicopter arrived a few minutes too late. It may be nothing to worry about. You'd expect that the captain would know enough to get everyone off except for his own people. We're concerned, of course, but there isn't anything we can do."

"I asked him personally to do this, Judge. Me."

Welcome to the real world, Mr. President, Moore thought. The chief executive had been lucky—he'd never had to send men to their deaths. Moore reflected that it was something easy to consider beforehand, less easy to get used to. He had affirmed death sentences from his seat on an appellate bench, and that had not been easy—even for men who had richly deserved their fates.

"Well, we'll just have to wait and see, Mr. President. The source this data comes from is more important than any one operation."

"Very well. What about Senator Donaldson?"

"He agreed to our suggestion. This aspect of the operation has worked out very well indeed."

"Do you really expect the Russians to buy it?" Pelt asked.

"We've left some nice bait, and we'll jerk the line a little to get their attention. In a day or two we'll see if they nibble at it. Henderson is one of their all-stars—his code name is Cassius—and their reaction to this will tell us just what sort of disinformation we can pass through him. He could turn out to be very useful, but we'll have to watch out for him. Our KGB colleagues have a very direct method for dealing with doubles."

"We don't let him off the hook unless he earns it," the president said coldly.

Moore smiled. "Oh, he'll earn it. We own Mr. Henderson."

THE FIFTEENTH DAY

FRIDAY, 17 DECEMBER

Ocracoke Inlet

There was no moon. The three-ship procession entered the inlet
at five knots, just after midnight to take advantage of the extra-
high spring tide. The *Pogy* led the formation since she had the
shallowest draft, and the *Dallas* trailed the *Red October*. The
coast guard stations on either side of the inlet were occupied
by naval officers who had relieved the "coasties."

Ryan had been allowed atop the sail, a humanitarian gesture
from Ramius that he much appreciated. After eighteen hours
inside the *Red October* Jack had felt confined, and it was good
to see the world—even if it was nothing but dark empty space.
The *Pogy* showed only a dim red light that disappeared if it
was looked at for more than a few seconds. He could see the
water's feathery wisps of foam and the stars playing hide-and-
seek through the clouds. The west wind was a harsh twenty
knots coming off the water.

Borodin was giving terse, monosyllabic orders as he conned

the submarine up a channel that had to be dredged every few months despite the enormous jetty which had been built to the north. The ride was an easy one, the two or three feet of chop not mattering a whit to the missile sub's 30,000-ton bulk. Ryan was thankful for this. The black water calmed, and when they entered sheltered waters a Zodiac-type rubber boat zoomed towards them.

"Ahoy *Red October!*" a voice called in the darkness. Ryan could barely make out the gray lozenge shape of the Zodiac. It was ahead of a tiny patch of foam formed by the sputtering outboard motor.

"May I answer, Captain Borodin?" Ryan asked, getting a nod. "This is Ryan. We have two casualties aboard. One's in bad shape. We need a doctor and a surgical team right away! Do you understand?"

"Two casualties, and you need a doc, right." Ryan thought he saw a man holding something to his face, and thought he heard the faint crackle of a radio. It was hard to tell in the wind. "Okay. We'll have a doc flown down right away, *October. Dallas* and *Pogy* both have medical corpsmen aboard. You want 'em?"

"Damn straight!" Ryan replied at once.

"Okay. Follow *Pogy* two more miles and stand by." The Zodiac sped forward, reversed course, and disappeared in the darkness.

"Thank God for that," Ryan breathed.

"You are be—believer?" Borodin asked.

"Yeah, sure." Ryan should not have been surprised by the question. "Hell, you gotta believe in something."

"And why is that, Commander Ryan?" Borodin was examining the *Pogy* through oversized night glasses.

Ryan wondered how to answer. "Well, because if you don't, what's the point of life? That would mean Sartre and Camus and all those characters were right—all is chaos, life has no meaning. I refuse to believe that. If you want a better answer, I know a couple priests who'd be glad to talk to you."

Borodin did not respond. He spoke an order into the bridge microphone, and they altered course a few degrees to starboard.

The Dallas

A half mile aft, Mancuso was holding a light-amplifying night scope to his eyes. Mannion was at his shoulder, struggling to see.

"Jesus Christ," Mancuso whispered.

"You got that one right, Skipper," Mannion said, shivering in his jacket. "I'm not sure I believe it either. Here comes the Zodiac." Mannion handed his commander the portable radio used for docking.

"Do you read?"

"This is Mancuso."

"When our friend stops, I want you to transfer ten men to her, including your corpsman. They report two casualties who need medical attention. Pick good men, Commander, they'll need help running the boat—just make damned sure they're men who don't talk."

"Acknowledged. Ten men including the medic. Out." Mancuso watched the raft speed off to the *Pogy.* "Want to come along, Pat?"

"Bet your ass, uh, sir. You planning to go?" Mannion asked.

Mancuso was judicious. "I think Chambers is up to handling *Dallas* for a day or so, don't you?"

On shore, a naval officer was on the phone to Norfolk. The coast guard station was crowded, almost entirely with officers. A fiberglass box sat next to the phone so that they could communicate with CINCLANT in secrecy. They had been here only two hours and would soon leave. Nothing could appear out of the ordinary. Outside, an admiral and a pair of captains watched the dark shapes through starlight scopes. They were as solemn as men in a church.

Cherry Point, North Carolina

Commander Ed Noyes was resting in the doctor's lounge of the naval hospital at the U.S. Marine Corps Air Station, Cherry Point, North Carolina. A qualified flight surgeon, he had the duty for the next three nights so that he'd have four days off over Christmas. It had been a quiet night. This was about to change.

"Doc?"

Noyes looked up to see a marine captain in MP livery. The doctor knew him. Military police delivered a lot of accident cases. He set down his *New England Journal of Medicine*.

"Hi, Jerry. Something coming in?"

"Doc, I got orders to tell you to pack everything you need for emergency surgery. You got two minutes, then I take you to the airfield."

"What for? What kind of surgery?" Noyes stood.

"They didn't say, sir, just that you fly out somewheres, alone. The orders come from topside, that's all I know."

"Damn it, Jerry, I have to know what sort of surgery it is so I know what to take!"

"So take everything, sir. I gotta get you to the chopper."

Noyes swore and went into the trauma receiving room. Two more marines were waiting there. He handed them four sterile sets, prepackaged instrument trays. He wondered if he'd need some drugs and decided to grab an armful, along with two units of plasma. The captain helped him on with his coat, and they moved out the door to a waiting jeep. Five minutes later they pulled up to a Sea Stallion whose engines were already screaming.

"What gives?" Noyes asked the colonel of intelligence inside, wondering where the crew chief was.

"We're heading out over the sound," the colonel explained. "We have to let you down on a sub that has some casualties aboard. There's a pair of corpsmen to assist you, and that's all I know, okay?" It had to be okay. There was no choice in the matter.

The Stallion lifted off at once. Noyes had flown in them often enough. He had two hundred hours piloting helicopters, another three hundred in fixed-wing aircraft. Noyes was the kind of doctor who'd discovered too late that flying was as attractive a calling as medicine. He went up at every opportunity, often giving pilots special medical care for their dependents to get backseat time in an F-4 Phantom. The Sea Stallion, he noted, was not cruising. It was running flat out.

Pamlico Sound

The *Pogy* came to a halt about the time the helicopter left Cherry Point. The *October* altered course to starboard again and halted even with her to the north. The *Dallas* followed suit. A minute after that the Zodiac reappeared at the *Dallas'* side, then approached the *Red October* slowly, almost wallowing with her cargo of men.

"Ahoy *Red October!*"

This time Borodin answered. He had an accent but his English was understandable. "Identify."

"This is Bart Mancuso, commanding officer of USS *Dallas*. I have our ship's medical representative aboard and some other men. Request permission to come aboard, sir."

Ryan saw the *starpom* grimace. For the first time Borodin really had to face up to what was happening, and he would have been less than human to accept it without some kind of struggle.

"Permission is—yes."

The Zodiac edged right up to the curve of the hull. A man leaped aboard with a line to secure the raft. Ten men clambered off, one breaking away to climb up the submarine's sail.

"Captain? I'm Bart Mancuso. I understand you have some hurt men aboard."

"Yes," Borodin nodded, "the captain and a British officer, both shot."

"Shot?" Mancuso was surprised.

"Worry about that later," Ryan said sharply. "Let's get your doc working on them, okay?"

"Sure, where's the hatch?"

Borodin spoke into the bridge mike, and a few seconds later a circle of light appeared on deck at the foot of the sail.

"We haven't got a physician, we have an independent duty corpsman. He's pretty good, and *Pogy*'s man will be here in another couple minutes. Who are you, by the way?"

"He is a spy," Borodin said with palpable irony.

"Jack Ryan."

"And you, sir?"

"Captain Second Rank Vasily Borodin. I am—first officer, yes? Come over into the station, Commander. Please excuse me, we are all very tired."

"You're not the only ones." There wasn't that much room. Mancuso perched himself on the coaming. "Captain, I want you to know we had a bastard of a time tracking you. You are to be complimented for your professional skill."

The compliment did not elicit the anticipated response from Borodin. "You were able to track us. How?"

"I brought him along, you can meet him."

"And what are we to do?"

"Orders from shore are to wait for the doc to arrive and dive. Then we sit tight until we get orders to move. Maybe a day, maybe two. I think we could all use the rest. After that, we get you to a nice safe place, and I will personally buy you the best damned Italian dinner you ever had." Mancuso grinned. "You get Italian food in Russia?"

"No, and if you are accustomed to good food, you may find *Krazny Oktyabr* not to your liking."

"Maybe I can fix that. How many men aboard?"

"Twelve. Ten Soviet, the Englishman, and the spy." Borodin glanced at Ryan with a thin smile.

"Okay." Mancuso reached into his coat and came out with a radio. "This is Mancuso."

"We're here, Skipper," Chambers replied.

"Get some food together for our friends. Six meals for twenty-five men. Send a cook over with it. Wally, I want to show these men some good chow. Got it?"

"Aye aye, Skipper. Out."

"I got some good cooks, Captain. Shame this wasn't last week. We had lasagna, just like momma used to make. All that was missing was the Chianti."

"They have vodka," Ryan observed.

"Only for spies," Borodin said. Two hours after the shootout Ryan had had the shakes badly, and Borodin had sent him a drink from the medical stores. "We are told that your submarine men are greatly pampered."

"Maybe so," Mancuso nodded. "But we stay out sixty or seventy days at a time. That's hard enough, don't you think?"

"How about we go below?" Ryan suggested. Everyone agreed. It was getting cold.

Borodin, Ryan and Mancuso went below to find the Americans on one side of the control room and the Soviets on the other, just like before. The American captain broke the ice.

"Captain Borodin, this is the man who found you. Come here, Jonesy."

"It wasn't very easy, sir," Jones said. "Can I get to work?

Can I see your sonar room?"

"Bugayev." Borodin waved the ship's electronics officer over. The captain-lieutenant led the sonarman aft.

Jones took one look at the equipment and muttered, "Kludge." The face plates all had louvers on them to let out the heat. God, did they use vacuum tubes? Jones wondered. He pulled a screwdriver from his pocket to find out.

"You speak English, sir?"

"Yes, a little."

"Can I see the circuit diagrams for these, please?"

Bugayev blinked. No enlisted man, and only one of his *michmanyy,* had ever asked for it. Then he took the binder of schematics from its shelf on the forward bulkhead.

Jones matched the code number of the set he was checking with the right section of the binder. Unfolding the diagram, he noted with relief that ohms were ohms, all over the world. He began tracing his finger along the page, then pulled the cover panel off to look inside the set.

"Kludge, megakludge to the max!" Jones was shocked enough to lapse into Valspeak.

"Excuse me, what is this 'kludge'?"

"Oh, pardon me, sir. That's an expression we use in the navy. I don't know how to say it in Russian. Sorry." Jones stifled a grin as he went back to the schematic. "Sir, this one here's a low-powered high-frequency set, right? You use this for mines and stuff?"

It was Bugayev's turn to be shocked. "You have been trained in Soviet equipment?"

"No, sir, but I've sure heard a lot of it." Wasn't this obvious? Jones wondered. "Sir, this is a high-frequency set, but it doesn't draw a lot of power. What else is it good for? A low-power FM set you use for mines, for work under ice, and for docking, right?"

"Correct."

"You have a gertrude, sir?"

"Gertrude?"

"Underwater telephone, sir, for talking to other subs." Didn't this guy know anything?

"Ah, yes, but it is located in control, and it is broken."

"Uh-huh." Jones looked over the diagram again. "I think I

can rig a modulator on this baby, then, and make it into a gertrude for ya. Might be useful. You think your skipper would want that, sir?"

"I will ask." He expected Jones to stay put, but the young sonarman was right behind him when he went to control. Bugayev explained the suggestion to Borodin while Jones talked to Mancuso.

"They got a little FM set that looks just like the old gertrudes in sonar school. We have a spare modulator in stores, and I can probably rig it up in thirty minutes, no sweat," the sonarman said.

"Captain Borodin, do you agree?" Mancuso asked.

Borodin felt as if he were being pushed too fast, even though the suggestion made perfectly good sense. "Yes, have your man do it."

"Skipper, how long we gonna be here?" Jones asked.

"A day or two, why?"

"Sir, this boat looks kinda thin on creature comforts, you know? How 'bout I grab a TV and a tape machine? Give 'em something to look at, you know, sort of give 'em a quick look at the USA?"

Mancuso laughed. They wanted to learn everything they could about this boat, but they had plenty of time for that, and Jones' idea looked like a good way to ease the tension. On the other hand, he didn't want to incite a mutiny on his own sub. "Okay, take the one from the wardroom."

"Right, Skipper."

The Zodiac delivered the *Pogy*'s corpsman a few minutes later, and Jones took the boat back to the *Dallas*. Gradually the officers were beginning to engage in conversation. Two Russians were trying to talk to Mannion and were looking at his hair. They had never met a black man before.

"Captain Borodin, I have orders to take something out of the control room that will identify—I mean, something that comes from this boat." Mancuso pointed. "Can I take that depth gauge? I can have one of my men rig a substitute." The gauge, he saw, had a number.

"For what reason?"

"Beats me, but those are my orders."

"Yes," Borodin replied.

Mancuso ordered one of his chiefs to perform the job. The

chief pulled a crescent wrench from his pocket and removed the nut holding the needle and dial in place.

"This is a little bigger than ours, Skipper, but not by much. I think we have a spare. I can flip it backwards and scribe in the markings, okay?"

Mancuso handed his radio over. "Call it in and have Jonesy bring the spare back with him."

"Aye, Cap'n." The chief put the needle back in place after setting the dial on the deck.

The Sea Stallion did not attempt to land, though the pilot was tempted. The deck was almost large enough to try. As it was, the helicopter hovered a few feet over the missile deck, and the doctor leaped into the arms of two seamen. His supplies were tossed down a moment later. The colonel remained in the back of the chopper and slid the door shut. The bird turned slowly to move back southwest, its massive rotor raising spray from the waters of Pamlico Sound.

"Was that what I think it was?" the pilot asked over the intercom.

"Wasn't it backwards? I thought missile subs had the missiles aft of the sail. Those were in front of the sail, weren't they? I mean, wasn't that the rudder sticking up behind the sail?" the copilot responded quizzically.

"It was a Russian sub!" the pilot said.

"What?" It was too late to see, they were already two miles away. "Those were our guys on the deck. They weren't Russians."

"Son of a bitch!" the major swore wonderingly. And he couldn't say a thing. The colonel of division intelligence had been damned specific about that: "You don't see nothin', you don't hear nothin', you don't think nothin', and you goddamned well don't ever say nothin'."

"I'm Doctor Noyes," the commander said to Mancuso in the control room. He had never been on a submarine before, and when he looked around he saw a compartment full of instruments all in a foreign language. "What ship is this?"

"Krazny Oktyabr," Borodin said, coming over. In the centerpiece of his cap there was a gleaming red star.

"What the hell is going on here?" Noyes demanded.

"Doc," Ryan took him by the arm, "you have two patients aft. Why not let's worry about them?"

Noyes followed him aft to sick bay. "What's going on here?" he persisted more quietly.

"The Russians just lost a submarine," Ryan explained, "and now she belongs to us. And if you tell anybody—"

"I read you, but I don't believe you."

"You don't have to believe me. What kind of cutter are you?"

"Thoracic."

"Good," Ryan turned into sick bay, "you have a gunshot wound victim who needs you bad."

Williams was lying naked on the table. A sailor came in with an armful of medical supplies and set them on Petrov's desk. The *October*'s medical locker had a supply of frozen plasma, and the two corpsmen already had two units running into the lieutenant. A chest tube was in, draining into a vacuum bottle.

"We got a nine-millimeter in this man's chest," one of the corpsmen said after introducing himself and his partner. "He's had a chest tube in the last ten hours, they tell me. The head looks worse than it is. Right pupil is a little blown, but no big deal. The chest is bad, sir. You'd better take a listen."

"Vitals?" Noyes fished in his bag for a stethoscope.

"Heart is 110 and thready. Blood pressure's eighty over forty."

Noyes moved his stethoscope around Williams' chest, frowning. "Heart's in the wrong place. We have a left tension pneumothorax. There must be a quart of fluid in there, and it sounds like he's heading for congestive failure." Noyes turned to Ryan. "You get out of here. I've got a chest to crack."

"Take care of him, Doc. He's a good man."

"Aren't they all," Noyes observed, stripping off his jacket. "Let's get scrubbed, people."

Ryan wondered if a prayer would help. Noyes looked and talked like a surgeon. Ryan hoped he was. He went aft to the captain's cabin, where Ramius was sleeping with the drugs he'd been given. The leg had stopped bleeding, and evidently one of the corpsmen had checked on it. Noyes could work on him next. Ryan went forward.

Borodin felt he had lost control and didn't like it, though it was something of a relief. Two weeks of constant tension plus the nerve-wrenching change in plans had shaken the officer more than he would have believed. The situation now was unpleasant—the Americans were trying to be kind, but they were so damned overpowering! At least the *Red October*'s officers were not in danger.

Twenty minutes later the Zodiac was back again. Two sailors went topside to unload a few hundred pounds of frozen food, then helped Jones with his electronic gear. It took several minutes to get everything squared away, and the seamen who took the food forward came back shaken after finding two stiff bodies and a third frozen solid. There had not been time to move the two recent casualties.

"Got everything, Skipper," Jones reported. He handed the depth gauge dial to the chief.

"What is all of this?" Borodin asked.

"Captain, I got the modulator to make the gertrude." Jones held up a small box. "This other stuff is a little color TV, a video cassette recorder, and some movie tapes. The skipper thought you gentlemen might want something to relax with, to get to know us a little, you know?"

"Movies?" Borodin shook his head. "Cinema movies?"

"Sure," Mancuso chuckled. "What did you bring, Jonesy?"

"Well, sir, I got *E.T.*, *Star Wars*, *Big Jake*, and *Hondo*." Clearly Jones wanted to be careful what parts of America he introduced the Russians to.

"My apologies, Captain. My crewman has limited taste in movies."

At the moment Borodin would have settled for *The Battleship Potemkin*. The fatigue was really hitting him hard.

The cook bustled aft with an armload of groceries. "I'll have coffee in a few minutes, sir," he said to Borodin on his way to the galley.

"I would like something to eat. None of us has eaten in a day," Borodin said.

"Food!" Mancuso called aft.

"Aye, Skipper. Let me figure this galley out."

Mannion checked his watch. "Twenty minutes, sir."

"We have everything we need aboard?"

"Yes, sir."

Jones bypassed the pulse control on the sonar amplifier and wired in the modulator. It was even easier than he'd expected. He had taken a radio microphone from the *Dallas* along with everything else and now connected it to the sonar set before powering the system up. He had to wait for the set to warm up. Jones hadn't seen this many tubes since he'd gone out on TV repair jobs with his father, and that had been a long time ago.

"*Dallas*, this is Jonesy, do you copy?"

"Aye." The reply was scratchy, like a taxicab radio.

"Thanks. Out." He switched off. "It works. That was pretty easy, wasn't it?"

Enlisted man, hell! And not even trained on Soviet equipment! the *October*'s electronics officer thought. It never occurred to him that this piece of equipment was a near copy of an obsolete American FM system. "How long have you been a sonarman?"

"Three and a half years, sir. Since I dropped out of college."

"You learn all this in three years?" the officer asked sharply.

Jones shrugged. "What's the big deal, sir? I've been foolin' with radios and stuff since I was a kid. You mind if I play some music, sir?"

Jones had decided to be especially nice. He had only one tape of a Russian composer, the Nutcracker Suite, and had brought that along with four Bachs. Jones liked to hear music while he prayed over circuit diagrams. The young sonarman was in Hog Heaven. All the Russian sets he had listened to for three years—now he had their schematics, their hardware, and the time to figure them all out. Bugayev continued to watch in amazement as Jones' fingers did their ballet through the manual pages to the music of Tchaikovsky.

"Time to dive, sir," Mannion said in control.

"Very well. With your permission, Captain Borodin, I will assist with the vents. All hatches and openings are . . . shut." The diving board used the same light-array system as American boats, Mancuso noticed.

Mancuso took stock of the situation one last time. Butler and his four most senior petty officers were already tending to the nuclear tea kettle aft. The situation looked pretty good, considering. The only thing that could really go badly wrong would be for the *October*'s officers to change their minds. The

Dallas would be keeping the missile sub under constant sonar observation. If she moved, the *Dallas* had a ten-knot speed advantage with which to block the channel.

"The way I see it, Captain, we are rigged for dive," Mancuso said.

Borodin nodded and sounded the diving alarm. It was a buzzer, just like on American boats. Mancuso, Mannion, and the Russian officer worked the complex vent controls. The *Red October* began her slow descent. In five minutes she was resting on the bottom, with seventy feet of water over the top of her sail.

The White House

Pelt was on the phone to the Soviet embassy at three in the morning. "Alex, this is Jeffrey Pelt."

"How are you, Dr. Pelt? I must offer my thanks and that of the Soviet people for your action to save our sailor. I was informed a few minutes ago that he is now conscious, and that he is expected to recover fully."

"Yes, I just learned that myself. What's his name, by the way?" Pelt wondered if he had awakened Arbatov. It didn't sound like it.

"Andre Katyskin, a cook petty officer from Leningrad."

"Good, Alex, I am informed that USS *Pigeon* has rescued nearly the entire crew of another Soviet submarine off the Carolinas. Her name, evidently, was *Red October*. That's the good news, Alex. The bad news is that the vessel exploded and sank before we could get them all off. Most of the officers, and two of our officers, were lost."

"When was this?"

"Very early yesterday morning. Sorry about the delay, but *Pigeon* had trouble with the radio, as a result of the underwater explosion, they say. You know how that sort of thing can happen."

"Indeed." Pelt had to admire the response, not a trace of irony. "Where are they now?"

"The *Pigeon* is sailing to Charleston, South Carolina. We'll have your crewmen flown directly to Washington from there."

"And this submarine exploded? You are sure?"

"Yeah, one of the crewmen said they had a major reactor

accident. It was just good luck that *Pigeon* was there. She was heading to the Virginia coast to look at the other one you lost. I think your navy needs a little work, Alex," Pelt observed.

"I will pass that along to Moscow, Doctor," Arbatov responded dryly. "Can you tell us where this happened?"

"I can do better than that. We have a ship taking a deep-diving research sub down to look for the wreckage. If you want, you can have your navy fly a man to Norfolk, and we'll fly him out to check it for you. Fair enough?"

"You say you lost two officers?" Arbatov played for time, surprised at the offer.

"Yes, both rescue people. We did get a hundred men off, Alex," Pelt said defensively. "That's something."

"Indeed it is, Dr. Pelt. I must cable Moscow for instructions. I will be back to you. You are at your office?"

"Correct. Bye, Alex." He hung up and looked at the president. "Do I pass, boss?"

"Work a little bit on the sincerity, Jeff." The president was sprawled in a leather chair, a robe over his pajamas. "They'll bite?"

"They'll bite. They sure as hell want to confirm the destruction of the sub. Question is, can we fool 'em?"

"Foster seems to think so. It sounds plausible enough."

"Hmph. Well, we have her, don't we?" Pelt observed.

"Yep, I guess that story about the GRU agent was wrong, or else they kicked him off with everybody else. I want to see that Captain Ramius. Jeez! Pulling a reactor scare, no wonder he got everybody off the ship!"

The Pentagon

Skip Tyler was in the CNO's office trying to relax in a chair. The coast guard station on the inlet had had a low-light television, the tape from which had been flown by helicopter to Cherry Point and from there by Phantom jet fighter to Andrews. Now it was in the hands of a courier whose automobile was just pulling up at the Pentagon's main entrance.

"I have a package to hand deliver to Admiral Foster," an ensign announced a few minutes later. Foster's flag secretary pointed him to the door.

"Good morning, sir! This is for you, sir." The ensign handed Foster the wrapped cassette.

"Thank you. Dismissed."

Foster inserted the cassette in the tape player atop his office television. The set was already on, and the picture appeared in several seconds.

Tyler was standing beside the CNO as it focused. "Yep."

"Yep," Foster agreed.

The picture was lousy—no other word for it. The low-light television system did not give a very sharp picture since it amplified all of the ambient light equally. This tended to wash out many details. But what they saw was enough: a very large missile submarine whose sail was much farther aft than the sails on anything a Western country made. She dwarfed the *Dallas* and *Pogy*. They watched the screen without a word for the next fifteen minutes. Except for the wobbly camera, the picture was about as lively as a test pattern.

"Well," Foster said as the tape ended, "we got us a Russian boomer."

"How 'bout that?" Tyler grinned.

"Skip, you were up for command of *Los Angeles*, right?"

"Yes, sir."

"We owe you for this, Commander, we owe you a lot. I did some checking the other day. An officer injured in the line of duty does not necessarily have to retire unless he is demonstrably unfit for duty. An accident while returning from working on your boat is line of duty, I think, and we've had a few ship commanders who were short a leg. I'll go to the president myself on this, son. It will mean a year's work getting back in the groove, but if you still want your command, by God, I'll get it for you."

Tyler sat down for that. It would mean being fitted for a new leg, something he'd been considering for months, and a few weeks getting used to it. Then a year—a good year—relearning everything he needed to know before he could go to sea . . . He shook his head. "Thank you, Admiral. You don't know what that means to me—but, no. I'm past that now. I have a different life, and different responsibilities now, and I'd just be taking someone else's slot. Tell you what, you let me get a look at that boomer, and we're even."

"That I can guarantee." Foster had hoped he'd respond that way, had been nearly sure of it. It was too bad, though. Tyler, he thought, would have been a good candidate for his own flag except for the leg. Well, nobody ever said the world was fair.

The Red October

"You guys seem to have things under control," Ryan observed. "Does anybody mind if I flake out somewhere?"

"Flake out?" Borodin asked.

"Sleep."

"Ah, take Dr. Petrov's cabin, across from the medical office."

On his way aft Ryan looked in Borodin's cabin and found the vodka bottle that had been liberated. It didn't have much taste, but it was smooth enough. Petrov's bunk was not very wide or very soft. Ryan was past caring. He took a long swallow and lay down in his uniform, which was already so greasy and dirty as to be beyond hope. He was asleep in five minutes.

The Sea Cliff

The air-purifier system was not working properly, Lieutenant Sven Johnsen thought. If his sinus cold had lasted a few more days he might not have noticed. The *Sea Cliff* was just passing ten thousand feet, and they couldn't tinker with the system until they surfaced. It was not dangerous—the environmental control systems had as many built-in redundancies as the Space Shuttle—just a nuisance.

"I've never been so deep," Captain Igor Kaganovich said conversationally. Getting him here had been complicated. It had required a Helix helicopter from the *Kiev* to the *Tarawa*, then a U.S. Navy Sea King to Norfolk. Another helicopter had taken him to the USS *Austin*, which was heading for 33N 75W at twenty knots. The *Austin* was a landing ship dock, a large vessel whose aft end was a covered well. She was usually used for landing craft, but today she carried the *Sea Cliff*, a three-man submarine that had been flown down from Woods Hole, Massachusetts.

"Does take some getting used to," Johnsen agreed, "but when you get down to it, five hundred feet, ten thousand feet, doesn't make much difference. A hull fracture would kill you just as fast, just down here there'd be less residue for the next boat to try and recover."

"Keep thinking those happy thoughts, sir," Machinist's Mate First Class Jesse Overton said. "Still clear on sonar?"

"Right, Jess." Johnsen had been working with the machinist's mate for two years. The *Sea Cliff* was their baby, a small, rugged research submarine used mainly for oceanographic tasks, including the emplacement or repair of SOSUS sensors. On the three-man sub there was little place for bridge discipline. Overton was not well educated or very articulate—at least not politely articulate. His skill at maneuvering the minisub was unsurpassed, however, and Johnsen was just as happy to leave that job to him. It was the lieutenant's task to manage the mission at hand.

"Air system needs some work," Johnsen observed.

"Yeah, the filters are about due for replacement. I was going to do that next week. Coulda' done it this morning, but I figured the backup control wiring was more important."

"Guess I have to go along with you on that. Handling okay?"

"Like a virgin." Overton's smile was reflected in the thick Lexan view port in front of the control seat. The *Sea Cliff's* awkward design made her clumsy to maneuver. It was as though she knew what she wanted to do, just not quite how she wanted to do it. "How wide's the target area?"

"Pretty wide. *Pigeon* says after the explosion the pieces spread from hell to breakfast."

"I believe it. Three miles down, and a current to spread it around."

"The boat's name is *Red October*, Captain? A *Victor*-class attack submarine, you said?"

"That is your name for the class," Kaganovich said.

"What do you call them?" Johnsen asked. He got no reply. What was the big deal? he wondered. What did the name of the class matter to anybody?

"Switching on locater sonar." Johnsen activated several systems, and the *Sea Cliff* pulsed with the sound of the high-frequency sonar mounted on her belly. "There's the bottom." The yellow screen showed bottom contours in white.

"Anything sticking up, sir?" Overton asked.

"Not today, Jess."

A year before they had been operating a few miles from this spot and nearly been impaled on a Liberty ship, sunk around 1942 by a German U-boat. The hulk had been sitting up at an angle, propped up by a massive boulder. That near collision would surely have been fatal, and it had taught both men caution.

"Okay, I'm starting to get some hard returns. Directly ahead, spread out like a fan. Another five hundred feet to the bottom."

"Right."

"Hmph. There's one big piece, 'bout thirty feet long, maybe nine or ten across, eleven o'clock, three hundred yards. We'll go for that one first."

"Coming left, lights coming on now."

A half-dozen high-intensity floodlights came on, at once surrounding the submersible in a globe of light. It did not penetrate more than ten yards in the water, which ate up the light energy.

"There's the bottom, just where you said, Mr. Johnsen," Overton said. He halted the powered descent and checked for buoyancy. Almost exactly neutral, good. "This current's going to be tough on battery power."

"How strong is it?"

"Knot an' a half, maybe more like two, depending on bottom contours. Same as last year. I figure we can maneuver an hour, hour an' a half, tops."

Johnsen agreed. Oceanographers were still puzzling over this deep current, which seemed to change direction from time to time in no particular pattern. Odd. There were a lot of odd things in the ocean. That's why Johnsen got his oceanography degree, to figure some of the buggers out. It sure beat working for a living. Being three miles down wasn't work, not to Johnsen.

"I see somethin', a flash off the bottom right in front of us. Want I should grab it?"

"If you can."

They couldn't see it yet on any of the *Sea Cliff*'s three TV monitors, which looked straight ahead, forty-five degrees left and right of the bow.

"Okay." Overton put his right hand on the waldo control. This was what he was really best at.

"Can you see what it is?" Johnsen asked, fiddling with the TV.

"Some kinda instrument. Can you kill the number one flood, sir? It's dazzlin' me."

"Wait one." Johnsen leaned forward to kill the proper switch. The number one floodlight provided illumination for the bow camera, which went immediately blank.

"Okay, baby, now let's just hold steady . . ." The machinist's mate's left hand worked the directional propeller controls; his right was poised in the waldo glove. Now he was the only one who could see the target. Overton's reflection was grinning at itself. His right hand moved rapidly.

"Gotcha!" he said. The waldo took the depth-gauge dial a diver had magnetically affixed to the *Sea Cliff*'s bow prior to setting out from the *Austin*'s dock bay. "You can hit the light again, sir."

Johnsen flicked it on, and Overton maneuvered his catch in front of the bow camera. "Can ya see what it is?"

"Looks like a depth gauge. Not one of ours, though," Johnsen observed. "Can you make it out, Captain?"

"Da," Kaganovich said at once. He let out a long breath, trying to sound unhappy. "It is one of ours. I cannot read the number, but it is Soviet."

"Put it in the basket, Jess," Johnsen said.

"Right." He maneuvered the waldo, placing the dial in a basket welded on the bow, then getting the manipulator arm back to its rest position. "Getting some silt. Let's pick up a little."

As the *Sea Cliff* got too close to the bottom the wash from her propellers stirred up the fine alluvial silt. Overton increased power to get back to a twenty-foot height.

"That's better. See what the current is doin', Mr. Johnsen? Good two knots. Gonna cut our bottom time." The current was wafting the cloud to port, rather quickly. "Where's the big target?"

"Dead ahead, hundred yards. Let's make sure we see what that is."

"Right. Going forward . . . There's something, looks like a butcher knife. We want it?"

"No, let's keep going."

"Okay, range?"

"Sixty yards. Ought to be seeing it soon."

The two officers saw it on TV the same time Overton did. Just a spectral image at first, it faded like an afterimage in one's eye. Then it came back.

Overton was the first to react. "Damn!"

It was more than thirty feet long and appeared perfectly round. They approached from its rear and saw the main circle and within it four smaller cones that stuck out a foot or so.

"That's a missile, Skipper, a whole fuckin' Russkie nuclear missile!"

"Hold position, Jess."

"Aye aye." He backed off on the power controls.

"You said she was a *Victor,*" Johnsen said to the Soviet.

"I was mistaken." Kaganovich's mouth twitched.

"Let's take a closer look, Jess."

The *Sea Cliff* moved forward, up the side of the rocket body. The Cyrillic lettering was unmistakable, though they were too far off to make out the serial numbers. There was a new treasure for Davey Jones, an SS-N-20 Seahawk, with its eight five-hundred-kiloton MIRVs.

Kaganovich was careful to note the markings on the missile body. He'd been briefed on the Seahawk immediately before flying from the *Kiev*. As an intelligence officer, he ordinarily knew more about American weapons than their Soviet counterparts.

How convenient, he thought. The Americans had allowed him to ride in one of their most advanced research vessels whose internal arrangements he had already memorized, and they had accomplished his mission for him. The *Red October* was dead. All he had to do was get that information to Admiral Stralbo on the *Kirov* and the fleet could leave the American coast. Let them come to the Norwegian Sea to play their nasty games! See who would win them up there!

"Position check, Jess. Mark the sucker."

"Aye." Overton pressed a button to deploy a sonar transponder that would respond only to a coded American sonar signal. This would guide them back to the missile. They would return later with their heavy-lift rig to put a line on the missile and haul it to the surface.

"That is the property of the Soviet Union," Kaganovich pointed out. "It is in—under international waters. It belongs to my country."

"Then you can fuckin' come and get it!" snapped the American seaman. He must be an officer in disguise, Kaganovich thought. "Beg pardon, Mr. Johnsen."

"We'll be back for it," Johnsen said.

"You'll never lift it. It is too heavy," Kaganovich objected.

"I suppose you're right." Johnsen smiled.

Kaganovich allowed the Americans their small victory. It

could have been worse. Much worse. "Shall we continue to search for more wreckage?"

"No, I think we'll go back up," Johnsen decided.

"But your orders—"

"My orders, Captain Kaganovich, were to search for the remains of a *Victor*-class attack submarine. We found the grave of a boomer. You lied to us, Captain, and our courtesy to you ends at this point. You got what you wanted, I guess. Later we'll be back for what we want." Johnsen reached up and pulled the release handle for the iron ballast. The metal slab dropped free. This gave the *Sea Cliff* a thousand pounds of positive buoyancy. There was no way to stay down now, even if they wanted to.

"Home, Jess."

"Aye aye, Skipper."

The ride back to the surface was a silent one.

The USS Austin

An hour later, Kaganovich climbed to the *Austin*'s bridge and requested permission to send a message to the *Kirov*. This had been agreed upon beforehand, else the *Austin*'s commanding officer would have refused. Word on the dead sub's identity had spread fast. The Soviet officer broadcast a series of code words, accompanied by the serial number from the depth-gauge dial. These were acknowledged at once.

Overton and Johnsen watched the Russian board the helicopter, carrying the depth-gauge dial.

"I didn't like him much, Mr. Johnsen. *Keptin Kaganobitch*. The name sounds like a terminal studder. We snookered him, didn't we?"

"Remind me never to play cards with you, Jess."

The Red October

Ryan woke up after six hours to music that seemed dreamily familiar. He lay in his bunk for a minute trying to place it, then slipped his feet into his shoes and went forward to the wardroom.

It was *E.T.* Ryan arrived just in time to see the credits scrolling up the thirteen-inch TV set sitting on the forward end of the wardroom table. Most of the Russian officers and three

Americans had been watching it. The Russians were all dabbing their eyes. Jack got a cup of coffee and sat at the end of the table.

"You liked it?"

"It was magnificent!" Borodin proclaimed.

Lieutenant Mannion chuckled. "Second time we ran it."

One of the Russians started speaking rapidly in his native language. Borodin translated for him. "He asks if all American children act with such—Bugayev, *svobodno?*"

"Free," Bugayev translated, incorrectly but close enough.

Ryan laughed. "I never did, but the movie was set in California—people out there are a little crazy. The truth is, no, kids don't act like that—at least I've never seen it, and I have two. At the same time, we do raise our kids to be a lot more independent than Soviet parents do."

Borodin translated, and then gave the Russian response. "So, all American children are not such hooligans?"

"Some are. America is not perfect, gentlemen. We make lots of mistakes." Ryan had decided to tell the truth insofar as he could.

Borodin translated again. The reactions around the table were a little dubious.

"I have told them this movie is a child's story and should not be taken too seriously. This is so?"

"Yes, sir," Mancuso, who had just come in, said. "It's a kid's story, but I've seen it five times. Welcome back, Ryan."

"Thank you, Commander. I take it you have things under control."

"Yep. I guess we all needed the chance to unwind. I'll have to write Jonesy another commendation letter. This really was a good idea." He waved at the television. "We have lots of time to be serious."

Noyes came in. "How's Williams?" Ryan asked.

"He'll make it." Noyes filled his cup. "I had him open for three and a half hours. The head wound was superficial—bloody as hell, but head wounds are like that. The chest was a close one, though. The bullet missed the pericardium by a whisker. Captain Borodin, who gave that man first aid?"

The *starpom* pointed to a lieutenant. "He does not speak English."

"Tell him that Williams owes him his life. Putting that chest tube in was the difference. He would have died without it."

"You're sure he'll make it?" Ryan persisted.

"Of course he'll make it, Ryan. That's what I do for a living. He'll be a sick boy for a while, and I'd feel better if we had him in a real hospital, but everything's under control."

"And Captain Ramius?" Borodin asked.

"No problem. He's still sleeping. I took my time sewing it up. Ask him where he got his first aid training."

Borodin did. "He said he likes to read medical books."

"How old is he?"

"Twenty-four."

"Tell him if he ever wants to study medicine, I'll tell him how to get started. If he knows how to do the right thing at the right time, he might just be good enough to do it for a living."

The young officer was pleased by this comment and asked how much money a doctor could make in America.

"I'm in the service, so I don't make very much. Forty-eight thousand a year, counting flight pay. I could do a lot better on the outside."

"In the Soviet Union," Borodin pointed out, "doctors are paid about the same as factory workers."

"Maybe that explains why your docs are no good," Noyes observed.

"When will the captain be able to resume command?" Borodin asked.

"I'm going to keep him down all day," Noyes said. "I don't want him to start bleeding again. He can start moving around tomorrow. Carefully. I don't want him on that leg too much. He'll be fine, gentlemen. A little weak from the blood loss, but he'll recover fully." Noyes made his pronouncements as though he were quoting physical laws.

"We thank you, Doctor," Borodin said.

Noyes shrugged. "It's what they pay me for. Now can I ask a question? What the hell is going on here?"

Borodin laughed, translating the question for his comrades. "We will all become American citizens."

"And you're bringing a sub along with you, eh? Son of a gun. For a while there I thought this was some sort of—I don't know, something. This is quite a story. Guess I can't tell it to anybody, though."

"Correct, Doctor." Ryan smiled.

"Too bad," Noyes muttered as he headed back to sick bay.

Moscow

"So, Comrade Admiral, you report success to us?" Narmonov asked.

"Yes, Comrade General Secretary," Gorshkov nodded, surveying the conference table in the underground command center. All of the inner circle were here, along with the military chiefs and the head of the KGB. "Admiral Stralbo's fleet intelligence officer, Captain Kaganovich, was permitted by the Americans to view the wreckage from aboard one of their deep-submergence research vessels. The craft recovered a fragment of wreckage, a depth-gauge dial. These objects are numbered, and the number was immediately relayed to Moscow. It was positively from *Red October*. Kaganovich also inspected a missile blasted loose from the submarine. It was definitely a Seahawk. *Red October* is dead. Our mission is accomplished."

"By chance, Comrade Admiral, not by design," Mikhail Alexandrov pointed out. "Your fleet failed in its mission to *locate* and destroy the submarine. I think Comrade Gerasimov has some information for us."

Nikolay Gerasimov was the new KGB chief. He had already given his report to the political members of this group and was eager to release it to these strutting peacocks in uniform. He wanted to see their reactions. The KGB had scores to settle with these men. Gerasimov summarized the report he had from agent Cassius.

"Impossible!" Gorshkov snapped.

"Perhaps," Gerasimov conceded politely. "There is a strong probability that this is a very clever piece of disinformation. It is now being investigated by our agents in the field. There are, however, some interesting details which support this hypothesis. Permit me to review them, Comrade Admiral.

"First, why did the Americans allow our man aboard one of their most sophisticated research submarines? Second, why did they cooperate with us at all, saving our sailor from the *Politovskiy* and *telling* us about it? They let us see our man immediately. Why? Why not keep our man, use him, and dispose of him? Sentimentality? I think not. Third, at the same time they picked this man up their air and fleet units were harassing our fleet in the most blatant and aggressive manner. This suddenly stopped, and a day later they were tripping over their own feet in their efforts to assist in our 'search and rescue.'"

"Because Stralbo wisely and courageously decided to refrain from reacting to their provocations," Gorshkov replied.

Gerasimov nodded politely again. "Perhaps so. That was an intelligent decision on the admiral's part. It cannot be easy for a uniformed officer to swallow his pride so. On the other hand, I speculate that it is also possible that about this time the Americans received this information which Cassius passed on to us. I further speculate that the Americans were fearful of our reaction were we to suspect that they had perpetrated this entire affair as a CIA operation. We know now that several imperialist intelligence services are inquiring as to the reason for this fleet operation.

"Over the past two days we have been doing some fast checking of our own. We find," Gerasimov consulted his notes, "that there are twenty-nine Polish engineers at the Polyarnyy submarine yard, mainly in quality control and inspection posts, that mail and message-handling procedures are very lax, and the Captain Ramius did not, as he supposedly threatened in his letter to Comrade Padorin, sail his submarine into New York harbor, but was rather in a position a thousand kilometers south when the submarine was destroyed."

"That was an obvious piece of disinformation on Ramius' part," Gorshkov objected. "Ramius was both baiting us and deliberately misleading us. For that reason we deployed our fleet at all of the American ports."

"And never did find him," Alexandrov noted quietly. "Go on, Comrade."

Gerasimov continued. "Whatever port he was supposedly heading for, he was over five hundred kilometers from any of them, and we are certain that he could have reached any of them on a direct course. In fact, Comrade Admiral, as you reported in your initial briefing, he could have reached the American coast within seven days of leaving port."

"To do that, as I explained at length last week, would have meant traveling at maximum speed. Missile submarine commanders prefer not to do this," Gorshkov said.

"I can understand it," Alexandrov observed, "in view of the fate of the *Politovskiy*. But you would expect a traitor to the *Rodina* to run like a thief."

"Into the trap we set," Gorshkov replied.

"Which failed," Narmonov commented.

"I do not claim that this story is true, nor do I claim it is even a likely one at this point," Gerasimov said, keeping his voice detached and clinical, "but there is sufficient circumstantial evidence supporting it that I must recommend an indepth investigation by the Committee for State Security touching on all aspects of this affair."

"Security in my yards is a naval and GRU matter," Gorshkov said.

"No longer." Narmonov announced the decision reached two hours earlier. "The KGB will investigate this shameful business along two lines. One group will investigate the information from our agent in Washington. The other will proceed on the assumption that the letter from—allegedly from—Captain Ramius was genuine. If this was a traitorous conspiracy, it could only have been possible because Ramius was able under current regulations and practices to choose his own officers. The Committee for State Security will report to us on the desirability of continuing this practice, on the current degree of control ship captains have over the careers of their officers, and over Party control of the fleet. I think we will begin our reforms by allowing officers to transfer from one ship to another with greater frequency. If officers stay in one place too long, obviously they may develop confusion in their loyalties."

"What you suggest will destroy the efficiency of my fleet!" Gorshkov pounded on the table. It was a mistake.

"The People's fleet, Comrade Admiral," Alexandrov corrected. "The Party's fleet." Gorshkov knew where that idea came from. Narmonov still had Alexandrov's support. That made the comrade general secretary's position secure, and that meant the positions of other men around this table were not. Which men?

Padorin's mind revolted at the suggestion from the KGB. What did those bastard spies know about the navy? Or the Party? They were all corrupt opportunists. Andropov had proven that, and the Politburo was now letting this whelp Gerasimov attack the armed services, which safeguarded the nation against the imperialists, had saved it from Andropov's clique, and had never been anything but the stalwart servants of the Party. But it does all fit, doesn't it? he thought. Just as Khrushchev had deposed Zhukov, the man who made his succession possible when Beria was done away with, so these bastards would now play the KGB against the uniformed men who had made their positions safe in the first place . . .

"As for you, Comrade Padorin," Alexandrov went on.

"Yes, Comrade Academician." For Padorin there was no apparent escape. The Main Political Administration had passed final approval on Ramius' appointment. If Ramius were indeed a traitor, then Padorin stood condemned for gross misjudgment, but if Ramius had been an unknowing pawn, then Padorin along with Gorshkov had been duped into precipitous action.

Narmonov took his cue from Alexandrov. "Comrade Admiral, we find that your secret provisions to safeguard the security of the submarine *Red October* were successfully implemented—unless, that is, Captain Ramius was blameless and scuttled the ship himself along with his officers and the Americans who were doubtless trying to steal it. In either case, pending the KGB's inspection of the parts recovered from the wreck, it would appear that the submarine did not fall into enemy hands."

Padorin blinked several times. His heart was beating fast, and he could feel a twinge of pain in his left chest. Was he being let off? Why? It took him a second to understand. He was the political officer, after all. If the Party was seeking to reestablish political control over the fleet—no, to reassert what never had been lost—then the Politburo could not afford to depose the Party's representative in high command. This would make him the vassal of these men, Alexandrov especially. Padorin decided that he could live with that.

And it made Gorshkov's position extremely vulnerable. Though it would take some months, Padorin was sure that the Russian fleet would have a new chief, one whose personal power would not be sufficient to make policy without Politburo approval. Gorshkov had become too big, too powerful, and the Party chieftains did not wish to have a man with so much personal prestige in high command.

I have my head, Padorin thought to himself, amazed at his good fortune.

"Comrade Gerasimov," Narmonov went on, "will be working with the political security section of your office to review your procedures and to offer suggestions for improvements."

So, now he became the KGB's spy in high command? Well, he had his head, his office, his dacha, and his pension in two years. It was a small price to pay. Padorin was more than content.

THE SIXTEENTH DAY

SATURDAY, 17 DECEMBER

The East Coast

The USS *Pigeon* arrived at her dock in Charleston at four in the morning. The Soviet crewmen, quartered in the crew's mess, had become a handful for everyone. As much as the Russian officers had worked to limit contact between their charges and their American rescuers, this had never really been possible. To state it simply, they had been unable to block the call of nature. The *Pigeon* had stuffed her visitors with good navy chow, and the nearest head was a few yards aft. On the way to and from the facilities, the *Red October*'s crewmen met with American sailors, some of whom were Russian-speaking officers disguised as enlisted men, others of whom were Russian language specialists in the enlisted rates flown out just as the last load of Soviets had arrived aboard. The fact that they were aboard a putatively hostile vessel and had found friendly Russian-speaking men had been overpowering for many of the young conscripts. Their remarks had been recorded on hidden tape machines for later examination in Washington. Petrov and the three junior officers had been slow to catch on, but when they did they took to escorting the men to the toilet in relays, like protective parents. What they were not able to prevent was an intelligence officer in a bosun's uniform making an offer of asylum: anyone who wished to remain in the United States would be permitted to do so. It took ten minutes for the information to spread throughout the crew.

When it came time for the American crewmen to eat, the Russian officers could hardly prohibit contact, and it turned out that the officers themselves got very little to eat, so busy were they patrolling the mess tables. To the bemused surprise of their American counterparts, they were forced to decline repeated invitations to the *Pigeon*'s wardroom.

The *Pigeon* docked carefully. There was no hurry. As the gangway was set in place, the band on the dock played a selection of Soviet and American airs to mark the cooperative nature of the rescue mission. The Soviets had expected that their arrival would be a quiet one given the time of day. They were mistaken in this. When the first Soviet officer was halfway down the gangway, he was dazzled by fifty high-intensity television lights and the shouted questions of television reporters routed out of bed to meet the rescue ship and so have a bright piece of Christmas season news for the morning network broadcasts. The Russians had never encountered anything like Western newsmen before, and the resulting cultural collision was total chaos. Reporters singled out the officers, blocking their paths to the consternation of marines trying to keep control of things. To a man the officers pretended not to know a word of English, only to find that an enterprising reporter had brought along a Russian language professor from the University of South Carolina in Columbia. Petrov found himself stumbling through politically acceptable platitudes in front of a half-dozen cameras and wishing the entire affair were the bad dream it seemed to be. It took an hour to get every Russian sailor aboard the three buses chartered for the purpose and off to the airport. Along the way cars and vans filled with news crews raced alongside the buses, continuing to annoy the Russians with camera lights and further shouted questions that no one could understand. The scene at the airport was not much different. The air force had sent down a VC-135 transport, but before the Russians could board it they again had to jostle their way through a sea of reporters. Ivanov found himself confronted with a Slavic language expert whose Russian was marred by a horrendous accent. Boarding took another half hour.

A dozen air force officers got everyone seated and passed out cigarettes and liquor miniatures. By the time the VIP transport reached twenty thousand feet, it was a very happy flight. An officer spoke to them over the intercom system, explaining what was to happen. Medical checks would be made of everyone. The Soviet Union would be sending a plane for them the next day, but everyone hoped their stay might be extended a day or two so that they might experience American hospitality in full. The flight crew outdid itself, telling their passengers the history of every landmark, town, village, interstate highway, and truck stop on the flight route, proclaiming through the interpreter the wish of all Americans for peaceful, friendly relations with the Soviet Union, expressing the professional admiration of the U.S. Air Force for the courage of the Soviet seamen, and mourning the deaths of the officers who had courageously lingered behind, allowing their men to go first. The whole affair was a masterpiece of duplicity aimed at overwhelming them, and it began to succeed.

The aircraft flew low over the Washington suburbs while approaching Andrews Air Force Base. The interpreter explained that they were flying over middle-class homes that belonged to ordinary workers in government and local industry. Three more buses awaited them on the ground, and instead of driving on the beltway around Washington, D.C., the buses drove directly through town. American officers on each bus apologized for the traffic jams, telling the passengers that nearly every American family has one car, many two or more, and that people only use public transportation to avoid the nuisance of driving. The *nuisance* of driving one's own car, the Soviet seaman thought in amazement. Their political officers might later tell them that this was a total lie, but who could deny the thousands of cars on the road? Surely this could not all be a sham staged for the benefit of a few sailors on an hour's notice? Driving through southeast D.C. they noted that black people owned cars—scarcely had room to park them all! The bus continued down the Mall, with the interpreters voicing the hope that they would be allowed to see the many museums open to everyone. The Air and Space Museum, it was mentioned, had a moon rock brought back by the Apollo astronauts ... The Soviets saw the joggers in the Mall and the thousands of people casually strolling around. They jabbered among themselves as the buses turned north to Bethesda through the nicer sections of northwest Washington.

At Bethesda they were met by television crews broadcasting live over all three networks and by friendly, smiling U.S. Navy doctors and corpsmen who led them into the hospital for medical checks.

Ten embassy officials were there, wondering how to control the group but politically unable to protest the attention given their men in the spirit of détente. Doctors had been brought in from Walter Reed and other government hospitals to give each man a quick and thorough medical examination, particularly to check for radiation poisoning. Along the way each man found himself alone with a U.S. Navy officer who asked politely if that individual might wish to stay in the United States, pointing out that each man making this decision would be required to make his intentions known in person to a representative of the Soviet embassy—but that if he wished to do so, he would be permitted to stay. To the fury of the embassy officials, four men made this decision, one recanting after a confrontation with the naval attaché. The Americans had been careful to have each meeting videotaped so that later accusations of intimidation could be refuted at once.

When the medical checks were completed—thankfully, radiation exposure levels had been slight—the men were again fed and bedded down.

Washington, D.C.

"Good morning, Mr. Ambassador," the president said. Arbatov noted that again Dr. Pelt was standing at his master's side behind the large antique desk. He had not expected this meeting to be a pleasant one.

"Mr. President, I am here to protest the attempted kidnapping of our seamen by the United States government."

"Mr. Ambassador," the president responded sharply, "in the eyes of a former district attorney, kidnapping is a vile and loathsome crime, and the government of the United States of

America will not be accused of such a thing—certainly not in this office! We have not, do not, and never will kidnap people. Is that clear to you, sir?"

"Besides which, Alex," Pelt said less forcefully, "the men to whom you refer would not be alive were it not for us. We lost two good men rescuing your servicemen. You might at least express some appreciation for our efforts to save your crew, and perhaps make a gesture of sympathy for the Americans who lost their lives in the process."

"My government notes the heroic effort of your two officers, and does wish to express its appreciation and that of the Soviet people for the rescue. Even so, gentlemen, deliberate efforts have been made to entice some of those men to betray their country."

"Mr. Ambassador, when your trawler rescued the crew of our patrol plane last year, officers of the Soviet armed forces offered money, women, and other enticements to our crewmen if they would give out information or agree to stay behind in Vladivostok, correct? Don't tell me that you have no knowledge of this. You know that's how the game is played. At the time we did not object to this, did we? No, we were sufficiently grateful that those six men were still alive, and now, of course, all of them are back at work. We remain grateful for your country's humanitarian concern for the lives of ordinary American citizens. In this case, each officer and enlisted man was told that he could stay if he wished to do so. No force of any kind was used. Each man wishing to remain here was required by us to meet with an official of your embassy so as to give you a fair chance to explain to him the error of his ways. Surely this is fair, Mr. Ambassador. We made no offers of money or women. We do not buy people, and we damned well do not— ever—kidnap people. Kidnappers are people I put in jail. I even managed to have one executed. Don't you ever accuse me of that again," the president concluded righteously.

"My government insists that all of our men be returned to their homeland," Arbatov persisted.

"Mr. Ambassador, any person in the United States, regardless of his nationality or the manner of his arrival, is entitled to the full protection of our law. Our courts have ruled on this many times, and under our law no man or woman may be compelled to do something against his will without due process.

The subject is closed. Now, I have a question for you. What was a ballistic missile submarine doing three hundred miles from the American coast?"

"A missile submarine, Mr. President?"

Pelt lifted a photograph from the president's desk and handed it to Arbatov. Taken from the tape recorder on the *Sea Cliff*, it showed the SS-N-20 sea-launched ballistic missile.

"The name of the submarine is—was *Red October*," Pelt said. "It exploded and sank three hundred miles from the coast of South Carolina. Alex, we have an agreement between our two countries that no such vessel will approach either country to within five hundred miles—eight hundred kilometers. We want to know what that submarine was doing there. Don't try to tell us that this missile is some kind of fabrication—even if we had wanted to do such a foolish thing, we wouldn't have had the time. That's one of your missiles, Mr. Ambassador, and the submarine carried nineteen more just like it." Pelt deliberately misstated the number. "And the government of the United States asks the government of the Soviet Union how it came to be there, in violation of our agreement, while so many other of your ships are so close to our Atlantic coast."

"That must be the lost submarine," Arbatov offered.

"Mr. Ambassador," the president said softly, "the submarine was not lost until Thursday, seven days after you told us about it. In short, Mr. Ambassador, your explanation of last Friday does not coincide with the facts we have physically established."

"What accusation are you making?" Arbatov bristled.

"Why, none, Alex," the president said. "If that agreement is no longer operative, then it is no longer operative. I believe we discussed that possibility last week also. The American people will know later today what the facts are. You are sufficiently familiar with our country to imagine their reaction. I will have an explanation. For the moment, I see no further reason for your fleet to be off our coast. The 'rescue' has been successfully concluded, and the further presence of the Soviet fleet can only be a provocation. I want you and your government to consider what my military commanders are telling me right now—or if you prefer, what your commanders would be telling General Secretary Narmonov if the situation were reversed. I will have an explanation. Without one I can reach one of only a few conclusions—and those are conclusions I would prefer not to choose from. Send that message to your government, and tell them that since some of your men have opted to stay here, we'll probably find out what was really happening in short order. Good day."

Arbatov left the office, turning left to leave by the west entrance. A marine guard held the door open, a polite gesture that stopped short of his eyes. The ambassador's driver, waiting outside in a Cadillac limousine, held the door open for him. The driver was chief of the KGB's political intelligence section at that organization's Washington station.

"So," he said, checking traffic on Pennsylvania Avenue before making a left turn.

"So, the meeting went exactly as I had predicted, and now we can be absolutely certain why they are kidnapping our men," Arbatov replied.

"And that is, Comrade Ambassador?" the driver prompted. He did not let his irritation show. Only a few years before this Party hack would not have dared temporize with a senior KGB officer. It was a disgrace, what had happened to the Committee for State Security since the death of Comrade Andropov. But things would be set right again. He was certain of that.

"The president all but accused us of sending the submarine deliberately to their shore in violation of our secret 1979 protocol. They are holding our men to interrogate them, to take their heads apart so that they can learn what the submarine's orders were. How long will that take the CIA? A day? Two?" Arbatov shook his head angrily. "They may know already—a few drugs, a woman, perhaps, to loosen their tongues. The president also invited Moscow to imagine what the Pentagon hotheads are telling him to think! And telling him to do. No mystery there, is there? They will say we were rehearsing a surprise nuclear attack—perhaps even executing one! As if we were not working harder than they to achieve peaceful coexistence! Suspicious fools, they are fearful about what has happened, and even more angry."

"Can you blame them, Comrade?" the driver asked, taking all of this in, filing, analyzing, composing his independent report to Moscow Center.

"And he said that there was no further reason for our fleet to be off their coast."

"How did he say this? Was it a demand?"

"His words were soft. Softer than I expected. This concerns me. They are planning something, I think. Rattling a saber makes noise, drawing it does not. He demands an explanation for this entire affair. What do I tell him? What *was* happening?"

"I suspect that we will never know." The senior agent did know—the original story, that is, incredible as it was. That the navy and the GRU could allow such a fantastic error to take place had amazed him. The story from agent Cassius was scarcely less mad. The driver had passed it on to Moscow himself. Was it possible that the United States and the Soviet Union were both victims of a third party? An operation gone awry, and the Americans trying to find out who was responsible and how it was done so that they might try to do it themselves? That part of the story made sense, but did the rest? He frowned at the traffic. He had orders from Moscow Center: if this was a CIA operation, he was supposed to find out immediately. He didn't believe it was. If so the CIA was being unusually effective in covering it. Was it possible to cover such a complex operation? He didn't think so. Regardless, he and his colleagues would be working for several weeks to penetrate any cover there was, to find out what was being said in Langley and in the field, while other KGB sections did the same throughout the world. If the CIA had penetrated the Northern Fleet's high command he'd find out. Of that he was confident. He could almost wish they had done so. The GRU would be responsible for the disaster, and would be disgraced after profiting from the KGB's loss of prestige a few years back. If he was reading the situation correctly, the Politburo was turning the KGB loose on the GRU and the military, allowing Moscow Center to initiate its own independent investigation of the affair. Regardless of what was found, the KGB would come out ahead and deflate the armed services. One way or another, his organization would discover what had taken place, and if it was damaging to his rivals, so much the better . . .

When the door closed behind the Soviet ambassador, Dr. Pelt opened a side door to the Oval Office. Judge Moore came in.

"Mr. President, it's been a while since I've had to do things like hide in closets."

"You really expect this to work?" Pelt said.

"Yes, I do now," Moore settled comfortably into a leather chair.

"Isn't this a little shaky, Judge?" Pelt asked. "I mean, running an operation this complex?"

"That's the beauty of it, Doctor, we're not running anything. The Soviets will be doing that for us. Oh, sure, we'll have a lot of our people prowling around Eastern Europe asking a lot of questions. So will Sir Basil's fellows. The French and the Israelis already are, because we've asked them if they know what's happening with the stray missile sub. The KGB will find out quickly enough and wonder why the four main Western intelligence agencies are all asking the same questions—instead of pulling into their shells like they'd expect them to if this were our operation.

"You have to appreciate the dilemma the Soviets face, a choice between two equally unattractive scenarios. On the one hand, they can choose to believe that one of their most trusted professional officers has committed high treason on an unprecedented scale. You've seen our file on Captain Ramius. He's the Communist version of an eagle scout, a genuine New Soviet Man. Add to that the fact that a defection conspiracy necessarily involves a number of equally trusted officers. The Soviets have a mind block against believing that individuals of this type will ever leave the Workers' Paradise. That seems paradoxical, I admit, given the strenuous efforts they expend to keep people from leaving their country, but it's true. Losing a ballet dancer or a KGB agent is one thing—losing the son of a Politburo member, an officer with nearly thirty years of unblemished service, is quite another. Moreover, a naval captain has a lot of privileges; you might call his defection the equivalent of a self-made millionaire leaving New York to live in Moscow. They simply will not believe it.

"On the other hand, they can believe the story we planted through Henderson, which is also unattractive but is supported by a good deal of circumstantial evidence, especially our efforts to entice their crewmen to defect. You saw how furious they are about that. The way they think, this is a gross violation of the rules of civilized behavior. The president's forceful reaction to our discovery that this was a missile submarine is also evidence that favors Henderson's story."

"So what side will they come down on?" the president asked.

"That, sir, is a question of psychology more than anything else, and Soviet psychology is very hard for us to read. Given the choice between the collective treason of ten men and an outside conspiracy, my opinion is that they will prefer the latter. For them to believe that this really was defection—well, it would force them to reexamine their own beliefs. Who likes to do that?" Moore gestured grandly. "The latter alternative means that their security has been violated by outsiders, but being a victim is more palatable than having to recognize the intrinsic contradictions of their own governing philosophy. On top of that we have the fact that the KGB will be running the investigation."

"Why?" Pelt asked, caught up in the judge's plot.

"In either case, a defection or a penetration of naval operational security, the GRU would have been responsible. Security of the naval and military forces is their bailiwick, the more so with the damage done to the KGB after the departure of our friend Andropov. The Soviets can't have an organization investigating itself—not in their intelligence community! So, the KGB will be looking to take its rival service apart. From the KGB's perspective, outside instigation is the far more attractive alternative; it makes for a bigger operation. If they confirm Henderson's story and convince everyone that it's true— and they will, of course—it makes them look all that much better for having uncovered it."

"They will confirm the story?"

"Of course they will! In the intelligence business if you look hard enough for something, you find it, whether it's really there or not. Lord, we owe this Ramius fellow more than he will ever know. An opportunity like this doesn't come along once in a generation. We simply can't lose."

"But the KGB will emerge stronger," Pelt observed. "Is that a good thing?"

Moore shrugged. "Bound to happen eventually. Unseating and possibly killing Andropov gave the military services too much prestige, just like with Beria back in the fifties. The Soviets depend on political control of their military as much as we do—more. Having the KGB take their high command apart gets the dirty work done for them. It had to happen anyway, so it's just as well that we can profit by it. There's only a few more things we have to do."

"Such as?" the president asked.

"Our friend Henderson will leak information in a month or so saying that we had a submarine tracking *Red October* all the way from Iceland."

"But why?" Pelt objected. "Then they'll know that we were lying, that all the excitement over the missile sub was a lie."

"Not exactly, Doctor," Moore said. "Having a missile sub this close to our coast remains a violation of the agreement, and from their point of view we have no way of knowing why she was there—until we interrogate the crewmen remaining behind, who will probably tell us little of value. The Soviets will expect that we have not been completely truthful with them on this affair. The fact that we were trailing their sub and were ready to destroy it at any time gives them the evidence of our duplicity that they'll be looking for. We'll also say that *Dallas* monitored the reactor incident on sonar, and that will explain the proximity of our rescue ship. They know, well, they certainly suspect, that we have concealed something. This will mislead them about what it was we really concealed. The Russians have a saying for this. They call it wolf meat. And they will launch an extensive operation to penetrate our operation, whatever it is. But they will find nothing. The only people in the CIA who know what is really going on are Greer, Ritter, and myself. Our operations people have orders to *find out* what was going on, and that's all that can leak out."

"What about Henderson, and how many of our people know about the submarine?" the president asked.

"If Henderson spills anything to them he'll be signing his own death warrant. The KGB deals severely with double agents, and would not believe that we tricked him into delivering false information. He knows it, and we'll be keeping a close eye on him in any case. How many of our people know about the sub? A hundred perhaps, and the number will increase somewhat— but remember that they think we now have two dead Soviet subs off our coast, and they have every reason to believe that whatever Soviet sub equipment turns up in our labs has been recovered from the ocean floor. We will, of course, be reactivating the *Glomar Explorer* for just that purpose. They'd be suspicious if we didn't. Why disappoint them? Sooner or later they just might figure the whole story out, but by that time the stripped hulk will be at the bottom of the sea."

"So, we can't keep this a secret forever?" Pelt asked.

"Forever's a long time. We have a plan for the possibility. For the immediate future the secret should be fairly safe, what with only a hundred people in on it. In a year, minimum, more likely two or three, they may have accumulated enough data to suspect what has happened, but by that time there won't be much physical evidence to point to. Moreover, if the KGB discovers the truth, will they *want* to report it? Were the GRU to find out, they certainly would, and the resulting chaos within their intelligence community would also work to our benefit." Moore took a cigar from a leather holder. "As I said, Ramius has given us a fantastic opportunity on several levels. And the beauty of it is that we don't have to do much of anything. The Russians will be doing all the legwork, looking for something that isn't there."

"What about the defectors, Judge?" the president asked.

"They, Mr. President, will be taken care of. We know how to do this, and we rarely have a complaint about the CIA's hospitality. We'll take some months to debrief them, and at the same time we'll be preparing them for life in America. They'll get new identities, reeducation, cosmetic surgery if necessary, and they'll never have to work another day as long as they live—but they will want to work. Almost all of them do. I expect the navy will find places for them, paid consultants for their submarine warfare department, that sort of thing."

"I want to meet them," the president said impulsively.

"That can be arranged, sir, but it will have to be discrete," Moore cautioned.

"Camp David, that ought to be secure enough. And Ryan, Judge, I want him taken care of."

"Understood, sir. We're bringing him along rather quickly already. He has a big future with us."

Tyuratam, USSR

The reason *Red October* had been ordered to dive long before dawn was orbiting the earth at a height of eight hundred kilometers. The size of a Greyhound bus, Albatross 8 had been sent aloft eleven months earlier by a heavy-lift booster from the Cosmodrome at Tyuratam. The massive satellite, called a RORSAT, for radar ocean reconnaissance satellite, was specifically designed for maritime surveillance.

Albatross 8 passed over Pamlico Sound at 1131 local time. Its on-board programming was designed to trace thermal receptors over the entire visible horizon, interrogating everything in sight and locking on any signature that fit its acquisition parameters. As it continued on its orbit and passed over elements of the U.S. fleet, the *New Jersey*'s jammers were aimed upward to scramble its signal. The satellite's tape systems dutifully recorded this. The jamming would tell the operators something about American electronic warfare systems. As Albatross 8 crossed the pole, the parabolic dish on its front tracked in on the carrier signal of another bird, the *Iskra* communications satellite.

When the reconnaissance satellite located its higher flying cousin, a laser side-link transmitted the contents of the Albatross' tape bank. The *Iskra* immediately relayed this to the ground station at Tyuratam. The signal was also received by a fifteen-meter dish located in western China which was operated by the U.S. National Security Agency in cooperation with the Chinese, who used the data received for their own purposes. The Americans transmitted it via their own communications satellite to NSA headquarters at Fort Meade, Maryland. At almost the same time the digital signal was examined by two teams of experts five thousand miles apart.

"Clear weather," a technician moaned. *"Now* we get clear weather!"

"Enjoy it while you can, Comrade." His neighbor at the next console was watching data from a geosynchronous weather satellite that monitored the Western Hemisphere. Knowing the weather over a hostile country can have great strategic value. "There's another cold front approaching their coast. Their winter has been like ours. I hope they are enjoying it."

"Our men at sea will not." The technician mentally shuddered at the thought of being at sea in a major storm. He'd taken a Black Sea cruise the previous summer and become hopelessly seasick. "Aha! What is this? Colonel!"

"Yes, Comrade?" The colonel supervising the watch came over quickly.

"See here, Comrade Colonel." The technician traced a finger on the TV screen. "This is Pamlico Sound, on the central coast of the United States. Look here, Comrade." The thermal image of the water on the screen was black, but as the technician adjusted the display it changed to green with two white patches, one larger than the other. Twice the large one split into two segments. The image was of the surface of the water, and some of the water was half a degree warmer than it should have been. The differential was not constant, but it did return enough to prove that something was adding heat to the water.

"Sunlight, perhaps?" the colonel asked.

"No, Comrade, the clear sky gives even sunlight to the entire area," the technician said quietly. He was always quiet when he thought he was on to something. "Two submarines, perhaps three, thirty meters under the water."

"You are certain?"

The technician flipped on a switch to display the radar picture, which showed only the corduroy pattern of small waves.

"There is nothing *on* the water to generate this heat, Comrade Colonel. Therefore it must be something *under* the water. The time of year is wrong for mating whales. It can only be nuclear submarines, probably two, perhaps three. I speculate, Colonel, that the Americans have been sufficiently frightened by the deployment of our fleet to seek shelter for their missile submarines. Their missile sub base is only a few hundred kilometers south. Perhaps one of their *Ohio*-class boats have taken shelter here and is being protected by a hunter sub, as ours are."

"Then he will soon move out. Our fleet is being recalled."

"Too bad, it would be good to track him. This is a rare opportunity, Comrade Colonel."

"Indeed. Well done, Comrade Academician." Ten minutes later the data had been transmitted to Moscow.

Soviet Naval High Command, Moscow

"We will make use of this opportunity, Comrade," Gorshkov said. "We are now recalling our fleet, and we will allow several submarines to remain behind to gather electronic intelligence. The Americans will probably lose several in the shuffle."

"Quite likely," the chief of fleet operations said.

"The *Ohio* will go south, probably to their submarine base at Charleston or Kings Bay. Or north to Norfolk. We have *Konovalov* at Norfolk, and *Shabilikov* off Charleston. Both will stay in place for several days, I think. We must do something right to show the politicians that we have a real navy. Being able to track on an *Ohio* would be a beginning."

"I'll have the orders out in fifteen minutes, Comrade." The chief of operations thought this was a good idea. He had not liked the report of the Politburo meeting that he'd gotten from Gorshkov—though if Sergey were on his way out, he would be in a good place to take over the job...

The New Jersey

The RED ROCKET message had arrived in Eaton's hand only moments before: Moscow had just transmitted a lengthy operational letter via satellite to the Soviet fleet. Now the Russians were in a real fix, the commodore thought. Around them were three carrier battle groups—the *Kennedy, America,* and *Nimitz*—all under Josh Painter's command. Eaton had them in sight, and had operational control of the *Tarawa* to augment his own surface action group. The commodore turned his binoculars on the *Kirov*.

"Commander, bring the group to battle stations."

"Aye." The group operations officer lifted the tactical radio mike. "Blue Boys, this is Blue King. Amber Light, Amber Light, execute. Out."

Eaton waited four seconds for the *New Jersey*'s general quarters alarm to sound. The crew raced to their guns.

"Range to *Kirov*?"

"Thirty-seven thousand six hundred yards, sir. We've been sneaking in a laser range every few minutes. We're dialed in, sir," the group operations officer reported. "Main battery turrets are still loaded with sabots, and gunnery's been updating the solution every thirty seconds."

A phone buzzed next to Eaton's command chair on the flag bridge.

"Eaton."

"All stations manned and ready, Commodore," the battleship's captain reported. Eaton looked at his stopwatch.

"Well done, Captain. We've got the men drilled very well indeed."

In the *New Jersey*'s combat information center the numerical displays showed the exact range to the *Kirov*'s mainmast. The logical first target is always the enemy flagship. The only question was how much punishment the *Kirov* could absorb—and what would kill her first, the gun rounds or the Tomahawk missiles. The important part, the gunnery officer had been saying for days, was to kill the *Kirov* before any aircraft could interfere. The *New Jersey* had never sunk a ship all on her own. Forty years was a long time to wait.

"They're turning," the group operations officer said.

"Yep, let's see how far."

The *Kirov*'s formation had been on a westerly course when the signal arrived. Every ship in the circular array turned to starboard, all together. Their turns stopped when they reached a heading of zero-four-zero.

Eaton set his glasses down in the holder. "They're going home. Let's inform Washington and keep the men at stations for a while."

Dulles International Airport

The Soviets outdid themselves getting their men away from the United States. An Aeroflot Illyushin IL-62 was taken out of regular international service and sent directly from Moscow to Dulles. It landed at sunset. A near copy of the British VC-10, the four-engine aircraft taxied to the remotest service area for refueling. Along with some other passengers who did not deplane to stretch their legs, a spare flight crew was brought along so that the plane could immediately return home. A pair of mobile lounges drove from the terminal building two miles to the waiting aircraft. Inside them the crewmen of the *Red October* looked out at the snow-dusted countryside, knowing this was their final look at America. They were quiet, having been roused from bed in Bethesda and taken by bus to Dulles only an hour earlier. This time no reporters harassed them.

The four officers, nine *michmanyy*, and the remaining enlisted crew were split into distinct groups as they boarded. Each group was taken to a separate part of the aircraft. Each officer and *michman* had his own KGB interrogator, and the debriefing began as the aircraft started its takeoff roll. By the time the Illyushin reached cruising altitude most of the crewmen were asking themselves why they had not opted to remain behind with their traitorous countrymen. These interviews were decidedly unpleasant.

"Did Captain Ramius act strangely?" a KGB major asked Petrov.

"Certainly not!" Petrov answered quickly, defensively. "Didn't you know our submarine was sabotaged? We were lucky to escape with our lives!"

"Sabotaged? How?"

"The reactor systems. I am the wrong one to ask on this, I am not an engineer, but it was I who detected the leaks. You see, the radiation film badges showed contamination, but the engine room instruments did not. Not only was the reactor tampered with, but all of the radiation-sensing instruments were disabled. I saw this myself. Chief Engineer Melekhin had to rebuild several to locate the leaking reactor piping. Svyadov can tell this better. He saw it himself."

The KGB officer was scribbling notes. "And what was your submarine doing so close to the American coast?"

"What do you mean? Don't you know what our orders were?"

"What were your orders, Comrade Doctor?" The KGB officer stared hard into Petrov's eyes.

The doctor explained, concluding, "I saw the orders. They were posted for all to see, as is normal."

"Signed by whom?"

"Admiral Korov. Who else?"

"Did you not find those orders a little strange?" the major asked angrily.

"Do you question your orders, Comrade Major?" Petrov summoned up some spine. "*I* do not."

"What happened to your political officer?"

In another space Ivanov was explaining how the *Red October* had been detected by American and British ships. "But Captain Ramius evaded them brilliantly! We would have made it except for that damned reactor accident. You must find who did that to us, Comrade Captain. I wish to see him die myself!"

The KGB officer was unmoved. "And what was the last thing the captain said to you?"

"He ordered me to keep control of my men, not to let them speak with Americans any more than necessary, and he said that the Americans would never get their hands on our ship." Ivanov's eyes teared at the thought of his captain and his ship, both lost. He was a proud and privileged young Soviet man, the son of a Party academician. "Comrade, you and your people must find the bastards who did this to us."

"It was very clever," Svyadov was recounting a few feet away. "Even Comrade Melekhin only found it on his third attempt, and he swore vengeance on the men who did it. I saw it myself," the lieutenant said, forgetting that he never had, really. He explained in detail, to the point of drawing a diagram of how it had been done. "I don't know about the final accident. I was just coming on duty then. Melekhin, Surzpoi, and Bugayev worked for hours attempting to engage our auxiliary power systems." He shook his head. "I tried to join them, but Captain Ramius forbade it. I tried again, against orders, but Comrade Petrov prevented me."

Two hours over the Atlantic the senior KGB interrogators met aft to compare notes.

"So, if this captain was acting, he was devilishly good at it," the colonel in charge of the initial interrogations summarized. "His orders to his men were impeccable. The mission orders were announced and posted as is normal—"

"But who among these men knows Korov's signature? And we can't very well ask Korov, can we?" a major said. The commander of the Northern Fleet had died of a cerebral hemorrhage two hours into his first interrogation in the Lubyanka, much to everyone's disappointment. "It could have been forged in any case. Do we have a secret submarine base in Cuba? And what of the death of the *zampolit?*"

"The doctor is sure it was an accident," another major answered. "The captain thought he had struck his head, but he had actually broken his neck. I feel they should have radioed for instructions, though."

"A radio silence order," the colonel said. "I checked. This is entirely normal for missile submarines. Was this Captain Ramius skilled in unarmed combat? Might he have murdered the *zampolit?*"

"A possibility," mused the major who had questioned Petrov. "He was not trained in such things, but it is not hard to do."

The colonel did not know whether to agree. "Do we have any evidence that the crew thought a defection was being attempted?" All heads shook negatively. "Was the submarine's operational routine otherwise normal?"

"Yes, Comrade Colonel," a young captain said. "The surviving navigation officer, Ivanov, says that the evasion of imperialist surface and sub forces was effected perfectly—exactly in accordance with established procedures, but executed brilliantly by this Ramius fellow over a period of twelve hours. I have not even suggested that treason might be involved. Yet." Everyone knew that these sailors would be spending time in the Lubyanka until each head had been picked clean.

"Very well," the colonel said, "up to this point we have no indication of treason by the officers of the submarine? I thought not. Comrades, you will continue your interrogations in a gentler fashion until we arrive in Moscow. Allow your charges to relax."

The atmosphere on the aircraft gradually became more pleasant. Snacks were served, and vodka to loosen the tongues and encourage comradely good fellowship with the KGB officers, who were drinking water. The men all knew that they would be imprisoned for some time, and this fate was accepted with what to a Westerner would be surprising fatalism. The KGB would be working for weeks to reconstruct every event on the submarine from the time the last line was cast off at Polyarnyy to the moment the last man entered the *Mystic*. Other teams of agents were already working worldwide to learn if what happened to the *Red October* was a CIA plot or the plot of some other intelligence service. The KGB would find its answer, but the colonel in charge of the case was beginning to think the answer did not lie with these seamen.

The Red October

Noyes allowed Ramius to walk the fifteen feet from sick bay to the wardroom under supervision. The patient did not look very good, but this was largely because he needed a wash and a shave, like everyone else aboard. Borodin and Mancuso assisted him into his seat at the head of the table.

"So, Ryan, how are you today?"

"Good, thank you, Captain Ramius." Ryan smiled over his

coffee. In fact he was hugely relieved, having for the past several hours been able to leave the question of running the sub to the men who actually knew something about it. Though he was counting the hours until he could get out of the *Red October,* for the first time in two weeks he was neither seasick nor terrified. "How is your leg, sir?"

"Painful. I must learn not to be shot again. I do not remember saying to you that I owe you my life, as all of us do."

"It was my life, too," Ryan replied, a little embarrassed.

"Good morning, sir!" It was the cook. "May I fix you some breakfast, Captain Ramius?"

"Yes, I am very hungry."

"Good! One U.S. Navy breakfast. Let me get some fresh coffee, too." He disappeared into the passageway. Thirty seconds later he was back with fresh coffee and a place setting for Ramius. "Ten minutes on the breakfast, sir."

Ramius poured a cup of coffee. There was a small envelope in the saucer. "What is this?"

"Coffee Mate," Mancuso chuckled. "Cream for your coffee, Captain."

Ramius tore open the packet, staring suspiciously inside before dumping the contents into the cup and stirring.

"When do we leave?"

"Sometime tomorrow," Mancuso answered. The *Dallas* was going to periscope depth periodically to receive operational orders and relaying them to the *October* by gertrude. "We learned a few hours ago that the Soviet fleet is heading back northeast. We'll know for sure by sundown. Our guys are keeping a close eye on them."

"Where do we go?" Ramius asked.

"Where did you tell them you were going?" Ryan wanted to know. "What exactly did your letter say?"

"You know about the letter—how?"

"We know—that is, I know about the letter, but that's all I can say, sir."

"I told Uncle Yuri that we were sailing to New York to make a present of this ship to the president of the United States."

"But you didn't head for New York," Mancuso objected.

"Certainly not. I wished to enter Norfolk. Why go to a civilian port when a naval base is so close? You say I should tell Padorin the truth?" Ramius shook his head. "Why? Your coast is so large."

Dear Admiral Padorin, I'm sailing for New York . . . No wonder they went ape! Ryan thought.

"We go to Norfolk or Charleston?" Ramius asked.

"Norfolk, I think," Mancuso said.

"Didn't you know they'd send the whole fleet after you?" Ryan snapped. "Why send the letter at all?"

"So they will know," Ramius answered. "So they will know. I did not expect that anyone would locate us. There you surprised us."

The American skipper tried to smile. "We detected you off the coast of Iceland. You were luckier than you imagine. If we'd sailed from England on schedule, we'd have been fifteen miles closer in shore, and we would have had you cold. Sorry, Captain, but our sonars and sonar operators are very good. You can meet the man who first tracked you later. He's working with your man Bugayev at the moment."

"*Starshina,*" Borodin said.

"Not an officer?" Ramius asked.

"No, just a very good operator," Mancuso said, surprised. Why would anyone want an officer to stand watch on sonar gear?

The cook came back in. His idea of the standard U.S. Navy breakfast was a large platter with a slab of ham, two eggs over easy, a pile of hash browns, and four slices of toast, with a container of apple jelly.

"Let me know if you want more, sir," the cook said.

"This is a normal breakfast?" Ramius asked Mancuso.

"Nothing unusual about it. I prefer waffles myself. Americans eat big breakfasts." Ramius was already attacking his. After two days without a normal meal and all the blood loss from his leg wound, his body was screaming for food.

"Tell me, Ryan," Borodin was lighting a cigarette, "what is it in America that we will find most amazing?"

Jack motioned to the captain's plate. "Food stores."

"Food stores?" Mancuso asked.

"While I was sitting on *Invincible* I read over a CIA report on people who come over to our side." Ryan didn't want to say *defectors.* Somehow the word sounded demeaning. "Supposedly the first thing that surprises people, people from your part of the world, is going through a supermarket."

"Tell me about them," Borodin ordered.

"A building about the size of a football field—well, maybe a little smaller than that. You go in the front door and get a shopping cart. The fresh fruits and vegetables are on the right, and you gradually work your way left through the other departments. I've been doing that since I was a kid."

"You say fresh fruits and vegetables? What about now, in winter?"

"What about winter?" Mancuso said. "Maybe they cost a little more, but you can always get fresh produce. That's the one thing we miss on the boats. Our supply of fresh produce and milk only lasts us about a week."

"And meat?" Ramius asked.

"Anything you want," Ryan answered. "Beef, pork, lamb, turkey, chicken. American farmers are very efficient. The United States feeds itself and has plenty left over. You know that, the Soviet Union buys our grain. Hell, we pay farmers not to grow things, just to keep the surplus under control." The four Russians were doubtful.

"What else?" Borodin asked.

"What else will surprise you? Nearly everyone has a car. Most people own their own homes. If you have money, you can buy nearly anything you want. The average family in America makes something like twenty thousand dollars a year, I guess. These officers all make more than that. The fact of the matter is that in our country if you have some brains—and all of you men do—and you are willing to work—and all of you men are—you will live a comfortable life even without any help. Besides, you can be sure that the CIA will take good care of you. We wouldn't want anybody to complain about our hospitality."

"And what will become of my men?" Ramius asked.

"I can't say exactly, sir, since I've never been involved in this sort of thing myself. I would guess that you will be taken to a safe place to relax and unwind. People from the CIA and the navy will want to talk to you at length. That's no surprise, right? I told you this before. A year from now you will be doing whatever you choose to do."

"And anybody who wants to take a cruise with us is welcome to," Mancuso added.

Ryan wondered how true this was. The navy would not want to let any of these men on a 688-class boat. It might give one of them information valuable enough to enable him to return home and keep his head.

"How does a friendly man become a CIA spy?" Borodin asked.

"I am not a spy, sir," Ryan said again. He couldn't blame them for not believing him. "Going through graduate school I got to know a guy who mentioned my name to a friend of his in the CIA, Admiral James Greer. Back a few years ago I was asked to join a team of academics that was called in to check up on some of the CIA's intelligence estimates. At the time I was happily engaged writing books on naval history. At Langley—I was there for two months during the summer—I did a paper on international terrorism. Greer liked it, and two years ago he asked me to go to work there full time. I accepted. It was a mistake," Ryan said, not really meaning it. Or did he? "A year ago I was transferred to London to work on a joint intelligence evaluation team with the British Secret Service. My normal job is to sit at a desk and figure out the stuff that field agents send in. I got myself roped into this because I figured out what you were up to, Captain Ramius."

"Was your father a spy?" Borodin asked.

"No, my dad was a police officer in Baltimore. He and my mother were killed in a plane crash ten years ago."

Borodin expressed his sympathy. "And you, Captain Mancuso, what made you a sailor?"

"I wanted to be a sailor since I was a kid. My dad's a barber. I decided on submarines at Annapolis because I thought it looked interesting."

Ryan was watching something he had never seen before, men from two different places and two very different cultures trying to find common ground. Both sides were reaching out, seeking similarities of character and experience, building a foundation for understanding. This was more than interesting. It was touching. Ryan wondered how difficult it was for the Soviets. Probably harder than anything he had ever done— their bridges were burned. They had cast themselves away from everything they had known, trusting that what they found would be better. Ryan hoped they would succeed and make their transition from Communism to freedom. In the past two days he had come to realize what courage it took for men to defect. Facing a gun in a missile room was a small matter compared with walking away from one's whole life. It was strange how easily Americans put on their freedoms. How difficult would it be for these men who had risked their lives to adapt to something that men like Ryan so rarely appreciated? It was people like these who had built the American Dream, and people like these who were needed to maintain it. It was odd that such men should come from the Soviet Union. Or perhaps not so odd, Ryan thought, listening to the conversation going back and forth in front of him.

THE SEVENTEENTH DAY

SUNDAY, 19 DECEMBER

The Red October

"Eight more hours," Ryan whispered to himself. That's what they had told him. An eight-hour run to Norfolk. He was back at the rudder diving-plane controls by his own request. Operating them was the only thing he knew how to do, and he had to do something. The *October* was still badly shorthanded. Nearly all of the Americans were helping out in the reactor and engine spaces aft. Only Mancuso, Ramius, and himself were in control. Bugayev, with the help of Jones, was monitoring the sonar equipment a few feet away, and the medical people were still worrying over Williams in sick bay. The cook was shuttling back and forth with sandwiches and coffee, which Ryan found disappointing, probably because he had been spoiled by Greer's.

Ramius was half sitting on the rail that surrounded the periscope pedestal. The leg wound was not bleeding, but it had to be hurting more than the man admitted since he was letting Mancuso check the instruments and handle the navigation.

"Rudder amidships," Mancuso ordered.

"Midships," Ryan turned the wheel back to the right to center it, checking his rudder angle indicator. "Rudder is amidships, steady on course one-two-zero."

Mancuso frowned at his chart, nervous at being forced to pilot the massive submarine in so cavalier a manner. "You have to be careful around here. The sandbar keeps building up from the southerly littoral drift, and they have to dredge it every few months. The storms this area's been having can't have helped much." Mancuso went back to look through the periscope.

"I am told this is a dangerous area," Ramius said.

"The graveyard of the Atlantic," Mancuso confirmed. "A lot of ships have died along the Outer Banks. Weather and current conditions are bad enough. The Germans are supposed to have had a hell of a time here during the war. Your charts don't show it, but there's hundreds of wrecks spotted on the bottom." He went back to the chart table. "Anyway, we give this place a nice wide berth, and we don't turn north till about here." He traced a line on the chart.

"These are your waters," Ramius agreed.

They were in a loose three-boat formation. The *Dallas* was leading them out to sea, the *Pogy* was trailing. All three boats were traveling flooded-down, their decks nearly awash, with no one on their bridge stations. All visual navigation was being done by periscope. No radar sets were operating. None of the three boats was making any electronic noise. Ryan glanced casually at the chart table. They were beyond the inlet proper, but the chart was marked with sandbars for several more miles.

Nor were they using the *Red October*'s caterpillar drive system. It had turned out to be almost exactly what Skip Tyler had predicted. There were two sets of tunnel impellers, a pair about a third of the way back from the bow and three more just aft of midships. Mancuso and his engineers had examined the plans with great interest, then commented at length on the quality of the caterpillar design.

For his part, Ramius had not wanted to believe that he had been detected so early on. Mancuso had ultimately produced Jones with his personal map to show the *October*'s estimated course off Iceland. Though a few miles off the ship's log, it was too close to have been a coincidence.

"Your sonar must be better than we expected," Ramius

grumbled a few feet from Ryan's control station.

"It is pretty good," Mancuso allowed. "Better yet, there's Jonesy—he's the best sonarman I've ever had."

"So young, and so smart."

"We get a lot of them that way," Mancuso smiled. "Never as many as we'd like, of course, but our kids are all volunteers. They know what they're getting into. We're picky about who we take, and then we train the hell out of 'em."

"Conn, sonar." It was Jones' voice. "*Dallas* is diving, sir."

"Very well." Mancuso lit a cigarette as he went to the intercom phone. He punched the button for engineering. "Tell Mannion we need him forward. We'll be diving in a few minutes. Yeah." He hung up and went back to the chart.

"You have them for more than three years, then?" Ramius asked.

"Oh, yeah. Hell, otherwise we'd be letting them go right after they're fully trained, right?"

Why couldn't the Soviet Navy get and retain people like this? Ramius thought. He knew the answer all too well. The Americans fed their men decently, gave them a proper mess room, paid them decently, gave them trust—all the things he had fought twenty years for.

"You need me to work the vents?" Mannion said, coming in.

"Yeah, Pat, we'll dive in another two or three minutes."

Mannion gave the chart a quick look on his way to the vent manifold.

Ramius hobbled to the chart. "They tell us that your officers are chosen from the bourgeois classes to control ordinary sailors from the working class."

Mannion ran his hands over the vent controls. There sure were enough of them. He'd spent two hours the previous day figuring the complex system out. "That's true, sir. Our officers do come from the ruling class. Just look at me," he said deadpan. Mannion's skin was about the color of coffee grounds, his accent pure South Bronx.

"But you are a black man," Ramius objected, missing the jibe.

"Sure, we're a real ethnic boat." Mancuso looked through the periscope again. "A Guinea skipper, a black navigator, and a crazy sonarman."

"I heard that, sir!" Jones called out rather than use the intercom speaker. "Gertrude message from *Dallas*. Everything looks okay. They're waiting for us. Last gertrude message for a while."

"Conn, aye. We're clear, finally. We can dive whenever you wish, Captain Ramius," Mancuso said.

"Comrade Mannion, vent the ballast tanks," Ramius said. The *October* had never actually surfaced and was still rigged for dive.

"Aye aye, sir." The lieutenant turned the topmost rank of master switches on the hydraulic controls.

Ryan winced. The sound made him think of a million toilets being flushed at once.

"Five degrees down on the planes, Ryan," Ramius said.

"Five degrees down, aye." Ryan pushed forward on the yoke. "Planes five degrees down."

"She's slow going down," Mannion observed, watching the handpainted depth-gauge replacement. "So durn big."

"Yeah," Mancuso said. The needle passed twenty meters.

"Planes to zero," Ramius said.

"Planes to zero angle, aye." Ryan pulled back on the control. It took thirty seconds for the submarine to settle. She seemed very slow to respond to the controls. Ryan had thought that submarines were as responsive as aircraft.

"Make her a little light, Pat. Enough that it takes a degree of down to hold her level," Mancuso said.

"Uh-huh." Mannion frowned, checking the depth gauge. The ballast tanks were now fully flooded, and the balancing act would have to be done with the much smaller trim tanks. It took him five minutes to get the balance exactly right.

"Sorry, gentlemen. I'm afraid she's too big to dial in quick," he said, embarrassed with himself.

Ramius was impressed but too annoyed to show it. He had expected the American captain to take longer than this to do it himself. Trimming a strange sub so expertly on his first try . . .

"Okay, now we can come around north," Mancuso said. They were two miles past the last charted bar. "Recommend new course zero-zero-eight, Captain."

"Ryan, rudder left ten degrees," Ramius ordered. "Come to zero-zero-eight."

"Okay, rudder left ten degrees," Ryan responded, keeping

one eye on the rudder indicator, the other on the gyro compass repeater. "Come to oh-oh-eight."

"Caution, Ryan. He turns slowly, but once turning you must use much backward—"

"Opposite," Mancuso corrected politely.

"Yes, opposite rudder to stop him on proper course."

"Right."

"Captain, do you have rudder problems?" Mancuso asked. "From tracking you it seemed that your turning circle was rather large."

"With the caterpillar it is. The flow from the tunnels strikes the rudder very hard, and it flutters if you use too much rudder. On our first sea trials, we had damage from this. It comes from—how do you say—the come-together of the two caterpillar tunnels."

"Does this affect operations with the propellers?" Mannion asked.

"No, only with the caterpillar."

Mancuso didn't like that. It didn't really matter. The plan was a simple, direct one. The three boats would make a straight dash to Norfolk. The two American attack boats would leapfrog forward at thirty knots to sniff out the areas ahead while the *October* plodded along at a constant twenty.

Ryan began to ease his rudder as the bow came around. He waited too long. Despite five degrees of right rudder, the bow swung right past the intended course, and the gyro repeater clicked accusingly on every third degree until it stopped at zero-zero-one. It took another two minutes to get back on the proper course.

"Sorry about that. Steady on zero-zero-eight," he finally reported.

Ramius was forgiving. "You learn fast, Ryan. Perhaps one day you will be a true sailor."

"No thanks! The one thing I've learned on this trip is that you guys earn every nickel you get."

"Don't like subs?" Mannion chuckled.

"No place to jog."

"True. Unless you still need me, Captain, I'm ready to go aft. The engine room's awful shorthanded," Mannion said.

Ramius nodded. Was he from the ruling class? the captain wondered.

The V. K. Konovalov

Tupolev was heading back west. The fleet order had instructed everyone but his *Alfa* and one other to return home at twenty knots. Tupolev was to move west for two and half hours. Now he was on a reciprocal heading at five knots, about the top speed the *Alfa* could travel without making much noise. The idea was that his sub would be lost in the shuffle. So, an *Ohio* was heading for Norfolk—or Charleston more probably. In any case, Tupolev would circle quietly and observe. The *Red October* was destroyed. That much he knew from the ops order. Tupolev shook his head. How could Marko have done such a thing? Whatever the answer, he had paid for his treason wit' his life.

The Pentagon

"I'd feel better if we had some more air cover," Admiral Foster said, leaning against the wall.

"Agreed, sir, but we can't be so obvious, can we?" General Harris asked.

A pair of P-3Bs was now sweeping the track from Hatteras to the Virginia Capes as though on a routine training mission. Most of the other Orions were far out at sea. The Soviet fleet was already four hundred miles offshore. The three surface groups had rejoined and were now ringed by their submarines. The *Kennedy, America,* and *Nimitz* were five hundred miles to their east, and the *New Jersey* was dropping back. The Russians would be watched all the way home. The carrier battle groups would be following them all the way to Iceland, keeping a discrete distance and maintaining air groups at the fringe of their radar coverage continuously, just to let them know that the United States still cared. Aircraft based in Iceland would track them the rest of the way home.

HMS *Invincible* was now out of operation and about halfway home. American attack subs were returning to normal patrol patterns, and all Soviet subs were reported to be off the coast, though this data was sketchy. They were traveling in loose packs and the noise generated made tracking difficult for the patrolling Orions, which were short of sonobuoys. Still and all, the operation was about over, the J-3 judged.

"You heading for Norfolk, Admiral?" Harris asked.

"Thought I might get together with CINCLANT, a post-action conference, you understand," Foster said.

"Aye aye, sir," Harris said.

The New Jersey

She was traveling at twelve knots, with a destroyer fueling on either beam. Commodore Eaton was in the flag plot. It was all over and nothing had happened, thank God. The Soviets were now a hundred miles ahead, within Tomahawk range but well beyond everything else. All in all, he was satisfied. His force had operated successfully with the *Tarawa,* which was now headed south to Mayport, Florida. He hoped they'd be able to do this again soon. It had been a long time since a flag officer on a battleship had had a carrier respond to his command. They had kept the *Kirov* force under continuous surveillance. If there had been a battle, Eaton was convinced that they'd have handled Ivan. More importantly, he was certain that Ivan knew it. All they awaited now was the order to return to Norfolk. It would be nice to be back home for Christmas. He figured his men had earned it. Many of the battleship's men were oldtimers, and nearly everyone had a family.

The Red October

Ping. Jones noted the time on his pad and called out, "Captain, just got a ping from *Pogy.*"

The *Pogy* was now ten miles ahead of the *October* and *Dallas.* The idea was that after she got ahead and listened for ten minutes, a single ping from her active sonar would signal that the ten miles to the *Pogy* and the twenty or more miles beyond her were clear. The *Pogy* would drift slowly to confirm this, and a mile to the *October*'s east the *Dallas* went to full speed to leapfrog ten miles beyond the other attack sub.

Jones was experimenting with the Russian sonar. The active gear, he'd found, was not too bad. The passive systems he didn't want to think about. When the *Red October* had been lying still in Pamlico Sound, he'd been unable to track in on the American subs. They had also been still, with their reactors only turning generators, but they had been no more than a mile away. He was disappointed that he'd not been able to locate them.

The officer with him, Bugayev, was a friendly enough guy. At first he'd been a little standoffish—as if he were a lord and I were a serf, Jones thought—until he'd seen how the skipper treated him. This surprised Jones. From what little he knew of Communism, he had expected everyone to be fairly equal. Well, he decided, that's what I get from reading *Das Kapital* in a freshman poli-sci course. It made a lot more sense to look at what Communism built. Garbage, mostly. The enlisted men didn't even have their own mess room. Wasn't that some crap! Eating your meals in your bunk rooms!

Jones had taken an hour—when he was supposed to be sleeping—to explore the submarine. Mr. Mannion had joined him. They started in the bunkroom. The individual footlockers didn't lock—probably so that officers could rifle through them. Jones and Mannion did just that. There was nothing of interest. Even the sailor porn was junk. The poses were just plain dumb, and the women—well, Jones had grown up in California. Garbage. It was not at all hard for him to understand why the Russians wanted to defect.

The missile had been interesting. He and Mannion opened an inspection hatch to examine the inside of the missile. Not too shabby, they thought. There was a little too much loose wiring, but that probably made testing easier. The missile seemed awfully big. So, he thought, that's what the bastards have been aiming at us. He wondered if the navy would hold onto a few. If it was ever necessary to flip some at old Ivan, might as well include a couple of his own. *Dumb* idea, Jonesy, he said to himself. He didn't ever want those goddamned things to fly. One thing was for sure: everything on this bucket would be stripped off, tested, taken apart, tested again—and he was the navy's number one expert on Russian sonar. Maybe he'd be present during the analysis . . . It might be worth staying in the navy a few extra months for.

Jones lit a cigarette. "Want one of mine, Mr. Bugayev?" He held his pack out to the electronics officer.

"Thank you, Jones. You were in university?" The lieutenant took the American cigarette that he'd wanted but been too proud to ask for. It was dawning on him slowly that this enlisted man was his technical equal. Though not a qualified watch officer, Jones could operate and maintain sonar gear as well as anyone he'd known.

"Yes, sir." It never hurt to call officers sir, Jones knew. Especially the dumb ones. "California Institute of Technology. Five semesters completed. A average. I didn't finish."

"Why did you leave?"

Jones smiled. "Well, sir, you gotta understand that Cal Tech is, well, kinda a funny place. I played a little trick on one of my professors. He was working with strobe lights for high-speed photography, and I rigged a little switch to work the room lights off the strobe. Unfortunately there was a short in the switch, and it started this little electrical fire." Which had burned out a lab, destroying three months of data and fifteen thousand dollars of equipment. "That broke the rules."

"What did you study?"

"I was headin' for a degree in electrical engineering, with a strong minor in cybernetics. Three semesters to go. I'll get it, then my masters, then my doctorate, and then I'll go back to work for the navy as a civilian."

"Why are you a sonar operator?" Bugayev sat down. He had never spoken like this with an enlisted man.

"Hell, sir, it's fun! When something's going on—you know, a war game, tracking another sub, like that—*I* am the skipper. All the captain does is react to the data I give him."

"And you like your commander?"

"Sure thing! He's the best I've had—I've had three. My skipper's a good guy. You do your job okay, and he doesn't hassle you. You got something to say to him, and he listens."

"You say you will go back to college. How do you pay for it? They tell us that only the ruling class sons go to university."

"That's crap, sir. In California if you're smart enough to go, you go. In my case, I've been saving my money—you don't spend much on a sub, right?—and the navy pitches in, too. I got enough to see me all the way through my masters. What's your degree in?"

"I attended a higher naval school. Like your Annapolis. I would like to get a proper degree in electronics," Bugayev said, voicing his own dream.

"No sweat. I can help you out. If you're good enough for Cal Tech, I can tell you who to talk to. You'd like California. That is the place to live."

"And I wish to work on a real computer," Bugayev went on, wishful.

Jones laughed quietly. "So, buy yourself one."

"Buy a computer?"

"Sure, we got a couple of little ones, Apples, on *Dallas*. Cost you about, oh, two thousand for a nice system. That's a lot less than what a car goes for."

"A computer for two thousand dollars?" Bugayev went from wishful to suspicious, certain that Jones was leading him on.

"Or less. For three grand you can get a really nice rig. Hell, you tell Apple who you are, and they'll probably give it to you for free, or the navy will. If you don't want an Apple, there's the Commodore, TRS-80, Atari. All kinds. Depends on what you want to use it for. Look, just one company, Apple, has sold over a million of 'em. They're little, sure, but they're real computers."

"I have never heard of this—Apple?"

"Yeah, Apple. Two guys started the company back when I was in junior high. Since then they've sold a million or so, like I said—and they are some kinda rich! I don't have one myself—no room on a sub—but my brother has his own computer, an IBM-PC. You still don't believe me, do you?"

"A working man with his own computer? It is hard to believe." He stabbed out the cigarette. American tobacco was a little bland, he thought.

"Well, sir, then you can ask somebody else. Like I said, *Dallas* has a couple of Apples, just for the crew to use. There's other stuff for fire control, navigation, and sonar, of course. We use the Apples for games—you'll *love* computer games, for sure. You've never had fun till you've tried Choplifter— and other things, education programs, stuff like that. Honest, Mr. Bugayev, you can walk into most any shopping center and find a place to buy a computer. You'll see."

"How do you use a computer with your sonar?"

"That would take a while to explain, sir, and I'd probably have to get permission from the skipper." Jones reminded himself that this guy was still the enemy, sort of.

The V. K. Konovalov

The *Alfa* drifted slowly at the edge of the continental shelf, about fifty miles southeast of Norfolk. Tupolev ordered the reactor plant chopped back to about five percent of total output, enough to operate the electrical systems and little else. It also made his submarine almost totally quiet. Orders were passed by word of mouth. The *Konovalov* was on a strict silent ship routine. Even ordinary cooking was forbidden. Cooking meant moving metal pots on metal grates. Until further notice, the crew was on a diet of cheese sandwiches. They spoke in whispers when they spoke at all. Anyone who made noise would attract the attention of the captain, and everyone aboard knew what that meant.

SOSUS Control

Quentin was reviewing data sent by digital link from the two Orions. A crippled missile boat, the USS *Georgia*, was heading into Norfolk after a partial turbine failure, escorted by a pair of attack boats. They had been keeping her out, the admiral had said, because of all the Russian activity on the coast, and the idea now was to get her in, fixed, and out as quickly as possible. The *Georgia* carried twenty-four Trident missiles, a noteworthy fraction of the country's total deterrent force. Repairing her would be a high priority item now that the Russians were gone. It was safe to bring her in, but they wanted the Orions first to check and see if any Soviet submarines had lingered behind in the general confusion.

A P-3B was cruising at nine hundred feet about fifty miles southeast of Norfolk. The FLIR showed nothing, no heat signature on the surface, and the MAD gear detected no measurable disturbance in the earth's magnetic field, though one aircraft's flight path took her within a hundred yards of the *Alfa*'s position. The *Konovalov*'s hull was made of non-magnetic titanium. A sonobuoy dropped seven miles to the south of her position also failed to pick up the sound of her reactor plant. Data was being transmitted continuously to Norfolk, where Quentin's operations staff entered it into his computer. The problem was, not all of the Soviet subs had been accounted for.

Well, the commander thought, that figures. Some of the
boats had taken the opportunity to creep away from their charted
loci. There was the odd chance, he had reported, that one or
two strays were still out there, but there was no evidence of
this. He wondered what CINCLANT had working. Certainly
he had seemed awfully pleased with something, almost eu-
phoric. The operation against the Soviet fleet had been handled
pretty well, what he'd seen of it, and there was that dead *Alfa*
out there. How long until the *Glomar Explorer* came out of
mothballs to go and get that? He wondered if he'd get a chance
to look the wreck over. What an opportunity!

Nobody was taking the current operation all that seriously.
It made sense. If the *Georgia* were indeed coming in with a
sick engine she'd be coming slow, and a slow *Ohio* made about
as much noise as a virgin whale determined to retain her status.
And if CINCLANTFLT were all that concerned about it, he
would not have detailed the delousing operation to a pair
of P-3s piloted by reservists. Quentin lifted the phone and
dialed CINCLANTFLT Operations to tell them again that
there was no indication of hostile activity.

The Red October

Ryan checked his watch. It had been five hours already. A long
time to sit in one chair, and from a quick glance at the chart
it appeared that the eight-hour estimate had been optimistic—
or he'd misunderstood them. The *Red October* was tracing up
the shelf line and would soon begin to angle west for the
Virginia Capes. Maybe it would take another four hours. It
couldn't be too soon. Ramius and Mancuso looked pretty tired.
Everybody was tired. Probably the engine room people most
of all—no, the cook. He was ferrying coffee and sandwiches
to everyone. The Russians seemed especially hungry.

The Dallas/The Pogy

The Dallas passed the *Pogy* at thirty-two knots, leapfrogging
again, with the *October* a few miles aft. Lieutenant Commander
Wally Chambers, who had the conn, did not like being blind
on the speed run of thirty-five minutes despite word from the
Pogy that everything was clear.

The *Pogy* noted her passage and turned to allow her lateral array to track on the *Red October*.

"Noisy enough at twenty knots," the *Pogy*'s sonar chief said to his companions. *"Dallas* doesn't make that much at thirty."

The V. K. Konovalov

"Some noise to the south," the *michman* said.

"What, exactly?" Tupolev had been hovering at the door for hours, making life unpleasant for the sonarmen.

"Too soon to say, Comrade Captain. Bearing is not changing, however. It is heading this way."

Tupolev went back to the control room. He ordered power reduced further in the reactor systems. He considered killing the plant entirely, but reactors took time to start up and there was no telling yet how distant the contact might be. The captain smoked three cigarettes before going back to sonar. It would not do at all to make the *michman* nervous. The man was his best operator.

"One propeller, Comrade Captain, an American, probably a *Los Angeles,* doing thirty-five knots. Bearing has changed only two degrees in fifteen minutes. He will pass close aboard, and—wait . . . His engines have stopped." The forty-year-old warrant officer pressed the headphones against his ears. He could hear the cavitation sounds diminish, then stop entirely as the contact faded away to nothing. "He has stopped to listen, Comrade Captain."

Tupolev smiled. "He will not hear us, Comrade. Racing and stopping. Can you hear anything else? Might he be escorting something?"

The *michman* listened to the headphones again and made some adjustments on his panel. "Perhaps . . . there is a good deal of surface noise, Comrade, and I—wait. There seems to be some noise. Our last target bearing was one-seven-one, and this new noise is . . . one-seven-five. Very faint, Comrade Captain—a ping, a single ping on active sonar."

"So." Tupolev leaned against the bulkhead. "Good work, Comrade. Now we must be patient."

The Dallas

Chief Laval pronounced the area clear. The BQQ-5's sensitive receptors revealed nothing, even after the SAPS system had been used. Chambers maneuvered the bow around so that the single ping would go out to the *Pogy,* which in turn fired off her own ping to the *Red October* to make sure the signal was received. It was clear for another ten miles. The *Pogy* moved out at thirty knots, followed by the U.S. Navy's newest boomer.

The V. K. Konovalov

"Two more submarines. One single screw, the other twin screw, I think. Still faint. The single-screw submarine is turning much more rapidly. Do the Americans have twin-screw submarines, Comrade Captain?"

"Yes, I believe so." Tupolev wondered about this. The difference in signature characteristics was not all that pronounced. They'd see in any case. The *Konovalov* was creeping along at two knots, one hundred fifty meters beneath the surface. Whatever was coming seemed to be coming right for them. Well, he'd teach the imperialists something after all.

The Red October

"Can anybody spell me at the wheel?" Ryan asked.

"Need a stretch?" Mancuso asked, coming over.

"Yeah. I could stand a trip to the head, too. The coffee's about to bust my kidneys."

"I relieve you, sir." The American captain moved into Ryan's seat. Jack headed aft to the nearest head. Two minutes later he was feeling much better. Back in the control room, he did some knee bends to get circulation back in his legs, then looked briefly at the chart. It seemed strange, almost sinister, to see the U.S. coast marked in Russian.

"Thank you, Commander."

"Sure." Mancuso stood.

"It is certain that you are no sailor, Ryan." Ramius had been watching him without a word.

"I have never claimed to be one, Captain," Ryan said agreeably. "How long to Norfolk?"

"Oh, another four hours, tops," Mancuso said. "The idea's to arrive after dark. They have something to get us in unseen, but I don't know what."

"We left the sound in daylight. What if somebody saw us then?" Ryan asked.

"I didn't see anything, but if anybody was there, all he'd have seen was three sub conning towers with no numbers on them." They had left in daylight to take advantage of a "window" in Soviet satellite coverage.

Ryan lit another cigarette. His wife would give him hell for this, but he was tense from being on the submarine. Sitting at the helmsman's station left him with nothing to do but stare at the handful of instruments. The sub was easier to hold level than he had expected, and the only radical turn he had attempted showed how eager the sub was to change course in any direction. Thirty-some-thousand tons of steel, he thought—no wonder.

The Pogy/The Red October

The *Pogy* stormed past the *Dallas* at thirty knots and continued for twenty minutes, stopping eleven miles beyond her—and three miles from the *Konovalov,* whose crew was scarcely breathing now. The *Pogy*'s sonar, though lacking the new BC-10/SAPS signal-processing system, was otherwise state of the art, but it was impossible to hear something that made no noise at all, and the *Konovalov* was silent.

The *Red October* passed the *Dallas* at 1500 hours after receiving the latest all-clear signal. Her crew was tired and looking forward to arriving at Norfolk two hours after sundown. Ryan wondered how quick'y he could fly back to London. He was afraid that the CIA would want to debrief him at length. Mancuso and the crewmen of the *Dallas* wondered if they'd get to see their families. They weren't counting on it.

The V. K. Konovalov

"Whatever it is, it is big, very big, I think. His course will take him within five kilometers of us."

"An *Ohio,* as Moscow said," Tupolev commented.

"It sounds like a twin-screw submarine, Comrade Captain," the *michman* said.

"The *Ohio* has one propeller. You know that."

"Yes, Comrade. In any case, he will be with us in twenty minutes. The other attack submarine is moving at thirty-plus knots. If the pattern holds, he will proceed fifteen kilometers beyond us."

"And the other American?"

"A few kilometers seaward, drifting slowly, like us. I do not have an exact range. I could raise him on active sonar, but that—"

"I am aware of the consequences," Tupolev snapped. He went back to the control room.

"Tell the engineers to be ready to answer bells. All men at battle stations?"

"Yes, Comrade Captain," the *starpom* replied. "We have an excellent firing solution on the American hunter sub—the one moving, that is. The way he runs at full speed makes it easy for us. The other we can localize in seconds."

"Good, for a change," Tupolev smiled. "You see what we can do when circumstances favor us?"

"And what shall we do?"

"When the big one passes us, we will close and ream his asshole. They have played their games. Now we shall play ours. Have the engineers increase power. We will need full power shortly.

"It will make noise, Comrade," the *starpom* cautioned.

"True, but we have no choice. Ten percent power. The *Ohio* cannot possibly hear that, and perhaps the near hunter sub won't either."

The Pogy

"Where did that come from?" The sonar chief made some adjustments on his board. "Conn, sonar, I got a contact, bearing two-three-zero."

"Conn, aye," Commander Wood answered at once. "Can you classify?"

"No, sir. It just came up. Reactor plant and steam noises, real faint, sir. I can't quite read the plant signature . . ." He flipped the gain controls to maximum. "Not one of ours. Skipper, I think maybe we got us an *Alfa* here."

"Oh, great! Signal *Dallas* right now!"

The chief tried, but the *Dallas,* running at thirty-two knots, missed the five rapid pings. The *Red October* was now eight miles away.

The Red October

Jones' eyes suddenly screwed shut. "Mr. Bugayev, tell the skipper I just heard a couple of pings."

"Couple?"

"More 'n one, but I didn't get a count."

The Pogy

Commander Wood made his decision. The idea had been to send the sonar signals on a highly directional, low-power basis so as to minimize the chance of revealing his own position. But the *Dallas* hadn't picked that up.

"Max power, Chief. Hit *Dallas* with everything."

"Aye aye." The chief flipped his power controls to full. It took several seconds until the system was ready to send a hundred-kilowatt blast of energy.

Ping ping ping ping ping!

The Dallas

"Wow!" Chief Laval exclaimed. "Conn, sonar, danger signal from *Pogy!*"

"All stop!" Chambers ordered. "Quiet ship."

"All stop." Lieutenant Goodman relayed the orders a second later. Aft, the reactor watch reduced steam demand, increasing the temperature in the reactor. This allowed neutrons to escape out of the pile, rapidly slowing the fission reaction.

"When speed gets to four knots, go to one-third speed," Chambers told the officer of the deck as he went aft to the sonar room. "Frenchie, I need data in a hurry."

"Still going too fast, sir," Laval said.

The Red October

"Captain Ramius, I think we should slow down," Mancuso said judiciously.

"The signal was not repeated," Ramius disagreed. The second directional signal had missed them, and the *Dallas* had not relayed the danger signal yet because she was still traveling too fast to locate the *October* and pass it along.

The Pogy

"Okay, sir, *Dallas* has killed power."

Wood chewed on his lower lip. "All right, let's find the bastard. Yankee search, Chief, max power." He went back to control. "Man battle stations." An alarm went off two seconds later. The *Pogy* had already been at increased readiness, and within forty seconds all stations were manned, with the executive officer, Lieutenant Commander Tom Reynolds, as fire control coordinator. His team of officers and technicians were waiting for data to feed into the Mark 117 fire control computer.

The sonar dome in the *Pogy*'s bow was blasting sound energy into the water. Fifteen seconds after it started the first return signal appeared on Chief Palmer's screen.

"Conn, sonar, we have a positive contact, bearing two-three-four, range six thousand yards. Classify probable *Alfa* class from his plant signature," Palmer said.

"Get me a solution!" Wood said urgently.

"Aye." Reynolds watched the data input as another team of officers was making a paper and pencil plot on the chart table. Computer or not, there had to be a backup. The data paraded across the screen. The *Pogy*'s four torpedo tubes contained a pair of Harpoon antiship missiles and two Mark 48 torpedoes. Only the torpedoes were useful at the moment. The Mark 48 was the most powerful torpedo in the inventory; wire-guided— and able to home in with its own active sonar—it ran at over fifty knots and carried a half-ton warhead. "Skipper, we got a solution for both fish. Running time four minutes, thirty-five seconds."

"Sonar, secure pinging," Wood said.

"Aye aye. Pinging secured, sir." Palmer killed power to the active systems. "Target elevation-depression angle is near zero, sir. He's about at our depth.

"Very well, sonar. Keep on him." Wood now had his target's position. Further pinging would only give it a better idea of his own.

The Dallas

"Pogy was pinging something. They got a return, bearing one-nine-one, about," Chief Laval said. "There's another sub out there. I don't know what. I can read some plant and steam noises, but not enough for a signature."

The Pogy

"The boomer's still movin', sir," Chief Palmer reported.

"Skipper," Reynolds looked up from the paper tracks, "her course takes her between us and the target."

"Terrific. All ahead one-third, left twenty degrees rudder." Wood moved to the sonar room while his orders were carried out. "Chief, power up and stand by to ping the boomer hard."

"Aye aye, sir." Palmer worked his controls. "Ready, sir."

"Hit him straight on. I don't want him to miss this time."

Wood watched the heading indicator on the sonar plot swing. The *Pogy* was turning rapidly, but not rapidly enough to suit him. The *Red October*—only he and Reynolds knew that she was Russian, though the crew was speculating like mad—was coming in too fast.

"Ready, sir."

"Hit it."

Palmer punched the impulse control.

Ping ping ping ping ping!

The Red October

"Skipper," Jones yelled. "Danger signal!"

Mancuso jumped to the annunciator without waiting for Ramius to react. He twisted the dial to All Stop. When this was done he looked at Ramius. "Sorry, sir."

"All right." Ramius scowled at the chart. The phone buzzed a moment later. He took it and spoke in Russian for several seconds before hanging up. "I told them that we have a problem but we do not know what it is."

"True enough." Mancuso joined Ramius at the chart. Engine noises were diminishing, though not quickly enough to suit the American. The *October* was quiet for a Russian sub, but this was still too noisy for him.

"See if your sonarman can locate anything," Ramius suggested.

"Right." Mancuso took a few steps aft. "Jonesy, find what's out there."

"Aye, Skipper, but it won't be easy on this gear." He already had the sensor arrays working in the direction of the two escorting attack subs. Jones adjusted the fit of his headphones and started working on the amplifier controls. No signal processors, no SAPS, and the transducers weren't worth a damn! But this wasn't the time to get excited. The Soviet systems had to be manipulated electromechanically, unlike the computer-controlled ones he was used to. Slowly and carefully, he altered the directional receptor gangs in the sonar dome forward, his right hand twirling a cigarette pack, his eyes shut tight. He didn't notice Bugayev sitting next to him, listening to the same input.

The Dallas

"What do we know, Chief?" Chambers asked.

"I got a bearing and nothing else. *Pogy*'s got him all dialed in, but our friend powered back his engine right after he got lashed, and he faded out on me. *Pogy* got a big return off him. He's probably pretty close, sir."

Chambers had only moved up to his executive officer's posting four months earlier. He was a bright, experienced officer and a likely candidate for his own command, but he was only thirty-three years old and had only been back in submarines for those four months. The year and a half prior to that he'd been a reactor instructor in Idaho. The gruffness that was part of his job as Mancuso's principal on-board disciplinarian also shielded more insecurity than he would have cared to admit. Now his career was on the line. He knew exactly how important this mission was. His future would ride on the decisions he was about to make.

"Can you localize with one ping?"

The sonar chief considered this for a second. "Not enough for a shooting solution, but it'll give us something."

"One ping, do it."

"Aye." Laval worked on his board briefly, triggering the active elements.

The V. K. Konovalov

Tupolev winced. He had acted too soon. He should have waited until they were past—but then if he had waited that long, he would have had to move, and now he had all three of them hovering nearby, almost still.

The four submarines were moving only fast enough for depth control. The Russian *Alfa* was pointed southeast, and all four were arrayed in a roughly trapezoidal fashion, open end seaward. The *Pogy* and the *Dallas* were to the north of the *Konovalov,* the *Red October* was southeast of her.

The Red October

"Somebody just pinged her," Jones said quietly. "Bearing is roughly northwest, but she isn't making enough noise for us to read her. Sir, if I had to make a bet, I'd say she was pretty close."

"How do you know that?" Mancuso asked.

"I heard the pulse direct—just one ping to get a range, I think. It was from a BQQ-5. Then we heard the echo off the target. The math works out a couple of different ways, but smart money is he's between us and our guys, and a little west. I know it's shaky, sir, but it's the best we got."

"Range ten kilometers, perhaps less," Bugayev commented.

"That's kinda shaky, too, but it's as good a starting place as any. Not a whole lot of data. Sorry, Skipper. Best we can do," Jones said.

Mancuso nodded and returned to control.

"What gives?" Ryan asked. The plane controls were pushed all the way forward to maintain depth. He had not grasped the significance of what was going on.

"There's a hostile submarine out there."

"What information do we have?" Ramius asked.

"Not much. There's a contact northwest, range unknown, but probably not very far. I know for sure it's not one of ours. Norfolk said this area was cleared. That leaves one possibility. We drift?"

"We drift," Ramius echoed, lifting the phone. He spoke a few orders.

The *October*'s engines were providing the power to move

the submarine at a fraction over two knots, barely enough to maintain steerage way and not enough to maintain depth. With her slight positive buoyancy, the *October* was drifting upward a few feet per minute despite the plane setting.

The Dallas

"Let's move back south. I don't like the idea of having that *Alfa* closer to our friend than we are. Come right to one-eight-five, two-thirds," Chambers said finally.

"Aye aye," Goodman said. "Helm, right fifteen degrees rudder, come to new course one-eight-five. All ahead two thirds."

"Right fifteen degrees rudder, aye." The helmsman turned the wheel. "Sir, my rudder is right fifteen degrees, coming to new course one-eight-five."

The *Dallas'* four torpedo tubes were loaded with three Mark 48s and a decoy, an expensive MOSS (mobile submarine simulator). One of her torpedoes was targeted on the *Alfa*, but the firing solution was vague. The "fish" would have to do some of the tracking by itself. The *Pogy*'s two torpedoes were almost perfectly dialed in.

The problem was that neither boat had authority to shoot. Both attack submarines were operating under the normal rules of engagement. They could fire in self-defense only and defend the *Red October* only by bluff and guile. The question was whether the *Alfa* knew what the *Red October* was.

The V. K. Konovalov

"Steer for the *Ohio*," Tupolev ordered. "Bring speed to three knots. We must be patient, comrades. Now that the Americans know where we are they will not ping us again. We will move from our place quietly."

The *Konovalov*'s bronze propeller turned more quickly. By shutting down some nonessential electrical systems, the engineers were able to increase speed without increasing reactor output.

The Pogy

On the *Pogy*, the nearest attack boat, the contact faded, degrading the directional bearing somewhat. Commander Wood debated whether or not to get another bearing with active sonar but decided against it. If he used active sonar his position would be like that of a policeman looking for a burglar in a dark building with a flashlight. Sonar pings could well tell his target more than they told him. Using passive sonar was the normal routine in such a case.

Chief Palmer reported the passage of the *Dallas* down their port side. Both Wood and Chambers decided not to use their underwater telephones to communicate. They could not afford to make any noise now.

The Red October

They had been creeping along for a half hour now. Ryan was chain-smoking at his station, and his palms were sweating as he struggled to maintain his composure. This was not the sort of combat he had been trained for, being trapped inside a steel pipe, unable to see or hear anything. He knew that there was a Soviet submarine out there, and he knew what her orders were. If her captain realized who they were—then what? The two captains, he thought, were amazingly cool.

"Can your submarines protect us?" Ramius asked.

"Shoot at a Russian sub?" Mancuso shook his head. "Only if he shoots first—at them. Under the normal rules, we don't count."

"What?" Ryan was stunned.

"You want to start a war?" Mancuso smiled, as though he found this situation amusing. "That's what happens when warships from two countries start exchanging shots. We have to smart our way out of this."

"Be calm, Ryan," Ramius said. "This is our usual game. The hunter submarine tries to find us, and we try not to be found. Tell me, Captain Mancuso, at what range did you hear us off Iceland?"

"I haven't examined your chart closely, Captain," Mancuso mused. "Maybe twenty miles, thirty or so kilometers."

"And then we were traveling at thirteen knots—noise increases faster than speed. I think we can move east, slowly, without being detected. We use the caterpillar, move at six knots. As you know, Soviet sonar is not so efficient as American. Do you agree, Captain?"

Mancuso nodded. "She's your boat, sir. May I suggest northeast? That ought to put us behind our attack boats inside an hour, maybe less."

"Yes." Ramius hobbled over to the control board to open the tunnel hatches, then went back to the phone. He gave the necessary orders. In a minute the caterpillar motors were engaged and speed was increasing slowly.

"Rudder right ten, Ryan," Ramius said. "And ease the plane controls."

"Rudder right ten, sir, easing the planes, sir." Ryan carried the orders out, glad that they were doing something.

"Your course is zero-four-zero, Ryan," Mancuso said from the chart table.

"Zero-four-zero, coming right through three-five-zero." From the helmsman's seat he could hear the water swishing down the portside tunnel. Every minute or so there was an odd rumble that lasted three or four seconds. The speed gauge in front of him passed through four knots.

"You are frightened, Ryan?" Ramius chuckled.

Jack swore to himself. His voice had wavered. "I'm a little tired, too."

"I know it is difficult for you. You do well for a new man with no training. We will be late to Norfolk, but we shall get there, you will see. Have you been on a missile boat, Mancuso?"

"Oh, sure. Relax, Ryan. This is what boomers do. Somebody comes lookin' for us, we just disappear." The American commander looked up from the chart. He had set coins at the estimated positions of the three other subs. He considered marking it up more but decided not to. There were some very interesting notations on this coastal chart—like programmed missile-firing positions. Fleet intelligence would go ape over this sort of information.

The *Red October* was moving northeast at six knots now. The *Konovalov* was coming southeast at three. The *Pogy* was heading south at two, and the *Dallas* south at fifteen. All four submarines were now within a six-mile-diameter circle, all converging on about the same point.

The V. K. Konovalov

Tupolev was enjoying himself. For whatever reason, the Americans had chosen to play a conservative game that he had not expected. The smart thing, he thought, would have been for one of the attack boats to close in and harrass him, allowing the missile sub to pass clear with the other escort. Well, at sea nothing was ever quite the same twice. He sipped at a cup of tea as he selected a sandwich.

His sonar *michman* noted an odd sound in his sonar set. It only lasted a few seconds, then was gone. Some far-off seismic rumble, he thought at first.

The Red October

They had risen because of the *Red October*'s positive trim, and now Ryan had five degrees of down-angle on the diving planes to get back down to a hundred meters. He heard the captains discussing the absence of a thermocline. Mancuso explained that it was not unusual for the area, particularly after violent storms. They agreed that it was unfortunate. A thermal layer would have helped their evasion.

Jones was at the aft entrance of the control room, rubbing his ears. The Russian phones were not very comfortable. "Skipper, I'm getting something to the north, comes and goes. I haven't gotten a bearing lock on it."

"Whose?" Mancuso asked.

"Can't say, sir. The active sonar isn't too bad, but the passive stuff just isn't up to the drill, Skipper. We're not blind, but close to it."

"Okay, if you hear something, sing out."

"Aye aye, Captain. You got some coffee out here? Mr. Bugayev sent me for some."

"I'll have a pot sent in."

"Right." Jones went back to work.

The V. K. Konovalov

"Comrade Captain, I have a contact, but I do not know what it is," the *michman* said over the phone.

Tupolev came back, munching on his sandwich. *Ohio*s had

been acquired so rarely by the Russians—three times to be exact, and in each case the quarry had been lost within minutes—that no one had a feel for the characteristics of the class.

The *michman* handed the captain a spare set of phones. "It may take a few minutes, Comrade. It comes and goes."

The water off the American coast, though nearly isothermal, was not entirely perfect for sonar systems. Minor currents and eddies set up moving walls that reflected and channeled sound energy on a nearly random basis. Tupolev sat down and listened patiently. It took five minutes for the signal to come back.

The *michman*'s hand waved. "Now, Comrade Captain."

His commanding officer looked pale.

"Bearing?"

"Too faint, and too short to lock in—but three degrees on either bow, one-three-six to one-four-two."

Tupolev tossed the headphones on the table and went forward. He grabbed the political officer by the arm and led him quickly to the wardroom.

"It's *Red October!*"

"Impossible. Fleet Command said that his destruction was confirmed by visual inspection of the wreckage." The *zampolit* shook his head emphatically.

"We have been tricked. The caterpillar acoustical signature is unique, Comrade. The Americans have him, and he is out there. We must destroy him!"

"No. We must contact Moscow and ask for instructions."

The *zampolit* was a good Communist, but he was a surface ship officer who didn't belong on submarines, Tupolev thought.

"Comrade Zampolit, it will take several minutes to approach the surface, perhaps ten or fifteen to get a message to Moscow, thirty more for Moscow to respond at all—and then they will request *confirmation!* An hour in all, two, three? By that time *Red October* will be gone. Our original orders are operative, and there is no time to contact Moscow."

"But what if you are wrong?"

"I am not wrong, Comrade!" the captain hissed. "I will enter my contact report in the log, and my recommendations. If you forbid this, I will log that also! I am right, Comrade. It will be your head, not mine. Decide!"

"You are certain?"

"*Certain!*"

"Very well." The *zampolit* seemed to deflate. "How will you do this?"

"As quickly as possible, before the Americans have a chance to destroy us. Go to your station, Comrade." The two men went back to the control room. The *Konovalov*'s six bow torpedo tubes were loaded with Mark C 533-millimeter wire-guided torpedoes. All they needed was to be told where to go.

"Sonar, search forward on all active systems!" the captain ordered.

The *michman* pushed the button.

The Red October

"Ouch." Jones' head jerked around. "Skipper, we're being pinged. Port side, midships, maybe a little forward. Not one of ours, sir."

The Pogy

"Conn, sonar, the *Alfa*'s got the boomer! The *Alfa* bearing is one-nine-two."

"All ahead two-thirds," Wood ordered immediately.

"All ahead two-thirds, aye."

The *Pogy*'s engines exploded into life, and soon her propeller was thrashing the black water.

The V. K. Konovalov

"Range seven thousand, six hundred meters. Elevation angle zero," the *michman* reported. So, this was the submarine they had been sent to hunt, he thought. He had just donned a headset that allowed him to report directly to the captain and fire control officer.

The *starpom* was the chief fire control supervisor. He quickly entered the data into the computer. It was a simple problem of target geometry. "We have a solution for torpedoes one and two."

"Prepare to fire."

"Flooding tubes." The *starpom* flipped the switches himself, reaching past the petty officer. "Outer torpedo tube doors are open."

"Recheck firing solution!" Tupolev said.

The Pogy

The *Pogy*'s sonar chief was the only man to hear the transient noise.

"Conn, sonar, *Alfa* contact—she just flooded tubes, sir! Target bearing is one-seven-nine."

The V. K. Konovalov

"Solution confirmed, Comrade Captain," the *starpom* said.

"Fire one and two," Tupolev ordered.

"Firing one . . . Firing two." The *Konovalov* shuddered twice as compressed air charges ejected the electrically powered torpedoes.

The Red October

Jones heard it first. "High-speed screws port side!" he said loudly and clearly. "Torpedoes in the water port side!"

"Ryl nalyeva!" Ramius ordered automatically.

"What?" Ryan asked.

"Left, rudder left!" Ramius pounded his fist on the rail.

"Left full, do it!" Mancuso said.

"Left full rudder, aye." Ryan turned the wheel all the way and held it down. Ramius was spinning the annunciator to flank speed.

The Pogy

"Two fish running," Palmer said. "Bearing is changing right to left. I say again, torpedo bearing changing right to left rapidly on both fish. They're targeted on the boomer."

The Dallas

The *Dallas* heard them, too. Chambers ordered flank speed and a turn to port. With torpedoes running his options were limited, and he was doing what American practice taught, heading someplace else—very fast.

The Red October

"I need a course!" Ryan said.

"Jonesy, give me a bearing!" Mancuso shouted.

"Three-two-zero, sir. Two fish heading in," Jones responded at once, working his controls to nail the bearing down. This was no time to screw up.

"Steer three-two-zero, Ryan," Ramius ordered, "if we can turn so fast."

Thanks a lot, Ryan thought angrily, watching the gyrocompass click through three-five-seven. The rudder was hard over, and with the sudden increase in power from the caterpillar motors, he could feel feedback flutter through the wheel.

"Two fish heading in, bearing is three-two-zero, I say again bearing is constant," Jones reported, much cooler than he felt. "Here we go, guys..."

The Pogy

Her tactical plot showed the *October,* the *Alfa,* and the two torpedoes. The *Pogy* was four miles north of the action.

"Can we shoot?" the exec asked.

"At the *Alfa?*" Wood shook his head emphatically. "No, dammit. It wouldn't make a difference anyway."

The V. K. Konovalov

The two Mark C torpedoes were charging at forty-one knots, a slow speed for this range, so that they could be more easily guided by the *Konovalov*'s sonar system. They had a projected six-minute run, with one minute already completed.

The Red October

"Okay, coming through three-four-five, easing the rudder off," Ryan said.

Mancuso kept quiet now. Ramius was using a tactic that he didn't particularly agree with, turning into the fish. It offered a minimum target profile, but it gave them a simpler geometric intercept solution. Presumably Ramius knew what Russian fish could do. Mancuso hoped so.

"Steady on three-two-zero, Captain," Ryan said, eyes locked

on the gyro repeater as though it mattered. A small voice in his brain congratulated him for going to the head an hour earlier.

"Ryan, down, maximum down on the diving planes."

"All the way down." Ryan pushed the yoke to the stops. He was terrified, but even more frightened of fouling up. He had to assume that both commanders knew what they were about. There was no choice for him. Well, he thought, he did know one thing. Guided torpedoes can be tricked. Like radar signals that are aimed at the ground, sonar pulses can be obscured, especially when the sub they are trying to locate is near the bottom or the surface, areas where the pulses tend to be reflected. If the *October* dove she could lose herself in an opaque field—presuming she got there fast enough.

The V. K. Konovalov

"Target aspect has changed, Comrade Captain. Target is now smaller," the *michman* said.

Tupolev considered this. He knew everything there was on Soviet combat doctrine—and knew that Ramius had written a good deal of it. Marko would do what he taught all of us to do, Tupolev thought. Turn into the oncoming weapons to minimize target cross-section and dive for the bottom to become lost in the confused echoes. "Target will be attempting to dive into the bottom-capture field. Be alert."

"Aye, Comrade. Can he reach the bottom quickly enough?" the *starpom* asked.

Tupolev racked his brain for the *October*'s handling characteristics. "No, he cannot dive that deep in so short a time. We have him." Sorry, my old friend, but I have no choice, he thought.

The Red October

Ryan cringed each time the sonar lash echoed through the double hull. "Can't you jam that or something?" he demanded.

"Patience, Ryan," Ramius said. He had never faced live warheads before but had exercised this problem a hundred times in his career. "Let him know he has us first."

"Do you carry decoys?" Mancuso asked.

"Four of them, in the torpedo room, forward—but we have no torpedomen."

Both captains were playing the cool game, Ryan noted bitterly from inside his terrified little world. Neither was willing to show fright before his peer. But they were both trained for this.

"Skipper," Jones called, "two fish, bearing constant at three-two-zero—they just went active. I say again, the fish are now active—shit! they sound just like 48s. Skipper, they sound like Mark 48 fish."

Ramius had been waiting for this. "Yes, we stole the torpedo sonar from you five years ago, but not your torpedo engines. *Bugayev!*"

In the sonar room, Bugayev had powered up the acoustical jamming gear as soon as the fish were launched. Now he carefully timed his jamming pulses to coincide with those from the approaching torpedoes. The pulses were dialed into the same carrier frequency and pulse repetition rate. The timing had to be precise. By sending out slightly distorted return echoes, he could create ghost targets. Not too many, nor too far away. Just a few, close by, and he might be able to confuse the fire control operators on the attacking *Alfa*. He thumbed the trigger switch carefully, chewing on an American cigarette.

The V. K. Konovalov

"Damn! He's jamming us." The *michman,* noting a pair of new pips, showed his first trace of emotion. The fading pip from the true contact was now bordered with two new ones, one north and closer, the other south and farther away. "Captain, the target is using Soviet jamming equipment."

"You see?" Tupolev said to the *zampolit.* "Use caution now," he ordered his *starpom.*

The Red October

"Ryan, all up on planes!" Ramius shouted.

"All the way up." Ryan yanked back, pulling the yoke hard against his belly and hoping that Ramius knew what the hell he was doing.

"Jones, give us time and range."

"Aye." The jamming gave them a sonar picture plotted on the main scopes. "Two fish, bearing three-two-zero. Range to number one is 2,000 yards, to number two is 2,300—I got a depression angle on number one! Number one fish is heading down a little, sir." Maybe Bugayev wasn't so dumb after all, Jones thought. But they had two fish to sweat . . .

The Pogy

The *Pogy*'s skipper was enraged. The goddamned rules of engagement prevented him from doing a goddamned thing, except, maybe—

"Sonar, ping the sonuvabitch! Max power, blast the sucker!"

The *Pogy*'s BQQ-5 sent timed wave fronts of energy lashing at the *Alfa*. The *Pogy* couldn't shoot, but maybe the Russian didn't know that, and maybe this lashing would interfere with their targeting sonar.

The Red October

"Any time now—one of the fish has capture, sir. I don't know which." Jones moved the phones off one ear, his hand poised to slap the other off. The homing sonar on one torpedo was now tracking them. Bad news. If these were like Mark 48s . . . Jones knew all too well that those things didn't miss much. He heard the change in the Doppler shift of the propellers as they passed beneath the *Red October*. "One missed, sir. Number one missed under us. Number two is heading in, ping interval is shortening." He reached over and patted Bugayev on the shoulder. Maybe he really was the on-board genius that the Russians said he was.

The V. K. Konovalov

The second Mark C torpedo was cutting through the water at forty-one knots. This made the torpedo-target closing speed about fifty-five. The guidance and decision loop was a complex one. Unable to mimic the computer homing system on the American Mark 48, the Soviets had the torpedo's targeting sonar report back to the launching vessel through an insulated wire. The *starpom* had a choice of sonar data with which to guide the torpedoes, that from the sub-mounted sonar or that from the torpedoes themselves. The first fish had been duped by the ghost images that the jamming had duplicated on the torpedo sonar frequency. For the second, the *starpom* was using the lower-frequency bow sonar. The first one had missed low, he knew now. That meant that the target was the middle pip. A quick frequency change by the *michman* cleared the sonar picture for few seconds before the jamming mode was altered. Coolly and expertly, the *starpom* commanded the second torpedo to select the center target. It ran straight and true.

The five-hundred-pound warhead struck the target a glancing blow aft of midships, just forward of the control room. It exploded a millisecond later.

The Red October

The force of the explosion hurled Ryan from his chair, and his head hit the deck. He came to from a moment's unconsciousness with his ears ringing in the dark. The shock of the explosion had shorted out a dozen electrical switchboards, and it was several seconds before the red battle lights clicked on. Aft, Jones had flipped his headphones off just in time, but Bugayev, trying to the last second to spoof the incoming torpedo, had not. He was rolling in agony on the deck, one eardrum ruptured, totally deafened. In the engine spaces men were scrambling back to their feet. Here the lights had stayed on, and Melekhin's first action was to look at the damage-control status board.

The explosion had occurred on the outer hull, a skin of light steel. Inside it was a water-filled ballast tank, a beehive of cellular baffles seven feet across. Located beyond the tank were high-pressure air flasks. Then came the *October*'s battery and the inner pressure hull. The torpedo had impacted in the center of a steel plate on the outer hull, several feet from any weld joints. The force of the explosion had torn a hole twelve feet across, shredded the interior ballast tank baffles, and ruptured a half-dozen air flasks, but already much of its force had been dissipated. The final damage was done to thirty of the large nickle-cadmium battery cells. Soviet engineers had placed these here deliberately. They had known that such a placement would make them difficult to service, difficult to recharge, and worst of all expose them to seawater contamination. All this had been accepted in light of their secondary purpose as additional armor for the hull. The *October*'s batteries saved her. Had it not been for them, the force of the explosion would have been spent on the pressure hull. Instead it was greatly reduced by the layered defensive system which had no Western counterpart. A crack had developed at the weld joint on the inner hull, and water was spraying into the radio room as though from a high-pressure hose, but the hull was otherwise secure.

In control, Ryan was soon back in his seat trying to determine if his instruments still worked. He could hear water splashing into the next compartment forward. He didn't know what to do. He did know it would be a bad time to panic, much as his brain screamed for the release.

"What do I do?"

"Still with us?" Mancuso's face looked satanic in the red lights.

"No goddammit, I'm dead—what do I do?"

"Ramius?" Mancuso saw the captain holding a flashlight taken from a bracket on the aft bulkhead.

"Down, dive for bottom." Ramius took the phone and called engineering to order the engines stopped. Melekhin had already given the order.

Ryan pushed his controls forward. In a goddamned submarine that's got a goddamned hole punched in it, they tell you to go *down!* he thought.

The V. K. Konovalov

"A solid hit, Comrade Captain," the *michman* reported. "His engines stopped. I hear hull creaking noises, his depth is changing." He tried some additional pings but got nothing. The explosion had greatly disturbed the water. There were rumbling echoes of the initial explosion reverberating through the sea. Trillions of bubbles had formed, creating an "ensonified zone" around the target that rapidly obscured it. His active pings were reflected back by the cloud of bubbles, and his passive listing ability was greatly reduced by the recurring rumbles. All he knew for sure was that one torpedo had hit, probably the second. He was an experienced man trying to decide what was noise and what was signal, and he had reconstructed most of the events correctly.

The Dallas

"Score one for the bad guys," the sonar chief said. The *Dallas* was running too fast to make proper use of her sonar, but the explosion was impossible to miss. The whole crew heard it through the hull.

In the attack center Chambers plotted their position two miles from where the *October* had been. The others in the compartment looked at their instruments without emotion. Ten of their shipmates had just been hit, and the enemy was on the other side of the wall of noise.

"Slow to one-third," Chambers ordered.

"All ahead one-third," the officer of the deck repeated.

"Sonar, get me some data," Chambers said.

"Working on it, sir." Chief Laval strained to make sense of what he heard. It took a few minutes as the *Dallas* slowed to under ten knots. "Conn, sonar, the boomer took one hit. I don't hear her engines . . . but there ain't no breakup noises. I say again, sir, no breakup noises."

"Can you hear the *Alfa?*"

"No, sir, too much crud in the water."

Chamber's face screwed into a grimace. You're an officer, he told himself, they pay you to think. First, what's happening? Second, what do you do about it? Think it through, then act.

"Estimated distance to target?"

"Something like nine thousand yards, sir," Lieutenant Goodman said, reading the last solution off the fire control computer. "She'll be on the far side of the ensonified zone."

"Make your depth six hundred feet." The diving officer passed this on to the helmsman. Chambers considered the situation and decided on his course of action. He wished Mancuso and Mannion were here. The captain and navigator were the other two members of what passed for the *Dallas'* tactical management committee. He needed to exchange some ideas with other experienced officers—but there weren't any.

"Listen up. We're going down. The disturbance from the explosion will stay fairly steady. If it moves at all, it'll go up. Okay, we'll go under it. First we want to locate the boomer. If she isn't there, then she's on the bottom. It's only nine hundred feet here, so she could be on the bottom with a live crew. Whether or not she's on the bottom, we gotta get between her and the *Alfa*." And, he thought on, if the *Alfa* shoots then, I kill the fucker, and rules of engagement be damned. They had to trick this guy. But how? And where was the *Red October?*

The Red October

She was diving more quickly than expected. The explosion had also ruptured a trim tank, causing more negative buoyancy than they had at first allowed for.

The leak in the radio room was bad, but Melekhin had noted the flooding on his damage control board and reacted immediately. Each compartment had its own electrically powered pump. The radio room pump, supplemented by a master-zone pump that he had also activated, was managing, barely, to keep up with the flooding. The radios were already destroyed, but no one was planning to send any messages.

"Ryan, all the way up, and come right full rudder," Ramius said.

"Right full rudder, all the way up on the planes," Ryan said. "We going to hit the bottom?"

"Try not to," Mancuso said. "It might spring the leak worse."

"Great," Ryan growled back.

The *October* slowed her descent, arcing east below the ensonified zone. Ramius wanted it between himself and the *Alfa*. Mancuso thought that they might just survive after all. In that case he'd have to give this boat's plans a closer look.

The Dallas

"Sonar, give me two low-powered pings for the boomer. I don't want anybody else to hear this, Chief."

"Aye." Chief Laval made the proper adjustments and sent the signals out. "All right! Conn, sonar, I got her! Bearing two-zero-three, range two thousand yards. She is not, repeat *not,* on the bottom, sir."

"Left fifteen degrees rudder, come to two-zero-three," Chambers ordered.

"Left fifteen degrees rudder, aye!" the helmsman sang out. "New course two-zero-three. Sir, my rudder is left fifteen degrees."

"Frenchie, tell me about the boomer!"

"Sir, I got . . . pump noises, I think . . . and she's moving a little, bearing is now two-zero-one. I can track her on passive, sir."

"Thompson, plot the boomer's course. Mr. Goodman, we

still have that MOSS ready for launch?"

"Aye aye," responded the torpedo officer.

The V. K. Konovalov

"Did we kill him?" the *zampolit* asked.

"Probably," Tupolev answered, wondering if he had or not. "We must close to be certain. Ahead slow."

"Ahead slow."

The Pogy

The *Pogy* was now within two thousand yards of the *Konovalov*, still pinging her mercilessly.

"He's moving, sir. Enough that I can read passive," Sonar Chief Palmer said.

"Very well, secure pinging," Wood said.

"Aye, pinging secured."

"We got a solution?"

"Locked in tight," Reynolds answered. "Running time is one minute eighteen seconds. Both fish are ready."

"All ahead one-third."

"All ahead one-third, aye." The *Pogy* slowed. Her commanding officer wondered what excuse he might find for shooting.

The Red October

"Skipper, that was one of our sonars that pinged us, off north-north-east. Low-power ping, sir, must be close."

"Think you can raise her on gertrude?"

"Yes sir!"

"Captain?" Mancuso asked. "Permission to communicate with my ship?"

"Yes."

"Jones, raise her right now."

"Aye. This is Jonesy calling Frenchie, do you copy?" The sonarman frowned at the speaker. "Frenchie, answer me."

The Dallas

"Conn, sonar, I got Jonesy on the gertrude."

Chambers lifted the control room gertrude phone. "Jones,

this is Chambers. What is your condition?"

Mancuso took the mike away from his man. "Wally, this is Bart," he said. "We took one midships, but she's holding together. Can you run interference for us?"

"Aye aye! Starting right now, out." Chambers replaced the phone. "Goodman, flood the MOSS tube. Okay, we'll go in behind the MOSS. If the *Alfa* shoots at it, we take her out. Set it to run straight for two thousand yards, then turn south."

"Done. Outer door open, sir."

"Launch."

"MOSS away, sir."

The decoy ran forward at twenty knots for two minutes to clear the *Dallas,* then slowed. It had a torpedo body whose forward portion carried a powerful sonar transducer that ran off a tape recorder and broadcast the recorded sounds of a 688-class submarine. Every four minutes it changed over from loud operation to silent. The *Dallas* trailed a thousand yards behind the decoy, dropping several hundred feet below its course track.

The *Konovalov* approached the wall of bubbles carefully, with the *Pogy* trailing to the north.

"Shoot at the decoy, you son of a bitch," Chambers said quietly. The attack center crew heard him and nodded grim agreement.

The Red October

Ramius judged that the ensonified zone was now between him and the *Alfa.* He ordered the engines turned back on, and the *Red October* proceeded on a north-easterly course.

The V. K. Konovalov

"Left ten degrees rudder," Tupolev ordered quietly. "We'll come around the dead zone to the north and see if he is still alive when we turn back. First we must clear the noise."

"Still nothing," the *michman* reported. "No bottom impact, no collapse noises . . . New contact, bearing one-seven-zero . . . Different sound, Comrade Captain, one propeller . . . Sounds like an American."

"What heading?"

"South, I think. Yes, south . . . The sound's changing. It is American."

"An American sub is decoying. We ignore it."

"Ignore it?" the *zampolit* said.

"Comrade, if you were heading north and were torpedoed, would you then head south? Yes, you would—but not Marko. It is too obvious. This American is decoying to try to take us away from him. Not too clever, this one. Marko would do better. And he would go north. I know him, I know how he thinks. He is now heading north, perhaps northeast. They would not decoy if he was dead. Now we know that he is alive but crippled. We will find him, and finish him," Tupolev said calmly, fully caught up in the hunt for *Red October*, remembering all he had been taught. He would prove now that he was the new master. His conscience was still. Tupolev was fulfilling his destiny.

"But the Americans—"

"Will not shoot, Comrade," the captain said with a thin smile. "If they could shoot, we would already be dead from the one to the north. They cannot shoot without permission. They must *ask* for permission, as we must—but we already have the permission, and the advantage. We are now where the torpedo struck him, and when we clear the disturbance we will find him again. Then we will have him."

The Red October

They couldn't use the caterpillar. One side was smashed by the torpedo hit. The *October* was moving at six knots, driven by her propellers, which made more noise than the other system. This was much like the normal drill of protecting a boomer. But the exercise always presupposed that the escorting attack boats could shoot to make the bad guy go away . . .

"Left rudder, reverse course," Ramius ordered.

"What?" Mancuso was astounded.

"Think, Mancuso," Ramius said, looking to be sure that Ryan carried out the order. Ryan did, not knowing why.

"Think, Commander Mancuso," Ramius repeated. "What has happened? Moskva ordered a hunter sub to remain behind, probably a *Politovskiy*-class boat, the *Alfa* you call him. I know all their captains. All young, all, ah, aggressive? Yes, aggressive. He must know we are not dead. If he knows this, he will pursue us. So, we go back like a fox and let him pass."

Mancuso didn't like this. Ryan could tell without looking.

"We cannot shoot. Your men cannot shoot. We cannot run from him—he is faster. We cannot hide—his sonar is better. He will move east, use his speed to contain us and his sonar to locate us. By moving west, we have the best chance to escape. This he will not expect."

Mancuso still didn't like it, but he had to admit it was clever. Too damned clever. He looked back down at the chart. It wasn't his boat.

The Dallas

"The bastard went right past. Either ignored the decoy or flat didn't hear it. He's abeam of us, we'll be in his baffles soon," Chief Laval reported.

Chambers swore quietly. "So much for that idea. Right fifteen degrees rudder." At least the *Dallas* had not been heard. The submarine responded rapidly to the controls. "Let's get behind him."

The Pogy

The *Pogy* was now a mile off the *Alfa*'s port quarter. She had the *Dallas* on sonar and noted her change of course. Commander Wood simply did not know what to do next. The easiest solution was to shoot, but he couldn't. He contemplated shooting on his own. His every instinct told him to do just this. The *Alfa* was hunting Americans . . . But he couldn't give in to his instinct. Duty came first.

There was nothing worse than overconfidence, he reflected bitterly. The assumption behind this operation had been that there wouldn't be anybody around, and even if there were the attack subs would be able to warn the boomer off well in advance. There was a lesson in this, but Wood didn't care to think about it just now.

The V. K. Konovalov

"Contact," the *michman* said into the microphone. "Ahead, almost dead ahead. Using propellers and going at slow speed. Bearing zero-four-four, range unknown."

"Is it *Red October?*" Tupolev asked.

"I cannot say, Comrade Captain. It could be an American. He's coming this way, I think."

"Damn!" Tupolev looked around the control room. Could they have passed the *Red October?* Might they already have killed him?

The Dallas

"Does he know we're here, Frenchie?" Chambers asked, back in sonar.

"No way, sir." Laval shook his head. "We're directly behind him. Wait a minute . . ." The chief frowned. "Another contact, far side of the *Alfa*. That's gotta be our friend, sir. Jesus! I think he's heading this way. Using his wheels, not that funny thing."

"Range to the *Alfa?*"

"Under three thousand yards, sir."

"All ahead two thirds! Come left ten degrees!" Chambers ordered. "Frenchie, ping, but use the under-ice sonar. He may not know what that is. Make him think we're the boomer."

"Aye aye, sir!"

The V. K. Konovalov

"High-frequency pinging aft!" the *michman* called out. "Does not sound like an American sonar, Comrade."

Tupolev was suddenly puzzled. Was it an American to seaward? The other one on his port quarter was certainly American. It had to be the *October*. Marko was still the fox. He had lain still, letting them go past, so that he could shoot at them!

"All ahead full, left full rudder!"

The Red October

"Contact!" Jones sang out. "Dead ahead. Wait . . . It's an *Alfa!* She's close! Seems to be turning. Somebody pinging her on the other side. Christ, she's *real* close. Skipper, the *Alfa* is not a point source. I got signal separation between the engine and the screw."

"Captain," Mancuso said. The two commanders looked at one another and communicated a single thought as if by telepathy. Ramius nodded.

"Get us range."

"Jonesy, ping the sucker!" Mancuso ran aft.

"Aye." The systems were fully powered. Jones loosed a single ranging ping. "Range fifteen hundred yards. Zero elevation angle, sir. We're level with her."

"Mancuso, have your man give us range and bearing!" Ramius twisted the annunciator handle savagely.

"Okay, Jonesy, you're our fire control. Track the mother."

The V. K. Konovalov

"One active sonar ping to starboard, distance unknown, bearing zero-four-zero. The seaward target just ranged on us," the *michman* said.

"Give me a range," Tupolev ordered.

"Too far aft of the beam, Comrade. I am losing him aft."

One of them was the *October*—but which? Could he risk shooting at an American sub? No!

"Solution to the forward target?"

"Not a good one," the *starpom* replied. "He's maneuvering and increasing speed."

The *michman* concentrated on the western target. "Captain, contact forward is not, repeat not Soviet. Forward contact is American."

"*Which* one?" Tupolev screamed.

"West and northwest are both American. East target unknown."

"Keep the rudder at full."

"Rudder is full," the helmsman responded, holding the wheel over.

"The target is behind us. We must lock on and shoot as we turn. Damn, we are going too fast. Slow to one-third speed."

The *Konovalov* was normally quick to turn, but the power reduction made her propeller act like a brake, slowing the maneuver. Still, Tupolev was doing the right thing. He had to point his torpedo tubes near the bearing of the target, and he had to slow rapidly enough for his sonar to give him accurate firing information.

The Red October

"Okay, the *Alfa* is continuing her turn, now heading right to left . . . Propulsion sounds are down some. She just chopped power," Jones said, watching the screen. His mind was working furiously computing course, speed, and distance. "Range is now twelve hundred yards. She's still turning. We doin' what I think?"

"Looks that way."

Jones set the active sonar on automatic pinging. "Have to see what this turn does, sir. If she's smart she'll burn off south and get clear first."

"Then pray she ain't smart," Mancuso said from the passageway. "Steady as she goes!"

"Steady as she goes," Ryan said, wondering if the next torpedo would kill them.

"Her turn is continuing. We're on her port beam now, maybe her port bow." Jones looked up. "She's going to get around first. Here come the pings."

The *Red October* accelerated to eighteen knots.

The V. K. Konovalov

"I have him," the *michman* said. "Range one thousand meters, bearing zero-four-five. Angle zero."

"Set it up," Tupolev ordered his exec.

"It will have to be a zero-angle shot. We're swinging too rapidly," the *starpom* said. He set it up as quickly as he could. The submarines were now closing at over forty knots. "Ready for tube five only! Tube flooded, door—open. Ready!"

"Shoot!"

"Fire five!" The *starpom*'s finger stabbed the button.

The Red October

"Range down to nine hundred—high-speed screws dead ahead! We have one torpedo in the water dead ahead. One fish, heading right in!"

"Forget it, track the *Alfa!*"

"Aye, okay, the *Alfa*'s bearing two-two-five, steadying down. We need to come left a little, sir."

"Ryan, come left five degrees, your course is two-two-five."

"Left five rudder, coming to two-two-five."

"The fish is closing rapidly, sir," Jones said.

"Screw it! Track the *Alfa*."

"Aye. Bearing is still two-two-five. Same as the fish."

The combined speed ate up the distance between the submarines rapidly. The torpedo was closing the *October* faster still, but it had a safety device built in. To prevent them from blowing up their own launch platform, torpedoes could not arm until they were five hundred to a thousand yards from the boat that launched them. If the *October* closed the *Alfa* fast enough, she could not be hurt.

The *October* was now passing twenty knots.

"Range to the *Alfa* is seven hundred fifty yards, bearing two-two-five. The torpedo is close, sir, a few more seconds." Jones cringed, staring at the screen.

Klonk!

The torpedo struck the *Red October* dead center in her hemispherical bow. The safety lock still had another hundred meters to run. The impact broke it into three pieces, which were batted aside by the accelerating missile submarine.

"A dud!" Jones laughed. "Thank you, God! Target still bearing two-two-five, range is seven hundred yards."

The V. K. Konovalov

"No explosion?" Tupolev wondered.

"The safety locks!" The *starpom* swore. He'd had to set it up too fast.

"Where is the target?"

"Bearing zero-four-five, Comrade. Bearing is constant," the *michman* replied, "closing rapidly."

Tupolev blanched. "Left full rudder, all ahead flank!"

The Red October

"Turning, turning left to right," Jones said. "Bearing is now two-three-zero, spreading out a little. Need a little right rudder, sir."

"Ryan, come right five degrees."

"Rudder is right five," Jack answered.

"No, rudder ten right!" Ramius countermanded his order. He had been keeping a track with pencil and paper. And he knew the *Alfa*.

"Right ten degrees," Ryan said.

"Near-field effect, range down to four hundred yards, bearing is two-two-five to the center of the target. Target is spreading out left and right, mostly left," Jones said rapidly. "Range . . . three hundred yards. Elevation angle is zero, we are level with the target. Range two hundred fifty, bearing two-two-five to target center. We can't miss, Skipper."

"We're gonna hit!" Mancuso called out.

Tupolev should have changed depth. As it was he depended on the *Alfa*'s acceleration and maneuverability, forgetting that Ramius knew exactly what these were.

"Contact spread way the hell out—instantaneous return, sir!"

"Brace for impact!"

Ramius had forgotten the collision alarm. He yanked at it only seconds before impact.

The *Red October* rammed the *Konovalov* just aft of midships at a thirty-degree angle. The force of the collision ruptured the *Konovalov*'s titanium pressure hull and crumpled the *October*'s bow as if it were a beer can.

Ryan had not braced hard enough. He was thrown forward, and his face struck the instrument panel. Aft, Williams was catapulted from his bed and caught by Noyes before his head hit the deck. Jones' sonar systems were wiped out. The missile submarine bounded up and over the top of the *Alfa*, her keel grating across the upper deck of the smaller vessel as the momentum carried her forward and upward.

The V. K. Konovalov

The *Konovalov* had had full watertight integrity set. It did not make a difference. Two compartments were instantly vented to the sea, and the bulkhead between the control room and the after compartments failed a moment later from hull deformation. The last thing that Tupolev saw was a curtain of white foam coming from the starboard side. The *Alfa* rolled to port, turned by the friction of the *October*'s keel. In a few seconds the submarine was upside down. Throughout her length men and gear tumbled about like dice. Half the crew were already drowning. Contact with the *October* ended at this point, when the *Konovalov*'s flooded compartments made her drop stern first toward the bottom. The political officer's last conscious act was to yank at the disaster beacon handle, but it was to no

avail: the sub was inverted, and the cable fouled on the sail.
The only marker on the *Konovalov*'s grave was a mass of
bubbles.

The Red October

"We still alive?" Ryan's face was bleeding profusely.

"Up, up on the planes!" Ramius shouted.

"All the way up." Ryan pulled back with his left hand,
holding his right over the cuts.

"Damage report," Ramius said in Russian.

"Reactor system is intact," Melekhin answered at once.
"The damage control board shows flooding in the torpedo
room—I think. I have vented high-pressure air into it, and the
pump is activated. Recommend we surface to assess damage."

"*Da!*" Ramius hobbled to the air manifold and blew all
tanks.

The Dallas

"Jesus," the sonar chief said, "somebody hit somebody. I got
breakup noises going down and hull-popping noises going up.
Can't tell which is which, sir. Both engines are dead."

"Get us up to periscope depth quick!" Chambers ordered.

The Red October

It was 1654 local time when the *Red October* broke the surface
of the Atlantic Ocean for the first time, forty-seven miles southeast of Norfolk. There was no other ship in sight.

"Sonar is wiped out, Skipper." Jones was switching off his
boxes. "Gone, crunched. We got some piddly-ass lateral hy-
drophones. No active stuff, not even the gertrude."

"Go forward, Jonesy. Nice work."

Jones took the last cigarette from his pack. "Any time, sir—
but I'm gettin' out next summer, depend on it."

Bugayev followed him forward, still deafened and stunned
from the torpedo hit.

The *October* was sitting still on the surface, down by the
bow and listing twenty degrees to port from the vented ballast
tanks.

The Dallas

"How about that," Chambers said. He lifted the microphone. "This is Commander Chambers. They killed the *Alfa!* Our guys are safe. Surfacing the boat now. Stand by the fire and rescue party!"

The Red October

"You okay, Commander Ryan?" Jones turned his head carefully. "Looks like you broke some glass the hard way, sir."

"You don't worry till it stops bleeding," Ryan said drunkenly.

"Guess so." Jones held his handkerchief over the cuts. "But I sure hope you don't always drive this bad, sir."

"Captain Ramius, permission to lay to the bridge and communicate with my ship?" Mancuso asked.

"Go, we may need help with the damage."

Mancuso got into his jacket, checking to make sure his small docking radio was still in the pocket where he had left it. Thirty seconds later he was atop the sail. The *Dallas* was surfacing as he made his first check of the horizon. The sky had never looked so good.

He couldn't recognize the face four hundred yards away, but it had to be Chambers.

"Dallas, this is Mancuso."

"Skipper, this is Chambers. You guys okay?"

"Yes! But we may need some hands. The bow's all stove in and we took a torpedo midships."

"I can see it, Bart. Look down."

"Jesus!" The jagged hole was awash, half out of the water, and the submarine was heavily down by the bow. Mancuso wondered how she could float at all, but it wasn't the time to question why.

"Come over here, Wally, and get the raft out."

"On the way. Fire and rescue is standing by, I—there's our other friend," Chambers said.

The *Pogy* surfaced three hundred yards directly ahead of the *October*.

"Pogy says the area's clear. Nobody here but us. Heard that

one before?" Chambers laughed mirthlessly. "How about we radio in?"

"No, let's see if we can handle it first." The *Dallas* approached the *October*. Within minutes Mancuso's command submarine was seventy yards to port, and ten men on a raft were struggling across the chop. Up to this time only a handful of men aboard the *Dallas* had known what was going on. Now everyone knew. He could see his men pointing and talking. What a story they had.

Damage was not as bad as they had feared. The torpedo room had not flooded—a sensor damaged by the impact had given a false reading. The forward ballast tanks were permanently vented to the sea, but the submarine was so big and her ballast tanks so subdivided that she was only eight feet down at the bow. The list to port was only a nuisance. In two hours the radio room leak had been plugged, and after a lengthy discussion among Ramius, Melekhin, and Mancuso it was decided that they could dive again if they kept their speed down and did not go below thirty meters. They'd be late getting to Norfolk.

THE EIGHTEENTH DAY

MONDAY, 20 DECEMBER

The Red October

Ryan again found himself atop the sail thanks to Ramius, who said that he had earned it. In return for the favor, Jack had helped the captain up the ladder to the bridge station. Mancuso was with them. There was now an American crew below in the control room, and the engine room complement had been supplemented so that there was something approaching a normal steaming watch. The leak in the radio room had not been fully contained, but it was above the waterline. The compartment had been pumped out, and the *October*'s list had eased to fifteen degrees. She was still down by the bow, which was partially compensated for when the intact ballast tanks were blown dry. The crumpled bow gave the submarine a decidedly asymmetrical wake, barely visible in the moonless, cloud-laden sky. The *Dallas* and the *Pogy* were still submerged, somewhere aft, sniffing for additional interference as they neared Capes Henry and Charles.

461

Somewhere farther aft an LNG (liquified natural gas) carrier was approaching the passage, which the coast guard had closed to all normal traffic in order to allow the floating bomb to travel without interference all the way to the LNG terminal at Cove Point, Maryland—or so the story went. Ryan wondered how the navy had persuaded the ship's skipper to fake engine trouble or somehow delay his arrival. They were six hours late. The navy must have been nervous as all hell until they had finally surfaced forty minutes earlier and been spotted immediately by a circling Orion.

The red and green buoy lights winked at them, dancing on the chop. Forward he could see the lights of the Chesapeake Bay Bridge-Tunnel, but there were no moving automobile lights. The CIA had probably staged a messy wreck to shut it down, maybe a tractor-trailer or two full of eggs or gasoline. Something creative.

"You've never been to America before," Ryan said, just to make conversation.

"No, never to a Western country. Cuba once, many years ago."

Ryan looked north and south. He figured they were inside the capes now. "Well, welcome home, Captain Ramius. Speaking for myself, sir, I'm damned glad you're here."

"And happier that you are here," Ramius observed.

Ryan laughed out loud. "You can bet your ass on that. Thanks again for letting me up here."

"You have earned it, Ryan."

"The name's Jack, sir."

"Short for John, is it?" Ramius asked. "John is the same as Ivan, no?"

"Yes, sir, I believe it is." Ryan didn't understand why Ramius' face broke into a smile.

"Tug approaching." Mancuso pointed.

The American captain had superb eyesight. Ryan didn't see the boat through his binoculars for another minute. It was a shadow, darker that the night, perhaps a mile away.

"*Sceptre,* this is tug *Paducah.* Do you read? Over."

Mancuso took the docking radio from his pocket. "*Paducah,* this is *Sceptre.* Good morning, sir." He was speaking in an English accent.

"Please form up on me, Captain, and follow us in."

"Jolly good, *Paducah*. Will do. Out."

HMS *Sceptre* was the name of an English attack submarine. She must be somewhere remote, Ryan thought, patrolling the Falklands or some other faraway location so that her arrival at Norfolk would be just another routine occurrence, not unusual and difficult to disprove. Evidently they were thinking about some agent's being suspicious of a strange sub's arrival.

The tug approached to within a few hundred yards, then turned to lead them in at five knots. A single red tuck light showed.

"I hope we don't run into any civilian traffic," Mancuso said.

"But you said the harbor entrance was closed," Ramius said.

"Might be some guy in a little sailboat out there. The public has free passage through the yard to the Dismal Swamp Canal, and they're damned near invisible on radar. They slip through all the time."

"This is crazy."

"It's a free country, Captain," Ryan said softly. "It will take you some time to understand what free really means. The word is often misused, but in time you will see just how wise your decision was."

"Do you live here, Captain Mancuso?" Ramius asked.

"Yes, my squadron is based in Norfolk. My home is in Virginia Beach, down that way. I probably won't get there anytime soon. They're going to send us right back out. Only thing they can do. So, I miss another Christmas at home. Part of the job."

"You have a family?"

"Yes, Captain. A wife and two sons. Michael, eight, and Dominic, four. They're used to having daddy away."

"And you, Ryan?"

"Boy and a girl. Guess I will be home for Christmas. Sorry, Commander. You see, for a while there I had my doubts. After things get settled down some I'd like to get this whole bunch together for something special."

"Big dinner bill," Mancuso chuckled.

"I'll charge it to the CIA."

"And what will the CIA do with us?" Ramius asked.

"As I told you, Captain, a year from now you will be living your own lives, wherever you wish to live, doing whatever you wish to do."

"Just so?"

"Just so. We take pride in our hospitality, sir, and if I ever get transferred back from London, you and your men are welcome in my home at any time."

"Tug's turning to port." Mancuso pointed. The conversation was taking too maudlin a turn for him.

"Give the order, Captain," Ramius said. It was, after all, Mancuso's harbor.

"Left five degrees rudder," Mancuso said into the microphone.

"Left five degrees rudder, aye," the helmsman responded. "Sir, my rudder is left five degrees."

"Very well."

The *Paducah* turned into the main channel, past the *Saratoga*, which was sitting under a massive crane, and headed towards a mile-long line of piers in the Norfolk Naval Shipyard. The channel was totally empty, just the *October* and the tug. Ryan wondered if the *Paducah* had a normal complement of enlisted men or a crew made entirely of admirals. He would not have given odds either way.

Norfolk, Virginia

Twenty minutes later they were at their destination. The Eight-Ten Dock was a new dry dock built to service the *Ohio*-class fleet ballistic missile submarines, a huge concrete box over eight hundred feet long, larger than it had to be, covered with a steel roof so that spy satellites could not see if it were occupied or not. It was in the maximum security section of the base, and one had to pass several security barriers of armed guards— marines, not the usual civilian guards—to get near the dock, much less into it.

"All stop," Mancuso ordered.

"All stop, aye."

The *Red October* had been slowing for several minutes, and it was another two hundred yards before she came to a complete halt. The *Paducah* curved around to starboard to push her bow round. Both captains would have preferred to power their own way in, but the damaged bow made maneuvering tricky. The diesel-powered tug took five minutes to line the bow up properly, headed directly into the water-filled box. Ramius gave the engine command himself, the last for this submarine. She eased forward through the black water, passing slowly under the wide roof. Mancuso ordered his men topside to handle the lines tossed them by a handful of sailors on the rim of the dock, and the submarine came to a halt exactly in its center. Already the gate they had passed through was closing, and a canvas cover the size of a clipper's mainsail was being drawn across it. Only when cover was securely in place were the overhead lights switched on. Suddenly a group of thirty or so officers began screaming like fans at a ballgame. The only thing left out was the band.

"Finished with the engines," Ramius said in Russian to the crew in the maneuvering room, then switched to English with a trace of sadness in his voice. "So. We are here."

The overhead traveling crane moved down toward them and stopped to pick up the brow, which it brought around and laid carefully on the missile deck forward of the sail. The brow was hardly in place when a pair of officers with gold braid nearly to their elbows walked—ran—across it. Ryan recognized the one in front. It was Dan Foster.

The chief of naval operations saluted the quarterdeck as he got to the edge of the gangway, then looked up at the sail. "Request permission to come aboard, sir."

"Permission is—"

"Granted," Mancuso prompted.

"Permission is granted," Ramius said loudly.

Foster jumped aboard and hurried up the exterior ladder on the sail. It wasn't easy, since the ship still had a sizable list to port. Foster was puffing as he reached the control station.

"Captain Ramius, I'm Dan Foster." Mancuso helped the CNO over the bridge coaming. The control station was suddenly crowded. The American admiral and the Russian captain shook hands, then Foster shook Mancuso's. Jack came last.

"Looks like the uniform needs a little work, Ryan. So does the face."

"Yeah, well, we ran into some trouble."

"So I see. What happened?"

Ryan didn't wait for the explanation. He went below without

excusing himself. It wasn't his fraternity. In the control room
the men were standing around exchanging grins, but they were
quiet, as if they feared the magic of the moment would evaporate all too quickly. For Ryan it already had. He looked for
the deck hatch and climbed up through it, taking with him
everything he'd brought aboard. He walked up the gangway
against traffic. No one seemed to notice him. Two hospital
corpsmen were carrying a stretcher, and Ryan decided to wait
on the dock for Williams to be brought out. The British officer
had missed everything, having only been fully conscious for
the past three hours. As Ryan waited he smoked his last Russian
cigarette. The stretcher, with Williams tied onto it, was man-
handled out. Noyes and the medical corpsmen from the subs
tagged along.

"How are you feeling?" Ryan walked alongside the stretcher
toward the ambulance.

"Alive," Williams said, looking pale and thin. "And you?"

"What I feel under my feet is solid concrete. Thank God
for that!"

"And what he's going to feel is a hospital bed. Nice meeting
you, Ryan," the doctor said briskly. "Let's move it, people."
The corpsmen loaded the stretcher into an ambulance parked
just inside the oversized doors. A minute later it was gone.

"You Commander Ryan, sir?" a marine sergeant asked after
saluting.

Ryan returned the salute. "Yes."

"I have a car waiting for you, sir. Will you follow me,
please?"

"Lead on, Sergeant."

The car was a gray navy Chevy that took him directly to
the Norfolk Naval Air Station. Here Ryan boarded a helicopter.
By now he was too tired to care if it were a sleigh with reindeer
attached. During the thirty-five-minute trip to Andrews Air
Force Base Ryan sat alone in the back, staring into space. He
was met by another car at the base and driven straight to Langley.

CIA Headquarters

It was four in the morning when Ryan finally entered Greer's
office. The admiral was there, along with Moore and Ritter.

The admiral handed him something to drink. Not coffee, Wild Turkey bourbon whiskey. All three senior executives took his hand.

"Sit down, boy," Moore said.

"Damned well done." Greer smiled.

"Thank you." Ryan took a long pull on the drink. "Now what?"

"Now we debrief you," Greer answered.

"No, sir. Now I fly the hell home."

Greer's eyes twinkled as he pulled a folder from a coat pocket and tossed it in Ryan's lap. "You're booked out of Dulles at 7:05 A.M. First flight to London. And you really should wash up, change your clothes, and collect your Skiing Barbie."

Ryan tossed the rest of the drink off. The sudden slug of whiskey made his eyes water, but he was able to refrain from coughing.

"Looks like that uniform got some hard use," Ritter observed.

"So did the rest of me." Jack reached inside the jacket and pulled out the automatic pistol. "This got some use, too."

"The GRU agent? He wasn't taken off with the rest of the crew?" Moore asked.

"You *knew* about him? You knew and you didn't get word to me, for Christ's sake!"

"Settle down, son," Moore said. "We missed connections by half an hour. Bad luck, but you made it. That's what counts."

Ryan was too tired to scream, too tired to do much of anything. Greer took out a tape recorder and a yellow pad full of questions.

"Williams, the British officer, is in a bad way," Ryan said, two hours later. "The doc says he'll make it, though. The sub isn't going anywhere. Bow's all crunched in, and there's a pretty nice hole where the torpedo got us. They were right about the *Typhoon*, Admiral, the Russians built that baby strong, thank God. You know, there may be people left alive on that *Alfa* . . ."

"Too bad," Moore said.

Ryan nodded slowly. "I figured that. I don't know that I like it, sir, leaving men to die like that."

"Nor do we," Judge Moore said, "nor do we, but if we were to rescue someone from her, well, then everything we've—

everything you've been through would be for nothing. Would you want that?"

"It's a chance in a thousand anyway," Greer said.

"I don't know," Ryan said, finishing off his third drink and feeling it. He had expected Moore to be uninterested in checking the *Alfa* for signs of life. Greer had surprised him. So, the old seaman had been corrupted by this affair—or just by being at the CIA—into forgetting the seaman's code. And what did this say about Ryan? "I just don't know."

"It's a war, Jack," Ritter said, more kindly than usual, "a real war. You did well, boy."

"In a war you do well to come home alive," Ryan stood, "and that, gentlemen, is what I plan to do, right now."

"Your things are in the head." Greer checked his watch. "You have time to shave if you want."

"Oh, almost forgot." Ryan reached inside his collar to pull out the key. He handed it to Greer. "Doesn't look like much, does it? You can kill fifty million people with that. 'My name is Ozymandias, king of kings! Look on my works, ye mighty, and despair!'" Ryan headed for the washroom, knowing he had to be drunk to quote Shelley.

They watched him disappear. Greer switched off the tape machine, looking at the key in his hand. "Still want to take him to see the president?"

"No, not a good idea," Moore said. "Boy's half smashed, not that I blame him a bit. Get him on the plane, James. We'll send a team to London tomorrow or the next day to finish the debriefing."

"Good." Greer looked into his empty glass. "Kind of early in the day for this, isn't it?"

Moore finished off his third. "I suppose. But then it's been a fairly good day, and the sun's not even up yet. Let's go, Bob. We have an operation of sorts to run."

Norfolk Naval Shipyard

Mancuso and his men boarded the *Paducah* before dawn and were ferried back to the *Dallas*. The 688-class attack submarine sailed immediately and was back underwater before the sun rose. The *Pogy*, which had never entered port, would complete her deployment without her corpsman aboard. Both submarines had orders to stay out thirty more days, during which their crewmen would be encouraged to forget everything they had seen, heard, or wondered about.

The *Red October* sat alone with the dry dock draining around her, guarded by twenty armed marines. This was not unusual in the Eight-Ten Dock. Already a select group of engineers and technicians was inspecting her. The first items taken off were her cipher books and machines. They would be in National Security Agency headquarters at Fort Meade before noon.

Ramius, his officers, and their personal gear were taken by bus to the same airfield Ryan had used. An hour later they were in a CIA safe house in the rolling hills south of Charlottesville, Virginia. They went immediately to bed except for two men, who stayed awake watching cable television, already amazed at what they saw of life in the United States.

Dulles International Airport

Ryan missed the dawn. He boarded a TWA 747 that left Dulles on time, at 7:05 A.M. The sky was overcast, and when the aircraft burst through the cloud layer into sunlight, Ryan did something he had never done before. For the first time in his life, Jack Ryan fell asleep on an airplane.

ABOUT THE AUTHOR

He has had a private chat with the President of the United States who proclaimed himself to be an avid fan of *The Hunt for Red October*. He has lunched with the White House staff. His novel has been a top seller at the Pentagon. Yet the author in question is neither a former intelligence nor naval officer. Rather, Tom Clancy is an insurance broker from a small town in Maryland whose only previously published writing was a letter to the editor and a three-page article about the MX missile. Clancy always wanted to write a suspense novel, and a newspaper article about a mutiny on a Soviet frigate gave him the initial idea for *Red October*. He did extensive research about Soviet–American naval strategies and submarine technology. Then, in the time he could spare from his insurance business, Clancy sat down at his typewriter and wrote. The rest is history ... and now Clancy is at work on a major new novel.

Bestselling Thrillers — action-packed for a great read

___ $3.95 0-425-07671-7 **ROLE OF HONOR** John Gardner
___ $3.95 0-425-07657-1 **DAI-SHO** Marc Olden
___ $3.50 0-425-07324-6 **DAU** Ed Dodge
___ $3.95 0-425-08158-3 **RED SQUARE** Edward Topol and
Fridrikh Neznansky
___ $4.50 0-425-08383-7 **THE HUNT FOR RED OCTOBER**
Tom Clancy
___ $3.95 0-425-08301-2 **AIRSHIP NINE** Thomas H. Block
___ $3.95 0-441-37033-0 **IN HONOR BOUND**
Gerald Seymour
___ $3.95 0-441-01972-2 **AMERICAN REICH** Douglas Muir
___ $3.50 0-441-10550-5 **CIRCLE OF DECEIT**
Walter Winward
___ $3.50 0-441-27316-5 **GAME OF HONOR** Tom Lewis
___ $3.95 0-441-47128-5 **LAST MESSAGE TO BERLIN**
Philippe van Rjndt
___ $3.50 0-515-08337-2 **DEATHWATCH** Elleston Trevor
___ $3.95 0-515-08415-8 **QUILLER** Adam Hall

Prices may be slightly higher in Canada.

THE PENGUIN CLASSICS

FOUNDER EDITOR (1944–64): E. V. RIEU

EDITOR:

Betty Radice

GIOVANNI BOCCACCIO was born in 1313, either in Florence or Certaldo (a town in Florentine territory). His father, a prosperous merchant banker with the Compagnia dei Bardi, entertained notions of his son following in his footsteps, and between the years 1325–8 sent his son to Naples to learn the trade; he himself moved there in 1327 when he was appointed general manager of the Neapolitan branch. When he realized that Boccaccio had no vocation for banking he arranged for him to study canon law. This was equally unsuccessful and after a few years Boccaccio gave up his legal studies and devoted his time to literature. At this period Naples, under the Angevin king, Robert of Anjou, was one of the major intellectual and cultural centres of Italy. To judge from references in his Latin Epistles, Boccaccio considered this the happiest period of his life. For political and economic reasons he was forced to return to Florence in 1341. His experiences during the Black Death (1347–9) are recorded in the introduction to the *Decameron*, and when he met Petrarch in 1350 he had probably begun work on it. He had already gained a reputation as a man of letters in Florence, and the government sent him on several minor missions. In 1354 and 1365 he was sent to the Papal Court at Avignon, and in 1367 to Rome in order to congratulate Urban V on the return of the papacy from the Babylonian Captivity. He revisited Naples twice in 1355 and 1362: but each time he came away saddened, unable to recapture his lost youth. He moved to Certaldo and spent the last thirteen years of his life there, dying in 1375, just over a year after Petrarch. Boccaccio wrote several other works, including *Elegia di madonna Fiammetta*, described as 'the first modern psychological novel'.

G. H. MCWILLIAM is Professor of Italian at Leicester University and a former Fellow of Trinity College, Dublin. A leading authority on the work of Ugo Betti, he has written and broadcast on several other Italian authors, including Dante, Boccaccio, and Verga. His previous translations include plays and poems by Betti, Pirandello, Svevo, and Quasimodo. In 1962 the Italian Government awarded him the silver medal for his services to Italian culture.

Giovanni Boccaccio

THE DECAMERON

TRANSLATED
WITH AN INTRODUCTION BY
G. H. McWILLIAM

Penguin Books

Penguin Books Ltd, Harmondsworth, Middlesex, England
Penguin Books, 625 Madison Avenue, New York, New York 10022, U.S.A.
Penguin Books Australia Ltd, Ringwood, Victoria, Australia
Penguin Books Canada Ltd, 2801 John Street, Markham, Ontario, Canada L3R 1B4
Penguin Books (N.Z.) Ltd, 182–190 Wairau Road, Auckland 10, New Zealand

—

This translation first published 1972
Reprinted 1973, 1975, 1976, 1977, 1978, 1980, 1981

—

—

Made and printed in Great Britain by
Hazell Watson & Viney Ltd,
Aylesbury, Bucks
Set in Monotype Bembo

CONTENTS

THIRD DAY

FOURTH DAY

FIFTH DAY

SIXTH DAY

SEVENTH DAY

EIGHTH DAY

NINTH DAY

TENTH DAY

TRANSLATOR'S INTRODUCTION

I

Giovanni Boccaccio was born in the summer of 1313, probably in Florence but possibly in Certaldo, a town in Florentine territory which forms the setting for the famous story of Friar Cipolla (*Decameron*, VI, x). The identity of Boccaccio's mother has never been established, but the assertion that she was a Frenchwoman, and that he was born in Paris, is now almost universally discounted. His father was a prosperous Florentine merchant-banker, who at some time between the years 1325 and 1328 sent his adolescent son to study the rudiments of banking and commerce in Naples. Boccaccio's father was a director of the celebrated Florentine banking concern, the Compagnia dei Bardi, of whose Neapolitan branch he was appointed general manager in the autumn of 1327. It was not long before he discovered that his son had no real vocation for a business career, and he therefore arranged for him to turn instead to the study of canon law, a subject which Giovanni found no less irksome and distasteful than his abortive commercial apprenticeship. Within a few years, doubtless to the despair of his father, he abandoned his legal studies and embarked upon a literary career.

Under the rule of the erudite King Robert of Anjou, Naples was at this time one of the major intellectual centres in the Italian peninsula, and Boccaccio, by virtue of his connections with Florentine bankers, who were the prop and mainstay of the Angevin monarchy (as of other European monarchies of the period), gained ready access to Neapolitan high society and participated actively in the carefree and sophisticated life of King Robert's court. The years he spent in Naples were crucial to the development of his artistic sensibility. It was there that he laid the foundations of his immense erudition, which underpins the whole of his literary work and was later to earn him an outstanding reputation as a humanist.

From the scattered references to Naples that are found in Boccaccio's Latin epistles, it is evident that he regarded his sojourn in that city as the happiest and most rewarding period of his life. It was therefore with deep reluctance that in 1341 he was compelled, through a combination of political and economic factors, to leave Naples and return to Florence. He tells us in the Introduction to the *Decameron* that he was in Florence during the Great Plague of 1348, but the evidence for this is not entirely conclusive. His first meeting with Petrarch, whom he looked upon with an esteem not far short of idolatry, took place in 1350, at which time he was probably at work on the *Decameron*, having already completed all but one of his important remaining works in the vernacular, which had not only brought him a considerable reputation as a man of letters but had helped him to achieve a position of some importance in Florentine political and diplomatic circles. He was sent by the Florentine commune on a number of relatively minor missions, including two to the Papal court at Avignon (in 1354 and 1365) and one to Rome in 1367 to offer homage to Urban V on the return of the papacy from its 'Babylonish captivity'. In 1355, and again in 1362, he briefly revisited his old haunts in Naples, but on each occasion he returned to Florence bitterly disillusioned, having failed to recapture the spirit which had animated his youthful attachment to the Neapolitan social and literary scene.

The last thirteen years of Boccaccio's life were spent in Certaldo, and it was there that he died in 1375, just over a year after the death of Petrarch.

II

It should be emphasized that even if the *Decameron* had never been written, Boccaccio would still occupy a position of fundamental importance in the history of European literature for his so-called minor works, of which one (*Elegia di madonna Fiammetta*) has been described as the first modern psychological novel, another (*Comedia delle Ninfe fiorentine*) is the forerunner of the pastoral literature of the Renaissance, and two others (*Filostrato* and *Teseida*) supplied Chaucer with the source-material for his *Troilus and Criseyde* and *Knight's Tale* respectively. Moreover, with the encyclopaedic Latin works to which, under the guidance and encouragement of Petrarch, he devoted the last twenty years or so of his life, Boccaccio established a reputation as one of the leading humanists of the fourteenth century. It was because of these Latin treatises, in fact, and not because of the *Decameron* or any of his other vernacular works, that he was revered for at least a century after his death.

But it is of course the *Decameron* with which Boccaccio's name has been primarily associated for the past five hundred years, and which countless major and minor European writers have plundered for the raw material of their own artistic creations. One of the chief talking points among Boccaccio's critics is the question of whether the *Decameron* is a product of the Middle Ages or of the Renaissance. The view that Boccaccio is a representative of the Renaissance was succinctly formulated by the famous Italian nineteenth-century critic, Francesco De Sanctis, in his assertion that 'Dante brings one epoch to a close, Boccaccio opens up another', and the same critic even went so far as to call Boccaccio 'the Voltaire of the fourteenth century'. But in recent years, with the deepening of our knowledge of the Middle Ages, this view of Boccaccio has been substantially modified, and it is nowadays more usual to regard Boccaccio as a medieval writer, the *Decameron* being looked upon as the secular epic of the age whose religious and philosophical ideals are most magnificently expressed in the poetry of Dante. The *Decameron* has indeed been called a 'human comedy', complementing the *Divine Comedy* of Dante. But whereas it is perfectly obvious that Dante is a medieval writer, Boccaccio's position is by no means so clear-cut.

Those who regard the *Decameron* as a product of the Middle Ages claim (with reason) that the features of the work which the nineteenth-century critics pointed to admiringly as evidence of Boccaccio's Renaissance spirit are seen on closer inspection to have their roots in medieval culture. Boccaccio's fierce denunciation of the corruption and malpractices of ecclesiastics is closely paralleled in Dante, and it was perfectly common for medieval writers to hold priests and friars up to ridicule. Nor does one need to assume, because Boccaccio exalts the pleasures of the flesh, that he is resolutely turning his back on the Middle Ages. After all, he derived at least nine-tenths of his stories from medieval sources, and as Professor Whitfield pithily reminds us, 'wine and women is an old story, not reserved for the rebirth of learning'.* Furthermore, in those passages of the *Decameron* where Boccaccio theorizes about Fortune, his position is much closer to that of medieval writers like St Thomas Aquinas and Dante than to that of Renaissance theorists like Pico della Mirandola or Machiavelli. And even his theoretical statements about love, and his idealization of women, have strong precedents in the literature of the Middle Ages, in particular in *De Arte Honeste Amandi* of Andreas Cappellanus and in the poetry of the *dolce stil novo*, the school of poets to which Dante and Guido Cavalcanti belonged. Finally, the structure of the *Decameron* is distinctly medieval by virtue of its division into ten parts, each sub-divided into ten smaller parts, the distinct change of mood which takes place after the allegorically significant third and ninth days, the division of the storytellers into three men and seven women, and so on. This elaborately worked out structure, which finds its counterpart in the architecture of the great Gothic cathedrals, places Boccaccio in much closer affinity, from a purely formal viewpoint, with Dante than with Machiavelli or Ariosto.

And yet there is no denying that the spirit of the *Decameron* is by and large forward-looking. The chief indications of this are to be found in Boccaccio's attitude to religion on the one hand and to women on the other. So far as religion is concerned, while he pays conventional, orthodox respect to the Christian deity, he resolutely attacks all forms of superstition and bases his attitude to life and religious belief upon reason and experience. It is not so much a sceptical attitude that he adopts, as a rational clearheadedness, a determination to draw his own conclusions from observable facts and from his knowledge of how people behave in certain situations. The scathing attacks he delivers on such medieval practices as the cult of new saints and the worship of holy relics go far beyond any of the pronouncements on such issues to be found in the writings of his predecessors.

Finally, Boccaccio's attitude to love (as distinct from his theoretical observations on the subject), and his obvious adoration of women in their physical reality, are much closer to the Renaissance viewpoint than to the ethos of the Middle Ages. The right true end of love, for

* See p. 66 of *A Short History of Italian Literature* (Penguin Books, 1960).

Boccaccio, is its physical consummation, not a situation in which the lover gazes ecstatically upon his untouchable mistress, as though she were the ark of the covenant. Boccaccio's heroines are, with very few exceptions, creatures of flesh and blood rather than symbols of some higher, abstract quality of the spirit. And although there are plenty of instances of illicit physical love in the literature of the Middle Ages, they are almost invariably accompanied by a note of condemnation, with hellfire crackling vigorously away just round the corner. With one or two striking exceptions, such as the story of the widow and the scholar (VIII, vii), the misogyny characteristic of the medieval raconteur is notably absent from the Decameron. Boccaccio never condemns the physical union of people who are in love. One may even say that he has elevated physical love to a principle of life. He takes the view that copulation is a pleasurable activity, without any disagreeable side-effects such as punishments and torments post mortem. Yet the actual descriptions of people making love to one another are on the whole stylized and remarkably astringent, for Boccaccio is first and foremost a magnificent storyteller, who realizes that the most important ingredients of a good story are a lively and eloquent style, an interesting plot, and characters who can be instantly visualized in the mind of the reader.

III

It is widely but erroneously believed that the Decameron has never been fully rendered into English. Boccaccio's translators are said to have blenched to a man (or in at least one case, to a woman) at the prospect of describing in the English tongue what actually took place in the Tunisian desert between the saintly young hermit, Rustico, and the pious young virgin and earnest seeker after truth, Alibech (III, x). And many other passages from the work are said to have been consistently bowdlerized or expurgated to render it acceptable to a hypersensitive and puritanical English-reading public.

It is easy to see how the misconception has arisen if one takes the trouble to inspect the various translations of the Decameron that have been published in England and America from the early seventeenth century down to the twentieth. The treatment of the tenth tale of the

Third Day offers a fascinating insight into the English national character, as well as providing some indication of the way in which our attitude, as a nation, towards the description and discussion of the sexual act (as distinct from its legitimate or illicit enjoyment) has undergone slight but significant change, especially in the course of the last eighty years or so. We shall return to the Alibech case later on, and we shall also be considering some other crucial passages from the *Decameron*, with a view to deciding which parts of Boccaccio's monumental masterpiece have presented the chief problems to his English translators, and whether yet another translation is either necessary or desirable.

But let us first of all review, as briefly as possible, the various English translations of the *Decameron*, indicating the year in which they were published and giving the name of the translator in those cases where it is known. For one of the curious facts about English versions of the *Decameron* is the number of mute, inglorious Miltons to be found in the ranks of its translators. All of the earliest versions are by anonymous hands, and it was not until the middle of the nineteenth century that an anglicizer of the *Decameron* (he can hardly be called an English translator, as he rejoiced in the fine old Irish name of Kelly) was prepared to reveal his identity. At first glance, one is tempted to speculate that all these anonymous translators were clergymen, labouring in the untroubled, bucolic calm of English rural rectories, and silently relishing Boccaccio's denunciation of a corrupt Roman Church and of the manifold sharp practices of a celibate priesthood and celibate religious orders. However that may be, it is clear that until comparatively recently a certain stigma was attached, in the puritan English consciousness, to anyone translating so palpably licentious a work as the *Decameron*, even if the translator took care to state in his preface – as one of them did – that 'whenever [he] met with any thing that seemed immodest or loose, [he had] studied so to manage the Expression, and conceal the Matter, that the fair Sex may read it without blushing'.

A second curious fact about English versions of the *Decameron* is that it was not until two hundred and fifty years after Boccaccio's death (and four years after the death of Shakespeare) that the first apparently complete translation was published. This was the justly celebrated anonymous translation of 1620, which has been attributed, on what I believe to be insufficient evidence, to John Florio. But whilst the 1620 translation is a magnificent specimen of Jacobean prose, its high-handed treatment of the original text produces a number of shortcomings, to some of which we shall subsequently refer. Eighty-two years elapsed before the appearance of a new translation (also anonymous, though there are grounds for believing that the translator's name was John Savage), this being the version published in 1702, whose title-page reads: 'Il Decamerone. One hundred ingenious novels: written by John Boccaccio, The first Refiner of the Italian Language. Now done into English, and accommodated to the Gust of the present Age.' Again, we shall see later on how the Gust of the Age was reflected in the translator's handling of Boccaccio's text. In 1741 a third anonymous version was published, and in his preface the translator (posthumously identified as Charles Balguy, a physician who practised at Peterborough) severely censures his two predecessors for the liberties they had taken with the Italian, 'altering every thing according to the people's own taste and fancy', so that 'a great part of both bears very little resemblance to the original'. But the degree of his own fidelity to the original may be judged by his subsequent remark that 'Boccace is so licentious in many places, that it requires some management to preserve his wit and humour, and render him tolerably decent. This I have attempted with the loss of two novels, which I judged incapable of such treatment; and am apprehensive, it may still be thought by some people, that I have rather omitted too little, than too much.' Between the date of its first publication and the middle of the present century, this 1741 version was several times reissued with slight or major modifications, sometimes without any acknowledgement whatever to the original translator. The editor of the text printed in 1804 clearly considered that the 1741 translator had 'omitted too little' for he carried out a further process of expurgation. But the 1741 text is restored, with minor alterations and a half-hearted attempt to supply the two missing *novelle*, in a version printed in 1822 whose title-page proclaims it as a 'new edition; in which are restored many passages omitted in former editions'. This claim is not borne out by the text, which, apart from the emasculated renderings of the two missing *novelle*, is almost a word-for-word reproduction of the 1741 version with one or two significant excisions. But this was perhaps to be expected of an editor who in his preface had written that 'It must be admitted that the previous life of Boccaccio was not the most regular or the most exemplary. His work, and particularly the *Decameron*, bespeak him a man too loose in his manners, and who did not always pay a due respect to sacred things.'

It was in 1855 that a substantially new translation was published, and that, for the first time, the translator's name was revealed on the title-page. 'Bohn's Extra Volume' for that year was a revised translation of the *Decameron* by W. K. Kelly, who in his preface refers to the 1741 version on which his own translation is based, but claims that: 'Every page, almost every line, has undergone considerable modifications: large omissions have been supplied . . .' But although the quality of the translation is markedly better than that of the 1741 version, two large omissions which Kelly failed to supply were the *Proemio* and the *Conclusione dell'autore*, neither of which, for reasons that are hard to determine, had so far appeared in any English version. Nor did they appear in the version published in 1872, despite its claim to be a 'Complete translation, restoring those passages omitted in former editions'. This 1872 version is in fact the 1741 version all over again, except that, as in 1822 and in Kelly's translation of 1855, some attempt is made to restore the two missing *novelle*. But the seriousness of this attempt may be gauged by the editor's prefatory note, in which, combining a wanton disregard for accuracy with a dash of unintended humour, he writes that: 'The first English Translation of Boccaccio appeared in 1620–25, in folio. But that and all succeeding translations are imperfect, wanting Novel X of the THIRD Day, and Novel X of the NINTH Day. The present edition will be found to be COMPLETE, although a few passages are in French or Italian.'

In 1886, more than 500 years after Boccaccio's death, the English reader was finally enabled to read the whole of the *Decameron* in the splendidly scrupulous but curiously archaic translation of John Payne. It is true that Payne's translation, replete with copious and for the most part illuminating footnotes, was printed for the Villon Society by private subscription and for private circulation only, but his work

marks a major breakthrough in a centuries-old tradition of English
reticence *vis-à-vis* Boccaccio's great masterpiece. The two missing
stories are accurately translated into English for the first time, many of
Boccaccio's *double-entendres* are tastefully and wittily explained to the
reader in the footnotes, whilst both the *Proemio* and the *Conclusione
dell'autore* at last make their appearance in English dress. Except for
John Payne's addiction to a sonorous and self-conscious Pre-
Raphaelite vocabulary, his version of the *Decameron* could well have
acquired definitive status and spared the labours of some of his
successors in the field.

In 1895, the 1741 version appeared yet again in an elegant four-
volume edition introduced by Alfred Wallis and preceded by a
publishers' note in which it is claimed that 'many passages hitherto
needlessly abridged have been amended, and among other restora-
tions may be mentioned the "Proem", the "Conclusion", and the
reply to his critics and censors with which Boccaccio commences the
Fourth Day. With the exception of part of one novel, given in the
French rendering of Antoine Le Maçon, the whole of the *Decameron*
is here presented in English.' It is clear from this that John Payne's
elegant and faithful rendering of 1886 had entirely escaped the
publishers' notice. But their claim to have filled the gaps in the 1741
version – a service for which they 'acknowledge their obligations'
to a Mr S. W. Orson – is on the whole justified, though with certain
minor reservations.

In 1896, yet another anonymous version of the *Decameron* appeared,
claiming on its title-page to be a 'New Translation from the Italian'
and the 'First Complete English Edition'. As we have seen, the
second of these claims is totally spurious, and although a cursory
reading of the text might suggest that the translation is indeed a new
one, it turns out on closer inspection to be a somewhat unsubtle, not
to say plagiaristic, reworking of previous versions, with the addition
of vulgarly erotic overtones (thus piling Pelion on Ossa) in such
stories as that of the monk and the abbot (I, iv) and that of Messer
Lizio's daughter and her attachment to the song of the nightingale
(V, iv).

In the present century, three further completely new translations of
the *Decameron* have seen publication. By far the most important of

these was the version by J. M. Rigg, first published in 1903, the chief virtues of which are its overall fidelity to the original text and its heightened and elegant style, which is particularly suited to the more formal passages in the *Decameron*, such as the introduction, the framework in general, the occasional philosophical digressions, the long speeches cast in deliberately rhetorical mould, and those stories (to be found more especially in the Fourth and Tenth Days) which to some extent depend for their effect upon the perfection of their form. But Rigg is not nearly so confident in his handling of the straightforward dialogue and colloquial speech to be found in the majority of Boccaccio's stories, and he employs a vocabulary that is old-fashioned or even obsolete in many places, though his language is not nearly so startlingly archaic as John Payne's.

Rigg's translation was reissued at regular intervals and appeared in the Everyman's Library series, with an introduction by Edward Hutton, in 1930. And it was in that year also that the other two twentieth-century translations of the *Decameron* were first published. One of these was the work of the Italo-American novelist and literary biographer, Frances Winwar, to whom belongs the distinction of being (so far as we are able to tell) Boccaccio's first woman translator in the English-speaking world. The other translation published in 1930 was by Richard Aldington.

Frances Winwar's translation was introduced to the reader by one Burton Rascoe, who began his brief prefatory note with the words: 'Giovanni Boccaccio was a bastard born in Paris during the year 1313.' From this we may deduce that Mr Rascoe believed in plain-speaking and was no great shakes as a Boccaccio scholar, but he does refer to Rigg's version of the *Decameron*, saying that while it was admirable in many respects it was 'somewhat stiff, archaic and "literary"'. And he goes on to state that 'in making the present translation for this edition Frances Winwar, herself a novelist, has endeavoured to render Boccaccio's fluid Tuscan vernacular into a correspondingly simple and fluid conventional English'. The fact is of course that simplicity is not one of the distinguishing features of Boccaccio's fluid Tuscan vernacular, and Miss Winwar's translation, whilst fairly accurate and eminently readable, fails to do justice to those more ornate and rhetorical passages in the work, where a formal and 'literary' style such as that adopted by Rigg is much more appropriate. Miss Winwar's translation is not complete, for the *Proemio* is unaccountably omitted.

Finally we come to the Aldington translation, which has more faults than the servant of Friar Cipolla, and which it would be kindest to pass over in silence, except that for a large number of contemporary English readers it alone has served as their means of judging Boccaccio's worth. Aldington's version of the *Decameron* is littered with schoolboy errors, on the lines of 'I had better arms round your neck than you thought' (II, vi), where Boccaccio had written *'io t'ho avuti miglior bracchi alla coda che tu non credevi'* – a simple case of confusing *braccio* ('arm') with *bracco* ('hound'). Aldington has an uncanny knack of mistaking first-person endings for third-person endings, and seems blissfully unaware of the subtle distinction between subjunctives and indicatives, so that, for instance, *'quasi tutti dovessero dal toccamento di questo corpo divenir sani'* (II, i) becomes 'almost all of whom became well when they touched Arrigo's body'. But not only does Aldington frequently distort and sometimes wholly reverse Boccaccio's meaning, he also transmutes Boccaccio's rhythmical, majestic prose into a language that is jolting and totally commonplace. Where the texture of Boccaccio's prose is rich and complex, that of Aldington's version is plain and threadbare, so that anyone reading it might be forgiven for thinking that Boccaccio was a kind of sub-standard fourteenth-century Somerset Maugham.

Our catalogue is now complete, and we may summarize the position by saying that the English translations of the *Decameron* are nine in number, of which four (those of 1620, 1702, 1741, and 1896) were published anonymously. The remaining five are those of Kelly (1855), Payne (1886), Rigg (1903), Winwar (1930), and Aldington (1930). In what follows, I shall use the date of publication in referring to the anonymous versions, and the translator's name in referring to the others. I shall also use the date of publication when referring to any of the three translations (those of 1804, 1822, and 1895) which are simple revisions of the 1741 version.

Let us now return to the strange adventures of Alibech (III, x). In 1620, she disappears without trace, her story having been replaced by a prolix, tedious, and edifying account of the wooing of a Danish princess, at the conclusion of which the translation reads: 'This Novell of Dioneus, was commended by all the company, and so much the rather, because it was free from all folly and obscoeneness.' The tale of the fair Serictha was taken, not from Boccaccio, but from Belleforest's *Histoires tragiques*, and, needless to say, it is quite out of keeping with the habitual dionysiac flights of Dioneo's fancy. Even Salviati, in his post-Tridentine edition of Boccaccio's hundred tales, had not felt it necessary to expunge the doings of Alibech completely, though it is true that his asterisks lie thick upon the pages of this particular story.

There is still no sign of Alibech in 1702, for in dispensing entirely with the *cornice*, the translator killed two birds with one stone, and substituted for the tale of Alibech the story of Filippo Balducci with which Boccaccio replied to his critics in the introduction to the Fourth Day. Nor does she appear in 1741, for hers was one of the two stories which the translator judged incapable of tolerably decent rendition. It was not until 1822, in fact, that an English publisher was prepared to acknowledge Alibech's existence, but no sooner does Alibech ask the hermit to explain how the devil's reincarceration is to be managed, than the text reverts to the original Italian, which remains the language of the translation until the outbreak of the fire at Capsa. There is a wry footnote, however, which states that 'the translators regret that the disuse into which magic has fallen, makes it impossible to render the technicals of that mysterious art into tolerable English: they have therefore found it necessary to insert several passages in the original Italian. To those who are acquainted with the French language the version of a few passages by Mirabeau, will be sufficient to throw some light on these difficulties'. The footnote then continues with the French version to which the translators refer.

The notion that pornography is permissible, provided it appears in a language that only a minority of your readers can understand, was one that found favour with other translators, including Kelly, who proceeds in English as far as the genuflection of the two protagonists before he too runs for cover in the Italian text, giving a French translation at the foot of the page. The British Museum's copy of

Kelly's translation has had a page torn out at this point, and a similar fate has befallen the Museum's copy of the 1872 edition. But other libraries have been less vulnerable to this form of unofficial censorship. The copy of Kelly's translation in the library of Trinity College, Dublin, shows that he too reverts to English at the point in the narrative where Rustico is rescued from his unenviable dilemma, whilst the Bodleian Library's copy of the 1872 edition, a version that claims to restore all passages previously omitted, shows that the editor reprints verbatim the 1822 account of the Alibech saga, including its footnote lamenting the disuse of magic.

It was John Payne who, in 1886, true to his scholarly regard for the principles of accuracy and completeness, first divulged to English readers (or at any rate to those who could afford to subscribe to the publications of the Villon Society) the precise nature of the pious mission to which Alibech and Rustico devoted their youthful energies. The whole story is faithfully rendered in Payne's quaint, archaic prose, of which the following brief specimen will possibly suffice by way of illustration: 'Certes, father mine, this same devil must be an ill thing and an enemy in very deed of God, for that it irketh hell itself, let be otherwhat, when he is put back therein.'

Despite John Payne's courageous example, a further half century was to elapse before the pillars of Hercules were again transgressed, and the doings of Alibech and Rustico were revealed to the English reader at large. In 1895, as the publishers had forewarned in their prefatory note, Mr Orson's new translation of Alibech's desert pilgrimage gives way in mid-story to Le Maçon's sixteenth-century French version, and only resurfaces when the fire breaks out at Capsa. In 1896, in spite of the obvious relish with which the translator approaches the erotic sequences in several of the other *novelle*, the central passage of Alibech's story is given in French, without either footnote or explanation. Even Rigg, whose translation is in other respects no less scrupulous than Payne's, leaves the whole of the passage, from the genuflection of the two main characters to the outbreak of the fire at Capsa, in the original Italian, to the beginning of which is appended a footnote reading: 'No apology is needed for leaving, in accordance with precedent, the subsequent detail untranslated.'

Both of the new translations published in 1930 (Winwar's in

America, and Aldington's in England) provide reasonably faithful English renderings of the whole of the tale of Alibech and Rustico, though it has to be borne in mind that Miss Winwar's version was not immediately available to the general public, as it first appeared in two immensely elegant and expensively produced quarto volumes, under the auspices of the Limited Editions Club of New York, and a further eight years elapsed before it was issued in a format destined for general circulation, whilst Aldington's translation also appeared first in an expensive and lavishly illustrated edition.

Thus it has taken the best part of six hundred years for one of Boccaccio's most celebrated stories to become generally available in the English language. To anyone who is familiar with the *Decameron* as a whole, it may seem rather strange that so comparatively innocent a story should have been so persistently singled out for special treatment, but there are reasons for this, as I think we shall see. There are many stories in the *Decameron* which are no less erotic than that of Alibech – the tales, for example, of Caterina and the nightingale (V, iv), or of Peronella and the tub (VII, ii) – and there are certainly stories which are much more gross or indecent than anything we encounter in the tenth of the Third Day. Here one thinks in particular of the Rabelaisian humour, *ante litteram*, of the trick played on Master Simone by Bruno and Buffalmacco (VIII, ix), and of the abortive attempt by the priest, Father Gianni, to turn his comrade's wife into a mare (IX, x).

This last story is of course the second of the two *novelle* which the 1741 translator judged incapable of preservation. But Father Gianni had already turned up in the two earlier versions, though admittedly in a modified form. And thereby hangs a tale . . .

The 1620 English translation of the *Decameron* is based almost exclusively upon a combination of Le Maçon's French translation, first published in 1545, and the famous edition of Salviati, first published in 1582, in which an ingenious attempt is made to mould Boccaccio's work into a shape acceptable to the ethic of the Counter-Reformation. In pursuing this object, Salviati makes regular use of three devices in particular. In the first place, he will omit words or phrases or whole sentences and replace them with an asterisk. Secondly he will make alterations or additions to the text, at the same time indicating that a change has been made by using an alternative type style. Thirdly he adds marginal glosses to the text whenever he considers them necessary. As a result of Salviati's revision, everything in Boccaccio's text that might have been construed as blasphemous, profane, critical of the Church and its institutions, or offensive to Christian morality, was meticulously removed. The story of the monk and the abbot (I, iv) becomes the story of a young man and his superior, and is enacted, not in a monastery, but in a heathen temple dedicated to false religion. 'The wicked hypocrisy of the religious' (I, vi) becomes 'The wicked avarice of judges'. An abbot (II, iii) is turned into a knight. The story of the Pisan judge (II, x) is set 'some hundred years before Tuscany and Liguria adopted the Christian faith' (*'forse cento anni, avanti che la Toscana, e la Liguria venissero alla cristiana fede'*), and it is not his wife who is stolen by the Monegasque pirate, Paganino, but his mistress, who is described near the beginning of the story as 'a widow . . . who with only one other man had strayed from the path of virtue' (*'una vedova . . . che solamente con un altro huomo haveva commesso fallo'*). The convent, in the tale of Masetto da Lamporecchio (III, i), is transformed into a harem. The ending of the story of Ricciardo and Catella (III, vi) is altered in such a way that, shortly after their encounter in the bagnio, Catella dies of grief, and Ricciardo of remorse. Friar Alberto (IV, ii) becomes plain Alberto, and visits the vain and foolish Venetian lady in the form not of the Angel Gabriel but of Cupid. Friar Cipolla on the other hand (VI, x) retains his title, but is presented as an impostor, and his feather is not the Angel Gabriel's but a feather from the phoenix in Noah's Ark, whilst the coals over which St Lawrence was roasted become the coals on which this mythical phoenix was burned. The tale of the nun and the abbess (IX, ii), like the tale of Masetto, is set in an oriental harem. But the contortions which Salviati performs in the ninth story of the Ninth Day are truly remarkable. This is the tale of the two young men, Joseph of Antioch and Melissus of Lajazzo, who went to Jerusalem to seek advice from King Solomon. Since Solomon was a respected biblical figure, Salviati felt constrained to describe Boccaccio's king as 'Solomon, King of Britain' (*'Salamone Re di Brettagna'*), and to alter the young men's route accordingly, making them call at Naples and ride through France.

The changes I have listed form no more than a small sample of Salviati's massive expurgation of Boccaccio's text. The relevance of Salviati's version of the *Decameron* to our present discussion is that a large number of his revisions were accepted by the anonymous author of the 1620 English version. Since the latter was a Protestant, however, he was far less concerned than Salviati to conceal Boccaccio's frequent attacks upon the Roman church and clergy, but in the story of Father Gianni, he follows Salviati fairly closely. Gianni is no longer a priest, but simply 'an honest man . . . of poor condition'. Salviati, incidentally, inserts a pious marginal gloss to this story, stating that the author as usual is deriding the use of magic, and mocking those who believe in such things. The spell of Gianni Lotteringhi's wife in the story of the werewolf (VII, i) prompts Salviati to make a similar marginal comment. How then does Salviati explain the highly efficacious magic in the story of Messer Torello (X, ix), who is transported by Saladin's wizard in the space of a single night from Egypt to Pavia? Simply by reminding the reader that in a work of fiction anything is possible, and that in any case, Saladin was a pagan: '*Non si lasci il lettore indurre a credere, che queste cose sien vere, ma ricordisi, che sono novelle, e di quelle ciance, delle quali son pieni tutti i libri de' romanzi: e non si scordi, che 'l Saladino era pagano.*'* The only conclusion to be drawn from this disingenuous marginal comment, when set beside Salviati's other glosses, is that pagan magic, unlike Christian magic, may sometimes achieve its purpose.

But to return to Father Gianni. In 1620, we find that the secularized Gianni is transforming his companion's wife, not into a mare, but into a mule, and the spell is broken before the tail is applied. Nor does he fare any better in 1702, but at least he recovers his ecclesiastical status. This is in turn denied him in an English version of the tale that appeared a few years later in Alexander Smith's *History of the most Noted Highway-Men, Foot-Pads, House-Breakers, Shop-Lifts and Cheats*, where he turns up in the guise of the highwayman,

---

*'The reader should not allow himself to be persuaded into thinking that these things are real, but should remember that they are stories, and the sort of nonsense with which all tales of chivalry are filled to overflowing: nor should he forget that Saladin was a pagan.'

Thomas Rumbold, who for the sum of fifty guineas agrees to trans-form the shrewish wife of an innkeeper into a mare. In 1741, as already noted, Father Gianni disappears altogether, but he turns up again in 1822, where two key sentences which Salviati had replaced by asterisks are given in the original Italian. The bewildered English reader is not left entirely in the dark, however, as there is a footnote containing the relevant section from La Fontaine's French reworking of Boccaccio's story. Kelly, in his 1855 version, omits the two key sentences altogether, along with other important details of the incantatory process, so that it is difficult for the reader to tell what is happening. The 1872 translator follows the same procedure as in 1822 so far as the two key sentences are concerned, and he also attempts to supply what Kelly has omitted elsewhere. But his know-ledge of Italian was clearly inadequate to the task, for his version asserts that 'next, he felt her stomach, and finding it firm and round, he made her rise up and stand erect, saying, "this will make a good mare's chest"'.

As in the case of Alibech, so in the case of Father Gianni, it was John Payne who first supplied the monoglot Englishman with an accurate account of the proceedings, and his example was to be followed by all three of Boccaccio's twentieth-century translators. Meanwhile the 1895 version contained a new translation of Father Gianni's story, presumably the work of Mr Orson, but the central episode is modified, and loses its concreteness and energy. Orson omits certain details whilst adding certain others, and the use which he makes of innuendo in place of Boccaccio's direct and forthright descriptive statement deprives the story of whatever merit it pos-sessed. (It can only be defended, presumably, as a particularly fine specimen of literary obscenity.) The 1896 translator also produces a new version, but connoisseurs of Boccaccio's vivid horticultural imagery will be interested to note that the expression *l'umido radicale* is here translated as 'the humid radical'.

Why is it that Boccaccio's English translators have clearly been less inhibited by the story of Father Gianni than by that of Alibech and Rustico? Without excluding other explanations, I want to suggest that there are two reasons for this. In the first place, the story of Alibech depends for its humorous effect upon its gentle derision of certain fundamental Christian beliefs. It is, in a word, profane, whereas the story of Father Gianni is merely obscene, and its connection with Mother Church can be broken by the simple expedient of secularizing the chief character. In the second place, the story of Alibech has no known literary antecedents, whereas stories involving the transformation of human beings into animals were fairly commonplace in medieval literature, as they were in classical literature. The example of Apuleius, a writer whom Boccaccio greatly admired, springs readily to mind, and there are at least five other accounts in medieval literature of the metamorphosis of a girl into a mare. So that whereas the story of Father Gianni forms part of a well documented and widely accepted literary tradition, the story of Alibech appears to have been a product of Boccaccio's own making.

When Salviati addressed himself to the task of revising the *Decameron*, he was chiefly concerned, as the editors of the 1573 expurgated Giunti edition had already been concerned before him, with three possible areas of embarrassment: namely, the impropriety of many of the tales, the criticism (whether open or implied) of the Church and its institutions, and the blasphemous or profane elements that are scattered liberally throughout Boccaccio's text. Salviati and other Italian expurgators devoted far more attention to the last two of these areas than they did to the first, so that whereas a mild oath or an innocuous reference to a priest will invariably be suppressed or replaced, a licentious or erotic episode will often be allowed to remain in its entirety, especially if it has classical antecedents. The ending of the story of Peronella (VII, ii), which Salviati leaves severely alone, is a case in point.

The attitude of Boccaccio's English translators – at any rate until towards the end of the nineteenth century – is very different, as I think we have already seen. But there is one area, that of blasphemy or profanity, in which the English translators and the Italian expurgators meet on common ground. This can be illustrated by the treatment accorded, in Counter-Reformation Italy and Protestant England alike, to the sixth story of the Sixth Day, where it is ingeniously proved that the Baronci are the oldest family in Florence. The Baronci were notoriously ill-favoured, and in Boccaccio's story a young man called Michele Scalza proves their antiquity by claiming that they were formed when God was still learning the rudiments of His craft. This would not do at all for Salviati, whose emendation of the text at this point is reflected in numerous English versions. The 1620 translator was so shocked by the story that he replaced it with another, bearing the title: 'A Yong and ingenious Scholler, being unkindly reviled and smitten by his ignorant Father, and through the procurement of an unlearned Vicare; afterward attained to be doubly revenged on him.' In 1702, Scalza is reported as saying: 'I have nothing then to prove but the Antiquity of the Baronchi's. This will be evident by that Prometheus made them in time when he first began to learn to Paint, and made others after he was Master of his Art.' In 1741, we find Scalza saying: 'You must understand therefore that they were formed when nature was in its infancy, and before she was perfect at her work,' and this became the standard way of translating the passage until John Payne set matters right in 1886. Payne anglicizes the Baronci, calling them 'the Cadgers', and in a footnote he claims that Baronci is 'the Florentine name for what we should call professional beggars'. Later in the same footnote, Payne points out (one presumes with tongue firmly in cheek) that 'this story has been a prodigious stumbling-block to former translators, not one of whom appears to have had the slightest idea of Boccaccio's meaning'. The original blasphemy is also restored in 1895, but not in 1896, where Scalza says: 'Nature, then, you will allow, was in its first and earliest state when they were created'. Finally, all three of Boccaccio's twentieth-century translators revert to Scalza's original statement.

Among other peculiarities (far too numerous to record in their entirety) of English translations of the *Decameron*, we may cite the treatment accorded to the story of Pietro di Vinciolo (V, x), and to that of Friar Cipolla (VI, x). The first of these concerns a sodomitical husband and his discovery of his attractive wife's no less attractive young lover beneath a chicken-coop. Boccaccio derived the story from Apuleius and so arranged the plot that the goals of all three characters were ultimately fulfilled. But in the 1620 English version there is no reference whatever to the husband's unnatural proclivities, and by comparison with the original, the translation falls more than a little flat. Some idea of this may be obtained from the concluding lines, which read as follows: 'After supper, the youth was sent away in friendly manner, and Pedro was alwayes afterward more loving to his Wife, then formerly hee had beene, and no complaint passed on either side, but mutuall joy and Household contentment, such as ought to bee betweene Man and Wife.' Nor is this all, for the 1620 translator follows the example of Le Maçon in prefixing a moral to all of the stories. The tale of Andreuccio, for example, (II, v), is interpreted by the 1620 translator as 'Comprehending, how needful a thing it is, for a man that travelleth in affaires of the world, to be provident and well advised, and carefully to keepe himself from the crafty and deceitfull allurements of Strumpets'. But the moral he attaches to the story of Pietro di Vinciolo is even more astonishing, for Boccaccio is now alleged to be 'Reprehending the cunning of immodest women, who by abusing themselves, do throw evill aspersions on all their Sexe'.

In 1702, the ending of Pietro's story moves a little closer to the original, for the translation reads: 'I cannot pretend to tell you what the Husband and Wife did afterwards, but it was said the next day in Perugia, that the Husband spent the Night as agreeably as his Wife'. In 1741, however, all reference to Pietro's liking for the company of his fellows is once again removed, and after a muted description of the quarrel between husband and wife, and of the convivial supper *à trois*, the story ends with the words 'This however I remember, that the next morning, in the publick market place, the young man could not positively say whether the wife or the husband had the better of the argument'.

But as Dante reminds us, in a reference to the souls of the sodomitical in the fifteenth canto of *Inferno*:

> *Saper d'alcuno è buono;*
> *degli altri fia laudabile tacerci,*
> *ché il tempo saria corto a tanto suono.*★

Let us turn instead to the story of Friar Cipolla, which presents more problems to the translator than any other tale in the whole of the *Decameron*, and of which no satisfactory English version has ever

★ "'Some," he replies, "it will be well to name;
   The rest we must pass over, for sheer dearth
   Of time – 'twould take too long to mention them."'
(*The Divine Comedy* – 1: *Hell*, trans. Dorothy Sayers, Penguin, 1949, p. 165.)

been published. As we have already seen, his feather and coals, largely at the instance of Salviati, were subjected to a curious transmogrification in the 1620 version, but in all the later English translations they recover their original identity. It is in Cipolla's sermon, however, and especially his account of his wanderings, that formidable problems confront Boccaccio's translators. How is one to deal with the lengthy catalogue of seemingly far-flung places, all of which, as Boccaccio's Italian editors (including Branca) never tire of assuring us, correspond to localities in and around the city of Florence? John Payne, normally so assiduous and resourceful in finding English equivalents for Boccaccio's proper nouns, ducked the problem entirely by failing to translate the names of the places that Cipolla claimed to have visited, and appending a series of footnotes, one of which boldly asserts that 'One of the commentators, with characteristic carelessness, states that the places mentioned in the preachment of Fra Cipolla (an amusing specimen of the patter-sermon of the mendicant friar of the middle ages, that ecclesiastical Cheap Jack of his day) are all names of streets or places in Florence, a statement which, it is evident to the most cursory reader, is altogether inaccurate.' Rigg's translation also resorts to footnotes, but unlike Payne, Rigg accepts the view that the place-names are all connected with Florence.

Difficult as it is to find English equivalents for Cipolla's nonsensical place-names, his account of his dealings with the Patriarch of Jerusalem, and the list of sacred relics which he claims to have acquired from that venerable dignitary of the Church, pose even more serious problems. The relic described by Cipolla as '*una delle coste del Verbum-caro-fatti-alle-finestre*' assumes far more curious forms in the English translations than even Boccaccio himself can ever have contemplated in his wildest fantasies. The gross error committed by the 1620 translator ('one of the ribbes of the Verbum Caro, fastened to one of the Windowes') was repeated with monotonous regularity by later translators and editors. The rib was still fastened to one of the windows in 1741, 1804, 1822, and Kelly's version of 1855. John Payne came a little nearer the mark with an absolutely literal translation ('one of the ribs of the Verbum Caro Get-thee-to-the-windows') accompanied by the inevitable footnote. The rib was then re-fastened to one of the windows in 1895, and again in 1896, but it was rescued once more in 1903 by Rigg, who, like John Payne, adopted a literal translation ('hie thee to the casement') and explained the deplorably weak pun in a footnote. Frances Winwar also translates fairly literally ('a rib of the Verbum-Caro Look-out-of-the-Window'), but Aldington, whether through ignorance, perverseness, or subtle design, calls it 'a rib of the Verbum Caro made at the factory'.

No work by any Italian writer has been translated so often, either wholly or in part, as the *Decameron*. Quite apart from the nine separate English versions that have been published, there are so many English translations or adaptations of individual stories, or groups of stories, that their total number defies computation. And no other Italian writer has supplied English literature with so rich a store of narrative material.

The reasons for Boccaccio's perennial appeal to the English translator or reader are not far to seek, although it is clear that the aura of equivocation surrounding the name of Boccaccio was not invariably the most important factor by any means. His earliest translators, in fact, directed their attention to those tales which remained strictly within the bounds of propriety and afforded the maximum amount of moral uplift to their hearers. The sixteen tales from the *Decameron* that appear in Painter's *The Palace of Pleasure*, first published in 1566, are carefully selected, and judiciously doctored, to present Boccaccio as a rigid moralist, and it was not until the nineteenth century was drawing to a close that the English reader was first made acquainted with the full range of Boccaccio's narrative versatility. Before the appearance of John Payne's magniloquent English version in 1886, Boccaccio's taste for the erotic and the profane had been consistently glossed over or toned down in varying degrees by his English translators, so that it would be quite wrong to attribute his enduring popularity to this particular aspect of his work. Boccaccio's gifts as a storyteller, his phenomenal and absolute mastery in a genre of which there are few if any outstanding examples in English literature, (a genre which nourishes and sustains other forms of literature such as the drama and narrative poetry), provide a more plausible explanation of his extraordinary *fortuna* in the Anglo-Saxon world.

All the same, when one considers the problems which the *Decameron* poses for the would-be translator, it is perhaps surprising that the task has been attempted so often. On the one hand, there are those long, elaborate, beautifully balanced sentences, with their trailing clusters of dependent clauses, frequently so arranged as to reproduce the characteristic hendecasyllabic rhythms of Italian poetry, and employing all the stylistic devices of medieval rhetoric. On the other hand, one has a whole series of vivid and racy colloquialisms, to be found more especially in the tales that are set in the more humble social milieux of medieval Italy. The variations and complexities of Boccaccio's style and language are limitless, and no translator can ever hope to do them full justice. But because, like Everest, the *Decameron* is there, and because it is inconceivable that a truly satisfactory English translation of this great European masterpiece will ever be produced, there will always be someone who is foolhardy enough to attempt the task, even if he is familiar with Dante's sombre warning from the first book of the *Convivio*:

*Nulla cosa per legame musaico armonizzata si può dalla sua loquela in altra trasmutare senza rompere tutta la sua dolcezza e armonia.**

Canterbury, April 1971.   G. H. MCWILLIAM

* 'Nothing that is harmonized by the bond of the Muse can be transformed from its own language into another without upsetting all its sweetness and harmony.'

Here begins the book called Decameron, *otherwise known as Prince Galahalt, wherein are contained a hundred stories, told in ten days by seven ladies and three young men.*

PREFACE

To take pity on people in distress is a human quality which every man and woman should possess, but it is especially requisite in those who have once needed comfort, and found it in others. I number myself as one of these, because if ever anyone required or appreciated comfort, or indeed derived pleasure therefrom, I was that person. For from my earliest youth until the present day, I have been inflamed beyond measure with a most lofty and noble love, far loftier and nobler than might perhaps be thought proper, were I to describe it, in a person of my humble condition. And although people of good judgement, to whose notice it had come, praised me for it and rated me much higher in their esteem, nevertheless it was exceedingly difficult for me to endure. The reason, I hasten to add, was not the cruelty of my lady-love, but the immoderate passion engendered within my mind by a craving that was ill-restrained. This, since it would allow me no proper respite, often caused me an inordinate amount of distress. But in my anguish I have on occasion derived much relief from the agreeable conversation and the admirable expressions of sympathy offered by friends, without which I am firmly convinced that I should have perished. However, the One who is infinite decreed by immutable law that all earthly things should come to an end. And it pleased Him that this love of mine, whose warmth exceeded all others, and which had stood firm and unyielding against all the pressures of good intention, helpful advice, and the risk of danger and open scandal, should in the course of time diminish of its own accord. So that now, all that is left of it in my mind is the delectable feeling which Love habitually reserves for those who refrain from venturing too far upon its deepest waters. And thus what was once a source of pain has now become, having shed all discomfort, an abiding sensation of pleasure.

But though the pain has ceased, I still preserve a clear recollection of the kindnesses I received in the past from people who, prompted by feelings of goodwill towards me, showed a concern for my sufferings. This memory will never, I think, fade for as long as I live. And since it is my conviction that gratitude, of all the virtues, is most highly to be commended and its opposite condemned, I have resolved, in order not to appear ungrateful, to employ what modest talents I possess in making restitution for what I have received. Thus, now that I can claim to have achieved my freedom, I intend to offer some solace, if not to those who assisted me (since their good sense or good fortune will perhaps render such a gift superfluous), at least to those who stand in need of it. And even though my support, or if you prefer, my encouragement, may seem very slight (as indeed it is) to the people concerned, I feel nonetheless that it should for preference be directed where it seems to be most needed, because that is the quarter in which it will be more effective and, at the same time, more readily appreciated.

And who will deny that such encouragement, however small, should much rather be offered to the charming ladies than to the men? For the ladies, out of fear or shame, conceal the flames of passion within their fragile breasts, and a hidden love is far more potent than one which is worn on the sleeve, as everyone knows who has had experience of these matters. Moreover they are forced to follow the whims, fancies and dictates of their fathers, mothers, brothers and husbands, so that they spend most of their time cooped up within the narrow confines of their rooms, where they sit in apparent idleness, wishing one thing and at the same time wishing its opposite, and reflecting on various matters, which cannot possibly always be pleasant to contemplate. And if, in the course of their meditations, their minds should be invaded by melancholy arising out of the flames of longing, it will inevitably take root there and make them suffer greatly, unless it be dislodged by new interests. Besides which, their powers of endurance are considerably weaker than those that men possess.

When men are in love, they are not affected in this way, as we can see quite plainly. They, whenever they are weighed down by melancholy or ponderous thoughts, have many ways of relieving or expelling them. For if they wish, they can always walk abroad, see and hear many things, go fowling, hunting, fishing, riding and gambling, or attend to their business affairs. Each of these pursuits has the power of engaging men's minds, either wholly or in part, and diverting them from their gloomy meditations, at least for a certain period: after which, some form of consolation will ensue, or the affliction will grow less intense.

So in order that I may to some extent repair the omissions of Fortune, which (as we may see in the case of the more delicate sex) was always more sparing of support wherever natural strength was more deficient, I intend to provide succour and diversion for the ladies, but only for those who are in love, since the others can make do with their needles, their reels and their spindles. I shall narrate a hundred stories or fables or parables or histories or whatever you choose to call them, recited in ten days by a worthy band of seven ladies and three young men, who assembled together during the plague which recently took such heavy toll of life. And I shall also include some songs, which these seven ladies sang for their mutual amusement.

In these tales will be found a variety of love adventures, bitter as well as pleasing, and other exciting incidents, which took place in both ancient and modern times. In reading them, the aforesaid ladies will be able to derive, not only pleasure from the entertaining matters therein set forth, but also some useful advice. For they will learn to recognize what should be avoided and likewise what should be pursued, and these things can only lead, in my opinion, to the removal of their affliction. If this should happen (and may God grant that it should), let them give thanks to Love, which, in freeing me from its bonds, has granted me the power of making provision for their pleasures.

FIRST DAY

Here begins the First Day of the Decameron, *wherein first of all the author explains the circumstances in which certain persons, who presently make their appearance, were induced to meet for the purpose of conversing together, after which, under the rule of* Pampinea, *each of them speaks on the subject they find most congenial.*

Whenever, fairest ladies, I pause to consider how compassionate you all are by nature, I invariably become aware that the present work will seem to you to possess an irksome and ponderous opening. For it carries at its head the painful memory of the deadly havoc wrought by the recent plague, which brought so much heartache and misery to those who witnessed, or had experience of it. But I do not want you to be deterred, for this reason, from reading any further, on the assumption that you are to be subjected, as you read, to an endless torrent of tears and sobbing. You will be affected no differently by this grim beginning than walkers confronted by a steep and rugged hill, beyond which there lies a beautiful and delectable plain. The degree of pleasure they derive from the latter will correspond directly to the difficulty of the climb and the descent. And just as the end of mirth is heaviness,★ so sorrows are dispersed by the advent of joy.

This brief unpleasantness (I call it brief, inasmuch as it is contained within few words) is quickly followed by the sweetness and the pleasure which I have already promised you, and which, unless you were told in advance, you would not perhaps be expecting to find after such a beginning as this. Believe me, if I could decently have taken you whither I desire by some other route, rather than along a path so difficult as this, I would gladly have done so. But since it is impossible without this memoir to show the origin of the events you

★Proverbs xiv, 13.

will read about later, I really have no alternative but to address myself to its composition.

I say, then, that the sum of thirteen hundred and forty-eight years had elapsed since the fruitful Incarnation of the Son of God, when the noble city of Florence, which for its great beauty excels all others in Italy, was visited by the deadly pestilence. Some say that it descended upon the human race through the influence of the heavenly bodies, others that it was a punishment signifying God's righteous anger at our iniquitous way of life. But whatever its cause, it had originated some years earlier in the East, where it had claimed countless lives before it unhappily spread westward, growing in strength as it swept relentlessly on from one place to the next.

In the face of its onrush, all the wisdom and ingenuity of man were unavailing. Large quantities of refuse were cleared out of the city by officials specially appointed for the purpose, all sick persons were forbidden entry, and numerous instructions were issued for safeguarding the people's health, but all to no avail. Nor were the countless petitions humbly directed to God by the pious, whether by means of formal processions or in any other guise, any less ineffectual. For in the early spring of the year we have mentioned, the plague began, in a terrifying and extraordinary manner, to make its disastrous effects apparent. It did not take the form it had assumed in the East, where if anyone bled from the nose it was an obvious portent of certain death. On the contrary, its earliest symptom, in men and women alike, was the appearance of certain swellings in the groin or the armpit, some of which were egg-shaped whilst others were roughly the size of the common apple. Sometimes the swellings were large, sometimes not so large, and they were referred to by the populace as *gavòccioli*. From the two areas already mentioned, this deadly *gavòcciolo* would begin to spread, and within a short time it would appear at random all over the body. Later on, the symptoms of the disease changed, and many people began to find dark blotches and bruises on their arms, thighs, and other parts of the body, sometimes large and few in number, at other times tiny and closely spaced. These, to anyone unfortunate enough to contract them, were just as infallible a sign that he would die as the *gavòcciolo* had been earlier, and as indeed it still was.

Against these maladies, it seemed that all the advice of physicians and all the power of medicine were profitless and unavailing. Perhaps the nature of the illness was such that it allowed no remedy: or perhaps those people who were treating the illness (whose numbers had increased enormously because the ranks of the qualified were invaded by people, both men and women, who had never received any training in medicine), being ignorant of its causes, were not prescribing the appropriate cure. At all events, few of those who caught it ever recovered, and in most cases death occurred within three days from the appearance of the symptoms we have described, some people dying more rapidly than others, the majority without any fever or other complications.

But what made this pestilence even more severe was that whenever those suffering from it mixed with people who were still unaffected, it would rush upon these with the speed of a fire racing through dry or oily substances that happened to be placed within its reach. Nor was this the full extent of its evil, for not only did it infect healthy persons who conversed or had any dealings with the sick, making them ill or visiting an equally horrible death upon them, but it also seemed to transfer the sickness to anyone touching the clothes or other objects which had been handled or used by its victims.

It is a remarkable story that I have to relate. And were it not for the fact that I am one of many people who saw it with their own eyes, I would scarcely dare to believe it, let alone commit it to paper, even though I had heard it from a person whose word I could trust. The plague I have been describing was of so contagious a nature that very often it visibly did more than simply pass from one person to another. In other words, whenever an animal other than a human being touched anything belonging to a person who had been stricken or exterminated by the disease, it not only caught the sickness, but died from it almost at once. To all of this, as I have just said, my own eyes bore witness on more than one occasion. One day, for instance, the rags of a pauper who had died from the disease were thrown into the street, where they attracted the attention of two pigs. In their wonted fashion, the pigs first of all gave the rags a thorough mauling with their snouts after which they took them between their teeth and shook them against their cheeks. And within a short time they began to writhe as though they had been poisoned, then they both dropped dead to the ground, spreadeagled upon the rags that had brought about their undoing.

These things, and many others of a similar or even worse nature, caused various fears and fantasies to take root in the minds of those who were still alive and well. And almost without exception, they took a single and very inhuman precaution, namely to avoid or run away from the sick and their belongings, by which means they all thought that their own health would be preserved.

Some people were of the opinion that a sober and abstemious mode of living considerably reduced the risk of infection. They therefore formed themselves into groups and lived in isolation from everyone else. Having withdrawn to a comfortable abode where there were no sick persons, they locked themselves in and settled down to a peaceable existence, consuming modest quantities of delicate foods and precious wines and avoiding all excesses. They refrained from speaking to outsiders, refused to receive news of the dead or the sick, and entertained themselves with music and whatever other amusements they were able to devise.

Others took the opposite view, and maintained that an infallible way of warding off this appalling evil was to drink heavily, enjoy life to the full, go round singing and merrymaking, gratify all of one's cravings whenever the opportunity offered, and shrug the whole thing off as one enormous joke. Moreover, they practised what they preached to the best of their ability, for they would visit one tavern after another, drinking all day and night to immoderate excess; or alternatively (and this was their more frequent custom), they would do their drinking in various private houses, but only in the ones where the conversation was restricted to subjects that were pleasant or entertaining. Such places were easy to find, for people behaved as though their days were numbered, and treated their belongings and their own persons with equal abandon. Hence most houses had become common property, and any passing stranger could make himself at home as naturally as though he were the rightful owner. But for all their riotous manner of living, these people always took good care to avoid any contact with the sick.

In the face of so much affliction and misery, all respect for the laws of God and man had virtually broken down and been extinguished in our city. For like everybody else, those ministers and executors of the laws who were not either dead or ill were left with so few subordinates that they were unable to discharge any of their duties. Hence everyone was free to behave as he pleased.

There were many other people who steered a middle course between the two already mentioned, neither restricting their diet to the same degree as the first group, nor indulging so freely as the second in drinking and other forms of wantonness, but simply doing no more than satisfy their appetite. Instead of incarcerating themselves, these people moved about freely, holding in their hands a posy of flowers, or fragrant herbs, or one of a wide range of spices, which they applied at frequent intervals to their nostrils, thinking it an excellent idea to fortify the brain with smells of that particular sort; for the stench of dead bodies, sickness, and medicines seemed to fill and pollute the whole of the atmosphere.

Some people, pursuing what was possibly the safer alternative, callously maintained that there was no better or more efficacious remedy against a plague than to run away from it. Swayed by this argument, and sparing no thought for anyone but themselves, large numbers of men and women abandoned their city, their homes, their relatives, their estates and their belongings, and headed for the countryside, either in Florentine territory or, better still, abroad. It was as though they imagined that the wrath of God would not unleash this plague against men for their iniquities irrespective of where they happened to be, but would only be aroused against those who found themselves within the city walls; or possibly they assumed that the whole of the population would be exterminated and that the city's last hour had come.

Of the people who held these various opinions, not all of them died. Nor, however, did they all survive. On the contrary, many of each different persuasion fell ill here, there, and everywhere, and having themselves, when they were fit and well, set an example to those who were as yet unaffected, they languished away with virtually no one to nurse them. It was not merely a question of one citizen avoiding another, and of people almost invariably neglecting their neighbours and rarely or never visiting their relatives, addressing them only from a distance; this scourge had implanted so great a terror in the hearts of men and women that brothers abandoned brothers, uncles their nephews, sisters their brothers, and in many cases wives deserted their husbands. But even worse, and almost incredible, was the fact that fathers and mothers refused to nurse and assist their own children, as though they did not belong to them.

Hence the countless numbers of people who fell ill, both male and female, were entirely dependent upon either the charity of friends (who were few and far between) or the greed of servants, who remained in short supply despite the attraction of high wages out of all proportion to the services they performed. Furthermore, these latter were men and women of coarse intellect and the majority were unused to such duties, and they did little more than hand things to the invalid when asked to do so and watch over him when he was dying. And in performing this kind of service, they frequently lost their lives as well as their earnings.

As a result of this wholesale desertion of the sick by neighbours, relatives and friends, and in view of the scarcity of servants, there grew up a practice almost never previously heard of, whereby when a woman fell ill, no matter how gracious or beautiful or gently bred she might be, she raised no objection to being attended by a male servant, whether he was young or not. Nor did she have any scruples about showing him every part of her body as freely as she would have displayed it to a woman, provided that the nature of her infirmity required her to do so; and this explains why those women who recovered were possibly less chaste in the period that followed.

Moreover a great many people died who would perhaps have survived had they received some assistance. And hence, what with the lack of appropriate means for tending the sick, and the virulence of the plague, the number of deaths reported in the city whether by day or night was so enormous that it astonished all who heard tell of it, to say nothing of the people who actually witnessed the carnage. And it was perhaps inevitable that among the citizens who survived there arose certain customs that were quite contrary to established tradition.

It had once been customary, as it is again nowadays, for the women relatives and neighbours of a dead man to assemble in his house in order to mourn in the company of the women who had been closest to him; moreover his kinsfolk would forgather in front of his house along with his neighbours and various other citizens, and there would be a contingent of priests, whose numbers varied according to the quality of the deceased; his body would be taken thence to the church in which he had wanted to be buried, being borne on the shoulders of his peers amidst the funeral pomp of candles and dirges. But as the ferocity of the plague began to mount, this practice all but disappeared entirely and was replaced by different customs. For not only did people die without having many women about them, but a great number departed this life without anyone at all to witness their going. Few indeed were those to whom the lamentations and bitter tears of their relatives were accorded; on the contrary, more often than not bereavement was the signal for laughter and witticisms and general jollification – the art of which the women, having for the most part suppressed their feminine concern for the salvation of the souls of the dead, had learned to perfection. Moreover it was rare for the bodies of the dead to be accompanied by more than ten or twelve neighbours to the church, nor were they borne on the shoulders of worthy and honest citizens, but by a kind of gravedigging fraternity, newly come into being and drawn from the lower orders of society. These people assumed the title of sexton, and demanded a fat fee for their services, which consisted in taking up the coffin and hauling it swiftly away, not to the church specified by the dead man in his will, but usually to the nearest at hand. They would be preceded by a group of four or six clerics, who between them carried one or two candles at most, and sometimes none at all. Nor did the priests go to the trouble of pronouncing solemn and lengthy funeral rites, but, with the aid of these so-called sextons, they hastily lowered the body into the nearest empty grave they could find.

As for the common people and a large proportion of the bourgeoisie, they presented a much more pathetic spectacle, for the majority of them were constrained, either by their poverty or the hope of survival, to remain in their houses. Being confined to their own parts of the city, they fell ill daily in their thousands, and since they had no one to assist them or attend to their needs, they inevitably perished almost without exception. Many dropped dead in the open streets, both by day and by night, whilst a great many others, though dying in their own houses, drew their neighbours' attention to the fact more by the smell of their rotting corpses than by any other means. And what with these, and the others who were dying all over the city, bodies were here, there and everywhere.

Whenever people died, their neighbours nearly always followed a single, set routine, prompted as much by their fear of being contaminated by the decaying corpse as by any charitable feelings they may have entertained towards the deceased. Either on their own, or with the assistance of bearers whenever these were to be had, they extracted the bodies of the dead from their houses and left them lying outside their front doors, where anyone going about the streets, especially in the early morning, could have observed countless numbers of them. Funeral biers would then be sent for, upon which the dead were taken away, though there were some who, for lack of biers, were carried off on plain boards. It was by no means rare for more than one of these biers to be seen with two or three bodies upon it at a time; on the contrary, many were seen to contain a husband and wife, two or three brothers and sisters, a father and son, or some other pair of close relatives. And times without number it happened that two priests would be on their way to bury someone, holding a cross before them, only to find that bearers carrying three or four additional biers would fall in behind them; so that whereas the priests had thought they had only one burial to attend to, they in fact had six or seven, and sometimes more. Even in these circumstances, however, there were no tears or candles or mourners to honour the dead; in fact, no more respect was accorded to dead people than would nowadays be shown towards dead goats. For it was quite apparent that the one thing which, in normal times, no wise man had ever learned to accept with patient resignation (even though it struck so seldom and unobtrusively), had now been brought home to the feeble-minded as well, but the scale of the calamity caused them to regard it with indifference.

Such was the multitude of corpses (of which further consignments were arriving every day and almost by the hour at each of the churches), that there was not sufficient consecrated ground for them to be buried in, especially if each was to have its own plot in accordance with long-established custom. So when all the graves were full, huge trenches were excavated in the churchyards, into which new arrivals were placed in their hundreds, stowed tier upon tier like ships' cargo, each layer of corpses being covered over with a thin layer of soil till the trench was filled to the top.

But rather than describe in elaborate detail the calamities we experienced in the city at that time, I must mention that, whilst an ill wind was blowing through Florence itself, the surrounding region was no less badly affected. In the fortified towns, conditions were similar to those in the city itself on a minor scale; but in the scattered hamlets and the countryside proper, the poor unfortunate peasants and their families had no physicians or servants whatever to assist them, and collapsed by the wayside, in their fields, and in their cottages at all hours of the day and night, dying more like animals than human beings. Like the townspeople, they too grew apathetic in their ways, disregarded their affairs, and neglected their possessions. Moreover they all behaved as though each day was to be their last, and far from making provision for the future by tilling their lands, tending their flocks, and adding to their previous labours, they tried in every way they could think of to squander the assets already in their possession. Thus it came about that oxen, asses, sheep, goats, pigs, chickens, and even dogs (for all their deep fidelity to man) were driven away and allowed to roam freely through the fields, where the crops lay abandoned and had not even been reaped, let alone gathered in. And after a whole day's feasting, many of these animals, as though possessing the power of reason, would return glutted in the evening to their own quarters, without any shepherd to guide them.

But let us leave the countryside and return to the city. What more remains to be said, except that the cruelty of heaven (and possibly, in some measure, also that of man) was so immense and so devastating that between March and July of the year in question, what with the fury of the pestilence and the fact that so many of the sick were inadequately cared for or abandoned in their hour of need because the healthy were too terrified to approach them, it is reliably thought that over a hundred thousand human lives were extinguished within the walls of the city of Florence? Yet before this lethal catastrophe fell upon the city, it is doubtful whether anyone would have guessed it contained so many inhabitants.

Ah, how great a number of splendid palaces, fine houses, and noble dwellings, once filled with retainers, with lords and with ladies, were bereft of all who had lived there, down to the tiniest child! How numerous were the famous families, the vast estates, the notable fortunes, that were seen to be left without a rightful successor! How many gallant gentlemen, fair ladies, and sprightly youths, who would have been judged hale and hearty by Galen, Hippocrates and Aesculapius (to say nothing of others), having breakfasted in the morning with their kinsfolk, acquaintances and friends, supped that same evening with their ancestors in the next world!

The more I reflect upon all this misery, the deeper my sense of personal sorrow; hence I shall refrain from describing those aspects which can suitably be omitted, and proceed to inform you that these were the conditions prevailing in our city, which was by now almost emptied of its inhabitants, when one Tuesday morning (or so I was told by a person whose word can be trusted) seven young ladies were to be found in the venerable church of Santa Maria Novella, which was otherwise almost deserted. They had been attending divine service, and were dressed in mournful attire appropriate to the times. Each was a friend, a neighbour, or a relative of the other six, none was older than twenty-seven or younger than eighteen, and all were intelligent, gently bred, fair to look upon, graceful in bearing, and charmingly unaffected. I could tell you their actual names, but refrain from doing so for a good reason, namely that I would not want any of them to feel embarrassed, at any time in the future, on account of the ensuing stories, all of which they either listened to or narrated themselves. For nowadays, laws relating to pleasure are somewhat restrictive, whereas at that time, for the reasons indicated above, they were exceptionally lax, not only for ladies of their own age but also for much older women. Besides, I have no wish to supply envious tongues, ever ready to censure a laudable way of life, with a chance to besmirch the good name of these worthy ladies with their lewd and filthy gossip. And therefore, so that we may perceive distinctly what each of them had to say, I propose to refer to them by names which are either wholly or partially appropriate to the qualities of each. The first of them, who was also the eldest, we shall call Pampinea, the second Fiammetta, Filomena the third, and the fourth Emilia; then we shall name the fifth Lauretta, and the sixth Neifile, whilst to the last, not without reason, we shall give the name of Elissa.

Without prior agreement but simply by chance, these seven ladies found themselves sitting, more or less in a circle, in one part of the church, reciting their paternosters. Eventually, they left off and heaved a great many sighs, after which they began to talk among themselves on various different aspects of the times through which they were passing. But after a little while, they all fell silent except for Pampinea, who said:

'Dear ladies, you will often have heard it affirmed, as I have, that no man does injury to another in exercising his lawful rights. Every person born into this world has a natural right to sustain, preserve, and defend his own life to the best of his ability – a right so freely acknowledged that men have sometimes killed others in self-defence, and no blame whatever has attached to their actions. Now, if this is permitted by the laws, upon whose prompt application all mortal creatures depend for their well-being, how can it possibly be wrong, seeing that it harms no one, for us or anyone else to do all in our power to preserve our lives? If I pause to consider what we have been doing this morning, and what we have done on several mornings in the past, if I reflect on the nature and subject of our conversation, I realize, just as you also must realize, that each of us is apprehensive on her own account. This does not surprise me in the least, but what does greatly surprise me (seeing that each of us has the natural feelings of a woman) is that we do nothing to requite ourselves against the thing of which we are all so justly afraid.

'Here we linger for no other purpose, or so it seems to me, than to count the number of corpses being taken to burial, or to hear whether the friars of the church, very few of whom are left, chant their offices at the appropriate hours, or to exhibit the quality and quantity of our sorrows, by means of the clothes we are wearing, to all those whom we meet in this place. And if we go outside, we shall see the dead and the sick being carried hither and thither, or we shall see people, once condemned to exile by the courts for their misdeeds, careering wildly about the streets in open defiance of the law, well knowing that those appointed to enforce it are either dead or dying; or else we shall find ourselves at the mercy of the scum of our city who, having scented our blood, call themselves sextons and go prancing and bustling all over the place, singing bawdy songs that add insult to our injuries. Moreover, all we ever hear is "So-and-so's dead" and "So-and-so's dying"; and if there were anyone left to mourn, the whole place would be filled with sounds of wailing and weeping.

'And if we return to our homes, what happens? I know not whether your own experience is similar to mine, but my house was once full of servants, and now that there is no one left apart from my maid and myself, I am filled with foreboding and feel as if every hair of my head is standing on end. Wherever I go in the house, wherever I pause to rest, I seem to be haunted by the shades of the departed, whose faces no longer appear as I remember them but with strange and horribly twisted expressions that frighten me out of my senses.

'Accordingly, whether I am here in church or out in the streets or sitting at home, I always feel ill at ease, the more so because it seems to me that no one possessing private means and a place to retreat to is left here apart from ourselves. But even if such people are still to be found, they draw no distinction, as I have frequently heard and seen for myself, between what is honest and what is dishonest; and provided only that they are prompted by their appetites, they will do whatever affords them the greatest pleasure, whether by day or by night, alone or in company. It is not only of lay people that I speak, but also of those enclosed in monasteries, who, having convinced themselves that such behaviour is suitable for them and is only unbecoming in others, have broken the rules of obedience and given themselves over to carnal pleasures, thereby thinking to escape, and have turned lascivious and dissolute.

'If this be so (and we plainly perceive that it is), what are we doing here? What are we waiting for? What are we dreaming about? Why do we lag so far behind all the rest of the citizens in providing for our safety? Do we rate ourselves lower than all other women? Or do we suppose that our own lives, unlike those of others, are bound to our bodies by such strong chains that we may ignore all those things which have the power to harm them? In that case we are deluded and mistaken. We have only to recall the names and the condition of the young men and women who have fallen victim to this cruel pestilence, in order to realize clearly the foolishness of such notions.

'And so, lest by pretending to be above such things or by becoming complacent we should succumb to that which we might possibly avoid if we so desired, I would think it an excellent idea (though I do not know whether you would agree with me) for us all to get away from this city, just as many others have done before us, and as indeed they are doing still. We could go and stay together on one of our various country estates, shunning at all costs the lewd practices of our fellow citizens and feasting and merrymaking as best we may without in any way overstepping the bounds of what is reasonable.

'There we shall hear the birds singing, we shall see fresh green hills and plains, fields of corn undulating like the sea, and trees of at least a thousand different species; and we shall have a clearer view of the heavens, which, troubled though they are, do not however deny us their eternal beauties, so much more fair to look upon than the desolate walls of our city. Moreover the country air is much more refreshing, the necessities of life in such a time as this are more abundant, and there are fewer obstacles to contend with. For although the farmworkers are dying there in the same way as the townspeople here in Florence, the spectacle is less harrowing inasmuch as the houses and people are more widely scattered. Besides, unless I am mistaken we shall not be abandoning anyone by going away from here; on the contrary, we may fairly claim that we are the ones who have been abandoned, for our kinsfolk are either dead or fled, and have left us to fend for ourselves in the midst of all this affliction, as though disowning us completely.

'Hence no one can reproach us for taking the course I have advocated, whereas if we do nothing we shall inevitably be confronted with distress and mourning, and possibly forfeit our lives into the bargain. Let us therefore do as I suggest, taking our maidservants with us and seeing to the dispatch of all the things we shall need. We can move from place to place, spending one day here and another there, pursuing whatever pleasures and entertainments the present times will afford. In this way of life we shall continue until such time as we discover (provided we are spared from early death) the end decreed by Heaven for these terrible events. You must remember, after all, that it is no more unseemly for us to go away and thus preserve our own honour than it is for most other women to remain here and forfeit theirs.'

Having listened to Pampinea's suggestion, the other ladies not only applauded it but were so eager to carry it into effect that they had already begun to work out the details amongst themselves, as though they wanted to rise from their pews and set off without further ado. But Filomena, being more prudent than the others, said:

'Pampinea's arguments, ladies, are most convincing, but we should not follow her advice as hastily as you appear to wish. You must remember that we are all women, and every one of us is sufficiently adult to acknowledge that women, when left to themselves, are not the most rational of creatures, and that without the supervision of some man or other their capacity for getting things done is somewhat restricted. We are fickle, quarrelsome, suspicious, cowardly, and easily frightened; and hence I greatly fear that if we have none but ourselves to guide us, our little band will break up much more swiftly, and with far less credit to ourselves, than would otherwise be the case. We would be well advised to resolve this problem before our departure.'

Then Elissa said:

'It is certainly true that man is the head of woman, and that without a man to guide us it rarely happens that any enterprise of ours is brought to a worthy conclusion. But where are we to find these men? As we all know, most of our own menfolk are dead, and those few that are still alive are fleeing in scattered little groups from that which we too are intent upon avoiding. Yet we cannot very well go away with total strangers, for if self-preservation is our aim, we must so arrange our affairs that wherever we go for our pleasure and repose, no trouble or scandal should come of it.'

Whilst the talk of the ladies was proceeding along these lines, there came into the church three young men, in whom neither the horrors of the times nor the loss of friends or relatives nor concern for their own safety had dampened the flames of love, much less extinguished them completely. I have called them young, but none in fact was less than twenty-five years of age, and the first was called Panfilo, the second Filostrato, and the last Dioneo. Each of them was most agreeable and gently bred, and by way of sweetest solace amid all this turmoil they were seeking to catch a glimpse of their lady-loves, all three of whom, as it happened, were among the seven we have mentioned, whilst some of the remaining four were closely related to one or other of the three. No sooner did they espy the young ladies than they too were espied, whereupon Pampinea smiled and said:

'See how Fortune favours us right from the beginning, in setting before us three young men of courage and intelligence, who will readily act as our guides and servants if we are not too proud to accept them for such duties.'

Then Neifile, whose face had turned all scarlet with confusion since she was the object of one of the youth's affections, said:

'For goodness' sake do take care, Pampinea, of what you are saying! To my certain knowledge, nothing but good can be said of any one of them, and I consider them more than competent to fulfil the office of which we were speaking. I also think they would be good, honest company, not only for us, but for ladies much finer and fairer than ourselves. But since it is perfectly obvious that they are in love with certain of the ladies here present, I am apprehensive lest, by taking them with us, through no fault either of theirs or of our own, we should bring disgrace and censure on ourselves.'

'That is quite beside the point,' said Filomena. 'If I live honestly and my conscience is clear, then people may say whatever they like; God and Truth will take up arms in my defence. Now, if only they were prepared to accompany us, we should truly be able to claim, as Pampinea has said, that Fortune favours our enterprise.'

Filomena's words reassured the other ladies, who not only withdrew their objections but unanimously agreed to call the young men over, explain their intentions, and inquire whether they would be willing to join their expedition. And so, without any further discussion, Pampinea, who was a blood relation to one of the young men, got up and walked towards them. They were standing there gazing at the young ladies, and Pampinea, having offered them a cheerful greeting, told them what they were proposing to do, and asked them on behalf of all her companions whether they would be prepared to join them in a spirit of chaste and brotherly affection.

The young men thought at first that she was making mock of them, but when they realized she was speaking in earnest, they gladly agreed to place themselves at the young ladies' disposal. So that there should be no delay in putting the plan into effect, they made provision there and then for the various matters that would have to be attended to before their departure. Meticulous care was taken to see that all necessary preparations were put in hand, supplies were sent on in advance to the place at which they intended to stay, and as dawn was breaking on the morning of the next day, which was a Wednesday, the ladies and the three young men, accompanied by one or two of the maids and all three manservants, set out from the city. And scarcely had they travelled two miles from Florence before they reached the place at which they had agreed to stay.

The spot in question was some distance away from any road, on a small hill that was agreeable to behold for its abundance of shrubs and trees, all bedecked in green leaves. Perched on its summit was a palace, built round a fine, spacious courtyard, and containing loggias, halls, and sleeping apartments, which were not only excellently proportioned but richly embellished with paintings depicting scenes of gaiety. Delectable gardens and meadows lay all around, and there were wells of cool, refreshing water. The cellars were stocked with precious wines, more suited to the palates of connoisseurs than to sedate and respectable ladies. And on their arrival the company discovered, to their no small pleasure, that the place had been cleaned from top to bottom, the beds in the rooms were made up, the whole house was adorned with seasonable flowers of every description, and the floors had been carpeted with rushes.

Soon after reaching the palace, they all sat down, and Dioneo, a youth of matchless charm and readiness of wit, said:

'It is not our foresight, ladies, but rather your own good sense, that has led us to this spot. I know not what you intend to do with your troubles; my own I left inside the city gates when I departed thence a short while ago in your company. Hence you may either prepare to join with me in as much laughter, song and merriment as your sense of decorum will allow, or else you may give me leave to go back for my troubles and live in the afflicted city.'

Pampinea, as though she too had driven away all her troubles, answered him in the same carefree vein.

'There is much sense in what you say, Dioneo,' she replied. 'A merry life should be our aim, since it was for no other reason that we were prompted to run away from the sorrows of the city. However, nothing will last for very long unless it possesses a definite form. And since it was I who led the discussions from which this fair company has come into being, I have given some thought to the continuance of our happiness, and consider it necessary for us to choose a leader, drawn from our own ranks, whom we would honour and obey as our superior, and whose sole concern will be that of devising the means whereby we may pass our time agreeably. But so that none of us will complain that he or she has had no opportunity to experience the burden of responsibility and the pleasure of command associated with sovereign power, I propose that the burden and the honour should be assigned to each of us in turn for a single day. It will be for all of us to decide who is to be our first ruler, after which it will be up to each ruler, when the hour of vespers approaches, to elect his or her successor from among the ladies and gentlemen present. The person chosen to govern will be at liberty to make whatever arrangements he likes for the period covered by his rule, and to prescribe the place and the manner in which we are to live.'

Pampinea's proposal was greatly to everyone's liking, and they unanimously elected her as their queen for the first day, whereupon Filomena quickly ran over to a laurel bush, for she had frequently heard it said that laurel leaves were especially worthy of veneration and that they conferred great honour upon those people of merit who were crowned with them. Having plucked a few of its shoots, she fashioned them into a splendid and venerable garland, which she set upon Pampinea's brow, and which thenceforth became the outward symbol of sovereign power and authority to all the members of the company, for as long as they remained together.

Upon her election as their queen, Pampinea summoned the servants of the three young men to appear before her together with their own maidservants, who were four in number. And having called upon everyone to be silent, she said:

'So that I may begin by setting you all a good example, through which, proceeding from good to better, our company will be enabled to live an ordered and agreeable existence for as long as we choose to remain together, I first of all appoint Dioneo's manservant, Parmeno, as my steward, and to him I commit the management and care of our household, together with all that appertains to the service of the hall. I desire that Panfilo's servant, Sirisco, should act as our buyer and treasurer, and carry out the instructions of Parmeno. As well as attending to the needs of Filostrato, Tindaro will look after the other two gentlemen in their rooms whenever their own manservants are prevented by their offices from performing such duties. My own maidservant, Misia, will be employed full-time in the kitchen along with Filomena's maidservant, Licisca, and they will prepare with diligence whatever dishes are prescribed by Parmeno. Chimera and Stratilia, the servants of Lauretta and Fiammetta, are required to act as chambermaids to all the ladies, as well as seeing that the places we frequent are neatly and tidily maintained. And unless they wish to incur our royal displeasure, we desire and command that each and every one of the servants should take good care, no matter what they should hear or observe in their comings and goings, to bring us no tidings of the world outside these walls unless they are tidings of happiness.'

Her orders thus summarily given, and commended by all her companions, she rose gaily to her feet, and said:

'There are gardens here, and meadows, and other places of great charm and beauty, through which we may now wander in search of our amusement, each of us being free to do whatever he pleases. But on the stroke of tierce*, let us all return to this spot, so that we may breakfast together in the shade.'

The merry company having thus been dismissed by their newly elected queen, the young men and their fair companions sauntered slowly through a garden, conversing on pleasant topics, weaving fair garlands for each other from the leaves of various trees, and singing songs of love.

After spending as much time there as the queen had allotted them,

*The canonical office recited at the third hour of the day, in other words at about 9 a.m.

they returned to the house to find that Parmeno had made a zealous beginning to his duties, for as they entered the hall on the ground floor, they saw the tables ready laid, with pure white tablecloths and with goblets shining bright as silver, whilst the whole room was decorated with broom blossom. At the queen's behest, they rinsed their hands in water, then seated themselves in the places to which Parmeno had assigned them.

Dishes, daintily prepared, were brought in, excellent wines were at hand, and without a sound the three manservants promptly began to wait upon them. Everyone was delighted that these things had been so charmingly and efficiently arranged, and during the meal there was pleasant talk and merry laughter from all sides. Afterwards, the tables were removed, and the queen sent for musical instruments so that one or two of their number, well versed in music, could play and sing, whilst the rest, ladies and gentlemen alike, could dance a *carole*. At the queen's request, Dioneo took a lute and Fiammetta a viol, and they struck up a melodious tune, whereupon the queen, having sent the servants off to eat, formed a ring with the other ladies and the two young men, and sedately began to dance. And when the dance was over, they sang a number of gay and charming little songs.

In this fashion they continued until the queen decided that the time had come for them to retire to rest, whereupon she dismissed the whole company. The young men went away to their rooms, which were separated from those of the ladies, and found that, like the hall, they too were full of flowers, and that their beds were neatly made. The ladies made a similar discovery in theirs, and, having undressed, they lay down to rest.

The queen rose shortly after nones*, and caused the other ladies to be roused, as also the young men, declaring it was harmful to sleep too much during the day. They therefore betook themselves to a meadow, where the grass, being protected from the heat of the sun, grew thick and green, and where, perceiving that a gentle breeze was stirring, the queen suggested that they should all sit on the green grass in a circle. And when they were seated, she addressed them as follows:

'As you can see, the sun is high in the sky, it is very hot, and all is silent except for the cicadas in the olive-trees. For the moment, it

---

*The fourth of the day offices of the Church, corresponding to 3 p.m.

would surely be foolish of us to venture abroad, this being such a cool and pleasant spot in which to linger. Besides, as you will observe, there are chessboards and other games here, and so we are free to amuse ourselves in whatever way we please. But if you were to follow my advice, this hotter part of the day would be spent, not in playing games (which inevitably bring anxiety to one of the players, without offering very much pleasure either to his opponent or to the spectators), but in telling stories – an activity that may afford some amusement both to the narrator and to the company at large. By the time each one of you has narrated a little tale of his own or her own, the sun will be setting, the heat will have abated, and we shall be able to go and amuse ourselves wherever you choose. Let us, then, if the idea appeals to you, carry this proposal of mine into effect. But I am willing to follow your own wishes in this matter, and if you disagree with my suggestion, let us all go and occupy our time in whatever way we please until the hour of vespers.'

The whole company, ladies and gentlemen alike, were in favour of telling stories.

'Then if it is agreeable to you,' said the queen, 'I desire that on this first day each of us should be free to speak upon whatever topic he prefers.'

And turning to Panfilo, who was seated on her right, she graciously asked him to introduce the proceedings with one of his stories. No sooner did he receive this invitation than Panfilo began as follows, with everyone listening intently:

FIRST STORY

Ser Cepperello deceives a holy friar with a false confession, then he dies; and although in life he was a most wicked man, in death he is reputed to be a Saint, and is called Saint Ciappelletto.

It is proper, dearest ladies, that everything done by man should begin with the sacred and admirable name of Him that was maker of all things. And therefore, since I am the first and must make a beginning to our story-telling, I propose to begin by telling you of one of His marvellous works, so that, when we have heard it out, our hopes will rest in Him as in something immutable, and we shall forever praise His name. It is obvious that since all temporal things are transient and mortal, so they are filled and surrounded by troubles, trials and tribulations, and fraught with infinite dangers which we, who live with them and are part of them, could without a shadow of a doubt neither endure, nor defend ourselves against, if God's special grace did not lend us strength and discernment. Nor should we suppose that His grace descends upon and within us through any merit of our own, for it is set in motion by His own loving kindness, and is obtained by the pleas of people who like ourselves were mortal, and who, by firmly doing His pleasure whilst they were in this life, have now joined Him in eternal blessedness. To these, as to advocates made aware, through experience, of our frailty (perhaps because we have not the courage to submit our pleas personally in the presence of so great a judge) we present whatever we think is relevant to our cause. And our regard for Him, who is so compassionate and gener- ous towards us, is all the greater when, the human eye being quite unable to penetrate the secrets of divine intelligence, common opinion deceives us and perhaps we appoint as our advocate in His majestic presence one who has been cast by Him into eternal exile. Yet He from whom nothing is hidden, paying more attention to the purity of the supplicant's motives than to his ignorance or to the banishment of the intercessor, answers those who pray to Him exactly as if the advocate were blessed in His sight. All of which can clearly be seen in the tale I propose to relate; and I say clearly because it is concerned, not with the judgement of God, but with that of men.

It is said, then, that Musciatto Franzesi, having become a fine gentle- man after acquiring enormous wealth and fame as a merchant in France, was obliged to come to Tuscany with the brother of the French king, the Lord Charles Stateless, who had been urged and encouraged to come by Pope Boniface. But finding that his affairs, as is usually the case with merchants, were entangled here, there, and everywhere, and being unable quickly or easily to unravel them, he decided to place them in the hands of a number of different people. All this he succeeded in arranging, except that he was left with the problem of finding someone capable of recovering certain loans which he had made to various people in Burgundy. The reason for his dilemma was that he had been told the Burgundians were a quarrelsome, thoroughly bad and unprincipled set of people; and he was quite unable to think of anyone he could trust, who was at the same time sufficiently villainous to match the villainy of the Burgundians. After devoting much thought to this problem, he suddenly recalled a man known as Ser Cepperello, of Prato, who had been a frequent visitor to his house in Paris. This man was short in stature and used to dress very neatly, and the French, who did not know the meaning of the word Cepperello, thinking that it signified *chapel*, which in their language means 'garland', and because as we have said he was a little man, used to call him, not Ciappello, but Ciappelletto: and everywhere in that part of the world, where few people knew him as Ser Cepperello, he was known as Ciappelletto.*

This Ciappelletto was a man of the following sort: a notary by profession, he would have taken it as a slight upon his honour if one of his legal deeds (and he drew up very few of them) were discovered to be other than false. In fact, he would have drawn up free of charge as many false documents as were requested of him, and done it more willingly than one who was highly paid for his services. He would take great delight in giving false testimony, whether asked for it or not. In those days, great reliance was placed in France upon sworn declarations, and since he had no scruples about swearing falsely, he used to win, by these nefarious means, every case in which he was required to swear upon his faith to tell the truth. He would take particular pleasure, and a great amount of trouble, in stirring up enmity, discord and bad blood between friends, relatives and anybody else; and the more calamities that ensued, the greater would be his rapture. If he were invited to witness a murder or any other criminal act, he would never refuse, but willingly go along; and he often found

---

*In order to follow this long-winded explanation of the character's name, the English reader should bear in mind that *-etto*, like *-ello*, is a diminutive suffix, and that Boccaccio probably thought the name Cepperello was derived from *ceppo* ('log'), whereas it was almost certainly a diminutive form of Ciapo, or Jacopo. The point is that Cepperello ('little log') was a far more appropriate name for this incorrigible ruffian than Ciappelletto ('chaplet').

himself cheerfully assaulting or killing people with his own hands. He was a mighty blasphemer of God and His Saints, losing his temper on the tiniest pretext, as if he were the most hot-blooded man alive. He never went to church, and he would use foul language to pour scorn on all of her sacraments, declaring them repugnant. On the other hand, he would make a point of visiting taverns and other places of ill repute, and supplying them with his custom. Of women he was as fond as dogs are fond of a good stout stick; in their opposite, he took greater pleasure than the most depraved man on earth. He would rob and pilfer as conscientiously as if he were a saintly man making an offering. He was such a prize glutton and heavy drinker, that he would occasionally suffer for his over-indulgence in a manner that was highly indecorous. He was a gambler and a card-sharper of the first order. But why do I lavish so many words upon him? He was perhaps the worst man ever born. Yet for all his villainy, he had long been protected by the power and influence of Messer Musciatto, on whose account he was many a time treated with respect, both by private individuals, whom he frequently abused, and by the courts of law, which he was forever abusing.

So that when Musciatto, who was well acquainted with his way of living, called this Ser Ciappelletto to mind, he judged him to be the very man that the perverseness of the Burgundians required. He therefore sent for him and addressed him as follows:

'Ser Ciappelletto, as you know, I am about to go away from here altogether, but I have some business to settle, amongst others with the Burgundians. These people are full of tricks, and I know of no one better fitted than yourself to recover what they owe me. And so, since you are not otherwise engaged at present, if you will attend to this matter I propose to obtain favours for you at court, and allow you a reasonable portion of the money you recover.'

Ser Ciappelletto, who was out of a job at the time and ill-supplied with worldly goods, seeing that the man who had long been his prop and stay was about to depart, made up his mind without delay and said (for he really had no alternative) that he would do it willingly. So that when they had agreed on terms, Ser Ciappelletto received powers of attorney from Musciatto and letters of introduction from the King, and after Musciatto's departure he went to Burgundy, where scarcely anybody knew him. And there, in a gentle and amiable fashion that ran contrary to his nature, as though he were holding his anger in reserve as a last resort, he issued his first demands and began to do what he had gone there to do. Before long, however, while lodging in the house of two Florentine brothers who ran a money-lending business there and did him great honour out of their respect for Musciatto, he happened to fall ill; whereupon the two brothers promptly summoned doctors and servants to attend him, and provided him with everything he needed to recover his health. But all their assistance was unavailing, because the good man, who was already advanced in years and had lived a disordered existence, was reported by his doctors to be going each day from bad to worse, like one who was suffering from a fatal illness. The two brothers were filled with alarm, and one day, alongside the room in which Ser Ciappelletto was lying, they began talking together.

'What are we to do about the fellow?' said one to the other. 'We've landed ourselves in a fine mess on his account, because to turn him away from our house in his present condition would arouse a lot of adverse comment and show us to be seriously lacking in common sense. What would people say if they suddenly saw us evicting a dying man after giving him hospitality in the first place, and taking so much trouble to have him nursed and waited upon, when he couldn't possibly have done anything to offend us? On the other hand, he has led such a wicked life that he will never be willing to make his confession or receive the sacraments of the Church; and if he dies unconfessed, no church will want to accept his body and he'll be flung into the moat like a dog. But even if he makes his confession, his sins are so many and so appalling that the same thing will happen, because there will be neither friar nor priest who is either willing or able to give him absolution; in which case, since he will not have been absolved, he will be flung into the moat just the same. And when the townspeople see what has happened, they'll create a commotion, not only because of our profession which they consider iniquitous and never cease to condemn, but also because they long to get their hands on our money, and they will go about shouting: "Away with these Lombard dogs that the Church refuses to accept"; and they'll come running to our lodgings and perhaps, not content with stealing our goods, they'll take away our lives into the bargain. So we shall be in a pretty fix either way, if this fellow dies.'

Ser Ciappelletto, who as we have said was lying near the place where they were talking, heard everything they were saying about him, for he was sharp of hearing, as invalids invariably are. So he called them in to him, and said:

'I don't want you to worry in the slightest on my account, nor to fear that I will cause you to suffer any harm. I heard what you were saying about me and I agree entirely that what you predict will actually come to pass, if matters take the course you anticipate; but they will do nothing of the kind. I have done our good Lord so many injuries whilst I lived, that to do Him another now that I am dying will be neither here nor there. So go and bring me the holiest and ablest friar you can find, if there is such a one, and leave everything to me, for I shall set your affairs and my own neatly in order, so that all will be well and you'll have nothing to complain of.'

Whilst deriving little comfort from all this, the two brothers nevertheless went off to a friary and asked for a wise and holy man to come and hear the confession of a Lombard who was lying ill in their house. They were given an ancient friar of good and holy ways who was an expert in the Scriptures and a most venerable man, towards whom all the townspeople were greatly and specially devoted, and they conducted him to their house.

On reaching the room where Ser Ciappelletto was lying, he sat down at his bedside, and first he began to comfort him with kindly words, then he asked him how long it was since he had last been to confession. Whereupon Ser Ciappelletto, who had never been to confession in his life, replied:

'Father, it has always been my custom to go to confession at least once every week, except that there are many weeks in which I go more often. But to tell the truth, since I fell ill, nearly a week ago, my illness has caused me so much discomfort that I haven't been to confession at all.'

'My son,' said the friar, 'you have done well, and you should persevere in this habit of yours. Since you go so often to confession, I can see that there will be little for me to hear or to ask.'

'Master friar,' said Ser Ciappelletto, 'do not speak thus, for how-

ever frequently or regularly I confess, it is always my wish that I
should make a general confession of all the sins I can remember committing from the day I was born till the day of my confession. I
therefore beg you, good father, to question me about everything, just
as closely as if I had never been confessed. Do not spare me because I
happen to be ill, for I would much rather mortify this flesh of mine
than that, by treating it with lenience, I should do anything that
could lead to the perdition of my soul, which my Saviour redeemed
with His precious blood.'

These words were greatly pleasing to the holy friar, and seemed to
him proof of a well-disposed mind. Having warmly commended Ser
Ciappelletto for this practice of his, he began by asking him whether
he had ever committed the sin of lust with any woman. To which,
heaving a sigh, Ser Ciappelletto replied:

'Father, I am loath to tell you the truth on this matter, in case I
should sin by way of vainglory.'

To which the holy friar replied:

'Speak out freely, for no man ever sinned by telling the truth,
either in confession or otherwise.'

'Since you assure me that this is so,' said Ser Ciappelletto, 'I will
tell you. I am a virgin as pure as on the day I came forth from my
mother's womb.'

'Oh, may God give you His blessing!' said the friar. 'How nobly
you have lived! And your restraint is all the more deserving of praise
in that, had you wished, you would have had greater liberty to do the
opposite than those who, like ourselves, are expressly forbidden by
rule.'

Next he asked him whether he had displeased God by committing
the sin of gluttony; to which, fetching a deep sigh, Ser Ciappelletto
replied that he had, and on many occasions. For although, apart from
the periods of fasting normally observed in the course of the year by
the devout, he was accustomed to fasting on bread and water for at
least three days every week, he had drunk the water as pleasurably
and avidly (especially when he had been fatigued from praying or
going on a pilgrimage) as any great bibber of wine; he had often
experienced a craving for those dainty little wild herb salads that
women eat when they go away to the country; and sometimes the

thought of food had been more attractive to him than he considered proper in one who, like himself, was fasting out of piety. Whereupon the friar said:

'My son, these sins are natural and they are very trivial, and therefore I would not have you burden your conscience with them more than necessary. No matter how holy a man may be, he will be attracted by the thought of food after a long period of fasting, and by the thought of drink when he is fatigued.'

'Oh!' said Ser Ciappelletto. 'Do not tell me this to console me, father. As you are aware, I know that things done in the service of God must all be done honestly and without any grudge; and if anyone should do otherwise, he is committing a sin.'

The friar, delighted, said to him:

'I am contented to see you taking such a view, and it pleases me greatly that you should have such a good and pure conscience in this matter. But tell me, have you ever been guilty of avarice, by desiring to have more than was proper, or keeping what you should not have kept?'

To which Ser Ciappelletto replied:

'Father, I would not wish you to judge me ill because I am in the house of these money-lenders. I have nothing to do with their business; indeed I had come here with the express intention of warning and reproaching them, and dissuading them from this abominable form of money-making; and I think I would have succeeded, if God had not stricken me in this manner. However, I would have you know that my father left me a wealthy man, and when he was dead, I gave the greater part of his fortune to charity. Since then, in order to support myself and enable me to assist the Christian poor, I have done a small amount of trading, in the course of which I have desired to gain, and I have always shared what I have gained with the poor, allocating one half to my own needs and giving the other half to them. And in this I have had so much help from my Creator that I have continually gone from strength to strength in the management of my affairs.'

'You have done well,' said the friar, 'but tell me, how often have you lost your temper?'

'Oh!' said Ser Ciappelletto, 'I can assure you I have done that very often. But who is there who could restrain himself, when the whole day long he sees men doing disgusting things, and failing to observe God's commandments, or to fear His terrible wrath? There have been many times in the space of a single day when I would rather have been dead than alive, looking about me and seeing young people frittering away their time, telling lies, going drinking in taverns, failing to go to church, and following the ways of the world rather than those of God.'

'My son,' said the friar, 'this kind of anger is justified, and for my part I could not require you to do penance for it. But has it ever happened that your anger has led you to commit murder or to pour abuse on anyone or do them any other form of injury?'

To which Ser Ciappelletto replied:

'Oh, sir, however could you, that appear to be a man of God, say such a thing? If I had thought for a single moment of doing any of the things you mention, do you suppose I imagine that God would have treated me so generously? Those things are the business of cut-throats and evildoers, and whenever I have chanced upon one of their number, I have always sent him packing, and offered up a prayer for his conversion!'

'May God give you His blessing,' said the friar, 'but now, tell me, my son: have you ever borne false witness against any man, or spoken ill of people, or taken what belonged to others without seeking their permission?'

'Never, sir, except on one occasion,' replied Ser Ciappelletto, 'when I spoke ill of someone. For I once had a neighbour who, without the slightest cause, was forever beating his wife, so that on this one occasion I spoke ill of him to his wife's kinsfolk, for I felt extremely sorry for that unfortunate woman. Whenever the fellow had had too much to drink, God alone could tell you how he hammered her.'

Then the friar said:

'Let me see now, you tell me you were a merchant. Did you ever deceive anyone, as merchants do?'

'Faith, sir, I did,' said Ser Ciappelletto. 'But all I know about him is that he was a man who brought me some money that he owed me for a length of cloth I had sold him. I put the money away in a box without counting it, and a whole month passed before I discovered there were four pennies more than there should have been. I kept them for a year with the intention of giving them back, but I never saw him again, so I gave them away to a beggar.'

'That was a trivial matter,' said the friar, 'and you did well to dispose of the money as you did.'

The holy friar questioned him on many other matters, but always he answered in similar vein, and hence the friar was ready to proceed without further ado to give him absolution. But Ser Ciappelletto said:

'Sir, I still have one or two sins I have not yet told you about.'

The friar asked him what they were, and he said:

'I recall that I once failed to show a proper respect for the Holy Sabbath, by making one of my servants sweep the house after nones on a Saturday.'

'Oh!' said the friar. 'This, my son, is a trifling matter.'

'No, father,' said Ser Ciappelletto, 'you must not call it trifling, for the Sabbath has to be greatly honoured, seeing that this was the day on which our Lord rose from the dead.'

Then the friar said:

'Have you done anything else?'

'Yes, sir,' replied Ser Ciappelletto, 'for I once, without thinking what I was doing, spat in the house of God.'

The friar began to smile, and said:

'My son, this is not a thing to worry about. We members of religious orders spit there continually.'

'That is very wicked of you,' said Ser Ciappelletto, 'for nothing should be kept more clean than the holy temple in which sacrifice is offered up to God.'

In brief, he told the friar many things of this sort, and finally he began to sigh, and then to wail loudly, as he was well able to do whenever he pleased.

'My son,' said the holy friar. 'What is the matter?'

'Oh alas, sir,' replied Ser Ciappelletto, 'I have one sin left to which I have never confessed, so great is my shame in having to reveal it; and whenever I remember it, I cry as you see me doing now, and feel quite certain that God will never have mercy on me for this terrible sin.'

'Come now, my son,' said the holy friar, 'what are you saying? If all the sins that were ever committed by the whole of mankind, together with those that men will yet commit till the end of the world, were concentrated in one single man, and he was as truly repentant and contrite as I see you to be, God is so benign and merciful that He would freely remit them on their being confessed to Him; and therefore you may safely reveal it.'

Then Ser Ciappelletto said, still weeping loudly:

'Alas, father, my sin is too great, and I can scarcely believe that God will ever forgive me for it, unless you intercede with your prayers.'

To which the friar replied:

'You may safely reveal it, for I promise that I will pray to God on your behalf.'

Ser Ciappelletto went on weeping, without saying anything, and the friar kept encouraging him to speak. But after Ser Ciappelletto, by weeping in this manner, had kept the friar for a very long time on tenterhooks, he heaved a great sigh, and said:

'Father, since you promise that you will pray to God for me, I will tell you. You are to know then that once, when I was a little boy, I cursed my mother.' And having said this, he began to weep loudly all over again.

'There now, my son,' said the friar, 'does this seem so great a sin to you? Why, people curse God the whole day long, and yet He willingly forgives those who repent for having cursed Him. Why then should you suppose He will not forgive you for this? Take heart and do not weep, for even if you had been one of those who set Him on the cross, I can see that you have so much contrition that He would certainly forgive you.'

'Oh alas, father,' said Ser Ciappelletto, 'what are you saying? My dear, sweet mother, who carried me day and night for nine months in her body, and held me more than a hundred times in her arms! It was too wicked of me to curse her, and the sin is too great; and if you do not pray to God for me, it will never be forgiven me.'

Perceiving that Ser Ciappelletto had nothing more to say, the friar absolved him and gave him his blessing. He took him for a very saintly man indeed, being fully convinced that what Ser Ciappelletto had said was true; but then, who is there who would not have been convinced, on hearing a dying man talk in this fashion? Finally, when all this was done, he said to him:

'Ser Ciappelletto, with God's help you will soon be well again. But in case it were to happen that God should summon your blessed and well-disposed soul to His presence, are you willing for your body to be buried in our convent?'

To which Ser Ciappelletto replied:

'Yes, father. In fact, I would not wish to be elsewhere, since you have promised that you will pray to God for me. Besides, I have always been especially devoted to your Order. So when you return to your convent, I beg you to see that I am sent that true body of Christ which you consecrate every morning on the altar. For although I am unworthy of it, I intend with your permission to take it, and afterwards to receive the holy Extreme Unction, so that, having lived as a sinner, I shall at least die as a Christian.'

The holy man said that he was greatly pleased, that the words were well spoken, and that he would see it was brought to him at once; and so it was.

The two brothers, who strongly suspected that Ser Ciappelletto was going to deceive them, had posted themselves behind a wooden partition which separated the room where Ser Ciappelletto was lying from another, and as they stood there listening they could easily follow what Ser Ciappelletto was saying to the friar. When they heard the things he confessed to having done, they were so amused that every so often they nearly exploded with mirth, and they said to each other:

'What manner of man is this, whom neither old age nor illness, nor fear of the death which he sees so close at hand, nor even the fear of God, before whose judgement he knows he must shortly appear, have managed to turn from his evil ways, or persuade him to die any differently from the way he has lived?'

Seeing, however, that he had said all the right things to be received for burial in a church, they cared nothing for the rest.

Shortly thereafter Ser Ciappelletto made his communion, and, failing rapidly, he received Extreme Unction. Soon after vespers on the very day that he had made his fine confession, he died. Whereupon the two brothers made all necessary arrangements, using his own money to see that he had an honourable funeral, and sending news of his death to the friars and asking them to come that evening to observe the customary vigil, and the following morning to take away the body.

On hearing that he had passed away, the holy friar who had received his confession arranged with the prior for the chapter-house bell to be rung, and to the assembled friars he showed that Ser Ciappelletto had been a saintly man, as his confession had amply proved. He expressed the hope that through him the Lord God would work many miracles, and persuaded them that his body should be received with the utmost reverence and loving care. Credulous to a man, the prior and the other friars agreed to do so, and that evening they went to the place where Ser Ciappelletto's body lay, and celebrated a great and solemn vigil over it; and in the morning, dressed in albs and copes, carrying books in their hands and bearing crosses before them, singing as they went, they all came for the body, which they then carried back to their church with tremendous pomp and ceremony, followed by nearly all the people of the town, men and women alike. And when it had been set down in the church, the holy friar who had confessed him climbed into the pulpit and began to preach marvellous things about Ser Ciappelletto's life, his fasts, his virginity, his simplicity and innocence and saintliness, relating among other things what he had tearfully confessed to him as his greatest sin, and describing how he had barely been able to convince him that God would forgive him, at which point he turned to reprimand his audience, saying:

'And yet you miserable sinners have only to catch your feet in a wisp of straw for you to curse God and the Virgin and all the Saints in heaven.'

Apart from this, he said much else about his loyalty and his purity of heart. And in brief, with a torrent of words that the people of the town believed implicitly, he fixed Ser Ciappelletto so firmly in the minds and affections of all those present that when the service was over, everyone thronged round the body to kiss his feet and his hands, all the clothes were torn from his back, and those who succeeded in grabbing so much as a tiny fragment felt they were in Paradise itself. He had to be kept lying there all day, so that everyone could come and gaze upon him, and on that same night he was buried with honour in a marble tomb in one of the chapels. From the next day forth, people began to go there to light candles and pray to him, and later they began to make votive offerings and to decorate the chapel with figures made of wax, in fulfilment of promises they had given.

The fame of his saintliness, and of the veneration in which he was held, grew to such proportions that there was hardly anyone who did not pray for his assistance in time of trouble, and they called him, and call him still, Saint Ciappelletto. Moreover it is claimed that through him God has wrought many miracles, and that He continues to work them on behalf of whoever commends himself devoutly to this particular Saint.

It was thus, then, that Ser Cepperello of Prato lived and died, becoming a Saint in the way you have heard. Nor would I wish to deny that perhaps God has blessed and admitted him to His presence. For albeit he led a wicked, sinful life, it is possible that at the eleventh hour he was so sincerely repentant that God had mercy upon him and received him into His kingdom. But since this is hidden from us, I speak only with regard to the outward appearance, and I say that this fellow should rather be in Hell, in the hands of the devil, than in Paradise. And if this is the case, we may recognize how very great is God's loving kindness towards us, in that it takes account, not of our error, but of the purity of our faith, and grants our prayers even when we appoint as our emissary one who is His enemy, thinking him to be His friend, as though we were appealing to one who was truly holy as our intercessor for His favour. And therefore, so that we, the members of this joyful company, may be guided safely and securely by His grace through these present adversities, let us praise the name of Him with whom we began our storytelling, let us hold Him in reverence, and let us commend ourselves to Him in the hour of our need, in the certain knowledge that we shall be heard.

And there the narrator fell silent.

SECOND STORY

A Jew called Abraham, his curiosity being aroused by Jehannot de Chevigny, goes to the court of Rome; and when he sees the depravity of the clergy, he returns to Paris and becomes a Christian.

The ladies were full of praise for Panfilo's story, parts of which they had found highly amusing. Everyone had listened closely, and when it came to an end Neifile, sitting next to Panfilo, was asked by the queen to continue the proceedings with a story of her own. Neifile, whose manners were no less striking than her beauty, replied with a smile that she would gladly do so, and began in this fashion:

Panfilo has shown us in his tale that God's loving kindness is unaffected by our errors, when they proceed from some cause which it is impossible for us to detect; and I in mine propose to demonstrate to you how this same loving kindness, by patiently enduring the shortcomings of those who in word and deed ought to be its living witness and yet behave in a precisely contrary fashion, gives us the proof of its unerring rightness; my purpose being that of strengthening our conviction in what we believe.

As I was once informed, fair ladies, there lived in Paris a great merchant, a worthy man called Jehannot de Chevigny, who was extremely honest and upright and ran a flourishing textile business. He was particularly friendly with an enormously rich Jew called Abraham, who was himself a merchant and an extremely upright and honest man. In view of Abraham's honesty and integrity, Jehannot began to have serious regrets that the soul of so worthy, good and wise a man should go to its perdition because it was lacking in proper faith. So he began in an amiable manner to urge him to abandon the erroneous ways of Judaism and embrace the true Christian faith, which being sound and holy was, as he could see for himself, steadily growing and prospering; whereas in contrast his own religion was manifestly declining and coming to nought.

The Jew replied that he considered no faith to be sound and holy except the Jewish, and that he had been born into that one, and meant to live and die in it; nor was there anything that would shift him from his resolve. This reply did not however deter Jehannot, a few days later, from renewing his appeal and showing him, in the sort of homespun language for which most merchants have a natural bent, on what grounds our faith was superior to the Jewish. And although Abraham was very learned in Jewish doctrine, nevertheless, either because of his great friendship for Jehannot or possibly because he was stirred by the words which the Holy Ghost put into the mouth of this ignoramus, he began to be highly entertained by Jehannot's explanations. But his belief was unshaken, and he would not allow himself to be converted.

The more stubbornly he resisted, the more Jehannot continued to pester him, until finally the Jew, overcome by such incessant importunity, said:

'Now listen, Jehannot, you would like me to become a Christian, and I am prepared to do so on one condition: that first of all I should go to Rome, and there observe the man whom you call the vicar of God on earth, and examine his life and habits together with those of his fellow cardinals; and if they seem to me such that, added to your own arguments, they lead me to the conclusion that your faith is superior to mine, as you have taken such pains to show me, then I shall do as I have promised; but if things should turn out differently, I shall remain a Jew as I am at present.'

When Jehannot heard this, he was thrown into a fit of gloom, and said to himself: 'I have wasted my energies, which I felt I had used to good effect, thinking I had converted the man; for if he goes to the court of Rome and sees what foul and wicked lives the clergy lead, not only will he not become a Christian, but, if he had already turned Christian, he would become a Jew again without fail.' And turning to Abraham, he said.

'Come now, my friend, why should you want to put yourself to the endless trouble and expense involved in going all the way from here to Rome? Besides, for a rich man like yourself, the journey both by sea and land is full of dangers. Do you suppose you will not find anyone here to baptize you? If by chance you have any doubts concerning the faith as I have outlined it to you, where else except in Paris will you find greater and more learned exponents of Christian doctrine, capable of answering your questions and resolving your difficulties? Hence in my opinion this journey of yours is quite unnecessary. You must remember that the Church dignitaries in Rome are no different from the ones you have seen and can still see here, except that they are the better for being closer to the chief shepherd. And so if you will take my advice, you will save your energy for a pilgrimage on some later occasion, when perhaps I will keep you company.'

'Jehannot,' replied the Jew, 'I believe it to be just as you say it is, but to put the matter in a nutshell, if you really want me to do as you have urged me with so much insistence, I am fully prepared to go there. Otherwise, I shall do nothing about it.'

'Go then, and good luck to you,' said Jehannot, seeing that the Jew had made up his mind. He was quite certain that Abraham would never become a Christian, once he had seen the court of Rome; but since it would make no difference, he did not insist any further.

The Jew mounted a horse, and rode off with all possible speed to the court of Rome, where on his arrival he was warmly welcomed by his Jewish friends. And there he settled down, without telling anybody why he had come, and cautiously began to observe the behaviour of the Pope, the cardinals, the other Church dignitaries, and all the courtiers. Being a very perceptive person, he discovered, by adding the evidence of his own eyes to information given him by others, that practically all of them from the highest to the lowest were flagrantly given to the sin of lust, not only of the natural variety, but also of the sodomitic, without the slightest display of shame or remorse, to the extent that the power of prostitutes and young men to obtain the most enormous favours was virtually unlimited. In addition to this, he clearly saw that they were all gluttons, wine-bibbers, and drunkards without exception, and that next to their lust they would rather attend to their bellies than to anything else, as though they were a pack of animals.

Moreover, on closer inspection he saw that they were such a collection of rapacious money-grubbers that they were as ready to buy and sell human, that is to say, Christian blood as they were to trade for profit in any kind of divine object, whether in the way of sacraments or of church livings. In this activity, they had a bigger turnover and more brokers than you could find on any of the Paris markets including that of the textile trade. They had applied the name of 'procuration' to their unconcealed simony, and that of 'sustentation' to their gluttony, as if (to say nothing of the meaning of the words) God were ignorant of the intentions of their wicked minds and would allow Himself to be deceived, as men are, by the mere names of things.

All this, together with many other things of which it is more prudent to remain silent, was highly distasteful to the Jew, who was a sober and respectable man. And so, feeling he had seen enough, he decided to return to Paris, which he did. On hearing of his arrival, Jehannot, thinking nothing to be less likely than that his friend should have turned Christian, came to his house, where they made a great fuss of each other. And after Abraham had rested for a few days, Jehannot asked him what sort of an opinion he had formed about the Holy Father and the cardinals and the other members of the papal court. Whereupon the Jew promptly replied:

'A bad one, and may God deal harshly with the whole lot of them. And my reason for telling you so is that, unless I formed the wrong impression, nobody there who was connected with the Church seemed to me to display the slightest sign of holiness, piety, charity, moral rectitude or any other virtue. On the contrary, it seemed to me that they were all so steeped in lust, greed, avarice, fraud, envy, pride, and other like sins and worse (if indeed that is possible), that I regard the place as a hotbed of diabolical rather than divine activities. And as far as I can judge, it seems to me that your pontiff, and all of the others too, are doing their level best to reduce the Christian religion to nought and drive it from the face of the earth, whereas they are the very people who should be its foundation and support.

'But since it is evident to me that their attempts are unavailing, and that your religion continues to grow in popularity, and become more splendid and illustrious, I can only conclude that, being a more holy and genuine religion than any of the others, it deservedly has the Holy Ghost as its foundation and support. So whereas earlier I stood firm and unyielding against your entreaties and refused to turn Christian, I now tell you quite plainly that nothing in the world could prevent me from becoming a Christian. Let us therefore go to the church where, in accordance with the traditional rite of your holy faith, you shall have me baptized.'

When Jehannot, who was expecting precisely the opposite conclusion, heard him saying this, he was the happiest man that ever lived. And he went with him to Nôtre Dame de Paris, and asked the clergy there to baptize Abraham. This they did, as soon as they heard that he himself desired it: Jehannot stood as his sponsor, and gave him the name of John. And afterwards he engaged the most learned teachers to instruct him thoroughly in our religion, which he quickly mastered, thereafter becoming a good and worthy man, holy in all his ways.

THIRD STORY

Melchizedek the Jew, with a story about three rings, avoids a most dangerous trap laid for him by Saladin.

Neifile's story was well received by all the company, and when she fell silent, Filomena began at the queen's behest to address them as follows:

The story told by Neifile reminds me of the parlous state in which a Jew once found himself. Now that we have heard such fine things said concerning God and the truth of our religion, it will not seem inappropriate to descend at this juncture to the deeds and adventures of men. So I shall tell you a story which, when you have heard it, will possibly make you more cautious in answering questions addressed to you. It is a fact, my sweet companions, that just as folly often destroys men's happiness and casts them into deepest misery, so prudence extricates the wise from dreadful perils and guides them firmly to safety. So clearly may we perceive that folly leads men from contentment to misery, that we shall not even bother for the present to consider the matter further, since countless examples spring readily to mind. But that prudence may bring its reward, I shall, as I have promised, prove to you briefly by means of the following little tale:

Saladin, whose worth was so great that it raised him from humble beginnings to the sultanate of Egypt and brought him many victories over Saracen and Christian kings, had expended the whole of his treasure in various wars and extraordinary acts of munificence, when a certain situation arose for which he required a vast sum of money. Not being able to see any way of obtaining what he needed at such short notice, he happened to recall a rich Jew, Melchizedek by name, who ran a money-lending business in Alexandria, and would certainly, he thought, have enough for his purposes, if only he could be persuaded to part with it. But this Melchizedek was such a miserly fellow that he would never hand it over of his own free will, and the Sultan was not prepared to take it away from him by force. However, as his need became more pressing, having racked his brains to discover some way of compelling the Jew to assist him, he resolved to use force in the guise of reason. So he sent for the Jew, gave him a cordial reception, invited him to sit down beside him, and said:

'O man of excellent worth, many men have told me of your great wisdom and your superior knowledge of the ways of God. Hence I would be glad if you would tell me which of the three laws, whether the Jewish, the Saracen, or the Christian, you deem to be truly authentic.'

The Jew, who was indeed a wise man, realized all too well that Saladin was aiming to trip him up with the intention of picking a quarrel with him, and that if he were to praise any of the three more than the others, the Sultan would achieve his object. He therefore had need of a reply that would save him from falling into the trap, and having sharpened his wits, in no time at all he was ready with his answer.

'My lord,' he said, 'your question is a very good one, and in order to explain my views on the subject, I must ask you to listen to the following little story:

'Unless I am mistaken, I recall having frequently heard that there was once a great and wealthy man who, apart from the other fine jewels contained in his treasury, possessed a most precious and beautiful ring. Because of its value and beauty, he wanted to do it the honour of leaving it in perpetuity to his descendants, and so he announced that he would bequeath the ring to one of his sons, and that whichever of them should be found to have it in his keeping, this man was to be looked upon as his heir, and the others were to honour and respect him as the head of the family.

'The man to whom he left the ring, having made a similar provision regarding his own descendants, followed the example set by his predecessor. To cut a long story short, the ring was handed down through many generations till it finally came to rest in the hands of a man who had three most splendid and virtuous sons who were very obedient to their father, and he loved all three of them equally. Each of the three young men, being aware of the tradition concerning the ring, was eager to take precedence over the others, and they all did their utmost to persuade the father, who was now an old man, to leave them the ring when he died.

'The good man, who loved all three and was unable to decide which of them should inherit the ring, resolved, having promised it to each, to try and please them all. So he secretly commissioned a master-craftsman to make two more rings, which were so like the first that even the man who had made them could barely distinguish them from the original. And when he was dying, he took each of his sons aside in turn, and gave one ring to each.

'After their father's death, they all desired to succeed to his title and estate, and each man denied the claims of the others, producing his ring to prove his case. But finding that the rings were so alike that it was impossible to tell them apart, the question of which of the sons was the true and rightful heir remained in abeyance, and has never been settled.

'And I say to you, my lord, that the same applies to the three laws which God the Father granted to His three peoples, and which formed the subject of your inquiry. Each of them considers itself the legitimate heir to His estate, each believes it possesses His one true law and observes His commandments. But as with the rings, the question as to which of them is right remains in abeyance.'

Saladin perceived that the fellow had ingeniously side-stepped the trap he had set before him, and he therefore decided to make a clean breast of his needs, and see if the Jew would come to his assistance. This he did, freely admitting what he had intended to do, but for the fact that the Jew had answered him so discreetly.

Melchizedek gladly provided the Sultan with the money he required. The Sultan later paid him back in full, in addition to which he showered magnificent gifts upon him, made him his lifelong friend, and maintained him at his court in a state of importance and honour.

FOURTH STORY

A monk, having committed a sin deserving of very severe punishment, escapes the consequences by politely reproaching his abbot with the very same fault.

No sooner did Filomena stop talking, having reached the end of her tale, than Dioneo, who was sitting next to her and already knew it was his turn to address them because of the order in which they were speaking, began in the following manner without awaiting further instructions from the queen:

Sweet ladies, if I have properly understood your unanimous intention, we are here in order to bring pleasure to each other with our storytelling. I therefore contend that each must be allowed (as our queen agreed just now that we might) to tell whatever story we think most likely to amuse. So having heard how Abraham's soul was saved through the good advice of Jehannot de Chevigny, and how Melchizedek employed his wisdom in defending his riches from the wily manoeuvres of Saladin, I intend, without fear of your disapproval, to give you a brief account of the clever way in which a monk saved his body from very severe punishment.

In Lunigiana, which is not all that far from where we are now, there is a monastery that once had a greater supply of monks and of saintliness than it nowadays has, and in it there was a young monk whose freshness and vitality neither fasts nor vigils could impair. One day, about noon, when all the other monks were asleep, he chanced to be taking a solitary stroll round the walls of the monastery, which lay in a very lonely spot, when his eyes came to rest on a strikingly beautiful girl, perhaps some local farmhand's daughter, who was going about the fields collecting wild herbs. No sooner did he see her, than he was fiercely assailed by carnal desire.

He went up to her and engaged her in conversation, passing from subject to subject till he came to an understanding with her and took her back to his cell, making sure that no one was watching. But being carried away by the vigour of his passion, he threw all caution to the winds, and whilst he was cavorting with the girl, the Abbot, who happened to have risen from his siesta and was quietly walking past the monk's cell, heard the racket that the pair were creating. So that he might recognize the voices, he crept softly up to the door of the cell, stood there listening, and came to the definite conclusion that one of the voices was a woman's. His first impulse was to order the door to be opened, but he then decided to deal with the matter differently and returned to his room, where he waited for the monk to come out.

The monk, albeit he had taken the greatest of pleasure and delight in the young woman's company, suspected nonetheless that something was amiss, for it had seemed to him that he could hear the shuffling of feet in the corridor. He had therefore applied his eye to a tiny aperture, from which he had obtained an excellent view of the Abbot, standing there listening. He was thus well aware that the Abbot had had the opportunity of knowing that the girl was in his cell, and consequently he was very worried, for he knew he would be punished severely on account of all this. But without betraying his anxiety to the girl, he quickly ran his mind over various expedients to see if he could chance upon one that might do him some good, and hit upon a novel piece of mischief, which would have precisely the effect he was seeking. Pretending to the girl that he thought they had spent sufficient time together, he said to her:

'I am just going to find a way of letting you out of here without your being seen. So stay here and make no sound till I return.'

He then emerged from his cell and, having locked the door, went straight to the Abbot's room and handed him his key, this being the usual practice whenever any monk was going out. Then without so much as batting an eyelid, he said:

'Sir, this morning I was not able to bring in all the faggots that were cut for me, so with your permission I should like to go to the wood and have them brought in.'

The Abbot, thinking that the monk knew nothing of the fact that he had seen him, was glad of the chance to find out more about the offence he had committed, and he gladly accepted the key and gave him his ready permission. After watching the monk go away, he began to consider whether it would be better for him to open the man's cell in the presence of all the monks and let them bear witness to his disgrace, so that they would have no reason to complain against him later when he punished the fellow, or first to hear the girl's account of the affair. On reflecting that she might be a respectable woman or the daughter of some man of influence, not wishing to make the mistake of putting such a lady to shame by displaying her to all of the monks, he decided he would first go and see who she was and then make up his mind. So he quietly made his way to the cell, opened the door, entered, and locked the door behind him.

When she saw the Abbot coming in, the girl was terrified out of her wits, and began to weep for shame. Master Abbot, having looked her up and down, saw that she was a nice, comely wench, and despite his years he was promptly filled with fleshly cravings, no less intense than those his young monk had experienced. And he began to say to himself: 'Well, well! Why not enjoy myself a little, when I have the opportunity? After all, I can have my fill of sorrow and afflictions whenever I like. This is a fine-looking wench, and not a living soul knows that she is here. If I can persuade her to play my game, I see no reason why I shouldn't do it. Who is there to know? No one will ever find out, and a sin that's hidden is half forgiven. I may never get another chance as good as this. It's always a good idea, in my opinion, to accept any gift that the Good Lord places in our path.' Having said all this to himself, and completely reversed his original intention in going there, he went up to the girl and gently began to console her and tell her not to cry. One subject led to another, and eventually he came round to explaining what he had in mind.

The girl, who was not exactly made of iron or of flint, fell in very readily with the Abbot's wishes. He took her in his arms and kissed her a few times, then lowered himself on to the monk's little bed. But out of regard, perhaps, for the weight of his reverend person and the tender age of the girl, and not wishing to do her any injury, he settled down beneath her instead of lying on top, and in this way he sported with her at considerable length.

Meanwhile the monk, who had only pretended to go to the wood, had hidden himself in the corridor, and when he saw the Abbot entering the cell by himself, he felt quite reassured, being convinced that everything was proceeding according to plan. And when he perceived that the Abbot had locked himself in, he was left in no doubt whatsoever. Emerging from his hiding-place, he quietly crept up to a chink in the wall, through which he saw and heard all that the Abbot was doing and saying.

The Abbot, deciding he had spent enough time with the girl, locked her in the cell and returned to his room. And after a while, hearing the monk and supposing he had just returned from the wood, he determined to give him a jolly good scolding and have him locked up, so that he alone would possess the prize they had captured. So he sent for the monk, put on a stern face, reprimanded him most severely, and ordered him to be locked in the punishment-cell.

Without hesitating for a moment, the monk replied:

'Sir, I have not yet been long enough in the Order of Saint Benedict to have had a chance of acquainting myself with all its special features, and you had failed until just now to show me that monks have women to support, as well as fasts and vigils. But now that you have pointed this out, I promise that if you will forgive me just this once, I will never again commit the same error. On the contrary, I shall always follow your good example.'

The Abbot, who was no fool, quickly realized that the monk had outwitted him and, moreover, seen what he had done. Being tarred with the same brush, he was loath to inflict upon the monk a punishment of which he himself was no less deserving. So he pardoned the monk and swore him to secrecy concerning what he had seen, then they slipped the girl out unobtrusively, and we can only assume that they afterwards brought her back at regular intervals.

FIFTH STORY

The Marchioness of Montferrat, with the aid of a chicken banquet and a few well-chosen words, restrains the extravagant passion of the King of France.

As they listened to Dioneo's story, the ladies at first felt some embarrassment, which showed itself in the modest blushes that appeared on all their faces. Then, glancing at one another and barely managing to restrain their laughter, they giggled as they listened. When it came to an end, however, they gently rebuked him with a few well-chosen words, in order to show that stories of that kind should not be told when ladies were present. Then the queen turned to Fiammetta, who was sitting on the grass next to him, and indicated that it was her turn to continue. Whereupon, with a cheerful smile towards the queen, she gracefully began:

Whereas men, if they are very wise, will always seek to love ladies of higher station than their own, women, if they are very discerning, will know how to guard themselves from accepting the advances of a man who is of more exalted rank. For which reason, and also because of the pleasure I feel at our having, through our stories, begun to demonstrate the power of good repartee, I have been prompted to show you, fair ladies, in the story that I have to tell, how through her words and actions a gentlewoman avoided this pitfall and guided her suitor clear of its dangers.

The Marquis of Montferrat was a man of outstanding worth, who had sailed as Gonfalonier of the Church with a Christian host on a Crusade to the Holy Land. And one day, during a conversation about his merits at the court of King Philippe Le Borgne, who was also preparing to leave France to join the Crusade, a courtier observed that there was not a wedded couple under the sun to compare with the Marquis and his lady; for just as the Marquis was a paragon of all the knightly virtues, so the lady was more beautiful and worthy of esteem than any other woman in the world.

These words left such a deep impression on the French king's mind, that without having ever seen the lady, he at once became fervently enamoured of her, and decided that under no circumstances would he embark for the Crusade at any other port but Genoa, so that, by travelling overland, he would have a plausible pretext for paying the Marchioness a visit. In this way he thought he would succeed, since the Marquis would be absent, in bringing his desires to fruition.

He lost no time in putting his deep-laid scheme into effect. Having sent all his men on ahead, he set out with a small retinue of nobles, and as they approached the territory of the Marquis, he sent word to the lady, a day in advance, that she was to expect him for breakfast on the following morning. Being an intelligent and judicious woman, she sent back a message to say that she was glad to have been singled out for this uniquely great favour, and that the King would be very welcome. She then began to wonder why such a great king should be calling upon her in her husband's absence. Nor was she wrong in the conclusion that she reached, namely, that he was being drawn thither by the fame of her beauty. Nevertheless, with her habitual nobility of spirit she made ready to entertain him; and after summoning all the few remaining gentlemen of rank, acting upon their advice she issued instructions for the necessary preparations to be made, at the same time insisting that she alone would arrange the banquet and devise its menu. Without a moment's delay, she collected together all the hens that could be found in the neighbourhood, and ordered her cooks to prepare a series of dishes, using these alone, for the royal banquet.

The King arrived on the day he had appointed, and was warmly and honourably received by the lady. On meeting her for the first time, he was greatly amazed to find that she was even more beautiful, intelligent and gentle-mannered than he had been led to expect from the words of the courtier, and he was lavish with his compliments, for he had become all the more inflamed with passion on finding that the lady exceeded his expectations. After he had rested for a while in rooms that had been richly appointed with all the furnishings appropriate to the reception of so great a king, it was time for the banquet, and the King sat with the Marchioness at one table, whilst the remaining guests were entertained at other tables according to their rank and quality.

The King, being served with many dishes one after another and with choice and precious wines, and gazing contentedly from time to time at the beautiful Marchioness, was filled with intense pleasure. But as one dish was followed by the next, he began to feel somewhat perplexed, for he could not help noticing that although the courses were different, each and every one of them consisted solely of chicken. He was well enough acquainted with that particular region to know that it should be well stocked with a variety of game, and by sending the lady advance notice of his arrival he had given her ample time to organize a hunt. But although he was greatly surprised by all this, he had no desire to give her any cause for embarrassment, except for putting in a word about her chickens. So smiling broadly, he turned towards her and said:

'Madam, is it only hens that flourish in these parts, and not a single cock?'

The Marchioness, who understood his question perfectly, saw this as exactly the kind of Heaven-sent opportunity she had hoped for in order to make clear her intentions. On hearing the King's inquiry, she turned boldly towards him and replied:

'No, my lord, but our women, whilst they may differ slightly from each other in their rank and the style of their dress, are made no differently here than they are elsewhere.'

On hearing this, the King saw clearly the reason for the banquet of chickens, and the virtue that lay concealed beneath her little homily. He realized that honeyed words would be wasted on a lady of this sort, and that force was out of the question. And thus, in the same way that he had foolishly become inflamed, so now he wisely decided that he was honour-bound to extinguish the ill-conceived fires of his passion. Fearing her replies, he teased her no further, but applied himself to his meal, by now convinced that all hope was lost. And as soon as he had finished eating, in order to compensate for his dishonourable coming by his swift departure, he thanked her for her generous hospitality and departed for Genoa, with the lady wishing him God-speed.

SIXTH STORY

*With a clever remark, an honest man exposes the wicked hypocrisy of the
religious.*

All the ladies applauded the courage of the Marchioness and the eloquent rebuff she had given to the King of France. Then in deference
to the wishes of the queen, Emilia, who was seated next to Fiammetta,
started boldly to speak:

I likewise will describe a stinging rebuke, but one which was administered by an honest layman to a grasping friar, with a gibe no less
amusing than it was laudable.

Not long ago then, dear young ladies, there was in our city a
Franciscan, an inquisitor on the look-out for filthy heretics, who
whilst trying very hard, as they all do, to preserve an appearance of
saintly and tender devotion to the Christian faith, was no less expert
at tracking down people with bulging purses than at seeking out those
whom he deemed to be lacking in faith. His diligence chanced to put
him on the trail of a certain law-abiding citizen, endowed with far
more money than commonsense, who one day, not from any lack of
faith but simply in the course of an innocent conversation with his
friends, came out with the remark that he had a wine of such a quality
that Christ himself would have drunk it.

The worthy soul had been drinking too much perhaps, or possibly
he was over-excited, but unfortunately his words were reported to the
inquisitor, who on hearing that the man had large estates and a tidy
sum of money, hastily proceeded *cum gladiis et fustibus** to draw up
serious charges against him. This, he thought, would have the effect,
not so much of lessening his victim's impiety, as of lining his own
pockets with florins, which was what in fact happened. Having issued
a summons, he asked the man whether the charges against him were
correct. The good man admitted that they were, and explained the
circumstances, whereupon this devout and venerable inquisitor of St
John Golden-Mouth said:

* 'with swords and staves' (Matthew xxvi, 47).

'So you turned Christ into a drinker, did you, and a connoisseur of choice wines, as if he were some tosspot or drunken tavern-crawler like one of yourselves? And now you eat humble-pie, and try to pass the whole thing off as something very trifling. But that is where you are mistaken. The fire is what you deserve when we come to take action against you, as indeed we must.'

The friar addressed these words to him, and a great many more, with a menacing look all over his features, as though the fellow were an Epicurean denying the immortality of the soul. In brief, he struck such terror into him, that the poor man arranged for certain go-betweens to grease the friar's palm with a goodly amount of St John Golden-Mouth's ointment (a highly effective remedy against the disease of galloping greed common among the clergy, and especially among Franciscans, who look upon money with distaste), so that the inquisitor would deal leniently with him.

The ointment he used is highly efficacious (though it is not mentioned by Galen in any of his treatises on medicine), and he applied it so liberally and effectively that the fire with which he had been threatened was graciously commuted to the wearing of a cross, which made him look as if he were about to set off on a Crusade. In order to make his badge more attractive, the friar stipulated that the cross should be yellow on a black ground. And apart from this, having pocketed the money, he kept him for several days under open arrest, ordering him by way of penance to attend mass every morning in Santa Croce and report to him every day at the hour of breakfast, after which he was free to do as he pleased for the rest of the day.

The man carried out his instructions to the letter, and one morning at mass he happened to be listening to the Gospel when he heard these words being sung: 'For every one you shall receive an hundredfold, and shall inherit everlasting life.' He committed the words firmly to memory, and at the usual hour he presented himself as instructed before the inquisitor, whom he found already at table. The inquisitor asked him whether he had listened to mass that morning, and he promptly replied that he had. Whereupon the inquisitor said:

'Do you have any doubts, or questions you wish to ask, about anything you heard during the service?'

'To be sure,' the good man replied, 'I have no doubts about any of the things I heard, indeed I firmly believe them all to be true. But one of the things I heard made me feel very sorry for you and your fellow friars, and I still feel very sorry when I think what an awful time you are all going to have in the life to come.'

'And what was it,' asked the inquisitor, 'which caused you to feel so sorry for us?'

'Sir,' the good man replied, 'it was that passage from the Gospel which says that for every one you shall receive an hundredfold.'

'That is true,' said the inquisitor. 'But why should this have perturbed you so?'

'Sir,' replied the good man, 'I will tell you. Every day since I started coming here, I have seen a crowd of poor people standing outside and being given one and sometimes two huge cauldrons of vegetable-water which, being surplus to your needs, is taken away from you and the other friars here in the convent. So if you are going to receive a hundred in the next world for every one you have given, you will have so much of the stuff that you will all drown in it.'

The other friars sitting at the inquisitor's table all burst out laughing, but the inquisitor himself, on hearing their guzzling hypocrisy exposed in this fashion, flew into a towering rage. And but for the fact that the affair had already brought him discredit, he would have laid further charges against the man for the way his amusing remark had held both him and the other lazy rogues up to ridicule. So he angrily told him to go about his business, and not to show his face there again.

SEVENTH STORY

Bergamino, with the help of a story about Primas and the Abbot of Cluny, tellingly chides Can Grande della Scala for a sudden fit of parsimony.

Emilia's story, and the vivacious manner of its telling, provoked the laughter of the whole company, including the queen, and everybody applauded the crusader's novel interpretation of the gospel. When the laughter subsided and they were all quiet again, Filostrato, whose turn it was to tell a story, began to speak as follows:

Excellent ladies, it is a fine thing to strike a sitting target. But when an archer takes sudden aim, and hits an unusual object that has suddenly appeared from nowhere, his achievement is well-nigh miraculous. It is not unduly difficult, for anyone so inclined, to discuss, criticize and admonish the clergy for their foul and corrupt way of life, which in many ways resembles a sitting target of evil. And although our honest man did well to pierce the self-esteem of the inquisitor by pointing out the hypocrisy of friars who offer in alms to the poor what they should be giving to the pigs or throwing down the drain, I feel that the hero of my story (for which I have taken my cue from the previous tale) is the more worthy of praise; for this man censured a great prince, Can Grande della Scala, for a quite unwonted and sudden fit of miserliness, by telling a charming tale in which he represented, through others, what he wanted to say about himself and Can Grande. My story runs as follows:

It is a matter of very common knowledge throughout the greater part of the world that Can Grande della Scala, upon whom Fortune smiled in so many of his deeds, was one of the most outstanding and magnificent princes that Italy has known since the Emperor Frederick the Second. He once arranged to hold a splendid and marvellous festival at Verona to which many people would be coming from all over the place, in particular court-entertainers of various kinds. But for reasons of his own, he suddenly changed his mind about it, offered token presents to those who had come, and sent them all packing. The only person to receive neither present nor *congé* was a certain Bergamino, a conversationalist of quite extraordinary wit and brilliance, who lingered on in the hope that it would eventually turn out to his advantage. But Can Grande had the fixed idea that whatever he gave to this man would be more surely wasted than if he had thrown it into the fire. He did not, however, say anything personally to Bergamino about this, nor did he have him told by others.

Several days went by, and Bergamino, receiving neither a summons to the Duke's table nor any request for his professional services, began to feel the crippling expense of staying at the inn with his servants and horses, and fell into a state of melancholy. But he waited just the same, thinking it would be unwise of him to leave. In his luggage he

had three fine rich robes, which had been given to him by other
noble lords, so that he would cut a graceful figure at the festivities.
And since the innkeeper was demanding payment, he first gave him
one of these, and then, after staying a while longer, he was compelled
to give him the second, since otherwise he would have had to leave
the inn altogether. Then he began to live off the third, having decided
to stay until he had seen how long it would last, and then go
away.

Now while he was living off this third robe, he happened one day
to be standing with a very gloomy expression on his face, in front of
the table where Can Grande was dining. More out of a desire to tease
him than to be entertained by any of his witticisms, Can Grande
looked towards him and said:

'Bergamino, what is the matter? You are looking so sad! Say
something to us.'

Without a moment's reflection, yet with all the fluency of a speech
prepared long in advance, Bergamino suddenly came out with a
story relevant to his own case, which ran as follows:

'My lord, I must begin by telling you that Primas was a very great
grammarian and had no equal as a quick and gifted versifier. These
two qualities made him so famous and respected, that even though he
was not known everywhere by sight, his name and reputation were
such that there was hardly anybody who did not know who Primas
was.

'Now it happened that once, while he was living at Paris in a state
of poverty (which was the way he mostly lived, for his abilities were
little appreciated by those who were rich enough to help him), he
heard mention of a certain abbot of Cluny, who was believed to have
a higher revenue from his estates than any other prelate in God's
Church, with the exception of the Pope. He heard people saying
wonderful and magnificent things about this abbot, for instance that
he always held open court and that nobody who called upon him was
ever refused food and drink, provided only that he asked for it
while the Abbot was at table. When Primas heard this, he decided,
being a man who enjoyed seeing gentlemen and princes, that he
would go and discover for himself how splendidly the Abbot lived,
and he enquired how far it was from Paris to his residence. On being

told it was a distance of about six miles, Primas calculated that by setting out early in the morning he could reach the place in time for breakfast.

'He ascertained which road he should take, but since nobody else appeared to be going there, he was afraid that he might be unlucky enough to lose his way, and arrive at some spot where a meal would not be so easy to come by. So in order to be on the safe side, he decided, by way of insuring himself against tota l lack of sustenance, to take along three loaves, reflecting at the same time that he would always be able to find water to drink, although this commodity was not much to his taste. And so he set out, with the loaves stuffed inside his tunic, and made such excellent progress that he arrived before breakfast at the place where the Abbot was living. Once inside, he took a good look round, and saw that a great number of tables had been set, the kitchen was a hive of activity, and various other dining arrangements had been put in hand, whereupon he thought to himself: "This man is truly as excellent as people say." He spent a little more time surveying the scene, and then, since the meal was now ready, the Abbot's steward ordered in the water for them to wash their hands, after which he seated them all at table. By a pure coincidence, the place where Primas was seated happened to be directly opposite the door of the room from which the Abbot would emerge as he came into the hall to dine.

'It was a custom of the house that neither wine nor bread nor any other food or drink was ever placed on the tables till the Abbot came and occupied his seat. So when the steward had got everybody settled, he sent word to the Abbot that the meal was ready and they were awaiting his pleasure.

'The Abbot ordered a servant to open the door of his room so that he could proceed into the hall, but as he was on his way in, he looked straight ahead, and the first man he happened to catch sight of was Primas, who was very scruffily dressed and unknown to him by sight. No sooner did the Abbot see him, than a malicious thought suddenly crossed his mind, of a sort he had never entertained before, and he said to himself: "Why should I give my hospitality to the likes of this fellow?" And turning on his heel, he ordered the door of his room to be shut, and asked his attendants whether any of them knew the identity of the uncouth fellow who was seated at table opposite the door of his room. But nobody knew who he was.

'Primas had worked up an appetite from his walk and was not in the habit of going without food, so after waiting for a while and seeing no sign of the Abbot's return, he took out one of the three loaves he had brought with him, and started to eat. Meanwhile the Abbot ordered one of his servants to go and see whether the man was still there.

' "Yes, sir," replied the servant. "What is more, he is eating a loaf of bread, which he must have brought with him."

' "Then let him eat his own food, if he has some," said the Abbot, "for he shall eat none of ours today."

'The Abbot would have preferred that Primas should go away of his own accord, for he felt it would be discourteous to order him to leave. Having eaten the first loaf, there being still no sign of the Abbot, Primas began to eat the second. This fact also was reported to the Abbot, who had sent to see whether he was still there.

'Finally, since the Abbot showed no sign of coming, Primas, having finished the second loaf, started to eat the third. This too was reported to the Abbot, who began to ponder the matter and say to himself: "Now what on earth has got into me today? Why have I suddenly become such a miser? Why should I feel so much contempt for this unknown visitor? For years I have provided food for any man who cared to eat it, without inquiring whether he was a peasant or a gentleman, poor or rich, merchant or swindler. With my own eyes, I have seen any number of rogues devouring my food, and I have never felt as I do today about this fellow. No ordinary man can have caused me to be afflicted with such meanness. This fellow I regard as a knave must be someone important, for me to have set my heart so firmly against offering him my hospitality."

'Having said this to himself, he was anxious to know who the man might be. And when he discovered it was Primas, who had come there to see if the tales of his generosity were true, the Abbot felt thoroughly ashamed, for he had long been aware of the reputation Primas enjoyed as a man of excellent worth. Being desirous of making amends, he went out of his way to do him honour. After having fed him in a manner appropriate to his renown, he saw that he was richly clothed, provided him with money and a saddle-horse, and offered him the freedom of his household. Well satisfied, Primas thanked the Abbot as heartily as he could, before returning on horseback to Paris, whence he had set out on foot.'

Can Grande, being a man of some intelligence, had no need to hear any more in order to see exactly what Bergamino was driving at. And with a broad smile, he said to him:

'Bergamino, you have given an apt demonstration of the wrongs you have suffered. You have shown us your worth, my meanness, and what it is that you want from me. To tell you the truth, I was never seized before with the meanness I have lately felt on your account. But I shall drive it away with the stock that you yourself have furnished.'

Can Grande saw that the innkeeper's account was settled, then dressed Bergamino most sumptuously in one of his own robes, provided him with money and a saddle-horse, and offered him the freedom of his household for the rest of his stay.

EIGHTH STORY

With a few prettily spoken words, Guiglielmo Borsiere punctures the avarice of Ermino de' Grimaldi.

Next to Filostrato was sitting Lauretta, who, knowing that she was expected to speak without waiting to be bidden, allowed the applause for Bergamino's cleverness to subside, then gracefully began as follows:

The previous story, dear friends, implants in me a desire to tell you how, in similar fashion and not without fruitful effects, a worthy courtier derided the covetous habits of a very rich merchant. Although the burden of my tale is similar to the last, that is no reason for you to find it less agreeable, when you consider how much good eventually came of it.

In Genoa, then, a long time ago, there lived a gentleman called Ermino de' Grimaldi, who was generally acknowledged, on account of his vast wealth and huge estates, to be by far the richest citizen in the Italy of his day. Not only was he richer than any man in Italy, he was incomparably greedier and more tight-fisted than every other grasper or miser in the whole wide world. For he would entertain on a shoestring, and in contrast to the normal habits of the Genoese (who are wont to dress in the height of fashion), he would sooner go about in rags than spend any money on his personal appearance. Nor was his attitude to food and drink any different. It was therefore not surprising that he had lost the surname of Grimaldi and was simply known to one and all as Ermino Skinflint.

Now, it so happened that whilst this fellow, by spending not a penny, was busily increasing his fortune, there arrived in Genoa a worthy courtier, Guiglielmo Borsiere by name, who was refined of manner and eloquent of tongue, altogether different from the courtiers of today. For to the eternal shame of those who nowadays lay claim, despite their corrupt and disgraceful habits, to the title and distinction of lords and gentlemen, our modern courtiers are better described as asses, brought up, not in any court, but on the dungheap of all the scum of the earth's iniquities. In former times, their function usually consisted, and all their efforts were expended, in making peace whenever disputes or conflicts arose between two nobles, negotiating treaties of marriage, friendship or alliance, restoring tired minds and amusing the courts with fine and graceful witticisms, and censuring the failings of miscreants with pungent, fatherly strictures, all of which they would do for the slenderest of rewards. Whereas nowadays they spend the whole of their time in exchanging scandal with each other, sowing discord, describing acts of lewdness and ribaldry, or worse still, practising them in the presence of gentlemen. Or else they will justly or falsely accuse one another of wicked, disgusting and disreputable conduct, and entice noble spirits with false endearments to do what is evil and sinful. And the man who is held in the greatest esteem, who is most highly honoured and richly rewarded by our base and wretched nobles, is the one whose speech and actions are the most reprehensible. All of which is greatly and culpably to the shame of the modern world, and proves very clearly that the present generation has been stripped of all the virtues, and left to wallow abjectly in a cesspit of vices.

But to return to what I had begun to say before my righteous anger carried me somewhat further astray than I had intended, the aforesaid Guiglielmo received a warm and ready welcome from all the best families in Genoa. And after he had spent a number of days in the city, and listened to several accounts of Ermino's greed and miserliness, he was eager to see what manner of man he was.

Ermino had already been told what an excellent fellow Guiglielmo Borsiere was, and since, for all his meanness, he still preserved a glimmer of civility, he received him very sociably, with cheerful countenance, and began to converse with him on various different topics. As they talked, he conveyed him, along with certain other Genoese who were present, to a splendid house he had recently caused to be built for his use. And having shown him all over the building, he said:

'Well now, Guiglielmo, as one who has seen and heard many things in his time, could you perhaps suggest a thing that no man has ever seen, which I could commission to be painted in the main hall of this house of mine?'

To which Guiglielmo, on hearing him talk in this unseemly fashion, replied:

'Sir, I do not think I could suggest a thing that no man has ever seen, unless it were a fit of the sneezes or something of that sort. But if you like, I can certainly suggest a thing I do not believe that you yourself have ever seen.'

'Ah,' said Ermino, who was not expecting the answer he was about to be given, 'then I beg you to tell me what it is.'

Whereupon Guiglielmo promptly replied:

'Let Generosity be painted there.'

When Ermino heard this word, he was so overcome with shame, that his character was suddenly and almost totally transformed.

'Guiglielmo,' he said, 'I shall have it painted there in such a way that neither you nor anyone else will ever again have cause to tell me that I have not seen and known it.'

Guiglielmo's remark had such a potent effect upon Ermino that from that day forth he became the most courteous and generous gentleman in the Genoa of his time, and was respected above all others, not only by his fellow-citizens, but by visitors to the city.

NINTH STORY

The King of Cyprus is transformed, on receiving a sharp rebuke from a lady of Gascony, from a weakling into a man of courage.

The queen's final word of command was reserved for Elissa, who, without pausing to hear it, began all merrily as follows:

It has frequently come about, young ladies, that a single word, uttered more often by chance than with studied intent, has sufficed to cure a person of something against which various strictures and any number of punishments have proved ineffectual. This fact is very well brought out in the story told by Lauretta, and I too propose to show it to you in another tale, which shall be very brief. For good stories may always come in useful, and you should lend them an attentive ear, no matter who does the telling.

I say, then, that during the reign of the first king of Cyprus, after the conquest of the Holy Land by Godfrey of Bouillon, it happened that a gentlewoman of Gascony made a pilgrimage to the Sepulchre, and having arrived in Cyprus on her return journey, she was brutally assaulted by a pack of ruffians. Her sorrow at this deed was inconsolable, and she resolved to go and lay a complaint before the King. But she was told that she would be wasting her time, for the King was of such a weak and craven disposition, that not only would he allow others' wrongs to go unpunished by the law, but like a despicable coward he would suffer all manner of insults offered to his own royal person. So much so, indeed, that whenever anybody had an axe to grind, he would relieve his feelings by shaming or insulting the King.

On hearing this, the woman lost all hope of being revenged, but she decided, as some small compensation for her woes, to taunt this king with his faint-heartedness. So she presented herself in tears before him, and said:

'My lord, I do not come before you in the expectation of any redress for the wrong inflicted upon me. But by way of reparation for my injury, I beg you to instruct me how you manage to endure the wrongs which, as I am led to understand, are inflicted upon you, so that I might learn from you to bear my own with patience. God knows that, if I could, I would willingly make you a present of it, since you find these things so easy to support.'

The King, who until that moment had been so slow and passive, reacted as though he had been roused from sleep. Beginning with the injury done to this lady, which he avenged most harshly, he thenceforth became the implacable scourge of all those who did anything to impugn the honour of his crown.

TENTH STORY

Master Alberto of Bologna neatly turns the tables on a lady who was intent upon making him blush for being in love with her.

Once Elissa was silent, only the tale of the queen remained to be told, and she began with womanly grace to address them as follows:

Just as the sky, worthy young ladies, is bejewelled with stars on cloudless nights, and the verdant fields are embellished with flowers in the spring, so good manners and pleasant converse are enriched by shafts of wit. These, being brief, are much better suited to women than to men, as it is more unseemly for a woman to speak at inordinate length, when this can be avoided, than it is for a man. Yet nowadays, to the universal shame of ourselves and all living women, few or none of the women who are left can recognize a shaft of wit when they hear one, or reply to it even if they recognize it. For this special skill, which once resided in a woman's very soul, has been replaced in our modern women by the adornment of the body. She who sees herself tricked out in the most elaborate finery, with the largest number of gaudy stripes and speckles, believes that she should be much more highly respected and more greatly honoured than other women, forgetting that if someone were to dress an ass in the same clothes or simply load them on its back, it could still carry a great deal more than she could, nor would this be any reason for paying it greater honour than you would normally accord to an ass.

I am ashamed to say it, since in condemning others I condemn myself: but these over-dressed, heavily made-up, excessively ornamented females either stand around like marble statues in an attitude of dumb indifference, or else, on being asked a question, they give such stupid replies that they would have been far better advised to remain silent. And they delude themselves into thinking that their inability to converse in the company of gentlemen and ladies proceeds from their purity of mind. They give the name of honesty to their dull-wittedness, as though the only honest women are those who speak to no one except their maids, their washerwomen, or their pastrycooks. Whereas if, as they fondly imagine, this had been Nature's intention, she would have devised some other means for restricting their prattle.

In this as in other things one must, it is true, take account of the time and the place and the person with whom one is speaking. For it sometimes happens that men or women, thinking to make a person blush through uttering some little pleasantry, and having under-estimated the other person's powers, find the blush intended for their opponent recoiling upon themselves. Wherefore, in order that you may learn to be on your guard, and also in order that people should not associate you with the proverb commonly heard on everyone's lips, namely that women are always worsted in any argument, I desire that the tale which it falls to me to relate, and which completes our storytelling for today, should be one which will make you conversant with these matters. Thus you will be able to show that you are different from other women, not only for the noble qualities of your minds, but also for the excellence of your manners.

Not many years ago, there lived in Bologna a brilliant physician of almost universal renown, and perhaps he is alive to this day, whose name was Master Alberto. Although he was an old man approaching seventy, and the natural warmth had almost entirely departed from his body, his heart was so noble that he was not averse to welcoming the flames of love. One day, whilst attending a feast, he had seen a strikingly beautiful woman, a widow whose name, according to some accounts, was Malgherida de' Ghisolieri. He was mightily attracted by the lady, and, no differently than if he had been in the prime of his youth, he felt those flames so keenly in his mature old breast, that he never seemed able to sleep at night, unless in the course of the day he had seen the fair lady's fine and delectable features. Hence he began to pass regularly up and down in front of the lady's house, sometimes on foot and sometimes on horseback, depending on his mood. And accordingly both she and several other ladies quickly divined his motive, and often jested with one another to see a man of such great age and wisdom caught in the toils of love. For the good ladies seemed to suppose that the delightful sensations of love could take root and thrive in no other place than the frivolous hearts of the young.

Master Alberto continued to pass up and down, and one Sunday, whilst the lady happened to be seated outside her front-door with a number of other ladies, they caught sight of him in the distance, coming in their direction. Whereupon they all resolved, with the lady's agreement, to receive him and do him honour, and then make fun of him for this great passion of his. And that was precisely what they did. For they all stood up and invited him to accompany them into a cool walled garden, where they plied him with excellent wines and sweetmeats, and eventually they asked him, charmingly and with good grace, how it came about that he had fallen in love with this fair lady, when he was well aware that she was being courted by many a handsome, well-bred and sprightly young admirer. On hearing himself chided so politely, the doctor replied, smiling broadly:

'My lady, the fact that I am enamoured should not excite the wonder of anyone who is wise, and especially not your own, because you are worthy of my love. For albeit old men are naturally deficient in the powers required for lovemaking, they do not necessarily lack a ready will, or a just appreciation of what should be loved. On the contrary, in this respect their longer experience gives them an advantage over the young. The hope which sustains an old man like myself in loving one who is loved, as you are, by many young men, is founded on what I have often observed in places where I have seen ladies eating lupins and leeks whilst taking a meal out of doors. For although no part of the leek is good, yet the part which is less objectionable and more pleasing to the palate is the root, which you ladies are generally drawn by some aberration of the appetite to hold in the hand while you eat the leaves, which are not only worthless, but have an unpleasant taste. How am I to know, my lady, whether you are not equally eccentric in choosing your lovers? For if this were so, I should be the one you would choose, and the others would be cast aside.'

The gentlewoman, who along with the others was feeling somewhat abashed, replied:

'Master Alberto, you have given us a charming and very sound reproof for our presumptuousness. Your love is nonetheless precious to me, since it proceeds from so patently wise and excellent a man. And therefore, saving my honour, you are free to ask of me what you will, and regard it as yours.'

The doctor stood up with his companions, thanked the lady, took his leave of her amid much laughter and merriment, and departed.

Thus the lady, thinking she would score a victory, underestimated the object of her raillery and was herself defeated. And if you ladies are wise, you will guard against following her example.

* * *

Already the sun was dipping towards the west, and the heat of the day had largely abated, when the stories told by the seven young ladies and the three young men were found to be at an end. Accordingly their queen addressed them, in gracious tones, as follows:

'For the present day, dear friends, my reign is complete except for giving you another queen, who shall decide for herself how her time and ours should be spent in seemly pleasures on the morrow. And albeit some little time still appears to be left until nightfall, I believe this to be the most suitable hour at which to begin all the days that ensue, since preparations can thus be made for whatever the new queen considers appropriate with regard to the following day. For we are unlikely to make proper provision for the future unless some thought is devoted beforehand to the matter. And therefore, with due reverence to the One who gives life to all things, and with an eye to our common good, I decree that on this coming day the queen who will govern our realm shall be Filomena, a young lady of excellent judgement.'

Having spoken these words, she rose to her feet and removed her laurel garland, which she reverently placed upon Filomena; after which, first she herself, then all the other maidens, and the young men too, hailed Filomena as their queen and pledged themselves with good grace to her sovereignty.

Filomena blushed a little for modesty on finding that she had been crowned as their queen. But recalling the words so recently uttered by Pampinea, and not wishing to appear obtuse, she plucked up courage, and first of all she confirmed the appointments made by Pampinea, and gave instructions as to what should be done for the following morning, as well as for supper that evening, due account being taken of the place in which they were staying. Then she began to address the company as follows:

'Dearest companions, albeit Pampinea, more out of kindness of heart than for any merit of my own, has made me your queen, I do not intend, in shaping the manner in which we should comport ourselves, merely to follow my personal judgement, but rather to blend my judgement with yours. In order that you may know what I have in mind, and thus be at liberty to suggest additions or curtailments to my programme, I propose to expound it to you briefly. Unless I am mistaken, I would say that the formalities observed today by Pampinea were both laudable and pleasing. And so, until such time as we should find them wearisome, whether through constant repetition or for some other reason, I consider they ought to remain unaltered.

'Having thus confirmed the procedure for the activities upon which we have now embarked, we can rise from this place, and go off in search of our amusement. And when the sun is about to set, we shall sup out of doors, and then we shall have a few songs and other entertainments, after which it will be time to go to bed. Tomorrow morning we shall rise early, whilst it is yet cool, and once more we shall go off somewhere and engage in whatever pastime each of us may prefer. In due course we shall return, as we did today, in order to breakfast together. We shall then dance for a while, and when we have risen from our siesta, we shall return and resume our storytelling, from which I consider that a great deal of pleasure and of profit is derived.

'I do however wish to initiate a practice which Pampinea, because she was elected late as our queen, was unable to introduce: namely, to restrict the matter of our storytelling within some fixed limit which will be defined for you in advance, so that each of us will have time to prepare a good story on the subject prescribed.

'Ever since the world began, men have been subject to various tricks of Fortune, and it will ever be thus until the end. Let each of us, then, if you have no objection, make it our purpose to take as our theme *those who after suffering a series of misfortunes are brought to a state of unexpected happiness.*'

This rule was commended by all the company, gentlemen and ladies alike, and they agreed to be bound by it. But Dioneo said, when the rest had finished talking:

'My lady, like all the others, I too say that the rule you have given us is highly attractive and laudable. But I would ask you to grant me a special privilege, which I wish to have conferred upon me for as long as our company shall last, namely, that whenever I feel so inclined, I may be exempted from this law obliging us to conform to the subject agreed, and tell whatever story I please. But so that none shall think I desire this favour because I have but a poor supply of stories, I will say at once that I am willing always to be the last person to speak.'

The queen, knowing what a jovial and entertaining fellow he was, and clearly perceiving that he was only asking this favour so that, if the company should grow weary of hearing people talk, he could enliven the proceedings with some story that would move them to laughter, cheerfully granted his request, having first obtained the consent of the others. She then stood up, and they all sauntered off towards a stream of crystal-clear water, which descended the side of a hill and flowed through the shade of a thickly wooded valley, its banks lined with smooth round stones and verdant grasses. On reaching the stream, they stepped barefoot and with naked arms into the water and began to engage in various games with each other. But when it was nearly time for supper, they made their way back to the house, and there they supped merrily together.

After supper, instruments were sent for, and the queen decreed that a dance should begin, which Lauretta was to lead whilst Emilia was to sing a song, accompanied on the lute by Dioneo. No sooner did she hear the queen's command than Lauretta promptly began to dance,

and she was joined by the others, whilst Emilia sang the following
song in amorous tones:

> 'In mine own beauty take I such delight
>   That to no other love could I
>   My fond affections plight.
>
> 'Since in my looking-glass each hour I spy
>   Beauty enough to satisfy the mind,
>   Why seek out past delights, or new ones try
>   When all content within my glass I find?
>   What other sight so pleasing to mine eyes
>   Is there that I might see
>   Which further I could prize?
>
> 'My sweet reflection never fades away;
>   My consolation ever is
>   To see it every day.
>   It lies beyond the tongue's expressing
>   To celebrate a joy so fine;
>   None understands this bliss who has not burned
>   With a delight like mine.
>
> 'The longer I reflect upon those same
>   Eyes that stare from mine own face back to me,
>   The fiercer burns the flame.
>   I yield it all my heart, it renders back
>   All that I gave; I taste the bliss
>   It promised me; and hope yet more to have.
>   Ah, who has loved like this!'

Albeit the words of this little song caused not a few to ponder its
meaning, they all joined cheerfully in the choruses. When it was over,
they danced and sang some other short pieces, and then, as the night
was short and much of it already spent, the queen was pleased to
bring the first day to an end. Having called for torches to be lit, she
ordered her companions to retire to rest till the following morning,
and this command, returning to their several rooms, they duly
obeyed.

Here ends the First Day of the Decameron

SECOND DAY

Here begins the Second Day, wherein, under the rule of Filomena, the discussion turns upon those who after suffering a series of misfortunes are brought to a state of unexpected happiness.

The sun, having already ushered in the new day, was casting its light into every corner, and the birds singing gaily among the green boughs were announcing its presence to the ear, when the seven ladies and the three young men rose with one accord from their slumbers. Entering the gardens, they went from one part to another, and amused themselves for a long time by wandering unhurriedly over the dew-flecked lawns and weaving pretty garlands of flowers. And as they had done on the previous day, so they did on this. Having breakfasted in the open air, they danced a little and then retired to rest. Rising in the afternoon at about the hour of nones, as their queen had requested, they came to the little green meadow, where they seated themselves in a circle around her. She, looking most shapely and attractive, sat there with her laurel crown on her head, gazing in turn at each of her companions, and eventually she requested Neifile to open the day's proceedings by telling the first story. Whereupon, without waiting for further encouragement, Neifile cheerfully began in the following manner:

FIRST STORY

Martellino, having pretended to be paralysed, gives the impression that he has been cured by being placed on the body of Saint Arrigo. When his deception is discovered, he is beaten, arrested, and very nearly hanged: but in the end he saves his skin.

It has often happened, dearest ladies, that a man who has attempted to hold people up to ridicule, especially in matters worthy of reverence, has merely found himself humiliated, sometimes suffering injury into the bargain. Hence, in deference to the queen's wishes, and by way of introduction to our theme, I propose in this story of mine to tell you what happened to a fellow-citizen of ours who, after running into serious trouble, escaped far more lightly than he had anticipated.

Not long ago there lived at Treviso a German, whose name was Arrigo. He was just a poor fellow who carried people's heavy goods for hire, yet everyone regarded him as a man of honest and very saintly ways. Whether it is true or not I cannot say, but the Trevisans claim that when he died, all the bells of the cathedral in Treviso began to ring of their own accord. This was taken as a miracle, and everyone said that Arrigo must be a Saint. The whole of the populace therefore converged on the house in which his corpse was lying, and from there they conveyed it to the cathedral, treating it as though it were indeed the body of a Saint. People who were lame or blind or paralysed were taken to the church, along with others suffering from any kind of illness or infirmity, in the belief that they would all be cured by contact with Arrigo's body.

In the middle of all this turmoil, with people rushing hither and thither, three fellow-citizens of ours, whose names were Stecchi, Martellino, and Marchese, happened to arrive in Treviso. These three used to do the rounds of the various courts, where they would entertain their audiences by putting on disguises and making all manner of gestures, by means of which they could impersonate anyone they pleased. They had never been to Treviso before, and were surprised to find so much commotion. But when they heard the reason, they immediately wanted to go and see for themselves. After calling at an inn, where they left their belongings, Marchese said:

'We ought to go and inspect this Saint. But I can't see how we are to reach him, because from what I have heard, the square is swarming with Germans, to say nothing of the armed men stationed there by the ruler to prevent disturbances. And in any case, the church itself is said to be crammed with so many people, that it can hardly take another living soul.'

'Don't be put off by a little thing like that,' said Martellino, who was eager to see what was going on. 'I shall certainly find a way of reaching the Saint's body.'

'How?' said Marchese.

'Like this,' Martellino replied. 'I'll disguise myself as a paralytic, and pretend I can't walk. Then with you propping me up on one side and Stecchi on the other, you will both go along giving the impression that you're taking me to be healed by the Saint. When they see us coming, everyone will step aside and let us through.'

Marchese and Stecchi thought this a splendid idea, so all three of them promptly left the inn and went to a lonely spot, where Martellino contorted not only his hands, fingers, arms and legs, but also his mouth, his eyes and the whole of his face, becoming such a horrifying spectacle that no one would have taken him for anything other than a genuine case of hopeless and total bodily paralysis. In this state he was taken up by Marchese and Stecchi, and they headed for the church, with pity written all over their faces, humbly beseeching all those blocking their path to make way, for the love of God. They persuaded people to move without any trouble, and in brief, to the accompaniment of almost continuous cries of 'Make way! Make way!', and with all eyes turned in their direction, they arrived at the place where the body of Saint Arrigo was lying. There were some gentlemen standing round the body, and they quickly took hold of Martellino and laid him across it, so that it might help him regain the use of his limbs.

Martellino lay there motionless for a while, with all eyes fixed upon him to see what would happen. Then, like the skilled performer that he was, he began to go through the motions of straightening out one of his fingers, then a hand, then an arm, and so on until he had unwound himself completely. When the people saw this, they applauded Saint Arrigo so rowdily that a roll of thunder would have passed unnoticed.

Now it happened that there was a Florentine standing nearby, and although he was very well acquainted with Martellino, he had failed to recognize him when he was first led in, because of the grotesqueness of his appearance. But when he saw him standing up straight, he knew at once who it was, and he burst out laughing and said:

'God damn the fellow! Who would have thought, to see him arriving, that he was not really paralysed at all!'

'What?' exclaimed a number of Trevisans, who had overheard the Florentine's words. 'Do you mean to say he was not paralysed?'

'Heaven forbid!' the Florentine replied. 'He has always stood as straight as the rest of us. But as you could see just now, he has this extraordinary knack of disguising himself in any manner he chooses.'

There was no need to say any more, for on hearing this they forced their way to the front, and began to shout:

'Take hold of that blaspheming swindler! He comes here pretending to be a cripple, poking fun at our Saint and making fools of us when he wasn't really crippled at all!'

And so saying, they seized him and dragged him away; then they took him by the hair, tore every stitch of clothing from his back, and started to punch and to kick him. In fact, everybody within sight was bearing down upon him, or so it seemed to Martellino.

'Mercy, for the love of God!' he cried, defending himself as best he could. But it was of no use, for more and more people were piling on top of him every minute.

When Marchese and Stecchi saw what was happening, they began to have serious misgivings. Fearing for their own safety, they dared not go to Martellino's assistance, but on the contrary they yelled 'Kill him!' as loudly as anybody else, at the same time trying to devise some way of rescuing him from the hands of the mob. And he would certainly have been killed but for a quick piece of thinking on the part of Marchese, who made his way as swiftly as possible to the captain in charge of the watch, drawn up in strength outside the church, and said to him:

'For God's sake, come quickly! There's a villain over here who has cut my purse, and robbed me of a hundred gold florins at the very least. Arrest him! Please don't let him run off with my money!'

On hearing this, a dozen or more of the officers rushed over to the place where poor Martellino was having his brains beaten out, and after forcing their way through the crowd with enormous difficulty, they removed him all bruised and battered from their clutches, and hauled him off to the magistrate's palace.

A number of people followed him all the way, still angry with him for hoodwinking them, and when they heard he had been arrested as a cutpurse, they too began to claim that he had stolen their purses, thinking this as fair a way as any of making life unpleasant for him. The magistrate, who was of a harsh disposition, no sooner heard these accusations than he took him aside and began to interrogate him on the matter. But Martellino gave him facetious answers, as though quite unconcerned at his arrest. This upset the judge, who had him fastened to the strappado, and ordered him to be given a series of good hard blows, with the intention of extracting a confession from him before having him hanged. When they let him down, and the judge asked him whether the accusations brought against him were true, he replied, since a straight denial would have been useless:

'Sir, I am ready to confess the truth. But make each of my accusers say when and where I cut his purse, and I will tell you whether or not I did it.'

'A good idea!' said the judge, and he ordered several of them to be summoned. One of them claimed that his purse had been stolen a week before, another said six days, another four, and some of them said they had been robbed that very day. Whereupon Martellino retorted:

'Sir, they are all a lot of bare-faced liars, and I can prove it to you, because I only arrived in this city for the first time a couple of hours ago. I wish to God I had never set foot in it at all! As soon as I arrived, I went to have a look at the body of this Saint, where I had the ill-luck to be given a good drubbing, as you can see for yourself. Ask the customs officer at the city gates, consult his register, ask my landlord, and they will all bear out what I have told you. And if you find I am telling the truth, I beg you to listen no further to these vicious perjurers. Please don't let me be tortured and put to death.'

Meanwhile, with the matter proceeding along these lines, word had reached Marchese and Stecchi that the judge was giving him a rough handling and had already put him on the strappado. 'We have made a fine mess of things,' they said, shaking with fright. 'We have taken him out of the frying-pan, and dropped him straight in the fire.' Being determined to leave no stone unturned, they tracked down their landlord, and explained to him what had happened. The landlord, who was highly amused at their tale, took them to see a man called

Sandro Agolanti, a Florentine living in Treviso who had considerable influence with the ruler of the city. Having acquainted him with all the facts, the landlord joined the other two in pleading with him to intervene on Martellino's behalf.

Sandro laughed heartily, then he went off to see the prince, and persuaded him to send for Martellino. The men who were sent to fetch him found him still standing in front of the judge, wearing nothing but a shirt, and trembling all over with fear and dismay because the judge would not listen to anything that was said in his defence. Indeed, since he happened to have some sort of grudge against Florentines, he was quite determined to have him hanged, and stubbornly refused to hand him over until he was compelled to do so. When Martellino came before the ruler, he gave him a full account of what had happened, and begged him as a supreme favour to let him go about his business; for until he was safely back in Florence, he would always feel that he had a noose round his neck. The ruler went into fits of laughter to hear of such remarkable goings on and ordered each of them to be provided with a new suit of clothes. Thus all three emerged from this dreadful ordeal better than they ever expected, and returned home safe and sound.

SECOND STORY

Rinaldo d'Asti is robbed, turns up at Castel Guiglielmo, and is provided with hospitality by a widow. Then, having recovered his belongings, he returns home safe and sound.

Neifile's account of Martellino's adventures brought gales of laughter from the ladies and the young men, especially Filostrato, who, being seated next to Neifile, was bidden by the queen to tell the next story. He began straightway, as follows:

Fair ladies, the story that takes my fancy is one that contains a judicious mixture of piety, calamity and love. Possibly it has no more to recommend it than its usefulness, but it will be especially helpful to people wandering through the uncertain territories of Love, where those who have not made a regular habit of saying St Julian's paternoster, even though they have good beds, may find themselves uncomfortably lodged.

During the reign of the Marquis Azzo of Ferrara, a merchant whose name was Rinaldo d'Asti was returning home after dispatching certain business in Bologna. He had already passed through Ferrara, and was riding towards Verona, when he fell in with three men who, though they had the appearance of merchants, were in fact brigands of a particularly desperate and disreputable sort. With these he struck up conversation, and rashly agreed to ride along in their company.

On seeing that he was a merchant, who was probably carrying a certain amount of money with him, these men resolved to rob him at the earliest opportunity. But in order not to arouse his suspicions, they assumed an air of simplicity and respectability, restricting their conversation to the subject of loyalty and other polite topics, and went out of their way to appear humble and obliging towards him. He consequently thought himself very fortunate to have met them, for he was travelling alone except for a single servant on horseback. As they went along, with the conversation passing as usual from one thing to another, they got on to the subject of the prayers that people address to God, and one of the bandits turned to Rinaldo and said:

'What about you, sir? What prayer do you generally say when you are travelling?'

'To tell the truth,' Rinaldo replied, 'in matters of this kind I am rather simple and down-to-earth. I am one of the old-fashioned sort who likes to call a spade a spade, and I don't know many prayers. All the same, when I am travelling it is my custom never to leave the inn of a morning without reciting an Our Father and a Hail Mary for the souls of St Julian's father and mother, after which I pray to God and the Saint to give me a good lodging for the night to come. On many a day, in the course of my travels, I have met with great dangers, only to survive them all and find myself at nightfall in a safe place and a comfortable lodging. Now I firmly believe this favour to have been obtained for me from God by St Julian, in whose honour I recite my prayer; and if on any morning I neglected to say it, I would feel I could do nothing right the whole day, and would come to some harm before the evening.'

'Did you say it this morning?' said the man who had asked him the question.

'I did indeed,' replied Rinaldo.

The man, who by this time knew what was going to happen, said to himself: 'A fat lot of good it will do you, for I reckon you are going to have a poor night's lodging if all goes according to plan.' Then he turned to Rinaldo and said:

'I too have travelled a great deal, and although I have heard many people speak highly of this Saint, I have never prayed to him myself. Nevertheless, I have always managed to find good quarters. Perhaps we shall see this evening which of us is the better lodged: you, who have said the prayer, or I, who have not said it. Mind you, I *do* use another one instead, either the *Dirupisti* or the *Intemerata* or the *De Profundis*, all of which are extremely effective, or so my old grandmother used to tell me.'

And so they went along, talking of this and that, with the three men biding their time and waiting for a suitable place to carry their villainous plan into effect. The day was drawing to a close when, at a concealed and deserted river-crossing on the far side of the fortress-town called Castel Guiglielmo, the three bandits took advantage of the lateness of the hour to launch their attack and rob him of everything he possessed, including his horse. Before leaving, they turned to him as he stood there in nothing but his shirt, and called out:

'Now see whether the prayer you said to St Julian will give you as good a night's lodging as our own saint will provide for us.' They then crossed the river, and rode off.

Rinaldo's wretch of a servant did nothing to assist his master on seeing him attacked, but turned his horse round and galloped all the way to Castel Guiglielmo without stopping. It was already dark by the time he entered the town, so he conveniently forgot the whole business, and put up for the night at an inn.

Rinaldo, bare-footed and wearing only a shirt, was at his wits' end, for the weather was very cold, it was snowing hard the whole time, and it was getting darker every minute. Shivering all over, his teeth chattering, he began to look round for a sheltered spot where he could spend the night without freezing to death. But since there had been a war in the countryside a short time previously and everything had been burnt to the ground, there was no shelter to be seen anywhere, and so he set off for Castel Guiglielmo, walking at a brisk pace on account of the cold. He had no idea whether his servant had fled to the fortress or to some other town, but he thought that, once inside the walls, God would surely send him some sort of relief.

He still had over a mile to go when night came on with a vengeance, and when he finally arrived it was so late that the gates were locked, the drawbridges were up, and he was unable to gain admittance. Feeling depressed and miserable, he looked round with tears in his eyes to see whether there was a place where he would at least find some protection from the snow, and he happened to catch sight of a house that jutted out appreciably from the top of the castle walls, so he decided to go and take refuge beneath it till daybreak. When he reached the spot, he discovered there was a postern underneath the overhang, and although the door was locked, at its base he heaped a quantity of straw which was lying nearby, and settled down upon it. He was thoroughly fed up, and complained at regular intervals to St Julian, saying that this was no way to treat one of his faithful devotees. St Julian had not lost sight of him, however, and before very long he was to see that Rinaldo was comfortably settled.

In the castle there was a widow, lovelier of body than any other woman in the world, with whom the Marquis Azzo was madly in love. He had set her up there as his mistress, and she was living in the very house beneath which Rinaldo had taken refuge. As it happened, the Marquis had arrived at the castle on that very day with the intention of spending the night with her, and had made secret arrangements to have a sumptuous supper prepared, and to take a bath in the lady's house beforehand. Everything was ready, and she was only waiting for the Marquis to turn up, when a servant happened to arrive at the gate, bringing the Marquis a message requiring him to leave immediately. So he sent word to the lady that he would not be coming, then hastily mounted his horse and rode away. The lady, feeling rather disconsolate and not knowing what to do with herself, decided she would have the bath which had been prepared for the Marquis, after which she would sup and go to bed. And so into the bath she went.

As she lay there in the bath, which was near the postern on the other side of which our unfortunate hero had taken shelter, she could hear the wails and moans being uttered by Rinaldo, who sounded from the way his teeth were chattering as if he had been turned into a stork. She therefore summoned her maid, and said:

'Go upstairs, look over the wall, and see who it is on the other side of this door. Find out who he is and what he is doing there.'

The maid went up, and by the light of the stars she saw him sitting there just as we have described him, bare-footed and wearing only his shirt, and quivering all over like a jelly. She asked him who he was, and Rinaldo, who was shaking so much that he could hardly articulate, told her his name and explained as briefly as possible how and why he came to be there. He then implored her, in an agonized voice, to do whatever she could to prevent his being left there all night slowly freezing to death.

The maid, feeling very sorry for him, returned to her mistress and told her the whole story. The lady too was filled with pity, and, remembering that she had a key for that particular door, which the Marquis occasionally used for his clandestine visits, she said to the maid:

'Go and let him in, but do it quietly. We have this supper here, and no one to eat it. And we can easily put him up, for there's plenty of room.'

The maid warmly commended her mistress's charity, then she went and opened the door and let him in. Perceiving that he was almost frozen stiff, the lady of the house said to him:

'Quickly, good sir, step into that bath whilst it is still warm.'

He willingly obeyed, without waiting to be bidden twice. His whole body was refreshed by its warmth, and he felt as if he were returning from death to life. The lady had him supplied with clothes that had once belonged to her husband, who had died quite recently, and when he put them on they fitted him to perfection. As he awaited further instructions from the lady, he fell to thanking God and St Julian for rescuing him from the cruel night he had been expecting, and leading him to what appeared a good lodging.

Meanwhile the lady had taken a brief rest, having first ordered a huge fire to be lit in one of the rooms, to which she presently came, asking what had become of the gentleman.

'He's dressed, ma'am,' replied the maid, 'and he's ever so handsome, and seems a very decent and respectable person.'

'Then go and call him,' said the woman, 'and tell him to come here by the fire and have some supper, for I know he has not had anything to eat.'

On entering the room, Rinaldo, judging from her appearance that she was a lady of quality, greeted her with due reverence and thanked her with all the eloquence at his command for the kindness she had done him. When she saw him and heard him speak, the lady concluded that her maid had been right, and she welcomed him cordially, installed him in a comfortable chair beside her own in front of the fire, and asked him what had happened and how he came to be there, whereupon Rinaldo told her the whole story in detail.

The lady had already heard bits of the story after the arrival of Rinaldo's servant at the castle, and so she fully believed everything he told her. She in turn told him what she knew about his servant, adding that it would be easy enough to find him next morning. But by now the table was laid for supper, and Rinaldo, after washing his hands with the lady, accepted her invitation to sit down and eat at her side.

He was a fine, tall, handsome fellow in the prime of manhood, with impeccably good manners, and the lady cast many an appreciative glance in his direction. As she had been expecting to sleep with the Marquis, her carnal instincts were already aroused, and after supper she got up from the table and consulted with her maid to find out whether she thought it a good idea, since the Marquis had let her down, to make use of this unexpected gift of Fortune. The maid, knowing what her mistress had in mind, encouraged her for all she was worth, with the result that the lady returned to Rinaldo, whom she had left standing alone by the fire, and began to ogle him, saying:

'Come, Rinaldo, why are you looking so unhappy? What's the good of worrying about the loss of a horse and a few clothes? Do relax and cheer up. I want you to feel completely at home here. In fact, I will go so far as to say that seeing you in those clothes, I keep thinking you are my late husband, and I've been wanting to take you in my arms and kiss you the whole evening. I would certainly have done so, but I was afraid you might take it amiss.'

On hearing these words and perceiving the gleam in the lady's eyes, Rinaldo, who was no fool, advanced towards her with open arms, saying:

'My lady, I shall always have you to thank for the fact that I am alive, and when I consider the fate from which you delivered me, it would be highly discourteous of me if I did not attempt to further your inclinations to the best of my ability. Kiss and embrace me, therefore, to your heart's content, and I shall be more than happy to return the compliment.'

There was no need for any further preliminaries. The lady, who was all aflame with amorous desire, promptly rushed into his arms. Clasping him to her bosom, she smothered him with a thousand eager kisses and received as many in return, then they both retired into her bedroom, where they lost no time in getting into bed, and before the night was over they satisfied their longings repeatedly and in full measure.

They arose as soon as dawn began to break, for the lady was anxious not to give cause for scandal. Having provided him with some very old clothes and filled his purse with money, she then explained which road he must take on entering the fortress in order to find his servant, and finally she let him out by the postern through which he had entered, imploring him to keep their encounter a secret.

As soon as it was broad day and the gates were opened, he entered the castle, giving the impression he was arriving from a distance, and rooted out his servant. Having changed into the clothes that were in his portmanteau, he was about to mount his servant's horse, when as if by some divine miracle the three brigands were brought into the castle, after being arrested for another crime they had committed shortly after robbing him on the previous evening. They had made a voluntary confession, and consequently Rinaldo's horse, clothing and money were restored to him, and all he lost was a pair of garters, which the robbers were unable to account for.

Thus it was that Rinaldo, giving thanks to God and St Julian, mounted his horse and returned home safe and sound, whilst the three robbers went next day to dangle their heels in the north wind.

THIRD STORY

Three young men squander their fortunes, reducing themselves to penury. A nephew of theirs, left penniless, is on his way home when he falls in with an abbot, whom he discovers to be the daughter of the King of England. She later marries him and makes good all the losses suffered by his uncles, restoring them to positions of honour.

The whole company, men and ladies alike, listened with admiration to the adventures of Rinaldo d'Asti, commending his piety and giving thanks to God and St Julian, who had come to his rescue in the hour of his greatest need. Nor, moreover, was the lady considered to have acted foolishly (even though nobody openly said so) for the way she had accepted the blessing that God had left on her doorstep. And while everyone was busy talking, with half-suppressed mirth, about the pleasant night the lady had spent, Pampinea, finding herself next to Filostrato and realizing rightly that it would be her turn to speak next, collected her thoughts together and started planning what to say. And upon receiving the queen's command, she began, in a manner no less confident than it was lively, to speak as follows:

Excellent ladies, if the ways of Fortune are carefully examined, it will be seen that the more one discusses her actions, the more remains to be said. Nor is this surprising, when you pause to consider that she controls all the affairs we unthinkingly call our own, and that consequently it is she who arranges and rearranges them after her own inscrutable fashion, constantly moving them now in one direction, now in another, then back again, without following any discernible plan. The truth of this assertion is clearly illustrated by everything that happens in the space of a single day, as well as being borne out by some of the previous stories. Nevertheless, since our queen has decreed that we should speak on this particular theme, I shall add to the tales already told a story of my own, from which my listeners will

possibly derive some profit, and which in my opinion ought to prove
entertaining.

In our city there once lived a nobleman named Messer Tebaldo,
who according to some people belonged to the Lamberti family,
whilst others maintain he was an Agolanti, perhaps for the simple
reason that Tebaldo's son later followed a profession with which the
Agolanti family has always been associated and which it practises to
this day. But leaving aside the question to which of the two families
he belonged, I can tell you that he was one of the wealthiest nobles
of his time, and that he had three sons, of whom the first was called
Lamberto, the second Tebaldo, and the third Agolante. These three
had grown into fine and mettlesome youths, the eldest being not yet
eighteen, when Messer Tebaldo died very rich, and they inherited all
of his lands, houses and movables.

Finding they had come into a vast amount of money and possessions, they began to indulge in a reckless orgy of spending, heedless of
everything except their own pleasure. They employed a veritable
army of servants, kept large numbers of thoroughbred horses,
hounds and hawks, entertained continuously, gave presents, and
entered the lists at jousts and tournaments. They engaged, not only in
all the activities befitting a gentleman, but also in any others falling
within the range of their youthful inclinations. However, they had
not been leading this sort of life for long when the fortune left to
them by their father dwindled to nothing, and since their income was
inadequate to meet their commitments, they began to pawn and sell
their possessions. So busily were they occupied in selling one thing
after another, that they were scarcely aware of being almost bankrupt,
until one day their eyes, which had been kept closed by riches, were
opened by poverty.

Lamberto therefore called the others together and pointed to the
contrast between their father's splendour and their own sorry condition. He reminded them how rich they had been, and how they had
fallen into poverty on account of their extravagance. And he encouraged them, with all the strength at his command, to join with him in
selling what little they still possessed and to go away, before their
destitution became even more apparent. They agreed to do so, and

without the slightest attempt at leave-taking or any other ceremony, they set out from Florence and travelled without pause until they arrived in England. There they took a small house in London, and, reducing their spending to an absolute minimum, they began to lend money at a high rate of interest, and their business prospered so well that within a few years they amassed a huge fortune.

In consequence they were able to return one by one to Florence, where they re-purchased a large part of their possessions, buying many other things in addition, and they all married. Since they were still lending money in England, they sent a young nephew of theirs, called Alessandro, to manage the business there, whilst they themselves remained in Florence. Having forgotten the parlous condition to which they had previously been reduced by their recklessness, and despite the fact that they now had families to support, they spent with less restraint than ever, borrowing large sums of money, and piling up huge debts with every merchant in Florence. For a few years they managed to meet their expenses with the help of the money remitted to them by Alessandro, who had opened up an extremely profitable line of business by offering mortgages to barons on their castles and other properties.

The three brothers spent lavishly, and, since they could always count on England, they borrowed money whenever they ran short. But suddenly, a totally unexpected war broke out in England between the King and one of his sons, splitting the whole of the island into two rival factions, as a result of which the castles of the barons were taken out of Alessandro's control, and all his other assets were frozen. But he remained in the island in the hope that son and father would make peace at any moment, in which case he might recover not only all his capital, but the outstanding interest as well. Meanwhile, in Florence, the three brothers made no attempt whatever to curb their enormous expenditure, but borrowed more and more each day.

But as the years went by one after another, and their expectations were seen to be bearing no fruit, the three brothers lost their sources of credit, and immediately afterwards, since their creditors were demanding payment, they were thrown into prison. Their assets were realized to meet their debts, but the amount they raised was insufficient, and so they remained in prison, leaving their wives and little children to wander off in rags, some taking to the country, some going to one place, some to another, with nothing but a lifetime of poverty ahead of them.

Alessandro, after waiting several years in England for a peace that never came, thought it not only pointless but positively dangerous to stay there any longer, and decided to return to Italy. He set out all alone on his journey, but as he was leaving Bruges he happened to see, also leaving the city, an abbot dressed in white, who was attended by many monks and preceded by a large number of retainers and a substantial baggage train. Bringing up the rear were two worthy knights, relatives of the king, with whom Alessandro was personally acquainted. And so, having made his presence known, they readily received him as one of their company.

As he jogged along beside the two knights, Alessandro made polite inquiries concerning the identity of the monks who were riding ahead with this large retinue of servants, and asked where they were all going.

'The person riding up front,' replied one of the knights, 'is a young relative of ours who has just been appointed Abbot of one of the largest abbeys in England. But because he is below the minimum age prescribed by law for this great office, we are going with him to Rome in order to ask the Holy Father to give him dispensation for his excessive youth and confirm him in office. But we wish to keep the matter a secret.'

The new abbot rode on, sometimes going ahead, sometimes falling back behind his retinue, in the style regularly to be observed in gentlemen of quality when they are travelling, until eventually he found himself level with Alessandro, who was very young, exceedingly good-looking and well-built, and the most well-mannered, agreeable and finely-spoken person you can imagine. The Abbot's first glimpse of Alessandro gave him more genuine pleasure than anything he had ever seen in his life. Calling him to his side, he began to converse amicably with him, asking who he was, whence he had come, and whither he was bound. Alessandro answered all his questions, frankly revealing the exact state of his affairs and placing himself at the Abbot's entire disposal for whatever small service he might be able to render.

The Abbot, on hearing his fine, precise way of talking and observing his manners more closely, judged him to be a gentleman despite the lowly nature of his past occupation, and became even more enraptured with him. Being filled with compassion by the tale of Alessandro's misfortunes, he began to console him in tones of deep affection, telling him not to lose hope; for if he kept his courage, God would not only restore him to the position from which he had been toppled by Fortune, but set him even higher. The Abbot then said that he too was making for Tuscany, and invited Alessandro to join his party. Alessandro thanked him for his kind words, and declared his readiness to do whatever he was asked.

So the Abbot rode on, becoming more and more fascinated by what he saw of Alessandro. And after a few days, they arrived at a small town, not very richly endowed with inns, where the Abbot wished to put up for the night. Alessandro persuaded the Abbot to dismount at a place run by a very good friend of his, and saw that he was given a room in the most comfortable part of the house. By this time, Alessandro, being a very experienced traveller, had become a sort of major-domo to the Abbot, and he searched high and low to find accommodation in the town for the whole of the Abbot's retinue, lodging some in one place, some in another. By the time he returned to the inn, the Abbot had supped, the hour was very late, and everyone had gone off to bed. He asked the landlord where he could sleep, and the landlord replied:

'I really don't know. As you can see, the place is completely full, and my family and I are having to sleep on benches. But in the Abbot's room there are some cupboards for storing grain. If you like, I'll show you where they are and fix you up some sort of bed in there to sleep the night on as best you can.'

'How am I to squeeze into the Abbot's room?' said Alessandro. 'You know how tiny it is. There wasn't even any space in there for a single one of his monks to lie on the floor. If only I had noticed those cupboards when the Abbot's bed-curtains were drawn! His monks could have slept in those, and I could have lodged where the monks are staying.'

'Well, that's how matters stand,' said the landlord. 'Once you resign yourself to it, you'll sleep like a top in there. The Abbot is asleep, and the curtains are drawn in front of his bed. I'll slip in quietly, and put down a nice mattress for you to sleep on.'

When he saw that it could all be arranged without disturbing the Abbot, Alessandro fell in with the scheme, and, making as little noise as possible, he bedded down where the landlord had suggested.

The Abbot, far from being asleep, was locked in meditation on the subject of certain newly aroused longings of his. He had overheard the conversation between Alessandro and the landlord, and was listening, too, when Alessandro turned in for the night.

'God has answered my prayers,' said the Abbot delightedly to himself. 'If I do not seize this opportunity, it may be a long time before another comes my way.' Having firmly made up his mind, he waited for complete silence to descend on the inn, then he called out to Alessandro in a low voice, and, firmly brushing aside the latter's numerous excuses, persuaded him to undress and lie down at his side. The Abbot placed one of his hands on Alessandro's chest, and then, to Alessandro's great astonishment, began to caress him in the manner of a young girl fondling her lover, causing Alessandro to suspect, since there seemed to be no other explanation for his extraordinary behaviour, that the youth was possibly in the grip of some impure passion. But either by intuition, or because of some movement on Alessandro's part, the Abbot understood at once what he was thinking, and began to smile. Then, hastily tearing off the shirt he was wearing, he took Alessandro's hand and placed it on his bosom, saying:

'Drive those silly thoughts out of your head, Alessandro. Lay your hand here, and see what I am hiding.'

And placing his hand on the Abbot's bosom, Alessandro discovered a pair of sweet little rounded breasts, as firm and finely shaped as if they were made of ivory. It dawned on him at once that this was a woman, and without awaiting further invitation he immediately took her in his arms. But just as he was about to kiss her, she said:

'Wait! Before you come any closer, there is something I want to tell you. As you can gather, I am not a man, but a woman. I am also a virgin, and I set out from home in order to obtain the Pope's permission for my marriage. I know not whether to call it your good fortune or my misfortune, but from the moment I saw you, the other day, I burned with a love deeper than woman has ever experienced for any man. Hence I am resolved to have you as my husband rather than any other. But if you do not want to marry me, you must leave me at once and return to your own place.'

Alessandro had no idea who she was, but in view of the size of her retinue he judged her to be a rich noblewoman, and could see for himself that she was very beautiful. So without wasting too much time in thought, he replied that if this was what she desired, he was only too ready to oblige.

She then sat up in bed, handed him a ring, and made him plight her his troth beneath a small picture of Our Lord, after which they fell into each other's arms, and for the rest of the night they disported themselves to their great and mutual pleasure. They decided carefully what they should do, and when it was daybreak, Alessandro arose and, retracing his steps, stole away from the room without anyone realizing where he had passed the night. Then, reeling with happiness, he set out once more with the Abbot and her retinue, and several days later they arrived in Rome.

They had been staying in the city for only a few days when the Abbot, attended by Alessandro and the two knights, was received in audience by the Pope. Having paid him their respects in the appropriate fashion, the Abbot began:

'As you, Holy Father, must know better than all others, whoever desires to live a good and honest life is obliged to shun as best he may every possible motive for behaving otherwise. I myself, being one who desires to live a thoroughly honest life, have come all this way in the clothes you see me wearing, ostensibly to seek Your Holiness's blessing for my marriage. But in reality, I have fled, taking with me a considerable part of the treasures belonging to my father, the King of England, for he was planning to marry me to the King of Scotland, who is a very old man whereas I myself am a young girl, as you can see. What caused me to run away, was not so much the King of Scotland's age, as the fear that, once married to him, my youthful frailty might tempt me into contravening God's laws and staining the honour of my royal-blooded father.

'In this frame of mind, I was on my way hither when God, who alone knows best how to measure our needs, being stirred as I believe by His compassion, set before my eyes the person He decreed should be my husband. The one I refer to is the young man' – and she pointed to Alessandro – 'whom you see standing here at my side. It may well be that he is less pure-blooded than a person of royal birth, but both in bearing and in character he is a worthy match for any great lady. He, therefore, is the man I have taken; it is him alone that I want, and no matter what my father or anyone else may have to say on the subject, I will never accept any other. The ostensible aim of my journey has thus been removed. But I desired to complete it, for two reasons: firstly, to meet Your Holiness and visit the venerable and sacred places in which this city abounds; and secondly, so that through your good offices I could make public, before you and the whole world, the marriage that Alessandro and I have contracted with God as our only witness. What is pleasing to God and to me should not be disagreeable to you, and I therefore beg you in all humility to give us your blessing, armed with which, since you are God's vicar, we should be more certain of His entire approval. And thus we may live our lives together, till death us do part, to the greater glory not only of God but also of yourself.'

On hearing that his wife was the daughter of the King of England, Alessandro could scarcely contain his astonishment and happiness. But the two knights were even more astonished, and they were so furious that they would have done Alessandro an injury, and possibly the lady as well, if they had been anywhere else but in the Pope's presence. The Pope, for his part, was greatly astonished both by the lady's attire and by her choice of a husband. But he realized there was no turning back, and decided to grant her request. He could see, however, that the knights were seething with rage, and so first of all he pacified them and reconciled them with Alessandro and the lady, then he gave orders for what was to be done.

For the appointed day, the Pope arranged a magnificent ceremony to which he had invited all the cardinals and a large number of other great nobles, and he summoned the couple into their presence. The lady, dressed in regal robes and looking very gracious and beautiful, was greeted with unanimous and well-deserved praise, as also was Alessandro, who carried his fine clothes with such a natural and dignified air that, honourably attended by the two knights, he looked more like a royal prince than a young man who had once been engaged in money-lending. Without further ado, the Pope had them taken solemnly through the marriage ceremony from the beginning, then a sumptuous wedding-feast was held, after which he dismissed them with his blessing.

On leaving Rome, it was the wish of both Alessandro and his bride that they should make for Florence, where their story had already been noised abroad. There the townspeople received them with all possible honour, and the three brothers were released from prison on the petition of the lady, who had seen that all their creditors were paid. She then settled the brothers and their wives once more in their estates, after which Alessandro and his wife took their leave of all concerned, and taking Agolante with them, they set out from Florence for Paris, where they were honourably received by the King. From Paris, the two knights went on ahead to England, where they worked on the King to such good effect that he pardoned the princess and gave a magnificent welcome both to her and to his son-in-law, on whom, with great pomp and ceremony, he shortly afterwards conferred a knighthood, creating him Earl of Cornwall for good measure.

Being a very astute and capable man, Alessandro brought great benefit to the island by reconciling father and son, consequently winning the affection and gratitude of the entire population. At the same time, Agolante recovered all their money down to the last penny, and returned to Florence immensely rich, having first been given a knighthood by Earl Alessandro. As for the Earl, he lived a life of great renown with his lady. Indeed, there are those who maintain that, partly through his own ability and intelligence, and partly with the help of his father-in-law, he later conquered Scotland and was crowned her king.

FOURTH STORY

Landolfo Rufolo is ruined and turns to piracy; he is captured by the Genoese and shipwrecked, but survives by clinging to a chest, full of very precious jewels; finally, having been succoured by a woman on Corfu, he returns home rich.

When she saw that Pampinea had brought her story to its triumphant close, Lauretta, who was seated next to her, took up her cue without a pause and began to speak as follows:

Fairest ladies, it is in my opinion impossible to envisage a more striking act of Fortune than the spectacle of a person being raised from the depths of poverty to regal status, which is what happened, as we have been shown by Pampinea's story, in the case of her Alessandro. And since, from now on, nobody telling a story on the prescribed subject can possibly exceed those limits, I shall not blush to narrate a tale which, whilst it contains greater misfortunes, does not however possess so magnificent an ending. I realize of course, when I think of the previous story, that my own will be followed less attentively. But since it is the best I can manage, I trust that I shall be forgiven.

Few parts of Italy, if any, are reckoned to be more delightful than the sea-coast between Reggio and Gaeta. In this region, not far from Salerno, there is a strip of land overlooking the sea, known to the inhabitants as the Amalfi coast, which is dotted with small towns, gardens and fountains, and swarming with as wealthy and enterprising a set of merchants as you will find anywhere. In one of these little towns, called Ravello, there once lived a certain Landolfo Rufolo, and although Ravello still has its quota of rich men, this Rufolo was a very rich man indeed. But being dissatisfied with his fortune, he sought to double it, and as a result he nearly lost every penny he possessed, and his life too.

This Rufolo, then, having made the sort of preliminary calculations that merchants normally make, purchased a very large ship, loaded it with a mixed cargo of goods paid for entirely out of his own pocket, and sailed with them to Cyprus. But on his arrival, he discovered that several other ships had docked there, carrying precisely the same kind of goods as those he had brought over himself. And for this reason, not only did he have to sell his cargo at bargain prices, but in order to complete his business he was practically forced to give the stuff away, thus being brought to the verge of ruin.

Being extremely distressed about all this, not knowing what to do, and finding himself reduced overnight from great wealth to semi-poverty, he decided he would make good his losses by privateering, or die in the attempt. At all events, having set out a rich man, he was determined not to return home in poverty. And so, having found a buyer for his merchantman, he combined the proceeds with the money he had raised on his cargo, and purchased a light pirate-vessel, which he armed and fitted out, choosing only the equipment best suited for the ship's purpose. He then applied himself to the systematic looting of other people's property, especially that of the Turks.

In his new rôle, he met with far more success than he had encountered in his trading activities. Within the space of about a year, he raided and seized so many Turkish ships that, quite apart from having regained what he had lost in trading, he discovered that he was considerably more than twice as wealthy as before. He thus had enough, he now realized, to avoid the risk of repeating his former mistake, and once he had persuaded himself to rest content with what he had, he made up his mind to call it a day and return home with the loot. Being wary of commercial ventures, he did not bother to invest his money, but simply steered a homeward course, at breakneck speed, in the tiny ship with which he had collected his spoils. He had come as far as the Archipelago, when he found himself sailing one evening directly into the teeth of a southerly gale, and his frail craft was barely able to cope with the mountainous seas. So he put into a cove on the leeward side of a small island, with the intention of waiting for more favourable winds. He had not been there long, however, when two large Genoese carracks, homeward-bound from Constantinople, struggled into the bay to escape the same storm from which Landolfo had taken shelter. The crews of the Genoese ships recognized Landolfo's vessel, which they already knew from various rumours to be loaded with booty. And being by nature a rapacious, money-grabbing set of people, they blocked his way of escape and made their preparations for seizing the prize. First they put ashore a party of well-armed men with crossbows, who were strategically placed so that no one was able to leave Landolfo's vessel without running into a barrage of arrows. Then they launched cutters, by means of which, aided by the current, they drew themselves towards Landolfo's little ship. This they captured without losing a man, after a brief and half-hearted struggle, and they took her crew prisoner. Landolfo was left wearing nothing but a threadbare old doublet and taken aboard one of their ships, and after everything of value had been removed from his vessel, they sent it to the bottom.

The next day, the wind changed quarter, and the two ships hoisted their sails and set a westerly course. For the whole of that day they made good progress, but in the evening a gale began to blow, producing very heavy seas and separating the two carracks from each other. By a stroke of ill-luck, the ship in which the wretched, destitute Landolfo was travelling was driven by the force of the gale on to the coast of the island of Cephalonia, where she ran aground with a tremendous crash, split wide open, and like a piece of glass being flung against a wall, was smashed to smithereens. As is usually the case when this happens, the sea was rapidly littered with an assortment of floating planks, chests and merchandise. And although it was pitch dark and there was a heavy swell, the poor wretches who had survived the wreck, or those of them who could swim, began to cling to whatever object happened to float across their path.

One of their number was poor Landolfo, who had in fact been calling out all day for death to come and take him, for he felt he would rather die than return home poverty-stricken. But now that he was staring death in the face, he was frightened by the prospect, and like the others he too clung to the first spar that came within his reach, in the hope that by remaining afloat for a little longer, God might somehow come to his rescue.

Settling himself astride the spar as best he could, he clung on till daybreak, meanwhile being tossed hither and thither by sea and wind. When dawn came, he cast his eyes around him, but all he could see was clouds and water, and a chest floating on the sea's surface. To his great consternation, this chest floated every so often into his vicinity, causing him to fear lest it should collide into him and do him an injury. So whenever it came too near, he summoned up the meagre strength he still possessed, and pushed it away as best he could with his hands.

But as luck would have it, the sea was struck by a sudden squall, which sent the chest hurtling into Landolfo's spar, upending it and inevitably causing Landolfo to lose his grip and go under. When he re-surfaced, he found that he was some distance away from the spar, and was afraid that he would never reach it, for he was exhausted and only his panic was keeping him afloat. He therefore made for the chest, which was quite close at hand, and dragging himself up on its lid, he sprawled across it and held it steady with his arms. And in this fashion, buffeted this way and that by the sea, with nothing to eat and far more to drink than he would have wished, not knowing where he was and seeing nothing but water, he survived for the whole of that day and the following night.

By the next day, Landolfo had almost turned into a sponge when, either through the will of God or the power of the wind, he arrived off the coast of the island of Corfu. Clinging grimly to the edges of the chest with both hands, just as we see a man in danger of drowning attaching himself firmly to anything within reach, he was sighted by a peasant woman, who happened to be scouring and polishing her pots and pans in the sand and salt-water.

At first, being unable to make out what creature it was that was approaching the shore, she started back with a cry of alarm. He said nothing to her, for he was quite unable to speak and scarcely able to see. But as the current bore him closer to the shore, she could make out the shape of the chest, and peering more intently, she first of all recognized a pair of arms stretched across its lid, after which she picked out the face and realized it was a human being. Prompted by compassion, she waded some distance out into the sea, which was now quite calm, took him by the hair and dragged him to the shore, chest and all. There, with an effort, she unhooked his hands from the chest, which she placed on the head of her young daughter who was with her, whilst she herself carried Landolfo away like a baby and put him into a hot bath. She rubbed away so vigorously at him and poured so much hot water over him, that eventually he began to thaw out and recover some of his lost strength. And when she judged it to be the right moment, she took him from the bath and refreshed him with a quantity of good wine and nourishing food. After she had nursed him to the best of her ability for several days, his recovery was complete and he took stock of his surroundings. The good woman therefore decided it was time to hand over his chest, which she had been keeping for him, and to tell him that from now on he must fend for himself. And this she did.

He could remember nothing about any chest, but he nevertheless accepted it when the good woman offered it to him, for he thought it could hardly be so valueless that it would not keep him going for a few days. His hopes were severely jolted when he discovered how light it was, but all the same, when the woman was out of the house, he forced it open to see what was inside, and discovered that it contained a number of precious stones, some of them loose and others mounted. Being quite knowledgeable on the subject of jewels, he realized from the moment he saw them that they were extremely valuable, and his spirits rose higher than ever. He praised God for once again coming to his rescue, but since Fortune had dealt him two cruel blows in rapid succession, and might conceivably deal him a third, he decided he would have to proceed with great caution if he wanted to convey these things safely home. So he wrapped them up as carefully as he could in some old rags, told the woman that if she liked, she could keep the chest, since he no longer had any use for it, and asked her to let him have a sack in exchange.

The good woman gladly complied with his request, and after he had thanked her profusely for the assistance she had rendered, he slung his sack over his shoulder and went on his way, first taking a boat to Brindisi and then making his way gradually up the coast as far as Trani, where he met some cloth-merchants who hailed from his native town. Without mentioning the chest, he gave them an account of all his adventures, and they felt so sorry for him that they fitted him out with new clothes, lent him a horse, and sent him back with company to Ravello, whither he was intent on returning at all costs.

Secure at last in Ravello, he gave thanks to God for leading him safely home, untied his little sack, and made what was virtually his first real inspection of its contents. The stones he possessed were, he discovered, so valuable and numerous, that even if he sold them at less than their market value, he would be twice as rich as when he had set out. So that, having taken steps to dispose of his gems, he sent, by way of payment for services received, a tidy sum of money to the good woman of Corfu who had fished him out of the sea. And likewise, he sent a further sum to the people at Trani who had given him the new clothes. He was no longer interested in commerce, so he kept the remainder of the money and lived in splendour for the rest of his days.

FIFTH STORY

Andreuccio of Perugia comes to buy horses in Naples, where in the course of a single night he is overtaken by three serious misfortunes, all of which he survives, and he returns home with a ruby.

The stones found by Landolfo – began Fiammetta, whose turn it was to tell the next story – have put me in mind of a tale almost as full of perils as the one narrated by Lauretta. But it differs from hers in that its dangers arose in the space of a single night, as you shall hear, whereas in Lauretta's story they were perhaps spread over several years.

I was once informed that there lived in Perugia a young man whose name was Andreuccio di Pietro, a horsedealer, who, having heard good reports of the Neapolitan horse-trade, stuffed five hundred gold florins in his purse and, though he had never left home before, set out for Naples with one or two other merchants. He arrived one Sunday evening as darkness was falling, and the next morning, having been told by his innkeeper how to get there, he went to the market. He saw a great many horses, to a number of which he took a liking, and he made offers for several of them without however being able to strike a single bargain. But in order to indicate his willingness to buy, he kept pulling out his purse bulging with florins, and waving it about in full view of all the passers-by, thus displaying a lack of both caution and experience.

While he was conducting his business in this manner and holding out his money for inspection, it happened that a young Sicilian woman passed by, without attracting his attention. She was not only very beautiful, but willing to do any man's bidding for a modest fee, and when she saw the purse she immediately fell to thinking how contented she would be if she could lay her hands on the money. However, she walked straight on.

She was accompanied by an old woman, also Sicilian, who on seeing Andreuccio allowed her companion to go on ahead, whilst she herself rushed over to him and threw her arms around him in a display of affection. On seeing this, the young woman said nothing, but held herself aloof from the proceedings and waited for the other woman to catch her up. Andreuccio, having turned round and recognized the old woman, made a great fuss of her and extracted a promise that she would call and see him at his inn. After conversing briefly with him, she then went away, and Andreuccio returned to business, without however purchasing anything that morning.

The young woman, having spied Andreuccio's purse and noted how well her companion was acquainted with him, was determined to see if she could find some way of relieving him of the whole or a part of his cash. So she began to put out feelers, asking the older woman who he was, where he came from, what he was doing in Naples, and how it came about that she knew him. Andreuccio himself could hardly have furnished her with a more particular account of his affairs than the one given her by the old woman, for she had lived with Andreuccio over a long period in Sicily, and later in Perugia. Moreover she was also able to reveal where he was staying and why he had come to Naples.

Now that she was fully informed about his family and the names of his various relatives, the young woman devised an ingenious plan for achieving her object. On arriving home, she gave the old woman enough work to occupy her for the rest of the day, so that she could not keep her appointment with Andreuccio. Then she took aside a maidservant of hers, to whom she had given a thorough grounding in affairs of this sort, and towards evening she sent her to the inn where Andreuccio was staying. On arriving at the door of the inn, she happened to run across our hero, who was by himself, and she asked him where she could find Andreuccio. When he told her that he was the very man, she drew him aside and said:

'Sir, there is a gentlewoman of this city who would be glad of a few words with you, if you have no objection.'

When he heard this, Andreuccio immediately assumed, on looking himself up and down and thinking what a handsome fellow he was, that the woman must have fallen in love with him, as though he were the only good-looking youth at that time to be found in Naples. So he readily agreed, and asked where and when the lady would like to see him.

'You may come whenever you wish, sir,' said the maid. 'She is waiting for you at her house.'

'Lead the way then,' Andreuccio promptly replied. 'I'll follow you.' And without leaving any message at the inn, off he went.

The maid conveyed him to the lady's house, which was situated in a quarter called The Fleshpots, the mere name of which shows how honest a district it was. But Andreuccio neither knew nor suspected anything of all this, being of the opinion that he was on his way to see a gentlewoman in a perfectly respectable part of the city. Eventually, with the maid leading the way, they arrived at the lady's house, and Andreuccio went boldly in. The maid had already hailed her mistress with the words 'Andreuccio's here!', and as he mounted the stairs he saw the lady coming out on the landing to receive him.

She was still very young, tall in stature, with a very beautiful face, and her clothes and jewellery were a model of good taste. Just before Andreuccio reached her, she opened her arms wide and descended three steps to meet him. Then she clasped him round the neck and remained for some time without speaking, as though hindered by a surge of powerful emotion. Finally, her eyes filling with tears, she kissed his brow and said, in a somewhat faltering voice:

'Oh, Andreuccio my dear, how delighted I am to see you.'

Not knowing what to make of this barrage of affection, he replied, in tones of deep astonishment:

'My lady, the pleasure is mine.'

Then she took him by the hand, and led him up to the main room of her house, from whence, without another word, she passed with him into her bedroom, which was all fragrant with roses, orange-blossom and other pleasant odours. There he saw an exquisite curtained bed, a large number of dresses hanging from pegs, as is the custom in those parts, and other very beautiful, expensive-looking objects. He had never seen such finery before, and was firmly convinced that the lady must be nothing less than a genuine aristocrat.

Having made him sit by her side on a chest at the foot of the bed, she began to address him as follows:

'Andreuccio, I am quite sure you must be astonished at me for embracing you like this and bursting into tears, for you do not know me and it may be that you have never even heard of me before. But you are now to hear something that will possibly increase your astonishment, for the fact is that I am your sister. I have always longed to meet all of my brothers, and now that God has been good enough to allow me to see one of them, I shall no longer die disconsolate when the time comes for me to depart this life. But in case you know nothing of this, I will tell you all about it.

'Pietro, who is my father as well as yours, lived for many years in Palermo, as I suppose you may have heard. Being a good and amiable man, he was greatly loved there, and he is still loved there to this day by those who knew him. But of all his profound admirers, none loved him more than my mother, who was a widowed lady of gentle birth. Indeed, she loved Pietro so deeply, that she abandoned all fear of her father, her brothers and her good name, and their friendship became so intimate that it led to the birth of the person you see here now, sitting beside you.

'When I was still a little girl, Pietro's business called him away from Palermo and he returned to Perugia, leaving my mother and me to fend for ourselves, and as far as I have been able to discover, he never gave either of us another thought. For this reason, but for the fact that he was my father, I would be inclined to reproach him bitterly, considering (to say nothing of the affection he should have had for me, his own daughter, born neither of a serving-wench nor of any low-class woman) the ingratitude he displayed towards my mother. For she, prompted by her unswerving devotion, surrendered herself body and soul to this man, without so much as knowing who he was.

'But never mind about all that. Wrongs committed in the distant past are far easier to condemn than to rectify. At all events, the fact is that he abandoned me when I was still a tiny child in Palermo, where I eventually grew up, and my mother, being a wealthy woman, married me off to a worthy nobleman from Girgenti, who out of affection for my mother and myself came to live in Palermo. Being a staunch supporter of the Guelphs, he began to intrigue on behalf of King Charles of Naples. But before the plot could be sprung, it reached the ears of King Frederick, and we had to flee from Sicily just as I was about to become the greatest lady in the island. Of our huge store of possessions, we took away only those few things we were able to carry with us, and leaving behind our lands and palaces, we came as refugees to this country, where we found King Charles so well-disposed towards us that he made good some of the losses we had suffered on his account. He gave us estates and houses, and as you will see for yourself, he makes generous and regular provision for my husband, or in other words your brother-in-law. And that, my dear sweet brother, is how I came to be in Naples, where, thanks more to God than to yourself, I have met you at last.' And having said all this, sobbing with affection, she embraced him a second time and kissed him once again on the forehead.

She had told her tale very glibly and with great self-assurance, neither stammering at any point nor swallowing any of her words. For his part, Andreuccio remembered that his father really had been in Palermo, and he knew from his own experience how lightly young men are apt to regard the love of a woman. So what with her tears of affection, her fond embraces and her chaste kisses, he was more than satisfied that she was telling the truth. And when she had finished, he replied:

'I beg you not to take my amazement too much to heart, madam, for to tell you the truth I have never had the slightest knowledge of your existence. For some reason or other, my father never spoke of you and your mother, or if he did I never came to hear of it. But I am all the more delighted to find my sister in Naples, because I was feeling rather lonely here and the discovery was so unexpected. I myself am merely a small trader, but I know of no man, however exalted his station, who would not be equally delighted upon finding such a sister. There is one thing, though, that I would like you to explain: how did you know I was here?'

To which she replied:

'I learned about it this morning from a poor old woman, who often comes to see me because she spent a long time with our father in Palermo and Perugia; or at least she tells me she did. And if it weren't for the fact that I thought it more decorous for you to come to my own house than for me to visit you in another's, I would have called to see you hours ago.'

After saying this, she began to inquire about all of his relatives, naming each one individually, and Andreuccio, allowing himself to be led even further up the garden path, told her how they all were.

As it was a very hot evening, and they had been talking together for some little time, she sent for Greek wine and sweetmeats and saw that Andreuccio was given something to drink, after which he got up to go, saying it was time for supper. She refused to allow him to do any such thing: on the contrary, pretending to be deeply hurt, she flung her arms round his neck, saying:

'Alas, now I am quite certain how little you care for me! What else am I to think, when you are with a sister you have never seen before, in her own house, where you should have stayed from the moment you arrived, and now you want to leave me to go and have supper at some inn! Really! You are going to sup with me. My husband is not at home, for which I am very sorry, but though I am merely a woman, I am quite capable of supplying you with a little hospitality.'

Andreuccio, not knowing how else to reply, said:

'I care for you just as much as any man should care for his sister, but if I don't go back they will be waiting for me all evening to turn up for supper, and I shall cut a bad figure.'

Whereupon she said:

'Good heavens, as if I didn't have anyone in the house who could be sent to tell them not to expect you! But you would be doing a much greater kindness, and no more than your duty, if you were to send word to your companions that they should come and have supper here. And then afterwards, if you still insist on leaving, you could all go back to the inn together.'

Andreuccio replied that he would rather do without his companions that evening, and that he would place himself entirely at her disposal, if this was what she really wanted. She accordingly went through the motions of sending word to the inn that they should not expect him for supper. Then after a lot of further talk, they sat down to a splendid supper, consisting of several courses, which she cunningly prolonged until darkness had completely fallen. When they got up from table, Andreuccio said he would have to go, but she refused to hear of it under any circumstances, telling him that Naples was no place to wander about in at night, especially if one was a stranger, and that when she had sent word to the inn not to expect him for supper, she had told them he would not be sleeping there either.

He swallowed all this, and since, being taken in by appearances, he was enjoying her company, he stayed where he was. After supper, she engaged him, not without her reasons, in a protracted conversation about this and that, and when the night was well advanced she left Andreuccio to sleep in her room, with a page-boy to show him where to find anything he needed, whilst she herself retired into another room with her maidservants.

The heat was stifling, and so, on finding himself alone, Andreuccio stripped to his doublet and removed his hose and breeches, and laid them under his bolster. Nature demanded that he should relieve his belly, which was inordinately full, so he asked the page where he could do it, and the boy showed him a door in one of the corners of the room, saying:

'Go through there.'

Andreuccio passed jauntily through, and chanced to step on to a plank, which came away at its other end from the beam on which it was resting, so that it flew up in the air and fell into the lower regions, taking Andreuccio with it. Although he had fallen from a goodly height, he mercifully suffered no injury; but he got himself daubed from head to foot in the filthy mess with which the place was literally swimming.

Now in order to give you a clearer picture of what has preceded and what follows, I shall describe the sort of place it was. In a narrow alleyway, such as we often see between two houses, some boards, and a place to sit, had been rigged up on two beams, running across from one house to the next; and it was one of these boards that had collapsed under Andreuccio's weight.

So finding himself down there in the alley, Andreuccio, cursing his bad luck, began calling out to the boy. But as soon as he had heard him falling, the boy had hurried off to tell his mistress, who rushed into her room and made a rapid search for Andreuccio's clothes. These she found, together with his money, which being a doubting sort of fellow he stupidly carried with him wherever he went. And so it was that this woman of Palermo, this self-styled sister of a Perugian, obtained the prize for which she had laid her trap. Being no longer interested in Andreuccio, she quickly went and closed the door through which he had passed just before he fell.

Receiving no answer from the boy, Andreuccio began to call more loudly, but it was of no use. His suspicions being already aroused, he began, now that it was too late, to see how he had been hoodwinked, and having climbed a low wall dividing the alleyway from the road, he scrambled down into the street and went up to the front-door, which he was easily able to identify. He stood there for ages, vainly calling out, and shaking and beating the door for all he was worth. Finally, plainly perceiving the predicament he was in, he burst into tears and said to himself:

'Oh, poor me! What a sudden way to lose five hundred florins and a sister!'

He said a lot more besides, then began to shout and to pummel on the door all over again, creating such a disturbance that he woke a number of the people living nearby, who got up out of bed as they could not endure the racket. One of the woman's maids came to the window, all bleary-eyed, and said in tones of annoyance:

'Who is knocking down there?'

'Oh,' said Andreuccio, 'don't you recognize me? I am Andreuccio, the brother of Madonna Fiordaliso.'

'My good man,' she replied, 'if you have had too much to drink, go and sleep it off and come back in the morning. I don't know any Andreuccio; you are talking nonsense. Be off with you, for goodness' sake, and let us sleep.'

'What!' said Andreuccio. 'Talking nonsense, am I? You know very well I'm not. But if it's really true that Sicilians make a habit of discovering blood-relatives and then forgetting all about them, at least give me back the clothes I left there, and I'll go away gladly.'

'My good man,' she said, hardly able to contain her laughter, 'you must be dreaming.'

As she said this, she simultaneously withdrew her head and closed the window, whereupon Andreuccio, who no longer had the slightest doubt that he had lost everything, grew so distressed, that whereas he was very angry to begin with, he now became almost frantic with rage. Deciding that force was a more effective weapon than words for retrieving his belongings, he picked up a large stone and started all over again to rain on the door like a madman, this time with much greater energy.

Taking exception to his hammering, many of the neighbours previously roused from their beds now appeared at their windows, and regarding him as some troublemaker who had invented the things he was saying in order to make this good woman's life a misery, they began to shout in unison, like all the dogs in one particular district howling at a stray.

'This is a fine way to carry on,' they shouted, 'coming round here at this hour and knocking up honest women with your ridiculous tall stories. For heaven's sake clear off, man, and please let us get some sleep. If you have any business with the lady, leave it till the morning and stop annoying us like this in the middle of the night.'

Being, perhaps, encouraged by this chorus of abuse, a man concealed inside the house, who was the good woman's bully, and whom Andreuccio had as yet neither seen nor heard, came to the window and said, in a low, fierce, spine-chilling growl:

'Who's that down there?'

Andreuccio raised his head towards the point from which the growl was coming, and caught sight of a face which, so far as he could judge, clearly belonged to some mighty man or other, who had a thick black beard and was yawning and rubbing his eyes as though he had just been roused from a deep sleep.

'It's me,' replied Andreuccio, not without marked trepidation. 'The brother of the lady who lives here.'

The man did not wait for Andreuccio to finish, but adopting an even more threatening tone, he exclaimed:

'I don't know what restrains me from coming down there and giving you the biggest pasting you've ever had in your life, you miserable drunken idiot, making all this racket in the middle of the night and keeping everyone awake.' He then retired from view, and bolted the window.

Being better informed than Andreuccio about the sort of person he was, some of the neighbours addressed Andreuccio in hushed, compassionate tones, saying:

'For God's sake, be a good chap and take yourself off, unless you want to be killed down there tonight. Do go away for your own good.'

So Andreuccio, terrified out of his wits by the man's voice and appearance, and urged on by the advice of these people, whose words seemed to him to be prompted by Christian charity, set off with the intention of returning to the inn. He had no idea where he was, so he simply struck out in the direction from which, following in the maid-servant's footsteps, he had come on the previous day. All he felt certain of was that he would never see his money again and that he was the most wretched man alive.

However, he had not progressed very far when he became uncomfortably aware of the odour emanating from his person, and, deciding he had better make for the sea in order to have a wash, he turned off to the left and started to walk along a street known as the Ruga Catalana. As he was approaching the upper part of the city, he happened to see two people coming towards him carrying a lantern, and fearing lest they might turn out to be officers of the watch or a pair of cut-throats, he decided to avoid them by slipping quietly into a near-by hut. But the two men also came into the same hut, as though it were the very place they had been heading for. Once inside, one of them put down some iron tools he had been carrying over his shoulder, and they both began to inspect these and pass various comments about them. Presently, the first man said:

'What can be causing this unholy stench? I reckon it's the worst I've ever smelt.'

As he said this, they raised their lantern a little, and catching sight of poor Andreuccio, they let out a gasp of astonishment and demanded to know who he was.

Andreuccio at first said nothing, but when they took the light nearer to him and asked him what he was doing there, covered with filth in this manner, he told them the whole story of his adventures. The two men, who could well imagine where all this had taken place, said to each other:

'It must have happened round at Butch Belchfire's place.'

Then one of them said, addressing Andreuccio:

'Listen, friend, you may have lost your money, but you can thank God that you happened to fall and couldn't get back into the house. Because if you hadn't fallen, you can rest assured that as soon as you were asleep you would have been done in, and in that case you'd have lost your life as well as your money. What's the use of crying over spilt milk? You've about as much chance of plucking stars from the heavens as you have of recovering a single penny. But you may very well have your throat cut, if you ever breathe a word about it and he finds out.'

The two men then conferred briefly together, after which they said to him:

'Look, we're feeling sorry for you, and since we were on our way to do a little job, if you'd like to join us we can almost guarantee that your share of the proceeds will more than make up what you've lost.' And as he was feeling desperate, Andreuccio agreed to go with them.

Now, just a few hours earlier, the burial had taken place of an archbishop whose name was Messer Filippo Minutolo. He was the Archbishop of Naples, and he had been buried with some very valuable regalia and wearing a ruby on his finger, worth more than five hundred gold florins, which these two fellows were on their way to plunder. They disclosed their intentions to Andreuccio, and being more covetous than well-advised, he set off in their company. As they were on their way to the cathedral, with Andreuccio still putting forth a powerful odour, one of them said:

'Couldn't we find some place or other where this fellow could be washed, so that he didn't stink so appallingly?'

'Certainly,' said the other. 'Not far from here, there's a well, which always used to have a pulley and a big bucket at the top. Let's go there and give him a quick wash.'

On reaching the well, they found that the rope was still there, but the bucket had been removed. So they hit on the idea of tying him to the rope and lowering him into the well so that he could wash himself down below. When he had finished washing, he was to give the rope a tug, and they would haul him up again.

Shortly after they had lowered him into the well, some officers of the watch, feeling thirsty on account of the heat and also because they had been chasing somebody, happened to come to the well for a drink. When the other two saw them coming, they immediately took to their heels, making good their escape without being spotted by the officers.

Meanwhile Andreuccio, having completed his ablutions at the bottom of the well, gave a tug on the rope. The officers had taken off their surcoats and laid them on the ground beside their bucklers and pikestaffs, and they now began to haul away at the rope, thinking it had a bucket full of water attached to it.

When Andreuccio saw that he had nearly reached the top of the well, he let go the rope and threw himself on to the rim, clinging to it with both hands. On seeing this apparition, the officers were filled with sudden panic, and without a word they dropped the rope and began to run as fast as their legs would carry them. Andreuccio stared at them in blank amazement, and if he hadn't held on tightly, he would have fallen to the bottom, perhaps being killed or doing himself serious injury. However, he clambered out, and when he saw these weapons, he grew even more perplexed, for he knew they had not been left there by his companions. Bewailing his misfortune, and fearing lest anything worse should befall him, he decided to leave all these things where they were and clear off. So away he went without having the slightest idea where he was going.

As he was walking along, he came across his two companions, who were on their way back to the well to haul him out. They could hardly believe their eyes when they saw him coming, and they asked him who had helped him out. Andreuccio said he didn't know and gave them a detailed account of how it had happened, describing what he had found lying beside the well. Putting two and two together, they had a good laugh and told him why they had run away, and explained who it was that had hauled him out of the well. And without wasting any more words, the night already being half spent, they made their way to the cathedral, which they entered without any difficulty. On reaching the tomb, which was very big and made of marble, they got out their tools and lifted the enormously heavy lid, propping it up so that there was just enough room for a man to squeeze his way inside. When this operation was complete, one of them said:

'Who's going in?'

'I'm not,' said the other.

'And I'm not, either,' said the first. 'How about Andreuccio?'

'I won't do it,' said Andreuccio, whereupon both the others rounded on him saying:

'What do you mean, you won't do it? If you don't damned well get in there quickly, we'll give you such a hammering over the pate with these iron bars that we'll kill you stone dead.'

Shaking with fear, Andreuccio crawled into the tomb, thinking to himself as he did so: 'These two are making me go inside so as to leave me in the lurch. Once I've handed everything out, they'll go about their business while I'm still struggling my way out of the tomb, and I shall be left empty-handed.' He therefore decided that before doing anything else, he would make certain of his own share of the plunder. Remembering what they had said about the precious ring, as soon as he reached the floor of the vault he took the ring from the archbishop's finger and put it on his own, then he handed out the crosier, the mitre and the gloves, and having stripped the body down to the shift and handed everything out, he told them there was nothing left.

The others insisted that the ring should be there, and told him to make a thorough search. But he replied that he was unable to find it, and kept them waiting for some little time, pretending to look for it. And since, for their part, they were just as sharp-witted as Andreuccio, they told him to go on looking, and as soon as they got the chance they took away the prop supporting the lid. Then they made off, leaving Andreuccio imprisoned inside the tomb.

You can easily imagine the effect that all of this had upon Andreuccio. He tried again and again, using first his head and then his shoulders, to see if he could raise the lid, but he was merely wasting his energies, and in the end, in the depths of despair, he fainted and collapsed on the archbishop's corpse. If anyone could have seen them at that moment, he would have had a job to tell which of the two, the archbishop or Andreuccio, was the cadaver. But when Andreuccio came to his senses, he burst into copious tears, for he realized beyond any doubt that there were only two possible ends in store for him: either he would die of hunger and the noxious odours inside the tomb, covered all over in maggots from the dead body; or if some-one were to come and find him there, he would be hanged as a thief.

Whilst these unpleasant thoughts were running through his mind, feeling thoroughly down in the dumps, he heard a number of people talking and moving about in the cathedral, and quickly realized that they had come to carry out the work already completed by himself and his companions, whereupon he became considerably more alarmed. But having opened the tomb and propped up the lid, they began to argue about who should go inside, and no one was willing to do it. However, after much heated discussion, a priest came forward, saying:

'What are you afraid of? Do you think he is going to devour you? Dead men don't eat the living. I will go in myself.'

Having said this, he laid his chest on the edge of the tomb and swivelled round, thrusting his legs inside preparatory to descending, and with only his head sticking out.

When Andreuccio saw this, he stood up and grasped the priest by one of his legs, giving the priest the impression that he was about to be dragged down into the tomb. The priest no sooner felt this happening than he let out an ear-splitting yell and hurled himself bodily out of the tomb. The rest of the gang were terrified by this turn of events, and, leaving the tomb open, they all started running away as though they were being pursued by ten thousand devils.

When Andreuccio perceived what had happened, he was contented beyond his wildest hopes, and, clambering hastily out, he left the cathedral by the way he had come. By now it was almost daybreak, and as he was wandering aimlessly along with the ring on his finger, he eventually came to the waterfront. Shortly thereafter he stumbled across his inn, where he found that his companions and the innkeeper had been up all night, wondering what on earth had become of him. After telling them what had happened, he was urged by the inn-keeper to leave Naples at once. He promptly followed the innkeeper's advice, and returned to Perugia, having invested, in a ring, the money with which he had set out to purchase horses.

SIXTH STORY

Madonna Beritola, having lost her two sons, is found on an island with two roebucks and taken to Lunigiana, where one of her sons, having entered the service of her lord and master, makes love to the daughter of the house and is thrown into prison. After the Sicilian rebellion against King Charles, the son is recognized by his mother, he marries his master's daughter, he is reunited with his brother, and they are all restored to positions of great honour.

The whole company, ladies and young men alike, rocked with laughter over Fiammetta's account of Andreuccio's misfortunes, and then Emilia, on seeing that the story was finished and receiving a signal from the queen, began as follows:

The erratic course pursued by Fortune frequently leads to pain and irritation. But since our mental faculties, which are easily lulled to sleep by her blandishments, are aroused as often as a subject is openly discussed, I consider that nobody, whether he be happy or miserable, should ever object to hearing an account of her eccentricities, in that the first man will be placed on his guard and the second will receive some consolation. Accordingly, I propose to tell you a story, no less true than touching, on this same topic upon which such splendid things have already been said. And whilst my tale has a happy ending, the suffering contained therein was so intense and protracted, that I can scarcely believe it was ever entirely assuaged by the happiness that ensued.

You are to know, dear ladies, that Manfred, who was crowned King of Sicily after the death of the Emperor Frederick II, held few of his courtiers in higher esteem than a gentleman of Naples called Arrighetto Capece, who had a beautiful and noble wife, also Neapolitan, called Madonna Beritola Caracciolo. Arrighetto was in fact governing the island, when news reached him that King Charles I had defeated and killed Manfred at Benevento, and that the whole kingdom had gone over to the conqueror. Knowing that the Sicilians could never be trusted for long, and not wishing to become a subject of his master's enemy, he prepared to flee. But his plans were discovered by the Sicilians, who promptly took him prisoner and delivered him over to King Charles along with many other friends and servants of King Manfred. And shortly afterwards, the island itself was surrendered.

In the face of all this upheaval, not knowing what had become of Arrighetto, frightened by what had happened and fearing a possible attempt on her own honour, Madonna Beritola abandoned everything she possessed, and though pregnant and reduced to poverty, she fled by ship to Lipari with her son, Giusfredi, who was about eight years old. There she gave birth to a second son, whom she called The Outcast, and having hired a nurse, she embarked with all three on a tiny ship bound for Naples, with the intention of rejoining her family. But her plans misfired, for the ship was driven by strong winds to the island of Ponza, where they put in to a little bay and began to await more favourable weather for their voyage.

Like the others, Madonna Beritola went ashore there, and she sought out a deserted and remote spot on the island where, in complete solitude, she could give vent to her sorrow for the loss of her husband. This became a daily ritual of hers, until one day, as she was busy sorrowing, it happened that a pirate-galley arrived, taking the crew and everyone else unawares, and departed again after capturing the ship and all hands.

Having completed her daily lament, Madonna Beritola, following her usual practice, returned to the shore to look for her children. On finding nobody in sight she was at first perplexed, and then suddenly suspecting what had happened, she cast her eyes seaward and saw the galley, not yet very far distant, with the little ship in tow. Realizing all too clearly that she had now lost her children as well as her husband, and finding herself abandoned there, alone and destitute, without the slightest notion of how she was going to find them again, she fell in a dead faint on to the sand with the names of her husband and children on her lips.

There was nobody at hand to revive her with cold water or other remedies, and hence it was some time before she came to her senses. When, eventually, the strength returned to her poor exhausted body, bringing with it further tears and lamentations, she called out over and over again to her children and searched high and low for them in every cavern she could find. But when she saw that her efforts were useless and that the night was approaching, she began, prompted by an instinctive feeling that all was not entirely lost, to devote some attention to her own predicament. And, leaving the shore, she returned to the cave where she was in the habit of giving vent to her tears and sorrow.

She had had nothing to eat since midday, and a little after tierce on the following morning, having spent the night in great fear and incredible anguish, she was compelled to start eating grass in order to appease her hunger. Having fed herself to the best of her ability, she then started brooding, tearfully, about what was to become of her. And whilst in the midst of these various reflections, she caught sight of a doe, which came towards her and disappeared into a nearby cave, emerging shortly afterwards and then running away into the woods. Getting up from where she was sitting, she entered the cave from which the doe had emerged, and inside she saw two newly-born roebucks, no more than a few hours old, which seemed to her the sweetest and most charming sight it was possible to imagine. And since her own milk was not yet dry after her recent confinement, she picked them up tenderly and applied them to her breast. They showed no sign of refusing this favour, but took suck from her as though she were their own mother; and from then on they made no distinction between their mother and herself. Thus the lady felt she had found some company on this deserted island, and having become just as familiar with the doe as with the two roebucks, she resolved to remain there for the rest of her days on a diet of grass and water, bursting into tears whenever she remembered her past life with her husband and children.

As a result of leading this sort of life, the gentle woman had turned quite wild when, a few months later, a small Pisan ship happened to be driven in by a storm, casting anchor in the same little bay where she herself had arrived, and lying there for several days.

Now, aboard this ship there was a gentleman of the Malespina family called Currado, who was returning home from a pilgrimage with his worthy and devout lady after visiting all the holy places in the Kingdom of Apulia. One day, in order to relieve the monotony of the delay, he went ashore with his wife, some of his servants, and his dogs, and started exploring the island. And not very far from the place where Madonna Beritola was, Currado's dogs began giving chase to the two roebucks, which had now grown quite big and were out grazing. Pursued by the dogs, the two roebucks ran to the very cave where Madonna Beritola was sheltering.

Seeing what was happening, she got up, took hold of a stick, and drove the dogs back. Shortly afterwards, Currado and his lady, who had been following the dogs, arrived on the scene; and when they saw her standing there, all bronzed and emaciated, with long and unkempt hair, their astonishment, though much less than her own, was very great indeed. However, after Currado had complied with her entreaties to call off his dogs, they persuaded her, with a good deal of coaxing, to tell them who she was and what she was doing there, and she gave them a full account of her past life and all her misfortunes, ending by revealing her fierce determination to stay on the island. On hearing this, Currado, who had been very well acquainted with Arrighetto Capece, wept with compassion, and attempted to talk her out of her proud decision, offering to take her back to her home, or alternatively, to honour her as a sister and keep her in his own family, where she could stay until such time as God granted her a kindlier fate. However, she would have nothing to do with his proposals, and so he left her with his wife, bidding her to arrange for food to be brought, and, since the woman was all in rags, to let her have some of her own clothes to wear. But most important, she was to do all she could to bring her back to the ship.

On being left alone with Beritola, Currado's wife shed countless tears over the lady's misfortunes, then she gave instructions for food and clothes to be brought, which she had the greatest difficulty in persuading her to accept. And finally, after a stream of entreaties, with Madonna Beritola asserting that on no account would she go to any place in which she was known, she persuaded her to accompany them to Lunigiana, bringing with her the doe and the two roebucks. The doe had meanwhile, in fact, returned, and, to the no small astonishment of Currado's wife, it had greeted Beritola with a display of affection.

And so, once the weather had improved, Madonna Beritola embarked on the ship with Currado and his lady, taking with her the doe and the two roebucks, a circumstance which, since few people knew her real name, led to her being referred to as Cavriuola.* The winds were favourable, and they soon reached the mouth of the River Magra, where they left the ship and proceeded to Currado's estates in the hills.

After her arrival at the castle, Madonna Beritola, dressed in widow's weeds, began to live a humble, secluded and obedient life as a maid of honour to Currado's lady, at the same time continuing to treat her roebucks with affection and ensuring that they were properly fed.

Meanwhile, the pirates who had unwittingly abandoned Madonna Beritola at Ponza and seized the ship on which she had been travelling, had arrived at Genoa with all their captives. When the spoils were divided between the owners of the galley, it turned out that Madonna Beritola's nurse and the two children were assigned, along with a quantity of goods, to a certain Messer Guasparrino d'Oria, who sent the woman and the two boys to his house with the intention of employing them as slaves on household duties.

Being exceedingly distressed by the loss of her mistress and by the sorry state to which she saw herself and the two children reduced, the nurse wept over and over again. But she was a sensible and prudent woman despite her lowly station in life, and once she had realized that her tears were not going to help in freeing them all from slavery, she did all she could to comfort the children. Considering where they were, she thought it quite possible that the two boys would be molested if their identity were discovered. And moreover, she was hoping that sooner or later their luck would change, in which case, provided they were still alive, the children might regain the positions of honour they had lost. So she resolved not to tell anybody who they were until a suitable occasion presented itself, and meanwhile, whenever she was questioned on the matter, she would claim that the children were her own. Renaming the older boy Giannotto di Procida instead of Giusfredi and leaving the younger boy's name

* i.e. 'Doe'.

unaltered, she explained very carefully to Giusfredi why she had
changed his name and how dangerous it might be for him if he were
recognized. And she drummed this into him so often and with so
much persistence, that, being an intelligent boy, he followed the
instructions of his wise nurse to the letter.

And so the two boys and their nurse, badly clothed and worse shod,
continued for many years in Messer Guasparrino's house, patiently
performing all the most menial tasks it is possible to imagine. But
Giannotto was made of sterner stuff than slaves are made of, and by
the time he was sixteen the baseness of a servile existence had become
so repugnant to him that he abandoned Messer Guasparrino's household and enlisted as a seaman on galleys plying between Genoa and
Alexandria, after which he travelled far and wide without however
finding a single opportunity for advancement.

Finally, when he had almost lost hope of a change of fortune, his
wanderings led him to Lunigiana, where he chanced to enter the
service of Currado Malespina, whom he attended, to the latter's no
small satisfaction, with considerable efficiency. It was now some three
or four years since his departure from Messer Guasparrino's and he
had grown into a well-built, handsome young man. He had meanwhile heard that his father, whom he had supposed to be dead, was
still alive, but languishing under heavy guard in one of King Charles's
dungeons. And whilst he occasionally saw his mother, who was in
attendance on Currado's lady, he never recognized her, nor she him,
for they had both changed a great deal in the period that had elapsed
since they had last seen one another.

Now, whilst Giannotto was in Currado's service, it happened that a
daughter of Currado's, whose name was Spina, was left a widow by a
certain Niccolò da Grignano, and returned to her father's house.
Being a beautiful and very graceful girl of little more than sixteen,
she began to take an interest in Giannotto, and he in her, with the
result that they fell madly in love with one another. Their love was
soon consummated, and since it continued for several months undetected, they became excessively confident and were less cautious
than they should have been. And one day, while out walking in a
fine, thickly-wooded forest, Giannotto and the girl, forging on ahead
of their companions, came to a delectable spot all covered with grass

and flowers and surrounded by trees, and, thinking they had left the others far behind, they began to make love.

So great was their enjoyment that they lost all track of time, and they had been together for ages when the girl's mother arrived on the scene, to be followed a moment later by Currado. Dismayed beyond measure by what he saw, he ordered three of his servants, without giving any reasons, to seize the pair of them, bind them, and march them off to one of his castles. Then he stalked away, seething with distress and anger, and intent on having them ignominiously put to death.

The girl's mother was extremely upset, and regarded no punishment as too severe for her daughter's lapse. But she could not stand passively aside and allow them to suffer the kind of fate which, on piecing together certain of Currado's remarks, she realized he was intending to inflict on the culprits. So she hurried to catch up with her irate husband, and began pleading with him not to ruin his old age by killing his own daughter in a sudden fit of frenzy and soiling his hands with the blood of one of his servants. He could, she insisted, find some other way of placating his anger, such as having them incarcerated, so that, as they languished in prison, they would have a chance of repenting in full for their sinful behaviour. The saintly woman pressed these views and many others upon him with so much urgency, that she dissuaded him from killing them. And he ordered each of them to be imprisoned in different places, where they were to be closely guarded, receive a minimum of food, and suffer the maximum of discomfort, until such time as he decided otherwise. These instructions were promptly carried out, and I leave you to imagine the sort of life they led in their captivity, weeping incessantly and almost starving to death.

Now, when Giannotto and Spina had been languishing in these wretched conditions for more than twelve months, and Currado had dismissed them from his thoughts, it came about that King Peter of Aragon, with the aid of a subversive movement led by Messer Gian di Procida, stirred up a rebellion in Sicily and wrested the island from King Charles. Currado, being a Ghibelline, was overjoyed at the news, and when Giannotto heard about it from one of his gaolers, he heaved a deep sigh, and said:

'Oh, alas! for fourteen long years I have travelled the world in continual hardship, waiting only for this to happen! And now that it has come about, just to prove the vanity of all my hopes, I find myself here in this prison-cell, without the slightest prospect of being released until the day I die.'

'What are you talking about?' said the gaoler. 'Surely the affairs of mighty monarchs are no concern of yours? What was your business in Sicily?'

'It almost breaks my heart,' replied Giannotto, 'when I recall the business of my father. For although I was still a small boy when I fled from the island, yet I remember seeing him as its governor, when King Manfred was alive.'

'And who was this father of yours?' asked the gaoler.

'My father's name,' said Giannotto, 'can now be safely revealed, since I no longer have anything to fear from its disclosure. He was called (and if he is still alive he is still called) Arrighetto Capece, and my own name is not Giannotto but Giusfredi. Furthermore, I have not the slightest doubt that if I were a free man, I could return to Sicily and occupy, even now, a position of the highest importance.'

The good man asked no more questions, but at the first opportunity he referred the whole matter to Currado. And although, as he listened, Currado put on a show of indifference for the gaoler's benefit, he went straight to Madonna Beritola and asked her in a pleasant manner whether she and Arrighetto had ever had a son called Giusfredi. Bursting into tears the woman replied that if the older of her two sons was still alive, this indeed would be his name, and that he would now be twenty-two years old.

On hearing this, Currado concluded that the young man must be telling the truth, and it occurred to him that, in this case, he was in a position to perform an act of clemency that would repair both his own and his daughter's honour, namely to offer her to him in marriage. He therefore arranged a secret interview with Giannotto, in the course of which he interrogated him in detail on the whole of his past life. And having confirmed beyond any doubt that he was indeed Giusfredi, the son of Arrighetto Capece, he said:

'Giannotto, you are aware how great an injury you have done to me in the person of my own daughter. I treated you as a friend, and it was your duty as my servant never to do anything that would undermine my honour, or that of my family. Many another man, in my place, would have had you ignominiously put to death, but I could not bring myself to do such a thing. Now, since what you say is true, and you are a man of gentle birth, I desire with your consent to put an end to your suffering and release you from your wretched, captive existence, at the same time restoring both your own reputation and mine. As you are aware, my daughter Spina, for whom you formed so loving but improper an attachment, is a widow, and she has a good, large dowry. You are acquainted with her ways, and with her father and mother; of your own present condition, I say nothing. Therefore, if you are agreeable, I am willing to convert a dishonourable friendship into an honourable marriage, and allow you to live with her here in my house for as long as you wish to remain, as though you were my own son.'

Giannotto's fine physique had been wasted away by his imprisonment, but the innate nobility of his spirit was in no way impaired, and he still loved his lady as wholeheartedly as ever. So that, although he found himself in the other man's power, and wished for nothing better than what Currado was proposing, he had not the slightest hesitation in following the promptings of his noble heart.

'Currado,' he replied, 'neither the lust for power nor the desire for riches nor any other motive has ever led me to harbour treacherous designs against your person or property. I loved your daughter, I love her still, and I shall always love her, because I consider her a worthy object of my love. And if, in wooing her, I was acting in a manner that would commonly be regarded as dishonourable, the fault I committed was one which is inseparable from youth. In order to eradicate it, one would have to do away with youth altogether. Besides, it would not be considered half so serious as you and many others maintain, if old men would remember that they were once young, and if they would measure other people's shortcomings against their own and vice versa. I committed this fault, not as your enemy, but as your friend. It has always been my wish to do what you are now proposing, and if I had thought your consent would be forthcoming, I would have asked you long ago for your daughter's hand. Coming at this moment, when my expectations were at such a low ebb, your consent is all the more gratifying to me. But if your intentions do not match your words, please do not feed me with vain hopes. Send me back to my prison-cell and have me treated as cruelly as you like. Whatever you do to me, I shall always love Spina, and for her sake I shall always love and respect her father.'

Currado listened in amazement to Giannotto's words, which convinced him of both his courage and the warmth of his love, increasing his esteem for the young man. He therefore rose to his feet, embraced and kissed him, and gave orders without further ado for Spina to be brought there in secret.

She had turned all pale, thin and weak in prison, and like Giannotto, she almost seemed another person as, in Currado's presence and by mutual consent, they took the marriage vows according to our custom.

A few days later, having kept the whole matter secret and provided them with everything they could possibly need or desire, he decided it was time to break the glad tidings to their respective mothers, and summoning his lady and Cavriuola, he turned to the latter and said:

'What would you say, my lady, if I were to arrange for your elder son to be restored to you, as the husband of one of my daughters?'

'The only thing I could say,' replied Cavriuola, 'would be that if it were possible for me to be more obliged to you than I am already, then inasmuch as you would be giving me something I value more than my own life, my debt would be correspondingly large. And by restoring him to me in the way you describe, you would in some measure be rekindling my lost hopes.'

She then stopped and burst into tears, and Currado turned to his lady, saying:

'And what would you say, my dear, if I were to present you with such a son-in-law?'

'If it were pleasing to you,' the lady replied, 'I would not object to a vagrant for a son-in-law, let alone a man who is of noble birth.'

'Within a few days,' said Currado, 'I hope to have good news for you both.'

Meanwhile, the two young people were gradually putting flesh on their bones, and when Currado saw that they had quite recovered, he had them dressed in fine clothes, and turned to Giusfredi, saying:

'Would it not add greatly to your happiness to see your mother in this place?'

'My mother suffered such appalling misfortunes,' replied Giusfredi, 'that I cannot believe she has survived them. But if she has, I would be very glad indeed to see her, for with her advice I believe I could largely repair my fortunes in Sicily.'

Currado then summoned the two ladies, and they both smothered the new bride with affection, at the same time wondering what had happened to soften Currado's heart to the extent of uniting her in wedlock with Giannotto.

With Currado's words fresh in her memory, Madonna Beritola had meanwhile begun to stare intently at the young man. Suddenly, some occult force stirred within her, causing her to recollect the boyish features of her son's face. And without awaiting further proof of his identity, she rushed towards him and flung her arms about his neck. Her feelings of maternal joy and affection were so intense that she was unable to utter a word: on the contrary, she lost all the power of her five senses and collapsed in the arms of her son as though she were dead. Giannotto, for his part, was filled with amazement, for he could remember having seen her on many previous occasions in that same castle without ever having recognized her. Nevertheless, he now knew instinctively that she was his mother, and, bursting into tears and reproaching himself for his former indifference, he received her in his arms and kissed her with tenderness. Shortly afterwards, with the loving assistance of Spina and Currado's lady, who applied cold water and other remedies, Madonna Beritola recovered her senses and embraced her son all over again, weeping copiously and uttering a stream of gentle endearments. And, giving vent to her maternal affection, she kissed him a thousand times or more whilst he held her in his arms and gazed at her in awe and reverence.

When the chaste and joyful greetings had been repeated three or four times* to the no small pleasure and approval of the onlookers, and mother and son had exchanged the story of their adventures, Giusfredi turned to Currado, who, having already informed his friends about the marriage and received their delighted approval, had given orders for a sumptuous and splendid banquet, and he said:

*B. is here quoting the opening lines from Canto VII of Dante's *Purgatorio*.

'Currado, you have bestowed many favours upon me and you have long sheltered my mother under your roof. But so that we may use your good offices to the full, I now want to ask you to gladden my mother, my wedding-feast and myself by sending for my brother. As I have told you already, he and I were seized by pirates acting for Messer Guasparrino d'Oria, who is detaining him in his house in the rôle of a servant. And I would also like you to send somebody to Sicily who can bring us a clear picture of conditions there, and tell us whether my father, Arrighetto, is alive or dead, and whether, if he is alive, he is in good health.'

Giusfredi's request was well received by Currado, who immediately sent experienced couriers to Genoa and Sicily. The one who went to Genoa called on Messer Guasparrino and earnestly entreated him on Currado's behalf to send him The Outcast and his nurse, giving him a concise account of what Currado had done for Giusfredi and his mother.

'It is true,' said Messer Guasparrino, who was greatly astonished by this tale, 'that I would do anything in my power to please Currado. And for the past fourteen years, the boy you mention, and his mother, have certainly been under my roof. I will gladly send them to him, but you are to warn him from me not to pay too much attention to the tall stories of Giannotto, who now masquerades, if I understand you aright, under the name of Giusfredi. That young man is much more cunning than Currado seems to realize.'

He said no more, but having attended to the good man's lodging he secretly sent for the nurse and questioned her closely on the subject. She had already heard about the rebellion in Sicily, and on learning that Arrighetto was alive, she abandoned her former fear and told him the whole story, explaining her reasons for the action she had taken.

On finding that the nurse's account corresponded exactly with that of Currado's emissary, Messer Guasparrino began to take her story seriously. Being a very astute man, he took various steps to have it thoroughly checked, becoming more and more convinced of its veracity with every scrap of new evidence he discovered. Ashamed at having treated the boy so contemptuously, he made amends by bestowing a wife on him in the person of his pretty little eleven-year-old daughter, together with a huge dowry, for he was well aware of Arrighetto's past and present fame. After celebrating the event in great style, he embarked, along with the youth, his daughter, Currado's emissary, and the nurse, on a well-armed galliot, and sailed for Lerici, where he was met by Currado. Then, with the whole of his company, he proceeded to one of Currado's castles, not very far from there, where the great wedding-feast was about to be held.

The general rejoicing, whether that of the mother on seeing her son again, or that of the two brothers, or that with which all three greeted the faithful nurse, or that displayed by everyone towards Messer Guasparrino and his daughter and vice versa, or that of the whole company in the presence of Currado, his lady, his children and his friends, would be impossible to describe in words. And thus I leave it, ladies, to your imagination. But to crown it all, the Lord God, whose generosity knows no bounds once it is set in motion, arranged things so that news should arrive that Arrighetto was alive and in good health.

For amid the great rejoicing, when the guests, men and women, were still seated round the tables, having proceeded no further than the first course, Currado's other emissary returned from Sicily. Amongst other things, he narrated how Arrighetto had been held prisoner in Catania on the orders of King Charles, and how, after the country's insurrection against the King, the people had stormed the prison, killing his gaolers and setting him free. Since he was King Charles's bitterest opponent, they had then elected him their leader and joined him in pursuing and killing the French. For this reason, he had achieved a high reputation in the eyes of King Peter, who had reinstated him in all his possessions and titles. And so he now enjoyed a position of great honour and authority.

The messenger added that Arrighetto had welcomed him very warmly, being overjoyed beyond description to hear about his wife and son, of whom he had received no news since the time of his capture. He was in fact sending a brigantine with some gentlemen aboard, to come and fetch them, and they were due to arrive at any moment.

The envoy's announcement was greeted with prolonged cheering and rejoicing, and Currado promptly went out with some of his friends to meet the gentlemen who were coming to fetch Madonna

Beritola and Giusfredi; and after giving them a hearty welcome, he took them in to his banquet, less than half of which had so far been served.

Such was the delight of Beritola, Giusfredi and all the others on seeing them that they almost raised the roof with their greeting. But before sitting down to eat, the Sicilians conveyed Arrighetto's warmest greeting and deepest thanks to Currado and his lady for the hospitality they had offered to his wife and son, and pledged his readiness to assist them in any way within his power. They then turned to Messer Guasparrino, whose courteous action had taken them by surprise, and said they were quite certain that when Arrighetto came to know of the generous settlement he had made on The Outcast he would be just as grateful to him as he was to Currado, or possibly even more. Then without further ado, they turned with great gusto to the business of feasting the two brides and their respective bridegrooms.

Currado's entertainment of his son-in-law and his other friends and relatives was not confined to that day alone, but extended over many of the days that followed. When the feasting was over, and Madonna Beritola, Giusfredi and the others felt that the time had come for their departure, they went aboard the brig, taking Spina with them, and to the accompaniment of copious tears they took their leave of Currado, his wife, and Messer Guasparrino. The winds being favourable, they soon reached Sicily, and on their arrival at Palermo they were all, the two sons and their womenfolk alike, greeted by Arrighetto with a warmth that beggars description. There it is believed that they all lived long and happily, at peace with the Almighty and grateful for the blessings He had bestowed upon them.

SEVENTH STORY

The Sultan of Babylon sends his daughter off to marry the King of Algarve. Owing to a series of mishaps, she passes through the hands of nine men in various places within the space of four years. Finally, having been restored to her father as a virgin, she sets off, as before, to become the King of Algarve's wife.

The young ladies, who were feeling very sorry for Madonna Beritola, would possibly have dissolved into tears if Emilia's recital of the lady's woes had continued for very much longer. When, finally, the tale was finished, it was the queen's wish that Panfilo should take up the storytelling, and being very obedient he began forthwith as follows:

Delectable ladies, it is no easy matter for a man to decide what is in his best interests. For as we have often had occasion to observe, there are many who have considered that only their poverty stood between themselves and a secure, trouble-free life, and they have not only prayed to God for riches, but sought deliberately to acquire them, sparing themselves neither effort nor danger in the process. And no sooner have they succeeded, than the prospect of a substantial legacy has frequently caused them to be murdered by people who, before they had become rich, had never dreamed of doing them any harm. Others have risen from low estate to the dizzy heights of kingship through a thousand dangerous battles, spilling the blood of their nearest and dearest as they went along, thinking sovereign power represented the peak of happiness. But as they could have seen and heard for themselves, it was a happiness fraught with endless fear and worry, and at the cost of their lives they came to realize that the chalice at a royal table may sometimes be poisoned, even though it is made of gold. Again, there have been many people who have ardently yearned for bodily strength and beauty, whilst others have longed with equal intensity for bodily ornaments, only to discover too late that the very things they so unwisely desired were the cause of their death or unhappiness.

But in order not to become involved in a detailed review embracing the whole range of human desires, I will merely affirm that no man can, with complete confidence, elect any one of them as being wholly immune from the accidents of Fortune. For if we were to proceed at all times in a correct manner, we would have to resign ourselves to the acquisition and possession of whatever has been granted to us by the One who alone knows what we need and has the power to provide it for us. However, there are many ways in which people sin through their desires, and you, gracious ladies, sin above all in one particular way, which is in your desiring to be beautiful, inasmuch as, being dissatisfied with the attractions bestowed upon you by Nature, you go to extraordinary lengths in trying to improve them. And therefore I would like to tell you a story about a Saracen girl's ill-starred beauty, which in the space of about four years caused her to be newly married on nine separate occasions.

A long time ago, Babylon was ruled by a sultan called Beminedab, during whose reign it was unusual for anything to happen that was contrary to his wishes. Apart from numerous other children, both male and female, this man possessed a daughter called Alatiel, who, at that period, according to everybody who had set eyes on her, was the most beautiful woman to be found anywhere on earth. Now, the Sultan had recently been attacked by a great horde of Arabs, and inflicted a major defeat on his aggressors, receiving timely assistance from the King of Algarve, who asked the Sultan, as a special favour, to give him Alatiel as his wife. The Sultan agreed, and having seen her aboard a well-armed and well-appointed ship with a retinue of noblemen and noblewomen and a large quantity of elegant and precious accoutrements, he bade her a fond farewell.

Finding the weather favourable, the ship's crew put on full sail, and for several days after leaving Alexandria the voyage was prosperous. But one day, when they had passed Sardinia and were looking forward to journey's end, they ran into a series of sudden squalls, each of which was exceptionally violent, and these gave the ship such a terrible buffeting that passengers and crew were convinced time and again that the end had come. But they had plenty of spirit, and by exerting all their skill and energy they survived the onslaught of the mountainous seas for two whole days. However, as night approached for the third time since the beginning of the storm, which showed no sign of relenting but on the contrary was increasing in fury, they felt the ship foundering. Though in fact they were not far from the coast of Majorca, they had no idea where they were, because it was a dark night and the sky was covered with thick black clouds, and hence it was impossible to estimate their position either with the ship's instruments or with the naked eye.

It now became a case of every man for himself, and there was nothing for it but to launch a longboat, into which the ship's officers leapt, preferring to put their trust in that rather than in the crippled vessel. But they had no sooner abandoned ship than every man aboard followed their example and leapt into the longboat, undeterred by the fact that the earlier arrivals were fighting them off with knives in their hands. Thus, in trying to save their lives, they did the exact opposite; for the longboat was not built for holding so many people in weather of this sort and it sank, taking everybody with it.

Meanwhile, the ship itself, though torn open and almost waterlogged, was driven swiftly along by powerful winds until eventually it ran aground on a beach on the island of Majorca. By this time, the only people still aboard were the lady and her female attendants, and they were all lying there like dead creatures, paralysed with terror by the raging tempest. The ship's impetus was so great that it thrust its way firmly into the sand before coming to rest a mere stone's throw from the shore, and since the wind was no longer able to move it, there it remained for the rest of the night, to be pounded by the sea.

By the time it was broad daylight, the storm had abated considerably, and the lady, who was feeling practically half-dead, raised her head and began, weak as she was, to call out to her servants one after another. But it was all to no purpose, because they were too far away to hear. On receiving no response and seeing nobody about, she wondered what on earth had happened, and began to be filled with considerable alarm. She staggered to her feet to discover that her maids of honour and the other women were lying about all over the place, and she attempted to rouse each of them in turn by calling to them at the top of her voice. But few of them showed any signs of life because they had all been laid low by their terror and the heavings of their stomachs, and her own fears were accordingly increased.

Nevertheless, since she was all alone and possessed no idea of her whereabouts, she felt in need of someone to talk to, and so she went round prodding the ones who were still alive and forced them to their feet, only to discover that none of them had any idea what had happened to all the men aboard. And when they saw that the ship was aground and full of water, they all started crying as though they would burst.

It was not until mid-afternoon that they were able to make their plight apparent to anybody on the shore or elsewhere in the vicinity who would come to their assistance. Halfway through the afternoon, in fact, a nobleman whose name was Pericone da Visalgo happened to pass that way as he was returning from one of his estates. He was riding along on horseback with several of his men, and when he saw the ship he immediately guessed what had happened. So he ordered one of his servants to try and clamber aboard without further delay and bring him a report on how matters stood. The servant had quite a struggle, but eventually he boarded the ship, where he found the young gentlewoman, frightened out of her senses, hiding with her handful of companions in the forepeak. On seeing him, the women burst into tears and repeatedly pleaded for mercy, but when they perceived that neither he nor they could understand what the other party was saying, they tried to explain their predicament by means of gestures.

Having sized up the situation to the best of his ability, the servant reported his findings to Pericone, who promptly arranged for the women to be brought ashore along with the most valuable of those items on the ship that could be salvaged, and escorted them all to his castle, where he restored the women's spirits by arranging for them to be fed and rested. He could see, from the richness of their apparel, that he had stumbled across some great lady of quality, and he quickly gathered which of them she must be because she was the sole centre of the other women's attention. The lady was pallid and extremely dishevelled-looking as a result of her exhausting experiences at sea, but it seemed to Pericone that she possessed very fine features, and for this reason he resolved there and then that if she had no husband he would marry her, and that, if marriage proved to be out of the question, he would make her his mistress.

Pericone, who was a very powerful, vigorous-looking fellow, caused the lady to be waited upon hand and foot, and when, after a few days, she had fully recovered, he found that she was even more beautiful than he had ever thought possible. He was greatly pained by the fact that they were unable to communicate with each other, and that he could not therefore discover who she was. Nevertheless, being immensely taken with her beauty, he behaved lovingly and agreeably towards her in an endeavour to persuade her to do his pleasure without a struggle. But it was no use: she refused to have anything to do with him; and meanwhile Pericone's ardour continued to increase.

The lady had no idea where she was, but she quickly gathered from their mode of living that the people she was staying with were Christians, and she could see little purpose, even if she had known her whereabouts, in revealing her identity. From the way Pericone was behaving, she knew that sooner or later, whether she liked it or not, she would be compelled to let him have his way with her, but meanwhile she was proudly resolved to turn a blind eye to her sorrowful predicament. To the three surviving members of her female retinue, she gave instructions that they should never disclose their identity to anyone until such time as they were in a position that offered them a clear prospect of freedom. Furthermore, she implored them to preserve their chastity, declaring her own determination to submit to no man's pleasure except her husband's – a sentiment that was greeted with approval by the three women, who said they would do their utmost to follow her instructions.

As the days passed, and Pericone came into closer proximity with the object of his desires, his advances were more firmly rejected, and the flames of his passion raged correspondingly fiercer. Realizing that his flattery was getting him nowhere, he decided to fall back on ingenuity and subterfuge, holding brute strength in reserve as a last resort. He had noticed more than once that the lady liked the taste of wine, which, since it is prohibited by her religion, she was unaccustomed to drinking, and by using this in the service of Venus, he thought it possible that she would yield to him. And so one evening, having feigned indifference concerning the matter for which she had paraded so much distaste, he held a splendid banquet with all the

trappings of a great festive occasion, at which the lady was present.
The meal was notable for its abundance of good food, and Pericone
arranged with the steward who was serving the lady to keep her well
supplied with a succession of different wines. The steward carried out
his instructions to the letter, and the lady, being caught off her
guard and carried away by the agreeable taste of the wines, drank
more than was consistent with her decorum. Forgetting all the
misfortunes she had experienced, she became positively merry, and
when she saw some women dancing in the Majorcan manner, she
herself danced Alexandrian fashion.

On seeing this, Pericone felt that he would soon obtain what he
wanted, and calling for further large quantities of food and drink, he
caused the banquet to continue until the small hours of the morning.
Finally, when the guests had departed, he accompanied the lady,
alone, into her room. Without the least show of embarrassment,
being rather more flushed with wine than tempered by virtue, she
then undressed in Pericone's presence as though he were one of her
maidservants, and got into bed. Pericone lost no time in following
her example. Having snuffed out all the lights, he quickly scrambled
in from the other side and lay down beside her, and taking her into
his arms without meeting any resistance on her part, he began making
amorous sport with her. She had no conception of the kind of horn
that men do their butting with, and when she felt what was happening, it was almost as though she regretted having turned a deaf ear
to Pericone's flattery and could not see why she had waited for an
invitation before spending her nights so agreeably. For it was she
herself who was now issuing the invitation, and she did so several
times over, not in so many words, since she was unable to make
herself understood, but by way of her gestures.

Great indeed was their mutual delight. But Fortune, not content
with converting her from a king's bride into a baron's mistress, thrust
a more terrible friendship upon her.

Pericone had a twenty-five-year-old brother, fair and fresh as a
garden rose, whose name was Marato. He had already seen
the lady and taken an enormous liking to her, and as far as he
could judge from her reactions, she seemed to be very fond of him
also. Thus the only thing that appeared to be standing between him

and the conquest he desired to make of her was the strict watch maintained by Pericone. He therefore devised a nefarious scheme which he lost no time in pursuing to its dreadful conclusion.

In the port of the town, there happened at that time to be a ship commanded by two young Genoese, with a full cargo for Klarenza in the Peloponnese. She was already under canvas, ready to put to sea with the first favourable wind, and Marato made an arrangement with her masters for himself and the lady to be taken aboard the following night. This done, he decided how he would have to proceed, and when it was dark he wandered unobtrusively into his brother's house, to which he had open access, and concealed himself inside.

He had meanwhile enlisted the aid of some trusted companions for his enterprise, and in the dead of night, having let them into the house, he led them to the place where Pericone and the woman were sleeping. Entering the room, they killed Pericone in his sleep and seized the lady, who woke up and started to cry, threatening her with death if she made any noise. Then, taking with them a considerable quantity of Pericone's most precious possessions, they departed without being heard and made their way to the quayside, where Marato boarded the ship with the lady, leaving his companions to go their separate ways.

The ship's crew, taking advantage of a strong and favourable wind, cast off and sailed swiftly away.

The lady was sorely distressed by this second catastrophe, coming as it did so soon after the first. But Marato, with the Heaven-sent assistance of St Stiffen-in-the-hand, began consoling her to such good effect that she soon returned his affection and forgot all about Pericone. She had hardly begun to feel settled, however, before Fortune, not content, it seemed, with her previous handiwork, engineered yet another calamity. As we have almost grown tired of repeating, the woman had the body of an angel and a temperament to match, and the two young masters of the vessel fell so violently in love with her that they could concentrate on nothing else except how best they might make themselves useful and agreeable to her, at the same time taking care not to let Marato see what they were up to.

On discovering that they were both in love with the same woman, they talked the matter over in secret and agreed to make the lady's conquest a mutual affair, as though love were capable of being shared out like merchandise or profits. For some time their plans were thwarted because they found that Marato kept a close watch on her. But one day, when the ship was sailing along like the wind and Marato was standing on the stern facing seaward without the least suspicion of their intentions, they both crept up on him, seized him quickly from behind, and hurled him into the sea. By the time anybody so much as noticed that Marato had fallen overboard, they had already sailed on for over a mile, and the lady, hearing what had happened and seeing no way of going to his rescue, began to fill the whole ship with the sounds of her latest affliction.

The two gallants immediately rushed to her assistance, and with the aid of honeyed words and extravagant promises, few of which she understood, they attempted to pacify her. What she was bemoaning was not so much the loss of Marato as her own sorry plight, and so after she had listened to a stream of fine talk, repeated twice over, she seemed considerably less distraught. The two brothers then got down to a private discussion to decide which of them was to take her off to bed. Each man claimed priority over the other, and having failed to reach any agreement on the matter they began to argue fiercely between themselves. Nor did their quarrel stop with the exchange of verbal abuse. Losing their tempers, they reached for their knives and hurled themselves furiously upon one another, and before the ship's crew could separate the pair, they had both inflicted a number of stab-wounds, from which one man died instantly whilst the other emerged with serious injuries to various parts of his body. The lady was sorely distressed by all this, for she could see that she was now alone on the ship with nobody to turn to for help or advice, and she was greatly afraid lest the relatives and companions of the two men should vent their rage upon her. However, partly because of the injured man's pleas on her behalf, partly because they soon arrived at Klarenza, the danger to her person was short-lived. On their arrival, she disembarked with the injured man, and went to live with him at an inn, whence the story of her great beauty spread rapidly through the city, eventually reaching the ears of the Prince of Morea, who was living in Klarenza at that time. He therefore demanded to see her, and on discovering her to be more beautiful than she had been reported, he immediately fell so ardently in love with her that he could think of nothing else.

When he learnt about the circumstances of her arrival in the city, he saw no reason why he should not be able to have her. And indeed, once the wounded man's relatives discovered that the Prince was putting out inquiries, they promptly sent her off to him without asking any questions. The Prince was highly delighted, but so also was the lady, who considered that she had now escaped from a most dangerous situation. On finding that she was endowed with stately manners as well as beauty, the Prince calculated, since he could obtain no other clue to her identity, that she must be a woman of gentle birth, and his love for her was accordingly redoubled. And not only did he keep her in splendid style, but he treated her as though she were his wife rather than his mistress.

On comparing her present circumstances with the awful experiences through which she had passed, the lady considered herself very fortunately placed. Now that she was contented and completely recovered, her beauty flourished to such a degree that the whole of the eastern empire seemed to talk of nothing else. And so it was that the Duke of Athens, a handsome, powerfully-proportioned youth who was a friend and relative of the Prince, was smitten with a desire to see her, and under the pretext of paying the Prince one of his customary visits, he came with a splendid and noble retinue to Klarenza, where he was received with honour amid great rejoicing.

A few days later, the two men fell to conversing about this woman's beauty, and the Duke asked whether she was so marvellous an object as people claimed.

'Far more so,' replied the Prince. 'But instead of accepting my word for it, I would rather that you judged with your own eyes.'

Thereupon the Prince invited the Duke to follow him, and they made their way to the lady's apartments. Having been warned of their approach, she received them with great civility, her face radiant with happiness. She seated herself between the two men, but the pleasure of conversing with her was denied them because she understood little or nothing of their language. And so each man stared in fascination upon her, in particular the Duke, who could scarcely believe that she was a creature of this earth. Little realizing, as he gazed at her, that he was imbibing the poison of love through the medium of his eyes, and fondly believing that he could satisfy his pleasure merely by looking at her, he was completely bowled over by her beauty and fell violently in love with her.

When he and the Prince had taken their leave of her, and he had an opportunity to indulge in a little quiet reflection, he came to the conclusion that the Prince must be the happiest man on earth, in possessing so beautiful a plaything. Many and varied were the thoughts that passed through his mind until eventually, his blazing passion gaining the upper hand over his sense of honour, he decided that whatever the consequences, he would remove this pleasure-giving object from the Prince and do all in his power to make it serve his own happiness.

Being determined to move swiftly, he thrust aside all regard for reason and fair play, and concentrated solely on cunning. And one day, in the furtherance of his evil designs, he made arrangements with one of the Prince's most trusted servants, Ciuriaci by name, to have all his horses and luggage placed secretly in readiness for a sudden departure. During the night, he and a companion, both fully armed, were silently admitted by the aforesaid Ciuriaci into the Prince's bedroom. It was a very hot night, and although the woman was asleep, the Prince was standing completely naked at a window over-looking the sea, taking advantage of a breeze that was blowing from that quarter. The Duke, having told his companion beforehand what he had to do, stole quietly across the room as far as the window, drove a dagger into the Prince's back with so much force that it passed right through his body, and catching him quickly in his arms he hurled him out of the window.

Now the palace stood very high above sea-level, and the window at which the Prince had been standing overlooked a cluster of houses that had been laid in ruins by the violence of the sea. It was but rarely, if ever, that anybody went there, and consequently, as the Duke had already foreseen, no one's attention was attracted by the body of the Prince as it fell.

On seeing this deed accomplished, the Duke's companion quickly produced a noose that he had brought along for the purpose, and pretending to embrace Ciuriaci, he threw it round his neck, and drew it tight so that Ciuriaci could not make any noise. He was then joined by the Duke, and they strangled the man before hurling him out to join his master. This done, they satisfied themselves that neither the lady nor anybody else had heard them, and then the Duke picked up a lantern, carried it over to the bed, and silently uncovered the woman, who was sleeping soundly. Having exposed her whole body, he gazed upon her in rapt fascination, and although he had admired her when she was clothed, now that she was naked his admiration was greater beyond all comparison. The flames of his desire burned correspondingly fiercer, and unperturbed by the crime he had just committed, he lay down at her side, his hands still dripping with blood, and made love to the woman, who was half-asleep and believed him to be the Prince.

Eventually, after spending some time with her, he rose giddily to his feet and summoned a few of his men, whom he commanded to hold the lady in such a way that she could not make any noise. Then he conducted her through the secret door by way of which he had entered, and, having settled her on horseback with a minimum of noise, he set out with all his men in the direction of Athens. Since he was already married, however, it was not in Athens itself that he deposited this unhappiest of women, but at a very beautiful palace of his, not far from the city, overlooking the sea. Here he established her in secluded splendour, and saw that she was provided with everything she needed.

On the following day, the Prince's courtiers had waited until the late afternoon for their master to rise from his bed. But when they still heard no sound, they pushed open his bedroom-doors, which were not locked, and found the room deserted. They thereupon assumed that he had gone away somewhere in secret in order to spend a few days in the delightful company of this fair mistress of his, and they gave no further thought to the matter.

It was thus that matters stood, when on the very next day a local idiot, who had strayed into the ruins where the bodies of the Prince and Ciuriaci were lying, dragged Ciuriaci forth by the rope round his neck and started pulling him through the streets. On recognizing who it was, the people were greatly astonished, and talked the idiot into leading them to the place from which he had dragged the body, where, to the enormous grief of the whole city, they also found the body of the Prince. After burying him with full honours, they took steps to discover who was responsible for this unspeakable crime, and on finding that the Duke of Athens had departed secretly and was nowhere to be found, they rightly concluded that he must be the culprit and that he must have carried off the lady as well. So that, having hastily elected their dead ruler's brother as their new prince, they urged him with all the eloquence at their command to take his revenge. And when further evidence came to light, proving that their suspicions were correct, the Prince summoned friends, kinsfolk and servants from various places to come to his support and he quickly assembled a huge and powerful army, with which he set out to make war on the Duke of Athens.

When the Duke received word of the operations, he too mobilized all his armed forces for his defence, and many powerful outsiders came to his assistance, including two who were sent by the Emperor of Constantinople, namely his son, Constant, and his nephew, Manuel. These latter, arriving at the head of large and well-drilled contingents, received a warm welcome from the Duke. But the welcome they received from the Duchess was even warmer, because she was Constant's sister.

With the prospect of war becoming daily more imminent, the Duchess chose a convenient moment to invite the two men to her room, where, talking without stopping amid floods of tears, she told them the whole story, explaining the reasons for the war and exposing the wrong practised upon her by the Duke on account of this woman, of whose existence he imagined her to be ignorant. Bewailing her lot in no uncertain terms, she begged them, for the sake of the Duke's honour and her own happiness, to take whatever measures they could devise for setting matters to rights.

The young men were already fully informed about the whole business, and so without asking too many questions they consoled her to the best of their ability and gave her every ground for optimism. Then, having discovered from the Duchess where the lady was staying, they took their leave of her. Since they had often heard glowing accounts of this woman's marvellous beauty, they were naturally anxious to see her, and they therefore asked the Duke if he would introduce her to them. The Duke agreed to do so, forgetting the fate which had befallen the Prince after granting a similar favour. And the following morning, having ordered a magnificent banquet to be prepared in a beautiful garden on the estate where the lady was living, he took the two men and a handful of other friends to dine with her.

On sitting down in her company, Constant began to stare at her in blank amazement, vowing to himself that he had never seen anything so beautiful, and that no one could possibly reproach the Duke, or anybody else, for resorting to treachery and other dishonest means in order to gain possession of so fair an object. Moreover, his admiration increased with every look he cast in her direction, so that eventually the same thing happened to him as had previously happened to the Duke. And when the time came for him to leave, he was so much in love with her that he dismissed the war completely from his mind and concentrated his thoughts on planning a way of abducting her, at the same time taking good care not to reveal his love to anyone.

But whilst he was struggling with his passion, the time arrived for marching against the Prince, who by now had almost reached the Duke's territories. Accordingly, at a given signal, the Duke set out from Athens with Constant and all the others, and they took up combat positions along certain stretches of the frontier so as to halt the Prince's advance. Constant's thoughts and sentiments continued to focus on the woman, and now that the Duke was no longer near her, he fancied that he had an excellent opportunity for obtaining what he wanted. And so a few days after their arrival at the frontier, he pretended to be seriously ill so that he would have a pretext for returning to Athens. He then handed over all his powers to Manuel, and with the Duke's permission he returned to Athens to stay with his sister. A few days later, having steered the conversation round to the sense of injury under which she was labouring on account of the Duke's mistress, he told her that if she so desired he could be of considerable assistance to her in this affair, in that he could have the woman removed from where she was staying and taken elsewhere.

Thinking that Constant was motivated by brotherly love and not by his love for the woman, the Duchess said that she would be only too pleased, provided it could be carried out in such a way that the Duke never discovered that she had given her consent to the scheme. Constant reassured her completely on this point, and accordingly the Duchess gave him permission to proceed in whatever way he considered best.

The first thing he did was to fit out a fast boat in secret, which one evening, having informed his men on board what they were to do, he sent to a spot near the garden of the place where the lady was living. Then he went there with another group of his men, to be amicably received by her retainers as well as by the lady herself, who, at her visitor's suggestion, accompanied Constant and his companions into the garden, whilst her servants trailed along behind. As though he wished to impart some message from the Duke, he then led her off alone in the direction of a gate, overlooking the sea, which had already been unlocked by one of his accomplices. At a given signal, the boat nosed her way inshore, and having had the lady seized and bundled quickly aboard, he turned to her servants, saying:

'Unless you want to be killed, don't move or make any sound. It is not my intention to steal the Duke's mistress, but to remove the injury he does to my sister.'

Since nobody dared offer any reply, Constant embarked with his men, settled himself next to the lady, who was crying, and ordered them to cast off and start rowing. And they plied their oars to such good effect that just before dawn on the following day they arrived at Aegina.

Going ashore there in order to rest, Constant amused himself in the company of the lady, who was bitterly bewailing her ill-starred beauty. Then they boarded the ship once again, and a few days later they arrived at Chios, where Constant decided to remain, for he thought he would be safe there from his father's strictures and from the possibility of having to surrender the stolen woman. For several days, the fair lady bemoaned her misfortune. Eventually, however, she responded to Constant's efforts at consoling her, and began, as on previous occasions, to derive pleasure from the fate to which Fortune had consigned her.

And this was how matters stood when Osbech, who was at that time the King of the Turks and who was constantly at war with the

Emperor, happened to pass through Smyrna, where he learned that Constant was leading a dissolute life on Chios with some stolen mistress of his, leaving himself wide open to attack. Arriving by night with a squadron of light warships, Osbech quietly entered the town with his men, took numerous people captive from their beds before they were aware of their enemies' arrival, and slaughtered those who had woken up in time to seize their arms. The invaders then set the whole town on fire, and having loaded their booty and prisoners on to the ships, they returned to Smyrna.

On reviewing the spoils of the expedition immediately after their return, Osbech, who was a young man, was delighted to discover the fair lady, whom he recognized as the one who had been taken, along with Constant, as she was lying asleep in her bed. So he promptly married her, and after celebrating the nuptials he happily devoted himself, for the next few months, to the pleasures of the marriage-bed.

Now, during the period immediately preceding these happenings, the Emperor had been negotiating a pact with the King of Cappadocia, Basano, whereby the latter was to descend with his forces on Osbech from one direction whilst the Emperor attacked him with his own troops from the other. He had not yet been able to bring the negotiations to a successful conclusion, however, because of his unwillingness to concede some of the more outrageous of Basano's demands. But on hearing what had happened to his son, he was so indignant that he immediately agreed to the King of Cappadocia's terms, and urged him to attack Osbech as soon as he possibly could, meanwhile making his own preparations for marching against him from the opposite direction.

When he heard about this, rather than allow himself to be sandwiched between two mighty rulers, Osbech assembled his army and marched against the King of Cappadocia, leaving his fair lady at Smyrna under the close supervision of a faithful retainer and friend. Some time later, he confronted and engaged the King of Cappadocia, and in the ensuing battle he was killed, whilst his army was defeated and put to flight. Flushed with victory, Basano began to advance unopposed on Smyrna, and all the people on his route did homage to him as their conqueror.

Meanwhile, the retainer in whose care Osbech had left his fair lady,

Antioco by name, had been so overwhelmed by her beauty that he
had betrayed the trust of his friend and master, and although he was
getting on in years, he had fallen in love with her. He was familiar
with her language, and this pleased her immensely because for several
years she had been more or less forced to lead the life of a deaf-mute
as she could neither understand what anybody was saying nor make
herself understood. With love spurring him on, Antioco began in the
first few days to take so many liberties with her that before long they
ceased to care about their lord and master who had gone off soldiering
to the wars, and not only did they become good friends, they also
became lovers. And as they lay between the sheets, they had a very
happy time of it together.

But when they heard that Osbech had been defeated and killed,
and that Basano was on his way there, carrying all before him, they
decided with one accord not to await his arrival. Taking with them a
substantial quantity of Osbech's most valuable possessions, they fled
together in secret and came to Rhodes. But they had not been living
there for very long when Antioco became mortally ill. With him at
the time there happened to be staying a Cypriot merchant, a bosom
friend of his whom he loved dearly, and realizing that his life was
drawing to its close, he decided to bequeath his property to him,
along with his beloved mistress. And so shortly before he died, he
summoned them both to his bedside, and said:

'I see quite plainly that my strength is failing, which saddens me
greatly because life has never been sweeter to me than of late. There is
one thing, however, that reconciles me to my fate, for I shall find
myself dying – if die I must – in the arms of the two people I love
best in the whole world: yours, my dear dear friend, and those of this
woman whom I have loved more deeply than I love myself, from the
earliest days of our acquaintance. All the same, it worries me to think
that when I am gone, she might be left here alone in a strange place,
with nobody to turn to for help or advice. And I should be all the
more worried if it were not for the knowledge of your own presence,
for I believe that you will cherish her, for my sake, as tenderly as you
would cherish me. In the event of my death, therefore, I commit her
and all my property to your charge, and with all my power I entreat
you to handle them both in whatever way you think most likely to

console my immortal spirit. And I beseech you, dear sweet lady, not to forget me when I am dead, so that in the next world I can claim to be loved in this world by the fairest woman ever fashioned by nature. Promise me faithfully that you will carry out these two requests of mine, and I shall undoubtedly die contented.'

As they listened to these words, both the lady and his merchant friend shed many a tear. When he had finished speaking, they soothed him and gave him their word of honour that in the event of his death they would do as he had asked. Very soon afterwards he passed away, and they saw that he was given an honourable funeral.

A few days later, having completed all his business in Rhodes and being desirous of taking ship on a Catalan carrack that was about to sail for Cyprus, the Cypriot merchant inquired of the fair lady what she was proposing to do, telling her that for his part, he was compelled to return to Cyprus. The lady said that if he had no objection, she would gladly accompany him, because she had hoped that out of his affection for Antioco, he would treat and regard her as a sister. The merchant assured her of his willingness to do whatever she asked, and with the object of protecting her from any harm that might befall her before they reached Cyprus, he passed her off as his wife. Having embarked on the ship, therefore, they were assigned to a small cabin on the poop-deck, and in order to maintain appearances, he bedded down with her in the same narrow little bunk. What happened next was something that neither of them had bargained for when leaving Rhodes, because what with the darkness, the enforced idleness, and the warmth of the bed, all of which are powerful stimulants, they were each consumed with an almost equally intense longing, and without sparing a thought for the love and friendship they owed to the dead Antioco, they began to excite each other, with the result that by the time they reached the Cypriot's home-port of Paphos, they had become husband and wife in good earnest. And for some time after their arrival in Paphos, they lived together in the merchant's house.

Now it so happened that there came to Paphos, on some business or other, a gentleman called Antigono, who was old in years and even older in wisdom. He was not a very rich man, because although he had undertaken numerous commissions in the service of the King of Cyprus, Fortune had never been particularly kind to him. One day, as he was walking past the house where the fair lady was living, at a time when the Cypriot merchant was away on a trading mission in Armenia, this Antigono happened to catch sight of the lady at one of the windows. Since she was very beautiful, he began to stare at her, and it occurred to him that he had seen her on some previous occasion, but try as he would he could not remember where.

For a long time now, the fair lady had been a plaything in the hands of Fortune, but the moment was approaching when her trials would be over. When she espied Antigono, she recalled having seen him at Alexandria, where he once occupied a position of some importance in her father's service. Knowing that her merchant was away, and being suddenly filled with the hope that there might be some possibility of returning once more to her regal status with the help of this man's advice, she sent for him at the earliest opportunity. When he called upon her, she shyly asked whether she was right in thinking him to be Antigono of Famagusta. Antigono said that he was, adding:

'I have an idea, ma'am, that I have seen you before, but I cannot for the life of me remember where. Pray be good enough, therefore, if you have no objection, to remind me who you are.'

On hearing that this was indeed the man she had assumed him to be, the lady burst into tears and threw her arms round his neck, and presently she asked her highly astonished visitor whether he had ever seen her in Alexandria. No sooner had she put the question than Antigono recognized her as the Sultan's daughter Alatiel, whom everybody believed to be drowned at sea, and he prepared to make her the ceremonial bow that was her due. But she would not allow this and asked him instead to come and sit down with her for a while. Complying, Antigono asked her in reverential tones how, when and whence she had come to Cyprus, and told her that the whole Egyptian nation had been convinced, for many years, that she had been drowned at sea.

'I wish to goodness they were right,' said the lady, 'and I think my father would share my opinion if he were ever to discover the sort of life I have led.' And so saying, she started crying prodigiously all over again, whereupon Antigono said to her:

'My lady, it is too soon for you to go upsetting yourself like this. Tell me about your misfortunes, if you like, and about the life you have been living. Possibly we shall find that the point has been reached where we shall be able, with God's help, to devise some happy outcome to your dilemma.'

'Antigono,' the fair lady replied, 'the other day, when I first saw you, it was as if I was seeing my own father. Prompted by the love and tenderness that I have an obligation to bear him, I revealed my presence to you, when I could have remained concealed. Yours is the first familiar face I have encountered for many years, and there are few people I could possibly be so contented to see. To you, therefore, as though you were my father, I shall reveal the story of my appalling misfortunes, which I have never related to anyone before. If, when you have heard what I have to say, you see any possibility of restoring me to my former state, I beseech you to explore it; if not, I must ask you never to tell a living soul that you have either seen me or heard anything about me.'

And so saying, never ceasing to weep, she told him about everything that had happened to her since the day on which she was shipwrecked off Majorca, whereupon Antigono too began to weep with compassion, and after considering the matter at some length, he said:

'My lady, since your identity has remained a secret throughout the course of your misadventures, I shall have no difficulty in restoring you to a higher place than ever in your father's affection, and you will then go to marry the King of Algarve, as originally arranged.'

When she inquired how it was to be managed, he explained to her in detail what she was to do. And to avoid all further delay and any further complications, Antigono returned at once to Famagusta and went to see the King, addressing him thus:

'My lord, if it pleases you, you can at the same time cover yourself with glory and render a most valuable service to one who has grown poor while acting on your behalf. I refer of course to myself.'

The King asked him to explain, and Antigono replied:

'The fair young daughter of the Sultan, who was long reputed to have been drowned at sea, has arrived in Paphos. For many years, she has endured extreme hardship in the struggle to preserve her honour, she has been reduced to comparative poverty, and she wishes to return to her father. If you were to send her back to the Sultan under my escort, it would redound greatly to your credit, and I would be sure of a rich reward. It is unlikely, moreover, that the Sultan will ever forget your charitable deed.'

His regal magnanimity having been stirred, the King readily gave his consent, and he dispatched a guard of honour to accompany the lady to Famagusta, where he and the Queen welcomed her amid scenes of indescribable rejoicing and magnificent pomp and splendour. And when she was asked by the King and Queen to tell them about her adventures, she replied exactly as she had been instructed by Antigono.

A few days later, at her own request, the King sent her back to the Sultan under the guardianship of Antigono, providing her with a distinguished retinue of fine gentlemen and ladies-in-waiting, and needless to say, the Sultan gave her a tremendous welcome, which he extended also to Antigono and the whole of her retinue. After she had rested for a while, the Sultan demanded to know how it came about that she was still alive, where she had been living all this time, and why she had never sent word of what she was doing.

Remembering Antigono's instructions to the tiniest detail, the lady then addressed her father as follows:

'Father, some twenty days after my departure, our ship was disabled by a raging tempest, and ran aground at night on the shores of the western Mediterranean, near a place called Aiguesmortes. I never discovered what happened to all the men who were in the ship. All I can remember is that when the dawn arrived, I truly felt as if I was rising from the dead. The local people had already espied the wreck, and they came running from miles around in order to plunder it. I was put ashore with two of my maidservants, who were instantly snatched by young men and carried off in different directions, and that was the last I saw or heard of them. I myself, after putting up stout resistance, was overpowered by two young men and hauled away by my tresses, weeping bitterly all the time. But just as they were crossing a road in order to drag me into a thick forest, four men happened to pass that way on horseback, and when my captors saw them coming, they instantly let me go and took to their heels.

'On seeing this, the four men, who to judge from their appearance seemed to hold positions of authority, rode swiftly up and asked me a lot of questions, to which I gave as many answers. But it was impossible to make ourselves understood. After talking together for some little while, they took me up on one of their horses and conducted me to a convent of nuns who practised these men's religion. I do not know what it was that they said to the nuns, but at any rate I was kindly received by everybody, and I was always treated with great respect. Whilst there, I joined them in the devout worship of St Stiffen, for whom the women of that country possess a deep affection. But after staying with them for some time, and acquiring a discreet knowledge of their language, I was asked who I was and where I had come from. Knowing where I was, I feared to tell them the truth lest they should expel me as an enemy of their religion, and so I replied that I was the daughter of a fine nobleman of Cyprus, who was sending me to be married in Crete when we were driven by a storm on to those shores and shipwrecked.

'For fear of meeting a worse fate, I imitated their customs regularly, in various ways. Eventually, I was asked by the oldest of these women, whom the others refer to as the Abbess, whether I wished to return to Cyprus, and I replied that there was nothing I desired more. However, being concerned for my honour, she was unwilling to entrust me to anyone coming to Cyprus until about two months ago, when certain French gentlemen, some of them related to the Abbess, arrived there with their wives. And when she heard that they were going to visit the Sepulchre, where the man they look upon as God was buried after being killed by the Jews, she placed me under their care and asked them to hand me over to my father on reaching Cyprus.

'It would take too long to describe how greatly I was honoured and how warmly I was welcomed by these noblemen and their wives. Suffice it to say that we all took ship, and that several days later we reached Paphos, where I found myself facing a dilemma, because there was nobody there who knew me and I had no idea what to say to these gentlemen, who were anxious to carry out the venerable lady's instructions and hand me over to my father.

'However, it was the will of Allah, who was possibly feeling sorry for me, that just as we stepped ashore at Paphos Antigono should be standing on the quayside. I promptly called out to him, and using our own language so that neither the gentlemen nor their wives would follow what I was saying, I told him to welcome me as his daughter. He promptly complied, made a tremendous fuss of me, and strained his modest resources to the limit in ensuring that those noblemen and their ladies were suitably entertained. He afterwards conveyed me to the King of Cyprus, and I could never adequately describe how honourably I was received or how much trouble the King took in returning me to you here in Alexandria. And now, if there is anything else that remains to be said, let it be told by Antigono, to whom I have recounted the story of my adventures over and over again.'

'My lord,' said Antigono, turning to the Sultan, 'her story corresponds in every detail with the account she has given me on many occasions, as well as with the assurances I received from the noblemen in whose company she came to Cyprus. One thing only she has refrained from mentioning because it would not have been appropriate for her to do so, and I shall tell you what it is. Those good people who brought her to Cyprus paid glowing tribute to the honest life she had led while living with the nuns, they were full of praise for her virtue and her excellent character, and when the time came for them to commit her to my charge and bid her a fond farewell, they all, gentlemen and ladies alike, burst into floods of tears. Were I to provide you with a full account of what they said to me on this particular subject, I could go on talking all day and all night without coming to the end of it. I trust, however, that these few remarks will suffice to convince you that, as their words showed and as I have been able to observe for myself, no other living monarch can claim to possess such a beautiful, virtuous and courageous daughter.'

The Sultan was absolutely delighted to hear these tidings, and prayed repeatedly that Allah would grant him an opportunity to make a proper restitution to those who had done honour to his daughter, in particular the King of Cyprus who had restored her to him in such splendid style. A few days later, having ordered sumptuous presents to be prepared for Antigono, he gave him leave to return to Cyprus, at the same time dispatching letters and special envoys to convey his heartfelt thanks to the King for the favours he had bestowed upon his daughter.

Then finally, since it was his wish to make an end of what was begun, or in other words that she should become the King of Algarve's wife, he wrote informing him of all that had happened, adding that, if he still desired to marry her, he should send his envoys to fetch her. The King of Algarve was delighted with these tidings, sent a suitably distinguished party to act as her escort, and upon her arrival he gave her a joyous welcome. And so, despite the fact that eight separate men had made love to her on thousands of different occasions, she entered his bed as a virgin and convinced him that it was really so. And for many years afterwards she lived a contented life as his queen. Hence the saying: 'A kissed mouth doesn't lose its freshness, for like the moon it always renews itself.'

EIGHTH STORY

The Count of Antwerp, being falsely accused, goes into exile and leaves his two children in different parts of England. Unknown to them, he returns to find them comfortably placed. Then he serves as a groom in the army of the King of France, and having established his innocence, is restored to his former rank.

The ladies heaved many a sigh over the fair lady's several adventures: but who knows what their motives may have been? Perhaps some of them were sighing, not so much because they felt sorry for Alatiel, but because they longed to be married no less often than she was. However, leaving this question aside, when they had all finished laughing at Panfilo's final words, from which the queen assumed his tale to be finished, she turned to Elissa and enjoined her to continue the proceedings with a story of her own. And being only too happy to oblige, Elissa began as follows:

The field through which we are roaming today is exceedingly broad, and it would be very easy for anyone to try his skill there, not only once but a dozen times, since Fortune has stocked it so abundantly with her marvels and afflictions. But to choose a single story from among the infinite number that could be narrated, I shall begin by telling you that when the Roman imperial authority passed from French into German hands, the two nations became sworn enemies and made bitter and continuous war upon one another. Accordingly, in order to defend their own country and attack the other, the King of France and his son mobilized all their kingdom's resources, including those of their friends and kinsfolk, and assembled a huge army to march against their enemies. But before proceeding any further, not wishing to leave their country ungoverned, and knowing that Gualtieri, Count of Antwerp, was a noble, intelligent man and a most loyal friend and servant to their cause, and thinking, moreover, that although he was well skilled in the art of war, his talents would be even better employed in the subtleties of state government, they left him to rule over the whole of the kingdom of France as their viceroy, and went upon their way.

And so it was that Gualtieri settled down to the wise and orderly performance of his duties, always consulting the Queen and her daughter-in-law on all matters of importance, for although they had been left under his custody and jurisdiction, he treated them as far as possible with the same degree of deference that he would have displayed towards his rulers and superiors. This Gualtieri was about forty years old, physically very handsome, and as agreeable and courteous a nobleman as you could ever imagine. Moreover, apart from being the most elegantly dressed, he was more refined and graceful in bearing than any other knight of his times.

Now, it so happened that while the King of France and his son were away at the wars we have mentioned, Gualtieri's wife died, leaving him a widower with two small children, a boy and a girl. And whilst he was continuing to hold court with the aforesaid ladies, frequently sounding out their opinions on weighty matters of state, the wife of the King's son cast her eyes upon him, and being hugely taken with his handsome looks and agreeable manners, she fell violently and secretly in love. Considering her own unspoilt, youthful appearance and the fact that he was not tied to any woman, she thought it would be an easy matter to obtain what she wanted, and since only her shame seemed to be standing in her way, she decided to be rid of it and lay her cards on the table. And so one day, finding herself alone and feeling the time to be ripe, she summoned him to her room under the pretext of discussing affairs of state.

Being quite unprepared for what was to follow, the Count answered her summons without the slightest delay. Having entered the room, he found himself alone with the lady, and at her request he sat down beside her on a sofa. He then asked her, twice, why she had summoned him, but each time the lady remained silent. Finally, driven on by her passion, she blushed a deep crimson and, almost on the point of tears, trembling from head to toe, she started hesitantly to speak:

'Sweet friend and master, dearest one of all, since you are wise you will readily acknowledge that men and women are remarkably frail, and that, for a variety of reasons, some are frailer than others. It is therefore right and proper that before an impartial judge, people of different social rank should not be punished equally for committing an identical sin. For nobody would, I think, deny that if a member of the poorer classes, obliged to earn a living through manual toil, were to surrender blindly to the promptings of love, he or she would be far more culpable than a rich and leisured lady who lacked none of the necessary means to gratify her tiniest whim.

'I consider, then, that circumstances such as these must go a long way towards excusing any woman who allows herself to be enmeshed in the toils of love; and if, in addition, she has chosen a judicious and valiant lover on whom to bestow her affection, she no longer needs any justification whatever. Now, since it is my opinion that both of these prerequisites are present in my own case, and since, moreover, I possess additional incentives for loving, such as my youth and my husband's absence, they must inevitably operate in my favour and elicit your sympathy for my impetuous passion. And if they carry as much influence as they ought to carry with a man of your experience, I appeal to you for your advice and assistance.

'The fact is that I am unable, in my husband's absence, to withstand the promptings of the flesh and the powers of Love, which are so irresistible that even the strongest of men, not to mention frail women like myself, have often succumbed to them in the past and will always continue to do so. Living in the lap of luxury as I do, with nothing to occupy me, I have allowed my thoughts to dwell upon the pleasures of the senses, and fallen hopelessly in love. I realize of course that if this were to become known, it would be regarded as highly improper; but if it is kept secret I can't really see any harm in it, especially since the God of Love has seen fit not to deprive me of my good judgement in the business of choosing a lover. On the contrary, he has greatly enhanced it by showing me that you, my lord, are worthy in all respects to be loved by a lady of my condition. For unless I am greatly deceived, you are the most handsome, agreeable, elegant and judicious knight to be found anywhere in the Kingdom of France; and just as I can claim to be without a husband, you for your part are without a wife. In the name, therefore, of the immense love that I bear you, I entreat you not to deny me your own, but to take pity on my youth, which I assure you is melting away for you like ice beside a fire.'

These last words brought such a spate of tears in their train, that although she had intended to entreat him still further, she was bereft of the power of speech. And lowering her eyes, she allowed her head to fall upon his breast, weeping incessantly and very nearly swooning with emotion.

Being a knight of unimpeachable loyalty, the Count began to take her severely to task for this insane passion and to repulse the lady, who was already on the point of throwing her arms about his neck. With many an oath, he declared that he would sooner allow himself to be quartered than permit any such harm to be done to his master's honour, whether by himself or anyone else.

No sooner did the lady hear this than she forgot all about loving him and flew into a savage temper.

'So!' she said. 'Am I to be spurned in this fashion by an upstart knight? It seems you want to break my heart, but I shall break yours, so help me God, or have you hounded off the face of the earth.'

Whereupon she ran her hands through her hair, leaving it all rumpled and dishevelled, after which she tore open the front of her dress, at the same time calling out in a loud voice:

'Help! Help! The Count of Antwerp is trying to ravish me!'

When he saw what was happening, the Count was far more concerned about the envious proclivities of the courtiers than reassured by his own clear conscience in the matter; and for this reason he feared that the lady's wicked lies would carry greater conviction than his own protestations of innocence. He therefore hurried out of the room, got quickly away from the palace, and fled to his own house, whence, without pausing for further reflection, he took horse with his children and set off at breakneck speed in the direction of Calais.

The lady's caterwauling brought several people running, and when they saw her and heard what she was shouting about, they were convinced she was telling the truth, more especially because they now assumed that the Count had long been exploiting his charm and his elegant ways for no other purpose. There followed a wild rush to the Count's residence, with the intention of placing him under arrest. But on finding that he was not at home, they ransacked the whole of the premises and then razed them to the ground.

When the story, embroidered with various obscenities, reached the King and his son in the field, they were greatly distressed, and condemned the Count and his descendants to perpetual exile, promising huge rewards for his capture, dead or alive.

Meanwhile the Count, full of misgivings for having turned his innocence into apparent guilt by his hurried departure, arrived at Calais with his children, having succeeded in concealing his identity and escaping recognition. He then crossed rapidly to England, and proceeded, raggedly dressed, towards London. But before entering the city, he talked at great length with the two little children, laying great stress on two points in particular: first, that they must patiently support the state of poverty into which, through no fault of their own, Fortune had cast them along with their father; and second, that if they valued their lives, they must always be on their guard against telling anyone where they had come from or who their father was.

The boy, who was called Louis, was about nine years old, whilst the girl, whose name was Violante, was about seven, and considering their tender age, they paid the closest possible attention to their father's instructions, as they were later to prove. In order to make their task easier, the Count decided it would be necessary to change their names, and this he did, calling the boy Perotto and the girl Giannetta. And on arriving, poorly dressed, in London, they began to go round begging for alms, in the manner of the French vagrants that we see here in Italy.

And it was when they were begging outside a church one morning, that a great lady, the wife of one of the King of England's marshals, happened to catch sight of the Count and his two children as she was coming away from her devotions. On asking where he came from and whether the two children were his, he replied that he was from Picardy and that he was indeed their father. But he had been compelled to leave home with the children and lead a vagabond existence because of a crime that an elder son of his had committed.

The lady, who was of a kindly nature, ran her eyes over the girl and took a great liking to her, for she was a pretty little thing and had an air of gentility about her.

'Good sir,' said the lady. 'If you would like to leave this little girl with me, I will gladly look after her, for she is a pretty looking child. And if she turns out as well as she promises, when the time comes I shall arrange a good marriage for her.'

This request greatly pleased the Count, who promptly gave his consent, and with tears in his eyes he handed over his daughter, warmly commending her to the lady's care. He was well aware of the lady's identity, and now that he had found a good home for the child, he decided not to remain there any longer. And so, begging as he went, he made his way with Perotto to the other side of the island, finding the journey very tiring as he was unused to travelling on foot. Eventually he arrived in Wales, where there was another of the King's marshals, a man who lived in great style and kept a large number of servants, and to this man's castle the Count, either by himself or with his son, would frequently go in order to obtain something to eat.

There were several children at the castle, of whom some belonged to the Marshal himself and others were the sons of the local gentry, and whilst they were competing with each other in children's sports, like running and jumping, Perotto began to mix with them, performing equally as well or better than any of the others in every game they played. His prowess attracted the attention of the Marshal, who, taking a great liking to the child's manner and general behaviour, demanded to know who he was.

On being told that he was the son of a pauper who sometimes came into the castle begging for alms, the Marshal sent someone to ask whether he could keep him; and although it distressed him to part with the child, the Count, who was praying that such a thing might happen, willingly handed him over.

Now that both his son and his daughter were well bestowed, the Count decided to tarry no longer in England. So he crossed the sea to Ireland as best he could and eventually arrived at Strangford, where he entered the service of one of the feudatories of a rural baron, performing all the usual tasks of a groom or a servant. And there he remained for many years, unrecognized by anyone, and compelled to endure great hardship and discomfort.

Meanwhile, Violante, who was now called Giannetta, was being brought up by the gentlewoman in London, becoming a great favourite, not only of the lady and her husband, but of everyone else in the house and indeed of all those who knew her, and as she grew up she became so beautiful that she was a marvel to behold. Nor could anyone deny, on observing how impeccably she comported herself, that she deserved all the honour and blessings that her future might bring. Since receiving the girl from her father, the gentlewoman had never succeeded in discovering anything about him apart from what he had told her, and she now decided that the time had come for her to estimate the girl's rank as best she could, and find her a suitable husband.

But knowing her to be a woman of gentle birth, doing penance for another's sin through no fault of her own, the Lord above, who rewards all according to their deserts, arranged matters otherwise. One must in fact conclude that He alone, out of His loving kindness, made possible the train of events which followed, in order to prevent this nobly-born maiden from falling into the hands of a commoner.

The lady with whom Giannetta was living possessed an only son, who was dearly loved by both his parents, not only because he was their son but also because, being an outstandingly well-bred, talented, courageous and fine-bodied youth, he was eminently worthy of their affection. He was some six years older than Giannetta, and when he noticed how exceedingly beautiful and graceful she was becoming, he fell so deeply in love with her that he had eyes for no one else. But

because he supposed her to be of low estate, he dared not ask his
parents to allow him to marry her. Moreover, since he was afraid of
being reproached with falling in love with a commoner, he did all he
could to keep his love a secret, and thus he was afflicted with sharper
pangs than any he would have suffered had he brought it into the
open.

Eventually, his suffering became so acute that he fell very seriously
ill. A number of physicians were summoned in turn to his bedside,
but in spite of carrying out test after test on one thing after another,
they were unable to diagnose his ailment, and all of them despaired
of finding a cure. The boy's father and mother were so weighed down
with grief and worry that they almost collapsed under the strain.
They begged him over and over again, in tones of deep affection, to
tell them what was the matter, but by way of answer he would
merely sigh deeply or tell them that he felt himself burning all
over.

One day, he was being attended by a doctor who, though very
young, was also very clever. The doctor was holding him by the
wrist, taking his pulse, when Giannetta, who waited hand and foot on
the invalid for his mother's sake, entered the room in which the youth
was lying. When he saw her coming in, the flames of passion flared
up in the young man's breast, and although he neither spoke nor
moved, his pulse began to beat more strongly. The doctor noted this
at once, but concealing his surprise he remained silent, waiting to see
how long his pulse would continue to beat so rapidly.

As soon as Giannetta left the room, the young man's pulse returned
to normal, whereupon the doctor concluded that he was halfway
towards solving the mystery of the youth's illness. He waited for a
while, and then, still holding his patient by the wrist, he sent for
Giannetta, pretending that he wanted to ask her a question. She came
at once, and no sooner did she enter the room than the youth's
pulse began to race all over again: and when she departed, it subsided.

The doctor was therefore fully confirmed in his suspicions, and
having risen to his feet, he took the youth's parents aside, saying:

'Your son's health cannot be restored by any doctor, for it rests in
the hands of Giannetta. As I have discovered through certain unmistakable symptoms, the young man is ardently in love with her,

though as far as I can tell, she herself is unaware of the fact. But you will now know what measures to apply if you want him to recover.'

On hearing this, the nobleman and his lady were greatly relieved, for at least there was now a possibility that he could be cured. But they were very disturbed at the prospect, however remote it might seem, of being forced to accept Giannetta as their daughter-in-law. So when the doctor had left, they made their way to the invalid's bedside.

'My son,' said the lady, 'I would never have imagined you capable of desiring something and not telling your mother, especially when you could see that your health was suffering through not having what you wanted. You may be quite sure, indeed you should have known all along, that I would do anything to make you happy, even if it meant stretching the rules a little. However, since you have refused to take me into your confidence, Our Heavenly Father has seen fit to intervene on your behalf, thus displaying more pity towards you than you were prepared to concede to yourself. And, so that you would not die from your malady, He has shown me the reason for this illness of yours, which turns out to be nothing more than the excessive love you bear towards some young woman or other. It was really quite unnecessary for you to feel ashamed about revealing it, for this sort of thing is perfectly natural in someone of your age. Indeed, if you were not in love, I would think very poorly of you. Do not hide things from me, my son, but acquaint me freely with all your wishes. Get rid of all the sadness and anxiety that are causing your illness, and look on the bright side of things. You can be quite certain that I will move Heaven and earth to see that you have whatever you need to make you happy, for your happiness means more to me than anything else in the world. Cast aside all your shame and your fear, and tell me what I can do to make this love of yours prosper. And if I don't put heart and soul into it and arrange matters to your liking, you can consider me the cruellest mother that ever brought a son into the world.'

On first hearing these words, the young man was thrown into a state of confusion, but after reflecting that nobody was in a better position than his mother to procure his happiness, he conquered his embarrassment, and said:

'If I kept my love a secret, madam, that was only because I have noticed that most people, after reaching a certain age, try to forget that they were ever young. But now that I can see what a tolerant mother you are, not only will I not deny what you claim to have noticed, but I will tell you who the girl is, on condition that you do everything in your power to keep your promise and thus make it possible for me to recover.'

The lady, being over-confident in her ability to arrange things in a way she should never have even considered, willingly replied that he should feel quite free to take her fully into his confidence. For she would take immediate steps to ensure that he obtained what he wanted.

'Madam,' said the youth, 'you find me in my present condition because of the excellent beauty and impeccable manners of our Giannetta, or rather owing to my inability to make her notice, still less reciprocate, my feelings for her, and because I never dared reveal them to a living soul. And unless you can find some means of making good the promise you have given me, you may rest assured that my days are numbered.'

'My poor boy,' said the lady, thinking it preferable to encourage rather than reproach him. 'What a thing to become so upset about! Now calm yourself and leave everything to me, because you are going to get better.'

Being filled with new hope, the youth very quickly showed signs of making a splendid recovery, to the immense satisfaction of his mother, who decided she would now attempt to make good her promise. So one day she took Giannetta aside, and adopting a light-hearted tone, asked her very tactfully whether she had a lover.

'Oh, my lady,' replied Giannetta, blushing all over. 'It would not be at all proper for a poor girl like me, exiled from her home and living in another's service, to indulge in such a luxury as love.'

'Well,' said the lady, 'if you don't possess a lover, we are going to give you one, so that you can lead a merry life and enjoy your beauty to the full. It isn't right for a lovely girl like you to be without a lover.'

'My lady,' answered Giannetta, 'ever since the day you took me from my father, you have brought me up as your own daughter, and therefore I ought never to oppose any of your wishes. But I can't possibly agree to do this, and I think I am right to refuse. I intend to love no man unless he be my lawful spouse, and if you wish to present me with a husband, well and good. Since my sole remaining family heirloom is my honour, I am determined to safeguard and preserve it for as long as I live.'

Giannetta's reply seemed to present a serious obstacle to the plans the lady had devised for keeping her promise to her son, though in her heart of hearts, being a sensible woman, she greatly admired the girl's sentiments.

'Come now, Giannetta,' she said. 'Supposing His Royal Highness the King of England, who is a dashing young nobleman, wished to enjoy the love of an exquisitely beautiful girl like yourself, would you deny it to him?'

To which Giannetta promptly replied:

'The King could take me by force, but I would never consent freely unless his intentions were honourable.'

The lady, realizing how strong a character the girl possessed, pressed the matter no further, but decided to put her to the test. And so she informed her son that as soon as he was better, she would lock them in a room together so that he could try and bend her to his will, adding that it seemed undignified for her to go bowing and scraping on her son's behalf, as though she were a procuress, to one of her own ladies-in-waiting.

The young man was not at all pleased with this idea, and his condition immediately took a severe turn for the worse. On seeing this, the lady took Giannetta into her confidence, only to find that she was more adamant than ever. So she acquainted her husband with what she had done, and although both of them thought it a grave step to take, they mutually decided to let him marry her, preferring their son to be alive with an unsuitable wife than dead without any wife at all. And after a great deal of further heart-searching, they announced their consent.

This made Giannetta very happy, and she thanked God from the depths of her devout heart for not deserting her; nor, despite everything, did she once reveal that she was anyone other than a Picard's daughter.

The young man recovered, married the girl thinking himself the happiest of men, and proceeded to enjoy her to his heart's content.

Meanwhile, Perotto, who had remained in Wales in the household of the King of England's Marshal, had likewise become a favourite of his lord and master. He was an outstandingly handsome and fearless youth, and there was no one in the island who could match his skill at jousts, tournaments and other contests of arms. Everybody called him Perotto the Picard, and his fame resounded through the length and breadth of the country.

And just as God had not forgotten his sister, so too He showed that He had not lost sight of Perotto. For a great plague descended on that region, carrying off half the population and causing a large number of the remainder to take refuge in other parts, so that the country appeared to be totally deserted. The victims of the plague included Perotto's master and mistress, their son, and several of his master's brothers, grandchildren and other relatives, so that only a daughter of marriageable age survived, together with some members of the household, among them Perotto. Once the plague had abated somewhat, the young woman, knowing Perotto to be strong and capable, and having received encouragement and advice from her few surviving neighbours, made him her husband and proclaimed him master of all the goods and property she had inherited. Nor was it long before the King of England, having heard of the Marshal's death and knowing the worth of Perotto the Picard, appointed him his marshal in the dead man's place.

And that, in brief, was what happened to the two innocent children of the Count of Antwerp after he was forced to abandon them.

More than eighteen years had elapsed since his hurried departure from Paris when the Count, who was now an old man and still living in Ireland, having led a truly wretched life and endured all manner of hardships, was seized by a longing to discover what had become of his children. His physical appearance, as he could see for himself, had changed beyond all recognition, but because of the years he had spent in manual toil he felt much fitter now than when he was young and living a life of leisure. And so, very poor and badly dressed, he left the person in whose household he had served for all those years, returned to England, and made for the place where he had left

Perotto. Much to his delight and amazement, he discovered that his son was now a marshal and a great lord, and that he was a vigorous, fine-looking fellow. But he did not want to reveal himself before learning what had become of Giannetta.

He therefore set out once more, and never stopped until he arrived in London, where he made discreet inquiries about the lady with whom he had left his daughter and the life she was now leading. On discovering that Giannetta was married to the lady's son, he almost wept for joy. And now that he had traced both his children and found them so comfortably established, he forgot about all of his earlier misfortunes. Being anxious to see her, he began to loiter near her house in the guise of a pauper, until one day he was noticed by Giannetta's husband, whose name, by the way, was Giachetto Lamiens. Seeing how poor and decrepit he looked, Giachetto took pity on the old man and ordered one of his servants to bring him into the house and provide him with something to eat for charity's sake, which the servant readily did.

Giannetta had already presented Giachetto with several children, of whom the eldest was no more than eight, and they were the prettiest and most delightful infants imaginable. When they saw the Count at his meal, they all gathered round and made a fuss of him, as though impelled by some mysterious instinct which told them that this was their grandfather. Knowing them to be his grandchildren, the old man began to show them his affection and fondle them, with the result that the children were unwilling to come away, however much their tutor cajoled and threatened them. Hearing the commotion, Giannetta left the room she was in, came to where the Count was sitting, and spoke sharply to the children, threatening to chastise them if they did not obey their tutor's instructions. The children began to cry, protesting that they wanted to stay with this worthy fellow who loved them more than their tutor, whereupon the lady and the Count smiled broadly at one another.

The Count had risen to his feet, not in the manner of a father greeting his daughter but rather in the role of a pauper paying his respects to a fine lady, and as soon as he set eyes upon her, his heart was filled with a marvellous joy. But she never suspected for a moment who he was, either then or later, for he was thin and elderly-looking, and what with his beard, his greying hair and his dark complexion, he no longer seemed the same person. But on seeing how reluctant the children were to be parted from the old man, and how dismally they wailed whenever any attempt was made to dislodge them, the lady told their tutor to leave them for the present where they were.

It was while the children were playing with this worthy fellow that Giachetto's father, who now loathed Giannetta, happened to return home and hear the whole story from their tutor.

'Let them stay where they are,' he said, 'and to hell with them. It's obvious which side of the family they take after, for they are descended from a tramp on their mother's side, and it's hardly surprising if they feel at home in a tramp's company.'

The Count overheard these words, and was deeply wounded. But he simply shrugged his shoulders, and suffered the insult as patiently as he had borne countless others.

Although Giachetto was displeased when he heard the children making such a fuss of the worthy fellow, or in other words the Count, he was nevertheless so fond of them that, rather than see them cry, he gave instructions that if the man was willing to stay, he should be offered some job or other in the household. The Count gladly agreed to stay, but pointed out that the only thing he was good at was looking after horses, which he had been accustomed to handling all his life. A horse was therefore allotted to him, and when he had finished grooming it, he would occupy himself in keeping the children amused.

Whilst Fortune was treating the Count of Antwerp and his children in the manner we have just described, it happened that the King of France died, and was succeeded by the son whose wife had been responsible for the Count's exile. The old King had negotiated a series of truces with the Germans, and now that the last of these had expired, the new King reopened hostilities with a vengeance. The King of England, having recently become a relative of his, offered him assistance in the form of a large expeditionary force under the command of his marshal, Perotto, and Giachetto Lamiens, the son of the second marshal. Our worthy fellow, or the Count, was a member of Giachetto's contingent, for a long time serving in the army as a groom without ever being recognized; and being an able man, he made himself extremely useful by giving timely advice and performing various tasks over and above his normal duties.

During the war, the Queen of France happened to fall seriously ill, and realizing instinctively that she was about to die, she repented of all her sins, making a devout confession before the Archbishop of Rouen, who was famous for his excellence and saintliness. Among her other sins, she told him of the great wrong that had been perpetrated on the Count of Antwerp at her own instigation. Nor was she content solely with telling the Archbishop, but she gave a true account of the whole affair in the presence of many other gentlemen, requesting them to use their good offices with the King in order to secure the rehabilitation of the Count if he was still alive, or if he was dead, of his children. Not long afterwards she died, and was buried with full regal honours.

When the King was told about her confession, he heaved many an anguished sigh over the wrongs to which this excellent man had been so unjustly subjected. He then issued an edict, which was published far and wide, both throughout the army and elsewhere, to the effect that he would pay substantial rewards to anyone bringing him information concerning the whereabouts of the Count of Antwerp or any of his children. Because of the Queen's confession – so the edict continued – the King held him to be innocent of the charges which had led to his exile, and it was his intention, not only to restore him to his former position, but to grant him still higher honours. Rumours of the announcement reached the ears of the Count, who was still working as a groom, and when he had confirmed them he went at once to Giachetto and asked him to arrange a meeting with Perotto so that he could show them what the King was looking for.

When all three of them had come together, the Count said to Perotto, who was already thinking of announcing his identity:

'Perotto, Giachetto here is married to your sister, and never received any dowry from her. In order, therefore, that your sister should not remain without a dowry, I propose that he alone should claim these huge rewards that the King is offering. This he will do by declaring you to be the Count of Antwerp's son, his wife to be your sister Violante, and myself to be your father, the Count of Antwerp.'

On hearing this, Perotto looked intently at the old man, and it dawned upon him that this was indeed his father. Dissolving into tears, the threw himself at the Count's feet and embraced him, saying:

'Father, what a joy it is to see you!'

Giachetto, having listened to the Count's words and witnessed Perotto's response, was so delighted and astonished that he hardly knew where to put himself. But being convinced that it was all true, and bitterly ashamed for occasionally having spoken harshly to the groom or Count, he too burst into tears and sank to his knees at the old man's feet, humbly begging his pardon for all the wrongs he had done him. Whereupon the Count, having first of all persuaded him to stand up again, assured him very graciously that he was forgiven.

When the three of them had finished telling one another about their adventures, weeping and laughing endlessly together, Perotto and Giachetto offered to supply the Count with new clothes, but he could in no way be persuaded to accept them. On the contrary, he was determined that Giachetto, once he had claimed the promised reward, should present him exactly as he was, in his groom's clothing, so that the King would feel all the more ashamed for what had happened.

Giachetto therefore presented himself to the King along with the Count and Perotto, and offered to produce the Count and his children if and when, in accordance with the terms of the edict, the reward was forthcoming. The King promptly ordered all three portions to be displayed, making Giachetto's eyes pop out with astonishment, and told him he could take away the reward whenever he had made good his offer to show him the Count and his children.

Giachetto then turned and made way for his groom and Perotto.

'My lord,' he said. 'Here are the father and son. The daughter, who is my wife, is not here at present, but God willing you will see her soon.'

On hearing this, the King stared at the Count, and although his features were greatly altered, after surveying him at length he none-theless knew him again. Restraining his tears with an effort, he raised the Count from his knees to his feet, and kissed and embraced him. And after having warmly greeted Perotto, he ordered that the

Count should instantly be provided with all the clothes, servants, horses and accoutrements that were proper to his noble rank. This was no sooner said than done, and moreover the King did much honour also to Perotto and insisted on hearing a full account of his past adventures.

When Giachetto accepted the three enormous rewards for locating the Count and his children, the Count said to him:

'Take away these gifts so generously endowed by His Royal Highness, and remember to tell your father that your children, who are his grandchildren as well as mine, are not descended from a tramp on their mother's side.'

Giachetto took away the treasure, and arranged for his wife and his mother to come to Paris. Perotto's wife came too, and they all stayed with the Count, who entertained them on a truly lavish scale, having been reinstated in all his lands and property, and granted higher rank than he had ever had before. Then they all obtained the Count's leave to return to their respective homes, whilst he remained to the end of his days in Paris, covering himself with ever greater glory.

NINTH STORY

Bernabò of Genoa is tricked by Ambrogiuolo, loses his money, and orders his innocent wife to be killed. She escapes, however, and, disguising herself as a man, enters the service of the Sultan. Having traced the swindler, she lures her husband to Alexandria, where Ambrogiuolo is punished and she abandons her disguise, after which she and Bernabò return to Genoa, laden with riches.

Elissa's touching tale being at an end and her duty done, their queen, the tall and lovely Filomena, than whom none possessed more pleasing and cheerful a countenance, composed herself and said:

'The contract we made with Dioneo must be honoured, and since only he and I are left to speak, I shall tell my story first, and Dioneo, who laid special claim to that privilege, will be the last to address us.' And having said this, she began as follows:

There is a certain proverb, frequently to be heard on the lips of the people, to the effect that a dupe will outwit his deceiver – a saying which would seem impossible to prove but for the fact that it is borne out by actual cases. And therefore, dearest ladies, I would like, without overstepping the limits of our theme, to show you that the proverb is indeed true. Nor should you find my story unpalatable, for it will teach you to be on your guard against deceivers.

A number of very prosperous Italian merchants were once staying at the same inn in Paris, a city which people of their sort frequently have cause to visit for one reason or another. One evening, after they had all dined merrily together, they began talking about this and that, one subject led to another, and they eventually came round to discussing the womenfolk they had left behind in Italy.

'I don't know what my wife gets up to,' laughed one of them, 'but I do know this, that whenever I meet a girl here in Paris who takes my fancy, I have as much fun with her as I can manage, and forget about my wife.'

'I do the same,' said the second man, 'because whether or not I believe my wife is behaving herself, she will be making the most of her opportunities. So it's a case of tit for tat. Do as you would be done by, that's my motto.'

The third man was of more or less similar opinion. And indeed, it looked as though they were unanimous in agreeing that the women they had left behind would not be allowing the grass to grow under their feet.

Only one of them, a Genoese called Bernabò Lomellin, took a different line, maintaining that he, on the contrary, was blessed with a wife who was possibly without equal in the whole of Italy, for not only was she endowed with all the qualities of the ideal woman, but she also possessed many of the accomplishments to be found in a knight or esquire. She was extremely good looking and still very young, she was lithe and lissom, and there was no womanly pursuit, such as silk embroidery and the like, in which she did not outshine all other members of her sex. Furthermore, he claimed it was impossible to find a page or servant who waited better or more efficiently at a gentleman's table, for she was a paragon of intelligence and good manners, and the very soul of discretion. He then turned to her other accomplishments, praising her skill at horse-riding, falconry, reading, writing and book-keeping, at all of which she was superior to the average merchant. And finally, after a series of further eulogies, he came round to the subject they were discussing, stoutly maintaining that she was the most chaste and honest woman to be found anywhere on earth. Consequently, even if he stayed away for ten years or the rest of his life, he felt quite certain that she would never play fast and loose in another man's company.

Among the people present at this discussion, there was a young merchant from Piacenza called Ambrogiuolo, who, on hearing the last of Bernabò's laudatory assertions about his lady, began roaring with laughter and jokingly asked him whether it was the Emperor himself who had granted him this unique privilege.

Faintly annoyed, Bernabò replied that this favour had been conceded to him, not by the Emperor, but by God, who was a little more powerful than the Emperor.

Then Ambrogiuolo said:

'Bernabò, I do not doubt for a moment that you believe what you say to be true. But as far as I can judge, you have not devoted much attention to the study of human nature. For if you had, you surely possess enough intelligence to have discovered certain things that would cause you to think twice before making such confident assertions. When the rest of us spoke so freely about our womenfolk, we were merely facing facts, and so as not to let you run away with the idea that we suppose our wives to be any different from yours, I would like to pursue this subject a little further with you.

'I have always been told that man is the most noble of God's mortal creatures, and that woman comes second. Moreover, man is generally considered the more perfect, and the evidence of his works confirms that this is so. Being more perfect, it inevitably follows that he has a stronger will, and this too is confirmed by the fact that women are invariably more fickle, the reasons for which are to be found in certain physical factors which I do not propose to dwell upon.

'Man, then, has the stronger will. Yet quite apart from being unable to resist any woman who makes advances to him, he desires any woman he finds attractive, and not only does he desire her, but he will do everything in his power to possess her. And this is how he carries on, not just once a month, but a thousand times a day. What chance then do you think a woman, fickle by nature, can have against all the entreaties, the blandishments, the presents, and the thousand other expedients to which any intelligent lover will resort? Do you think she is going to resist him? Of course not, and you know it, no matter what you claim to the contrary. Why, you told us yourself that your wife is a woman, made of flesh and blood like the rest, in which case her desires are no different from any other woman's, and her power to resist these natural cravings cannot be any greater. So that, however virtuous she may be, it's quite possible that she acts like all the others. And whenever a thing is possible, one should not discount it prematurely or affirm its opposite, as you are doing.'

Bernabò's reply was brief and to the point.

'I am a merchant, not a philosopher,' he said, 'and I shall give you a merchant's answer. I am well aware that the sort of thing you describe can happen in the case of foolish women who are without any sense of shame. But the more judicious ones are so eager to safeguard their honour that they become stronger than men, who are indifferent to such matters. And my wife is one of these.'

'If, of course,' said Ambrogiuolo, 'a horn, bearing witness to their doings, were to sprout from their heads whenever they were unfaithful, then I think that the number of unfaithful women would be small. Not only do they not grow any horns, however, but the judicious ones leave no visible trace of their activities. There can't be any shame or loss of honour without clear evidence, and so if they can keep it a secret, either they get on with it or they desist because they are weak in the head. You can rest assured that the only chaste woman is either one who never received an improper proposal or one whose own proposals were always rejected. Even though I know that there are cogent and logical arguments to support this assertion, I would not be spelling it out with so much confidence were it not for the fact that I have often had occasion to prove it for myself with any number of women. And I will tell you this, that if I were anywhere near this ever-so-saintly lady of yours, I shouldn't think it would take me long to lead her where I have led others in the past.'

'We could go on arguing like this indefinitely,' said Bernabò, who was by this time thoroughly incensed. 'You would say one thing, I would say another, and in the end we would get precisely nowhere. But since you claim that they are all so compliant and that you are so clever, I am prepared, in order to convince you of my lady's integrity, to place my head on the block if you ever persuade her to meet your wishes in this respect. And if you don't succeed, all I want you to lose is a thousand gold florins.'

'Bernabò,' replied Ambrogiuolo, who was warming to his subject, 'I wouldn't know what to do with your head, if I were to win. But if you really want to see proof of what I have been saying, you can put up five thousand florins of your own, which is less than you'd pay for a new head, against my thousand. And whereas you did not fix any term, I will undertake to go to Genoa and have my way with this lady of yours within three months from the day I leave Paris. By way of proof, I shall return with some of her most intimate possessions, and I shall furnish you with so many relevant particulars that you will be forced to admit the truth of it with your own lips. I make one condition, however, and that is that you promise me on your word of honour neither to come to Genoa during this period nor to give her any hint in your letters of what is afoot.'

Bernabò declared himself to be quite satisfied with these terms, and however much the other merchants present, knowing that the affair could have serious repercussions, tried to prevent it from going any further, the passions of the two men were so strongly aroused that, contrary to the wishes of the others, they drew up a form of contract with their own hands which was binding on both parties.

When the bond was sealed, Bernabò remained in Paris whilst Ambrogiuolo came by the quickest possible route to Genoa. Having discovered where the lady lived, he spent the first few days after his arrival in making discreet enquiries about her way of life, and since the information he gathered more than confirmed the description he had been given by Bernabò, he began to feel he was on a fool's errand. However, he became friendly with a poor woman, who regularly visited the house and enjoyed the lady's deep affection. Being unable to persuade her to assist him in any other way, he bribed her to have him taken into the house inside a chest, made according to his own specifications, which found its way not only into the house but into the lady's very bedroom. Following Ambrogiuolo's instructions, the good woman pretended that it was on its way to some other place, and obtained the lady's permission to leave it for a day or two in her room for safe keeping.

When night had descended, and Ambrogiuolo was satisfied that the lady was asleep, he prised the chest open with certain tools of his and stepped silently forth into the room, where a single lamp was burning. He then began, by the light of the lamp, to inspect the arrangement of the furniture, the paintings, and everything else of note that the room contained, and committed it all to memory.

Next, having approached the bed and found the lady with a little girl beside her, both soundly asleep, he uncovered her from head to toe and saw that she was every bit as beautiful without any clothes as when she was fully dressed. But her body contained no unusual mark of any description except for the fact that below her left breast there was a mole, surrounded by a few strands of fine, golden hair. Having noted this, he silently covered her up again, although on seeing how beautiful she was he was sorely tempted to hazard his life and lie down beside her. However, having heard tales of her unbending strictness and her violent distaste for that sort of thing, he decided not to risk it. Roaming about the room at his leisure for most of the night, he removed a purse and a long cloak from a strong-box, together with some rings and one or two ornamental belts, all of which he stowed away in the chest before retiring into it himself and clamping down the lid again from the inside. And in this way he spent two whole nights there without the lady noticing that anything was amiss.

The good woman, following his instructions, returned on the morning of the third day for her chest, and had it taken back to its original place. Ambrogiuolo let himself out, and having paid the woman the sum he had promised her, he hurried back to Paris with his ill-gotten gains, arriving well within the agreed time-limit. He then called together the merchants who had been at the discussion when the bets were placed, and in Bernabò's presence he announced that since he had made good his boast he had won the wager. By way of proof, he began by describing the shape of the bedroom and the pictures it contained, then he showed them the things he had brought back with him, claiming that they had been given to him by the lady herself.

Bernabò conceded that his description of the room was correct, and furthermore he admitted that he did indeed recognize the exhibits as having once belonged to his lady. But he pointed out that Ambrogiuolo could have learnt about the arrangement of the room from one of the servants, and obtained these objects in similar fashion. So that, unless further evidence was forthcoming, he did not feel that the claim was substantiated.

'In all conscience, this should have been quite sufficient,' Ambrogiuolo retorted. 'But since you want me to provide further evidence, I will do so. And I will tell you that just below her left breast, your wife Zinevra has a sizeable little mole surrounded by about half-a-dozen fine golden hairs.'

When Bernabò heard this, he felt as though he had been stabbed through the heart, such was the pain that assailed him. His whole face changed, so that even if he had not uttered a word, it would have been quite obvious that what Ambrogiuolo had said was true.

'Gentlemen,' he said, after a long pause. 'What Ambrogiuolo says is true, and therefore, since he has won the wager, he may come whenever he likes in order to collect his due.' And the next day, Ambrogiuolo was paid in full.

Bernabò left Paris, and came hurrying back to Genoa with murder in his heart. But as he was approaching his destination, he decided to go no further, halting instead at an estate of his some twenty miles from the city. He then sent a retainer of his whom he greatly trusted to Genoa, with two horses and a letter telling his wife he had returned, and asking her to come and join him under this man's escort. And he secretly instructed the servant that on reaching the most suitable place, he was to kill her without showing any mercy and return to him alone.

When the retainer reached Genoa, he handed over the letter and delivered his master's message, being welcomed by the lady with great rejoicing; and next morning, they mounted their horses and set out for Bernabò's estate in the country. As they were riding along together, conversing on various topics, they came to a very deep ravine, a lonely spot with precipitous crags and trees all round it, which seemed to the retainer the ideal place to carry out his master's orders without any risk of detection. He therefore drew his dagger and seized the lady's arm, saying:

'Commend your soul to God, my lady, for this is the place where you must die.'

On seeing the dagger and hearing these words, the lady was completely terror-stricken.

'For God's sake, have mercy!' she cried. 'Before putting me to death, tell me what I ever did to you, that you should want to kill me.'

'My lady,' he replied. 'To me you have never done anything; but you must have done something or other to your husband, for he ordered me to kill you without mercy in the course of our journey. And if I fail to carry out his instructions, he has threatened to have me hanged by the neck. You know very well how much I depend upon him, and how impossible it would be for me to disobey him. God knows I feel sorry for you, but I have no alternative.'

The lady began to weep.

'Oh, for the love of God, have mercy!' she said. 'Don't allow yourself to murder someone who never did you any harm, just for the sake of obeying an order. As God is my witness, I have never given my husband the slightest cause for taking my life. But leaving that aside, you have it within your power to satisfy your master without offending God or laying a finger upon me. All you have to do is to take these outer garments I am wearing and leave me a cloak and a doublet. You can then return to our lord and master with the clothes and tell him you have killed me. And I swear to you, upon the life you will have granted me, that I will disappear and go away somewhere so that neither he nor you nor the people of these parts will ever hear of me again.'

The retainer was by no means eager to kill her, and was easily moved to compassion. And so, having taken the clothes, he gave her a tattered old doublet of his and a cloak to put on, left her some money she was carrying, and begged her to disappear entirely from those parts. He then abandoned her in the valley on foot and returned to his master, informing him that not only had his orders been carried out, but he had left her dead body surrounded by a pack of wolves.

Some time afterwards, Bernabò returned to Genoa, but once the story had leaked out, he never succeeded in living it down.

The lady, abandoned and forlorn, disguised herself as best she could, and when it was dark she went to a nearby cottage, where she obtained some things from an old woman and altered the doublet, shortening it to make it fit. She also converted her shift into a pair of knee-length breeches, cut her hair, and having transformed her appearance completely so that she now looked like a sailor, she made her way down to the coast, where she happened to encounter the master of a ship lying some distance offshore, a Catalan gentleman called Señor En Cararch, who had come ashore at Albenga to take on supplies of fresh water. Engaging him in conversation, she persuaded him to sign her on as his cabin-boy, calling herself Sicurano da Finale, and once they had gone aboard, the gentleman supplied her with some smarter clothes to wear. And she served him so well and so efficiently that he grew very attached to her.

Now it so happened that not long afterwards, the Catalan docked in Alexandria with a cargo which included some peregrine falcons that he was taking to the Sultan. These he duly delivered, after which he was occasionally invited to dine at the royal table, and the Sultan, on observing the ways of Sicurano, who was still in attendance upon him, was greatly impressed with the youth and asked the Catalan if he would allow him to keep him. Although he was loath to let him go, the Catalan gave his consent, and it was not very long before Sicurano's able performance of his duties had earned him the same degree of favour and affection from the Sultan that he had enjoyed with his previous master.

Now, at a certain season of the year, it was the custom to hold a trade-fair within the Sultan's domain at Acre, where merchants, both Christian and Saracen, used to congregate in large numbers. And in order to protect the merchants and their merchandise, the Sultan always used to send, in addition to his other officials, one of his court-dignitaries with a contingent of guardsmen. And so it was that when the time for the fair drew near, the Sultan thought that he would send Sicurano to discharge this function, as he already had an excellent knowledge of the language; and this he did.

Sicurano duly arrived in Acre, therefore, as captain in charge of the special guard whose duties were to protect the merchants and their merchandise. And as he went round on tours of inspection, discharging his functions with diligence and skill, he came across a number of merchants from Sicily, Pisa, Genoa, Venice and other parts of Italy, with whom he readily made friends out of a nostalgic feeling for the country of his birth.

Now, it so happened that on one of these occasions, having dismounted at the stall of some Venetian merchants, in the midst of various other valuable objects he caught sight of a purse and an ornamental belt, which he promptly recognized as his own former belongings. Concealing his astonishment, he politely asked who owned them and whether they were for sale.

One of the merchants attending the fair was Ambrogiuolo of Piacenza, who had arrived there on a Venetian ship with a large quantity of goods, and on hearing that the captain of the guard was asking who owned the articles in question, he stepped forward, grinning all over his face.

'Sir,' he said, 'these things belong to me, and they are not for sale. But if you like them, I will gladly make you a present of them.'

When Sicurano saw him laughing, he suspected that the fellow had somehow seen through his disguise, but keeping a straight face, he asked:

'Why do you laugh? Is it because you see me, a soldier, inquiring about these female commodities?'

'No, sir,' replied Ambrogiuolo. 'That is not the reason. I am laughing about the way I acquired them.'

'Oh,' said Sicurano. 'Then perhaps, if the explanation is not too improper, you will be good enough to tell us about it.'

'Sir,' replied Ambrogiuolo. 'These things were given to me, along with various others, by a gentlewoman of Genoa called Donna Zinevra, the wife of Bernabò Lomellin. It was after I had slept with her for the night, and she asked me to keep them as a token of her love. And I was laughing just now because I was reminded of the foolishness of her husband, who was insane enough to wager five thousand gold florins against a thousand that I would not succeed in seducing his lady. I won the wager of course, and I am given to understand that the husband, who should have punished himself for his stupidity instead of punishing his wife for doing what all other women do, returned from Paris to Genoa and had her put to death.'

On hearing these words, Sicurano understood at once why Bernabò had been so enraged with her, and realized that this was the fellow who was responsible for all her woes. And she vowed to herself that he would not remain unpunished.

Sicurano therefore pretended to be greatly amused by his story and skilfully cultivated his friendship, so that when the fair was over, Ambrogiuolo packed up all his goods and at Sicurano's invitation went with him to Alexandria, where Sicurano had a warehouse built for him and placed a large sum of money at his disposal. And Ambrogiuolo, seeing that it was greatly to his profit, was only too ready to stay there.

Being anxious to offer Bernabò clear proof of his wife's innocence, Sicurano never rested until, with the assistance of one or two influential Genoese merchants in the city and a variety of ingenious pretexts, he had enticed him to come to Alexandria. Bernabò was by now in a state of poverty, and Sicurano secretly commissioned some of his friends to shelter him and keep him out of the way until such time as he felt he could put his plans into effect.

Sicurano had already persuaded Ambrogiuolo to repeat his story in front of the Sultan, who had greatly relished it. But now that Bernabò had arrived, he wanted to see the business through as quickly as possible, and took the earliest opportunity to induce the Sultan to summon Ambrogiuolo and Bernabò to his presence, so that, in Bernabò's hearing, Ambrogiuolo could be coerced by fair means or foul to confess the truth concerning his boast with regard to Bernabò's wife.

So Ambrogiuolo and Bernabò duly appeared before the Sultan, who glared fiercely at Ambrogiuolo and ordered him to tell the truth about the manner in which he had won the five thousand gold florins from Bernabò. Among the many people present was Sicurano, whom Ambrogiuolo trusted more than anybody, but Sicurano glared even more fiercely at him and threatened him with dire tortures if he refused to speak out. Ambrogiuolo was therefore terrified whichever way he looked, and after being subjected to a little further persuasion, not anticipating any punishment other than the restitution of the five thousand gold florins and the articles he had stolen, he described in detail to Bernabò and all the others present exactly what had happened.

No sooner had he finished speaking than Sicurano, acting as though he were the Sultan's public prosecutor, rounded on Bernabò.

'And you?' he said. 'What was your reaction to these falsehoods concerning your lady?'

'I was overcome with rage at the loss of my money,' replied Bernabò, 'and also with shame at the damage to my honour that I thought my wife had committed. And so I had her killed by one of my retainers, and according to his own account, she was immediately devoured by a pack of wolves.'

Sicurano then addressed the Sultan, who, though he had been listening carefully and taking it all in, was still in the dark about Sicurano's motives in requesting and arranging this meeting.

'My lord,' he said. 'It will be quite obvious to you what a fine swain and a fine husband that good lady was blessed with. For the swain deprives her of her honour by besmirching her good name with lies, at the same time ruining her husband. And the husband, paying more attention to another man's falsehoods than to the truth that years of experience should have taught him, has her killed and eaten by wolves. Moreover, both the suitor and the husband love and respect her so deeply that they are able to spend a long time in her company without even recognizing her. But in order that you shall be left in no possible doubt concerning the merits of these two gentlemen, I am ready, provided that you will grant me the special favour of pardoning the dupe and punishing the deceiver, to make the lady appear, here and now, before your very eyes.'

The Sultan, who was prepared to allow Sicurano a completely free hand in this affair, gave his consent and told him to produce the lady. Bernabò, being firmly convinced that she was dead, was unable to believe his ears, whilst Ambrogiuolo, for whom things were beginning to look desperate, was afraid in any case that he was going to have more than a sum of money to pay, and could not see that it would affect him either one way or the other if the lady really were to turn up. But if anything he was even more astonished than Bernabò.

No sooner had the Sultan agreed to Sicurano's request than Sicurano burst into tears and threw himself on his knees at the Sultan's feet, at the same time losing his manly voice and the desire to persist in his masculine rôle.

'My lord,' he said, 'I myself am the poor unfortunate Zinevra, who for six long years has toiled her way through the world disguised as a man, a victim of the false and wicked calumnies of this traitor Ambrogiuolo and of the niquitous cruelty of this man who handed her over to be killed by one of his servants and eaten by wolves.'

Tearing open the front of her dress and displaying her bosom, she made it clear to the Sultan and to everyone else that she was indeed a woman. Then she rounded on Ambrogiuolo, haughtily demanding to know when he had ever slept with her, as he had claimed. But Ambrogiuolo, seeing who it was, simply stood there and said nothing, as though he were too ashamed to open his mouth.

The Sultan, who had always believed her to be a man, was so astonished on seeing and hearing all this, that he kept thinking that he must be dreaming and that his eyes and ears were deceiving him. But once he had recovered from his astonishment and realized that it was true, he lauded Zinevra to the skies for her virtuous way of life, her constancy, and her strength of character. And having ordered feminine clothes of the finest quality to be brought, and provided her with a retinue of ladies, he complied with her earlier request and spared Bernabò from the death he assuredly merited. On recognizing his wife, Bernabò threw himself in tears at her feet asking her forgiveness, and although he deserved no such favour, she graciously conceded it and helped him up again, clasping him in a fond and wifely embrace.

The Sultan next commanded that Ambrogiuolo should instantly be taken to some upper part of the city, tied to a pole in the sun, smeared with honey, and left there until he fell of his own accord; and this was done. He then decreed that all of Ambrogiuolo's possessions, which amounted in value to more than ten thousand doubloons, should be handed over to the lady. And for his own part, he put on a splendid feast, at which Bernabò, being Lady Zinevra's husband, and the most excellent Lady Zinevra herself were the guests of honour. And in addition he presented her with jewels, gold and silver plate, and money, all of which came to a further ten thousand doubloons in value.

He meanwhile commissioned a ship to be specially fitted out for their use, and once the feast held in their honour was concluded, he gave them leave to return to Genoa whenever it suited their purpose. And when they sailed into Genoa, weak with joy and laden with riches, a magnificent welcome awaited them, especially Lady Zinevra, whom everyone had thought to be dead. And thereafter, for as long as she lived, she was held in high esteem and regarded as a paragon of virtue.

As for Ambrogiuolo, on the very day that he was tied to the pole and smeared with honey, he was subjected to excruciating torments by the mosquitoes, wasps and horseflies which abound in that country, and not only was he slain, but every morsel of his flesh was devoured. Hanging by their sinews, his whitened bones remained there for ages without being moved, an eloquent testimony of his wickedness to all who beheld them. And thus it was that the dupe outwitted his deceiver.

TENTH STORY

Paganino of Monaco steals the wife of Messer Ricciardo di Chinzica, who, on learning where she is, goes and makes friends with Paganino. He asks him to restore her to him, and Paganino agrees on condition that he obtains her consent. She refuses to go back with Messer Ricciardo, and after his death becomes Paganino's wife.

Every member of the worthy company complimented the queen most warmly for telling so excellent a story, especially Dioneo, who was the sole remaining speaker of the day. And when he had finished singing its praises, he addressed them as follows:

Fair ladies, there was one feature of the queen's story which has caused me to substitute another tale for the one I was intending to relate. I refer to the stupidity of Bernabò, and of all other men who are given to thinking, as he apparently was, that while they are gadding about in various parts of the world with one woman after another, the wives they left behind are simply twiddling their thumbs. I will grant you that things turned out nicely for Bernabò, but we, who spend our lives in the company of women from the cradle upwards, know perfectly well what they enjoy doing most. In telling you this story, I shall demonstrate the foolishness of such people as Bernabò. And at the same time, I shall show the even greater foolishness of those who, overestimating their natural powers, resort to specious reasoning to persuade themselves that they can do the impossible, and who attempt to mould other people in their own image, thus flying in the face of nature.

There once lived, in Pisa, a very wealthy judge called Messer Ricciardo di Chinzica, who had rather more brain than brawn, and who, thinking perhaps he could satisfy a wife with those same talents that he brought to his studies, went to a great deal of trouble to find himself a wife who was both young and beautiful; whereas, had he been capable of giving himself such good advice as he gave to others, he should have avoided marrying anyone with either of the attributes in question. He succeeded in his quest, however, for Messer Lotto Gualandi agreed to let him marry a daughter of his called Bartolomea, who was one of the prettiest and most charming young ladies in Pisa, a city where most of the women look as ugly as sin. The judge brought her home with an air of great festivity, and although the wedding was celebrated in truly magnificent style, on the first night he only managed to come at her once in order to consummate the marriage, and even then he very nearly fell out of the game before it was over. And next morning, being a skinny and a withered and a spineless sort of fellow, he had to swallow down *vernaccia**, energy-tablets and various other restoratives to pull himself round.

Now, this judge fellow, having thus obtained a better notion of his powers, began to teach her a calendar which schoolchildren are apt to consult, of the sort that was once in use at Ravenna†. For he made it clear to her that there was not a single day that was not the

* A famous Italian sweet white wine.

† Ravenna was said to have as many churches as the number of days in the year, with the result that the town celebrated an extraordinary number of Saints' days.

feast of one or more Saints, out of respect for whom, as he would demonstrate by devious arguments, man and woman should abstain from sexual union. To the foregoing, he added holidays of obligation, the four Ember weeks, the eves of the Apostles and a numerous array of subsidiary Saints, Fridays and Saturdays, the sabbath, the whole of Lent, certain phases of the moon, and various special occasions, possibly because he was under the impression that one had to take vacations from bedding a woman, in the same way that he sometimes took vacations from summing up in the law-courts. For a long time (much to the chagrin of his lady, whose turn came round once a month at the most) he abided by this régime, always keeping a close watch on her lest anyone else should teach her as good a knowledge of the working-days as he had taught her of the holidays.

One summer, during a heat-wave, Messer Ricciardo happened to be seized by a longing to go and relax in the fresh air at a very fine villa of his near Montenero, and he took his fair lady with him. And during their stay, in order to provide her with a little recreation, he arranged a day's fishing, he and the fishermen taking out one boat whilst she and some other ladies went along to watch from a second. But as he became absorbed in what he was doing, they drifted several miles out to sea almost before they realized what was happening.

While their concentration was at its peak, a small galley came upon the scene commanded by Paganino da Mare, a notorious pirate of the time, who having caught sight of the two boats came sailing towards them. They turned and fled, but before they could reach safety, Paganino overtook the boat containing the women, and on catching sight of the fair lady, he disregarded everything else and took her aboard his galley before making off again under the very eyes of Messer Ricciardo, who had meanwhile reached the shore. Needless to say, our friend the judge was extremely distressed on seeing all this, for he was jealous of the very air that she breathed. And all he could do now was to wander about Pisa and other places, bemoaning the wickedness of the pirates, without having any idea who it was that had kidnapped his wife or where she had been taken.

Paganino reckoned himself very fortunate when he saw how beautiful she was, and since he was unmarried, he made up his mind to keep her. But she was weeping bitterly, and so he poured out a stream of endearments in an attempt to console her, and when night descended, having come to the conclusion that he had been wasting his time all day with words, he turned to comforting her with deeds, for he was not the sort of man to pay any heed to calendars, and he had long since forgotten about feasts and holy days. So effective were the consolations he provided, that before they had reached Monaco, the judge and his laws had faded from the lady's memory, and life with Paganino was a positive joy. And after he had brought her to Monaco, in addition to consoling her continuously night and day, Paganino treated her with all the respect due to a wife.

When, some time afterwards, information reached Messer Ricciardo of his lady's whereabouts, he was passionately resolved to go and fetch her in person, being convinced that he alone could handle the affair with the necessary tact. He was quite prepared to pay whatever ransom was demanded, and took ship for Monaco, where he caught sight of her soon after his arrival. But she had seen him, too, and that same evening she warned Paganino and informed him of her husband's intentions.

Next morning, Messer Ricciardo saw Paganino and engaged him in conversation, losing no time in getting on friendly and familiar terms with him, while Paganino, pretending not to know who he was, waited to see what he was proposing to do. At the earliest opportunity, Messer Ricciardo disclosed the purpose of his visit as concisely and politely as he could, then asked Paganino to hand the lady over, naming whatever sum he required by way of ransom.

'Welcome to Monaco, sir,' replied Paganino, smiling broadly. 'And as to your request, I will answer you briefly, as follows. It is true that I have a young lady in my house, but I couldn't say whether she is your wife or some other man's wife, for I do not know you, and all I know about the lady is that she has been living with me for some time. I have taken a liking to you, however, and since you appear to be honest, I will take you to see her, and if you are indeed her husband, as you claim to be, she will no doubt recognize you. If she confirms your story and wants to go with you, you are such an amiable sort of fellow that I am content to leave the amount of the ransom to your own good judgement. But if your story isn't true, it would be dishonest of you to try and deprive me of her, for I am a young man and no less entitled than anyone else to keep a woman, especially this one, for she is the nicest I ever saw.'

'Of course she is my wife,' said Messer Ricciardo. 'You will soon be convinced when you take me to see her, for she will fling her arms round my neck immediately. I could ask for nothing better than the arrangement you suggest.'

'In that case,' said Paganino, 'let us proceed.'

And so off they went to Paganino's house, where they entered a large room and Paganino sent for the lady, who came in from another room, composed in appearance and neatly dressed, and walked over to where the two men were standing. But she took no more notice of Messer Ricciardo than if he were some total stranger coming into the house as Paganino's guest. On seeing this, the judge was greatly astonished, for he had been expecting her to greet him with a display of frenzied rejoicing. 'Perhaps,' he thought, 'the melancholy and prolonged suffering to which I have been subjected, ever since I lost her, have wrought such a change in my appearance that she no longer knows who I am.' He therefore addressed her as follows:

'Madam, it was a costly idea of mine to take you fishing with me, for nobody ever experienced so much sorrow as I have endured from the day I lost you, and now it appears, from the coldness of your greeting, that you do not even recognize me. Don't you see that I am your Messer Ricciardo? Don't you understand that I came to Monaco fully prepared to offer this gentleman whatever ransom he required, so that I could have you back again and take you away from this house? And are you perhaps unaware that he has been good enough to tell me that he'll hand you over for whatever sum I choose to pay?'

The lady turned towards him, with the faintest suggestion of a smile on her lips.

'Are you addressing me, sir?' she asked. 'You must surely be mistaking me for someone else, for as far as I can recall, I have never seen you before in my life.'

'Oh, come now,' said Messer Ricciardo. 'Take a good look at me, and if you choose to remember properly, you will soon see that I am your husband, Ricciardo di Chinzica.'

'You will forgive me for saying so, sir,' said the lady, 'but it is not so proper as you imagine for me to stare at you. And in any case, I have already looked at you sufficiently to know that I have never seen you before.'

Messer Ricciardo supposed her to be doing this because she was afraid of Paganino, in whose presence she was perhaps reluctant to admit that she recognized him. And so, after a while, he asked Paganino if he would kindly allow him to speak with her alone in her room. Paganino agreed, on condition that he made no attempt to kiss her against her will, and he told the lady to go with Messer Ricciardo into her room, listen to what he had to say, and reply as freely as she pleased.

Thus the lady and Messer Ricciardo went into her room, closed the door behind them, and sat down.

'Oh, my dearest,' said Messer Ricciardo, 'my dear, sweet darling, my treasure, now do you remember your Ricciardo who loves you more than life itself? No? How is this possible? Can I have changed so much? Oh, my pretty one, do take another little look at me.'

The lady, who had begun to laugh, interrupted his babbling, saying:

'You are well aware that I possess a sufficiently good memory to know that you are my husband, Messer Ricciardo di Chinzica. But you showed very little sign of knowing *me*, when I was living with you, because if, either then or now, you were as wise as you wish to pretend, you should certainly have had the gumption to realize that a fresh and vigorous young woman like myself needs something more than food and clothes, even if modesty forbids her to say so. And you know how little of that you provided.

'If you were more interested in studying the law than in keeping a wife, you should never have married in the first place. Not that you ever seemed to me to be a judge. On the contrary, you had such an expert knowledge of feasts and festivals, to say nothing of fasts and vigils, that I thought you must be a town-crier. And I can tell you this, that if you had given as many holidays to the workers on your estates as you gave to the one whose job it was to tend my little field, you would never have harvested a single ear of corn. But by the merciful will of God, who took pity on my youth, I chanced upon the man with whom I share this room, where holy days – the ones you used to celebrate so religiously, being more devoted to pious works than to the service of the ladies – have never been heard of. And not only has that door remained firmly shut against sabbaths, Fridays, vigils, Ember Days and Lent (which is such a long drawn-out affair), but work goes on all the time here day and night, so that the place is a positive hive of activity. Why, this very morning, the bell for matins had barely stopped ringing before he was up and about, and I can't begin to tell you how busy we were. Hence I intend to remain with him, and work while I am still young, and save up all those fasts and holy days so that I can turn to them, along with pilgrimages, when I am an old woman. As for you, be so good as to clear off as soon as you can, and have as many holidays as you like, but not with me.'

As he listened to these words, Messer Ricciardo suffered the agonies of the damned, and when he saw that she had finished, he said:

'Oh, my dearest, how can you say such things? Have you lost all regard for your honour and that of your parents? Do you mean to say you prefer to stay on here, living in mortal sin as this man's strumpet, rather than to live in Pisa as my wife? When this fellow grows tired of you, he will turn you out and make you an object of ridicule, whereas I will always cherish you, and you will always be the mistress of my house whatever happens. Do you mean to cast aside your honour and forsake one who loves you more than life itself, simply because of this immoderate and unseemly appetite of yours? Oh, my treasure, don't say these things any more, come away with me. Now that I know what you want, I'll make a special effort in the future. Do change your mind, my precious, and come back to me, for my life has been sheer misery ever since the day you were taken away from me.'

'As to my honour,' the lady replied, 'I mean to defend what remains of it as jealously as anyone. I only wish my parents had displayed an equal regard for it when they handed me over to you! But since they were so unconcerned about my honour then, I do not intend to worry about their honour now. And if I am living in mortal sin, it can be pestle sin too for all I care, so stop making such a song and dance about it. And let me tell you this, that I feel as though

I am Paganino's wife here. It was in Pisa that I felt like a strumpet, considering all that rigmarole about the moon's phases and all those geometrical calculations that were needed before we could bring the planets into conjunction, whereas here Paganino holds me in his arms the whole night long and squeezes and bites me, and as God is my witness, he never leaves me alone.

'You say you will make an effort. But how? By doing things in three easy stages, and springing to attention with a blow from a cudgel? I've noticed, of course, what a fine, strong fellow you've become since I saw you last. Be off with you, and put your efforts into staying alive, for it seems to me that you won't survive much longer, you have such a sickly and emaciated look about you. Oh, and another thing. Even if Paganino leaves me (and he seems to have no such intention, provided I want to stay), I would never come back to you in any case, because if you were to be squeezed from head to toe there wouldn't be a thimbleful of sauce to show for it. Life with you was all loss and no gain as far as I was concerned, so if there were to be a next time, I would be trying my luck elsewhere. Once and for all, then, I repeat that I intend to stay here, where there are no holy days and no vigils. And if you don't clear off quickly I shall scream for help and claim you were trying to molest me.'

On seeing that the situation was hopeless, and realizing for the first time how foolish he had been to take a young wife when he was so impotent, Messer Ricciardo walked out of the room, feeling all sad and forlorn, and although he had a long talk with Paganino, it made no difference whatever. And so finally, having achieved precisely nothing, he left the lady there and returned to Pisa, where his grief threw him into such a state of lunacy that whenever people met him in the street and put any question to him, the only answer they got was: 'There's never any rest for the bar.' Shortly afterwards he died, and when the news reached Paganino, knowing how deeply the lady loved him, he made her his legitimate wife. And without paying any heed to holy days or vigils or observing Lent, they worked their fingers to the bone and thoroughly enjoyed themselves. So it seems to me, dear ladies, that our friend Bernabò, by taking the course he pursued with Ambrogiuolo, was riding on the edge of a precipice.

*   *   *

This story threw the whole company into such fits of laughter that there was none of them whose jaws were not aching, and the ladies unanimously agreed that Dioneo was right and that Bernabò had been an ass. But now that the tale was ended, the queen waited for the laughter to subside, and then, seeing that it was late and everyone had told a story, and realizing that her reign had come to an end, she removed the garland from her own head in the usual way, and, placing it on Neifile's, she said to her with a laugh:

'Dear sister, I do hereby pronounce you sovereign of our tiny nation.' And then she returned to her place.

Neifile blushed a little on receiving this honour, so that her face was like the rose that blooms at dawn in early summer, whilst her eyes, which she had lowered slightly, glittered and shone like the morning star. There followed a round of respectful applause, in token of the joy and goodwill of her companions, and when the clapping had subsided and she had recovered her composure, she seated herself in a slightly more elevated position, and said to them:

'I have no wish to depart from the excellent ways of my predecessors, of whose government you have shown your approval by your obedience. But since I really am your queen, I shall acquaint you briefly with my own proposals, and if they meet with your consent we shall carry them into effect.

'As you know, tomorrow is Friday and the next day is Saturday, both of which, because of the food we normally eat on those two days, are generally thought of as being rather tedious. Moreover, Friday is worthy of special reverence because that was the day of the Passion of Our Lord, who died that we might live, and I would therefore regard it as perfectly right and proper that we should all do honour to God by devoting that day to prayer rather than storytelling. As for Saturday, it is customary on that day for the ladies to wash their hair and rinse away the dust and grime that may have settled on their persons in the course of their week's endeavours. Besides, in deference to the Virgin Mother of the Son of God, they are wont to fast on Saturdays, and to refrain from all activities for the rest of the day, as a mark of respect for the approaching sabbath. Since, therefore, it would be impossible on a Saturday to profit to the full from the routine upon which we have embarked, I think we would be well advised to abstain from telling stories on that day also.

'It will then be four days since we came to stay here, and in order to avoid being joined by others, I think it advisable for us to move elsewhere. I have already thought of a place for us to go, and made the necessary arrangements.

'Our discourse today has taken place within very broad limits. But by the time we assemble after our siesta on Sunday afternoon at our new abode, you will have had more time for reflection, and I have therefore decided, since it will be all the more interesting if we restrict the subject-matter of our stories to a single aspect of the many facets of Fortune, that our theme should be the following: *People who by dint of their own efforts have achieved an object they greatly desired or recovered a thing previously lost.* Let each of us, therefore, think of something useful, or at least amusing, to say to the company on this topic, due allowance being made for Dioneo's privilege.'

The queen's speech met with general approval, and her proposal was unanimously adopted. She then summoned her steward, and having explained where he should place the tables for that evening, instructed him fully concerning his duties for the remainder of her reign. This done, she rose to her feet, her companions followed her example, and she gave them leave to amuse themselves in whatever way they pleased.

And so the ladies made their way with the three young men to a miniature garden, where they whiled away their time agreeably before supper. They then had supper, in the course of which there was much laughter and merriment, and when they had risen from table, at the queen's request Emilia began to dance whilst Pampinea sang the following song, the others joining in the chorus:

'If 'twere not I, what woman would sing,
  Who am content in everything?

'Come, Love, the cause of all my joy,
  Of all my hope and happiness,
  Come let us sing together:
  Not of love's sighs and agony
  But only of its jocundness

And its clear-burning ardour
In which I revel, joyfully,
As if thou wert a god to me.

'Love, the first day I felt thy fire
Thou sett'st before mine eyes a youth
Of such accomplishment
Whose able strength and keen desire
And bravery could none, in truth,
Find any complement.
With thee I sing, Lord Love, of this,
So much in him lies all my bliss.

'And this my greatest pleasure is:
That he loves me with equal fire,
Cupid, all thanks to thee;
Within this world I have my bliss
And I may in the next, entire,
I love so faithfully,
If God who sees us from above
Will grant this boon upon our love.'

When this song was finished, they sang a number of others, danced many dances and played several tunes. But eventually the queen decided it was time for them to go to bed, and they all retired to their respective rooms, carrying torches to light them on their way. For the next two days, they attended to those matters about which the queen had spoken earlier, and looked forward eagerly to Sunday.

Here ends the Second Day of the Decameron

THIRD DAY

Here begins the Third Day, wherein, under the rule of Neifile, the discussion turns upon people who by dint of their own efforts have achieved an object they greatly desired, or recovered a thing previously lost.

On the following Sunday, when already the dawn was beginning to change from vermilion to orange with the approach of the sun, the queen arose and summoned all her companions. Some time earlier, the steward had dispatched most of the things they required to their new quarters, together with servants to make all necessary preparations for their arrival. And once the queen herself had set out, he promptly saw that everything else was loaded on to the baggage train, as though he were striking camp, and then departed with the rest of the servants who had remained behind with the ladies and gentlemen.

Meanwhile the queen, accompanied and followed by her ladies and the three young men, and guided by the song of perhaps a score of nightingales and other birds, struck out westward at a leisurely pace along a little-used path carpeted with grass and flowers, whose petals were gradually opening to greet the morning sun. After walking no more than two miles, she brought them, long before tierce was half spent, to a most beautiful and ornate palace, which was situated on a slight eminence above the plain. Entering the palace, they explored it from end to end, and were filled with admiration for its spacious halls and well-kept, elegant rooms, which were equipped with everything they could possibly need, and they came to the conclusion that only a gentleman of the highest rank could have owned it. And when they descended to inspect the huge, sunlit courtyard, the cellars stocked with excellent wines, and the well containing abundant supplies of fresh, ice-cold water, they praised it even more. The whole place was decked with seasonable flowers and cuttings, and by way of repose they seated themselves on a loggia overlooking the central court. Here they were met by the steward, who had thoughtfully laid on a supply of delectable sweetmeats and precious wines for their refreshment.

After this, they were shown into a walled garden alongside the palace, and since it seemed at first glance to be a thing of wondrous beauty, they began to explore it in detail. The garden was surrounded and criss-crossed by paths of unusual width, all as straight as arrows and overhung by pergolas of vines, which showed every sign of yielding an abundant crop of grapes later in the year. The vines were all in flower, drenching the garden with their aroma, which, mingled with that of many other fragrant plants and herbs, gave them the feeling that they were in the midst of all the spices ever grown in the East. The paths along the edges of the garden were almost entirely hemmed in by white and red roses and jasmine, so that not only in the morning but even when the sun was at its apex one could walk in pleasant, sweet-smelling shade, without ever being touched by the sun's rays. It would take a long time to describe how numerous and varied were the shrubs growing there, or how neatly they were set out: but all the ones that have aught to commend them and flourish in our climate were represented in full measure. In the central part of the garden (not the least, but by far the most admirable of its features), there was a lawn of exceedingly fine grass, of so deep a green as to almost seem black, dotted all over with possibly a thousand different kinds of gaily-coloured flowers, and surrounded by a line of flourishing, bright green orange- and lemon-trees, which, with their mature and unripe fruit and lingering shreds of blossom, offered agreeable shade to the eyes and a delightful aroma to the nostrils. In the middle of this lawn there stood a fountain of pure white marble, covered with marvellous bas-reliefs. From a figure standing on a column in the centre of the fountain, a jet of water, whether natural or artificial I know not, but sufficiently powerful to drive a mill with ease, gushed high into the sky before cascading downwards and falling with a delectable plash into the crystal-clear pool below. And from this pool, which was lapping the rim of the fountain, the water passed through a hidden culvert and then emerged into finely constructed artificial channels surrounding the lawn on all sides. Thence it flowed along similar channels through almost the whole of the beautiful garden, eventually gathering at a single place from which it issued forth from the garden and descended towards the plain as a pure clear stream, furnishing ample power to two separate mills on its downward course, to the no small advantage of the owner of the palace.

The sight of this garden, and the perfection of its arrangement, with its shrubs, its streamlets, and the fountain from which they originated, gave so much pleasure to each of the ladies and the three young men that they all began to maintain that if Paradise were constructed on earth, it was inconceivable that it could take any other form, nor could they imagine any way in which the garden's beauty could possibly be enhanced. And as they wandered contentedly through it, making magnificent garlands for themselves from the leaves of the various trees, their ears constantly filled with the sound of some twenty different kinds of birds, all singing as though they were vying with one another, they became aware of yet another delightful feature, which, being so overwhelmed by the others, they had so far failed to notice. For they found that the garden was liberally stocked with as many as a hundred different varieties of perfectly charming animals, to which they all starting drawing each other's attention. Here were some rabbits emerging from a warren, over there hares were running, elsewhere they could observe some deer lying on the ground, whilst in yet another place young fawns were grazing. And apart from these, they saw numerous harmless creatures of many other kinds, roaming about at leisure as though they were quite tame, all of which added greatly to their already considerable delight.

When, however, they had wandered about the garden for some little time, sampling its various attractions, they instructed the servants to arrange the tables round the fountain, and then they sang half-a-dozen canzonets and danced several dances, after which, at the queen's command, they all sat down to breakfast. Choice and dainty dishes, exquisitely prepared, were set before them in unhurried succession, and when they rose from table, merrier than when they had started, they turned once more to music, songs and dancing. Eventually, however, as the hottest part of the day was approaching, the queen decided that those who felt so inclined should take their siesta. Some of them accordingly retired, but the rest were so overwhelmed by the beauty of their surroundings that they remained where they were and whiled away their time in reading romances or playing chess or throwing dice whilst the others slept.

But a little after nones, they all went and refreshed their faces in cool water before assembling, at the queen's request, on the lawn near the fountain, where, having seated themselves in the customary manner, they began to await their turn to tell a story on the topic the queen had proposed. The first of their number to whom she entrusted this office was Filostrato, who began as follows:

FIRST STORY

Masetto of Lamporecchio pretends to be dumb, and becomes a gardener at a convent, where all the nuns vie with one another to take him off to bed with them.

Fairest ladies, there are a great many men and women who are so dense as to be firmly convinced that when a girl takes the white veil and dons the black cowl, she ceases to be a woman or to experience feminine longings, as though the very act of making her a nun had caused her to turn into stone. And if they should happen to hear of anything to suggest that their conviction is ill-founded, they become quite distressed, as though some enormous and diabolical evil had been perpetrated against nature. It never enters their heads for a moment, possibly because they have no wish to face facts, that they themselves are continually dissatisfied even though they enjoy full liberty to do as they please, or that idleness and solitude are such powerful stimulants. Again, there are likewise many people who are firmly convinced that digging and hoeing and coarse food and hardy living remove all lustful desires from those who work on the land, and greatly impair their intelligence and powers of perception. But, since the queen has bidden me to speak, I would like to tell you a little tale, relevant to the topic she has prescribed, which will show you quite clearly that all these people are sadly mistaken in their convictions.

In this rural region of ours, there was and still is a nunnery, greatly renowned for its holiness, which I shall refrain from naming for fear of doing the slightest harm to its reputation. At this convent, not long ago, at a time when it housed no more than eight nuns and an abbess, all of them young, there was a worthy little man whose job it was to look after a very beautiful garden of theirs. And one day, being dissatisfied with his remuneration, he settled up with the nuns' steward and returned to his native village of Lamporecchio.

On his return, he was warmly welcomed by several of the villagers, among them a young labourer, a big, strong fellow called Masetto, who, considering that he was of peasant stock, possessed a remarkably handsome physique and agreeable features. Since the good man, whose name was Nuto, had been away from the village for some little time, Masetto wanted to know where he had been, and when he learned that Nuto had been living at a convent, he questioned him about his duties there.

'I tended a fine, big garden of theirs,' Nuto replied, 'in addition to which, I sometimes used to go and collect firewood, or I would fetch water and do various other little jobs of that sort. But the nuns gave me such a paltry wage that it was barely sufficient to pay for my shoe-leather. Besides, they are all young and they seem to me to have the devil in them, because whatever you do, it is impossible to please them. Sometimes, in fact, I would be working in the garden when one of them would order me to do one thing, another would tell me to do something else, and yet another would snatch the very hoe from my hands, and tell me I was doing things the wrong way. They used to pester me to such an extent that occasionally I would down tools and march straight out of the garden. So that eventually, what with one thing and another, I decided I'd had enough of the place and came away altogether. Just as I was leaving, their steward asked me whether I knew of anyone who could take the job on, and I promised to send somebody along, provided I could find the right man, but you won't catch me sending him anybody, not unless God has provided the fellow with the strength and patience of an ox.'

As he listened, Masetto experienced such a longing to go and stay with these nuns that his whole body tingled with excitement, for it was clear from what he had heard that he should be able to achieve what he had in mind. Realizing, however, that he would get nowhere by revealing his intentions to Nuto, he replied:

'How right you were to come away from the place! What sort of a life can any man lead when he's surrounded by a lot of women? He might as well be living with a pack of devils. Why, six times out of seven they don't even know their own minds.'

But when they had finished talking, Masetto began to consider what steps he ought to take so that he could go and stay with them. Knowing himself to be perfectly capable of carrying out the duties mentioned by Nuto, he had no worries about losing the job on that particular score, but he was afraid lest he should be turned down because of his youth and his unusually attractive appearance. And so, having rejected a number of other possible expedients, he eventually thought to himself: 'The convent is a long way off, and there's nobody there who knows me. If I can pretend to be dumb, they'll take me on for sure.' Clinging firmly to this conjecture, he therefore dressed himself in pauper's rags and slung an axe over his shoulder, and without telling anyone where he was going, he set out for the convent. On his arrival, he wandered into the courtyard, where as luck would have it he came across the steward, and with the aid of gestures such as dumb people use, he conveyed the impression that he was begging for something to eat, in return for which he would attend to any wood-chopping that needed to be done.

The steward gladly provided him with something to eat, after which he presented him with a pile of logs that Nuto had been unable to chop. Being very powerful, Masetto made short work of the whole consignment, and then the steward, who was on his way to the wood, took Masetto with him and got him to fell some timber. He then provided Masetto with an ass, and gave him to understand by the use of sign-language that he was to take the timber back to the convent.

The fellow carried out his instructions so efficiently that the steward retained his services for a few more days, getting him to tackle various jobs that needed to be done about the place. One day, the Abbess herself happened to catch sight of him, and she asked the steward who he was.

'The man is a poor deaf-mute, ma'am, who came here one day begging for alms,' said the steward. 'I saw to it that he was well fed, and set him to work on various tasks that needed to be done. If he turns out to be good at gardening, and wants to stay, I reckon we would do well out of it, because we certainly need a gardener, and this is a strong fellow who will always do as he's told. Besides, you wouldn't need to worry about his giving any cheek to these young ladies of yours.'

'I do believe you're right,' said the Abbess. 'Find out whether he knows what to do, and make every effort to hold on to him. Provide him with a pair of shoes and an old hood, wheedle him, pay him a few compliments, and give him plenty to eat.'

The steward agreed to carry out her instructions, but Masetto was not far away, pretending to sweep the courtyard, and he had overheard their whole conversation. 'Once you put me inside that garden of yours,' he said to himself, gleefully, 'I'll tend it better than it's ever been tended before.'

Now, when the steward had discovered what an excellent gardener he was, he gestured to Masetto, asking him whether he would like to stay there, and the latter made signs to indicate that he was willing to do whatever the steward wanted. The steward therefore took him on to the staff, ordered him to look after the garden, and showed him what he was to do, after which he went away in order to attend to the other affairs of the convent, leaving him there by himself. Gradually, as the days passed and Masetto worked steadily away, the nuns started teasing and annoying him, which is the way people frequently behave with deaf-mutes, and they came out with the foulest language imaginable, thinking that he was unable to hear them. Moreover, the Abbess, who was possibly under the impression that he had lost his tail as well as his tongue, took little or no notice of all this.

Now one day, when Masetto happened to be taking a rest after a spell of strenuous work, he was approached by two very young nuns who were out walking in the garden. Since he gave them the impression that he was asleep, they began to stare at him, and the bolder of the two said to her companion:

'If I could be sure that you would keep it a secret, I would tell you about an idea that has often crossed my mind, and one that might well work out to our mutual benefit.'

'Do tell me,' replied the other. 'You can be quite certain that I shan't talk about it to anyone.'

The bold one began to speak more plainly.

'I wonder,' she said, 'whether you have ever considered what a strict life we have to lead, and how the only men who ever dare set foot in this place are the steward, who is elderly, and this dumb gardener of ours. Yet I have often heard it said, by several of the ladies who have come to visit us, that all other pleasures in the world are mere trifles by comparison with the one experienced by a woman when she goes with a man. I have thus been thinking, since I have nobody else to hand, that I would like to discover with the aid of this dumb fellow whether they are telling the truth. As it happens, there couldn't be a better man for the purpose, because even if he wanted to let the cat out of the bag, he wouldn't be able to. He wouldn't even know how to explain, for you can see for yourself what a mentally retarded, dim-witted hulk of a youth the fellow is. I would be glad to know what you think of the idea.'

'Dear me!' said the other. 'Don't you realize that we have promised God to preserve our virginity?'

'Pah!' she said. 'We are constantly making Him promises that we never keep! What does it matter if we fail to keep this one? He can always find other girls to preserve their virginity for Him.'

'But what if we become pregnant?' said her companion. 'What's going to happen then?'

'You're beginning to worry about things before they've even happened. We can cross that bridge if and when we come to it. There'll be scores of different ways to keep it a secret, provided we control our own tongues.'

'Very well, then,' said the other, who was already more eager than the first to discover what sort of stuff a man was made of. 'How do we set about it?'

'As you see,' she replied, 'it is getting on for nones, and I expect all our companions are asleep. Let's make sure there's nobody else in the garden. And then, if the coast is clear, all we have to do is to take him by the hand and steer him across to that hut over there, where he shelters from the rain. Then one of us can go inside with him while the other keeps watch. He's such a born idiot that he'll do whatever we suggest.'

Masetto heard the whole of this conversation, and since he was quite willing to obey, the only thing he was waiting for now was for one of them to come and fetch him. The two nuns had a good look round, and having made certain that they could not be observed, the one who had done all the talking went over to Masetto and woke him up, whereupon he sprang instantly to his feet. She then took him by the hand, making alluring gestures to which he responded with big broad, imbecilic grins, and led him into the hut, where Masetto needed very little coaxing to do her bidding. Having got what she wanted, she loyally made way for her companion, and Masetto, continuing to act the simpleton, did as he was asked. Before the time came for them to leave, they had each made repeated trials of the dumb fellow's riding ability, and later on, when they were busily swapping tales about it all, they agreed that it was every bit as pleasant an experience as they had been led to believe, indeed more so. And from then on, whenever the opportunity arose, they whiled away many a pleasant hour in the dumb fellow's arms.

One day, however, a companion of theirs happened to look out from the window of her cell, saw the goings-on, and drew the attention of two others to what was afoot. Having talked the matter over between themselves, they at first decided to report the pair to the Abbess. But then they changed their minds, and by common agreement with the other two, they took up shares in Masetto's holding. And because of various indiscretions, these five were subsequently joined by the remaining three, one after the other.

Finally, the Abbess, who was still unaware of all this, was taking a stroll one very hot day in the garden, all by herself, when she came across Masetto stretched out fast asleep in the shade of an almond-tree. Too much riding by night had left him with very little strength for the day's labours, and so there he lay, with his clothes ruffled up in front by the wind, leaving him all exposed. Finding herself alone, the lady stood with her eyes riveted to this spectacle, and she was seized by the same craving to which her young charges had already succumbed. So, having roused Masetto, she led him away to her room, where she kept him for several days, thus provoking bitter complaints from the nuns over the fact that the handyman had suspended work in the garden. Before sending him back to his own quarters, she repeatedly savoured the one pleasure for which she had always reserved her most fierce disapproval, and from then on she demanded regular supplementary allocations, amounting to considerably more than her fair share.

Eventually, Masetto, being unable to cope with all their demands, decided that by continuing to be dumb any longer he might do himself some serious injury. And so one night, when he was with the Abbess, he untied his tongue and began to talk.

'I have always been given to understand, ma'am,' he said, 'that whereas a single cock is quite sufficient for ten hens, ten men are hard put to satisfy one woman, and yet here am I with nine of them on my plate. I can't endure it any longer, not at any price, and as a matter of fact I've been on the go so much that I'm no longer capable of delivering the goods. So you'll either have to bid me farewell or come to some sort of an arrangement.'

When she heard him speak, the lady was utterly amazed, for she had always believed him to be dumb.

'What is all this?' she said. 'I thought you were supposed to be dumb.'

'That's right, ma'am, I was,' said Masetto, 'but I wasn't born dumb. It was owing to an illness that I lost the power of speech, and, praise be to God, I've recovered it this very night.'

The lady believed him implicitly, and asked him what he had meant when he had talked about having nine on his plate. Masetto explained how things stood, and when the Abbess heard, she realized that every single one of the nuns possessed sharper wits than her own. Being of a tactful disposition, she decided there and then that rather than allow Masetto to go away and spread tales concerning the convent, she would come to some arrangement with her nuns in regard to the matter.

Their old steward had died a few days previously. And so, with Masetto's consent, they unanimously decided, now that they all knew what the others had been doing, to persuade the people living in the neighbourhood that after a prolonged period of speechlessness, his ability to talk had been miraculously restored by the nuns' prayers and the virtues of the saint after whom the convent was named, and they appointed him their new steward. They divided up his various functions among themselves in such a way that he was able to do them all justice. And although he fathered quite a number of nunlets and monklets, it was all arranged so discreetly that nothing leaked out until after the death of the Abbess, by which time Masetto was getting on in years and simply wanted to retire to his village on a fat pension. Once his wishes became known, they were readily granted.

Thus it was that Masetto, now an elderly and prosperous father who was spared the bother of feeding his children and the expense of their upbringing, returned to the place from which he had set out with an axe on his shoulder, having had the sense to employ his youth to good advantage. And this, he maintained, was the way that Christ treated anybody who placed a pair of horns upon His crown.

SECOND STORY

A groom makes love to King Agilulf's wife. Agilulf finds out, keeps quiet about it, tracks down the culprit, and shears his hair. The shorn man shears all the others, thus avoiding an unpleasant fate.

There were some parts of Filostrato's tale that caused the ladies to blush, others that provoked their laughter, and as soon as it had come to an end, the queen requested Pampinea to take up the storytelling. She accordingly began as follows, laughing all over her face:

Some people, having discovered or heard a thing of which they were better left in ignorance, are so foolishly anxious to publish the fact that sometimes, in censuring the inadvertent failings of others with the object of lessening their own dishonour, they increase it out of all proportion. And I now propose, fair ladies, to illustrate the truth of this assertion by describing a contrary state of affairs, wherein the wisdom of a mighty monarch was matched by the guile of a man whose social standing was possibly inferior to that of Masetto.

When Agilulf became King of the Lombards, he followed the example set by his predecessors and chose the city of Pavia, in Lombardy, as the seat of his kingdom. He had meanwhile married Theodelinda, who was the beautiful widow of the former Lombard king, Authari, and although she was a very intelligent and virtuous woman, she once had a most unfortunate experience with a suitor of hers. For during a period when the affairs of Lombardy, owing to the wise and resolute rule of this King Agilulf, were relatively calm and prosperous, one of the Queen's grooms, a man of exceedingly low birth, gifted out of all proportion to his very humble calling, who was as tall and handsome as the King himself, happened to fall hopelessly in love with his royal mistress.

Since his low station in life had not blinded him to the fact that this passion of his was thoroughly improper, he had the good sense not to breathe a word about it to anyone, nor did he even dare to cast tell-tale glances in the lady's direction. But although he was quite resigned to the fact that he would never win her favour, he could at least claim that his thoughts were directed towards a lofty goal. And being scorched all over by the flames of love, he excelled every one of his companions by the zealous manner in which he performed any trifling service that might conceivably bring pleasure to the Queen. Thus it came about that whenever the Queen was obliged to go out on horseback, she preferred to ride the palfrey that was under his care, rather than any of the others. On these occasions, the fellow considered himself to be in his seventh heaven, and he would remain close beside her stirrup, almost swooning with joy whenever he was able simply to brush against the lady's clothes.

However, one frequently finds in affairs of this sort that the weakening of expectation goes hand in hand with a strengthening of the initial passion, and that is exactly what happened in the case of this poor groom. So much so, in fact, that having no glimmer of hope to sustain him, he found it increasingly difficult to keep his secret yearnings under control, and since he was unable to rid himself of his passion, he kept telling himself that he would have to die. In reflecting on the ways and means, he was determined to die in such a manner that his motive, in other words his love for the Queen, would be inferred from the circumstances leading up to his death. And at the same time, he resolved that these circumstances should offer him an opportunity of trying his luck and seeing whether he could bring his desires either wholly or partially to fruition. Knowing that it would be quite futile to start either confiding in the Queen or writing letters to acquaint her with his love, he thought he would explore the possibility of entering her bed by means of a stratagem. He had already discovered that the King was not in the habit of invariably sleeping with her, and hence the one and only stratagem that might conceivably succeed was for him to find some way of impersonating the King so that he could approach her quarters and gain admittance to her bedchamber.

Accordingly, with the aim of discovering how the King was dressed and what procedure he followed when paying the Queen a visit, the groom concealed himself for several nights running in the King's palace, in a spacious hall situated between the respective royal bedchambers. And during one of these nocturnal vigils, he saw the King emerge from his room in an enormous cloak, with a lighted torch in one hand and a stick in the other. Walking over to the Queen's room, the King knocked once or twice on the door with his stick, whereupon he was instantly admitted and the torch was removed from his hand. Some time later, the King retired in like fashion to his own quarters, and the groom, who had been keeping a careful watch, decided that he too would have to adopt this same ritual. He therefore procured a torch and a stick, and a cloak similar to the one he had seen the King wearing, and having soaked himself thoroughly in a hot bath so that there should be no possibility of his giving offence to the Queen or arousing her suspicions by smelling of the stable, he transported these articles to the great hall and concealed himself in his usual place.

When he sensed that everyone was asleep, and that the time had finally come for him to gratify his longing or perish nobly in the attempt, he kindled a small flame with the aid of a flint and steel that he had brought along for the purpose, lit his torch, and, wrapping himself carefully up in the folds of the cloak, walked over to the door of the bedchamber and knocked twice with his stick. The door was opened by a chambermaid, still half asleep, who took the light and put it aside, whereupon without uttering a sound he stepped inside the curtain, divested himself of his cloak, and clambered into the bed where the Queen was sleeping. Knowing that the King, whenever he was angry about anything, was in the habit of refusing all discourse, he drew the Queen lustfully into his arms with a show of gruff impatience, and without a single word passing between them, he repeatedly made her carnal acquaintance. He was most reluctant to depart, but nevertheless he eventually arose, fearing lest by overstaying his welcome the delight he had experienced should be turned into sorrow, and having donned his cloak and retrieved his torch, he stole wordlessly away and returned as swiftly as possible to his own bed.

He could hardly have reached his destination when, to the Queen's utter amazement, the King himself turned up in her room, climbed into bed, and offered her a cheerful greeting.

'Heavens!' she said, emboldened to speak by his affable manner. 'Whatever has come over you tonight, my lord? You no sooner leave me, after enjoying me more passionately than usual, than you come back and start all over again! Do be careful, now.'

On hearing these words, the King immediately came to the conclusion that the Queen had been taken in by an outward resemblance to his own physique and manner. But he was a wise man, and since neither the Queen nor anybody else appeared to have noticed the deception, he had no hesitation in deciding to keep his own counsel. Many a stupid man would have reacted differently, and exclaimed: 'It was not I. Who was the man who was here? What happened? Who was it who came?' But this would only have led to complications, upsetting the lady when she was blameless and sowing the seeds of a desire, on her part, to repeat the experience. And besides, by holding his tongue his honour remained unimpaired, whereas if he were to talk he would make himself look ridiculous.

And so, showing little sign of his turbulent inner feelings either in his speech or in his facial expression, the King answered her as follows:

'Do you think, my dear, that I am incapable of returning to you a second time after being here once already?'

'Oh no, my lord,' the lady replied. 'But all the same, I beg you to take care of your constitution.'

'Your advice is sound, and I intend to follow it,' said the King. 'I shall go away again, and bother you no further tonight.'

And so, boiling with anger and indignation because of the trick that had clearly been played upon him, he put on his cloak again and departed, bent upon tracking the culprit quietly down, for the King supposed that he must be a member of the household, in which case, no matter who the fellow was, he would still be within the palace walls.

Accordingly, having equipped himself with a small lantern shedding very little light, he made his way to a dormitory above the palace-stables containing a long row of beds, where nearly all of his servants slept. And since he calculated that the author of the deed to which the lady had referred would not yet have had time to recover a normal pulse and heartbeat after his exertions, the King began at one end of the dormitory and went silently along the row, placing his hand on each man's chest in order to discover whether his heart was still pounding.

Although all the others were sleeping soundly, the one who had been with the Queen was still awake. And when he saw the King approaching, he realized what he was looking for and grew very frightened, with the result that the pounding of his heart, already considerable because of his recent labours, was magnified by his fear. He was convinced that the King would have him instantly put to death if he were to notice the way his heart was racing, and reflected on various possible courses of action. Eventually, however, on observing that the King was unarmed, he decided he would pretend to be asleep and wait for the King to make the first move.

Having examined a large number of the sleepers without finding the man he was looking for, the King came eventually to the groom, and on discovering that his heart was beating strongly, he said to himself: 'This is the one.' Since, however, he had no wish to broadcast his intentions, all he did was to shear away a portion of the hair on one side of the man's head, using a pair of scissors that he had brought along for the purpose. In those days, men wore their hair very long, and the King left this mark so that he could identify him by it next morning. He then departed from the scene, and returned to his own room.

The groom had witnessed the whole episode, and being of a sharp disposition, he realized all too clearly why he had been marked in this particular fashion. He therefore leapt out of bed without a moment's delay, and having laid his hands on one of several pairs of shears that happened to be kept in the stable for grooming the horses, he silently made the rounds of all the sleeping forms in the dormitory and cut everybody's hair in precisely the same way as his own, just above the ear. Having completed his mission without being detected, he crept back to bed and went to sleep.

When he arose the next morning, the King gave orders for the palace gates to remain closed until his whole household had appeared before him, and they duly assembled in his presence, all of them bareheaded. The King then began to inspect them with the intention of picking out the man whose hair he had shorn, only to discover, to his amazement, that the hair on most of their heads had been cut in exactly similar fashion.

'This fellow I'm looking for may be low-born,' he said to himself, 'but he clearly has all his wits about him.'

Then, realizing that he could not achieve his aim without raising a clamour, and not wishing to bring enormous shame upon himself for the sake of a trifling act of revenge, he decided to deal with the culprit by issuing a stern word of warning and showing him that his deed had not passed undetected.

'Whoever it was who did it,' he said, addressing himself to the whole assembly, 'he'd better not do it again. And now, be off with you.'

Many another man would have wanted to have all of them strung up, tortured, examined and interrogated. But in so doing, he would have brought into the open a thing that people should always try their utmost to conceal. And even if, by displaying his hand, he had secured the fullest possible revenge, he would not have lessened his shame but greatly increased it, as well as besmirching the fame of his lady.

Not unnaturally, the King's little speech caused quite a stir amongst his listeners, and a long time subsequently elapsed before they grew tired of discussing between themselves what it could have meant. But nobody divined its import except the one man for whom it was intended, and he was far too shrewd ever to throw any light on the subject while the King was still alive, nor did he ever risk his life again in performing any deed of a similar nature.

THIRD STORY

Under the pretext of going to confession and being very pure-minded, a lady who is enamoured of a young man induces a solemn friar to pave the way unwittingly for the total fulfilment of her desires.

Pampinea was now silent, and the bravery and prudence of the groom were praised by most of her listeners, who likewise applauded the wisdom of the King. Then the queen turned to Filomena, enjoining her to continue, whereupon Filomena began to speak, gracefully, as follows:

The story I propose to relate, concerning the manner in which a sanctimonious friar was well and truly hoodwinked by a pretty woman, should prove all the more agreeable to a lay audience inasmuch as the priesthood consists for the most part of extremely stupid men, inscrutable in their ways, who consider themselves in all respects more worthy and knowledgeable than other people, whereas they are decidedly inferior. They resemble pigs, in fact, for they are too feeble-minded to earn an honest living like everybody else, and so they install themselves wherever they can fill their stomachs.

It is not only in obedience to the command I have received, dear ladies, that I shall tell you this story. I also wish to impress upon you that even the clergy, to whom we women pay far too much heed on account of our excessive credulity, are capable of being smartly deceived, as indeed they sometimes are, both by men and by one or two of ourselves.

A few short years ago, in our native city, where fraud and cunning prosper more than love or loyalty, there was a noblewoman of striking beauty and impeccable breeding, who was endowed by Nature with as lofty a temperament and shrewd an intellect as could be found in any other woman of her time. Although I could disclose her name, along with those of the other persons involved in this story, I have no intention of doing so, for if I did, certain people still living would be made to look utterly contemptible, whereas the whole matter should really be passed off as a huge joke.

This lady, being of gentle birth and finding herself married off to a master woollen-draper because he happened to be very rich, was unable to stifle her heartfelt contempt, for she was firmly of the opinion that no man of low condition, however wealthy, was deserving of a noble wife. And on discovering that all he was capable of, despite his massive wealth, was distinguishing wool from cotton, supervising the setting up of a loom, or debating the virtues of a particular yarn with a spinner-woman, she resolved that as far as it lay within her power she would have nothing whatsoever to do with his beastly caresses. Moreover she was determined to seek her pleasure elsewhere, in the company of one who seemed more worthy of her affection, and so it was that she fell deeply in love with an extremely eligible man in his middle thirties. And whenever a day passed without her having set eyes upon him, she was restless for the whole of the following night.

However, the gentleman suspected nothing of all this, and took no notice of her; and for her part, being very cautious, she would not venture to declare her love by dispatching a maidservant or writing him a letter, for fear of the dangers that this might entail. But having perceived that he was on very friendly terms with a certain priest, a rotund, uncouth individual who was nevertheless regarded as an outstandingly able friar on account of his very saintly mode of life, she calculated that this fellow would serve as an ideal go-between for her and the man she loved. And so, after reflecting on the strategy she would adopt, she paid a visit, at an appropriate hour of the day, to the church where he was to be found, and having sought him out, she asked him whether he would agree to confess her.

Since he could tell at a glance that she was a lady of quality, the friar gladly heard her confession, and when she had got to the end of it, she continued as follows:

'Father, as I shall explain to you presently, there is a certain matter about which I am compelled to seek your advice and assistance. Having already told you my name, I feel sure you will know my family and my husband. He loves me more dearly than life itself, and since he is enormously rich, he never has the slightest difficulty or hesitation in supplying me with every single object for which I display a yearning. Consequently, my love for him is quite unbounded, and if my mere thoughts, to say nothing of my actual behaviour, were to run contrary to his wishes and his honour, I would be more deserving of hellfire than the wickedest woman who ever lived.

'Now, there is a certain person, of respectable outward appearance, who unless I am mistaken is a close acquaintance of yours. I really couldn't say what his name is, but he is tall and handsome, his clothes are brown and elegantly cut, and, possibly because he is unaware of my resolute nature, he appears to have laid siege to me. He turns up infallibly whenever I either look out of a window or stand at the front door or leave the house, and I am surprised, in fact, that he is not here now. Needless to say, I am very upset about all this, because his sort of conduct frequently gives an honest woman a bad name, even though she is quite innocent.

'I have made up my mind on several occasions to inform my brothers about him. But then it has occurred to me that men are apt to be tactless in their handling of these matters, and when they receive a dusty answer they start bandying words with one another and eventually somebody gets hurt. So in order to avoid unpleasantness and scandal, I have always held my tongue. Since, however, you appear to be a friend of his, I decided I would break my silence, for after all it is perfectly proper for you to censure people for this kind of behaviour, no matter whether they are your friends or total strangers. For the love of God, therefore, I implore you to speak to him severely and persuade him to refrain from his importunities. There are plenty of other women who doubtless find this sort of thing amusing, and who will enjoy being ogled and spied upon by him, but I personally have no inclination for it whatsoever, and I find his behaviour exceedingly disagreeable.'

And having reached the end of her speech, the lady bowed her head as though she were going to burst into tears.

The reverend friar realized immediately who it was to whom she was referring, and having warmly commended her purity of mind (for he firmly believed she was telling the truth), he promised to take all necessary steps to ensure that the fellow ceased to annoy her. Moreover, knowing her to be very rich, he expounded the advantages of charitable deeds and almsgiving, and told her all about his needy condition, whereupon the lady said:

'Please do restrain him, for the love of God; and if he should deny it, by all means tell him who it was who informed you and complained to you about it.'

Then, having completed her confession and received her penance, suddenly remembering the friar's injunctions to her on the subject of almsgiving, she casually stuffed his palm with money and requested him to say a few masses for the souls of her departed ones, after which she got up from where she was kneeling at his feet, and made her way home.

Shortly afterwards, the gentleman in question paid one of his regular visits to the reverend friar, and after they had conversed together for a while on general topics, the friar drew him to one side and reproached him in a very kindly sort of way for the amorous glances which, as the lady had given him to understand, he believed him to be casting in her direction.

Not unnaturally, the gentleman was amazed, for he had never so much as looked at the lady and it was very seldom that he passed by her house. But when he started to protest his innocence, the friar interrupted him.

'Now it's no use pretending to be shocked,' he said, 'or wasting your breath denying it, because you simply haven't a leg to stand on. This is no piece of idle gossip that I picked up from her neighbours. I had it from the lady's own lips, when she came here complaining bitterly about your behaviour. And apart from the fact that a man of your age ought to know better than to engage in such frivolous activities, I might inform you that I have never come across any woman possessing a more violent distaste for irresponsible conduct of that sort. So, out of regard for your own reputation and the lady's peace of mind, be so good as to desist and leave her in peace.'

The gentleman, being rather more perceptive than the reverend friar, was not exactly slow to appreciate the lady's cleverness, and putting on a somewhat sheepish expression, he promised not to bother her any more. But after leaving the friar, he made his way towards the house of the lady, who was keeping continuous vigil at a tiny little window so that she would see him if he happened to pass by. When she saw him coming, she smiled at him so prettily that he was able to conclude beyond all doubt that his interpretation of the friar's words was correct. And from that day forward, proceeding with the maximum of prudence and conveying the impression that he was engaged in some other business entirely, he became a regular visitor to the neighbourhood, thereby deriving much pleasure and affording the lady considerable delight and satisfaction. It was not long, however, before the lady, having by now ascertained that her fondness for him was reciprocated, became eager to stimulate his passion and demonstrate how deeply she loved him. At the first available opportunity, therefore, she returned to the reverend friar, and, kneeling in the church at his feet, she burst into tears.

On seeing this, the friar asked her in soothing tones what new affliction was troubling her.

'Father,' replied the lady, 'my new affliction is none other than that accursed friend of yours, of whom I complained to you the other day. I honestly believe he was born to tempt me into doing something that I shall regret for the rest of my days. And in that case, I shall never have the courage to kneel before you again.'

'What!' said the friar. 'Do you mean to say he is still annoying you?'

'He certainly is,' said the lady. 'Indeed, he appears to have taken exception to my complaining to you about him, and ever since, as though out of pure malice, he has been turning up seven times more often than he did before. Would to God that he was satisfied with parading up and down and staring at me, but yesterday he had the bare-faced impertinence to send a maidservant to me, in my own house, with his nonsensical prattle, and he sent me a belt and a purse, as though I didn't have enough belts and purses already. It made me absolutely furious, indeed it still does, and if I had not been afraid of committing a sin and hence incurring your displeasure, I would have stirred up a scandal there and then. So far, however, I have managed to restrain myself, because I did not wish to do or say anything without informing you first.

'As for the belt and the purse, I immediately handed them back to the woman who brought them, telling her to return them to her employer, and sent her off with a flea in her ear. But then it occurred to me that she might keep them for herself and tell him I had accepted them, and so I called her back and snatched them out of her hands in a blazing temper. I decided to bring them along to you instead, so that you could hand them back and tell him I have no need of his goods, because thanks both to God and to my husband, I possess so many belts and purses that I could bury myself under them. And I am sorry to have to say it, father, but if he doesn't stop pestering me after this, I shall tell my husband and brothers, come what may. For if needs be, I would much rather have him take a severe hiding than allow him to besmirch my good name. And that's all there is to it, father.'

She was still sobbing uncontrollably when, having come to the end of her speech, she extracted a very splendid, expensive-looking purse from beneath her cloak together with a gorgeous little belt, and hurled them into the lap of the friar, who, being fully taken in by her story, was feeling exceedingly distressed and accepted them without any question.

'Daughter,' he said, 'I am not surprised that you are so upset by what has happened, and I certainly cannot blame you. On the contrary, I am full of admiration for the way you have followed my advice in this affair. He has obviously failed to keep the promise he gave me the other day, when I first took him to task. Nevertheless, I believe that this latest outrage of his, following in the wake of his earlier misdemeanours, will enable me to give him such a severe scolding that he will not trouble you any further. In the meantime, you must with God's blessing contain your anger and refrain from informing any of your relatives, because that could bring him altogether too heavy a punishment. Never fear that this will harm your good name, for I shall always be here to bear unwavering witness, whether before God or before men, to your virtuous nature.'

The lady gave the appearance of being somewhat mollified, and then, knowing how covetous he and his fellow friars were, she moved on to another subject.

'Father,' she said, 'for the past few nights I have been dreaming about various departed relatives of mine, and they all appear to be suffering dreadful torments and continually asking for alms, especially my mother, who seems to be in such a state of affliction and misery that it would break your heart to see her. I think she is suffering abominably at seeing me persecuted like this by that enemy of God, and hence I should like you to pray for their souls and say the forty masses of St Gregory, so that God may release them from this scourging fire.' And so saying, she slipped a florin into his hand.

The reverend friar gleefully pocketed the money, and having poured out a torrent of fine words and pious tales to reinforce her godliness, he gave her his blessing and let her go.

Unaware that he had been hoodwinked, the friar watched her depart and then summoned his friend, who realized as soon as he arrived, from the friar's agitated appearance, that he was about to receive some news from the lady, and waited to hear what the friar had to say. The latter repeated all that he had said to him previously, and for the second time, angrily and without mincing his words, gave him a severe scolding for what the lady alleged he had done.

Being as yet unsure of which way the friar was going to jump, the gentleman denied having sent the purse and the belt, speaking without much conviction so as not to undermine the friar's belief in the story, just in case he had heard it from the lady herself.

The friar practically exploded with rage.

'What!' he said. 'Can you really have the effrontery to deny it, you scoundrel? Here, take a look at them – she brought them to me herself, with her eyes full of tears – and tell me whether or not you recognize them!'

The gentleman put on a display of acute embarrassment.

'Yes, indeed I do,' he said. 'I admit that it was wrong of me, and now that I fully appreciate her inclinations, I guarantee that you won't be troubled again.'

The words now started to flow in good earnest, and eventually the blockhead of a friar handed over the purse and the belt to his friend. Finally, after preaching him a lengthy sermon and getting him to promise that he would call a halt to his importunities, he sent him about his business.

The gentleman was feeling absolutely delighted, for not only did it appear quite certain that the lady loved him, but he had also received a handsome present. On leaving the friar, he went and stood in a sheltered place from which he showed his lady that both of the items were now in his possession, all of which made her very happy, the more so because her scheme appeared to be working better and better. All that she was waiting for now, in order to bring her work to a successful conclusion, was for her husband to go away somewhere, and not long afterwards it so happened that he was indeed called away on business to Genoa.

The next morning, after he had ridden off on horseback, the lady paid yet another visit to the reverend friar, filling his ears with sobs and lamentations.

'Father,' she said. 'I simply cannot bear it any longer. However, since I did promise you the other day that I wouldn't do anything without telling you first, I have come now to offer you my apologies in advance. And lest you should imagine that my tears and complaints are unjustified, I want to tell you what that friend of yours, or rather, that devil incarnate, did to me early this morning, a little before matins.

'I don't know what unfortunate accident led him to discover that my husband went away to Genoa yesterday morning, but during the night, at the hour I mentioned, he forced his way into the grounds and climbed up a tree to my bedroom-window, which overlooks the garden. He had already opened the window and was about to enter the room, when I awoke with a start, leapt out of bed, and began to scream. And I would have continued to scream but for the fact that he announced who he was and implored me to stop for your sake and for the love of God. Not wishing to cause you any distress, I stopped screaming, and since he was not yet inside, I rushed to the window, naked as on the day I was born, and slammed it in his face, after which I think the rogue must have taken himself off, because I heard no more of him. Now, I leave you to judge whether this sort of thing is either pleasant or permissible, but I personally have no intention of allowing him to get away with it any longer. In fact, I've already put up with more than enough of his antics for your sake.'

The lady's story threw the friar into such a state of turmoil that all he could do by way of reply was to ask her, over and over again, whether she was quite sure that it had not been some other man.

'Merciful God!' she replied. 'I ought to know the man by now! It was he, I tell you, and if he denies it, don't you believe him.'

'Daughter,' replied the friar, 'all I can say is that he has taken an unpardonable liberty and carried things beyond all reasonable bounds, and you took the proper course in sending him off as you did. But I would implore you, since God has protected you from dishonour, that just as you have followed my advice on the two previous occasions, you should do so again this time. Do not, in other words, complain to any of your kinsfolk, but leave things to me, and I shall see whether I can restrain this headstrong devil, whom I had always thought of as such a saintly person. If I can succeed in taming the beast that possesses him, all well and good. If I can't, then you have my blessing and my permission to follow your instinct and take whatever measures you consider most appropriate.'

'Very well, then,' said the lady. 'I have no wish to upset you, and therefore I shall follow your instructions just once more. But you'd better see that he takes care not to pester me again, because I promise you that if there's any more of it, I shan't be coming back to you.' And without saying another word, she turned her back on the friar and strode away.

She had hardly left the church when the gentleman arrived and was summoned by the friar, who drew him aside and gave him the fiercest scolding anyone ever had, calling him a disloyal traitor and a perjurer.

Having twice previously had occasion to observe the eventual drift of these reprimands, the man was careful not to commit himself, but simply tried to wheedle an explanation out of the friar by interpolating ambiguous comments, his first words being:

'Why are you creating such a fuss? Anyone would think I had crucified Christ.'

'For shame, you villain!' exclaimed the friar. 'Just listen to the man! He talks for all the world as if a year or two had passed, blotting out the memory of his wickedness and depravity. Can you have forgotten the offence you perpetrated in the short time that has elapsed since matins? Where were you this morning, a little before dawn?'

'I don't recall where I was,' replied the gentleman. 'But it didn't take you long to find out.'

'It certainly did not,' said the friar. 'I presume you were under the impression, since the husband was away, that the good lady would promptly welcome you into her arms. By heavens, sir, you're a fine gentleman! No mistake about it. A nocturnal prowler, a garden invader, and a tree climber, all rolled into one! Do you think you're going to conquer this lady's integrity through sheer impudence, clambering up trees to windows in the small hours? There's nothing in the world that she loathes more profoundly than these importunities of yours, and yet you still persist with them. Even supposing, however, that she had not made her attitude perfectly plain, you appear to have taken a fat lot of notice of my admonitions. Now, just listen to me. It isn't because she loves you that she has refrained, so far, from telling anyone about your importunities, but merely because I pleaded with her not to speak out. But she will not hold her peace any longer. I have given her my permission, if you annoy her just once more, to take whatever action she thinks best. What are you going to do if she informs her brothers?'

Having gathered all the information he needed, the gentleman pacified the friar to the best of his ability with a string of specious promises, and went about his business. Next morning, at the hour of matins, having broken into the garden, scaled the tree, and found the window open, he entered the bedroom, and before you could say knife he was lying in the arms of his fair mistress. And as she had been awaiting his arrival with intense longing, she gave him a rapturous welcome.

'A thousand thanks to our friend the friar,' she said, 'for instructing you so impeccably how to get here.'

Then, each enjoying the other to the accompaniment of many a hilarious comment about the stupid friar's naïveté, and random jibes about such draperly concerns as slubbing and combing and carding, they gambolled and frolicked until they very nearly died of bliss. After this first encounter, having devoted some little thought to the subject, they arranged matters in such a way that, without having further recourse to their friend the friar, they slept together no less pleasurably on many later occasions. And I pray to God that in the bountifulness of His mercy He may very soon conduct me, along with all other like-minded Christian souls, to a similar fate.

FOURTH STORY

Dom Felice teaches Friar Puccio how to attain blessedness by carrying out a certain penance, and whilst Friar Puccio is following his instructions, Dom Felice has a high old time with the penitent's wife.

When, having reached the end of her story, Filomena lapsed into silence, Dioneo added a few well-turned phrases of his own, warmly commending both the anonymous lady and the prayer with which Filomena had rounded off her narrative. Then the queen, laughing, looked towards Panfilo and said:

'Now, Panfilo, let us have some agreeable trifle to add to our enjoyment.'

Having promptly expressed his willingness to comply with her command, Panfilo began as follows:

Madam, many are those who, whilst they are busy making strenuous efforts to get to Paradise, unwittingly send some other person there in their stead; and not very long ago, as you are now about to hear, this happy fate befell a lady living in our city.

Close beside the Church of San Pancrazio, or so I have been told, there once lived a prosperous, law-abiding citizen called Puccio di Rinieri, who was totally absorbed in affairs of the spirit, and on reaching a certain age, became a tertiary in the Franciscan Order, assuming the name of Friar Puccio. In pursuit of these spiritual interests of his, since the other members of his household consisted solely of a wife and maidservant, which relieved him of the necessity of practising a profession, he attended church with unfailing regularity. Being a simple, well-intentioned soul, he recited his paternosters, attended sermons, went to mass, and turned up infallibly whenever lauds were being sung by the lay-members. Moreover, he practised fasting and other forms of self-discipline, and it was rumoured that he was a member of the flagellants.

His wife, who was called Monna Isabetta, was still a young woman of about twenty-eight to thirty, and she was as shapely, fair and fresh-complexioned as a round, rosy apple, but because of her

husband's godliness and possibly on account of his age, she was continually having to diet, so to speak, for much longer periods than she
would have wished. Thus it frequently happened, that when she was
in the mood for going to bed, or, in other words, playing games with
him, he would treat her to an account of the life of Our Lord, following this up with the sermons of Brother Nastagio or the Plaint of the
Magdalen or other pieces in a similar vein.

And that was how matters stood when a certain Dom Felice, a
handsomely-built young man who was one of the conventual monks
at San Pancrazio, returned from a sojourn in Paris. This Dom Felice
was a man of acute intelligence and profound learning, and Friar
Puccio assiduously cultivated his friendship. And because, in addition
to being very good at resolving all of Friar Puccio's spiritual problems, Dom Felice went out of his way, knowing the sort of person he
was, to give him the impression that he was exceedingly saintly, Friar
Puccio formed the habit of taking him home and offering him lunch,
or supper, according to the time of day. And in order to please her
husband, Monna Isabetta became equally friendly with him and did
all she possibly could to make him feel at home.

In the course of his regular visits to Friar Puccio's house, the monk
therefore had every opportunity to observe this shapely little wife,
blooming with vitality, and being quick to realize what it was that
she lacked most, he decided, in order to spare Friar Puccio the trouble,
that he would do his level best to supply it. And so, taking good care
not to arouse the Friar's suspicions, he began to cast meaningful
glances in her direction, with the result that he kindled in her breast a
yearning that corresponded to his own. On perceiving her response to
his advances, the monk seized the earliest opportunity to acquaint her
verbally with his intentions. But although he found her very willing
to give effect to his proposals, it was impossible to do so because she
would not risk an assignation with the monk in any other place
except her own house, and her own house was ruled out because
Friar Puccio never went away from the town, all of which made the
monk very disconsolate.

However, after devoting a great deal of thought to the subject, he
lighted upon a foolproof method for keeping company with the lady
in her own house, even though Friar Puccio happened to be under the

same roof. And one day, when Friar Puccio called round to see him, he spoke to him as follows:

'It has been obvious to me for some time, Friar Puccio, that your one overriding ambition in life is to achieve saintliness, but you appear to be approaching it in a roundabout way, whereas there is a much more direct route which is known to the Pope and his chief prelates, who, although they use it themselves, have no desire to publicize its existence. For if the secret were to leak out, the clergy, who live for the most part on the proceeds of charity, would immediately disintegrate, because the lay public would no longer give them their support, whether by way of almsgiving or in any other form. However, you are a friend of mine and you have been very good to me, and if I could be certain that you would not reveal it to another living soul, and that you wanted to give it a trial, I would tell you how it is done.'

Being anxious to learn all about it, Friar Puccio began by earnestly begging Dom Felice to teach him the secret, then he swore that he would never, without Dom Felice's express permission, breathe a word about it to anyone, at the same time declaring that provided it was the sort of thing he could manage, he would apply himself to it with a will.

'Since you have given me your promise,' said the monk, 'I will let you in on the secret. There is one thing, though, that I must emphasize. True, the doctors of the Church maintain that any person who wishes to attain blessedness should perform the penance I am about to describe. But listen carefully. I do not say that after doing the penance you will automatically cease to be a sinner. What will happen is this, that all the sins you have committed up to the moment of doing the penance will be purged and remitted as a result. And as for those you commit afterwards, they will never be counted as deadly sins, but on the contrary they will be erased by holy water, as happens already in the case of the venial ones.

'Now, let us proceed. It is necessary, first and foremost, for the penitent to confess his sins with very great thoroughness immediately before beginning the penance; and next, he must start to fast and practise a most rigorous form of abstinence, this to continue for forty days, during which you must abstain, not only from the company of other women, but even from touching your own wife. In addition, it is necessary to have some place in your own house from which you can look up at the heavens after night has fallen, and to which you will proceed at compline, having first positioned a very broad plank there in such a way that you can stand with your back resting against it, and keeping your feet on the floor, extend your arms outwards in an attitude of crucifixion; and by the way, if you want to support them on a couple of wall-pegs, that'll be perfectly all right. With your eyes fixed on the heavens, you must maintain this same posture, without moving a muscle, until matins. If you happened to be a scholar, you would, during the course of the night, be obliged to recite certain special prayers which I would give you to learn; but since you are not, you will have to say three hundred paternosters and three hundred Hail Marys in honour of the Trinity. As you gaze towards Heaven, you must constantly bear in mind that God created Heaven and earth. And at the same time, you must concentrate on the Passion of Christ, for you will be re-enacting His own condition on the cross.

'As soon as you hear the bell ringing for matins, you may, if you wish, proceed to your bed and lie down, fully dressed, for a short sleep. Later in the morning you must go to church, listen to at least three masses, and say fifty paternosters followed by the same number of Hail Marys. Then you must attend unobtrusively to your business, if you have any, after which you will take lunch, and report at the church just before vespers in order to recite certain prayers, of which I shall provide you with written copies. (These are absolutely vital, if you want the thing to work.) Finally, at compline, you return to the beginning, and follow the same procedure all over again. I once did all this myself, and I assure you that there is every prospect, if you follow these instructions and put plenty of devotion into it, that before your penance comes to an end you will be experiencing a wonderful sensation of eternal blessedness.'

'This is not too heavy a task,' said Friar Puccio, 'nor does it last very long. It should be quite possible to get the thing done, and I therefore propose, God willing, to make a start this coming Sunday.'

After leaving Dom Felice he went straight home, where, having obtained the monk's permission beforehand, he explained everything to his wife in minute detail.

The lady grasped the monk's intentions all too clearly, particularly when she heard about the business of standing still without moving a muscle until matins. Thinking it an excellent arrangement, she told her husband that she heartily approved of the idea, and also of any other measures he took for the good of his soul, adding that in order to persuade God to make his penance profitable she would join him in fasting, but there she would draw the line.

Thus the whole thing was settled, and on the following Sunday Friar Puccio began his long penance, during which Master Monk, by prior arrangement with the lady, came to supper with her nearly every evening at an hour when he could enter the house unobserved, always bringing with him large quantities of food and drink. Then, after supper, he would sleep with her all night until matins, when he would get up and leave, and Friar Puccio would return to bed.

The place where Friar Puccio had elected to do his penance was adjacent to the room where the lady slept, from which it was separated only by a very thin wall. And one night, when Master Monk was cutting too merry a caper with the lady and she with him, Friar Puccio thought he could detect a certain amount of vibration in the floorboards. When, therefore, he had recited a hundred of his paternosters, he came to a stop, and without leaving his post, he called out to his wife and demanded to know what she was doing.

His wife, who had a talent for repartee, and who at that moment was possibly riding bareback astride the nag of St Benedict or St John Gualbert, replied:

'Heaven help me, dear husband, I am shaking like mad.'

'Shaking?' said Friar Puccio. 'What is the meaning of all this shaking?'

His wife shrieked with laughter, for she was a lively, energetic sort of woman, and besides, she was probably laughing for a good reason.

'What?' she replied. 'You don't know its meaning? Haven't I heard you saying, hundreds of times: "He that supper doth not take, in his bed all night will shake"?'

Since she had already given him the impression that she was

fasting, Friar Puccio readily assumed this to be the cause of her sleeplessness, which in turn accounted for the way she was tossing and turning in bed.

'Wife,' he replied, in all innocence, 'I told you not to fast, but you would insist. Try not to think about it. Try and go to sleep. You're tossing about so violently in the bed that you're shaking the whole building.'

'Don't worry about me,' said his wife. 'I know what I'm doing. Just you keep up the good work, and I'll try and do the same.'

So Friar Puccio said no more, but turned his attention once again to his paternosters. From that night onward, Master Monk and the lady made up a bed in another part of the house, in which they cavorted to their hearts' content until the time came for the monk to leave, when the lady would return to her usual bed, being joined there shortly afterwards by Friar Puccio as he staggered in from his penance.

Thus, while the Friar carried on with his penance, his wife carried on with the monk, pausing now and then to deliver the same merry quip:

'You make Friar Puccio do penance, but we are the ones who go to Paradise.'

The lady was of the opinion that she had never felt better in her life, and having been compelled to diet by her husband for so long, she acquired such a taste for the monk's victuals that when Friar Puccio reached the end of his long penance, she found a way of banqueting with the monk elsewhere. And for a long time thereafter, she continued discreetly to enjoy such repasts.

To return to my opening remarks then, this was how it came about that Friar Puccio did penance with the intention of reaching Paradise, to which on the contrary he sent both the monk, who had shown him how to get there quickly, and his wife, who shared his house but lived in dire need of something which Master Monk, being a charitable soul, supplied her with in great abundance.

FIFTH STORY

Zima presents a palfrey to Messer Francesco Vergellesi, who responds by granting him permission to converse with his wife. She is unable to speak, but Zima answers on her behalf, and in due course his reply comes true.

The ladies shook with laughter over Panfilo's story of Friar Puccio, and when he had finished, the queen, with womanly grace, called upon Elissa to continue. Whereupon, speaking rather haughtily, not from affectation but from habit long established, Elissa began to address them as follows:

Many people imagine, because they know a great deal, that other people know nothing; and it frequently happens that when they think they are hoodwinking others, they later discover that they have themselves been outwitted by their intended victims. Consequently I consider it is quite insane for anyone to put another person's powers of intelligence to the test when he has no need to do so. But since, possibly, there are those who would not share my opinion, I should like, without straying from the topic of our discussion, to tell you what happened once to a certain nobleman of Pistoia.

The nobleman in question was called Messer Francesco, and belonged to the Vergellesi family of Pistoia. He was a very wealthy and judicious man, and he was also shrewd, but at the same time he was exceedingly mean. On being appointed Governor of Milan, he laid in all the paraphernalia appropriate to his new rank before setting out for that city, but was unable however to find a palfrey handsome enough to suit his requirements, and this caused him no small concern.

Now, in Pistoia at that time there was a very rich young man of humble birth called Ricciardo, who because of his well-groomed, elegant appearance was generally referred to by all the townspeople as Zima, or in other words, the Dandy. For a long time he had loved and wooed, without success, the exceedingly beautiful and virtuous wife of Messer Francesco, and it so happened that this man owned one of the finest palfreys in Tuscany, to which he was deeply attached because of its beauty. And since it was common knowledge that he was madly fond of Messer Franscesco's wife, someone told Messer Francesco that if he asked for the palfrey he was bound to get it on account of Zima's devotion to his lady.

Spurred on by his greed, Messer Francesco sent for Zima and asked him to sell him the palfrey, in the expectation that Zima would hand it over for nothing.

'Sir,' replied Zima, liking the sound of the nobleman's request, 'if you were to offer me everything you possess in the world you could not buy my palfrey: but you could certainly have it as a gift, whenever you liked, on this one condition, that before you take possession of it, you allow me, in your presence, to address a few words to your good lady in sufficient privacy for my words to be heard by her and by nobody else.'

Prompted by his avarice, and hoping to make a fool of the other fellow, the nobleman agreed to Zima's proposal, adding that he could talk to her for as long as he liked. And having left him to wait in the great hall of his palace, he went to his wife's room, explained to her how easy it would be to win the palfrey, and obliged her to come and listen to Zima; but she was to be very careful not to utter so much as a single word in reply to anything he said.

Although she strongly resented being involved in this arrangement, nevertheless, since she was obliged to do her husband's bidding, the lady agreed and followed him into the great hall in order to hear what Zima had to say. Zima took the nobleman aside to confirm the terms of their agreement, then went to sit with the lady in a corner of the hall that was well beyond everyone else's hearing.

'Illustrious lady,' he began, 'since you are not imperceptive, you will undoubtedly have become well aware, long before now, that I am deeply in love with you, not only because of your beauty, which without any question surpasses that of every other woman I ever saw, but also on account of your laudable manners and singular virtues, any one of which would be sufficient to capture the heart of the noblest man alive. It is thus unnecessary for me to offer you a long-winded account of my love for you. Suffice it to say that no man ever loved any woman more deeply or more ardently, and that I shall continue to do so unfailingly for as long as life sustains this poor, suffering body of mine, and longer still; for if, in the life hereafter, people love as they do on earth, I shall love you for ever. Consequently, you may rest assured that there is nothing you possess, be it precious or trifling, that you can regard as so peculiarly your own or count upon so infallibly under all circumstances as my humble self, and the same applies to all my worldly goods. But so that you may be fully persuaded that this is so, I assure you that I would deem it a greater privilege to be commissioned by you to perform some service that was pleasing to you, than to have the whole world under my own command and ready to obey me.

'Since, as you perceive, I belong to you unreservedly, it is not without reason that I will venture to address my pleas to your noble heart, which is the one true source of all my peace, all my contentment, and all my well-being. Dearest beloved, since I am yours and you alone have the power to fortify my soul with some vestige of hope as I languish in the fiery flames of love, I beseech you, as your most humble servant, to show me some mercy and mitigate the harshness you have been wont to display towards me in the past. Your compassion will console me, enabling me to claim that it is to your beauty that I owe, not only my love, but also my very life, which will assuredly fail unless your proud spirit yields to my entreaties, and then indeed people will be able to say that you have killed me. Now, leaving aside the fact that my death would not enhance your reputation, I believe, also, that your conscience would occasionally trouble you and you would be sorry for having been the cause of it, and sometimes, when you were even more favourably disposed, you would say to yourself: "Alas, how wrong it was of me not to take pity on my poor Zima!" But this repentance of yours, coming too late, would only serve to heighten your distress.

'Therefore, in order to forestall so regrettable an outcome, instead of allowing me to die, take pity on me whilst there is still time, for in you alone lies the power of making me the happiest or the most wretched man alive. It is my hope and my belief that you will not be so unkind as to allow death to be my reward for such passionate devotion, and that you will gladly consent to my humble entreaty, thus restoring my failing spirits, which have turned quite faint with awe in your gracious presence.'

At this point, his words trailed off into silence and he began to heave enormous sighs, after which his eyes shed a certain number of tears and he settled back into his chair to await the noble lady's answer.

Though she had previously remained unmoved by Zima's protracted courtship, his tilting at the jousts, his *aubades*, and all the other ways in which he had demonstrated his devotion, the lady was certainly stirred now by the tender words of affection addressed to her by this passionate suitor, so that, for the first time in her life, she began to understand what it meant to be in love. And despite the fact that, in obedience to her husband's instructions, she said nothing, she was unable to restrain herself from uttering one or two barely perceptible sighs, thus betraying what she would willingly have made clear to Zima, had she been able to reply.

Having waited for some time, only to discover that no answer was forthcoming, Zima was at first perplexed, but gradually began to realize how cleverly the nobleman had played his hand. Even so, as he continued to gaze upon her face, he noticed that every so often her eyes would dart a gleam in his direction, and this, together with the fact that she was obviously having some difficulty in restraining her sighs, filled him with hope and inspired him to improvise a second line of approach. And thus, mimicking the lady's voice whilst she sat and listened, he began to answer his own plea, speaking as follows:

'My poor, dear Zima, you may rest assured that I have been aware for some time of the intensity and completeness of your devotion, and what you have just said has made it all the more obvious to me. I am glad of your love, as is only natural, and I would not wish you to suppose, because I have seemed harsh and cruel, that my outward appearance reflected my true feelings towards you. On the contrary, I have always loved you and held you higher than any other man in my affection, but I was obliged to behave as I did for fear both of my husband and of damaging my good name. However, the time is now approaching when I shall be able to show you clearly how much I love you, at the same time offering you some reward for your past and present devotion towards me. Take heart, then, and be of good cheer, for Messer Francesco will leave within the next few days to become Governor of Milan, a fact of which you, who have given him your handsome palfrey for my sake, are already aware. And in the name of the true love I bear you, I give you my solemn promise that within a few days of his departure you will be able to come to me, and we shall bring our love to its total and pleasurable consummation.

'However, since there will be no further opportunity for us to discuss the matter, I must explain without further ado that one day in the near future you will see two towels hanging in the window of my room, which overlooks the garden. On that same evening, after darkness has fallen, you are to come to me, entering by way of the garden-gate and taking good care not to let anyone see you. There you will find me waiting for you, and we shall spend the whole night having all the joy and pleasure of one another that we desire.'

Having impersonated the lady whilst he said all this, Zima now began to speak on his own behalf.

'My dearest,' he answered, 'your kind reply has filled all of my faculties with such a surfeit of happiness that I am scarcely able to express my gratitude. But even if I could go on talking for as long as I wished, it would still be impossible for me to thank you as fully as my feelings dictate and your kindness deserves. I will therefore leave it to your own excellent judgement to imagine what I vainly long to put into words, merely pausing to assure you that I will carry out your instructions to the letter. I will then perhaps be better placed to appreciate the full extent of your generosity towards me, and I will spare no effort to show you all the gratitude of which I am capable. For the present, then, there is nothing further that remains to be said; and hence I will bid you farewell, my dearest, and may God grant you all those joys and blessings that you most eagerly desire.'

The lady never uttered a single word from beginning to end of this interview, and when it was over, Zima got up and began to return in the direction of the nobleman, who, seeing Zima on his feet, walked towards him laughing.

'Well?' he said. 'Don't you agree that I kept my promise?'

'I do not, sir,' Zima replied, 'for you promised that you would allow me to talk to your good lady and you have had me talking to a marble statue.'

This reply greatly pleased the nobleman, who, whilst he had always had a high opinion of the lady, now thought even better of her.

'From now on,' he said, 'that palfrey you owned belongs to me.'

'Quite so,' Zima replied. 'And for all the good it did me to insist on this favour of yours, I might as well have presented it to you without conditions in the first place. Indeed, I wish to God I had, because now you have bought the palfrey and I have got nothing to show for it.'

The nobleman was highly amused by all this, and now that he was supplied with a palfrey, he set out a few days later on the road to Milan and his governorship.

Left at home to her own devices, the lady recalled Zima's words, reflecting how deeply he loved her and how, for her sake, he had given away his palfrey; and on observing him from the house as he passed regularly up and down, she said to herself: 'What am I doing? Why am I throwing away my youth? This husband of mine has gone off to Milan and won't be returning for six whole months. When is he ever going to make up for lost time? When I'm an old woman? Besides, when will I ever find such a lover as Zima? I'm all by myself, and there's nobody to be afraid of. I don't see why I shouldn't enjoy myself whilst I have the chance. I won't always have such a good opportunity as I have at present. Nobody will ever know about it, and even if he were to find out, it's better to do a thing and repent of it than do nothing and regret it.'

The outcome of all this soul-searching was that one day she hung two towels in the window overlooking the garden, in the way Zima had indicated. Zima was overjoyed to see them, and after nightfall he cautiously made his way, unaccompanied, to the lady's garden-gate, which he found unlocked. Thence he proceeded to a second door, leading into the house itself, where he found the gentlewoman waiting for him.

When she saw him coming, she rose to meet him, and welcomed him with open arms. Embracing her and kissing her a hundred thousand times, he followed her up the stairs and they went directly to bed, where they tasted love's ultimate joys. And although this was the first time, it was by no means the last, for not only during the nobleman's absence in Milan but also after his return Zima visited the house again on numerous other occasions, to the exquisite pleasure of both parties.

SIXTH STORY

Ricciardo Minutolo loves the wife of Filippello Sighinolfo, and on hearing of her jealous disposition he tricks her into believing that Filippello has arranged to meet his own wife on the following day at a bagnio and persuades her to go there and see for herself. Later she learns that she has been with Ricciardo, when all the time she thought she was with her husband.

Elissa had nothing further to add, and after they had praised the skill of Zima, the queen called upon Fiammetta to proceed with the next story.

'Willingly, my lady,' replied Fiammetta, laughing gaily; and so she began:

I should like to move away a little from our own city (which is no less fertile in stories for all occasions than in everything else), and tell you something, as Elissa has done already, of events in the world outside. Let us therefore proceed to Naples, and I shall describe how one of those prudes, who profess such a loathing for love, was led by her lover's ingenuity to taste the fruits of love before she even noticed they had blossomed. You will thus, at one and the same time, be forearmed against things that could happen, and entertained by those that actually did.

In the ancient city of Naples, which is perhaps as delectable a city as any to be found in Italy, there once lived a young patrician, immensely rich and blue-blooded, whose name was Ricciardo Minutolo. Although he was married to a charming and very lovely young wife, he fell in love with a lady who by common consent was far more beautiful than any other woman in Naples. A paragon of virtue, she was called Catella, and was married to a young nobleman called Filippello Sighinolfo, whom she loved and cherished more dearly than anything else in the world.

So although Ricciardo Minutolo was in love with this Catella and did all the right things for winning a lady's favour and affection, he was unable to make the slightest impression upon her, and had almost reached the end of his tether. Even if he had known how to free himself from the bonds of love, he was quite incapable of doing so, and yet he could neither die nor see any point in living. And one day, as he languished away in this manner, it happened that certain kins-women of his urged him very strongly to call a halt to his philander-ing, pointing out that he was wasting his energies because Catella loved no man except Filippello, towards whom she was so jealously devoted that she suspected the very birds flying through the air, lest they should whisk him away from her.

On learning of Catella's jealousy, Ricciardo suddenly thought of a possible way to gratify his longings. He began to pretend that, having abandoned all hope of winning Catella's affection, he had fallen in love with another lady, and that it was now for her sake that he tilted and jousted and did all the things he had formerly done for Catella. Nor did it take him very long before he convinced nearly everyone in Naples, including Catella, that he was madly in love with this other lady. And so successful was he in sustaining this fiction, that Catella herself, not to mention various other people who had previously snubbed him on account of the attentions he was paying her, began to offer him the same civil, neighbourly greeting, whenever she met him, that she accorded to others.

Now it so happened that one day, during a spell of hot weather, several parties of the Neapolitan nobility, in accordance with local custom, set off for an outing along the sea-coast, where they would lunch and sup before returning home. And on discovering that Catella had gone there with a party of ladies, Ricciardo got together a little group of his own and made for the same place, which he no sooner reached than he received an invitation to join Catella's party. This he accepted after a certain show of reluctance, as though he were not at all anxious to press himself on their company. The ladies then began, with Catella joining in the fun, to pull Ricciardo's leg on the subject of his latest lady-love, whereupon he pretended to take violent offence, thus supplying them with further food for gossip. Eventually, as is the custom on such occasions, several of the ladies wandered off one by one in different directions, until only a handful of them, including Catella, were left behind with Ricciardo, who at a certain point threw off a casual reference to some affair that her husband was supposed to be having. Catella was promptly seized by an attack of jealousy, and her whole body began to throb with a burning desire to know what Ricciardo was talking about. She sat and brooded for a while, but in the end, unable to contain her feelings any longer, she implored Ricciardo, in the name of the lady he loved above all others, to be so good as to explain his remark about Filippello.

'Since you have implored me for *her* sake,' he told her, 'I dare not refuse you anything, no matter what it may be. I am therefore prepared to tell you about it, but you must promise me never to breathe a word of it either to your husband or to anyone else until you have confirmed the truth of my story. This you can do quite easily, and if you like, I will show you how.'

The lady took him up on this offer, which convinced her all the more that he was telling the truth, and swore to him that her lips would remain sealed. They then drew aside from the others so that they would not be overheard.

'Madam,' Ricciardo began, 'if I were still in love with you, as I once was, I would not have the heart to tell you anything that might possibly bring you distress; but since my love for you is now a thing of the past, I shall have fewer misgivings in disclosing exactly what is afoot. I do not know whether Filippello ever took offence at my being in love with you, or whether he mistakenly thought that you reciprocated my love; at all events, he never gave me any such impression. But now, having waited perhaps until such time as he thought me least likely to suspect, he appears to be intent on doing me the same service as he doubtless fears I have done to him: in other words, he is having an affair with my wife. From what I have been able to discover, he has been courting her for some time with the utmost secrecy, sending her a number of messages, all of which she has referred to me; and she has been replying in accordance with my instructions.

'But this very morning, before setting out from home to come here, I found my wife engaged in earnest conversation with some woman whom I instantly recognized for what she was, and so I called my wife and asked her what this person wanted. "It's that brute of a Filippello," she said. "By sending him replies and raising his hopes, you have encouraged him to pester me, and now he says he must know at all costs what I am proposing to do. He tells me that he could make arrangements for us to meet in secret at a bagnio in the city, and he refuses to take no for an answer. If it weren't for the fact that you have forced me to lead him on in this way, for reasons best known to yourself, I would have taught him so painful a lesson that he would never have had the courage to look in my direction again." When I heard this, I felt that the fellow was going too far and was no longer to be suffered, and it seemed to me that I should inform you about it, so that you might know how he rewards that unswerving fidelity of yours which once was almost the death of me.

'Lest you were to imagine, however, that this was all a fairy story, and so as to let you see the whole thing for yourself if you so desired, I prevailed upon my wife to tell the woman, who was still waiting for her answer, that she would present herself at the bagnio tomorrow afternoon around nones, when everyone is asleep. And the woman went away, looking very pleased with herself.

'Now, I don't suppose you imagine I was going to send her to the bagnio. But if I were you, I would see to it that he found *me* there instead of the lady he was expecting; and after playing him on the hook for a while, I would let him perceive who it was he had been consorting with, and regale him with all the abuse he deserved. If you do as I suggest, it is my belief that he will be put to so much shame that we shall both be avenged for his evil designs at a single blow.'

As is usually the way with people who suffer from jealousy, Catella immediately swallowed the whole story without bothering to consider the kind of person who was telling it or whether he could be deceiving her, and began to connect this tale of Ricciardo's with certain things that had happened in the past. Flying into a sudden rage, she said that she would certainly do as he suggested, because after all, it would cost so little effort on her part. And if Filippello really were to turn up, she was determined to make him feel so ashamed of himself that he would never look at another woman again without being stricken with guilt.

Ricciardo was pleased with her reaction, and, feeling that he was making good progress with his scheme, he added a number of other details to reinforce her belief in his story, at the same time extracting a faithful promise that she would never reveal the source of her information.

Next morning, Ricciardo presented his compliments to the good woman who supervised the bagnio that he had mentioned to Catella, explained his intentions, and asked her to give him all the assistance she could. And since she was greatly beholden to him, she willingly agreed to cooperate, and arranged with Ricciardo what she was to do and say.

In the building where the bagnio was situated, the woman had one room that was extremely dark, there being no window to let in the light. And following Ricciardo's instructions, she prepared this room for him and caused it to be furnished with her most comfortable bed, upon which, after he had lunched, Ricciardo lay down and began to wait for Catella to arrive.

Meanwhile, on the previous evening, the lady in question had returned home in high dudgeon after hearing Ricciardo's tale, by which she had allowed herself to be much too easily convinced. Shortly afterwards, Filippello also returned home, and being pre-occupied with other matters, he treated her with rather less than his customary affection. This made her considerably more suspicious, and she began saying to herself: 'He's obviously thinking of the woman he is planning to have fun and games with tomorrow, but he's in for a big disappointment.' And this reflection, together with the thought of what she would say to him after their assignation, kept her awake for most of the night.

But to cut a long story short, when it was nones Catella collected her personal maid and proceeded, without a second thought, to the bagnio which Ricciardo had told her about.

On her arrival, she chanced upon the good woman in charge of the establishment, and asked her whether Filippello had been there during the course of the day, to which the woman replied, as instruct-ed by Ricciardo:

'Are you the lady who was to come and speak with him?'

'I am,' Catella replied.

'Then go straight in,' said the woman. 'He's waiting for you.'

Catella, heavily veiled, and hotly in pursuit of something she would not have wished to find, got the woman to take her to the room where Ricciardo was waiting, and locked the door from the inside. On seeing her coming, Ricciardo rose joyfully to his feet, took her in his arms, and whispered:

'Welcome, my dearest.'

In her anxiety to prove that she really was the person he was expecting, Catella kissed and hugged and made a great fuss of him, at the same time refraining from speaking in case he should recognize her voice.

The room was exceedingly dark, a circumstance which suited both parties, and it was impossible, even after staying there for any length of time, to make things out with any degree of clarity. Ricciardo quickly guided her to the bed, however, and there they remained for a very long time to their immense and mutual pleasure and delight, though neither ventured to utter a word for fear of being recognized.

But eventually, Catella felt that the time had come to release her pent up indignation, and blazing with passionate anger she exclaimed:

'Ah! how wretched is the lot of women, and how misplaced the love that many of them bear their husbands! Alas, woe is me! For eight years I have loved you more than my very life, and now I find that you are totally absorbed in a passionate attachment to some other woman. Oh, you unspeakable villain! Who do you think you have just been cavorting with? You have been with the woman who has been lying beside you for the past eight years, the woman you have been deceiving for God knows how long with your false endearments, pretending to love her when all the time you were in love with another.

'You faithless scoundrel, I am not Ricciardo's wife, but Catella; listen to my voice, and you'll soon realize who I really am. Oh, how I long to be back again in the light of day, so that I can put you to the shame you so richly deserve, you filthy, loathsome beast. Alas! who have I been loving so devotedly for all these years? A faithless cur, who thinks he has a strange woman in his arms, and lavishes more caresses and amorous attention upon me in the brief time I have spent with him here than in the whole of the rest of our married life.

'You unprincipled lout, I must say you have given a splendid display of manly vigour here today, in contrast with the feeble, worn-out, lack-lustre manner that you always adopt in your own house. But thanks be to God, it was your own land you were tilling and not some other man's, as you fondly imagined. It is no wonder that you kept me at a distance last night: you were planning to disburden yourself elsewhere, and you wanted to arrive fresh and strong at the jousting. But with God's help, I saw to it that the stream took its natural course.

'Why do you not answer me, you villain? Why don't you say something? Have my words deprived you of the power of speech? In God's name, I don't know how I manage to refrain from plucking your eyes out. You thought you were going to conceal your infidelity very cunningly, didn't you? But you didn't succeed, by God, because I'm just as clever as you are, and I've had better hounds on your tail than you bargained for.'

Ricciardo was inwardly relishing this sermon, and without offering any reply he embraced and kissed her, and caressed her more passionately than ever, whereupon she began to harangue him afresh.

'Oh, yes! Now you think you are going to get round me with your false caresses, you disgusting beast. But if you think you can pacify and console me, you're very much mistaken. I shall never be consoled for this outrage until I have denounced you to every single one of our friends, neighbours and relatives.

'Well now, villain, am I not as beautiful as Ricciardo Minutolo's wife? Am I not as nobly bred as she? Why don't you answer me, you foul beast? What has she got that I haven't? Stay away from me, keep your filthy hands to yourself; you have done quite enough tilting for one day. Oh, I am well aware that you could impose your will on me by brute force, now that you know who I am; but with God's grace I shall see that you go hungry. Indeed, I cannot understand what prevents me from sending for Ricciardo, who loved me more dearly than his very life, and yet was never able to claim that I so much as looked at him once. I see no reason why I shouldn't, because after all, you thought you had his wife here, and it would have been all the same to you if you really had. So if I were to have him, you could hardly hold it against me.'

Now, the words flowed thick and fast, and the lady's sense of grievance was very great. But in the end, Ricciardo, on reflecting how much trouble might ensue if he let her go away without undeceiving her, decided to disclose who he was. He therefore took her in his arms, holding her tightly so that she could not escape, and said:

'Sweet my soul, do not upset yourself so. What I was unable to achieve by mere wooing, Love has taught me to obtain by deception. I am your Ricciardo.'

No sooner did Catella hear these words and recognize his voice than she tried to leap out of bed, only to find that she was unable to move. She then prepared to scream, but Ricciardo placed a hand over her mouth, saying:

'My lady, it is impossible now to undo what has happened, even if you were to scream for the rest of your life. Besides, if you scream, or if you ever make this known to anyone, two things will ensue. The first (which ought to cause you no small concern) is that your honour and good name will be laid in ruins, because no matter how much you insist that I tricked you into coming here, I shall say that you are lying. Indeed, I shall maintain that I induced you to come by promising you money and presents, and that the reason you are making such a song and dance about it is simply that you were annoyed because your gains fell short of your expectations. I need hardly remind you that people are more inclined to believe in bad intentions than in good ones, and hence my account will carry no less conviction than yours. In the second place, your husband and I will become mortal enemies, and it could just as easily happen that he is killed by me as I by him, in which case you would inevitably spend the rest of your days in grief and mourning.

'Light of my life, do not at one and the same time bring dishonour upon yourself and jeopardize the lives of your husband and me by setting us at each other's throats. You are not the first woman to have been deceived, nor will you be the last, and in any case I had no intention of depriving you of anything. I was impelled to do it by excess of love, and indeed I am prepared to love you and serve you in all humility for the rest of my days. For a long time past, I and everything I possess have been yours, and all my power and influence have been at your disposal; but henceforth I intend to place them more completely than ever at your command. You are a wise woman, and I am certain that you will act now with that same good sense that you are wont to display in other matters.'

Catella wept bitterly while Ricciardo was speaking, and though she was exceedingly annoyed and upset, she was nonetheless able to see that he was right, and realized that events could easily follow the course he predicted.

'Ricciardo,' she said. 'I do not know how God can ever provide me with sufficient strength to bear the wicked deception you have practised upon me. I have no wish to raise a clamour in this place, to which I was led by my own simplicity and excessive jealousy. But you may rest assured that I shall never be happy until I see myself avenged in some way or other for the wrong you have done me. Now let me go, and get out of here! You have had what you wanted, you have tortured me to your heart's content, and now you can go. For heaven's sake, go!'

On seeing that she was still far from mollified, Ricciardo, who was determined not to leave her until she had recovered her equanimity, set about the task of appeasing her with a stream of honeyed endearments. And he exhorted and cajoled and beseeched her to such good effect that she eventually succumbed and forgave him, after which, by mutual consent, they tarried together at some length to their inordinate delight.

And so it was that from that day forward, the lady abandoned the stony attitude she had previously displayed to Ricciardo, and began to love him with all the tenderness in the world. And by proceeding with the greatest of discretion, they enjoyed their love together on many a later occasion. May God grant that we enjoy ours likewise.

SEVENTH STORY

Tedaldo, exasperated with his mistress, goes away from Florence. Returning after a long absence disguised as a pilgrim, he talks to the lady, induces her to acknowledge her error, and liberates her husband, who has been convicted of murdering Tedaldo and is about to be executed. He then effects a reconciliation between the husband and his own brothers; and thereafter he discreetly enjoys the company of his mistress.

On lapsing into silence, Fiammetta was congratulated by all present, and the queen, being anxious not to lose any time, promptly called upon Emilia to tell her story. So Emilia began:

For my own part, I intend to return to our own city, from which the last two speakers chose to depart, and show you how a citizen of ours regained his lost mistress.

In Florence, then, there once lived a noble youth named Tedaldo degli Elisei, who, having fallen passionately in love with the wife of a certain Aldobrandino Palermini, a lady of impeccable breeding called Monna Ermellina, duly earned the reward of his persistent devotion. But Fortune, the enemy of those who prosper, undermined his happiness, inasmuch as the lady, having already begun to grant her favours to Tedaldo, suddenly decided for no apparent reason to withhold them from him entirely. Not only would she not listen to any of the messages he caused her to receive, but she absolutely refused to acknowledge his existence, thus casting him into a state of profound and excruciating melancholy. Since, however, he had carefully concealed this love-affair of his, no one guessed the reason for his sorrow.

Feeling that he had lost the lady's favours through no fault of his own, he tried in every possible way to retrieve them, only to discover that all his efforts were unavailing. And because he had no wish to allow her the satisfaction of seeing him suffer on her account, he resolved to vanish from the scene. Having scraped together all the money he could obtain, he departed in secret without informing any of his friends or relatives except for one companion of his who knew all about the affair, and went to Ancona, assuming the name of Filippo di Sanlodeccio. In Ancona, he made the acquaintance of a wealthy merchant with whom he obtained employment, travelling with him to Cyprus on one of his ships, and the merchant was so impressed by his character and abilities that he not only paid him a handsome salary but gave him a share in the business and placed him in charge of a sizeable portion of his affairs. To these, he devoted so much skill and diligence that within a few years he had made a name for himself as an able and prosperous merchant. And whilst his thoughts frequently returned to his cruel mistress and he still experienced sharp pangs of love and longed to see her again, he was so strong-willed that for seven years he succeeded in conquering his feelings.

But one day, in Cyprus, he happened to hear someone singing a song that he himself had composed, recounting the love that he bore to his mistress, her love for him, and the pleasure he had of her. And thinking it impossible that she should have forgotten him, he was stricken with such a burning desire to see her again that he could endure it no longer, and decided to return to Florence. Having wound up his affairs, he travelled with a servant as far as Ancona, where he waited for all his belongings to arrive and then shipped them to Florence, to a friend of his partner in Ancona, after which he himself followed with his servant, disguised as a pilgrim returning from the Holy Sepulchre; and when they arrived in Florence, they put up at a small inn run by two brothers, which was not far away from the lady's house. The first thing he did was to hurry over to her house in the hope of seeing her, but he found that all the windows and doors were barred and bolted, which led him to fear that she might be dead, or that she had moved elsewhere.

Deeply perturbed, he walked on until he reached the house of his kinsfolk, in front of which he saw four of his brothers, all of whom, to his great astonishment, were dressed in black. And knowing that he would not easily be recognized, on account of the marked changes in his clothing and physical appearance, he walked boldly up to the local shoemaker and asked him why these men were wearing black.

'They are wearing black,' replied the shoemaker, 'because within the past fortnight a brother of theirs called Tedaldo, who disappeared from the neighbourhood many years ago, was found murdered. As far as I can gather, they have proved in court that his murderer was a certain Aldobrandino Palermini, who has now been arrested. It seems that the murdered man was in love with Palermini's wife, and had returned here in disguise to be with her.'

Tedaldo was greatly astonished that anyone could resemble him so closely as to be mistaken for his own person, whilst the news of Aldobrandino's plight distressed him deeply. On making further inquiries he discovered that the lady was alive and well, and since it was now dark, he returned to the inn, his mind in a positive whirl. After dining in the company of his servant, he was shown up to his sleeping quarters, which were situated almost at the very top of the building. But because his mind was so active and his bed so uncomfortable, and also perhaps because of the meagreness of his supper,

Tedaldo was unable to drop off to sleep. He was still wide awake when, halfway through the night, he thought he could hear people entering the building by way of the roof; and shortly afterwards, through the cracks in the bedroom door, a glimmer of light became visible.

He therefore crept silently across to the door and began to peep through the crack in order to discover what was happening, and caught sight of a very pretty girl carrying the light and being met by three men who had descended from the roof. They all exchanged certain greetings, then one of the men addressed the girl as follows:

'We've nothing more to fear, thank God, because we've learnt for certain that Tedaldo Elisei's brothers have proved he was killed by Aldobrandino Palermini, who has made a confession. The sentence has already been signed, but all the same we'll have to keep this thing quiet, because if it ever leaks out that we did it, we'll be in the same sorry plight as Aldobrandino.'

This announcement was greeted by the woman with evident relief, and they all retired to bed in the lower part of the house.

Having overheard the whole of this, Tedaldo began to reflect how fatally easy it was for people to cram their heads with totally erroneous notions. His thoughts turned first of all to his brothers, who had gone into mourning and buried some stranger in his own stead, after which they had been impelled by their false suspicions to accuse this innocent man and fabricate evidence so as to have him brought under sentence of death. This in turn led him to reflect upon the blind severity of the law and its administrators, who in order to convey the impression that they are zealously seeking the truth, often have recourse to cruelty and cause falsehood to be accepted as proven fact, hence demonstrating, for all their proud claim to be the ministers of God's justice, that their true allegiance is to the devil and his iniquities. Finally, Tedaldo turned his thoughts to the question of how he could save Aldobrandino, and decided upon the course of action he would have to adopt.

When he got up next morning, he left his servant behind and made his way, at what seemed a suitable hour, to the house of his former mistress. Since the door happened to be open, he went in, and there, sitting on the floor in a little room downstairs, he found his lady-love,

all tearful and forlorn. Scarcely able to restrain himself from crying at
this piteous spectacle, he walked over to where she was sitting.

'Madam,' he said, 'do not torment yourself: your troubles will
soon be over.'

On hearing his voice, the lady looked up at him and sobbed, saying:

'Good sir, you appear to be a pilgrim and a stranger; how can you
know anything of my troubles and torments?'

'Madam,' replied the pilgrim, 'I come from Constantinople and I
have just arrived in this city, to which I was sent by God to convert
your tears into joy and deliver your husband from death.'

'But if you come from Constantinople,' said the woman, 'and if
you have only just arrived, how can you know anything of me or my
husband?'

Starting from the beginning, the pilgrim provided a full account of
Aldobrandino's predicament and told her exactly who she was, how
long she had been married, and many other things that he knew concerning her private affairs. This recital greatly astonished the lady,
who took him to be some kind of prophet and knelt down at his feet,
beseeching him in God's name, if he really had come to save Aldobrandino, to do so quickly before it was too late.

'Stand up, my lady,' said the pilgrim, assuming a very saintly air,
'and cry no more. Listen closely to what I am about to say, and take
good care never to repeat it to anyone. God has revealed to me that
your tribulation arises from a certain sin you once committed, which
He intends that you should purge, partially at any rate, by means of
this present affliction. He is very anxious that you should make
amends for it, because otherwise you would assuredly be plunged into
much greater suffering.'

'I have committed many sins, sir,' said the lady, 'and I do not know
which particular one it is that the Lord God desires me to atone for
out of all the rest. So if you know which one it is, please tell me, and
I shall do whatever I can to make amends for it.'

'I know very well what it is, madam,' said the pilgrim. 'And I shall
now ask you a few questions about it, not for my own benefit, but
merely to enable you to acknowledge the sin of your own free will,
and repent more fully. But let us come to the point. Tell me, do you
remember whether you ever had a lover?'

On hearing this question, the lady fetched a deep sigh and was greatly amazed, for she was under the impression that nobody had ever discovered her secret, albeit there had been a certain amount of gossip since the murder of the man who had been buried for Tedaldo, because of certain things which had been said, rather unwisely, by the friend in whom Tedaldo had confided.

'It is obvious,' she replied, 'that God reveals all of men's secrets to you, and I therefore see no reason for attempting to conceal my own. In my younger days, I was indeed deeply in love with the unfortunate young man whose death has been imputed to my husband. I was enormously grieved to hear that he was dead, and I have wept countless tears over him, for although I assumed an air of haughty indifference towards him before he went away, neither his departure nor his long absence nor even his unfortunate death has been able to dislodge him from my heart.'

'You were never in love with this hapless youth who has died,' said the pilgrim, 'but with Tedaldo Elisei. However, tell me: what reason did you have for snubbing him? Did he ever offend you?'

'Oh, no!' replied the lady. 'He certainly never offended me. My aloofness was prompted by the words of an accursed friar, to whom I once went for confession. When I told him how much I loved this man and described the intimacy of our relationship, he gave me such a severe scolding that I have never recovered from the shock to this day, for he told me that unless I mended my ways I would be consigned to the devil's mouth at the bottom of the abyss and exposed to the torments of hellfire. I was so frightened by all this that I firmly made up my mind never to have anything more to do with him. So as to remove all temptation, I refused from then on to accept any of his letters or messages. I suppose he eventually gave up and went away in despair. But if he had persevered a little longer, I am sure I would have relented, for I could see that he was wasting away like snow in the rays of the sun, and I was longing to break my resolve.'

'Madam,' said the pilgrim, 'it is this sin alone which lies at the root of all your suffering. I know for a fact that Tedaldo never coerced you in the slightest. When you fell in love with him, you did so of your own accord because you found him attractive. It was with your full consent that he began to visit you and enjoy your intimate favours, and your delight in him was so obvious from your words and deeds that, though he already loved you before, you intensified his love a thousandfold. And if this was so (as I know it was), what possible reason could prompt you to withdraw yourself so inflexibly from him? You should have thought about all these things beforehand, and if you felt it was wrong, if you felt you were going to have to repent, you should not have had anything to do with him in the first place. The point is this, that when he became yours, so you became his. Inasmuch as he belonged to you, you were perfectly free to discard him whenever you wished. But since, at the same time, you belonged to him, it was quite improper of you, indeed it was robbery on your part, to remove yourself from him against his will.

'Now, I would have you know that I myself am a friar. I am therefore familiar with all their ways, and it is not unfitting for me, as it would be for a layman, to express myself somewhat freely about them for your benefit. I do this, and I do it willingly, so that you will know them better in the future than you appear to have done in the past.

'There was once a time when friars were very saintly and worthy men, but those who lay claim nowadays to the title and reputation of friar have nothing of the friar about them except the habits they wear. Even these are not genuine friars' habits, because whereas the people who invented friars decreed that the habit should be close-fitting, coarse, and shabby, and that, by clothing the body in humble apparel, it should symbolize the mind's disdain for all the things of this world, your present-day friars prefer ample habits, generously cut and smooth of texture, and made from the finest of fabrics. Indeed, they now have elegant and pontifical habits, in which they strut like peacocks through the churches and the city-squares without compunction, just as though they were members of the laity showing off their robes. And like the fisherman who tries to take a number of fish from the river with a single throw of his casting-net, so these fellows, as they wrap themselves in the capacious folds of their habits, endeavour to take in many an over-pious lady, many a widow, and many another simpleton of either sex, this being their one overriding concern. It would therefore be more exact for me to say that these fellows do not wear friars' habits, but merely the colours of their habits.

'Moreover, whereas their predecessors desired the salvation of men, the friars of today desire riches and women. They have taken great pains, and still do, to strike terror into simple people's hearts with their loud harangues and specious parables, and to show that sins may be purged through almsgiving and mass-offerings. In this way, having taken refuge in the priesthood more out of cowardice than piety and in order to escape hard work, they are supplied with bread by one man and wine by another, whilst a third is persuaded to part with donations for the souls of his departed ones.

'It is of course true that prayers and almsgiving purge sins. But if only the donors were familiar with the sort of people to whom they were handing over their money, they would either keep it for themselves or cast it before a herd of swine. These so-called friars are well aware that the fewer the people who share a great treasure, the better off they are, and so each of them strives by blustering and intimidation to exclude others from whatever he is anxious to retain for his own exclusive use. They denounce men's lust, so that when the denounced are out of the way, their women will be left to the denouncers. They condemn usury and ill-gotten gains, so that people will entrust them with their restitution, and this enables them to make their habits more capacious and procure bishoprics and the other major offices of the Church, using the very money which, according to them, would have led its owners to perdition.

'Whenever anyone reproaches them with these and countless other wicked ways of theirs, they consider themselves acquitted from every charge, however serious, simply by replying: "Do as we say, not as we do." To hear them talk, one would think it was easier for the sheep to be strong-willed and law-abiding than it is for the shepherds. But this specious answer of theirs does not fool everyone by any means, and a great many of them know it.

'The friars of today want you to do as they say, or in other words fill their purses with money, confide your secrets to them, remain chaste, practise patience, forgive all wrongs, and take care to speak no evil, all of which are good, seemly and edifying goals to pursue. But why? Simply so that they can do the things they will be prevented from doing if they are done by the laity. Who will deny that laziness cannot survive without money to support it? If we were to spend our money on our own pleasures, the friar would no longer be able to idle away his time in the cloisters; if we were to go pursuing the ladies, the friars would be put out of business; if we failed to practise patience and forgive all wrongs, the friar would no longer have the effrontery to call upon us in our own homes and corrupt our families. But why should I elaborate every point in detail? Every time they come out with that hoary old excuse of theirs, they condemn themselves in the eyes of all intelligent men and women. Why do they not choose to remain within their own walls, if they feel themselves unable to behave in a chaste and godly manner? Or if they really must rub shoulders with the laity, why do they not follow that other holy text from the Gospel: "Then Christ began to act and to teach"? Let them set an example, before they start preaching to the rest of us. In my time I've seen a thousand of them laying siege, paying visits and making love, not only to ordinary women but to nuns in convents; and some of them were the ones who ranted loudest from the pulpit. Are these, then, the people whose advice we should follow? Anyone is free to do so if he likes, but God knows whether he will be acting wisely.

'However, even supposing we granted that the friar who censured you was right in this instance, and that to break one's marriage vows is a very grave offence, is it not far worse to steal? Is it not far worse to murder a man or send him wandering through the world in exile? Everyone will agree that it is, because after all, for a woman to have intimate relations with a man is a natural sin, but to rob him or to kill him or expel him is to act from evil intention.

'That you did indeed rob Tedaldo I have already proved to you just now, for you removed yourself from him when you belonged to him of your own free will. Secondly, I would suggest that you did your utmost to murder him, for it would not have been surprising, in view of the cruel way you treated him, if he had taken his own life; and in the eyes of the law, the accessory to a crime is as guilty as the person who actually commits it. Finally, it cannot be denied that you were responsible for condemning him to wander through the world for seven whole years in exile. So that on any one of the three articles to which I have referred, you committed a far greater sin than by your intimacy with him. But let us consider the matter more closely. Could it be that Tedaldo deserved all he received? He certainly did not, as you yourself have already conceded; and besides, I know that he loves you more dearly than his very life.

'Nothing was ever so warmly revered, so greatly extolled, or so highly exalted as you were by him above all other women, whenever he could speak of you without giving rise to suspicion. To you alone he entrusted the whole of his well-being, the whole of his honour, the whole of his freedom. Was he not a noble youth? Was he not as handsome as any of his fellow citizens? Was he not outstanding in those activities and accomplishments that pertain to the young? Was he not loved, esteemed, and given a ready welcome by all who met him? This, too, you will be willing to concede.

'What possible reason could you have had, then, for heeding the insane ravings of a stupid, envious little friar and deciding to treat him so cruelly? Why is it, I wonder, that certain women make the mistake of holding themselves aloof from men and looking down upon them? If they would only consider their own natures, and stop to think of how much more nobility God has conceded to man than to any of the other animals, they would undoubtedly be proud of a man's love and hold him in the highest esteem, and do everything in their power to please him, so that he would never grow tired of loving them. Did you do all this? No, because you allowed yourself to be swayed by the words of a friar who must without a doubt have been some soup-guzzling pie-muncher, and who in all probability intended to install himself in the place from which he was intent on dislodging another.

'This, then, was the sin which divine justice, all of whose dealings are perfectly balanced, would not allow to remain unpunished. You tried without good reason to remove yourself from Tedaldo; and likewise your husband's life, without good reason, has been placed in jeopardy and remains in jeopardy on Tedaldo's account, whilst you yourself have been cast into sorrow. If you want to release yourself from this affliction, here is what you must promise, or rather, what you must do: if it were ever to happen that Tedaldo returned here from his lengthy exile, you must restore to him your favour, your love, your goodwill and intimate friendship, and reinstate him in the position he occupied before you so foolishly heeded that lunatic friar.'

Here the pilgrim finished speaking, and meanwhile the lady had listened in rapt attention to every word he had uttered, for she felt his arguments to be very sound and was convinced, having heard him say so, that her affliction really stemmed from that one sin of hers.

'Friend of God,' she said, 'I know full well that what you say is true, and you have taught me a great deal about friars, all of whom I have hitherto regarded as Saints. I can see that I undoubtedly committed a serious error in behaving as I did towards Tedaldo, and if it lay within my power I would willingly make amends in the way you suggest. But how is this to be done? Tedaldo cannot ever return here again; he is dead. So what is the point of my giving you a pledge that I cannot keep?'

'Madam,' said the pilgrim. 'God has revealed to me that Tedaldo is not dead at all, but alive and well, and if only he enjoyed your favour he would also be happy.'

'But you must surely be mistaken,' said the lady. 'I saw him lying dead from a number of stab-wounds on my own doorstep, and held him in these arms and shed countless tears on his poor dead face, which possibly accounts for the malicious gossip that has been put about.'

'No matter what you may say, madam,' said the pilgrim, 'I assure you that Tedaldo is alive. And provided that you give me the pledge and intend to keep it, there is every hope of your seeing him soon.'

'I will do it, and willingly,' said the lady. 'Nothing would bring me greater joy than to see my husband released unharmed and Tedaldo alive.'

Tedaldo now decided that the time had come to make himself known to the lady and reassure her about her husband.

'Madam,' he said, 'in order to set your mind at rest about your husband, I shall have to tell you an important secret, which you must take care never to reveal for as long as you live.'

Since they were alone in a very remote part of the house (the lady being quite disarmed by the pilgrim's appearance of saintliness), Tedaldo drew forth a ring which he had religiously preserved and which the lady had given him on their last night together, and held it out for her to see, saying:

'Do you know this ring, madam?'

The lady recognized it at once.

'I do indeed, sir,' she replied. 'I gave it long ago to Tedaldo.'

The pilgrim thereupon stood up straight, and having thrown off his cloak and removed his hood, he addressed her in a Florentine accent, saying:

'And do you know me, too?'

When the lady saw that it was Tedaldo, she was utterly astonished, and began to tremble with fright, as though she were seeing a ghost. Far from rushing forward to welcome a Tedaldo who had returned from Cyprus, she shrank back in terror from a Tedaldo who had seemingly risen from the grave.

'Do not be afraid, my lady,' he said. 'I really am your Tedaldo. I am alive and well, and whatever you and my brothers may believe, I never died and was never murdered.'

Somewhat reassured by the sound of his voice, the lady looked at him more closely, and having convinced herself that he really was Tedaldo, she burst into tears, flung her arms about his neck, and kissed him, saying:

'Tedaldo, my sweet Tedaldo, you are welcome!'

'My lady,' said Tedaldo, after embracing and kissing her, 'there is no time now to exchange more intimate greetings. I must go and arrange for Aldobrandino to be restored to you safe and sound, and trust that you will hear good news of my endeavours before tomorrow evening. Indeed, I fully expect by tonight to hear that he is safe, in which case I should like to come and tell you all about it in a more leisurely way than I have time for at present.'

Donning once again his pilgrim's cloak and hood, he kissed the lady a second time, assured her that everything would be all right, and left her. He then proceeded to the place where Aldobrandino, more preoccupied with the dread of his impending doom than with the hope of his future release, was being held prisoner. And having been admitted to Aldobrandino's cell by the prison-warders, who assumed that he had come to minister to the condemned man, he sat down beside him, saying:

'Aldobrandino, I am a friend, sent here to save you by God, who has been moved to pity by your innocence. If, therefore, out of reverence to Him you will grant me the trifling favour that I am about to ask of you, it is certain that by tomorrow evening, instead of languishing here under sentence of death, you will hear the news of your acquittal.'

'Good sir,' Aldobrandino replied, 'I neither know you nor recall ever having seen you before, but since you show concern for my safety, you must indeed be a friend. It is perfectly true that I did not commit the crime for which it is said that I must be condemned to death, even though I have sinned in many other ways, which possibly explains my present predicament. In all reverence to God, however, I can tell you this: that if He were to have mercy on me now, there is nothing, whether great or small, that I would not do, and do willingly, let alone promise. Ask of me what you please, then, for you may be quite certain that if I should happen to be released I shall honour my word to the letter.'

'All I want you to do,' replied the pilgrim, 'is to pardon Tedaldo's four brothers for landing you in this plight in the mistaken belief that you murdered their brother, and, provided that they ask you to forgive them, to treat them as your own kith and kin.'

'Only the person who has been wronged,' replied Aldobrandino, 'knows how sweet and how intense is the desire for revenge. But in order that God may take thought for my salvation, I shall willingly forgive them; indeed, I do forgive them, here and now. And if I ever emerge from this place with my life and liberty, I shall act in a way that will certainly meet with your approval.'

This reply satisfied the pilgrim, and without enlightening him any further he departed, strongly urging him to be of good cheer and assuring him that before the next day was over he would hear the news of his deliverance.

After leaving Aldobrandino, he made his way to the law-courts and obtained a private interview with the most senior official.

'Sir,' he began, 'no man, especially in your position, should ever shrink from the task of uncovering the truth, so that, when a crime is committed, punishment may be inflicted on the guilty and not on the innocent. So as to ensure that this is done, thus bringing credit to yourself and retribution to those who have earned it, I have been prompted to call upon you. As you know, you have brought Aldobrandino Palermini to trial, you think you have discovered convincing proof that he is the man who murdered Tedaldo Elisei, and you are about to pronounce sentence upon him. But the evidence is false beyond any shadow of a doubt, and I believe I can prove it to you between now and midnight by handing over the young man's real murderers.'

The worthy official was already feeling sorry for Aldobrandino, and gladly gave ear to the words of the pilgrim, who furnished him with such a wealth of corroborative detail that he had the two inn-keeping brothers and their servant arrested, without a struggle, shortly after they had retired to bed. Being determined to get at the truth of the matter, he would have put them to the torture, but they broke down and made a full confession, individually at first and then all together, saying that they were the people who had murdered Tedaldo Elisei, who was a complete stranger to them. On being asked the reason, they said it was because he had been pestering one of their wives whilst they were away from the inn, and that he had tried to ravish her.

Having heard about their confession, the pilgrim took his leave of the official and made his way back to the house of Monna Ermellina, which he entered unobserved. All the servants had gone to bed, and he found her waiting up alone for him, equally desirous of hearing good news about her husband and of being fully reunited with Tedaldo. He went up to her, smiling happily, and said:

'My darling mistress, be of good cheer, for it is certain that Aldobrandino will be restored to you here tomorrow, safe and sound.' And in order to prove to her that it was so, he told her of all he had done.

Monna Ermellina was the happiest woman who ever lived, for twice in quick succession the impossible had happened: in the first place she had got Tedaldo back again, alive and well, after genuinely thinking she had mourned him as dead, and in the second she had seen Aldobrandino delivered from danger when she thought that within a few days she would be having to mourn his death also. And so, passionately hugging Tedaldo and smothering him with kisses, she retired with him to bed, where, to their mutual and delectable joy, they gladly and graciously made their peace with one another.

A little before daybreak, Tedaldo arose, having apprised the lady of his intentions and repeated his plea that she should keep everything secret, and putting on his pilgrim's garb, he left the house, so as to be ready at a moment's notice to act on Aldobrandino's behalf.

As soon as dawn arrived, the magistrates, confident that all the relevant facts were now in their possession, set Aldobrandino at liberty; and a few days later they had the delinquents beheaded at the scene of the murder. Aldobrandino was overjoyed to find himself at liberty, and so too were his wife and all his friends and relatives. Knowing full well that the whole thing was due to the efforts of the pilgrim, they offered him their hospitality for as long as he chose to remain in the city. And having brought him to their house, they fêted and feasted him without being able to stop, especially the lady, since she alone knew who it was she was honouring. But before very long, having learned that his brothers were being held up to ridicule on account of Aldobrandino's release and that they had armed themselves in fear and trembling, he decided that the time had come to reconcile the two sides, and reminded Aldobrandino of his promise. Aldobrandino readily agreed to carry it out, and the pilgrim persuaded him to arrange a sumptuous banquet for the following day, to which he was to invite not only his own relatives and womenfolk but also the four brothers and their wives. Moreover, the pilgrim offered to call on the four brothers in person and invite them to the reunion and banquet on Aldobrandino's behalf.

Aldobrandino gave his consent, whereupon the pilgrim immediately went to call upon the four brothers, and having told them as much as they needed to know, he eventually persuaded them without difficulty, using impeccable arguments, to ask Aldobrandino's forgiveness and patch up their differences with him. He then invited them to take their wives along to Aldobrandino's banquet on the following morning, and the brothers, being convinced of his good faith, gladly agreed to do so.

Next morning, therefore, at the hour of breakfast, Tedaldo's four brothers, still dressed in black and accompanied by some friends of theirs, presented themselves at the house of Aldobrandino, who was waiting to greet them. And in the presence of all the people who had been invited by Aldobrandino to join them in the festivities, they laid their weapons on the ground and threw themselves on Aldobrandino's mercy, asking him to forgive them for the way they had treated him. Aldobrandino received them with affection, his eyes full of tears, and having kissed each one of them on the mouth, he quickly said what he had to say and pardoned them for the wrongs he had suffered. They then made way for their wives and sisters, who were all dressed in mourning, and were given a gracious welcome by Monna Ermellina and the other ladies. Then all the guests, gentlemen and ladies alike, sat down to a splendid meal, excellent in every respect save for the general air of reticence engendered by the recent bereavement which Tedaldo's kinsfolk had suffered, and which was made more apparent by the sombre clothes they were wearing. For this very reason, in fact, some people had condemned the pilgrim's scheme for holding the banquet, and Tedaldo, who was well aware of their objections, felt that the time had now come to spring his surprise and disperse the mists of melancholy. He therefore rose to his feet while the others were still eating their dessert, and said:

'All that this banquet requires to bring it to life is the presence of Tedaldo. He has been here all the time, as it happens, but since you have failed to notice him, I want to point him out.'

Then, throwing off his cloak and all his pilgrim's clothing, he stood before them wearing a tunic of green taffeta, to be inspected and scrutinized at great length, and with no small display of astonishment, before anyone ventured to believe that he really was Tedaldo. Seeing how incredulous they looked, Tedaldo identified the families to which they belonged, told them about various things that had happened to them, and described his own adventures, whereupon his brothers and the other men rushed to embrace him, all weeping with joy, and the ladies followed their example, kinsfolk and others alike, with the sole exception of Monna Ermellina.

'Ermellina!' exclaimed Aldobrandino. 'What is this that I see? Why are you not greeting Tedaldo, like the other ladies?'

'I would greet him more willingly,' she replied, in everyone's hearing, 'than any of the ladies who have done so already, because it was thanks to him that you have been restored to me, and thus my debt to him is greater than anyone's. But I refrain because of the mischievous things that were said when we were mourning the man we mistook for Tedaldo.'

'Away with you!' said Aldobrandino. 'Do you suppose I pay any attention to gossip-mongers? He has amply proved that the stories were untrue by securing my release, and I never believed them in the first place. Up you get, quickly; go and embrace him.'

The lady could desire nothing better, and was not slow to obey her husband's instructions. Rising from her place, she threw her arms about his neck, as the other ladies had done, and gave him an ecstatic welcome.

Tedaldo's brothers were delighted by Aldobrandino's magnanimous gesture, as were all the other gentlemen and ladies who were present; and so it was that every trace of the doubts implanted in certain people's minds by the rumours was expelled.

Now that everyone had given Tedaldo a handsome welcome, he himself stripped his brothers of their mourning, tore asunder the sombre dresses that their wives and sisters were wearing, and ordered different clothes to be brought. And when all were newly attired, they made merry with a number of songs, dances and other entertainments, so that in contrast to its subdued beginning the banquet had a noisy ending. Nor was this all, for they immediately made their way to Tedaldo's house, singing and dancing as they went, and dined there that evening. And without varying the order of their festivities, they kept the party going for several days in succession.

For some time, the Florentines thought of Tedaldo as a man who had miraculously risen from the grave. Many people, including his own brothers, were left with a faint suspicion in their minds that he was not really Tedaldo at all. Even now, in fact, they were not entirely convinced, and they would possibly have remained unconvinced for a long time afterwards, but for the fact that some days later they accidentally discovered who the murdered man was.

It happened like this. One day, a group of soldiers from Lunigiana were passing the house, and when they caught sight of Tedaldo they rushed towards him, exclaiming:

'Good old Faziuolo!'

Tedaldo informed them, in the presence of his brothers, that they were mistaking him for another, and as soon as they heard his voice they became embarrassed and gave him their apologies.

'God's truth!' they said. 'You are the living image of a mate of ours called Faziuolo da Pontremoli, who came here about a fortnight or so ago and has never been heard of since. It's no wonder we were surprised by the clothes you're wearing, because he was just a common soldier like ourselves.'

On hearing this, Tedaldo's eldest brother interrupted to ask what sort of clothes this Faziuolo of theirs had been wearing. Their description fitted the facts so precisely, that what with this and other indications, it became quite obvious that the murdered man was not Tedaldo, but Faziuolo; and thenceforth, neither Tedaldo's brothers nor anyone else harboured any further doubts about him.

Tedaldo, who had made a fortune during his absence, remained constant in his love, whilst for her part his mistress never rebuffed him again. And by proceeding with discretion, they long enjoyed their love together. May God grant that we enjoy ours likewise.

EIGHTH STORY

Ferondo, having consumed a special powder, is buried for dead. The Abbot who is cavorting with his wife removes him from his tomb, imprisons him, and makes him believe he is in Purgatory. He is later resurrected, and raises as his own a child begotten on his wife by the Abbot.

Emilia had thus reached the end of her story, which in spite of its length was not unfavourably received. On the contrary, they all maintained that it had been briefly told, considering the number and variety of the incidents it had touched upon. And now the queen, making her wishes evident by a brief nod in the direction of Lauretta, induced her to begin:

Dearest ladies, I find myself confronted by a true story, demanding to be told, which sounds far more fictitious than was actually the case, and of which I was reminded when I heard of the man who was buried and mourned in mistake for another. My story, then, is about a living man who was buried for dead, and who later, on emerging from his tomb, was convinced that he had truly died and been resurrected – a belief that was shared by many other people, who consequently venerated him as a Saint when they should have been condemning him as a fool.

In Tuscany, then, there was and still is a certain abbey, situated, as so many of them are, a little off the beaten track. Its newly-appointed abbot was a former monk who was a veritable saint of a man in all his ways except for his womanizing, a hobby that he pursued so discreetly that very few people suspected, let alone knew about it, and hence he was considered to be very saintly and upright in every respect.

Now, this abbot happened to become closely acquainted with a very wealthy yeoman called Ferondo, an exceedingly coarse and unimaginative fellow whose company he suffered only because Ferondo's simple ways were sometimes a source of amusement. From associating with Ferondo, the Abbot made the discovery that he was married to a very beautiful woman, and he fell so ardently in love with her that she occupied his thoughts day and night, and he could concentrate on nothing else. But when he further discovered that Ferondo, for all his fatuousness and stupidity in every other respect, was extremely sensible in his devotion to this wife of his, and kept a careful watch upon her, the Abbot was driven to the brink of despair. Nevertheless, being very shrewd, he managed on occasion to persuade Ferondo to bring her to the abbey, when they would all go for a pleasant stroll together in the grounds and the Abbot would converse with them in a highly polite and articulate manner about the blessedness of the life eternal and the saintly deeds of various men and women of the past. Because of this, the lady was seized with the desire of going to him for confession, and she asked and obtained Ferondo's permission to do so.

And thus, much to the delight of the Abbot, the lady came to him in order to be confessed. First of all, however, having seated herself at his feet, she addressed him as follows:

'Sir, if God had given me a real husband, or no husband at all, perhaps it would be easy for me to set out under your guidance along the path you were telling us about, which leads to the life eternal. Considering the sort of man Ferondo is, and the moronic way he behaves, I am no better off than a widow. Yet I am a married woman, inasmuch as, while he lives, I cannot have any other husband except this half-witted oaf who for no reason whatever guards me with such extraordinary and excessive jealousy that my life with him is one long torment and misery. And so, before going any further with my confession, I humbly beseech you, with all my heart, to advise me what to do about it. For unless I take this as the starting point of my endeavours to lead a better life, no amount of confessing or of other pious deeds will do me any good.'

These sentiments were very much to the liking of the Abbot, who felt that Fortune had placed his greatest desire within sight of fulfilment.

'My daughter,' he said, 'I consider it a great affliction for a beautiful and sensitive woman like you to have a half-witted husband, but I consider it an even greater affliction to have a husband who is jealous; and since you are saddled with both, I can well believe what you say about your torment and misery. Without going into too many details, there is only one piece of advice, only one remedy, that I can suggest: namely, that Ferondo must be cured of his jealousy. What is more, I am able to provide him with the very medicine he needs, if only you have the necessary will to keep what I tell you a secret.'

'Have no fear on that account, Father,' said the lady, 'for I would sooner die than repeat anything you had asked me to keep to myself. But how is this cure to be effected?'

'If we want him to recover,' replied the Abbot, 'then obviously he will have to go to Purgatory.'

'But how can he go there if he's still alive?'

'He will have to die, that is how he will go there. And when he has had enough punishment to purge him of this jealousy of his, we shall recite certain prayers asking God to bring him back to life, and God will attend to it.'

'Am I to be left a widow, then?'

'Yes, for a while. But you must take good care not to remarry, because if you did, God would take it amiss. And besides, you would have to go back to Ferondo when he returned from Purgatory, and he would be more jealous than ever.'

'It sounds all right to me, provided it cures this malady of his, so that I no longer have to spend my whole life under lock and key. Do whatever you think best.'

'Right you are,' said the Abbot. 'But what reward are you prepared to offer me for rendering you so useful a service?'

'Whatever you ask, Father, provided I have it to give,' she replied. 'But what possible reward could a mere woman like myself offer to a man in your position?'

'Madam,' said the Abbot, 'you can do as much for me as I am about to do for you. Just as I am making preparations for your welfare and happiness, so you can do something that will lead to my freedom and salvation.'

'In that case,' said the lady, 'I am quite willing to do it.'

'All you need to do,' said the Abbot, 'is to give me your love and let me enjoy you. I am burning all over; I am pining for you.'

'Oh, Father!' exclaimed the lady, who was hardly able to believe her ears. 'Whatever are you asking me to do? I always took you for a Saint. Is this the sort of request that a saintly man should be making to a lady who goes to him for advice?'

'Do not be so astonished, my treasure,' said the Abbot. 'No loss of saintliness is involved, for saintliness resides in the soul, and what I am asking of you is merely a sin of the body. But be that as it may, your beauty is so overpowering that love compels me to speak out. And what I say is this, that when you consider that your beauty is admired by a Saint, you have more reason to be proud of it than other women, because Saints are accustomed to seeing the beauties of heaven. Furthermore, even though I am an Abbot, I am a man like the others, and as you can see I am still quite young. It should not be too difficult for you to comply with my request; on the contrary, you ought to welcome it, because whilst Ferondo is away in Purgatory, I will come and keep you company every night and provide you with all the solace that he should be giving you. Nobody will suspect us, because my reputation stands at least as high with everyone else as it formerly did with you. Do not cast aside this special favour which is sent to you by God, for you can have something that countless women yearn for, and if you are sensible enough to accept my advice, it will be yours. Moreover, I possess some fine, precious jewels, and I intend that you alone should have them. Do not therefore refuse, my dearest, to do me a service that I will do for you with the greatest of pleasure.'

Not knowing how to refuse him, yet feeling it was wrong to grant his request, the lady fixed her gaze upon the ground. The Abbot knew that she had heard him, and when he saw her at a loss for an answer, he felt she was already half-converted. He therefore followed up his previous arguments with a torrent of new ones, and by the time he had finished talking, he had convinced her that it was all for the best. And so in bashful tones she placed herself entirely at his service, adding that she could do nothing until Ferondo had gone to Purgatory.

'In that case,' said the Abbot, beaming with joy, 'we shall see that he goes there at once. Send him along to see me tomorrow, or the following day.'

Whereupon he furtively slipped a magnificent ring into her hand, and sent her away. The lady was delighted with her present, and looked forward to receiving others. And having rejoined her companions, she regaled them with marvellous accounts of the Abbot's saintliness as they made their way home together.

A few days later, Ferondo called at the abbey, and no sooner did the Abbot see him than he decided to pack him off to Purgatory. So he sought out a wondrous powder which had been given him in the East by a mighty prince, who maintained that it was the one used by the Old Man of the Mountain whenever he wanted to send people to his paradise in their sleep or bring them back again. The prince had further assured him that by varying the dose, one could render people unconscious for longer or shorter periods, during which they slept so profoundly that nobody would ever guess that they were still alive. Without letting Ferondo see what he was doing, the Abbot measured out a quantity sufficient to put him to sleep for three days, poured it into a glass of somewhat cloudy wine, and gave it to him to drink whilst they were still in his cell. He then led him off to the cloister, where he and several of his monks began to amuse themselves at Ferondo's expense and make fun of his imbecilities. Before very long, however, the powder began to take effect, and Ferondo, being suddenly overcome by a powerful sensation of drowsiness, fell asleep where he was standing and collapsed to the ground unconscious.

The Abbot, feigning consternation at this occurrence, got someone
to loosen his clothing, sent for cold water and had it sprinkled over
Ferondo's face, and ordered various other remedies to be applied, as
though he were intent on restoring the life and feeling of which he
had been deprived by his stomach-wind or whatever else it was that
had felled him. But on seeing that he failed to come round despite all
their efforts, and on testing his pulse and finding it had stopped, the
Abbot and his monks unanimously concluded that he must be dead.
So somebody was sent to inform his wife and kinsfolk, and they all
came rushing to the scene. And when his wife and kinswomen had
finished weeping, the Abbot caused him to be laid to rest in a tomb,
in the clothes he was wearing.

Ferondo and his wife had a little boy, and when she returned home,
she told the child that she intended to stay there for the rest of her days.
Thus she remained in Ferondo's house, and applied herself to the task
of looking after the child and administering the fortune left behind by
her husband.

Meanwhile, the Abbot quietly rose from his bed in the middle of
the night, and with the assistance of a Bolognese monk whom he
trusted implicitly and who had arrived that same day from Bologna,
he dragged Ferondo from the tomb and moved him into a vault,
totally devoid of any light, which served as a place of confinement for
monks who had broken their vows. Having removed the clothes
Ferondo was wearing and dressed him in a monastic habit, they left
him lying on a bundle of straw until such time as he should come to
his senses. And in the meantime, unbeknown to anyone else, the
Bolognese monk waited for Ferondo to come round, having been
told what to do by the Abbot.

Next day, the Abbot, accompanied by one or two of his monks,
called on the lady to pay her his respects, and found her dressed in
black and full of woe. After offering her a few words of comfort, he
quietly reminded her of her promise, and the lady, having caught
sight of another fine ring on the Abbot's finger, and realizing that she
was now a free agent, unhindered by Ferondo or anyone else, told
him that she was ready to honour it and arranged for him to call
there after dark that evening.

After dark, therefore, the Abbot decked himself out in Ferondo's clothes and set off for her house accompanied by his monk. Having spent the whole night in her arms with enormous pleasure and delight, he returned a little before matins to the abbey, and from then on he went regularly back and forth on the same errand. It occasionally happened that people would chance upon the Abbot as he wended his way to and fro, and they concluded that it must be Ferondo's ghost, wandering through the district doing penance. So that, in the course of time, various strange legends grew up among the simple countryfolk, and some of these reached the ears of Ferondo's wife, who was not mystified in the slightest.

When Ferondo recovered his senses, without having the faintest idea where he was, the Bolognese monk burst in upon him brandishing a bunch of sticks; and with a terrifying roar, he seized hold of him and gave him a severe thrashing. Weeping and howling, Ferondo kept repeating the same question:

'Where am I?'

'You are in Purgatory,' replied the monk.

'What?' said Ferondo. 'Do you mean to say I am dead, then?'

'You certainly are,' said the monk; whereupon Ferondo started bemoaning his fate and weeping over the plight of his wife and child, coming out with the most extraordinary statements imaginable.

The monk then brought him some food and drink, and Ferondo gasped with astonishment, saying:

'Do dead people eat?'

'Yes,' said the monk. 'As a matter of fact, the food I am giving you was sent this morning to the church by the woman who was your wife, with a request that masses should be said for your soul. And it is God's wish that you should have it here and now.'

'God bless her little heart!' exclaimed Ferondo. 'I did love her a lot of course, before I died. Why, I used to hold her in my arms all night, and I never stopped kissing her. And when the mood took me, I did more besides.'

His appetite being enormous, he then began to eat and drink, but the wine was not entirely to his liking.

'God damn the woman!' he exclaimed. 'This wine she's given to the priest didn't come from the cask alongside the wall.'

He continued with his meal, however, and when he had finished, the monk brandished his bunch of sticks once again, seized him a second time, and gave him another severe hiding.

'Hey!' yelled Ferondo, making the dickens of a protest. 'What are you doing this to me for?'

'Because the Almighty has given strict orders that you are to be beaten twice every day.'

'For what reason?'

'Because you were jealous of your wife, who was the finest woman in the whole district.'

'Alas, how right you are,' said Ferondo. 'She was also the sweetest; aye, sweeter than a sugar-plum. But I would never have been jealous if I had known I was giving offence to the Almighty.'

'You should have thought of that while you were still on the other side,' said the monk. 'You should have mended your ways before it was too late. And if you ever happen to return, be very careful to remember what I am doing now, and never be jealous again.'

'Eh? But surely the dead don't ever return, do they?'

'Some do, if God so wills it.'

'Well, I'm blessed!' said Ferondo. 'If I ever go back, I shall be the best husband in the world. I'll never beat her, nor scold her either, except about the wine she sent this morning. Which reminds me: she didn't send a single candle, and I was forced to eat in the dark.'

'She did send some,' said the monk, 'but they were used up during the masses.'

'Ah, yes,' said Ferondo, 'that'll be what has happened. Anyway, if I go back, I shall definitely allow her to do as she pleases. But tell me, why should *you* be doing this to me? Who are you?'

'I also am dead,' replied the monk. 'I lived in Sardinia, and because I lauded my master to the skies for his jealousy, God has decreed that I should be punished by supplying you with food and drink and these thrashings until He decides what to do with us next.'

'Is there anybody else here, apart from ourselves?' asked Ferondo.

'Yes, thousands,' said the monk. 'But you cannot see or hear them, any more than they can see or hear you.'

'And how far are we away from home?'

'Oho! Far more miles than one of our turds would travel.'

'Crikey! that's a fair distance. I should think we must have left the earth behind entirely.'

This kind of gibberish, together with his food rations and his regular beatings, kept Ferondo going for ten whole months during which the Abbot was highly assiduous and enterprising in his visits to the fair lady, with whom he had the jolliest time imaginable. But accidents will happen, and the lady eventually became pregnant, promptly told the Abbot about it, and they both agreed that Ferondo must be recalled at once from Purgatory and reunited with his wife, who undertook to convince him that it was he who had got her with child.

So the following night, the Abbot went to Ferondo's cell, and disguising his voice, he called to him and said:

'Ferondo, be of good cheer, for God has decreed that you should go back to earth, where, after your return, your wife will present you with a son. See that the child is christened Benedict, for it is in answer to the prayers of your reverend Abbot and your wife, and because of His love for St Benedict, that God has done you this favour.'

This announcement was received by Ferondo with great glee.

'I am very glad to hear it,' he said. 'God bless Mister Almighty and the Abbot and St Benedict and my cheesy-weesy, honey-bunny, sweetie-pie of a wife.'

Having put sufficient powder in Ferondo's wine to send him to sleep for about four hours, the Abbot dressed him in his proper clothes again and quietly restored him, with the aid of his monk, to the tomb in which he had originally been laid to rest.

A little after dawn next morning, Ferondo came to his senses and noticed a chink of light coming through a crack in the side of the tomb. Not having seen any light for ten whole months, he concluded that he must be alive, and started to shout:

'Open up! Open up!'

At the same time, he began to press his head firmly against the lid of the tomb, and not being very secure, it yielded and he started to push it aside Meanwhile the monks, who had just finished reciting their matins, hurried to the scene, and when they recognized Ferondo's voice and saw him emerging from the tomb, they were all terrified by the novelty of the occurrence and ran off to inform the Abbot.

The Abbot pretended to be rising from prayer.

'My sons,' he said, 'be not afraid. Take up the cross and the holy water and follow me. Let us go and see what God's omnipotence has in store for us.' And away he strode.

Ferondo, who was as white as a sheet on account of his prolonged incarceration in total darkness, had meanwhile emerged from the tomb, and on seeing the Abbot approaching, he hurled himself at his feet, saying:

'Father, I have been rescued from the torments of Purgatory and restored to life, and it was revealed to me that my release was brought about by your prayers, together with those of my wife and St Benedict. God bless you, therefore, and make you prosper, now and forever more!'

'God be praised for His omnipotence!' exclaimed the Abbot. 'Now that He has sent you back again, just you run along, my son, and comfort your good lady, for she has done nothing but weep since the day you departed this life. And take good care, from now on, to serve God and hold on to His friendship.'

'That's good advice, sir, and no mistake,' said Ferondo. 'Leave things to me. I love her so much that I'll give her a great big kiss the moment I find her.'

The Abbot pretended to marvel greatly over what had happened, and as soon as he was alone with his monks, he had them all devoutly chanting the *Miserere*.

When Ferondo returned to his village, everyone he met ran away from him in horror, and his wife was no less frightened of him than the rest, but he called them all back, assuring them that he had been restored to life. And once they recovered from the initial shock and saw that he really was alive, they bombarded him with questions, to all of which he replied as though he had been transformed into some kind of soothsayer, providing them with information about the souls of their kinsfolk and inventing all manner of marvellous tales about what went on in Purgatory. Moreover, he supplied the assembled populace with an account of the revelation he had received, before his return, from the Arse-angel Bagriel's own lips.

Having returned home with his wife and retaken possession of his property, he got her with child, or so he thought at any rate. He had been recalled not a moment too soon, for after a pregnancy that happened to be long enough to confirm the vulgar error which supposes that women carry their babies for exactly nine months, his wife gave birth to a son, which was christened Benedetto Ferondi.

Since nearly everyone was convinced that he really had been brought back from the dead, Ferondo's return and his tall stories immeasurably enhanced the Abbot's reputation for saintliness. And for his own part, because of the countless hidings he had received on account of his jealousy, Ferondo stopped being jealous and became a reformed character, so that the expectations held out to the lady by the Abbot were fulfilled to the letter. Of this she was very glad, and thereafter she lived no less chastely with her husband than she had in the past, except that, whenever the occasion arose, she gladly renewed her intimacy with the Abbot, who had ministered to her greatest needs with such unfailing skill and diligence.

NINTH STORY

Gilette of Narbonne, having cured the King of France of a fistula, asks him for the hand of Bertrand of Roussillon in marriage. Bertrand marries her against his will, then goes off in high dudgeon to Florence, where he pays court to a young woman whom Gilette impersonates, sleeping with him and presenting him with two children. In this way, he finally comes to love her and acknowledge her as his wife.

When Lauretta's tale had ended, the queen, not wishing to revoke Dioneo's privilege, and realizing that she herself was the only person left to speak, began without waiting to be urged. And with all her considerable charm she addressed her companions as follows:

How is anyone to tell a better story than the one we have just heard from Lauretta? It was certainly fortunate for us that hers was not the first, for otherwise we would have derived little pleasure from the ones that followed, which is what I fear will happen with the last two stories of today. However, for what it is worth, I am going to tell you the story that occurs to me as relevant to the topic we proposed.

In the kingdom of France, there once lived a nobleman who was called Isnard, Count of Roussillon, and who, being something of an invalid, always kept a doctor, named Master Gerard of Narbonne, at his beck and call. The Count had only one child, a little boy of exceedingly handsome and pleasing appearance called Bertrand, who was brought up with other children of his own age, among them the daughter of the doctor I have mentioned, whose name was Gilette. Gilette was head over heels in love with this Bertrand, being more passionately attached to him than was strictly proper in a girl of so tender an age, so that when, on the death of the Count, Bertrand was committed to the guardianship of the King and had to go away to Paris, she was driven to the brink of despair. Shortly afterwards, her own father died, and if she could have found a plausible excuse, she would gladly have gone to Paris in order to visit Bertrand. But she could see no way of doing it without causing a scandal, for she had inherited the whole of her father's fortune, and was kept under constant surveillance.

Even after reaching marriageable age, she still could not forget Bertrand, and without offering any explanation she rejected numerous suitors whom her kinsfolk had urged her to marry.

Now, because she had heard that Bertrand had become an exceedingly handsome young man, the flames of her love were raging more fiercely than ever when she happened to hear that the King of France had been suffering from a chest-tumour, which, because it had been treated maladroitly, had left him with a fistula that was causing him endless trouble and discomfort. Numerous doctors had been consulted, but he had not yet succeeded in finding a single one who was able to cure him. On the contrary, they had merely made matters worse, with the result that the King had abandoned all hope of recovery, and was refusing to accept further advice or treatment from anyone.

The girl was filled with joy to hear these tidings, for she realized that not only did they give her a legitimate reason for going to Paris, but, if the illness of the King was what she thought it was, she would have little difficulty in obtaining Bertrand's hand in marriage. Using the knowledge she had acquired in the past from her father, she proceeded to make up a powder from certain herbs that were good for the ailment she had diagnosed, then she rode off to Paris. Before doing anything else, she contrived to see Bertrand, after which she obtained an audience of the King and asked his permission to examine his malady. Not knowing how to refuse a young woman of such evident charm and beauty, the King allowed her to do so, and she knew at once that she could make him better.

'Sire,' she said, 'if you are willing, with God's help I can cure you of this malady within the space of a week, without causing you any bother or discomfort.'

The King refused to take her seriously, saying to himself: 'How could a young woman succeed in doing something that has defeated the skill and knowledge of the world's greatest physicians?' He therefore thanked her for her good intentions, adding that he had resolved to decline all further medical advice.

'Sire,' said the girl, 'you are sceptical of my powers because I am young and because I am a woman; but I would have you know that my powers of healing do not depend so much upon my knowledge as upon the assistance of God and the expertise of my late father, Master Gerard of Narbonne, who in his day was a famous physician.'

'Who knows?' thought the King to himself. 'Perhaps this woman has been sent to me by God. Why not find out what she can do? After all, she claims she can cure me in next to no time without causing me any discomfort.' And by reasoning thus, he persuaded himself that he should put her claims to the test.

'Young woman,' he said. 'Suppose we were to break our resolve, only to find that you fail to effect a cure? What penalty would you consider appropriate?'

'Sire,' replied the girl. 'Keep me under guard, and if I do not cure you within a week, order me to be burned. But what reward shall I have if I make you better?'

'If you do that,' replied the King, 'then since you appear to be unmarried, we shall provide you with a fine and noble husband.'

'Sire,' said the girl, 'I would certainly like you to give me a husband, but only the one I shall ask for, and you may rest assured that I shall not ask you for one of your sons or any other royal personage.'

The King gave her his promise forthwith, and the girl began to apply her remedy, restoring him to health with time to spare. Whereupon the King, feeling he had quite recovered, said to her:

'Young woman, you have clearly won yourself a husband.'

'In that case, sire,' she replied, 'I have won Bertrand of Roussillon, with whom I have been deeply in love since the days of my childhood.'

It was no laughing matter to the King that he should be obliged to give her Bertrand. But not wishing to break the promise he had given her, he sent for him and said:

'Bertrand, you are now fully trained and mature, and it is our pleasure that you should return to govern your lands, taking with you the young lady whom we have decided you should marry.'

'And who, my lord, may this young lady be?' asked Bertrand.

'She is the one who has restored our health with her physic,' replied the King.

Bertrand knew the girl, and had thought her very beautiful on seeing her again. But knowing that her lineage was in no way suited to his own noble ancestry, he was highly indignant, and said:

'But surely, sire, you would not want to marry me to a she-doctor. Heaven forbid that I should ever accept a woman of that sort for a wife.'

'The young lady has demanded your hand in marriage as her reward for restoring our health,' said the King. 'Surely you would not want us to break the promise we have given her.'

'Sire,' said Bertrand, 'You have the power to take away everything I possess, and hand me over to anyone you may choose, for I am merely your humble vassal. But I can assure you that I shall never rest content with such a match.'

'Of course you will,' said the King, 'for she is beautiful, intelligent, and deeply in love with you. Hence we are confident that you will be much happier with her than you would ever have been with a lady of loftier birth.'

Bertrand said no more, and the King gave orders for a splendid wedding feast to be arranged. And so, much against his will, on the appointed day and in the presence of the King, Bertrand married the girl who loved him more dearly than her very life. Having already made up his mind what he should do, as soon as the wedding was

over he sought the King's permission to depart, saying that he wished
to return to his own estates and consummate his marriage there. So
he duly set out on horseback, but instead of going to his estates he
came to Tuscany, where he learned that the Florentines were waging
war against the Sienese, and resolved to offer them his assistance. The
Florentines welcomed him with open arms and placed him in command of a sizeable body of men, paying him a good stipend, and for a
long time thereafter he remained in their service.

His bride was far from happy with the turn events had taken, and
in the hope of persuading him to return to his estates by her wise
administration, she went to Roussillon, where all the people received
her as their rightful mistress. Since there had been no Count to
govern the territory for some little time, she was faced on her arrival
with nothing but confusion and chaos. But being a capable woman,
she applied herself with great diligence to the task in hand, and soon
had everything restored to order, thus winning the profound respect
and devotion of her subjects, who were enormously pleased by her
endeavours and strongly critical of the Count because of his indifference towards her.

Having fully restored the Count's domain to order, the lady communicated this fact to her husband by way of two knights, beseeching
him to inform her whether it was on her account that he was deserting
his lands, in which case she would go away in order to please him. He
answered them very brusquely, saying:

'She may do whatever she likes. For my own part, I shall go back
to live with her when she wears this ring upon her finger, and when
she is carrying a child of mine in her arms.'

The ring was very dear to him, and he never let it stray from his
finger on account of certain magical powers which he had been told
that it possessed.

The knights realized that it was virtually impossible for the lady to
comply with either of these harsh conditions, but no amount of
reasoning on their part could shift him from his resolve, and they
therefore returned to their mistress to acquaint her with his answer.
Their tidings filled her with dismay, but after giving some thought to
the matter she decided to try and find out how and where these two
things might be accomplished, thus enabling her to win back her

husband. Having carefully considered what she must do, she called together a group of the leading notables of those parts, gave them a highly succinct and moving description of all she had done out of her love for the Count, and pointed out the results of her endeavours. Then she told them that she had no intention of protracting her stay if this entailed the Count's continued exile; on the contrary, she meant to spend the rest of her days in making pilgrimages and performing works of charity for the good of her soul. Finally, she asked them to take over the defence and administration of the territory, and to inform the Count that she had left him its exclusive and unencumbered title; then she vanished from the scene, having resolved never to set foot in Roussillon again.

As she spoke, her worthy hearers shed countless tears and pleaded with her over and over again to change her mind and stay with them, but all to no avail. Having bidden them farewell, she set out with one of her maidservants and a man who was her cousin, both of whom were dressed, like herself, in pilgrim's garb, and taking with her a goodly quantity of money and precious jewels. She had told no one where she was going, but in fact she made straight for Florence without pausing to rest. On her arrival, she chanced upon a little inn that was kept by a kindly widow, and there she quietly took up her abode in the guise of a poor pilgrim, eager for news of her husband.

It so happened that on the very next day, she saw Bertrand go riding past the inn on horseback with his men, and although she recognized him quite distinctly, she nonetheless enquired who he was from the good lady of the inn.

'He is a foreign nobleman,' replied the hostess. 'His name is Count Bertrand, he is a great favourite with the Florentines because of his affable and gentlemanly nature, and he is head over heels in love with a young lady living nearby, who is nobly bred but poor. The fact is that she is a most virtuous girl, who has not yet married on account of her poverty, but lives with her mother, a lady of great wisdom and probity. Indeed, but for this mother of hers, it is quite possible that the Count would already have had his way with the girl.'

The Countess committed everything to memory, and after giving further thought to each of the things she had heard and building a mental picture of the affair as a whole, she decided on her course of action. And one day, having discovered the name and address of the lady and this daughter of hers who was loved by the Count, she made her way unobtrusively to their house, wearing her pilgrim's habit. The poverty of the two women was immediately apparent to the Countess, who greeted them and asked the lady if she could talk to her in private.

The gentlewoman rose to her feet, assuring her that she was ready to listen, and led her into another room, where they sat down.

'Madam,' said the Countess, 'you and your daughter would appear to have fallen on hard times, and I too am dogged by ill luck. But if you so desired, you could perhaps repair your fortunes as well as my own at one and the same time.'

The lady replied that nothing would please her better than to repair her fortunes without compromising her honour.

'It is essential that I should be able to trust you,' continued the Countess, 'because if you were to betray my confidence, you would ruin everything, for all three of us.'

'You may confide in me as much as you like,' said the gentlewoman, 'for you may rest assured that I shall never betray you.'

The Countess then disclosed her true identity and related the whole history of her love from its earliest beginnings, telling her tale so touchingly that the gentlewoman, who had already gleaned some knowledge of the matter from elsewhere, was convinced that she was telling the truth and began to take pity on her. Having told her all the facts, the Countess continued:

'This, then, is the tale of my misfortunes. As you have heard, there are two things I must obtain if I am to have my husband. And I know of no one who can help me to obtain them except yourself, if it is true, as I have been led to believe, that my husband the Count is deeply in love with your daughter.'

'I know not, madam, whether the Count is in love with my daughter,' replied the gentlewoman. 'He claims to be, certainly, but how will this make it easier for me to assist you?'

'I will tell you,' said the Countess, 'but first of all I want to explain how I intend to repay your assistance. I see that your daughter is beautiful and of marriageable age, but it seems, both from what I have been told and from the evidence of my own eyes, that the impossibility of making a good marriage for her compels you to keep her at home. I therefore propose to reward your services by promptly supplying her, from my own resources, with whatever dowry you think she needs for an honourable marriage.'

The lady, being destitute, was attracted by this offer. But she was also proud of spirit, and she replied:

'Pray explain to me, madam, in what way I can assist you. If it is honourable for me to further your plans, I shall be glad to do so, and afterwards you may reward me in whatever way you please.'

Whereupon the Countess said:

'What I require you to do is to send some trustworthy person to inform my husband, the Count, that your daughter is prepared to place herself entirely at his disposal, but only on condition that he proves to her that his love is as deep and genuine as he claims; this she will never believe until he sends her the ring which he wears upon his hand and to which she understands that he is deeply attached. If he sends her the ring, you will hand it over to me, and then you will send him a message to the effect that your daughter is ready to do his bidding, and you will cause him to come here in secret and, all unsuspecting, lie with me instead of your daughter. Perhaps by the grace of God I shall become pregnant, and later on, with my husband's ring on my finger and my husband's child in my arms, I will regain his love and live with him as a wife should live with a husband. And it will all be thanks to you.'

In the eyes of the gentlewoman, this was no trivial request, for she was afraid lest her daughter's name be brought into disrepute. But after due reflection, she came to the conclusion that it was right and proper for her to assist the good lady to retrieve her husband, for she would be acting in pursuit of a worthy objective. And therefore, placing her trust in the transparent goodness and honesty of the Countess, she not only promised to do what was required, but within the space of a few days, proceeding with all necessary secrecy and caution, she had obtained possession of the ring from the Count (who was somewhat reluctant to part with it), and achieved the remarkable feat of putting the Countess to bed with him in place of her own daughter.

In the course of their earliest embraces, to which the Count devoted considerable ardour, God so willed that the lady should conceive two sons, as became manifest when the time arrived for her to bring them forth. This was not the only occasion, however, on which the gentlewoman arranged for the Countess to enjoy her husband's love, for she devised many other such encounters, proceeding with so much secrecy that nobody ever came to know about them. The Count went on believing that he had been consorting, not with his wife, but with the girl he loved; and before leaving her in the morning, he would present her with beautiful and precious jewels, all of which the Countess took special care to preserve.

Once she perceived that she was pregnant, the Countess no longer desired to trouble the gentlewoman any further, and said to her:

'By the grace of God, my lady, and thanks to your assistance, I now have what I wanted, and hence it is time for me to do whatever you want me to do, so that I may take my leave.'

The gentlewoman insisted that so long as the Countess was contented with what she had achieved, then she too was satisfied, and that she had not assisted her in the hope of obtaining any reward, but merely because she had felt it her duty to support so worthy a cause.

'I fully understand,' said the Countess. 'And for my own part, I have no intention of granting you any reward. I shall give you whatever you ask of me because the cause is worthy and I feel obliged to support it.'

The gentlewoman was sorely embarrassed, but her needs were great, and she asked for a hundred pounds so that she could marry her daughter. On hearing her ask for so modest a sum, the Countess, sensing her embarrassment, gave her five hundred pounds, together with a quantity of fine and precious jewels that probably amounted in value to the same sum again. The gentlewoman, quite overcome, thanked the Countess as warmly as she could, after which the Countess took her leave of her and returned to the inn.

So that Bertrand should have no further reason for sending messages or paying visits to her house, the gentlewoman took her daughter away with her to live with relatives in the country. And shortly afterwards, Bertrand was recalled by his nobles and returned home, having been assured that the Countess had gone away.

On hearing that he had left Florence and returned to his estates, the Countess was overjoyed. She herself remained in Florence until the time came for her confinement, when she gave birth to twin sons who were the image of their father. She took special care to have them properly nursed, and when she considered the time to be ripe, she set out with the children and succeeded in reaching Montpellier without being recognized. There she rested for a few days, making inquiries concerning the Count and his whereabouts, and on learning that he would be holding a magnificent feast for his lords and ladies on All Saints' Day in Roussillon, she too made her way there, still attired in the pilgrim's garb to which she had by now become accustomed.

Arriving at the Count's palace, she heard all the lords and ladies talking together prior to sitting at table, and so she made her way up to the hall, still wearing the same clothes and carrying the two infants in her arms, and threaded her way through the guests until, catching sight of the Count, she flung herself at his feet and burst into tears, saying:

'My lord, behold your unfortunate bride, who has suffered the pangs of a long and bitter exile so that you could return and settle in your ancestral home. I now beseech you, in God's name, to observe the conditions you imposed upon me through the agency of those two knights I sent to you. Here in my arms I carry, not merely one of your children, but two; and here is your ring. So the time has come for you to honour your promise and accept me as your wife.'

The Count could scarcely believe his ears, yet had to admit that the ring was his and that the children, since they resembled him so exactly, must also be his. All he could find to say was:

'How can this have happened?'

To the utter astonishment of the Count and all the others present, the Countess then related the whole of her story from beginning to end. Well knowing that she was telling the truth, and seeing what a handsome pair of children her remarkable persistence and intelligence had produced, the Count could no longer feel hostile towards her, and he not only honoured his promise but endeared himself to his lords and ladies (who were all entreating him to accept and welcome her as his lawful spouse) by helping the Countess to her feet, smothering her with kisses and embraces, and recognizing her as his lawful wife, at the same time acknowledging the children to be his. And having caused her to change into robes befitting her rank, he gave up the rest of the day to feasting and merrymaking, to the no small pleasure of those present and all of his vassals who came to hear of it. The festivities continued for several days, and from that time forth, never failing to honour the Countess as his lawful wedded wife, he loved her and held her in the greatest esteem.

TENTH STORY

Alibech becomes a recluse, and after being taught by the monk, Rustico, to put the devil back in Hell, she is eventually taken away to become the wife of Neerbal.

Dioneo had been following the queen's story closely, and on perceiving that it was finished, knowing that he was the only speaker left, he smiled and began without waiting to be bidden:

Gracious ladies, you have possibly never heard how the devil is put back into Hell, and hence, without unduly straying from the theme of your discussions for today, I should like to tell you about it. By learning how it is done, there may yet be time perhaps for you to save our souls from perdition, and you will also discover that, even though Love is more inclined to take up his abode in a gay palace and a dainty bedchamber than in a wretched hovel, there is no denying that he sometimes makes his powers felt among pathless woods, on rugged mountains, and in desert caves; nor is this surprising, since all living things are subject to his sway.

Now, to come to the point, there once lived in the town of Gafsa, in Barbary, a very rich man who had numerous children, among them a lovely and graceful young daughter called Alibech. She was not herself a Christian, but there were many Christians in the town, and one day, having on occasion heard them extol the Christian faith and the service of God, she asked one of them for his opinion on the best and easiest way for a person to 'serve God', as they put it. He answered her by saying that the ones who served God best were those who put the greatest distance between themselves and earthly goods, as happened in the case of people who had gone to live in the remoter parts of the Sahara.

She said no more about it to anyone, but next morning, being a very simple-natured creature of fourteen or thereabouts, Alibech set out all alone, in secret, and made her way towards the desert, prompted by nothing more logical than a strong adolescent impulse. A few days later, exhausted from fatigue and hunger, she arrived in the heart of the wilderness, where, catching sight of a small hut in the distance, she stumbled towards it, and in the doorway she found a holy man, who was astonished to see her in those parts and asked her what she was doing there. She told him that she had been inspired by God, and that she was trying, not only to serve Him, but also to find someone who could teach her how she should go about it.

On observing how young and exceedingly pretty she was, the good man was afraid to take her under his wing lest the devil should catch him unawares. So he praised her for her good intentions, and having given her a quantity of herb-roots, wild apples and dates to eat, and some water to drink, he said to her:

'My daughter, not very far from here there is a holy man who is much more capable than I of teaching you what you want to know. Go along to him.' And he sent her upon her way.

When she came to this second man, she was told precisely the same thing, and so she went on until she arrived at the cell of a young hermit, a very devout and kindly fellow called Rustico, to whom she put the same inquiry as she had addressed to the others. Being anxious to prove to himself that he possessed a will of iron, he did not, like the others, send her away or direct her elsewhere, but kept her with him in his cell, in a corner of which, when night descended, he prepared a makeshift bed out of palm-leaves, upon which he invited her to lie down and rest.

Once he had taken this step, very little time elapsed before temptation went to war against his willpower, and after the first few assaults, finding himself outmanoeuvred on all fronts, he laid down his arms and surrendered. Casting aside pious thoughts, prayers, and penitential exercises, he began to concentrate his mental faculties upon the youth and beauty of the girl, and to devise suitable ways and means for approaching her in such a fashion that she should not think it lewd of him to make the sort of proposal he had in mind. By putting certain questions to her, he soon discovered that she had never been intimate with the opposite sex and was every bit as innocent as she seemed; and he therefore thought of a possible way to persuade her, with the pretext of serving God, to gratify his desires. He began by delivering a long speech in which he showed her how powerful an enemy the devil was to the Lord God, and followed this up by impressing upon her that of all the ways of serving God, the one that He most appreciated consisted in putting the devil back in Hell, to which the Almighty had consigned him in the first place.

The girl asked him how this was done, and Rustico replied:

'You will soon find out, but just do whatever you see me doing for the present.' And so saying, he began to divest himself of the few clothes he was wearing, leaving himself completely naked. The girl followed his example, and he sank to his knees as though he were about to pray, getting her to kneel directly opposite.

In this posture, the girl's beauty was displayed to Rustico in all its glory, and his longings blazed more fiercely than ever, bringing about the resurrection of the flesh. Alibech stared at this in amazement, and said:

'Rustico, what is that thing I see sticking out in front of you, which I do not possess?'

'Oh, my daughter,' said Rustico, 'this is the devil I was telling you about. Do you see what he's doing? He's hurting me so much that I can hardly endure it.'

'Oh, praise be to God,' said the girl, 'I can see that I am better off than you are, for I have no such devil to contend with.'

'You're right there,' said Rustico. 'But you have something else instead, that I haven't.'

'Oh?' said Alibech. 'And what's that?'

'You have Hell,' said Rustico. 'And I honestly believe that God has sent you here for the salvation of my soul, because if this devil continues to plague the life out of me, and if you are prepared to take sufficient pity upon me to let me put him back into Hell, you will be giving me marvellous relief, as well as rendering incalculable service and pleasure to God, which is what you say you came here for to begin with.'

'Oh, Father,' replied the girl in all innocence, 'if I really do have a Hell, let's do as you suggest just as soon as you are ready.'

'God bless you, my daughter,' said Rustico. 'Let us go and put him back and then perhaps he'll leave me alone.'

At which point he conveyed the girl to one of their beds, where he instructed her in the art of incarcerating that accursed fiend.

Never having put a single devil into Hell before, the girl found the first experience a little painful, and she said to Rustico:

'This devil must certainly be a bad lot, Father, and a true enemy of God, for as well as plaguing mankind, he even hurts Hell when he's driven back inside it.'

'Daughter,' said Rustico, 'it will not always be like that.' And in order to ensure that it wouldn't, before moving from the bed they put him back half a dozen times, curbing his arrogance to such good effect that he was positively glad to keep still for the rest of the day.

During the next few days, however, the devil's pride frequently reared its head again, and the girl, ever ready to obey the call to duty and bring him under control, happened to develop a taste for the sport, and began saying to Rustico:

'I can certainly see what those worthy men in Gafsa meant when they said that serving God was so agreeable. I don't honestly recall ever having done anything that gave me so much pleasure and satisfaction as I get from putting the devil back in Hell. To my way of thinking, anyone who devotes his energies to anything but the service of God is a complete blockhead.'

She thus developed the habit of going to Rustico at frequent intervals, and saying to him:

'Father, I came here to serve God, not to idle away my time. Let's go and put the devil back in Hell.'

And sometimes, in the middle of their labours, she would say:

'What puzzles me, Rustico, is that the devil should ever want to escape from Hell. Because if he liked being there as much as Hell enjoys receiving him and keeping him inside, he would never go away at all.'

By inviting Rustico to play the game too often, continually urging him on in the service of God, the girl took so much stuffing out of him that he eventually began to turn cold where another man would have been bathed in sweat. So he told her that the devil should only be punished and put back in Hell when he reared his head with pride, adding that by the grace of Heaven, they had tamed him so effectively that he was pleading with God to be left in peace. In this way, he managed to keep the girl quiet for a while, but one day, having begun to notice that Rustico was no longer asking for the devil to be put back in Hell, she said:

'Look here, Rustico. Even though your devil has been punished and pesters you no longer, my Hell simply refuses to leave me alone. Now that I have helped you with my Hell to subdue the pride of your devil, the least you can do is to get your devil to help me tame the fury of my Hell.'

Rustico, who was living on a diet of herb-roots and water, was quite incapable of supplying her requirements, and told her that the taming of her Hell would require an awful lot of devils, but promised to do what he could. Sometimes, therefore, he responded to the call, but this happened so infrequently that it was rather like chucking a bean into the mouth of a lion, with the result that the girl, who felt that she was not serving God as diligently as she would have liked, was found complaining more often than not.

But at the height of this dispute between Alibech's Hell and Rustico's devil, brought about by a surplus of desire on the one hand and a shortage of power on the other, a fire broke out in Gafsa, and Alibech's father was burnt to death in his own house along with all his children and every other member of his household, so that Alibech inherited the whole of his property. Because of this a young man called Neerbal who had spent the whole of his substance in sumptuous living, having heard that she was still alive, set out to look for her, and before the authorities were able to appropriate her late father's fortune on the grounds that there was no heir, he succeeded in tracing her whereabouts. To the great relief of Rustico, but against her own wishes, he took her back to Gafsa and married her, thus inheriting a half-share in her father's enormous fortune.

Before Neerbal had actually slept with her, she was questioned by the women of Gafsa about how she had served God in the desert, and she replied that she had served Him by putting the devil back in Hell, and that Neerbal had committed a terrible sin by stopping her from performing so worthy a service.

'How do you put the devil back in Hell?' asked the women.

Partly in words and partly through gestures, the girl showed them how it was done, whereupon the women laughed so much that they are laughing yet; and they said:

'Don't let it worry you, my dear. People do the job every bit as well here in Gafsa, and Neerbal will give you plenty of help in serving the Lord.'

The story was repeated throughout the town, being passed from one woman to the next, and they coined a proverbial saying there to the effect that the most agreeable way of serving God was to put the devil back in Hell. The dictum later crossed the sea to Italy, where it survives to this day.

And so, young ladies, if you stand in need of God's grace, see that you learn to put the devil back in Hell, for it is greatly to His liking and pleasurable to the parties concerned, and a great deal of good can arise and flow in the process.

*   *   *

So aptly and cleverly worded did Dioneo's tale appear to the virtuous ladies, that they shook with mirth a thousand times or more. And when he had brought it to a close, the queen, acknowledging the end of her sovereignty, removed the laurel from her head and placed it very gracefully on Filostrato's, saying:

'Now we shall discover whether the wolf can fare any better at leading the sheep than the sheep have fared in leading the wolves.'

On hearing this, Filostrato laughed and said: 'Had you listened to me, the wolves would have taught the sheep by now to put the devil back in Hell, no less skilfully than Rustico taught Alibech. But you have not exactly been behaving like sheep, and therefore you must not describe us as wolves. However, you have placed the kingdom in my hands, and I shall govern it as well as I am able.'

'Allow me to tell you, Filostrato,' replied Neifile, 'that if you men had tried to teach us anything of the sort, you might have learned some sense from us, as Masetto did from the nuns, and retrieved the use of your tongues when your bones were rattling from exhaustion.'

On perceiving that the ladies had as many scythes as he had arrows, Filostrato abandoned his jesting and turned to the business of ruling his kingdom. Summoning the steward, he asked him to explain how matters stood, after which he discreetly gave him his instructions, consisting of what he thought would be appropriate and agreeable to the company as a whole. He then turned to the ladies, saying:

'Charming ladies, ever since I was able to distinguish good from evil, it has been my unhappy lot, owing to the beauty of one of your number, to find myself perpetually enslaved to Love. I have humbly and obediently followed all of his rules to the very best of my ability, only to find that I have invariably been forsaken to make way for another. Things have gone from bad to worse for me, and I do not suppose they will improve to my dying day. I therefore decree that the subject of our discussions for the morrow should be none other than the one which applies most closely to myself, namely, *those whose love ended unhappily*. For my part, I expect my own love to have a thoroughly unhappy ending, nor was it for any other reason that I was given (by one who knew what he was talking about) the name★ by which you address me.' And having uttered these words, he rose to his feet and dismissed them all till suppertime.

The garden was so lovely and delectable, that none of them chose to stray beyond its confines in search of greater pleasure in other parts. On the contrary, since the sun was now much cooler and no longer made hunting a chore, some of the ladies set off in pursuit of the hares and roebucks and other animals in the garden, that had been startling them by leaping a hundred times or more into their midst as they sat and talked. Dioneo and Fiammetta began to sing a song about Messer Guiglielmo and the Lady of Vergiù, whilst Filomena and Panfilo settled down to a game of chess. So intently were they all engaged upon their several activities, that the time passed by unnoticed, and when the hour of supper came, it caught them unawares. The tables were then placed round the edge of the beautiful fountain, and there, to their immense delight, they supped in the cool of the evening.

★B. intended the name Filostrato (Philostratos) to convey the meaning: 'vanquished by Love'.

No sooner had the tables been removed than Filostrato, wishing to keep to the path which the ladies crowned before him had taken, called upon Lauretta to dance and sing them a song.

'My lord,' she said, 'the only songs I know are the ones I have composed myself, and of those I remember, none is especially apt for so merry a gathering as this. But if you would like me to sing you one, I will gladly oblige.'

'Nothing of yours could be other than pleasing and beautiful,' replied the king. 'Sing it, therefore, exactly as you wrote it.'

And so, in mellifluous but somewhat plaintive tones, Lauretta began as follows, and the other ladies repeated the refrain after each verse:

> 'None has need for lamentation
> More than have I
> Who, alas, all sick for love
> In vain do sigh.
>
> 'He who moves the stars and heavens
> Decreed me at my birth
> Light, lovely, graceful, fair to see,
> To show men here on earth
> Some sign of that eternal grace
> That shines for ever in His face.
>   But I went all unprized
>   Because of men's unknowing
>   And mortal imperfection
>   Spurned and despised!
>
> 'One man once loved me dearly.
> In his embrace
> He held me, and in all his thoughts
> I held high place.
> My eyes with love inflamed him
> And all my time I spent,
> Which flew by all so lightly,
> In tender blandishment.
>   But now I am forsaken;
>   From me, alas, he's taken.

'And now there came before me
A youth all proud and vain
Though noble reputation
Gave him a valiant name.
He took me, and false fancies,
Alas for me!
Made him a jealous gaoler:
Gone liberty!
  And I, who came to earth
  To bring mankind delight
  Learned to despair, almost,
  Gone all my mirth!

'I curse my wretched fate
When I agreed
To change to wedding clothes
From widow's weeds.
Though they were dark, perhaps,
My life was fair; but now
I live a weary life,
With far less honour, too.
  Oh cursed wedding-tie!
  Before I took those vows
  That brought me to this pass
  Would God had let me die!

'Oh, sweetest love, with whom
I once was so content!
From where you stand, with Him
To whom our souls are sent,
Ah, spare some pity for me
For I cannot remove
Your memory which burns me
With all the pain of love!
  Ah, pray that I may soon return
  To those sweet climes for which I yearn!'

Here Lauretta ended her song, to which all had listened raptly and
construed in different ways. There were those who took it, in the
Milanese fashion, to imply that a good fat pig was better than a
comely wench. But others gave it a loftier, more subtle and truer
meaning, which this is not the moment to expound.

The king then called for lighted torches to be set at regular intervals amongst the lawns and flowerbeds, and at his behest, Lauretta's song was followed by many others until every star that had risen was beginning its descent, when, thinking it time for them all to retire, he bade them goodnight and sent them away to their various rooms.

Here ends the Third Day of the Decameron

FOURTH DAY

Here begins the Fourth Day, wherein, under the rule of Filostrato, *the discussion turns upon those whose love ended unhappily.*

Dearest ladies, both from what I have heard on the lips of the wise, and from what I have frequently read and observed for myself, I always assumed that only lofty towers and the tallest of trees could be assailed by envy's fiery and impetuous blast; but I find that I was mistaken. In the course of my lifelong efforts to escape the fierce onslaught of those turbulent winds, I have always made a point of going quietly and unseen about my affairs, not only keeping to the lowlands but occasionally directing my steps through the deepest of deep valleys. This can very easily be confirmed by anyone casting an eye over these little stories of mine, which bear no title and which I have written, not only in the Florentine vernacular and in prose, but in the most homely and unassuming style it is possible to imagine. Yet in spite of all this, I have been unable to avoid being violently shaken and almost uprooted by those very winds, and was nearly torn to pieces by envy. And thus I can most readily appreciate the truth of the wise men's saying, that in the affairs of this world, poverty alone is without envy.

Judicious ladies, there are those who have said, after reading these tales, that I am altogether too fond of you, that it is unseemly for me to take so much delight in entertaining and consoling you, and, what is apparently worse, in singing your praises as I do. Others, laying claim to greater profundity, have said that it is not good for a man of my age to engage in such pursuits as discussing the ways of women and providing for their pleasure. And others, showing deep concern for my renown, say that I would be better advised to remain with the Muses in Parnassus, than to fritter away my time in your company.

Moreover, there are those who, prompted more by spitefulness than commonsense, have said that I would be better employed in earning myself a good meal than in going hungry for the sake of producing nonsense of this sort. And finally there are those who, in order to belittle my efforts, endeavour to prove that my versions of the stories I have told are not consistent with the facts.

By gusts of such a kind as these, then, by teeth thus sharp and cruel, distinguished ladies, am I buffeted, battered, and pierced to the very quick whilst I soldier on in your service. As God is my witness, I take it all calmly and coolly; and though I need no one but you to defend me, I do not intend, all the same, to spare my own energies. On the contrary, without replying as fully as I ought, I shall proceed forthwith to offer a simple answer to these allegations. For I have not yet completed a third of my task, and since my critics are already so numerous and presumptuous, I can only suppose that unless they are discredited now, they could multiply so alarmingly before I reached the end that the tiniest effort on their part would be sufficient to demolish me. And your own influence, considerable though it may be, would be powerless to prevent them.

But before replying to any of my critics, I should like to strengthen my case by recounting, not a complete story (for otherwise it might appear that I was attempting to equate my own tales with those of that select company I have been telling you about), but a part of one, so that its very incompleteness will set it apart from the others. For the benefit of my assailants, then, I say that some time ago, there lived in our city a man called Filippo Balducci, who despite his lowly condition was as prosperous, knowledgeable, and capable a fellow as you could ever wish to meet. He was deeply in love with the lady who was his wife, and since she fully reciprocated his love, their marriage was peaceful, and they went out of their way to make each other's lives completely happy.

Now it so happened, as it happens to us all eventually, that the good lady departed this life, leaving nothing of herself to Filippo but their only son, who was then about two years old.

No man was ever more sorely distressed by the loss of the thing he loved than Filippo by the death of his wife. On finding himself bereft of the companion he adored, he firmly resolved to withdraw from the world and devote his life to the service of God, taking his little son with him. He therefore gave all he possessed to charity, and made his way forthwith to the slopes of Mount Asinaio, where he installed himself in a tiny little cave with his son, fasting and praying and living on alms. At all times, he took very great care not to let him see any worldly things, or even to mention their existence, lest they should distract him from his devotions. On the contrary, he was forever telling him about the glory of the life eternal, of God, and of the Saints, and all he taught him was to pray devoutly. He kept this up for a number of years, never permitting the boy to leave the cave or to see any living thing except for his father.

Every so often, the good man came to Florence, where various kindly people supplied him with things he needed, and then he returned to his cave. But one day, his son, who by this time was eighteen years old, happened to ask Filippo, who had reached a ripe old age, where he was going. Filippo told him that he was going to Florence, whereupon the youth said:

'Father, you are an old man now, and not as strong as you used to be. Why not take me with you on one of your excursions to Florence, introduce me to those charitable and devout people, and let me meet your friends? I am young, and stronger than you are, and if you do as I suggest, in future you'll be able to send me to Florence whenever we need anything, and you can stay here.'

On reflecting that this son of his was now grown up and no longer likely to be attracted to worldly things because he was so inured to the service of God, the worthy man said to himself: 'The fellow's talking sense.' And since he had to go to Florence anyway, he took him with him.

When the young man saw the palaces, the houses, the churches and all the other things that meet the eye in such profusion throughout the city, he could not recall ever having seen such objects before and was filled with amazement. He questioned his father about many of them and asked him what they were called.

Once his father had answered one of his questions, his curiosity was satisfied and he went on to ask about something else. And so they went along, with the son asking questions and the father replying, until they chanced upon a party of elegantly dressed and beautiful young ladies, who were coming away from a wedding; and no sooner did the young man see them, than he asked his father what they were.

'My son,' replied his father, 'keep your eyes fixed on the ground and don't look at them, for they are evil.'

'But what are they called, father?' inquired his son.

Not wishing to arouse any idle longings in the young man's breast, his father avoided calling them by their real name, and instead of telling him that they were women, he said:

'They are called goslings.'

Now, the extraordinary thing about it was that the young man, who had never set eyes on one of these objects before, took no further interest in the palaces, the oxen, the horses, the asses, the money, or any of the other things he had encountered, and promptly replied:

'Oh, father, do please get me one of those goslings.'

'Alas, my son, hold your tongue,' said his father. 'I tell you they are evil.'

'Do you mean to say evil looks like this?'

'Yes.'

'You can say what you like, father, but I don't see anything evil about them. As far as I am concerned, I don't think I have ever in my whole life seen anything so pretty or attractive. They are more beautiful than the painted angels that you have taken me to see so often. O alas! if you have any concern for my welfare, do make it possible for us to take one of these goslings back with us, and I will pop things into its bill.'

'Certainly not,' said his father. 'Their bills are not where you think, and require a special sort of diet.' But no sooner had he spoken than he realized that his wits were no match for Nature, and regretted having brought the boy to Florence in the first place.

But I have no desire to carry this tale any further, and I shall now direct my attention to the people for whose ears it was intended.

As you will recall, young ladies, some of my critics claim that it is wrong of me to take so much trouble to please you, and that I am altogether too fond of you. To these charges I openly plead guilty: it is quite true that I am fond of you and that I strive to please you. But what, may I ask, do they find so surprising about it, when you consider that a young man who had been nurtured and reared within the confines of a tiny cave on a bleak and lonely mountainside, with no other companion except his father, no sooner caught sight of you than all his desires, all his curiosity, all the leanings of his affection were centred upon you, and you alone? Nor, delectable ladies, was he yet aware of the amorous kisses, the sweet caresses, and the blissful embraces that you so often bestow upon us, for a man has merely to fix his eyes upon you to be captivated by your graceful elegance, your endearing charm, and your enchanting beauty, to say nothing of your womanly decorum.

Am I to be abused by these people, then, am I to be mauled and mangled for liking you and striving to please you, when Heaven has given me a body with which to love you and when my soul has been pledged to you since childhood because of the light that gleams in your eyes, the honeyed sounds that issue from your lips, and the flames that are kindled by your sighs of tender compassion? When you consider that even an apprentice hermit, a witless youth who was more of a wild animal than a human being, liked you better than anything he had ever seen, it is perfectly clear that those who criticize me on these grounds are people who, being ignorant of the strength and pleasure of natural affection, neither love you nor desire your love, and they are not worth bothering about.

As for those who keep harping on about my age, they are clearly unaware of the fact that although the leek's head is white, it has a green tail. But joking apart, all I would say to them is that even if I live to be a hundred, I shall never feel any compunction in striving to please the ones who were so greatly honoured, and whose beauty was so much admired, by Guido Cavalcanti and Dante Alighieri in their old age, and by Cino da Pistoia in his dotage. And but for the fact that I would be transgressing the normal bounds of polite debate, I would invoke the aid of history-books and show they are filled with examples from antiquity of outstanding men, who, in their declining years, strove with might and main to give pleasure to the ladies. If my critics are ignorant of this, let them go and repair the gaps in their knowledge.

As for my staying with the Muses in Parnassus, I fully concede the soundness of this advice, but all the same one cannot actually live with the Muses, any more than they can live with us. And if, when he strays from their company, a man takes pleasure in seeing that which resembles them, this is no reason for reproaching him. The Muses are ladies, and although ladies do not rank as highly as Muses, nevertheless they resemble them at first sight, and hence it is natural, if only for this reason, that I should be fond of them. Moreover, ladies have caused me to compose a thousand lines of poetry in the course of my life, whereas the Muses never caused me to write any at all. It is true that they have helped me, and shown me *how* to write; and it is possible that they have been looking over my shoulder several times in the writing of these tales, however unassuming they may be, perhaps because they acknowledge and respect the affinity between the ladies and themselves. And so, in composing these stories, I am not straying as far from Mount Parnassus or from the Muses as many people might be led to believe.

But what are we to say to those who are moved so deeply by my hunger that they advise me to procure myself a good meal? All I know is this, that whenever I ask myself what their answer would be if I had to beg a meal from them, I conclude that they would tell me to go and sing for it. And indeed, the poets have always found more to sustain them in their songs, than many a rich man has found in his treasures. The pursuit of poetry has helped many a man to live to a ripe old age, whereas countless others have died young by seeking more to eat than they really needed. All that remains to be said, then, is that these people are perfectly free to turn me away if I should ever come asking them for anything. Thank God, I am not yet starving in any case; and even if I were, I know, in the words of the Apostle, both how to abound and to suffer need.* Let them attend to their own business, then, and I shall attend to mine.

Finally, I would be greatly obliged to the people who claim that these accounts are inaccurate if they would produce the original versions, and if these turn out to be different from my own, I will grant their reproach to be just, and endeavour to mend my ways. But so long as they have nothing but words to offer, I shall leave them to their opinions, stick to my own, and say the same things about them as they are saying about me.

And there, gentle ladies, I will rest my case for the moment. Being

*Philippians iv, 12.

confident that God and you yourselves will assist me, I shall proceed patiently on my way, turning my back on these winds and letting them blow as hard as they like. For whatever happens, my fate can be no worse than that of the fine-grained dust, which, when a gale blows, either stays on the ground or is carried aloft, in which case it is frequently deposited upon the heads of men, upon the crowns of kings and emperors, and even upon high palaces and lofty towers, whence, if it should fall, it cannot sink lower than the place from which it was raised.

Moreover, whilst I have always striven to please you with all my might, henceforth I shall redouble my efforts towards that end, secure in the knowledge that no reasonable person will deny that I and other men who love you are simply doing what is natural. And in order to oppose the laws of nature, one has to possess exceptional powers, which often turn out to have been used, not only in vain, but to the serious harm of those who employ them.

I for one confess that I do not have such powers at my disposal, nor do I desire them; and even if I were to possess them, I would sooner transfer them to others than use them myself. So let the critics hold their tongues, and if they are unable to radiate any warmth, let them freeze, let them pursue the pleasures that appeal to their jaded palates, and leave me to enjoy my own in the brief life that we are given.

But we have digressed considerably, fair ladies, and now it is time for us to return whence we departed, and proceed on our established course.

Already the sun had extinguished every star in the heavens and expelled night's humid shadows from the earth, when Filostrato got up and caused his companions to be roused. Betaking themselves to the garden, they resumed their various pastimes, and in due course they breakfasted in the place where they had supped the night before. Whilst the sun was at its zenith they took their siesta, and, after they had risen, they seated themselves beside the beautiful fountain as usual. Filostrato then instructed Fiammetta to tell the first story of the day; and without waiting to be bidden twice, she began, in tones of womanly grace, to speak as follows:

FIRST STORY

Tancredi, Prince of Salerno, kills his daughter's lover and sends her his heart in a golden chalice; she besprinkles the heart with a poisonous liquid, which she then drinks, and so dies.

Cruel indeed is the topic for discussion assigned to us today by our king, especially when you consider that, having come here to fortify our spirits, we are obliged to recount people's woes, the telling of which cannot fail to arouse compassion in speaker and listener alike. Perhaps he has done it in order to temper in some degree the gaiety of the previous days; but whatever his motive, it is not for me to alter his decree, and I shall therefore relate an occurrence that was not only pitiful, but calamitous, and fully worthy of our tears.

Tancredi, Prince of Salerno, was a most benevolent ruler, and kindly of disposition, except for the fact that in his old age he sullied his hands with the blood of passion. In all his life he had but a single child, a daughter, and it would have been better for him if he had never had any at all.

He was as passionately fond of this daughter as any father who has ever lived, and being unable to bring himself to part with her, he refused to marry her off, even when she was several years older than the usual age for taking a husband. Eventually, he gave her to a son of the Duke of Capua, but shortly after her marriage she was left a widow and returned to her father. In physique and facial appearance, she was as beautiful a creature as there ever was; she was youthful and vivacious, and she possessed rather more intelligence than a woman needs. In the house of her doting father she led the life of a great lady, surrounded by comforts of every description. But realizing that her father was so devoted to her that he was in no hurry to make her a second marriage, and feeling that it would be shameless to approach him on the subject, she decided to see whether she could find herself a secret lover who was worthy of her affections.

In her father's court, she encountered many people of the kind to be found in any princely household, of whom some were nobly bred and others not. Having studied the conduct and manners of several of these, she was attracted to one above all the rest – a young valet of her father's called Guiscardo, who was a man of exceedingly humble birth but noble in character and bearing. By dint of seeing him often, before very long she fell madly and secretly in love with him, and her admiration of his ways grew steadily more profound. As for the young man himself, not being slow to take a hint, from the moment he perceived her interest in him he lost his heart to her so completely that he could think of virtually nothing else.

And so they were secretly in love with each other. The young woman was longing to be with him, and being unwilling to confide in anyone on the subject of her love, she thought of a novel idea for informing him how they could meet. Having written him a letter, explaining what he was to do in order to be with her on the following day, she inserted it into a length of reed, which later on she handed to Guiscardo, saying as though for the fun of it:

'Turn it into a bellows-pipe for your serving-wench, so that she can use it to kindle the fire this evening.'

Guiscardo took it and went about his business, reflecting that she could hardly have given it to him or spoken as she had without some special motive. As soon as he returned home, he examined the reed, saw that it was split, opened it, and found her letter inside. And when he had read it and taken careful note of what he was to do, he was the happiest man that ever lived, and set about making his preparations for going to see her in the way she had suggested.

Inside the mountain on which the Prince's palace stood, there was a cavern, formed at some remote period of the past, which was partially lit from above through a shaft driven into the hillside. But since the cavern was no longer used, the mouth of the shaft was almost entirely covered over by weeds and brambles. There was a secret staircase leading to the cavern from a room occupied by the lady, on the ground-floor of the palace, but the way was barred by a massive door. So many years had passed since the staircase had last been used, that hardly anybody remembered it was still there; but Love, to whose eyes nothing remains concealed, had reminded the enamoured lady of its existence.

For several days, she had been struggling to open this door by herself, using certain implements of her own as picklocks so that no one should perceive what was afoot. Having finally got it open, she had descended alone into the cavern, seen the shaft, and written to Guiscardo, giving him a rough idea of the distance between the top of the shaft and the floor of the cavern, and telling him to try and use the shaft as his means of access. With this object in view, Guiscardo promptly got hold of a suitable length of rope, tied various knots and loops in it to allow him to climb up and down, and the following night, without breathing a word to anyone, he made his way to the shaft, wearing a suit of leather to protect himself from the brambles. Firmly tying one end of the rope to a stout bush that had taken root at the mouth of the opening, he lowered himself into the cavern and waited for the lady to come.

In the course of the following day, the princess dismissed her ladies-in-waiting on the pretext of wanting to sleep, and having locked herself in her chamber, she opened the door and descended into the cavern, where she found Guiscardo waiting. After giving each other a rapturous greeting, they made their way into her chamber, where they spent a goodly portion of the day in transports of bliss. Before parting, they agreed on the wisest way of pursuing their lovemaking in future so that it should remain a secret, and then Guiscardo returned to the cavern, whilst the princess, having bolted the door behind him, came forth to rejoin her ladies-in-waiting.

During the night, Guiscardo climbed back up the rope, made his way out through the aperture by which he had entered, and returned home. And now that he was conversant with the route, he began to make regular use of it.

But their pleasure, being so immense and so continuous, attracted the envy of Fortune, who brought about a calamity, turning the joy of the two lovers into tears and sorrow.

From time to time, Prince Tancredi was in the habit of going alone to visit his daughter, with whom he would stay and converse for a while in her chamber and then go away. And one day, after breakfast, he came down to see her, entering her room without anyone hearing or noticing, only to discover that the princess (whose name was Ghismonda) had gone into her garden with all her ladies-in-waiting. Not wishing to disturb her whilst she was enjoying her walk in the garden, he sat down to wait for her on a low stool at a corner of her bed. The windows of the room were closed, and the bed-curtains had been drawn aside, and Tancredi rested his head against the side of the bed, drew the curtain round his body as though to conceal himself there on purpose, and fell asleep.

Whilst he was asleep, Ghismonda, who unfortunately had made an appointment with Guiscardo for that very day, left her attendants in the garden and stole quietly into the room, locking herself in without perceiving that anyone was there. Having opened the door for Guiscardo, who was waiting for her, they then went to bed in the usual way; but whilst they were playing and cavorting together, Tancredi chanced to wake up, and heard and saw what Guiscardo and his daughter were doing. The sight filled him with dismay, and at first he wanted to cry out to them, but then he decided to hold his peace and, if possible, remain hidden, so that he could carry out, with greater prudence and less detriment to his honour, the plan of action that had already taken shape in his mind.

The two lovers remained together for a considerable time, as was their custom, without noticing Tancredi; and when they felt it was time for them to part, they got up from the bed and Guiscardo returned to the cavern. She too left the room, and Tancredi, though he was getting on in years, clambered through a window and lowered himself into the garden without being seen, returning thence in deep distress to his own apartment.

On Tancredi's orders, Guiscardo was taken prisoner by two guards soon after dark that very night, just as he was emerging, hindered by the suit of leather he was wearing, from the hole in the ground. He was then conducted in secret to Tancredi, who almost burst into tears on seeing him, and said:

'Guiscardo, my benevolence towards you deserved a better reward than the shameful deed I saw you committing today, with my own eyes, against that which belongs to me.'

By way of reply, all that Guiscardo said was:

'Neither you nor I can resist the power of Love.'

Tancredi then ordered him to be placed under secret guard in one of the inner rooms, and this was done.

Ghismonda knew nothing of this, and after breakfast on the next day, Tancredi, who had been thinking all manner of strange and terrible thoughts, paid his usual call upon his daughter in her chamber. And having locked the door behind him, his eyes filled with tears, and he said to her:

'Never having doubted your virtue and honesty, Ghismonda, it would never have occurred to me, whatever people might have said, that you would ever so much as think of yielding to a man who was not your husband. But now I have actually seen you doing it with my own eyes, and the memory of it will always torment me during what little remains of my old age.

'Moreover, since you felt bound to bring so much dishonour upon yourself, in God's name you might at least have chosen someone whose rank was suited to your own. But of all the people who frequent my court, you have to choose Guiscardo, a youth of exceedingly base condition, whom we took into our court and raised from early childhood mainly out of charity. Your conduct has faced me with an appalling dilemma, inasmuch as I have no idea how I am to deal with you. I have already come to a decision about Guiscardo, who is under lock and key, having been arrested last night on my orders as he was emerging from the cavern; but God knows what I am to do with you. I am drawn in one direction by the love I have always borne you, deeper by far than that of any other father for a daughter; but on the other hand I seethe with all the indignation that the folly of your actions demands. My love prompts me to forgive you; my indignation demands that I should punish you without mercy, though it would be against my nature to do so. But before I reach any decision, I should like to hear what you have to say for yourself on the subject.' And so saying, he lowered his gaze and began to wail as though he were a child who had been soundly beaten.

Realizing, from what her father had said, that not only had her secret been discovered but Guiscardo was captured, Ghismonda was utterly overcome with sorrow, and needed all the self-control she possessed to prevent herself from screaming and sobbing as most other women would have done. But her proudness of heart more than made up for her shattered spirits, and by a miraculous effort of will, she remained impassive, and rather than make excuses for herself, she resolved to live no longer, being convinced that her Guiscardo was already dead.

She therefore allowed no trace of contrition or womanly distress to cloud her features, but addressed her father in a firm, unworried voice, staring him straight in the face without a single tear in her eyes.

'Tancredi,' she said, 'I am resolved neither to contradict you nor to implore your forgiveness, because denial would be pointless and I want none of your clemency. Nor do I have the slightest intention of appealing either to your better nature or to your affection. On the contrary, I propose to tell you the whole truth, setting forth convincing arguments in defence of my good name, and afterwards I shall act unflinchingly in accordance with the promptings of my noble heart. It is true that I loved Guiscardo, and that I love him still. I shall continue to love him until I die, which I expect to do very soon. And if people love each other beyond the grave, I shall never cease to love him. I was prompted to act as I did, not so much by my womanly frailty as by your lack of concern to marry me, together with his own outstanding worth. You are made of flesh and blood, Tancredi, and it should have been obvious to you that the daughter you fathered was also made of flesh and blood, and not of stone or iron. Although you are now an old man, you should have remembered, indeed you should still remember, the nature and power of the laws of youth. And although much of your own youth was spent in pursuit of military glory, you should nonetheless have realized how the old and the young are alike affected by living in comfort and idleness.

'As I have said, since you were the person who fathered me, I am made of flesh and blood like yourself. Moreover, I am still a young woman. And for both of these reasons, I am full of amorous longings, intensified beyond belief by my marriage, which enabled me to discover the marvellous joy that comes from their fulfilment. As I was incapable of resisting these forces, I made up my mind, being a woman in the prime of life, to follow the path along which they were leading, and I fell in love. But though I was prepared to commit a natural sin, I was determined to spare no effort to ensure that neither your good name nor mine should suffer any harm. To this end, I was assisted by compassionate Love and benign Fortune, who taught me the means whereby I could secretly achieve the fulfilment of my desires. No matter who told you about my secret, no matter how you came to discover it, I do not deny that the thing has happened.

'I did not take a lover at random, as many women do, but deliberately chose Guiscardo in preference to any other, only conceding my love to him after careful reflection; and through the patience and good judgement of us both, I have long been enjoying the gratification of my desires. It seems, however, that you prefer to accept a common fallacy rather than the truth, for you reproach me more bitterly, not for committing the crime of loving a man, but for consorting with a person of lowly rank, thus implying that if I had selected a nobleman for the purpose, you would not have had anything to worry about. You clearly fail to realize that in this respect, your strictures should be aimed, not at me, but at Fortune, who frequently raises the unworthy to positions of eminence and leaves the worthiest in low estate.

'But leaving this aside, consider for a moment the principles of things, and you will see that we are all of one flesh and that our souls were created by a single Maker, who gave the same capacities and powers and faculties to each. We were all born equal, and still are, but merit first set us apart, and those who had more of it, and used it the most, acquired the name of nobles to distinguish them from the rest. Since then, this law has been obscured by a contrary practice, but nature and good manners ensure that its force still remains unimpaired; hence any man whose conduct is virtuous proclaims himself a noble, and those who call him by any other name are in error.

'Consider each of your nobles in turn, compare their lives, their customs and manners with those of Guiscardo, and if you judge the matter impartially, you will conclude that he alone is a patrician whilst all these nobles of yours are plebeians. Besides, it was not through hearsay that Guiscardo's merit and virtues came to my notice, but through your good opinion of him, together with the evidence of my own eyes. For was it not you yourself who sang his praises more loudly than any, claiming for him all the qualities by which one measures a man's excellence? Nor were you mistaken by any means, for unless my eyes have played me false, I have seen him practise the very virtues for which you commended him, in a manner more wonderful than your words could express. So that if I was deceived in my estimate of Guiscardo, it was you alone who deceived me.

'If, then, you maintain that I gave myself to a man of base condi-tion, you are wrong. If, on the other hand, you were to describe him as poor, then perhaps you would be right, and you should hang your head in shame for the paltry rewards you bestowed on so excellent a servant. But in any case, a man's nobility is not affected by poverty, as it is by riches. Many kings, many great princes, were once poor; many a ploughman or shepherd, not only in the past but in the present, was once exceedingly wealthy.

'As for the last of your dilemmas, concerning how you are to deal with me, you can dismiss it from your thoughts entirely. If you are intent, in your extreme old age, upon behaving as you never behaved in your youth, and resorting to cruelty, then let your cruelty be aimed at me, for it was I who caused this so-called sin to be committed. I am resolved not to plead for clemency, and I swear that unless you do the same to me as you have already done, or intend to do, to Guiscardo, these hands of mine will do it for you.

'Now get you hence to shed your tears among the women, and if you think we have earned your cruelty, see that you slaughter us both at one and the same time.'

Although Tancredi knew that his daughter had a will of iron, he doubted her resolve to translate her words into action. So he went away and decided that whilst he would dismiss all thought of venting his rage on Ghismonda, he would cool her ardent passion by taking revenge on her paramour. He therefore ordered the two men who were guarding Guiscardo to strangle him noiselessly that same night, after which they were to take out his heart and bring it to him; and they carried out his orders to the letter.

Early next day, the Prince called for a fine, big chalice made of gold, and having placed Guiscardo's heart inside it, he ordered one of his most trusted servants to take it to his daughter, bidding him utter these words as he handed it over: 'Your father sends you this to comfort you in the loss of your dearest possession, just as you have comforted him in the loss of his.'

After her father had left, Ghismonda, unflinching in her harsh resolve, had called for poisonous herbs and roots, which she then distilled and converted into a potion, so that, if things turned out as she feared, she would have it ready to hand. And when the servant came to her with her father's gift and recited the message, she accepted it with great composure and removed the lid, no sooner seeing the heart and hearing the servant's words than she knew for certain that this was the heart of Guiscardo.

So she looked up at the servant, and said to him:

'Nothing less splendid than a golden sepulchre would have suited so noble a heart; in this respect, my father has acted wisely.'

Having spoken these words, she raised it to her lips and kissed it, then continued:

'Throughout my life, which is now approaching its end, I have had constant reminders of my father's devoted love, but never so patent a token as this. And in thanking him for the last time, I bid you tell him how grateful I was for so priceless a gift.'

Then she turned to the chalice, which she was holding firmly in her two hands, and gazing down upon Guiscardo's heart, she said:

'Ah! dear, sweet vessel of all my joys, cursed be the cruelty of him who has compelled me to see you with the eyes of my body, when it was enough that I should keep you constantly in the eyes of my mind! Your life has run the brief course allotted to it by Fortune, you have reached the end to which all men hasten, and in leaving behind the trials and tribulations of our mortal life, you have received at the hands of your enemy a burial worthy of your excellence. Your funeral rites lacked nothing but the tears of the woman you loved so dearly; but so that you should not be without them, God impelled my pitiless father to send you to me, and I shall cry for you even though I had resolved to die with tearless eyes and features unclouded by fear. And the instant my tears are finished I shall see that my soul is united with that other soul which you kept in your loving care. How could I wish for a better or surer companion as I set forth towards the unknown? I feel certain that his soul still lingers here within you, waiting for mine and surveying the scenes of our mutual happiness, and that our love for one another is as deep and enduring as ever.'

She said no more, but leaned over the chalice, suppressing all sound of womanly grief, and began to cry in a fashion wondrous to behold, her tears gushing forth like water from a fountain; and she implanted countless kisses upon the lifeless heart.

Her ladies-in-waiting, by whom she was surrounded, were at a loss to know what heart this was, nor were they able to make any sense of her words, but they too began to cry in unison, being filled with compassion for their mistress. They pleaded with her to explain why she was weeping, but to no avail; and for all their strenuous efforts, they were unable to console her.

But when she had cried as much as she deemed sufficient, she raised her head from the chalice, and after drying her eyes, she said:

'Oh, heart that I love so dearly, now that I have fully discharged my duties towards you, all that remains to be done is to bring my soul and unite it with yours.'

Having pronounced these words, she called for the phial containing the potion she had prepared on the previous day, and, pouring it into the chalice, where the heart lay bathed in her own abundant tears, she raised the mixture to her lips without any show of fear and drank it. After which, still holding on to the chalice, she climbed on to her bed, arranged herself as decorously as she could, and placing the heart of her dead lover close to her own, she silently waited for death.

Her ladies-in-waiting had no idea what potion it was that she had drunk, but her speech and actions were so strange that they had sent to inform Tancredi of all that was happening, and he, fearing the worst, had hurried down at once to his daughter's chamber, arriving there just as she had settled herself upon the bed. On seeing the state she was in, he tried to console her with honeyed words, and burst into floods of tears, but the time for pity was past, and Ghismonda said to him:

'Save those tears of yours for a less coveted fate than this of mine, Tancredi, and shed them not for me, for I do not want them. Who ever heard of anyone, other than yourself, who wept on achieving his wishes? But if you still retain some tiny spark of your former love for me, grant me one final gift, and since it displeased you that I should live quietly with Guiscardo in secret, see that my body is publicly laid to rest beside his in whatever spot you chose to cast his remains.'

The vehemence of his sobbing prevented the Prince from offering any reply, and the young woman, sensing that she was about to breathe her last, clasped the dead heart tightly to her bosom, saying:

'God be with you all, for I now take my leave of you.'

Then her vision grew blurred, she lost the use of her senses, and she left this life of sorrow behind her.

Thus the love of Guiscardo and Ghismonda came to its sad conclusion, as you have now heard. And as for Tancredi, after shedding countless tears and making tardy repentance for his cruelty, he saw that they were honourably interred together in a single grave, amid the general mourning of all the people of Salerno.

SECOND STORY

Friar Alberto, having given a lady to understand that the Angel Gabriel is in love with her, assumes the Angel's form and goes regularly to bed with her, until, in terror of her kinsfolk, he leaps out of the window and takes shelter in in the house of a pauper; the latter disguises him as a savage and takes him on the following day to the city square, where he is recognized and seized by his fellow friars, and placed under permanent lock and key.

Fiammetta's story had more than once brought tears to the eyes of the other ladies present, but the king seemed quite unmoved by it, for when it came to an end he looked at them sternly and said:

'I would think it a small price to pay if I were to give my life in exchange for one half of the bliss Ghismonda had with Guiscardo. Nor should any of you consider this surprising, because I die a thousand deaths in the course of every hour that I live, without being granted the tiniest portion of bliss in return. But leaving my affairs to take care of themselves for the moment, I will ask Pampinea to continue the proceedings by relating some gruesome tale that has a bearing on my own sorry state. And if she follows Fiammetta's example, I shall doubtless begin to feel one or two dewdrops descend on the fire that rages within me.'

On hearing herself singled out as the next speaker, Pampinea, knowing that her own feelings were a better guide than the king's words to the mood of her companions, was more inclined to amuse them than to satisfy the king in aught but his actual command; and so she decided that without straying from the agreed theme, she would narrate a story to make them laugh, and began thus:

There is a popular proverb which runs as follows: 'He who is wicked and held to be good, can cheat because no one imagines he would.' This saying offers me ample scope to tell you a story on the topic that has been prescribed, and it also enables me to illustrate the extraordinary and perverse hypocrisy of the members of religious orders. They go about in those long, flowing robes of theirs, and when they are asking for alms, they deliberately put on a forlorn expression and are all humility and sweetness; but when they are reproaching you with their own vices, or showing how the laity achieve salvation by almsgiving and the clerics by almsgrabbing, they positively deafen you with their loud and arrogant voices. To hear them talk, one would think they were excused, unlike the rest of us, from working their way to Heaven on their merits, for they behave as though they actually own and govern the place, assigning to every man who dies a position of greater or lesser magnificence there according to the quantity of money he has bequeathed to them in his will. Hence they are pulling a massive confidence trick, of which they themselves, if they really believe what they say, are the earliest victims; but the chief sufferers are the people who take these claims of theirs at their face value.

If only I were allowed to go into the necessary details, I would soon open many a simpleton's eyes to the sort of thing these fellows conceal beneath the ample folds of their habits. However, for the time being we must hope that God will punish their lies by granting to each and every one of them a fate similar to that which befell a certain Franciscan, by no means young in years, who was reputed in Venice to be one of the finest that Assisi had ever attracted to its cause. His story is one that I am especially pleased to relate, because you are all feeling saddened by hearing of Ghismonda's death, and perhaps I can restore your spirits a little by persuading you to laugh and be merry.

In the town of Imola, excellent ladies, there once lived a depraved and wicked fellow by the name of Berto della Massa. The townspeople learned from experience that his dealings were crooked, and he brought himself into so much disrepute that there was not a single person in the whole of Imola who was prepared to believe a word he uttered, no matter whether he was speaking the truth or telling a lie. He therefore perceived that Imola no longer afforded him any outlet for his roguery, and as a last resort he moved to Venice, where the scum of the earth can always find a welcome. There he decided to go in for some different kind of fraud from those he had practised elsewhere, and from the moment of his arrival, as though conscience-stricken by the crimes he had committed in the past, he gave people the impression that he was a man of quite extraordinary humility. What was more, having transformed himself into the most Catholic man who ever lived, he went and became a Franciscan, and styled himself Friar Alberto of Imola. Having donned the habit of his Order, he gave every appearance of leading a harsh, frugal existence, began to preach the virtues of repentance and abstinence, and never allowed a morsel of meat or a drop of wine to pass his lips unless they came up to his exacting standards.

Nobody suspected for a moment that he had been a thief, pander, swindler and murderer before suddenly blossoming into a great preacher; nor had he abandoned any of these vices, for he was simply biding his time until an opportunity arose for him to practise them in secret. His crowning achievement was to get himself ordained as a priest, and whenever he was celebrating mass in the presence of a large congregation, he would shed copious tears for the Passion of the Saviour, being the sort of man who could weep as much as he pleased at little cost to himself.

In short, what with his sermons and shedding of tears, he managed to hoodwink the Venetians so successfully that hardly anyone there made a will without depositing it with him and making him the trustee. Many people handed over their money to him for safe keeping, and he became the father-confessor and confidential adviser to the vast majority of the men and women of the city. Having thus been transformed from a wolf into a shepherd, he acquired a reputation for saintliness far greater than any St Francis had ever enjoyed in Assisi.

Now it happened that a frivolous and scatterbrained young woman, whose name was Monna Lisetta da Ca' Quirino, the wife of a great merchant who had sailed away to Flanders aboard one of his galleys, came to be confessed by this holy friar of ours accompanied by a number of other ladies. Being a Venetian, and therefore capable of talking the hind leg off a donkey, she had only got through a fraction of her business, kneeling all the time at his feet, when Friar Alberto demanded to know whether she had a lover.

'What, Master Friar?' she exclaimed, giving him a withering look. 'Have you no eyes in your head? Does it seem to you that my charms are to be compared to those of these other women? I could have lovers to spare if I wanted them, but my charms are not at the service of every Tom, Dick or Harry who happens to fall in love with them. How often do you come across anyone as beautiful as I? Why, even if I were in Heaven itself, my charms would be thought exceptional.'

But this was only the beginning, and she droned on interminably, going into such raptures about this beauty of hers that it was painful to listen to her.

Friar Alberto had sensed immediately that she was something of a half-wit, and realizing that she was ripe for the picking, he fell passionately in love with her there and then. This was hardly the moment, however, for whispering sweet nothings in her ear, and in order to show her how godly he was, he got up on to his high horse, reproached her for being vainglorious and made her listen to a great deal more of his balderdash. The lady retorted by calling him an ignoramus, and asserting that he was incapable of distinguishing one woman's beauty from another's. And since he did not want to irritate her unduly, Friar Alberto, having heard the rest of her confession, allowed her to proceed on her way with the others.

After biding his time for a few days, he went with a trusted companion to call upon Monna Lisetta at her own house, and, having got her to take him into a room where nobody could see what he was doing, he threw himself on his knees before her, saying:

'Madam, in God's name I beseech you to forgive me for talking to you as I did on Sunday last, when you were telling me about your beauty. That same night, I was punished so severely for my insolence that I have been laid up in bed ever since, and was only able to rise again today for the first time.'

'Who was it who punished you, then?' asked Lady Numskull.

'I will tell you about it,' said Friar Alberto. 'When I was praying in my cell that night, as I invariably do, I suddenly saw a great pool of radiant light, and before I was able to turn round and discover its source, I caught sight of an incredibly handsome young man, standing over me with a heavy stick in his hand. He grabbed me by the scruff of the neck, dragged me to the floor at his feet, and beat me so severely that my body was an aching mass of weals and bruises. When I asked him why he had done it, he replied: "Because, earlier today, you had the infernal cheek to speak ill of Monna Lisetta's celestial charms, and apart from God himself there is no one I love so dearly." I then asked him who he was, and he told me that he was the Angel Gabriel. "Oh, sir," said I, "I beg you to forgive me." "Very well," said he, "I shall forgive you, but on this sole condition, that you pay a personal call on the lady at your earliest opportunity and offer her your apologies. And should she refuse to accept them, I shall come back here again and give you such a hiding that you will never recover from it." He then went on to tell me something else, but I dare not tell you what it was unless you forgive me first.'

Being somewhat feeble in the upper storey, Lady Bighead believed every word and felt positively giddy with joy. She paused a little, then said:

'You see, Friar Alberto? I told you my charms were celestial. However, so help me God, I do feel sorry for you, and in order to spare you any further injury I shall pardon you forthwith, but only on condition that you tell me what it was that the Angel said next.'

'Since I am forgiven, madam, I will gladly tell you,' he replied. 'However, I must ask you to take great care never to repeat it to another living soul, because by so doing you will ruin everything and you will no longer be the luckiest woman alive, as you assuredly are at present.

'The Angel Gabriel asked me to tell you that he had taken such a liking to you that he would have come to spend the night with you on several occasions except for the fact that you might have been frightened. He now charges me to inform you that he would like to come to you on some night in the near future and spend a little time in your company. But since he is an angel and would not be able to

touch you if he were to come in his own angelic form, he says that
for your own pleasure he would prefer to come in the form of a man.
He therefore desires that you should let him know when, and in
whose form, you would like him to come, and he will carry out your
instructions to the letter. Hence you have every reason to regard
yourself as the most blessed woman on earth.'

Lady Noodle said she was delighted to hear that the Angel Gabriel
was in love with her, for she herself was greatly devoted to him and
never failed to light a fourpenny candle in his honour whenever she
came across a painting in which he was depicted. So far as she was
concerned, he would be welcome to visit her whenever he pleased,
but only if he promised not to desert her for the Virgin Mary, of
whom it was said that he was a great admirer, as seemed to be borne
out by the fact that in all the paintings she had seen of him, he was
invariably shown kneeling in front of the Virgin. As for the form in
which he should visit her, she would leave the choice entirely to him
so long as he was careful not to give her a fright.

'You speak wisely, madam,' said Friar Alberto, 'and I shall certainly
arrange for him to do as you suggest. But I want to ask you a great
favour and one that will cost you nothing, namely, that you should
instruct him to use this body of mine for the purpose of his visit. The
reason is this, that when he enters my body, he will remove my soul
and set it down in Heaven, where it will stay for the whole of the
time he remains in your company.'

'What a good idea!' said Lady Birdbrain. 'It will make up for the
blows he gave you on my account.'

'Very well, then,' said Friar Alberto. 'Now remember to leave
your door unlocked for him tonight, because otherwise, since he will
be arriving inside a human body, he will be unable to get in.'

The woman assured him that it would be done, and Friar Alberto
took his leave of her. As soon as he had gone, she strutted up and down
sticking her head so high in the air that her smock rose clear of her
bottom, and thinking that the hour for the Angel Gabriel's visit
would never come, so slowly did the time seem to pass.

Meanwhile, Friar Alberto, working on the assumption that his role
would be that of a paladin rather than an angel during the night
ahead, began to gorge himself on sweetmeats and various other

delicacies so as to ensure that he would not be easily thrown from his mount. And as soon as darkness had fallen, having received permission to be absent, he departed with a companion and went to the house of a lady-friend which he had used as his base before when setting out to sow his wild oats. At what he judged a suitable hour, he made his way thence, suitably disguised, to Monna Lisetta's house; and having let himself in, he transfigured himself into an angel with the aid of certain gewgaws that he had brought along for the purpose. Then he climbed the stairs and strode into her bedroom.

When she saw this pure white object advancing towards her, the woman fell upon her knees before it. The Angel gave her his blessing, helped her to her feet, and motioned her to get into bed. This she promptly did, being only too ready to obey, and the Angel lay down at his votary's side.

Friar Alberto was a powerful, handsomely-proportioned fellow at the peak of physical fitness, and his approach to the bedding of Monna Lisetta, who was all soft and fresh, was altogether different from the one employed by her husband; hence he flew without wings several times before the night was over, causing the lady to shriek with delight at his achievements, which he supplemented with a running commentary on the glories of Heaven. Then, shortly before dawn, having made arrangements to visit her again, he collected his trappings and returned to his companion, with whom the mistress of the house had generously bedded down for the night so that he would not be afraid of the dark.

After breakfast, the lady went with her maidservant to call upon Friar Alberto and brought him tidings of the Angel Gabriel, describing what he was like, repeating all the things he had told her about the glories of the Life Eternal, and filling out her account with wondrous inventions of her own.

'Madam,' said Friar Alberto, 'I know not how you fared with him. But I do know that when he came to see me last night and I gave him your message, he immediately took my soul and set it down amid a multitude of flowers and roses, more wonderful to behold than anything that was ever seen on earth. And there I remained until matins this morning, in one of the most delectable places ever created by God. As for my actual body, I haven't the slightest idea what became of it.'

'But that's exactly what I am telling you,' said the lady. 'Your body spent the whole night in my arms with the Angel Gabriel inside it. And if you don't believe me, take a look under your left breast, where I gave the Angel such an enormous kiss that it will leave its mark there for the best part of a week.'

'In that case,' said Friar Alberto, 'I shall undress myself later today – which is a thing I have not done for a very long time – in order to see whether you are telling the truth.'

The woman chattered away for a good while longer before returning once more to her own house, which from then on Friar Alberto visited regularly without encountering let or hindrance.

One day, however, Monna Lisetta was chatting with a neighbour of hers, and their conversation happened to touch upon the subject of physical beauty. She was determined to prove that no other woman was as beautiful as herself, and, being a prize blockhead, she remarked:

'You would soon cease to prattle about the beauty of other women if I were to tell you who has fallen for mine.'

At this, her neighbour's curiosity was thoroughly aroused, and, well knowing the sort of woman with whom she was dealing, she replied:

'You may well be right, my dear, but you can hardly expect to convince me unless I know who it is that you are talking about.'

'My good woman,' retorted Monna Lisetta, who was quick to take offence, 'I should not be telling you this, but my admirer is the Angel Gabriel, who loves me more than his very self. And he informs me that it is all because I am the most beautiful woman on the face of the earth, or the face of the water for that matter.'

Her neighbour wanted to burst out laughing there and then, but being eager to draw Monna Lisetta out a little further on the subject, she continued to keep a straight face.

'God bless my soul!' she exclaimed. 'If your admirer is the Angel Gabriel, my dear, and if he tells you this, then it must be perfectly true. But I never imagined the angels did this sort of thing.'

'That is where you are mistaken,' said the lady. 'I swear to you by God's wounds that he does it better than my husband, and he informs me that they do it up there as well. But he has fallen in love with me because he thinks me more beautiful than any of the women in Heaven, and he is forever coming down to keep me company. So there!'

On leaving Monna Lisetta, her friend could scarcely contain her eagerness to repeat what she had heard, and at the earliest opportunity, whilst attending a party with a number of other ladies, she recounted the whole of the story from beginning to end. These ladies passed the tale on to their husbands and to various of their female acquaintances, and thus within forty-eight hours the news was all over Venice. Unfortunately, however, the brothers of Monna Lisetta's husband were among those to whose ears the story came, and they firmly made up their minds, without breathing a word to the lady herself, to run this angel to earth and discover whether he could fly. And for several nights running they lay in wait for his coming.

Some tiny hint of what had occurred chanced to reach the ears of Friar Alberto, who, having called upon the lady one night with the intention of giving her a scolding, had scarcely stripped off his clothes before her brothers-in-law, who had seen him arrive at the house, were hammering at the door and trying to force it open. Hearing the noise and guessing what it signified, Friar Alberto leapt out of bed, and seeing that there was nowhere to hide, he threw open a window overlooking the Grand Canal and took a flying leap into the water.

Friar Alberto was a good swimmer, and because the water was deep he came to no harm. Having swum across the canal, he dashed through the open door of a house on the other bank, and pleaded with its tenant, an honest-looking fellow, to save his life for the love of God, spinning him some yarn to account for his arrival there at such a late hour in a state of nudity.

The honest man took pity on him, and since he was in any case obliged to go and attend to certain affairs of his, he tucked the Friar up in his own bed and told him to stay there until he returned. And having locked him in, he went about his business.

On forcing their way into her room, the lady's in-laws discovered that the Angel Gabriel had flown, leaving his wings behind. They were feeling discountenanced, to say the least, and bombarded the woman with a torrent of violent abuse, after which they left her there, alone and disconsolate, and returned home with the Angel's bits and pieces.

Meanwhile, in the clear light of morning, the honest man happened to be passing through the Rialto district when he heard people talking about how the Angel Gabriel, having gone to spend the night with Monna Lisetta, had been discovered there by her in-laws, whereupon he had hurled himself into the canal in a fit of terror, thereafter vanishing without trace. The man immediately realized that the person in question was none other than the one he was sheltering under his roof, and having returned to the house, he persuaded the Friar, after turning a deaf ear to a string of tall stories, to admit that this was indeed the case. The man then insisted on being paid fifty ducats in exchange for keeping the Friar's whereabouts secret from the lady's in-laws, and the two of them devised a way for the payment to be made.

Once the money had been handed over, Friar Alberto was anxious to get away from the place, and the honest man said to him:

'There is only one way of doing it, but it won't work unless you are willing to cooperate. Today we are holding a carnival, to which everyone has to bring a partner wearing some form of disguise, so that one man will be dressed up as a bear, another as a savage, and so on and so forth. To round off the festivities, there is to be a sort of fancy-dress hunt, or *caccia*, in St Mark's Square, after which all the people disperse, going off wherever they choose and taking their partners with them. Now if, instead of lying low here until someone gets wind of your whereabouts, you were to let me take you along in one of these disguises, after the ceremony I could leave you off wherever you wished. Apart from this, I can think of no other way for you to escape from here without being recognized, because the lady's in-laws have realized that you must have gone to ground somewhere in this part of the city, and their men are keeping watch over the whole neighbourhood, ready to seize hold of you the moment you appear.'

Although he baulked at the notion of going about the streets in a disguise of this sort, Friar Alberto was so terrified of the lady's in-laws that he allowed himself to be persuaded, and he told the fellow where he wanted to be taken, leaving him to work out the actual details.

The man applied a thick layer of honey to the Friar's body, after which he covered him with downy feathers from head to foot. He then tied a chain round his neck, put a mask over his face, and placed a club in one of his hands, whilst to the Friar's other hand he tethered two enormous dogs which he had collected earlier from the slaughter-house. Meanwhile, he sent an accomplice to the Rialto to announce that anyone wishing to see the Angel Gabriel should hurry along to St Mark's Square – which goes to show how far you can trust a Venetian.

Once these preparations were complete, the man waited a little longer and brought the Friar forth, getting him to lead the way whilst he held on to him from behind by means of the chain. Eventually, having stirred up a great commotion along the route and provoked the question 'Whoever is it?' from all the people he met, he drove his captive into the square. And what with all the crowds following in his wake, and those who had flocked from the Rialto after hearing the announcement, there were so many people in the square that it was impossible to count them. Upon his arrival, the man had tied his savage to a pillar in an elevated and conspicuous position, and was now pretending to wait for the mock-hunt, or *caccia*, to begin, whilst the Friar, since he was smeared with honey, was being pestered by hordes of gnats and gadflies.

When he saw that the square was more or less filled to capacity, the man stepped towards his savage as though to release him. But instead of setting him free, he tore the mask from Friar Alberto's face, pro-claiming:

'Ladies and gentlemen, since the pig refuses to put in an appearance, there is not going to be any *caccia*. But so that you will not feel that your coming here was a waste of time, I want you to see the Angel Gabriel, who descends by night from Heaven to earth to amuse the women of Venice.'

As soon as his mask was removed, Friar Alberto was immediately recognized by all the onlookers, who jeered at him in unison, calling him by the foulest names and shouting the filthiest abuse ever to have been hurled at any scoundrel in history, at the same time pelting his face with all the nastiest things they could lay their hands upon. They kept this up without stopping, and would have gone on all night but for the fact that half-a-dozen or so of his fellow friars, having heard what was going on, made their way to the scene. The first thing they did on arriving was to throw a cape over his shoulders, after which they set him free and escorted him back, leaving a tremendous commotion in their wake, to their own quarters, where they placed him under lock and key. And there he is believed to have eked out the rest of his days in wretchedness and misery.

Thus it was that this arch-villain, whose wicked deeds went unnoticed because he was held to be good, had the audacity to transform himself into the Angel Gabriel. In the end, however, having been turned from an angel into a savage, he got the punishment he deserved, and repented in vain for the crimes he had committed. May it please God that a similar fate should befall each and every one of his fellows.

THIRD STORY

Three young men fall in love with three sisters and elope with them to Crete. The eldest sister kills her lover in a fit of jealousy; the second, by giving herself to the Duke of Crete, saves her sister's life but is in turn killed by her own lover, who flees with the eldest sister. The murder is imputed to the third lover and the third sister, who are arrested and forced to make a confession. Fearing execution, they bribe their gaolers and flee, impoverished, to Rhodes, where they die in penury.

On finding that Pampinea had reached the end of her story, Filostrato brooded for a while, then turned to her and said:

'The ending of your story was not without a modicum of merit, from which I drew a certain satisfaction. But there was far too much matter of a humorous kind in the part that preceded it, and this I would have preferred to do without.'

He then turned to Lauretta, and said:

'Madam, pray proceed with a better tale if possible.'

'You are being much too unkind toward lovers,' she replied, laughing, 'if all you demand is an unhappy ending to their adventures. However, for the sake of obedience I shall tell you a story about three lovers, all of whom met an unpleasant fate before they were able to enjoy their separate loves to the full.'

Then she began:

Young ladies, as you are perfectly well aware, all vices can bring enormous sorrow to those who practise them, and in many cases they also bring affliction to others. But it seems to me that the one that leads us into danger more swiftly than any other is the vice of anger. For anger is nothing more than a sudden, thoughtless impulse, which, set in motion by a feeling of resentment, expels all reason, plunges the mind's eye into darkness, and sets our hearts ablaze with raging fury. And although men are not immune from this particular vice, and some men are more prone to it than others, nevertheless it has been observed to produce its most catastrophic effects among the ladies, for they catch fire more easily, their anger burns more fiercely, and they are carried away by it without offering more than a token resistance.

Nor is this fact surprising, for if we examine the matter closely, we shall see that fire, by its very nature, is more likely to be kindled in those things which are light in weight and soft in texture than in harder and heavier objects. And if the gentlemen will forgive me for saying so, we are invariably more delicate than they are, as well as being much more capricious.

Bearing in mind, then, that we have a natural propensity to fly into a temper, that our cheerfulness and mildness of manner have a pleasing and very soothing effect upon our menfolk, and that anger and fury can bring about so much peril and anguish, I intend to strengthen our will to resist this vice by telling this story of mine, which, as I have already said, concerns the love of three young men and three young women, and which shows how, through the anger of one of these latter, their happiness was transformed into complete and utter misery.

Marseilles, as you know, is an ancient and illustrious city on the coast of Provence, and it used to boast a larger number of wealthy citizens and great merchants than appears to be the case nowadays. One of these was a certain N'Arnald Civada, who, despite his exceedingly humble origins, had built himself a firm reputation as an honest merchant and amassed a huge fortune, both in money and capital goods. His wife presented him with a number of children, of whom the eldest three were girls, whilst all the rest were boys. Two of the girls were fifteen-year-old twins, the third was fourteen, and marriages had been arranged for all three by their kinsfolk, who were simply waiting for the return of N'Arnald from Spain, whither he had gone with a consignment of merchandise. The names of the first two girls were Ninetta and Maddalena; the third was called Bertella.

Ninetta was loved, with the devotion of his entire being, by a young man called Restagnone, who was poor but of noble birth. The girl reciprocated his love, and they had managed to devise a way of consummating it without revealing the fact to a living soul. They had already been enjoying the fruits of their love for quite some time when two young men called Folco and Ughetto, who were mutual friends and whose fathers had died, leaving them very wealthy, happened to fall in love with Maddalena and Bertella respectively.

It was Ninetta who first drew Restagnone's attention to this, and having confirmed that it was so, he cudgelled his brains for a way of using the young men's loves to repair his own fortunes. Having struck up an acquaintance with them, he made a practice of taking them, sometimes individually and sometimes together, to visit the three young ladies. And one day, when he felt that he was on sufficiently friendly and familiar terms with the two young men, he invited them round to his house, and said to them:

'My dear young friends, we have now become well enough acquainted for you to perceive the strength of my affection towards you, and to realize that I would work no less zealously in the pursuit of your interests than I would in pursuing my own. Because of my deep affection for you, I am going to lay before you a certain proposal of mine, which you will be free to reject or act upon as you think proper. If you have been speaking the truth, and if I rightly interpret what I have observed of your conduct over a great many days and nights, you burn with passionate love for the two young ladies whose sister is the object of my own no less ardent devotion. Being firmly resolved to assuage these fiery torments of ours, I have concocted a very sweet and pleasant remedy, which, provided you give your consent, will assuredly do the trick. Allow me to explain.

You young men are very rich and I am not. If you will give me a third share in your combined wealth, and decide whereabouts in the world you would like us to go and live happily with our ladies, I will undertake without fail to persuade the three sisters to come with us to the place we have chosen, bringing with them a substantial part of their father's fortune. Each of us will have his own lady, and we shall be able to live as three brothers, more contented than any other men on earth. That is my proposal, and now it is up to you to decide whether you are going to act upon it or turn it down.'

The two youths were exceedingly lovesick, and once they had heard that they were to have their ladies, they had no difficulty in making up their minds, telling Restagnone that if things turned out in the manner he had described, they were ready to do as he asked. A few days after receiving this answer from the two young men, Restagnone found himself alone with Ninetta, with whom every so often he was able to consort, but only at great inconvenience. Having dallied with her for a while, he told her about the discussion he had had with the young men, and plied her with numerous arguments in an effort to win her over to his scheme. This, however, was a relatively easy matter, for she was even more anxious than he was that they should be able to meet freely, without the constant fear of being discovered. And after pledging him her full support and assuring him that her sisters would follow her advice, especially in this particular matter, she asked him to make all necessary preparations as quickly as possible. Restagnone returned to the two youths, who pressed him a great deal on the subject of their earlier discussion, and he told them that as far as their ladies were concerned the whole thing was settled. Having chosen Crete as the place to which they should go, they sold certain properties of theirs under the pretext of using the proceeds for a trading expedition, converted everything else they possessed into hard cash, purchased a brigantine, which they provisioned in secret on a lavish scale, and waited for the appointed day to come. For her part, Ninetta, who had a very clear notion of the wishes of her two sisters, described the scheme to them in such glowing colours and fired them with so much enthusiasm that they thought they would never live long enough to see it carried out. When the night finally arrived for them to go aboard the brigantine, the three sisters opened up a huge chest belonging to their father and took a large amount of money and jewellery from it, which they carried quietly away from the house according to plan. Their three lovers were waiting for them, and all six hurried aboard the brigantine, which immediately weighed anchor and put out to sea. After an unbroken voyage, they arrived next evening in Genoa, where the new lovers enjoyed the first delectable fruits of their love.

Having taken on all the fresh provisions they needed, they put to sea again, making their way unimpeded from one port to the next until, a week later, they arrived in Crete. There, not far from Candia, they purchased vast and magnificent estates, upon which they built houses of great beauty and splendour. And what with their large retinue of servants, their dogs, their birds, and their horses, they began to live like lords, banqueting and merrymaking and rejoicing in the company of their ladies, the most contented men on God's earth.

This, then, was their way of life. But as we all know from experience, a surfeit of good things often leads to sorrow, and now that Restagnone, who had once been very much in love with Ninetta, was able to possess her whenever he liked without fear of discovery, he began to have second thoughts about her, with the result that his love began to wane. Furthermore, he was powerfully attracted to a beautiful and gently bred young woman of the neighbourhood whom he had glimpsed at a banquet, and he began to court her with the maximum of zeal, paying her extravagant compliments and putting on entertainments for her benefit. When Ninetta perceived what was happening, she was so distraught with jealousy that he was unable to make a move without her getting wind of it and pelting him with so much abuse and hostility that she made Restagnone's life a misery as well as her own.

In the same way, however, that a surfeit of good things generates distaste, so the withholding of a desired object sharpens the appetite, and Ninetta's resentment merely served to fan the flames of Restagnone's new-born love. Whether or not he eventually succeeded in possessing his beloved, we shall never know. But at all events somebody or other convinced Ninetta that he had, and she fell into a state of deep melancholy, which rapidly gave way to anger and finally to blazing fury. All her former love for Restagnone was transformed into bitter hatred, and in a paroxysm of rage she resolved to murder him and thus avenge the affront she believed him to have offered her. Having called in an old Greek woman who was expert in the preparation of poisons, she persuaded her by means of gifts and promises to concoct a lethal potion. And one evening, without giving the matter a second thought, she served this up to Restagnone, who was feeling thirsty because of the heat and was totally off his guard. The drink was so potent that it finished him off before matins, and the news of his death was sent to Folco, Ughetto, and their ladies. Without knowing that he had been poisoned, they joined their own bitter tears to those of Ninetta, and saw that he was given an honourable burial.

But a few days later, it happened that because of some other piece of villainy, the old woman who had concocted the poisonous potion for Ninetta was arrested. Under torture, she confessed to this particular crime along with the others she had committed, and supplied a full account of what had happened. The Duke of Crete said nothing about it to anyone, but one night he threw a cordon round Folco's palace, quietly arrested Ninetta, and took her away without a struggle. There was no need to resort to torture, for he very quickly learned from Ninetta everything he wanted to know about Restagnone's death.

Folco and Ughetto had been secretly informed by the Duke of the reason for Ninetta's arrest, and they in turn informed their ladies. All four were greatly distressed, and spared no effort to save Ninetta from being burnt at the stake, which was the punishment to which they realized she would be condemned, as she richly deserved. But the Duke was determined that justice should take its course, and it seemed that there was nothing they could do to make him change his mind.

Maddalena was a strikingly beautiful young woman, and for some little time she had been the object of the Duke's affection. She had never given him the slightest encouragement, but she now thought that by placating his desires she would be able to rescue her sister from the fire, and she informed him through a trusted messenger that she was ready to do his bidding on two conditions: first, that her sister should be returned to her unharmed; and secondly, that the whole matter should be kept secret. On receipt of the message, the sound of which was much to his liking, the Duke devoted a great deal of thought to it and in the end agreed to its terms, sending back word to that effect. And one evening, with the young woman's prior consent, he had Folco and Ughetto arrested on the pretext of hearing their version of the affair, and secretly went to spend the night with Maddalena. First, however, he had tied Ninetta up in a sack and made it appear that he intended to dump her in the sea, instead of which he took her with him and presented her to her sister by way of payment for his night of pleasure. Next morning, before leaving, he begged Maddalena not to look upon this first night of their love as the last they would spend together, and implored her to send her guilty sister away so that he should not be taken to task and compelled to put her on trial all over again.

That same morning, Folco and Ughetto were released, having been told that Ninetta had been executed by drowning in the course of the night. Believing this to be true, they returned home to comfort their ladies in the death of their sister, and although Maddalena made every effort to conceal her from Folco, he nevertheless discovered, much to his astonishment, that she was there. His suspicions were immediately aroused, for he had already heard it said that the Duke was in love with Maddalena, and he demanded to know how it came about that Ninetta was in the house.

Maddalena spun him a long-winded tale in an effort to explain, but he was too shrewd to be taken in by much of what she was saying, and kept pressing her to tell him the truth. She talked and talked, but in the end she had to tell him. Folco was overcome with dismay, and in a fit of blazing fury he drew out his sword and killed her, turning a deaf ear to her pleas for mercy. Fearing the Duke's wrath and retribution, he left her dead body where it lay and went off in search of Ninetta, whom he greeted with a false show of gaiety, saying:

'Let us go at once to the place where your sister has decided that I should take you, so that you won't fall into the Duke's hands a second time.'

Ninetta, who trusted him implicitly, was a frightened woman, and was only too anxious to make good her escape. By now it was already dark, and without stopping to bid her sister farewell, she and Folco set out, taking with them all the money he could lay his hands upon, which did not amount to very much. On reaching the sea-coast they took to a boat, and that was the last that was ever heard of them.

Next morning, when Maddalena's body was discovered, the Duke was immediately informed of the murder by certain people who had long regarded Ughetto with hatred and envy. The Duke, who was deeply in love with Maddalena, rushed to the house breathing fire and slaughter, arrested Ughetto and his lady, and forced them (though they were as yet ignorant of what had happened) to confess that they were jointly responsible with Folco for Maddalena's death.

In view of this confession, they were afraid, not without reason, that they would be put to death, and so they very cleverly bribed the men appointed to guard them by handing over a certain sum of money which they always kept hidden in the house for when it might be needed. There was no time to lose, and leaving behind all their possessions, they boarded a ship with their gaolers and fled under cover of darkness to Rhodes, where shortly thereafter they ended their days in poverty and distress.

And so it was that Restagnone's reckless love and Ninetta's anger brought ruin, not only to themselves, but also to others.

FOURTH STORY

Gerbino, violating a pledge given by his grandfather King William, attacks a ship belonging to the King of Tunis with the object of abducting the latter's daughter. She is killed by those aboard the ship, he kills them, and afterwards he is beheaded.

Her story having come to an end, Lauretta was now silent whilst various members of the company turned to their neighbours, lamenting the fate of the lovers. Some of them blamed it all on Ninetta's anger, but opinion was divided on this point, and they were still debating the pros and cons among themselves when the king, who all this time had seemed rapt in meditation, looked up and gave Elissa a signal to proceed. And in tones of humility she began, as follows:

Winsome ladies, there are many who believe that Love looses his arrows only when kindled by the eyes, and who regard with contempt anyone who maintains that a person may fall in love on the strength of verbal report. In this belief they are mistaken, as will be seen very clearly in a story I propose to relate, from which you will observe that hearsay not only caused two people to fall in love without ever having seen one another, but also swept each of the lovers to a tragic death.

According to the Sicilians, William the Second, King of Sicily, had two children: a son who was called Ruggieri, and a daughter whose name was Gostanza. Ruggieri died before his father, leaving a son named Gerbino, who, having been carefully reared by his grandfather, grew up to be a strikingly handsome young man and won great renown for his daring and courtesy. His fame was not confined to Sicily itself, but echoed round various parts of the world, flourishing above all in Barbary, which at that time happened to be a tributary to the King of Sicily. The marvellous tales that were told of Gerbino's courtesy and valour reached the ears of a great many people, including a daughter of the King of Tunis – a lady who, in the opinion of all who had seen her, was one of the loveliest creatures ever fashioned by Nature, as well as being the most gracious, and endowed with a truly noble heart. Being very receptive to tales of gallant men, she lovingly treasured the various accounts that filtered through to her on the subject of Gerbino's valorous exploits, and was fascinated by them to such a degree that she formed a mental picture of the sort of man he was, falling passionately in love with him; and nothing gave her greater pleasure than to talk about Gerbino and to listen whenever his name was mentioned by others.

Conversely, astounding reports of her own beauty and excellence had spread amongst other places to Sicily, where they came to the notice of Gerbino, who, far from remaining indifferent, derived no small pleasure from them and began to burn with a love the equal of her own.

Though he longed to see her, he lacked a plausible reason for seeking his grandfather's leave to visit Tunis, and he therefore charged every friend of his who went there to do all he possibly could in the way of drawing attention to his secret and devoted love, and return with tidings of the lady. One of these friends discharged his mission very skilfully, for by posing as a merchant and taking her a quantity of jewels for her to look at, he succeeded in apprising her fully of Gerbino's passionate devotion and in placing him, together with everything he possessed, entirely at her service. The lady's eyes shone with pleasure as she received the envoy and listened to his message, and having assured him that her own regard for Gerbino was no less passionate than his for her, she sent him one of her most valuable jewels as a token of her burning affection. No precious object ever brought greater delight to the person to whom it was sent than this jewel gave to Gerbino, who, using the same messenger, wrote her many letters and sent her the most marvellous presents. And it was understood between them that whenever Fortune offered them a suitable occasion, they would meet and become properly acquainted.

The affair had been dragging on in this fashion for somewhat longer than either of them would have wished, with the young lady pining away in Tunis and Gerbino doing the same in Sicily, when the King of Tunis suddenly announced his intention of marrying her to the King of Granada. This news distressed her enormously, for it meant that not only would a vast distance separate her from her lover but to all intents and purposes she would be kept entirely out of his reach; and if she had been able to devise any way of doing so, she would willingly have run away from her father to forestall such a calamity, and sailed across to Gerbino.

When Gerbino heard of the marriage, he too suffered the agonies of the damned, and vowed repeatedly to himself that if she were to travel to her husband by sea and a suitable opportunity arose, he would carry her off by main force.

Rumours of their love and of Gerbino's resolution came to the ears of the King of Tunis, who was apprehensive of the young man's determination and courage, and when the time for his daughter's departure approached he sent word of his intentions to King William, informing him that as soon as he had his assurance that neither Gerbino nor any of his associates would interfere with his plans, he would carry them into effect. King William, who was getting on in years, had no inkling of Gerbino's love for the lady, and never supposed for a moment that this was the reason why he was being asked for such an assurance. So he freely granted the King of Tunis's request, and sent him his glove as a token of his royal word. Once he had received this pledge, the King of Tunis had a fine, big ship fitted out in the port of Carthage, saw that it was provisioned with everything that the people who were to sail in her would need, and made sure it was embellished and equipped in a suitable style for conveying his daughter to Granada, after which there was nothing left for him to do but sit back and wait for favourable weather.

On observing all this activity and knowing its purpose, the young lady had secretly dispatched one of her servants to Palermo and commissioned him to deliver her greetings to the gallant Gerbino, informing him that she was to leave within a few days for Granada. Thus it would now be seen whether he was as daring a man as people reported, and whether he loved her as deeply as he had so often claimed.

The man whom she entrusted with the embassy carried out her instructions to the letter and returned to Tunis. Gerbino, who had heard all about his grandfather's pledge to the King of Tunis, was at a loss to know how he should react to the lady's message; but under the promptings of his love, not wishing to appear a coward, he hurried off to Messina, where he took over a pair of light galleys and rapidly put them into fighting trim. He then signed on a crew of stouthearted men for each of the vessels, and sailed to Sardinian waters, through which he calculated that the lady's ship would have to pass.

Nor were his calculations very wide of the mark, for within a few days of his arrival in those waters, the lady's ship came sailing up on a light breeze, not far distant from the place where he was waiting to intercept her. On catching sight of the ship, Gerbino turned to address his companions.

'Gentlemen,' he said. 'If you are as gallant as I conceive you to be, I doubt whether there is a single one of you who has never been in love. It is my conviction that no mortal being who is without experience of love can ever lay claim to true excellence. And if you are in love, or have ever been in love, it will not be difficult for you to understand what it is that I desire. For I am in love, gentlemen, and it was love that impelled me to engage you for the task that lies before us. The object of my love dwells out there upon that ship, which not only holds that which I desire above all else, but is crammed to the gunwales with treasure. If you are brave, and fight manfully, it will not be too difficult for us to take possession of these riches. My only claim upon the spoils of our victory is the lady for whose love I have taken up arms. Everything else I freely concede to you here and now. Let us set forth, then, and assail the ship whilst Fortune smiles upon us. God favours our enterprise, for He has stilled all breezes, and the ship is lying out there at our mercy.'

The dashing youth need not have wasted so many words, for the Messinese who were with him, being avid for plunder, already had visions of themselves performing the deed to which Gerbino was inciting them with his oratory. So that when he reached the end of his speech, they filled the air with a thunderous roar of approval, trumpets were sounded, and they all took up their weapons. Then they steered for the ship, plying their oars with gusto.

The ship was totally becalmed, and when the people aboard her saw the galleys approaching in the distance, they prepared to repel all boarders.

On reaching the ship, Gerbino called upon her officers to come aboard the galleys, unless they wanted a battle on their hands.

Having proclaimed who they were and discovered what it was that their attackers were demanding, the Saracens asserted that what they were doing was in breach of the royal pledge, the granting of which they confirmed by displaying King William's glove. At the same time, they made it perfectly clear that they would neither surrender nor give anything away without a fight. Gerbino, who had caught sight of the lady as she stood on the ship's poop, looking infinitely more beautiful than he had pictured her, grew more inflamed with passion than ever before, and when the glove was produced he retorted that since there were no falcons around at that particular moment, the glove was superfluous, adding that if they refused to hand over the lady, they had better look to their weapons. Hostilities commenced without further ado, each side raining arrows and stones upon the other, and in this manner they fought for a long time, doing one another a fair amount of damage. In the end, finding that he was making little headway, Gerbino lowered a small boat that they had brought from Sardinia, set it on fire, and manoeuvred it into a position alongside the ship with the aid of both of his galleys. Perceiving this, and knowing they were faced with the alternative of being roasted alive or surrendering, the Saracens brought the King's daughter up on deck from her cabin, where she had been giving vent to copious tears, and led her to the ship's prow. And having called upon Gerbino to witness the deed, they slaughtered her before his very eyes, whilst all the time she was screaming for help and pleading for mercy. They then cast her body into the sea with the words:

'Take her thus, for we are left with no choice but to let you have her in the form your treachery deserves.'

Upon seeing this act of cruelty, Gerbino seemed to abandon every instinct of self-preservation and edged right alongside the ship, oblivious to stones or arrows. Clambering aboard in defiance of impossible odds, he started laying about him with his sword, cutting down Saracens without mercy on all sides, as though he were a starving lion falling upon a herd of young bullocks and tearing and ripping them apart one after another, intent on appeasing its anger rather than its hunger. By now the fire was spreading rapidly through the ship, and having dispatched a large number of his opponents, Gerbino got his seamen to salvage all they could in return for their services and then abandoned ship, having gained a victory that was anything but rewarding.

He then saw to the recovery from the sea of the fair lady's body, which he mourned over at length, shedding a great many tears. And on returning to Sicily he had it honourably buried on the tiny island of Ustica, which is almost opposite Trapani, whence he returned home sadder than any other man on earth.

When the King of Tunis learned what had happened, he sent ambassadors to King William, dressed in black robes, to protest against his failure to observe his pledge. They explained precisely how it had been broken, to the no small consternation of the King, who, seeing no way of denying them the justice they were demanding, ordered Gerbino to be arrested. And with his own lips, whilst every one of his barons endeavoured to dissuade him, he sentenced Gerbino to death and had him beheaded in his presence, preferring to lose his only grandson rather than gain the reputation of being a monarch whose word was not to be trusted.

Thus, therefore, in the tragic manner I have described and within the space of a few days, the two young lovers met a violent end without ever having tasted the fruits of their love.

FIFTH STORY

Lisabetta's brothers murder her lover. He appears to her in a dream and shows her where he is buried. She secretly disinters the head and places it in a pot of basil, over which she weeps for a long time every day. In the end her brothers take it away from her ,and shortly thereafter she dies of grief.

When Elissa's story came to an end, the king bestowed a few words of praise upon it and then called upon Filomena to speak next. Being quite overcome with compassion for the hapless Gerbino and his lady-love, she fetched a deep sigh, then began as follows:

This story of mine, fair ladies, will not be about people of so lofty a rank as those of whom Elissa has been speaking, but possibly it will prove to be no less touching, and I was reminded of it by the mention that has just been made of Messina, which was where it all happened.

In Messina, there once lived three brothers, all of them merchants who had been left very rich after the death of their father, whose native town was San Gemignano. They had a sister called Lisabetta, but for some reason or other they had failed to bestow her in marriage, despite the fact that she was uncommonly gracious and beautiful.

In one of their trading establishments, the three brothers employed a young Pisan named Lorenzo, who planned and directed all their operations, and who, being rather dashing and handsomely proportioned, had often attracted the gaze of Lisabetta. Having noticed more than once that she had grown exceedingly fond of him, Lorenzo abandoned all his other amours and began in like fashion to set his own heart on winning Lisabetta. And since they were equally in love with each other, before very long they gratified their dearest wishes, taking care not to be discovered.

In this way, their love continued to prosper, much to their common enjoyment and pleasure. They did everything they could to keep the affair a secret, but one night, as Lisabetta was making her way to Lorenzo's sleeping-quarters, she was observed, without knowing it, by her eldest brother. The discovery greatly distressed him, but being a young man of some intelligence, and not wishing to do anything that would bring discredit upon his family, he neither spoke nor made a move, but spent the whole of the night applying his mind to various sides of the matter.

Next morning he described to his brothers what he had seen of Lisabetta and Lorenzo the night before, and the three of them talked the thing over at considerable length. Being determined that the affair should leave no stain upon the reputation either of themselves or of their sister, he decided that they must pass it over in silence and pretend to have neither seen nor heard anything until such time as it was safe and convenient for them to rid themselves of this ignominy before it got out of hand.

Abiding by this decision, the three brothers jested and chatted with Lorenzo in their usual manner, until one day they pretended they were all going off on a pleasure-trip to the country, and took Lorenzo with them. They bided their time, and on reaching a very remote and lonely spot, they took Lorenzo off his guard, murdered him, and buried his corpse. No one had witnessed the deed, and on their return to Messina they put it about that they had sent Lorenzo away on a trading assignment, being all the more readily believed as they had done this so often before.

Lorenzo's continued absence weighed heavily upon Lisabetta, who kept asking her brothers, in anxious tones, what had become of him, and eventually her questioning became so persistent that one of her brothers rounded on her, and said:

'What is the meaning of this? What business do you have with Lorenzo, that you should be asking so many questions about him? If you go on pestering us, we shall give you the answer you deserve.'

From then on, the young woman, who was sad and miserable and full of strange forebodings, refrained from asking questions. But at night she would repeatedly utter his name in a heart-rending voice and beseech him to come to her, and from time to time she would burst into tears because of his failure to return. Nothing would restore her spirits, and meanwhile she simply went on waiting.

One night, however, after crying so much over Lorenzo's absence that she eventually cried herself off to sleep, he appeared to her in a dream, pallid-looking and all dishevelled, his clothes tattered and decaying, and it seemed to her that he said:

'Ah, Lisabetta, you do nothing but call to me and bemoan my long absence, and you cruelly reprove me with your tears. Hence I must tell you that I can never return, because on the day that you saw me for the last time, I was murdered by your brothers.'

He then described the place where they had buried him, told her not to call to him or wait for him any longer, and disappeared.

Having woken up, believing that what she had seen was true, the young woman wept bitterly. And when she arose next morning, she resolved to go to the place and seek confirmation of what she had seen in her sleep. She dared not mention the apparition to her brothers, but obtained their permission to make a brief trip to the country for pleasure, taking with her a maidservant who had once acted as her go-between and was privy to all her affairs. She immediately set out, and on reaching the spot, swept aside some dead leaves and started to excavate a section of the ground that appeared to have been disturbed. Nor did she have to dig very deep before she uncovered her poor lover's body, which, showing no sign as yet of decomposition or decay, proved all too clearly that her vision had been true. She was the saddest woman alive, but knowing that this was no time for weeping, and seeing that it was impossible for her to take away his whole body (as she would dearly have wished), she laid it to rest in a more appropriate spot, then severed the head from the shoulders as best she could and enveloped it in a towel. This she handed into her maidservant's keeping whilst she covered over the remainder of the corpse with soil, and then they returned home, having completed the whole of their task unobserved.

Taking the head to her room, she locked herself in and cried bitterly, weeping so profusely that she saturated it with her tears, at the same time implanting a thousand kisses upon it. Then she wrapped the head in a piece of rich cloth, and laid it in a large and elegant pot, of the sort in which basil or marjoram is grown. She next covered it with soil, in which she planted several sprigs of the finest Salernitan basil, and never watered them except with essence of roses or orange-blossom, or with her own teardrops. She took to sitting permanently beside this pot and gazing lovingly at it, concentrating the whole of her desire upon it because it was where her beloved Lorenzo lay concealed. And after gazing raptly for a long while upon it, she would bend over it and begin to cry, and her weeping never ceased until the whole of the basil was wet with her tears.

Because of the long and unceasing care that was lavished upon it, and also because the soil was enriched by the decomposing head inside the pot, the basil grew very thick and exceedingly fragrant. The young woman constantly followed this same routine, and from time to time she attracted the attention of her neighbours. And as they had heard her brothers expressing their concern at the decline in her good looks and the way in which her eyes appeared to have sunk into their sockets, they told them what they had seen, adding:

'We have noticed that she follows the same routine every day.'

The brothers discovered for themselves that this was so, and having reproached her once or twice without the slightest effect, they caused the pot to be secretly removed from her room. When she found that it was missing, she kept asking for it over and over again, and because they would not restore it to her she sobbed and cried without a pause until eventually she fell seriously ill. And from her bed of sickness she would call for nothing else except her pot of basil.

The young men were astonished by the persistence of her entreaties, and decided to examine its contents. Having shaken out the soil, they saw the cloth and found the decomposing head inside it, still sufficiently intact for them to recognize it as Lorenzo's from the curls of his hair. This discovery greatly amazed them, and they were afraid lest people should come to know what had happened. So they buried the head, and without breathing a word to anyone, having wound up their affairs in Messina, they left the city and went to live in Naples.

The girl went on weeping and demanding her pot of basil, until eventually she cried herself to death, thus bringing her ill-fated love to an end. But after due process of time, many people came to know of

the affair, and one of them composed the song which can still be
heard to this day:

> Whoever it was,
> Whoever the villain
> That stole my pot of herbs, etc.

SIXTH STORY

*Andreuola loves Gabriotto. She tells him of a dream she has had, and he tells
her of another. He dies suddenly in her arms, and whilst she and a maidservant of hers are carrying him back to his own house, they are arrested by
the officers of the watch. She explains how matters stand, and the chief
magistrate attempts to ravish her, but she wards him off. Her father is
informed, her innocence is established, and he secures her release. Being
determined not to go on living in the world, she enters a nunnery.*

The story related by Filomena was much appreciated by the ladies,
for they had heard this song on a number of occasions without ever
succeeding, for all their inquiries, in discovering why it had been
written. It was now Panfilo's turn, and as soon as the king had heard
the concluding words of the previous tale, he instructed him to proceed. Panfilo therefore began:

The dream referred to n the last story offers me a pretext for
narrating a tale in which two dreams are mentioned, both of them
relating to a future event as distinct from something, as in Lisabetta's
case, that had already taken place. Moreover, no sooner were they
described by the people who had experienced them than both dreams
came true. For the fact is, dear ladies, that every living being suffers
from the common affliction of seeing various things in his sleep. And
although whilst he is asleep they all seem absolutely real, and after
waking up he judges some to be real, others possible, and a portion
of them totally incredible, nevertheless you will find that many of
them come true in the end.

This explains why a lot of people have just as much faith in their
dreams as they would have in the things they see when they are wide

awake, and why their dreams are sufficient of themselves to make them cheerful if they have seen something encouraging, or sorrowful if they have been frightened. At the other extreme there are those who refuse to believe in dreams until they discover that they have fallen into the very predicament of which they were forewarned. In my opinion, neither of these attitudes is commendable, because dreams are neither true every time nor always false. That they are not all true, each of us has frequently had occasion to discover; that they are not all false has been demonstrated a little while ago in Filomena's story, and, as I said earlier, I intend to show it in my own. For I maintain that if one conducts one's life virtuously, there is no reason to be afraid of any dream that encourages one to behave differently or to abandon one's good intentions because of it: and if one harbours perverse and wicked intentions, however much one's dreams appear favourable to these and encourage one to pursue them by presenting auspicious omens, none of them should be believed, whilst full credence should be given to those which predict the opposite. But let us turn now to the story.

In the city of Brescia there once lived a nobleman called Messer Negro da Pontecarrara. He had several children, including a daughter whose name was Andreuola, and although she was an exceedingly beautiful young woman, she was as yet unmarried. Andreuola chanced to fall in love with a neighbour of hers called Gabriotto, a man of low estate but full of admirable qualities, as well as being handsome and pleasing in appearance. Aided and abetted by her maidservant, the girl not only succeeded in apprising Gabriotto of her love but had him conveyed regularly into a beautiful garden in the grounds of her father's house, to the mutual joy of the two parties concerned. And so that this delectable love of theirs should never be torn asunder save by the hand of death, they secretly became husband and wife.

They continued to make love by this furtive means until one night, as she lay asleep, the girl had a dream in which she seemed to see herself in the garden with Gabriotto, giving and getting intense pleasure as she held him in her arms: and whilst they were thus occupied, she seemed to see a dark and terrible thing issuing from his body, the form of which she could not make out. The thing appeared to take hold of Gabriotto, and, by exerting some miraculous force, to tear him away from her despite all she could do to prevent it. It then vanished below ground, taking him with it, and they never set eyes upon one another again. Her sorrow was so intense that it woke her up, and although, now that she was awake, she felt relieved that she had merely been imagining all this, she was nevertheless filled with terror because of the dreadful things she had dreamt about. And for this reason, knowing that Gabriotto was anxious to visit her that evening, she did everything in her power to ensure that he stayed away. The following night, however, seeing that he was determined to come, she received him in the garden as usual. The roses were in flower, and she plucked a large number, some red and others white, before going to join him at the edge of a magnificent, crystal-clear fountain situated in the garden. There they disported themselves merrily together for a long while, and afterwards Gabriotto asked her why she had forbidden him to come on the previous evening, whereupon the girl explained to him about the dream she had experienced during the night before, and told him about the forebodings it had aroused in her.

On hearing her explanation, Gabriotto burst out laughing and told her that it was very silly to take any notice of dreams, since they were caused either by overeating or undereating, and they invariably turned out to be meaningless. Then he said:

'If I were the sort of person who takes dreams seriously, I would not have come to see you, not so much because of your own dream but because of one that I too experienced on the night before last. In it, I seemed to be out hunting in a fine and pleasant wood, and I captured the most beautiful and fetching little doe you ever saw. It was whiter than the driven snow, and it quickly grew so attached to me that it followed me about everywhere. For my part, I was apparently so fond of the animal that I put a golden collar round its neck and kept it on a golden chain to prevent it from straying.

'But then I dreamt that, whilst the doe was asleep, resting its head upon my chest, a coal-black greyhound appeared as if from nowhere, starving with hunger and quite terrifying to look upon. It advanced towards me, and I seemed powerless to resist, for it sank its teeth into my left side and gnawed away until it reached my heart, which it appeared to tear out and carry off in its jaws. The pain of it was so excruciating that I came to my senses, and the first thing I did on awakening was to run my hand over my left side just to make sure that it was still intact; but on discovering that I had come to no harm, I laughed at myself for being so credulous. But in any case, what does it signify? I have had the same kind of dream before, and much more terrifying ones, and they have never affected my life in the slightest degree, either one way or the other. So let us forget all about them and concentrate on enjoying ourselves.'

If the girl was already feeling frightened on account of her own dream, her fears were magnified on learning about Gabriotto's. She did her best to conceal them, however, for she did not wish to upset him. Although she took some solace in returning his kisses and caresses, she was filled with mysterious forebodings and kept looking into his face more often than usual. And every so often she cast her eyes round the garden to make sure that there was no sign of any black thing approaching.

As they lingered there together, Gabriotto suddenly heaved a tremendous sigh, enfolded her in his arms, and said:

'Alas, my dearest, comfort me, for I am dying.' And so saying, he fell back to the ground and lay motionless upon the grass.

On seeing this, the girl drew her fallen lover to her bosom, and, choking back her tears with an effort, she exclaimed:

'Oh, my precious husband! Alas! What is the matter?'

Gabriotto did not reply, but simply lay there gasping for breath and perspiring all over, and shortly thereafter he gave up the ghost.

You can all imagine the girl's distress and agony, for she loved him more dearly than her very self. Bursting into floods of tears, she called out to him over and over again, but all to no avail; and eventually, having run her fingers over the whole of his body and discovered that he was completely cold, she was forced to acknowledge that he was dead. Stricken with anguish, not knowing what to do or say, her tears streaming down her cheeks, she ran to fetch her maidservant, who knew all about her affair with Gabriotto, and poured out all the sorrow and misery she was feeling.

The two women wept for some time, gazing down together upon

Gabriotto's lifeless features, and then the girl said to her maid-servant:

'Now that God has taken this man away from me, I shall live no longer. But before I proceed to kill myself, I want us to do all things necessary to preserve my good name, to keep our love a secret, and to ensure that his body, from which his noble spirit has departed, will receive a proper burial.'

'Do not talk of killing yourself, my daughter,' said the maidservant. 'For though you may have lost him in this life, if you kill yourself you will lose him in the next life as well, because you will end up in Hell, which is the last place I would expect to find the soul of so virtuous a youth as Gabriotto. It is far better that you should be of good cheer and give some thought to assisting his soul by means of prayers and other good works, just in case he needs them on account of some peccadillo he may have committed. As to burying his body, the quickest way would be to do it here and now in the garden. Nobody will ever find out, because nobody knows that he was ever here. But if you do not like this idea, let us carry him from the garden and leave him outside, where he will be found in the morning and taken to his own house to be buried by his kinsfolk.'

Though she was filled with despair and wept the whole time, the girl was not deaf to her maidservant's advice. Rejecting the first of her suggestions, she seized upon the second, saying:

'I am sure that God would not wish me to permit so precious a youth, a man whom I love so deeply and to whom I am married, to be buried like a dog or left lying in the street. I have given him my own tears, and I am determined that he shall have the tears of his kinsfolk. What is more, I am beginning to see how we can manage it.'

She promptly sent the maid to fetch a length of silk cloth which was kept in one of her strongboxes, and when she returned with it they spread it on the ground and placed Gabriotto's body upon it. Then, weeping continuously, she rested his head on a cushion, closed his lips and his eyelids, made him a wreath out of roses, and filled all the space around him with the other roses they had gathered. And turning to her maidservant, she said:

'It is not far from here to his house, and so you and I are going to carry him to his front-door and leave him there, just as we have arranged him. Soon it will be day, and they will take him indoors. It won't be any consolation to his family, but for me at least, in whose arms he has died, it will bring some small pleasure.'

And so saying, she threw herself upon him once again, her tears streaming freely down her cheeks. She lay there sobbing for a long while until eventually, heeding her maidservant's repeated and anxious reminders that the dawn was approaching, she dragged herself to her feet. Then, removing from her finger the ring with which Gabriotto had married her, she threaded it on to his, saying through her tears:

'Dear husband, if your spirit is witness to my tears, and if there is any consciousness or feeling left in the human body after its soul has departed, receive fondly this final gift from the woman you loved so greatly when you were living on earth.'

No sooner had she said this, than she swooned and fell yet again upon his body. After a while she came to her senses and stood up, and then she and the maidservant took up the piece of cloth upon which his body was lying, went forth from the garden, and proceeded in the direction of his house. But as they were making their way along the street with his dead body, they had the misfortune to be discovered and stopped by the officers of the watch, who happened at that precise moment to be passing through the district on their way to investigate some other mishap.

After what had happened, Andreuola was more eager to die than to go on living, and, on recognizing the officers of the watch, she addressed them frankly and said:

'I know who you are, and realize that it would be futile for me to try and escape. I am quite prepared to come with you and explain all this before the magistrates. But if any of you should venture to lay a finger on me, or to remove anything from this man's body, you may rest assured that I shall denounce you.'

And so no hand was laid upon her, and she was led away with Gabriotto's body to the palace of the *podestà*.

The *podestà*, in other words the chief magistrate, having been roused from sleep, ordered her to be brought to his private quarters, where he questioned her about the circumstances of the case. He then got certain physicians to carry out a post mortem so as to ascertain that the good man had not been murdered, whether by poison or by any other means, and they unanimously confirmed that he had died a natural death from asphyxia, caused by the bursting of an abscess located in the region of his heart.

Feeling that the girl was not entirely blameless, despite the physicians' report, the magistrate made a pretence of offering her a favour that was not within his power to bestow, telling her that if she would yield to his pleasures, he would set her at liberty. On getting no response from her, he exceeded all the bounds of decorum and attempted to take her by force. But Andreuola, seething with indignation and summoning every ounce of her strength, defended herself vigorously and hurled him aside with a torrent of haughty abuse.

When it was broad day, the affair was reported to Messer Negro, who, sick with anxiety, set out with numerous friends for the palace of the *podestà*, where, having heard the whole story from the lips of the chief magistrate himself, he protested about the seizure of his daughter and demanded her release.

The chief magistrate, thinking it preferable to make a clean breast of his attempt on the girl rather than to wait for her to denounce him, began by praising her for her constancy, in proof of which he went on to describe how he had behaved towards her. On discovering how resolute she was, he had fallen deeply in love with her. And if it was agreeable to Messer Negro, who was her father, and also to the young lady herself, he would gladly take her for his wife, notwithstanding the fact that she had previously been married to a man of lowly condition.

Whilst they were talking in this fashion, Andreuola came into her father's presence, and, bursting into tears, threw herself on her knees before him.

'Father,' she cried, 'I suppose it is quite unnecessary for me to tell you about my reckless behaviour and about the tragedy that has befallen me, for I am sure you will already have been informed about these things. My sole request – and it is one that I make in all humility – is that you should pardon my transgression in taking as my husband, and without your knowledge, the man who was more pleasing to me than any other. Nor do I crave this forgiveness in order that my life shall be spared, but so that I may die as your daughter and not as your enemy.'

She thereupon collapsed in tears at his feet, and Messer Negro too began to cry, for he was by nature generous and affectionate, and he was getting on in years. And so, with tears in his eyes, he helped her tenderly to her feet, saying:

'My daughter, it was always my dearest wish that you should marry a man whom I considered worthy of you; and if you did indeed choose such a man, and he was pleasing to you, then I could have wished for nothing better. All the same, I am saddened to think that you did not trust me sufficiently to tell me about him, the more so on discovering that you have lost him even before I had any inkling of the matter. But still, since this is the way of it, I intend that he should be paid the same respect, now that he is dead, that I would willingly have paid to him for your sake if he were still alive; in other words, I intend to honour him as my son-in-law.' And, turning to his sons and kinsfolk, he instructed them to see that suitably splendid and honourable arrangements were put in hand for Gabriotto's funeral.

News of what had happened had meanwhile reached the ears of the young man's kinsfolk, who had now arrived upon the scene together with nearly all the men and women in the city. The body was therefore laid upon Andreuola's piece of silk cloth in the midst of all her roses and placed in the centre of the courtyard, where it publicly received the tears, not only of Andreuola and of Gabriotto's kinswomen, but of nearly all the women in the city and many of the men. And it was from the palace yard, in the style not of a plebeian but of a patrician, that his remains were taken with very great reverence to their burial, borne on the shoulders of the highest nobles in the land.

After the funeral, the chief magistrate repeated his previous offer and Messer Negro talked the matter over with his daughter, but she would have nothing to do with it. And within the space of a few days, it being her father's will that her own wishes should be scrupulously observed in this respect, she and her maidservant entered a convent of great renown for its sanctity, where they thenceforth lived long and virtuously as nuns.

SEVENTH STORY

Simona loves Pasquino; they are together in a garden; Pasquino rubs a sage-leaf against his teeth, and dies. Simona is arrested, and, with the intention of showing the judge how Pasquino met his death, she rubs one of the same leaves against her own teeth, and dies in identical fashion.

When Panfilo had dispatched his tale, the king, showing no trace of compassion for Andreuola, made it clear by looking towards Emilia that he wished her to add her tale to the ones already told; and without the least demur, she began:

My dear companions, having heard Panfilo's story I am impelled to narrate one that is dissimilar to his in every respect, except that, just as Andreuola lost her lover in a garden, so did the girl of whom I am obliged to speak. Like Andreuola, she too was arrested, but she freed herself from the arm of the law, not through physical strength or unwavering virtue, but by her untimely and unexpected death. As we have already had occasion to remark, whilst Love readily sets up house in the mansions of the aristocracy, this is no reason for concluding that he declines to govern the dwellings of the poor. On the contrary, he sometimes chooses such places for a display of strength no less awe-inspiring than that used by a mighty overlord to intimidate the richest of his subjects. Though the proof will not be conclusive, this assertion will in large measure be confirmed by my story, which offers me the pleasing prospect of returning to your fair city, whence, in the course of the present day, ranging widely over diverse subjects and directing our steps to various parts of the world, we have strayed so far afield.

Not so very long ago, then, there lived in Florence a young woman called Simona, a poor man's daughter, who, due allowance being made for her social condition, was exceedingly gracious and beautiful. Although she was obliged to earn every morsel that passed her lips by working with her hands, and obtained her livelihood by spinning wool, she was not so faint-hearted as to close her mind to Love, which for some time had been showing every sign of wishing to enter her thoughts via the agreeable words and deeds of a youth no more highly placed than herself, who was employed by a wool-merchant to go round and distribute wool for spinning. Having thus admitted Love to her thoughts in the pleasing shape of this young man, whose name was Pasquino, she was filled with powerful yearnings but was too timid to do anything about them. And as she sat at her spinning and recalled who had given her the wool, she heaved a thousand sighs more torrid than fire for every yard of woollen thread that she wound round her spindle. For his part, Pasquino developed a special interest in seeing that his master's wool was properly spun, and, acting as though the finished cloth was to consist solely of the wool that Simona was spinning, and no other, he encouraged her far more assiduously than any of the other girls. The young woman responded well to Pasquino's encouragement. She cast aside a good deal of her accustomed modesty and reserve, whilst he acquired greater daring than was usual for him, so that eventually, to their mutual pleasure and delight, their physical union was achieved. This sport they found so much to their liking that neither waited to be asked to play it by the other, but it was rather a question whenever they met of who was going to be first with the invitation.

With their pleasure thus continuing from one day to the next and waxing more impassioned in the process, Pasquino chanced to say to Simona that he would dearly like her to contrive some way of meeting him in a certain garden, whither he was anxious for her to come so that they could feel more relaxed together and less apprehensive of discovery.

Simona agreed to do it, and one Sunday, immediately after lunch, having given her father to understand that she was going to the Pardoning Festival at San Gallo, she made her way with a companion of hers called Lagina to the garden Pasquino had mentioned. When she got there, she found him with a friend of his whose name was Puccino, but who was better known as Stramba, or Dotty Joe. Stramba hit it off with Lagina from the very beginning, and so Simona and Pasquino left them together in one part of the garden and withdrew to another to pursue their own pleasures.

In that part of the garden to which Simona and Pasquino had retired, there was a splendid and very large clump of sage, at the foot of which they settled down to amuse themselves at their leisure. Some time later, having made frequent mention of a picnic they were intending to take, there in the garden, after they had rested from their exertions, Pasquino turned to the huge clump of sage and detached one of its leaves, with which he began to rub his teeth and gums, claiming that sage prevented food from sticking to the teeth after a meal.

After rubbing them thus for a while, he returned to the subject of the picnic about which he had been talking earlier. But before he had got very far, a radical change came over his features, and very soon afterwards he lost all power of sight and speech. A few minutes later he was dead, and Simona, having witnessed the whole episode, started crying and shrieking and calling out to Stramba and Lagina. They promptly rushed over to the spot, and when Stramba saw that not only was Pasquino dead, but his face and body were already covered with swellings and dark blotches, he exclaimed:

'Ah! you foul bitch, you've poisoned him!'

He made such a din that he was heard by several of the people living in the neighbourhood of the garden, and they rushed to see what it was all about. On finding this fellow lying there, dead and swollen, and hearing Stramba taking it out on Simona and accusing her of having tricked Pasquino into taking poison, whilst the girl herself, grief-stricken because of the sudden death of her lover, was so obviously at a loss for an explanation, they all concluded that Stramba's version of what had happened must be correct.

She was therefore seized and taken to the palace of the *podestà*, shedding copious tears all the way. Stramba had by this time been joined by two other friends of Pasquino, who were known as Atticciato and Malagevole, or in other words, Potbelly and Killjoy, and the three of them stirred up so much fuss that a judge was persuaded to interrogate her forthwith about the circumstances of Pasquino's death. But being unable to conceive how Simona could have practised any deceit, or how she could possibly be guilty, he insisted that she should accompany him to the site of the occurrence, so that, by getting her to show him the manner of it and seeing the dead body for himself, he could form a clearer impression of the matter than he had been able to obtain from her words alone.

Without creating any disturbance, he therefore had her conveyed to the spot where Pasquino's body lay, still swollen up like a barrel, and shortly afterwards he went there himself. Gazing at the body in astonishment, he asked her to show him precisely how it had happened, whereupon Simona walked over to the clump of sage, and, having told the judge what they had been doing together so as to place him fully in possession of the facts, she did as Pasquino had done, and rubbed one of the sage-leaves against her teeth.

Simona's actions were greeted with hoots of derision by Stramba, Atticciato, and Pasquino's other friends and acquaintances, who told the judge that they were pointless and frivolous, and denounced her wickedness with greater vehemence, at the same time demanding that she be burnt at the stake, since no lesser punishment would be appropriate for so terrible a crime. The poor creature was petrified, not only on account of her sorrow at losing her lover, but also because of her fear of suffering the punishment demanded by Stramba. But suddenly, as the result of having rubbed the sage-leaf against her teeth, she met the very same fate as the one that had stricken Pasquino, to the no small amazement of all those present.

Oh, happy souls, who within the space of a single day were granted release from your passionate love and your mortal existence! And happier still, if your destination was shared! And happy beyond description, if love is possible after death, and you love one another in the after-life as deeply as you did on earth! But happiest of all, so far as we, who have survived her, are able to judge, is the soul of Simona herself, since Fortune preserved her innocence against the testimony of Stramba and Atticciato and Malagevole – who were certainly worth no more than a trio of carders, and possibly even less – and, by causing her to die in the same way as her lover, found a more seemly way of ending her misery. For not only was she able to clear herself from their slanderous allegations, but she went to join the soul of her beloved Pasquino.

The judge, along with all the others present, was hardly able to believe his eyes, and remained rooted to the spot for some little time, not knowing what to say. But eventually, he recovered his wits, and said:

'The sage is evidently poisonous, which is rather unusual, to say the least. Before it should claim any further victims, let it be hacked down to its roots and set on fire.'

In the judge's presence, the man in charge of the garden proceeded to carry out these instructions, but he had no sooner felled the giant clump than the reason for the deaths of the two poor lovers became apparent.

Crouching beneath the clump of sage, there was an incredibly large toad, by whose venomous breath they realized that the bush must have been poisoned. Nobody dared to approach it, and so they surrounded it with a huge pyre, and cremated it alive together with the sage-bush. So ended the investigation of His Worship into the death of poor Pasquino, whose swollen body, together with that of his beloved Simona, was subsequently buried by Stramba and Atticciato and Guccio Imbratta and Malagevole in the Church of St Paul, which happened to be the parish to which the two dead lovers belonged.

EIGHTH STORY

Girolamo loves Salvestra; he is prevailed upon by his mother to go to Paris, and on his return he finds Salvestra married. Having secretly entered her house, he lies down and dies at her side; his body is taken to a church, where Salvestra lies down beside him, and she too dies.

When Emilia's tale had wound to a close, Neifile, having been bidden to speak by the king, began as follows:

Excellent ladies, to my way of thinking there are those who imagine that they know more than others when in fact they know less, and hence they presume to set up this wisdom of theirs against not only the counsels of their fellow men, but also the laws of nature. No good has ever come of their presumption, and from time to time it has done an enormous amount of harm. Now, there is nothing in the whole of nature that is less susceptible to advice or interference than Love, whose qualities are such that it is far more likely to burn itself out of its own free will than be quenched by deliberate pressure. And so it occurs to me that I should tell you a story about a lady who, in the belief that she could remove, from an enamoured heart, a love which had possibly been planted there by the stars, sought to be wiser than she actually was, and by flaunting her cleverness in a matter that was beyond her competence, succeeded at one and the same time in driving both Love and life from the body of her son.

According to the tales of our elders, there once lived in our city a very powerful and wealthy merchant whose name was Leonardo Sighieri, who had a son from his wife called Girolamo, and who, after the child was born, carefully put all his affairs in order and departed this life. The boy's interests were skilfully and scrupulously managed by his guardians, acting in conjunction with his mother. He grew up with the children of other families in the neighbourhood, and became very attached to a little girl of his own age, who was the daughter of a tailor. As they grew older, their friendship ripened into a love so great and passionate that Girolamo could not bear to let her out of his sight, and her own regard for him was certainly no less extreme. On perceiving this, the boy's mother took him to task several times, and even punished him for it. But on finding that he could not be deterred, she took the matter up with the boy's guardians, being convinced that because of her son's great wealth she could, as it were, turn a plum into an orange.

'This boy of ours,' she told them, 'who has only just reached the age of fourteen, is so enamoured of a local tailor's daughter, Salvestra by name, that if we do not separate them we shall perhaps wake up one morning to find that he has married her without telling anyone about it, and I shall never be happy again. If on the other hand he sees her marrying another, he will pine away. And so it would seem to me that in order to nip the affair in the bud, you ought to pack him off to some distant part of the world in the service of the firm. For if he is prevented from seeing the girl over a long period, she will vanish from his thoughts and we shall then be able to marry him to some young lady of gentle breeding.'

The guardians agreed with the lady's point of view and assured her that they would do all in their power to carry out her proposal. And having sent for the boy at the firm's premises, one of them began talking to him in tones of great affection, saying:

'My boy, you are quite a big fellow now, and it would be a good thing for you to start attending to your own affairs. We would therefore be very happy if you were to go and stay for a while in Paris, where you will not only see how a sizable part of your business is managed, but you will also, by mixing with all those lords and barons and nobles who abound in that part of the world, become a much better man, and acquire greater experience and refinement, than by remaining here. And then you can return to Florence.'

Having listened carefully, the lad gave them a short answer, saying that he would have none of it, since he considered he had as much right as anyone else to remain in Florence. His worthy mentors made several further attempts to persuade him, but being unable to extract any different answer, they reported back to the mother. She was livid with anger, and gave him a fierce scolding, not because he did not want to go to Paris but on account of his love for Salvestra. But then, soothing him with honeyed words, she began to pay him compliments and to coax him gently into following the advice of his guardians. And she played her cards so skilfully that in the end he agreed that he should go and stay there, but only for twelve months, and so it was arranged.

Still passionately in love, Girolamo went off to Paris, where he was detained by a series of delaying tactics for two whole years. On returning to Florence, more deeply in love than before, he was mortified to discover that his beloved Salvestra was married to a worthy young man who was by trade a tentmaker. Since there was nothing he could do about it, he tried to reconcile himself to the situation; and having inquired into where she was living, he began to walk up and down in the manner of a lovelorn youth outside her house, being convinced that she could not have forgotten him, any more than he had forgotten her. But this was not the case, for as the young man very soon perceived, to his no small sorrow, she no more remembered him than if she had never seen him before, and if she did indeed recollect anything at all, she certainly never showed it. Nevertheless the young man did everything he could to make her acknowledge him again; but feeling that he was getting nowhere, he resolved to speak to her in private, even if he were to die in the attempt.

Having inquired of a person living nearby regarding the disposition of the rooms, he secretly let himself in to the house one evening whilst she and her husband were attending a wake with some neighbours of theirs, and concealed himself behind some flysheets that were stretched across a corner of her bedroom. There he waited until they had returned home and retired to bed, and when he was sure that her husband was asleep, he crept over to that part of the room where he had seen Salvestra lying down, placed his hand on her bosom, and said:

'Are you asleep already, my dearest?'

The girl, who was not asleep, was about to scream when the young man hastily added:

'For pity's sake, do not scream, for it is only your Girolamo.'

On hearing this, she trembled from head to toe, and said:

'Oh, merciful heavens, do go away Girolamo. We are no longer children, and the time has passed for proclaiming our love from the house-tops. As you can see, I am married, and therefore it is no longer proper for me to care for any other man but my husband. Hence I beseech you in God's name to get out of here. If my husband were to hear you, even supposing nothing more serious came of it, it would certainly follow that I could never live in peace with him again, whereas up to now he has loved me and we live calmly and contentedly together.'

To hear her talking like this, the young man was driven to the brink of despair. He reminded her of the times they had spent in each other's company and of the fact that his love for her had never diminished despite their separation. He poured out a stream of entreaties and promised her the moon. But he was unable to make the slightest impression.

All he wanted to do now was to die, and so finally, invoking the great love he bore her, he pleaded with her to let him lie down at her side so that he could get warm, pointing out that his limbs had turned numb with cold whilst he was waiting for her. He assured her that he would neither talk to her nor touch her, and promised to go away as soon as he had warmed himself a little.

Feeling rather sorry for him, Salvestra agreed to let him do it, but only if he kept his promises. So the young man lay down at her side without attempting to touch her, and, concentrating his thoughts on his long love for her, on her present coldness towards him and on the dashing of his hopes, he resolved not to go on living. Without uttering a word, he clenched his fists and held his breath until finally he expired at her side.

After a while, wondering what he was doing and fearing lest her husband should wake up, the girl made a move.

'Girolamo,' she whispered, 'it's time for you to be going.'

On receiving no answer, she assumed that he had fallen asleep. So she stretched out her hand to wake him up and began to prod him, but found to her great astonishment that he was as cold as ice to the touch. She then prodded him more vigorously but it had no effect, and after trying once more she realized that he was dead. The discovery filled her with dismay and for some time she lay there without the slightest notion what to do.

In the end she decided to put the case to her husband without saying who was involved, and ask his opinion about what the people concerned ought to do about it; and having woken him up, she described her own recent experience as though it had happened to someone else, then asked him what advice he would give supposing it had happened to her.

To this, the worthy soul replied that in his view, the fellow who was dead would have to be taken quietly back to his own house and left there, and that no resentment should be harboured against the woman, who did not appear to him to have done any wrong.

'In that case,' said the girl, 'we shall have to do likewise.' And taking his hand, she brought it into contact with the young man's body, whereupon he leapt to his feet in utter consternation, lighted a lamp, and, without entering into further discussion with his wife, dressed the body in its own clothes. And without further ado, he lifted it on to his shoulders and carried it, confident in his own innocence, to the door of Girolamo's house, where he put it down and left it.

Next morning, when the young man's corpse was discovered lying on the doorstep, a great commotion was raised, in particular by the mother. The body was carefully examined all over, but no trace of a wound or a blow could be found, and it was the general opinion of the physicians that he had died of grief, as indeed he had. His remains were taken into a church, to which the sorrowing mother came with numerous kinswomen and neighbours, and they all began to weep and keen over his body, as is customary in our part of the world.

Whilst the tears and lamentations were at their height, the worthy man in whose house Girolamo had died turned to Salvestra and said: 'Just cover your head in a mantle and go over to the church where Girolamo was taken. Mingle with the women, and listen to what they are saying about this business, and I will do the same among the men, so that we may find out whether anything is being said against us.'

The girl readily assented, for she was stirred to pity now that it was too late and was eager to gaze upon the dead features of the man who had been unable to persuade her, whilst he was still alive, to grant him so much as a single kiss. And so off she went to the church.

What a wonderful thing Love is, and how difficult it is to fathom its deep and powerful currents! The girl's heart, which had remained sealed to Girolamo for as long as he was smiled upon by Fortune, was unlocked by his far from fortunate death. The flames of her former love were rekindled, and no sooner did she catch sight of his dead face than they were all instantly transformed into so much compassion that she edged her way forward, wrapped in her mantle, through the cluster of women mourners, coming to a halt only when she was almost on top of the corpse itself. Then with a piercing scream, she flung herself upon the dead youth, and if she failed to drench his face with her tears, that was because, almost as soon as she touched him, she died, like the young man, from a surfeit of grief.

The women, who had thus far failed to recognize her, crowded round to console her and urge her to her feet, but since she did not respond they tried to lift her themselves, only to discover that she was quite still and rigid. And when they finally succeeded in raising her, they saw at one and the same time that it was Salvestra and that she was dead. The women now had double cause for weeping, and they all began wailing again much more loudly than before.

The news spread through the church to the men outside and reached the ears of her husband, who happened to be standing in their midst. Having burst into tears, he simply went on crying, oblivious to the efforts of various bystanders to console and comfort him; but eventually he told several of them about what had occurred the night before between this young man and his wife, thus clearing up the mystery of their deaths, and everyone was filled with enormous sorrow.

The dead girl was taken up and decked out in all the finery with which we are wont to adorn the bodies of the dead, then she was laid on the selfsame bier upon which the young man was already lying. For a long time they mourned her, and afterwards the two bodies were interred in a single tomb: and thus it was that those whom Love had failed to join together in life were inseparably linked to each other in death.

NINTH STORY

Guillaume de Roussillon causes his wife to eat the heart of her lover, Guillaume de Cabestanh, whom he has secretly murdered. When she finds out, she kills herself by leaping from a lofty casement to the ground below, and is subsequently buried with the man she loved.

The king had no intention of interfering with Dioneo's privilege, and when, having planted no small degree of compassion in the hearts of her companions, Neifile's story came to its conclusion, there being no others left to speak, he began as follows:

Since you are so deeply moved, tender ladies, by the recital of lovers' woes, the tale that presents itself to me must inevitably arouse as much pity among you as the previous one, for the people whose misfortunes I shall describe were of loftier rank, and their fate was altogether more cruel.

You must know, then, that according to the Provençals, there once lived in Provence two noble knights, each of whom owned several castles and had a number of dependants. The name of the first was Guillaume de Roussillon, whilst the other was called Guillaume de Cabestanh. Since both men excelled in feats of daring, they were bosom friends and made a point of accompanying one another to jousts and tournaments and other armed contests, each bearing the same device.

Although the castles in which they lived were some ten miles apart, Guillaume de Cabestanh chanced to fall hopelessly in love with the charming and very beautiful wife of Guillaume de Roussillon, and, notwithstanding the bonds of friendship and brotherhood that united the two men, he managed in various subtle ways to bring his love to the lady's notice. The lady, knowing him to be a most gallant knight, was deeply flattered, and began to regard him with so much affection that there was nothing she loved or desired more deeply. All that remained for him to do was to approach her directly, which he very soon did, and from then on they met at frequent intervals for the purpose of making passionate love to one another.

One day, however, they were incautious enough to be espied by the lady's husband, who was so incensed by the spectacle that his great love for Cabestanh was transformed into mortal hatred. He firmly resolved to do away with him, but concealed his intentions far more successfully than the lovers had been able to conceal their love.

His mind being thus made up, Roussillon happened to hear of a great tournament that was to be held in France. He promptly sent word of it to Cabestanh and asked him whether he would care to call upon him, so that they could talk it over together and decide whether or not to go and how they were to get there. Cabestanh was delighted to hear of it, and sent back word to say that he would come and sup with him next day without fail.

On receiving Cabestanh's message, Roussillon judged this to be his opportunity for killing him. Next day, he armed himself, took horse with a few of his men, and lay in ambush about a mile away from his castle, in a wood through which Cabestanh was bound to pass. After a long wait, he saw him approaching, unarmed, and followed by two of his men, who were likewise unarmed, for he never suspected for a moment that he was running into danger. Roussillon waited until Cabestanh was at close range, then he rushed out at him with murder and destruction in his heart, brandishing a lance above his head and shouting: 'Traitor, you are dead!' And before the words were out of his mouth he had driven the lance through Cabestanh's breast.

Cabestanh was powerless to defend himself, or even to utter a word, and on being run through by the lance he fell to the ground. A moment later he was dead, and his men, without stopping to see who had perpetrated the deed, turned the heads of their horses and galloped away as fast as they could in the direction of their master's castle.

Dismounting from his horse, Roussillon cut open Cabestanh's chest with a knife, tore out the heart with his own hands, and, wrapping it up in a banderole, told one of his men to take it away. Having given strict orders that no one was to breathe a word about what had happened, he then remounted and rode back to his castle, by which time it was already dark.

The lady had heard that Cabestanh was to be there that evening for supper and was eagerly waiting for him to arrive. When she saw her husband arriving without him she was greatly surprised, and said to him:

'And how is it, my lord, that Cabestanh has not come?'

To which her husband replied:

'Madam, I have received word from him that he cannot be here until tomorrow.'

Roussillon left her standing there, feeling somewhat perturbed, and when he had dismounted, he summoned the cook and said to him:

'You are to take this boar's heart and see to it that you prepare the finest and most succulent dish you can devise. When I am seated at table, send it in to me in a silver tureen.'

The cook took the heart away, minced it and added a goodly quantity of fine spices, employing all his skill and loving care and turning it into a dish that was too exquisite for words.

When it was time for dinner, Roussillon sat down at the table with his lady. Food was brought in, but he was unable to do more than nibble at it because his mind was dwelling upon the terrible deed he had committed. Then the cook sent in his special dish, which Roussillon told them to set before his lady, saying that he had no appetite that evening.

He remarked on how delicious it looked, and the lady, whose appetite was excellent, began to eat it, finding it so tasty a dish that she ate every scrap of it.

On observing that his lady had finished it down to the last morsel, the knight said:

'What did you think of that, madam?'

'In good faith, my lord,' replied the lady, 'I liked it very much.'

'So help me God,' exclaimed the knight, 'I do believe you did. But I am not surprised to find that you liked it dead, because when it was alive you liked it better than anything else in the whole world.'

On hearing this, the lady was silent for a while; then she said:

'How say you? What is this that you have caused me to eat?'

'That which you have eaten,' replied the knight, 'was in fact the heart of Guillaume de Cabestanh, with whom you, faithless woman that you are, were so infatuated. And you may rest assured that it was truly his, because I tore it from his breast myself, with these very hands, a little before I returned home.'

You can all imagine the anguish suffered by the lady on hearing such tidings of Cabestanh, whom she loved more dearly than anything else in the world. But after a while, she said:

'This can only have been the work of an evil and treacherous knight, for if, of my own free will, I abused you by making him the master of my love, it was not he but I that should have paid the penalty for it. But God forbid that any other food should pass my lips now that I have partaken of such excellent fare as the heart of so gallant and courteous a knight as Guillaume de Cabestanh.'

And rising to her feet, she retreated a few steps to an open window, through which without a second thought she allowed herself to fall.

The window was situated high above the ground, so that the lady was not only killed by her fall but almost completely disfigured.

The spectacle of his wife's fall threw Roussillon into a panic and made him repent the wickedness of his deed. And fearing the wrath of the local people and of the Count of Provence, he had his horses saddled and rode away.

By next morning the circumstances of the affair had become common knowledge throughout the whole of the district, and people were sent out from the castles of the lady's family and of Guillaume de Cabestanh to gather up the two bodies, which were later placed in a single tomb in the chapel of the lady's own castle amid widespread grief and mourning. And the tombstone bore an inscription, in verse, to indicate who was buried there and the manner and the cause of their deaths.

TENTH STORY

The wife of a physician, mistakenly assuming her lover, who has taken an opiate, to be dead, deposits him in a trunk, which is carried off to their house by two money-lenders with the man still inside it. On coming to his senses, he is seized as a thief, but the lady's maidservant tells the judge that it was she who put him in the trunk, thereby saving him from the gallows, whilst the usurers are sentenced to pay a fine for making off with the trunk.

Now that the king had finished, only Dioneo was left to address the company. Knowing this to be so, and having already been asked by the king to proceed, he began as follows:

These sorrowful accounts of ill-starred loves have brought so much affliction to my eyes and heart (to say nothing of yours, dear ladies) that I have been longing for them to come to an end. Unless I were to add another sorry tale to this gruesome collection (and Heaven forbid that I should), they are now, thank God, over and done with. And instead of lingering any longer on so agonizing a topic, I shall make a start on a better and rather more agreeable theme, which will possibly offer some sort of guide to the subject we ought to discuss on the morrow.

Fairest maidens, I will have you know that in the comparatively recent past there lived in Salerno a very great surgeon called Doctor Mazzeo della Montagna, who, having reached a ripe old age, married a beautiful and gently bred young lady of that same city. No other woman in Salerno was kept so lavishly supplied as Mazzeo's wife with expensive and elegant dresses, jewellery, and all the other things a woman covets; but the fact is that for most of the time she felt chilly, because the surgeon failed to keep her properly covered over in bed.

Now, you may remember my telling you about Messer Ricciardo di Chinzica, and of the way he taught his wife to observe the feasts of the various Saints. This old surgeon did much the same thing, for he pointed out to the girl that you needed heaven knows how many days to recover after making love to a woman, and spouted a lot of similar nonsense, all of which made her wretchedly unhappy. But as she was a woman of considerable spirit and intelligence, she resolved to put the family jewels in cotton wool and wear out some other man's gems. Having gone out into the streets, she cast a critical eye over a number of young bloods, eventually finding one who was exactly to her liking, and she made him the sole custodian of her hopes, heart, and happiness. On perceiving her interest in him, the young man was powerfully smitten, and wholeheartedly reciprocated her love.

His name was Ruggieri d'Aieroli, and he was of noble birth. But he led such a disreputable life, and mixed with so many undesirable characters, that he had alienated all his friends and relatives, none of whom wished him any good or wanted anything to do with him. He was notorious throughout Salerno for his acts of larceny and for other highly unsavoury activities, about which the lady was more or less indifferent because she liked him for other reasons. Using a maid-servant as a go-between, she so arranged matters that she and her lover were united, but after they had been making love together for a while she began to censure his way of life and to entreat him for her sake to reform his ways. And in order to make it worth his while to do so, she furnished him from time to time with various sums of money.

Taking good care not to be discovered, they had been meeting in this fashion for some time when it happened that a man with a diseased leg was placed under the Doctor's care. Having examined the ailment, the Doctor informed the man's kinsfolk that unless he re-moved a gangrenous bone in the patient's leg, it would have to be amputated altogether, otherwise he would die. At the same time, whilst the removal of the bone offered every chance of a cure, there was no guarantee that the operation would be successful. The man's family accepted the surgeon's advice along with the reservations he had expressed, and handed the patient into his keeping.

The operation was to be performed towards evening, and that same morning, realizing that the invalid would be unable to with-stand the pain unless he were doped beforehand, the doctor issued a special prescription providing for the distillation of a certain liquid which he intended to administer to the patient in order to put him to sleep for as long as the pain and the operation were likely to last. And having had it delivered to his house, he put it down on a window-ledge in his bedroom without bothering to tell anyone what it was.

That evening, just as the surgeon was about to go to his patient, a messenger arrived from some very close friends of his at Amalfi, telling him that he was to abandon everything and go there at once because of a serious brawl in which a number of people had suffered injury.

Postponing the operation on the leg until the following morning, the surgeon got into a boat and went to Amalfi, whereupon the lady, knowing that he would be away from home for the rest of the night, secretly sent for Ruggieri in her usual way and showed him into her bedroom, locking him inside until certain other people in the house had retired for the night.

Whether because of having had a tiring day or because he had eaten food containing a lot of salt or because of some peculiarity of his constitution, Ruggieri, whilst he was waiting in the bedroom for his mistress, suddenly felt enormously thirsty. And catching sight of the bottle of medicine which the doctor had left on the window-ledge, he mistook it for drinking water, raised it to his lips, and drank it down to the last drop. Almost at once he was filled with a feeling of great drowsiness, and shortly afterwards he fell fast asleep.

At the earliest opportunity, the lady came up to the bedroom, and on finding Ruggieri asleep she began to prod him and whisper to him to get up. But it was no use; he neither answered nor moved a muscle. And so the lady, growing somewhat impatient, gave him a more violent shove, saying:

'Get up, lazybones. If you wanted to sleep, you should have gone to your own house to do it instead of coming round here.'

The lady's shove toppled Ruggieri from the chest on which he was lying, and he fell to the floor, showing no more sign of life than if he were a corpse. The lady was rather frightened, and she began to try and raise him, then shook him more vigorously and tweaked his nose and pulled his beard. But it was all to no purpose: he was sleeping like a log.

The lady now began to fear that he was dead, and in her panic she started pinching him viciously and holding a lighted candle against his skin, but it was no use. And hence, being no physician herself even though she was married to one, she was quite convinced that he must be dead. Since there was nothing in the world that she loved so much, her distress can readily be imagined. Not daring to make any noise, she began to weep in silence over his body and lament her ghastly misfortune.

After a while, however, being afraid that she might lose her reputation on top of losing her lover, the lady saw that she must immediately devise some means for getting his body out of the house. Having no idea how she should go about it, she called out softly to her maid, showed her the dilemma she was in, and asked her what they ought to do. The maid was greatly astonished, and she too began shaking and pinching him, but when she saw that he was without any feeling, she agreed with her mistress that he really was dead, and said that he would have to be put out of the house.

'But where on earth can we leave him,' inquired the lady, 'so as to prevent people suspecting, when he is discovered in the morning, that this was the house from which he was taken?'

'Ma'am,' replied the maid, 'late this evening I caught sight of a trunk standing outside the shop of our neighbour, the carpenter. It was not a very large trunk, but if it is still there it will come in nice and handy, because we can put the body inside, stab him two or three times with a dagger, and leave him there. No matter who finds him in the trunk, they will have no reason for supposing that he came from here rather than from somewhere else. In fact, since he was such an unruly sort of youth, they will think that he was murdered by one of his enemies as he was about to commit some crime or other, and then stuffed inside the trunk.'

The lady said that no power on earth would persuade her to stab him, but that otherwise the maid's proposal seemed to her a good one, and she sent her to see whether the trunk was still in the same place. Having confirmed that it was, the maid, who was a sturdy young woman, lifted Ruggieri on to her shoulders with the help of her mistress. And with the lady walking on ahead to make sure no one was coming, they got him to the trunk, put him inside, closed the lid, and left him there.

Now, a few days earlier, two young men had moved into a house a little further along the street. They were money-lenders, always on the lookout for ways of making pots of money and saving a few coppers, and since they were short of furniture and had noticed the trunk lying there the previous day, they had agreed that if it was still there after dark, they would carry it off to their own house.

In the dead of night they came out of their house, found the trunk, and without stopping to examine it closely (though it did seem a little heavy), they carried it quickly back to their house and dumped it in the first convenient place, which happened to be immediately beside a room where their womenfolk were sleeping. And without bothering to see that it was in a secure position, they left it there and went off to bed.

Ruggieri slept for a very long time, but eventually he digested the potion, its effects wore off, and just before matins he woke up. But although he had emerged from sleep and recovered the use of his senses, his mind was still blurred, and in fact it was some days before he shook off his state of bewilderment. On opening his eyes and finding that he could not see anything, he groped about with his hands and discovered that he was inside this trunk, whereupon he began to ponder and mutter to himself, saying: 'What's all this? Where am I? Am I asleep, or awake? I have a clear recollection of entering my lady's bedchamber this evening, and now I appear to be inside some sort of chest. What does it mean? Can it be that the doctor returned home, or that something equally unexpected happened, causing my mistress to conceal me here whilst I was asleep? Why of course, that's the explanation, that's it exactly.'

And so he kept quiet and listened to see whether he could hear anything. But after remaining stock-still for some considerable time, feeling rather uncomfortable inside the trunk, which was none too big, and getting a pain in the side on which he was lying, he decided to turn over. This operation he performed with such a degree of skill that in pressing his back against one of the sides of the trunk, which had not been placed on an even keel, he caused it to topple over and fall with a resounding crash, waking up the women who were asleep in the adjoining room and giving them such a fright that they hardly dared to breathe, let alone open their mouths.

Ruggieri received quite a shock when the trunk toppled over, but on finding that it had burst open in falling, he preferred to clamber out rather than stay where he was, just in case anything worse was about to happen to him. Being at his wits' end, and not knowing where he was, he began to fumble his way round the premises in order to see whether he could find a door or a staircase that would offer him a way of escaping.

The women heard these fumbling sounds as they lay there awake, and they began calling out: 'Who's there?' Being unable to recognize their voices, Ruggieri offered no reply, and so the women started calling to the two young men, who, because they had gone to bed so late, were soundly asleep and had heard nothing of all the racket.

Feeling more frightened than ever, the women got out of bed and ran to the windows, shouting: 'Burglars! Burglars!' And so several of their neighbours rushed into the house from various directions, some by way of the roof, some by the front-door, and others by the entrance at the rear. And the noise reached such a pitch that even the young men woke up and scrambled out of bed.

On finding himself in the midst of all this commotion, Ruggieri very nearly collapsed with astonishment. He was in no condition to make a dash for it, and in any case he could see that escape was impossible; so he was seized and handed over to the chief magistrate's officers, who had meanwhile rushed to the scene, having been attracted by all the noise. He was then taken before the chief magistrate, and since he had a very bad reputation he was immediately put to the torture and forced to confess that he had broken into the money-lenders' house with intent to rob, whereupon the magistrate resolved to have him hanged by the neck at the earliest opportunity.

During the course of the morning, the news that Ruggieri had been caught red-handed burgling the money-lenders' house spread like wildfire through the whole of Salerno. And when the lady and her maid came to hear of it, they were so bewildered and astonished that they almost began to think that instead of actually doing what they had done the night before they had merely been dreaming. What was more, the lady was nearly out of her mind with anxiety at the thought of the danger that Ruggieri was in.

Halfway through the morning, the doctor returned from Amalfi and sent someone to fetch his potion so that he could operate on his patient, and when the bottle was found to be empty he made a great commotion and protested that he could not leave anything in his own house without people interfering with it.

The lady, who had troubles of her own to think about, lost her temper with him and said:

'I wonder what you would say if something really terrible had happened, when you create so much fuss over a spilled bottle of water? Isn't there plenty more of it about?'

'My dear,' said the surgeon, 'you seem to think that it was ordinary water, but that is not the case. On the contrary, it was a potion specially prepared for putting people to sleep.'

He then told her what he needed it for, and it immediately dawned upon the lady that Ruggieri must have drunk the potion, which explained why they had thought he was dead.

'We knew nothing of all that,' she said. 'You'll have to make yourself some more of it.'

Seeing that he had no alternative, the surgeon sent out for a second bottle of the stuff, and shortly afterwards the maid, who on the lady's instructions had gone out to discover what people were saying about Ruggieri, returned to her mistress, saying:

'Everyone is saying awful things about him, ma'am, and as far as I was able to discover, there is not one of his friends or relatives who has lifted a finger to save him or has any intention of doing so. Everyone is quite convinced that the judge will have him hanged tomorrow. But there's another thing I want to tell you, and that is that I think I have discovered how he came to be in the money-lenders' house. Just listen, and I'll tell you. You know the carpenter, don't you, in front of whose shop we found the trunk to put Ruggieri in? Well, he was having a heated argument just now with a man to whom it appears that the trunk belonged. The man was demanding to be paid for his trunk, and the carpenter was denying he had sold it, saying that on the contrary it had been stolen from him during the night. And the man said: "It's not true. You sold it to the two young money-lenders. They told me so themselves, for I spotted the trunk on going into their house early this morning, when Ruggieri was being arrested." "They are lying," said the carpenter, "for I never sold it to them. They must have stolen it from me last night. Let us go round and see them." So off they went by mutual agreement to the money-lenders' house, and I came back here. As you can see, I think this explains how Ruggieri was taken to the place where he was discovered. But I still can't make out how he came to life again.'

The lady now understood exactly what had happened. She told the maid about her conversation with the Doctor, and begged her to help in freeing Ruggieri, telling her that she was in a position, if she so wished, to save Ruggieri and preserve the reputation of her mistress at one and the same time.

'Tell me what I have to do, ma'am,' said the maid, 'and I'll do it gladly, no matter what it involves.'

The lady, who saw that there was no time to lose, quickly improvised a plan of campaign and expounded it carefully to the maid, who first of all went straight to the Doctor and, bursting into tears, said to him:

'Sir, I have done you a serious wrong, and I must ask you to forgive me.'

'And what may that be?' asked the surgeon.

'Sir,' replied the maid, continuing to weep, 'it concerns Ruggieri d'Aieroli. You know what a headstrong lad he is? Well, he took a fancy to me, and what with my fear of him on the one hand and my love for him on the other, a month or two ago I was obliged to become his mistress. When he discovered you were not going to be here last night, he talked me into allowing him into your house to sleep with me in my room. He said he was thirsty, but I hadn't a drop of wine or water to offer him. I couldn't go downstairs without being seen by your good lady, who was in the drawing room, but I remembered having seen a bottle of water in your bedroom, and so I ran to fetch it, gave it him to drink, and put the bottle back again where I had found it. They tell me you've been playing merry hell about it, and I freely confess that it was wrong of me to do it, but then everybody makes a blunder occasionally. I can only say that I am very sorry, not only for doing what I did, but also for Ruggieri's sake, because he is about to lose his life over it. I therefore beseech you with all my heart to forgive me and let me go and see what I can do to help Ruggieri.'

Angry though he was to hear what she had done, the Doctor had difficulty in keeping a straight face.

'You have been hoist with your own petard,' he replied. 'For you thought you had a young man who would shake your skin-coat well and truly last night, instead of which you had a slug-abed. Now go and see about saving your lover, and take good care in future not to bring him into the house again, otherwise I shall make you pay for it twice over.'

Feeling that she had emerged with flying colours from the first of her engagements, the maid hurried round as quickly as possible to the prison and wheedled the gaoler into letting her speak to Ruggieri. And after telling him what he was to say to the judge if he wanted to be saved, she actually succeeded in getting the judge himself to grant her a hearing.

The judge saw that she was a tasty-looking dish, and thought he would have just one little nibble before listening to what she had to say. Knowing that she would obtain a better hearing, the girl did not object in the slightest, and when the snack was finished she picked herself up and said:

'Sir, you are holding Ruggieri d'Aieroli here on a charge of theft, but you've arrested the wrong man.'

She then told him the whole story from beginning to end, explaining how she, who was his mistress, had let him into the doctor's house, and how she had unwittingly given him the opiate to drink, and how she had stuffed him inside the trunk thinking him to be dead. After this she told him about the conversation she had overheard between the master-carpenter and the trunk's owner, thus showing him how Ruggieri had ended up in the house of the money-lenders.

Seeing that it was an easy matter to verify her story, the judge first of all enquired of the surgeon whether what she had said about the potion was true, and discovered that it was. He then summoned the carpenter, the owner of the trunk, and the money-lenders, and after listening to a string of tall stories from the money-lenders, he found that they had stolen the trunk during the night and brought it into their house. Finally he sent for Ruggieri and asked him where he had lodged the previous evening. Ruggieri replied that he had no idea where he had lodged, but that he clearly remembered going to lodge with Doctor Mazzeo's maid, in whose bedroom he had drunk some water because he was very thirsty; what happened to him after that he was unable to say, except that he had woken up in the money-lenders' house to find himself inside a trunk.

The judge was greatly entertained by what he had heard, and made Ruggieri and the maid and the carpenter and the money-lenders repeat their stories several times over. In the end, pronouncing Ruggieri innocent, he ordered the money-lenders to pay a fine of ten gold florins, and set Ruggieri at liberty. You can all imagine what a relief this was for Ruggieri, and of course his mistress was absolutely delighted. She later celebrated his release in the company of Ruggieri himself, and along with the dear maid who had wanted to stick him with a knife, they had many a good laugh about it together. Their love continued to flourish, affording them greater and greater pleasure – which is what I should like to happen to me, except that I would not want to be stuffed inside a trunk.

* * *

If the earlier stories had saddened the fair ladies' hearts, this last one of Dioneo's caused so much merriment, especially the bit about the judge and his little nibble, that it drove away the melancholy engendered by the others.

But perceiving that the sun was beginning to yellow and that his reign had come to a close, the king offered the fair ladies a most handsome apology for having foisted so disagreeable a theme as the misfortunes of lovers upon them. Having made his excuses, he stood up and removed the laurel wreath from his head. All the ladies wondered to which of them it would be given, and eventually he set it down with a flourish upon the fine blonde head of Fiammetta, saying:

'I now bequeath you this crown, knowing that you are better able than any other to restore the spirits of our fair companions tomorrow after the rigours of the present day's proceedings.'

Fiammetta, who had long, golden curls that cascaded down over delicate, pure white shoulders, a softly rounded face that glowed with the authentic hues of white lilies and crimson roses, a pair of eyes in her head that gleamed like a falcon's, and a sweet little mouth with lips like rubies, answered Filostrato with a smile, saying:

'I accept it with pleasure, Filostrato; and so that you may the more keenly appreciate the error of your ways, I desire and decree forthwith that each of us should be ready on the morrow to recount *the adventures of lovers who survived calamities or misfortunes and attained a state of happiness.*'

Fiammetta's proposal met with general approval, and after summoning the steward and making appropriate arrangements, she rose to her feet and gaily dismissed the whole company till supper-time.

So they all wandered off to amuse themselves until supper in whatever way they pleased, some of them remaining in the garden, of whose beauties one did not easily tire, whilst others ventured beyond its confines and made for the windmills, whose sails were turning in the evening breeze.

When it was time for supper, they forgathered as usual beside the beautiful fountain, and partook of a most delicious meal, excellently served. Then, having risen from table, they devoted themselves to singing and dancing in their customary fashion, with Filomena leading the revels, and the queen said:

'Filostrato, it is not my intention to depart from the ways of my predecessors. Like them, I too intend to command that a song should be sung, and since I am sure that your songs will be no less gloomy than your stories, I desire that you should choose one and sing it to us now, so that no day other than this will be blighted by your woes.'

Filostrato replied that he would be only too willing to obey, and launched immediately into a song, the words of which ran as follows:

> 'With fitting tears, I show
>   The mourning heart bereaved,
>   Its faith in Love deceived.
>
> 'Love, who first fixed into my heart
>   She for whom now I sigh in vain,
>   You showed me her so full of grace
>   That I held light each bitter pain
>   Which came to torment me
>   So everlastingly.
>   I know my error now;
>   Not without grief, I vow.

'I comprehend that false deceit
And see how, while I thought that she
Seemed to allow my love, she'd found
Another servant, spurning me.
   Ah, then I could not see
   My future misery!
   But she the other took
   And me for him forsook.

'A mournful song swelled through my heart
When I perceived that I was spurned,
That dwells there still; and oft I curse
Faith, hope, love and the hour I learned
   Her noble beauteousness
   Whose radiance doth oppress
   My dying soul, which yet
   Cannot those charms forget.

'Bereft of every comfort now,
Oh, Lord of love, to you I cry;
I burn with such a torment here
That for a less I'd crave to die.
   Come Death, then, end my life
   With all its cruel strife;
   Strike down my misery!
   I shall the better be.

'No other way nor other ease
Remains to soothe my grief but death.
Grant me this, Love, and end my woes;
Take from me now my wretched breath.
   All joy is gone from me,
   No pleasure's left for me;
   Make then my death content her
   As the new love you sent her.

'My song, if none should learn to sing
Thee over, I take little care;
No one can sing thee as I can.
Only, to Love one message bear:
   Beg him, since life was all
   Loathsome to me, and vile,

To safer haven take
Me for his honour's sake.'

Filostrato's mood, and the reason, were made abundantly clear by the words of his song. And perhaps the face of one of the ladies dancing would have clarified the matter still further if the shades of darkness, which had meanwhile descended, had not concealed the blush which spread across her cheeks as he was singing.

Many other songs followed, until finally it was time for them to go to bed, whereupon, by the queen's command, they all retired to their rooms.

Here ends the Fourth Day of the Decameron

FIFTH DAY

Here begins the Fifth Day, wherein, under the rule of Fiammetta, are discussed the adventures of lovers who survived calamities or misfortunes and attained a state of happiness.

The whole of the East was already suffused with white, and the heavens of the Western world were shot through by the rays of the rising sun, when Fiammetta was roused from sleep by the melodious songs of the birds in the trees, chanting their joyous greetings to the dawn. She arose and sent for all the other ladies and the three young men, then sauntered down with her companions to the fields, where, walking over the dew of the broad and grassy plain, she conversed agreeably with the others upon this and that, till the sun had climbed well into the sky. But as the heat of the sun's rays grew more intense, she retraced her steps, and on reaching the house she saw that her companions were refreshed from the gentle exertions of their walk with excellent wines and sweetmeats, after which they whiled away their time till breakfast in the delectable garden. No detail had been overlooked by their resourceful steward in the preparation of the meal, to which in due course, at the bidding of the queen, after singing some canzonets and one or two *ballades*, they gaily addressed themselves. One by one, they disposed of the various dishes with relish, and when the meal was over, mindful of the practice already established, they danced and sang to the music of instruments. The queen then dismissed them till after the siesta hour, whereat some of them went away to sleep, whilst the others remained in the garden to savour its pleasures.

But shortly after nones, at the queen's command, they all forgathered as usual beside the fountain. And having seated herself in a position of honour, the queen fixed her gaze upon Panfilo, smiled, and bade him tell the first of the day's stories, all of which were to end happily. Panfilo readily agreed, and began as follows:

FIRST STORY

Cymon acquires wisdom through falling in love with Iphigenia, whom he later abducts on the high seas. After being imprisoned at Rhodes, he is released by Lysimachus, with whom he abducts both Iphigenia and Cassandra whilst they are celebrating their nuptials. They then flee with their ladies to Crete, whence after their marriage they are summoned back with their wives to their respective homes.

Delectable ladies, I can think of many stories with which I could aptly make a beginning to so joyful a day as this. But there is one in particular that strikes me as specially pleasing, for not only will it enable you to perceive the happy goal to which our discussions will from now on be directed, but it will also allow you to appreciate the sacredness, the power, and the beneficial effects of the forces of Love, which so many people, ignorant of what they are saying, mistakenly treat with contempt and abuse. All of which, unless I am mistaken, you will find most agreeable, for I take it that you are yourselves in love.

In the chronicles of the ancient Cypriots, then, we read that there once lived in the island of Cyprus a very noble gentleman, Aristippus by name, who was richer in worldly possessions than any other man in the country. And if Fortune had not presented him with one particular source of affliction, he would have accounted himself the happiest man alive. This consisted in the fact that one of his children, a youth of outstandingly handsome appearance and perfect physique, was to all intents and purposes an imbecile, whose case was regarded as hopeless. His true name was Galesus, but since the sum total of his tutor's persistent efforts, his father's cajolings and beatings, and all the ingenuity of various others, had failed to drum a scrap of learning or good manners into his head, on the contrary leaving him coarsely inarticulate and with the manners rather of a wild beast than a human being, he had earned himself the unflattering nickname of Cymon, which in their language has the same sort of meaning as 'simpleton' in ours. His hopeless condition was a matter of very grave concern to his father, who, despairing of any improvement and not wishing to have the source of his affliction constantly before him, ordered him to go and live with his farmworkers in the country. Cymon was only too pleased to obey, for to his way of thinking the customs and practices of country yokels were far more congenial than life in the city.

So Cymon went away to the country, where one afternoon, whilst going about his rustic business on one of his father's estates, with a stick on his shoulder, he chanced to enter a wood, renowned in those parts for its beauty, the trees of which were thickly leaved as it happened to be the month of May. As he was walking through the wood, guided as it were by Fortune, he came upon a clearing surrounded by very tall trees, in a corner of which there was a lovely cool fountain. Beside the fountain, lying asleep on the grass, he saw a most beautiful girl, attired in so flimsy a dress that scarcely an inch of her fair white body was concealed. From the waist downwards she was draped in a pure white quilt, no less diaphanous than the rest of her attire, and at her feet, also fast asleep, lay two women and a man, who were the young lady's attendants.

On catching sight of this vision, Cymon stopped in his tracks, and leaning on his stick, began to stare at her, rapt in silent admiration, as though he had never before set eyes upon the female form. And deep within his uncouth breast, which despite a thousand promptings had remained stubbornly closed to every vestige of refined sentiment, he sensed the awakening of a certain feeling which told his crude, uncultured mind that this girl was the loveliest object that any mortal being had ever seen. He now began to consider each of her features in turn, admiring her hair, which he judged to be made of gold, her brow, nose and mouth, her neck and arms; and especially her bosom, which was not yet very pronounced. Having suddenly been transformed from a country bumpkin into a connoisseur of beauty, he longed to be able to see her eyes, but they were closed in heavy slumber, from which the girl gave no apparent sign of awakening. Several times he was on the point of rousing her so that he might observe them, but as she seemed far more beautiful than any woman he had ever seen, he supposed that she might be a goddess, and he had sufficient mother wit to appreciate that divine things require more respect than those pertaining to earth. He therefore refrained, and waited for her to wake up of her own accord; and though he grew tired of waiting, he was filled with such strange sensations of pleasure that he was unable to tear himself away.

A long time elapsed before the girl, whose name was Iphigenia, raised her head and opened her eyes. Her attendants were still asleep, and on catching sight of Cymon standing before her, leaning on his stick, she was greatly astonished. She recognized him at once, for Cymon was known to almost everyone in those parts, not only because of the contrast between his handsome appearance and boorish manner, but also on account of his father's rank and riches.

'Cymon!' she exclaimed. 'What brings you here to the woods at this time of day?'

Cymon made no reply, but stood there gazing into her eyes, which seemed to shine with a gentleness that filled him with a feeling of joy such as he had never known before. When she saw him staring at her, Iphigenia was afraid that his rusticity might impel him to act in a way that would bring dishonour upon her, and having awakened her maidservants, she rose to her feet, saying:

'Cymon, I bid you good day.'

'I shall come with you,' Cymon replied.

Still feeling somewhat apprehensive, the girl refused his company, but did not succeed in shaking him off till he had escorted her all the way to her door. He then proceeded to his father's house, where he declared that he would on no account return to the country. His father and family were greatly displeased about this, but allowed him to stay in the hope of discovering what had caused him to change his mind.

Now that Cymon's heart, which no amount of schooling had been able to penetrate, was pierced by Love's arrow through the medium of Iphigenia's beauty, he suddenly began to display a lively interest in one thing after another, to the amazement of his father, his whole family, and everyone else who knew him. He first of all asked his father's permission to wear the same sort of clothes as his brothers, including all the frills with which they were in the habit of adorning themselves, and to this his father very readily agreed. He then began to associate with young men of excellence, observing the manners befitting a gentleman, more especially those of a gentleman in love, and within a very short space of time, to everyone's enormous stupefaction, he not only acquired the rudiments of learning but became a paragon of intelligence and wit. Furthermore (and this again was a consequence of his love for Iphigenia), he abandoned his coarse and rustic accent, adopting a manner of speech that was more seemly and civilized, and even became an accomplished singer and musician, whilst in horse-riding and in martial prowess, whether on sea or land, he distinguished himself by his skill and daring.

In short, (without going into further detail about his various accomplishments), in the space of four years from the day he had fallen in love, he turned out to be the most graceful, refined, and versatile young man in the island of Cyprus.

What, then, are we to say, fair ladies, of this young man? Surely, all we need say is that the lofty virtues instilled by Heaven in Cymon's valiant spirit were chained together and locked away by envious Fortune in a very small section of his heart, and that her mighty bonds had been shattered and torn apart by a much more powerful force, in other words that of Love. Being a rouser of sleeping talents, Love had rescued those virtues from the darkness in which they had lain so cruelly hidden and forced them into the light, clearly displaying whence he draws, and whither he leads, those creatures who are subject to his rule and illumined by his radiance.

Although, in common with many another young man in love, Cymon was inclined in some ways to carry his love for Iphigenia to extremes, nevertheless Aristippus, on reflecting that Love had turned his son from a donkey into a man, not only treated him with patience and tolerance but encouraged him to go further, and taste Love's pleasures to the full. But Cymon (who refused to be called Galesus because he recalled that Iphigenia had addressed him by his nickname) was determined to achieve the object of his yearning by honourable means, and made several attempts to persuade Iphigenia's father, Cypsehus, to grant him her hand in marriage, only to be told on each occasion that Cypsehus had already promised her to Pasimondas, a young nobleman of Rhodes, and had no intention of breaking his word.

When the time came for Iphigenia's marriage contract to be

honoured, and her husband sent to fetch her, Cymon said to himself: 'Ah, Iphigenia! now is the time for me to prove how deeply I love you! Through you I have achieved manhood, and if I succeed in winning you, beyond doubt I shall achieve greater glory than any of the gods. And win you I certainly shall, or I shall perish.' Being thus resolved, he furtively enlisted the help of certain young nobles who were friends of his, made secret arrangements to fit out a ship with everything one needed for a naval battle, and put out to sea, where he hove to and waited for the vessel which was to convey Iphigenia to her husband in Rhodes. And after her husband's friends had been sumptuously entertained by her father, they escorted her aboard, pointed the ship's prow in the direction of Rhodes, and departed.

On the following day, Cymon, who was very much on the alert, caught up with them in his own vessel, and standing on the prow, he hailed the crew of Iphigenia's ship in a loud voice:

'Lower your sails and heave to, or prepare to be overwhelmed and sunk!'

Cymon's opponents had brought up weapons from below and were making ready to defend themselves, so he followed up his words by seizing a grappling-iron and hurling it on to the stern of the Rhodian ship as it was pulling swiftly away, thus bringing his bows hard up against the enemy's poop. Without waiting to be joined by his comrades, he leapt aboard the Rhodians' ship like a raging lion as though contemptuous of all opposition. Spurred on by his love, he set about his adversaries with astonishing vigour, striking them down with his cutlass, one after another, like so many sheep. On seeing this the Rhodians laid down their arms, and more or less in chorus gave themselves up as his prisoners.

Then Cymon said to them:

'Young men, it was not the desire for plunder, nor any hatred towards you personally, that impelled me to leave Cyprus and subject you to armed attack on the high seas. My motive was the acquisition of something which I value most highly, and which it is very easy for you to surrender to me peaceably. I refer to Iphigenia, whom I love more than anything else in the world. Since I was unable to obtain her from her father by friendly and peaceable means, Love has compelled me to seize her from you in this hostile fashion, by force of arms. And now I intend to be to her such as your master, Pasimondas, was to have been. Give her to me, then, and proceed with God's grace on your voyage.'

The young men, more from necessity than the kindness of their hearts, handed over the weeping Iphigenia to her captor.

'Noble lady,' said Cymon, on perceiving her tears, 'do not distress yourself. It is your Cymon that you see before you. The constant love I have borne you gives me far more right to possess you than the plighted troth of Pasimondas.'

Having seen that Iphigenia was taken aboard, he returned to his own ship and allowed the Rhodians to go with all their possessions intact.

The winning of so precious a prize made Cymon the happiest man on earth. After spending some time consoling his tearful mistress, he persuaded his companions that they should not return to Cyprus for the present, and they all agreed to steer their ship towards Crete, where Cymon and most of the others had family ties, both recently made and long established, as well as numerous friends and acquaintances. And for this very reason they thought it safe to go there with Iphigenia.

They had reckoned without the fickleness of Fortune, however, for no sooner had she handed the lady into Cymon's keeping, than she converted the boundless joy of the enamoured youth into sad and bitter weeping.

Scarcely four hours had elapsed since Cymon and the Rhodians had parted company, when, with the approach of night, to which Cymon was looking forward with a keener pleasure than any he had ever experienced, an exceptionally violent storm arose, filling the sky with dark clouds and turning the sea into a raging cauldron. It thus became impossible for those aboard to see what they were doing or steer a proper course, or to keep their balance sufficiently long to perform their duties.

Needless to say, Cymon was greatly aggrieved by all this. The gods had granted his desire, but only, it seemed, to fill him with dread at the prospect of dying, which without Iphigenia he would have faced with cheerful indifference. His companions were equally woebegone, but the saddest one of all was Iphigenia, who was shedding copious tears and trembled with fear at every buffeting of the waves. Between her tears she bitterly cursed Cymon's love and censured his temerity, declaring that this alone had brought about the raging tempest, though it could also have arisen because Cymon's desire to marry her was contrary to the will of the gods, who were determined, not only to deny him the fruits of his presumptuous longing, but to make him witness her demise before he, too, died a miserable death.

These laments she continued to pour forth, along with others of still greater vehemence, until, with the wind blowing fiercer all the time, the seamen at their wits' end, and everyone ignorant of the course they were steering, they arrived off the island of Rhodes. Not realizing where they were, they did everything in their power to make a good landfall, and thus prevent loss of life.

Fortune was kindly to their endeavours, and guided them into a tiny bay, to which the Rhodians released by Cymon on the previous day had brought their own vessel a little while before. Dawn was breaking as they entered the bay, turning the sky a little brighter, and no sooner did they become aware that they were at the island of Rhodes than they perceived the very ship from which they had parted company, lying no more than a stone's throw away from their own. Cymon was dismayed beyond measure by this discovery, and fearing just such a fate as eventually overtook him, he called upon his crew to spare no effort in getting away from there and allowing Fortune to carry them wherever she pleased, since she could hardly choose a worse place than the one they were in. They strove with might and main to make good their escape, but without success, for a fierce gale was blowing directly against them, which not only prevented them from leaving the bay but drove them of necessity to the shore.

They eventually ran aground and were recognized by the Rhodian sailors, who by now were already ashore. One of these hurried off to inform the young Rhodian nobles, who had meanwhile made their way to a nearby town, that the ship carrying Cymon and Iphigenia had, like their own, been driven into the bay by the storm.

Overjoyed by these tidings, the young Rhodians assembled a large number of the townspeople and instantly returned to the shore. Cymon and his companions had meanwhile disembarked, intending to seek refuge in some neighbouring woods, but before they could do so they were all seized, along with Iphigenia, and led away to the town. Here they were held until Lysimachus, the chief magistrate of Rhodes in that particular year, came from the city and marched them all off to prison under a specially heavy armed escort, as arranged by Pasimondas, who had lodged a complaint with the Senate of Rhodes as soon as the news had reached him.

And so it came about that the hapless Cymon lost his beloved Iphigenia almost as soon as he had won her, with nothing to show for his pains except one or two kisses. As for Iphigenia, she was given hospitality by various noble ladies of Rhodes, who restored her spirits from the shock of her abduction and the fatigue she had suffered in the tempest; and she remained with them until the day appointed for her wedding.

Pasimondas urged with all his eloquence that Cymon and his companions should be put to death, but their lives were spared on account of having set the young Rhodians at liberty on the previous day, and they were condemned to spend the rest of their lives in prison. And there, as may readily be imagined, they led a wretched existence, and despaired of ever knowing happiness again.

It was whilst Pasimondas was pressing zealously ahead with the preparations for his forthcoming marriage that Fortune, as though to make amends for the sudden blow she had dealt to Cymon's hopes, devised a novel way of procuring him his liberty. Pasimondas had a brother, younger but no less eligible than himself, whose name was Ormisdas, and who for some time had been seeking to marry a beautiful young noblewoman of the city called Cassandra, with whom Lysimachus, the chief magistrate, was very deeply in love. But the marriage had been several times postponed because of some unexpected turn of events.

Now, seeing that he was about to hold a huge reception to celebrate his own wedding, Pasimondas thought it would be an excellent idea to arrange for Ormisdas to be married at the same time, thus avoiding a second round of spending and feasting. He therefore re-opened discussions with Cassandra's kinsfolk and brought them to a successful conclusion, all the parties agreeing that on the day that Pasimondas married Iphigenia, Ormisdas should marry Cassandra.

Lysimachus, having heard of this arrangement, was greatly distressed, for it now appeared that all his hopes of marrying Cassandra, provided that Ormisdas did not marry her first, had suddenly vanished. He was wise enough, however, to conceal the agony he was suffering, and began to study various ways and means of preventing the marriage from taking place, eventually concluding that the only possible solution was to abduct her.

This seemed a feasible proposition because of the office he held, although if he had held no office at all he would have thought it a far less dishonourable course to take. But in short, after lengthy reflection his sense of honour gave way to his love, and he resolved, come what may, to carry Cassandra off. On giving thought to the sort of companions he would need for effecting his design, and planning the strategy he should adopt, he remembered that he was holding Cymon prisoner, together with all his men, and it occurred to him that for an enterprise such as this it would be impossible to find a better or more loyal accomplice.

So during the night he had Cymon secretly conveyed to his chamber, and introduced the subject in this fashion:

'Not only, Cymon, do the gods most freely and generously distribute their largesse amongst men, they also have exceedingly subtle ways of putting our merits to the test. And those whom they discover to be firm and constant in all circumstances, since they are the worthiest, are singled out for the highest rewards. The gods desired surer proofs of your excellence than you were able to display when living in the house of your father, whom I know to be immensely rich. And having first of all transformed you (or so I have been told) from an insensate beast into a man through the keen stimulus of Love, they are now intent upon seeing whether, after a severe ordeal and the discomforts of imprisonment, you are any less resolute than when you briefly enjoyed the spoils of victory. Nothing they have previously granted you, however, can have brought you so much joy and happiness as the thing which, if your courage has not deserted you, they are preparing to offer to you now. And in order to restore your strength, and put fresh heart into you, I intend to explain what it is.

'Pasimondas, who gloats over your undoing and fervently advocates your death, is making every effort to bring forward the celebration of his nuptials to your beloved Iphigenia, and thus enjoy the prize which Fortune had no sooner been content to bestow upon you than she angrily snatched away from you again. If he should succeed, and if you are as deeply in love as I suspect, I can readily imagine the pain you will suffer, for on that same day his brother, Ormisdas, is proposing to do the same to me by marrying Cassandra, whom I love more dearly than anything else in the world. If we are to prevent Fortune from dealing us so heavy and calamitous a blow, it seems to me that she has left us with no other recourse except the stoutness of our hearts and the strength of our right hands, with which we must seize our swords and fight our way to our ladies, you to carry off Iphigenia for the second time and I to carry off Cassandra for the first. If, therefore, you value the prospect of recovering your lady (not to mention your liberty, which must in any case mean little to you without Iphigenia), the gods have placed the means within your reach, provided you will join me in my enterprise.'

These words restored Cymon's depleted spirits to the full, and his answer was quickly forthcoming.

'Lysimachus,' he said, 'if this scheme of yours procures me the reward of which you have spoken, you could not have chosen a more resolute or loyal comrade. Therefore entrust me with whatever task you desire me to perform, and you will marvel at the energy I devote to your cause.'

'Two days hence,' said Lysimachus, 'the brides will cross their husbands' threshold for the first time. As dusk is falling, we shall go to the house, you with your companions and I with certain of mine whom I trust implicitly, and make our way inside by armed force. We shall then seize the ladies from the midst of the assembled guests, and carry them off to a ship which I have caused to be fitted out in secret, killing anyone who should have the temerity to stand in our way.'

Cymon agreed to the plan, and lay quietly in prison until the appointed time.

When the wedding-day arrived, it was marked by magnificent pomp and splendour, and the house of the two brothers was filled throughout with sounds of revelry and rejoicing. Lysimachus, having completed all his preparations, handed out weapons to Cymon and his companions, as well as to his own friends, and these they concealed beneath their robes. He then delivered a lengthy harangue to fire them with enthusiasm for his plan, and when he judged the time to be ripe, he divided them into three separate groups, one of which he prudently dispatched to the harbour so that no one could prevent them from embarking when the time came for them to leave. Having led the other two parties to the house of Pasimondas, he posted one of them at the main entrance to frustrate any attempt to lock them inside or bar their retreat, whilst with the other, including Cymon, he charged up the stairs. On reaching the hall, where the two brides were already seated and about to dine along with numerous other ladies, they marched boldly forward and hurled the tables to the floor. Then each of the two men seized his lady and handed her over to his companions, instructing them to carry them off at once to the waiting ship.

The brides began to cry and scream, the other ladies and the servants followed suit, and the whole place was filled in an instant with uproar and wailing. But Cymon and Lysimachus and their companions, having drawn their swords, made their way unopposed to the head of the staircase, everyone standing aside to let them pass. As they were descending the stairs, they were met by Pasimondas, who had been attracted by all the noise and came up wielding a heavy stick; but he was struck such a fierce blow over the head by Cymon that a good half of it was severed from his body, and he dropped dead at the feet of his assailant. In rushing to his brother's assistance, the hapless Ormisdas was likewise slain by one of Cymon's lusty blows, whilst a handful of others who ventured to approach were set upon and beaten back by the rest of the invaders.

Leaving the house full of blood, tumult, tears, and sadness, they made their way unimpeded to the ship, keeping close together and carrying their spoils before them. Having handed the ladies aboard, Cymon and Lysimachus followed with their comrades just as the shore began to fill with armed men who were coming to the rescue of the two ladies. But they plied their oars with a will, and made good their escape.

On arriving in Crete they were given a joyous welcome by a large number of their friends and relatives, and after they had married their ladies and held a great wedding-feast, they gaily enjoyed the spoils of their endeavours.

In Rhodes and in Cyprus their deeds gave rise to great commotion and uproar, which took some time to subside. But in the fullness of time, their friends and relatives interceded on their behalf in both these places, and made it possible for Cymon and Lysimachus, after a period of exile, to return to Cyprus and Rhodes with Iphigenia and Cassandra respectively. And each lived happily ever after with his lady in the land of his birth.

SECOND STORY

Gostanza, in love with Martuccio Gomito, hears that he has died, and in her despair she puts to sea alone in a small boat, which is carried by the wind to Susa; she finds him, alive and well, in Tunis, and makes herself known to him, whereupon Martuccio, who stands high in the King's esteem on account of certain advice he had offered him, marries her and brings her back with a rich fortune to Lipari.

Perceiving that Panfilo's story was at an end, the queen, having warmly commended it, directed Emilia to proceed with one of hers, and Emilia began as follows:

It is only natural that we should rejoice on seeing an enterprise crowned with rewards appropriate to the sentiments that inspired it. And since it is proper for true love to be rewarded in the long run with joy rather than suffering, it gives me far greater pleasure to obey the queen, and speak upon the present topic, than it gave me yesterday to address myself to the one prescribed for us by the king.

You are to know then, dainty ladies, that near Sicily there is a small island called Lipari, on which, not very long ago, there lived a most beautiful girl, Gostanza by name, who belonged to one of the noblest families on the island. With this girl, a young man called Martuccio Gomito, who also lived on the island, and who, apart from being an outstanding craftsman, was exceedingly handsome and well-mannered, fell in love. And Gostanza reciprocated his love so wholeheartedly that she was never happy when he was out of her sight. Desiring to make her his wife, Martuccio requested her father's consent, but was told that since he was too poor he couldn't have her.

Martuccio, indignant at seeing himself rejected on the grounds of his poverty, commissioned a small sailing-ship with certain friends and relatives of his, and vowed never to return to Lipari until he was a rich man. Having put to sea, he began to play the pirate along the coasts of Barbary, plundering every vessel that was weaker than his own. He had all the luck that was going for as long as he kept his ambition within reasonable bounds. But it was not enough that Martuccio and his companions should have quickly amassed a small fortune for themselves; their appetite for riches was enormous, and in trying to assuage it they encountered a flotilla of Saracen ships, by which, after lengthy resistance, they were captured and plundered. Most of Martuccio's men were dumped into the sea, and their ship was sunk, but Martuccio himself was hauled off to Tunis, where he was left to languish in a prison-cell.

Word was meanwhile brought to Lipari, not merely by one or two but by several different people, that Martuccio and all the men aboard his ship had been drowned.

When she heard that Martuccio and his companions were dead, the girl, who had been distressed beyond measure by his departure, wept incessantly and resolved to put an end to her life. Lacking the courage to do herself violently to death, she hit upon a novel but no less certain way of killing herself; and one night, she secretly left her father's house and made her way to the harbour, where she chanced upon a tiny fishing-boat, lying some distance away from the other vessels. Its owners having gone ashore just a little while earlier, the boat was still equipped with its mast, its sail, and its oars. And since, like most of the women on the island, she had learnt the rudiments of seamanship, she stepped promptly aboard, rowed a little way out to sea, and hoisted the sail, after which she threw the oars and rudder overboard and placed herself entirely at the mercy of the wind. She calculated that one of two things would inevitably happen: either the boat, being without ballast or rudder, would capsize in the wind, or it would be driven aground somewhere and smashed to pieces. In either case she was certain to drown, for she would be unable to save herself even if she wanted to. So having wrapped a cloak round her head, she lay down, weeping, on the floor of the boat.

But her calculations proved quite wrong, for the wind blew so gently from the north that the sea was barely disturbed, the boat maintained an even keel, and towards evening on the following day she drifted ashore near a town called Susa, a hundred miles or so beyond Tunis.

The girl was not aware that she was more ashore than afloat, for she had not raised her head once from the position in which it was lying, nor had she any intention of doing so, whatever happened.

As luck would have it, when the boat ran aground there was a poor woman on the shore, taking in nets that had been left in the sun by the fishermen for whom she worked. On seeing the boat, she wondered how the fishermen aboard could have let it run aground under full sail, and assumed that they must be asleep. So she went up to the boat, but the only person she could see was this young woman, lying there fast asleep. Having called to her several times, she eventually got her to wake up, and since she could see that the girl was a Christian from the clothes she was wearing, she asked her in Italian how it came about that she had landed in that particular spot, and in that particular boat, all by herself.

Hearing herself addressed in Italian, the girl wondered whether she had been driven back to Lipari by a change of wind. She started to her feet and looked around, and on seeing that she was grounded on a coastline that was totally unfamiliar to her, she asked the good woman where she was.

'You are near Susa, in Barbary, my daughter,' the woman replied. On learning where she was, the girl, dismayed that God had denied her the death she was seeking, was afraid lest worse should befall her. Not knowing what to do, she sat down beside the keel of the boat and burst into tears. On seeing this, the good woman took pity upon her and persuaded her, after a good deal of coaxing, to go with her to her little cottage, where she treated her so kindly that Gostanza told her how she came to be there. The woman realized that she must be hungry, and so she placed some dry bread, water, and a quantity of fish before her, and with much difficulty persuaded her to eat a little.

Then Gostanza asked her who she was, and how she came to speak such fluent Italian, whereupon the good woman told her that she was from Trapani, that her name was Carapresa, and that she was employed by some fishermen, who were Christians.

The girl was feeling very sorry for herself, but on hearing the name Carapresa (which means 'precious gain'), without knowing why, she took it as a good omen. For some strange reason she began to feel more hopeful, and was no longer so anxious to put an end to herself. Without disclosing who she was or whence she came, she earnestly entreated the good woman, in God's name, to have mercy on her youth and advise her how to save herself from coming to any harm.

The woman was a kindly soul, and after leaving her for a while in the cottage whilst she quickly gathered up her nets, she returned and wrapped her from head to foot in her own cloak, then took her with her to Susa. And on arriving in the town, she said:

'Gostanza, I am going to take you to the house of a very kind Saracen lady, who employs me regularly on various errands. She is elderly and tender-hearted: I shall commend you to her as warmly as I possibly can, and I am quite certain that she will gladly take you in and treat you as a daughter. Once you are under her roof, you are to serve her as loyally as you can, so as to win and retain her favour until such time as God may send you better fortune.'

Carapresa was as good as her word. When the lady, who was getting on in years, had heard her story, she looked into Gostanza's eyes, burst into tears, gathered her in her arms and kissed her on the forehead. Then she led her by the hand into the house, where she lived with certain other women, isolated from all male company. The women worked with their hands in various ways, producing a number of different objects made of silk, palm, and leather, and within a few days, the girl, having learned to make some of these objects, was sharing the work with the others. Her benefactress and the other ladies were remarkably kind and affectionate towards her, and before very long they had taught her to speak their language.

Now, whilst the girl was living at Susa, having long been given up as dead by her family, it happened that the King of Tunis, whose name was Mulay Abd Allah, was threatened by a powerful young grandee, who came from Granada, and who claimed that the kingdom of Tunis belonged to him. And having assembled an enormous army, he marched against the King to drive him from the realm.

Tidings of these events came to the ears of Martuccio Gomito as he lay in prison, and as he was well versed in the language of the Saracens, on learning that the King of Tunis was making strenuous efforts to defend himself, he said to one of the men who were guarding him and his companions:

'If I could speak to the King, I am sure I could advise him how to win this war of his.'

The gaoler reported Martuccio's words to his superior, who immediately passed them on to the King. The King therefore ordered Martuccio to be brought before him, and asked him what advice he had in mind.

'My lord,' replied Martuccio, 'years ago I spent some time in this country of yours, and if I rightly observed the tactics you employ in battle, it seems that you leave the brunt of the fighting to your archers. If, therefore, one could devise a way of cutting off the enemy's supply of arrows whilst leaving your own men with arrows to spare, I reckon that your battle would be won.'

'If this could be done,' replied the King, 'without a doubt I should be confident of winning.'

'My lord,' said Martuccio, 'it can certainly be done if you have a mind to do it. Listen, and I shall tell you how. You must see that the bows of your archers are fitted with much finer string than that which is normally used. You must then have arrows specially made, the notches of which will only take this finer string. All of this must be done in great secrecy so that the enemy knows nothing about it, otherwise he would take suitable counter-measures. The reason for my advice is this: as you know, when your enemy's archers have fired all their arrows, and your own men have fired theirs, each side will have to gather up the other's arrows for the battle to continue. But the arrows fired by your archers will be useless to the enemy because their bow-strings will be too thick to fit the small notches, whereas your own men will have no difficulty at all in using the enemy's arrows because a fine string can perfectly well be fitted in a thick notch. Thus your own men will have an abundant supply of arrows, and the others will have none at all.'

Being a man of some intelligence, the King approved of Martuccio's plan and carried it out to the letter, thereby winning the war. Martuccio was therefore raised to a high position in the King's favour, and consequently grew rich and powerful.

Tidings of these events spread throughout the country, and when it was reported to Gostanza that Martuccio Gomito, whom she had long supposed to be dead, was in fact alive, her love for him, which by now was beginning to fade from her heart, was suddenly rekindled, blazing more fiercely than ever, and all her lost hopes were revived. She therefore recounted all her vicissitudes to the good lady with whom she was living, and told her that she desired to go to Tunis, so that she might feast her eyes upon that which her ears had made them eager to behold. Her request was warmly approved by the lady, who, treating her as a daughter, took her by sea to Tunis, where she and Gostanza were honourably received in the house of one of the lady's kinswomen.

They had brought Carapresa with them, and the lady sent her to find out all she could about Martuccio. When she returned with the news that Martuccio was alive and of high estate, the lady resolved to go in person to Martuccio and inform him of the arrival of his beloved Gostanza. And so one day, she called upon Martuccio, and said to him:

'Martuccio, a servant of yours from Lipari has turned up at my house, and desires to talk to you there in private. Since he did not wish me to entrust his mission to others, I have come to inform you in person.'

Martuccio thanked the lady, and followed her back to her house.

The girl was so delighted to see him that she nearly died. Carried away by her feelings, she ran up to him and flung her arms round his neck; then she burst into tears, unable to speak because of her joy and the bitter memory of her past misfortunes.

When he saw who it was, Martuccio was at first struck dumb with astonishment, but then he began to sigh, and said:

'Oh, Gostanza, can it really be you? I was told, long ago, that you had vanished from Lipari, never to be heard of again.' And this was all he could say before he, too, burst into tears, took her tenderly in his arms, and kissed her.

Gostanza described to him all that had happened to her, and told him of the honour paid to her by the noble lady with whom she had been staying. Martuccio spent some time conversing with her, after which he left her and went to the King, his master, to whom he gave a full account, not only of his own vicissitudes but also those of the girl, adding that he intended, by the King's leave, to marry her according to the Christian rite.

The King, who was filled with amazement, summoned the girl to his presence; and having heard her confirm Martuccio's story with her own lips, he said:

'Then you have certainly earned the right to marry him.'

He then called for sumptuous and splendid gifts to be brought, and divided them between Gostanza and Martuccio, granting them leave to arrange matters between themselves in whatever way they pleased.

The gentlewoman with whom Gostanza had been staying was nobly entertained by Martuccio, who thanked her for all she had done to assist Gostanza, gave her such presents as were suitable to a person of her rank, and commended her to God, after which she and Gostanza took their leave of one another, shedding many tears. By the King's leave, they then embarked on a small sailing-ship, taking Carapresa with them, and with the aid of a prosperous wind they came once more to Lipari, where there was such great rejoicing that no words could ever describe it.

There, Martuccio and Gostanza were married, celebrating their nuptials in great pomp and splendour; and they spent the rest of their lives in the tranquil and restful enjoyment of the love they bore one another.

THIRD STORY

Pietro Boccamazza flees with Agnolella; they encounter some brigands; the girl takes refuge in a forest, and is conducted to a castle; Pietro is captured by the brigands, but escapes from their clutches, and after one or two further adventures, he reaches the castle where Agnolella is, marries her, and returns with her to Rome.

There was not one member of the company who failed to applaud Emilia's story, which the queen no sooner discovered to be at an end than she turned to Elissa and bade her to continue. Elissa was only too eager to obey, and began as follows:

The tale that presents itself to me, gracious ladies, concerns a calamitous night that was once experienced by two young people slightly lacking in good sense; but since it was followed by many a day of happiness, hence falling within our terms of reference, I should like to tell you about it.

Not long ago, in the city of Rome – which was once the head and is now the rump of the civilized world – there lived a young man called Pietro Boccamazza, belonging to an illustrious Roman family, who fell in love with a charming and very beautiful girl called Agnolella, the daughter of a certain Gigliuozzo Saullo, who, though a plebeian, was much respected by his fellow-citizens. So skilfully did he press his suit that the girl soon came to love him in equal measure. Spurred on by the intensity of his love, and no longer willing to endure the pangs of his desire, Pietro asked for her hand in marriage. But when his kinsfolk discovered what he was proposing to do, they all descended on him and took him severely to task, at the same time letting it be known to Gigliuozzo Saullo that he should on no account take Pietro seriously, otherwise they would never acknowledge him as their friend or kinsman.

Having thus been prevented from attaining his desire by the only means he could think of, Pietro all but died of grief. If he could only have secured Gigliuozzo's consent, he would have defied every one of his relatives and married the girl whether they liked it or not. But in any case he was determined, provided he had her support, to see this affair through to the end; and having learned through the medium of a third party that her approval was forthcoming, he arranged with her that they should elope from Rome together. So one morning, having made all necessary preparations, Pietro got up very early, saddled a pair of horses, and rode away with her in the direction of Anagni, where there were certain friends of his whom he trusted implicitly. Since they were afraid that they might be pursued, they had no time to stop and celebrate their nuptials, so they simply murmured sweet nothings to one another as they rode along, and exchanged an occasional kiss.

Now, the route they were taking was not very familiar to Pietro, and when they were about eight miles away from Rome, instead of turning right, they turned off along a road to the left. Scarcely had they ridden for two miles along this road when they found themselves close to a castle, from which, as soon as they were sighted, a dozen soldiers emerged. Just as they were about to be intercepted by the soldiers, the girl saw them coming and let out a shriek, saying:

'Quickly, Pietro, let's fly; they are coming for us.'

Employing all her strength, she pulled her nag's head sharply round in the direction of a huge forest; and clinging to the saddle for dear life, she dug her spurs into the animal's sides, whereupon the nag, being thus goaded, carried her off into the forest at a brisk gallop.

Pietro, who had been busy gazing into the girl's eyes instead of watching where he was going, was slower than she to catch sight of the soldiers, and he was still looking about him to discover from which direction they were coming when he was fallen upon, caught, and forced to dismount. They asked him who he was, and when he told them, they began to confer among themselves, saying: 'This fellow's a friend of the Orsini, our enemies. What better way to show them our contempt than to take away his clothes and his nag, and string him up from one of these oak trees.' This idea commanded their unanimous approval, and they ordered Pietro to strip.

As he was undressing, knowing only too well what was in store for him, it happened that a company of soldiers, at least two dozen strong, descended on them with shouts of 'Kill them! Kill them!' In their confusion, the others abandoned Pietro and looked to their defence; but on finding themselves greatly outnumbered, they took to their heels, with their assailants in full pursuit. When Pietro saw this, he promptly gathered up his belongings, leapt on to his steed, and galloped away as fast as he could along the path by which the girl had already fled.

But on finding no sign of a track through the forest, or even the imprint of a horse's hoof, he was overcome with despair, and as soon as he judged himself to be beyond the reach of his captors and their assailants, he burst into tears and began to meander through the forest, calling her name in all directions. But there was no reply, and, not daring to retrace his steps, he rode on without having the slightest notion of where he was going. To add to his misery, he was afraid, not only on his own account but also on the girl's, of all the wild beasts that are generally to be found lurking in forests, and in his mind's eye he constantly saw her being suffocated by bears or devoured by wolves.

And so our luckless Pietro careered all day long through the forest, shouting and calling, sometimes going round in circles when he thought he was proceeding in a straight line, until eventually, what with shouting and weeping and feeling afraid and not having eaten, he was so exhausted that he could go no further. Finding that darkness had fallen, and not knowing what else he could do, he dismounted from his nag, tethered it to a large oak, and then climbed the tree to avoid being devoured in the night by wild beasts. The night was clear, and before very long the moon had risen, but for fear of tumbling from his perch Pietro dared not fall asleep. This would in any case have been impossible because he was far too dejected and concerned for Agnolella's safety, and so his only alternative was to stay awake, groaning and cursing and bewailing his misfortune.

Meanwhile the girl, who as we have stated was fleeing with no destination in mind, simply let her nag carry her wherever it chose, and soon she had penetrated so far into the forest that she could no longer discern the way by which she had entered. So she spent the whole day just as Pietro had done, threading her way through the wildwood, pausing occasionally to rest, weeping and calling out incessantly, and bemoaning her terrible fate.

Finally, as dusk was falling and there was still no sign of Pietro, she stumbled upon a narrow path, along which her nag proceeded to trot, and after riding along it for over two miles, she saw a cottage ahead of her in the distance, to which she made her way as speedily as possible, there to find a kindly man of very ancient appearance, with a wife little younger than himself.

On seeing that she was by herself, they exclaimed:

'Alas, child, whatever are you doing in these parts, all alone, at this hour?'

Through her tears, the girl told them that she had lost her companion in the forest, and asked them how far it was to Anagni.

'This road doesn't lead to Anagni, my child,' the good man replied. 'It's a dozen miles or so from here to Anagni.'

Whereupon Agnolella said:

'Then is there a house nearby where I could spend the night?'

'None that you could reach before dark,' he answered.

To which the girl said:

'For the love of God, would you be so kind, since I cannot go elsewhere, to let me stay here for the night?'

'Young woman,' he replied, 'we should be happy for you to spend the night with us, but at the same time we must warn you that these parts are infested, day and night, by bands of cut-throats who fight among themselves and every so often wreak damage and hardship upon us. If we had the misfortune to be invaded by one of these bands whilst you were here, on seeing what a pretty young woman you are they would affront and manhandle you, and we could not lift a finger to help. We want you to know about this so that if such a thing were to happen, you would harbour no resentment against us.'

The old man's words filled the girl with alarm, but seeing that the hour was so late, she replied:

'God willing, we shall all be spared from any such calamity, but even if such a fate were to befall me, it is a much lesser evil to be misused by men than to be torn to pieces by wild beasts in the forest.'

And so saying, she dismounted and went inside the poor man's dwelling, where she supped frugally with them on what little food they had in the house, after which, still fully clothed, she settled down exhausted with the others on their tiny little bed. And there she lay, sobbing the whole night long and bewailing the misfortunes of herself and Pietro, to whom she could only suppose that the worst must have happened.

A little before dawn, she heard a loud trampling of horses' hooves, so she got up and made her way in to a spacious yard at the rear of the cottage. Along one of its sides, she saw a great pile of hay, in which she decided to hide, so that if these strangers came to the cottage, she would not be so easily found. No sooner had she finished concealing herself, than the horsemen, a large band of marauders, arrived at the door of the cottage. Having forced the old people to open the door, they pushed their way inside, where they found the girl's nag still fully saddled, and demanded to know who was there.

Seeing no sign of the girl, the good man replied:

'There is no one here apart from ourselves. But this nag, whoever it ran away from, turned up here yesterday evening, and we brought it into the house so that it would not be devoured by wolves.'

'In that case,' the gang's leader replied, 'since he doesn't belong to anyone we shall take him along with us.'

The bandits dispersed through the cottage, and some of them found their way into the yard, where they put off their lances and wooden shields. But one of their number, having nothing better to do, happened to hurl his lance into the hay, coming within an ace of killing the hidden girl, who all but gave herself away as the head of the lance skimmed her left breast, passing so close to her body that it tore through her clothes. She very nearly let out a great scream, fearing that she would come to serious harm, but remembered just in time where she was and kept quiet, trembling from head to foot.

The men roamed freely about the house in small groups, and having cooked themselves some goat's meat and one or two other things they had brought with them, they ate and drank to their hearts' content. They then went about their business, taking the girl's nag with them, and when they were at a safe distance from the cottage, the good man turned to his wife, and said:

'Whatever became of the young woman who came to us yesterday evening? I haven't set eyes on her from the time we got up.'

The good woman said she had no idea, and went off to look for her.

On realizing that the men had gone away, the girl clambered out of the hay. The old man was greatly relieved to discover that she had not fallen into their clutches, and since it was now growing light he said to her:

'Now that the day is breaking, we shall go with you, if you like, to a castle which is only five miles away, where you will find yourself in good hands. You'll have to walk, though, because that bunch of rogues who have just left took your nag away with them.'

Resigning herself to the loss of her nag, the girl begged them in God's name to conduct her to the castle; whereupon they set out, and arrived there when the hour of tierce was about half spent.

The castle belonged to a member of the Orsini family called Liello di Campo di Fiore, whose wife, a devout and exceedingly worthy woman, happened at that time to be staying there. On seeing Agnolella, she recognized her instantly and gave her a cordial welcome, and insisted on knowing precisely how she came to be there. The girl told her the whole story from start to finish.

The lady, who also knew Pietro because he was a friend of her husband, was greatly distressed to learn what had happened, and on hearing where he had been seized, she was convinced that he must be dead.

So she said to the girl:

'Since you have no idea what has become of Pietro, you must stay here with me until such time as I can send you safely back to Rome.'

Pietro had meanwhile stayed put in the branches of the oak, feeling as miserable as sin, and towards midnight he saw at least a score of wolves approaching. On seeing the nag, they crept up on him from all sides, but the nag heard them coming, and, tossing his head, broke loose from his tether and started to run away. Since he was surrounded, he could not get very far, so he set about the wolves with his teeth and his hooves, holding them at bay for quite some time till eventually they forced him to the ground, throttled the life out of him, and tore out his innards. They all began to gorge upon their prey, and having picked the carcase clean, they went away leaving nothing but the bones. Pietro was thrown into despair by this spectacle, for to him the nag was a sort of comrade, a prop and stay in his afflictions, and he began to think that he would never succeed in leaving the forest alive.

He continued to keep a lookout on all sides, however, and a little before dawn, when he was all but freezing to death up there in the oak, he caught sight of a huge fire, about a mile from where he was sheltering. So as soon as daylight had come he descended from his perch, feeling distinctly apprehensive, and made off in that direction. On reaching the spot he found a number of shepherds sitting and making merry round the fire, and they took pity on him and asked him to join them. When he had eaten and warmed himself at the fire, having given them an account of his misfortunes and explained how it was that he came to be wandering alone through the forest, he asked them whether there was any village or township thereabouts to which he might go.

The shepherds replied that some three miles away there was a castle belonging to Liello di Campo di Fiore, and that Liello's wife was at present living there. Overjoyed, Pietro asked whether any of the shepherds would guide him as far as the castle, and two of them volunteered to do so. On reaching the castle, Pietro met various people he knew, and whilst he was trying to arrange for them to go out and search for the girl in the forest, he was told that Liello's wife wanted to see him. He promptly answered her summons, and on finding that she had Agnolella with her, he was the happiest man that was ever born.

He was positively longing to take her in his arms, but was too embarrassed to do so in the presence of the lady. And if his own joy knew no bounds, the girl was no less delighted on seeing him.

The noble lady took him in and made him very welcome, and having heard the tale of his adventures from his own lips, she spoke to him severely for attempting to defy the wishes of his kinsfolk. But on seeing that he was quite unrepentant, and that the girl was eager to marry him, she said to herself: 'Why should I go to all this trouble? They are in love, they understand one another, both are friends of my husband, and their intentions are honourable. Besides, it seems to me that they have God's blessing, for one of them has been saved from being hanged, the other from being killed by a lance, and both of them from being devoured by wild beasts. So let them do as they wish.' She therefore turned to them, and said:

'If you have really set your hearts on becoming husband and wife, so be it; you shall have my blessing, the wedding can be celebrated here at Liello's expense, and after you are married you can safely leave it to me to make peace between you and your kinsfolk.'

So there they were married, and Pietro's enormous joy was only surpassed by that of Agnolella. The noble lady gave them as splendid a wedding as could possibly be arranged in her mountain retreat, and it was there that they tasted the first exquisite fruits of their love.

Some days later, guarded by a powerful escort, they returned with the lady on horseback to Rome, where, on finding that Pietro's kinsfolk were greatly angered by what he had done, she succeeded in restoring him to their good graces. And afterwards, he and Agnolella lived to a ripe old age in great peace and happiness.

FOURTH STORY

Ricciardo Manardi is discovered by Messer Lizio da Valbona with his daughter, whom he marries, and remains on good terms with her father.

Elissa, falling silent, listened as her companions lauded her tale, and the queen called upon Filostrato to tell his story. Laughing, he began as follows:

I have been teased so many times, and by so many of you, for obliging you to tell cruel stories and making you weep, that I feel obliged to make some slight amends for the sorrow I caused, and tell you something that will make you laugh a little. Hence I propose to tell you a very brief tale about a love which, apart from one or two sighs and a moment of fear not unmixed with embarrassment, ran a smooth course to its happy conclusion.

Not long ago then, excellent ladies, there lived in Romagna a most reputable and virtuous gentleman called Messer Lizio da Valbona, who, on the threshold of old age, had the good fortune to be presented by his wife, Madonna Giacomina, with a baby daughter. When she grew up, she outshone all the other girls in those parts for her charm and beauty, and since she was the only daughter left to her father and mother, they loved and cherished her with all their heart, and guarded her with extraordinary care, for they had high hopes of bestowing her in marriage on the son of some great nobleman.

Now, to the house of Messer Lizio there regularly came a handsome and sprightly youth called Ricciardo de' Manardi da Brettinoro, with whom Messer Lizio spent a good deal of his time; and he and his wife would no more have thought of keeping him under surveillance than if he were their own son. Whenever he set eyes on the girl, Ricciardo was struck by her great beauty, her graceful bearing, her charming ways and impeccable manners, and, seeing that she was of marriageable age, he fell passionately in love with her. He took great pains to conceal his feelings, but the girl divined that he was in love with her, and far from being offended, to Ricciardo's great delight she began to love him with equal fervour. Though frequently seized with the longing to speak to her, he was always too timid to do so until one day, having chosen a suitable moment, he plucked up courage and said to her:

'Caterina, I implore you not to let me die of love for you.'

'Heaven grant,' she promptly replied, 'that you do not allow me to die first for love of you.'

Ricciardo was overjoyed by the girl's answer, and, feeling greatly encouraged, he said to her:

'Demand of me anything you please, and I shall do it. But you alone can devise the means of saving us both.'

Whereupon the girl said:

'Ricciardo, as you see, I am watched very closely, and for this reason I cannot think how you are to come to me. But if you are able to suggest anything I might do without bringing shame upon myself, tell me what it is, and I shall do it.'

Ricciardo turned over various schemes in his mind, then suddenly he said:

'My sweet Caterina, the only way I can suggest is for you to come to the balcony overlooking your father's garden, or better still, to sleep there. Although it is very high, if I knew that you were spending the night on the balcony, I would try without fail to climb up and reach you.'

'If you are daring enough to climb to the balcony,' Caterina replied, 'I am quite sure that I can arrange to sleep there.'

Ricciardo assured her that he was, whereupon they snatched a single kiss and went their separate ways.

It was already near the end of May, and on the morning after her conversation with Ricciardo, the girl began complaining to her mother that she had been unable to sleep on the previous night because of the heat.

'What are you talking about, child?' said her mother. 'It wasn't in the least hot.'

To which Caterina said:

'Mother, if you were to add "in my opinion", then perhaps you would be right. But you must remember that young girls feel the heat much more than older women.'

'That is so, my child,' said her mother, 'but what do you expect me to do about it? I can't make it hot or cold for you, just like that. You have to take the weather as it comes, according to the season. Perhaps tonight it will be cooler, and you will sleep better.'

'God grant that you are right,' said Caterina, 'but it is not usual for the nights to grow any cooler as the summer approaches.'

'Then what do you want us to do about it?' inquired the lady.

'If you and father were to consent,' replied Caterina, 'I should like to have a little bed made up for me on the balcony outside his room, overlooking the garden. I should have the nightingale to sing me off to sleep, it would be much cooler there, and I should be altogether better off than I am in your room.'

Whereupon her mother said:

'Cheer up, my child; I shall speak to your father about it, and we shall do whatever he decides.'

The lady reported their conversation to Messer Lizio, who, perhaps because of his age, was inclined to be short-tempered.

'What's all this about being lulled to sleep by the nightingale?' he exclaimed. 'She'll be sleeping to the song of the cicadas if I hear any more of her nonsense.'

Having heard what he had said, on the following night, more to spite her father than because she was feeling hot, Caterina not only stayed awake herself but, by complaining incessantly of the heat, also prevented her mother from sleeping.

So next morning, her mother went straight to Messer Lizio, and said:

'Sir, you cannot be very fond of this daughter of yours. What difference does it make to you whether she sleeps on the balcony or not? She didn't get a moment's rest all night because of the heat. Besides, what do you find so surprising about a young girl taking pleasure in the song of the nightingale? Young people are naturally drawn towards those things that reflect their own natures.'

'Oh, very well,' said Messer Lizio. 'Take whichever bed you please, and set it up for her on the balcony with some curtains round it. Then let her sleep there and hear the nightingale singing to her heart's content.'

On hearing that her father had given his permission, the girl promptly had a bed made up for her on the balcony; and since it was her intention to sleep there that same night, she waited for Ricciardo to come to the house, and gave him a signal, already agreed between them, by which he understood what was expected of him.

As soon as he had heard his daughter getting into bed, Messer Lizio locked the door leading from his own room to the balcony, and then he too retired for the night.

When there was no longer any sound to be heard, Ricciardo climbed over a wall with the aid of a ladder, then climbed up the side of the house by clinging with great difficulty to a series of stones projecting from the wall. At every moment of the ascent, he was in serious danger of falling, but in the end he reached the balcony unscathed, where he was silently received by the girl with very great rejoicing. After exchanging many kisses, they lay down together and for virtually the entire night they had delight and joy of one another, causing the nightingale to sing at frequent intervals.

Their pleasure was long, the night was brief, and though they were unaware of the fact, it was almost dawn when they eventually fell asleep without a stitch to cover them, exhausted as much by their merry sport as by the nocturnal heat. Caterina had tucked her right arm beneath Ricciardo's neck, whilst with her left hand she was holding that part of his person which in mixed company you ladies are too embarrassed to mention.

Dawn came, but failed to wake them, and they were still asleep in

the same posture when Messer Lizio got up out of bed. Remembering that his daughter was sleeping on the balcony, he quietly opened
the door, saying:

'I'll just go and see whether Caterina has slept any better with the
help of the nightingale.'

Stepping out on to the terrace, he gently raised the curtain surrounding the bed and saw Ricciardo and Caterina, naked and uncovered, lying there asleep in one another's arms, in the posture just
described.

Having clearly recognized Ricciardo, he left them there and made
his way to his wife's room, where he called to her and said:

'Be quick, woman, get up and come and see, for your daughter
was so fascinated by the nightingale that she has succeeded in way-
laying it, and is holding it in her hand.'

'What are you talking about?' said the lady.

'You'll see, if you come quickly,' said Messer Lizio.

The lady got dressed in a hurry, and quietly followed in Messer
Lizio's footsteps until both of them were beside the bed. The curtain
was then raised, and Madonna Giacomina saw for herself exactly how
her daughter had taken and seized hold of the nightingale, whose
song she had so much yearned to hear.

The lady, who considered that she had been seriously deceived in
Ricciardo, was on the point of shouting and screaming abuse at him,
but Messer Lizio restrained her, saying:

'Woman, if you value my love, hold your tongue! Now that she
has taken him, she shall keep him. Ricciardo is a rich young man, and
comes of noble stock. We could do a lot worse than have him as our
son-in-law. If he wishes to leave this house unscathed, he will first
have to marry our daughter, so that he will have put his nightingale
into his own cage and into no other.'

The lady was reassured to see that her husband was not unduly
perturbed by what had happened, and on reflecting that her daughter
had enjoyed a good night, was well-rested, and had caught the
nightingale, she held her peace.

Nor did they have long to wait before Ricciardo woke up, and on
seeing that it was broad daylight, he almost died of fright and called to
Caterina, saying:

'Alas, my treasure, the day has come and caught me unawares! What is to happen to us?'

At these words, Messer Lizio stepped forward, raised the curtain, and replied:

'What you deserve.'

On seeing Messer Lizio, Ricciardo nearly leapt out of his skin and sat bolt upright in bed, saying:

'My lord, in God's name have mercy on me. I know that I deserve to die, for I have been wicked and disloyal, and hence you must deal with me as you choose. But I beseech you to spare my life, if that is possible. I implore you not to kill me.'

'Ricciardo,' said Messer Lizio, 'this deed was quite unworthy of the love I bore you and the firm trust I placed in you. But what is done cannot be undone, and since it was your youth that carried you into so grievous an error, in order that you may preserve not only your life but also my honour, you must, before you do anything else, take Caterina as your lawful wedded wife. And thus, not only will she have been yours for this night, but she will remain yours for as long as she lives. By this means alone will you secure your freedom and my forgiveness; otherwise you can prepare to meet your Maker.'

Whilst this conversation was taking place, Caterina let go of the nightingale, and having covered herself up, she burst into tears and implored her father to forgive Ricciardo, at the same time beseeching Ricciardo to do as Messer Lizio wished, so that they might long continue to enjoy such nights as this together in perfect safety.

All this pleading was quite superfluous, however, for what with the shame of his transgression and his urge to atone on the one hand, and his desire to escape with his life on the other (to say nothing of his yearning to possess the object of his ardent love), Ricciardo readily consented, without a moment's hesitation, to do what Messer Lizio was asking.

Messer Lizio therefore borrowed one of Madonna Giacomina's rings, and Ricciardo married Caterina there and then without moving from the spot, her parents bearing witness to the event.

This done, Messer Lizio and his wife withdrew, saying:

'Now go back to sleep, for you doubtless stand in greater need of resting than of getting up.'

As soon as her parents had departed, the two young people fell once more into each other's arms, and since they had only passed half a dozen milestones in the course of the night, they added another two to the total before getting up. And for the first day they left it at that.

After they had risen, Ricciardo discussed the matter in greater detail with Messer Lizio, and a few days later he and Caterina took appropriate steps to renew their marriage vows in the presence of their friends and kinsfolk. Then, amid great rejoicing, he brought her to his house, where the nuptials were celebrated with dignity and splendour. And for many years thereafter he lived with her in peace and happiness, caging nightingales by the score, day and night, to his heart's content.

FIFTH STORY

Before he dies, Guidotto da Cremona consigns to Giacomino da Pavia a young girl, who later on, in Faenza, is wooed by Giannole di Severino and Minghino di Mingole; these two come to blows, but when the girl is identified as Giannole's sister, she is given in marriage to Minghino.

In listening to the tale of the nightingale, all the ladies laughed so much that it was some time after Filostrato had finished before they managed to contain their mirth. But when their laughter had died away, the queen said:

'Without a doubt, Filostrato, though you plunged us all into sorrow yesterday, you have tickled our ribs so much today that we cannot hold it against you any longer.'

Then, turning to Neifile, she asked her to tell her story, and Neifile cheerfully began, as follows:

Since Filostrato crossed the borders of Romagna for the subject of his tale, I too shall take the liberty of roaming for a while in that part of the world.

In the town of Fano, then, there once lived two Lombards, of whom the first was called Guidotto da Cremona and the second Giacomino da Pavia. No longer young, they had spent the greater part of their lives in warring and soldiering, and on his deathbed, Guidotto, who had no children of his own and trusted Giacomino more than any other friend or relative, committed to his comrade's care a little girl of his, who was about ten years of age. He also bequeathed him all his worldly possessions, and having talked to him at length about his affairs, he departed this life.

Now, around that period, the town of Faenza, which for many years had been ravaged by war and other calamities, was restored to somewhat more stable conditions, and anyone wishing to return was freely permitted to do so. Hence Giacomino, who had once lived in Faenza and had grown attached to the place, returned there with all his belongings, taking with him the girl entrusted to him by Guidotto, whom he loved and treated as a daughter.

As she grew older, the girl became singularly beautiful, being better looking than any other young woman then living in Faenza; and with her beauty were united a virtuous disposition and graceful manners. She thus began to attract the gaze of various admirers, and in particular of two very handsome and well-connected young men, who fell so violently in love with her that their jealousy and hatred of each other surpassed all bounds. The first of these was called Giannole di Severino, the second Minghino di Mingole, and neither would have hesitated for a moment to marry the girl, who had now reached the age of fifteen, if the consent of his kinsfolk had been forthcoming. But since this was not the case, each of them resolved to seize possession of her by whatever means he could devise.

Giacomino had in his house an elderly maidservant and a serving-man called Crivello, a highly sociable and entertaining sort of fellow, with whom Giannole became very friendly. Choosing the right moment Giannole told Crivello all about his love for the girl, imploring him to assist him in attaining his desire, and promising to reward him handsomely in return.

'Now look,' said Crivello, 'there is only one possible way in which I could be of service to you, and that consists in waiting for Giacomino to dine away from home and then letting you in to the room where she happens to be. If I were to broach the subject to her orally, she would never stop to listen. If this plan appeals to you, I promise to see it through, and I shall be as good as my word, after which it will be up to you to make the most of your opportunities.'

Giannole assured him that this was all he desired, and there, for the time being, the matter rested.

For his part, Minghino had made friends with the maidservant, working upon her to such good effect that she had delivered several messages to the girl and almost fired her with Minghino's love. Moreover she had promised to convey him to her as soon as Giacomino chanced for any reason to be away from the house for the evening.

A few days after his conversation with Giannole, Crivello persuaded Giacomino to accept an invitation to supper at the house of one of his friends; and having passed the word to Giannole, he arranged that on receiving a certain signal Giannole was to come to the front door, which he would find unlocked. Meanwhile the maidservant, knowing nothing of all this, sent word to Minghino that Giacomino was going out to supper, and told him to stay near the house so that, when she gave him the signal, he could come and be let in.

Neither of the two lovers knew anything of the other's movements, and soon after dusk, each of them, being suspicious of his rival, set out with a number of armed companions so as to be certain of carrying off the prize. Since they were obliged to wait for the signal, Minghino and his men stationed themselves in a house nearby belonging to one of his friends, whilst Giannole bided his time with his companions some little distance away from the girl's house.

Once Giacomino was out of the way, Crivello and the maidservant made strenuous efforts to send each other packing.

'Why don't you go to bed?' said Crivello. 'What are you pottering about the house for at this hour?'

'What about you?' said the maidservant, 'Why not go and wait for your master? What are you hanging about here for, now that you've had your supper?'

Thus neither could persuade the other to go away, and Crivello, realizing that the hour agreed upon with Giannole had come, said to himself: 'Why should I worry about her? If she doesn't keep her mouth shut, so much the worse for her.'

And so, having given the prearranged signal, he went to open the door for Giannole, who promptly arrived with two of his companions and made his way inside. Finding the girl in the hall, they seized her in order to carry her off, but she began to struggle and scream at the top of her voice, and the maidservant followed her example. On hearing all the noise, Minghino rushed to the spot with his companions to find the girl already being dragged through the doorway; whereupon they all drew their swords, and with shouts of 'Ah, traitors, you are dead! You shan't get away with this! What's the meaning of this outrage?' they started raining blows on their opponents. Meanwhile a number of people from the neighbouring houses, having taken up lanterns and weapons, had rushed out into the street in order to see what the noise was about, and begun to hurl abuse at the girl's assailants. And with their assistance, Minghino managed after a long struggle to snatch the girl away from Giannole and put her back inside the house. The affray continued until the officers of the *podestà* arrived on the scene and arrested a large number of the combatants including Minghino, Giannole, and Crivello, all of whom were led away to prison.

By the time Giacomino returned home, peace had been restored. And though he was greatly perturbed by what had happened, on looking into the matter and discovering that the girl was in no way to blame, he was partially reassured. At the same time he resolved, so as to prevent the same thing happening all over again, to have the girl married at the earliest opportunity.

Next morning he received a deputation from the kinsfolk of the two parties concerned, who had apprised themselves of the facts and were well aware of the parlous situation in which the arrested youths would find themselves if Giacomino were to seek the retribution he had every right to demand. With honeyed words, they begged him to suit his actions, not so much to the injury he had received from the young men's thoughtlessness, as to the love and goodwill which they were convinced that he bore to themselves, his humble suppliants. Then they offered, on behalf not only of themselves but also of the young men who had perpetrated the deed, to make whatever amends Giacomino cared to specify.

Giacomino's answer was quickly given, for in the course of his life he had seen many worse things than this, and he was not the sort of man to harbour resentment.

'Gentlemen,' he said, 'even i f I were in my native city, and not in yours, I count myself the sort of friend who would never do anything that was contrary to your wishes, either in the present instance or in any other. Besides, I am more than ever bound to respect your wishes in this matter inasmuch as you have wronged one of yourselves, for this young woman comes neither from Cremona nor Pavia, as many people may possibly have supposed, but from Faenza, though neither she nor I nor the person who entrusted her to my care ever discovered whose daughter she was. Hence I am fully prepared to do as you ask.'

The worthy men were surprised to learn that the girl was a native of Faenza, and having thanked Giacomino for taking so generous a view of the matter, they asked him to be so kind as to explain how she had come under his control, and how he knew that she was from Faenza.

Giacomino said to them:

'Guidotto da Cremona, who was a friend and comrade of mine, informed me on his deathbed that when this town was captured by the Emperor Frederick, and everything was being plundered, he and his companions entered a house and found it full of booty. All the inhabitants had fled except for this girl, who would be about two years old at the time, and as he was going up the stairs, she called him "father". He felt sorry for the child, and together with all the valuables from the house, he took her with him to Fano. And in Fano, as he was dying, he appointed me her guardian and bequeathed to me everything he possessed, on the understanding that when she grew up I would see that she was married, handing over his fortune to her by way of dowry. She is now of marriageable age, but I have not yet succeeded in finding a suitable husband for her. The sooner I can do so the better, for I've no wish to suffer the things I suffered last night all over again.'

One of the people present was Guiglielmino da Medicina, who had been with Guidotto at the time of this escapade, and remembered quite clearly whose house Guidotto had plundered. Seeing the owner of the house standing there with the others, he went up to him and said:

'Bernabuccio, do you hear what Giacomino says?'

'Yes,' said Bernabuccio, 'and I was just thinking about it, because during those upheavals I lost a little girl of the age that Giacomino mentioned.'

'Then it must be the same girl,' said Guiglielmino, 'for I was once in a place where I heard Guidotto describing the house he had looted, and I recognized it as yours. Try and remember whether the child had any mark by which you could identify her, and get them to look for it. I am certain you will find that she is your daughter.'

Having pondered for a while, Bernabuccio remembered that she ought to have a small scar above her left ear in the shape of a cross – the remains of an abscess which he had had removed shortly before his house was looted. So without further ado he went up to Giacomino, who was still standing on his doorstep, and asked him to take him into the house and let him see the girl.

Giacomino readily took him inside, and introduced him to the girl. As soon as Bernabuccio set eyes on her, he could see that she was the living image of the child's mother, who was still a good-looking woman. Not content with this, however, he asked Giacomino if he would kindly allow him to lift the hair above the girl's left ear, and Giacomino told him to go ahead.

Bernabuccio went up to the girl, who was feeling rather embarrassed by all this, and having raised her hair with his right hand, he caught sight of the cross-shaped scar. Now that he knew for certain that she was his daughter, he burst into tears and enfolded her in a tender embrace, albeit the girl attempted to hold him at a distance; and turning to Giacomino he said:

'Brother, this is my daughter; it was my house that was plundered by Guidotto, and in the heat of the moment my wife, the child's mother, left her behind. Later that day, my house was set on fire, and we had always supposed until now that the child was burned to death.'

On hearing this the girl, having taken account of his age and the fact that his words rang true, was prompted by some mysterious impulse to relax in his arms and tenderly mingle her tears with his.

Bernabuccio instantly sent for her mother and for other women relatives, as well as for her brothers and sisters, and having presented her to each of them in turn and told them the story, he took her back to his house amid great rejoicing and the exchange of a thousand embraces, Giacomino being well content that he should have her. Tidings of these events were brought to the *podestà*, an excellent fellow, who, knowing that Giannole, whom he was holding prisoner, was the son of Bernabuccio and the girl's blood-brother, decided to deal with him leniently and overlook the offence he had committed. What was more, he took a personal interest in the affair, and in consultation with Bernabuccio and Giacomino he induced Giannole and Minghino to make peace with one another. Then, to the enormous satisfaction of Minghino's kinsfolk, he announced that the girl, whose name was Agnesa, was to be married to Minghino; and having set the two young men at liberty, he also released Crivello and the others who had been implicated in the matter.

Shortly afterwards Minghino, overjoyed, celebrated his nuptials in truly magnificent style and conveyed his bride to his house, thereafter living many years with her in peace and prosperity.

SIXTH STORY

Gianni of Procida is found with the girl he loves, who had been handed over to King Frederick. He and the girl are tied to a stake, and are about to be burnt when he is recognized by Ruggieri de Loria. He is then set free, and afterwards they are married.

Neifile's story found much favour with the ladies, and when it came to an end, the queen called on Pampinea to tell them one of hers. Her face upraised and smiling, she forthwith began:

Mighty indeed, dear ladies, are the powers of Love, inducing lovers, as they do, to endure great hardships and expose themselves to extraordinary and incredible risks. Ample confirmation of this is to be found in many of the stories already told, both today and on other occasions, but nevertheless I should like to prove it once again with this tale of a young lover's courage.

On Ischia, which is an island very near Naples, there once lived an exceedingly charming and beautiful girl called Restituta, the daughter of Marin Bòlgaro, a nobleman of the island. She was loved to the

point of distraction by a young man from Procida, a small island
close to Ischia, whose name was Gianni, and she in turn was in love
with him. Not content with going from Procida to Ischia every day
to catch a glimpse of his beloved, Gianni would frequently make the
crossing by night, swimming there and back if no boat was available,
so that, even if he could see nothing else, he could at least gaze upon
the walls of her house.

Thus they were deeply in love with each other, but one summer's
day, as the girl was wandering by herself along the shore, prising
sea-shells from the rocks with a small knife, she chanced upon a tiny
cove, hemmed in by cliffs, where a number of young Sicilians, on
their way from Naples, had landed from their frigate in order to
relax in the shade and take fresh water from a nearby spring.

The girl failed to notice them, and when they perceived how
beautiful she was, seeing that she was all alone, the youths resolved to
seize her and carry her off. Nor did they waste any time in giving
effect to their resolve, but promptly took hold of the girl, and, though
she screamed and shouted, bundled her aboard their ship. They then
sailed away, but on arriving in Calabria, they fell to arguing among
themselves over which of them was to take possession of the girl, each
of them wanting her for himself. Being unable to reach any sort of
agreement, they decided, rather than make matters worse and bring
ruin upon themselves for the sake of a girl, to give her to King
Frederick of Sicily, who was then a young man, much addicted to
pretty things of that sort. And this they did on reaching Palermo.

The girl was greatly prized by the King on account of her beauty,
but as he was feeling somewhat indisposed, he ordered that until such
time as he recovered she should be lodged with a retinue in a sumptuous villa in one of his gardens, known as La Cuba; and these
instructions were carried out.

The girl's abduction gave rise to a great furore in Ischia, but the
worst part about it was that they had no idea who it was that had
carried her off. Gianni, who was the person most deeply affected by
her disappearance, knew better than to hang about waiting for news
in Ischia, and , having ascertained the direction taken by her captors,
he hired a frigate of his own, in which, as swiftly as possible, he scoured
the whole of the coast from Cape Minerva to Scalea in Calabria,

making inquiries about the girl wherever he went. Finally, at Scalea, he was told she had been taken by Sicilian sailors to Palermo, and thither he made his way as speedily as he could. On discovering, after searching high and low for her, that she had been given to the King and was being kept by him in La Cuba, he was greatly perturbed and not only despaired of retrieving her but almost gave up hope of ever seeing her again.

Nevertheless, sustained by Love, he sent away the frigate and remained in Palermo, for it was clear that nobody in those parts knew who he was. He frequently walked past La Cuba, and one day, to the great joy both of himself and the girl, they caught sight of each other as she was standing at a window. Seeing that the street was deserted, Gianni got as near to her as he could manage, spoke to her, and was told by the girl of the means he would have to adopt if he wanted to talk to her in greater privacy. He then went away, having first surveyed with care the surrounding area. Biding his time till long after darkness had fallen, he returned to the spot, and by climbing over a wall that would not have afforded a perch to a woodpecker, he made his way into the garden. There he found a long pole, and, having, in accordance with the girl's instructions, propped it against a window, he hauled himself up to it without any trouble.

Feeling that her honour was by now as good as lost, the girl, who in the past had treated him rather cruelly in her determination to preserve it, had made up her mind to gratify his every desire, for she could think of no man who had a greater right to possess her, and moreover she was hopeful of persuading him to effect her release; she had therefore left the window open, to ensure that he had immediate access to her.

Finding the window open, Gianni clambered silently into the room and lay down beside the girl, who was not asleep by any means. Before they did anything else, the girl apprised him fully of her intentions, imploring him with all her heart to release her from captivity and take her away. Gianni assured her that nothing would give him greater pleasure, and that, on taking his leave of her, he would without fail make such arrangements as would enable him, on his next visit, to convey her to safety.

They then enfolded one another in a blissful embrace, and partook of the greatest pleasure that Love can supply, repeating the experience several times over until they unwittingly fell asleep in each other's arms.

Shortly before daybreak, the King, who had taken an instant liking to the girl and was now feeling better, called her to mind, and resolved, despite the lateness of the hour, to go and spend some time in her company; so he quietly made his way to La Cuba with one of his retainers. On entering the building, he went straight to the room where he knew the girl to be sleeping and got the servants to open the door without making a sound. Preceded by a huge, blazing torch, he walked into the room, only to discover, on looking at the bed, that Gianni and the girl were lying there asleep and naked in one another's arms. This spectacle rendered him speechless with horror and distress, and he was so enraged that he could scarcely forbear from drawing a dagger from his belt and killing them where they lay. But on reflecting that it would be a most cowardly deed for any man, let alone a king, to kill two people lying naked and asleep, he held himself in check, and resolved instead to have them publicly burnt at the stake. Turning to the single companion who was with him, he said:

'What think you of this shameless hussy, in whom I once reposed my hopes?'

He then inquired of his companion whether he could recognize this young man, who had had the impudence to come and perpetrate such an outrage on the King in his own house, and the man replied that he could not recall having ever set eyes on the youth.

So the King stormed out of the room, and ordered that the two lovers, naked as they were, should be seized and tied up; and as soon as daylight came, they were to be brought to the main square in Palermo and bound, back to back, to a stake, there to remain till the hour of tierce, so that they could be seen by the whole of the populace, after which they were to be burnt alive in accordance with their deserts. These instructions given, he returned to Palermo and retired in high dudgeon to his room.

As soon as the King had left, several men burst in on the two lovers, and not only woke them up, but swiftly seized and bound them without any pity. As may readily be imagined, on seeing what was happening to them the two young people were greatly alarmed, and, fearing they would be put to death, they burst into tears and bitterly reproached themselves. In accordance with the King's command, they were taken to Palermo and tied to a stake in the square; and before their eyes faggots were stacked in readiness for them to be burnt alive at the hour the King had decreed.

All the men and women of Palermo immediately hurried to the square in order to see the two lovers: and whilst the men stood and gazed at the girl, unanimously praising her shapeliness and beauty, so the women were all clustering round the youth, expressing their warm approval of his fine figure and handsome features. But the pair of hapless lovers hung their heads in shame and bewailed their misfortune, expecting at any moment to be cruelly consumed by the fire.

Whilst they were thus being held until the hour fixed for their execution, news of their offence was bruited abroad and reached the ears of Ruggieri de Loria, a man of inestimable worth, who at that time was the Admiral of the Royal Fleet. Curious to see who they were, he made his way towards the place where they stood bound to the stake, and, on reaching the spot, he looked at the girl and found her exceedingly beautiful. He then directed his gaze at the youth, whom he recognized without too much trouble, and moving a little nearer he asked him whether he was Gianni of Procida.

Gianni raised his eyes, and, recognizing the Admiral, he replied:

'My lord, I was indeed the man of whom you speak, but I am about to be that person no longer.'

Whereupon the Admiral asked what had brought him to such a pass, and Gianni replied:

'Love, and the wrath of the King.'

The Admiral persuaded him to elaborate, and having heard the whole story from Gianni's own lips, he turned to go. But Gianni called him back, and said:

'Alas, my lord, procure me a favour, if this be possible, from the person who set me here.'

Ruggieri asked what favour he had in mind, and Gianni said:

'I see that I must die, and very soon. Wherefore, seeing that I have been set here back to back with this young woman, whom I loved more dearly than life itself, being loved no less deeply in return, I should like us to be turned face to face, so that I may have the consolation of gazing into her eyes as I depart.'

'With pleasure!' exclaimed Ruggieri, with a laugh. 'And i f I have my way, you shall see so much of her that before you die you'll be sorry you ever asked such a favour.'

Leaving Gianni, he spoke to the men charged with carrying out the sentence, and ordered them not to proceed any further without new instructions from the King, to whom he forthwith made his way. And although he perceived that the King was extremely distraught, he was not to be deterred from speaking his mind.

'My lord,' he said, 'what injury have you suffered from the two young people you have sentenced to be burnt down there in the square?'

The King told him, and Ruggieri continued:

'They have done wrong, and well deserve to be punished, but not by you; for although wrongdoing requires a punishment, good deeds require a reward, to say nothing of pardon and clemency. Do you realize who these people are that you are so eager to put to death at the stake?'

The King replied that he did not know them, whereupon Ruggieri said:

'Then I shall make it my business to tell you, so that you will see how unwise it is for you to let yourself be carried away by your anger . The young man is the son of Landolfo of Procida, blood-brother to Messer Gianni of Procida, through whose efforts you became King and master of this island. The girl is the daughter of Marin Bòlgaro, without whose power and influence Ischia would be lost to you tomorrow. What is more, these two youngsters have long been in love with one another, and it was not out of any disrespect towards your royal highness, but rather through being constrained by their love, that they committed this sin of theirs – if sin is a suitable word to describe the things young people do in the cause of love. Why, then, should you wish to have them put to death, when you ought to be entertaining them right royally and bestowing precious gifts upon them?'

On realizing that Ruggieri must be speaking the truth, the King was not only filled with horror over what he was proposing to do, but bitterly regretted the action he had already taken. So he promptly sent word that the two young lovers were to be released from the stake and brought into his presence. These orders were carried out, and after inquiring fully into their condition, the King decided that he must make amends, through largesse and hospitality, for the indignity he had caused them to suffer. He therefore had them newly clothed in courtly attire, and arranged, by their mutual consent, for Gianni and the girl to be married. And finally he sent them back, well content and laden with magnificent presents, to the place from which they had come. There they were received with tremendous rejoicing, and long thereafter lived in joy and happiness together.

SEVENTH STORY

Teodoro falls in love with Violante, the daughter of his master, Messer Amerigo. He gets her with child, and is sentenced to die on the gallows. But whilst he is being whipped along the road to his execution, he is recognized by his father and set at liberty, after which he and Violante become husband and wife.

All the ladies were on tenterhooks, anxiously wondering whether the two lovers would be burnt, and on learning that they had escaped, they all rejoiced and offered thanks to God. Then, having heard the end of the story, the queen entrusted the telling of the next to Lauretta, who cheerfully began as follows:

Fairest ladies, there once lived in the island of Sicily, during the reign of good King William, a nobleman called Messer Amerigo Abate of Trapani, who was blessed with many possessions, including a large number of children. He was therefore in need of servants, and when certain galleys arrived from the Levant belonging to Genoese pirates, who had captured a great many children along the Armenian coast, he purchased a number of them, believing them to be Turkish. For the most part they appeared to be of rustic, shepherd stock, but there was one, Teodoro by name, who seemed gently bred and better looking than any of the others.

Though he was treated as a servant, Teodoro was brought up in the house along with Messer Amerigo's children, and as he grew older, being prompted by his innate good breeding rather than by the accident of his menial status, he acquired so much poise and so agreeable a manner that Messer Amerigo granted him his freedom. Supposing him to be a Turk, Messer Amerigo had him baptized and re-named Pietro, and placed him in charge of his business affairs, taking him deeply into his confidence.

Side-by-side with Messer Amerigo's other children, there grew up a daughter of his called Violante, a dainty young beauty who, as her father was not in a hurry to marry her off, chanced to fall in love with Pietro. But whilst she loved him, and held his conduct and achievements in high esteem, she was too shy to tell him so directly. Love spared her this trouble, however, for Pietro, having cast many a furtive glance in her direction, fell so violently in love with her that he felt unhappy whenever she was out of his sight. Since he could not help feeling that what he was doing was wrong, he was greatly afraid lest anyone should discover his secret; but the girl, who was by no means averse to his company, divined his feelings towards her, and, in order to bolster his confidence, she let it appear that she was delighted, as indeed she was. And on this footing their relationship rested for some considerable time, neither of them venturing to say anything to the other, much as they mutually desired to do so. Consumed by the flames of love, they longed for one another with equal ardour till Fortune, as though deciding that they should be united, found a way for them to dispel the fears and apprehensions by which they were impeded.

About a mile away from Trapani itself, Messer Amerigo kept a very charming property, to which his wife, with their daughter and various other ladies and maidservants, frequently went by way of recreation. Having gone there one day when the weather was very hot, taking Pietro with them, they suddenly found that the sky had become overcast with thick dark clouds, such as we occasionally observe in the course of the summer. And so the lady, not wishing to be caught there by the storm, set off with her companions along the road leading back to Trapani, making all the haste they could. But Pietro and Violante, being young and fit, soon found themselves well ahead of the girl's mother and the other ladies, perhaps because they were prompted no less by their love than by fear of the weather. And when they had drawn so far ahead of the others that they were almost out of sight, there was a series of thunderclaps, immediately followed by a very heavy hailstorm, from which the lady and her companions took shelter in the house of a farm-labourer.

Pietro and the girl, having nowhere more convenient to take refuge, entered an old, abandoned cottage that was almost totally in ruins; and, having both squeezed in beneath the fragment of roof that still remained intact, they were forced by the inadequacy of their shelter to huddle up close to one another. The contact of their bodies made them pluck up the courage to disclose their amorous yearnings, Pietro being the first to broach the subject by saying:

'Would to God that this hailstorm would never come to an end, so that I could remain here for ever!'

'That would suit me very well,' said the girl.

Having uttered these words, they went on to hold and squeeze one another's hands, after which they proceeded to embrace and then to exchange kisses, while the hailstorm continued.

But to cut a long story short, by the time the weather improved they had tasted Love's ultimate delights and arranged to meet again in secret for their mutual pleasure.

The cottage was not far from the city gate, and once the storm was over they went and waited there for the lady, and returned with her to the house. Every so often, employing the maximum of secrecy and discretion, they would meet again, to their considerable enjoyment, in the same place as before. But what happened in the end was that the girl became pregnant, much to the dismay of both parties, whereupon she took various measures to frustrate the course of nature and miscarry, but all to no effect.

Pietro, in fear of his life, made up his mind to flee, and told her so. But on hearing this, the girl said:

'If you go away, I shall kill myself without fail!'

To which Pietro, who was deeply in love with her, replied:

'But, my lady, how can you possibly want me to remain here? Our offence will be brought to light by your pregnancy. And whereas you will be readily forgiven, I shall be the poor wretch who has to suffer the penalty for your sin and my own.'

'My sin will be only too obvious, Pietro,' she replied, 'but rest assured that your own will never be discovered unless you reveal it yourself.'

Whereupon Pietro said:

'Since you have given me this promise, I shall stay; but take good care not to break it.'

The girl did all she possibly could to conceal her condition, but one day, seeing that she could hide it no longer on account of the swelling of her body, she went to her mother in floods of tears and made a full confession, imploring her to rescue her from harm.

The lady was utterly appalled, and admonished her severely, demanding to know how it had come about. So as to protect Pietro, the girl invented a tale containing a garbled version of the facts, which the lady believed, and in order to conceal her daughter's transgression she sent her away to a property of theirs in the country. Messer Amerigo very rarely set foot in this particular place, and her mother never thought for a moment that he would be going there, but just as the time came for the girl to be delivered, it so happened that on his way back from a hawking expedition he was passing directly beside the room where his daughter was in labour. Much to his astonishment, he heard the girl shrieking, as women are wont to do at such times, and he therefore walked straight in to inquire what was going on.

On seeing her husband arrive, the lady rose to her feet in dismay and explained what had happened to their daughter. But being less credulous than his wife, he maintained it was not possible for the girl to be ignorant of who had got her with child, and said he would ferret out the facts, come what may. Let her tell him the truth, therefore, and she would be restored to his favour; otherwise, she could expect to be put to death without mercy.

The lady did her utmost to persuade her husband to rest content with the story which she herself had accepted, but it was no use. Brandishing his sword, he rushed over in a towering rage to the bedside of his daughter, who meanwhile, as her mother was conversing with her father, had given birth to a son, and he said:

'Either you reveal the name of this child's father, or you shall die forthwith.'

Fearing she would be killed, the girl broke her promise to Pietro and made a clean breast of everything that had passed between them, whereupon the knight raved and stormed like a madman, and barely managed to restrain himself from putting her to death. However, after speaking his mind in no uncertain terms, he remounted his horse and rode off to Trapani, where he lodged a complaint with the Viceroy, a certain Messer Currado, about the injury Pietro had done him. Since he was unprepared for this turn of events, Pietro was promptly taken into custody, and on being put to the torture, he made a full confession.

A few days later the Viceroy sentenced him to be whipped through the town and then hanged by the neck. And in order to ensure that the two lovers and their child should all perish at the same time, Messer Amerigo, whose anger was by no means appeased by the destruction of Pietro, mixed some poison with wine in a goblet and handed it to one of his servants together with an unsheathed dagger, saying:

'Go with this goblet and this dagger to Violante, and tell her in my name that she is to die forthwith by whichever of the two means she prefers, the poison or the steel. Tell her she is to do it at once, otherwise I shall see that she is burnt alive, as she deserves, in the presence of every man and woman in the town. This done, you are to take the child which was born to her the other day, dash its head against a wall, and cast it away to be devoured by the dogs.'

As soon as the cruel father had passed this savage sentence on his daughter and grandchild, the servant, who was more disposed to evil than to good, took his leave.

Meanwhile Pietro, having been condemned to die, was being whipped along to the gallows by a troop of soldiers, when the leaders of the procession took it into their heads to pass in front of an inn where three Armenian noblemen were staying. These latter were ambassadors from the King of Armenia, on their way to Rome in order to negotiate with the Pope on very important matters connected with a crusade that was about to be launched. Having broken their journey at Trapani for a few days' rest and relaxation, they had been lavishly entertained by the noblemen of the town, and by Messer Amerigo in particular. And on hearing Pietro's escort passing the inn, they came to a window and peered out.

One of the three ambassadors, an elderly gentleman who wielded great authority and whose name was Phineas, fixed his gaze on Pietro, who was stripped to the waist with his hands tied behind his back, and perceived that on his chest there was a large red spot, which was not painted on the skin but imprinted there by nature, being what the women in this part of the world describe as a strawberry mark. On seeing this, he was at once reminded of a son of his who had been abducted by pirates from the shore at Lajazzo some fifteen years earlier and had never been heard of since. Having made a mental estimate of the age of the poor wretch who was being scourged, he calculated that his son, if he were still alive, would be roughly the same age. Hence, because of the mark on the youth's chest, he began to suspect that this was his own son; and he thought to himself that if this were indeed the case, the youth would still remember his name and that of his father, as well as one or two words of the Armenian language.

So when the youth came within earshot, Phineas called out: 'Theodor!'

As soon as he heard this cry, Pietro raised his head, whereupon Phineas addressed him in Armenian, saying:

'Where do you come from? Whose son are you?'

The soldiers escorting him halted in deference to the great man, allowing Pietro to reply:

'I am from Armenia, my father's name was Phineas, and I was brought here as a child by strangers.'

On hearing these words, Phineas knew for certain that this was the son he had lost. With tears in his eyes, he descended with his companions and ran through the ranks of the soldiers to embrace him. He then removed the exquisite silken cloak he was wearing, threw it over the young man's shoulders, and asked the leader of the execution-party to be good enough to wait there until he received the order to proceed. The man readily agreed to do so.

Phineas was already aware of the reason for which the young man was being led away to his death, for it had been bruited all over the town, and he therefore hurried off with his companions and their retinue to Messer Currado, whom he addressed as follows:

'Sir, this fellow whom you are sending to die as a slave is my own son, a freeman, and he is prepared to plight his troth to the girl he is alleged to have robbed of her virginity. I beg you therefore to postpone the execution until it is known whether she will have him as her husband, for otherwise you may find that you have acted illegally.'

On hearing that the youth was the son of Phineas, Messer Currado was filled with astonishment. Having uttered one or two apologetic phrases concerning the waywardness of Fortune, he agreed that Phineas had proved his case, and got him to return forthwith to the inn. He then sent for Messer Amerigo and told him what had happened.

Believing his daughter and grandchild to be already dead, Messer Amerigo was the most repentant man on earth, for he realized full well that if only she were still alive, it would be possible to set the whole affair to rights. However, just in case his instructions had not been carried out, and he was still in time to countermand them, he sent a message post-haste to the place where his daughter was.

The messenger found that the servant who had been sent by Messer Amerigo, having set the knife and poison in front of the girl, was bombarding her with abuse for taking so long to make up her mind, and trying to coerce her into choosing between the two. But on hearing his master's latest command, he stopped tormenting her, returned to Messer Amerigo, and told him how matters stood. Feeling greatly relieved, Messer Amerigo made his way to the place where Phineas was staying, and, choking back his tears, he apologized as best he could for what had happened, declaring that if Theodor wished to marry his daughter, he would be delighted to let him have her.

Phineas gladly accepted his apologies, and replied:

'I intend that my son should marry your daughter. And if he should raise any objection to doing so, let the sentence passed upon him be carried out.'

Being thus in agreement, Phineas and Messer Amerigo went to Pietro, who, though delighted at having found his father again, was still in great fear of being put to death, and they inquired into his own wishes on the subject.

On hearing that Violante would marry him if he so wished, Theodor was filled with such transports of joy that he had the sensation of passing from Hell into Heaven at a single bound; and he said that if this was what the two fathers were proposing, he could only regard it as the greatest of favours.

They therefore sent someone to ascertain the wishes of the girl herself, who after some time, having learned what had happened to Theodor and what was being proposed, ceased to be the saddest woman alive, awaiting only death to put an end to her misery. Giving some credence to the messenger's words, she began to take a slightly rosier view of her circumstances, and replied that if she were to follow her own inclinations in the matter, nothing would make her happier than to marry Theodor; but at all events she would do whatever her father ordered.

By mutual consent, therefore, the girl's betrothal was announced and a very great feast was held, to the immense pleasure of all the townspeople. Putting her infant son out to nurse, the girl recovered her strength, and before very long she appeared more lovely than ever. On rising from her confinement, she presented herself to Phineas, whose return from Rome everyone had meanwhile been awaiting, and greeted him with all the reverence due to a father. Phineas, delighted to have acquired so beautiful a daughter-in-law, saw to it that their nuptials were celebrated in the grand manner, with much feasting and merrymaking, and from then on he always looked upon Violante as his daughter. A few days after the nuptials, he took ship with her, his son, and his infant grandson, and sailed away with them to Lajazzo, where the two lovers lived in comfort and happiness for the rest of their days.

EIGHTH STORY

In his love for a young lady of the Traversari family, Nastagio degli Onesti squanders his wealth without being loved in return. He is entreated by his friends to leave the city, and goes away to Classe, where he sees a girl being hunted down and killed by a horseman, and devoured by a brace of hounds. He then invites his kinsfolk and the lady he loves to a banquet, where this same girl is torn to pieces before the eyes of his beloved, who, fearing a similar fate, accepts Nastagio as her husband.

No sooner did Lauretta fall silent, than at the bidding of the queen Filomena began as follows:

Adorable ladies, just as our pity is commended, so is our cruelty severely punished by divine justice. And in order to prove this to you, as well as to give you an incentive for banishing all cruelty from your hearts, I should like to tell you a story as delightful as it is full of pathos.

In Ravenna, a city of great antiquity in Romagna, there once used to live a great many nobles and men of property, among them a young man called Nastagio degli Onesti, who had inherited an incredibly large fortune on the deaths of his father and one of his uncles. Being as yet unmarried, he fell in love, as is the way with young men, with a daughter of Messer Paolo Traversari, a girl of far more noble lineage than his own, whose love he hoped to win by dint of his accomplishments. But though these were very considerable, and splendid, and laudable, far from promoting his cause they appeared to damage it, inasmuch as the girl he loved was persistently cruel, harsh and unfriendly towards him. And on account possibly of her singular beauty, or perhaps because of her exalted rank, she became so haughty and contemptuous of him that she positively loathed him and everything he stood for.

All of this was so difficult for Nastagio to bear that he was frequently seized, after much weeping and gnashing of teeth, with the longing to kill himself out of sheer despair. But, having stayed his hand, he would then decide that he must give her up altogether, or learn if possible to hate her as she hated him. All such resolutions were unavailing, however, for the more his hopes dwindled, the greater his love seemed to grow.

As the young man persisted in wooing the girl and spending money like water, certain of his friends and relatives began to feel that he was in danger of exhausting both himself and his inheritance. They therefore implored and advised him to leave Ravenna and go to live for a while in some other place, with the object of curtailing both his wooing and his spending. Nastagio rejected this advice as often as it was offered, but they eventually pressed him so hard that he could not refuse them any longer, and agreed to do as they suggested. Having mustered an enormous baggage-train, as though he were intending to go to France or Spain or some other remote part of the world, he mounted his horse, rode forth from Ravenna with several of his friends, and repaired to a place which is known as Classe, some three miles distant from the city. Having sent for a number of tents and pavilions, he told his companions that this was where he intended to stay, and that they could all go back to Ravenna. So Nastagio pitched his camp in this place, and began to live in as fine and lordly a fashion as any man ever born, from time to time inviting various groups of friends to dine or breakfast with him, as had always been his custom.

Now, it so happened that one Friday morning towards the beginning of May, the weather being very fine, Nastagio fell to thinking about his cruel mistress. Having ordered his servants to leave him to his own devices so that he could meditate at greater leisure, he sauntered off, lost in thought, and his steps led him straight into the pinewoods. The fifth hour of the day was already spent, and he had advanced at least half a mile into the woods, oblivious of food and everything else, when suddenly he seemed to hear a woman giving vent to dreadful wailing and ear-splitting screams. His pleasant reverie being thus interrupted, he raised his head to investigate the cause, and discovered to his surprise that he was in the pinewoods. Furthermore, on looking straight ahead he caught sight of a naked woman, young and very beautiful, who was running through a dense thicket of shrubs and briars towards the very spot where he was standing. The woman's hair was dishevelled, her flesh was all torn by the briars and brambles, and she was sobbing and screaming for mercy. Nor was this all, for a pair of big, fierce mastiffs were running at the girl's heels, one on either side, and every so often they caught up with her and savaged her. Finally, bringing up the rear he saw a swarthy-looking knight, his face contorted with anger, who was riding a jet-black steed and brandishing a rapier, and who, in terms no less abusive than terrifying, was threatening to kill her.

This spectacle struck both terror and amazement into Nastagio's breast, to say nothing of compassion for the hapless woman, a sentiment that in its turn engendered the desire to rescue her from such agony and save her life, if this were possible. But on finding that he was unarmed, he hastily took up a branch of a tree to serve as a cudgel, and prepared to ward off the dogs and do battle with the knight. When the latter saw what he was doing, he shouted to him from a distance:

'Keep out of this, Nastagio! Leave me and the dogs to give this wicked sinner her deserts!'

He had no sooner spoken than the dogs seized the girl firmly by the haunches and brought her to a halt. When the knight reached the spot he dismounted from his horse, and Nastagio went up to him saying:

'I do not know who you are, or how you come to know my name; but I can tell you that it is a gross outrage for an armed knight to try and kill a naked woman, and to set dogs upon her as though she were a savage beast. I shall do all in my power to defend her, of that you may be sure.'

Whereupon the knight said:

'I was a fellow-citizen of yours, Nastagio, my name was Guido degli Anastagi, and you were still a little child when I fell in love with this woman. I loved her far more deeply than you love that Traversari girl of yours, but her pride and cruelty led me to such a pass that, one day, I killed myself in sheer despair with this rapier that you see in my hand, and thus I am condemned to eternal punishment. My death pleased her beyond measure, but shortly thereafter she also died, and because she had sinned by her cruelty and by gloating over my sufferings, and was quite unrepentant, being convinced that she was more of a saint than a sinner, she too was condemned to the pains of Hell. No sooner was she cast into Hell than we were both given a special punishment, which consisted in her case of fleeing before me, and in my own of pursuing her as though she were my mortal enemy rather than the woman with whom I was once so deeply in love. Every time I catch up with her, I kill her with this same rapier by which I took my own life; then I slit her back open, and (as you will now observe for yourself) I tear from her body that hard, cold heart to which neither love nor pity could ever gain access, and together with the rest of her entrails I cast it to these dogs to feed upon.

'Within a short space of time, as ordained by the power and justice of God, she springs to her feet as though she had not been dead at all, and her agonizing flight begins all over again, with the dogs and myself in pursuit. Every Friday at this hour I overtake her in this part of the woods, and slaughter her in the manner you are about to observe; but you must not imagine that we are idle for the rest of the week, because on the remaining days I hunt her down in other places where she was cruel to me in thought and deed. As you can see for yourself, I am no longer her lover but her enemy, and in this guise I am obliged to pursue her for the same number of years as the months of her cruelty towards me. Stand aside, therefore, and let me carry out the judgement of God. Do not try to oppose what you cannot prevent.'

On hearing these words, Nastagio was shaken to the core, there was scarcely a single hair on his head that was not standing on end, and he stepped back to fix his gaze on the unfortunate girl, waiting in fear and trembling to see what the knight would do to her. This latter, having finished speaking, pounced like a mad dog, rapier in hand, upon the girl, who was kneeling before him, held by the two mastiffs, and screaming for mercy at the top of her voice. Applying all his strength, the knight plunged his rapier into the middle of her breast and out again at the other side, whereupon the girl fell on her face, still sobbing and screaming, whilst the knight, having laid hold of a dagger, slashed open her back, extracted her heart and every-thing else around it, and hurled it to the two mastiffs, who devoured it greedily on the instant. But before very long the girl rose suddenly to her feet as though none of these things had happened, and sped off in the direction of the sea, being pursued by the dogs, who kept tearing away at her flesh as she ran. Remounting his horse, and seizing his rapier, the knight too began to give chase, and within a short space of time they were so far away that Nastagio could no longer see them.

For some time after bearing witness to these events, Nastagio stood rooted to the spot out of fear and compassion, but after a while it occurred to him that since this scene was enacted every Friday, it ought to prove very useful to him. So he marked the place and returned to his servants; and when the time seemed ripe, he sent for his friends and kinsfolk, and said to them:

'For some little time you have been urging me to desist from wooing this hostile mistress of mine and place a curb on my extravagance, and I am willing to do so on condition that you obtain for me a single favour, which is this: that on Friday next you arrange for Messer Paolo Traversari and his wife and daughter and all their womenfolk, together with any other lady you care to invite, to join me in this place for breakfast. My reason for wanting this will become apparent to you on the day itself.'

They thought this a very trifling commission for them to undertake, and promised him they would do it. On their return to Ravenna, they invited all the people he had specified. And although they had a hard job, when the time came, in persuading Nastagio's beloved to go, she nevertheless went there along with the others.

Nastagio saw to it that a magnificent banquet was prepared, and had the tables placed beneath the pine trees in such a way as to surround the place where he had witnessed the massacre of the cruel lady. Moreover, in seating the ladies and gentlemen at table, he so arranged matters that the girl he loved sat directly facing the spot where the scene would be enacted.

The last course had already been served, when they all began to hear the agonized yells of the fugitive girl. Everyone was greatly astonished and wanted to know what it was, but nobody was able to say. So they all stood up to see if they could find out what was going on, and caught sight of the wailing girl, together with the knight and the dogs. And shortly thereafter they came into the very midst of the company.

Everyone began shouting and bawling at the dogs and the knight, and several people rushed forward to the girl's assistance; but the knight, by repeating to them the story he had related to Nastagio, not only caused them to retreat but filled them all with terror and amazement. And when he dealt with the girl in the same way as before, all the ladies present (many of whom, being related either to the suffering girl or to the knight, still remembered his great love and the manner of his death) wept as plaintively as though what they had witnessed had been done to themselves.

When the spectacle was at an end, and the knight and the lady had gone, they all began to talk about what they had seen. But none was stricken with so much terror as the cruel maiden loved by Nastagio, for she had heard and seen everything distinctly and realized that these matters had more to do with herself than with any of the other guests, in view of the harshness she had always displayed towards Nastagio; consequently, she already had the sensation of fleeing before her enraged suitor, with the mastiffs tearing away at her haunches.

So great was the fear engendered within her by this episode, that in order to avoid a similar fate she converted her enmity into love; and, seizing the earliest opportunity (which came to her that very evening), she privily sent a trusted maidservant to Nastagio, requesting him to be good enough to call upon her, as she was ready to do anything he desired. Nastagio was overjoyed, and told her so in his reply, but added that if she had no objection he preferred to combine his pleasure with the preservation of her good name, by making her his lawful wedded wife.

Knowing that she alone was to blame for the fact that she and Nastagio were not already married, the girl readily sent him her consent. And so, acting as her own intermediary, she announced to her father and mother, to their enormous satisfaction, that she would be pleased to become Nastagio's wife. On the following Sunday Nastagio married her, and after celebrating their nuptials they settled down to a long and happy life together.

Their marriage was by no means the only good effect to be produced by this horrible apparition, for from that day forth the ladies of Ravenna in general were so frightened by it that they became much more tractable to men's pleasures than they had ever been in the past.

NINTH STORY

In courting a lady who does not return his love, Federigo degli Alberighi spends the whole of his substance, being left with nothing but a falcon, which, since his larder is bare, he offers to his lady to eat when she calls to see him at his house. On discovering the truth of the matter, she has a change of heart, accepts him as her husband, and makes a rich man of him.

Once Filomena had finished, the queen, finding that there was no one left to speak apart from herself (Dioneo being excluded from the reckoning because of his privilege), smiled cheerfully and said:

It is now my own turn to address you, and I shall gladly do so, dearest ladies, with a story similar in some respects to the one we have just heard. This I have chosen, not only to acquaint you with the power of your beauty over men of noble spirit, but so that you may learn to choose for yourselves, whenever necessary, the persons on whom to bestow your largesse, instead of always leaving these matters to be decided for you by Fortune, who, as it happens, nearly always scatters her gifts with more abundance than discretion.

You are to know, then, that Coppo di Borghese Domenichi, who once used to live in our city and possibly lives there still, one of the most highly respected men of our century, a person worthy of eternal fame, who achieved his position of pre-eminence by dint of his character and abilities rather than by his noble lineage, frequently took pleasure during his declining years in discussing incidents from the past with his neighbours and other folk. In this pastime he excelled all others, for he was more coherent, possessed a superior memory, and spoke with greater eloquence. He had a fine repertoire, including a tale he frequently told concerning a young Florentine called Federigo, the son of Messer Filippo Alberighi, who for his deeds of chivalry and courtly manners was more highly spoken of than any other squire in Tuscany. In the manner of most young men of gentle breeding, Federigo lost his heart to a noble lady, whose name was Monna Giovanna, and who in her time was considered one of the loveliest and most adorable women to be found in Florence.

And with the object of winning her love, he rode at the ring, tilted, gave sumptuous banquets, and distributed a large number of gifts, spending money without any restraint whatsoever. But since she was no less chaste than she was fair, the lady took no notice, either of the things that were done in her honour, or of the person who did them.

In this way, spending far more than he could afford and deriving no profit in return, Federigo lost his entire fortune (as can easily happen) and reduced himself to poverty, being left with nothing other than a tiny little farm, which produced an income just sufficient for him to live very frugally, and one falcon of the finest breed in the whole world. Since he was as deeply in love as ever, and felt unable to go on living the sort of life in Florence to which he aspired, he moved out to Campi, where his little farm happened to be situated. Having settled in the country, he went hunting as often as possible with his falcon, and, without seeking assistance from anyone, he patiently resigned himself to a life of poverty.

Now one day, while Federigo was living in these straitened circumstances, the husband of Monna Giovanna happened to fall ill, and, realizing that he was about to die, he drew up his will. He was a very rich man, and in his will he left everything to his son, who was just growing up, further stipulating that, if his son should die without legitimate issue, his estate should go to Monna Giovanna, to whom he had always been deeply devoted.

Shortly afterwards he died, leaving Monna Giovanna a widow, and every summer, in accordance with Florentine custom, she went away with her son to a country estate of theirs, which was very near Federigo's farm. Consequently this young lad of hers happened to become friendly with Federigo, acquiring a passion for birds and dogs; and, having often seen Federigo's falcon in flight, he became fascinated by it and longed to own it, but since he could see that Federigo was deeply attached to the bird, he never ventured to ask him for it.

And there the matter rested, when, to the consternation of his mother, the boy happened to be taken ill. Being her only child, he was the apple of his mother's eye, and she sat beside his bed the whole day long, never ceasing to comfort him. Every so often she asked him whether there was anything he wanted, imploring him to tell her what it was, because if it was possible to acquire it, she would move heaven and earth to obtain it for him.

After hearing this offer repeated for the umpteenth time, the boy said:

'Mother, if you could arrange for me to have Federigo's falcon, I believe I should soon get better.'

On hearing this request, the lady was somewhat taken aback, and began to consider what she could do about it. Knowing that Federigo had been in love with her for a long time, and that she had never deigned to cast so much as a single glance in his direction, she said to herself: 'How can I possibly go to him, or even send anyone, to ask him for this falcon, which to judge from all I have heard is the finest that ever flew, as well as being the only thing that keeps him alive? And how can I be so heartless as to deprive so noble a man of his one remaining pleasure?'

Her mind filled with reflections of this sort, she remained silent, not knowing what answer to make to her son's request, even though she was quite certain that the falcon was hers for the asking.

At length, however, her maternal instincts gained the upper hand, and she resolved, come what may, to satisfy the child by going in person to Federigo to collect the bird, and bring it back to him. And so she replied:

'Bear up, my son, and see whether you can start feeling any better. I give you my word that I shall go and fetch it for you first thing tomorrow morning.'

Next morning, taking another lady with her for company, his mother left the house as though intending to go for a walk, made her way to Federigo's little cottage, and asked to see him. For several days, the weather had been unsuitable for hawking, so Federigo was attending to one or two little jobs in his garden, and when he heard, to his utter astonishment, that Monna Giovanna was at the front-door and wished to speak to him, he happily rushed there to greet her.

When she saw him coming, she advanced with womanly grace to meet him. Federigo received her with a deep bow, whereupon she said:

'Greetings, Federigo!' Then she continued: 'I have come to make amends for the harm you have suffered on my account, by loving me more than you ought to have done. As a token of my esteem, I should like to take breakfast with you this morning, together with my companion here, but you must not put yourself to any trouble.'

'My lady,' replied Federigo in all humility, 'I cannot recall ever having suffered any harm on your account. On the contrary I have gained so much that if ever I attained any kind of excellence, it was entirely because of your own great worth and the love I bore you. Moreover I can assure you that this visit which you have been generous enough to pay me is worth more to me than all the money I ever possessed, though I fear that my hospitality will not amount to very much.'

So saying, he led her unassumingly into the house, and thence into his garden, where, since there was no one else he could call upon to chaperon her, he said:

'My lady, as there is nobody else available, this good woman, who is the wife of the farmer here, will keep you company whilst I go and see about setting the table.'

Though his poverty was acute, the extent to which he had squandered his wealth had not yet been fully borne home to Federigo; but on this particular morning, finding that he had nothing to set before the lady for whose love he had entertained so lavishly in the past, his eyes were well and truly opened to the fact. Distressed beyond all measure, he silently cursed his bad luck and rushed all over the house like one possessed, but could find no trace of either money or valuables. By now the morning was well advanced, he was still determined to entertain the gentlewoman to some sort of meal, and, not wishing to beg assistance from his own farmer (or from anyone else, for that matter), his gaze alighted on his precious falcon, which was sitting on its perch in the little room where it was kept. And having discovered, on picking it up, that it was nice and plump, he decided that since he had nowhere else to turn, it would make a worthy dish for such a lady as this. So without thinking twice about it he wrung the bird's neck and promptly handed it over to his housekeeper to be plucked, dressed, and roasted carefully on a spit. Then he covered the table with spotless linen, of which he still had a certain amount in his possession, and returned in high spirits to the garden, where he announced to his lady that the meal, such as he had been able to prepare, was now ready.

The lady and her companion rose from where they were sitting and made their way to the table. And together with Federigo, who waited on them with the utmost deference, they made a meal of the prize falcon without knowing what they were eating.

On leaving the table they engaged their host in pleasant conversation for a while, and when the lady thought it time to broach the subject she had gone there to discuss, she turned to Federigo and addressed him affably as follows:

'I do not doubt for a moment, Federigo, that you will be astonished at my impertinence when you discover my principal reason for coming here, especially when you recall your former mode of living and my virtue, which you possibly mistook for harshness and cruelty. But if you had ever had any children to make you appreciate the power of parental love, I should think it certain that you would to some extent forgive me.

'However, the fact that you have no children of your own does not exempt me, a mother, from the laws common to all other mothers. And being bound to obey those laws, I am forced, contrary to my own wishes and to all the rules of decorum and propriety, to ask you for something to which I know you are very deeply attached – which is only natural, seeing that it is the only consolation, the only pleasure, the only recreation remaining to you in your present extremity of fortune. The gift I am seeking is your falcon, to which my son has taken so powerful a liking, that if I fail to take it to him I fear he will succumb to the illness from which he is suffering, and consequently I shall lose him. In imploring you to give me this falcon, I appeal, not to your love, for you are under no obligation to me on that account, but rather to your noble heart, whereby you have proved yourself superior to all others in the practice of courtesy. Do me this favour, then, so that I may claim that through your generosity I have saved my son's life, thus placing him forever in your debt.'

When he heard what it was that she wanted, and realized that he could not oblige her because he had given her the falcon to eat, Federigo burst into tears in her presence before being able to utter a single word in reply. At first the lady thought his tears stemmed more from his grief at having to part with his fine falcon than from any other motive, and was on the point of telling him that she would prefer not to have it. But on second thoughts she said nothing, and waited for Federigo to stop crying and give her his answer, which eventually he did.

'My lady,' he said, 'ever since God decreed that you should become the object of my love, I have repeatedly had cause to complain of Fortune's hostility towards me. But all her previous blows were slight by comparison with the one she has dealt me now. Nor shall I ever be able to forgive her, when I reflect that you have come to my poor dwelling, which you never deigned to visit when it was rich, and that you desire from me a trifling favour which she has made it impossible for me to concede. The reason is simple, and I shall explain it in few words.

'When you did me the kindness of telling me that you wished to breakfast with me, I considered it right and proper, having regard to your excellence and merit, to do everything within my power to prepare a more sumptuous dish than those I would offer to my ordinary guests. My thoughts therefore turned to the falcon you have asked me for and, knowing its quality, I reputed it a worthy dish to set before you. So I had it roasted and served to you on the trencher this morning, and I could not have wished for a better way of disposing of it. But now that I discover that you wanted it in a different form, I am so distressed by my inability to grant your request that I shall never forgive myself for as long as I live.'

In confirmation of his words, Federigo caused the feathers, talons and beak to be cast on the table before her. On seeing and hearing all this, the lady reproached him at first for killing so fine a falcon, and serving it up for a woman to eat; but then she became lost in admiration for his magnanimity of spirit, which no amount of poverty had managed to diminish, nor ever would. But now that her hopes of obtaining the falcon had vanished she began to feel seriously concerned for the health of her son, and after thanking Federigo for his hospitality and good intentions, she took her leave of him, looking all despondent, and returned to the child. And to his mother's indescribable sorrow, within the space of a few days, whether through his disappointment in not being able to have the falcon, or because he was in any case suffering from a mortal illness, the child passed from this life.

After a period of bitter mourning and continued weeping, the lady was repeatedly urged by her brothers to remarry, since not only had she been left a vast fortune but she was still a young woman. And though she would have preferred to remain a widow, they gave her so little peace that in the end, recalling Federigo's high merits and his latest act of generosity, namely to have killed such a fine falcon in her honour, she said to her brothers:

'If only it were pleasing to you, I should willingly remain as I am; but since you are so eager for me to take a husband, you may be certain that I shall never marry any other man except Federigo degli Alberighi.'

Her brothers made fun of her, saying:

'Silly girl, don't talk such nonsense! How can you marry a man who hasn't a penny with which to bless himself?'

'My brothers,' she replied, 'I am well aware of that. But I would sooner have a gentleman without riches, than riches without a gentleman.'

Seeing that her mind was made up, and knowing Federigo to be a gentleman of great merit even though he was poor, her brothers fell in with her wishes and handed her over to him, along with her immense fortune. Thenceforth, finding himself married to this great lady with whom he was so deeply in love, and very rich into the bargain, Federigo managed his affairs more prudently, and lived with her in happiness to the end of his days.

TENTH STORY

Pietro di Vinciolo goes out to sup with Ercolano, and his wife lets a young man in to keep her company. Pietro returns, and she conceals the youth beneath a chicken coop. Pietro tells her that a young man has been discovered in Ercolano's house, having been concealed there by Ercolano's wife, whose conduct she severely censures. As ill luck would have it, an ass steps on the fingers of the fellow hiding beneath the coop, causing him to yell with pain. Pietro rushes to the spot and sees him, thus discovering his wife's deception. But in the end, by reason of his own depravity, he arrives at an understanding with her.

When the queen's tale had reached its conclusion, they all praised God for having given Federigo so fitting a reward, and then Dioneo, who was not in the habit of waiting to be asked, began straightway as follows:

Whether it is an accidental failing, stemming from our debased morals, or simply an innate attribute of men and women, I am unable to say; but the fact remains that we are more inclined to laugh at scandalous behaviour than virtuous deeds, especially when we ourselves are not directly involved. And since, as on previous occasions, the task I am about to perform has no other object than to dispel your melancholy, enamoured ladies, and provide you with laughter and merriment, I shall tell you the ensuing tale, for it may well afford enjoyment even though its subject matter is not altogether seemly. As you listen, do as you would when you enter a garden, and stretch forth your tender hands to pluck the roses, leaving the thorns where they are. This you will succeed in doing if you leave the knavish husband to his ill deserts and his iniquities, whilst you laugh gaily at the amorous intrigues of his wife, pausing where occasion warrants to commiserate with the woes of her lover.

Not so very long ago, there lived in Perugia a rich man called Pietro di Vinciolo, who, perhaps to pull the wool over the eyes of his fellow-citizens or to improve the low opinion they had of him, rather than because of any real wish to marry, took to himself a wife. But the unfortunate part about it, considering his own proclivities, was that he chose to marry a buxom young woman with red hair and a passionate nature, who would cheerfully have taken on a pair of husbands, let alone one, and now found herself wedded to a man whose heart was anywhere but in the right place.

Having in due course discovered how matters stood, his wife, seeing that she was a fair and lusty wench, blooming with health and vitality, was greatly upset about it, and every so often she gave him a piece of her mind, calling him the foulest names imaginable. She was miserable practically the whole time, but one day, realizing that if she went on like this her days might well be ended before her husband's ways were mended, she said to herself: 'Since this miserable sinner deserts me to go trudging through the dry with clogs on, I'll get someone else to come aboard for the wet. I married the wretch, and brought him a good big dowry, because I knew he was a man and thought he was fond of the kind of thing that other men like, as is right and proper that they should. If I hadn't thought he was a man, I should never have married him. And if he found women so repugnant, why did he marry me in the first place, knowing me to be a woman? I'm not going to stand for it any longer, I have no desire to turn my back on the world, nor have I ever wanted to, otherwise I'd have gone into a nunnery; but if I have to rely on this fellow for my fun and games, the chances are that I'll go on waiting until I'm an old woman. And what good will it do me then, in my old age, to look back and complain about the way I wasted my youth, which this husband of mine teaches me all too well how to enjoy? He has shown me how to lead a pleasurable life, but whereas in his case the pleasure can only be condemned, in my own it will commend itself to all, for I shall simply be breaking the laws of marriage, whereas he is breaking those of Nature as well.'

These, then, were the wife's ideas, to which she doubtless gave further thought on other occasions, and in order to put them into effect, she made the acquaintance of an old bawd who to all outward appearances was as innocent as Saint Verdiana feeding the serpents, for she made a point of attending all the religious services clutching her rosary, and never stopped talking about the lives of the Fathers of the Church and the wounds of St Francis, so that nearly everyone regarded her as a saint. Choosing the right moment, the wife took her fully into her confidence, whereupon the old woman said:

'The Lord above, my daughter, who is omniscient, knows that you are very well advised, if only because you should never waste a moment of your youth, and the same goes for all other women. To anyone who's had experience of such matters, there's no sorrow to compare with that of having wasted your opportunities. After all, what the devil are we women fit for in our old age except to sit round the fire and stare at the ashes? No woman can know this better than I, or prove it to you more convincingly. Now that I am old, my heart bleeds when I look back and consider the opportunities I allowed to go to waste. Mind you, I didn't waste all of them – I wouldn't want you to think I was a half-wit – but all the same I didn't do as much as I should have. And God knows what agony it is to see myself reduced now to this sorry state, and realize that if I wanted to light a fire, I couldn't find anyone to lend me a poker.

'With men it is different: they are born with a thousand other talents apart from this, and older men do a far better job than younger ones as a rule; but women exist for no other purpose than to do this and to bear children, which is why they are cherished and admired. If you doubt my words, there's one thing that ought to convince you, and that is that a woman's always ready for a man, but not vice-versa. What's more, one woman could exhaust many men, whereas many men can't exhaust one woman. And since this is the purpose for which we are born, I repeat that you are very well advised to pay your husband in his own coin, so that when you're an old woman your heart will have no cause for complaint against your flesh.

'You must help yourself to whatever you can grab in this world, especially if you're a woman. It's far more important for women than for men to make the most of their opportunities, because when we're old, as you can see for yourself, neither our husbands nor any other man can bear the sight of us, and they bundle us off into the kitchen to tell stories to the cat, and count the pots and pans. And what's worse, they make up rhymes about us, such as "When she's twenty give her plenty. When she's a gammer, give her the hammer," and a lot of other sayings in the same strain.

'But I won't detain you any longer with my chit-chat. You've told me what you have in mind, and I can assure you right away that you couldn't have spoken to anyone in the world who was better able to help. There's no man so refined as to deter me from telling him what's required of him, nor is there any so raw and uncouth as to prevent me from softening him up and bending him to my will. So just point out the one you would like, and leave the rest to me. But one thing I would ask you to remember, my child, and that is to offer me some token of your esteem, for I'm a poor old woman, and from now on I want you to have a share in my indulgences and all the paternosters I recite, so that God may look with favour on the souls of your departed ones.'

Having said her piece, she came to an understanding with the young lady that if she should come across a certain young man who frequently passed through that part of the city, and of whom she was given a very full description, she would take all necessary steps. The young woman then handed over a joint of salted meat, and they took their leave of one another.

Within the space of a few days, the youth designated by the lady was ushered secretly into her apartments by the beldam, and thereafter, at frequent intervals, several others who had taken the young woman's fancy were similarly introduced to her. And although she was in constant fear of being discovered by her husband, she made the fullest possible use of her opportunities.

One evening, however, her husband having been invited to supper by a friend of his called Ercolano, the young woman commissioned the beldam to fetch her one of the most handsome and agreeable youths in Perugia, and her instructions were duly carried out. But no sooner were she and the youth seated at the supper-table than her husband, Pietro, started clamouring at the door to be let in.

The woman was convinced, on hearing this, that her final hour had come. But all the same she wanted to conceal the youth if possible, and not having the presence of mind to hide him in some other part of the house, she persuaded him to crawl beneath a chicken-coop in the lean-to adjoining the room where they were dining, and threw a large sack over the top of it, which she had emptied of its contents earlier in the day. This done, she quickly let in her husband, to whom she said as he entered the house:

'You soon gobbled down that supper of yours.'

'We never ate a crumb of it,' replied Pietro.

'And why was that?' said his wife.

'I'll tell you why it was,' said Pietro. 'No sooner had Ercolano, his wife and myself taken our places at table than we heard someone sneezing, close beside where we were sitting. We took no notice the first time it happened, or the second, but when the sneezing was repeated for the third, fourth and fifth times, and a good many more besides, we were all struck dumb with astonishment. Ercolano was in a bad mood anyway because his wife had kept us waiting for ages before opening the door to let us in, and he rounded on her almost choking with fury, saying: "What's the meaning of this? Who's doing all that sneezing?" He then got up from the table, and walked over to the stairs, beneath which there was an alcove boarded in with timber, such as people very often use for storing away bits and pieces when they're tidying up the house.

'As this was the place from which Ercolano thought the sneezes were coming, he opened a little door in the wainscoting, whereupon the whole room was suddenly filled with the most appalling smell of sulphur, though a little while before, when we caught a whiff of sulphur and complained about it, Ercolano's wife said: "It's because I was using sulphur earlier in the day to bleach my veils. I sprinkled it into a large bowl so that they would absorb the fumes, then placed it in the cupboard under the stairs, and it's still giving off a faint smell." After opening the little door and waiting for the fumes to die down a little, Ercolano peered inside and caught sight of the fellow who'd being doing all the sneezing, and was still sneezing his head off because of the sulphur. But if he'd stayed there much longer he would never have sneezed again, nor would he have done anything else for that matter.

'When he saw the man sitting there in the cupboard, Ercolano turned to his wife and shouted: "Now I see, woman, why you kept us waiting so long at the door just now, without letting us in; but I'll make you pay for it, if it's the last thing I do." On hearing this, since it was perfectly obvious what she had been doing, his wife got up from the table without a word of explanation and took to her heels, and what became of her I have no idea. Not having noticed that his wife had fled, Ercolano called repeatedly on the man who was sneezing to come out, but the fellow was already on his last legs and couldn't be persuaded to budge. So Ercolano grabbed him by one of his feet, dragged him out, and ran for a knife in order to kill him, at which point, since I was afraid we would all be arrested, myself included, I leapt to my feet and saved him from being killed or coming to any harm. As I was defending him from Ercolano, my shouts brought several of the neighbours running to the scene, and they picked up the youth, who was no longer conscious, and carried him out of the house, but I've no idea where they took him. All this commotion put paid to our supper, so that, as I said, not only did I not gobble it down, but I never ate a crumb of it.'

On hearing this tale, his wife perceived that other women, even though their plans occasionally miscarried, were no less shrewd than herself, and she was strongly tempted to speak up in defence of Ercolano's wife. But thinking that by censuring another's misconduct she would cover up her own more successfully, she said:

'What a nice way to behave! What a fine, God-fearing specimen of womanhood! What a loyal and respectable spouse! Why, she had such an air of saintliness that she looked as if butter wouldn't melt in her mouth! But the worst part about it is that anyone as old as she is should be setting the young so fine an example. A curse upon the hour she was born! May the Devil take the wicked and deceitful hussy, for allowing herself to become the general butt and laughing-stock of all the women of this city! Not only has she thrown away her own good name, broken her marriage vows, and forfeited the respect of society, but she's had the audacity, after all he has done for her, to involve an excellent husband and venerable citizen in her disgrace, and all for the sake of some other man. So help me God, women of her kind should be shown no mercy; they ought to be done away with; they ought to be burnt alive and reduced to ashes.'

But at this point, recollecting that her lover was concealed beneath the chicken-coop in the very next room, she started coaxing Pietro to go to bed, saying it was getting late, whereupon Pietro, who had a greater urge to eat than to sleep, asked her whether there was any supper left over.

'Supper?' she replied. 'What would I be doing cooking supper, when you're not at home to eat it? Do you take me for the wife of Ercolano? Be off with you to bed, and give your stomach a rest, just for this once.'

Now, earlier that same evening, some of the labourers from Pietro's farm in the country had turned up at the house with a load of provisions, and had tethered their asses in a small stable adjoining the lean-to, without bothering to water them. Being frantic with thirst, one of the asses, having broken its tether, had strayed from the stable and was roaming freely about the premises, sniffing in every nook and cranny to see if it could find any water. And in the course of its wanderings, it came and stood immediately beside the coop under which the young man lay hidden.

Since the young man was having to crouch on all fours, one of his hands was sticking out slightly from underneath the coop, and as luck would have it (or rather, to his great misfortune) the ass brought one of its hooves to rest on his fingers, causing him so much pain that he started to shriek at the top of his voice. Pietro, hearing this, was filled with astonishment, and, realizing that the noise was coming from somewhere inside the house, he rushed from the room to investigate. The youth was still howling, for the ass had not yet shifted its hoof from his fingers and was pressing firmly down upon him all the time. 'Who's there?' yelled Pietro as he ran to the coop, lifting it up to reveal the young man, who, apart from suffering considerable pain from having his fingers crushed beneath the hoof of the ass, was trembling with fear from head to foot in case Pietro should do him some serious injury.

Pietro recognized the young man as one he had long been pursuing for his own wicked ends, and demanded to know what he was doing there. But instead of answering his question, the youth pleaded with him for the love of God not to do him any harm.

'Get up,' said Pietro. 'There's no need to worry, I shan't do you any harm. Just tell me what you're doing here, and how you got in.'

The young man made a clean breast of the whole thing, and Pietro, who was no less pleased with his discovery than his wife was filled with despair, took him by the hand and led him back into the room, where the woman was waiting for him in a state of indescribable terror. Pietro sat down, looked her squarely in the face, and said:

'When you were heaping abuse on Ercolano's wife just now, and saying that she ought to be burnt alive, and that she was giving women a bad name, why didn't you say the same things about yourself? And if you wanted to keep yourself out of it, what possessed you to say such things about her, when you knew full well that you were tarred with the same brush? The only reason you did it, of course, was because all you women are alike. You go out of your way to criticize other people's failings so as to cover up your own. Oh, how I wish that a fire would descend from Heaven and burn the whole revolting lot of you to ashes!'

On finding that all she had to contend with, in the first flush of his anger, was a string of verbal abuse, and noting how delighted he seemed to be holding such a good-looking boy by the hand, the wife plucked up courage and said:

'It doesn't surprise me in the least that you want a fire to descend from Heaven and burn us all to ashes, seeing that you're as fond of women as a dog is fond of a hiding, but by the Holy Cross of Jesus you'll not have your wish granted. However, now that you've raised the subject, I'd like to know what you're grumbling about. It's all very well for you to compare me to Ercolano's wife, but at least he gives that sanctimonious old trollop whatever she wants, and treats her as a wife should be treated, which is more than can be said for you. I grant you that you keep me well supplied with clothes and shoes, but you know very well how I fare for anything else, and how long it is since you last slept with me. And I'd rather go barefoot and dressed in rags, and have you treat me properly in bed, than have all those things to wear and a husband who never comes near me. For the plain truth is, Pietro, that I'm no different from other women, and I want the same that they are having. And if you won't let me have it, you can hardly blame me if I go and get it elsewhere. At least I do you the honour not to consort with stable-boys and riff-raff.'

Pietro saw that she could go on talking all night, and since he was not unduly interested in his wife, he said:

'Hold your tongue now, woman, and leave everything to me. Be so good as to see that we're supplied with something to eat. This young man looks as though he's had no more supper this evening than I have.'

'Of course he hasn't had any supper,' said his wife. 'We were no sooner seated at table than you had to come knocking at the door.'

'Run along, then,' said Pietro, 'and get us some supper, after which I'll arrange matters so that you won't have any further cause for complaint.'

On perceiving that her husband was so contented, the wife sprang to her feet and quickly relaid the table. And when the supper she had prepared was brought in, she and the youth and her degenerate husband made a merry meal of it together.

How exactly Pietro arranged matters, after supper, to the mutual satisfaction of all three parties, I no longer remember. But I do know that the young man was found next morning wandering about the piazza, not exactly certain with which of the pair he had spent the greater part of the night, the wife or the husband. So my advice to you, dear ladies, is this, that you should always give back as much as you receive; and if you can't do it at once, bear it in mind till you can, so that what you lose on the swings, you gain on the round-abouts.

*   *   *

Dioneo's story was thus concluded, and if the ladies' laughter was restrained, this was more out of modesty than because it had failed to amuse them. But now the queen, perceiving that her sovereignty had come to an end, rose to her feet; and transferring the laurel crown from her own head to that of Elissa, she said to her:

'Madam, it is now for you to command us.'

Elissa, having accepted the honour, proceeded as before, first of all arranging with the steward about what was to be done during her term of office, and then, to the general satisfaction of the company, she addressed them as follows:

'Already we have heard many times how various people, with some clever remark or ready retort, or some quick piece of thinking, have been able, by striking at the right moment, to draw the teeth of their antagonists or avert impending dangers. This being so splendid a topic, and one which may also be useful, I desire that with God's help our discussion on the morrow should confine itself to the following: *those who, on being provoked by some verbal pleasantry, have returned like for like, or who, by a prompt retort or shrewd manoeuvre, have avoided danger, discomfiture or ridicule.*'

This proposal was warmly approved by one and all, and so the queen, having risen to her feet, dismissed the whole company till suppertime.

On seeing that the queen had risen, the honourable company did likewise; then all of them turned their attention, in the usual way, to whatever pleased them most. But when the cicadas' song was no longer to be heard, everyone was called back, and they all sat down to supper. Of this they partook in a gay and festive spirit, and when the meal was over they proceeded to sing and make music. Emilia having begun to dance, Dioneo was called upon to sing them a song, and he promptly came out with: 'Monna Aldruda, lift up your tail, for marvellous tidings I bring.' Whereupon all the ladies began to laugh, especially the queen, who ordered him to stop and sing them another.

'My lady,' said Dioneo, 'if I had a drum, I'd sing you "Skirts up, Monna Lapa", or "The grass beneath the privet grows", or, if you preferred, "The waves of the sea are my torment". But I haven't a drum, so take your pick from among these others. Would you like "Out you come to wither away, like to the flower that blossoms in May"?'

'No,' said the queen, 'sing us something else.'

'In that case,' said Dioneo, 'I'll sing you "Monna Simona, put wine in your cask. Not till October, sir, she said".'

'Oh, confound you,' said the queen, with a laugh, 'if you're going to sing, choose something nice. We don't want to hear that one.'

'Come, my lady,' said Dioneo, 'Don't take offence. Which do you like best? I know a thousand of them, at least. Would you like "I never have enough of my little bit of stuff", or "Ah! be gentle, husband dear", or "I bought myself a cock for a hundred pounds"?'

All the ladies laughed except the queen, who was beginning to grow impatient with him.

'No more of your nonsense, Dioneo,' she said. 'Sing us something pleasant, or you'll learn what it means to provoke my anger.'

Dioneo, hearing these words, curtailed his idle chatter and promptly began to sing the following song:

'Cupid, the beauteous light
  That shines forth from my mistress' eyne
  Has made me both her slave and thine.

'Moved by the splendour of those lovely eyes
  Which first thy flame did kindle in my heart,
    Their gaze transfixing mine,
  I understood what lofty virtue lies
  In thee, for her fair countenance hath art
    In my esteem to shine,
  So that no virtue known can with her vie,
  Which gives me all the more a cause to sigh.

'Therefore, my dear Lord, I have lately grown
  One of thy servants, and obedient wait
    Clemency from thy might.
  Yet I know not if my whole state is known –
  That high desire thou didst initiate
    And, too, that faith so bright
  In her, that doth my mind so utterly possess
  That this apart I crave no other happiness.

'And so I pray thee, gentle Lord of mine,
  That thou wilt show her this, and let her feel
    Some inkling of thy power
  To do me some small service, since I pine
  Consumed with love, and in its torments reel,
    And wither hour by hour;
  I beg thee, when thou canst, do this for me,
  And when thou goest, would I might come with thee!'

When, by his silence, Dioneo showed them that his song was finished, the queen, having warmly commended it, called for many others to be sung. But it was now very late, and the queen, perceiving that the cool of the night had banished the warmth of the day, bade them all go and sleep to their hearts' content till the morning.

Here ends the Fifth Day of the Decameron

SIXTH DAY

Here begins the Sixth Day, wherein, under the rule of Elissa, the discussion turns upon those who, on being provoked by some verbal pleasantry, have returned like for like, or who, by a prompt retort or shrewd manoeuvre, have avoided danger, discomfiture or ridicule.

The moon, poised in the centre of the heavens, had lost her radiance, and the whole of our hemisphere was already suffused with the fresh light of dawn, when the queen arose and summoned her companions. Leaving their fair abode, they sauntered over the dew, conversing together on one subject after another, and discussing the merits and demerits of the stories so far narrated, at the same time laughing anew over the various adventures therein related, until, as the sun rose higher and the air grew warmer, they decided with one accord to retrace their steps, whereupon they turned about and came back to the house.

The tables being already laid, with fragrant herbs and lovely flowers strewn all around, they followed the queen's bidding and addressed themselves to their breakfast before the heat of the day should become too oppressive. And after making a merry meal of it, they first of all sang some gay and charming songs, after which some of their number retired to sleep, whilst others played chess or threw dice. And Dioneo, along with Lauretta, began to sing a song about Troilus and Cressida.

When the time came for them to reassemble, the queen saw that they were all summoned in the usual way, and they seated themselves round the fountain. But just as the queen was about to call for the first story, something happened which had never happened before, namely, that she and her companions heard a great commotion, issuing from the kitchen, among the maids and men-servants. So the steward was summoned, and, on being asked who was shouting and what the quarrel was about, he replied that it was some dispute between Licisca and Tindaro. He was unable to explain its cause, as he had no sooner arrived on the scene to restore order than he had been called away by the queen. She therefore ordered him to fetch Licisca and Tindaro to her at once, and when they came before her, she demanded to know what they were quarrelling about.

Tindaro was about to reply, when Licisca, who was no fledgeling and liked to give herself airs, rounded on him with a withering look, spoiling for an argument, and said:

'See here, you ignorant lout, how can you dare to speak first, when I am present? Hold your tongue and let me tell the story.'

She then turned back to the queen, and said:

'Madam, this fellow thinks he knows Sicofante's wife better than I do. I've known her for years, and yet he has the audacity to try and convince me that on the first night Sicofante slept with her, John Thomas had to force an entry into Castle Dusk, shedding blood in the process; but I say it is not true, on the contrary he made his way in with the greatest of ease, to the general pleasure of the garrison. The man is such a natural idiot that he firmly believes young girls are foolish enough to squander their opportunities whilst they are waiting for their fathers and brothers to marry them off, which in nine cases out of ten takes them three or four years longer than it should. God in Heaven, they'd be in a pretty plight if they waited all that long! I swear to Christ (which means that I know what I'm saying) that not a single one of the girls from my district went to her husband a virgin; and as for the married ones, I could tell you a thing or two about the clever tricks they play upon their husbands. Yet this great oaf tries to teach me about women, as though I were born yesterday.'

While Licisca was talking, the ladies were laughing so heartily that you could have pulled all their teeth out. Six times at least the queen had told her to stop, but all to no avail: she was determined to have her say. And when she had come to the end of her piece, the queen turned, laughing, to Dioneo, and said:

'This is a dispute for you to settle, Dioneo. Be so good, therefore, when we come to the end of our storytelling, to pronounce the last word on the subject.'

'Madam,' Dioneo swiftly replied, 'the last word has already been spoken. In my opinion, Licisca is right. I believe it is just as she says; and Tindaro is a fool.'

Hearing this, Licisca burst out laughing, and, turning back to Tindaro, she said:

'There! What did I tell you? Now get along, and stop thinking you know more than I do, when you're hardly out of your cradle. Thanks be to God, I haven't lived for nothing, believe you me!'

But for the fact that the queen sternly commanded her to be silent, told her not to shout or argue any more unless she wanted to be whipped, and sent her back to the kitchen with Tindaro, there would have been nothing else to do for the rest of the day but listen to her prattle. And when they had withdrawn, the queen enjoined Filomena to tell the first story, whereupon Filomena began gaily, as follows:

FIRST STORY

A knight offers to take Madonna Oretta riding through the realm of narrative, but makes such a poor job of it that she begs him to put her down.

Tender ladies, as stars bedeck the heavens on cloudless nights, and in the spring the green meadows are adorned with flowers, and hillsides with saplings newly come into leaf, so likewise are graceful manners and polite discourse enriched by shafts of wit. These, being brief, are much better suited to women than to men, since it is more unseemly for a woman to make long speeches than it is for a man.

But for some reason or other, whether because we are lacking in intelligence or because all the women of our generation were born under an unlucky star, few if any women now remain who can produce a witticism at the right moment, or who, on hearing a witticism uttered, can understand its meaning. Since Pampinea has already spoken at some length on this subject, I do not propose to elaborate further upon it. But in order to show you how exquisite these sayings can be if proffered at the right moment, I should like to tell you about the courteous way in which a lady imposed silence upon a certain knight.

As many of you will know, either through direct personal acquaintance or through hearsay, a little while ago there lived in our city a lady of silver tongue and gentle breeding, whose excellence was such that she deserves to be mentioned by name. She was called Madonna Oretta, and she was the wife of Messer Geri Spina. One day, finding herself in the countryside like ourselves, and proceeding from place to place, by way of recreation, with a party of knights and ladies whom she had entertained to a meal in her house earlier in the day, one of the knights turned to her, and, perhaps because they were having to travel a long way, on foot, to the place they all desired to reach, he said:

'Madonna Oretta, if you like I shall take you riding along a goodly stretch of our journey by telling you one of the finest tales in the world.'

'Sir,' replied the lady, 'I beseech you most earnestly to do so, and I shall look upon it as a great favour.'

Whereupon this worthy knight, whose swordplay was doubtless on a par with his storytelling, began to recite his tale, which in itself was indeed excellent. But by constantly repeating the same phrases, and recapitulating sections of the plot, and every so often declaring that he had 'made a mess of that bit', and regularly confusing the names of the characters, he ruined it completely. Moreover, his mode of delivery was totally out of keeping with the characters and the incidents he was describing, so that it was painful for Madonna Oretta to listen to him. She began to perspire freely, and her heart missed several beats, as though she had fallen ill and was about to give up the ghost. And in the end, when she could endure it no longer, having perceived that the knight had tied himself inextricably in knots, she said to him, in affable tones:

'Sir, you have taken me riding on a horse that trots very jerkily. Pray be good enough to set me down.'

The knight, who was apparently far more capable of taking a hint than of telling a tale, saw the joke and took it in the cheerfullest of spirits. Leaving aside the story he had begun and so ineptly handled, he turned his attention to telling her tales of quite another sort.

SECOND STORY

By means of a single phrase, Cisti the Baker shows Messer Geri Spina that he is being unreasonable.

Madonna Oretta's timely remark was warmly commended by all the men and ladies present, and then the queen ordered Pampinea to continue in the same vein. Pampinea therefore began, as follows:

Fair ladies, I cannot myself decide whether Nature is more at fault in furnishing a noble spirit with an inferior body, or Fortune in allotting an inferior calling to a body endowed with a noble spirit, as happened in the case of Cisti, our fellow-citizen, and many other people of our own acquaintance. This Cisti was a man of exceedingly lofty spirit, and yet Fortune made him a baker.

I would assuredly curse Nature and Fortune alike, if I did not know for a fact that Nature is very discerning, and that Fortune has a thousand eyes, even though fools represent her as blind. Indeed, it is my conviction that Nature and Fortune, being very shrewd, follow the practice so common among mortals, who, uncertain of what the future will bring, make provision for emergencies by burying their most precious possessions in the least imposing (and therefore least suspect) part of their houses, whence they bring them forth in the hour of their greatest need, their treasure having been more securely preserved in a humble hiding place than if it had been kept in a sumptuous chamber. In the same way, the two fair arbiters of the world's affairs frequently hide their greatest treasure beneath the shadow of the humblest of trades, so that when the need arises for it to be brought forth, its splendour will be all the more apparent. This is amply borne out by a brief anecdote I should now like to relate, concerning an episode, in itself of no great importance, in which Cisti the Baker opened the eyes of Messer Geri Spina to the truth, and of which I was reminded by the tale we have just heard about Madonna Oretta, who was Messer Geri's wife.

I say, then, that when Pope Boniface, who held Messer Geri in the highest esteem, sent a delegation of his courtiers to Florence on urgent papal affairs, they took lodging under Messer Geri's roof; and almost every morning, for one reason or another, it so happened that Messer Geri and the Pope's emissaries were obliged by the nature of their business to walk past the Church of Santa Maria Ughi, beside which Cisti had his bakery, where he practised his calling in person.

Though Fortune had allotted to Cisti a very humble calling, she had treated him so bountifully that he had become exceedingly rich; but it would never have occurred to him to exchange this occupation for any other, for he lived like a lord, and in addition to numerous other splendid possessions, he kept the finest cellar of wines, both red and white, to be found anywhere in Florence or the surrounding region. On noticing that Messer Geri passed by his door every morning with the Pope's emissaries, it occurred to Cisti that since the season was very hot he might as well do them the kindness of offering them some of his delicious white wine. But, being sensible of the difference in rank between himself and Messer Geri, he considered it would be presumptuous of him to issue an invitation and resolved to arrange matters in such a way that Messer Geri would come of his own accord.

And so every morning, wearing a gleaming white doublet and a freshly laundered apron, which made him look more like a miller than a baker, Cisti appeared in his doorway at the hour in which Messer Geri and the emissaries were due to pass by, and called for a shiny metal pail of fresh water and a brand new little Bolognese flagon containing a quantity of his best white wine, together with a pair of wineglasses, that gleamed as brightly as if they were made of silver. He then seated himself in the doorway, and just as they were passing, he cleared his throat a couple of times and began to drink this wine of his with so much relish that he would have brought a thirst to the lips of a corpse.

Messer Geri, having witnessed this charade on two successive mornings, turned to him on the third, and said:

'How does it taste, Cisti? Is it good?'

'Indeed it is, sir,' Cisti replied, springing to his feet, 'But how am I to prove how exquisite it tastes, unless you sample it for yourself?'

Now, whether because of the heat, or as a result of expending more energy than usual, or through observing Cisti drinking with so much gusto, Messer Geri had conceived such a keen thirst that he turned, smiling, to the emissaries, and said:

'My lords, we would do well to test the quality of this gentleman's wine; perhaps it will be such as to give us no cause for regret.'

He thereupon led them over to Cisti, who promptly arranged for a handsome bench to be brought out from his bakery and invited them to sit down. Their servants then stepped forward to wash the wineglasses, but Cisti said:

'Stand aside, my friends, and leave this office to me, for I am no less skilled at serving wine than at baking bread. And if you are expecting to taste so much as a single drop, you are going to be disappointed.'

And so saying, he washed four handsome new glasses with his own hands, called for a small flagon of his best wine, and, taking meticulous care, filled the glasses for Messer Geri and his companions, none of whom had tasted such an exquisite wine for years. Messer Geri affirmed that the wine was excellent, and for the remainder of the emissaries' stay in Florence, he called there nearly every morning with them to sample it afresh.

When their mission was completed and the emissaries were about to depart, Messer Geri held a magnificent banquet, to which he invited a number of the most distinguished citizens of Florence. He also sent an invitation to Cisti, who could by no means be persuaded to accept. So he ordered one of his servants to take a flask, ask Cisti to fill it with wine, and serve half a glass of it to each of the guests during the first course.

The servant, who was possibly feeling somewhat annoyed that he had never been allowed to sample the wine, took along a huge flask, and when Cisti saw it, he said:

'Messer Geri has not sent you to me, my lad.'

The servant kept assuring him that he had, but could obtain no other answer. So he returned to Messer Geri and told him what Cisti had said.

'Go back to him,' said Messer Geri, 'and tell him that I *am* sending you to him; and if he gives you the same answer, ask him to whom I am sending you.'

The servant returned to Cisti, and said:

'I can assure you, Cisti, that it is to you that Messer Geri sends me.'

'And I can assure you, my lad,' Cisti replied, 'that you are wrong.'

'To whom is he sending me then?' asked the servant.

'To the Arno,' replied Cisti.

When the servant reported this conversation to Messer Geri, his eyes were immediately opened to the truth, and he asked the servant to show him the flask. On being shown the flask, he said:

'Cisti is perfectly right.' And having given the servant a severe scolding, he ordered him to return with a flask of more modest proportions.

On seeing this second flask, Cisti said:

'Now I know that he has sent you to me.' And he filled it up for him contentedly.

Later that same day, Cisti filled a small cask with wine of the same vintage and had it tenderly conveyed to Messer Geri's house, after which he called on Messer Geri in person, and said:

'Sir, I would not want you to suppose that I was taken aback on seeing the large flask this morning. But since you appeared to have forgotten what I have shown you with the aid of my small flagons during these past few days, namely, that this is not a wine for servants, I thought I would refresh your memory. However, since I have no intention of storing it for you any longer, I have now sent you every single drop of it, and henceforth you may dispose of it as you please.'

Messer Geri set great store by Cisti's gift, and thanked him as profusely as the occasion seemed to warrant. And from that day forth he held him in high esteem and regarded him as a friend of his for life.

THIRD STORY

With a quick retort, Monna Nonna de' Pulci puts a stop to the unseemly banter of the Bishop of Florence.

When Pampinea came to the end of her story, Cisti's reply was warmly applauded by all those present, and so too was his generosity, after which the queen was pleased to call upon Lauretta, who gaily began to speak, as follows:

Lovesome ladies, there is much truth in what both Pampinea and

Filomena have been saying about the beauty of repartee and our own lack of skill in its use. It is unnecessary to repeat their arguments, but I should like to remind you that apart from what has already been said on this subject, the nature of wit is such that its bite must be like that of a sheep rather than a dog, for if it were to bite the listener like a dog, it would no longer be wit but abuse. The remark made by Madonna Oretta, and Cisti's retort, were excellent examples of the genre.

It is of course true, in the case of repartee, that when someone bites like a dog after having, so to speak, been bitten by a dog in the first place, his reaction does not seem as reprehensible as it would have been had he not been provoked; and one therefore has to be careful over how, when, on whom, and likewise where one exercises one's wit. To these matters, one of our prelates paid so little attention on one occasion, that he received no less painful a bite than he administered; and I should now like to tell you, in a few words, how this came about.

While Messer Antonio d'Orso, a wise and worthy prelate, was Bishop of Florence, there came to the city a Catalan nobleman called Messer Dego della Ratta, who was Marshal to King Robert of Naples. Being a fine figure of a man, and inordinately fond of women, Messer Dego pursued a number of the Florentine ladies, for one of whom, a ravishing beauty, he conceived a particular liking, and she happened to be the niece of the Bishop's brother.

Having learnt that the lady's husband, though he came of a good family, was very greedy and corrupt, he came to an arrangement with him whereby he would give him five hundred gold florins for allowing him to sleep for one night with his wife. But what he actually did was to gild five hundred coins of silver, called *popolini*, which were in everyday use at that period, and, having slept with the man's wife against her will, he handed these over to the husband. Subsequently the story became common knowledge, so that the scoundrelly husband was not only cheated but held up to ridicule. And the Bishop, being a wise man, feigned complete ignorance of the whole affair.

The Bishop and the Marshal were frequently to be seen in one another's company, and one day, it being the feast of St John, they happened to be riding side by side down the street along which the *palio** is run, casting an eye over the ladies, when the Bishop spotted a young woman (now, alas, no longer with us, having died in middle age during this present epidemic), whose name was Monna Nonna de' Pulci. You all know the person I mean – she was the cousin of Messer Alesso Rinucci, and at the time of which I am speaking she was a fine-looking girl in the flower of youth, well-spoken and full of spirit, who had recently been married and set up house in the Porta San Piero quarter. The Bishop pointed her out to the Marshal, then he rode up beside her, clapped his hand on the Marshal's shoulder, and said:

'How do you like this fellow, Nonna? Do you think you could make a conquest of him?'

It seemed to Monna Nonna that the Bishop's words made her out to be less than virtuous, or that they were bound to damage her reputation in the eyes of those people, by no means few in number, in whose hearing they were spoken. So that, less intent upon vindicating her honour than upon returning blow for blow, she swiftly retorted:

'In the unlikely event, my lord, of his making a conquest of me, I should want to be paid in good coin.'

These words stung both the Marshal and the Bishop to the quick, the former as the author of the dishonest deed involving the niece of the Bishop's brother, and the latter as its victim, inasmuch as she was one of his own relatives. And without so much as looking at one another, they rode away silent and shamefaced, and said no more to Monna Nonna on that day.

In this case, therefore, since the girl was bitten first, it was not inappropriate that she should make an equally biting retort.

*An annual horse-race, still held at Siena.

FOURTH STORY

Currado Gianfigliazzi's cook, Chichibio, converts his master's anger into laughter with a quick word in the nick of time, and saves himself from the unpleasant fate with which Currado had threatened him.

When Lauretta was silent, and they had all paid glowing tribute to Monna Nonna, the queen called upon Neifile to tell the next story, whereupon Neifile began:

Amorous ladies, whilst a ready wit will often bring a swift phrase, apposite and neatly turned, to the lips of the speaker, it sometimes happens that Fortune herself will come to the aid of people in distress by suddenly putting words into their mouths that they would never have been capable of formulating when their minds were at ease; which is what I propose to show you with this story of mine.

As all of you will have heard and seen for yourselves, Currado Gianfigliazzi has always played a notable part in the affairs of our city. Generous and hospitable, he lived the life of a true gentleman, and, to say nothing for the moment of his more important activities, he took a constant delight in hunting and hawking. One day, having killed a crane with one of his falcons in the vicinity of Peretola, finding that it was young and plump, he sent it to an excellent Venetian cook of his, whose name was Chichibio, telling him to roast it for supper and to see that it was well prepared and seasoned.

Chichibio, who was no less scatterbrained than he looked, plucked the crane, stuffed it, set it over the fire, and began to cook it with great care. But when it was nearly done, and giving off a most appetizing smell, there came into the kitchen a fair young country wench, called Brunetta, who was the apple of Chichibio's eye. And on sniffing the smell of cooking and seeing the crane roasting on the spit, she coaxed and pleaded with him to give her one of the legs. By way of reply, Chichibio burst into song:

'I won't let you have it, Donna Brunetta, I won't let you have it, so there!'

This put Donna Brunetta's back up, and she said:

'I swear to God that if you don't let me have it, you'll never have another thing out of me!' In short, they had quite a lengthy set-to, and in the end, not wishing to anger his girl, Chichibio cut off one of the crane's legs and gave it to her.

A little later, the crane was set before Currado and his guests, and much to his surprise, Currado found that one of the legs was missing. So he sent for Chichibio and asked him what had happened to it. Being a Venetian, and hence a good liar, Chichibio promptly replied:

'My lord, cranes have only the one leg.'

Whereupon Currado flew into a rage, and said:

'What the devil do you mean, cranes have only the one leg? Do you think I've never seen a crane before?'

'What I mean, sir,' continued Chichibio, 'is that they have only the one leg. We'll go and see some live ones, if you like, and I'll show you.'

Not wishing to embarrass his visitors, Currado decided not to pursue the matter, but said:

'I've never seen a one-legged crane before, nor have I ever heard of one. But since you have offered to show me, you can do so tomorrow morning, and then I shall be satisfied. But I swear to you by the body of Christ that if you fail to prove it, I shall see that you are given such a hiding that you will never forget my name for as long as you live.'

There the matter rested for that evening, but next morning, as soon as it was light, Currado, whom a night's sleep had done nothing to pacify, leapt out of bed, still seething with anger, and ordered his horses to be saddled. And, having obliged Chichibio to mount an old jade, he led the way to a river bank where cranes were usually to be seen in the early morning, saying:

'We shall soon see which of us was lying last night.'

On perceiving that Currado was still as angry as ever, and that he would now have to prove what he had said, Chichibio, who had no idea how he was going to do it, rode along behind Currado in a state of positive terror. If he could have run away he would gladly have done so, but since this was out of the question, he kept gazing ahead of him, behind him, and to each side, and wherever he looked he imagined he could see cranes standing on two feet.

However, just as they were approaching the river, Chichibio

caught sight of well over a dozen cranes, all standing on one leg on the river bank, which is their normal posture when they are asleep. So he quickly pointed them out to Currado, saying:

'Now you can see quite plainly, sir, that I was telling you the truth last night when I said that cranes have only the one leg. Take a look at the ones over there.'

'Wait a bit,' said Currado, 'and I'll show you they have two.' And moving a little closer to them, he yelled: 'Oho!' whereupon the cranes lowered their other leg, and after taking a few strides, they all began to fly away. Currado then turned to Chichibio, saying:

'What do you say to that, you knave? Do they have two legs, or do they not?'

Chichibio was almost at his wits' end, but in some mysterious way he suddenly thought of an answer.

'They do indeed, sir,' he said, 'but you never shouted "Oho!" to the one you had last night, otherwise it would have shoved its second leg out, as these others have done.'

Currado was so delighted with this answer that all his anger was converted into jollity and laughter.

'You're right, Chichibio,' he said. 'Of course, I should have shouted.'

This then, was how Chichibio, with his prompt and amusing reply, avoided an unpleasant fate and made his peace with his master.

FIFTH STORY

Messer Forese da Rabatta and Master Giotto, the painter, returning from Mugello, poke fun at one another's disreputable appearance.

The ladies were highly amused by Chichibio's reply, and in deference to the queen's wishes, as soon as Neifile had stopped, Panfilo began:

Dearest ladies, whilst it is true that Fortune occasionally conceals abundant treasures of native wit in those who practise a humble trade, as was demonstrated just now by Pampinea, it is equally true that Nature has frequently planted astonishing genius in men of monstrously ugly appearance.

This was plainly to be observed in two citizens of ours, about whom I now propose to say a few words. The first, who was called Messer Forese da Rabatta, being deformed and dwarf-like in appearance, with a plain snub-nosed face that would have seemed loathsome alongside the ugliest Baronci* who ever lived, was a jurist of such great distinction that many scholars regarded him as a walking encyclopedia of civil law. The second, whose name was Giotto, was a man of such outstanding genius that there was nothing in the whole of creation that he could not depict with his stylus, pen, or brush. And so faithful did he remain to Nature (who is the mother and the motive force of all created things, via the constant rotation of the heavens), that whatever he depicted had the appearance, not of a reproduction, but of the thing itself, so that one very often finds, with the works of Giotto, that people's eyes are deceived and they mistake the picture for the real thing.

Hence, by virtue of the fact that he brought back to light an art which had been buried for centuries beneath the blunders of those who, in their paintings, aimed to bring visual delight to the ignorant rather than intellectual satisfaction to the wise, his work may justly be regarded as a shining monument to the glory of Florence. And all the more so, inasmuch as he set an example to others by wearing his celebrity with the utmost modesty, and always refused to be called a master, even though such a title befitted him all the more resplendently in proportion to the eagerness with which it was sought and usurped by those who knew less than himself or by his own pupils. But for all the greatness of his art, neither physically nor facially was he any more handsome than Messer Forese.

Turning now to our story, I should first point out that both Messer Forese and Giotto owned properties in the region of Mugello. And one summer, when the law courts were closed for the vacation, Messer Forese had gone to visit this property of his, and was returning to Florence astride an emaciated old hack, when whom should he meet up with along the road but the aforementioned Giotto, who was likewise returning from a visit to his property. Giotto was no better accoutred than himself, his mount was just as decrepit, and,

*The allusion will be clarified in the story that follows.

since they were both getting on in years and travelling at a snail's pace, they rode along together.

However, they happened to be caught in a sudden downpour such as we often experience in summer, and they took shelter as soon as they could in the house of a peasant, who was known to both men and was in fact a friend of theirs. But after a while, since the rain showed no sign of stopping and they wanted to reach Florence by nightfall, they borrowed a pair of shabby old woollen capes from the peasant, along with a couple of hats that were falling to bits from old age, these being the best he could provide, and resumed their journey.

After they had travelled some distance, by which time they were soaked to the skin and bespattered all over by the steady spray of mud that hacks kick up with their hooves (none of which is calculated to improve anyone's appearance), the weather cleared up a little, and the two men, having ridden for a long time in silence, began to converse with one another.

As Messer Forese was riding along listening to Giotto, who was a very fine talker, he turned to inspect him, shifting his gaze from Giotto's flank to his head and then to the rest of his person, and on perceiving how thoroughly unkempt and disreputable he looked, giving no thought to his own appearance he burst out laughing, and said:

'Giotto, supposing we were to meet some stranger who had never seen you before, do you think he would believe that you were the greatest painter in the world?'

To which Giotto swiftly replied:

'Sir, I think he would believe it if, after taking a look at you, he gave you credit for knowing your ABC.'

On hearing this, Messer Forese recognized his error, and perceived that he was hoist with his own petard.

SIXTH STORY

Michele Scalza proves to certain young men that the Baronci are the most noble family in the whole wide world, and wins a supper.

The ladies were still laughing over Giotto's swift and splendid retort when the queen called for the next story from Fiammetta, who began as follows:

Young ladies, Panfilo's mention of the Baronci, with whom, possibly, you are less well acquainted than he is, has reminded me of a story demonstrating their great nobility, and since it falls within the scope of our agreed topic, I should like to relate it to you.

In our city, not so very long ago, there was a young man called Michele Scalza, who was the most entertaining and agreeable fellow you could ever wish to meet, and he was always coming out with some new-fangled notion or other, so that the young men of Florence loved to have him with them when they were out on the spree together.

Now, one day, he was with some friends of his at Montughi, and they happened to start an argument over which was the most ancient and noble family in Florence. Some maintained it was the Uberti, some the Lamberti, and various other names were tossed into the discussion, more or less at random.

Scalza listened to them for a while, then he started grinning, and said:

'Get along with you, you ignorant fools, you don't know what you're talking about. The most ancient and noble family, not only in Florence but in the whole wide world, is the Baronci. All the philosophers are agreed on this point, and anyone who knows the Baronci as well as I do will say the same thing. But in case you think I'm talking about some other family of that name, I mean the Baronci who live in our own parish of Santa Maria Maggiore.'

His companions, who had been expecting him to say something quite different, poured scorn on this idea, and said:

'You must be joking. We know the Baronci just as well as you do.'

'I'm not joking,' said Scalza. 'On the contrary I'm telling you the gospel truth. And if there's anyone present who would care to wager a supper to be given to the winner and six of his chosen companions, I'll gladly take him up on it. And just to make it easier for you, I'll abide by the decision of any judge you choose to nominate.'

Whereupon one of the young men, who was called Neri Mannini, said:

'I am ready to win this supper.' And having mutually agreed to appoint Piero di Fiorentino, in whose house they were spending the day, as the judge, they went off to find him, being followed by all the others, who were eager to see Scalza lose the wager so that they could pull his leg about it.

They told Piero what the argument was all about, and Piero, who was a sensible young man, listened first to what Neri had to say, after which he turned to Scalza, saying:

'And how do you propose to prove this claim you are making?'

'Prove it?' said Scalza. 'Why, I shall prove it by so conclusive an argument that not only you yourself, but this fellow who denies it, will have to admit that I am right. As you are aware, the older the family, the more noble it is, and everyone agreed just now that this was so. Since the Baronci are older than anyone else, they are *ipso facto* more noble; and if I can prove to you that they really are older than anybody else, I shall have won my case beyond any shadow of a doubt.

'The fact of the matter is that when the Lord God created the Baronci, He was still learning the rudiments of His craft, whereas He created the rest of mankind after He had mastered it. If you don't believe me, picture the Baronci to yourselves and compare them to other people; and you will see that whereas everybody else has a well-designed and correctly proportioned face, the Baronci sometimes have a face that is long and narrow, sometimes wide beyond all measure, some of them have very long noses, others have short ones, and there are one or two with chins that stick out and turn up at the end, and with enormous great jaws like those of an ass; moreover, some have one eye bigger than the other, whilst others have one eye lower than the other, so that taken by and large, their faces are just like the ones that are made by children when they are first learning to draw. Hence, as I've already said, i t is quite obvious that the Lord God created them when He was still learning His craft. They are therefore older than anybody else, and so they are more noble.'

When Piero, the judge, and Neri, who had wagered the supper, and all the others, recalling what the Baronci looked like, had heard Scalza's ingenious argument, they all began to laugh and to declare that Scalza was right, that he had won the supper, and that without a doubt the Baronci were the most ancient and noble family, not only in Florence, but in the whole wide world.

And that is why Panfilo, in wanting to prove the ugliness of Messer Forese, aptly maintained that he would have looked loathsome alongside a Baronci.

SEVENTH STORY

Madonna Filippa is discovered by her husband with a lover and called before the magistrate, but by a prompt and ingenious answer she secures her acquittal and causes the statute to be amended.

Fiammetta had finished speaking, and everyone was still laughing over the novel argument used by Scalza to ennoble the Baronci above all other families, when the queen called upon Filostrato to tell them a story; and so he began:

Worthy ladies, a capacity for saying the right things in the right place is all very well, but to be able to say them in a moment of dire necessity is, in my opinion, a truly rare accomplishment. With this ability, a certain noblewoman of whom I propose to speak was so liberally endowed, that not only did she provide laughter and merriment to her listeners, but, as you shall presently hear, she disentangled herself from the meshes of an ignominious death.

In the city of Prato, there used to be a statute, no less reprehensible, to be sure, than it was severe, which without exception required that every woman taken in adultery by her husband should be burned alive, whether she was with a lover or simply doing it for money.

While this statute was in force, a case arose in which a certain noble lady, beautiful and exceedingly passionate by nature, whose name was Madonna Filippa, was discovered one night in her own bedchamber by her husband, Rinaldo de' Pugliesi, in the arms of Lazzarino de' Guazzagliotri, a handsome young noble of that city, with whom she was very deeply in love, and who loved her in return. Rinaldo, seeing them together, was greatly dismayed, and could scarcely prevent himself from rushing upon them and killing them; and but for the fact that he feared the consequences to himself, he would have followed the promptings of his anger, and done them to death.

Having been restrained by his caution from taking precipitate action, he could not however be restrained from desiring the death of his wife, and since it would have been unlawful for him to kill her with his own hands, he was determined to invoke the city statute. And so, having more than sufficient evidence to prove her guilt, he denounced her on the very next morning without inquiring any further into the matter, and took out a summons.

Now, a woman who is genuinely in love is apt to be quite fearless, and Rinaldo's wife was no exception. And although many of her friends and relatives advised her against such a course, she firmly resolved to answer the summons, confess the truth, and die a courageous death, rather than run away like a coward, thus being forced to live in exile for defying the court, and proving herself unworthy of a lover such as the man in whose arms she had lain the night before. So that, attended by a numerous throng of men and women, all encouraging her to protest her innocence, she went before the *podestà*, looked him squarely between the eyes, and asked him in a firm voice what it was that he required of her.

On gazing at this woman and observing that she was very beautifu l and impeccably well-bred, to say nothing of the fortitude of spirit to which her words bore witness, the *podestà* was touched with compassion for her, being afraid lest she should confess and thus compe l him, if he wished to preserve his authority, to have her put to death. Nevertheless, being unable to avoid questioning her about what she was alleged to have done, he said:

'Madam, as you see, Rinaldo your husband is here, and he has lodged a complaint against you, claiming that he has taken you in adultery; he is therefore demanding that I should punish you, as prescribed by one of our statutes, by having you put to death. But this I cannot do unless you confess, and therefore I must warn you to be very careful how you answer. Now tell me, is your husband's accusation true?'

Without flinching in the slightest, the lady replied in a most fetching sort of voice:

'Sir, it is true that Rinaldo is my husband, and that he found me last night in Lazzarino's arms, wherein, on account of the deep and perfect love I bear towards him, I have lain many times before; nor shall I ever deny it. However, as I am sure you will know, every man and woman should be equal before the law, and laws must have the consent of those who are affected by them. These conditions are not fulfilled in the present instance, because this law only applies to us poor women, who are much better able than men to bestow our favours liberally. Moreover, when this law was made, no woman gave her consent to it, nor was any woman even so much as consulted. It can therefore justly be described as a very bad law.

'If, however, to the detriment of my body and your soul, you wish to give effect to this law, that is your own affair. But before you proceed to pass any judgement, I beseech you to grant me a small favour, this being that you should ask my husband whether or not I have refused to concede my entire body to him, whenever and as often as he pleased.'

Without waiting for the *podestà* to put the question, Rinaldo promptly replied that beyond any doubt she had granted him whatever he required in the way of bodily gratification.

'Well then,' the lady promptly continued, 'if he has always taken as much of me as he needed and as much as he chose to take, I ask you, Messer Podestà, what am I to do with the surplus? Throw it to the dogs? Is it not far better that I should present it to a gentleman who loves me more dearly than himself, rather than allow it to turn bad or go to waste?'

The nature of the charge against the lady, coupled with the fact that she was such a well-known figure in society, had brought almost all the citizens of Prato flocking to the court, and when they heard the charming speech she made in her defence, they rocked with mirth and, as with a single voice, they all exclaimed that the lady was right and that it was well spoken. And at the *podestà*'s suggestion, before they left the court, they amended the harsh statute so that in future it would apply only to those wives who took payment for being unfaithful to their husbands.

After making such a fool of himself, Rinaldo departed from the scene feeling quite mortified; and his wife, now a free and contented woman, having, so to speak, been resurrected from the flames, returned to her house in triumph.

EIGHTH STORY

Fresco urges his niece not to look at herself in the glass, if, as she has claimed, she cannot bear the sight of horrid people.

As they listened to Filostrato's tale, the ladies at first felt a trifle embarrassed, and showed it by the blush of modesty that appeared on their cheeks; but then they began to exchange glances with one another, and, scarcely able to contain their laughter, they heard the rest of it with their faces wreathed in smiles. When it came to an end, the queen turned to Emilia and called upon her to speak next; and Emilia, heaving a sigh as though she had just been awakened from a pleasant dream, began as follows:

Fair young ladies, having been absorbed for quite a while in distant reverie, I shall now bestir myself to obey the queen's command, and recount a tale, much shorter perhaps than the one I would have told you if I had had all my wits about me, concerning the foolish error of a young woman, and how it was corrected by an amusing remark of her uncle's, though she was far too dense to appreciate its significance.

There was once a certain gentleman called Fresco da Celatico, and he had a niece whose pet-name was Cesca. Whilst she had a good figure and a pretty face (though it was far from being one of those angelic faces that we not infrequently come across), she had such a high opinion of herself and gave herself so many airs that she fell into the habit of criticizing everything and everyone she ever set eyes upon, never thinking for a moment of her own defects, even though she was the most disagreeable, petulant, and insipid young woman imaginable, and nothing could be done to please her. Moreover, her pride was so enormous that even in a scion of the French royal family it would have been excessive. And whenever she walked along the street, she was continually wrinkling up her nose in disgust, as though a nasty smell was assailing her nostrils every time she saw or met anyone.

Now, leaving aside her many other tiresome and disagreeable mannerisms, and coming to the point, she happened one day to return from a walk, and, finding Fresco at home, she flounced into a chair at his side, simpering like a spoilt child, and fretting and fuming. Fresco cast her a quizzical look, and said:

'Cesca, why do you come home so early, when today is a feast day?'

'The truth is,' Cesca replied, affecting a thoroughly world-weary air, 'that I have come home early because I doubt whether I have ever seen such a tiresome and disagreeable set of people as the ones who are walking our streets today. Every man and woman that I meet is utterly repellent to me, and I don't believe there is a woman anywhere in the world who is so upset by the sight of horrid people as I am. So I came home early to spare myself the torment of looking at them.'

Whereupon Fresco, who found the fastidious airs of his niece highly distasteful, said to her:

'If you can't bear the sight of horrid people, my girl, I advise you, for your own peace of mind, never to look at yourself in the glass.'

But the girl, whose head was emptier than a hollow reed even though she imagined herself to be as wise as Solomon, might have been a carcase of mutton for all she understood of Fresco's real meaning, and she told him that she intended to look in the glass just like any other woman. So she remained as witless as before, and she is still the same to this day.

NINTH STORY

With a barbed saying, Guido Cavalcanti politely delivers an insult to certain Florentine gentlemen who had taken him by surprise.

The queen, perceiving that Emilia had dashed off her story and that she herself was the sole remaining speaker apart from the person who was privileged to speak last of all, began to address the company as follows:

Sweet ladies, although you have deprived me of at least two of the stories that I had thought of telling you today, I still have another in reserve, towards the end of which there occurs a *bon mot* that is more subtle, perhaps, than any of the ones we have heard so far.

I must first of all remind you that in days gone by, our city was noted for certain excellent and commendable customs, all of which have now disappeared, thanks to the avarice which, increasing as it does with the growing prosperity of the city, has driven them all away. One of these customs was that in various parts of Florence a limited number of the gentlemen in each quarter of the city would meet regularly together in one another's houses for their common amusement. Only those people who could afford to entertain on a suitably lavish scale were admitted to these coteries, and they took it in turn to play the host to their companions, each of them being allotted his own special day for the purpose. Distinguished visitors to Florence were frequently invited to these gatherings, and so too were a number of the citizens. At least once every year they all wore the same kind of dress, whilst on all the more important anniversaries they rode together through the city, and sometimes they tilted together, especially on the principal feasts or when the news of some happy event had reached the city, such as a victory in the field.

Among these various companies, there was one that was led by Messer Betto Brunelleschi, into whose ranks Messer Betto and his associates had striven might and main to attract Messer Cavalcante de' Cavalcanti's son, Guido. And not without reason, for apart from the fact that he was one of the finest logicians in the world and an expert natural philosopher (to none of which Betto and his friends attributed very much importance), Guido was an exceedingly charming and sophisticated man, with a marked gift for conversation, and he outshone all his contemporaries in every activity pertaining to a gentleman that he chose to undertake. But above and beyond all this he was extremely rich, and could entertain most sumptuously those people whom he happened to consider worthy of his hospitality.

However, Messer Betto had never succeeded in winning him over, and he and his companions thought this was because of his passion for speculative reasoning, which occasionally made him appear somewhat remote from his fellow beings. And since he tended to subscribe to the opinions of the Epicureans, it was said among the common herd that these speculations of his were exclusively concerned with whether it could be shown that God did not exist.

Now, one day, Guido had walked from Orsammichele along the Corso degli Adimari as far as San Giovanni, which was a favourite walk of his because it took him past those great marble tombs, now to be found in Santa Reparata, and the numerous other graves that lie all around San Giovanni. As he was threading his way among the tombs, between the porphyry columns that stand in that spot and the door of San Giovanni, which was locked, Messer Betto and his friends came riding through the piazza of Santa Reparata, and on seeing Guido among all these tombs, they said:

'Let's go and torment him.'

And so, spurring their horses and making a mock charge, they were upon him almost before he had time to notice, and they began to taunt him, saying:

'Guido, you spurn our company; but supposing you find that God doesn't exist, what good will it do you?'

Finding himself surrounded, Guido promptly replied:

'Gentlemen, in your own house you may say whatever you like to me.'

Then, placing a hand on one of the tombstones, which were very tall, he vaulted over the top of it, being very light and nimble, and landed on the other side, whence, having escaped from their clutches, he proceeded on his way.

Betto and his companions were left staring at one another, then they began to declare that he was out of his mind, and that his remark was meaningless, because neither they themselves nor any of the other citizens, Guido included, owned the ground on which they were standing. But Messer Betto turned to them, and said:

'You're the ones who are out of your minds, if you can't see what he meant. In a few words he has neatly paid us the most back-handed compliment I ever heard, because when you come to consider it, these tombs are the houses of the dead, this being the place where the dead are laid to rest and where they take up their abode. By describing it as our house, he wanted to show us that, by comparison with himself and other men of learning, all men who are as uncouth and unlettered as ourselves are worse off than the dead. So that, being in a graveyard, we are in our own house.'

Now that Guido's meaning had been pointed out to them, they all felt suitably abashed, and they never taunted him again. And from that day forth, they looked upon Messer Betto as a paragon of shrewdness and intelligence.

TENTH STORY

Friar Cipolla promises a crowd of country folk that he will show them a feather of the Angel Gabriel, and on finding that some bits of coal have been put in its place, he proclaims that these were left over from the roasting of Saint Lawrence.

His nine companions having each told a story, Dioneo knew without waiting for any formal command that it was now his own turn to speak. He therefore silenced those of his companions who were praising Guido's clever retort, and began:

Charming ladies, although I have the privilege of speaking on any subject I may choose, I do not propose to depart from the topic on which all of you have spoken so appositely today. On the contrary, following in your footsteps, I intend to show you how one of the friars of Saint Anthony, by a quick piece of thinking, neatly side-stepped a trap which had been laid for him by two young men. And if I speak at some length, so as to tell the whole story as it should be told, this ought not to disturb you unduly, for you will find, if you look up at the sun, that it is still in mid heaven.

Certaldo, as you may possibly have heard, is a fortified town situated in the Val d'Elsa, in Florentine territory, and although it is small, the people living there were at one time prosperous and well-to-do. Since it was a place where rich pickings were to be had, one of the friars of Saint Anthony used to visit the town once every year to collect the alms which people were foolish enough to donate to his Order. He was called Friar Cipolla,* and he always received a warm welcome there, though this was doubtless due as much to his name as to the piety of the inhabitants, for the soil in those parts produces onions that are famous throughout the whole of Tuscany.

This Friar Cipolla was a little man, with red hair and a merry face, and he was the most sociable fellow in the world. He was quite illiterate, but he was such a lively and excellent speaker, that anyone hearing him for the first time would have concluded, not only that he was some great master of rhetoric, but that he was Cicero in person, or perhaps Quintilian. And there was scarcely a single man or woman in the whole of the district who did not regard him as a friend, familiar or well-wisher.

During one of his regular annual visits to Certaldo, on a Sunday morning in the month of August, when all the good folk from the neighbouring hamlets were gathered in the parish church for mass, Friar Cipolla, choosing a suitable moment, came forward and said:

'Ladies and gentlemen, as you know, every year it is your custom to send to the poor of the Lord Saint Anthony a portion of your wheat and oats, varying in amount from person to person according to his ability and devotion, so that the blessed Saint Anthony will protect your oxen, asses, pigs and sheep from harm. Moreover it is customary, in particular for those of you who are enrolled as members of our confraternity, to pay those modest sums which fall due every year at this time, and it is precisely to collect these contributions of yours that my superior, Master Abbot, has sent me among you. And so, with God's blessing, when you hear the bells ring after nones, you will assemble outside the church, where as usual I shall preach the

* i.e. 'onion'.

sermon and you will kiss the cross. But in addition to this, since I know how deeply devoted you all are to the Lord Saint Anthony, I shall show you, by way of special favour, a most sacred and beautiful relic, which I myself brought back from a visit I once paid to the Holy Land across the sea; and this is one of the feathers of the Angel Gabriel, which was left behind in the bedchamber of the Virgin Mary when he came to annunciate her in Nazareth.'

And at this point he ended his homily and returned to the mass.

Now, among the large congregation present in the church when Friar Cipolla made this announcement, were a pair of very wily young fellows, one of whom was called Giovanni del Bragoniera and the other Biagio Pizzini. Having had a good laugh together over Friar Cipolla's relic, they decided, though they were his good friends and boon companions, to have a little fun with this feather at the Friar's expense. They knew that Friar Cipolla was to breakfast with a friend that morning in the citadel, and so they waited until he was safely seated at table, then made their way down into the street, whence they proceeded to the inn where the Friar was staying, their intention being that Biagio should engage Friar Cipolla's servant in conversation whilst Giovanni rummaged through the Friar's belongings and removed this feather, or whatever it was, so that later in the day they could see how he explained its disappearance to the populace.

Friar Cipolla had a servant, variously known as Guccio Balena, or Guccio Imbratta, or Guccio Porco, who was such a coarse fellow that he could have given lessons in vulgarity to Lippo Topo* himself, and whom Friar Cipolla frequently used to make fun of in conversation with his cronies, saying:

'My servant has nine failings, any one of which, had it been found in Solomon or Aristotle or Seneca, would have sufficed to vitiate all the ingenuity, all the wisdom, and all the saintliness they ever possessed. So you can imagine what this fellow must be like, considering that he hasn't a scrap of ingenuity, wisdom or saintliness, and possesses all nine.'

Friar Cipolla had put these nine failings into rhyme, so that whenever he was asked what they were, he replied:

*A cartoonist of moderate artistic talent, famous for the grotesqueness of his caricatures.

'I'll tell you: he's untruthful, distasteful and slothful; negligent, disobedient, and truculent; careless, witless and graceless. Apart from this, he has one or two other little foibles, that are best passed over in silence. But the funniest thing about him is that wherever he goes, he's always wanting to find himself a wife and rent a house; and because he has a big, black, greasy beard, he thinks he's very handsome and seductive, and that every woman he meets is desperately in love with him; and if he were left to his own devices, he'd be so busy chasing the girls that he could lose his breeches and be none the wiser. All the same I must confess that he's a great help to me, because he won't allow me to be burdened with anybody's secrets, but always insists on sharing them with me; and if anyone asks me a question, he's so afraid I won't be able to answer that he does it for me, putting in a quick "yes" or a quick "no" as the occasion appears to merit.'

This, then, was the man Friar Cipolla had left behind at the inn, with strict instructions not to allow anyone to touch his belongings, in particular his saddlebags, which contained his sacred bits and pieces.

But no nightingale was ever as happy on the branch of a tree as Guccio Imbratta in the kitchen of an inn, especially if there happened to be a serving-wench in the offing. And having caught a glimpse of a stocky little kitchen-maid, who was plump and coarse and bow-legged, with a pair of paps like a couple of dung-baskets and a face like a Baronci, her skin plastered in sweat, grease and soot, he left Friar Cipolla's things to take care of themselves, and like a vulture descending on carrion, down he swooped. Although it was August, he took a seat beside the fire and struck up a conversation with the girl, whose name was Nuta, telling her that he was a gentleman by proxy, that he had more florins than anyone could count, not excluding the ones he had to pay out, which were even more in number, and that not even his master could do and say so many fine things as he. Moreover, paying no heed to the cowl he was wearing, which had enough grease on it to season the soup-cauldron of Altopascio,* or to his patched and tattered doublet, which was smeared with filth round the collar and under the armpits, and stained all over in more colours than a length of cloth from India or Tartary, or to his shoes, that were falling to bits, or to his hose, that were gaping at the seams, he told

*An abbey near Lucca, renowned for its generous doles of soup.

her, as though he were the Lord of Chatillon himself, that he would buy her some fine new clothes, set her up in comfort, release her from her drudgery, and, whilst she wouldn't have much to call her own, give her something to look forward to at any rate. But all these promises, and a great many more, though uttered with a good deal of affection, were as insubstantial as the air itself, and like most of the projects he undertook, they came to nothing.

Finding Guccio Porco thus occupied with Nuta, the two young men were delighted, since it meant that half their job was already done. And so they made their way unhindered to Friar Cipolla's room, the door of which was unlocked; and having let themselves in, the very first thing they laid hands upon was the saddlebag containing the feather. On opening the bag, they found a small casket wrapped in a length of taffeta, and when they raised the lid, and found that it contained one of the tail feathers of a parrot, they concluded that this must be the one he had promised to display to the people of Certaldo.

And without a doubt he could easily have got away with it in those days, because the luxuries of Egypt had not yet infiltrated to any marked degree into Tuscany, as they were later to do on a very wide scale, to the ruination of the whole of Italy. A few people in Tuscany were aware that such things existed, but they were almost totally unknown in Certaldo, where, since the lives of the people still conformed to the honest precepts of an earlier age, not only had they never seen any parrots, but the vast majority had never even heard of them.

Delighted, then, with their discovery, the young men removed the feather from the casket, and in its place, so as not to leave the casket empty, they put a few pieces of coal, which they had found lying in a corner of the room. They then closed the lid, and, leaving everything just as they had found it, they made off, undetected, with the feather, chortling with glee, and waited to see what Friar Cipolla, on finding the coals instead of the feather, would have to say for himself.

When mass was over, the simple folk who were in the church, having heard that they would be seeing the feather of the Angel Gabriel after nones, had returned to their homes and passed the news on to all their friends and neighbours. And after they had eaten their midday meal, they thronged the citadel in such vast numbers, all agog to see the feather, that they scarcely had sufficient room to move their limbs.

Having eaten a hearty breakfast and taken a short siesta, Friar Cipolla arose shortly after nones, and on perceiving that a great multitude of peasants had come to see the feather, he sent word to Guccio Imbratta that he was to come up to the citadel, bringing with him the bells and the saddle-bags. So Guccio tore himself away from the kitchen and from Nuta, and made his way up at a leisurely pace. His body was swollen up like a balloon with all the water he had been drinking, and so he arrived there puffing and panting; but having, in accordance with Friar Cipolla's instructions, taken up his stance in the church doorway, he began to ring the bells with great gusto.

When the entire populace was assembled in front of the church, Friar Cipolla began to preach his sermon, never suspecting for a moment that any of his things had been tampered with. He harangued his audience at great length, carefully stressing what was required of them, and on reaching the point where he was to display the Angel Gabriel's feather, he first recited the *Confiteor* and caused two torches to be lit; then, throwing back the cowl from his head, he carefully unwound the taffeta and drew forth the casket, which, after a few words in praise and commendation of the Angel Gabriel and his relic, he proceeded to open. When he saw that it was full of coal, Guccio Balena was the last person he suspected of playing him such a trick, for he knew him to be incapable of rising to such heights of ingenuity. Nor did he even blame the man for being so careless as to allow others to do it, but inwardly cursed his own stupidity in entrusting his things to Guccio's care, knowing full well, as he did, that he was negligent, disobedient, careless and witless. Without changing colour in the slightest, however, he raised his eyes and hands to Heaven, and in a voice that could be heard by all the people present, he exclaimed:

'Almighty God, may Thy power be forever praised!'

Then, closing the casket and turning to the people, he said:

'Ladies and gentlemen, I must explain to you that when I was still very young, I was sent by my superior into those parts where the sun appears, with express instructions to seek out the privileges of the

Porcellana,* which, though they cost nothing to seal and deliver, bring far more profit to others than to ourselves.

'So away I went, and after setting out from Venison, I visited the Greek Calends, then rode at a brisk pace through the Kingdom of Algebra and through Bordello, eventually reaching Bedlam, and not long afterwards, almost dying of thirst, I arrived in Sardintinia. But why bother to mention every single country to which I was directed by my questing spirit? After crossing the Straits of Penury, I found myself passing through Funland and Laughland, both of which countries are thickly populated, besides containing a lot of people. Then I went on to Liarland, where I found a large number of friars belonging to various religious orders including my own, all of whom were forsaking a life of discomfort for the love of God, and paying little heed to the exertions of others so long as they led to their own profit. In all these countries, I coined a great many phrases, which turned out to be the only currency I needed.

'Next I came to the land of Abruzzi, where all the men and women go climbing the hills in clogs, and clothe pigs in their own entrails; and a little further on I found people carrying bread on staves, and wine in pouches, after which I arrived at the mountains of the Basques, where all the waters flow downwards.

'In short, my travels took me so far afield that I even went to Parsnipindia, where I swear by this habit I am wearing that I saw the feathers flying – an incredible spectacle for anyone who has never witnessed it. And if any of you should doubt my words, Maso del Saggio will bear me out on this point, for he has set up a thriving business in that part of the world, cracking nuts and selling the shells retail.

'But being unable to find what I was seeking, or to proceed any further except by water, I retraced my steps and came at length to the Holy Land, where in summertime the cold bread costs fourpence a loaf, and the hot is to be had for nothing. There I met the Reverend Father Besokindas Tocursemenot, the most worshipful Patriarch of Jerusalem, who, out of deference to the habit of the Lord Saint

---

*Like many of the other mystifying phrases in Cipolla's sermon, the 'privileges of the Porcellana' probably connote the practice of sodomy, a vice to which monks and friars were traditionally susceptible.

Anthony, which I have always worn, desired that I should see all the holy relics he had about him. These were so numerous, that if I were to give you a complete list, I would go on for miles without reaching the end of it. But so as not to disappoint the ladies, I shall mention just a few of them.

'First of all he showed me the finger of the Holy Ghost, as straight and firm as it ever was; then the forelock of the Seraph that appeared to Saint Francis; and a cherub's fingernail; and one of the side-bits of the Word-made-flash-in-the-pan; and an article or two of the Holy Catholic faith; and a few of the rays from the star that appeared to the three Magi in the East; and a phial of Saint Michael's sweat when he fought with the Devil; and the jawbone of Death visiting Saint Lazarus; and countless other things.

'And because I was able to place freely at his disposal certain sections of the Rumpiad in the vernacular, together with several extracts from Capretius, which he had long been anxious to acquire, he gave me a part-share in his holy relics, presenting me with one of the holes from the Holy Cross, and a small phial containing some of the sound from the bells of Solomon's temple, and the feather of the Angel Gabriel that I was telling you about, and one of Saint Gherardo da Villamagna's sandals, which not long ago in Florence I handed on to Gherardo di Bonsi, who holds him in the deepest veneration; and finally, he gave me some of the coals over which the blessed martyr Saint Lawrence was roasted. All these things I devoutly brought away with me, and I have them to this day.

'True, my superior has never previously allowed me to exhibit them, until such time as their authenticity was established. However, by virtue of certain miracles they have wrought, and on account of some letters he has received from the Patriarch, he has now become convinced that they are genuine, and has granted me permission to display them in public. But I am afraid to entrust them to others, and I always take them with me wherever I go.

'Now, the fact is that I keep the feather of the Angel Gabriel in a casket to prevent it being damaged, and in another casket I keep the coals over which Saint Lawrence was roasted. But the two caskets are so alike that I often pick up the wrong one, which is what has happened today; for whereas I intended to bring along the one containing the feather, I have brought the one with the coals. Nor do I consider this a pure accident; on the contrary I am convinced that it was the will of God, and that it was He who put the casket of coals into my hands, for I have just remembered that the day after tomorrow is the Feast of Saint Lawrence. And since it was God's intention that I should show you the coals over which he was roasted, and thus rekindle the devotion which you should all feel towards Saint Lawrence in your hearts, He arranged that I should take up, not the feather which I had meant to show you, but the blessed coals that were extinguished by the humours of that most sacred body. You will therefore bare your heads, my blessed children, and step up here in order to gaze devoutly upon them.

'But before you do so, I must tell you that all those who are marked with the sign of the cross by these coals may rest assured that for a whole year they will never be touched by fire without getting burnt.'

And so saying, he chanted a hymn in praise of Saint Lawrence, opened up the casket, and displayed the coals. For some little time, the foolish multitude gazed open-mouthed upon them in awe and wonderment, then they all pressed forward in a great throng round Friar Cipolla, and, giving him larger offerings than usual, they begged him one and all to touch them with the coals.

So Friar Cipolla took the coals between his fingers and began to scrawl the biggest crosses he could manage to inscribe on their white smocks and on their doublets and on the shawls of the women, declaring that however much the coals were worn down in making these crosses, they recovered their former shape when restored to the casket, as he had often had occasion to observe.

At considerable profit to himself, therefore, having daubed crosses on all the citizens of Certaldo, Friar Cipolla neatly turned the tables on the people who had sought to make a fool of him by taking away his feather. Having attended his sermon and observed the ingenious manner in which he had turned the situation to his advantage with his preposterous rigmarole, the two young men laughed until they thought their sides would split. And when the crowd had dispersed, they went up to him, shaking with mirth, and told him what they had done, at the same time handing back the feather, which proved the following year to be no less lucrative to him than the coals had been on this occasion.

★   ★   ★

The whole company was vastly pleased and entertained by Dioneo's tale, and they all laughed heartily over Friar Cipolla, especially at his pilgrimage and at the relics, both the ones he had seen and those he had brought back with him. On perceiving that it was finished, and that her reign, too, had come to an end, the queen stood up, and removing her crown, she placed it on Dioneo's head, saying with a laugh:

'The time has come, Dioneo, for you to discover what a burden it is to have ladies under your control and guidance. Be our king, therefore, and rule us wisely, so that when your reign is ended, we shall have cause to sing your praises.'

Dioneo accepted the crown, and replied with a laugh:

'I daresay you have often seen kings whose worth is far greater than mine – on a chessboard, I mean. But without a doubt, if you were to obey me as a true king ought to be obeyed, I should see that you received a measure of that joy without which no entertainment is ever truly pleasurable and complete. But enough of this idle chatter. I shall rule as best I can.'

And having, in accordance with their usual practice, sent for the steward, he gave him clear instructions about the duties he was to perform during the remainder of his sovereignty, after which he said:

'Worthy ladies, our discussions have ranged so widely over the field of human endeavour, and touched upon such a variety of incidents, that if Mistress Licisca had not come here a short while ago and said something which offered me a subject for our deliberations on the morrow, I suspect I should have had a hard job to find a suitable theme. As you will have heard, she told us that none of the girls in her neighbourhood had gone to her husband a virgin; and she added that she knew all about the many clever tricks played by married women on their husbands. But leaving aside the first part, which even a child could have told you, I reckon that the second would make an agreeable subject for discussion; and hence, taking our cue from Mistress Licisca, I should like us to talk tomorrow about *the*

tricks which, either in the cause of love or for motives of self-preservation,
women have played upon their husbands, irrespective of whether or not they
were found out.'

Some of the ladies felt that it would be unseemly for them to
discuss a subject of this sort, and asked him to propose another, but the
king replied:

'Ladies, I know as well as you do that the theme I have prescribed
is a delicate one to handle; but I am not to be deterred by your
objections, for I believe that the times we live in permit all subjects
to be freely discussed, provided that men and women take care to do
no wrong. Are you not aware that because of the chaos of the present
age, the judges have deserted the courts, the laws of God and man are
in abeyance, and everyone is given ample licence to preserve his life
as best he may? This being so, if you go slightly beyond the bounds
of decorum in your conversation, with the object, not of behaving
improperly but of giving pleasure to yourselves and to others, I do
not see how anyone in the future can have cause to condemn you for
it.

'Besides, it seems to me that this company of ours has comported
itself impeccably from the first day to this, despite all that we have
heard, and with God's help it will continue to do so. Furthermore,
everybody knows that you are all highly virtuous, and I doubt
whether even the fear of dying could make you any less so, to say
nothing of a little pleasurable discourse.

'But the real point is this, that if anyone were to discover that you
had refrained at any time from discussing these little peccadilloes, he
might well suspect that you had a guilty conscience about them, and
that this was why you were so reluctant to talk about them. Apart
from which, you would be paying me a nice compliment if, having
elected me as your king and law-giver, you were to refuse to speak on
the subject I prescribe, especially when you consider how obedient I
was to all of you. Set aside these scruples, then, which ill become such
healthy minds as your own, and let each of you put her best foot forward and think of some entertaining story to relate.'

Having listened to Dioneo's arguments, the ladies agreed to fall in
with his scheme, whereupon he gave permission to them all to occupy
their time until supper in whatever way they pleased.

The sun was still very high, for the day's discussions had been relatively brief, and so Elissa, seeing that Dioneo had started a game of dice with the other young men, drew all the ladies aside, and said:

'Ever since we came here, I have been wanting to take you to a place where none of you, so far as I know, has ever been, called the Valley of the Ladies. It is not far away from here, but this is the first opportunity I have had (the sun being still very high) of taking you to see it. So if you would all like to come, I am quite sure that once you are there you will not be in the least disappointed.'

The ladies agreed to go with her, and without saying anything to the young men, they sent for one of their maidservants, and set out; nor had they gone much more than a mile, when they came to the Valley of the Ladies. This they entered by way of a very narrow path, along one side of which there flowed a beautifully clear stream, and they found it to be as delectable and lovely a place, especially since the weather was so hot, as could possibly be imagined. And according to the description I was given later by one of their number, the floor of the Valley was perfectly circular in shape, for all the world as if it had been made with compasses, though it seemed the work of Nature rather than of man. It was little more than half a mile in circumference, and surrounded by half-a-dozen hills, all comparatively low-lying, on each of whose summits one could discern a palace, built more or less in the form of a pretty little castle. The sides of the hills ranged downwards in a regular series of terraces, concentrically arranged like the tiers of an amphitheatre, their circles gradually diminishing in size from the topmost terrace to the lowest.

Of these slopes, the ones facing south were covered all over in vines, olives, almonds, cherries, figs, and many other species of fruit trees, whilst those which faced north were thickly wooded with young oaks, ashes, and various other trees, all as green and straight as you could imagine. The plain itself, to which there was no other means of access than the path by which the ladies had entered, was filled with firs, cypresses, bay-trees, and a number of pines, all of which were so neatly arranged and symmetrically disposed that they looked as if they had been planted by the finest practitioner of the forester's craft. And when the sun was overhead, few or none of its rays penetrated their foliage to the ground beneath, which was one continuous lawn of tiny blades of grass interspersed with flowers, many of them purple in colour.

But the thing that afforded them no less pleasure was a stream cascading down over the living rock of a gorge separating two of the surrounding hills, which produced a most delectable sound as it descended and looked from a distance as though it was issuing forth under pressure in a powdery spray of fine quicksilver. On reaching the floor of the valley, it flowed swiftly along a neat little channel to the centre of the plain, where it formed a tiny lake like one of those fishponds that prosperous townspeople occasionally construct in their gardens. The lake was not very deep, so that if a man were to stand in it, the water would have come up no further than his chest; and since it was free of all impurities, its bed showed up vividly as a stretch of very fine gravel, every fragment of which could have been counted by anyone with sufficient patience and nothing better to do. But apart from the bed of the lake, on looking into the water one could see a number of fishes darting in all directions, which were not only delightful but wondrous to behold. The lake had no other banks than the floor of the valley itself, and all around its edges the grass grew much more thickly through being so close to the water. And it was drained by a second little channel, through which the stream flowed out of the valley and so downwards to its lower reaches.

This, then, was the place to which the young ladies came; and after they had gazed all around and extolled its marvellous beauty, seeing the limpid pool shimmering there before them they made up their minds, since it was very hot and they were in no danger of being observed, to go for a swim. And having ordered their maid to go back and keep watch along the path by which they had entered the valley, and bring them warning if anyone should come, all seven of them undressed and took to the water, which concealed their chaste white bodies no better than a thin sheet of glass would conceal a pink rose. And when they were in the water, which remained as crystal-clear as before, they began as best they could to swim hither and thither in pursuit of the fishes, which had nowhere to hide, and tried to seize hold of them with their hands.

In this sport they persisted for a while, and after they had caught some of the fish, they emerged from the pool and put on their clothes again. And being unable to bestow higher praise upon the place than that which they had already accorded to it, feeling that it was time to make their way back again, they set forth at a gentle pace, talking all the while of its beauty. It was as yet quite early when they arrived at the palace, where they found the young men still playing dice in the place where they had left them, and Pampinea greeted them with a laugh, saying:

'We have stolen a march upon you today.'

'What?' said Dioneo. 'Do you mean to say you have begun to do these things even before you talk about them?'

'Yes, Your Majesty,' said Pampinea. And she gave him a lengthy description of the place from which they had come, telling him how far away it was, and what they had been doing there.

On hearing her account of the place's beauty, the king was anxious to see it for himself, and he straightway ordered supper to be served. This they all proceeded to eat with a great deal of relish, and when it was over, the three young men and their servants deserted the ladies and made their way to the Valley. None of them had been there before, and all things considered, they concluded admiringly that it was one of the loveliest sights in the world. And when they had bathed and dressed, since the hour was very late they went straight back home, where they found the ladies dancing a *carole* to an air being sung by Fiammetta. They joined them in the dance, and when it was finished, having taken up the subject of the Valley of the Ladies, they talked at length in praise of its beauty.

And so the king sent for the steward, and ordered him to see that things were set out for them next morning in that very place, and that beds were carried there in case anyone should want to sleep or lie down in the middle part of the day. Then he called for lights to be brought, together with wine and sweetmeats, and when they had taken a little refreshment, he ordered everyone to join in the dancing. At his request, Panfilo began the first dance, whereupon the king turned to Elissa and in pleasing tones he said:

'Fair lady, just as you honoured me today with the crown, so I wish to honour you this evening with the privilege of singing to us. Sing to us therefore, and let your song be about the one you prefer to all the rest.'

Elissa, with a smile, readily consented and began to sing in dulcet tones as follows:

> 'Love, if I ever from thy claws break free
> I think no other hook will tangle me.
>
> 'I entered in thy war, a fair young maid,
> Believing it was perfect peace benign,
> And all my arms upon the ground I laid,
> Thinking to find thy honour like to mine.
>   But thou, disloyal tyrant,
>   Leapt'st out at me instead
>   In armour fiercely girded
>   With talons cruel outspread.
>
> 'And now, all bound around with chains of thine,
> To him who for my very death was born
> Thou gav'st me prisoner; and now I pine
> Within his grasp, and in distraction mourn.
>   His lordship is so cruel
>   That all my tears and cries
>   Go unregarded, while, alas,
>   I waste away with sighs.
>
> 'The wind has swept away my every prayer;
> E'en now, when my cruel torment grows so high,
> None listens to them, none will give them ear;
> My life is hateful, yet how may I die?
>   Since I lie in thy bondage
>   Have pity, Lord, on me,
>   Do for me what I cannot
>   And set my spirit free.
>
> 'But if thou canst not grant me this, alas,
> Cut all those bonds of hope that bind me fast.
> I pray thee, Lord, at least to grant me this,
> For if thou dost, my faith is that at last
>   I may regain that beauty
>   That once I had by right
>   And, sorrow banished, deck me
>   With flowers of red and white.'

When Elissa, fetching a most pathetic sigh, had brought her song to a close, albeit everyone puzzled over the words no one was able to say who it was that had caused her to sing such a song. The king, however, who was in good mettle, sent for Tindaro and ordered him to bring out his cornemuse, to the strains of which he caused several reels to be danced. But when a goodly portion of the night was spent, he told them, one and all, to retire to bed.

Here ends the Sixth Day of the Decameron

SEVENTH DAY

Here begins the Seventh Day, wherein, under the rule of
Dioneo, *are discussed the tricks which, either in the cause of*
love or for motives of self-preservation, women have played
upon their husbands, irrespective of whether or not they were
found out.

Every star had vanished from the eastern heavens, excepting that
alone which we call Lucifer, which was still glowing in the whitening
dawn, when the steward arose and made his way with a large
baggage-train to the Valley of the Ladies, there to arrange everything
in accordance with his master's orders and instructions. And after his
departure it was not long before the king also arose, having been
awakened by the noise of the servants loading the animals, and caused
all the ladies and the other young men to be roused.

Nor were the sun's rays shining as yet in all their glory, when the
whole company set forth; and it seemed to them that they had never
heard the nightingales and other birds sing so gaily as they appeared to
sing that morning. Their songs accompanied them all the way to the
Valley of the Ladies, where they were greeted by a good many more,
so that all the birds seemed to be rejoicing at their coming.

On roaming through the Valley and surveying it for a second time,
they thought it even more beautiful than on the day before, inasmuch
as the hour showed off its loveliness to better advantage. And when
they had broken their fast with good wine and delicate sweetmeats,
so as not to be outdone by the birds they too burst into song, whereupon the Valley joined forces with them, repeating every note that
was uttered; and to these songs of theirs, sweet new notes were added
by all the birds, as though they were determined not to be out-
matched.

When it was time to eat, they took their places at the tables, which
in deference to the king's wishes had been set beneath the leafy bay-
trees and the other fine trees fringing the delectable pool, and as they

ate they could see the fishes swimming about the lake in enormous shoals, which attracted not only their attention but also an occasional comment. At the end of the meal, the tables were cleared and taken away, and they began to sing even more merrily than before, then played upon their instruments and danced one or two *caroles*.

Their discreet steward had meanwhile made up several beds in different parts of the little valley, surrounding them with drapes of French cretonne and bedecking them with canopies, and the king gave leave to those who so desired to retire for their siesta; and those who had no desire to sleep were free to amuse themselves to their hearts' content in the various ways to which they were accustomed. In due course, when the time came for them to address themselves once more to their story-telling, they all got up and proceeded to seat themselves on rugs which, in accordance with the king's instructions, had been laid upon the grass beside the lake, in a spot not far away from where they had breakfasted. Then the king ordered Emilia to open the proceedings, and with a broad smile, she gaily began to speak, as follows:

FIRST STORY

Gianni Lotteringhi hears a tapping at his door in the night; he awakens his wife, and she leads him to believe it is a werewolf, whereupon they go and exorcize it with a prayer, and the knocking stops.

My lord, I should have counted myself very fortunate if you had chosen some person other than myself to introduce so splendid a topic as the one on which we are called upon to speak; but since you desire me to set a reassuring example to the other ladies, I shall willingly do so. I shall endeavour, dearest ladies, to say something that might prove useful to you in the future, for if other women are no different from myself, we are easily frightened, and in particular by werewolves. Heaven knows that I am unable to explain what these creatures might be, nor have I ever found any woman who could, but we are frightened of them just the same. However, if you should ever encounter one, you will henceforth be able to drive it away, for by listening carefully to my story you will learn a fine and godly prayer which is tailored to the purpose.

There once lived in Florence, in the quarter of San Pancrazio, a master-weaver whose name was Gianni Lotteringhi, a man more successful in his calling than sensible in other matters, for although he was a simple sort of fellow, he was regularly elected as the leader of the laud-singers at Santa Maria Novella, and had to conduct their rehearsals, and he was often given other such trifling little duties, so that all in all he had a mighty high opinion of himself; yet the only reason these functions were entrusted to him was that, being comfortably off, he frequently used to supply the friars with a good meal.

These latter, since they often wrung a pair of hose or a cloak or a scapular out of him, taught him some good prayers and gave him copies of the Paternoster in the vernacular and the song of Saint Alexis and the lament of Saint Bernard and the laud of Lady Matilda and a whole lot of other drivel, all of which he greatly prized, and preserved with the greatest of loving care for the good of his soul.

Now, this man had a most charming and beautiful wife, a woman of great intelligence and perspicacity, whose name was Monna Tessa, the daughter of Mannuccio dalla Cuculia. Realizing that she had a nincompoop for a husband, she fell in love with Federigo di Neri Pegolotti, a handsome fellow in the full vigour of his youth, and he with her, and she made arrangements through one of her maid-servants for Federigo to come and keep her company at a splendid villa belonging to her husband in Camerata, where she used to spend the whole of the summer, and to which Gianni would occasionally come in the evening in order to sup with her and stay overnight before returning next morning to his place of business or sometimes to his laud-singers.

Federigo desired nothing better, and one day, when the coast was clear, he made his way up to the villa as prearranged, a little before vespers. Gianni was not expected that evening, so Federigo was thoroughly at his ease; and to his immense pleasure, he was able to sup there and spend the night with the lady, who lay in his arms and taught him a good half dozen of her husband's lauds before the night was over.

But neither she nor Federigo intended that this first time should also be the last, and since it was imprudent to send the maid to fetch him every time, they came to the following arrangement: that every day, on his way to or from a villa of his that stood a little further up the road, he should keep an eye on the vineyard alongside her house, where he would see the skull of an ass perched on top of one of the stakes of the vines. If he saw that the face was turned in the direction of Florence, he would come to her after dark that evening without fail and in complete safety, and if the door was locked he would knock three times and she would come and let him in; but if he saw that the face of the skull was pointing towards Fiesole he would stay away, because it would mean that Gianni was at home. And by using this system they were able to meet together regularly.

But on one of these occasions when Federigo was due to come and take supper with Monna Tessa, and she had roasted a pair of fat capons in his honour, it so happened that, much to the lady's chagrin, Gianni turned up unexpectedly, very late in the evening. She and her husband supped on a small quantity of salted meat which she had cooked separately; and meanwhile she got her maid to wrap the two roast capons in a white tablecloth together with a quantity of new-laid eggs and a flask of choice wine, and carry them into her garden, which it was possible to reach without going through the house, and where every so often she and Federigo used to sup. And she told the maid to leave all these things at the foot of a peach-tree that stood at the edge of a pretty little meadow.

But she was so enraged by what had happened that she forgot to tell the maid to wait until Federigo arrived, so as to inform him that Gianni was at home and that he was to take away the things from the garden. And so not long after she and Gianni had gone to bed, and the maid had also retired for the night, Federigo came and tapped gently at the door, which was so near to the bedroom that Gianni heard it immediately, and so did the lady. But so that Gianni could have no possible reason to suspect her, she pretended to be asleep.

Federigo waited a little, then knocked a second time, whereupon Gianni began to wonder what it was all about and gave his wife a little poke, saying:

'Tessa, do you hear what I hear? It sounds like someone tapping at our door.'

His wife, who had heard it much more clearly than he had, made a show of waking up, and murmured:

'Mm? What's that you say?'

'I said,' Gianni replied, 'that it sounds like someone tapping at our door.'

'Tapping?' she said. 'Oh, heavens, Gianni dear, d'you know what it'll be? It'll be the werewolf that's been frightening me out of my senses for these past few nights. I was so terrified that every time I heard it I stuck my head under the bedclothes and kept it there until it was broad daylight.'

'Come now, don't be afraid, my dear,' said Gianni. 'If that's all it is, there's no need to worry, because before we got into bed I recited the *Te lucis* and the *Intemerata* and various other excellent prayers, and I also made the sign of the cross from corner to corner of the bed in the name of the Father, the Son and the Holy Ghost, so no matter how powerful this werewolf may be, it can't do us any harm.'

In case Federigo should become suspicious of her and take offence, Monna Tessa decided that, come what may, she must get up out of bed and apprise him of the fact that Gianni was there, and so she said to her husband:

'That's all very well. You can spout as many words as you like, but as far as I'm concerned I shan't feel safe or secure until we exorcize it, and now that you are here we can do it.'

'Exorcize it?' said Gianni. 'How are we to do that?'

'I know exactly how to exorcize it,' said his wife, 'because the day before yesterday, when I went to the pardoning at Fiesole, I came across a hermitess, who as God is my witness, Gianni dear, is the most saintly woman you ever met, and when she saw how terrified I was of the werewolf, she taught me a fine and godly prayer, telling me that she had tried it many a time before becoming a recluse, and that it had always worked for her. Heaven knows that I would never have sufficient courage to try it out by myself, but now that you are here, I want us to go and exorcize it.'

Gianni thought this an excellent idea, and so they both got up out of bed and tiptoed over to the door, on the other side of which

Federigo, his suspicions already aroused, was still waiting. On reaching the door, Gianni's wife said to him:

'As soon as I give you the word, have a good spit.'

'Right you are,' said Gianni.

Then the lady began the exorcism, saying:

'Werewolf, werewolf, black as any crow, you came here with your tail erect, keep it up and go; go into the garden, and look beneath the peach, and there you'll find roast capons, and a score of eggs with each; raise the flask up to your lips, and take a swig of wine; then get you gone and hurt me not, nor even Gianni mine.' And so saying, she turned to her husband, and said:

'Spit, Gianni.' And Gianni spat.

Federigo, who was standing outside and heard every syllable, had stopped feeling jealous, and despite all his frustration he had to hold his sides to prevent himself from bursting into laughter. And in a low murmur, as Gianni was doing his spitting, he groaned:

'The teeth!'

When Monna Tessa had exorcized the werewolf three times in this same fashion, she and her husband returned to bed.

Federigo had come with an empty stomach, for he had been expecting to sup with his mistress. But having clearly grasped the meaning of the words of the prayer, he made his way into the garden, where at the foot of the large peach-tree he found the two capons and the wine and the eggs, which he took back with him to his house, there to make a splendid and leisurely meal of it all. And on many a later occasion, when he was with his mistress, they had a good laugh together over this incantation of hers.

It is true that some people maintain that the lady had in fact turned the skull of the ass towards Fiesole, and that a farmhand, passing through the vineyard, had poked his stick inside it and given it a good twirl, so that it ended up facing towards Florence, hence causing Federigo to think that she wanted him to come. According to this second account, the words of the lady's prayer went like this: 'Werewolf, werewolf, leave us be; the ass's head was turned, but not by me; I curse the one who did it, and I think you will agree; for I'm here with my dear Gianni, as anyone can see.' And so Federigo beat a hasty retreat, and lost his supper that evening as well as his lodging.

However, there is a neighbour of mine, a very old woman, who tells me that both accounts are correct if there is any truth in a story which she was told when she was still a child, and that the second version refers, not to Gianni Lotteringhi, but to a man from Porta San Piero called Gianni di Nello, who was just as great a dunderhead as Gianni Lotteringhi.

I therefore leave it to you, dear ladies, to choose the version you prefer, or perhaps you would like to accept both, for as you have heard, they are extremely effective in situations like the one I have described. Commit them to memory, then, for they may well stand you in good stead in times to come.

SECOND STORY

Peronella hides her lover in a tub when her husband returns home unexpectedly. Her husband has sold the tub, but she tells him that she herself has already sold it to a man who is inspecting it from the inside to see whether it is sound. Leaping forth from the tub, the man gets the husband to scrape it out and carry it back to his house for him.

Emilia's story was received with gales of laughter, and everyone agreed that the prayer was indeed a fine and godly one. When the tale was finished, the king ordered Filostrato to follow, and so he began:

Adorable ladies, so numerous are the tricks that men, and husbands in particular, play upon you, that whenever any woman happens to play one on her husband, you should not only be glad to hear about it but you should also pass it on to as many people as you can, so that men will come to realize that women are just as clever as they are. All of which is bound to work out to your own advantage, for when a man knows that he has clever people to deal with, he will think twice before attempting to deceive them.

Who can be in any doubt, therefore, that when husbands come to learn of what we shall be saying today on this subject, they will have every reason to refrain from trifling with you, knowing that if you so desired you could do the same to them? And for this reason, it is my intention to tell you about the trick which a young woman, though she was of lowly condition, played on the spur of the moment upon her husband, in order to save her own skin.

Not so long ago, in Naples, a poor man took to wife a charming and beautiful girl, whose name was Peronella. He was a bricklayer by trade, and earned a very low wage, but this, together with the modest amount she earned from her spinning, was just about sufficient for them to live on.

Now one day, Peronella caught the eye of a sprightly young gallant, who, finding her exceedingly attractive, promptly fell in love with her, and by using all his powers of persuasion, he succeeded in gaining her acquaintance. So that they could be together, they came to this arrangement: that since her husband got up early every morning to go to work or to go and look for a job, the young man should lie in wait until he saw him leaving the house; and as the district where she lived, which was called Avorio, was very out-of-the-way, as soon as the husband had left, he should go in to her. And in this way they met very regularly.

But one particular morning, shortly after the good man had left the house and Giannello Scrignario (such was the young gallant's name) had gone inside to join Peronella, the husband, who was usually away for the whole day, returned home. Finding the door locked on the inside, he knocked, and after he had knocked he said to himself:

'May the Lord God be forever praised; for though He has willed that I should be poor, at least He has given me the consolation of a good, chaste girl for a wife. See how quick she was to lock the door after I left, so that no one should come in and give her any trouble.'

Now, Peronella knew it was her husband from his way of knocking, and she said:

'O alas, Giannello my love, I'm done for! That's my husband, curse the fellow, who for some reason or other has come back home. I've never known him to return at this hour before; perhaps he saw you coming in. But whatever the reason, for God's sake hop into this tub over here while I go and let him in and find out what has brought him home so early in the day.'

Giannello promptly got into the tub, whereupon Peronella went and opened the door to her husband, and, pulling a long face, she said:

'What's got into you this morning, coming back home so early? It looks to me, seeing that you're carrying your tools, as if you've decided to take the day off, in which case what are we going to live on? How are we to buy anything to eat? Do you think I'm going to let you pawn my Sunday dress and my other little bits and pieces? Here I am, stuck in this house from morning till night and working my fingers to the bone, so that we shall at least have sufficient oil to keep our lamp alight! Oh, what a husband! I haven't a single neighbour who doesn't gape and laugh at me for slaving away as I do; and yet you come back here twiddling your thumbs when you ought to be out working.'

At this point she burst into tears, then started all over again, saying:

'O alas, woe is me, why was I ever born, what did I do to deserve such a husband! I could have had a decent, hard-working young fellow, and I turned him down to marry this worthless good-for-nothing, who doesn't appreciate what a good wife I am to him. All the other wives have a jolly good time: they have two or three lovers apiece, and they whoop it up under their husbands' noses, whereas for poor little me, just because I am a respectable woman and find that sort of thing distasteful, there's nothing but misery and ill luck. I just can't understand why I don't take one or two lovers, as other women do. It's time you realized, husband, that if I wanted to misbehave, I'd soon find someone to do it with, for there are plenty of sprightly young fellows who love and admire me, and who have offered me large sums of money, or dresses and jewels if I preferred, but not being the daughter of that kind of woman, I never had it in me to accept. And what is my reward? A husband who slopes back home when he ought to be out working.'

'Oh, for Heaven's sake, woman,' said her husband, 'stop making such a song and dance about it. I know how virtuous you are, and as a matter of fact I saw the proof of it this very morning. The fact is that I went to work, but what you don't seem to realize, and I didn't either, is that today is the feast of Saint Galeone and everybody's on holiday, and that's the reason I came home so early. But even so I've made sure that we shall have enough food to last us for over a month. You know that tub that's been cluttering up the house for ages? Well, I've sold it for five silver ducats to this man waiting here on the doorstep.'

Whereupon Peronella said:

'That really does put the lid on it. One would think that since you are a man and get about a good deal, you ought to know the value of things; yet you sell a tub for five silver ducats, which I, a mere woman who hardly ever puts her nose outside the front door, seeing what a nuisance it was to have it in the house, have just sold to an honest fellow here for seven. He's inside the tub now, as a matter of fact, seeing whether it is sound.'

When he heard this, her husband was delighted, and turning to the man who had come to collect the tub, he said:

'Run along now, there's a good fellow. You heard what my wife said. She's sold it for seven, and all you would offer me for it was five.'

'So be it,' said the good fellow, and away he went.

And Peronella said to her husband:

'Now that you are here, you'd better come up and settle this with him yourself.'

Giannello was listening with both ears to see whether there was anything he had to guard against or attend to, and on hearing Peronella's words, he leapt smartly out of the tub. And with a casual sort of air, as though he had heard nothing of the husband's return, he called out:

'Are you there, good woman?'

Whereupon the husband, who was just coming up, said:

'Here I am, what can I do for you?'

'Who the hell are you?' said Giannello. 'It's the woman who was selling me this tub that I wanted to speak to.'

'That's all right,' said the good man. 'You can deal with me: I'm her husband.'

So Giannello said:

'The tub seems to be in pretty good shape, but you appear to have left the lees of the wine in it, for it's coated all over with some hard substance or other that I can't even scrape off with my nails. I'm not going to take it unless it's cleaned out first.'

So Peronella said:

'We made a bargain, and we'll stick to it. My husband will clean it out.'

'But of course,' said the husband. And having put down his tools and rolled up his sleeves, he called for a lamp and a scraping tool, lowered himself into the tub, and began to scrape away. Peronella, as though curious to see what he was doing, leaned over the mouth of the tub, which was not very wide, and resting her head on her arm and shoulder, she issued a stream of instructions, such as: 'Scrape it here, and here, and over there,' and 'Have another go at this little bit here.'

While she was busy instructing and directing her husband in this fashion, Giannello, who had not fully gratified his desires that morning before the husband arrived, seeing that he couldn't do it in the way he wished, contrived to bring it off as best he could. So he went up to Peronella, who was completely blocking up the mouth of the tub, and in the manner of a wild and hot-blooded stallion mounting a Parthian mare in the open fields, he satisfied his young man's passion, which no sooner reached fulfilment than the scraping of the tub was completed, whereupon he stood back, Peronella withdrew her head from the tub, and the husband clambered out.

Then Peronella said to Giannello:

'Here, take this lamp, my good man, and see whether the job's been done to your satisfaction.'

Having taken a look inside the tub, Giannello told her it was all right, and that he was satisfied. He then handed seven silver ducats to the husband, and got him to carry it round to his house.

THIRD STORY

Friar Rinaldo goes to bed with his godchild's mother; her husband finds them together in the bedroom, and they give him to understand that the Friar was charming away the child's worms.

Filostrato's reference to the Parthian mare was not so abstruse as to prevent the alert young ladies from grasping its meaning and having a good laugh, albeit they pretended to be laughing for another reason. But when the king saw that the story was finished, he called upon Elissa to speak, and she promptly obeyed, beginning as follows:

Winsome ladies, Emilia's exorcizing of the werewolf has reminded me of a story about another incantation, and although it is not so fine a tale as hers, it is the only one I can think of for the moment that is relevant to our theme, and I shall therefore relate it to you.

You are to know that there once lived in Siena a dashing young man of respectable parentage, Rinaldo by name, who had fallen desperately in love with the very beautiful wife of a wealthy neighbour of his. Having convinced himself that if only he could find a way of conversing with her in private he would obtain all he wanted from her, he resolved, since the woman was pregnant and he could think of no other pretext, to offer himself as the child's godfather; so having made friends with the woman's husband, he put this proposition to him in as tactful a way as he could manage, and it was all agreed.

Having thus strengthened his hand by becoming the godfather to Madonna Agnesa's child, which gave him a slightly more plausible excuse for conversing with her, he conveyed to her in so many words what had long been apparent to her from the gleam in his eyes. But his words made little impression on the lady, though she was not displeased to have heard them.

Not long afterwards, for reasons best known to himself, Rinaldo decided to become a friar, and there were clearly some good pickings to be had, for he persevered in that profession. Although at first he put aside his love for his neighbour's wife and gave up one or two of his other vices, nevertheless in the course of time, without abandoning the habit of his Order, he reverted to his former ways; and he began to take a pride in his appearance, wear expensively tailored cassocks, affect an air of sprightliness and elegance in all his doings, compose canzonets and sonnets and *ballades*, sing various songs, and engage in countless other activities of a similar nature.

But why do I ramble on about this Friar Rinaldo of ours? Is there a single one of these friars who behaves any differently? Ah, scandal of this corrupt and wicked world! It doesn't worry them in the least that they appear so fat and bloated, that a bright red glow suffuses their cheeks, that their clothes are smooth as velvet, and that in all their dealings they are so effeminate; yet they are anything but dovelike, for they strut about like so many proud peacocks with all their feathers on display. Furthermore, their cells are stuffed with jars filled with unguents and electuaries, with boxes full of various sweetmeats, with phials and bottles containing oils and liquid essences, and with casks brimming over with Malmsey and Greek and other precious wines, so that to any impartial observer they look more like scent shops or grocery stores than the cells of friars. But what is worse, they are not ashamed to admit that they suffer from gout, as though it were not widely known and recognized that regular fasting, a meagre and simple diet, and a sober way of life make people lean and slender, and for the most part healthy. Or at least, if they produce infirmity, this does not take the form of gout, for which the remedy usually prescribed is continence and all the other features of a humble friar's existence. Moreover, they think we are too stupid to realize that a frugal life, lengthy vigils, prayer and self-restraint ought to give to people a pale and drawn appearance, and that neither Saint Dominic nor Saint Francis had four cloaks apiece, or swaggered about in habits that were elegantly tailored and finely woven, but clad themselves in coarse woollen garments of a natural colour, made to keep out the cold. However, God will doubtless see that they, and the simple souls who keep them supplied with all these things, receive their just deserts.

As I was saying, then, Friar Rinaldo was filled once more with all his earlier cravings, and began to pay regular visits to the mother of his godchild. And having become more self-confident, he entreated her to grant his wishes with greater persistence than ever.

One day, Friar Rinaldo importuned her so repeatedly that the good lady, finding herself under so much pressure and thinking him more handsome, perhaps, than he had seemed to her in the past, resorted to the expedient that all women fall back upon when they are itching to concede what is being asked of them, and said:

'Come now, Friar Rinaldo! Do you mean to say that friars indulge in that sort of thing?'

'Madam,' he replied, 'from the moment I am rid of this habit, which I can slip off with the greatest of ease, I shall no longer seem a friar to you, but a man who is made no differently from the rest.'

The lady puckered her lips in a smile, and said:

'Heaven help me, you are my child's godfather; how could you suggest such a thing? It would be awfully wicked; in fact I was always told it was one of the worst sins anyone could commit, otherwise I should be only too willing to do as you suggest.'

'If that's the only thing that deters you,' said Friar Rinaldo, 'then you're just being silly. I don't say it isn't a sin, but God forgives greater sins than this to those who repent. However, tell me this, to whom is this child of yours more closely related: myself, who held him at his baptism, or your husband, by whom he was begotten?'

'My husband, naturally,' she replied.

'Exactly,' said the friar, 'and doesn't your husband go to bed with you?'

'Of course he does,' the lady replied.

'Well then,' said the friar, 'since your husband's more closely akin to the child than I am, surely I can do the same.'

Since logic was not one of her strong points, and she needed little persuasion in any case, the lady either believed or pretended to believe that the Friar was speaking the truth, and she replied:

'How could anyone refute so sensible an argument?'

After which, notwithstanding the fact that he was her child's godfather, she allowed him to have his will of her. And thereafter, having taken the first step, they forgathered very frequently, for his sponsorship of the child made it easy for him to come and go without arousing suspicion.

On one of these occasions, having called at the lady's house with one of his fellow friars, to discover that she was alone except for the child and a very pretty and attractive little maidservant, he packed his companion off to the attic to teach the wench the Lord's Prayer, whilst he and the lady, who was holding her little boy by the hand, made their way into her bedroom, locking the door behind them. And having settled down on a sofa, they began to have a merry time of it together.

But while they were carrying on in this fashion, the child's father happened to return home, and before anyone realized he was there, he was knocking at the door of the bedroom and calling for his wife.

Hearing his voice, Madonna Agnesa said:

'Oh my God, I'm done for, that's my husband. Now he's bound to discover why you and I are always so friendly.'

'That's true enough,' said Friar Rinaldo, who had nothing on except his vest, having discarded his habit and his hood. 'If only I had my clothes on, we could invent some explanation. But if you open the door and he sees me like this, no excuse can possibly do any good.'

Then the woman had a sudden inspiration. 'You get dressed,' she said, 'and as soon as you've got your clothes on, take your godson in your arms and listen carefully to what I shall say to him, so that you can back me up later. But in the meantime, leave everything to me.'

Scarcely had the good man finished knocking at the door, when his wife replied:

'All right, I'm coming.' And, getting up, she went and opened the bedroom door, looking a picture of innocence.

'Oh, husband,' she said, 'I tell you it was God who sent our neighbour Friar Rinaldo to us today, for if he hadn't come, we should certainly have lost our child.'

'What's this?' exclaimed the poor fool of a husband, turning white as a sheet.

'Oh, husband,' said the woman, 'a short while ago, the child fell into a sudden faint, and I thought he must be dead. I was so terrified that I could neither move nor speak, but just at that moment our neighbour Friar Rinaldo turned up. He took the child in his arms and said: "Neighbour, these are worms that he has in his body, and if they were to come any closer to his heart, they could easily be the death of him. But don't you worry, because I am going to cast a spell on them and kill them all off, and before I leave this house the child will be as fit and well as you have ever known him." He wanted you to recite some special prayers, but the maid couldn't find you, so he got a companion of his to recite them in the highest part of the house, while he and I came in here with the child. And since it is only the mother who can be of service in matters of this sort, we locked ourselves in so that we shouldn't be disturbed. He still has the child in his arms, and all he's waiting for now, I think, is to hear from his companion that the prayers have been said, and then the spell will be complete, for already the child is quite himself again.'

The simple soul believed all this nonsense, being so overwhelmed by his concern for the child that he never stopped to think that his wife could be deceiving him. And fetching a deep sigh, he said:

'I want to go and see him.'

'Don't go to him yet,' said the woman, 'or you'll ruin what's been done. Wait here while I go and see whether it's all right for you to come in, and I'll give you a call.'

Friar Rinaldo, who had overheard the entire conversation and put on his clothes with time to spare, took the child in his arms, and when he had arranged things to his liking, he called out:

'Is that the father's voice I can hear out there, my dear?'

'It is indeed,' our simple friend replied.

'In that case,' said Friar Rinaldo, 'come along in.'

The simpleton went in, and Friar Rinaldo said to him:

'Here, take this child, who has been restored to health by the grace of God, when at one time I never thought you would see him alive at vespers. I suggest that you commission a wax figure, the same size as the child, and have it placed to the glory of God in front of the statue of Saint Ambrose, through whose merits God has granted you this favour.'

On catching sight of its father, the boy ran up and made a great fuss of him, as small children do, whereupon the father took him in his arms, and, with tears flowing down his cheeks as though he were snatching him up from the grave, he began to rain kisses on the child and thank his neighbour for saving his life.

Friar Rinaldo's companion had meanwhile taught the pretty little maidservant not merely one Lord's Prayer but possibly as many as four, and had presented her with a white linen purse that had been given to him by a nun, thus making her his devotee. When he heard the simpleton calling to his wife at the door of her bedroom, he quietly went and stood in a place from which he could see and hear all that was going on; and on finding that everything was proceeding so smoothly, he came downstairs, entered the bedroom, and said:

'I've recited all four of those prayers that you asked me to say, Friar Rinaldo.'

'Brother,' said Friar Rinaldo, 'you've done an excellent job and I admire your stamina. I personally managed to recite only two before my neighbour turned up. But through our combined efforts the Lord God has granted our request, and the child is cured.'

Then the simpleton called for choice wines and sweetmeats, and regaled his neighbour and the other friar with exactly the sort of pick-me-up they needed, after which he accompanied them to the door and bade them a grateful farewell. And without any delay he had the waxen image made, and sent it to be hung with the others in front of the statue of Saint Ambrose, but not the one from Milan.*

FOURTH STORY

Tofano locks his wife out of the house one night, and his wife, having pleaded with him in vain to let her in, pretends to throw herself down a well, into which she hurls an enormous stone. Tofano emerges from the house and rushes to the well, whereupon she steals inside, bolts the door on her husband, and rains abuse upon him at the top of her voice.

No sooner did the king perceive that Elissa's story was at an end, than he turned towards Lauretta, indicating that he wanted her to speak next; and without hesitation she began as follows:

*The saint referred to in this story is not St Ambrose, but a Dominican friar of Siena, the Blessed Ambrogio Sansedoni, who was posthumously honoured by the Commune of Siena in 1288 when a chapel was devoted to his memory.

O Love, how manifold and mighty are your powers! How wise your counsels, how keen your insights! What philosopher, what artist could ever have conjured up all the arguments, all the subterfuges, all the explanations that you offer spontaneously to those who nail their colours to your mast? Every other doctrine is assuredly behindhand in comparison with yours, as may clearly be seen from the cases already brought to our notice. And to these, fond ladies, I shall now add yet another, by telling you of the expedient adopted by a woman of no great intelligence, who to my way of thinking could only have been motivated by Love.

In the city of Arezzo, then, there once lived a man of means, Tofano by name, who, having taken to wife a woman of very great beauty, called Monna Ghita, promptly grew jealous of her without any reason. On perceiving how jealous he was, the lady took offence and repeatedly asked him to explain the reason, but since he could only reply in vague and illogical terms, she resolved to make him suffer in good earnest from the ill which hitherto he had feared without cause.

Having observed that a certain young man, a very agreeable sort of fellow to her way of thinking, was casting amorous glances in her direction, she secretly began to cultivate his acquaintance. And when she and the young man had carried the affair to the point where it only remained to translate words into deeds, she once again took the initiative and devised a way of doing it. She had already discovered that one of her husband's bad habits was a fondness for drink, and so she began not only to commend him for it, but to encourage him deliberately whenever she had the chance. With a little practice, she quickly acquired the knack of persuading him to drink himself into a stupor, almost as often as she chose, and once she saw that he was blind drunk, she put him to bed and forgathered with her lover. This soon became a regular habit of theirs, and they met together in perfect safety. Indeed, the lady came to rely so completely on the fellow's talent for drinking himself unconscious that she made bold, not only to admit her lover to the premises, but on occasion to go and spend a goodly part of the night with him at his own house, which was no great distance away.

The amorous lady had been doing this for quite some time when her unfortunate husband happened to notice that although she encouraged him to drink, she herself never drank at all, which made him suspect (as was indeed the case) that his wife was making him drunk so that she could do as she pleased when he was asleep. In order to prove whether this was so, he returned home one evening, having refrained from drinking for the whole day, and pretended to be as drunk as a lord, scarcely able to speak or stand on his feet. Being taken in by all this, and concluding that he would sleep like a log without imbibing any more liquor, his wife quickly put him to bed, then left the house and made her way, as on previous occasions, to the house of her lover, where she stayed for half the night.

Hearing no sound from his wife, Tofano got up, went and bolted the door from the inside, and stationed himself at the window so that he would see her coming back and let her know that he had tumbled to her mischief; and there he remained until she returned. Great indeed was the woman's distress when she came home to find that she was locked out, and she began to apply all her strength in an effort to force the door open.

Tofano put up with this for a while, then he said:

'You're wasting your energies, woman. You can't possibly get in. Go back to wherever it is that you've been until this hour of the night, and rest assured that you won't return to this house till I've made an example of you in front of your kinsfolk and neighbours.'

Then his wife began to plead with him for the love of God to let her in, saying that she had not been doing anything wrong, as he supposed, but simply keeping vigil with a neighbour of hers, who could neither sleep the whole night because it was too long, nor keep vigil in the house by herself.

Her pleas were totally unavailing, for the silly ass was clearly determined that all the Aretines should learn about his dishonour, of which none of them had so far heard anything. And when she saw that it was no use pleading with him, the woman resorted to threats, and said:

'If you don't let me in, I shall make you the sorriest man on earth.'

To which Tofano replied:

'And how are you going to do that?'

The lady had all her wits about her, for Love was her counsellor, and she replied:

'Rather than face the dishonour which in spite of my innocence you threaten me with, I shall hurl myself into this well, and when they find me dead inside it, they will all think that it was you who threw me into it when you were drunk; and so either you will have to run away, lose everything you possess, and live in exile, or you will have your head chopped off for murdering your wife, which in effect is what you will have done.'

But having made up his stupid mind, Tofano was not affected in the slightest by these words, and so his wife said:

'Now look here, I won't let you torment me any longer; may God forgive you, I'll leave my distaff here, and you can put it back where it belongs.'

The night was so dark that you could scarcely see your hand in front of your face, and having uttered these words, the woman groped her way towards the well, picked up an enormous stone that was lying beside it, and with a cry of 'God forgive me!' she dropped it into the depths. The stone struck the water with a tremendous thump, and when Tofano heard this he was firmly convinced that she had thrown herself in. So he seized the pail and its rope, rushed headlong from the house, and ran to the well to assist her. His wife was lying in wait near the front door, and as soon as she saw him running to the well, she stepped inside the house, bolted the door, and went to the window, where she stood and shouted:

'You should water down your wine when you're drinking it, and not in the middle of the night.'

When he heard her voice, Tofano saw that he had been outwitted and made his way back to the house. And on finding that he couldn't open the door, he ordered her to let him in.

Whereas previously she had addressed him in little more than a whisper, his wife now began to shout almost at the top of her voice, saying:

'By the cross of God, you loathsome sot, you're not going to come in here tonight. I will not tolerate this conduct of yours any longer. It's time I showed people the sort of man you are and the hours you keep.'

Being very angry, Tofano too began to shout, pouring out a stream of abuse, so that the neighbours, men and women alike, hearing all this racket, got up out of bed and appeared at their windows, demanding to know what was going on.

The woman's eyes filled with tears, and she said: 'It's this villain of a man, who returns home drunk of an evening, or else he falls asleep in some tavern or other and then comes back at this hour. I've put up with it for God knows how long and remonstrated with him until I was blue in the face. But I can't put up with it any longer, and so I've decided to take him down a peg or two by locking him out, to see whether he will mend his ways.'

Tofano on the other hand, like the fool that he was, explained precisely what had happened, and came out with a whole lot of threats and abuse, whereupon his wife spoke up again, saying to the neighbours:

'You see the sort of man he is! What would you say if I were in the street and he was in the house, instead of the other way round? In God's faith I've no doubt you would believe what he was saying. So you can see what a crafty fellow he is. He accuses me of doing the very thing that he appears to have done himself. He thought he could frighten me by dropping something or other down the well; but I wish to God that he really had thrown himself in, and drowned himself at the same time, so that all the wine he's been drinking would have been well and truly diluted.'

The neighbours, men and women alike, all began to scold Tofano, putting the blame on him alone and reviling him for slandering his poor wife; and in brief, they created such an uproar that it eventually reached the ears of the woman's kinsfolk.

Her kinsfolk hurried to the scene, and having listened to the accounts of several of the neighbours, they took hold of Tofano and hammered him till he was black and blue. They then went into the house, collected all the woman's belongings, and took her back with them, threatening Tofano with worse to follow.

Seeing what a sorry plight he had landed himself in on account of his jealousy, Tofano, since he was really very fond of his wife, persuaded certain friends of his to intercede on his behalf with the lady's kinsfolk, with whom he succeeded in making his peace and arranging for her to come back to him. And not only did he promise her that he would never be jealous again, but he gave her permission to amuse herself to her heart's content, provided she was sensible enough not to let him catch her out. So, like the stupid peasant, he first was mad and then was pleasant. Long live love, therefore, and a plague on all skinflints!

FIFTH STORY

A jealous husband disguises himself as a priest and confesses his wife, by whom he is given to understand that she loves a priest who comes to her every night. And whilst the husband is secretly keeping watch for him at the front door, the wife admits her lover by way of the roof and passes the time in his arms.

Thus Lauretta brought her tale to an end, and after everyone had commended the lady for treating her reprobate husband as he deserved, the king, not wanting to waste any time, turned to Fiammetta and graciously entrusted her with the telling of the next story; and she therefore began, as follows:

Illustrious ladies, I too am prompted, after listening to the previous tale, to tell you about a jealous husband, for in my estimation they deserve all the suffering their wives may inflict upon them, especially when they are jealous without reason. And if the lawgivers had taken all things into account, I consider that in this respect the punishment they prescribed for wives should have been no different from that which they prescribe for the person who attacks another in self-defence. For no young wife is safe against the machinations of a jealous husband, who will stop at nothing to bring about her destruction.

After being cooped up for the whole week looking after the house and the family, like everyone else she yearns on Sundays for peace and comfort, and wants to enjoy herself a little, just as farm-labourers do, or the workers in the towns, or the magistrates on the bench; just as God did, in fact, when on the seventh day He rested from all His labours. And indeed, it is laid down in both canon and civil law, which aim to promote the glory of God and the common good of the people, that working days should be distinguished from days of rest. But jealous husbands will have none of this: on the contrary, when other women are enjoying their day of rest, their own wives are more wretched and miserable than ever, for they are kept more securely under lock and key; and only those poor creatures who have had to put up with this sort of treatment can describe how exhausting it all is. To sum up, therefore, no matter what a wife may do to a husband who is jealous without cause, she is surely to be commended rather than condemned.

But turning now to the story, there once lived in Rimini a very rich merchant and landowner, who, having married an exceedingly beautiful woman, became inordinately jealous of her. He had no other reason for this except that, because he loved her a great deal and thought her very beautiful and knew that she did everything she could to please him, he concluded that every other man must feel the same about her, and also that she would take just as much trouble to please other men as she did in pleasing her husband. And in his jealousy he kept such a constant watch upon her and guarded her so closely, that I doubt whether many of those condemned to death are guarded by their gaolers with the same degree of vigilance.

It wasn't just a question of her not being able to attend a party or a wedding, or go to church, or step outside her door for a single moment: he wouldn't even allow her to stand at the window or cast so much as a solitary glance outside the house. Her life thus became a complete misery, and her suffering was all the more difficult to bear in that she had done nothing to deserve it.

For her own amusement, finding herself persecuted so unfairly by her husband, the lady cast about her to see whether she could find any way of supplying him with a just and proper motive for his jealousy. Not being allowed to stand at the window, she was unable to offer signs of encouragement to any potential suitor who might be passing her way. But knowing there was a handsome and agreeable young man in the house next door, she calculated that if she could find a crack in the wall separating their two houses, she could keep on peering through it until an opportunity arose of speaking to the youth and offering him her love if he was prepared to accept it, after which, provided they could find some way of doing it, they could could come together once in a while. And in this way she could keep body and soul together until her husband came to his senses.

So when her husband was not at home, she went from room to room carefully inspecting the wall, until eventually, in a very remote part of the house, she came across a place where it was cracked. She peered through to the other side, and although she could not make very much out, she could see enough to realize that it was a bedroom, and she said to herself: 'If this turned out to be the bedroom of Filippo' (the name of the youth next door) 'there wouldn't be much left for me to do.' So she got one of her maidservants, who was feeling rather sorry for her, to keep watch whenever there was nobody about, and discovered that it was indeed the young man's bedroom, and that he slept there all by himself. By paying regular visits to the crack in the wall, and dropping tiny pieces of stone and straw through the opening whenever she could hear the young man on the other side, she eventually succeeded in getting him to come and investigate. Then she called to him in a low whisper, and the young man, recognizing her voice, replied; whereupon, since there was no likelihood of her being disturbed, she briefly told him what she had in mind. Overjoyed, the young man proceeded to widen the hole on his own side of the wall, which he did in such a way that nobody would notice, and from then on they would very often talk to each other there and touch one another's hands, though it was impossible to do more on account of the strict watch maintained by the jealous husband.

Now, seeing that Christmas was approaching, the lady told her husband that she would like, with his permission, to attend church on Christmas morning and go to confession and Holy Communion like any other Christian.

'And what sins have you committed,' said the jealous husband, 'that you want to go to confession?'

'Oh, really!' she exclaimed. 'Do you think I'm a saint, just because you keep me locked up? You know very well that I have my sins just as other people do, but I'm not going to reveal them to you, because you're not a priest.'

Her words made the husband suspicious, and he decided to try and find out what these sins were. So he granted her request, but told her that she could only go to their own chapel and not to any of the other churches. Moreover, she was to go there early in the morning, and be confessed, either by their own chaplain or by the priest whom the chaplain allotted to her, and not by anybody else, after which she was to come straight back to the house. The lady had a shrewd suspicion that it was some sort of trap, but asked no questions and replied that she would do as he wished.

On the morning of Christmas Day, the lady got up at dawn, and as soon as she was neatly dressed she went to the church her husband had specified. Meanwhile he too had risen and made his way to the same church, arriving there before she did. And having explained to the chaplain what he was proposing to do, he disguised himself in the robes of a priest, with a large hood that came down over his cheeks, like the ones that are often worn by priests; this he pulled forward a little, so as to conceal his features, then he seated himself in one of the pews.

On arriving at the church, the lady asked to speak to the chaplain. So the chaplain came, and when she told him that she wanted to be confessed, he said he was too busy, but would send her one of his fellow-priests. He then went away, and sent the jealous husband, unfortunately for him, to hear her confession. The husband walked solemnly up to her, and although the light was not very good and he had pulled the hood well down over his eyes, she knew immediately who it was, and said to herself: 'God be praised, the fellow's turned from a jealous husband into a priest; but never mind, I'll see that he gets what he's looking for.' And pretending not to recognize him, she seated herself at his feet.

Master Jealous had stuffed a few bits of gravel in his mouth so as to impede his speech and prevent his wife from recognizing his voice, and he thought that his disguise was so perfect in all other respects that she was bound to be taken in by it.

But to come now to the confession, among the things which the lady told him, having first of all pointed out that she was married, was that she had fallen in love with a priest, who came to her every night and slept with her.

When he heard this, the jealous husband felt as though a knife had been driven into his heart; and but for the fact that he was eager to know more about it, he would have abandoned the confession there and then, and taken himself off. However, he stood his ground, and said to her:

'What's this I hear? Doesn't your husband sleep with you?'

'Oh yes, Father,' she replied.

'In that case,' said the husband, 'how can the priest sleep with you as well?'

'Father,' said the lady, 'it's a mystery to me how the priest manages to do it, but there isn't a door in the house that is so securely locked that it doesn't spring open the moment he touches it. He tells me that before opening the door of my bedroom, he recites a certain formula that sends my husband straight off to sleep, and as soon as he hears him snoring, he opens the door, comes into the bedroom, and lies down at my side. And the system never fails.'

'Madam,' he said, 'this is an evil business, and you must put a stop to it at all costs.'

'Father,' said the lady, 'I don't think I could ever do that, for I love him too deeply.'

'Then I cannot give you absolution,' he said.

'I am sorry about that,' said the lady. 'But I didn't come here to tell lies, and if I thought I could do as you are asking, I should tell you so.'

'I am truly sorry for you, madam,' he said, 'for I see that your soul will be lost if this is allowed to continue. But I will do you a favour, and go to the trouble of saying certain special prayers to God on your behalf, which may possibly assist you. I shall send one of my seminarists to call on you, and you are to tell him whether or not my prayers have had any effect. And if they achieve their object, we can go on from there.'

'Oh, Father,' she said, 'don't send anyone to the house, because if my husband were to hear about it, he is so madly jealous that nothing in the world could dissuade him from believing that some great evil was afoot, and he'd be impossible to live with for a whole year.'

'Don't worry about that,' he said, 'for I shall make sure that everything is so discreetly arranged that you won't hear a word out of him.'

'If you can manage to do that,' said the lady, 'then I have no objection.' And after reciting the *Confiteor* and receiving her penance, she got up from where she was kneeling at his feet and went off to listen to the mass.

Fuming with rage, the luckless husband went away, abandoned his priestly disguise, and returned home, determined to find a way of catching this priest and his wife together, so that he could bring the pair of them to book. When his wife came back from the church, she saw from the expression on her husband's face that she had spoilt his Christmas for him; but he tried as best he could to conceal what he had done and what he thought he had discovered.

After breakfast, having made up his mind to spend the following night lying in wait near the front door to see whether the priest would turn up, he said to his wife:

'I have to go out to supper this evening, and I won't be back till the morning, so take good care to lock the front door, the landing door, and the bedroom door, and go to bed when you feel like it.'

'Very well,' said the lady.

As soon as she had the chance, she went to the hole in the wall and gave the usual signal, which Filippo no sooner heard than he came to the spot. She then gave him an account of what she had done that morning, and told him what her husband had said to her after breakfast, then she said:

'I'm certain he won't leave the house: he's just going to keep watch at the front door. So climb up on to the roof tonight and find your way in here, so that we can be together.'

The young man was delighted with this turn of events, and said:

'My lady, leave everything to me.'

As soon as it was dark, the jealous husband crept into hiding, armed to the teeth, in one of the rooms on the ground floor, and his wife, having locked all the doors, in particular the one on the landing so that her husband could not come up, bided her time in her room. When the coast was clear, the young man picked his way carefully over the roof from his own room to hers, and they got into bed, where they had a blissful time and a merry one together until dawn next morning, when he returned to his own house.

The husband, supperless, aching all over, and freezing to death, waited practically the whole night beside the front door with his weapons at the ready, to see whether the priest would turn up; and just before daybreak, being unable to keep his eyes open any longer, he dropped off to sleep in the ground-floor room.

A little before tierce he woke up to find the front door already unlocked, and pretending that he had just arrived home he went upstairs and had his breakfast. Shortly after breakfast he sent a young servant to his wife, disguised as the seminarist of the priest who had confessed her, to ask her whether 'that certain person' had called upon her again.

His wife, who recognized the messenger very easily, replied that he had failed to call for once, and that if he continued to absent himself she might very well forget all about him, although she would be sorry if this were to happen.

What more remains to be said? For night after night, the jealous husband lay in wait for the priest, and his wife lay in bed with her lover, till eventually, being unable to contain himself any longer, he flew into a tearing rage and demanded to know what his wife had said to the priest on the morning she had gone to confession. She told him that his question was neither fair nor proper, and refused to answer it, whereupon he exclaimed:

'Loathsome woman, whether you like it or not I know exactly what you said to him, and I absolutely insist on knowing the name of this priest with whom you're so infatuated and who uses magic spells to sleep with you every night, otherwise I shall slit your gullet.'

His wife told him it was untrue that she was infatuated with a priest.

'What!' he cried. 'Isn't that what you said to the priest who confessed you?'

'As a matter of fact I did,' said his wife. 'But I can't imagine how you came to be so well-informed. You must have been eavesdropping.'

'Never mind about that,' said her husband. 'Just tell me who this priest is, and be quick about it.'

His wife began to smile, and said:

'It's an edifying sight, I must say, when a mere woman leads an intelligent man by the nose, as though she were leading a ram by its horns to the slaughter. Not that you are all that intelligent, nor ever have been since the day you allowed the evil spirit of jealousy to enter your heart, without any obvious reason. And the more thick-headed and stupid you are, the lesser my achievement.

'Do you suppose, dear husband, that my eyes are as defective as your reasoning? Because if so, you're greatly mistaken. I recognized my confessor from the moment I set eyes on him, I know perfectly well it was you. I was determined to let you have what you were looking for, and I succeeded. But if you were as clever as you imagine, you would never have resorted to that sort of trick for discovering the secrets of your good little wife; nor would you have become a prey to idle suspicion, for you would have realized that she was confessing the truth to you without having sinned in the least.

'I told you I was in love with a priest: but is it not a fact that you, whom I am misguided enough to love, had turned into a priest? I told you he could open any door in the house when he wanted to come and sleep with me: but which of the doors in your own house has ever prevented you from coming to me, no matter where I happened to be? I told you the priest slept with me every night: but haven't you always slept with me? And as you know very well, every time you sent that seminarist of yours to me, you had slept elsewhere, and so I sent you word that the priest had not been with me. How could anybody, other than a man who had allowed himself to be blinded by his jealousy, have been witless enough not to understand all this? But in your case, what do you do? You spin me some yarn every evening about going out to supper and staying the night with friends, then hang about the house keeping an all-night vigil at the front door.

'Isn't it time that you took yourself in hand, started behaving like a man again, and stopped allowing yourself to be made such a fool of by someone who knows you as well as I do? Leave off keeping such a strict watch over me, because I swear to God that if I were to set my heart on making you a cuckold, I should have my fling and you'd be none the wiser.'

And so it was that the jealous wretch, having thought himself very clever in ferreting out his wife's secret, saw that he had made an ass of himself. Without saying anything by way of reply, he began to look upon his wife as a model of intelligence and virtue. And just as he had worn the mantle of the jealous husband when it was unnecessary, he cast it off completely now that his need for it was paramount. So his clever little wife, having, as it were, acquired a licence to enjoy herself, no longer admitted her lover by way of the roof as though he were some kind of cat, but showed him in at the front door. And from that day forth, by proceeding with caution, she spent many an entertaining and delightful hour in his arms.

SIXTH STORY

Whilst she is entertaining Leonetto, Madonna Isabella is visited by Messer Lambertuccio, who has fallen in love with her. Her husband returning unexpectedly, she sends Messer Lambertuccio running forth from the house with a dagger in his hand, and Leonetto is taken home a little later on by her husband.

Fiammetta's story was marvellously pleasing to the whole company, and everyone declared that the wife had taught the stupid man a most admirable lesson. But now that this tale was concluded, the king enjoined Pampinea to tell the next, and she began:

Many are those who naïvely maintain that Love impairs the intellect and that anyone falling in love is more or less turned into a fool. This, it seems to me, is a ridiculous assertion, as is amply proved by the stories we have heard so far, as well as by the one I now propose to relate.

In our fair city, where the good things of life are to be found in great abundance, there once lived a gently bred and exceedingly beautiful young woman, who was married to a nobleman of great worthiness and excellence. But just as it frequently happens that people grow tired of always eating the same food, and desire a change of diet, so this lady, being somewhat dissatisfied with her husband, fell in love with a young man called Leonetto, who, albeit his origins were humble, was extremely agreeable and accomplished. He too fell in love with her, and since it is unusual, as you know, for nothing to ensue when both of the parties are agreed, not much time elapsed before they consummated their love.

Now, because she was such a charming and beautiful woman, it happened that a gentleman called Messer Lambertuccio fell desperately in love with her, but as she thought him very tiresome and disagreeable, she could not be persuaded to love him on any account. The fellow kept pestering her with a stream of messages, however, and when these failed to have any effect, being a man of considerable influence, he threatened to ruin her if she refused to yield. Hence the lady was filled with fear and trembling, and knowing the sort of man he was, she brought herself to do his bidding. But having gone to stay, as we Florentines are apt to do in the summer, at her beautiful country villa, the lady, whose name was Madonna Isabella, sent word to Leonetto that he was to come and keep her company, since her husband had ridden off that morning, saying that he would be away for the next few days. Leonetto was overjoyed, and made his way to the villa post-haste.

Meanwhile, Messer Lambertuccio, hearing that the lady's husband was not at home, saddled his horse, rode unaccompanied to the villa, and knocked at the door.

The lady's maid, seeing who it was, immediately went to warn her mistress, who was in her bedroom with Leonetto, and having called her forth, she said:

'Messer Lambertuccio is downstairs, ma'am, and he's all alone.'

The lady was aggrieved beyond measure to hear of Lambertuccio's arrival, but as she was so afraid of him, she asked Leonetto if he would mind concealing himself for a while behind the curtains of the bed until such time as he should take his leave of her.

Leonetto, being no less terrified of the man than she was herself, hid behind the bed, and she told her maid to go and let Messer Lambertuccio in. This she did, and having ridden into the courtyard, he dismounted, tethered his palfrey to a ring, and came up the stairs. The lady came to meet him, smiling, at the head of the stairs, and having bidden him a cheerful welcome she asked him the nature of his business.

He embraced and kissed her, and said:

'My dearest, I heard that your husband was away, so I've come to keep you company for a while.' And without further preliminaries, they went into the bedroom, and Messer Lambertuccio, having locked the door, proceeded to bend her to his pleasure.

But whilst he was thus tarrying with the lady, to her utter amazement her husband happened to return. No sooner did the maid espy him approaching the villa, than she ran at once to her mistress's bedroom and said:

'It's the master, he's coming back, ma'am. He'll be down there in the yard by now, I should think.'

Finding herself with two men in the house, and knowing it was impossible to conceal the second because his horse was standing in the yard, the lady thought her hour had come. However, with extraordinary presence of mind she leapt out of bed and said to Messer Lambertuccio:

'Sir, if you love me in the slightest degree, and wish to save my life, do as I shall tell you. Take out your dagger, wave it about in your hand, and charge down the stairs like a madman, breathing fire and slaughter, and shouting: "I vow to God I'll catch up with him yet!" If my husband should try to stop you or ask you any questions, keep repeating these same words. And when you reach your horse, leap into the saddle and ride away without stopping for an instant.'

Messer Lambertuccio willingly agreed to do it, and having drawn his dagger, his face all flushed from his recent exertions, as well as from his anger at the husband's return, he carried out the lady's instructions to the letter. The husband, having already dismounted, was puzzling over the palfrey in the courtyard, and was just about to mount the stairs, when he saw Lambertuccio descending. And being taken aback by his words and the wild expression on his face, he said:

'What is the meaning of this, sir?'

But Messer Lambertuccio, having inserted his foot in the stirrup and vaulted into the saddle, uttered not a word, except: 'I swear to God I'll get him, wherever he may be!' And away he rode.

On mounting the staircase, the nobleman found his wife at the top, looking all distressed and terrified, and he said to her:

'What is going on? What has got into Messer Lambertuccio? For whom are these threats of his intended?'

Retreating towards the bedroom so that Leonetto would overhear, the lady replied:

'Oh husband, I've never had such a fright in all my life. Some young man or other came running into the house, with Messer Lambertuccio in pursuit, brandishing a dagger. He burst into my room, the door of which happened to be open, and trembling from head to foot, he said: "Madam, for God's sake save me from being killed and expiring in your arms." I stood up, and I was just about to ask him who he was and what it was all about when Messer Lambertuccio came charging up the stairs, shouting: "Blackguard, where are you?" I stood in the doorway to prevent him coming any further, and when he saw that I didn't want him to enter the room, he had the decency not to insist. And after a long rigmarole, he went rushing off down the stairs, as you saw for yourself.'

'You did the right thing, my dear,' said the husband. 'It would have been a very serious matter for us if anyone had been murdered under our own roof. And it was highly improper of Messer Lambertuccio to pursue a man who had taken refuge within these walls.'

He then asked what had become of the young man, and his wife replied:

'I have no idea where he can have hidden himself.'

So her husband called out:

'Where are you? Come on out, you're quite safe.'

Having overheard everything, Leonetto emerged from his hiding place with an expression of terror all over his features, which was not very surprising considering that he had indeed been frightened out of his wits, and the husband said to him:

'What is your business with Messer Lambertuccio?'

'Sir,' replied the young man, 'I have no business with him whatsoever, and that is why I firmly believe that he is out of his mind, or that he mistook me for somebody else, for no sooner did he see me, a little way down the road, than he drew his dagger and said: "Say your prayers, you blackguard." Without stopping to ask him the reason, I took to my heels and ran in here, where thanks to God and to this kind lady, I escaped from his clutches.'

Then the nobleman said:

'Come now, don't be afraid; I shall see you to your doorstep safe and sound, and then you can have some inquiries made, and discover what it is all about.'

After they had all had supper together, the husband conveyed the young man back to Florence on horseback, and saw him to his own front door. Later that evening, in accordance with instructions he had received from the lady, Leonetto spoke privately with Messer Lambertuccio, and so arranged matters that even though many more words were spoken on the subject, the nobleman never came to know of the trick that his wife had played upon him.

SEVENTH STORY

Lodovico discloses to Madonna Beatrice how deeply he loves her, whereupon she persuades her husband, Egano, to impersonate her in a garden, and goes to bed with Lodovico, who in due course gets up, goes into the garden, and gives Egano a hiding.

The stratagem adopted by Madonna Isabella, as recounted by Pampinea, drew gasps of astonishment from every member of the company. But the king now called upon Filomena to follow, and she said:

Lovesome ladies, unless I am much mistaken I think I can offer you no less splendid a story, which will not take long to relate.

You are to know, then, that in Paris there was once a Florentine nobleman, who on account of his straitened circumstances decided to become a merchant, in which capacity he was so successful that he made a huge fortune. His wife had borne him no more than a single child, to whom he had given the name of Lodovico, and because this child was more of a patrician's son than the son of a merchant, instead of launching him on a career in business the father had secured him a place in the French royal household, where he was brought up with other young nobles and acquired the manners and attributes of a gentleman.

One day, whilst Lodovico happened to be discussing with several other young men the rival merits of various beautiful ladies from

France, England, and other parts of the world, they were joined by a number of knights who had recently returned from the Holy Sepulchre. And one of these latter began to maintain that of all the women he had ever seen in the numerous places he had visited, he had never encountered anyone so beautiful as Madonna Beatrice, the wife of Egano de' Galluzzi, who lived in Bologna. Moreover, he claimed that those of his companions who, like himself, had seen the lady in Bologna, were entirely of the same opinion.

Having listened to this gentleman's words, Lodovico, who had never yet fallen in love, was inflamed with such a longing to see her that he could think of nothing else. And having firmly made up his mind to go to Bologna and see this lady, and to stay there for a while if she lived up to his expectations, he gave his father to understand that he wished to go to the Holy Sepulchre, and with the greatest of difficulty obtained his permission.

He therefore assumed the name of Anichino, and came to Bologna, where, as luck would have it, on the day following his arrival he saw the lady at a banquet, and discovered that her beauty was even greater than he had been led to believe. Hence he was swept completely off his feet, and resolved never to leave Bologna until he had won her love. Having given some thought to various possible ways of achieving this object, he discarded them one by one, and concluded that his only hope lay in finding employment with the lady's husband, who kept a large household of servants.

He therefore sold all his horses and arranged for his servants to be comfortably lodged, having ordered them to pretend not to know him; and having struck up an acquaintance with the landlord of his inn, he explained that he would like, if possible, to enter the service of some gentleman of standing, whereupon the landlord said:

'You are exactly the kind of attendant who would appeal to a nobleman, Egano by name, who lives in this city and keeps a great many servants. He makes a point of surrounding himself with good-looking fellows like yourself. I'll mention your name to him.'

The landlord was as good as his word, and by the time he had taken his leave of Egano, he had arranged for Anichino to enter his service, which suited Anichino down to the ground.

Now that he was living under Egano's roof, and frequently had occasion to see his lady, he began to serve his master so efficiently, and earned himself so high a place in his esteem, that Egano could do nothing without consulting him beforehand; and he placed not only his own person, but all of his affairs under Anichino's control.

Now one day Egano went out hawking, leaving Anichino at home, and Madonna Beatrice, who so far knew nothing of his love for her, albeit she had often had occasion to observe his ways and had formed a very good opinion of his character, invited him to play chess with her. Anichino, wishing to make her happy, played his pieces very skilfully and allowed her to beat him, which sent the lady into transports of joy. And when the lady's attendants, who had been watching the game, had all drifted away and left them alone together, Anichino fetched an enormous sigh.

The lady looked at him, and said:

'What's the matter, Anichino? Does it hurt you so much to be beaten?'

'My lady,' Anichino replied, 'I sighed for a much stronger reason than that.'

So the lady said:

'Alas, if I hold any place in your affection, do tell me what it is.'

At the mention of the place she held in his affection, Anichino, who loved her above everything else in the whole world, heaved a second sigh, much deeper than the first, whereupon the lady pleaded with him once again to explain the reason.

'My lady,' said Anichino, 'I am greatly afraid that you might be offended, if I were to tell you; and for all I know you might repeat it to some other person.'

'I shall certainly not take it amiss,' said the lady, 'and you may rest assured that no matter what you tell me, I shan't repeat a word of it to anyone without your permission.'

So Anichino said:

'Since you give me this assurance, I shall tell you all about it.' And controlling his tears with an effort, he told her who he was, the things he had heard about her, how and where he had fallen in love with her, how he had come to Bologna, and why he had entered her husband's service. Then he humbly asked her whether she could bring herself to take pity on him, and grant him the secret desire that burned so fiercely in his heart. But if she was unwilling to do this, he begged her to be content that he should love her, and allow him to continue in her service.

Ah, how singularly sweet is the blood of Bologna! How admirably you rise to the occasion in moments such as these! Sighs and tears were never to your liking: entreaties have always moved you, and you were ever susceptible to a lover's yearnings. If only I could find words with which to commend you as you deserve, I should never grow tired of singing your praises!

Whilst Anichino was speaking, the gentlewoman fixed her gaze upon him, and being fully convinced of his sincerity, she was so overcome by his protestations of love that she, too, began to sigh. And when her sighs had abated, she replied:

'Anichino, my dearest, be of good cheer; many are those that have wooed me, and that woo me to this day, but neither gifts nor promises nor fine words have ever succeeded in persuading me to fall in love with a single one of my admirers, whether he was a nobleman or a mighty lord or any other man; yet within the brief space of these few words of yours, you have made me feel that I belong far more to you than to myself. I consider that you have well and truly earned my love. I therefore concede it to you, and before the coming night is over, I promise that it will be yours to enjoy. In order to bring this about, see that you come to my room towards midnight. I shall leave the door open. You know the side of the bed on which I sleep: come to me there, and if I should be asleep, touch me so that I wake up, and then I shall give you the solace that you have so long desired. And to show you that I mean what I am saying, I want to give you a kiss.' Whereupon, throwing her arms round his neck, she gave him an amorous kiss, and Anichino did the like to her.

There, for the time being, the matter rested, and Anichino, having taken his leave of the lady, went off to attend to certain duties of his, ecstatically looking forward to the coming of the night. Egano returned home from his hawking, and as soon as he had supped, feeling weary, he retired to bed. The lady soon followed his example, and, as she had promised, she left the door of the bedroom ajar.

Thither, at the appointed hour, Anichino came, and having crept quietly into the room and bolted the door behind him, he made his way to the side of the bed where the lady usually slept. Placing his hand on her bosom, he found that she was not asleep, for she promptly clasped his hand between both her own, and, holding it tightly, she twisted and turned in the bed until she succeeded in waking Egano, to whom she said:

'I didn't want to say anything of this last night, because you seemed so tired; but tell me truthfully, of all the servants you have in the house, which do you regard as the finest, the most loyal, and the most deeply attached to his master?'

'My dear,' Egano replied, 'why do you ask such a question when you know very well that I have never had anyone I could trust so completely, or respect so profoundly, as I trust and respect Anichino?'

On learning that Egano had woken up, and hearing his own name being mentioned, Anichino made several attempts to withdraw his hand so that he could make good his escape, for he strongly suspected that the lady was going to give him away. But she was clasping his hand so firmly that it was impossible for him to retrieve it.

'I'll tell you why,' said the lady, in reply to Egano's question. 'My own opinion of Anichino was the same as yours; I too considered him the most faithful of your servants. But he has undeceived me, for yesterday, when you were out hawking and he stayed behind, he had the impudence, thinking it a good opportunity, to propose that I should minister to his pleasures. And so that I should have no diffi-culty in providing you with tangible and visible evidence of all this, I gave him my consent and told him that I would go into the garden, shortly after midnight, and wait for him at the foot of the pine-tree. I personally have no intention of going there, of course: but if you desire to know what a trustworthy servant he is, you can easily slip into one of my skirts, cover your head in a veil, and go down there to see whether he turns up, as I am certain he will.'

'I must certainly look into this,' said Egano. So he got out of bed, and, groping around in the darkness, he struggled into one of his wife's skirts as best he could and covered his head in a veil. Then he made his way down to the garden and stood at the foot of the pine-tree, waiting for Anichino to turn up.

As soon as she heard him leaving the bedroom, the lady got up and bolted the door from the inside.

After experiencing the biggest fright that he had ever had in his life, and struggling with all his might to free himself from the lady's grasp, and silently heaping a hundred thousand curses upon the lady and upon himself for loving her and trusting her, Anichino was positively overjoyed when, at the end of it all, he saw what she had done. As soon as the lady had returned to her bed, she urged him to strip off his clothes and get in beside her, and there they lay for quite some time together, to their mutual pleasure and delight.

When the lady thought it was time for Anichino to go, she persuaded him to get up and put on his clothes, saying:

'My darling treasure, find yourself a good stout stick and go down to the garden. Make it appear that you were putting my fidelity to the test, pretend to think that Egano is me, shower him with abuse, and give him a sound thrashing with the stick. Just think of the wonderful joy and amusement it'll bring to us both!'

So Anichino got up and made his way to the garden with a switch of silver willow in his hand, and just as he was approaching the pine-tree, Egano, seeing him coming, stood up and came to meet him, as though with the intention of bidding him a most cordial welcome. But Anichino said:

'So you came after all, did you, you filthy little whore? You thought me capable of wronging my master, did you? A thousand curses upon you!' And raising his stick, he began to beat him.

On hearing this outburst and catching sight of the stick, Egano took to his heels without saying a word, being closely pursued by Anichino, who kept on saying:

'Take that, you shameless hussy, and may God punish you as you deserve! Mark my words, I shall tell Egano of this tomorrow!'

Bruised and battered all over, Egano returned as fast as he could to his bedroom, and his wife asked him whether Anichino had come to the garden.

'Would to God that he hadn't,' said Egano, 'for he mistook me for you, beat me black and blue with a cudgel, and addressed me by the foulest names that any wicked woman was ever called. I must say I thought it very strange that he should have spoken to you as he did with the intention of dishonouring me. But I see now that, finding you so gay and sociable, he simply wanted to put you to the test.'

Then the lady said:

'Thanks be to God that he tested me with words, and saved his deeds for you! At least it can be said that his words tried my patience less severely than his deeds tried yours. But since he is so loyal to you, we should do him honour and hold him high in our esteem.'

'I agree with you entirely,' said Egano.

In view of what had happened, Egano came to the conclusion that he was blessed with the most faithful wife and the most loyal servant that any nobleman had ever possessed. And for this reason, whilst on many a future occasion they all three had a good laugh over the events of that particular night, at the same time it became far easier than it would otherwise have been for Anichino and the lady to do the thing that brought them pleasure and delight, at any rate for as long as Anichino chose to remain with Egano in Bologna.

EIGHTH STORY

A husband grows suspicious of his wife, and discovers that her lover comes to her at night, forewarning her of his arrival by means of a string attached to her toe. Whilst the husband is giving chase to the lover, his wife gets out of bed and puts another woman in her place, who receives a beating from the husband and has her tresses cut off. The husband then goes to fetch his wife's brothers, who, on discovering that his story is untrue, subject him to a torrent of abuse.

Filomena's listeners were all of the opinion that Madonna Beatrice had adopted a curiously subtle means of duping her husband, and everyone declared that Anichino must have had a terrible fright when the lady was holding him so tightly and he heard her saying that he had made advances to her. The king, however, seeing that Filomena had finished, turned to Neifile and said:

'Now it's your turn.'

Neifile smiled a little, then began:

Fair ladies, if I am to entertain you with a story as excellent as the ones with which you have been regaled by my predecessors, my task will indeed be difficult; but I hope, with God's aid, to give a good account of myself.

You are to know, then, that in our fair city there once lived a very rich merchant called Arriguccio Berlinghieri, who, like many of his counterparts of the present day, foolishly decided to marry into the aristocracy, and took to wife a young gentlewoman, quite unsuited to him, whose name was Monna Sismonda. And since, as is commonly the way with merchants, he was always going out and about and rarely stayed at home with his wife, she fell in love with a young man called Ruberto, who had been courting her for some little time.

Having become his mistress, she took such a delight in his company that she possibly grew a little careless, for Arriguccio, either because he had got wind of the affair or for some other reason, suddenly became exceedingly jealous, and, having stopped going out and about, he left all his other affairs hanging in abeyance, and devoted almost the whole of his time to keeping her under close surveillance. Nor would he ever drop off to sleep until he saw that she was safely abed. Consequently the lady was utterly mortified, because it was now quite impossible for her to be with her Ruberto.

But having given a great deal of thought to devising some means of consorting with her lover, and being under constant pressure from Ruberto himself to find a way out of this impasse, she eventually hit upon the following expedient: since her bedroom overlooked the street, and she had frequently had occasion to observe that Arriguccio, once he was asleep, slept like a log, she would ask Ruberto to come to the front door towards midnight and she would go and let him in. In this way she could spend some time in his arms whilst her husband was soundly asleep. But so that she would know that he had come, she contrived, in such a way that nobody would notice, to dangle a length of string from the bedroom window with its end almost touching the ground; at its other end, the string ran along the floor of the room to the bed, finishing up under the bedclothes, and as soon as she was in bed, she tied it to her big toe.

Ruberto was duly informed beforehand, and she further directed him that, on arriving at the house, he was to give the string a tug, and if her husband was asleep, she would release it and go downstairs to let him in; but if her husband was still awake, she would hold on to the string and haul it in, to let him know that he was to go away. This arrangement suited Ruberto down to the ground, and he made regular use of it, sometimes being able to see her and sometimes not.

They continued to use this ingenious device until one night, when the lady was asleep, Arriguccio happened to stretch his leg down the bed and catch his foot in the string. Having groped for it with his hand and discovered that it was attached to the lady's toe, he said to himself: 'This must clearly be some devilish trick or other.' And when he perceived that the string passed out by the window, he was quite convinced of it; so he gently detached it from the lady's toe, tied it to his own, and waited, alert and vigilant, to see what would happen.

Shortly afterwards, Ruberto came along and jerked the string as usual, giving Arriguccio a start. He had not tied it on properly, and so Ruberto, who had given it a good tug and was left with the string in his hands, assumed that he was to wait, which is what in fact he did.

Arriguccio, having leapt out of bed and buckled on his sword and dagger, rushed to the door to find out who this fellow was, and do him an injury. Now, for all that he was a merchant, Arriguccio was as strong and as fierce as a bull, and in opening the door he made a lot of noise, whereas his wife always opened it quietly. On hearing this, Ruberto, as he waited outside, rightly concluded that the person opening the door was Arriguccio, and so he promptly took to his heels, with Arriguccio in hot pursuit.

Eventually, after running for quite a while without shaking off his pursuer, Ruberto, who was also armed, drew his sword and faced about; and so they began to fight, with Arriguccio attacking and Ruberto defending himself.

Meanwhile, Arriguccio's wife, having woken up as he opened the door of the bedroom, had no sooner found that the string was missing than she realized that her stratagem had been discovered, and on hearing Arriguccio giving chase to Ruberto, she leapt out of bed. Foreseeing what was likely to happen, she summoned her maid, who knew all about the affair, and prevailed upon her to take her own place in the bed, at the same time entreating her to keep her identity a secret and patiently bear all the blows that Arriguccio might give her, for which service she would be so well rewarded that she would have no cause for complaint. And after extinguishing the light that was burning in the bedroom, she went away and concealed herself in another part of the house, and waited to see what would happen.

On hearing Arriguccio and Ruberto fighting with one another, the people living nearby rose from their beds and began to curse and swear at them; and so Arriguccio, for fear of being recognized, broke off the engagement and reluctantly made his way home, seething with anger, having failed either to identify the young man or to injure him in the slightest. And on reaching the bedroom, he began to shout and rave, saying:

'Where are you, strumpet? You thought you'd get away from me by putting out the light, did you? Well, you'd better think again!'

Then, going up to the bed, he took hold of the maidservant, thinking her to be his wife, and kicked and punched her with all the power he had in his feet and hands, until her face was black and blue all over, at the same time addressing her by the foulest names that an unchaste woman was ever called; and finally, he cut off her hair.

The maidservant wept bitterly, and with good reason, but although from time to time she cried out, saying 'Alas, for God's sake have mercy!' or 'Oh, please, no more!' her speech was so distorted by her sobbing, and Arriguccio was so demented with rage, that he failed to notice that the voice was not his wife's.

Having given her an unholy thrashing and cut off her hair, as we have already mentioned, he said:

'Vile hussy, I'll not soil my hands with you any further, but I shall go seek out your brothers and tell them about the fine way you behave. Furthermore, I shall tell them to come and deal with you as their honour requires, and take you away from here, because you're certainly not going to stay in this house any longer.' And having spoken these words, he stormed out of the room, bolted the door on the outside, and strode off, all alone, into the night.

Monna Sismonda had been listening the whole time, and as soon as she heard her husband leaving the house, she opened the bedroom door and re-lit the lamp, to discover her maidservant lying there, all bruised and battered, and crying her eyes out. Having consoled her as best she could, she led the girl back to her own room, where she covertly arranged for her to be nursed back to health and waited upon, and rewarded her so handsomely from Arriguccio's own coffers that the girl was more than contented.

No sooner was the maid safely bestowed in her room than Monna Sismonda returned, remade the bed, and tidied up the whole room so as to make it look as if no one had slept there. Having re-lit the main lamp, she dressed herself and combed her hair to give the impression that she had not yet gone to bed, then she lit another lamp, which she took out on to the landing with some of her sewing. She then sat down and began to sew, and waited to see how things would develop.

On leaving the house, Arriguccio had hurried round to his wife's brothers' house as fast as his legs would carry him, and hammered away at the door until someone came to let him in. Hearing that it was Arriguccio, the lady's three brothers and her mother got up out of bed, called for lights to be lit, and came down to ask him what had brought him to see them, all alone, at that hour of the night.

Arriguccio gave them a full account of all that he had found and all that he had done, beginning with his discovery of the string attached to Monna Sismonda's toe; and in order to prove his story beyond any shadow of a doubt, he handed over the hair which he had cut off (or so he thought) from his wife's head, adding that they were to come and fetch her and deal with her according to the dictates of their family honour, as he had no intention of permitting her to darken his doorstep again.

The lady's brothers, who believed every word of his story, were exceedingly angry, and, calling for torches to be lit, they set forth with Arriguccio and made their way to his house, determined to punish her severely. On seeing how incensed they were against her daughter, the mother burst into tears and began to follow them, pleading with each of them in turn not to be taken in so quickly by everything they heard without looking further into the matter. She pointed out that the husband might have some other reason for losing his temper and knocking her about, and that he might have trumped up these charges against her as a cover for his own misdeeds. Moreover, she was astonished that such a thing could have happened, knowing her daughter as she did, and having brought her up herself

from her infancy. And she made a great many more observations, all
of them in similar vein.

On arriving at Arriguccio's house, they all went inside and began
to ascend the stairs, and Monna Sismonda, hearing them coming,
called out:

'Who is it?'

Whereupon one of her brothers replied:

'You'll find out soon enough who it is, you brazen hussy.'

And so Monna Sismonda said:

'What can be the meaning of this? Good Lord, deliver us.' And
rising to her feet, she added:

'Brothers, how nice to see you. But what can have brought the
three of you here at this hour of the night?'

When they saw her sitting there with her sewing, and without a
mark on her face albeit Arriguccio had claimed that he had beaten
her black and blue all over, her brothers were somewhat taken aback,
and the vehemence of their anger was diminished. But having recovered from the initial shock, they demanded an explanation of
the complaint that Arriguccio had laid against her, threatening to
deal with her severely if she told them any lies.

'I don't know what I'm supposed to tell you,' said the lady, 'nor
do I know why Arriguccio should have complained to you about me.'

Arriguccio could do nothing but gape at her as though he had lost
his wits, for he could remember having punched her times without
number about the face, scratched it well and truly, and given her the
biggest hiding imaginable, yet as far as he could tell she bore no trace
whatever of all this.

But to cut a long story short, her brothers told her what Arriguccio
had said, mentioning the string and the thrashing he had given her
and all the other details, whereupon the lady turned to Arriguccio,
saying:

'Heavens above, husband, what is this that I hear? Why bring so
much shame upon yourself by making me out to be an adulteress,
when I am nothing of the sort, and claiming to have done something
cruel and wicked, when you haven't? You hadn't even set foot in the
house tonight until just now, let alone come anywhere near me!
When did you give me this beating? I have no recollection of it.'

'What!' exclaimed Arriguccio. 'Vile woman, did we not go to bed together this evening? Did I not return here, after giving chase to your lover? Did I not give you a hiding, and cut off your hair?'

To which his wife replied:

'You never went to bed in this house tonight. But let us leave that point aside, for I have only my own words to prove it, and take up what you said about giving me a hiding and cutting off my hair. You never gave me any hiding, as everybody here, including yourself, can see quite clearly by examining my person. Nor would I advise you ever to make so bold as to lay your hands on me, for, by the cross of God, I would deform your face for life. What's more, you never cut off my hair either, unless you did it without my noticing: let's just see now whether my hair has been cut off or not.'

And removing her veils, she displayed a fine head of hair, which showed no signs of having been trimmed.

When her brothers and her mother saw and heard all this, they rounded on Arriguccio, saying:

'What sort of a joke is this, Arriguccio? This doesn't correspond in the least to what you came and told us, and you're going to have a job to prove the rest of your story.'

Arriguccio stood transfixed, as if he were in a trance. Although he was bursting to speak, on seeing there was no truth in the very thing he thought he could prove, he made no attempt to say anything.

So the lady turned back to her brothers, and said:

'I see now, brothers, what his intentions were: he wanted me to tell you about the wicked and scoundrelly way he behaves, which is a subject I have never had any desire to discuss, but now I shall do so. I firmly believe that his story is true, that he did all the things he was telling you about, and that what happened was this:

'The worthy gentleman, to whom I had the misfortune to be given by you in marriage, who calls himself a merchant and wants people to think that he is more temperate than a monk and more chaste than a virgin (as indeed he should be) goes carousing nearly every night in the taverns, and consorting with one harlot after another; and meanwhile I have to sit here, as you found me when you arrived, and wait up half the night for him, and sometimes he never comes home at all until morning. It's my belief that he got himself blind drunk and bedded down with some strumpet or other, then woke up to find the string attached to her foot, after which he performed all those brave exploits he's been telling you about, and finally returned to his doxy, beat her up, and cut off her hair. Since he was still in his cups, he believed (as I'm sure he still does) that he'd done all this to me; and if you take a good look at his face, you'll see that he is still half drunk even now. But all the same, whatever he may have said about me, I would not want you to take it as anything other than the lunatic ravings of someone who is full of Dutch courage. And since I am prepared to forgive him, you must do the same.'

Having heard what her daughter had said, the mother now began to raise a clamour, saying:

'By the cross of God, daughter, we ought to do no such thing; on the contrary, this loathsome, ungrateful cur ought to be put to death. You were far too good for him in the first place. God in Heaven, you'd think he had picked you up out of the gutter! To hell with this small-time trader in horse manure, let him take his foul slander elsewhere! These country yokels, they move into town after serving as cut-throat to some petty rustic tyrant, and wander about the streets in rags and tatters, their trousers all askew, with a quill sticking out from their backsides, and no sooner do they get a few pence in their pockets than they want the daughters of noble gentlemen and fine ladies for their wives. And they devise a coat of arms for themselves, and go about saying: "I belong to such-and-such a family" and "My people did so-and-so". If only my sons had followed my advice! They could easily have married you into the finest family in Florence, with no more than a hunk of bread for a dowry, instead of which they had to give you to this perfect jewel of a man, who has the impudence, when he's married to the most chaste and respectable girl in the city, to wake us up in the middle of the night and call you a strumpet, as if we didn't know you. God's faith! if I had anything to do with it, he'd be given such a thrashing that he'd smart for the rest of his days.'

Then, turning to her sons, she said:

'Didn't I tell you all along that it couldn't be true? Have you heard how your poor sister is treated by this precious brother-in-law of yours? He's a tuppenny-ha'penny pedlar, that's what he is! If I were in your place, after hearing what he's said about her and what he's done to her, I'd never rest content till I'd scourged him from the face of the earth. And if I were a man, and not a woman, I wouldn't allow anyone to stop me. God punish the drunken villain! He ought to be ashamed of himself!'

Angered by what they had seen and heard, the young men turned on Arriguccio and called him all the names under the sun; and by way of conclusion, they said:

'We'll let you off lightly this time, seeing that you've had too much to drink. But as you value your life, take care never to disturb us again with your nonsensical stories, because if we hear any more from you, you can rest assured we shall pay you out twice over.' And with this dire warning they departed.

Arriguccio was left standing there, gazing into space like an idiot, and not knowing whether the things he had done were real or part of a dream. However, he said no more about it, but left his wife in peace, so that not only had she kept her wits about her and avoided the immediate danger, but she had also made it possible, from then on, to enjoy herself to her heart's content without any fear of her husband.

NINTH STORY

Lydia, wife of Nicostratus, falls in love with Pyrrhus, who sets her three tasks as a proof of her sincerity. She performs all three, in addition to which she makes love to Pyrrhus in her husband's presence, causing Nicostratus to believe that his eyes have been deceiving him.

Neifile's story was so much to their liking that the ladies could not be restrained from laughing and talking about it, even though the king, who had ordered Panfilo to narrate his own tale, called upon them several times to be silent. But as soon as they were quiet, Panfilo began as follows:

Venerable ladies, it is my conviction that there is no enterprise, however perilous or difficult it may be, that those who are fervently in love will not have the courage to undertake. And although this has been proved in many of the stories we have heard, nevertheless I believe that I can prove it better still with the one I now propose to relate, in which you will hear of a lady whose deeds were far more favoured by Fortune than tempered by common sense. Consequently I would not advise any of you to take the risk of following her example, seeing that Fortune is not always so kindly disposed, and that all men are not equally gullible.

In Argos, that most ancient city of Greece, whose kings brought it universal renown out of all proportion to its size, there was once a noble lord, Nicostratus by name, upon whom, on the threshold of old age, Fortune bestowed a wife of great distinction, no less bold than she was beautiful, whose name was Lydia.

Being a wealthy patrician, Nicostratus kept a large number of servants, hawks and hounds, and was passionately fond of hunting. One of his retainers, whose name was Pyrrhus, was a sprightly and elegant young man, handsomely proportioned, and skilled in every activity he chose to pursue, and Nicostratus loved and trusted him above all others.

With this young man, Lydia fell desperately in love, to such an extent that her thoughts were fixed upon him alone at every hour of the day and night. But Pyrrhus, either failing or not desiring to notice, showed a total lack of interest in her love, which filled the lady's heart with unspeakable sorrow. But being determined at all costs to acquaint him with her feelings, she summoned a maid of hers, named Lusca, whom she was able to trust implicitly, and said to her:

'Lusca, the favours you have had from me in the past should have sufficed to earn me your loyalty and obedience, and hence you must take good care that nobody ever hears what I am about to tell you, apart from the person to whom I shall ask you to repeat it. As you can see, Lusca, I am young and vigorous, and I am well supplied with all the things a woman could desire. In short, with one exception I have nothing to complain about, and the exception is this: that my husband is much older than myself, and consequently I am ill provided with the one thing that gives young women their greatest pleasure. And because I desire this thing no less than other women, I long ago made up my mind that since Fortune has been so unkind as to give me an elderly husband, I would repair her omissions myself, and devise the means of winning solace and salvation through my own efforts. So that my enjoyment therein should be no less complete than in other matters, I have decided that our Pyrrhus, since he is more worthy of my love than any other man, should supply my needs with his embraces, and such is the love that I bear him, that I am never content except when I am gazing or musing upon him. Unless I can forgather with him very soon, I firmly believe that I shall die. And therefore, as you value my life, you must acquaint him with my love in whatever way you think best, and ask him on my behalf to favour me with his company at such time as you shall go to fetch him.'

The maidservant willingly agreed to carry out her mistress's instructions; and at the first opportunity, having taken Pyrrhus aside, she conveyed the lady's message as best she could. Pyrrhus was greatly astonished to hear it, for he had never had the slightest inkling that the lady was in love with him, and suspected that she had sent the message in order to test his loyalty. So without mincing his words, he abruptly replied:

'Lusca, I cannot believe that these words have come from my lady, so be careful of what you are saying. Even if they really did come from her, I cannot believe that she meant me to take them seriously. But if she did, I should never dream of doing such an injury to my master, who already honours me more than I deserve. So take care never to speak to me of such matters again.'

Not to be deterred by the severity of his tone, Lusca replied:

'Pyrrhus, if my mistress commands me to speak to you of these or any other matters, I shall do so as often as she tells me, whether you like it or not, and all I can say is that you are an obstinate fool.'

Feeling somewhat galled by the answer that Pyrrhus had given her, she returned to her mistress, who, on hearing the result of her mission, simply wanted to lie down and die. However, a few days later she raised the subject once more with her maidservant, and said:

'Lusca, as you know, an oak is not felled by a single blow of the axe. So it seems to me that you should return to this man, who has such a curious way of proving his loyalty at my expense, and, choosing a suitable moment, make a full declaration of my passion and do everything you can to bring this affair to a happy conclusion. For if things are left in their present state, I shall pine away and he will think I was putting his fidelity to the test, so that, whereas I want him to love me, he will end up by hating me.'

The maidservant comforted her mistress, and when she found Pyrrhus in a cheerful and agreeable mood, she said to him:

'Pyrrhus, a few days ago I told you of the ardent flames of love with which my mistress is consumed on your account, and I now assure you for the second time that if you persist in treating her so cruelly, she cannot go on living for much longer. I therefore appeal to you to lay aside your scruples, and grant her the solace she desires. I have always thought you very sensible, but if you carry this stubbornness of yours any further, I shall begin to think you're a blockhead. What greater honour could you have than to be loved above all else by so noble and beautiful and wealthy a lady as this? Don't you realize how fortunate you are, to be offered so pleasant a remedy to the cravings of your youth, and so secure a refuge from all your material needs? Which of your equals will lead a more blissful life than your own, if only you will see reason? Which of them will you find so abundantly supplied with arms and horses, or with clothes and money, if only you will grant her your love?

'Open your heart to my appeals, and return to your senses. Remember how seldom it happens that Fortune greets the same man twice with smiling face and open arms! If such a man should fail to grasp her bounty with both hands, and later suffer poverty and distress, he will only have himself to blame, not Fortune. And another thing: the loyalty of servants to their masters is quite a different matter from the loyalty of friends and equals. In fact, so far as it lies within their power, servants should treat their masters no differently from the way their masters treat them. If you had a beautiful wife, or mother or daughter or sister, and Nicostratus took a liking to her, do you honestly think he would bother his head, as you are doing, with notions of loyalty? More fool you, if that is what you believe; for you can rest assured that if flattery and coaxing proved ineffectual, he would take her by force, and you'd be powerless to stop him. So let us treat them and their belongings as they would treat us and ours. Make the most of Fortune's blessings; don't spurn the lady, go out and meet her half-way, for you may be sure that if you fail to do so, not only will you bring about the certain death of your mistress, but you will reproach yourself so often for it that you too will want to die.'

Having already reflected at length on Lusca's original message, Pyrrhus had made up his mind that if she were to approach him again on the subject, his answer would be different, and he would do all in his power to please the lady, provided it could be proved that she was not simply putting his loyalty to the test. And so he replied as follows:

'Look here, Lusca, I agree with everything you say, but on the other hand I know my master to be very wise and very shrewd, and now that he has entrusted me with the conduct of all his affairs, I strongly suspect that Lydia is doing this with his advice and encouragement, so as to put me to the test. But if she will do three things to reassure me, she can count on me in future to do whatever she asks without a moment's hesitation. The three things I want her to do are these: first, she must kill Nicostratus' favourite sparrowhawk before his very eyes; second, she must send me a tuft of Nicostratus' beard; and lastly, she must send me one of the best teeth he has left in his jaw.'

These terms seemed harsh to Lusca and well nigh impossible to the lady. But Love, that great comforter and excellent teacher of guile, bolstered her resolve, and through her maidservant she sent him word that she would carry out all of his demands to the letter, and without undue delay. Moreover, since Pyrrhus seemed to think Nicostratus so intelligent, she informed him that she would make love to Pyrrhus under the old man's nose, and then persuade Nicostratus that he was suffering from hallucinations.

Pyrrhus therefore waited to see what the lady would do, and a few days later, when Nicostratus was entertaining certain gentlemen to a sumptuous banquet, this being a regular practice of his, the tables had no sooner been cleared away than Lydia issued forth from her chamber, wearing a dress of green velvet and a splendid array of jewels, and strode majestically into the hall where the gentlemen were. In full view of Pyrrhus and all the others, she then went up to the perch where the sparrowhawk, so greatly prized by Nicostratus, was standing, unhooked its chain as though intending to take it on her hand, and having seized it by the jesses, dashed its head against the wall and killed it.

Nicostratus yelled at her, saying: 'For pity's sake, woman, what have you done?' but she ignored him, and turning instead to the gentlemen with whom he had been dining, she said: 'Gentlemen, even if a king were to insult me, I should be hard put to avenge myself if I hadn't the courage to take my revenge on a sparrowhawk. I should like you to know that for some little time, this bird has been depriving me of all the attention that men should devote to their ladies' pleasure; for Nicostratus gets up every morning at the crack of dawn, mounts his horse, and with his sparrowhawk perched on his hand, he rides away to the open plains in order to watch it fly, leaving me, such as you see me, alone and ill content in my bed. Hence I have often longed to do the thing I have done just now, and all I was waiting for was an opportunity to do it in the presence of men who would judge my cause impartially, as I trust you gentlemen will.'

Supposing that her affection for Nicostratus was no less profound than her words appeared to imply, all the gentlemen started to laugh. And turning to Nicostratus, who was flushed with anger, they said:

'Well, well! How right the lady was to avenge her wrongs by killing the sparrowhawk!' And by dint of various witty remarks on the subject (the lady having meanwhile returned to her chamber), they converted Nicostratus' rage into laughter.

Pyrrhus, who had witnessed the whole of this episode, said to himself: 'The lady has set my love on a firm and noble footing. God grant that she may persevere, and thus conduct it to a happy conclusion.'

Having killed the sparrowhawk, Lydia bided her time, and a few days later, being closeted in her chamber with Nicostratus, she began to caress him and tease him, and he took her playfully by the hair, giving it a gentle pull. This provided her with the chance to fulfil the second of Pyrrhus' demands, and she promptly took hold of a small tuft of his beard, and, laughing the whole time, jerked it with so much violence that it came away entirely from his chin. When Nicostratus began to protest, she interrupted him, saying:

'What's the matter? Why do you pull such a face just because I've plucked some half-dozen hairs from your beard? I can't possibly have hurt you as much as you hurt me, when you were tugging at my hair just now.'

And so they continued jesting and sporting with one another, and the lady, having carefully preserved the tuft she had removed from his beard, sent it that same day to her beloved.

The third demand presented a rather more difficult problem, but Love had greatly sharpened the lady's wits, and since she was no dullard in the first place, she had already thought of a way of fulfilling it.

Now, Nicostratus had two young boys in his household, who, since they came of noble stock, had been entrusted to his care by their fathers so that they might learn good manners, and when Nicostratus was at table, one of them carved his meat whilst the other poured out his drink. Having sent for these two boys, the lady gave them to understand that they suffered from bad breath, and instructed them that, whenever they were waiting upon Nicostratus, they should hold their heads as far to one side as possible; but they were not to mention this matter to anyone.

The boys believed her, and began to do as the lady had told them, so that eventually she took Nicostratus aside, and said to him:

'Have you noticed what these boys do when they are waiting upon you?'

'I have indeed,' said Nicostratus, 'and in fact, I've been meaning to ask them why they do it.'

Whereupon the lady said:

'There's no need: I can tell you the reason. I've been keeping it to myself for ages as I didn't want to upset you, but now that others have begun to notice, it's time that you were told. All that's wrong is that you suffer from appallingly bad breath, and I've no idea why this should be, because you never used to have it. However, it is quite repulsive, and seeing that you have to consort with people of quality, we shall have to find some way of curing it.'

'What could be causing it, I wonder?' said Nicostratus. 'Can it be that one of my teeth is rotten?'

'That's quite possible,' said Lydia. Whereupon, having taken him over to a window, she got him to open his mouth, and after carefully inspecting both sides of his jaw, she exclaimed:

'Oh, Nicostratus, how can you have endured it for so long? There's a tooth over here, on this side of your mouth, that as far as I can see is not only decayed, but rotten to the very core, and if it stays there much longer it will certainly contaminate the ones on either side of it. I advise you to have it out, before the damage grows worse.'

'If that is your advice, I shall act upon it,' said Nicostratus. 'Send at once for a surgeon to come and take it out.'

'Heaven forbid,' replied the lady, 'that we should bother with a surgeon in a trifling matter of this sort. I feel quite capable of taking it out for you myself. Besides, these surgeons are quite barbaric when it comes to extracting people's teeth, and I couldn't possibly bear to see you suffering under the hands of any one of them. No, I absolutely insist on doing it myself, and then at least, if you're in too much pain, I shall stop at once, whereas a surgeon would take no notice.'

So she sent for the necessary implements, and cleared everybody out of the room except Lusca. She then locked the door, persuaded Nicostratus to lie down on a table, and, inserting the pincers in his mouth, clapped them to one of his teeth. And though he screamed with pain, one of the women held him firmly down whilst the other, employing all the manual strength she possessed, extracted the tooth, which she promptly hid away, replacing it with another, horribly decayed, that she had been holding in her hand. This she showed to Nicostratus, who was writhing in agony and very nearly half dead, saying:

'Just take a look at this tooth that you've been carrying around in your mouth for all this time.'

Nicostratus was completely taken in, and although the pain had been quite excruciating and he was rending the air with his plaints, nevertheless, now that the tooth was out, it seemed to him that he felt much better. And when they had soothed and mollified him, and the pain had abated, he got up and went away.

Taking up the tooth, the lady sent it forthwith to her lover, who, being by now convinced of her love, declared that he was ready to minister to all her pleasures. But the lady wished to reassure him still further, and albeit she could hardly wait for him to take her in his arms, she was determined to keep the promise she had given him. She therefore pretended to be ill, and one day, when Nicostratus came to visit her after breakfast, attended only by Pyrrhus, she asked him whether they would help her down to the garden so as to relieve the tedium of her sick-bed. So they conveyed her to the garden, Nicostratus supporting her on one side and Pyrrhus on the other, and set her down on a lawn at the foot of a beautiful pear-tree. And after sitting there together for a while, she turned to Pyrrhus, to whom she had sent word beforehand of what he was to do, and said:

'Pyrrhus, I long to have one or two of those pears. Climb the tree and throw some of them down.'

Pyrrhus, having swiftly clambered up, began to throw down some of the pears, and as he was doing so, he called out to Nicostratus, saying:

'For shame, sir, what are you doing? And you, my lady, how can you be so brazen as to allow it in my presence? Do you think I am blind? Until a moment ago you were very ill; how can you have recovered so rapidly? If you wanted to indulge in that sort of thing, you have plenty of fine bedrooms in the house – why don't you go and do it in one of those? It would surely be more seemly than doing it here in my presence.'

The lady turned to her husband, and said:

'What's Pyrrhus talking about? Is he quite mad?'

Whereupon Pyrrhus said:

'I'm not mad, my lady. Do you think I can't see you?'

Nicostratus gaped at him in blank astonishment, and said:

'Why, Pyrrhus, I think you must be dreaming.'

'No, my lord,' he replied, 'I am wide awake, and so are you, it appears. In fact, you're putting so much vigour into it that if this tree were to be given so hard a buffeting, there wouldn't be a single pear left on it.'

'What can this mean?' said the lady. 'Can he really be seeing what he professes to be seeing? Heaven help me, if only I were fit and strong, I should climb up there and see for myself what these marvels are that he claims to be witnessing.'

Meanwhile, Pyrrhus continued to pour forth a stream of similar remarks from his vantage-point in the pear-tree, until eventually Nicostratus ordered him to come down. And when he had reached the ground, Nicostratus said:

'What is it you claim to be seeing?'

'I do believe,' said Pyrrhus, 'that you take me for an idiot or a lunatic. Since you force me to speak, I saw you lying on top of your lady, and as soon as I started to descend, you got up and sat in the spot where you are sitting now.'

To which Nicostratus replied:

'You are certainly behaving like an idiot, for we haven't moved in the slightest since you climbed up the tree.'

'What's the use of arguing about it?' said Pyrrhus. 'I can only repeat that I saw you, and you were going to it merrily.'

Nicostratus grew visibly more astonished, until finally he said:

'I'm going to find out for myself whether this pear-tree is enchanted, and what kind of marvels you can see from its branches.' So up he climbed, and no sooner had he done so than Pyrrhus and his lady began to make love together, whereupon Nicostratus, seeing what they were about, shouted:

'Ah, vile strumpet, what are you doing? And you, Pyrrhus, after all the trust I placed in you!' And so saying, he began to climb down again.

'We are just sitting here quietly,' said Pyrrhus and the lady. But on seeing him descending, they returned to their former places. No sooner had Nicostratus descended and found them sitting where he had left them than he began to shower them with abuse.

'Why Nicostratus,' said Pyrrhus, 'I must confess that you were right after all, and that my eyes were deceiving me when I was up in the tree. My only reason for saying this is that I know for a fact that you too have had a similar illusion. If you think I am wrong, you have only to stop and reflect whether a woman of such honesty and intelligence as your good lady, even if she wished to stain your honour in this manner, would ever bring herself to do it before your very eyes. Of myself I say nothing, except that I would sooner allow myself to be drawn and quartered than even contemplate such an act, let alone do it in your presence. Hence it is quite obvious that whatever it is that is distorting our vision, it must emanate from the pear-tree. For nothing in the world would have dissuaded me from believing that you had lain here carnally with your lady, until I heard you claiming that I had apparently been doing something which I most certainly never did, nor even thought of doing for a moment.'

At this point, he was interrupted by the lady, who rose to her feet and said to her husband, in tones of considerable annoyance:

'The devil take you if you have such a low opinion of me as to suppose that, had I wanted to comport myself as scandalously as you claim to have seen, I should do it before your very eyes. You may rest assured that if I should ever feel the urge to do it, I shouldn't do it out here in the garden. On the contrary, I'd find myself a nice, comfortable bed, and arrange the whole thing so discreetly that if you ever got to know about it I should be very much surprised.'

Nicostratus now felt that they must both be speaking the truth, and that they could never have brought themselves to do such a thing in his presence. So he ceased his shouting and raving, and began to talk about the strangeness of the thing, and about the miraculous way in which a man's eyesight could be affected by climbing a tree.

But the lady pretended to be angry because of the aspersions that Nicostratus seemed to have cast on her character and intelligence, and she said:

'This pear-tree will certainly never bring shame upon me or any other woman again if I can help it. Run and fetch an axe, Pyrrhus, and, at one and the same time, avenge us both by chopping it down, though in point of fact it would be much better to cleave Nicostratus' skull with the axe for allowing the eyes of his intellect to be blinded so easily. For however much your eyes may have borne out what you were saying, Nicostratus, you should never have allowed your mind to accept it, or even to entertain the idea for a moment.'

So Pyrrhus very quickly went to fetch the axe, and chopped the pear-tree down. And no sooner was it felled than the lady turned to Nicostratus, saying:

'Now that I have seen the fall of my honour's adversary, all my anger has departed.'

Then, as Nicostratus was pleading with her to forgive him, she graciously consented to do so, bidding him never again to harbour such ignoble thoughts about his lady, who loved him more dearly than herself.

And so the poor deluded husband returned with her and her lover to the palace, within whose walls it thenceforth became easier for Pyrrhus and Lydia to meet, at regular intervals, for their common delight and pleasure. May God grant that we enjoy a similar fate!

TENTH STORY

Two Sienese fall in love with a woman of whose child one of them is the godfather. This man dies, returns to his companion from the afterworld in fulfilment of a promise he had given him, and describes what people do there.

All that now remained was for the king to tell his story, and as soon as he perceived that the ladies had stopped mourning over the fate of the innocent pear-tree, he began:

It goes without saying that a just king must be the first to observe those laws that he has himself prescribed, and that, if he fails to do so, he deserves rather to be punished as a slave than honoured as a king. And yet, almost of necessity, it now behoves me, as your king, to commit precisely this error and thus incur your censure. Yesterday evening, when I decreed the form that our discussions of today were to take, I fully intended to forego my privilege for once, submit to the same rule as yourselves, and address myself to the theme upon which you have all been speaking. But the story I was proposing to relate has now been told; and moreover, the subject has been so extensively and admirably discussed, that for my own part, however much I cudgel my brains, I cannot think of anything to say on this topic that will stand comparison with the things already said. Since, therefore, being obliged to infringe the law which I myself have made, I am worthy of punishment, I shall straightway declare that I am ready to make whatever amends may be required of me, and fall back upon my customary privilege.

Taking my cue, dearest ladies, from Elissa's compelling account of the godfather and the mother of his godchild, as well as from the extraordinary simplicity of the Sienese, I shall tell you a little tale about them, which has nothing to do with the tricks played by clever wives on their foolish husbands, but which, albeit much of it will strain your credulity, should nevertheless prove entertaining in parts.

There once lived, in the Porta Salaia district of Siena, two young men of the people, called Tingoccio Mini and Meuccio di Tura, who nearly always went about together and who, to all outward appearances, were quite devoted to one another. Being in the habit, like other folk, of going to church and listening to sermons, they had frequently heard about the glory and the suffering that awaited the souls of the dead, each according to his merits, in the world to come. But since they wanted to find out for certain about these matters, and could think of no other way of doing it, they promised one another that whichever of them died first would return, if possible, to the one who was still alive, and give him all the information he wanted; and they sealed this compact with a solemn oath.

Not long after making this promise, whilst the pair of them were still going about together in the way we have described, Tingoccio happened to become godfather to the infant son of a man called Ambruogio Anselmini, who lived with his wife, Monna Mita, in the district of Camporeggi.

Now, this Monna Mita was a woman of great beauty and attractiveness, and notwithstanding his sponsorship of the child, Tingoccio, who called to see her every now and then with Meuccio, fell in love with her. But he was not the only one, for Meuccio, having heard Tingoccio singing her praises and finding her very attractive, also fell in love with her. Neither man spoke to the other about his love for the lady, but each for a different reason. Tingoccio took care not to say anything to Meuccio because he had a guilty conscience about falling in love with the mother of his godchild, and would have been ashamed to have anyone know about it. But Meuccio kept it to himself for quite another reason, namely, that he realized how fond Tingoccio was of her, and therefore said to himself: 'If I take him into my confidence, he will be jealous of me; and since he is her child's godfather, and can talk to her whenever he likes, he will do his best to turn her against me, with the result that I shall never get anywhere with her.'

Things remained much as we have described them, with the two young men pining away for Monna Mita, until Tingoccio, who was in a better position to open his heart to the lady, played his cards so skilfully that he obtained what he wanted from her – a circumstance that did not escape the notice of Meuccio, who was anything but pleased about it. However, since he was hoping that his own desires would one day find fulfilment, and was anxious not to provide Tingoccio with the slightest cause to ruin his chances or interfere in any way with his plans, he pretended to know nothing.

And there, for the time being, the matter rested, Tingoccio being luckier than his comrade in his love for the lady. But the richness of the soil in Monna Mita's garden inspired Tingoccio to dig it over with so much energy and zeal that he contracted a fever from his labours, which left him so enfeebled that within the space of a few days, being unable to shake it off, he departed this life.

On the night of the third day after his unfortunate demise (being unable, perhaps, to make it any sooner), he kept his promise and appeared to Meuccio, who was lying in bed fast asleep. Tingoccio called out to him, and Meuccio woke up with a start, saying:

'Who are you?'

'I am Tingoccio,' he replied, 'and I have returned, as I promised, to bring you tidings of the other world.'

Having recovered from the shock of seeing him, Meuccio said:

'My brother, you are welcome.'

He then asked him whether, as he put it, he was 'lost', and Tingoccio replied:

'Lost? If a thing is lost, it can't be found; so what on earth would I be doing here, if I was lost?'

'That's not what I mean,' said Meuccio. 'What I want to know is whether you're among the souls of the damned, in the scourging fires of Hell.'

'Not exactly,' replied Tingoccio. 'But I'm being severely punished just the same, because of the sins I committed, and it's all very painful.'

Then Meuccio questioned him in detail about the punishments that were meted out there for each of the sins committed on earth, and Tingoccio described them one by one. And when Meuccio went on to ask him whether there was anything he could do for him, Tingoccio replied in the affirmative, saying that he should arrange for prayers and masses to be recited on his behalf, and for alms to be given, since these things were highly beneficial to the souls of the dead. All of this Meuccio readily agreed to do.

Just as Tingoccio was leaving, Meuccio remembered about Monna Mita, and raising his head a little, he said:

'By the way, Tingoccio: what punishment have they given you for making love to the mother of your godchild?'

Whereupon Tingoccio replied:

'My brother, as soon as I arrived down there, I was met by one who seemed to know all of my sins by heart, and who ordered me to proceed to the place where I am being severely punished for my misdeeds. There I found a large company of souls condemned to the same punishment as myself, and as I stood in their midst, I suddenly remembered how I had carried on with my godchild's mother. And since I was expecting to have to pay a much heavier penalty for this than the one I had been given, I began, even though I was being roasted in a fierce and enormous fire, to tremble all over with fear. On noticing this, one of my fellow sinners said: "Why do you tremble so when standing in the fire? Have you done something worse than the rest of us?" "Oh, my friend," said I, "it fills me with terror when I think of the judgement that awaits me for a dreadful sin I have committed." He then asked me which sin I was referring to, and I said: "I made love to the mother of my godchild, and went to it so heartily that I shed my pelt in the process." He had a good laugh over this, and said: "Be off with you, you fool! There's nothing special down here about the mother of a godchild." I was so relieved to hear it that I could have wept.'

The dawn was now approaching, so Tingoccio said:

'Farewell, Meuccio, I can't stay here any longer.' And all of a sudden he was gone.

Having learnt that there was nothing special down there about the mother of a godchild, Meuccio began to laugh at his own stupidity for having in the past spared several such ladies from his attentions. From that day forth, having shed his ignorance, he was a much wiser man in dealing with such matters. And if only Friar Rinaldo had known as much as Meuccio, there would have been no need for him to make up syllogisms when persuading Madonna Agnesa to minister to his pleasures.

*   *   *

The sun was descending in the west and a gentle breeze had risen, when the king, having brought his story to an end, removed the crown of laurel from his brow, there being no one else left to speak, and placed it upon the head of Lauretta, saying:

'With this, your namesake, madam, I crown you queen of our company. And now it is up to you, as our empress, to give such orders as you consider apt for our common entertainment and pleasure.'

He then returned to his place and sat down, and Lauretta, having become their queen, summoned the steward and ordered him to set the tables in the delectable valley at a somewhat earlier hour than usual, so that they could return at their leisure to the palace; and she also instructed him about the things he was to do during the rest of her reign.

This done, she turned to address the company, saying:

'Yesterday, Dioneo insisted that we should talk, today, about the tricks played upon husbands by their wives; and but for the fact that I do not wish it to be thought that I belong to that breed of snapping curs who immediately turn round and retaliate, I should oblige you, on the morrow, to talk about the tricks played on wives by their husbands. But instead of doing that, I should like each of you to think of a story about *the tricks that people in general, men and women alike, are forever playing upon one another*. This, I feel sure, will be no less agreeable a topic than the one to which we have today been addressing ourselves.'

Having spoken these words, she rose to her feet and dismissed the company until suppertime.

And so the whole company arose, gentlemen and ladies alike, and some of them began to wade, barefooted, in the limpid waters of the lake, whilst others went roaming off over the greensward to beguile the time amongst the tall, straight trees. Dioneo and Fiammetta sang a long duet about Palamon and Arcite. And so, in their several different ways, they whiled away the time to their entire delight and joy until the hour of supper, when they seated themselves at table beside the tiny lake. There they supped in gay and leisurely fashion with never a fly to trouble them, fanned by a gentle breeze that came from the surrounding hills, with the dulcet songs of a thousand birds delighting their ears.

No more than half the vesperal hour had elapsed when the tables were cleared away, and at the queen's behest, they wandered for a while through the delectable valley before slowly retracing their steps towards their lodging. Jesting and laughing not only about the things they had been saying earlier in the day, but many others also, in due course they arrived at the goodly palace a little before dark. There they dispelled the fatigue of their brief journey with the coolest of wines and the daintiest of sweetmeats, and in no time at all they were dancing *caroles* beside the beautiful fountain, accompanied sometimes by Tindaro on the cornemuse and sometimes by the music of other instruments.

Finally, however, the queen ordered Filomena to sing a song, and she began as follows:

> 'Alas, my life is desolate!
> For will I ne'er return
> Whence I departed all disconsolate?
>
> 'Certain I know not, such is the desire
> That burns within my breast
> There to return, alas, where once I was.
> Oh, my true love, who sets my heart afire,
> My one, my only rest,
> Tell me what I should do, my dearest lord;
> I dare ask none, nor know to whom to go
> To beg for hope and help except thyself,
> My soul is wounded so.
>
> 'I cannot well relate how great the pleasure
> Which so impassioned me
> That neither day nor night could yield me rest.
> My hearing, sight and touch, in strongest measure
> Were so increased in me
> That each sense lit new fires within my breast

Which burn and scorch me to the very core.
Save thee alone, no one can comfort me
Or my faint heart restore.

'Alas, come tell me when it is to be,
When will that time return
When I may come upon thee once again
And kiss those eyes which have so murdered me?
My love, for whom I yearn,
Tell me when thou wilt come, and tell me "soon",
And somewhat ease the pains Love made me bear.
Say thou wilt swiftly come, then linger here;
How long I do not care.

'If I perchance should hold thee once again,
I may not be the fool
That I have been before to let thee go.
My grasp this time I firmer will maintain;
Let Fate do what she will.
For I must satisfy my craving soul
With thy sweet lips: I have no more to say.
Therefore come quickly, come embrace me soon;
I sing to think you may!'

All of her companions surmised from this song that Filomena was engrossed in some new and exciting love; and since the words seemed to imply that she had gone beyond the mere exchange of amorous glances, some of those present, supposing her to have savoured the fruits of her love, were not a little envious. But when her song was finished, the queen, remembering that the following day was a Friday, graciously addressed the whole company as follows:

'Noble ladies, young gentlemen, tomorrow as you know is the day that is consecrated to the Passion of Our Lord, and you will doubtless recall that when Neifile was our queen, we observed it devoutly, abstaining from our agreeable discussions, not only on that day, but on the ensuing Saturday. Wherefore, being desirous to follow the good example which Neifile has set us, I feel that for the next two days it would be seemly for us to suspend our pleasant storytelling, as we did last week, and meditate upon the things that were done on those two days for the salvation of our souls.'

The queen's devout words commanded general approval, and so, a goodly portion of the night being already spent, she dismissed the whole company and they all betook themselves to their rest.

Here ends the Seventh Day of the Decameron

EIGHTH DAY

Here begins the Eighth Day, wherein, under the rule of Lauretta, are discussed the tricks that people in general, men and women alike, are forever playing upon one another.

On the Sunday morning, the rays of the rising sun had already appeared among the highest mountain peaks, the shades of night had departed, and all things were plainly visible, when the queen and her companions rose from their beds; and after sauntering for a while upon the dew-flecked lawns, they made their way, the hour of tierce being nearly half spent, to a nearby chapel, where they heard divine service. Returning to the palace, they breakfasted in gay and festive mood, and after they had sung and danced a little, they were dismissed by the queen, so that those who wished to go and rest were free to do so.

But in compliance with the wishes of the queen, once the sun was past its zenith they took their places beside the delectable fountain to proceed as usual with their storytelling, and at the queen's command Neifile began as follows:

FIRST STORY

Gulfardo borrows from Guasparruolo a sum of money equivalent to the amount he has agreed to pay the latter's wife in return for letting him sleep with her. He gives her the money, but later tells Guasparruolo, in her presence, that he has handed it back to his wife, and she has to admit it.

Since God has ordained that I should tell the first of our stories today, I am well content to do so. And since we have talked a great deal, fond ladies, of the tricks played by women upon men, I should like to tell you of one which was played by a man upon a woman, my intention being, not to censure the man for what he did or to claim that the woman was misused, but on the contrary to commend the man and censure the woman, and to show that men are just as capable of deceiving those who trust them, as of being deceived by those in whom they place their trust. Strictly speaking, however, the incident I am about to relate should not be termed a deception, but rather a reprisal. For a woman should act at all times with the greatest decorum, and guard her chastity with her life, on no account permitting herself to defile it; and although it is not always possible for us to observe this precept to the full on account of our frailty, nevertheless I declare that any woman who strays from the path of virtue for monetary gain deserves to be burnt alive, whereas the woman who yields to the forces of Love, knowing how powerful they are, deserves a lenient judge who will order her acquittal – which, as was pointed out to us the other day by Filostrato, is what happened to Madonna Filippa in Prato.

Now, in the city of Milan there was once a German soldier of fortune, a fearless fellow by the name of Gulfardo, who, unlike the majority of his countrymen, was extremely loyal to those in whose service he enrolled. And since he was always most scrupulous in repaying sums of money he had borrowed, he could find any number of merchants who were willing to lend him as much as he wanted, at a low rate of interest.

Since coming to live in Milan, he had fallen in love with a very beautiful woman called Madonna Ambruogia, the wife of a wealthy merchant, Guasparruolo Cagastraccio by name, with whom he was on the most friendly and familiar of terms, but neither her husband nor anyone else was aware of his love for the lady, for he proceeded at all times with the utmost discretion. And one day, he sent her a message, imploring her to grant him the sweet reward of his devotion, and affirming that he, for his part, was prepared to do whatever she might ask of him.

After much humming and hawing, the lady made up her mind, and informed Gulfardo that she was prepared to comply with his request on two conditions: firstly, that he must never breathe a word of it to anyone; and secondly, that since he was well off and she wanted to buy something for herself, he was to give her two hundred gold florins, and then she would always be at his service.

On hearing of the woman's rapacity, Gulfardo, who had always thought of her as a perfect lady, was incensed by her lack of decorum, and his fervent love was transmuted into a feeling more akin to hatred. Being resolved to beat her at her own game, he sent word that he would be only too willing to meet her wishes, and do everything else in his power to make her happy. She was therefore to let him know when she would like him to come to her, and he would bring her the money. And she could rest assured that nobody would hear of the matter, except for a comrade of his whom he greatly trusted, who was privy to all his affairs.

The lady, or strumpet rather, was delighted with this reply, and sent back word that in a few days' time Guasparruolo, her husband, had to go to Genoa on business, and as soon as he was out of the way she would let Gulfardo know and invite him to call.

Having waited for the right moment, Gulfardo went to Guasparruolo and said:

'I'm about to drive a bargain, for which I require two hundred gold florins. Would it be possible for you to lend them to me, at the same rate of interest as usual?'

Guasparruolo willingly agreed to lend him the money, and counted it out for him right away.

A few days later, Guasparruolo went off to Genoa as his wife had predicted, and she therefore sent word to Gulfardo that he should come to her, bringing the two hundred gold florins. So Gulfardo, taking his friend with him, went to the lady's house, where he found her waiting for him, and the first thing he did was to hand over the two hundred gold florins in his comrade's presence, saying:

'Here, take this money, my lady, and give it to your husband when he returns.'

The lady took the money, thinking Gulfardo had used this form of words simply so that his comrade should not suspect he was giving it to her by way of payment. And she replied:

'I shall see that he gets it, of course, but first I should like to make sure that it is all here.' Whereupon she emptied the florins out on to a table, and on finding, to her great satisfaction, that they came to exactly two hundred, she put them away in a safe place. She then went back to Gulfardo and conveyed him to her bedroom, where, not only on that occasion but on many others before her husband's return from Genoa, she placed her person freely at his disposal.

No sooner did Guasparruolo return from Genoa than Gulfardo, having made certain that his wife would be with him, called upon him with his companion, and said to him in the lady's presence:

'Guasparruolo, those two hundred gold florins you lent me the other day were not needed after all, as I was unable to complete the transaction. So I brought them straight back and handed them over to your wife. Do remember to cancel my debt, won't you?'

Turning to his wife, Guasparruolo asked her whether she had received the money, and since she could hardly deny the fact when the witness was staring her in the face, she said:

'Yes, I did indeed receive the money, but forgot to tell you about it.'

'That settles it, then. Don't worry, Gulfardo, I shall make quite sure that it's entered up in the books.'

Having made a fool of the lady, Gulfardo took his leave, and she gave her husband the ill-gotten proceeds of her depravity; and thus the sagacious lover had enjoyed the favours of his rapacious lady free of charge.

SECOND STORY

The priest of Varlungo goes to bed with Monna Belcolore, leaving her his cloak by way of payment; then, having borrowed a mortar from her, he sends it back and asks her to return the cloak which he had left with her as a pledge. The good woman hands it over, and gives him a piece of her mind.

The gentlemen and ladies alike were still applauding Gulfardo's treatment of the covetous Milanese lady when the queen turned, smiling, to Panfilo, and enjoined him to follow; so Panfilo began:

Fair ladies, it behoves me to relate a little story against a class of persons who keep on offending us without our being able to retaliate. I am referring to the priests, who have proclaimed a crusade against our wives, and who seem to think, when they succeed in laying one of them on her back, that they have earned full remission of all their sins, as surely as if they had brought the Sultan back from Alexandria to Avignon in chains. Whereas we poor dupes who belong to the laity cannot do the same to them, albeit we may vent our spleen against their mothers, sisters, mistresses and daughters with no less passion than the priests display when assailing our wives. But however that may be, I propose to tell you this tale of country love, more amusing for its ending than conspicuous for its length, from which you will be able to draw a useful moral, namely, that you shouldn't believe everything that a priest tells you.

I say then, that in Varlungo, which as all of you know or will possibly have heard is a hamlet, no great distance from here, there once lived a worthy priest, robust and vigorous in the service of the ladies, who, albeit he was none too proficient at reading books, always had a rich stock of good and holy aphorisms with which to entertain his parishioners under the elm every Sunday. And whenever the men of the parish were away from their homes, he was far more assiduous in calling on their wives than any of his predecessors, bringing them fairings and holy water and a candle-end or two, and giving them his blessing.

Now, among the many women in his parish who had taken his fancy, there was one in particular for whom he had a very soft spot indeed. Her name was Monna Belcolore, she was married to a farm-worker called Bentivegna del Mazzo, and without a doubt she was a vigorous and seductive-looking wench, buxom and brown as a berry, who seemed better versed in the grinder's art than any other girl in the village. When, moreover, she had occasion to play the tambourine, and sing 'A little of what you fancy does you good', and dance a reel or a jig, with a dainty little kerchief in her hand, she could knock spots off every single one of her neighbours. Master Priest was so enthralled by all these talents of hers that he was driven to distraction, and spent his whole time loitering about the village in the hope of seeing her. Whenever he caught sight of her in church on a Sunday morning, he would intone a *Kyrie* and a *Sanctus*, trying very hard to sound like a master cantor when in fact he was braying like an ass, whereas if she was nowhere to be seen he would hardly open his lips. But on the whole he managed to disguise his feelings, so that neither Bentivegna del Mazzo nor any of his neighbours noticed anything unusual in his behaviour.

With the object of getting to know Monna Belcolore better, every now and then he gave her presents, sometimes sending her a few cloves of fresh garlic, of which he grew the finest specimens thereabouts in his own garden, and sometimes a basket of beans, or a bunch of chives or shallots. If he met her in the street, he would look at her with a forlorn expression on his face, and whisper fond reproaches in her ear, but being a stubborn little thing, she pretended not to notice and passed him by with her nose in the air, so that Master Priest was getting precisely nowhere.

One day, however, while the priest was strolling aimlessly about the village, a little after noon, he happened to meet Bentivegna del Mazzo, who was driving a heavily laden ass before him. The priest hailed him and asked him where he was going, and Bentivegna replied:

'Faith, Father, to tell the honest truth I have some business to attend to in town, and I'm taking these things to the lawyer, Ser Bonaccorri da Ginestreto, so that he'll help me to answer this 'ere summings I've had from the tawny general to appear before the judge at the sizes.'

The priest was delighted.

'You do well, my son,' he said, 'Go now, with my blessing, and come back soon. And if you should happen to meet Lapuccio or Naldino, don't forget to ask them to bring me those leather thongs for my flails.'

Bentivegna promised he would see about it, and continued on his way towards Florence, while the priest, having decided that the time had come for him to call upon Belcolore and try his luck, set off at a spanking pace, never slowing up for a moment until he had arrived on her doorstep. As he entered the house, he called out:

'God bless all here! Is anyone at home?'

Belcolore was upstairs, and on hearing his voice she called down to him:

'Oh, Father, you are welcome! But why go traipsing round the village in this awful heat?'

'By the grace of God,' replied the priest, 'I've come to keep you company for a while, for I met your husband on his way to town.'

Belcolore came downstairs, took a seat, and began to sift a heap of cabbage seed that her husband had gathered earlier in the day.

'Come now, Belcolore,' said the priest, 'must you always drive me to despair like this?'

Belcolore began to laugh, and said: 'What have I done to you?'

'Nothing,' replied the priest. 'But the trouble is that there's something I'd like to do to you, something ordained by God, and you won't let me do it.'

'Bless my soul!' said Belcolore. 'Priests don't do that sort of thing.'

'We certainly do,' replied the priest. 'Why on earth shouldn't we? What's more, we do a much better job of it than other men, and do you know why? It's because we do our grinding when the millpond's full. So if you want to make hay while the sun shines, hold your tongue and let me get on with it.'

'What sort of hay do you mean?' said Belcolore. 'You priests are all the same, you're as tight-fisted as the very devil.'

'You only have to tell me what you want,' said the priest, 'and you shall have it. Would you like a pretty little pair of shoes, or a silk head-scarf, or a fine woollen waistband, or what?'

'That's a splendid choice, I must say!' exclaimed Belcolore. 'I already have all those things. But if you're really so fond of me, why not do me a little favour, and then I would do whatever you want?'

'Tell me what the favour is, and I'll do it gladly,' said the priest.

So Belcolore said:

'I have to go to Florence on Saturday to deliver some wool that I have spun, and get my spinning wheel mended. And if you'll lend me five pounds, which a man like you can easily afford, I shall call at the pawnbroker's and collect my black skirt and the waistband I wear on Sundays. I wore it on my wedding-day, you understand, and ever since I pawned it I haven't been able to go to church or anywhere else. Do me this one favour, and I'll be yours for evermore.'

'So help me God,' said the priest, 'I haven't the money with me, or I'd gladly let you have it. But you may depend on me to see that you get it by Saturday.'

'Oh yes,' said Belcolore, 'you all make these fine promises, and then you fail to keep any of them. Do you think you're going to treat me as you treated Biliuzza, who went away empty-handed and ended up walking the streets because of what you did to her? God's faith, you'll not fool me so easily. If you haven't the money with you, you can go and fetch it.'

'Oh come!' said the priest. 'Don't make me go all the way back for it now, when you can see for yourself that I'm rearing to get on with the job. By the time I returned, there might be someone here to thwart our plans, and Lord knows when I shall be in such fine fettle again as I am at present.'

'That's your own lookout,' she said. 'If you want to go, go; if not, take your fettle elsewhere.'

Seeing that she was not prepared to do his bidding without a *quid pro quo*, and had turned down his suggestion of a *sine custodia*, the priest said:

'I'll tell you what I'll do. Since you won't trust me to send you the money, I'll leave you this fine blue cloak of mine by way of surety.'

Belcolore looked up at him and said:

'Will you now? And how much is the cloak worth?'

'How much is it worth?' said the priest. 'Why, I'll have you know that it's made of pure Douai, not to say Trouai, and there are those in the parish who would claim that it's Quadrouai. I bought it less than a fortnight ago from Lotto, the old-clothes-merchant, for exactly seven pounds, and according to Buglietto d'Alberto, who as you know is an expert in such matters, it would have been cheap at half the price.'

'Is that so?' said Belcolore. 'So help me God, I would never have believed it. But anyway, let's have a look at it.'

Master Priest, who was champing at the bit, took off his cloak and gave it to her. And when she had put it safely away, she said:

'Let's go into the barn, Father. Nobody ever comes near the place.'

So off they went to the barn, where he smothered her with luscious kisses and made her a kinswoman of the Lord God. And after spending some time in amorous sport with her, he made his way back to the church in his surplice, as though he'd been officiating at a wedding.

By the time he arrived there, it began to dawn on him that all the candle-ends he could muster from a whole year's offerings would scarcely amount to a half of five pounds in value, and he could have kicked himself for being so stupid as to leave her his cloak. So he began to consider how he might retrieve it without having to pay.

Being a crafty sort of fellow, he soon thought of a very good way of getting it back, and it worked to perfection. On the following day, which happened to be a feast day, he sent the child of one of his neighbours to Monna Belcolore's house, asking her whether she would kindly lend him her stone mortar, because Binguccio dal Poggio and Nuto Buglietti were due to breakfast with him later in the morning, and he wanted to prepare a sauce.

Belcolore sent him the mortar, and when it was nearly time for breakfast and the priest knew that Bentivegna del Mazzo and Belcolore would be about to sit at table, he called his sacristan and said:

'Take this mortar back to Monna Belcolore, and say to her: "Father says thank you very much, and would you mind sending back the cloak that the boy left with you by way of surety."'

So the sacristan took the mortar along to Belcolore's house, where he found her sitting at table with Bentivegna, having breakfast; and having put the mortar down on the table, he gave her the priest's message.

When she heard him asking for the cloak, Belcolore tried to speak, but Bentivegna rounded on her angrily, saying:

'What's all this about taking sureties from the priest? Jesus Christ, I've a good mind to thrash the hide off you. Pox take you, woman, go and get the cloak and hand it back, and be quick about it. And just you remember from now on: if the priest wants anything, he's to have it, no matter what it is, even if he asks for our ass.'

Belcolore got up, grumbling and muttering to herself, and went to fetch the cloak, which she had tucked away in a chest at the foot of the bed. And as she handed it over to the sacristan, she said:

'Give the priest this message from me: "Belcolore says that she swears to God you won't be grinding any more of your sauces in her mortar, after the shabby way you've treated her over this one."'

The sacristan took the cloak back to the priest and gave him Belcolore's message, whereupon he burst out laughing and said:

'Next time you see her, tell her that if she doesn't lend me her mortar, I shan't let her have my pestle. It's no use having one without the other.'

Bentivegna supposed his wife had spoken as she did because of the scolding he had given her, and thought no more about it. But Belcolore was infuriated with the priest for having made such a fool of her, and refused to speak to him for the rest of the summer until the grape-harvest, by which time he had scared the life out of her so successfully by threatening to see that she was consigned to the very centre of Hell, that she made her peace with him over a bottle of must and some roast chestnuts. From then on, they had many a good guzzle together, and instead of giving her the five pounds, the priest put a new skin on her tambourine and tricked it out with a pretty little bell, which made her very happy.

THIRD STORY

Calandrino, Bruno and Buffalmacco set off in search of the heliotrope along the banks of the Mugnone. Thinking he has found it, Calandrino staggers home carrying an enormous load of stones, and his wife gives him a piece of her mind, causing him to lose his temper and beat her up. Then finally, he tells his companions what they have known all along.

The ladies laughed so heartily over Panfilo's tale that they are laughing yet, and when it was over, the queen called upon Elissa to follow him. And so, still laughing, she thus began:

Charming ladies, I know not whether, with this little story of mine, which is no less true than entertaining, I shall succeed in making you laugh as much as Panfilo has done with his, but at any rate I shall do my best.

Not long ago, there lived in our city, where there has never been any lack of unusual customs and bizarre people, a painter called Calandrino, a simple, unconventional sort of fellow, who was nearly always to be found in the company of two other painters, whose names were Bruno and Buffalmacco. These latter were a very jovial pair, but they were also shrewd and perceptive, and they went about with Calandrino because his simplemindedness and the quaintness of his ways were an endless source of amusement to them.

Also in Florence at that time there was a most agreeable, astute, and successful young man called Maso del Saggio, who, having heard one or two stories about Calandrino's simplicity, decided to have a little fun at his expense by playing some practical joke upon him, or putting some fantastic notion into his head.

So one day, happening to find him in the church of San Giovanni staring intently at the paintings and bas-reliefs of the canopy which had recently been erected above the high altar, he decided that this was the ideal time and place for doing what he had in mind. And having explained his intentions to a companion of his, they walked over to the place where Calandrino was sitting, and pretending not to notice him, they began to discuss the properties of various stones, of which Maso spoke with tremendous authority, as though he were a great and famous lapidary.

Hearing them talking together, Calandrino pricked up his ears, and after a while, seeing that their conversation was not intended to be private, he got up and joined them, much to the delight of Maso, who continued to hold forth until finally Calandrino asked him where these magical stones were to be found.

Maso replied that they were chiefly to be found in Nomansland, the territory of the Basques, in a region called Cornucopia, where the vines are tied up with sausages, and you could buy a goose for a penny, with a gosling thrown in for good measure. And in those parts there was a mountain made entirely of grated Parmesan cheese, on whose slopes there were people who spent their whole time making macaroni and ravioli, which they cooked in chicken broth and then cast it to the four winds, and the faster you could pick it up, the more you got of it. And not far away, there was a stream of Vernaccia wine, the finest that was ever drunk, without a single drop of water in it.

'That's a marvellous place, by the sound of it,' said Calandrino, 'but tell me, what do they do with all the chickens they cook?'

'They are all eaten by the Basques,' Maso replied.

Then Calandrino asked him whether he had ever been there himself, and Maso replied:

'Been there myself? If I've been there once, I've been there a thousand times at least.'

Whereupon Calandrino asked:

'How many miles away is it?'

'More than a milling, that spends the night trilling,' said Maso.

'In that case,' said Calandrino, 'it must be further than the Abruzzi.'

'It is indeed,' Maso replied, 'just a trifle.'

Seeing that Maso was saying this with a completely straight face, the simple-minded Calandrino took every word of it as gospel, and he said:

'It's too far away for me, then; but if it were nearer, I can assure you that one of these days I'd come with you, so as to see all that macaroni tumbling down, and feed my face on it. But do please tell me, are there none of these magical stones to be found in this part of the world?'

'Yes,' replied Maso. 'There are two kinds of stone that are very magical indeed. First of all we have the sandstones of Settignano and Montici, from which, when they are turned into millstones, we get all our flour; hence the popular saying, in the countries I was telling you about, that blessings come from God and millstones from Montici. But we have such a lot of these sandstones, that we think as little of them as they do of emeralds, of which they have whole mountains, higher than Monte Morello, that sparkle and glitter in the middle of the night, believe you me if they don't! And by the way, did you know that anyone who could master the art of setting millstones in rings, before a hole was bored in them, and who took them to the Sultan, could have anything he chose? Now, the second is a stone that we lapidaries call the heliotrope, which has the miraculous power of making people invisible when they are out of sight, provided they are carrying it on their person.'

'Amazing!' said Calandrino. 'But this second stone, where is it to be found?'

Maso replied that one could usually find decent specimens in the valley of the Mugnone, whereupon Calandrino said:

'How big are these stones? What colour are they?'

'The size varies,' Maso replied. 'Some of them are bigger and others smaller, but they are all very nearly black in colour.'

Having made a mental note of all that he had heard, Calandrino pretended that he had other things to attend to and took his leave of Maso, determined to go and look for one of these stones; but he decided that before doing so, he would have to inform Bruno and Buffalmacco, who were his bosom friends. He therefore went to look for them, so that they could all set forth at once in search of the stone before anyone else should come to hear about it, and he spent the whole of the rest of the morning trying to trace them.

Finally, in mid-afternoon, he suddenly remembered that they were working at the nunnery a little beyond the city-gate on the road to Faenza, so he abandoned everything he was doing and proceeded to the nunnery, running nearly all the way in spite of the tremendous heat. And having called them away from their painting, he said to them:

'Pay attention to me, my friends, and we can become the richest men in Florence, for I have heard on good authority that along the Mugnone there's a certain kind of stone, and when you pick it up you become invisible. I reckon we ought to go there right away, before anyone else does. We'll find it without a doubt, because I know what it looks like; and once we've found it, all we have to do is to put it in our purses and go to the money-changers, whose counters, as you know, are always loaded with groats and florins, and help ourselves to as much as we want. No one will see us; and so we'll be able to get rich quick, without being forced to daub walls all the time like a lot of snails.'

When Bruno and Buffalmacco heard this, they had a good laugh to themselves, stared one another in the face pretending to be greatly astonished, and told Calandrino that they thought it a splendid idea. Then Buffalmacco asked him what the stone was called, but Calandrino, being rather dense, had already forgotten its name, and so he replied:

'Why should we bother about the name, when we know about its special powers? Let's not waste any more time, but go and look for it now.'

'Very well,' said Bruno, 'but what do these stones look like?'

'They come in various shapes and sizes,' said Calandrino, 'but they're all the same colour, which is very nearly black. So what we have to do is to collect all the black stones we happen to see, until we come across the right one. Come on, let's get going.'

'Wait a minute,' said Bruno. And turning to Buffalmacco, he said:

'Calandrino appears to be talking sense, but there's no point in going there at this time of day, because the sun is shining straight down on the Mugnone and it will have dried all the stones, so that the ones that seem black in the early morning, before the sun gets at them, will be just as white as the others. Besides, as it's the middle of the week there'll be a lot of people along the Mugnone, and if they were to see us they might guess what we were up to, in which case they might follow our example, and come across the stone before we do. We don't want to kill the goose that lays the golden egg. Wouldn't you agree, Buffalmacco, that we ought to do this job in the early morning, so that we can distinguish the black stones from the white ones, and that we should wait until the weekend, when nobody will see us?'

Since Bruno's advice was supported by Buffalmacco, Calandrino agreed to wait, and it was arranged that on the following Sunday morning they would all go and look for the magic stone. Meanwhile Calandrino pleaded with them not to breathe a word of this to anyone, as it had been revealed to him in strict confidence, and he then went on to tell them what he had heard about the land of Cornucopia, declaring with many an oath that he was speaking the gospel truth. And when he had taken his leave of them, they put their heads together and agreed on their plan of campaign.

Calandrino looked forward eagerly to Sunday morning, and when it came, he got up at crack of dawn and went round to call for his friends. Then they all proceeded to the Mugnone by way of the Porta San Gallo and began to work their way downstream, looking for the stone. Being the keenest of the trio, Calandrino went on ahead, darting this way and that, and whenever he caught sight of a black stone he leapt on it, picked it up, and stuffed it down his shirt, while the other two trailed along behind, occasionally picking up an odd stone here and there. Before he had gone very far, Calandrino found that there was no more room in his shirt, so he gathered up the folds of his skirt, which was not cut in the Hainault style, attached them securely to his waist all round, and turned them into a capacious bag, which took him no long time to fill, after which he made a second bag out of his cloak, which in no time at all he had likewise filled up with stones.

Now that Calandrino was fully laden and the hour of breakfast was approaching, Bruno turned to Buffalmacco, as they had pre-arranged, and said:

'Where's Calandrino got to?'

Buffalmacco, who could see him quite plainly, turned to gaze in every direction, and then replied:

'I've no idea. He was here a moment ago, just a little way ahead of us.'

'A moment ago, indeed! I'll bet you he's at home by now, tucking in to his breakfast, after putting this crazy idea into our heads of searching for black stones along the Mugnone.'

'Well,' said Buffalmacco, 'I can't say I blame him for leaving us in the lurch like this, seeing that we were stupid enough to believe him in the first place. What a pair of blockheads we are! No one in his right mind would ever have believed all that talk about finding such a valuable stone in the Mugnone.'

Hearing them talk in this fashion, Calandrino concluded that he must have picked up the stone without knowing it, and that because of its special powers they were unable to see him, even though he was standing just a few yards away. He therefore decided, being delighted with his good fortune, to go back home; and without saying anything to the others, he turned about and started to return by the way he had come.

On seeing this, Buffalmacco turned to Bruno and said:

'What'll we do now? Why don't we go home, the same as he did?'

'Come on then,' Bruno replied. 'But I swear to God that I won't fall for any more of Calandrino's tricks. If he were as close to me now as he's been all morning, I'd give him such a rap on the heels with this pebble that he wouldn't forget this little hoax of his for the best part of a month.' No sooner were the words out of his mouth than he took aim and caught Calandrino squarely on the heel with the pebble, whereupon Calandrino, grimacing with pain, jerked his foot high in the air and began to puff and gasp for breath. But he nonetheless managed to hold his tongue, and continued on his way.

Then Buffalmacco took between his fingers one of the pebbles he had collected earlier, and said to Bruno:

'D'you see this nice sharp bit of flint? How I'd love to send it whizzing into Calandrino's back!' He then let it go, and it caught Calandrino a nasty blow in the small of the back. But to cut a long story short, they kept stoning Calandrino in this fashion, making various abusive remarks, all the way back along the Mugnone to the Porta San Gallo, where, having thrown away the rest of the stones they had collected, they paused to chat with the customs guards. These latter, having been let into the secret beforehand, had allowed Calandrino to pass unchallenged, and were splitting their sides with laughter.

Calandrino walked on without stopping until he reached his house, which was situated near the Canto alla Macina, and Fortune favoured the hoax to such an extent that at no point along his route, either beside the river or in the city streets, did anyone address a single word to him, though as a matter of fact he encountered very few people because nearly everyone was at breakfast.

Calandrino let himself into the house, staggering under his burden, but as luck would have it, his wife, a handsome-looking gentlewoman called Monna Tessa, was standing at the head of the stairs; and as she was somewhat annoyed with him for staying out so long, no sooner did she catch sight of him than she began to scold him, saying:

'A fine fellow you are, I must say, coming home to breakfast when everyone else has finished eating. Where the devil have you been?'

On realizing that she could see him, Calandrino was filled with anger and dismay, and began to shout:

'Blast you, woman, why did you have to be standing there? Now you've ruined everything, but I swear to God I'll be even with you yet.' And having ascended the stairs, he deposited his enormous collection of stones in one of the smaller rooms and rushed upon his wife like a madman. Catching her by the tresses, he hurled her to the ground at his feet and began to pummel her and kick her as hard as he could until she was bruised and battered all over from head to foot, whilst all the time she was pleading in vain for mercy and clasping her hands in a gesture of supplication.

Bruno and Buffalmacco, having tarried for a while at the city gate to have a good laugh with the watchmen, slowly set off to follow Calandrino at a distance, and when, on reaching his front door, they heard the sound of the terrible beating he was inflicting on his wife, they pretended they had only just returned and called out to him. Calandrino appeared at the window, flushed, panting, and covered in sweat, and asked them to come up. So up the stairs they went, scowling all over their faces, to find the room cluttered up with stones and the woman huddled in a corner, her hair dishevelled, her clothes torn, and her face covered with scratches and bruises, weeping her eyes out, whilst at the other side of the room Calandrino was sitting gasping for breath as though he were completely exhausted, his clothes in total disarray.

Having spent a little time surveying the scene, they said:

'What's all this, Calandrino? Are you planning to build a wall with all these stones we can see lying about?' And so as to add insult to injury, they continued:

'What's happened to Monna Tessa? It looks as though you've been giving her a beating. Whatever made you do that?'

What with the weight of all the stones he had carried, and the fury with which he had assailed his wife, and his despair over losing the fortune he had imagined to be within his grasp, Calandrino was so fatigued that he couldn't draw sufficient breath to utter a single word in reply. So Buffalmacco, having paused for a while, began all over again, saying:

'Look here, Calandrino, you had no right to play such a mean trick on us, just because you were feeling piqued about something or other. You talked us into going with you to look for this magic stone, and then, without so much as bidding us fare you well or fare you badly, you left us standing there along the Mugnone like a pair of boobies, and cleared off home. We're not exactly pleased with the way you've behaved: and you can rest assured that you'll never do this to us again.'

This was more than Calandrino could bear, so he summoned up all his energies and replied:

'Don't be angry, my friends, you're quite wrong about what happened. I actually found the stone, and if you don't believe me, I'll prove it. When you started asking one another where I was, I was standing less than ten yards away from you the whole time. And when I saw that you were making tracks for home and couldn't see me,

I walked ahead of you. As a matter of fact, I was just a little way in front of you all the way back to the city gate.'

He then gave them an account of everything they had said and done from beginning to end, and showed them the marks made by the stones on his heels and his back, after which he said:

'And I'll tell you another thing: as I was coming in at the city gate, loaded up to the eyebrows with all these stones you see here, nobody said a word to me, and you know for yourselves what those customs men are like, with their tedious and offensive manner of demanding to see everything. Besides, I met various friends and neighbours as I was coming along the road, who are always in the habit of bidding me good morning and offering me a drink, yet none of them uttered so much as a syllable, and they passed me by as though they hadn't seen me. But when I finally arrived home, I was met by this blasted devil of a woman; and because, as you know, all things lose their virtue in the presence of a woman, the spell was broken and she saw me. So instead of being the luckiest man in Florence, she's made me the unluckiest, which is why I beat her with all the strength I had in my hands. So help me God, I could slit the woman's throat for her. I curse the hour that I first set eyes on her, and the day she came into this house.'

And flying once more into a rage, he made as though to get up and give her another good thrashing.

As they listened to Calandrino's tale, Bruno and Buffalmacco feigned great astonishment, and nodded at regular intervals to confirm what he was saying, though it was all they could do to prevent themselves from bursting out laughing. But when they saw him rising furiously to his feet to beat his wife a second time, they rushed forward to restrain him, declaring that if anyone was to blame it was not the lady, but Calandrino himself, for he was well aware that women caused things to lose their virtue, and hadn't warned her beforehand not to show her face that day in his presence. Moreover it was God Himself, they argued, who had prevented him from taking this precaution, either because Calandrino was not destined to enjoy this singular piece of good fortune, or because he was intending to deceive his companions, to whom he should have revealed his discovery the moment he realized the stone was in his possession.

After a lot of palaver, they managed, with a great deal of effort, to conciliate the hapless lady and her husband, and they then departed, leaving him to sit and brood with his house full of stones.

FOURTH STORY

The Rector of Fiesole falls in love with a widow, but his love is not reciprocated. He goes to bed with her maid, thinking it to be the widow, and the lady's brothers cause him to be found there by his bishop.

When Elissa came to the end of her tale, which in the course of its telling had brought no small pleasure to the entire company, the queen turned to Emilia and indicated that she would like her to tell her own story next; so Emilia promptly began, as follows:

Worthy ladies, it has already been shown, as I recall, in several of the stories we have heard, that priests, friars, and clerics of all descriptions will stop at nothing to force themselves on our attention. But however much we may discuss this particular subject, more will remain to be said; and I therefore propose to tell you a story about a rector who was determined, come what may, to obtain the favours of a certain widow, whether she wanted to grant them to him or not. But being highly intelligent, the lady, who was of gentle birth, treated him according to his deserts.

As you all know, Fiesole, which stands on top of a hill, clearly visible from where we are now, is a city of great antiquity, and was once very large. Although it has now fallen into total ruin, it has never been without a bishop, and there is one living there to this day. Some years ago, a widow of gentle birth, called Monna Piccarda, had an estate there, not far from the main church; and since she was not the wealthiest of women, she resided there for almost the entire year, in a house of modest proportions, together with her two brothers, a pair of very worthy and polite young gentlemen.

Now, this lady went regularly to the nearby church, and since she was still a very beautiful and charming young woman, its rector fell so passionately in love with her that she alone commanded the whole of his attention. And in the end he waxed so bold as to acquaint the lady with his wishes, imploring her to be content that he should love her and to requite his ardent passion.

Though elderly in years, this rector had the mentality of a small child, being haughty and presumptuous, and possessing a mighty high opinion of himself. He was forever picking holes in people and making himself generally unpleasant, and was so pompous and tedious that he was disliked by everybody, but especially by this lady, who not only disliked but positively loathed him. But being an intelligent woman, as we have said, she replied:

'Sir, I am extremely flattered that you should love me. I am bound to love you in return, and I shall do so with all my heart, but there must never be anything unseemly about our love for one another. You are my spiritual father, you are a priest, and you are fast approaching your old age, all of which things require that you should lead a chaste and honourable life. Besides, I am no longer a young girl, able to take affairs of this sort in her stride, but a widow; and you know how essential it is that widows should follow the path of virtue. You must therefore excuse me, for I can never love you in the way you request, nor do I wish to be loved in this manner by you.'

Although he could obtain no other answer from her at this first encounter, the Rector was not the sort of man to be discouraged or defeated by a single rebuff, and with his habitual arrogance and effrontery he importuned her repeatedly by means of letters and messages, as well as by word of mouth whenever he saw her coming into church. And so the lady, finding that his attentions were becoming quite intolerable, resolved that she would teach him a salutary lesson, albeit she would do nothing without first consulting her brothers. She therefore told them all about the Rector's importunate behaviour, and explained what she was proposing to do about it. Having obtained their full consent, a few days later she went to the church as usual, and no sooner did the Rector catch sight of her than he came over to her and spoke to her in his customary, over-familiar manner.

When she saw him coming, the lady fixed her gaze upon him and gave him a cheerful smile. So the Rector led her to a secluded corner of the church, and plied her with his usual stream of endearments, whereupon the lady fetched a deep sigh and said:

'Sir, I have frequently heard it said that no fortress is sufficiently strong to withstand a perpetual siege, and I have now discovered, from my own experience, that this is perfectly true. For you have beleaguered me so completely with your tender words and countless acts of courtesy that you have forced me to break my former resolve. And seeing that you find me so much to your liking, I am willing to surrender.'

'Heaven be praised!' said the Rector, who could scarcely contain his joy. 'To tell you the truth, madam, I am amazed that you should have held out for so long, seeing that this has never happened to me with any woman before. And in fact, I have sometimes had occasion to reflect, that if women were made of silver, you couldn't turn them into coins, as they bend too easily. But no more of this: when and where can we be together?'

'Sweet my lord,' replied the lady, 'we can meet whenever you please, for I have no husband to whom I must give an account of my nights. But as to where we are going to meet, I have no idea.'

'Why not?' said the Rector. 'Why don't we meet in your house?'

'Sir,' replied the lady, 'as you know, I have two younger brothers, who bring their friends to the house at all hours of the day and night, and since my house is not very big, it would be quite impossible for us to meet there unless we were to stay completely silent, like deaf-mutes, without saying a word, and move about in the dark, as though we were blind. In this case, it would be feasible, for my brothers never invade my bedroom; but their own is immediately next to mine, and one can't even whisper without being heard.'

'That's no great problem,' said the Rector. 'Let's do as you suggest for a night or two, until I can think of a place where we can meet more freely.'

'I leave that to you, sir,' said the lady, 'but on one thing I must insist: that the affair remains a secret, and you never breathe a word of it to anyone.'

'Of that you may rest assured, madam,' replied the Rector. 'But when are we to meet? Can you arrange it for tonight?'

'Why, of course,' said the lady. And having explained to him how and when he was to come, she took her leave of him and returned home.

Now, this lady had a maidservant, who was none too young and had the ugliest and most misshapen face you ever saw. She had a huge, flat nose, a wry mouth, thick lips, big teeth, which were unevenly set, and a pronounced squint; moreover she was always having trouble with her eyes, and her complexion was a sort of yellowy green, so that she looked as though she had spent the summer, not at Fiesole, but at Senigallia.* Apart from this, she was hipshot on the right side, and walked with a slight limp. Her name was Ciuta, but because she was so ugly to look at, everyone called her Ciutazza†. And although her body was so misshapen, she was always prepared for a spot of mischief.

So the lady sent for her and said:

'Ciutazza, if you will do something for me tonight, I shall give you a fine new smock.'

At the mention of a smock, Ciutazza pricked up her ears and said:

'If you give me a smock, ma'am, I'll go through fire for you.'

'That's good,' said the lady. 'Now, what I want you to do is to sleep with a man tonight in my bed, and ply him with caresses. But you must take care not to utter a single word in case my brothers should hear you, for as you know, they sleep in the room next to mine. And tomorrow you shall have the new smock.'

'If need be,' said Ciutazza, 'I would sleep with half a dozen men, let alone one.'

After dark that evening, the Rector came to the house as arranged, and in accordance with the lady's plans, the two young men were in their own room, making a good deal of noise. The Rector entered the lady's bedroom without a sound, and groped his way through the dark, as instructed, to the bed, on which Ciutazza was already lying, having been carefully briefed by her mistress about what she was to do.

Master Rector, thinking it was the lady who was lying beside him, took Ciutazza in his arms and began to kiss her without saying a word, and Ciutazza returned the compliment. And so the Rector

* A town on the Adriatic coast, notorious in Boccaccio's day for malaria.
† The name 'Ciuta' in itself has a repulsive ring about it, which is magnified by the pejorative suffix -azza.

began to disport himself with her, taking possession of the prize he
had long been coveting.

Having thus brought the pair together, the lady directed her
brothers to put the rest of her plan into effect. They therefore stole
quietly out of their room and made their way towards the piazza;
and Fortune was even kinder to their scheme than they had hoped,
for since it was a very hot evening, the Bishop had been looking for
the two young men and was already on his way to their house for a
convivial chat and some liquid refreshment. As soon as he saw them
coming, he told them what he had in mind, and they all returned to
the house, where, to his no small pleasure, he sat with them in a cool
little courtyard in which numerous lanterns had been lit, and drank
some excellent wine of theirs.

When they had taken their fill, the young men said:

'Since you have been so kind as to honour us with your company
in our humble little abode, to which we were just about to invite you,
we should like you to take a look at something we are anxious to
show you.'

The Bishop readily agreed, and so one of the young men seized a
lighted torch and led the way, being followed by the Bishop and all
the rest of the company, to the room where Master Rector was
lying in bed with Ciutazza. In order to make up for lost time, the
Rector had been riding at a furious pace, and already, by the time all
these people arrived, he had covered at least three miles, so that, in
spite of the heat, feeling a little weary, he had dropped off to sleep
with Ciutazza in his arms.

So when the young man bearing the torch entered the room with
the Bishop and all the others in his wake, the first thing they saw was
the Rector lying there with Ciutazza in his arms. At that precise
moment, the Rector woke up, and seeing all these people standing
round him in the torchlight, he thrust his head under the bedclothes,
feeling thoroughly ashamed and confused. But the Bishop, taking
him severely to task, forced him to show his face and have a good
look at the person with whom he had been sleeping.

What with his discovery of the lady's deception, and the disgrace
that he felt he had suffered, the Rector was instantly transformed into
the saddest man who ever lived. The Bishop ordered him to dress, and

when he had done so, he was marched back to the church under heavy escort, there to suffer severe penance for the sin he had committed.

Before taking his leave of the lady's brothers, the Bishop asked them how it had come about that the Rector had gone to their house to sleep with Ciutazza, and the young men told him the whole story from beginning to end. On hearing what had happened, the Bishop warmly commended the lady and the two young men, who, not wishing to soil their hands with the blood of a priest, had treated the Rector as he deserved.

The Rector was forced by his bishop to do forty days' penance for his sin, but love and indignation prolonged his suffering to forty-nine days at the very least, to say nothing of the fact that for a long time afterwards, he was unable to walk down the street without being pointed at by small boys, who would taunt him with the words: 'There goes the man who went to bed with Ciutazza.' And this riled him so much that he was almost driven out of his mind.

This, then, was the way in which the worthy lady rid herself of the presumptuous Rector's insufferable attentions, and Ciutazza won herself a smock.

FIFTH STORY

Three young men pull down the breeches of a judge from the Marches whilst he is administering the law on the Florentine bench.

When Emilia had brought her story to an end, and the widow had been commended by all those present, the queen looked towards Filostrato, and said:

'Now it is your turn to speak.'

Filostrato promptly replied that he was ready to do so, and began as follows:

Delectable ladies, after hearing Elissa referring just now to the young man called Maso del Saggio, I have been prompted to discard the tale I was intending to relate in order to tell you one about Maso and some of his companions, which, though not improper, contains certain words that you ladies would hesitate to use. But since it is highly amusing, I am sure you would like to hear it.

As all of you will doubtless have heard, the chief magistrates of our city very often come from the Marches, and tend as a rule to be mean-hearted men, who lead such a frugal and beggarly sort of life that anyone would think they hadn't a penny to bless themselves with. And because of their inborn miserliness and avarice, they bring with them judges and notaries who seem to have been brought up behind a plough or recruited from a cobbler's shop rather than from any of the schools of law.

Now, one of these March-men came here once to take up his appointment as *podestà*, and among the numerous judges he brought with him, there was one called Messer Niccola da San Lepidio, who looked more like a coppersmith than anything else, and he was assigned to the panel of judges that tried criminal cases.

Now it frequently happens that people go to the law-courts who have no business to be there at all, and this was the case with Maso del Saggio, who had gone there one morning to look for a friend. His gaze being attracted to the place where this Messer Niccola was sitting, he was struck by the man's curious and witless appearance, and began to scrutinize him carefully. And amongst the many strange features that he noted, unbecoming in any person of tidy habits and gentle breeding, he saw that the fur of his judge's cap was thick with grime, that he had a quill-case dangling from his waist, and that his gown was longer than his robe. But the most remarkable thing of all, to Maso's way of thinking, was a pair of breeches, the crotch of which, when the judge was sitting down and his clothes gaped open in front owing to their skimpiness, appeared to come halfway down his legs.

Having seen all he wanted to see of the judge's breeches, he abandoned the search for his friend and set off on a different quest, this time for two companions of his called Ribi and Matteuzzo, who were no less high-spirited than Maso himself. And when he had tracked them down, he said to them:

'If my friendship means anything to you, come along with me to the law-courts, and I'll show you the most priceless booby you ever saw.'

So off he went with Ribi and Matteuzzo to the law-courts, where he showed them the judge and his breeches. Viewing this spectacle from the back of the court, they began to laugh, and on coming closer to the platform on which Master Judge was seated, they saw that it would be very easy for a person to conceal himself underneath. Moreover the plank on which the judge's feet were resting had a large hole in it, through which a hand and an arm could be thrust with the greatest of ease.

Maso therefore turned to his companions, and said:

'Let's pull those breeches right down for the fellow. We can do it quite easily.'

The other two had already seen how it could be done, and having arranged with one another what they were to say and do, they returned there the following morning. Despite the fact that the courtroom was crowded, Matteuzzo managed to crawl into the space beneath the platform without being seen, and positioned himself exactly below the spot where the judge's feet were resting. Then Maso went up to the judge on one side and seized the hem of his robe, whilst Ribi approached him from the other side and did the same.

'Sir,' Maso began. 'O sir, I beseech you in God's name not to let this petty thief, who is standing at the other side of you, escape from this courtroom before you have made him give me back the pair of thigh-boots he has stolen from me. He claims he didn't do it, and yet I saw him, less than a month ago, having them re-soled.'

Then Ribi shouted in his other ear:

'Don't you believe him, sir; he's a lying rogue, and because he knows that I've come to lay a complaint against him for stealing a saddlebag of mine, he comes out with this story about the thigh-boots, which I've had in my house for donkey's years. If you don't believe me, I can call any number of witnesses, such as the woman next door, who runs the fruit stall, and Grassa the tripe-merchant, and a dustman from Santa Maria a Verzaia, who saw him on his way home from town.'

Maso for his part was not prepared to leave all the talking to Ribi, but he too began to shout, and Ribi shouted even louder. And as the judge stood up and edged closer to them in order to follow what they were saying, Matteuzzo seized his opportunity, thrust his hand through the hole in the plank, took a firm hold on the seat of the judge's breeches, and pulled hard. The breeches came down forthwith, for the judge was a scraggy fellow, and very lean in the buttocks. Being at a loss to understand how this had come about, the judge tried to cover himself up by drawing his clothes across the front of his body and sitting down, but Maso and Ribi were still holding on to them at either side and shouting their heads off, saying:

'It's monstrous, sir, that you should refuse me a hearing, and try to withdraw without giving your verdict. Surely you don't need written evidence to decide a trifling matter of this sort.' And whilst they were saying all this, they held on to his clothes sufficiently long for everyone in court to perceive that he had lost his breeches. Then finally, Matteuzzo, having clung to them for some little time, released his hold and made good his escape from the courtroom without being seen, whilst Ribi, deciding he had done quite enough, exclaimed:

'I swear to God I'll appeal to the Senate.'

At the same time, Maso let go the judge's robe on his side, saying:

'I shan't go to any Senate. I'll keep coming back here, sir, until I find you in less of a muddle than you seem to be in this morning.'

Then they both made off in opposite directions as fast as their legs would carry them.

It was only at this point that Master Judge, having pulled up his breeches before all those present, as though he were just getting up out of bed, became aware of the deception and demanded to know what had become of the two men who were arguing about the thigh-boots and the saddlebag. But when they couldn't be found, he began to swear by the bowels of God that somebody should tell him whether it was the custom in Florence for a judge to have his breeches removed whilst sitting on the bench of justice.

When the *podestà*, for his part, was told what had happened, he practically threw a fit. But when it was pointed out by his friends that this had only been done in order to show him that the Florentines knew he had brought fools with him instead of judges so as to save money, he thought it best to hold his tongue, and nothing more was said about the matter.

SIXTH STORY

Bruno and Buffalmacco steal a pig from Calandrino. Pretending to help him find it again, they persuade him to submit to a test using ginger sweets and Vernaccia wine. They give him two sweets, one after the other, consisting of dog-stools seasoned with aloes, so that it appears that he has stolen the pig himself. And finally they extract money from him, by threatening to tell his wife about it.

Filostrato had no sooner completed his story, which aroused a great deal of laughter, than the queen called on Filomena to follow, whereupon she began, saying:

Gracious ladies, just as Filostrato was prompted to tell you the previous tale by hearing the name of Maso, in precisely the same way I too have been prompted by hearing the names of Calandrino and his companions to tell you another, which I believe you will find to your liking.

It is unnecessary for me to explain to you who Calandrino, Bruno and Buffalmacco were, for you have heard enough on that score in the earlier tale. So I shall omit the preliminaries, and tell you that Calandrino had a little farm not far from Florence, which he had received from his wife by way of a dowry. Among the other things he acquired from this farm, every year he used to obtain a pig there, and it was his regular custom to go to the country in December with his wife, slaughter the pig, and have it salted.

Now, it so happened that one year, when Calandrino's wife was not feeling very well, he went to the farm by himself to slaughter the pig. And when Bruno and Buffalmacco heard about this, knowing that his wife was remaining behind, they went to stay for a few days with a priest, who was a very great friend of theirs and lived near Calandrino's farm.

Calandrino had slaughtered the pig on the morning of the very day they arrived, and on seeing them with the priest, he called out to them, saying:

'I bid you a hearty welcome, my friends. Come along inside, and

I'll show you what an excellent farmer I am.' And having taken them into the farmhouse, he showed them the pig.

It was a very fine pig, as they could see for themselves, and when they learnt from Calandrino that he intended to salt it and take it back to his family, Bruno said:

'You must be out of your mind! Why not sell it, so that we can all have a good time on the proceeds? You can always tell your wife it's been stolen.'

'Not a chance,' said Calandrino. 'She wouldn't believe me, and she'd kick me out of the house. Now, stop pestering me, because I shall never do anything of the sort.'

They argued with him at great length, but it was no use. And after Calandrino had invited them to stay for supper with so reluctant an air that they decided not to accept, they all took their leave of him.

After leaving Calandrino, Bruno said to Buffalmacco:

'Why don't we steal that pig of his tonight?'

'But how are we to do that?' said Buffalmacco.

'I've already thought of a good way to do it,' said Bruno, 'provided that he doesn't move it to some other place.'

'In that case,' said Buffalmacco, 'let's do it. After all, why not? And when the deed is done, you and I, and our friend the priest here, will all make merry together.'

The priest was very much in favour of this idea, and so Bruno said:

'This thing calls for a certain amount of finesse. Now you know, Buffalmacco, don't you, that Calandrino is a mean sort of fellow, who's very fond of drinking when other people pay. So let's go and take him to the tavern, where the priest can pretend to play the host to the rest of us and pay for all the drinks. When he sees that he has nothing to pay, Calandrino will drink himself into a stupor, and then the rest will be plain sailing because there's no one else staying at the house.'

Everything turned out as Bruno had predicted. When Calandrino saw that the priest would not allow him to pay, he began to drink like a fish, and quaffed a great deal more than he needed to make him drunk. By the time he left the tavern, it was already very late, and not wishing to eat any supper, he staggered off home and went to bed, thinking he had bolted the door whereas in fact he had left it wide open.

Buffalmacco and Bruno went and had supper with the priest, and when the meal was over they stealthily made their way to Calandrino's house, taking with them certain implements so that they could break in at the spot that Bruno had decided on earlier in the day. On finding the door open, however, they walked in, collected the pig, and carted it off to the priest's house, where they stowed it away and went off to bed.

Next morning, having slept off the effects of the wine, Calandrino got up and went downstairs to find that his pig had gone and the door was open. So he went round asking various people whether they knew who had taken the pig, and being unable to find any trace of it, he began to make a great outcry, shouting: 'Alas! Woe is me! Somebody's stolen my pig!'

Meanwhile, Bruno and Buffalmacco got up and went round to Calandrino's to hear what he would have to say about the pig. And no sooner did he catch sight of them than he called out to them, almost in tears, saying:

'Alas, my friends, somebody's stolen my pig!'

Bruno then went up to him, and, speaking out of the corner of his mouth, he said:

'Fancy that! So you've had a bit of sense at last, have you?'

'Pah!' exclaimed Calandrino. 'I'm telling you the gospel truth.'

'That's the way,' said Bruno. 'Go on shouting like that, so that people will think it's really happened.'

Whereupon Calandrino began to shout even louder, saying:

'God's body, man, I tell you it's been stolen, it really has.'

'Excellent, excellent,' said Bruno. 'Keep it up, give the thing plenty of voice and make yourself heard, so as to make it sound convincing.'

'You'll drive me to perdition in a minute,' said Calandrino. 'Do I have to hang myself by the neck before I can convince you that it really has been stolen?'

'Get away with you!' said Bruno. 'How can that be, when I saw it there myself only yesterday? Are you trying to make me believe it's flown away?'

'It's gone, I tell you,' said Calandrino.

'Go on,' said Bruno, 'you're joking.'

'I swear to you I'm telling the truth,' said Calandrino. 'What am I to do now? I can't go back home without the pig. My wife will never believe me, but even if she does, she'll make my life a misery for the next twelve months.'

'Upon my soul,' said Bruno, 'it's a serious business, if you're speaking the truth. But as you know, Calandrino, I was telling you only yesterday that you ought to say this. I wouldn't like to think that you were fooling your wife and us at the same time.'

Calandrino protested loudly, saying:

'Ah! why are you so intent on driving me to despair and provoking me to curse God and all the Saints in Heaven? I tell you the pig was stolen from me in the night.'

'If that's the case,' said Buffalmacco, 'we'll have to see if we can find some way of getting it back.'

'How are we to do that?' asked Calandrino.

So Buffalmacco said:

'Whoever took your pig, we can be quite sure that he didn't come all the way from India to do it. It must have been one of your neighbours. So all you have to do is to bring them all together so that I can give them the bread and cheese test, and we'll soon see who's got it.'

'Oh, yes,' said Bruno, 'your bread and cheese will work miracles, I'm sure, on some of the fine folk who live around here. It's quite obvious that one of them has the pig. They'd guess what we were up to, and stay away.'

'What's to be done, then?' asked Buffalmacco.

'What we ought to do,' Bruno replied, 'is to use the best ginger sweets we can get hold of, along with some fine Vernaccia wine, and invite them round for a drink. They wouldn't suspect anything, and they'd all turn up. And it's just as easy to bless ginger sweets as it is to bless bread and cheese.'

'You certainly have a point there,' said Buffalmacco. 'What do you say, Calandrino? Shall we give it a try?'

'Of course,' said Calandrino. 'Let's do that, for the love of God. If only I could find out who took it, I shouldn't feel half so miserable about it!'

'That's settled then,' said Bruno. 'Now I'd be quite willing to go to Florence and get these things for you, if you'll give me the money.'

Calandrino gave him all the money he had, which amounted to about forty pence, and so Bruno went to Florence and called on a friend of his, who was an apothecary. Having bought a pound of the best ginger sweets he had in stock, he got him to make two special ones, consisting of dog-stools seasoned with fresh hepatic aloes; then he had these coated with sugar, like the rest, and so as not to lose them or confuse them with the others, he had a tiny mark put on them which enabled him to recognize them without any difficulty. And having bought a flask of fine Vernaccia, he returned to Calandrino's place in the country, and said to him:

'See to it that you invite all the people you suspect to come and drink with you tomorrow morning. It's a holiday, so they'll all come readily enough. Tonight, along with Buffalmacco, I shall cast a spell on the sweets, and bring them round to your house first thing tomorrow morning. I shall hand the sweets out myself, to save you the trouble, and I shall pronounce all the right words and do all the right things.'

Calandrino issued the invitations, and next morning a goodly crowd of people assembled round the elm in front of the church, of whom some were farm-workers and others were young Florentines who happened to be staying in the country. Then along came Bruno and Buffalmacco with a box of sweets and a flask of wine, and having got them to stand in a circle, Bruno made the following announcement:

'Gentlemen, I must explain to you why you are here, so that if you should take offence at anything that happens, you won't go and blame it on me. The night before last, Calandrino, who is here among us, was robbed of a fine fat pig, and he can't find out who has taken it. And since it could only have been taken by one of the people here, he wants to discover who it was by offering, to each of you in turn, one of these sweets to eat, together with a drink of this wine. I should explain to you right away that whoever has taken the pig will be unable to swallow the sweet – in fact, he will find it more bitter than poison, and spit it out. So before he is put to so much shame in the presence of all these people, perhaps it would be better for the person responsible to make a clean breast of it to the priest, and I can call the whole thing off.'

All of them were only too eager to eat one of the sweets, and so Bruno, having lined them up with Calandrino in the middle, started from one end and began to hand one out to each of them in turn. When he came to Calandrino, he picked up one of the sweets of the canine variety and placed it in the palm of his hand. Calandrino promptly tossed it into his mouth and began to chew on it, but no sooner did his tongue come into contact with the aloe than, finding the bitter taste quite intolerable, he spat it out again.

They were all keeping a close watch on one another to see who was going to spit out his sweet, and Bruno, who still had several more to distribute, carried on as though nothing had happened until he heard a voice behind him saying: 'Hey, Calandrino, what's the meaning of this?' Turning quickly round, and seeing that Calandrino had spat his out, he said:

'Wait a minute! Perhaps he spat it out for some other reason. Here, take another!' And picking up the second one, he thrust it into Calandrino's mouth before proceeding to hand out the ones he had left.

Bitter as Calandrino had found the first, the second seemed a great deal more so, but being ashamed to spit it out, he kept it in his mouth for a while. As he chewed away at it, tears as big as hazel-nuts began to roll down his cheeks until eventually, being unable to bear it any longer, he spat it out like the first.

Buffalmacco was meanwhile handing out drinks all round, with the assistance of Bruno. And when, along with all the others, they observed what had happened, everyone declared that Calandrino had obviously stolen the pig himself, and there were one or two who gave him a severe scolding about it.

However, when the crowd had dispersed, leaving Bruno and Buffalmacco alone with Calandrino, Buffalmacco turned to him and said:

'I was convinced all along that you were the one who had taken it. You were just pretending to us that it had been stolen so that you wouldn't have to buy us a few drinks out of the proceeds.'

Calandrino, who still had the bitter taste of the aloe in his mouth, swore to them that he had not taken the pig, but Buffalmacco said:

'Own up, man, how much did it fetch? Six florins?'

Calandrino was by now on the brink of despair, but Bruno said:

'You might as well know, Calandrino, that one of the fellows we were drinking and eating with this morning told me that you had a girl up here, that you kept her for your pleasure and gave her all the little titbits that came your way, and that he was quite certain you had sent her this pig of yours. You've become quite an expert at fooling people, haven't you? Remember the time you took us along the Mugnone? There we were, collecting those black stones, and as soon as you'd got us stranded up the creek without a paddle, you cleared off home, and then tried to make us believe that you'd found the thing. And now that you've given away the pig, or sold it rather, you think you can persuade us, by uttering a few oaths, that it's been stolen. But you can't fool us any more: we've cottoned on to these tricks of yours. As a matter of fact, that's why we took so much trouble with the spell we cast on the sweets; and unless you give us two brace of capons for our pains, we intend to tell Monna Tessa the whole story.'

Seeing that they refused to believe him, and thinking that he had enough trouble on his hands without letting himself in for a diatribe from his wife, Calandrino gave them the two brace of capons. And after they had salted the pig, they carried their spoils back to Florence with them, leaving Calandrino to scratch his head and rue his losses.

SEVENTH STORY

A scholar falls in love with a widow, who, being in love with someone else, causes him to spend a winter's night waiting for her in the snow. But on a later occasion, as a result of following his advice, she is forced to spend a whole day, in mid July, at the top of a tower, where, being completely naked, she is exposed to the flies and the gadflies and the rays of the sun.

Though the ladies shook with laughter over the hapless Calandrino, they would have laughed even more if the people who had stolen his pig had not relieved him also of his capons, which made them feel sorry for him. However, the story having come to an end, the queen called upon Pampinea to tell hers, and she began forthwith, as follows:

Dearest ladies, one cunning deed is often capped by another, and hence it is unwise to take a delight in deceiving others. Many of the stories already narrated have caused us to laugh a great deal over tricks that people have played on each other, but in no case have we heard of the victim avenging himself. I therefore propose to enlist your sympathy for an act of just retribution that was dealt to a fellow townswoman of ours, who very nearly lost her life when she was hoist with her own petard. Nor will it be unprofitable for you to hear this tale, for it will teach you to think twice before playing tricks on people, which is always a sensible precaution.

Not many years ago, there lived in Florence a young woman called Elena, who was fair of body, proud of spirit, very gently bred, and reasonably well endowed with Fortune's blessings. When her husband died prematurely, leaving her a widow, she made up her mind that she would never remarry, having fallen in love with a handsome and charming young man of her own choosing. And now that she was free from all other cares, she succeeded, with the assistance of a maidservant whom she greatly trusted, in passing many a pleasant hour in his arms, to the wondrous delight of both parties.

Now it happened that around that time, a young nobleman of our city called Rinieri, having spent some years studying in Paris with the purpose, not of selling his knowledge for gain as many people do, but of learning the reasons and causes of things (a most fitting pursuit for any gentleman), returned from Paris to Florence. There he was held in high esteem for his nobility and his learning, and he led the life of a gentleman.

But it frequently happens that the more keen a man's awareness of life's profundities, the more vulnerable he is to the forces of Love, and so it was in the case of this Rinieri. For one day, being in need of a little diversion, he went to a banquet, where his eyes came to rest upon this young woman, Elena, who was dressed (as our widows usually are) in black, and seemed to him the loveliest and most fascinating woman he had ever seen. He thought to himself that the man to whom God should grant the favour of holding her naked in his arms could truly claim that he was in Paradise. And having stolen many a cautious glance at the lady, knowing that so great and precious a prize could not be won without considerable effort, he firmly resolved to devote all his care and attention to pleasing the lady, so that he might win her love and savour her manifest beauty to the full.

The young woman, who was her own greatest admirer, was not in the habit of keeping her eyes fixed upon the ground, but darted coy glances in every direction and swiftly singled out those men who were showing an interest in her. And on catching sight of Rinieri, she laughed to herself and thought: 'I shan't have wasted my time in coming here today, for unless I am mistaken, I'm about to lead a simpleton by the nose.' She then began to look at him every so often out of the corner of her eye, and did her utmost to make it appear that she took an interest in him, being of the opinion, in any case, that the more men she could entice and conquer with her charms, the more highly would her beauty be prized, especially by the young man to whom, along with her love, she had given it.

The learned scholar, setting all philosophical meditations aside, filled his mind exclusively with thoughts of the lady; and thinking it would please her, he discovered where she lived and began to walk past her house at frequent intervals, inventing various pretexts for passing that way. For the reason already mentioned, this greatly encouraged the lady's vanity, and she pretended to be very flattered. And so at the first opportunity the scholar made friends with her maidservant, declared his love for the lady, and begged her to use her influence with her mistress so that he might win her favours.

The maid promised him the moon and reported their conversation to her mistress, who laughed so much that she nearly died. And she said:

'I wonder where he's left all that wisdom that he brought back with him from Paris? But never mind, let's give him what he's looking for. Next time he speaks to you, tell him that I love him far more than he loves me; but tell him that I have to protect my honour, so that I may hold up my head in the company of other women. And if he's as wise a man as they say he is, this ought to make him think more highly of me.'

Ah, what a poor, misguided wretch she must have been, dear ladies, to suppose that she could get the better of a scholar!

But to return to our narrative, the maid having delivered the lady's message, the scholar, overjoyed, proceeded to entreat her with greater warmth than before, writing letters to her and sending her presents, all of which she accepted. But the only answers he received were couched in the vaguest of terms; and in this fashion she toyed with him for some little time.

She meanwhile gave a full account of the affair to her lover, who took it rather amiss and displayed a certain amount of jealousy. And so at length, in order to show him that his jealousy was misconceived, she sent her maid to the scholar, who was bombarding her with entreaties, to tell him on her behalf that albeit since the day he had first declared his love, she had not had a single opportunity to grant his desires, she hoped it would be possible to forgather with him in the immediate future, during Christmastide. If, therefore, he would like to come to the courtyard of her house after dark on the evening of the day after Christmas, she would meet him there as soon as she conveniently could.

The scholar was the happiest man in Christendom, and having gone to her house at the time she had specified, he was taken by the maid to a courtyard, where he was locked in and began to wait for the lady.

Earlier that evening, the lady had invited her lover to the house, and after they had supped merrily together, she told him what she was proposing to do that night, adding:

'And you'll be able to see exactly how much I love this fellow, whom you were foolish enough to regard as your rival.'

These words brought great joy to the heart of her lover, who was impatient to see what the outcome would be.

Now, it so happened that earlier in the day there had been a heavy fall of snow, and it lay thick all over the place, so before the scholar had spent much time in the courtyard, he began to feel distinctly chilly. But since he was expecting relief at any moment, he suffered it all in patience.

After a while, the lady said to her lover:

'Let's go and spy on this precious rival of yours from the little window in the bedroom, and see what he has to say to the maid. I have just sent her down to have a few words with him.'

So off they went to the bedroom, from which they could look down on the courtyard without being seen, and they heard the maid addressing the scholar from another window.

'Rinieri,' she said, 'my mistress is positively at her wits' end, for one of her brothers called on her this evening and kept her talking for ages, after which he insisted on staying for supper, and he still hasn't left, though I think he'll be going quite soon. This explains why she hasn't been able to come to you; but she'll be down in a moment, and begs you not to be angry with her for having to wait so long.'

Thinking the maid's story was true, the scholar replied:

'Tell my lady that she is not to worry on my account until it is convenient for her to come. But tell her to come as soon as she can.'

The maid closed the window and retired to bed, whereupon the lady said to her lover:

'What do you say to that, my dearest? Do you think I'd keep him out there freezing to death if I cared for him, as you suspect?'

Her lover's doubts were by now almost totally dispelled, and she got into bed with him, where they disported themselves merrily and rapturously for hours on end, laughing and making fun of the hapless scholar.

The scholar was walking up and down the courtyard to keep himself warm, and since there was nowhere for him to sit down or take shelter, he kept cursing the lady's brother for tarrying so long with her. Whenever he heard a sound, he thought it must be the lady opening a door to let him in, but his hopes were dashed every time.

After cavorting with her lover till the early hours of the morning, the lady said:

'What do you think of this scholar, my darling? Which would you say was the greater: his wisdom, or my love for him? Will the cold I am causing him to suffer dispel the coldness that entered your heart when I spoke of him in jest to you the other day?'

'But of course, my precious,' replied the lover. 'Now I can see quite clearly that you care for me as deeply as I care for you, who are the true source of my well-being, my repose and my delight, and the haven of all my desires.'

'Then give me a thousand kisses at least,' said the lady, 'so that I may see whether you are telling me the truth.' Whereupon, clasping her firmly to his bosom, her lover kissed her, not a thousand times, but more than a hundred thousand. But after they had billed and cooed in this fashion for a while, the lady said:

'Come, let's get up and see whether those flames, in which this weird lover of mine was always claiming to be consumed, show any sign of diminishing.'

They accordingly got up and returned once more to the window, and on looking down into the yard, they saw the scholar performing a sort of eightsome reel in the snow, for which the sound of his chattering teeth provided the accompaniment. And because of the extreme cold, he was moving his feet at such a furious pace that they had never seen a dance to compare with it.

'What do you say to that, my sweetheart?' said the lady. 'Don't you think it clever of me to make men dance without the aid of trumpets or bagpipes?'

'I do indeed, my darling,' replied her lover, shaking with laughter.

Then the lady said:

'Let's go down to the door leading into the courtyard. You keep quiet while I talk to him, and we'll hear what he has to say. Perhaps it will be just as funny as it is to stand here and watch him.'

And so, having tiptoed out of the bedroom, they crept downstairs to the courtyard-door, and without opening it by so much as a fraction of an inch, the lady called out to the scholar in a low voice, through a tiny crack in the door.

On hearing her summons, the scholar gave thanks to God, wrongly concluding that she was about to let him in. And walking across to the door, he said:

'Here I am, my lady. Open up for the love of God, for I'm freezing to death.'

'Ah yes, you must be very cold,' said the lady. 'But can it really be so chilly as all that out there, simply because it's been snowing a little? It snows a great deal harder in Paris, or so I've been told. I can't let you in at present, because this accursed brother of mine, who came to supper with me yesterday evening, still hasn't gone. However, he'll be going soon, and when he does, I'll come and let you in right away. I had an awful job to tear myself away from him just now, so that I could come and encourage you not to take offence over having to wait.'

'But, madam,' said the scholar, 'I implore you for the love of God to let me in, so that I can take shelter, for there was never such a heavy fall of snow as this, and it's still coming down. Once you've let me in, I'll wait as long as you please.'

'Alas, my dearest, I can't do that,' said the lady. 'This door makes such a din when it's opened that my brother would be sure to hear it. But I'll see if I can persuade him to go away now, and then I'll come back to let you in.'

'Go quickly then,' said the scholar. 'And I beg you to make sure there's a nice big fire, so that I can warm myself up when I come in. I'm so cold that I scarcely have any feeling left in my body.'

'I don't see how that can be possible,' said the lady. 'You always claim in your letters that you are burning all over because of your love for me. But it's clear to me now that you must have been joking. However, I must go now. Wait here, and keep your fingers crossed.'

The lady's lover, having heard every syllable, was mightily pleased, and returned with his mistress to bed, where they slept very little, but spent virtually the entire night disporting themselves and making fun of the unfortunate scholar.

Perceiving that he had been duped, the scholar, whose teeth were chattering so vigorously that he seemed to have been turned into a stork, tried the door several times to see whether it would open, and searched all round the courtyard for some other way out. But finding none, he paced to and fro like a lion in a cage, cursing the severity of the weather, the perfidy of the lady, the inordinate length of the night, and his own stupidity. So indignant did he feel about the way he had been treated by the lady that his fervent and longstanding love was transformed into savage and bitter hatred, and his mind dwelt on various elaborate schemes for securing his revenge, which he now desired far more ardently than he had formerly yearned to hold her in his arms.

It seemed to him that the night would never end, but eventually the dawn began to appear, and the maidservant, following the instructions of her mistress, came down to open the courtyard gate. Pretending to be very sorry for him, she said:

'A curse on that brother of hers for coming here yesterday evening. He's kept us in suspense the entire night, and frozen you to the marrow. But you know how it is! Don't be disheartened, try again some other night, and perhaps you'll have better luck. My mistress is heartbroken that this should have happened, she really is.'

Though seething with indignation, the scholar was wise enough to know that menaces simply forearm the person who is threatened, and so, swallowing all the resentment that was striving within him for an outlet, he said to her in a quiet voice, without betraying the slightest hint of his anger:

'To be honest, it was the worst night I have ever spent, but I could see that the lady was in no way to blame, for she was so concerned about me that she came down in person to apologize and offer me her sympathy. And as you say, perhaps I shall have better luck some other night. So fare you well, and commend me to your mistress.'

Paralysed in every limb and every joint, he returned as best he could to his own house, where, feeling utterly exhausted, he flung himself on to his bed and fell fast asleep. Some time later, he woke up to find that he could scarcely move his arms or his legs, and having sent for physicians and told them about the chilling he had suffered, he placed himself under their care.

Though the physicians applied the most prompt and efficient remedies they could devise, it was some little time before they managed to restore his circulation and straighten out his limbs, and but for his youth and the advent of milder weather, he would never have recovered at all. However, having regained his health and vigour, he suppressed his hatred of the widow and pretended to be far more enamoured of her than he had ever been before.

Now, after a certain amount of time had elapsed, Fortune supplied the scholar with a chance to gratify his longing for revenge. For the young man who was the object of the widow's affection, paying no heed whatever to the love that she bore him, fell in love with another woman and resolved to have nothing more to do with her, so that she pined away in tears and bitter lamentations. But her maid, feeling very sorry for her and finding no way of assuaging the grief that had seized her mistress in the loss of her lover, conceived the foolish idea that the young man might be persuaded to return to his former love by the application of some form of magic. And since she supposed that the scholar, whom she regularly caught sight of in the neighbourhood as he passed by the house in his usual fashion, must be a great expert in the art of magic, she broached the idea to her mistress.

The lady was not very intelligent, and it never occurred to her that if the scholar had known anything about magic he would have used it on his own behalf. She therefore took the maid's suggestion seriously, and told her to go and find out at once whether he would do it. And in return for his assistance, she would promise him faithfully to give him whatever he wanted.

The maid scrupulously delivered the message, on hearing which the scholar was overjoyed, and said to himself: 'Praise be to God, for with His assistance, the time has come for me to punish the wicked hussy for the wrong she did me in exchange for all the love I bore her.' And turning to the maid, he said:

'Tell my lady not to worry about this, for even if her lover were in India, I should make him return to her at once and ask her forgiveness for flouting her wishes. Tell her that she has only to fix a time and a place, and I shall explain to her what she must do in order to remedy matters. And do please give her my kindest regards.'

The maid took his answer to her mistress, and it was arranged that they should meet in the church of Santa Lucia, near the Prato gate.

So there they met, the lady and the scholar, and as they conversed alone together, quite forgetting that this was the man she had almost conveyed to his death, she freely poured out all her troubles, told him what she desired, and begged him to come to her rescue, whereupon the scholar said:

'Madam, it is perfectly true that magic was one of the subjects I studied in Paris. I can assure you that I learned all there is to know about it, but since it is most distasteful to God, I made a vow never to practise it, either for my own or anyone else's benefit. However, my love for you is so intense that I find it impossible to refuse you anything, so even if I were to be consigned to Hell for this alone, I am ready to do it, since that is what you want of me. Nevertheless, I must warn you that this is a more difficult thing to achieve than perhaps you imagine, especially when a woman wishes to regain the love of a man or vice versa, for it cannot be done except by the person most closely involved. Moreover it is essential for this person to be very brave, for the operation must be carried out at night in a lonely place, with no other people present, and I do not know whether you are ready to comply with these conditions.'

Being more a slave to her love than a model of common sense, the lady replied:

'So powerful are the promptings of Love that I would do anything to possess again the man who has so cruelly forsaken me. But tell me, why do I have to be brave?'

'Madam,' replied the scholar, with devilish cunning, 'it will be my job to make an image, in tin, of the man whose love you wish to regain, and this I shall send to you in due course. Holding the image in your hand, you must make your way all alone, in the dead of night, when the moon is well on the wane, to a flowing stream, in which you must immerse yourself seven times, completely naked, after which, still naked, you must climb up a tree or on to the roof of some deserted building. Facing towards the north, with the image still in your hand, you must repeat seven times in succession a certain formula which I shall write down for you, whereupon you will be approached by two young ladies, as fair as you have ever seen, who will greet you amicably and ask you what it is that you want to be done. See that you explain your wishes to them as clearly and as fully as you can, and make sure that you give them the name of the right person. Once you've done that, they will go away, and you'll be able to descend to the place where you left your clothes, put them on again, and return home. And without a shadow of a doubt, by the middle of the following night your lover will come to you in tears, asking you to forgive and take pity on him. Thenceforth, I can assure you that he will never again desert you for another woman.'

The lady, hanging on his every word, was already, in her mind's eye, holding her lover once again in her arms, and half her troubles seemed to be over.

'You may rest assured,' she replied, 'that I shall carry out your instructions to the letter, and I know the very place to do it, for I have a farm along the upper reaches of the Arno which is very close to the banks of the river, and since we are now in the month of July it will be a pleasure to go for a bathe. Moreover, I recall that not far from the river there is a small tower, which is totally abandoned except for the fact that every so often the shepherds climb up the wooden ladder to a platform at the top, in order to scan the country-side for their lost sheep. The place is very deserted and out-of-the-way, and by climbing to the top of the tower, I hope to be in an ideal spot to do all you require.'

The scholar knew exactly where the lady's property and the little tower were situated, and being pleased to find that things were working according to plan, he said:

'I was never in those parts, madam, and hence I know neither the farm nor the tower of which you speak. But if your description is correct, there couldn't be a better place in the whole world. When the time is ripe, therefore, I shall send you the image and the magic formula; but I do urge you to remember, once your wish has been granted and you realize how well I have served you, to keep the promise you have given me.'

The lady assured him that she would do so without fail, and having taken her leave of him she returned to her house.

Delighted at the prospect of what was about to happen, the scholar fashioned an image with certain hieroglyphics upon it, and wrote down some nonsense concocted by himself to serve as a formula. These he sent in due course to the lady, bidding her to wait no longer, but to act upon his instructions on the very next night; then he secretly made his way with a servant to the house of one of his friends, which was not far away from the tower, in order to carry his plan into effect.

For her part, the lady set out with her maidservant and went to the farm. As soon as night had fallen, pretending that she was about to retire, she sent the maid off to bed, and in the dead of night, she stole softly out of the house and made her way to the bank of the Arno, near the tower of which she had spoken. Then, having peered in every direction and listened carefully to make sure that no one was about, she undressed, concealed her clothes under a bush, and dipped herself seven times in the river, clutching the image in her hand; after which, still holding the image, she made her way, naked, towards the tower.

Near the tower there was a clump of willows and other trees from which the scholar, having concealed himself there with his man-servant shortly after dark, had viewed the whole of these proceedings. When the lady, in all her naked beauty, was passing within an arm's length of where he lay hidden, he could see her white form piercing the shades of the night, and as he gazed upon her bosom and the other parts of her body, perceiving how lovely they were and thinking to himself what was shortly to happen to them, he could not help feeling sorry for her. Moreover, being suddenly assailed by the desires of the flesh, which caused a recumbent part of his person to stand, he was strongly tempted to sally forth from his hiding-place, seize her in his arms, and take his pleasure of her. So that, what with his pity on the one hand and his lust on the other, he very nearly gave himself away. But when he remembered who he was, the wrong he had suffered, the reason for it, and the person who had inflicted it upon him, his indignation was rekindled, dispelling all his pity and fleshly desires, and, clinging firmly to his resolve, he allowed her to proceed on her way.

Having climbed to the top of the tower, the lady turned to face the north and began to recite the words given to her by the scholar, who meanwhile, having followed her into the tower, had silently dis-mantled piece by piece the ladder leading up to the platform on which she was standing. And he was now waiting to see what she would say and do.

The lady repeated the formula seven times and began to await the arrival of the two fair maidens, but she had so long to wait that, apart from feeling far more chilly than she would have wished, she was still there when the dawn began to appear. Feeling somewhat aggrieved that things had not worked out as the scholar had told her, she said to herself: 'I strongly suspect he was trying to give me a night like the one I provided for him; but if that was his intention, he's chosen a feeble way of avenging himself, for the night he spent was at least three times as long, and the cold was far more severe.' But as she had no desire to be found up there in broad daylight, she now prepared to descend, only to discover that the ladder had gone.

She accordingly felt as though the world beneath her feet had suddenly been taken away, and fell in a dead faint on the platform of the tower, where she lay for some time before recovering her senses. On coming round, she began to weep and wail in a most heartrending fashion, and realizing all too well that this was the scholar's handiwork, she repented the wrong she had done, as well as the excessive trust she had placed in one whom she had every reason to look upon as her enemy. And whilst she was thus reproaching herself, a considerable time elapsed.

Eventually she looked all around her in search of some way to descend, but being unable to find any, she burst once more into tears and thought, bitterly, to herself: 'Oh, hapless woman, what will your brothers, your kinsfolk, your neighbours, and Florentine people in general have to say, when it is known that you were found in this spot, completely naked? Your fair repute will be seen as merely an empty façade; and if you try to brazen it out by giving some spurious explanation or other, you will be exposed by this accursed scholar, who knows all about your private affairs. Ah, poor wretch, that at one and the same moment you should have lost not only the young man you were foolish enough to love, but your good name into the bargain!' And her anguish grew to such a pitch that she was almost on the point of hurling herself from the tower to the ground.

The sun having now arisen, however, she moved a little closer to the wall on one side of the tower, thinking she might see some youngster driving his sheep in her direction, whom she could send to fetch her maidservant. But as she peeped over the rim, she caught sight of the scholar, who had just woken up after sleeping for a while under a bush.

'Good morning, madam,' he said. 'Have the young ladies arrived yet?'

On hearing these words, the lady burst into tears yet again, and begged him to come inside the tower so that she could speak to him.

The scholar very politely granted her request, and the lady, lying face downwards on the floor of the roof in such a way that only her head appeared in the aperture, addressed him, weeping plaintively and saying:

'You have certainly paid me back, Rinieri, for the unpleasant night

I caused you to spend, for although we are in the month of July, I was convinced, not having any clothes on, that I was going to freeze to death up here last night. But apart from this I've been crying so much over the trick I played on you and over being such a fool as to believe you, that it's a miracle I have any eyes left in my head. I therefore implore you, not for love of me, whom you have no reason to love, but for your own sake, as a gentleman, to let this suffice by way of revenge for the injury I did you, and bring me my clothes and let me down. Please don't deprive me of that which you could never restore to me even if you wished, in other words, my good name. For even if I did prevent you from spending one night with me, I can make amends for it whenever you like by letting you spend many another night with me in exchange for that one. Rest content with what you have done. Let it suffice you, as a gentleman, to have succeeded in avenging yourself and making me aware of the fact. Don't apply your strength against a mere woman: the eagle that conquers a dove has nothing to boast about. For the love of God and the sake of your honour, do have mercy on me.'

The scholar, indignantly reflecting on the injury she had done him, and perceiving her tears and her entreaties, was filled with pleasure and sorrow at one and the same time: the pleasure of that revenge which he had desired above all else, and the sorrow engendered by his compassionate nature at the sight of her distress. His compassion being unequal, however, to his craving for revenge, he replied:

'Madonna Elena, if by my entreaties (albeit I had not the power to flavour them with tears and honeyed words as you do your own) I had succeeded, on the night I spent freezing to death in that snow-filled courtyard of yours, in prevailing upon you to shelter me in any way at all, it would be an easy matter for me now to grant your request. But since you display so much more concern now for your good name than you ever showed in the past, and find it so unpleasant to stay up there in a state of nudity, why do you not direct these pleas of yours to the man in whose arms, as you well remember, you were pleased to spend that night, no less naked than you are now, listening to me as I tramped with chattering teeth through the snow in your yard? Why not ask him to assist you, why not ask him to bring you your clothes, why not ask him to set up the ladder for you to descend?

Why not turn to him to protect this good name of yours, since it is for his sake that you have placed it in jeopardy, not only now but a thousand times before?

'Why do you not call to him to come and help you? What could be more appropriate, since you belong to him? If he refuses to help and protect you, whom will he ever help and protect? Go on, you silly woman, call to him, and see whether your love for him and your intelligence, combined with his own, can save you from my stupidity. After all, did you not ask him, when you were cavorting together, whether he considered my stupidity or your love for him to be the greater? As for the generous offer you made just now to grant me your favours, I no longer desire them, and you couldn't very well deny them to me if I did. Save your nights for your lover, if you should happen to escape from here alive; you and he are welcome to them; one night was quite enough for me, and I have no intention of being fooled a second time.

'What is more, by cunningly mincing your words, you attempt through flattery to soften my heart towards you, calling me a gentleman, and quietly trying to dissuade me from punishing you for your wickedness, by appealing to my better nature. But the eyes of my mind will not be clouded now by your blandishments, as once they were by your perfidious promises. I know myself better now than I did earlier, for you taught me more about my own character in a single night than I ever learned during the whole of my stay in Paris.

'But even supposing I were a charitable man, you are not the sort of woman who deserves to be treated with charity. For a savage beast of your sort, death is the only fit punishment, the only just revenge, though admittedly, had I been dealing with a human being, I should already have done enough. So whilst I am not an eagle, yet, knowing that you are not a dove, but a poisonous snake, I intend to harry you with all the hatred and all the strength of a man who is fighting his oldest enemy. To call it revenge, however, is a misuse of words, for it is rather a punishment, inasmuch as revenge must exceed the offence and this will fall short of it. For when I consider how nearly you came to causing my death, it would not suffice for me to take your life by way of revenge, nor a hundred others like it, since I should only be killing a foul and wicked strumpet.

'For how, in the name of Lucifer, do you differ from any other miserable little whore, apart from having a tolerably pretty face, which in any case a few years hence will be covered all over in wrinkles? Yet it was not for lack of trying that you failed to murder a gentleman (as you called me just now), who can bring more benefit to humanity in a single day than a hundred thousand women of your sort can bring to it for as long as the world shall last. By suffering as you do now, then, you will possibly learn what it means to trifle with a man's affections, and to hold a man of learning up to ridicule; and if you should escape with your life, you will have good cause never to stoop to such folly again.

'But if you are so anxious to descend, why do you not throw yourself over the parapet? With God's help, you would break your neck, and so release yourself from the pain you seem to be suffering, at the same time making me the happiest man alive. That is all I have to say to you for the present. Now that I have managed to put you up there, let's see whether you are as clever at finding your way down as you were at making me look such a fool.'

Whilst the scholar was speaking, the hapless woman wept without stopping, time was passing, and the sun was climbing higher in the sky. But now that he was silent, she said:

'Ah! how could any man be so cruel! If you suffered so much on that accursed night, and my fault seemed so unpardonable, that neither my youth, my beauty, my bitter tears, nor my humble entreaties can evoke the tiniest crumb of pity, at least you should be touched to some extent, and hence prepared to treat me less severely, by the fact that I eventually trusted in you and told you all my secrets, thus allowing you to show me the error of my ways. For if I had not confided in you, you would not have been able to avenge yourself upon me, as you appear so eagerly to have wished.

'Alas! set your anger aside now, and grant me your forgiveness. If you will only forgive me and allow me to descend, I am prepared to forsake that faithless youth entirely, and you alone will be my lover and my lord, even though you despise my beauty, showing it to be fleeting and of little worth. But whatever you may say about it, or indeed about the beauty of any other woman, I can at least tell you this: that our beauty should be prized, if for no other reason than because it brings sweetness, joy, and solace to a man's youth; and you yourself are not old, by any means. Furthermore, however cruelly you treat me, I cannot believe that you would wish to see me suffer so ignominious a death as to throw myself down like a desperate woman before your very eyes – those eyes to which, unless you lied then as you do now, the sight of me was once so pleasing. Ah! in the name of God, have mercy on me, for pity's sake! The sun is becoming unbearably hot, and just as I suffered from the intense cold during the night, so now does the heat begin to distress me exceedingly.'

'Madam,' replied the scholar, who was only too delighted to converse with her, 'it was not because you loved me that you took me into your confidence, but to recover the love that you had lost, and hence you deserve to be treated even more harshly. Moreover you are out of your mind if you suppose that this was the only way I had of obtaining the revenge that I coveted. I had a thousand others, and I had placed a thousand snares around your feet whilst pretending to love you, so that even if this one had failed, you would inevitably have stumbled into another before very long. True, you could not have chosen to fall into a trap which would bring you greater shame and suffering than this, but then I laid it in this way, not in order to spare your pain, but to enhance my pleasure. And even supposing that all my little schemes had failed, I should still have had my pen, with which I should have lampooned you so mercilessly, and with so much eloquence, that when my writings came to your notice (as they certainly would), you would have wished, a thousand times a day, that you had never been born.

'The power of the pen is far greater than those people suppose who have not proved it by experience. I swear to God (and may He grant that my revenge will continue to be as sweet from now until its end as it has been in its beginning), that you yourself, to say nothing of others, would have been so mortified by the things I had written that you would have put out your eyes rather than look upon yourself ever again. It's no use reproaching the sea for having grown from a tiny stream.

'As for your love, or that you should belong to me, these are matters towards which, as I said before, I am utterly indifferent. Go on belonging, if you can, to the man you belonged to before, whom I now love as much as I formerly hated, considering the pretty pass to which you have been brought on his account. You women are always falling in love with younger men, and yearning for them to love you in return, because of their fresher complexions and darker beards, their jaunty gait, their dancing and their jousting; but when a man is properly mature, he has put such matters as these behind him, and knows a thing or two that these young fellows have yet to learn.

'Moreover, because a young man will cover more miles in a single day, he seems to you a better rider. But whereas I admit that he will shake your skin-coat with greater vigour, the older man, being more experienced, has a better idea of where the fleas are lurking. Besides, a portion that is small, but delicately flavoured, is infinitely preferable to a larger one that has no taste at all. And a hard gallop will tire and weaken a man, however young, whilst a gentle trot, though it may bring him somewhat later to the inn, will at least ensure that he is still in good fettle on arrival.

'Senseless creatures that you are, you fail to perceive how much evil may lie concealed beneath their handsome outward appearance. A young man is never content with one woman, but desires as many as he sets his eyes upon, thinking himself worthy of them all; hence his love can never be stable, as you can now bear witness all too clearly for yourself. Besides, they feel they have a right to be pampered and worshipped by their women, and take an enormous pride in boasting of their conquests – a failing which has caused many a woman to land in the arms of the friars, who keep their lips sealed about such matters. When you claim that your maid and I are the only people who know of your secret love, you are sadly mistaken. You deceive yourself if that is what you believe, for the people of the district where he lives, as well as of your own, talk about nothing else; but the person most closely involved is invariably the last to hear of these things. And you should also remember that young men will steal from you, whereas older men will give you presents.

'And so, having made a bad choice, you may remain his to whom you gave yourself, and leave me, whom you spurned, to another; for I have found a lady who is far more worthy of my love, and understands me better than you ever did. It seems that you do not believe me when I tell you, here and now, that I long to see you dead: but if you want proof of my words in the life hereafter, why not throw yourself to the ground without any further ado, in which case your soul, which I truly believe to be nestling already in the arms of the devil, will soon see whether or not your headlong fall has brought any tears to my eyes? But since you are unlikely to afford me so great a pleasure as this, I shall simply advise you, if you find yourself being scorched, to remember the freezing you gave me, and if you mix the hot with the cold, you will doubtless find the rays of the sun more bearable.'

On perceiving from the scholar's words that he was determined to wreak vengeance upon her, the hapless lady burst once more into tears, and said:

'Since nothing pertaining to me can move you to pity me, at least be moved by the love you bear this other lady, who is so much wiser than myself, and by whom you claim to be loved. Forgive me for her sake, fetch me my clothes so that I may dress, and let me come down.'

Whereupon the scholar burst out laughing, and observing that it was already well past the hour of tierce, he replied:

'Ah, how can I refuse your request, now that you have appealed to me in her name? Tell me where your clothes are, so that I can go and fetch them and arrange for you to descend.'

The lady took him seriously and, feeling somewhat reassured, described to him exactly where she had hidden her clothes, whereupon the scholar issued forth from the tower and ordered his servant not to move away from the spot, but to stay close to the tower and do his best to see that no one set foot inside it until he returned. And having given him these instructions, he made his way to his friend's house, where in due course, after eating a most leisurely meal, he retired for a siesta.

The lady continued to lie on the roof of the tower, foolishly entertaining some faint hope of a speedy end to her predicament, until, feeling exceedingly sore, she sat up and crawled over to that section of the parapet which afforded a little shade from the sun, where she settled down to wait with no other company than her own bitter thoughts. By turns brooding and weeping, now hoping and now despairing of the scholar's return with her clothes, her mind flitting from one doleful reflection to the next, she eventually succumbed to her grief, and since she had been awake for the whole of the previous night, she fell into a deep slumber.

The sun was positively blazing, and having reached its zenith, was beating freely down, with all its power, straight on to her soft and tender body and on to her unprotected head, so that not only did it scorch every part of her flesh that was exposed to its rays, but it caused her skin to split into countless tiny cracks and fissures. And so intense was the roasting she received that although she was soundly asleep, it forced her to wake up.

On finding she was being burnt, she attempted to move, whereupon she felt as if the whole of her scorched skin was being rent asunder like a piece of flaming parchment being stretched from both ends. Moreover (and this was not in the least surprising), she had such an excruciating pain in her head that she thought it would burst. The floor of the tower-roof was so hot that she could find nowhere to stand or sit down, and so she kept shifting her position the whole time, weeping incessantly. But apart from all this, there being not a breath of wind, the air was literally teeming with flies and gadflies, which, settling in the fissures of her flesh, stung her so ferociously that every sting was like a spear being thrust into her body. And hence she flailed her arms in all directions, heaping a constant stream of curses upon herself, her life, her lover, and the scholar.

Being thus goaded, tormented, and pierced to the very quick by the incalculable heat, the rays of the sun, the flies and gadflies, her hunger and above all her thirst, as well as by a thousand agonizing thoughts, she stood up straight and looked about her in the hope of seeing or hearing someone who could be summoned to her assistance, being by now prepared to do anything, come what may, to effect her release.

But here too she was dogged by ill luck. The peasants had all deserted the fields on account of the heat, and in any case nobody had been working near the tower that morning because they were staying at home to thresh the corn. So all she heard was the sound of cicadas, and the only moving thing in sight was the Arno, whose inviting waters did nothing to lessen her thirst, but only made it worse. And scattered about the countryside she could see houses and woods and shaded places, all of which played no less cruelly upon her desires.

What more are we to say of this hapless widow? What with the sun beating down from above, the torrid heat of the floor beneath her feet, and the flies and gadflies piercing her flesh all over, she was in such a sorry state that her body, whose whiteness had dispelled the shades of night just a few hours before, had now turned red as madder, and being liberally flecked with blood, it would have seemed, to anyone who saw it, the ugliest thing in the world.

There, then, she remained, bereft of all counsel and all hope, expecting rather to die than survive, until late in the afternoon, when the scholar, having risen from his siesta, returned to the tower to see how his lady was faring, and told his servant, who had not yet eaten, to go and procure himself a meal. On hearing him talking to the servant, the lady painfully dragged her weak, tormented body to the aperture, where she sat down, burst into tears, and said:

'Surely your revenge has exceeded all the bounds of reason, Rinieri. For whereas I made you freeze by night in my courtyard, you have roasted me on this tower by day, or rather burnt me to a cinder, and caused me to die of hunger and thirst in the process. I therefore beg you in God's name to come up here, and, since I do not have the courage to take my own life, to kill me yourself, for death is the one thing I desire above all else, such is the torture I am suffering. But if you are unwilling to concede me this favour, let me at least have a beaker of water so that I may moisten my mouth, which is so parched and dry that my tears will not suffice to bathe it.'

From the sound of her voice, the scholar realized all too plainly that her strength was failing. Furthermore, from that part of her body which was visible to him, he could see that she must be burnt by the sun from head to toe. All of which, together with the humble tone of her entreaties, caused him to feel a modicum of pity for her; but nevertheless he replied:

'Vile strumpet that you are, you shall not perish by these hands of mine, but by your own, if you really want to die; and you will have as much water from me to relieve you from the heat, as you gave me fire to restore me from the cold. My one great regret is that the illness I suffered on account of the cold required to be treated with stinking dung, whereas your own injuries, occasioned by the heat, can be treated with fragrant rose-water. And whereas I practically lost my life as well as the use of my limbs, you will merely be flayed by this heat, and emerge with your beauty unimpaired, like a snake that has sloughed off its skin.'

'Ah! woe is me,' cried the lady. 'I pray to God that only my worst enemies should acquire beauty by such means as this! But how could you be so cruel as to torture me in this fashion? What greater punishment could you or anyone else have inflicted upon me, if I had caused your entire kith and kin to die a lingering death? Of this at least I am certain, that no traitor who had put a whole city to the slaughter could have been more barbarously treated than I have, for not only do you cause me to be roasted in the sun and devoured by flies, but you refuse me a beaker of water, when even a condemned murderer on his way to the gallows will frequently be given wine to drink if only he asks for it. However, since I see you are determined to be quite ruthless, and my suffering cannot move you in the slightest, I shall now prepare to die with resignation, so that God may have mercy on my soul, and I pray that He will observe what you have done and judge you accordingly.'

Having uttered these words, she crawled in terrible agony, being convinced that she would never survive the intense heat, towards the centre of the platform, where, quite apart from her other torments, she felt that she would swoon from thirst at any moment. And all the time, she was wailing loudly and bemoaning her misfortunes.

Finally, however, with the approach of evening, the scholar, feeling he had done enough, sent for her clothes and wrapped them in his servant's cloak, after which he made his way to the hapless lady's house, where he found her maid sitting sadly and forlornly on the doorstep, not knowing what she should do.

'My good woman,' he said, 'tell me, what has become of your mistress?'

'Sir,' replied the maidservant, 'I cannot rightly say. I was convinced that I saw her going to bed last night, and thought I should find her there this morning. But she was nowhere to be seen, and I have no idea what has become of her. I am dreadfully worried about her, but perhaps you, sir, have brought me some news of her whereabouts?'

'Would to God,' replied the scholar, 'that I had been able to put you in the place where I have put your mistress, so that I could punish you for your sins as I have punished your mistress for hers! But I assure you that you shan't escape from my clutches until I have paid you back with so much interest that you'll never make a fool of any man again without remembering me first.'

Then, turning to his servant, he said:

'Give her these clothes and tell her to go and fetch her, if she wants to.'

The servant did as he was bidden, and the maid, having seized the clothes from his hands, and recognized them, turned pale with terror, strongly suspecting, in view of what she had been told, that they had murdered her. Scarcely able to prevent herself from screaming, she burst into tears, and, the scholar having now departed, she immediately set off at a run towards the tower, with the clothes under her arm.

That same afternoon, a swineherd from the lady's estate had had the misfortune to lose two of his pigs, and searching all over for them, he arrived at the tower shortly after the scholar had left. Peering into every nook and cranny to see whether his pigs were anywhere to be found, he heard the unfortunate lady's despairing moans, and climbing as far up the tower as he could, he called out:

'Who is it that is crying up there?'

Recognizing the swineherd's voice, the lady called to him by name, and said:

'Alas! go fetch my maid and tell her to come up here.'

'Oh my God!' he exclaimed, seeing who it was. 'How ever did you get up there, ma'am? Your maid has been searching high and low for you the whole day. But who would have thought of looking for you here?'

Seizing the ladder by the two uprights, he set it in the proper position and began to tie on the rungs by means of withies. As he was doing this, the maidservant arrived on the scene, and on entering the tower, no longer able to hold herself in check, she clapped her palms to the sides of her head and cried out:

'My poor, sweet mistress, where are you?'

On hearing the maidservant's voice, the lady called to her with all her strength, saying:

'Here I am, my sister. Up here. Don't cry, but just bring me my clothes, and quickly.'

No sooner did she hear the voice of her mistress, than her fears were almost entirely dispelled, and climbing the ladder, which by this time was all but repaired, she succeeded, with the swineherd's assistance, in reaching the platform, where, finding her mistress lying naked on the floor, utterly broken and exhausted, looking more like a burnt log than a human form, she dug her nails into her face and burst into tears, as though she were gazing down upon a corpse. However, the lady implored her for God's sake to be silent and help her to dress. And having learnt from the maid that no one knew where she had been, except for the swineherd and those who had brought her clothes, she felt somewhat relieved, and begged them for God's sake never to breathe a word about it to anyone.

The lady could not descend by herself, and so, after some little discussion, the swineherd hoisted her on to his shoulders and carried her safely down the ladder and out of the tower, leaving the maid-servant to make her own way down. But being in too much of a hurry, the poor maidservant missed her footing as she was descending the ladder, and fell to the ground, breaking her thigh in the process, whereupon she began to roar with agony like a wounded lion.

Having set the lady down on the grass, the swineherd returned to see what was wrong with the maidservant, and on finding she had broken her thigh, he brought her forth in the same fashion, setting her on the grass by the side of her mistress. When the lady saw that, on top of her other afflictions, the person on whose assistance she most depended had broken her thigh, she burst yet again into tears, weeping so bitterly that not only was the swineherd unable to console her, but he too started to cry.

But as the sun was by now beginning to set, and the hapless lady was anxious that they should be away from there before nightfall, she prevailed upon him to go back to his house, whence, having enlisted the aid of his wife and two of his brothers, he returned with a plank on which they placed the maidservant and conveyed her to the house. Meanwhile, the lady's spirits having been restored by a draught of cool water and a torrent of sympathy, the swineherd hoisted her once more on to his shoulders, and carried her home, setting her down in her own bedroom.

His wife prepared a bowl of gruel for the lady, after which she undressed her and put her to bed. Between them they arranged that both the lady and her maid should be taken to Florence later that same night, and this was duly done.

On returning to Florence, the lady, who was by no means deficient in guile, wove a completely fictitious account of how she and her maid had sustained their injuries, and persuaded her brothers, sisters, and everyone else that it had all come about through the machinations of evil spirits.

The physicians promptly set to work upon the lady, but since she shed the whole of her skin several times over because it kept sticking to the bedclothes, she suffered untold agony and torment before they succeeded in curing her of her raging fever and other infirmities. They also attended to the maidservant's thigh, which in due course mended itself.

In view of what she had been through, the lady gave no further thought to her lover, and from then on she wisely refrained from playing any more tricks or falling deeply in love with anyone. As for the scholar, when he heard that the maid had broken her thigh, he deemed his revenge sufficient, and went happily about his business and said no more about it.

This, then, was the foolish young lady's reward for supposing it was no more difficult to trifle with a scholar than with any other man, being unaware that scholars – not all of them, mind you, but the majority at any rate – know where the devil keeps his tail.

I advise you therefore to think twice, ladies, before you play such tricks, especially when you have a scholar to deal with.

EIGHTH STORY

A story concerning two close friends, of whom the first goes to bed with the wife of the second. The second man finds out, and compels his wife to lock the first man in a chest, on which he makes love to his friend's wife whilst he is trapped inside.

Grievous and painful as the recital of Elena's woes had been to the ladies, their compassion was restrained by the knowledge that she had partially brought them upon herself, though at the same time they considered the scholar to have been excessively severe and relentless, not to say downright cruel. However, now that Pampinea had come to the end of her story, the queen called next upon Fiammetta, who, all eager to obey, began as follows:

Charming ladies, since you appear to have been somewhat stricken by the harshness of the offended scholar, I consider this a suitable moment at which to soothe your outraged feelings with something slightly more entertaining; and I therefore propose to tell you a little tale about a young man who took a more charitable view of an injury he received, and devised a more harmless way of avenging himself. You will thereby be enabled to apprehend, that when a man seeks to avenge an injury, it should be quite sufficient for him to render an eye for an eye and a tooth for a tooth, without wanting to inflict a punishment out of all proportion to the original offence.

You are to know, then, that there once lived in Siena (or so I have heard) two highly prosperous young men of good plebeian families, of whom the first was called Spinelloccio Tavena and the second was called Zeppa di Mino, and they lived next door to one another in the district of Camollia. They always went about together, and to all outward appearances were as deeply attached to one another as if they were brothers. And both were married to very beautiful women.

Now, it happened that Spinelloccio spent a great deal of his time in Zeppa's house, and since Zeppa was not always at home, he made such good friends with Zeppa's wife that they became lovers, and it was a long time before anyone discovered their secret. One day, however, when Zeppa was at home and his wife was unaware of the fact, Spinelloccio called at his house, and, on being informed by the wife that Zeppa was out, he swiftly went up to the parlour, where, perceiving that she was all alone, he enfolded her in his arms and began to kiss her, and she greeted him in the same way. Although Zeppa saw all this happening, he held his tongue and remained hidden, so that he could see where their little game was going to end; and before long, to his utter dismay, he saw his wife and Spinelloccio, still clinging to one another, make their way into the bedroom and lock themselves in. Realizing, however, that neither by creating an uproar nor by interfering in any way was he going to reduce the extent of his injury, but that on the contrary his dishonour would thereby be increased, he applied his mind to devising some form of revenge that would satisfy his wounded pride without causing any scandal, and after pondering at some length, he thought he had discovered a way of doing it.

He remained in hiding for as long as Spinelloccio and his wife were together, but as soon as Spinelloccio had left, he walked into the bedroom, where he found his wife still putting the finishing touches to her headdress, which had fallen off whilst she was cavorting with her lover.

'Well, woman,' he said, 'and what may you be doing?'

'Can't you see?' she replied.

'Yes,' said Zeppa, 'I can see all right. And I've seen one or two other things that I would have preferred not to see at all.' He then took her to task over what she had been doing, and after making numerous excuses, she confessed in fear and trembling to those aspects of her relationship with Spinelloccio that she could not very well deny, then burst into tears and asked his forgiveness.

Whereupon Zeppa said to her:

'Now listen to me, woman. You've done wrong, and if you want me to forgive you, see that you do exactly as I am about to tell you. I want you to tell Spinelloccio that tomorrow morning, about the hour of tierce, he is to invent some excuse for quitting my company so that he can come back here to you; once he is here, I shall return home, and as soon as you hear me coming, you are to make him hide in this chest and lock him in, after which I shall give you the rest of your instructions. There's no need whatever for you to worry about doing all this. I give you my word that I shan't do him any harm.'

In order to please him, his wife agreed to do it, and gave Spinelloccio the message.

The following morning, Zeppa and Spinelloccio were roaming the streets together, and when it was nearly tierce, Spinelloccio, who had promised Zeppa's wife that he would call on her at that hour, said to his companion:

'I have to breakfast with a friend this morning, and I don't want to keep him waiting, so I think I'll be getting along.'

'You can't go to breakfast at this hour,' said Zeppa. 'It's too early.'

'That doesn't matter,' said Spinelloccio. 'I also have one or two things to discuss with him, so I still have to arrive there in good time.'

Having, therefore, taken leave of Zeppa, Spinelloccio doubled back on his tracks and was soon under Zeppa's roof in the company of his wife. But they had scarcely set foot inside the bedroom before Zeppa returned home, and as soon as the woman heard him coming, she pretended to be frightened out of her senses and, having persuaded Spinelloccio to take cover in the chest to which her husband had referred, she locked him inside it and left the room.

Zeppa came upstairs and asked her whether it was time for breakfast, and on being told that it was, he said:

'Spinelloccio is taking breakfast with a friend of his this morning, and he's left his wife all alone in the house. Go and call out to her from the window, and tell her to come and have breakfast with us.'

Still feeling apprehensive on her own account, the woman was only too ready to obey him, and promptly did as she was told. And so, after a good deal of coaxing, Spinelloccio's wife, hearing that her husband would not be returning home for breakfast, was persuaded by Zeppa's wife to come and join them. As soon as she set foot inside the house, Zeppa made a great fuss of her and took her tenderly by the hand. Then, having ordered his wife, in a low whisper, to go along to the kitchen, he led the other woman off into the bedroom, and no sooner had they crossed the threshold than he turned round and locked the door on the inside.

When she perceived that he had locked the door, the woman said:

'Come now, Zeppa, what is the meaning of this? Was this, then, your reason for inviting me here? I thought you loved Spinelloccio as a brother, I thought you were his loyal friend.'

Holding her firmly round the waist, Zeppa guided her closer to the chest in which her husband was confined, and said to her:

'Before you go complaining, my dear, listen to what I have to say to you. I loved Spinelloccio as a brother, and I still do, but yesterday I discovered, without his knowing it, that my trust in him had come to this, that he makes love just as freely to my wife as he does to you. Now, because I love him, the only revenge I propose to take is one that exactly matches the offence. He has possessed my wife, and I intend to possess you. If you refuse to co-operate, I shall certainly catch him out sooner or later, and since I have no intention of allowing his offence to go unpunished, I shall deal with him in such a way as to make both of your lives a perpetual misery.'

Having listened to Zeppa's story and questioned him closely about it, the woman was convinced that he was telling the truth, and she said:

'My dear Zeppa, if I have to bear the brunt of your revenge, so be it; but only if you will see that your wife harbours no resentment against me over this deed we are obliged to perform, just as I myself, in spite of what she has done to me, intend to harbour none against her.'

To which Zeppa replied:

'I shall certainly see to that; and what's more, I shall present you with as fair and precious a jewel as any you possess.' So saying, he took her in his arms and began to kiss her; and having laid her on the chest in which her husband was imprisoned, he sported with her upon it to his heart's content, and she with him.

Spinelloccio, who was inside the chest and had not only heard all that Zeppa had said but also his wife's reply and the fandango that shortly thereafter took place directly above his head, was torn with anguish, and felt at any moment he would die. But for his fear of Zeppa, he would have given his wife a severe scolding, even though he was under lock and key. In the end, however, recalling that he himself was to blame in the first place, that Zeppa was justified in doing this to him and that he had chosen a civil and comradely way of taking his revenge, Spinelloccio vowed that, if Zeppa was agreeable, they would thenceforth become greater friends than ever.

Having taken his fill of pleasure, Zeppa stepped down from the chest, and on being asked by the lady for the jewel he had promised, he opened the door and summoned his wife. The only words she uttered, on entering the room, were:

'My dear, you've paid me back in my own coin.' And as she said this, she laughed.

Then Zeppa said to her:

'Open up this chest.'

She duly obeyed, and turning to the lady, Zeppa pointed to the huddled figure of her husband, Spinelloccio, who was now revealed inside it.

It would be hard to decide which of the two was the more embarrassed: Spinelloccio, on seeing Zeppa standing over him and knowing that he knew what he had done; or the lady, on seeing her husband and realizing that he had heard and felt what she had been doing directly above his head.

However, Zeppa broke the silence, saying to the lady:

'Here's the jewel I promised to give you.'

Spinelloccio now emerged from the chest, and without making too much fuss, he said:

'Now we are quits, Zeppa. So let us remain friends, as you were saying just now to my wife. And since we have always shared everything in common except our wives, let us share them as well.'

Zeppa having consented to this proposal, all four breakfasted together in perfect amity. And from that day forth, each of the ladies had two husbands, and each of the men had two wives, nor did this arrangement ever give rise to any argument or dispute between them.

NINTH STORY

Being eager to 'go the course' with a company of revellers, Master Simone, a physician, is prevailed upon by Bruno and Buffalmacco to proceed by night to a certain spot, where he is thrown by Buffalmacco into a ditch and left to wallow in its filth.

When the ladies had quite finished commenting upon the two Sienese and their wife-sharing, the queen, who short of offending Dioneo was the only one left to address them, began as follows:

When you consider, fond ladies, how richly Spinelloccio deserved the trick played upon him by Zeppa, you will I think agree with what Pampinea was saying earlier, when she tried to show that one should not judge a person too harshly for playing a trick on another, if the victim is being hoist with his own petard, or if he is simply asking to be made a fool of. The case of Spinelloccio belongs to the first of these categories, and I now propose to tell you of a man who belonged to the second, for I consider that those who played the trick upon him are worthy rather of praise than of blame. The man to whom I refer was a physician, who came to Florence from Bologna, like the ass that he was, covered in vair from head to tail.

We are constantly seeing fellow-citizens of ours returning from Bologna as judges or physicians or lawyers, tricked out in long flowing robes of scarlet and vair, looking very grand and impressive, but failing to live up to their splendid appearance. Master Simone da Villa was a man of this sort, for his patrimony was far more copious than his learning, and when, a few years ago, he came to Florence dressed in scarlet robes with a fine-looking hood, and calling himself a doctor of medicine, he set up house in the street we now call Via del Cocomero.

Being, as we have said, newly arrived in Florence, this Master Simone made it a practice, among his other eccentricities, to ask whoever he happened to be with at the time about all the people he saw passing down the street; and he duly noted and remembered everything he was told about them, as though this information was essential in prescribing the right medicine for his patients.

Among the people who aroused his greatest curiosity were the two painters already mentioned twice here today, Bruno and Buffalmacco, who were neighbours of his and never out of one another's company. Since they seemed to him the jolliest and most carefree fellows in the world, as was indeed the case, he made various inquiries about their social condition, and everyone told him that these two men were painters, who hadn't a penny to bless themselves with. But as he was unable to conceive how they could possibly lead such merry lives without visible means of support, he came to the conclusion, having heard that they were very clever, that they must be drawing huge profits from a source that other people had no knowledge of. He therefore became eager to make friends with one of them at least, if not with both, and eventually succeeded in striking up an acquaintance with Bruno, who, realizing from the first that this physician was a blockhead, began to take a huge delight in the man's extraordinary simplicity, whilst the physician for his part found Bruno wondrously entertaining. Having invited Bruno to breakfast with him a few times, thereby assuming that he could treat him as a familiar, he told him how amazed he was that he and Buffalmacco, considering they were so poor, could lead such merry lives; and he pleaded with Bruno to explain to him how they did it. Taking the physician's words as yet another proof of his crass stupidity, Bruno burst out laughing, and on the principle that a silly question deserves a silly answer, he replied as follows:

'Master Simone, there are few people to whom I would reveal this secret of ours, but since you are a friend and I know you won't let it go any further, I shan't keep it all to myself. It's perfectly true that my comrade and I lead as full and contented a life as you suppose, and even more so. Yet if we had to rely on our painting, or on the income from our capital, we shouldn't have enough to pay the water-rates. Not that I want you to think that we live by stealing: no, we simply go the course, as the saying is, by which means we obtain all the pleasures and necessities of life without doing harm to anyone; and that is how, as you've noticed, we always manage to be so cheerful.'

The physician, hanging on his every word without knowing what he was talking about, was filled with amazement by all this, and promptly conceived a burning desire to discover what was meant by 'going the course'. So he begged and pleaded with him to explain it, declaring most emphatically that he would never tell another living soul.

'Good heavens, Master!' exclaimed Bruno. 'Do you realize what you are asking me to do? The secret you want me to reveal is so tremendous that if anyone were to find out I had told you, I could be ruined and driven from the face of the earth; I could even finish up in the jaws of the Lucifer at San Gallo. However, such is my veneration for your truly distinguished ineptitude that I am obliged to grant your every wish, and therefore I shall let you into the secret, but only on condition that you swear by the cross of Montesone to keep your promise, and never repeat it to anyone.'

The physician gave him the required assurance, and Bruno continued:

'Know then, my sweet Master, that not long ago there came to this city a great master in necromancy, whose name was Michael Scott, for he was a native of Scotland. He was entertained in princely style by many Florentine nobles, of whom only a handful are still alive, and when the time came for him to depart, they persuaded him to leave behind him two able disciples, whom he charged with the duty of ministering promptly to the pleasures of these nobles who had done him so much honour.

'These two men freely assisted the aforesaid nobles in certain love-affairs and other little escapades of theirs, and after a while, having taken a liking to the city and the ways of its people, they decided to settle here permanently. They soon acquired a goodly number of intimate friends in the city, without caring whether they were rich or poor, patrician or plebeian, provided only that they were men whose interests coincided with their own. And in order to please these friends of theirs, they founded a society of about five-and-twenty members, who were to meet at least twice a month in whatever place the pair of them should decide. When they are all assembled, each of the members makes a wish, and the two magicians see that it is granted that same night.

'Now, because Buffalmacco and I are on the most friendly and intimate of terms with these two men, they enrolled us in this society of theirs, and we've belonged to it ever since. I assure you that whenever we hold one of our meetings, it's a wonderful thing to behold the tapestries all round the walls of the banqueting hall, and the tables set in regal style, and the noble array of handsome-looking servants, both male and female, who are at the beck and call of every member of the company, and the bowls and the jugs, the flasks and the goblets, and the rest of the vessels from which we either eat or drink, all made of silver or of gold; and no less marvellous than all this, the abundance and variety of the dishes that are set before us one after the other, each of them suited to our own particular tastes.

'I could never describe to you the range and multiplicity of the dulcet sounds from countless instruments, and the melodious songs, that descend upon our ears at these gatherings. Nor could I tell you how many candles we burn at these banquets, or estimate the number of sweetmeats we consume, or the value of the wines that we drink. Neither would I want you to imagine, my dear wiseacre, that we attend these meetings in the clothes you normally see us wearing; even the most beggarly of the people present looks like an emperor, for we are decked out, one and all, in sumptuous robes and other finery.

'But over and above all these other delights, there are the beautiful women who are brought to us there, the moment we ask for them, from every corner of the earth. Not only would you see the Begum of Barbanicky, the Queen of the Basques, and the Sultana of Egypt, but also the Empress of Osbech, the Chitchatess of Norwake, the Semolina of Nomansland, and the Scalpedra of Narsia. But why bother to enumerate them all? You would see every queen in the world there, not even excluding the Skinkymurra of Prester John, who has horns sticking out of her anus: now there's a spectacle for you! And when they have wined and dined, these ladies trip the light fantastic for a little while, after which each of them retires to a bedroom with the man who asked for her to be brought.

'Now these rooms, mark you, are so glorious to behold that you'd swear you were in Paradise itself. Moreover they're as fragrant as the spice-jars in your dispensary when you're pounding the cumin, and the beds on which we lie are every bit as splendid as the Doge's bed in Venice. I leave you to imagine how busily these ladies work the treadle, and how nimbly they pull the shuttle through, to weave a fine close fabric. But the people who have the best time of all, in my opinion, are Buffalmacco and myself, because Buffalmacco invariably sends for the Queen of France, and I send for the Queen of England, who when all's said and done are two of the handsomest women on God's earth. So you can work it out for yourself whether we have good reason to be happier than other men, considering that we enjoy the love of two such queens as these, not to mention the fact that when we have need of a couple of thousand florins, they hand them over to us right away. And that's what we mean when we talk about going the course, for just as the corsair takes away other people's goods, we do the same; but whereas corsairs never restore their plunder, we give ours back as soon as we've put it to good use.

'Now that you've discovered what is meant, my precious Master, by going the course, you will see for yourself how important it is that you should keep it a secret; so there's no need for me to say any more on the subject.'

Master Simone, the extent of whose medical knowledge was sufficient, perhaps, to treat an infant for thrush, took everything Bruno had said as the gospel truth, and was inflamed with an intense longing to become a member of their society, as though this were the highest good to which any mortal being could possibly aspire. He accordingly told Bruno that he was no longer in the least surprised that they were always so cheerfully disposed; and it was with the greatest difficulty that he restrained himself from urging him to enrol him there and then, rather than waiting until he had plied him more generously with his hospitality, after which he could plead his cause with a better chance of success.

Having therefore held himself in check, he assiduously began to court Bruno's friendship, regularly inviting him to breakfast and supper, and displaying boundless affection towards him. And they spent so much time in one another's company that it began to look as though the physician was unable to exist without him.

Bruno counted his blessings, and in order not to appear ungrateful for the physician's lavish hospitality, he painted a Lenten mural for him on the wall of his dining-room and an *Agnus Dei* at the entrance to his bedroom and a chamber-pot over his front door, so that those people who needed to consult him could distinguish his house from the rest. Moreover, he decorated the loggia with a painting of the battle between the cats and the mice, which in the eyes of the physician was something of a masterpiece.

One morning, after failing to turn up to supper the previous evening, Bruno said to the physician:

'I was with the company last night, but as I'm tiring a little of the Queen of England, I got them to fetch me the Gumedra of the Great Khan of Altarisi.'

'Gumedra?' said the physician. 'What does that signify? I don't understand these titles.'

'I'm not a bit surprised, my dear Master,' said Bruno, 'for I've heard that neither Watercress nor Avadinner say anything on the subject.'

'You mean Hippocras and Avicenna,' said the physician.

'You may well be right,' said Bruno, 'for these names of yours mean about as much to me as mine do to you. However, the word Gumedra in the language of the Great Khan is equivalent to the word Empress in ours. And believe you me, she's really delicious! She'd soon make you forget all about your medicines and your pills and your poultices, I can tell you.'

From time to time, by recounting other tales of a similar kind, Bruno added further fuel to the flames of the physician's longings, until, very late one evening, when Bruno was busy painting the battle between the cats and the mice by the light of a lantern being held aloft by Master Simone, the physician decided that Bruno was by now sufficiently in his debt for him to bring his feelings into the open. And since they were alone in the house, he said:

'As God is my witness, Bruno, there isn't anyone on earth for whom I would do all the things I would do for you. Why, even if you were to ask me to go all the way from here to Peretola,* I almost believe I would do it. So I trust you will not take it amiss if I speak to you now as an intimate friend, and ask you a favour in strict confidence. As you know, you spoke to me not long ago about the doings of your

*A distance of about four miles.

merry company, and ever since that day, I've been positively dying to attend your meetings. I have good reason for wanting to come, as you'll see for yourself if I should happen to be invited, for I assure you here and now that if I don't get those magicians of yours to fetch the comeliest serving wench you've seen for many a long day, I deserve to be taken for an idiot. I fell passionately in love with the girl from the moment I clapped eyes on her, last year at Cacavincigli, and I swear to God that I offered her ten Bolognese groats, but she turned them down. So I implore you, from the bottom of my heart, to tell me what I have to do to become a member, and I beg you to use all your power and influence to bring it about, for I can assure you that you could never have a better or more loyal comrade, nor one who would bring you greater credit. I don't suppose, for instance, that any of your members is a doctor of medicine, and you can see for yourself what a handsome fellow I am, with a fine pair of shanks and a face like a rose. Besides, I know lots of good stories and some excellent songs. Would you like to hear one?' And without waiting for an answer, he burst into song.

Bruno was so amused by all this that he had a job to keep a straight face; and when the song was finished, the Master said:

'Well, Bruno, what do you think of that?'

'It's fantastic,' said Bruno. 'With a cacophonous voice like that, you could charm the vultures out of the trees.'

'If you hadn't heard it with your own ears,' said the Master, 'you wouldn't have believed it possible, would you?'

'I certainly wouldn't,' said Bruno.

'I know lots of others,' said the Master, 'but let's forget about those for the moment. Such as you see me, my father was a nobleman, though he lived in the country, and on my mother's side I was born into the Vallecchio family. Furthermore, as you will have seen, I have a finer collection of books, and a more splendid wardrobe, than any other doctor in Florence. God's faith! I have a robe that cost me nearly a hundred pounds in farthings, all told, ten years ago at the very least. So I do implore you to have me enrolled in your company; and if you get me in, God's faith! you can be as ill as you like, and I'll never charge you a penny for my services.'

Bruno was more than ever convinced, having listened to his

prattle, that the man was a complete nincompoop, and said to him:

'Shed a little more light up here, Master, and just be patient till I've finished putting the tails on these mice, then I'll give you my answer.'

When he had finished off the tails, Bruno pretended to be very worried by the doctor's request, and said:

'I know about the great things you would do for me, Master, but nevertheless the favour you are asking, though it may seem trivial to a man of your great intellect, is anything but simple to my way of thinking, and even if I were in a position to grant it, I know of no one in the world for whom I would do it, apart from yourself. And I would do it for you, not only because I love you as a brother, but because your words are seasoned with so much wisdom that they would startle a pious old lady out of her boots, let alone persuade me to change my mind; indeed, the more time I spend in your company, the wiser you appear. Besides, even if I had no other reason for loving you, I am bound to love you on seeing that you have lost your heart to such a beauty as the one you described. I must however point out that I am not as influential as you suppose in these matters, and it is not within my power to grant your request. But if you will give me your solemn pledge, as a gentleman and a moron, to keep my words a secret, I shall explain how you can achieve your aim without my assistance. And since you have all those fine books and the other things you were telling me about, I feel certain that your efforts will be crowned with success.'

'Have no fear, you may speak out,' said the Master. 'If you knew me a little better, you'd soon find out whether I can keep a secret or not. Why, when Messer Guasparruolo da Saliceto was on the magistrates' bench at Forlimpopoli, he confided nearly all his secrets to me, knowing they would be in safe keeping. And if you want me to prove it, I was the first man he told that he was about to marry Bergamina. Now what do you think of that?'

'That settles it,' said Bruno. 'If a man of that sort confided in you, I can certainly do the same. Now what you have to do is this. In this company of ours we have a captain and two counsellors, all of whom hold office for six months, and we know for certain that from the beginning of next month, Buffalmacco is to be captain and I am to

be one of the counsellors. Whenever there is any question of nomi-
nating and electing a new member, the captain's views carry a great
deal of weight, so I advise you to go out of your way to make friends
with Buffalmacco, and entertain him on a suitably lavish scale.
Buffalmacco's the sort of man who will take a powerful liking to you
from the moment he discovers how intelligent you are, and when
you've softened him up a little with your sparkling wit and those
priceless treasures of yours, you can put the question to him, and he
won't know how to refuse. I've already had a word with him about
you, and he's dying to make your acquaintance, so do as I've suggested, and then leave the rest to Buffalmacco and myself.'

'This plan of yours seems most excellent,' said the Master, 'for i f
Buffalmacco takes a delight in the company of the wise, he has only
to converse with me for a little while, and I guarantee that he will
never want to let me out of his sight. I have enough intelligence to
supply a whole city, and still remain a paragon of wisdom.'

Having thus arranged matters with Master Simone, Bruno recounted the whole tale in all its particulars to Buffalmacco, who was
so impatient to proceed to the task of supplying Master Simpleton
with the object of his quest, that every hour that passed seemed more
like a thousand.

Being inordinately eager to go the course, the physician never
relaxed until he had made Buffalmacco his friend, which he easily
succeeded in doing. He then began to treat him to the finest suppers
and breakfasts you could possibly imagine, to which Bruno was also
invited. For their part, Bruno and Buffalmacco assiduously courted
his company, and on finding themselves regaled with precious
wines and fat capons and an abundance of other excellent dishes at
Master Simone's table, they stuffed themselves like princes, and
turned up for a meal even when they were not invited, always giving
him to understand that they would not have done this for anyone
else.

Eventually however the Master made the same request to Buffalmacco that he had previously made to Bruno, whereupon Buffalmacco pretended to be very angry and subjected Bruno to a torrent of
abuse, saying:

'By the great tall God of Passignano, I swear I've a good mind to give you such a pasting over the face that your nose would end up in your boots, traitor that you are, for you alone can have revealed these secrets to the Master.'

But Bruno was stoutly defended by the physician, who swore and affirmed that he had heard about these things from another source, and eventually succeeded in mollifying Buffalmacco with a goodly quantity of his pearls of wisdom, after which Buffalmacco turned to him and said:

'It's quite plain that you've been at Bologna, my dear Master, and that you came back here with a pair of well-sealed lips. Moreover you obviously didn't learn your alphabet from a blackboard, as many an ignoramus has done, but from a blackamoor; and unless I'm mistaken, you were christened on a Sunday. Bruno tells me you were studying medicine up there in Bologna, but it seems to me that you studied how to capture men's minds, for what with your wisdom and your singular ways, you're a better exponent of that particular art than any other man I ever saw.'

But at this point he was interrupted by the physician, who turned to Bruno and said:

'What a thing it is to meet and converse with men of wisdom! Who but this worthy man would have been so prompt to read all my thoughts? You were not nearly so quick as Buffalmacco to appreciate my excellence; but you might at least tell him what I said to you when you told me he took a delight in the company of the wise: do you think I've been as good as my word?'

'Better,' said Bruno.

The Master then turned to Buffalmacco, saying:

'You'd have had a lot more to say if you'd seen me in Bologna, where there wasn't a single person, great or small, student or professor, who didn't worship the very ground beneath my feet, such was the pleasure I was able to give to each and every one of them with my wise and witty conversation. And I can tell you this, that whenever I opened my mouth, I made everybody laugh because I was so popular. When the time came for me to leave Bologna, they were all heartbroken and wanted me to stay. In fact they were so anxious to keep me there that they offered to let me do all the teaching in the faculty of medicine. But I declined the offer because I'd made up my mind to return to the huge estates that my family has always owned in this part of the world. And that was what I did.'

Whereupon Bruno said to Buffalmacco:

'There now, I told you so, but you wouldn't believe me. Holy Mother of Jesus! there's not a doctor in the land who knows more than he does about the urine of an ass, nor would you find his equal if you were to go all the way from here to the gates of Paris. Surely you'll agree to help him now.'

'Bruno is quite right,' said the physician, 'but people don't appreciate me here. You Florentines are not very bright on the whole; I only wish you could see me in my natural element, surrounded by my fellow-doctors.'

So Buffalmacco said:

'I must confess, Master, that you have a much better head on your shoulders than I ever gave you credit for. So speaking with all the deference that is due to a man of your great wisdom, I give you my equivocal promise that without fail I shall see that you are enrolled in our company.'

Now that he had been given this assurance, the doctor positively lavished hospitality on the two men, who enjoyed themselves enormously, persuading him to swallow the most fantastic pieces of nonsense; and they promised that he should have as his mistress the Countess of Cesspool, who was the finest thing to be found in the entire arse-gallery of the human race. When the doctor asked them who this Countess was, Buffalmacco replied:

'Ah, my pretty pumpkin, she's a very great lady, and there are few houses anywhere on earth in which she doesn't make her presence smelt; why, even the Franciscans pay their tributes to her on the big bass drum, to say nothing of the countless others she receives. And I can tell you this, that wherever she happens to be, she lets people know about it, even though she generally holds herself aloof. All the same, she swept past your front door the other night when she was on her way to the Arno to bathe her feet and get a breath of fresh air; but she spends most of her time at Laterina. You can regularly see her footmen going the rounds, all carrying a rod in one hand and a bucket in the other as symbols of her authority; and wherever you look you'll find many of her nobles, such as Baron Ffouljakes,

Lord Dung, Viscount Broomhandle, and the Earl of Loosefart, and others, with all of whom I believe you are acquainted, though perhaps you don't recall them just at present. This, then, if all goes according to plan, is the great lady in whose tender arms we shall place you, in which case you can forget about that girl from Cacavincigli.'

Having been born and bred in Bologna, the physician was unable to grasp the meaning of their words, and told them that the lady would suit him down to the ground. Nor did he have long to wait before the two painters brought him the news of his election to the company.

On the morning of the day appointed for the next meeting of the society, the Master invited the pair of them to breakfast, and after the meal he asked them how he was to get there, to which Buffalmacco replied:

'See here, Master, for reasons you are now about to hear, you will have to be very brave, otherwise you may run into trouble and make things very awkward for us. This evening, after dark, you must contrive to climb up on to one of the raised tombs that were erected just recently outside Santa Maria Novella, wearing one of your most sumptuous robes, for not only does the company require you to be nobly dressed when you are presented for the first time, but since you are gently bred, the Countess is proposing (or so we have been told, for we have never actually met her) to make you a Knight of the Bath at her own expense. And you are to remain on the tomb till we send for you.

'Now, so that you will know exactly what to expect, I should explain that we shall be sending a black creature with horns to come and fetch you, which, though not very large, will attempt to frighten you by parading up and down before you in the piazza, leaping high in the air, and making loud hissing noises. When it sees that you are not afraid, it will come silently towards you, and as soon as it has drawn near to where you are sitting, you must clamber boldly down from the tomb and, without invoking God or any of the Saints, leap on to its back. Once you are seated firmly on its back, you must fold your arms across your chest and leave them there, for you mustn't touch the beast with your hands.

'It will then move slowly off, and convey you to the place where we are all assembled; but I must stress here and now that if you invoke God or any of the Saints, or if you display any fear, you could be thrown off or dashed against something, and then you really will be in a mess. So unless you're quite sure that your courage won't desert you, I advise you not to come, for you would only do yourself an injury and bring no credit to ourselves.'

'You don't know me yet,' said the physician. 'Perhaps it's because I wear gloves and long robes that you doubt my courage. But if I were to tell you about some of my nocturnal escapades in Bologna, when I used to go after the women with my companions, you'd be lost in admiration. God's faith, I remember a night when there was one girl (a scraggy little baggage, what's more, no bigger than a midget) who refused to come with us, so after giving her a few good punches I picked her up bodily and carried her very nearly a stone's throw, and in the end I forced her to come. Then there was the time when I was all by myself except for my servant, and shortly after the Angelus I walked past the cemetery of the Franciscans, where a woman had been buried earlier in the day, and I wasn't the least bit afraid. So you have no need to worry on that score, because I'm as brave and as bold a man as you're ever likely to meet. As to my being nobly dressed for the occasion, I can tell you that I shall wear the scarlet robes in which I was commenced, and you'll soon discover whether the company will rejoice to see me, and whether I'm not elected captain before very long. Just wait till I arrive there this evening, and you'll see how things will go, for this Countess has never set eyes on me yet, and she's already so enamoured of me that she wants to make me a Knight of the Bath. Perhaps you think a knighthood wouldn't suit me, and that I shan't know what to do with it when I've got it; but leave it to me, and I'll show you!'

'That's all very well,' said Buffalmacco, 'but see that you don't let us down, either by not coming or by not being there when we send for you. The reason I say this is that the weather is cold, and you medical men are very sensitive to the cold.'

'Heaven forbid,' said the physician. 'I'm not one of your cold-blooded creatures; I don't mind the cold. In fact, whenever I get up in the night to relieve nature, as we all do at times, I very rarely throw anything over my nightshirt other than a fur coat. So you may rest assured that I shall be there.'

Bruno and Buffalmacco then departed, and when darkness was beginning to fall, the Master invented some excuse for leaving his wife, and having smuggled his splendid gown out of the house, he duly put it on and made his way to one of the aforementioned tombs, where, since it was a bitterly cold evening, he sat huddled on the marble, and began to await the arrival of the mysterious beast.

Buffalmacco, who was tall in stature and sturdy as an ox, had procured one of the masks that people used to wear at those special festivals that are nowadays no longer held; and having donned a coat of black fur, he got himself up to look exactly like a bear, except that his mask had the face of the devil and was furnished with horns. In this strange garb, with Bruno following at a safe distance in order to observe the proceedings, he made his way to the new piazza at Santa Maria Novella. And no sooner did he perceive that the learned doctor was there than he began to dance and leap all over the piazza, hissing, screaming and shrieking like one possessed.

When the Master saw and heard all this, every hair of his head stood on end and he began to tremble all over, just like a woman, except that he was far more frightened. He began to think he should have stayed at home, but now that he had come so far, he tried to put a bold face upon it, such was his eagerness to observe the marvels of which the two men had spoken.

After cavorting madly for some little time in the manner we have described, Buffalmacco appeared to calm down, and coming over to the tomb on which the Master was seated, he stopped and stood perfectly still. Being terrified out of his wits, the Master could not decide whether to mount the creature or remain where he was, but in the end, fearing lest the thing should attack him if he failed to climb on to its back, he chose the lesser of the two evils; and having clambered down from the tomb, he leapt on the creature's back, whispering 'God preserve me' as he did so. Once he was firmly seated, still trembling like a leaf, he folded his arms across his chest as instructed, whereupon Buffalmacco moved slowly off on all fours in the direction of Santa Maria della Scala, and carried him almost as far as the nunnery of Ripole.

Now at that time there were some ditches in those parts into which the farmers used to pour the offerings of the Countess of Cesspool, to enrich their lands. And when Buffalmacco reached this spot, he ambled up to the edge of one of the ditches, and, choosing the right moment, grabbed one of the doctor's feet and heaved him smartly off his back, casting him head first into the ditch. He then began to snarl in a most terrifying manner, leaping frantically all over the place, and eventually made his way past Santa Maria della Scala towards the meadow of Ognissanti, where he rejoined Bruno who had run away because he was unable to contain his laughter. And hugging one another with glee, they went and watched from a safe distance to see what the filth-bespattered doctor would do.

The worthy physician, finding himself in this unspeakably loathsome place, endeavoured to stand on his feet and grope his way out, but stumbled and fell in all directions before he finally succeeded in scrambling clear, sorrowing and forlorn, and covered in filth from head to toe, having parted company with his doctoral hood and swallowed several drams of the ditchwater. Then, scraping the stuff off with his hands as best he could, he made his way back to his house, not knowing what else he could do, and knocked at the door until his wife came down to let him in.

No sooner was he inside the house, reeking to high heaven, and the door had been closed behind him, than Bruno and Buffalmacco were listening at the keyhole to hear what sort of a reception the Master's wife would accord him. And as they stood there on the doorstep, all ears, they heard the lady giving him the biggest scolding that ever a poor devil received.

'God, what a fine state you are in!' she said. 'Went to see some other woman, and wanted to cut a dashing figure in your scarlet robe, I suppose? Were you not satisfied with me? Hell's bells, I could satisfy a whole parish, let alone you. I wish to Christ they had drowned you, instead of simply dumping you where you deserved. A splendid physician you are, I don't think, to abandon your wife and go chasing after other people's women at this time of night!'

To these reproaches she added countless others whilst the physician was giving himself a good wash, and never stopped tormenting him until well into the small hours.

Next morning, Bruno and Buffalmacco painted bruises on their torsoes to make it look as if they had been severely beaten, then made their way to the house of the physician, who was already up and about. A foul smell assailed their nostrils from the moment they set foot inside the house, for no amount of washing and scrubbing had been able to disperse all trace of it. When the doctor was told that they had called to see him, he advanced to meet them, bidding them good morning, but Bruno and Buffalmacco looked at him angrily, as they had prearranged, and replied:

'We shan't say the same to you. On the contrary, we pray to God that you'll have a terrible morning and end up with your throat cut, for you are the dirtiest traitor that ever lived. We put ourselves to endless trouble to see that you should be honoured and entertained, and what thanks do we get, apart from being practically slaughtered like a pair of dogs? Why, you could have driven an ass all the way to Rome with fewer blows than the ones we received last night on account of your treachery, not to mention the fact that we were very nearly expelled from the very company we'd arranged for you to join. And if you think we're making this up, take a look at our bodies.' At which point they bared their chests sufficiently long for him to catch a glimpse of the mass of bruises they had painted there, then instantly covered them up again.

The physician attempted to apologize, recounting the saga of his misfortunes and telling them how he had been thrown into the ditch, but Buffalmacco cut him short, saying:

'I wish he'd hurled you from the bridge into the Arno. Didn't we warn you beforehand not to mention God or any of the Saints?'

'I swear to God I did no such thing,' said the physician.

'Is that so?' said Buffalmacco. 'And I suppose you're going to tell us you weren't afraid, either. But our informant told us you were trembling like a leaf, and didn't know whether you were coming or going. You've led us right up the garden path, but we shan't allow anyone to impose on us again. And as for you, we shall see that you are treated with the contempt you deserve.'

The physician pleaded with them to forgive him, and strove to mollify them with all the eloquence at his command, imploring them not to bring disgrace upon him. And out of fear lest they should make a public laughing-stock of him, from that day forth he pampered and fêted them on a much more lavish scale than ever before.

So now you have heard how wisdom is imparted to anyone who has not acquired much of it at Bologna.

TENTH STORY

A Sicilian lady cleverly relieves a merchant of the goods he has brought to Palermo. He later returns there pretending to have brought a much more valuable cargo, and after having borrowed a sum of money from the lady, leaves her with nothing but a quantity of water and tow.

There is no need to inquire whether the ladies laughed heartily over certain of the passages from the queen's story: they laughed so much that the tears ran down their cheeks a dozen times at the very least. But when the tale was ended, Dioneo, knowing it was now his turn, addressed the company as follows:

Gracious ladies, it goes without saying that the more cunning a person is, the greater our satisfaction in seeing that person cunningly deceived. And hence, whilst the stories you have told have all been excellent, the one I propose to relate should afford you greater pleasure than any of the others, inasmuch as it concerns the duping of a lady who knew far more about the art of deception than any of the men or women who were beguiled in the tales we have heard so far.

In the seaports of all maritime countries, it used to be the practice, and possibly still is, that any merchant arriving there with merchandise, having discharged his cargo, takes it to a warehouse, which in many places is called the *dogana* and is maintained by the commune or by the ruler of the state. After presenting a written description of the cargo and its value to the officers in charge, he is given a storeroom where his merchandise is placed under lock and key; the officers then record all the details in their register under the merchant's name, and whenever the merchant removes his goods from bond, either wholly or in part, they make him pay the appropriate dues. It is by consulting this register that brokers, more often than not, obtain their information about the amount and value of the goods stored at the *dogana*, together with the names of the merchants to whom they belong. And when a suitable opportunity presents itself, they approach the merchants and arrange to barter, exchange, sell, or otherwise dispose of their merchandise.

Among the many seaports where this system prevailed was Palermo, in Sicily, which was also notable, and still is, for the number of women, lovely of body but hostile to virtue, who to anyone unfamiliar with their ways are frequently mistaken for great ladies of impeccable honesty. Their sole aim in life consists, not so much in fleecing men, as in skinning them wholesale, and whenever they catch sight of a merchant from foreign parts, they find out from the *dogana* register what goods he has deposited there and how much he is worth; after which, using all their charms and amorous wiles, and whispering honeyed words into the ears of their unsuspecting victim, they attempt to ensnare him into falling in love with them. In this way they have enticed a large number of merchants to part with a substantial proportion of their goods, and a great many others to hand over the entire lot, whilst some of them have been known to forfeit not only their merchandise, but their ships as well, and even their flesh and their bones, so daintily has the lady-barber known how to wield her razor.

To Palermo, then, not so very long ago, there came one of our young Florentines, Niccolò da Cignano by name, though he was generally known as Salabaetto, who had been sent there by his principals with a consignment of woollens, worth about five hundred gold florins, which were left over from the fair at Salerno. Having handed the invoice for these goods to the officers of the *dogana*, he put them into store, and without showing any great eagerness to dispose of them, he began to see what the city could offer him in the way of amusement.

Since he was a very handsome youth, of fair complexion, with blonde hair and a most shapely figure, it was not long before one of these lady-barbers, who styled herself Madonna Jancofiore, having gleaned some knowledge of his affairs, began to cast glances in his direction. The young man, perceiving this, and assuming her to be some fine lady who had fallen for his handsome looks, decided that he would have to be very careful in conducting this little amour, and without breathing a word about it to anyone, he took to walking past her house at frequent intervals. He was soon observed by the lady, who after kindling the flames of his passion for a few days by flashing her eyes at him and appearing as if she was pining away for his love, secretly sent one of her maidservants to call upon him. This woman, being well-versed in the arts of the procuress, spun him a long rigmarole and then, almost bursting into tears, informed him that her mistress was so taken up with his handsome looks and agreeable manners that she was unable to rest by day or night; she therefore hoped that he would agree to meet her in secret at some bagnio, there being nothing she more ardently desired; and finally, taking a ring from her purse, she handed it over to him with the lady's compliments.

When he heard this, Salabaetto was the happiest man who ever lived, and taking the ring, he brushed it against his eyelids, kissed it, and put it on his finger, telling the good woman that Madonna Jancofiore's love was fully reciprocated, since he loved her more than his very life, and that he was ready to meet her wherever and whenever she pleased.

The go-between returned with this answer to her mistress, and soon afterwards Salabaetto was informed that he was to wait for her at a certain bagnio on the following day after vespers. Without giving the slightest hint to anyone about where he was going, Salabaetto swiftly made his way to the bagnio at the appointed hour, and found that it was reserved for the lady. He had not been there long before two slave-girls arrived, one of whom was carrying a fine big feather mattress on her head, whilst the other had a huge basket filled with this, that, and the other. And having laid the mattress on a bed in one of the rooms of the bagnio, they covered it with a pair of sheets, fine as gossamer and edged all round with silk, over which they placed a quilt of whitest Cyprian buckram, together with two exquisitely embroidered pillows. They then undressed, got into the bath, and washed and scrubbed it all over until it gleamed.

Nor was it long before the lady herself arrived at the bagnio, attended by two more slave-girls. She no sooner saw Salabaetto than she rushed ecstatically forward to greet him, flung her arms round his neck, and smothered him with kisses; and after heaving several deep sighs, she said:

'My fascinating Tuscan, I know of no other man who could have brought me to do this. My heart is all on fire because of you.'

She then undressed, bidding him do the same, and they both stepped naked into the bath, attended by two of the slave-girls. Nor would she allow either of the girls to lay a hand upon him, but she herself washed Salabaetto from head to toe with marvellous care, using soap that was steeped in musk and cloves; and finally, she had herself washed and rubbed down by the two slave-girls.

This operation completed, the slave-girls fetched two sheets, white as snow and very finely woven, from which there came the fragrant smell of roses, so powerful that it seemed the bagnio was filled with roses and nothing else. Having wrapped Salabaetto in one of these and their mistress in the other, the slave-girls took them up and conveyed them both to the bed, where, when they had ceased to perspire, the sheets enfolding them were removed and they found themselves lying naked between the sheets of the bed. Silver phials, exquisitely wrought, were then produced from the basket, some filled with rose-water, others with the water of orange flowers or jasmine blossom, with which their bodies were liberally sprinkled by the slave-girls, after which they refreshed themselves for a while with precious wines and sweetmeats.

Salabaetto thought he was in Paradise, and devoured the lady a thousand times with his eyes, for she was assuredly a very beautiful woman. Every hour that passed seemed to him a hundred years as he waited for the slave-girls to depart so that he might find himself in her embrace. Eventually, however, at the lady's command, they withdrew from the room, leaving a lighted torch behind them, whereupon she and Salabaetto fell into one another's arms. And there they remained together for some little time, to the immense delight of Salabaetto, who imagined her to be wasting away out of her love for him.

At length the lady decided it was time for them to rise, so she summoned the slave-girls, who helped them to dress. They then took some further refreshment in the form of wine and sweetmeats, and washed their faces and hands in the flower-scented waters. And as they were on the point of leaving, the lady said to Salabaetto:

'If it pleases you, I should consider it a very great favour if you were to come to my house for supper this evening, and spend the night with me.'

Being thoroughly taken in by her beauty and her calculated charm, and firmly believing that she loved him to distraction, Salabaetto replied:

'Whatever pleases you, my lady, is infinitely pleasing to me. Ask of me what you will, therefore, whether this evening or at any other time, and I shall do it gladly.'

And so returning to her house, the lady arranged for an impressive array of her gowns and other paraphernalia to be put on display in her bedroom, and having given instructions for a magnificent supper to be prepared, she waited for Salabaetto to come. As soon as it was reasonably dark, he made his way to the house, where he received a rapturous welcome, and after a most convivial supper, impeccably served, she led him off into the bedroom. The air was heavy with the wondrous fragrance of eagle-wood, and looking round, he observed that the bed was profusely adorned with mechanical songbirds, and that masses of beautiful gowns were hanging from the walls on pegs. All these things together, and each in particular, led him to the firm conviction that she was a great and wealthy lady. For although he had heard one or two rumours portraying her in quite a different light, nothing in the world could persuade him that there was any truth in these reports; and even if the suspicion crossed his mind that she had beguiled men before, he could never imagine for a moment that the same thing would happen to him.

It would be impossible to describe his bliss as he lay all night in her arms, the flames of his love burning ever more fiercely; and when morning came, she fastened a dainty and beautiful little silver girdle round his waist, with a fine purse to go with it, and said to him:

'My darling Salabaetto, I implore you to remember that just as my person is yours to enjoy, so everything I have here is yours, and all that I can do is at your command.'

Salabaetto took her in his arms and kissed her, then walked jauntily forth from the house and made his way down to that part of the city where his fellow-merchants forgathered. From then on he consorted with her regularly without spending so much as a farthing, becoming ever more deeply enamoured. And when, eventually, he disposed of his woollen goods for ready money at a substantial profit, the good lady was immediately informed, though not by Salabaetto himself.

On the following evening, Salabaetto called to see her, and she began to jest and frolic with him, kissing and hugging him with such a show of burning passion that it seemed she would die of love in his arms. And she kept asking him to accept a pair of exquisite silver goblets, which Salabaetto refused to take, having at one time and another had presents from her worth at least thirty gold florins, without ever managing to persuade her to take so much as a silver groat in return. At length, however, when she had worked him up into a frenzy of excitement with her display of passion and generosity, she was called away from the room by one of her slave-girls, acting upon instructions received beforehand from her mistress. After a brief absence she returned, her eyes full of tears, and hurling herself face downwards on the bed, she began to give vent to the most piteous wailings that ever issued from a woman's lips, much to the astonishment of Salabaetto, who took her in his arms, and mingling his own tears with hers, he said:

'Ah, dearest heart of my body, what has happened to you so suddenly? What is the cause of all this sorrow? Ah! do tell me, my darling.'

After allowing Salabaetto to coax and cajole her for some little time, the lady replied:

'Alas, my sweet master, I know not what to do nor what to say. I have just received a letter from my brother, who writes from Messina, telling me that unless I send him a thousand gold florins without fail within the next seven days, by selling and pawning everything I have in the house, he will lose his head on the block. I have no idea how I am to find so large a sum at such short notice. If only I had a fortnight at my disposal, I should be able to raise twice the amount by collecting a certain sum of money that is owed to me, or I could sell one of the family estates. But since this is out of the question, I wish I'd been struck dead before this dreadful news had ever reached my ears . . .'

At which point she broke off, appearing sorely distressed, and the tears rolled down her cheeks in a never-ending torrent.

Salabaetto, who in the heat of his amorous passion had mislaid a substantial part of his wits, thought that her tears were genuine, and her words even more so. And he replied:

'Be of good cheer, my lady, for though I couldn't supply you with a thousand, I could certainly let you have five hundred gold florins, if you are sure you can repay me within the next fortnight. Fortunately for you, I managed only yesterday to dispose of my cargo of woollens, otherwise I shouldn't have been able to lend you a groat.'

'Do you mean to say,' said the lady, 'that you have been short of money? Why on earth didn't you ask me for some? I don't have a thousand, but I could easily have given you a hundred, and possibly two. And now that you have told me all this, I simply wouldn't have the heart to accept your offer of assistance.'

Deeply touched by these sentiments, Salabaetto replied:

'That is no reason for you to refuse, my lady. If my own need had been as great as yours, I should certainly have asked for your help.'

'Oh, my Salabaetto!' exclaimed the lady. 'I plainly perceive that your love for me is true and perfect, when without waiting to be asked for such a large sum of money, you freely offer to help me in my hour of need. And though I was all yours without this token of your love, from now on I shall assuredly belong to you even more completely; nor shall I ever forget that you saved my brother's life. God knows that I am reluctant to accept your offer, knowing that you are a merchant, and merchants do all their business with money. But I shall accept the money all the same, for my need is very urgent and I am quite confident that I shall be able to repay you in the near future. And as to the remainder of the sum I require, if I cannot find any swifter way of raising it, I shall place all these belongings of mine in pawn.' Whereupon she flung herself in tears across the bed, and buried Salabaetto's head in her bosom.

Salabaetto then set about consoling her as best he could, and after spending the night with her, he proved his generosity and devotion towards her by bringing her five hundred sparkling gold florins without waiting to be asked. These she accepted with laughter in her heart and tears in her eyes, promising to repay them as soon as she could, which was all that Salabaetto required by way of bond.

Now that she had her hands on the money, it became a different story altogether; for whereas he had always had free access to the lady whenever he pleased, she now began to fob him off with various excuses, so that nine times out of ten he was turned away from the house, and even when he did get in to see her, she no longer greeted him with the smiling countenance, the caresses, or the lavish hospitality to which he had previously been accustomed.

Not only did the lady fail to repay Salabaetto by the date she had promised, but a further month went by, then another, and when he asked her for his money, all he could get out of her was a string of excuses. Salabaetto now realized how cleverly he had been taken in by her villainy, and knowing that he could prove nothing against her (for he had no written evidence of the transaction, and there was no independent witness), he was exceedingly distressed and reproached himself bitterly for his foolishness. Moreover, he was too ashamed to lodge a complaint with the authorities, because he had been warned of her character beforehand and had only himself to blame if he was made a laughing-stock for behaving so stupidly. And when he received several letters from his principals ordering him to change the money and forward it to them, fearing lest his lapse should be discovered if he remained in Palermo any longer without obeying their instructions, he decided to leave. So he boarded a small ship, and instead of sailing to Pisa as he should have done, he went to Naples.

Now, there happened at that time to be living in Naples a compatriot of ours, Pietro dello Canigiano, who was treasurer to Her Highness the Empress of Constantinople – a man of great intelligence and shrewdness, and a very close friend of Salabaetto and his family. Knowing him to be the very soul of discretion, Salabaetto took him into his confidence a few days after his arrival, told him about what he had done and about the sad fate which had befallen him, and requested his assistance and advice in finding some means of livelihood in Naples, declaring that he had no intention of ever returning to Florence.

Saddened by what he had heard, Canigiano replied:

'A fine state of affairs, I must say; a fine way to carry on; a fine sense of loyalty you have shown to your employers. No sooner do you lay your hands on a large sum of money, than you squander the lot in riotous living. But what's done is done, and now we must look to the remedy.'

Since he had a shrewd head on his shoulders, Canigiano quickly saw what was to be done, and explained his plan to Salabaetto, who, thinking it an excellent idea, set about putting it into effect. He still had a little money of his own, and supplementing this with a loan from Canigiano, he ordered a number of bales of merchandise to be packed and tightly corded up, and having purchased and filled about a score of oil-casks, he loaded the entire consignment aboard a ship and returned to Palermo. There he presented the invoice for the bales to the officers of the *dogana*, to whom he also declared the value of the casks, and having made sure that they had registered everything under his own name, he placed the goods in store, saying that he wished to leave them there until the arrival of a further consignment of merchandise he was expecting.

On learning of his return and hearing that the goods he had brought were worth two thousand gold florins at the very least, without counting the goods still to come, which were valued at more than three thousand, Madonna Jancofiore, thinking she had set her sights too low, decided to repay him the five hundred florins so that she could get her claws on the greater portion of the five thousand, and sent word that she would like to see him.

When Salabaetto called upon her, she pretended to know nothing of the merchandise he had brought and gave him the warmest of welcomes, saying:

'Listen, my love; in case you were angry with me for not paying you back that money of yours punctually . . .'

But Salabaetto, having profited from his earlier mistakes, laughed and said:

'To tell the truth, my lady, I was very little displeased, for I would pluck the very heart from my body and give it to you, if I thought it would make you happy. But I should like you to judge for yourself how angry I am with you. So great and so particular is the love I bear you, that I have sold the greater part of my possessions, and now I have brought with me to Palermo a consignment of goods worth over two thousand florins. Moreover, I am expecting a further consignment from the West worth more than three thousand, and I intend to start a business in Palermo and settle here for good, for I consider myself more fortunate in loving you than any other lover in the world.'

'I do assure you, Salabaetto,' said the lady, 'that any success of yours gives me enormous pleasure, since I love you more dearly than my very life; and I am delighted that you have returned here with the intention of staying, for I hope we shall still have many a good time together. But I owe you a little apology for all those occasions, before you went away, when you wanted to come here and I was unable to see you, as well as for the times when you came and you were not so well received as usual. And I must also ask you to forgive me for not repaying your money by the date I had promised.

'You must remember that I was terribly sad and distressed at that particular time, and whenever a woman is in this condition, no matter how much she may love anyone, she cannot be as unfailingly cheerful and attentive towards him as he would like her to be. Besides, as you can hardly fail to realize, it is no easy matter for a woman to scrape together a thousand gold florins. We are always being fobbed off with lies, and people fail to keep their promises to us, with the result that we ourselves are compelled to tell lies to others. It was for this reason alone, and not through any ulterior motive, that I failed to pay you back. However, I did obtain the money shortly after you went away, and had I known your address, you may be quite sure that I would have sent it on to you; but since I didn't know where you were, I put it away for you in a safe place.'

Then, having called for a purse that contained the very florins he had given her, she placed it in his hand, saying:

'Count them and make sure they come to five hundred.'

Salabaetto had never felt so happy in his whole life, and having counted the florins and confirmed that they amounted to exactly five hundred, he tucked them away, saying:

'I know that you are telling me the truth, my lady. Indeed, you have done more than enough to prove it, and because of this, as also because of the love I bear you, I assure you that whenever you are in need of money in the future, and it is within my power to supply it,

you have only to ask and it shall be yours. Once I have set up my
business here in Palermo, you will see for yourself that this is no idle
promise.'

Having thus cemented his love for the lady by means of these
verbal protestations, Salabaetto began once more to play the gallant
with her, whilst for her part she entertained and solaced him for all
she was worth, pretending to love him to the point of distraction.
However, Salabaetto was determined that his own duplicity should
punish hers, and one evening, having received an invitation from her
earlier in the day to sup and spend the night with her, he turned up
at her house looking so distraught and miserable that it seemed he
was about to die at any moment. Jancofiore, hugging and kissing
him, began to question him about the reasons for his sadness, and
after allowing her to wheedle him for a while, he replied:

'I am utterly ruined, for the ship carrying the goods I was expecting
has been seized by Monegasque pirates. They are demanding a ransom of ten thousand gold florins, of which I have to pay a thousand,
and I haven't a penny to my name, because as soon as you paid me
back those five hundred florins, I sent them to Naples to be invested
in a consignment of linen which is now on its way to Palermo. If I
were to sell the goods I have in store here at the moment, I should lose
half their true value, because it's the wrong time to sell. On the other
hand, I can't find anyone here to lend me the money, because I am
still not well enough known in the city. Hence I have no idea what
to do or what to say; if I don't send the money soon, my merchandise
will be shipped to Monaco and I shall never see it again.'

These tidings were highly irritating to the lady, for it seemed she
was about to lose everything; but perceiving what she must do to
prevent the goods going to Monaco, she said:

'God knows I love you so dearly that I am very sorry to hear of
your misfortune; but what's the use of becoming so upset about it?
If I had the money to lend you, God knows that I should let you have
it here and now, but I haven't got it. It's true that I know of someone
who might help – the person who lent me the remaining five hundred
florins I needed the other month – but he charges a high rate of interest.
You'd have to pay him at least thirty per cent if you were to borrow
the money from him, and he would want something substantial by

way of security. Now I personally would be prepared for your sake to offer him all I possess, myself included, as security for whatever sum he will lend, but how are you going to guarantee the rest of the loan?'

Salabaetto was delighted, for he knew exactly what was prompting her to do him this favour, and perceived that it was she herself who would be lending him the money. So after he had thanked her, he told her that he would not be deterred by the exorbitant rate of interest, as he needed the money very badly; and he then went on to explain that by way of surety he would place the merchandise he had at the *dogana* to the credit of the person who was to lend him the money. However, he wished to retain the key to the warehouse, so as to be able to display his merchandise if anyone should ask him to do so, and also to ensure that his goods were not interfered with or exchanged or moved elsewhere.

The lady agreed that this was a wise precaution, and declared that a surety of this kind would be more than adequate. Early next morning, she sent for a broker who was privy to most of her secrets, and having explained the situation to him, she gave him a thousand gold florins, which the broker lent to Salabaetto, having first ensured that all the goods that Salabaetto had at the *dogana* were transferred to his own name. Various documents were signed and countersigned by the two men, and when all was settled between them, they went their separate ways to attend to their other affairs.

At the earliest opportunity, Salabaetto took ship with his fifteen hundred gold florins, and returned to Pietro dello Canigiano in Naples, whence he made full remittance to his principals in Florence for the woollens with which they had originally sent him to Palermo; and having paid Pietro and all his other creditors, he made merry with Canigiano over the trick he had played on the Sicilian woman, celebrating his success for several days on end. He then left Naples, and having decided to retire from commerce, made his way to Ferrara.

When Jancofiore learned that Salabaetto was no longer to be found in Palermo, her suspicions were aroused and she began to wonder what had become of him. After waiting for at least two months without seeing any sign of him, she got the broker to force a way in to the warehouse. And having first of all tested the casks, which were supposed to be full of oil, she discovered that they were filled with sea-water, apart from about a firkin of oil that was floating at the top of each cask, near the bung-hole. Then, untying the bales, she found that all except two (which consisted of woollens) were filled with tow. And in fact, to cut a long story short, the whole consignment was worth no more than two hundred florins.

On perceiving that she had been outwitted, Jancofiore lamented long and bitterly over the five hundred florins she had repaid, and even more over the thousand she had lent, frequently repeating to herself the old saw: 'Honesty's the better line, when dealing with a Florentine.' And so it was that, having burnt her fingers and covered herself in ridicule, she discovered that some people are every bit as knowing as others.

*   *   *

No sooner had Dioneo reached the end of his story, than Lauretta, knowing that the time had come for her to abdicate, commended the advice given by Pietro Canigiano, which to judge by its effects had been very sound; and having also praised the sagacity of Salabaetto, who was no less worthy of commendation for translating Pietro's advice into practice, she removed the laurel crown from her head and placed it upon Emilia's, saying with womanly grace:

'I know not, madam, whether you will make an agreeable queen, but we shall certainly have a fair one. See to it, then, that your actions are in keeping with your beauty.'

Lauretta then resumed her seat, leaving Emilia feeling somewhat ill at ease, not so much in having been made their queen as in hearing herself praised in public for something to which ladies are wont to attach most importance, and her face turned the colour of fresh roses at dawn. But having lowered her gaze until her blushes had receded, she summoned the steward and made appropriate arrangements for their activities of the morrow, after which she addressed them as follows:

'Delectable ladies, we may readily observe that when oxen have laboured in chains beneath the yoke for a certain portion of the day, their yoke is removed and they are put out to grass, being allowed to roam freely through the woods wherever they please. Similarly, we may perceive that gardens stocked with numerous different trees are much more beautiful than forests consisting solely of oaks. And therefore, having regard to the number of days during which our deliberations have been confined within a predetermined scheme, I consider that it would be both appropriate and useful for us to wander at large for a while, and in so doing recover the strength for returning once again beneath the yoke.

'Accordingly, when we resume our storytelling on the morrow, I do not propose to confine you to any particular topic; on the contrary, I desire that each of us should speak on whatever subject he chooses, it being my firm conviction that we shall find it no less rewarding to hear a variety of themes discussed than if we had restricted ourselves to one alone. Moreover, by doing as I have suggested, we shall all recruit our strength, and thus my successor will feel more justified in forcing us to observe our customary rule.'

The members of the company applauded the queen for proposing so sensible an arrangement; and rising from their places, they turned to various forms of relaxation, the ladies making garlands and otherwise amusing themselves whilst the young men sang songs and played games. In this way they whiled away their time until supper, to which in due course they gaily addressed themselves, sitting in a circle round the delectable fountain. And when supper was over they freely engaged in their usual pastimes of singing and dancing.

Finally the queen, out of deference to the ways of her predecessors, ordered Panfilo to sing a song, notwithstanding the fact that various members of the company had already sung several of their own accord. And so Panfilo promptly began, as follows:

'Love, I take such delight in thee,
  And find such joy and pleasure in thy name,
  That I am happy burning in thy flame.

'I feel such joy within my breast,
  Grown from the precious grace
  Which thou hast brought to me,
  So strong it cannot be suppressed
  But shines out from my face
  Declaring me to be

Enamoured joyfully –
Happy to stay and burn so nigh
To one in place and name so high!

'I cannot sing aloud in song
Or sketch forth with my hand
The joy, Love, that I know;
For to reveal it would be wrong,
That I well understand.
A torment it would grow;
But I am happy so.
All speech would be subdued and broken
'Ere one small part of it were spoken.

'Who is there who aright could guess
My arms would find that place
That they were clasped around?
None would believe my happiness
That I might bend my face
Whither I did, and found
Salvation sweet and grace.
Hence I with burning joy conceal
A rapture I may not reveal.'

Thus did Panfilo's song come to an end, and though everyone had joined wholeheartedly in the refrain, there was not a single person present who did not attend more carefully than usual to the words, striving to guess what Panfilo had implied he was obliged to conceal. And whilst several formed their own opinions as to his meaning, they were all well wide of the mark. But in the end the queen, perceiving that Panfilo's song was finished and that the young ladies and the gentlemen were showing clear signs of fatigue, ordered them all to retire to bed.

Here ends the Eighth Day of the Decameron

NINTH DAY

Here begins the Ninth Day, wherein, under the rule of Emilia, it is left to each member of the company to speak on whatever subject he chooses.

The light whose radiance dispels the shades of night had already softened into pale celestial hues the deep azure of the eighth heaven, and the flowerets in the meadows had begun to raise their drooping heads, when Emilia arose and caused the other young ladies to be called, and likewise the three young men. Answering her summons, they set off at a leisurely pace behind the queen, and made their way to a little wood, not very far from the palace. On entering the wood, they observed a number of roebucks, stags, and other wild creatures, which, as though sensing they were safe from the hunter on account of the plague, stood their ground as if they had been rendered tame and fearless. However, by approaching these creatures one after another as though intending to touch them, they caused them to run away and leap in the air; and in this way they amused themselves for some little time until, the sun being now in the ascendant, they thought it expedient to retrace their steps.

They were all wreathed in fronds of oak, and their hands were full of fragrant herbs or flowers, so that if anyone had encountered them, he would only have been able to say: 'Either these people will not be vanquished by death, or they will welcome it with joy.'

And so back they came, step by gradual step, singing, chattering, and jesting with one another as they walked along, and on reaching the palace they found everything neatly arranged and the servants all gay and festive. They then rested for a while, nor did they sit down at table before half-a-dozen canzonets, each of them more lively than the one preceding it, had been sung by the young men and the ladies; after which, having rinsed their hands in water, they were shown to their places at table by the steward, acting on instructions from the queen. The food was served, and they all ate merrily; and after rising from their meal, they danced and made music for a while until the queen gave permission, to those who so desired, to retire to rest.

At the customary hour, however, they were all seated in their usual places for the start of their discussions, and the queen, looking towards Filomena, bade her tell the first story of the day, whereupon Filomena smiled and began as follows:

FIRST STORY

Madonna Francesca is wooed by a certain Rinuccio and a certain Alessandro, but is not herself in love with either. She therefore induces the one to enter a tomb and pose as a corpse, and the other to go in and fetch him out, and since neither succeeds in completing his allotted task, she discreetly rids herself of both.

Since it is your wish, my lady, that I should be the first to sally forth into this broad and spacious arena to which we have been brought by your bounteous decree, I shall do so with the greatest of pleasure. And if I should acquit myself favourably therein, I daresay those who follow me will do as well as I, and even better.

In the course of our conversations, dear ladies, we have repeatedly seen how great and mighty are the forces of Love. Yet I do not think we have fully exhausted the subject, nor would we do so if we were to talk of nothing else for a whole year. And since Love not only leads lovers into divers situations fraught with mortal peril, but will even induce them to enter the houses of the dead in the guise of corpses, I should like to tell you a story on this very subject, by way of addition to those already told, from which you will not only comprehend the power of Love, but learn of the ingenious means employed by a worthy lady to rid herself of two unwanted admirers.

I say then that in the city of Pistoia, there was once a very beautiful widow, of whom, as chance would have it, two of our fellow-Florentines, who were living in Pistoia after being banished from Florence, became deeply enamoured. Their names were Rinuccio

Palermini and Alessandro Chiarmontesi, and each of them, unknown to the other, was secretly doing his utmost to win the lady's love.

The gentlewoman, whose name was Madonna Francesca de' Lazzari, was subjected to a steady stream of messages and entreaties from the two men, to which on occasion she had been incautious enough to lend a ready ear; and being unable to extricate herself, as she was prudent enough to wish, she conceived a plan for ridding herself from their importunities. This consisted in asking them to do her a service which, though not impossible, she thought that no one would ever perform, so that when they failed to carry it out she would have plausible and legitimate grounds for rejecting their advances; and her plan was this.

On the day the idea came into her head, the death had occurred in Pistoia of a man who, despite the nobility of his lineage, was reputed to be the greatest rogue who had ever lived, not only in Pistoia but in the whole world. Moreover, he was so deformed of body and his features were so hideously distorted that any stranger, on seeing him for the first time, would have been terrified out of his wits. He had been buried in a tomb outside the church of the Franciscans, and the lady, seeing this as a good opportunity to further her plans, summoned one of her maidservants and said:

'As you know, not a day passes without my being plagued and tormented from morning till night with the attentions of those two Florentines, Rinuccio and Alessandro. I have no intention of conceding my love to either of the two, and in order to be rid of them, I have made up my mind, since they are always so free with their promises, to test their sincerity by setting them both a task which I am certain they will fail to accomplish, and thus I shall put an end to their pestering.

'Now this is how I shall go about it. As you know, this morning, at the convent of the Franciscans, the burial took place of Scannadio (such was the name of the villain in question), the sight of whom was sufficient, when he was still alive, let alone now that he is dead, to frighten the bravest men in the land. So I want you first of all to go secretly to Alessandro, and say to him: "Madonna Francesca sends me to tell you that the time has come when you may have the love for which you have been craving, and that if you so desire you can go to her in the manner I shall now explain. For reasons you will be told about later, a kinsman of hers is obliged to convey to her house, tonight, the body of Scannadio, who was buried this morning. And since she is utterly repelled by the thought of harbouring this man's corpse under her own roof, she implores you to do her a great favour, namely that when darkness has fallen, you should enter Scannadio's tomb, put on his clothes, and lie there impersonating him till her kinsman comes to fetch you. Without saying a word or uttering any sound, you are to allow yourself to be taken from the tomb and brought to her house. She will be waiting there to receive you, and you will be able to stay with her for as long as you like, leaving everything else to her." If he agrees to do this, all well and good; but if he refuses, you are to tell him from me that I never want to set eyes on him again, and that if he values his life he will take good care not to send me any more of his messages or entreaties.

'You will then go to Rinuccio Palermini and say to him: "Madonna Francesca says she is ready to grant your every wish, provided you do her a great favour, namely that just before midnight tonight you go to the tomb where Scannadio was buried this morning, and without saying a word about anything you may see or hear, fetch his body gently forth and take it to her house. There you will discover why she wants you to do her this service, and you will have all you desire of her. But if you should refuse to do it, she charges you here and now never to send her any further messages or entreaties."'

The maidservant called on each of the men in turn and delivered the two messages exactly as instructed, in each case receiving the same answer, namely that they would venture into Hell itself, let alone a tomb, if she wanted them to do so. So the maid conveyed this answer to her mistress, who waited to see whether they were mad enough to carry out her request.

After dark, having waited until most people were asleep, Alessandro Chiarmontesi stripped down to his doublet and set forth from his house in order to take Scannadio's place in the tomb. But as he was on his way to the graveyard, he began to feel very frightened, and to say to himself: 'Why should I be such a fool? Where do I think I'm going? For all I know, her kinsfolk may have discovered I'm in love with her. Perhaps they think I've seduced her, and have forced her into this so that they can murder me inside the tomb. If that's the case, I shan't stand a dog's chance, nobody will be any the wiser, and they'll escape scot free. Or possibly, for all I know, it's a trap prepared for me by some enemy of mine, who persuaded her to do him this favour because she's in love with him.'

But then he thought: 'Let's suppose that neither of these things will happen, and her kinsfolk really do have to take me to her house. It's hardly likely they would want Scannadio's body in order to embrace it or put it to bed with the lady. On the contrary, one can only conclude that they want to wreak vengeance upon it in return for some wrong he has done them. She tells me not to make a sound, no matter what may happen; but what if they were to gouge my eyes out, or wrench out my teeth, or cut off my hands, or do me some other piece of mischief, where would I be then? How could I keep quiet? And yet if I open my mouth, they will recognize me and possibly give me a sound hiding. But even if they don't, I shall have achieved precisely nothing, because they won't leave me with the lady in any case. Besides, she will say that I have disobeyed her instructions, and will never have anything to do with me again.'

So powerfully did these reflections prey upon his mind that he was on the point of turning round and going back home. But his great love spurred him on, suggesting counter-arguments that were so persuasive that they brought him at length to the tomb. Having opened it up, he stepped inside, stripped the corpse, and donned Scannadio's clothes. Then, shutting himself inside the tomb, he lay down in the dead man's place, and his mind began to dwell on the kind of man he had been, and upon the weird things that were said to have happened at night in various quite ordinary places, not to mention cemeteries. Every hair of his head stood on end, and he was convinced that Scannadio would rise to his feet at any moment and slit his throat on the spot. But drawing sustenance from his fervent love, he subdued these as well as other gruesome thoughts, and, lying perfectly still as if he were the corpse, settled down to wait and see what would happen.

When midnight was approaching, Rinuccio set forth from his house to do the deed which his lady had commissioned him to perform. As he walked along, he was assailed by a multitude of thoughts on the various things that might happen to him, such as being caught red-handed by the watch with Scannadio's corpse on his shoulders, and being condemned to the stake as a sorcerer, or of incurring the hatred of Scannadio's kinsfolk if they should ever find out what he had done. And several other fears of a similar nature entered his head, by which he was all but deterred from going on.

But he took a firm grip on himself, saying: 'Here's a pretty state of affairs! Am I to say nay to the first request I receive from this noble lady, when I have loved her so deeply and still do, and when, moreover, she offers me her favours as my reward? No, I shall proceed to honour the promise I have given her, even if it means my certain death.' And so, putting his best foot forward, he came at length to the tomb, which he opened without any difficulty.

On hearing the tomb being opened, Alessandro was filled with terror, but managed nonetheless to remain perfectly still. Rinuccio clambered in, and thinking he was taking up the body of Scannadio, seized Alessandro by the feet, dragged him out, hoisted him on to his shoulders, and set off in the direction of the gentlewoman's house. It was such a dark night that he couldn't really see where he was going, and being none too particular about his burden, he frequently banged Alessandro's body against the edges of certain benches that were set at intervals along the side of the street.

The gentlewoman, being eager to see whether Rinuccio would fetch Alessandro, was standing with her maidservant at the window, forearmed with a suitable pretext for sending them both packing. But just as Rinuccio came up to her front door, he was challenged by the officers of the watch, who happened to be lying in ambush for an outlaw in that very part of the city. On hearing the sound of Rinuccio's laboured tread, they promptly produced a lantern to see what was afoot, and seizing their shields and their lances, they called out:

'Who goes there?'

Rinuccio realized at once who it was, and not having time to stop and compose his thoughts, he dropped Alessandro like a sack of coal and ran off as fast as his legs would carry him. Meanwhile Alessandro scrambled quickly to his feet, and though he was encumbered by the dead man's garments, which were inordinately long, he too took to his heels.

By the light of the officers' lantern, the lady had plainly observed Rinuccio carrying Alessandro on his shoulders, dressed in Scannadio's clothes, and was greatly amazed by this evident proof of their courage. But for all her amazement, she was convulsed with laughter when she saw Alessandro being dropped, and when she saw them running away. Delighted at the turn which events had taken, and giving thanks to God for ridding her from their tiresome attentions, she withdrew from the window and retired to her room, declaring to her maidservant that her two suitors must without a doubt be very much in love with her, as it seemed they had followed her instructions to the letter.

Rinuccio was heartbroken over what had happened, and cursed his evil luck, but instead of going home, he waited till the officers had gone, and returned to the place where he had dumped Alessandro. He then began to grope about on hands and knees in search of the body so that he could carry out the rest of his assignment, but being unable to find it, he assumed it had been taken away by the officers, and sadly made his way back home.

Not knowing what else he could do, Alessandro likewise returned home without ever having discovered who had fetched him from the tomb, feeling bitterly disappointed that things should have turned out so disastrously.

Next morning, when Scannadio's tomb was found open and there was no sign of the corpse (Alessandro having rolled it down into the lower depths), the whole of Pistoia was alive with rumours as to what exactly had happened, the more simple-minded concluding that Scannadio had been spirited away by demons.

Each of the lady's suitors informed her what he had done and what had happened, and, apologizing on this account for not carrying out her instructions to the full, demanded her forgiveness and her love. But she pretended not to believe them, and by curtly replying that she wanted no more to do with either of them, as they had failed to carry out her bidding, she neatly rid herself of both.

SECOND STORY

An abbess rises hurriedly from her bed in the dark when it is reported to her that one of her nuns is abed with a lover. But being with a priest at the time, the Abbess claps his breeches on her head, mistaking them for her veil. On pointing this out to the Abbess, the accused nun is set at liberty, and thenceforth she is able to forgather with her lover at her leisure.

When Filomena was silent, the good sense shown by the lady in ridding herself of those she had no wish to love was praised by the whole of the company, who one and all described not as love but as folly the daring presumption of the lovers. Then Elissa was graciously asked by the queen to continue, and she promptly began as follows:

Dearest ladies, the manner in which Madonna Francesca released herself from her affliction was indeed very subtle; but I should now like to tell you of a young nun who, with the assistance of Fortune, freed herself by means of a timely remark from the danger with which she was threatened. As you all know, a great many people are foolish enough to instruct and condemn their fellow creatures, but from time to time, as you will observe from this story of mine, Fortune deservedly puts them to shame. And that is what happened to the Abbess who was the superior of the nun whose deeds I am now about to relate.

You are to know, then, that in Lombardy there was once a convent, widely renowned for its sanctity and religious fervour, which housed a certain number of nuns, one of them being a girl of gentle birth, endowed with wondrous beauty, whose name was Isabetta. One day, having come to the grating to converse with a kinsman of hers, she fell in love with a handsome young man who was with him; and the young man, observing that she was very beautiful, and divining her feelings through the language of the eyes, fell no less passionately in love with her.

For some little time, to the no small torment of each, their love remained unfulfilled; but eventually, their desire for one another being equally acute, the young man thought of a way for him and his nun to forgather in secret; and with her willing consent he visited her not only once but over and over again, to their intense and mutual delight. This went on for some considerable time until one night, unbeknown either to himself or to Isabetta, he was seen by one of the other nuns as he left her cell and proceeded on his way. The nun told several of her companions, who at first were inclined to report Isabetta to the Abbess, a lady called Madonna Usimbalda, whose goodness and piety were a byword among all the nuns and everyone else who knew her. But on second thoughts they decided, so that their story should admit of no denial, to try and arrange for the Abbess to catch her red-handed with the young man. So they kept it to themselves, and secretly took it in turns to keep her under close and constant watch in order to take her *in flagrante*.

Now Isabetta knew nothing of all this, and one night, taking no special care, she happened to arrange for her lover to come. This he no sooner did than he was espied by the nuns whose business it was to keep watch, and after biding their time until well into the night, the nuns formed themselves into two separate groups, the first mounting guard at the entrance to Isabetta's cell whilst the second hurried off to the chamber of the Abbess. Their knocking at the door was promptly acknowledged by the Abbess, and so they called out to her, saying:

'Get up, Mother Abbess, come quickly! We've discovered Isabetta has a young man with her in her cell!'

The Abbess was keeping company that night with a priest, whom she frequently smuggled in to her room in a chest, and on hearing this clamour, fearing lest the nuns, in their undue haste and excess of zeal, should burst down the door of her chamber, she leapt out of bed as quick as lightning and dressed as best she could in the dark. Thinking, however, that she had taken up the folded veils which nuns wear on their heads and refer to as psalters, she happened to seize hold of the priest's breeches. And she was in such a tearing hurry, that without noticing her mistake, she clapped these on to her head instead of her psalter and sallied forth, deftly locking the door behind her and exclaiming:

'Where is this damnable sinner?'

Then in company with the others, who were so agog with excitement and so anxious to catch Isabetta in the act that they failed to notice what the Abbess had on her head, she arrived at the door of the cell, which, with a concerted heave, they knocked completely off its hinges. On bursting into the cell, they found the two lovers, who were lying in bed in one another's arms, and who, stunned by this sudden invasion, not knowing what to do, remained perfectly still.

The girl was immediately seized by the other nuns, and led away to the chapter-house by command of the Abbess. The young man meanwhile stayed where he was, and having put on his clothes, he waited to see how the affair would turn out, being resolved, if his girl should come to any harm, to do a serious mischief to as many of them as he could lay hold of, and to take her away from the convent altogether.

The Abbess, having taken her seat in the chapter-house in the presence of all the nuns, who only had eyes for the delinquent, began to administer the most terrible scolding that any woman was ever given, telling her that by her foul and abominable conduct, if it ever leaked out, she had defiled the sanctity, the honour, and the good name of the convent; and by way of addition to this torrent of abuse, she threatened her with the direst of penalties.

Knowing herself to be at fault, the girl was at a loss for an answer, so she simply stood there looking shy and embarrassed without saying a word, with the result that the others began to feel sorry for her. But as the strictures of the Abbess continued to flow thick and fast, she happened to raise her eyes and perceive what the Abbess had on her head, with the braces dangling down on either side.

Realizing what the Abbess had been up to, she took heart and said:

'By the grace of God, Mother Abbess, tie up your bonnet, and then you may say whatever you like to me.'

The Abbess, having no idea what she meant by this, said to her:

'What bonnet, you little whore? Are you going to have the effrontery to stand there making witty remarks? Do you think it funny to have behaved in this disgraceful manner?'

And so, for the second time, the girl said:

'I would ask you once again, Mother Abbess, to tie up your bonnet, and then you may address me in whatever way you please.'

Accordingly, several of the nuns looked up at the Abbess, and the Abbess likewise raised her hands to the sides of her head, so that they all saw what Isabetta was driving at. Whereupon the Abbess, recognizing that she was equally culpable and that there was no way of concealing the fact from all the nuns, who were gazing at her with their eyes popping out of their heads, changed her tune and began to take a completely different line, arguing that it was impossible to defend oneself against the goadings of the flesh. And she told them that provided the thing was discreetly arranged, as it had been in the past, they were all at liberty to enjoy themselves whenever they pleased.

Isabetta was then set at liberty, and she and the Abbess returned to their beds, the latter with the priest and the former with her lover. She thenceforth arranged for him to visit her at frequent intervals, undeterred by the envy of those of her fellow nuns, without lovers, who consoled themselves in secret as best they could.

THIRD STORY

Egged on by Bruno and Buffalmacco and Nello, Master Simone persuades Calandrino that he is pregnant. Calandrino then supplies the three men with capons and money for obtaining a certain medicine, and recovers from his pregnancy without giving birth.

When Elissa had completed her story, and all the ladies had given thanks to God for safely conducting the young nun to so sweet a haven after the buffeting she had received from her jealous companions, the queen called upon Filostrato to follow; and without waiting to be asked twice, he began:

Lovely ladies, that uncouth fellow from the Marches, the judge of whom I spoke to you yesterday, took from the tip of my tongue a story I was on the point of telling you concerning Calandrino. We have already heard a good deal about Calandrino and his companions, but since anything we may say about him is bound to enhance the gaiety of our proceedings, I shall now proceed to recount the tale I intended to tell you yesterday.

We all retain a vivid picture, from our earlier discussions, of Calandrino and the other people to whom I am obliged to refer in this story, so without any further ado I shall tell you that an aunt of Calandrino died, leaving him two hundred pounds in brass farthings. He accordingly started to talk of wanting to purchase a farm, and, acting as though he had ten thousand gold florins to spend, he approached every broker in Florence and entered into negotiations, all of which were abruptly broken off as soon as the price of the property was mentioned.

When Bruno and Buffalmacco came to hear of this, they told him again and again that he would do far better to spend the money with them, having a riotous time, than to go buying land, as if he needed it to make mud pies. But far from bringing Calandrino round to their own point of view, they were unable to wring so much as a solitary meal out of him.

One day, as they were grumbling to one another on the subject, they were joined by a fellow-painter of theirs, whose name was Nello, and the three of them decided they must find some way of stuffing themselves at Calandrino's expense. So without dilly-dallying, having come to an agreement on the strategy to adopt, they lay in wait next morning as Calandrino was leaving his house, and before he had gone very far along the road, Nello came up to him and said:

'Good morning, Calandrino.'

By way of answer, Calandrino said that he wished Nello a good morning and good year too, after which Nello, stepping back a little, began to look Calandrino intently in the face.

'What are you staring at?' said Calandrino.

'Has anything happened to you overnight?' said Nello. 'You look odd, somehow.'

Calandrino was immediately thrown into a panic, and said:

'Odd, you say? Lord! What do you think is the matter with me?'

'Oh, I don't say you're ill or anything,' said Nello. 'You look quite different, that's all. But perhaps it's merely my imagination.'

Nello then took his leave, and Calandrino, feeling very worried, but otherwise perfectly fit and well, proceeded on his way. However, Buffalmacco was lurking a little further along the road, and on seeing him leaving Nello, he walked up to him, bade him good morning, and asked him whether he was feeling all right.

'I'm not exactly sure,' Calandrino replied. 'I was talking to Nello just now, and he said I looked quite different. I wonder if there's anything wrong with me?'

'Oh, it's nothing,' said Buffalmacco. 'You just look half dead, that's all.'

Calandrino was beginning to feel decidedly feverish, when all of a sudden Bruno appeared on the scene, and the first thing he said was:

'What on earth's the matter, Calandrino? You look just like a corpse. Are you feeling all right?'

When he heard both of them saying the same thing, Calandrino was quite certain he was ill, and asked them in tones of deep alarm:

'What am I to do?'

So Bruno said:

'I reckon you ought to return home, go straight to bed, keep yourself well covered up, and send a specimen of your water to Master Simone, who as you know is a close friend of ours. He'll soon tell you what you have to do. We shall come with you, and if anything needs to be done, we'll attend to it.'

So together with Nello, who now came up and joined them, they returned with Calandrino to his house, where he made his way to his bedroom, feeling as though he were on his last legs, and said to his wife:

'Come and cover me up well; I'm feeling very poorly.'

He accordingly got into bed, and dispatched a servant-girl with a specimen of his water to Master Simone, whose surgery at that time was situated in the Mercato Vecchio, at the sign of the pumpkin.

Turning to his companions, Bruno said:

'You stay here with him, whilst I go and see what the doctor has to say, and fetch him back here if necessary.'

'Ah, yes, there's a good fellow!' said Calandrino. 'Go to him and find out for me how matters stand. Goodness knows what's going on inside my poor stomach: I feel awful.'

Bruno therefore set off for the doctor's, arriving there ahead of the girl carrying the specimen, and explained to Master Simone what they were up to. So that when the girl turned up with the specimen, Master Simone examined it and said to her:

'Go and tell Calandrino that he is to keep himself nice and warm.

I shall be coming round straightway to tell him what's wrong with him, and explain what he has to do.'

The girl delivered the message, and shortly afterwards the Master arrived with Bruno, sat down at Calandrino's bedside, and proceeded to take his pulse. Then after a while, in the hearing of Calandrino's wife, who was present in the room, he said:

'Look here, Calandrino, speaking now as your friend, I'd say that the only thing wrong with you is that you are pregnant.'

When Calandrino heard this, he began to howl with dismay, and turning to his wife, he exclaimed:

'Ah, Tessa, this is your doing! You always insist on lying on top. I told you all along what would happen.'

When she heard him say this, Calandrino's wife, who was a very demure sort of person, turned crimson with embarrassment, and lowering her gaze, left the room without uttering a word.

Meanwhile Calandrino continued to wail and moan, saying:

'Ah, what a terrible fate! What am I to do? How am I to produce this infant? Where will it come out? This woman's going to be the death of me now, with her insatiable lust, I can see that. May God make her as miserable as I desire to be happy. I swear that if I were fit and strong, which is far from being the case, I should get up from this bed and break every bone in her body. It serves me right, though; I should never have allowed her to lie on top: but if I ever get out of this alive, she certainly won't do it again, even if she's dying of frustration.'

Bruno and Buffalmacco and Nello were so vastly amused by Calandrino's outburst that it was all they could do to keep a straight face, although Master Simone guffawed so heartily that all his teeth could have been pulled out one after another. At length, however, on being urged and entreated by Calandrino for advice and assistance, the doctor said:

'Now there's no cause for alarm, Calandrino. By the grace of God we've diagnosed the trouble early enough for me to cure you quite easily in a matter of a few days. But it's going to cost you a pretty penny.'

'Get on with it then, doctor, for the love of God,' said Calandrino. 'I have two hundred pounds here with which I was going to buy a farm, but you can take the whole lot if necessary, provided I don't have to bear this child. I simply don't know how I could manage it, when I think of the great hullabaloo women make when they are having babies, even though they have plenty of room for the purpose. If I had all that pain to contend with, I honestly think I should die before I ever produced any child.'

'Just leave everything to me,' said the doctor. 'I shall prescribe a certain medicine for you, a distilled liquid that is most effective in cases of this sort, and highly agreeable to the palate, which will clear everything up in three days and leave you feeling fit as a fiddle. But in future you must be more sensible and desist from these foolish antics. Now in order to prepare this medicine, we shall need three brace of good fat capons, and you must give five pounds in small change to Bruno and the others, so that they can purchase the remaining ingredients we require. See that everything is brought round to my surgery, and tomorrow morning I shall send you the distilled beverage, which you are to start drinking at once, a good big glassful at a time.'

'Whatever you say, doctor,' said Calandrino. And handing over five pounds to Bruno, together with the money for the three brace of capons, he asked him to purchase the things he needed, apologizing for putting him to so much trouble.

The doctor then went away, and concocted a harmless medicinal draught, which he duly sent round to Calandrino. As for Bruno, having purchased the capons and various other essential delicacies, he made a hearty meal of them in company with the doctor and his two companions.

Calandrino took the medicine for three mornings running, then the doctor called to see him along with his three friends, and having taken Calandrino's pulse, he said:

'You're cured, Calandrino, without a shadow of a doubt; so there's no need for you to stay at home any longer. It's quite safe now for you to get up and do whatever you have to.'

So Calandrino got up and went happily about his business, and whenever he fell into conversation with anyone he bestowed high praise on Master Simone for his miraculous cure, which in only three days had effected a painless miscarriage. Bruno, Buffalmacco, and Nello were delighted with themselves for getting round Calandrino's avarice so cleverly, but they had not deceived Monna Tessa, who muttered and moaned to her husband about it for a long time afterwards.

FOURTH STORY

Cecco Fortarrigo gambles away everything he possesses at Buonconvento, together with the money of Cecco Angiulieri. He then pursues Cecco Angiulieri in his shirt claiming that he has been robbed, causes him to be seized by peasants, dons his clothes, mounts his palfrey, and rides away leaving Angiulieri standing there in his shirt.

All the members of the company roared with laughter on hearing what Calandrino had said about his wife; but when Filostrato had finished speaking, Neifile began, at the queen's behest, as follows:

Worthy ladies, but for the fact that it is more difficult for people to display their wisdom and their virtues than it is to show their folly and their vices, it would be so much wasted effort for them to reflect carefully before opening their mouths to speak; all of which has been amply demonstrated by the stupidity of Calandrino, who was under no obligation whatever, in order to recover from the malady from which in his simplicity he believed himself to be suffering, to hold forth about the secret pleasures of his wife in public. But the story of Calandrino brings to mind a tale of a totally different sort, wherein one man's cunning defeats the wisdom of another, to the latter's extreme distress and embarrassment; and I should now like to tell you about it.

In Siena, not many years ago, there lived two young men, who had both come of age and were both called Cecco, the one being the son of Messer Angiulieri and the other of Messer Fortarrigo. And whilst they failed to see eye-to-eye with each other on various matters, there was one respect at least – namely, their hatred of their respective fathers – in which they were in such total agreement that they became good friends and were often to be found in one another's company. But Angiulieri, who was as handsome a man as he was courteous, feeling that he was leading a poor sort of life in Siena on the meagre allowance he was given by his father, and hearing that the new papal ambassador in the March of Ancona was a certain cardinal who was very well disposed towards him, resolved to make his way there in the belief that by doing this he would better his lot. And having spoken to his father on the subject, he came to an arrangement with him whereby he would receive six months' allowance in advance, so that he could purchase new clothes and a good horse, and go there looking reasonably respectable.

No sooner did he begin to look round for someone to take with him as his servant than his plans reached the ears of Fortarrigo, who immediately called on Angiulieri and begged him with all the eloquence at his command to take him with him, saying that he would be willing to act as his servant, his valet, and his general factotum without requiring any other payment than his food and lodging. But Angiulieri refused his offer, not because he had the slightest doubt of his ability to perform these duties, but because Fortarrigo was an inveterate gambler and furthermore he occasionally got very drunk. Fortarrigo assured him that he would guard against both these weaknesses and swore repeatedly that he would keep his promise, to which he added such a torrent of entreaties that Angiulieri finally yielded and agreed to take him.

So early one morning they set forth together, reaching Buonconvento in time for breakfast. Since it was a very warm day, after breakfast Angiulieri asked the innkeeper to prepare a bed for him, and with Fortarrigo's assistance he got undressed and lay down to rest, telling Fortarrigo to call him at the hour of nones.

As soon as Angiulieri was asleep, Fortarrigo went straight to the tavern, where after a few drinks he started to gamble with one or two other people there, and within a short space of time he had lost every penny he possessed, along with every stitch of clothing he was wearing. Being anxious to recoup his losses, he made his way back in nothing but his shirt to the room where Angiulieri was resting, and, perceiving that he was fast asleep, took all the money from his purse and returned to the gaming-table, where he lost Angiulieri's money as well.

On waking up, Angiulieri stepped out of bed, put on his clothes, and made inquiries about Fortarrigo. But as he was nowhere to be found, he assumed that he had lapsed into his former habits and fallen asleep somewhere or other in a drunken stupor. He therefore resolved to abandon him, and having caused his palfrey to be saddled and laden with his luggage, his intention being to procure another servant at Corsignano, he prepared to set off. But when he came to pay his bill, only to discover that he hadn't a single penny in his purse, he made a terrible scene about it and the whole of the innkeeper's household was thrown into turmoil, with Angiulieri claiming that he had been robbed on the premises and threatening to have them all arrested and taken to Siena under escort. At that very moment, however, Fortarrigo appeared on the scene in his shirt, having come to take away Angiulieri's clothes as he had taken his money. And when he saw that Angiulieri was about to take to the road, he said:

'What's all this, Angiulieri? Do we have to go away already? Please stay a little longer. I pawned my doublet for thirty-eight shillings, and the man who has it will be bringing it back here any moment. I'm certain he'll let us have it for thirty-five if we pay him right away.'

A heated discussion then ensued, which was still in full spate when someone interrupted them and made it clear to Angiulieri that Fortarrigo was the person who had taken his money, by informing him exactly how much he had lost, whereupon Angiulieri very nearly threw a fit and would have killed Fortarrigo there and then but for the fact that his fear of the law was greater than his fear of God. So he showered him with abuse, and, threatening to have him hanged by the neck or to see that he was forbidden on pain of death to return to Siena, he mounted his horse.

Fortarrigo's response to this torrent of vituperation was to behave as though it was being directed, not at himself, but at somebody else. And he said:

'Come now, Angiulieri! We shan't get anywhere by throwing these little tantrums. Let's approach the matter sensibly: the fact is that we can have the doublet back for thirty-five shillings if we redeem it now, whereas if we wait for as much as a single day, he'll insist on being paid the full thirty-eight, which is what he gave me for it. His only reason for making me this concession is that I wagered the money on his advice. Come on, now! Why should we turn down an opportunity to save three shillings?'

Angiulieri was now growing positively distraught, especially when he saw that he was being stared at suspiciously by all the people around him, who seemed to be under the impression, not that Fortarrigo had gambled away Angiulieri's money, but that Angiulieri was still holding on to some of Fortarrigo's.

'What the hell do I care about your doublet?' he yelled. 'May you be hanged by the neck. Not only do you rob me and gamble away all my money, but you prevent me from leaving as well. And now you stand there making fun of me.'

Fortarrigo still persisted in acting as though Angiulieri's words were meant for someone else, and said to him:

'Ah, why do you want to make me forfeit the three shillings? Do you think I won't let you have the money back again? Come on now, pay up like a true friend. Why are you in such a hurry? We can still reach Torrenieri quite easily by nightfall. Go and find that purse of yours. I tell you I could never find another doublet that suited me as well as that one, not if I were to ransack the whole of Siena. And to think I let the fellow have it for thirty-eight shillings! It's worth every penny of forty, at least; so you're letting me down twice over.'

Distressed beyond all measure that the fellow, after stealing his money, should now have the gall to hold him up with his prattle, Angiulieri offered no reply, but turned his palfrey's head and set off along the road to Torrenieri. But Fortarrigo had thought of a cunning idea, and began to jog along behind him, still clad in nothing more than his shirt. For at least two miles he stuck to his tail, pleading with him over and over again on the subject of his doublet, and just as Angiulieri began to quicken his pace to avoid having to listen, Fortarrigo caught sight of a number of farm-workers in a field bordering the road some distance ahead. So he yelled to them at the top of his voice, saying:

'Stop him! Stop him!'

And so, brandishing their hoes and their spades, they blocked the road and stopped Angiulieri from going any further, supposing him to have robbed the shirt-clad figure who was stumbling along and shouting in his wake. And albeit Angiulieri explained to them how matters stood, and told them who he was, it made very little difference.

But Fortarrigo now arrived at the spot, and fixing Angiulieri with a withering look, he said:

'You miserable sneak-thief! I could just about kill you for running off with my belongings like this.'

Then, turning to the peasants, he said:

'Gentlemen, you can see the sort of state he left me in, sneaking off from the inn as he did, after gambling away everything he possessed! But with God's help and your own, I can say that I've salvaged something at least, and I shall always be grateful to you for your timely assistance.'

Angiulieri gave them an opposite version of what had happened, but they refused to listen. So Fortarrigo, with the help of the peasants, dragged Angiulieri from his palfrey to the ground, stripped the clothes off his back, and put them on himself. Then he mounted the horse, and leaving Angiulieri barefoot and naked except for his shirt, he made his way back to Siena, informing everyone he met that he had won Angiulieri's palfrey and clothes as the result of a wager.

Thus, instead of presenting himself as a rich man before the cardinal in the Marches, as he had intended, Angiulieri returned penniless to Buonconvento in his shirt. Nor, for the time being, did he have the courage to return to Siena, but having borrowed a suit of clothes, he mounted the jade on which Fortarrigo had been riding, and made his way to Corsignano, where he stayed with relatives until his father came once more to his assistance.

Although Fortarrigo's cunning upset the well-laid plans of Angiulieri on this occasion, he did not go unpunished, for Angiulieri paid him back later, when a suitable time and place presented themselves.

FIFTH STORY

*Calandrino falls in love with a young woman, and Bruno provides him with
a magic scroll, with which he no sooner touches her than she goes off with
him. But on being discovered with the girl by his wife, he finds himself in
very serious trouble.*

Neifile's story was of no great length, and when it drew to a close it
was passed off by the company without much laughter or comment.
The queen now turned to Fiammetta, ordering her to follow.
Fiammetta gaily replied that she would do so with pleasure, and
began:

Noble ladies, as you will doubtless be aware, the more one returns
to any given subject, the greater the pleasure it brings, provided the
person by whom it is broached selects the appropriate time and place.
And since we are assembled here for no other purpose than to rejoice
and be merry, I consider this a suitable time and a proper place
for any subject that will promote our joy and pleasure; for even if it
had been aired a thousand times already, we could return to it as
many times again, and it would still afford delight to us all.

Hence, albeit we have referred many times to the doings of Calandrino, they are invariably so amusing, as Filostrato pointed out a little
earlier, that I shall venture to add a further tale to those we have already heard about him. I could easily have told it in some other way,
using fictitious names, had I wished to do so; but since by departing
from the truth of what actually happened, the storyteller greatly
diminishes the pleasure of his listeners, I shall turn for support to my
opening remarks, and tell it in its proper form.

Niccolò Cornacchini, a wealthy fellow-citizen of ours, owned
various lands including a beautiful estate at Camerata, on which he
caused a fine and splendid mansion to be built, commissioning Bruno
and Buffalmacco to paint it throughout with frescoes. So enormous
was the task with which they were confronted, that they first enlisted
the aid of Nello and Calandrino, then they all got down to work.

Now, albeit one of the rooms contained a bed and other pieces of furniture, nobody was living on the premises except for an elderly housekeeper, and accordingly every so often one of Niccolò's sons, a young bachelor whose name was Filippo, was in the habit of turning up with some young lady or other, who would minister to his pleasures for a day or two and then be sent away.

On one of these visits, he arrived at the mansion with a girl, Niccolosa by name, who was kept by a scoundrelly fellow called Mangione in a house at Camaldoli, from whence he let her out on hire. This girl had a beautiful figure, dressed well, and, for a woman of her sort, was very polite and well-spoken. And one day, around noon, having emerged from the bedroom in a flimsy white shift, her hair tied up in a bun, she happened to be washing her hands and face at a well in the courtyard when Calandrino came to the well for some water.

He gave her a friendly greeting, which she acknowledged, then she began to stare at him, not because she found him the least bit attractive, but because she was fascinated by his odd appearance. Calandrino returned her gaze, and on seeing how beautiful she was, began to think of various excuses for not returning with the water to his companions. However, not knowing who she was, he was afraid to address her, and the girl, perceiving that he was still staring at her, mischievously rolled her eyes at him a couple of times and fetched a few little sighs, so that Calandrino instantly fell in love with her and stood rooted to the spot till she was called inside by Filippo.

On returning to his work, Calandrino did nothing but heave one huge sigh after another; and Bruno, who always kept an eye on him because he found him so entertaining, noticed this and said:

'What the devil's the matter, comrade Calandrino? You do nothing but sigh the whole time.'

'Comrade,' said Calandrino, 'if only I had someone to help me, I could be the happiest man alive.'

'What do you mean?' said Bruno.

'Don't tell a soul,' said Calandrino, 'but there's a girl down there who's lovelier than a nymph, and she's so much in love with me that you'd be astonished. I came across her just now when I went to fetch the water.'

'Good heavens!' said Bruno. 'You'd better be careful, in case it's Filippo's wife.'

'That's exactly who I think she is,' said Calandrino, 'for he called to her from the bedroom, and she went in to him. But anyway, what does it matter? For a girl like that, I'd slip one over on Jesus Christ, let alone Filippo. The truth is, comrade, that I'm so wild about her that I can't begin to tell you how I feel.'

Then Bruno said:

'I'll make one or two inquiries for you, comrade, and find out who she is. If she turns out to be Filippo's wife, I'll fix things up for you in a trice, because she happens to be a very close friend of mine. But how are we to prevent Buffalmacco from finding out? I never get a chance to speak to her except when he is with me.'

'I'm not worried about Buffalmacco,' said Calandrino, 'but we must keep it a secret from Nello, because Tessa is a kinswoman of his and he would ruin everything.'

'That's true,' said Bruno.

Now, Bruno knew perfectly well who she was, for he had seen her arriving at the house, and Filippo had told him in any case. So as soon as Calandrino downed tools for a moment to go and see whether he could catch a glimpse of the girl, Bruno told Nello and Buffalmacco all about Calandrino's sudden infatuation, and together they agreed what they should do about it.

As soon as Calandrino returned, Bruno whispered in his ear:

'Did you see her?'

'Ah, that I did!' Calandrino replied. 'She's struck me all of a heap.'

'I'll just go and see whether she's the one I think she is,' said Bruno, 'in which case you can safely leave everything to me.'

So Bruno went downstairs, and finding Filippo and the girl together, he carefully explained the sort of man that Calandrino was, and told them what he had said. He then arranged with each of them what they should do and say so that they could all have a merry time at Calandrino's expense over this little love-affair of his. And returning to Calandrino, he said:

'Just as I thought: it's Filippo's wife. So we shall have to tread very warily, because if Filippo gets wind of this affair, he'll spill so much of our blood that all the water in the Arno won't wash it away. But what message would you like me to give her, if I should have a chance to speak to her?'

'Faith!' replied Calandrino. 'You're to tell her first and foremost that I wish her a thousand bushels of the sort of love that fattens a girl; then you're to say that I'm her obedient servant, and if there's anything she needs . . . Do you follow me?'

'Indeed I do,' said Bruno. 'Leave everything to me.'

When suppertime came, they all abandoned work for the day and made their way downstairs to the courtyard, where Filippo and Niccolosa stood loitering about for Calandrino's benefit. Fixing his gaze on Niccolosa, Calandrino began to perform a whole series of curious antics, so blatantly obvious that even a blind man would have noticed. As for Niccolosa, in view of what Bruno had told her, she gave Calandrino every encouragement, and took the greatest delight in his eccentricities. And whilst all this was going on, Filippo was deep in conversation with Buffalmacco and the others, pretending not to notice.

After a while, however, much to Calandrino's annoyance, Filippo and the girl went away; and as they were on their way back to Florence, Bruno said to him:

'There's no doubt about it, Calandrino, you've got her in the palm of your hand. Holy Mother of God, if you were to bring along your rebeck and serenade her with one or two of those love-songs of yours, she'd be so eager to come to you that she'd hurl herself bodily through the window.'

'Do you really think so, comrade?' said Calandrino. 'Do you think I ought to fetch it?'

'I certainly do,' Bruno replied.

Whereupon Calandrino said:

'You wouldn't believe me today, when I told you. But you must admit, comrade, that when it comes to obtaining what I want, I know better than anybody else how to go about it. What other man could have persuaded a lady of her quality to fall in love with him so quickly? Could any of those young gallants have done it, who parade up and down the whole day long, spouting like a tap, and who wouldn't know how to gather three handfuls of nuts in a thousand years? Just wait till you see what I can do with my rebeck: you'll be amazed! You needn't think I'm past the age for this sort of thing, because I'm not, and she knows it. And once I lay my paws on her, she'll know it even better. God's truth! I'll sport with her so merrily that she'll cling to me like a mother besotted with her son.'

'Ah, yes!' said Bruno. 'You'll make a proper meal out of her. I can see you now, in my mind's eye, nibbling her sweet red lips and her rosy cheeks with those lute-peg teeth of yours, and then devouring her whole body, piece by succulent piece.'

On hearing these words, Calandrino felt as though he was already getting down to business, and he skipped and sang, being seized by such a transport of delight that he almost split his hide.

Next day he brought along his rebeck, to the strains of which, much to the delight of all the others, he sang a number of songs. But to cut a long story short, he became so frantically eager to see the girl as often as possible, that he did practically no work at all, for he would be dashing to and fro a thousand times a day, first to the windows, then to the door, then to the courtyard, in the hope of catching a glimpse of her. And for her part, the girl, astutely following Bruno's instructions, gave Calandrino as many opportunities to see her as she possibly could.

But Bruno also played the role of go-between, supplying Calandrino with answers to the messages he sent her, and from time to time delivering a note in Niccolosa's own hand. And whenever she was not actually there, as was more often than not the case, he got her to write letters to Calandrino in which, whilst holding out every hope that his devoted love would soon have its reward, she explained that she was staying at the house of her kinsfolk, where for the present it was impossible for him to see her.

Bruno and Buffalmacco kept a careful watch on the progress of the affair, being hugely entertained by Calandrino's antics; and every so often they persuaded him to hand over various objects which they claimed his lady had requested, such as an ivory comb, a purse, a small dagger, and other such trifles, in return bringing him some worthless little rings, which sent Calandrino into raptures. But apart from this they coaxed one or two good meals out of him, and he showed them various other little favours to encourage them in their efforts on his behalf.

Now, after being kept on tenterhooks in this manner for at least two months without making any further progress, Calandrino, seeing that the work was nearing completion, and realizing that unless he gathered the fruits of his love before the frescoes were finished he would never have another opportunity, began to solicit Bruno's aid with all the power at his command. So when she next came to stay at the house, Bruno made arrangements with Filippo and the girl about what they were to do, then he went to Calandrino and said:

'Look here, comrade, this woman has promised me a thousand times that she would give you what you wanted, but when it comes to the point she does nothing, and I strongly suspect that she's leading us by the nose. So unless you have any objection, as she won't keep her promises, we shall make her keep them whether she wants to or not.'

'Ah yes!' Calandrino replied. 'Let's do that, for the love of God, and do it quickly.'

'Are you bold enough to touch her with a scroll that I shall give you?' asked Bruno.

'Of course I am,' said Calandrino.

'In that case,' said Bruno, 'see that you let me have a small piece of parchment from a stillborn lamb, a live bat, three grains of incense, and a candle that has been blessed, and leave the rest to me.'

Calandrino accordingly spent the whole of that evening attempting by various ingenious means to catch a live bat, which he eventually succeeded in doing, and took it along to Bruno next morning, together with the other items he had specified. Bruno then withdrew to an inner room, filled the parchment with a series of meaningless hieroglyphics, and brought it back to Calandrino, saying:

'Now listen, Calandrino: if you touch her with this parchment, she will immediately come with you and do whatever you want. So if Filippo should go off anywhere today, you must contrive to approach her and touch her with the scroll, then make your way round the side of the house to the barn, which is the ideal spot for your purposes as no one ever goes near it. You'll find that she will follow you, and once she reaches the barn, you know exactly what you have to do.'

Calandrino was overjoyed, and seizing the parchment, he said: 'Just you leave it to me, comrade.'

Nello, against whom Calandrino was constantly on his guard, was enjoying the affair as much as anyone, and was every bit as eager to make a fool of him; so on Bruno's instructions he went down to Florence, called on Calandrino's wife, and said to her:

'You remember the hiding Calandrino gave you, Tessa, for no reason at all, on the day he came home from the Mugnone with all those stones? Well, now's your chance to be even with him, and if you fail to take it, you needn't regard me as your friend or your kinsman ever again. He's fallen in love with some woman up there at Camerata, and she's such a wanton little baggage that she's forever going off with him in private. They've arranged to meet today, as a matter of fact, so I want you to come and see, and punish him as he deserves.'

Monna Tessa was not at all amused by what she had heard, and leaping to her feet, she exclaimed:

'Ah, false villain, so this is how he treats me, is it? By all that's holy, he shan't get away with it, not if I can help it.'

Seizing her cloak, she promptly set forth, accompanied by a maid-servant, and made her way up to Camerata with Nello, walking at such a furious pace that he was scarcely able to keep up. However, long before she reached the mansion, Bruno saw her coming and said to Filippo:

'There's our friend coming now.'

Filippo therefore went to the part of the house where Calandrino and the others were working, and said:

'Gentlemen, I have some urgent business to attend to in Florence, so keep up the good work.' And taking his leave of them, he went and concealed himself in a place from which, without being observed, he would be able to see what Calandrino was doing.

As soon as Calandrino imagined Filippo to be well on his way to Florence, he descended to the courtyard, where, finding Niccolosa alone, he engaged her in conversation. She had been carefully briefed on what she was to do, and walking over to Calandrino, she treated him with greater familiarity than usual. Calandrino therefore touched her with the scroll, and immediately directed his steps towards the barn without saying a word. She followed him in, closed the door behind her, and threw her arms about his neck; then she pushed him over on to some straw that was lying on the floor and promptly sat astride his prostrate form, forcing his hands back against his shoulders. And without allowing him to bring his face close to hers, she gazed at him rapturously, saying:

'Oh, my sweet Calandrino, heart of my body, my dearest, my darling, my angel, how long I have been yearning to have you all to myself and hold you in my arms! You've swept me off my feet with your winning ways! You've captured my heart with that rebeck of yours! Is it really possible that I am holding you in my embrace?'

'Alas, my dearest,' said Calandrino, who was scarcely able to move. 'Let me up, so that I may kiss you.'

'Oh, but you are too hasty,' said Niccolosa. 'First let me have a good look at you. Let me feast my eyes upon your dear, sweet face.'

Bruno and Buffalmacco saw and heard everything that passed between them, having meanwhile joined Filippo in his hiding place. And just as Calandrino had freed his arms, and was on the point of kissing Niccolosa, along came Nello with Monna Tessa.

'I swear to God they are in there together,' he said, as they came up to the door of the barn. Fuming with rage, Calandrino's wife applied both her hands to the door and pushed it open. On entering the barn, she saw Calandrino lying there on his back, straddled by Niccolosa, who no sooner caught sight of Monna Tessa than she leapt to her feet and ran off to join Filippo.

Before Calandrino could get up, Monna Tessa pounced upon him and attacked him with her nails, clawing his face all over before seizing him by the hair and dragging him round the floor of the barn, saying:

'You filthy, despicable dog, so you'd do this to me, would you? A curse on all the love I ever bore you, demented old fool that you are. Don't you think you have enough to do, keeping the home fires burning, without going off to stoke up other people's? A fine lover you would make for anyone! Don't you know yourself, villain? Don't you realize, scoundrel, that if they were to squeeze you from head to toe, there wouldn't be enough juice to make a sauce? God's faith, it wasn't your wife who was getting you with child this time. May the Lord make her suffer, whoever she is, for she must surely be a depraved little hussy to take a fancy to a precious jewel like you.'

When he first saw his wife coming in, Calandrino was unsure whether he was dead or alive, and hadn't the courage to defend himself against her furious onslaught. But in the end, all torn and bleeding and dishevelled, he picked up his cape, staggered to his feet, and humbly entreated Monna Tessa not to shout unless she wanted him to be torn to pieces, for the woman who was with him was none other than the wife of the master of the house.

'I don't care who she is,' bawled Monna Tessa. 'May God punish her as she deserves.'

Pretending to have been attracted by all the noise, Bruno and Buffalmacco now appeared on the scene, having laughed themselves silly along with Filippo and Niccolosa as they watched this spectacle; and after much heated discussion, they pacified Monna Tessa and advised Calandrino to return to Florence and never show his face there again in case Filippo came to hear of what had happened and did him some serious mischief.

And so, scratched and torn to ribbons, Calandrino made his way back to Florence feeling all forlorn and dejected; and not having the courage to return to Camerata, he resigned himself to the torrent of strictures and abuse to which he was subjected day and night by Monna Tessa, and made an end to his love for Niccolosa, having supplied a feast of entertainment, not only for his companions, but for Filippo and Niccolosa as well.

SIXTH STORY

Two young men lodge overnight at a cottage, where one of them goes and sleeps with their host's daughter, whilst his wife inadvertently sleeps with the other. The one who was with the daughter clambers into bed beside her father, mistaking him for his companion, and tells him all about it. A great furore then ensues, and the wife, realizing her mistake, gets into her daughter's bed, whence with a timely explanation she restores the peace.

As on previous occasions, so also on this, the company was heartily amused by Calandrino's doings, which the ladies had no sooner finished debating than the queen called on Panfilo to address them; and he began as follows:

Laudable ladies, the name of Calandrino's lady-love reminds me of a tale about another Niccolosa, which I should now like to relate to you, for as you will see, it shows us how a good woman's presence of mind averted a serious scandal.

Not long ago, there lived in the valley of the Mugnone a worthy man who earned an honest penny by supplying food and drink to wayfarers; and although he was poor, and his house was tiny, he would from time to time, in cases of urgent need, offer them a night's lodging, but only if they happened to be people he knew.

Now, this man had a most attractive wife, who had borne him two children, the first being a charming and beautiful girl of about fifteen or sixteen, as yet unmarried, whilst the second was an infant, not yet twelve months old, who was still being nursed at his mother's breast.

The daughter had caught the eye of a gay and handsome young Florentine gentleman who used to spend much of his time in the countryside, and he fell passionately in love with her. Nor was it long before the girl, being highly flattered to have won the affection of so noble a youth, which she strove hard to retain by displaying the greatest affability towards him, fell in love with him. And neither of the pair would have hesitated to consummate their love, but for the fact that Pinuccio (for such was the young man's name) was not prepared to expose the girl or himself to censure.

At length however, his ardour growing daily more intense, Pinuccio was seized with a longing to consort with her, come what may, and it occurred to him that he must find some excuse for lodging with her father overnight, since, being conversant with the layout of the premises, he had good reason to think that he and the girl could be together without anyone ever being any the wiser. And no sooner did this idea enter his head than he promptly took steps to carry it into effect.

Late one afternoon, he and a trusted companion of his called Adriano, who knew of his love for the girl, hired a couple of pack-horses, and having laden them with a pair of saddlebags, filled probably with straw, they set forth from Florence; and after riding round in a wide circle they came to the valley of the Mugnone, some time after nightfall. They then wheeled their horses round to make it look as though they were returning from Romagna, rode up to the cottage of our worthy friend, and knocked at the door. And since the man was well acquainted with both Pinuccio and his companion, he immediately came down to let them in.

'You'll have to put us up for the night,' said Pinuccio. 'We had intended to reach Florence before dark, but as you can see, we've made such slow progress that this is as far as we've come, and it's too late to enter the city at this hour.'

'My dear Pinuccio,' replied the host, 'as you know, I can't exactly offer you a princely sort of lodging. But no matter: since night has fallen and you've nowhere else to go, I shall be glad to put you up as best I can.'

So the two young men dismounted, and having seen that their nags were comfortably stabled, they went into the house, where, since they had brought plenty to eat with them, they made a hearty supper along with their host. Now, their host had only one bedroom, which was very tiny, and into this he had crammed three small beds, leaving so little space that it was almost impossible to move between them. Two of the beds stood alongside one of the bedroom walls, whilst the third was against the wall on the opposite side of the room; and having seen that the least uncomfortable of the three was made ready for his guests, the host invited them to sleep in that for the night. Shortly afterwards, when they appeared to be asleep, though in reality they were wide awake, he settled his daughter in one of the other two beds, whilst he and his wife got into the third; and beside the bed in which she was sleeping, his wife had placed the cradle containing her infant son.

Having made a mental note of all these arrangements, Pinuccio waited until he was sure that everyone was asleep, then quietly left his bed, stole across to the bed in which his lady-love was sleeping, and lay down beside her. Although she was somewhat alarmed, the girl received him joyously in her arms, and they then proceeded to take their fill of that sweet pleasure for which they yearned above all else.

Whilst Pinuccio and the girl were thus employed, a cat, somewhere in the house, happened to knock something over, causing the man's wife to wake up with a start. Being anxious to discover what it was, she got up and groped her way in the dark towards that part of the house from which the noise had come.

Meanwhile Adriano also happened to get up, not for the same reason, but in order to obey the call of nature, and as he was groping his way towards the door with this purpose in view, he came in contact with the cradle deposited there by the woman. Being unable to pass without moving it out of his way, he picked it up and set it down beside his own bed; and after doing what he had to do, he returned to his bed and forgot all about it.

Having discovered the cause of the noise and assured herself that nothing important had fallen, the woman swore at the cat, and, without bothering to light a lamp and explore the matter further, returned to the bedroom. Picking her way carefully through the darkness, she went straight to the bed where her husband was lying; but on finding no trace of the cradle, she said to herself: 'How stupid I am! What a fine thing to do! Heavens above, I was just about to step into the bed where my guests are sleeping.' So she walked a little further up the room, found the cradle, and got into bed beside Adriano, thinking him to be her husband.

On perceiving this, Adriano, who was still awake, gave her a most cordial reception: and without a murmur he tacked hard to windward over and over again, much to her delight and satisfaction.

This, then, was how matters stood when Pinuccio, who had gratified his longings to the full and was afraid of falling asleep in the young lady's arms, abandoned her so as to go back and sleep in his own bed. But on reaching the bed to find the cradle lying there, he moved on, thinking he had mistaken his host's bed for his own, and ended up by getting into bed with the host, who was awakened by his coming. And being under the impression that the man who lay beside him was Adriano, Pinuccio said:

'I swear to you that there was never anything so delicious as Niccolosa. By the body of God, no man ever had so much pleasure with any woman as I have been having with her. Since the time I left you, I assure you I've been to the bower of bliss half a dozen times at the very least.'

The host was not exactly pleased to hear Pinuccio's tidings, and having first of all asked himself what the devil the fellow was doing in his bed, he allowed his anger to get the better of his prudence, and exclaimed:

'What villainy is this, Pinuccio? I can't think why you should have played me so scurvy a trick, but by all that's holy, I shall pay you back for it.'

Now, Pinuccio was not the wisest of young men, and on perceiving his error, instead of doing all he could to remedy matters, he said:

'Pay me back? How? What could you do to me?'

Whereupon the host's wife, thinking she was with her husband, said to Adriano:

'Heavens! Just listen to the way those guests of ours are arguing with one another!'

Adriano laughed, and said:

'Let them get on with it, and to hell with them. They had far too much to drink last night.'

The woman had already thought she could detect the angry tones of her husband, and on hearing Adriano's voice, she realized at once whose bed she was sharing. So being a person of some intelligence, she promptly got up without a word, seized her baby's cradle, and having picked her way across the room, which was in total darkness, she set the cradle down beside the bed in which her daughter was sleeping and scrambled in beside her. Then, pretending to have been aroused by the noise her husband was making, she called out to him and demanded to know what he was quarrelling with Pinuccio about. Whereupon her husband replied:

'Don't you hear what he says he has done to Niccolosa this night?'

'He's telling a pack of lies,' said the woman. 'He hasn't been anywhere near Niccolosa, for I've been lying beside her myself the whole time and I haven't managed to sleep a wink. You're a fool to take any notice of him. You men drink so much in the evening that you spend the night dreaming and wandering all over the place in your sleep, and imagine you've performed all sorts of miracles: it's a thousand pities you don't trip over and break your necks! What's Pinuccio doing there anyway? Why isn't he in his own bed?'

At which point, seeing how adroitly the woman was concealing both her own and her daughter's dishonour, Adriano came to her support by saying:

'How many times do I have to tell you, Pinuccio, not to wander about in the middle of the night? You'll land yourself in serious trouble one of these days, with this habit of walking in your sleep, and claiming to have actually done the fantastic things you dream about. Come back to bed, curse you!'

When he heard Adriano confirm what his wife had been saying, the host began to think that Pinuccio really had been dreaming after all; and seizing him by the shoulder, he shook him and yelled at him, saying:

'Wake up, Pinuccio! Go back to your own bed!'

Having taken all of this in, Pinuccio now began to thresh about as though he were dreaming again, causing his host to split his sides with laughter. But in the end, after a thorough shaking, he pretended to wake up; and calling to Adriano, he said:

'Why have you woken me up? Is it morning already?'

'Yes,' said Adriano. 'Come back here.'

Pinuccio kept up the pretence, showing every sign of being extremely drowsy, but in the end he left his host's side and staggered back to bed with Adriano. When they got up next morning, their host began to laugh and make fun of Pinuccio and his dreams. And so, amid a constant stream of merry banter, the two young men saddled and loaded their horses, and after drinking the health of their host, they remounted and rode back to Florence, feeling no less delighted with the manner than with the outcome of the night's activities.

From then on, Pinuccio discovered other ways of consorting with Niccolosa, who meanwhile assured her mother that he had certainly been dreaming. And thus the woman, who retained a vivid memory of Adriano's embraces, was left with the firm conviction that she alone had been awake on the night in question.

SEVENTH STORY

Talano d'Imolese dreams that his wife is savaged all about the throat and the face by a wolf, and tells her to take care; but she ignores his warning, and the dream comes true.

Panfilo's story being now at an end, the woman's presence of mind was applauded by one and all, after which the queen called upon Pampinea to tell hers, and she began as follows:

Delectable ladies, we have talked on previous occasions about the truths embodied in dreams, which many of us refuse to take seriously. But even though this topic has already been aired, I am determined to tell you a pithy little tale showing what happened not long ago to a neighbour of mine through ignoring a dream of her husband's in which she appeared.

I don't know whether you were ever acquainted with Talano d'Imolese, but he was a person of high repute, and was married to a young woman called Margarita, who, though exceedingly beautiful, was the most argumentative, disagreeable and self-willed creature on God's earth, for she would never heed other people's advice and regarded everyone but herself as an incompetent fool. This made life very difficult for Talano, but since he had no choice in the matter, he bore it all philosophically.

Now one night, when Talano happened to be staying with this wife of his at one of their country estates, he dreamt that he saw her wandering through some very beautiful woods, which were situated not far away from the house. As he watched, an enormous and ferocious wolf seemed to emerge from a corner of the woods and hurl itself at Margarita's throat, dragging her to the ground. She struggled to free herself, screaming for help, and when at length she managed to escape from its clutches, the whole of her throat and face appeared to be torn to ribbons. So when Talano got up next morning, he said to his wife:

'Woman, your cussedness has been the bane of my life since the day we were married; but all the same I should be sorry if you came to any harm, and therefore, if you'll take my advice, you won't venture forth from the house today.'

When she asked him the reason, he told her about his dream, whereupon she tossed her head in the air and said:

'Evil wishes beget evil dreams. You pretend to be very anxious for my safety, but you only dream these horrid things about me because you'd like to see them happen. You may rest assured that I shall never give you the satisfaction of seeing me suffer any such fate as the one you describe, whether on this day or any other.'

'I knew you would say that,' said Talano. 'A mangy dog never thanks you for combing its pelt. But you may think whatever you like. I only mentioned it for your own good, and once again I advise you to stay at home today, or at any rate to keep well away from those woods of ours.'

'Very well,' said the woman, 'I'll do as you say.'

But then she began to think to herself: 'Here's a crafty fellow! Do you see how he tries to frighten me out of going near the woods today? He's doubtless made an appointment there with some strumpet or other, and doesn't want me to find him. Ah, he'd do well for himself at a supper for the blind, but knowing him as I do, I should be a great fool to take him at his word. He certainly won't get away with this. I shall find out what business takes him to those woods, even if I have to wait there the whole day.'

No sooner had she reached the end of these deliberations than her husband left the house, whereupon she too left the house by a separate door and made her way to the woods without a moment's delay, keeping out of sight as much as possible. On entering the woods, she concealed herself in the thickest part she could find, and kept a sharp lookout on all sides so that she could see if anyone was coming.

Nothing was further removed from her thoughts than the prospect of seeing any wolves, but all of a sudden, whilst she was standing there in the way we have described, a wolf of terrifying size leapt out from a nearby thicket; on seeing which, she scarcely had time to exclaim 'Lord, deliver me!' before the wolf hurled itself at her throat, seized her firmly in its jaws, and began to carry her off as though she were a new-born lamb.

So tightly was the wolf holding on to her throat that she was unable to scream for help, nor was there anything else she could do; and hence the wolf, as it bore her away, would assuredly have strangled her but for the fact that it ran towards some shepherds, who yelled at the beast and forced it to release her. The poor, unfortunate woman was recognized by the shepherds, who carried her back to her house, and after long and intensive treatment at the hands of various physicians, she recovered. Her recovery was not complete, however, for the whole of her throat and a part of her face were so badly disfigured that whereas she was formerly a beautiful woman, she was thenceforth deformed and utterly loathsome to look upon. Hence she was ashamed to show herself in public, and shed many a bitter tear for her petulant ways and her refusal to give credence, when it would have cost her nothing, to her husband's prophetic dream.

EIGHTH STORY

Biondello plays a trick on Ciacco in regard of a breakfast, whereupon Ciacco discreetly avenges himself, causing Biondello to receive a terrible hiding.

Each and every member of the joyful company maintained that what Talano had seen in his sleep was no dream, but rather a vision, as it corresponded so exactly with what had actually taken place. But when they had all finished talking, the queen called upon Lauretta to follow, and so she began:

Judicious ladies, just as my predecessors today have almost without exception taken their cue from something already said, I too am prompted, by the account Pampinea gave us yesterday of the scholar's bitter vendetta, to tell you of another vendetta, which, whilst it was no laughing matter for its victim, was at the same time rather less brutal.

I would have you know, then, that in Florence there was once a man known to everyone as Ciacco, who was the greatest glutton that ever lived. Since his purse was unequal to the demands made upon it by his gluttony, and since he was also a highly cultivated person, never at a loss for something clever and amusing to say, he built a reputation for himself, not exactly as a jester but rather as a wit, and took to mixing with wealthy people possessing a taste for good food, with whom he regularly supped and breakfasted even when not invited.

In Florence, at the time of which I am speaking, there was a man called Biondello, who was a dapper little fellow, elegant to a fault and neater than a fly, with a coif surmounting a head of long, fair hair, exquisitely arranged so that not a single strand was out of place, and this man practised the same profession as Ciacco.

One morning, during Lent, Biondello was at the fishmarket buying a pair of huge lampreys for Messer Vieri de' Cerchi, when he was observed by Ciacco, who went up to him and said:

'Oho! What have we here?'

To which Biondello replied:

'The other three that were sent to Messer Corso Donati's yesterday evening, along with a sturgeon, were much finer specimens than these. He's invited one or two gentlemen to breakfast, and because he thought there might not be enough to go round, he got me to purchase these other two. Won't you be coming?'

'What a question to ask!' Ciacco replied. 'Of course I shall be coming.'

At what seemed to him an appropriate hour, Ciacco made his way to the house of Messer Corso, whom he found with several of his neighbours waiting to go to breakfast. When Messer Corso asked him the nature of his business, Ciacco replied:

'I have come, sir, in order to breakfast with you and your friends.'

'You are most welcome,' said Messer Corso. 'And since the meal is now ready, let us go and eat.'

So they all sat down at table, and after a first course of tunny and chick-peas they had some fried fish from the Arno, after which the meal came abruptly to an end.

On discovering that Biondello had deceived him, Ciacco was boiling with indignation, and resolved to pay him back in his own coin. A few days later he came across Biondello, who had meanwhile amused a number of people with the tale of his little hoax. No sooner did Biondello catch sight of Ciacco than he greeted him and asked, with a broad grin, what he had thought of Messer Corso's lampreys.

'That is a question,' replied Ciacco, 'which you will be far better able to answer yourself, before another week has passed.'

After leaving Biondello, Ciacco went to work without further ado, and having agreed upon terms with a crafty intermediary, he handed him an enormous wine-bottle, led him to a spot near the Loggia de' Cavicciuli, and pointing out to him a gentleman there called Messer Filippo Argenti – a huge, powerful, muscular-looking fellow, who was as haughty, hot-tempered, and quarrelsome a man as ever drew breath – he said:

'You are to go up to that man over there with this flask in your hand, and say to him: "Sir, I have been sent to you by Biondello, who asks if you will be so kind as to rubify this flask for him with some of your excellent red wine, as he wants to wet his whistle with his comrades." But be very careful not to let him lay his hands on you, otherwise you'll have a thin time of it and my plans will be ruined.'

'Do I have to say anything else?' said the intermediary.

'No,' said Ciacco. 'Now off you go, and when you've said your piece, return here to me with the flask and I shall pay you your fee.'

So the intermediary made his way across to Messer Filippo and delivered the message, which Messer Filippo no sooner heard than he concluded that Biondello, who was no stranger to him, was having a joke at his expense. Not being slow to take offence, he went all red in the face and said:

'Rubify? Wet his whistle? God curse the fellow, and you too!'

Whereupon he leapt to his feet and shot out an arm at the intermediary, intending to take him by the scruff of the neck. But the latter, being on his guard, was too quick for him and took to his heels. He then returned by a roundabout route to Ciacco, who had witnessed the whole scene, and told him what Messer Filippo had said.

Ciacco was delighted, and having paid the man his fee, went off in search of Biondello, never resting for a moment till he found him.

'Have you been to the Loggia de' Cavicciuli lately?' he asked him.

'No, I haven't,' replied Biondello. 'Why do you ask?'

'Because I've heard that Messer Filippo is looking for you,' said Ciacco. 'I couldn't tell you what it is he wants.'

'Good,' said Biondello. 'I'll go over there and converse with him a little.'

Biondello then took his leave, and Ciacco followed him at a discreet distance to see what would happen. Meanwhile Messer Filippo, having failed to catch the intermediary, had been left in a towering rage and was breathing fire and fury, being unable to make any sense of the man's words except that Biondello, at the prompting of some person or other, was making fun of him. And it was whilst he was fuming away in this manner that Biondello arrived on the scene.

No sooner did Messer Filippo set eyes on Biondello than he strode up to him and gave him a tremendous punch in the face.

'Oh alas, sir!' cried Biondello. 'What does this mean?'

'Scoundrel!' yelled Messer Filippo, tearing Biondello's coif to ribbons and hurling his hood to the ground, at the same time raining blows upon him. 'You'll see only too clearly what it means. I'll teach you to send people to me with all this talk of rubifying flasks and wetting your whistle. Do you suppose you can make fun of me as though I were a child?'

And so saying, he pounded Biondello's face with a pair of fists that seemed to be made of iron. Nor was this all, for he disarranged every hair on the poor fellow's head, and having rolled him over in the mud, tore all the clothes he was wearing to shreds. So zealously did he address himself to his task that from the first moment to the last Biondello was unable to utter so much as a single syllable, or to ask him why he was attacking him. He had certainly heard Messer Filippo talk about 'rubifying flasks' and 'wetting whistles', but what these phrases might signify he had no idea.

Having taken an almighty drubbing, he was eventually surrounded by a number of onlookers, who succeeded with the greatest difficulty in removing him, battered and bedraggled, from Messer Filippo's reach. They then explained why Messer Filippo had done it and admonished him for sending such a message, telling him that in future he should remember who Messer Filippo was and that he was not a man to be trifled with.

His eyes full of tears, Biondello protested his innocence, denying that he had ever sent anyone to Messer Filippo for wine. But there was little he could do about it now, and after making himself look a little more presentable he returned home, sorrowful and forlorn, rightly concluding that this was a piece of Ciacco's handiwork. Several days later, when the bruises had faded from his face and he once again began to show himself in public, one of the first people he happened to meet was Ciacco.

'Tell me, Biondello,' he asked, laughing, 'what opinion did you form of Messer Filippo's wine?'

'The same as the one you formed of Messer Corso's lampreys,' he replied.

Then Ciacco said:

'From now on it's up to you: if you should ever try to present me with another of those sumptuous meals, I shall supply you with one of these excellent drinks.'

Knowing it was easier for him to bear ill-will to Ciacco than to do him any actual harm, Biondello bade him a polite good day, and took care never to play any tricks on him again.

NINTH STORY

Two young men ask Solomon's advice, the first as to how he may win people's love, the second as to how he should punish his obstinate wife. Solomon replies by telling the former to love, and the latter to go to Goosebridge.

Not wishing to revoke Dioneo's privilege, the queen saw that she alone remained to tell a story, and when the ladies had finished laughing over the hapless Biondello, she cheerfully thus began:

Lovable ladies, if the order of things is impartially considered, it will quickly be apparent that the vast majority of women are through Nature and custom, as well as in law, subservient to men, by whose opinions their conduct and actions are bound to be governed. It therefore behoves any woman who seeks a calm, contented and untroubled life with her menfolk, to be humble, patient, and obedient, besides being virtuous, a quality that every judicious woman considers her especial and most valued possession.

Even if this lesson were not taught to us by the law, which in all things is directed to the common good, and by usage (or custom as we have called it), Nature proves it to us very plainly, for she has made us soft and fragile of body, timid and fearful of heart, compassionate and benign of disposition, and has furnished us with meagre physical strength, pleasing voices, and gently moving limbs. All of which shows that we need to be governed by others; and it stands to reason that those who need to be aided and governed must be submissive, obedient, and deferential to their benefactors and governors. But who are the governors and benefactors of us women, if they are not our menfolk? Hence we should always submit to men's will, and do them all possible honour, and any woman who behaves differently is worthy, in my opinion, not only of severe censure, but of harsh punishment.

I have expressed views of this kind on previous occasions, and I was confirmed in them a little while ago by what Pampinea told us about Talano's obstinate wife, to whom God sent the punishment that her husband was unable to visit upon her. I repeat, therefore, that in my judgement, all those women should be harshly and rigidly punished, who are other than agreeable, kindly, and compliant, as required by Nature, usage, and law.

Hence I should like to acquaint you with a piece of advice that was once proffered by Solomon, for it is a useful remedy in treating those who are afflicted by the malady of which I have spoken. It should not be thought that his counsel applies to all women, regardless of whether they require such a remedy, although men have a proverb which says: 'For a good horse and a bad, spurs are required; for a good woman and a bad, the rod is required.' Which words, being frivolously interpreted, all women would readily concede to be true; but I suggest that even in their moral sense they are no less admissible.

All women are pliant and yielding by nature, and hence for those who step beyond their permitted bounds the rod is required to punish their transgressions; and in order to sustain the virtue of the others, who practise restraint, the rod is required to encourage and frighten them.

But leaving all preaching aside, and coming to what I propose to tell you, I say that when the fame of Solomon's wisdom, having spread to the four corners of the earth, was at its highest peak, and it was known that he would share it unstintingly with anyone wishing to verify it in person, many people came to him from different parts of the world to ask his advice on matters of great privacy and complexity; and one of those who set out to go and consult him was a young man called Melissus, who was of a noble family and very rich, and was born and bred in the town of Lajazzo.

As he was on his way to Jerusalem, after leaving Antioch he chanced upon another young man, riding in the same direction, whose name was Joseph; and after a while, as is usually the way with travellers, they fell into conversation.

Heaving learned what manner of man this Joseph was, and whence he had come, he asked him where he was going and for what purpose. To which Joseph replied that he was going to seek Solomon's advice about how he should deal with his wife, who was the most perverse and stubborn woman on earth, and against whose wilfulness all his entreaties, endearments, and everything else had availed him nothing. Then he in turn asked Melissus whence he had come, where he was going, and why; and Melissus replied:

'I come from Lajazzo, and like yourself, I too suffer a misfortune. I am a rich young man, and I spend my substance in banqueting and entertaining my fellow-citizens, but the curious thing about it is that despite all this I cannot find a single man who wishes me well. And so I am going where you are going, to seek advice about what I must do to be loved.'

So the two companions journeyed on together, and on reaching Jerusalem, through the good offices of one of Solomon's lords, they were ushered into his presence and Melissus briefly explained the nature of his business. And all that Solomon said by way of reply was: 'Love'.

This said, Melissus was promptly shown the door, and Joseph explained his own reason for coming. But the only answer he received from Solomon was: 'Go to Goosebridge,' and the words were scarcely out of the King's mouth before Joseph, too, was removed from his presence. Outside, he found Melissus waiting for him, and told him about the answer he had been given.

After pondering upon these words without succeeding in extracting a meaning from them, or anything that might help to resolve their problems, the two young men, feeling they had been made to look foolish, began to make their way homewards. After travelling for several days, they came to a fine-looking bridge across a river; and since a lengthy baggage-train of mules and horses happened to be using the bridge, they were forced to wait till all the animals had crossed it.

When all but a few of them had done so, one of the mules took fright, in the way they frequently do, and refused to take another step. So one of the muleteers took hold of a stick and began to beat it, quite gently to begin with, in order to make it go across. But the mule, veering from one side of the road to the other and occasionally turning back, was utterly determined not to go on. This caused the muleteer to lose his temper completely, and he began to beat it with his stick quite unmercifully, raining a series of terrible blows on its head, its flanks, and its hindquarters, but all to no avail.

Melissus and Joseph, who were standing there watching all this, directed a stream of abuse at the muleteer, saying:

'Hey! villain, what are you doing? Do you want to kill the poor beast? Why don't you try talking nicely to him and leading him across gently? He'll come more quickly that way than by beating him as you are doing.'

'You know your horses and I know my mule,' replied the muleteer. 'Just you leave him to me.'

Having said this he began to beat the mule all over again, and administered so many blows to each of its flanks that the mule moved on, and the muleteer's point was made.

As the two young men were about to proceed on their way, Joseph saw a fellow sitting on the further side of the bridge and asked him what the place was called.

'Sir,' the good man replied, 'this place is called Goosebridge.'

No sooner did Joseph hear the name than he recalled the words of Solomon, and said to Melissus:

'I do declare, my friend, that the advice I had from Solomon may yet turn out to be sound and sensible. For it's perfectly plain to me now that I've never known how to beat my wife properly, and this muleteer has shown me what I must do.'

A few days later they came to Antioch, and Joseph invited Melissus to stay with him and rest for a few days before going on with his journey. Having met with an icy reception from his wife, Joseph told her to see that supper was prepared, taking her instructions from Melissus; and the latter, seeing that Joseph wanted him to do it, briefly explained what he would like to eat. But the woman, true to her old habits, did almost the exact opposite of what Melissus had prescribed; and when Joseph saw what she had done, he rounded on her angrily and said:

'Were you not told about the kind of supper you were to serve?'

The woman turned to him defiantly, and said:

'What are you talking about? Bah! get on with your supper, if you want it. I shall do as I think fit, not as I am told. And if you don't like it, you can lump it.'

Melissus was astounded by the woman's reply, and took great exception to it. And Joseph said: 'Woman, you are just the same as ever; but believe me, I shall make you change your ways.' Then, turning to Melissus, he said: 'We shall soon see, my friend, whether Solomon's advice was sound. Pray be good enough to stay and observe what I shall do, and look upon it as a game. If you should be tempted to interfere, remember what the muleteer said to us when we felt so sorry for his mule.'

'Since I am a guest in your house,' said Melissus, 'I have no intention of opposing your wishes.'

Having laid his hands on a good, stout stick of sapling oak, Joseph made his way to his wife's bedroom, to which she had retired, mumbling and muttering angrily to herself, from the supper-table. And grabbing her by the tresses, he flung her to the floor at his feet and began to belabour her cruelly.

The woman first began to shriek and then to threaten; but on finding that Joseph was totally unmoved by all this, she began, bruised and battered from head to toe, to plead with him in God's name to spare her life, saying she would never again do anything to displease him.

None of this had the slightest effect upon Joseph, who on the contrary tanned her hide with ever-increasing fury, dealing her hefty blows about the ribs, the haunches, and the shoulders until eventually he stopped from sheer exhaustion. And to cut a long story short, there was not a bone nor a muscle nor a sinew in the good woman's back that was not rent asunder.

His task completed, Joseph came back to Melissus and said to him:

'Tomorrow we shall see how Solomon's advice to go to Goose-bridge has stood up to the test.' Then, having rested for a while, he washed his hands and supped with Melissus; and in due course they both retired to bed.

Meanwhile his unfortunate wife picked herself up with great difficulty from the floor and collapsed on to her bed, where she slept as best she could till the following morning. And having risen very early, she sent to ask Joseph what he would like for breakfast.

Joseph had a good laugh with Melissus over this, and issued the necessary instructions. And when, in due course, they came down to breakfast, they found an excellent meal awaiting them, precisely as Joseph had ordered. Hence they were both full of praise for the advice which at first they had ill understood.

A few days later, Melissus took his leave of Joseph and returned home, where he told a wise man about what he had heard from Solomon; and the man said:

'He could not have given you a truer or a better piece of advice. You know perfectly well that you love no one, and that you dispense your hospitality and your favours, not because you love other people, but merely for pomp and pride. Love, therefore, as Solomon told you, and you will be loved.'

So that was how the shrew was punished, and how the young man came to be loved through loving others.

TENTH STORY

Father Gianni is prevailed upon by Neighbour Pietro to cast a spell in order to turn his wife into a mare; but when he comes to fasten on the tail, Neighbour Pietro, by saying that he didn't want a tail, completely ruins the spell.

This story of the queen's produced one or two murmurs from the ladies, and one or two laughs from the young men; but when they had quieted down, Dioneo began to address them as follows:

Charming ladies, the beauty of a flock of white doves is better enhanced by a black crow than by a pure white swan; and likewise the presence of a simpleton among a group of intelligent people will sometimes add brilliance and grace to their wisdom, as well as affording pleasure and amusement.

Accordingly, since you are all models of tact and discretion, whereas I am something of a fool, I ought to command a higher place in your affections, by augmenting the light of your excellence through my own shortcomings, than if I were to diminish it by my superior worth. And hence, in telling you the story I am about to relate, I must claim greater licence to present myself in my true colours, and crave your more patient indulgence, than if I were blessed with greater intelligence. I shall tell you a tale, then, of no great length, from which you will learn how carefully one must observe the instructions of those who do things with the aid of magic, and how the slightest failure to do so may ruin all the magician has achieved.

Some years ago, in Barletta, there was a priest called Father Gianni di Barolo, who, because he had a poor living and wished to supplement his income, took to carrying goods, with his mare, round the various fairs of Apulia, and to buying and selling. In the course of his travels, he became very friendly with a man called Pietro da Tresanti, who practised the same trade as his own, but with a donkey, and in token of his friendship and affection he always addressed him, in the Apulian fashion, as Neighbour Pietro. And whenever Pietro came to Barletta, Father Gianni always invited him to his church, where he shared his quarters with him and entertained him to the best of his ability.

For his own part, Neighbour Pietro was exceedingly poor and had a tiny little house in Tresanti, hardly big enough to accommodate himself, his donkey, and his beautiful young wife. But whenever Father Gianni turned up in Tresanti, he took him to his house and entertained him there as best he could, in appreciation of the latter's hospitality in Barletta. However, when it came to putting him up for the night, Pietro was unable to do as much for him as he would have liked, because he only had one little bed, in which he and his beautiful wife used to sleep. Father Gianni was therefore obliged to bed down on a heap of straw in the stable, alongside his mare and Pietro's donkey.

Pietro's wife, knowing of the hospitality which the priest accorded to her husband in Barletta, had offered on several occasions, when the priest came to stay with them, to go and sleep with a neighbour of hers called Zita Carapresa di Giudice Leo, so that the priest could sleep in the bed with her husband. But the priest wouldn't hear of it, and on one occasion he said to her:

'My dear Gemmata, don't trouble your head over me. I am quite all right, because whenever I choose I can transform this mare of mine into a fair young maid and turn in with her. Then when it suits me I turn her back into a mare. And that is why I'd never be without her.'

The young woman was astonished, believed every word of it, and told her husband, adding:

'If he's as good a friend as you say, why don't you get him to teach you the spell, so that you can turn me into a mare and run your business with the mare as well as the donkey? We should earn twice as much money, and when we got home you could turn me back into a woman, as I am now.'

Being more of a simpleton than a sage, Neighbour Pietro believed all this and took her advice to heart; and he began pestering Father Gianni for all he was worth to teach him the secret. Father Gianni did all he could to talk him out of his folly, but without success, and so he said to him:

'Very well, since you insist, tomorrow we shall rise, as usual, before dawn, and I shall demonstrate how it's done. To tell the truth, as you'll see for yourself, the most difficult part of the operation is to fasten on the tail.'

That night, Pietro and Gemmata were looking forward so eagerly to this business that they hardly slept a wink, and as soon as the dawn was approaching, they scrambled out of bed and called Father Gianni, who, having risen in his nightshirt, came to Pietro's tiny little bedroom and said:

'I know of no other person in the world, apart from yourself, for whom I would perform this favour, but as you continue to press me, I shall do it. However, if you want it to work, you must do exactly as I tell you.'

They assured him that they would do as he said. So Father Gianni picked up a lantern, handed it to Neighbour Pietro, and said:

'Watch me closely, and memorize carefully what I say. Unless you want to ruin everything, be sure not to utter a word, no matter what you may see or hear. And pray to God that the tail sticks firmly in place.'

Neighbour Pietro took the lantern and assured him he would do as he had said. Then Father Gianni got Gemmata to remove all her clothes and to stand on all fours like a mare, likewise instructing her not to utter a word whatever happened, after which he began to fondle her face and her head with his hands, saying:

'This be a fine mare's head.'

Then he stroked her hair, saying:

'This be a fine mare's mane.'

And stroking her arms, he said:

'These be fine mare's legs and fine mare's hooves.'

Then he stroked her breasts, which were so round and firm that a certain uninvited guest was roused and stood erect. And he said:

'This be a fine mare's breast.'

He then did the same to her back, her belly, her rump, her thighs and her legs: and finally, having nothing left to attend to except the tail, he lifted his shirt, took hold of the dibber that he did his planting with, and stuck it straight in the appropriate furrow, saying:

'And this be a fine mare's tail.'

Until this happened, Neighbour Pietro had been closely observing it all in silence, but he took a poor view of this last bit of business, and exclaimed:

'Oh, Father Gianni, no tail! I don't want a tail!'

The vital sap which all plants need to make them grow had already arrived, when Father Gianni, standing back, said:

'Alas! Neighbour Pietro, what have you done? Didn't I tell you not to say a word no matter what you saw? The mare was just about to materialize, but now you've ruined everything by opening your mouth, and there's no way of ever making another.'

'That suits me,' said Neighbour Pietro. 'I didn't want the tail. Why didn't you ask me to do it? Besides, you stuck it on too low.'

To which Father Gianni replied:

'I didn't ask you because you wouldn't have known how to fasten it on, the first time, as deftly as I.'

The young woman, hearing these words, stood up and said to her husband, in all seriousness:

'Pah! what an idiot you are! Why did you have to ruin everything for the pair of us? Did you ever see a mare without a tail? So help me God, you're as poor as a church mouse already, but you deserve to be a lot poorer.'

Now that it was no longer possible to turn the young woman into a mare because of the words that Neighbour Pietro had uttered, she put on her clothes again, feeling all sad and forlorn. Meanwhile her husband prepared to return to his old trade, with no more than a donkey as usual: then he and Father Gianni went off to the fair at Bitonto together, and he never asked the same favour of him again.

*　*　*

How the ladies laughed to hear this tale, whose meaning they had grasped more readily than Dioneo had intended, may be left to the imagination of those among my fair readers who are laughing at it still. However, the stories were now at an end, the sun's heat had begun to abate, and the queen, knowing that her sovereignty had run its course, rose to her feet and removed her crown. This she placed upon the head of Panfilo, who alone remained to be invested with the honour; and smiling she said:

'My lord, you are left with an arduous task, for since you are the last, you must make up for the failings of myself and my predecessors in the office to which you have now acceded. God grant you grace in this undertaking, as He has granted it to me in crowning you our king.'

Accepting with joy the honour she had bestowed upon him, Panfilo replied:

'Your own excellence, madam, and that of my other subjects, will ensure that my reign is no less worthy of praise than those that have preceded it.' Then, following the example of his predecessors, he made all necessary arrangements with the steward; after which he turned to address the waiting ladies:

'Enamoured ladies,' he said, 'our queen of today, Emilia, prudently left you at liberty to speak on whatever subject you chose, so that you might rest your faculties. But now that you are refreshed, I consider that we should revert to our customary rule, and I therefore want you all to think of something to say, tomorrow, on the subject of *those who have performed liberal or munificent deeds, whether in the cause of love or otherwise*. The telling and the hearing of such things will assuredly fill you with a burning desire, well disposed as you already are in spirit, to comport yourselves valorously. And thus our lives, which cannot be other than brief in these our mortal bodies, will be preserved by the fame of our achievements – a goal which every man who does not simply attend to his belly, like an animal, should not only desire but most zealously pursue and strive to attain.'

The theme proposed by Panfilo was unanimously approved by the joyful company, and by the leave of their new king they all arose from where they were sitting and applied themselves, each according to his taste, to their usual pastimes; and thus they whiled away the time until supper. To this they came in festive mood, and at the end of the meal, which was served with meticulous care and formal propriety, they rose from their places and proceeded to dance as usual. They then sang countless songs, more entertaining for the words than polished in the singing, till finally the king asked Neifile to sing one on her own account. And without further ado, in a clear and gladsome voice, she began charmingly to sing, as follows:

'I am so young I love to sing
 And take delight in the early spring
 Thanks to the sweet thoughts Love doth bring.

'I see in green fields as I go
 Yellow and red and white flowers blow,
 Briar-roses and fair lilies grow.

'And in all these his face I see
 Who has so taken hold of me
 His wish is mine eternally.

'And when one certain bloom I spy
 Which most recalls him to my eye
 I pluck and greet it lovingly,

'Kiss it, and thus show that I know
What my whole soul aspireth to
And where my heart desires to go:

'Then, with the rest, I place it there
Among a posy bound with care
With my own light and golden hair.

'That pleasure given by a flower
To mortal eyes through Nature's power
Is so bestowed on me that there

'I fancy my sweet love to be
Standing himself in front of me,
Whose person hath so kindled me.

'Never in words could be expressed
Its scent's effect upon my breast,
Of which my sighs are witnesses.

'They never harsh nor rough breathe forth
But warm and sweet, of greater worth
Than other ladies' here on earth,

'And make their way unto my love,
Who when he hears them straight doth move
To bring me bliss just as, in sooth,
I murmur, "Come to me, and prove
I never need despair thy love."'

The king and all the ladies heaped lavish praise upon Neifile's song; after which, since much of the night was already spent, the king decreed that everyone should go and rest until the morning.

Here ends the Ninth Day of the Decameron

TENTH DAY

Here begins the Tenth and Last Day, wherein, under the rule of Panfilo, the discussion turns upon those who have performed liberal or munificent deeds, whether in the cause of love or otherwise.

One or two cloudlets in the western sky were still suffused with crimson, whilst those in the east, caught in the rays of the approaching sun, were already brightly tipped with gold, when Panfilo got up and caused the ladies and his two companions to be roused. When all were present, he conferred with them and decided upon the place to which they should go to amuse themselves; he then set forth at a leisurely pace, accompanied by Filomena and Fiammetta, and followed by all the rest. For some little time they sauntered gaily along, talking about the lives they intended to lead in the future, and answering each other's questions, until, having walked a considerable distance, they found that the sun was becoming too hot for their comfort, and returned to the palace. Gathering round the fountain, they had some glasses rinsed in its limpid waters, and those among them who were thirsty drank their fill; after which they roamed freely through the garden, savouring its delectable shade, until the hour of breakfast. And when they had eaten and slept, as was their custom, they forgathered in a spot designated by the king, who called upon Neifile to tell the first story; whereupon she cheerfully began, as follows:

FIRST STORY

A worthy knight enters the service of the King of Spain, by whom he feels that he is ill-requited; so the King gives him irrefutable proof that the fault lies, not with himself, but with the knight's own cruel fortune, in the end rewarding him most handsomely.

I account it an especial favour, honourable ladies, that our king should have singled me out to speak first on so weighty a theme as that of munificence, which, even as the sun embellishes and graces the whole of the heavens, is the light and splendour of every other virtue. So I shall tell you a little story, which to my way of thinking is most delightful, and which surely cannot be other than profitable to recall.

You are to know, then, that of the many gallant knights who have graced our city for longer than I can remember, there was one in particular, Messer Ruggieri de' Figiovanni, who was possibly the finest of them all. Being both wealthy and stout of heart, and seeing that, because of the general tenor of Tuscan manners, there would be little or no opportunity for him to prove his worth by remaining in these parts, he made up his mind to spend some time with King Alphonso of Spain, who was better renowned for his prowess than any other ruler of his day. And so he set out with a most impressive array of armour and horses and a large retinue, and made his way to Alphonso's court in Spain, where the King accorded him a gracious welcome.

There accordingly he settled, and because of his princely style of living and the prodigious feats he accomplished in the field, he quickly made his mark as a man of valour.

But the longer he remained at Alphonso's court, the more it seemed to him, through closely observing the ways of the King, that he was granting castles, towns and baronies to one man after another with very little discretion, giving them to people who had done nothing to deserve them. Now, Messer Ruggieri was conscious of his own merits, and since nothing was given to him, he considered that his own standing was thereby greatly diminished. He therefore decided to leave, and went to the King to ask his permission to do so. The King granted his request, and presented him with a most handsome-looking mule, the finest that any man had ever ridden, for which Messer Ruggieri was grateful in view of the long journey ahead of him.

The King then instructed one of his confidential servants to arrange as best he could to accompany Messer Ruggieri throughout the first day of his journey without allowing him to suspect that he had been sent by the King, and to make a mental note of everything Ruggieri said about him, so that he could report it later word for word. And on the second morning he was to order Messer Ruggieri to return to the King.

The servant kept watch, and as soon as Messer Ruggieri left the city, attached himself to his entourage in as natural a manner as possible, giving him the impression that he too was going to Italy.

So they rode along together, with Messer Ruggieri seated astride the mule presented to him by the King, conversing on various topics with his new companion, until at a certain point, just before tierce, he said:

'I suppose we ought to stop and relieve the animals.' So they stopped at a suitable place, where all the animals relieved themselves with the exception of the mule. They then rode on, with the King's servant still listening carefully to the words of the knight, till they came to a watercourse, where, as they were watering their mounts, the mule staled into the river. On seeing this, Messer Ruggieri said:

'Ah! God curse you, beast! you're just like the gentleman who presented you to me.'

The King's servant noted these words, and though he noted many more in the course of their long day's journey together, he heard nothing else from Ruggieri's lips that was other than highly complimentary to the King. Next morning, as soon as they were mounted and about to set off again for Tuscany, the servant delivered the King's order to Messer Ruggieri, who immediately turned back.

Having already been informed of what Messer Ruggieri had said about the mule, the King summoned him to his presence, welcomed him with a broad smile, and asked him why he had compared him to the mule, or rather vice versa.

Messer Ruggieri replied, with the greatest of candour:

'My lord, I compared it to you for this reason, that just as you bestow your gifts where they are inappropriate, and withhold them where they would be justified, so the mule relieved itself, not in the right place, but in the wrong one.'

So the King said:

'Messer Ruggieri, it was not because I failed to recognize in you a most gallant knight, deserving of the highest honours, that I withheld my bounty from you and bestowed it on many others, who were insignificant by comparison with yourself. The blame rests not with me but with your fortune, which has prevented me from giving you your deserts. And I intend to prove to you that I am speaking the truth.'

'My lord,' replied Messer Ruggieri, 'the fact that you have not rewarded me is immaterial, for I never had any desire to multiply my wealth. What distresses me is the absence of any token of your esteem. However, I consider your explanation to be sound and reasonable, and though I am ready to see whatever you wish to show me, I accept your word and there's no need for you to prove it.'

The King then led him into a great hall, where, as he had arranged beforehand, there were two large chests, both of which were padlocked; and in the presence of a large gathering, he said:

'Messer Ruggieri, one of these chests contains my crown, my orb and my royal sceptre, along with many fine brooches, rings and jewelled belts of mine and every other precious stone I possess. The other is filled with earth. Choose whichever one you like, and it shall be yours to keep, and thus you shall see whether it was I or your fortune that failed to acknowledge your worth.'

Seeing that this was what the King desired him to do, Messer Ruggieri chose one of the chests. The King ordered it to be opened, and it was found to be full of earth. Whereupon the King laughed and said:

'As you can see for yourself, Messer Ruggieri, I was telling you the truth about your fortune; but your merits are such that I am bound to oppose her powers. I know that you have little inclination to become a Spaniard, and hence I have no wish to give you either towns or castles in my domain; but in defiance of your fortune, I want you to have the chest of which she deprived you, so that you may take it to your native land and justly boast among your fellow-citizens of your achievements, to which my gifts will bear witness.'

Messer Ruggieri accepted the chest, thanked the King in a manner befitting so generous a gift, and returned with it, well content, to Tuscany.

SECOND STORY

Ghino di Tacco captures the Abbot of Cluny, cures him of a stomach ailment, and then releases him. The Abbot returns to the court of Rome, where he reconciles Ghino with Pope Boniface and creates him a Knight Hospitaller.

After they had finished praising King Alphonso for the munificence he displayed towards the Florentine knight, the king, who had been mightily pleased by Neifile's account, called upon Elissa to tell the next story; and she promptly began, as follows:

Tender ladies, there is no denying that for a king to have acted munificently, and bestowed his munificence upon one who had served him well, is all very fine and commendable. But what are we to think when we are told about a member of the clergy whose munificence was all the more remarkable in that he bestowed it on a person whom no one would have blamed him for treating as his enemy? Surely we can only conclude that whereas the munificence of the King was a virtue, that of the priest was a miracle; for these latter are so incredibly mean that women are positively generous by comparison, and they fight tooth and nail against every charitable instinct. Moreover, whereas all men naturally crave to be avenged for wrongs they have received, we know from experience that the members of the clergy, though they preach submissiveness and warmly commend the pardoning of wrongs, surpass all other men in the zeal with which they conduct their vendettas. But in the story you are about to hear, you will plainly discover how one of their number revealed his munificence.

Ghino di Tacco, whose feats of daring and brigandage brought him great notoriety after being banished from Siena and incurring the enmity of the Counts of Santa Fiore, staged a rebellion in Radicofani against the Church of Rome; and having established himself in the town, he made sure that anyone passing through the surrounding territory was set upon and robbed by his marauders.

Now the ruling Pope in Rome was Boniface VIII, and to his court there came the Abbot of Cluny, who was reputed to be one of the richest prelates in the world. In the course of his stay there, however, he ruined his stomach, and was advised by the physicians to go to the baths at Siena, where he was certain to recover. And so, having obtained permission from the Pope, he set out for Siena, heedless of the reputation of Ghino, accompanied by a huge and splendid train of goods, baggage, horses and servants.

On learning of his approach, Ghino di Tacco spread out his nets, and without allowing so much as a single page-boy to escape, he cut off the Abbot with the whole of his retinue and belongings in a narrow gorge. This done, he dispatched his ablest lieutenant to the Abbot, suitably escorted, who very politely requested the Abbot, on his master's behalf, to be good enough to make his way to Ghino's fortress and dismount there. On hearing this, the Abbot flew into a terrible rage and replied that he had no intention of doing any such thing, as he had nothing to discuss with Ghino. In short, he was going to continue his journey, and would like to see anyone try to prevent him.

Whereupon Ghino's emissary, speaking in deferential tones, said to him:

'My lord, you have come to a place where except for the power of God we fear nothing, and where excommunications and interdicts are entirely ineffectual. Please be good enough, therefore, to comply with Ghino's wishes in this matter.'

Whilst these words were being exchanged, the whole place had been surrounded by brigands; and so the Abbot, realizing that he and his men were trapped, set off in high dudgeon with Ghino's emissary along the road leading to the fortress, together with all his goods and retinue. Having dismounted at a large house, he was lodged, on Ghino's instructions, in an extremely dark and uncomfortable little room, whereas all the others were given very comfortable quarters, each according to his rank, in various parts of the fortress. And as for the horses and all the Abbot's belongings, these were put in a safe place and left untouched.

Once this was done, Ghino went to the Abbot and said to him:

'My lord, I am sent by Ghino, of whom you are a guest, in order to ask whether you will be so good as to inform him where you were going, and for what reason.'

The Abbot, being a sensible man, had by this time swallowed his pride, and informed him where he was going and why, whereupon Ghino took his leave of him, and resolved to try and cure him without the aid of spa-waters. Having given instructions that the room should be closely guarded and that a large fire should be kept burning in the grate, he left the Abbot alone until the following morning, when he returned bringing him two slices of toasted bread wrapped in a spotless white cloth, together with a large glass of Corniglia wine from the Abbot's own stores. And he addressed the Abbot as follows:

'My lord, when Ghino was younger, he studied medicine, and he claims to have learnt that there is no better cure for the stomach-ache than the one he is about to administer, which begins with these things I have brought you. Take them, then, and be of good cheer.'

His hunger being greater than his appetite for jesting, the Abbot ate the bread and drank the wine, at the same time displaying his indignation. He then became very truculent, asked a number of questions, and issued a lot of advice; and he made a special point of asking to see Ghino.

Since much of what he had said was pointless, Ghino chose to ignore it; but to some of the Abbot's questions he gave polite answers, affirming that Ghino would visit him as soon as he could. Having given him this assurance, he took his leave, and a whole day elapsed before he returned, bringing the same quantity of toasted bread and Corniglia wine as before.

He kept him in this fashion for several days, until he perceived that the Abbot had eaten some dried beans, which he had deliberately left in the room after smuggling them in on an earlier visit.

He therefore asked the Abbot on Ghino's behalf whether his stomach seemed any better, to which the Abbot replied:

'It would seem to be all right, if only I were out of his clutches; and apart from that, my one great longing is to eat, so fully have his remedies restored me to health.'

Ghino therefore made arrangements for the Abbot's servants to furnish a stately chamber with the Abbot's own effects, and gave orders for a great banquet to be prepared, to which a number of the residents and all of the Abbot's retinue were invited. And next morning he went to the Abbot and said:

'My lord, since you are feeling well again, the time has come for you to leave the sick-room.' And taking him by the hand, he led him to the stately chamber and left him there with his own attendants, whilst he went off to make sure that the banquet would be truly magnificent.

The Abbot relaxed for a while in the company of his own folk, and described to them the sort of life he had been living, whereas they on the other hand declared of one accord that Ghino had entertained them lavishly. But the time having now arrived for them to eat, the Abbot and all the others were regaled with a succession of excellent dishes and superb wines, though Ghino still refrained from telling the Abbot who he was.

The Abbot was entertained in this way for several days running, but eventually Ghino gave instructions for all of his effects to be brought to a large room overlooking a courtyard where every one of the Abbot's horses was assembled, down to the most moth-eaten nag he possessed. He then called on the Abbot and asked him how he was feeling and whether he was strong enough to travel. The Abbot replied that he was as strong as an ox, that he had fully recovered from his stomach ailment, and that once he was out of Ghino's hands, his troubles would be over.

Then Ghino took the Abbot to the room in which his goods and the whole of his retinue were gathered, and, guiding him to a window whence he could see all his horses, he said:

'My lord Abbot, you must realize that gentle birth, exile, poverty, and the desire to defend his life and his nobility against numerous powerful enemies, rather than any instinctive love of evil, have driven Ghino di Tacco, whom you see before you, to become a highway robber and an enemy of the court of Rome. But because you seem a worthy gentleman, and because I have cured you of the malady affecting your stomach, I do not intend to treat you as I would treat any other person who fell into my hands, of whose possessions I would take as large a portion as I pleased. On the contrary, I propose that you yourself, having given due regard to my needs, should decide how much or how little of your property you would care to leave with me. All your goods are set out here before you, and from this window you can see your horses tethered in the courtyard. I therefore bid you take as much or as little as you please, and you are henceforth free to leave whenever you wish.'

The Abbot was astonished and delighted to hear such generous sentiments from the lips of a highway robber, and promptly shed his anger and disdain, being filled instead with a feeling of goodwill towards Ghino, whom he was now disposed to look upon as a bosom friend. And he rushed to embrace him, saying:

'I swear to God that in order to win the friendship of such a man as I now judge you to be, I should willingly endure far greater wrongs than any you appear to have done me hitherto. A curse upon Fortune, that has compelled you to pursue so infamous a calling!'

Then the Abbot singled out an essential minimum of his numerous belongings and his horses, and leaving all the rest to Ghino, he returned to Rome.

The Pope had heard all about the seizure of the Abbot, and took a very serious view of the matter; but the first question he asked on seeing him again was whether the baths had done him any good. To which the Abbot replied, with a smile:

'Holy Father, without going as far as the baths I came across an excellent physician, who cured me completely.' He then described the manner of his cure, much to the pontiff's amusement; and he went on to ask the Pope, under the promptings of his generous instincts, to grant him a certain favour.

The Pope, thinking he would ask for something quite different, readily agreed to grant his request, whereupon the Abbot said:

'Holy Father, the favour I intend to ask of you is that you restore my physician, Ghino di Tacco, to your good graces, for he is assuredly

one of the finest and worthiest men I have ever met. As to his
wicked ways, I believe them to be more the fault of Fortune than
his own; and if you will change his fortune by granting him the
wherewithal to live in a style appropriate to his rank, I am convinced
that within a short space of time, you will come to share my high
opinion of him.'

The Pope was a person of lofty sentiments, always well-disposed
towards men of excellence, and he said that if Ghino was as fine a
man as the Abbot claimed, he would gladly do as he was asked. And
he told the Abbot to arrange for Ghino to come to Rome, it being
perfectly safe for him to do so.

And so, in accordance with the Abbot's wishes, Ghino came to the
papal court under safe conduct. Nor had he been there long before
his worth was acknowledged by the Pope, who made peace with him
and granted him a large priory in the Order of the Hospitallers,
having first created him a Knight of that Order. This position he held
for the rest of his days, remaining a friend and servant of Mother
Church and the Abbot of Cluny.

THIRD STORY

*Mithridanes is filled with envy over Nathan's reputation for courtesy, and
sets out to murder him. He comes across Nathan by accident but fails to
recognize him, and after learning from Nathan's own lips the best way to
carry out his intentions, he finds Nathan in a copse, as arranged. When he
realizes who it is, he is filled with shame, and thenceforth becomes Nathan's
friend.*

The tale they had just been told, about an act of generosity performed
by a member of the clergy, was certainly felt by one and all to be
something akin to a miracle. But once the ladies had finished debating
its novelty, the king called upon Filostrato to proceed, and he forthwith began, as follows:

Noble ladies, great though the munificence of the King of Spain
undoubtedly was, and that of the Abbot of Cluny possibly without
precedent, you will perhaps be no less amazed to hear of a person

who, in order to extend his generosity to another man who was thirsting not only for his blood but for his very life, astutely arranged to give him what he was seeking. Moreover, as I propose to show you in this little story of mine, he would have succeeded therein if his adversary had chosen to accept his offer.

It is quite certain (if the word of various Genoese and of others who have been to those parts may be trusted) that in the region of Cathay there once lived a man of noble lineage, wealthy beyond compare, whose name was Nathan. This man owned a small estate not far from a road along which anyone travelling from the West to the East or vice versa was more or less obliged to pass, and since he was a person of lofty and generous sentiments, who desired to be known by his works, he gathered about him a number of architects and craftsmen, who within a short space of time built for him one of the finest and largest and richest palaces ever seen, and furnished it in excellent taste with all things meet for the reception and entertainment of gentlefolk. There he kept a splendid and numerous retinue of servants, and took pains to ensure that all those people who came and went were received and entertained in a most festive and agreeable manner. To this laudable custom he was so unswervingly attached that before very long his fame had spread, not only throughout the Orient, but to most parts of the western world as well.

When he had arrived at a ripe old age without ever wearying of dispensing his largesse, his reputation chanced to reach the ears of a young man called Mithridanes, who lived in that same part of the world, and who, feeling himself to be no less wealthy than Nathan, grew jealous of Nathan's fame and excellence, and resolved, through a display of greater liberality, either to nullify or darken the old man's name. And so, having built a palace similar to Nathan's, he began to entertain all those who came and went on a more lavish scale than any ever previously known, and there is no doubt that within a short time he became very famous.

Now one day, whilst the young man was sitting all alone in the main courtyard, a woman happened to enter the palace by one of the gates, ask him for alms, and be given them. She then returned by way of a second gate, approached him again, and was given a further sum of money. This happened twelve times in succession, and when she returned for the thirteenth time, Mithridanes said to her:

'My good woman, you are very persistent with this begging of yours.' But he gave her the alms just the same.

On hearing what he had said, the old woman exclaimed:

'Ah, how wonderful is the generosity of Nathan! For his palace has thirty-two gates, just like this one, and I passed through each of them in turn, asked him for alms, and obtained them every time, without his ever so much as hinting that he knew who I was. Yet here I have only to pass through thirteen before I am recognized and given a scolding.' And so saying, she went away and never returned.

Mithridanes took the old woman's words about Nathan as a slight on his own reputation, and flying into a violent rage, he exclaimed:

'Poor fool that I am! How can I ever hope to match Nathan's generosity in greater things, let alone surpass him as I sought, when even in the most trivial affairs I cannot even approach him? All my efforts will be quite futile until he is removed from the face of the earth. He shows no sign of dying from old age, so I shall have to do the job with my own hands, and the sooner the better.'

He then leapt angrily to his feet, and without revealing his intentions to a living soul, set out on horseback with a mere handful of companions; and after the third day he came to the place where Nathan lived. Evening was now approaching, and having bidden his companions to pretend he was a total stranger to them, and find themselves somewhere to stay pending further instructions, he was left to his own devices. Not very far from Nathan's fair palace he came across its owner, all alone and very plainly attired, taking a pleasant stroll in the cool of the evening; and not realizing who it was, he asked him whether he could direct him to Nathan's house.

'My son,' Nathan gaily replied, 'nobody in these parts could show you better than I how to get there. So if you have no objection, I'll take you there myself.'

The young man gladly accepted his offer, but told him that if possible he did not want Nathan to see him or to know that he was there.

'Since you want it to be so,' said Nathan, 'I shall attend to that as well.'

Mithridanes therefore dismounted, and, walking along with Nathan, who was very soon entertaining him with a stream of fine talk, he made his way to the beautiful palace.

On reaching the palace, Nathan got one of his servants to take the young man's horse, and, whispering into the servant's ear, instructed him to pass the word immediately through the entire household that no one was to tell the young man that he himself was Nathan. And this command was carried out.

Once they were inside the palace, he saw that Mithridanes was lodged in an exquisite room, to which no one was admitted except the servants he had deputed to wait upon him. And making the visitor feel completely at home there, Nathan himself kept him company.

Thus they spent the evening together, and although Mithridanes treated Nathan with the deference of a son conversing with a father, he was unable to refrain from asking him who he was.

'I am one of Nathan's menial servants,' replied Nathan, 'and although I have been with him ever since my infancy, he has never raised me above my present station; so that, even if everyone else praises him to the skies, I myself have little to thank him for.'

The old man's words raised hopes in Mithridanes of being able to carry out his evil purpose more safely and discreetly, especially when Nathan went on to ask him very politely to tell him who he was and the nature of his business in that part of the world, offering him all the advice and assistance he could give.

Mithridanes paused for some little time before replying, but eventually decided to take him into his confidence. After much beating about the bush he came to the point; and having sworn him to secrecy he requested his help and advice, revealing exactly who he was, why he was there, and what had prompted him to come.

On hearing Mithridanes speak, and learning of his cruel resolve, Nathan was extremely perturbed. But he was not deficient in courage, and scarcely paused for a moment before replying, without batting an eyelid:

'Your father was a man of excellent worth, Mithridanes, and you are clearly intent upon following his example by this lofty enterprise of yours, wherein you extend a generous hand to all who come to you. Moreover, I warmly commend your envy of Nathan, for if this form of jealousy were more widespread, the world, which is very miserly, would soon become a better place to live in. I shall certainly keep your intentions a secret, but rather than render you any great assistance, I can offer you some useful advice, which is this. Some half a mile from where we stand, you can see a copse where practically every morning Nathan goes for a long walk, entirely alone; it will be a simple matter for you to find him there and deal with him as you please. But if you kill him, and wish to make good your escape, you must leave the copse, not by the way you entered, but along the path you see over there to the left, for although it is a little more difficult, it will lead you home by a shorter and safer route.'

Having imparted this information to Mithridanes, Nathan took his leave, and Mithridanes secretly sent word to his companions, who had likewise found lodging in the palace, about where they were to wait for him on the following day. Meanwhile Nathan had no misgivings about the advice he had offered, and when the next day came, not having changed his mind in the slightest, he set off alone for the copse to meet his doom.

Mithridanes had no other weapons but a sword and a bow, and as soon as he had risen he girded them on, mounted his horse, and rode over to the copse, where from some distance away he espied the solitary figure of Nathan sauntering among the trees. He galloped towards him, but being resolved to see his face and hear him speak before attacking him, he seized him by the turban he was wearing and exclaimed:

'Greybeard, your hour has come!'

By way of answer, all that Nathan said was:

'In that case I have only myself to blame.'

On hearing his voice and observing his features, Mithridanes recognized him at once as the man who had been so hospitable and sociable towards him, and had given him such faithful advice; hence his fury immediately subsided and his anger gave way to a feeling of shame. And having thrown away his sword, which he had already drawn in readiness to strike, he dismounted from his horse and flung himself in tears at Nathan's feet, saying:

'How clearly, dearest father, do I perceive your liberality, seeing the ingenious way in which you have come to offer me the life which without any reason I was eager to take, as you discovered for yourself from my own lips. But God was more heedful than I of my obligations, and in this moment of supreme need He has opened my eyes, which vile envy had kept so tightly sealed. And because you have been so compliant towards my evil design, I am all the more conscious of the debt of penitence that I owe you. Avenge yourself upon me, therefore, in whatever way you think my crime deserves.'

Having helped Mithridanes to his feet, Nathan kissed and embraced him affectionately and said:

'My son, as to your evil design, as you call it, there is no need either to ask or to grant forgiveness, because you pursued it, not out of hatred but in order to be better thought of. Fear me not, then, and rest assured that in view of the loftiness of your motives, no other living person loves you as greatly as I, for you do not devote your energies to the accumulation of riches, as misers do, but to spending what you have amassed. Nor should you feel ashamed for having wanted to kill me to acquire fame, or imagine that I marvel to hear it. In order to extend their dominions, and hence their fame, the mightiest emperors and greatest kings have practised virtually no other art than that of killing, not just one person as you intended, but countless thousands, setting whole provinces ablaze and razing whole cities to the ground. So that if, to enhance your personal fame, it was only me that you wanted to kill, there was nothing marvellous or novel about what you were doing, which on the contrary was very commonplace.'

Without wishing to excuse himself, Mithridanes praised Nathan for presenting his wicked design in so seemly a light, and concluded by expressing his utter astonishment that Nathan had been prepared to supply him not only with the means but also with advice for achieving his object. Whereupon Nathan replied:

'Mithridanes, neither my compliance nor my advice should astonish you, for ever since I became my own master, and began to pursue those same ideals by which you too are now inspired, I have always sought, so far as it lay within my power, to grant the desires of anyone crossing my threshold. You came here with the desire of taking my life, and when I heard what it was that you wanted, so that you would not be the only person ever to leave my house empty-handed, I forthwith resolved to present it to you: and with this purpose in mind, I gave you the advice I considered most apt for taking my life without losing your own. Therefore I repeat: if this is what you want, I implore you to take my life and do whatever you please with it, for I can think of no better way of bestowing it. I have had the use of it now these eighty years, during which it has brought me all the pleasures and joys I could desire; and I realize that, like all other men and nearly everything under the sun, I am subject to the laws of Nature, and have very little of it left. Hence I consider it far preferable to give it away now, just as I have always given away and spent my treasures, than to cling to it until such time as Nature deprives me of it against my will.

'Even if one were to give away a hundred years, it would not amount to much of a gift; and surely it is a much more trivial matter to give away the six or eight years of my life that still remain to me. Take it then, if you want it, I do implore you; for during all the years I have lived here, I have never yet found anyone who wanted it, and if you do not take it, now that you have asked for it, I doubt whether I shall ever find anyone else. But even if I should happen to do so, I realize that the longer I keep it, the less valuable it becomes; take it therefore, I beg you, before it loses its worth entirely.'

'God forbid,' said Mithridanes, feeling deeply ashamed, 'that I should even contemplate taking so precious a thing as your life, as until just now I was thinking of doing, let alone that I should actually deprive you of it. Far from wanting to shorten its years, I would gladly augment them with some of my own, if such a thing were possible.'

'Supposing it were,' Nathan promptly replied, 'would you really oblige me to accept them, and thus serve you as I have never served another living soul, by taking something of yours, when I have never before taken anything from anyone?'

'Yes,' said Mithridanes, without a moment's hesitation.

'Then do as I suggest,' said Nathan. 'You remain here in my house, young as you are, and assume the name of Nathan, whilst I go to live in yours, and henceforth call myself Mithridanes.'

To which Mithridanes replied:

'If I were able to comport myself so impeccably as you do now, and as you have always done in the past, I should accept your offer without a second thought; but because I feel quite certain that my deeds would only diminish the fame of Nathan, and because I have no intention of impairing another's name for that to which I cannot myself aspire, I am obliged to refuse it.'

After conversing agreeably together on these and many other matters, they returned as Nathan wished to the palace, where for several days on end he entertained Mithridanes in sumptuous style, giving him every encouragement to persevere in his great and noble resolve. And when Mithridanes wanted to return home with his companions, Nathan let him go, having made it abundantly clear that his liberality could never be surpassed.

FOURTH STORY

Messer Gentile de' Carisendi comes from Modena and takes from the tomb the lady he loves, who has been buried for dead. She revives and gives birth to a male child, and later Messer Gentile restores her and the child to Niccoluccio Caccianimico, the lady's husband.

Miraculous indeed did it seem to all those present that anyone should be liberal with his own blood; and everyone agreed that Nathan's generosity had certainly exceeded that of the King of Spain or the Abbot of Cluny. But after they had debated the matter at some length, the king fixed his gaze on Lauretta, thus showing that he wanted her to tell the next story; and Lauretta began forthwith, as follows:

Fair young ladies, so goodly and magnificent are the things we have been told, so fully has the ground already been covered, that those of us who have not yet told our tales would surely be left with no area to explore, unless of course we turn to the deeds of lovers, wherein a most copious supply of tales on any topic is always to be found. For this reason, and also because matters of this sort are especially fascinating for people of our age, I should like to tell you of a generous deed performed by one who was in love. And if it is true that in order to possess the object of their love men will give away whole fortunes, set aside their enmities, and place their lives, their honour, and (what is more important) their reputation in serious jeopardy, then possibly you will conclude, all things considered, that his action was no less striking than some of the ones already described.

In Bologna, then, that illustrious city in the Lombard plain, there once lived a gentleman called Messer Gentile de' Carisendi, distinguished for his valour and noble blood, who whilst still in his youth became enamoured of a gentlewoman, Madonna Catalina by name, who was the wife of a certain Niccoluccio Caccianimico. But because his love for the lady was ill-requited he almost despaired of it and went away to Modena, where he had been appointed to the office of *podestà*.

At the time of which we are speaking, Niccoluccio was absent from Bologna, and his wife, being pregnant, was staying at an estate of his, some three miles distant from the city, where she had the misfortune to contract a sudden and cruel malady, whose effects were so powerful and serious that all sign of life in her was extinguished, and consequently she was adjudged, even by her physicians, to be dead. Since her closest women relatives claimed to have heard from her own lips that she had not been pregnant sufficiently long for the unborn creature to be perfectly formed, they troubled themselves no further on that score; and after shedding many tears, they buried her, just as she was, in a tomb in the local church.

The news of the lady's demise was immediately reported to Messer Gentile by one of his friends, and despite the fact that she had never exactly smothered him with her favours, he was quite overcome with sorrow. But at length he said to himself:

'So, Madonna Catalina, you are dead! You never accorded me so much as a single glance when you were alive; but now that you are dead, and cannot reject my love, I am determined to steal a kiss or two from you.'

Night had already fallen, and having made arrangements to depart in secret, he took horse with one of his servants, riding without pause till he came to the place where the lady was buried. Having opened up the tomb, he made his way cautiously inside, and lying down beside her, he drew his face to hers and kissed her again and again, shedding tears profusely as he did so.

But as every woman knows, no sooner does a man obtain one thing, especially if he happens to be in love, than he wants something else; and just as Messer Gentile had made up his mind to tarry there no longer, he said to himself: 'Ah! why should I not place my hand gently on her breast, now that I am here? I have never touched her before, and I shall never have another opportunity.'

And so, overcome by this sudden longing, he placed his hand on the lady's bosom, and after keeping it there for some little time, he thought he could detect a faint heartbeat. Whereupon, subduing all his fears, he examined her more closely and discovered that she was in fact still alive, though the actual signs of life were minimal and very weak. He then removed her from the tomb as gently as possible with the aid of his servant, and having set her across his saddle-bow, he conveyed her in secret to his house in Bologna.

His mother, a wise and resourceful woman, was living in the house, and on hearing her son's lengthy account of all that had happened she was filled with compassion and skilfully restored Catalina to life by putting her in a warm bath and then setting her in front of a well-stoked fire. On coming to her senses, she cast a deep sigh, and said:

'Alas! where am I now?'

'Don't worry,' the worthy lady replied, 'you are in good hands.'

When she had fully recovered her wits, she looked about her and discovered to her amazement that she was in totally strange surroundings with Messer Gentile standing before her. She turned to his mother and asked her to explain how she came to be there, whereupon Messer Gentile gave her a faithful account of all that had happened. At this she began to sob, but eventually she thanked him as best she could and implored him out of the love he had borne her and his sense of honour to do nothing to her in his house that would bring herself or her husband into discredit, and to let her return home as soon as daylight came.

'My lady,' replied Messer Gentile, 'no matter how deeply I may have yearned in former times, I have no intention either now or in the future (since God has granted me this favour of restoring you to life on account of the love I once bore you) of treating you otherwise than as a very dear sister, either here or anywhere else. But the office I performed tonight on your behalf deserves some kind of reward; and hence I trust you will not deny me the favour I am about to ask of you.'

The lady graciously signified her willingness to grant him the favour, provided it lay in her power to do so and there was nothing improper about it. So Messer Gentile said:

'My lady, all your kinsfolk and all the people in Bologna firmly believe you to be dead, so that no one in your house is expecting you. Hence I should like you to be so kind as to stay here quietly with my mother until I return from Modena, which will be quite soon. My reason for asking you this is that I propose to make a precious gift of you to your husband, in a formal ceremony to which all the leading citizens will be invited.'

The lady was longing to gladden her kinsfolk with the news of her return from the dead, but since she acknowledged her debt to Messer Gentile and saw nothing wrong in his request, she resolved to do as he had asked; and she pledged him her word to that effect.

Scarcely had she finished giving him her answer than she felt the first indications that she was about to be delivered of her child, and not long afterwards, with the tender assistance of Messer Gentile's mother, she gave birth to a handsome boy. This event increased a thousandfold the happiness both of Messer Gentile and herself; and after ordering that she should have everything she needed and that she was to be treated exactly as though she were his own wife, Messer Gentile returned in secret to Modena.

When the period of his office at Modena came to an end and he was on the point of returning to Bologna, he arranged that on the morning of his arrival a great and splendid banquet should be given at his house for a large number of the city's notables, including Niccoluccio Caccianimico. Upon his arrival he dismounted and went to join his guests, having first called on the lady to find that she was looking healthier and lovelier than ever, and that her small son was also fit and well. And then, with matchless cordiality, he showed his guests to the table and saw that they were regally dined and wined.

When the meal was approaching its end, Messer Gentile, having previously told the lady what he intended to do and arranged with her concerning the manner in which she was to comport herself, got up and addressed them as follows:

'Gentlemen, I recall having once been told that in Persia there is a custom, highly agreeable to my way of thinking, whereby when a person wishes to pay the highest honour to a friend, he invites him to his house and shows him the thing he holds most dear, whether it be his wife, his mistress, his daughter, or what you will, at the same time declaring that if it were possible to do so, he would even more readily show him the very heart from his body. And I propose that we should observe this selfsame custom here in Bologna.

'You have been good enough to honour my banquet with your presence, and I now intend to honour you in the Persian style by showing you the most precious thing I possess or am ever likely to possess. But before doing this, I would ask you to give me your opinion upon the problem that I am about to place before you. A certain person has in his house a good and most loyal servant, who suddenly falls seriously ill; the gentleman in question, without waiting for the ailing servant to breathe his last, has him thrown on to the street and takes no further interest in him; then a stranger comes along who, taking pity on the invalid, conveys him to his house, where, with much loving care and at much expense, he restores him to his former state of health. Now what I should like to know is whether, if the second gentleman keeps him and uses his services, the first has any reasonable ground for complaint or regret when he demands to have him back and is refused.'

Messer Gentile's noble guests, having discussed the various pros and cons amongst themselves, all reached the same conclusion; and since Niccoluccio Caccianimico was a gifted and eloquent speaker, they left it to him to deliver their reply.

Niccoluccio began by extolling the Persian custom, then said that he and his fellow guests were of the unanimous opinion that the first gentleman had no legal claim to the servant, because in the instance cited he had not only abandoned him but cast him away; and that on account of the good offices rendered by the second gentleman, it appeared he was entitled to regard the servant as his own, because in refusing to give him up, he was neither causing any trouble, nor offering any insult, nor doing any injury, to the first.

All the others sitting round the tables (and there was many a worthy gentleman among them) chorused their approval of the answer Niccoluccio had given; and Messer Gentile, delighted with this reply and with the fact that it had come from Niccoluccio himself, affirmed that he too shared their opinion. Then he said:

'The time has come for me to do you honour as I promised.' And summoning two of his servants, he sent them to the lady, whom he had caused to be regally attired and adorned, requesting that she be pleased to come and gladden the gentlemen with her presence. Taking her bonny infant in her arms, she descended, accompanied by the two servants, to the hall, where at Messer Gentile's bidding she sat down next to one of the gentlemen; and then he said:

'Gentlemen, this is the jewel that I cherish above all others, and intend to treasure always. See for yourselves whether you think I have good cause.'

The gentlemen paid her eloquent homage and warmly commended her, and having assured their host that he ought indeed to cherish her, they all began to gaze in her direction. Many of those present would have sworn she was the person she actually was, but for the fact that they understood her to be dead. But the one who gazed most intently of all upon her was Niccoluccio, who was dying to know who she was; and no sooner did his host move aside from the lady than his curiosity got the better of him and he asked her whether she was a Bolognese or a foreigner.

On hearing this question being put to her by her own husband, it was something of an effort for the lady to withhold a reply; but faithful to her instructions she remained silent. Another of the gentlemen asked her whether the infant was hers, and yet another inquired whether she was Messer Gentile's wife, but to neither did she offer any answer. However they were now rejoined by Messer Gentile, and one of his guests said to him:

'This jewel of yours is indeed very beautiful, but are we right in thinking she is dumb?'

'Gentlemen,' replied Messer Gentile, 'that she has hitherto re-mained silent is no small proof of her virtue.'

'You tell us then,' replied the other. 'Who is she?'

'I shall be only too happy to tell you,' he replied, 'provided that you all promise not to move from your places, no matter what I may say, until I have finished speaking.'

They all gave him their promise, and once the tables had been cleared, Messer Gentile took his seat alongside the lady and said:

'Gentlemen, this lady is the faithful and loyal servant to whom I was referring in the question I put to you just now. Being little prized by her own people, she was cast like something vile and useless into the gutter, whence I myself retrieved her, and by dint of my loving care I removed her from death's grasp with my own hands. In recognition of my pure affection for the lady, God has transformed her from a fearsome corpse into the lovely object that you see before you. But so that you may have a better idea of how this came about, I shall briefly explain the circumstances.'

And so, much to the amazement of his hearers, he gave a clear account of all that had happened from the time he had first fallen in love with the lady until that very hour, then added:

'Therefore, unless you have suddenly changed your opinion, and Niccoluccio especially, this lady belongs to me as of right, and no one can lawfully demand her return.'

To this assertion nobody offered any reply, but they all waited to discover what he was going to say next. Niccoluccio, along with one or two others and the lady herself, dissolved into tears; but Messer Gentile rose to his feet, took the tiny infant in his arms, and, leading the lady by the hand, walked up to Niccoluccio, saying:

'Stand up now, my friend: I shall not restore your wife to you, for she was cast out by your kinsfolk and her own; but I wish to present you with this lady, together with her little child, of whom you are assuredly the father, though I am his godfather, and when I held him at his christening I named him Gentile. Nor should you cherish her any the less for having spent the best part of three months under my roof; for I swear to you in the name of God (who possibly willed that I should fall in love with her so that my love would be the instrument of her deliverance) that she never led a more upright existence with her parents or with you yourself than the life she has lived here in this house under my mother's care.'

He then turned to the lady and said:

'I now release you, my lady, from every promise you gave me, and hereby deliver you to Niccoluccio.' And having left the lady and the child with Niccoluccio, he returned to his place.

Niccoluccio received his wife and son eagerly in his arms, his joy being all the greater for being so totally unexpected, and thanked Messer Gentile to the best of his power and ability. This touching scene moved all the other guests to tears, and they were full of praise for Messer Gentile, as indeed were all those who came to hear of his story.

The lady was welcomed home amid scenes of great rejoicing, and for a long time afterwards the people of Bologna regarded her with awe as someone who had returned from the dead. And as for Messer Gentile, for the rest of his life he remained a close friend of Niccoluccio as well as of the families of both Niccoluccio and his wife.

What are we to conclude then, gentle ladies? Are we to regard a king who gave away his crown and sceptre, an abbot who reconciled an outlaw to the Pope at no cost to himself, or an old man who exposed his throat to the dagger of his adversary, as being in any way comparable to one who performed so noble a deed as Messer Gentile? For here we have the case of a man in the ardent flush of youth, who, believing himself to be legally entitled to that which the negligence of others had discarded and which he had the good fortune to retrieve, not only kept his ardour under decent restraint, but on obtaining the very object which he had coveted with his whole being for so long, generously surrendered it. In all conscience, none of the instances previously cited seems to me comparable to this.

FIFTH STORY

Madonna Dianora asks Messer Ansaldo for a beautiful May garden in the month of January, and Messer Ansaldo fulfils her request after hiring the services of a magician. Her husband then gives her permission to submit to Messer Ansaldo's pleasure, but on hearing of the husband's liberality Messer Ansaldo releases her from her promise, whilst the magician excuses Messer Ansaldo from the payment of any fee.

Every member of the joyful company praised Messer Gentile to the very skies, after which the king called upon Emilia to follow: and with a confident air, as though she were longing to speak, she thus began:

Dainty ladies, no one can seriously deny that Messer Gentile acted munificently, but if anyone should claim that to do more would be impossible, it will not be too difficult to prove that they are wrong, as I propose to show you in this little story of mine.

In the province of Friuli, which is cold but richly endowed with beautiful mountains, numerous rivers, and limpid streams, there is a town called Udine, where once there lived a beautiful noblewoman called Madonna Dianora, who was married to a most agreeable and good-natured man, exceedingly wealthy, whose name was Gilberto. Because of her outstanding worth, this lady attracted the undying love of a great and noble lord called Messer Ansaldo Gradense, a man of high repute, famous throughout the land for his feats of arms and deeds of courtesy. But although he loved her fervently and did everything he possibly could to persuade her to requite his love, sending her numerous messages to this end, all his efforts were unavailing. Eventually the lady grew tired of the knight's entreaties, and seeing that however firmly she rejected his approaches he still persisted in loving and importuning her, she decided to rid herself of him once and for all by requesting him to do something for her that was both bizarre and, as she thought, impossible. So one day, she said to the woman who regularly came to see her on Messer Ansaldo's behalf:

'My good woman, you have repeatedly assured me that Messer Ansaldo loves me above all else, and offered me sumptuous gifts on his behalf, all of which I prefer that he should keep, for they could never induce me to love him or submit to his pleasure. If only I could be certain, however, that he loved me as much as you claim, I should undoubtedly bring myself to love him and do his bidding. So if he will offer me proof of his love by doing what I intend to ask of him, I shall be only too ready to obey his commands.'

'And what is it, ma'am,' the good woman asked, 'that you want him to do?'

'What I want is this,' replied the lady. 'In the month of January that is now approaching, I want a garden, somewhere near the town, that is full of green plants, flowers, and leafy trees, exactly as though it were the month of May. And if he fails to provide it, let him take good care never to send you or anyone else to me again. For if he should provoke me any further, I shall no longer keep this matter a secret as I have until now, but I shall seek to rid myself of his attentions by complaining to my husband and kinsfolk.'

On hearing about the lady's proposition, the gentleman naturally felt that she was asking him to do something very difficult, or rather well-nigh impossible, and realized that her only reason for demanding such a thing was to dash his hopes; but nevertheless he resolved that he would explore every possible means of furnishing her request. He therefore set inquiries afoot in various parts of the world to see whether anyone could be found to advise and assist him in the matter, and eventually got hold of a man who offered to do it by magic, provided he was well-enough paid. So Messer Ansaldo agreed to pay him a huge sum of money, and waited contentedly for the time the lady had appointed. And during the night preceding the calends of January, when the cold was very intense and everything was covered in snow and ice, the magician employed his skills to such good effect that in a beautiful meadow not far from the town, there appeared next morning, as all those who saw it bore witness, one of the fairest gardens that anyone had ever seen, with plants and trees and fruits of every conceivable kind. No sooner did Messer Ansaldo feast his eyes upon this spectacle than he caused a quantity of the finest fruits and flowers to be gathered and secretly presented to his lady, inviting her to come and see the garden she had asked for, so that she would not only realize how much he loved her, but recall the solemn pledge she had given and take steps to keep her word in the manner of a gentle-woman.

The lady had been hearing many reports of the wonderful garden, and when she saw the flowers and the fruits, she began to repent of her promise. But for all her repentance, being curious to observe so rare a phenomenon, she went with several other ladies of the town to see the garden, and after commending it greatly and betraying no little astonishment, she made her way home in the depths of despair, thinking of what it obliged her to do. So profound was her distress, in fact, that she was unable to conceal it, with the inevitable result that her husband, noticing how melancholy she looked, demanded to know the reason. For some little time she remained silent, being too embarrassed to say anything, but finally he forced her to tell him the whole story from beginning to end.

Gilberto was at first extremely angry, but after mature reflection, bearing in mind the purity of his wife's intentions, he put aside his anger and said:

'Dianora, no wise or virtuous woman should ever pay heed to messages of that sort, nor should she ever barter her chastity with anyone, no matter what terms she may impose. The power of words received by the heart through the ears is greater than many people think, and to those who are in love nearly everything becomes possible. Hence you did wrong, first of all to pay any heed to him and secondly to barter with him. But because I know you were acting from the purest of motives, I shall allow you, so as to be quit of your promise, to do something which possibly no other man would permit, being swayed also by my fear of the magician, whom Messer Ansaldo, if you were to play him false, would perhaps encourage to do us a mischief. I therefore want you to go to him, and endeavour in every way possible to have yourself released from this promise without loss of honour; but if this should prove impossible, just for this once you may give him your body, but not your heart.'

On hearing her husband speak thus, the lady burst into tears, maintaining that she wanted no such favour from him; but no matter how loudly she protested, Gilberto was adamant. And so next morning, just as dawn was breaking, the lady set out, by no means richly adorned, together with one of her maids; and preceded by two of her husband's retainers she made her way to Messer Ansaldo's house. Messer Ansaldo was astounded to hear that his lady had come, and leaping out of bed he summoned the magician and said to him:

'I want you to see for yourself how great a prize your skill has procured me.'

They then descended to meet her, and Messer Ansaldo greeted her courteously and reverentially, without any show of unbridled passion, after which they all made their way into a splendid apartment where a huge fire was burning. After having offered her somewhere to sit, Messer Ansaldo said:

'My lady, if the love I have so long borne you merits any reward, I beseech you to do me the kindness of telling me truthfully why you have come here at this hour of day with so few people to bear you company.'

To which the lady replied, confused and almost in tears:

'Sir, I am led here, not because I love you or because I pledged you my word, but because I was ordered to come by my husband, who, paying more regard to the labours of your unruly love than to his own or his wife's reputation, has constrained me to call upon you. And by his command I am ready to submit for this once to your every pleasure.'

Great as Messer Ansaldo's astonishment had been when the lady arrived, his astonishment on hearing her words was considerably greater; and because he was deeply moved by Gilberto's liberality, his ardour gradually turned to compassion.

'My lady,' he said, 'since it is as you say, God forbid that I should ever impair the reputation of one who shows compassion for my love. With your consent, therefore, whilst you are under my roof I shall treat you exactly as though you were my sister, and whenever you choose you shall be free to depart, provided that you convey to your husband all the thanks you deem appropriate for the immense courtesy he has shown me, and that you look upon me always in future as your brother and servant.'

The lady was pleased beyond measure to hear these words.

'Nothing could ever make me believe,' she said, 'in view of your impeccable manners, that my coming to your house would have any other sequel than the one which I see you have made of it, for which I shall always remain in your debt.'

Then, having taken her leave, she returned to Gilberto suitably attended and told him what had happened. And from that day forth, Gilberto and Messer Ansaldo became the closest of loyal friends.

After perceiving how liberally Gilberto had behaved towards Messer Ansaldo, and Messer Ansaldo towards the lady, the magician said to Messer Ansaldo, as the latter was about to present him with his fee:

'Heaven forbid that after observing Gilberto's generosity in respect of his honour, and yours in respect of your love, I should not be equally generous in respect of my reward. And since I know that you can put this sum of money to good use, I intend that you should keep it.'

Messer Ansaldo was thrown into confusion and tried in every way possible to make him accept the whole or part of the money, but his efforts were unavailing; and when the magician, having after the third day removed his garden, signified his intention of leaving, he bade him good luck and God-speed. And now that his heart was purged of the lustful passion he had harboured for the lady, he was thenceforth inspired to regard her with deep and decorous affection.

What is to be our verdict here, fond ladies? Are we to award pride of place to the instance of a lady who was all but dead, and a love already grown lukewarm through loss of expectation, in preference to the liberality of Messer Ansaldo, whose love was more fervent than ever, being as it were inflamed by greater expectation, and who was holding the prize he had so strenuously pursued in the very palm of his hand? In my view it would be quite absurd to suppose that the first of these generous deeds could be compared with the second.

SIXTH STORY

King Charles the Old, victorious in battle, falls in love with a young girl; but later he repents of his foolish fancy, and bestows both her and her sister honourably in marriage.

It would take far too long to recount in full the various discussions that now took place amongst the ladies as to whether Gilberto or Messer Ansaldo or the magician had displayed the greater liberality in the affair of Madonna Dianora. Suffice it to say that after the king had allowed them ample time to debate the question, he looked towards Fiammetta and ordered her to silence their arguments by telling her story, and without further ado she began as follows:

Illustrious ladies, I have always been of the opinion that in a gathering such as ours, we should talk in such general terms that the meaning of what we say should never give rise to argument among us through being too narrowly defined. Such arguments as these are better conducted among scholars in seats of learning than among ourselves, who have quite enough to do in coping with our distaffs and our spindles. And therefore, since the story I was going to tell you is possibly a little ambiguous and I see you squabbling over those we have already heard, I shall abandon it and tell you another, concerning the chivalrous action, not of any insignificant man, but of a valiant king, whose reputation was in no way diminished in consequence.

Now, all of you will frequently have heard mention of King Charles the Old, or in other words Charles the First, by whose magnificent enterprise, as well as by the glorious victory he later achieved against King Manfred, the Ghibellines were expelled from Florence and the Guelphs returned to the city. Hence it came about that a certain knight, called Messer Neri degli Uberti, left Florence with his entire household and a large fortune, bent upon taking refuge under the very nose of King Charles; and so as to seek a secluded spot, where he might live out his remaining years in peace, he went to Castellammare di Stabia, where, a stone's throw away from the other habitations in the area, amid the olives, hazels, and chestnuts that abound in those parts, he purchased an estate on which he built a fine and comfortable mansion. Beside the mansion he laid out a delectable garden, in the centre of which, there being a goodly supply of fresh water, he constructed a fine, clear fishpond in the Florentine style, which he stocked in his own good time with abundant supplies of fish.

His sole occupation being that of making his garden daily more attractive, it happened that King Charles, in the heat of summer, went to Castellammare to relax for a while, and on hearing of the beauty of Messer Neri's garden, he was anxious to inspect it. But knowing to whom it belonged, he decided that since the knight was a political adversary of his, he would make his visit informal, and sent word that on the following evening he desired to sup with him incognito in his garden, together with four companions.

Messer Neri took very kindly to this proposal, and having made preparations on a truly lavish scale, and arranged with his household what was to be done, he received the King in his fair garden as cordially as he possibly could. After inspecting and admiring the whole of Messer Neri's garden and his house, the King washed and sat down at one of the tables, which had been placed at the side of the pool. He then ordered Count Guy de Montfort, who was one of his four companions, to sit on his right and Messer Neri on his left, and directed the other three to wait upon him, taking their instructions from Messer Neri.

Dainty dishes were set before him, and wines of rare excellence, and the King was warmly appreciative of the way in which everything had been so tastefully and admirably planned, without anyone knowing he was there or making him feel embarrassed.

Whilst he was contentedly addressing his meal, and admiring the solitude of his surroundings, there came into the garden two young girls, each about fourteen years old, who were as fair as threads of gold, their hair a mass of ringlets surmounted by a garland of peri-winkle flowers, and looking more like angels than anything else, so fine and delicate were their features. Their bodies were clothed in sheer linen dresses, white as driven snow, with closely fitting bodices and bell-shaped skirts cascading down from their waists to their feet.

The girl in front was carrying upon her shoulders a pair of fishnets, which she held with her left hand, whilst in her right she carried a long pole. The girl behind had a frying-pan slung over her left shoulder, a bundle of sticks beneath her left arm, and a trivet in her left hand, whilst in her other hand she held a cruse of oil and a small lighted torch. The sight of these two girls filled the King with surprise, and he waited with interest to see what it might import.

The girls came forward, chaste and modest in their bearing, and curtsied to the King. Then they walked to the edge of the fishpond, where the one with the frying-pan put it down along with all the other things she was carrying and took the pole from her companion, after which they both waded into the pool till the water came up to their breasts.

One of Messer Neri's servants forthwith lit the fire on the bank of the pool, and pouring the oil into the frying-pan, he placed it on the trivet and waited for the girls to throw him out some fish. And whilst one of them poked about in the places where she knew the fish to be hiding, the other wielded her nets to such good purpose that within a short space of time, to the huge delight of the King who was watching their every movement, they caught fish by the score. Some of these they threw to the servant, who tossed them almost before they were dead into the frying-pan; but then they began to pick out some of the finest specimens, as they had been instructed, and to throw them up on the table in front of the King, the Count, and their father.

The sight of these fishes writhing about on the table was marvellously pleasing to the King, who in his turn picked some of them up and politely tossed them back to the girls. And in this fashion they sported for some little time until the servant had cooked the ones he had been given, which at Messer Neri's bidding were placed before the King, more by way of an entremets than as a specially choice or delectable dish.

On seeing that the fish had been cooked, the girls emerged from the pool, their fishing done, with their thin white dresses clinging to their flesh so as to conceal almost nothing of their dainty bodies. And having taken up each of the things they had brought with them, they walked shyly past the King and made their way back into the house.

The King, the Count, and the others who were waiting upon him had been eyeing the two girls most attentively, and each of them had secretly much admired their beauty and shapeliness, as well as their charm and impeccable manners, but it was upon the King that they made the deepest impression. Indeed, he had studied every part of their bodies with such rapt attention as they emerged from the water, that if anyone had pinched him at that moment he would not have noticed. The more he thought about them, without knowing who they were nor how they came to be there, the more he felt in his heart a burning desire to pleasure them, and because of this he knew full well that unless he was very careful he would soon be falling in love; nor could he decide which of the two he preferred, so closely did they resemble one another in every particular.

After he had pondered this question for a while, he turned to Messer Neri and asked him who the two maidens were, and Messer Neri replied:

'My lord, they are my twin daughters, of whom the one is called the lovely Ginevra and the other the fair Isotta.' The King heaped compliments upon them, exhorting him to bestow them in marriage, to which Messer Neri replied apologetically that he no longer had the wherewithal to do so.

By now the supper was nearly over, with only the fruit remaining to be served, and the two girls reappeared, clad in gowns of finest sendal and bearing two huge silver trays, piled high with all the different fruits that were in season, which they placed upon the table before the King. This done, they stepped back a little from the table, and began to sing a song beginning:

> The story of my plight, O Love,
> Could not be told in many words,

in such sweet and pleasant tones, that it seemed to the King, as he sat there listening and gazing with rapture upon them, that all nine orders of the angels had come down there to sing. But when their song was finished, they knelt before the King and respectfully asked his permission to withdraw, and although he was loath to see them go, he granted it with a show of cheerfulness.

The supper being now at an end, the King and his companions

remounted their horses, and having taken their leave of Messer Neri, they returned, conversing on many different topics, to the royal lodge, where the King continued to harbour his secret passion; nor was he able, however weighty the affairs of state which supervened, to forget the charm and beauty of the lovely Ginevra, for whose sake he also loved the sister who resembled her so closely. Indeed, he could think of practically nothing else, so hopelessly had he become entangled in the snares of love; and in order to see Ginevra, he invented various pretexts for paying frequent visits to the delectable garden of Messer Neri, with whom he formed close ties of friendship.

But eventually, having reached the end of his tether, he became convinced that he was left with no other alternative except to abduct not only Ginevra but both the girls from their father, and disclosed both his love and his intention to Count Guy, who, being a valiant nobleman, said to him:

'My lord, I am greatly astonished by what you have told me, the more so because I feel that I am better acquainted with your ways than any other man alive, having known you intimately ever since you were a child. I do not recall that you were ever infected by any such passion in your youth, when Love should all the more easily have gripped you in its talons; and hence, to hear that you have fallen hopelessly in love now that you are approaching old age is so strange to me, so bizarre, as to seem little short of a miracle. Moreover, if I had the task of reproaching you for it, I know very well what I should say to you, seeing that you are still on a warlike footing in a kingdom newly acquired, among an alien people, full of deceits and treachery, and that you are preoccupied with matters of the gravest importance which prevent you from sitting comfortably upon your throne; yet despite all this you have succumbed to the temptations of love.

'This is not the action of a magnanimous king, but rather of a weak-willed youth. But what is far more serious, you say you have decided that you must abduct his two daughters from this unfortunate knight, who honoured you in his house beyond his means, and in order to honour you the more, displayed them almost naked to you, thus testifying that he trusts you implicitly, and that he firmly believes you to be no ravening wolf, but a king.

'Can you have so soon forgotten that it was Manfred's abuse of his subjects' womenfolk that opened the gates of this realm to you? Was there ever an act of betrayal more deserving of eternal punishment than this, whereby you deprive a man who does you honour, not only of his good name, but of his source of hope and consolation? What will people say of you, if you do such a thing? Perhaps you think it would be a sufficient excuse to say: "I did it because he is a Ghibelline." But is it consistent with the justice of a king that those who look to him for protection, no matter who they may be, should receive this kind of treatment? Let me remind you, my lord, that you covered yourself with glory by conquering Manfred and defeating Conradin. But it is far more glorious to conquer oneself. And therefore, as you have to govern others, conquer these feelings of yours, curb this wanton desire, and do not allow the splendour of your achievements to be dimmed by any such deed as this.'

The Count's words pierced the King to the very core of his being, affecting him all the more deeply because he knew them to be true; and so after unloosing a fervent sigh or two, he said:

'My dear Count, it is certainly true that to the experienced soldier, all other enemies, however powerful, are exceedingly weak and easy to conquer by comparison with his own desires. But although I shall suffer great torment, and the effort required is incalculable, your words have spurred me on to such a degree that I am determined, before many days have elapsed, to show you by my deeds that, just as I can conquer others, I am likewise able to master myself.'

Nor did many days elapse from the time these words were spoken before the King, having meanwhile returned to Naples, resolved to deprive himself of all occasion for straying from the path of virtue, at the same time repaying Messer Neri's hospitality. And this he would do by bestowing the two girls in marriage as though they were his own daughters, even though it was hard for him to let others possess what he so ardently desired for himself. So with Messer Neri's ready consent he supplied them both with splendid dowries and forthwith bestowed them in marriage, giving the lovely Ginevra to Messer Maffeo da Palizzi, and the fair Isotta to Messer Guiglielmo della Magna, who were noble knights and mighty barons both. And after consigning them to their respective husbands, he retired in agonies of despair to Apulia, where by dint of constant effort he mortified his ardent longings to such good and purposeful effect that the chains of Love were shattered, and for as long as he lived he was never a slave to this kind of passion again.

There are doubtless those who will say that it was a trifling matter for a king to bestow two girls in marriage, and I will agree with them. But I say it was no trifle, but a prodigy, if we consider that this action was performed by a king in love, who married off the girl he loved without having taken or gathered a single leaf, flower or fruit from his love.

Thus then did this magnificent king comport himself, richly rewarding the noble knight, commendably honouring the girls he loved, and firmly subduing his own instinctive feelings.

SEVENTH STORY

On hearing that a young woman called Lisa has fallen ill on account of her fervent love for him, King Peter goes to comfort her, and later on he marries her to a young nobleman; and having kissed her on the brow, he thenceforth always calls himself her knight.

When Fiammetta had reached the end of her tale, and fulsome praise had been accorded to the heroic munificence of King Charles (albeit one of the ladies present, being a Ghibelline, refused to extol him), Pampinea at the king's behest began as follows:

Winsome ladies, no sensible person would disagree with what you have said about good King Charles, unless she had other reasons for disliking him; but since his deed has now reminded me of another, perhaps equally commendable, that was performed by an adversary of his for the sake of yet another young countrywoman of ours, I should like to tell you about it.

At the time when the French were driven from Sicily, there was living in Palermo a very rich Florentine apothecary called Bernardo Puccini, whose wife had borne him one child only, an exquisitely beautiful daughter who was now of marriageable age. King Peter of

Aragon, having made himself master of the island, was staging a magnificent tournament in Palermo with all his lords, and whilst he was jousting in the Catalan style,* it happened that Bernardo's daughter, whose name was Lisa, was viewing the proceedings from a window along with some other ladies. When she saw the King riding in the joust, she was filled with so much admiration that after watching him perform in one or two further contests she fell passionately in love with him. The festivities came to an end, and Lisa went about her father's house, unable to think of anything else but the lofty and splendid love to which she aspired. But that which grieved her most was the knowledge of her lowly condition, which left her with scarcely any hope that her love could be brought to a happy conclusion. Nevertheless she would not be deterred from loving the King, though for fear of making things worse for herself, she dared not reveal her love to a single living soul.

The King neither noticed nor cared about any of this, which made her affliction all the more difficult to bear. As her love continued to increase, so also did her melancholy, till eventually, being unable to endure it any longer, the beautiful Lisa fell ill and began to waste visibly away from one day to the next, like snow in the rays of the sun.

Her father and mother, who were heartbroken by the turn that events had taken, assisted her in every way they could, nursing her day and night, calling in various physicians, and plying her with medicines. But it was all to no avail, for the girl, having despaired of her love, had chosen not to go on living. Since, however, her father had offered to supply her every need, she suddenly got it into her head that before she died, if suitable means could be found, she would inform the King of her love and of her resolve to perish. So one day she asked her father to summon Minuccio d'Arezzo to her bedside.

This Minuccio was held to be one of the finest singers and musicians of his day, being always welcome at King Peter's court, and Bernardo, thinking that Lisa wished to hear him sing and play to her, sent him a message to that effect. Being an obliging sort of fellow, he promptly

* That is, according to the rules prescribed for tournaments held in Catalonia, which was annexed to Aragon in 1137.

came to see her, and after cheering her up a little with words of tender affection, he played her one or two melodious airs on his viol, then sang her some songs; all of which added fuel to the flames of the young lady's passion, whereas he had meant to comfort her.

The young lady then told Minuccio that she would like a few words with him in private, and when everyone else had withdrawn, she said to him:

'Minuccio, I have chosen you to be the loyal custodian of a secret of mine, trusting in the first place that you will never disclose it to anyone except the person whose name I shall give you; and secondly, that you will do all in your power to render me your assistance. This I beg of you.

'You are to know then, my dear Minuccio, that on the day that our lord King Peter held the great feast celebrating his accession to the throne, fate decreed that I should set my eyes upon him as he was jousting, and such was the fiery passion that he kindled in my soul that I have been brought to the sorry plight in which you see me. Since I know how ill it befits a king to return my love, which I can neither expel from my heart nor even suppress, and which is altogether too much for me to bear, I have chosen to die as the lesser evil, and die I shall.

'But the truth is that nothing would distress me more than to depart this life without first bringing my love to his notice, and since I know of no one better placed than yourself to inform him of my intentions, I wish to charge you with this mission, which I implore you to accept. And when you have carried it out you must let me know, so that I may be freed from these torments and die in peace.'

She then fell silent, having wept continuously as she said all this, and Minuccio, amazed no less by the nobility of her sentiments than by the cruelty of her resolve, which sorely troubled him, immediately thought of an apt way of furnishing her request.

'Lisa,' he said, 'I pledge you my word, by which you may rest assured that you will never be deceived. Moreover I shall offer you my assistance, in token of my admiration for this lofty enterprise wherein you have set your heart upon so mighty a king. And if you will be of good cheer, I hope to take such steps as I think will enable me, before three days have passed, to bring you tidings that will make you exceedingly happy. But so as not to waste any time, I shall go and make a start right away.'

Lisa promised to take a rosier view of the matter, and after repeating her entreaties all over again, she bade him farewell.

Minuccio then went away, and, having called on Mico da Siena, who was a very able versifier of those times, he talked him into composing the following little song:

> Bestir thyself, O Love, go to my lord,
> Recount to him the torments I endure;
> Tell him that death will soon be my reward,
> For I must hide my yearning out of awe.
>
> Visit the place where my lord dwells,
> With clasp'd hands, Love, I thee entreat;
> Tell him that evermore for him
> My heart yearns with a passion sweet.
> Because this fire inflames me so
> I fear that it will stop my breath;
> I know not when my sufferings
> Will bring me through desire to death
> Out of my fear and shame; ah me!
> Go, tell him of my malady.
>
> Love, ever since I fell in love
> With him, you always granted me
> More fear than courage; wherefore I
> Could never show it openly
> To him who takes away my breath,
> And death is hard as I lie dying.
> Perhaps he would not be displeased
> If he were conscious of my sighing
> And I could find the power to show
> To him the measure of my woe.
>
> Since it was not thy pleasure, Love,
> That I should ever make so bold
> As to lay bare my heart through words
> Or looks, or to my lord unfold
> My love; I beg you, master sweet,
> Go and remind him of that day

I saw him with his shield and lance
With other knights upon the way,
When I first languished for his sake
And when my heart began to break.

For these words Minuccio promptly devised a melody, which had a sweet and sorrowful lilt as befitted the text, and on the third day he turned up at court, where King Peter, who was still at breakfast, asked him to sing a song to the strains of his viol. He thereupon began to sing and play this melody in tones of such sweet harmony that all those present in the regal hall appeared to be spellbound, so silently and raptly did they listen, the King himself being more engrossed, perhaps, than any other.

When Minuccio's song was finished, the King asked him whence it had come, as he could not recall ever having heard it.

'My lord,' replied Minuccio, 'the words were written less than three days ago, and so too was the melody.' And when the King asked him for whom the song had been composed, he replied: 'This I dare not reveal to anyone other than yourself.'

The King was eager to be told, and once the tables were cleared he took Minuccio with him to his chamber, where Minuccio supplied him with a detailed account of all that he had heard. The King was overjoyed, sang the girl's praises, and declared that her fortitude was such as to demand his compassion. Minuccio was therefore to go to her on his behalf, comfort her, and tell her he would visit her that evening without fail, a little before vespers.

Delighted to be the bearer of such pleasant tidings, Minuccio went straightway to the girl with his viol, and as soon as they were alone together, related all that had happened. Then he sang her the song, accompanying himself on his viol.

The girl was so happy and contented by all this that she at once began to show marked signs of improvement, without anyone in the house knowing or suspecting the reason. And she began to count the hours until vespers, when she was to see her lord and master.

Being of a kindly and generous disposition, the King, having reflected at length upon what he had heard from Minuccio, and recalling the girl and her beauty very clearly, was stirred to even greater pity than before. Towards the hour of vespers he mounted his horse, giving the impression he was going on a jaunt, and rode to the place where the house of the apothecary stood. This latter had a very fine garden, and the King, having sent one of his attendants to ask for the gates to be opened, rode into the garden and dismounted. And after conversing with Bernardo for a while, he inquired about his daughter, asking him whether he had yet bestowed her in marriage, to which Bernardo replied:

'My lord, she is not yet married. As a matter of fact she has been very ill, and she still is, though she has taken a miraculous turn for the better this very afternoon.'

The King was quick to realize what this improvement signified, and said:

'In good truth, the world would be the poorer for the untimely loss of so lovely an object. Let us go and call upon her.'

A little while later, attended by Bernardo and only two companions, he made his way to the girl's room, which he no sooner entered than he walked straight up to the bed. The girl was sitting up a little in eager anticipation of his coming, and he took her by the hand, saying:

'What is the meaning of this, my lady? You are young, you should be bringing solace to others, instead of which you take to your sickbed. We would ask you to be good enough to cheer up, for our sake, so that you may quickly recover.'

On feeling herself being touched by the hands of the person she loved above all else, the girl, albeit a little embarrassed, was filled with so much pleasure that she might have been in Paradise itself; and haltingly she replied:

'My lord, it was only because I was trying to support a burden that was far too heavy for my feeble powers that I succumbed to this malady. But with your kind assistance, you shall soon see me rid of it.'

Only the King was able to grasp the covert meaning of Lisa's words. She rose still higher in his esteem, and several times over he inwardly swore at Fortune for making her the daughter of such a man as Bernardo. But after he had spent some time in her company, and consoled her even further, he took his leave.

The King's considerate gesture was widely commended, being looked upon as a signal honour for the apothecary and his daughter. Nor was any woman ever more contented with her lover than was

Lisa with the visit of the King; and within a few days, aided by the renewal of her hopes, she recovered her health and seemed more lovely than ever.

But now that she was well again, the King, having consulted with the Queen as to how he should reward so great a love, took horse one morning with a number of his lords, and rode to the house of the apothecary. Entering the garden, he sent for Bernardo and his daughter, and meanwhile the Queen also arrived there with many fine ladies, who received the girl in their midst with great rejoicing, marvellous to behold.

At length the King, with the Queen at his side, summoned the girl and said to her:

'Worthy young lady, through your great love for us you have won for yourself a great honour, which for our sake we trust you will accept. The honour is this, that since you are as yet unmarried, we desire you to take as your husband the person we shall nominate, it being nonetheless our intention always to style ourselves your loyal knight, and of all your love we require no more than a single kiss.'

The girl was so embarrassed that the whole of her face turned crimson, and in a low voice, making the King's pleasure her own, she replied:

'My lord, I am quite sure that if it were known that I was in love with you, most people would consider me to be mad, for they would think I had taken leave of my senses and was unaware of the distinction between your rank and mine. But God alone can see inside the hearts of mortals, and He knows that ever since I first became attracted to you, I have known full well that you are a king, that I am the daughter of Bernardo the apothecary, and that it ill becomes me to direct the ardour of my affections towards so lofty a goal. But as you know far better than I, when people fall in love they are guided, not by reason, but by their natural inclinations and desires. These I repeatedly opposed with all my strength until, no longer able to resist, I loved you then as I love you now and as I shall love you for-ever. And because I was always prepared, from the moment I fell in love with you, to make my wishes accord with your own, not only shall I be willing to accept and treasure the husband you choose to bestow upon me, who will bring me dignity and honour, but if you were to order me to walk through fire, and I thought it would please you, I should do it gladly. As for my having a king as my loyal knight, you know how well it would suit a person of my condition, and hence I will say no more on the subject; nor will I concede the single kiss that you require of my love, without the permission of my lady the Queen. For the great kindness, however, which you and the Queen have displayed towards me, may God give you thanks and reward you on my behalf, since I myself could never repay you.'

She said no more, but the answer she had given was greatly pleasing to the Queen, who was now persuaded that the girl was as wise as the King had affirmed. The King then summoned Lisa's parents, and on learning that they approved of what he was proposing, he sent for a certain young man called Perdicone, who was gently bred but poor, and placing some rings in his hand, induced him to marry the girl without any show of reluctance.

Nor was this all, for apart from the many precious jewels that he and the Queen presented to Lisa, the King forthwith appointed him lord of Ceffalù and Calatabellotta, two excellent and very lucrative estates, saying:

'These we grant you by way of dowry for your wife; and as for our intentions with regard to yourself, of these you will learn in due course.'

Then, turning to the girl, he said:

'Now we desire to take the fruit of your love which is our due.' And holding her head between his hands, he kissed her on the brow.

Perdicone, along with Lisa's father and mother, and Lisa herself, well content with what had happened, celebrated the wedding in truly magnificent style, and their marriage was a happy one.

As a good many people affirm, the King was most scrupulous to observe his compact with the girl, for he always styled himself her loyal knight for as long as he lived, and never entered the lists without displaying the favour she had sent him.

By deeds such as these, then, does a sovereign conquer the hearts of his subjects, furnish occasions to others for similar deeds, and acquire eternal renown. But among the rulers of today, there are few if any who train the bowstrings of their minds upon any such objective, most of them having been changed into pitiless tyrants.

EIGHTH STORY

Sophronia, thinking she has married Gisippus, has really married Titus Quintus Fulvius, with whom she goes off to Rome, where Gisippus turns up in abject poverty. Believing that Titus has snubbed him, he confesses to a murder so that he will be put to death. But Titus recognizes him, and claims that he himself has done the murder, in order to secure Gisippus' release. On perceiving this, the real murderer gives himself up, whereupon all three are released by Octavianus. Titus then bestows his sister upon Gisippus in marriage, and shares with him all he possesses.

Pampinea having finished her tale, King Peter was extolled by all the ladies, but more especially by the one who was a Ghibelline; then Filomena began, at the king's command, as follows:

Magnificent ladies, which of us is not aware that kings, if they be so inclined, can do all sorts of wondrous things, and that they above all others are called upon to display munificence? Those people do well, then, who possess ample means and do all that is expected of them; but we ought neither to marvel thereat, nor laud them to the skies, as we should the person who is equally munificent but of whom, his means being slender, less is expected. So that if you are impressed by the actions of kings, and expend so many words in extolling them, I have no doubt whatsoever that when similar actions to these, or nobler ones, are performed by people like ourselves, your delight will be all the greater, your praises all the more fulsome. And hence I am minded to tell you a story about two private citizens, who were friends, and about the laudable generosity that each of them displayed towards the other.

Now, at the time when Octavianus Caesar, before he was called Augustus, was ruling the Roman Empire in the office known as the triumvirate, there lived in Rome a gentleman called Publius Quintus Fulvius, who had a son called Titus Quintus Fulvius. This latter was exceptionally clever, and his father sent him to study philosophy in Athens, doing all in his power to commend him to a nobleman of that city called Chremes, who was a very old friend of his. Chremes lodged him under his own roof with a son of his called Gisippus, and Titus and Gisippus were both sent by Chremes to study under the guidance of a philosopher named Aristippus.

Being regularly in one another's company, the two young men discovered that they shared many interests in common, and this gave rise to a powerful sense of mutual friendship and brotherliness, which lasted for the rest of their lives. Indeed, it was only when they were together that either Titus or Gisippus could feel happy and relaxed. Having once embarked upon their studies, since both were endowed with equally high intelligence, they scaled the glorious heights of philosophy side by side, amid a hail of marvellous tributes. And in this way of life, to the enormous delight of Chremes, who treated both alike as his sons, they continued for three whole years, at the end of which it came about that Chremes, already an old man, passed from this world as all things eventually must. Nor were the friends and kinsfolk of Chremes able to decide which of the two deserved greater compassion in this sudden loss, for he had been a father to them both, and both were equally heart-broken.

A few months later, Gisippus was confronted by a deputation of his friends and relatives, who along with Titus persuaded him to take a wife, and they found him an incredibly lovely Athenian girl of impeccably noble breeding, some fifteen years of age, whose name was Sophronia.

One day, a little before the date appointed for the nuptials, Gisippus asked Titus, since he had not yet set eyes upon the girl, to come with him to see her. So they went to her house, and with the girl sitting between the two of them, Titus began to scrutinize her very closely, as though to form an estimate of the beauty of his friend's future wife. But such was the boundless pleasure he experienced in surveying each part of her body that he was lost in silent admiration, and, though he showed no sign of what he was feeling, he burned with a passion more ardent than any ever kindled by a woman in her lover's breast. However, after spending some little time with her, they took their leave and returned home.

On arriving at the house, Titus retired to his room alone and began to meditate upon the young woman's charms; and the longer he

brooded upon her, the fiercer his ardour became. Perceiving the state
he was in, he cast many a passionate sigh and began to commune with
himself, saying: 'Ah, Titus, what a beggarly way to behave! Where,
upon whom, do you set your hopes, your heart and your love?
Don't you realize that the hospitality you have received from
Chremes and his family, and the perfect friendship that unites you to
Gisippus, her future husband, require that you should treat this girl
with all the reverence owing to a sister? Will you allow yourself to be
carried away by the delusions of love, the specious visions of desire?
Open your eyes, you fool, and come to your senses. Make way for
reason, bridle your lascivious desires, curb your unwholesome
longings, and direct your thoughts elsewhere. Fight against your lust
from the outset, and conquer yourself while you still have time. It is
wrong for you to want this thing, it is dishonest; and even if you
were certain (which you are not) of achieving your object, you would
only have to think where the duty of a true friend lies, as you are
bound to do in any case, to dismiss the idea from your mind. What
will you do, then, Titus? If you want to do what is proper, abandon
this unseemly love.'

But then he remembered Sophronia's beauty, and took the opposite viewpoint, rejecting all his previous arguments. And he said to
himself: 'The laws of Love are more powerful than any others; they
even supplant divine laws, let alone those of friendship. How often
in the past have fathers loved their daughters, brothers their sisters, or
mothers their stepsons? These are far more reprehensible than the
man who loves the wife of his friend, for he is only doing what a
thousand others have done before him. Besides, I am young, and
youth is entirely subject to the power of Love. So that wherever Love
decides to lead me, I am bound to follow. Honesty is all very well for
older people, but I can only act in accordance with the dictates of
Love. The girl is so beautiful that no one could fail to love her; so
that if I, who am young, fall in love with her, who can justly reproach me? It is not because she belongs to Gisippus that I love her,
but purely for her own sake, and I should love her no matter to whom
she belonged. Here Fortune is at fault for having conceded her to my
friend Gisippus rather than to some other man. But if anyone has to
love her (as she must be loved, and deservedly so, on account of her

beauty), then Gisippus should be all the more pleased to discover that she is loved by me and not by another.'

But then, reproaching himself for being so foolish, he returned to the contrary viewpoint, and for the rest of the day and the ensuing night he veered perpetually back and forth between the two sets of arguments. And after spending several days and nights, gradually wearing himself to a thread over it, and going without food or sleep, he was driven to take to his bed in a state of exhaustion.

Great was the distress of Gisippus when, after observing Titus lost in deep thought for days on end, he now discovered that his friend was ill. Never leaving his side, he attempted to comfort him using all the skill and loving care in his power, and from time to time he earnestly entreated him to disclose the reason for his sickness and melancholy. Titus offered him a series of spurious explanations, none of which satisfied Gisippus, so that in the end, unable to withstand the pressure that Gisippus was continuing to apply upon him, he burst into tears. And heaving many a sigh, he answered him as follows:

'If only the gods had so willed it, Gisippus, I would much rather have died than continued to live, when I think how Fortune has driven me to the point where my virtue had to be put to the test, and where, to my very great shame, you have found it wanting. But I confidently expect to receive, before long, my just reward in the form of my death, and this will be dearer to me than to go on living with the memory of my baseness, which, since there is nothing I either could or should conceal from you, I shall tell you about, though I burn with shame to speak of it.'

And so, starting from the beginning, he explained the cause of his melancholy, describing the conflict that had raged between his contrasting thoughts, which of them had won the day, and how he was wasting away for love of Sophronia. Moreover he declared that since he knew his attitude to be wholly improper, he had resolved that he would die by way of penance, and believed he would shortly achieve this desirable aim.

On hearing what Titus had said, and observing how bitterly he wept, Gisippus was at first somewhat taken aback, for although his own passionate feelings towards the beautiful Sophronia were more restrained, he too was fascinated by her charms. But he instantly decided that his friend's life meant more to him than Sophronia, and being moved to tears by the tears of his comrade, he replied, sobbing continuously:

'If, Titus, you were less in need of reassurance, I should take you severely to task, seeing that you have abused our friendship by not telling me earlier of this overwhelming passion. Even if you felt that your thoughts were improper, that was no reason for concealing them from your friend, any more than if they were proper: for just as a true friend takes a delight in sharing his friend's proper thoughts, so he will attempt to wean him away from those that are improper. But enough of that for the present: let us turn to the question that I take to be the more urgent. The fact that you have fallen violently in love with Sophronia, my promised bride, does not surprise me in the least; indeed I should be most surprised if you hadn't, considering her beauty and your own loftiness of spirit, which renders you all the more susceptible to passionate feelings, the greater the excellence of the object that arouses your liking. And inasmuch as you do right to love Sophronia, at the same time you do wrong to complain about Fortune (though you make no mention of this) for conceding her to me, as though you felt that there would be nothing improper about loving her if she belonged to another. But if you are still as wise as you always were, you should be counting your lucky stars that she was given to me and not to anyone else. For had she belonged to another, no matter how proper your love may have been, he would have preferred to keep her to himself rather than allow you to love her, whereas in my case, if you consider me your friend, as I am, you must hope for a kindlier fate. And the reason is this, that ever since our friendship began, I cannot recall possessing anything that was not as much yours as it was mine.

'Just as I have shared my other possessions with you, so I would share Sophronia, if I were already married to her and no other solution were possible; but as the matter stands at present, I am able to ensure that she is yours alone, and that is what I intend to do. For I should be a poor sort of friend if I were unable to convert you to my own way of thinking when the thing can be so decorously arranged. It is perfectly true that Sophronia is my promised bride, that I love her a great deal, and that I was eagerly looking forward to our marriage; but because your love for her is greater, and because you desire more fervently than I to possess so precious an object, you may rest assured that she shall enter the bridal chamber, not as my wife, but as yours. Fret no more then, cast aside your gloom, retrieve your health, your spirits and your gaiety; and from this time forth, look forward cheerfully to the reward of your love – a love far worthier than mine ever was.'

To hear Gisippus speak in these terms, Titus was at one and the same time delighted and ashamed: delighted on account of the tempting picture Gisippus had drawn, and ashamed because commonsense argued that the greater the generosity of his friend, the more unseemly did it appear for him to make use of it. And so, with tears still rolling down his cheeks, he replied with an effort as follows:

'Gisippus, your true and generous friendship shows me very clearly where my duty lies. God forbid that I should ever accept from you as mine the wife that He has given you as a mark of your superior worth. Had He judged that she ought to be mine, neither you nor anyone else can deny that He would never have given her to you. Be content, therefore, that in His infinite wisdom He has chosen you as the recipient of His largesse, and leave me to waste away in the tears of woe He has allotted to one who is unworthy of such bounty; for either I shall conquer my grief, in which case you will be happy, or it will conquer me and I shall be released from my suffering.'

To which Gisippus replied:

'If, Titus, our friendship is such as to enable me to force your acquiescence in any single one of my decisions, or if it can induce you to consent of your own accord, now is the time when I intend to exploit it to the full; and if you are determined to reject my entreaties, I shall use whatever compulsion is necessary to protect the interests of a friend, and to make Sophronia yours. I know the havoc that the powers of Love can inflict, I know they have led, not one, but count-less lovers to an unhappy death; and I can see that they have taken so tight a hold upon you that there is no longer any question of your turning back, or of conquering your tears. If you were to go on like this you would perish, in which event there is no doubt that I should speedily follow you. So even if I had no other cause for loving you, your life is precious to me because my own life depends upon it. Sophronia shall be yours, then, for it will not be easy for you to find another that you like nearly so much, whereas I can easily divert my love to some other woman, and then we shall both be satisfied. I should not perhaps be so generous, if wives were so scarce and difficult to find as friends, but since I can find another wife, but not another friend, with the greatest of ease, I prefer, rather than to lose you, not to lose her exactly, but as it were to transfer her. For I shan't lose her by giving her to you, but simply hand her over to my second self, at the same time changing her lot for the better. So if my entreaties mean anything to you, I entreat you here and now to cast aside your sorrows and bring solace to us both. Take heart, and prepare to enjoy the bliss for which your ardent love is yearning.'

Titus was reluctant to consent to the idea that Sophronia should become his wife, and hence refused at first to have anything to do with it; but being prodded by his love on the one hand, and propelled by his friend's insistence on the other, he eventually faltered and said:

'See here, Gisippus, I cannot tell which of us would remain the more contented if I were to do the thing you implore me to do, seeing that you claim it would give you so much pleasure. But as your liberality is such as to disarm my natural shame, I shall do it. Of this you may be certain, however, that I do it in the knowledge that you are not only giving me the woman I love, but also saving my life. Thus does your compassion for my plight exceed my own, and I pray that the gods may grant me the means whereby I may yet make you honourable amends and show you how deeply I prize the blessing you have conferred upon me.'

When Titus had finished speaking, Gisippus said:

'If we want our plans to succeed, Titus, this is what I think we ought to do. As you know, it was only after long discussions between Sophronia's kinsfolk and my own that she became my promised bride, and hence, if I were suddenly to announce that I no longer wish to marry her, there would be an awful scandal and I would cause distress to both our families. This would not worry me in the least, if I could see her being married to you as a result. But if I were to leave her in the lurch like this, I fear that her kinsfolk would promptly marry her off to some other fellow, and not necessarily to you, in which case you will have lost Sophronia and I shall have gained nothing. So it seems to me that if you are in agreement I should carry on with what I have begun, fetch her back here as my wife, and celebrate the nuptials, after which you and Sophronia, by whatever secret means we shall devise, will sleep together as man and wife. Later on, when the time and the place are appropriate, we shall disclose how matters stand; if they like the idea, all well and good; but if they don't, they'll have to lump it, because by that time the deed will be done and there'll be no way of setting things in reverse.'

Titus agreed to the plan, and so Gisippus went ahead and welcomed Sophronia to his house as his bride, by which time Titus was strong and well again. A great feast was held, and when night had descended, the waiting maids left the new bride in her husband's bed and departed.

Now the rooms of Titus and Gisippus were adjacent, and it was possible to pass freely from the one to the other; so on entering his room, Gisippus extinguished all the lights, betook himself quietly to Titus, and bade him go sleep with his lady.

Titus was overcome with embarrassment, began to have second thoughts, and refused to go. But Gisippus, after remonstrating with him at length, sent him all the same, being no less prepared to do Titus' pleasure than he had claimed.

Having eased himself into the bed, Titus took the girl in his arms, and asked her in a voice no louder than a whisper whether she wanted to be his wife, as though playing some sort of game with her. The girl replied in the affirmative, thinking he was Gisippus, whereupon he placed a fine and precious ring on her finger, saying:

'And I want to be your husband.'

The marriage was then consummated, and thereafter Titus long continued to disport himself amorously with her, neither Sophronia nor anyone else ever suspecting that the person with whom she shared her bed was not Gisippus.

This, then, was where the marriage of Sophronia and Titus stood, when Titus was informed by letter that Publius, his father, had departed this life, and that hence he should return to Rome at once to attend to his affairs. So after consulting with Gisippus, he decided to leave Athens and take Sophronia with him, which he was neither prepared nor easily able to do without explaining everything to Sophronia.

So one day, they called her into the room and took her fully into their confidence, nor could she doubt that their story was true because of numerous things that had passed between Titus and herself. And having cast a withering look, first at one, then at the other, she burst into floods of tears, complaining bitterly of the trick Gisippus had played on her. But before anyone else in the house came to hear of it, she took refuge in the house of her father, to whom, as well as to her mother, she recounted the way in which she and they had been hoodwinked by Gisippus, pointing out that she was married, not to Gisippus as they supposed, but to Titus.

Sophronia's father, who took a very grave view of the matter, complained loud and long to his kinsfolk, as well as to the kinsfolk of Gisippus, and there was a huge palaver, followed in turn by a great deal of gossip. Gisippus incurred the hatred of both Sophronia's kinsfolk and his own, and everyone declared that he deserved to be not only censured but punished most severely. But he maintained that he had acted honourably and in such a way as to merit the gratitude of Sophronia's kinsfolk, inasmuch as he had married her to someone better than himself.

For his part, Titus heard all that was going on, and patiently bore the suffering it caused him. But eventually, knowing the Greeks had a habit of raising an enormous clamour and intensifying their threats until such time as they found someone to answer them back, when they would suddenly become not only humble but positively servile, he decided that their prattle could no longer be allowed to pass without a rejoinder. His Roman heart being wedded to the guile of an Athenian, he skilfully persuaded the kinsfolk of Gisippus and Sophronia to forgather in a temple, to which he came, accompanied only by Gisippus. And he addressed the people waiting there as follows:

'In the opinion of many philosophers, all human actions conform to the will and decree of the immortal gods, and hence there are those who maintain that whatever we mortals do here on earth, either now or in the future, is inevitable and preordained; whereas certain others apply this principle of necessity only to what is already past and done with. Now, if we examine these opinions with a modicum of care, we shall clearly perceive that the person who criticizes that which cannot be changed is behaving exactly as though he wishes to prove himself wiser than the gods, who, to the best of our knowledge and belief, control and govern us, and all things pertaining to us, by a process of eternal and infallible logic. Thus you may very readily perceive the senseless and bestial arrogance of those who criticize their inscrutable ways, just as you will appreciate with what strong and substantial chains those people deserve to be bound, who permit themselves to be carried away by such excess of daring. Among these latter, you yourselves are all, in my opinion, to be numbered, unless I have been misinformed as to what you have been saying, and are still saying, about Sophronia's having become my wife after you had given her to Gisippus; for you overlook the fact that she was destined, *ab aeterno* so to speak, not for Gisippus but for me, as we now know from the sequel. Since however it appears that the secret insight and inscrutable purpose of the gods are a subject too abstruse and difficult for many people to follow, I shall assume that the gods play no part whatever in our affairs, and confine myself to the logic of mortals, in appealing to which I shall be obliged to do two things that are wholly at odds with my nature: for in the first place I must praise myself a little, and in the second I must disparage or humiliate another. But since I have no intention of departing from the truth in either case, and since this is what the present occasion demands, I shall nonetheless proceed.

'Prompted more by anger than by reason, you complain about Gisippus, whom you abuse, attack and condemn with these perpetual murmurs or rather outcries of yours, simply because he arranged to give to me the wife whom you had arranged to give to him. But in my opinion he deserves the highest praise, for two reasons: first, because he acted in the manner of a true friend, and secondly because his wisdom in so doing was superior to your own. Now, I have no intention of explaining to you, here and now, that which the sacred laws of friendship require that a man should do for his friend, being content simply to have reminded you that the ties of friendship may be much more binding than those of blood or kinship. For our friends are of our own choosing, whereas our kinsfolk are those that Fortune has allotted to us. So if my life was more precious to Gisippus than your goodwill, none of you should marvel thereat, since I am his friend, or regard myself as such.

'But let us turn to the second reason, which, if I am to prove that he was wiser than you are, I shall have to expound to you at greater length; for you seem to know nothing of the providence of the gods, and to know far less about the consequences of friendship. I say, then, that it was your judgement, your counsel, and your resolve that Sophronia should be given to Gisippus, a young man and a philosopher; and Gisippus gave her to a young man and a philosopher. You wanted her to go to an Athenian, and Gisippus gave her to a Roman. You gave her to a noble youth, Gisippus to a nobler; you to a rich young man, Gisippus to a richer; you to a youth who loved her not, and scarcely even knew her, Gisippus to a youth who loved her above all other blessings, including life itself.

'But in order to see whether what I say is true, and whether Gisippus is worthier of greater commendation than yourselves, let us examine the evidence point by point. That I am a young man and a philosopher, like Gisippus, my countenance and my condition will readily attest, without pursuing the matter any further. We are both of the same age, and we have always kept abreast of one another in our studies. It is true that he is an Athenian, and I am a Roman. But should there be any dispute upon the rival merits of our cities, I would remind you that my own city is free, whilst his pays tribute; I would remind you that my city rules the entire world, whilst his is one of her vassals; and I would remind you that whereas my city is renowned for her soldiers, her statesmen, and her men of letters, it is only for the last of these that Gisippus can boast of his.

'Moreover, though you may look upon me here as a very humble scholar, I was not born of the dregs of the Roman populace. My private house in Rome, and the places of public resort, are filled with ancient statues of my ancestors, and you will find that the annals of the city abound with descriptions of the many triumphs celebrated on the Capitol by the Quintii. Nor has my family fallen into decay on account of its antiquity, for on the contrary the glory of our name shines more resplendently now than at any time in the past.

'Concerning my wealth, modesty forbids that I should speak, bearing in mind that poverty with honour has long been regarded by the noble citizens of Rome as a priceless legacy. But if, after the opinion of the common herd, poverty is to be condemned and riches commended, of these I have abundant store, not out of avarice but out of the kindness of Fortune. And whilst I am fully aware of the value which, quite rightly, you placed upon having Gisippus as your kinsman here in Athens, there is no reason why I should be less of an asset to you in Rome, seeing that you will discover me to be an excellent host to you there, as well as a valuable, solicitous and powerful patron, who will be only too ready to assist you, whether in your public or your personal concerns.

'Who, therefore, having set all prejudice aside and examined the matter dispassionately, would rate your counsels higher than those of my friend Gisippus? No one, to be sure. Thus Sophronia is rightly wedded to Titus Quintus Fulvius, and if anyone deplores or bemoans the fact, he is both misguided and misinformed. Possibly there are those who will say that Sophronia is complaining, not of being wedded to Titus, but of the manner in which she became his wife, secretly, by stealth, and without the knowledge of a single friend or relative. But there is nothing miraculous about this, nor is it the first time that such a thing has happened.

'I gladly leave aside those who have married against the wishes of their fathers; and those who have eloped with their lovers, becoming their mistresses rather than their wives; and those who have divulged their wedded state, not in so many words, but through pregnancy and childbirth, thus leaving their fathers with no alternative but to consent. This was not the case with Sophronia, who on the contrary was bestowed upon Titus by Gisippus in an orderly, discreet, and honourable manner. There are those who will say that Gisippus had no right to bestow her in marriage, but these are merely foolish and womanly scruples, the product of shallow reasoning. This is by no means the first occasion on which Fortune has used strange and wonderful ways to achieve her established aims. What do I care if a cobbler, not to mention a philosopher, manages some affair of mine in his own way, whether openly or furtively, so long as the end result is a good one? If the cobbler has been indiscreet, then admit-

tedly I must take good care not to let him meddle again in my
affairs, but at the same time I must thank him for the services he has
rendered. So that if Gisippus has married Sophronia well, to complain
of the man and his methods is a piece of gratuitous folly; and if you
suspect his judgement, thank him for what he has done, and see that
he is never given the chance to do it again.

'Nevertheless I must make it clear that I never sought, whether by
native cunning or deliberate fraud, to besmirch the honour and the
fame of your family in the person of Sophronia. Although I married
her in secret, I was no plunderer, intent on despoiling her of her
virginity, nor did I wish to possess her on dishonourable terms, like
one who was your enemy and who spurned your kinship. I wanted
her because I was ardently enamoured of her enchanting beauty and
superior worth. Yet I knew that had I sought your formal consent,
which you may feel I was obliged to obtain, it would not have been
forthcoming, since, loving her deeply as you do, you would have
feared that I would take her away to Rome.

'Accordingly I resorted to the secret measures that can now be
openly revealed, and I forced Gisippus, for my sake, to fall in with my
plans. Moreover, though I was passionately in love with her, it was
not as her lover that I conjoined myself to Sophronia, but as her
husband. For as she herself can truthfully bear witness, I kept my
distance until after I had wedded her by saying the necessary words
and placing the ring on her finger, and when I asked her whether she
would have me as her husband, she told me that she would. If she
feels she was deceived, she should not blame me, but herself, for
failing to ask me who I was. So the enormous crime, the terrible sin,
the unpardonable wrong committed by Gisippus, my devoted friend,
and by myself, her devoted admirer, was simply that Sophronia was
married to Titus Quintus in secret; for this reason alone do you tear
him to pieces, bombard him with threats, and sharpen your knives
against him. What more would you have done, had he given her to a
serf, a scoundrel, or a slave? Where would you have found the fetters,
the dungeons, or the tortures equal to his offence?

'But of this let us say no more for the present. Something has now
occured which I was not yet expecting, namely, that my father has
died and I am obliged to return to Rome; and because I wish to take

Sophronia with me, I have revealed to you that which otherwise I might have continued to conceal. If you are wise, you will cheerfully accept it, for had I wished to deceive or offend you, I could have disowned her and left her on your hands. But heaven forbid that the heart of a Roman should ever harbour so cowardly a design.

'Sophronia then is mine, not only by the consent of the gods and the authority of human law, but through the good sense of my friend Gisippus and the skilful manner of my wooing her. But it seems that you disapprove of this, possibly because you think yourselves wiser than the gods and your fellow-beings, for you obstinately persist in doing two things that are highly repugnant to me. In the first place you hold on to Sophronia when you have no right to do such a thing without my consent; and secondly you treat Gisippus, to whom you are deeply indebted, as your enemy. It is not my intention to prove to you still further how foolishly you are behaving, being content for the present to offer you some friendly advice: to wit, that you should forget about your grievances, set all your anger aside, and see that Sophronia is restored to me, so that I may depart from Athens in peace, as your kinsman, and live henceforth as one of yourselves. For of this you may be certain, that whether or not you like what has been done, if you fail to heed my advice I shall take Gisippus with me, and once I return to Rome, I shall make quite sure that she who is rightfully mine is restored to me, however much you may object. And you shall learn from experience what havoc can be wrought by the wrath of a Roman, once you have made him your lifelong enemy.'

Having said what he had to say, Titus, his features contorted with anger, rose to his feet; and taking Gisippus by the hand, he led him out of the temple, tossing his head from side to side and looking daggers at all the people present, as if to show how little he was daunted by their numbers.

The people he had left behind in the temple, in part persuaded by the force of his arguments, in part alarmed by his concluding words, decided of one accord that since Gisippus had turned them down, i t was better to have Titus as their kinsman than to have lost a kinsman in Gisippus and gained an enemy in Titus.

So they went and sought out Titus, and told him they were willing that Sophronia should be his, adding that they would be glad to have him as a dear kinsman and Gisippus as a good friend. And after celebrating their friendship and kinship in a style suited to the occasion, they went their separate ways. Sophronia was then restored to Titus, and being a sensible girl, she made a virtue of necessity and soon accorded Titus the love she had formerly had for Gisippus. And she went with him to Rome, where she was received with great honour.

Meanwhile Gisippus stayed on in Athens, but could no longer command much esteem among most of his fellow-citizens; and not long afterwards, through factional strife in the city, he was driven out of Athens, poor and destitute, and condemned to perpetual exile along with all the members of his family. Now that he was banished, before very long he became not only a pauper but a beggar, and made his way as best he could to Rome, in order to discover whether Titus still remembered him. On learning that Titus was alive and that all the Romans sang his praises, he found out where he was living, then went and stood outside his house. Eventually Titus made his appearance, and though Gisippus would not venture to address him because of his beggarly condition, he endeavoured to let himself be seen so that Titus might recognize and send for him. When, therefore, Titus passed him by without any show of recognition, Gisippus was convinced that he had been deliberately snubbed, and remembering all he had done for Titus in the past, he retreated from the scene in dudgeon and despair.

It was already dark when Gisippus, hungry and penniless, having nowhere to go and heartily wishing he were dead, strayed into a very lonely part of the city where he came across a large cave, into which he crept with the intention of sheltering there for the night. And on the cave's bare floor, ill-apparelled and exhausted by prolonged weeping, he fell fast asleep. Just before dawn, however, a pair of burglars came to this very cave with the proceeds of their night's activities, and having started to quarrel with one another, the more powerful of the two killed his companion and made off.

All of this was seen and heard by Gisippus, who, being himself intent upon dying, felt that he had now discovered a way of achieving his goal without resorting to suicide. So he stayed where he was until the praetorian guards, having quickly got wind of the affair, arrived at the scene of the crime and bundled him off into custody. He was then interrogated and confessed to the murder, adding that he had been unable to find his way out of the cave; whereupon the praetor, whose name was Marcus Varro, sentenced him to death by crucifixion, which in those days was the regular method of execution.

By a singular coincidence, at that very moment Titus turned up at the law court, and on staring the wretched prisoner in the face, having learned the reasons for the sentence, he recognized him at once as Gisippus. Titus wondered how the fortunes of Gisippus could have reached so low an ebb, and how on earth he came to be in Rome; but his chief concern was to assist his friend in his hour of need, and since he could see no other way of saving him except by shifting the blame from Gisippus to himself, he quickly stepped forward and exclaimed:

'Marcus Varro, recall the wretched fellow you have just condemned, for he is innocent. I have already offended the gods enough by striking the blow that killed the person whose body was found by your men this morning, without wishing to offend them now with the death of another innocent.'

Not only was Varro astonished to hear these words, but aggrieved that everyone in court should also have heard them; and since he was morally obliged to follow the course prescribed by the laws of the land, he had Gisippus brought back and said to him, in the presence of Titus:

'How could you be so foolish as to confess, without being forced, to a crime that you never committed, knowing full well that your life was at stake? You told us that you were the person who killed that fellow in the cave last night, and now this other man comes and says it was he and not you who did the killing.'

Gisippus looked up, saw that it was Titus, and realized at once that he was doing this for his deliverance, out of gratitude for the favour that Gisippus had done him in the past. And so, shedding many a piteous tear, he turned to the praetor and said:

'I assure you, Varro, that it was I who killed him. It is too late now for Titus to concern himself with my deliverance.'

Whereupon Titus for his part said:

'My lord, as you see, this fellow is a foreigner, and when they found him beside the body of the victim, he was unarmed. You have only to look at him to realize that it's his poverty that makes him want to die. Let him go, therefore, and give to me the punishment I deserve.'

Varro, marvelling at the persistence of the two men, was already of the opinion that neither of them was guilty, and just as he was deliberating how best to absolve them, there suddenly stepped forth a youth named Publius Ambustus, who was known to everyone in Rome as a hardened criminal and notorious thief, and who in fact was the real murderer. And knowing that neither of the two was guilty of the crime to which both were confessing, he was so overwhelmed by their innocence that out of pure compassion he went up to Varro and said:

'My lord, fate decrees that I should solve the enigma of these two men, though who the god is that cajoles and compels me from within to expose my iniquitous deed, I know not. Take note, then, that neither of the two is guilty of the crime to which they both confess. It was I, in fact, who killed the man this morning at sunrise, and as I was dividing the spoils of our night's activities with the fellow I murdered, I saw this poor wretch lying asleep in the cave. As for Titus, he has no need of me for a champion: everyone knows him to be an upright citizen, who would never stoop to such a deed as this. Release them therefore, and punish me in the manner prescribed by the laws.'

News of the affair had meanwhile reached the ears of Octavianus, who summoned the three men to his presence and demanded to know why each of them was so eager to be convicted of the murder, whereupon they all explained their motives in turn. And in the end he released all three, the first two because they were innocent, and the third for the sake of the others.

Titus then took hold of his friend Gisippus, and after scolding him severely for treating him so coldly and suspiciously, he made a great fuss of him and led him away to his house, where Sophronia, with tears of compassion, greeted him as a brother. And after Titus had to some extent restored his spirits, and clothed him once again in a manner befitting his nobility and excellence, he not only made him joint owner of all his treasures and possessions, but also presented him with a wife in the person of a young sister of his called Fulvia. Then he said to him:

'It is now up to you to decide, Gisippus, whether you want to stay here with me, or return to Greece with all the things I have given you.'

Prompted on the one hand by the fact that he was exiled from his native city, and on the other by his just regard for the precious friendship of Titus, Gisippus consented to become a citizen of Rome, where they lived long and happily together under the same roof, Gisippus with his Fulvia and Titus with his Sophronia; and if such a thing were conceivable, their friendship gained steadily in strength with every day that passed.

Friendship, then, is a most sacred thing, not only worthy of singular reverence, but eternally to be praised as the deeply discerning mother of probity and munificence, the sister of gratitude and charity, and the foe of hatred and avarice, ever ready, without waiting to be asked, to do virtuously unto others that which it would wish to be done unto itself. But very seldom in this day and age do we find two persons in whom its hallowed effects may be seen, this being the fault of men's shameful and miserly greed, which, being solely concerned with seeking its own advantage, has banished friendship to perpetual exile beyond earth's farthest limits.

Except for the power of friendship, what quantity of love or riches, what kinsman's bond, could have wrought so powerful an effect upon the heart of Gisippus as to persuade him, on witnessing the fervour, the tears, and the sighs of Titus, to concede to him the fair and gracious promised bride with whom he was himself in love? Except for the power of friendship, what laws, what threats, what fear of consequence, could have prevented the youthful arms of Gisippus, in darkened or deserted places, or in the privacy of his own bed, from embracing this delectable girl, occasionally perhaps at her own invitation? Except for the power of friendship, what prospect of superior rank, or rich reward, or material gain, could have made Gisippus so indifferent to the loss of his own and Sophronia's kinsfolk, so indifferent to the slanderous rumours of the populace, so indifferent to the jests and jibes of his fellow men, as to gratify his comrade's desire?

And on the other hand, what other force but friendship would have prompted Titus, eagerly and without vacillation, to place his life in jeopardy in order to save Gisippus from the cross of his own desiring, when no one would have blamed him for turning a blind eye to the affair? What other force but friendship would have prompted Titus promptly and generously to share his extensive wealth with Gisippus, whose own possessions had been seized from him by Fortune? What other force but friendship would have prompted Titus readily and zealously to bestow his own sister in marriage upon Gisippus, when he could see that he was penniless and utterly destitute?

Men may thus continue to desire throngs of relatives, hordes of brothers, and swarms of children, and as their wealth increases, so they may multiply the number of their servants. But what they will fail to perceive is that every one of these, no matter who he may be, is more apprehensive of the tiniest peril to himself than eager to save his father, brother, or master from a great calamity, whereas between two friends, the position is quite the reverse.

NINTH STORY

Messer Torello offers hospitality to Saladin, who is disguised as a merchant. A Crusade is launched, and before setting off Messer Torello instructs his wife that, failing his return, she may remarry by a certain date. He is taken prisoner, but his skill in training hawks brings him to the notice of the Sultan, who recognizes him, reminds him of their previous encounter, and entertains him most lavishly. And when Messer Torello falls ill, he is conveyed by magic in the space of a single night to Pavia, where his wife's second marriage is about to be solemnized. But he is recognized by his wife at the wedding-feast, whence he returns with her to his house.

When Filomena had finished speaking, and fulsome praise had been bestowed by one and all upon Titus for his magnificent gesture of gratitude, the king, wishing to reserve the last place for Dioneo, began to address them as follows:

Enchanting ladies, what Filomena says about friendship is undoubtedly true, and it was not without reason that she complained, in her closing remarks, of the scant regard in which friendship is held by the people of today. If we had come here to rectify or even to condemn the world's shortcomings, I would reinforce her words with a lengthy speech of my own. But since we have another end in view, it occurs to me that I might now acquaint you, in the form of a narrative, lengthy perhaps but agreeable throughout, with one of the munificent deeds performed by Saladin. For even though it may not be possible for any of us, through lack of means, to win the complete friendship of another by emulating the things of which you will hear in my tale, at least we may take a delight in being courteous to people, in the hope that sooner or later our actions will bring their reward.

You are to know, then, that during the reign of the Emperor Frederick I, the Christians launched a great Crusade to recover the Holy Land, and that according to certain reports, Saladin, an outstandingly able ruler who was Sultan of Babylon at that period, having heard about this Crusade some time in advance, resolved to see for himself what preparations the Christian princes were making, the better to defend himself against them. So he settled all his outstanding affairs in Egypt, and, giving the impression he was going on a pilgrimage, set forth in the guise of a merchant, with an escort consisting solely of two very senior and judicious counsellors and three attendants. Their tour of inspection took them through many Christian countries, and one day, in the late afternoon, they were riding through Lombardy before crossing the Alps, when, on the road from Milan to Pavia, they happened to meet a nobleman called Messer Torello, of Strà in the province of Pavia, who, along with his attendants, his dogs, and his falcons, was going to stay at a beautiful estate of his on the banks of the Ticino. As soon as Messer Torello caught sight of these men, he observed that they were foreigners of gentle birth, and desired to do them honour. So that when Saladin inquired of one of Torello's attendants how far it was to Pavia, and whether they could reach it by nightfall, Torello himself replied, before the servant had time to open his mouth:

'By the time you reach Pavia, gentlemen, it will be too late for you to enter the city.'

'Then perhaps you will be good enough,' said Saladin, 'since we are strangers in these parts, to tell us where we may find the best night's lodging.'

'With pleasure,' said Messer Torello. 'I was just about to send one of these attendants of mine on an errand to a spot not far from Pavia. I shall get him to accompany you, and he will take you to a place where you will lodge in great comfort.'

He then went up to the shrewdest of his attendants, told him what he had to do, and sent him off with Saladin's party. Meanwhile he himself rode rapidly on to his country house, where he arranged for the finest possible supper to be prepared and for tables to be set in the garden, after which he went and waited at the main gate for his guests to arrive. The attendant, conversing on many different subjects with his gently bred companions, led them by a circular route along various byways and eventually brought them, without their knowing it, to his master's estate.

As soon as Messer Torello saw them coming, he advanced on foot to meet them, and laughing heartily he said:

'Gentlemen, I bid you the warmest of welcomes.'

Being of a very astute disposition, Saladin realized that the worthy knight had not invited them when they first met for fear of their refusing, and that, so as to make it impossible for them to deny him their company that evening, he had cleverly beguiled them into coming to his house. And having returned Messer Torello's greeting, he said:

'Sir, if it were possible to complain of courteous men, we should have good cause for complaint against you, for to say nothing of taking us slightly out of our way, you have more or less constrained us to accept this handsome gesture of yours, when all we did to merit your civility was to exchange a single greeting with you.'

To which the knight, who was no less wise than he was eloquent, replied:

'If I may judge from your appearance, gentlemen, my civility is bound to be a poor thing by comparison with your deserts. But to tell the truth you could not have found a decent place to lodge outside Pavia. Do not be aggrieved, then, to have added a few more miles to your journey for the sake of a little less discomfort.'

As he was speaking, his servants gathered round the visitors, and as soon as they had dismounted, their horses were led away to the stables. Meanwhile Messer Torello conducted the three gentlemen to the rooms that had been prepared for them, where they were helped off with their riding-boots, after which Torello offered them refreshment in the form of deliciously cool wines, and detained them with agreeable talk until it was time to go to supper.

Saladin and his companions and attendants were all conversant with the Italian tongue, so that they had no difficulty in following Messer Torello or in making themselves understood, and they were all of the opinion that this knight was the most agreeable, civilized, and affable gentleman they had so far had occasion to meet.

For his own part, Messer Torello concluded that they were gentlemen of quality, much more distinguished than he had previously thought, and reproached himself for his inability to entertain them in company that evening, with a banquet of greater splendour. He therefore resolved that he would make amends next morning, and having explained to one of his servants what he had in mind, he sent him to Pavia, which never closed its gates and was very close at hand, with a message for his wife, a lady of great intelligence and exceptional spirit. This done, he led his visitors into the garden, and politely asked them who they were, whence they came, and where they were going, to which Saladin replied:

'We are Cypriot merchants, we come from Cyprus, and we are on our way to Paris to conduct certain business of ours.'

'Would to God,' said Messer Torello, 'that this country of ours produced gentlemen of a kind to compare with what I see of the merchants of Cyprus.'

On these and other matters they conversed for a while, until supper was served and Messer Torello invited them to take their places at table; and albeit the meal was impromptu, it was splendidly arranged and they dined exceedingly well. Nor had the tables long been cleared before Messer Torello, observing that his guests were tired, showed them to sumptuous beds in which to lie down and rest, and shortly thereafter he too retired to bed.

The servant he had sent to Pavia delivered the message to his lady, who, in a spirit more worthy of a prince than of a woman, promptly summoned a number of her husband's friends and servants, and set all preparations in train for a sumptuous banquet. And apart from seeing that invitations were delivered, by the light of torches, to many of the city's leading nobles, she laid in a supply of clothes and silks and furs, and carried out all the instructions her husband had sent her, down to the tiniest detail.

Next morning, when the gentlemen had risen, Messer Torello invited them to join him for an expedition on horseback, and having called for his falcons, he took his guests to a nearby stretch of shallow water and showed them how magnificently the birds could fly. But when Saladin inquired whether there was anyone who could take them to Pavia and direct them to the most comfortable inn, Messer Torello said:

'I myself will direct you, for I am obliged to go to Pavia in any case.'

The gentlemen believed him, gladly accepted his offer, and set off with him on the road to Pavia, where they arrived a little after tierce. Thinking they were being directed to the finest of the city's inns, they came with Messer Torello to his mansion, where already some fifty or more of the leading citizens were assembled to greet them, and these immediately gathered round them, seizing their reins and their stirrups. Saladin and his companions no sooner saw this than they realized all too well what it signified, and they said:

'Messer Torello, we did not ask for any such favour as this. You entertained us royally last night, far better than we had any right to expect, and therefore you could easily have left us now to proceed on our way.'

To which Messer Torello replied:

'If, gentlemen, I was able to do you a service last night, for that I was indebted, not so much to yourselves, but rather to Fortune, who overtook you at such an hour on the road that you had no alternative but to come to my humble dwelling; but for the service we shall do you this morning, I and all these gentlemen who surround you are beholden only to you, and if you think it courteous to deny us your company at breakfast, you are at liberty to do so.'

Acknowledging defeat, Saladin and his companions dismounted, and after being welcomed by the gentlemen, they were gaily conveyed to the rooms which had been sumptuously prepared to receive them. They then divested themselves of their travelling attire, and, having taken a little refreshment, made their way to the banqueting hall, where everything was magnificently arranged. Having washed their hands, with all due pomp and ceremony they were ushered to their places at table, where they were plied with numerous dishes, each of them so exquisitely served that if the Emperor himself had been present, it would not have been possible to entertain him more handsomely. And even though Saladin and his two companions were mighty lords, accustomed to extraordinary acts of homage, they nonetheless marvelled at this one, which, considering the quality of the knight, whom they knew to be no prince, but a private citizen, seemed to them as magnificent as any they had ever seen.

When the meal was over, the tables were cleared and they talked learnedly together until, at Messer Torello's suggestion, it being very hot, all the gentlemen of Pavia went home to take their siesta, leaving him alone with his three visitors. And so that none of his treasures should remain hidden from their eyes, he escorted them into another room and sent for his excellent lady. She was a tall and very beautiful woman, and, decked in sumptuous robes, flanked by her two small children, who looked for all the world like angels, she came before them and charmingly paid her respects. No sooner did she appear than the gentlemen rose to their feet, greeted her with deference, and invited her to sit in their midst, making much ado over her enchanting little children. And after entering upon a pleasant conversation with the three visitors, in the course of which Messer Torello got up and left them alone together, she graciously inquired whence they had come and whither they were bound, whereupon the gentlemen gave her the answer they had already given to Messer Torello.

The lady smiled, and said:

'Then I see that my woman's instinct may well have its uses, for I want to ask you a special favour, namely, that you will neither refuse nor despise the trifling gift that I shall cause to be brought to you. On the contrary, I beg you to accept it, but you must bear in mind that a woman's heart is not so large as a man's, and her gifts are correspondingly smaller. So I trust you will pay more heed to the donor's good intentions than to the size of the gift.'

She then sent for two pairs of robes for each of the guests, one lined with silk and the other with fur, all of a quality more suited to a prince than to any merchant or private citizen. And these she presented to the gentlemen, along with three silken jackets and smallclothes, saying:

'Take these robes: they are like the ones in which I have arrayed my husband. As for the other things, though they are worth little, you may well find them useful, seeing that you are distant from your womenfolk. You have come a long way and still have far to go, and merchants take a pride in their appearance.'

The gentlemen could scarcely believe their eyes. It was abundantly clear that Messer Torello was bent upon doing them every possible honour, and for a moment they suspected, seeing that the robes were more sumptuous than those of any merchant, that he had seen through their disguise. However, one of them answered the lady as follows:

'These things are so exquisite , madam, that it would be difficult for anyone to accept them. But how are we to refuse, when you press them upon us with so much eloquence?'

Thus her gift was accepted, and since Messer Torello had now returned, the lady took her leave of the three gentlemen and went away to see that their servants were likewise supplied with garments, of a style suited to their condition. Meanwhile, in response to the earnest entreaties of Messer Torello, the gentlemen agreed to spend the rest of the day with him, and after they had taken their siesta, they donned their new robes and toured the city on horseback with their host. And when it was time for supper, they were splendidly dined and wined in the company of numerous eminent citizens.

In due course they retired to bed, and when they rose at daybreak, they found that their tired old nags had been replaced by a trio of sturdy and splendid-looking palfreys, and that fresh, strong horses had also been provided for their servants; on seeing which, Saladin turned to his companions and said:

'I swear to God that there was never a more perfect gentleman than this, nor any more courteous or considerate. And if the kings of

Christendom are such excellent princes as this man is a knight, the
Sultan of Babylon will be powerless to resist a single one of them, let
alone all those we have seen preparing to march against him.' But
realizing that Messer Torello would not take no for an answer, they
thanked him most politely and mounted their horses.

Messer Torello, together with several of his friends, escorted the
gentlemen for a goodly distance along the road leading out of the
city. But eventually Saladin begged him to turn back, being unable to
tarry any longer, though it grieved him to part company with his
host, whom he had come by now to regard with the deepest affection.
And albeit Messer Torello was no less loath to part company with his
guests, he said:

'Since you want me to leave you, gentlemen, I shall do so. But
first I should like to say this: I know not who you are, nor do I wish
to know more than you are willing to tell me. But whoever you may
be, you cannot persuade me to believe that you are merchants. And
with that I bid you farewell.'

To which Saladin, having already taken his leave of Messer
Torello's companions, replied as follows:

'We may yet have the chance, sir, of showing you some of our
merchandise, and then you shall be persuaded well enough. But
meanwhile we bid you adieu.'

Saladin then rode off with his companions, being firmly resolved,
if his life were spared and he avoided defeat in the war with which he
was faced, to return the hospitality of Messer Torello in full. He
talked a great deal to his companions about Messer Torello and his
lady, and about all the things he had done for them, waxing more
eloquent in his praises on each occasion he returned to the subject.
And when, at the cost of no little fatigue, his tour of the West was
completed, he returned by sea with his companions to Alexandria,
where, now that he was fully apprised of the facts, he drew up his
plan of defence. Meanwhile Messer Torello had returned to Pavia, and
although he pondered at great length upon who these three men might
have been, he never arrived at the truth nor even came anywhere near
it.

When the time arrived for the Crusade, and the soldiers were
assembling everywhere in large numbers, Messer Torello, undeterred

by the tears and entreaties of his lady, firmly made up his mind to go with them. He therefore made all his preparations, and as he was about to ride away, he summoned his wife, whom he loved very deeply, and said to her:

'As you see, my lady, I am joining this Crusade, both for personal renown and the good of my soul. I leave our good name and our possessions in your hands; and since my return is far less certain than my departure, owing to any of a thousand accidents that may befall me, I want you to promise me this: that whatever should be my fate, failing positive news that I live, you will wait for a year and a month and a day before you remarry, beginning from this, the day of my departure.'

'Torello,' she replied, weeping most bitterly, 'how I am to bear all the sorrow into which I am plunged by your going away, I simply cannot tell. But if I am strong enough to survive it, and if anything should happen to you, rest assured that for as long as I live I shall be wedded to Messer Torello and his memory.'

'My lady,' said Messer Torello, 'I am convinced that you will do all in your power to keep such a promise; but you are young and beautiful, you come from a famous family, and as everyone knows, you are a woman of exceptional gifts. Hence I have no doubt that if I am reported as missing, many a fine gentleman will be seeking your hand from your brothers and kinsfolk, who will subject you to so much pressure, that whether you like it or not you will be forced to comply with their wishes. And that is why I do not ask you to wait any longer than the period I have stated.'

'I shall do my utmost to keep my promise,' said the lady. 'And even if I am forced to act differently, at least I shall follow these instructions of yours to the letter. But I pray to God that neither you nor I will be brought to any such extremity.'

Having uttered these words, the lady burst into tears and embraced Messer Torello. Then, taking a ring from her finger, she presented it to him saying:

'If I should happen to die before we meet again, remember me when you look upon this ring.'

Messer Torello accepted the ring, and having mounted his horse, he bade farewell to everyone and proceeded upon his way. On arriving with his followers at Genoa, he boarded a galley, and after a prosperous voyage he landed at Acre, where he joined the main body of the Christian host. But almost overnight the army was afflicted by a great and deadly fever, in the course of which, whether through good judgement or good fortune, Saladin captured nearly all the Christians who managed to survive, divided them up, and imprisoned them in various cities of his realm. Among those captured was Messer Torello, who was marched away to prison in Alexandria, where, since no one was aware of his importance and he was afraid to disclose his identity, he was compelled to apply himself to the training of hawks, a science which he had mastered to perfection. And when his prowess came to the notice of Saladin, he had him removed from captivity and appointed him his falconer.

Neither of them recognized the other, and Messer Torello, whom Saladin referred to simply as 'the Christian', constantly had the thought of Pavia at the back of his mind and attempted several times to escape, but without success. So that when a party of Genoese emissaries came to Saladin's court to arrange for the ransom of certain fellow-citizens of theirs, he resolved that before they departed he would write to his wife, letting her know he was alive and would return to her as soon as he could, and asking her to wait for him. And having written the letter, he earnestly begged one of the emissaries, whom he knew personally, to see that it was delivered to his uncle, who was the Abbot of San Pietro in Ciel d'Oro, at Pavia.

This being the way matters stood with Messer Torello, it happened that as Saladin was conversing with him one day on the subject of his hawks, Messer Torello began to smile and his mouth assumed a certain expression, of which Saladin had taken particular note when staying at his house in Pavia. Consequently Saladin called Messer Torello to mind, and after peering at the falconer more intently, he was almost sure that this man and Messer Torello were one and the same. So, changing the subject, he said:

'Tell me, Christian, in what part of the West do you live?'

'My lord,' replied Messer Torello, 'I am a Lombard, from a city called Pavia, and I am a poor man of low estate.'

When Saladin heard this, he was virtually certain that his surmise was correct, and gleefully thought to himself: 'God has now given me the chance to show this man how greatly I valued his kindness towards me.' However, he said no more on the subject, but gave orders for all his robes to be laid out on display in one of the rooms of the palace, into which he took Messer Torello, and said to him:

'Take a look at these clothes, Christian, and tell me whether you ever saw any of them before.'

Messer Torello began to inspect them, and albeit he caught sight of the garments his wife had presented to Saladin, it never entered his head that they could be the ones in question. However, he replied:

'My lord, I recognize none of them, though it's true that these two resemble certain robes which I myself once wore, and were also worn by three merchants who came to stay with me.'

Whereupon Saladin, unable to restrain himself any longer, threw his arms affectionately round Messer Torello's neck, saying:

'You are Messer Torello of Strà; I am one of the three merchants to whom your good lady presented these garments; and the time has now come to persuade you of the quality of my merchandise, as I promised you I would, God willing, on the day I departed.'

On hearing this, Messer Torello was delighted and ashamed at one and the same time, for on the one hand he was delighted to have had so eminent a guest under his roof, whilst on the other he was ashamed at the thought of having entertained him so frugally. But Saladin continued:

'Messer Torello, now that God has sent you here to me, you must no longer think of me as your master, but rather as your servant.'

After much rejoicing in each other's company, Saladin caused him to be dressed in regal robes, and having presented him to a gathering of the leading peers of his realm, and spoken at length of Messer Torello's excellence, he commanded that those of them who set any store by his favour should honour the person of Messer Torello as they would his own. And this was precisely what each of them did from that day forth, especially the two gentlemen who had stayed with Saladin in Messer Torello's house.

Messer Torello's sudden elevation to the pinnacle of renown took his mind away for a while from his affairs in Lombardy, the more so because he had every reason to believe that his letter had been safely delivered into the hands of his uncle.

But on the very day that the Christian host fell into Saladin's hands, a Provençal knight of no great repute, whose name was Messer Torello of Dignes, had died and was buried in the Christian camp; and since Messer Torello of Strà was famed for his nobility throughout the whole of the army, whenever anyone heard that Messer Torello was dead they at once assumed it was the latter of the two, and not the former, who was meant. Before they had a chance to perceive their mistake Messer Torello was taken prisoner, so that many Italians returned with tidings of his death, and there were those who had the audacity to assert that they had seen his corpse and attended his burial. And when this came to the knowledge of his wife and family, it brought enormous and incalculable sorrow, not only to them but to all who had known him.

We should be hard put to describe in few words the nature and extent of the grief, the sadness, and the heartache experienced by his lady. Suffice it to say that when, after mourning continuously for several months on end, the pangs of her sorrow began to abate, and her hand was being sought by the most powerful men in Lombardy, she was urged by her brothers and the rest of her kinsfolk to remarry. Time after time she refused, bursting into floods of tears whenever the subject was mentioned. Eventually however she was forced to accede to the wishes of her kinsfolk, but only on condition that she should remain unmarried till the period prescribed in her promise to Messer Torello had expired.

This, then, was how matters stood in Pavia with the lady when one day, about a week before she was due to be married, Messer Torello chanced to catch sight in Alexandria of a man he had seen embarking with the Genoese emissaries on the galley that was leaving for Genoa. He therefore sent for him, and asked him what sort of a voyage they had had, and when they had arrived at Genoa.

'My lord,' said the man, 'I left the galley in Crete, where I later heard that her voyage ended in disaster; for as she was approaching Sicily, she ran into a northerly gale which drove her on to the Barbary reefs, and everyone aboard was drowned, including two of my brothers.'

Messer Torello believed every word of this account, which happened to be all too accurate, and when he recalled that less than a week remained of the period he had asked his wife to await his return, and realized that nothing had been heard of him in Pavia, he was convinced that she was by now betrothed to another. So deep was the despair into which he was cast that he lost the desire to eat, took to his bed, and resolved to die.

When Saladin, who greatly loved Messer Torello, heard news of this, he came in person to see him. And having, by dint of earnest and repeated entreaties, discovered the reason for his sorrow and his malady, he censured him severely for not confiding in him earlier, then begged him to take heart, declaring that if Torello would cheer up he would arrange for him to be in Pavia on the date he had prescribed. And he explained how it was to be accomplished.

Messer Torello took Saladin at his word, and since he had frequently heard that this sort of thing was possible and had often been done before, he began to feel more optimistic and to urge Saladin that he should attend to it at once.

Saladin therefore enjoined one of his magicians, with whose skill he was already well acquainted, to seek out a way of transporting Messer Torello on a bed to Pavia, in the space of a single night. The magician replied that this would be done, but that for Torello's own good he must first of all put him to sleep.

This arranged, Saladin returned to Messer Torello, and finding him still entirely resolved to be in Pavia by the date agreed if this were possible, and to die if it were not, he addressed him as follows:

'God knows, Messer Torello, that I cannot blame you in the slightest for loving your wife so dearly and for being so concerned at the thought of losing her to another. For of all the ladies I ever recall having met, she is the one whose way of life, whose manners, and whose demeanour – to say nothing of her beauty, which will fade like the flower – seem to me most precious and commendable. Nothing would have given me greater joy, since Fortune has brought you to Alexandria, than for us to have spent the rest of our lives together here, ruling as equals over the kingdom I now govern. God has willed that these wishes of mine should not be granted, but now that you have taken it into your head to die unless you are back again in Pavia by the date you prescribed, I dearly wish that I had known of all this in time for me to restore you to your home with the dignity, the splendour, and the company that your excellence deserves. Since, however, I am not even allowed to do this, and you are determined to be in Pavia forthwith, I shall do my best to get you there in the manner I have told you of.'

'My lord,' said Messer Torello, 'quite apart from your words, your actions have supplied me with abundant proof of your benevolence towards me, which far exceeds all my deserts, and even if you had said nothing, I should have lived and died in the certain knowledge that what you say is true. But since my mind is made up on the subject, I beg you to act quickly in the manner you have proposed, for after tomorrow I shall no longer be expected.'

Saladin assured him that everything was settled; and on the next day, it being his intention to send him on his way that same evening, he caused a most beautiful and sumptuous bed to be prepared in one of the great halls of his palace. It was a bed fashioned in the style of the East, with mattresses covered all over in velvet and cloth of gold, and Saladin had it bedecked with a quilt, embroidered with enormous pearls and the finest of precious stones, geometrically arranged, which was looked upon later, in these parts, as a priceless treasure. And finally he had two pillows placed upon it, of a quality appropriate to the bed itself. This done, he ordered that Messer Torello, who had now recovered, should be clothed in a robe of the kind that Saracens wear, more opulent and splendid than any that was ever seen, whilst around his head he caused one of his longest turbans to be wound.

It was already late in the evening when Saladin, along with many of his lords, went to Messer Torello's room; and having sat down beside him, he began, almost in tears, to address him as follows:

'Messer Torello, the time is approaching for you to be severed from me, and since I can neither go with you nor send another in my place, being prevented from doing so by the manner of your travelling, I am forced to take my leave of you here and now, which is why I have come. But before bidding you farewell, I implore you in the name of our love and our friendship to remember me. And before our lives are spent, I beg you if possible to settle your affairs in Lombardy and come once more to visit me; for not only will I rejoice to see you, but I shall then be able to repair the omissions which your haste to depart imposes upon me. Until such time as this should come about, let it not weary you to visit me with your letters, and ask of me whatever you please, for you may be sure that there is no other person on earth whose wants I would supply more readily.'

Messer Torello, being unable to control his tears, was prevented from replying at any length. And so in few words he declared it was impossible for him ever to forget Saladin's courteous deeds and sterling worth, and that without fail he would do as Saladin had requested, whenever the opportunity arose. So Saladin enfolded him tenderly in his arms, kissed him, and, weeping copiously, wished him God-speed and withdrew. Then all his nobles took their leave of Messer Torello and accompanied Saladin to the hall where the bed had been set.

But the hour was now late, and the magician being anxious to conduct the affair to a speedy conclusion, a physician came to Messer Torello with a certain potion, which he persuaded him to drink, explaining that it would fortify him for what lay ahead. Soon afterwards he fell asleep, and as he slept he was conveyed on Saladin's orders to the sumptuous bed, upon which Saladin placed a large, beautiful and priceless crown, which he marked in such a way that in due course it was clearly seen to have been sent from Saladin to Messer Torello's wife. Then on Messer Torello's finger he placed a ring containing a large ruby, whose value, since it glowed and glittered like a flaming torch, was well-nigh impossible to assess. He next had Messer Torello girded with a sword, so richly ornamented that it, too, could not easily be valued. Nor was this all, for he pinned a brooch to Messer Torello's breast, studded with pearls whose like were never seen, and many other precious stones besides. And on either side of his sleeping form, he caused an enormous golden bowl, overflowing with doubloons, to be placed, whilst all around him he set numerous rings and belts and strings of pearls and other objects, which would take too long to describe. This done, he kissed Messer Torello once more, and told the magician to make haste, whereupon before his very eyes the bed and Messer Torello suddenly disappeared in their entirety, leaving Saladin behind to converse with his nobles about him.

As he had requested, Messer Torello was deposited, along with all the aforesaid jewels and finery, in the church of San Pietro in Ciel d'Oro at Pavia, where he still lay asleep when the bell was rung for matins and the sexton entered the church carrying a lantern. Being suddenly confronted with the sight of the opulent bed, he could hardly believe his eyes, and such was the terror by which he was seized that he turned on his heel and came running out of the church, much to the amazement of the Abbot and the monks, who demanded to know the reason. Whereupon the sexton told them what he had seen.

'Come now,' said the Abbot, 'it's not as if you were a child any more, or a newcomer to this church, to be frightened so easily. Let's all go and see what has startled you.'

So the Abbot and his monks, having kindled a number of lights, entered the church and saw this amazing and sumptuous bed, with the sleeping knight upon it. And just as they were casting a wary and timorous eye over all the princely jewels, standing well back from the bed, the power of the potion happened to expend itself, Messer Torello stirred, and a great, deep sigh escaped his lips.

On seeing this, the monks, and also the Abbot, were frightened out of their wits, and they all ran away crying 'Lord, deliver us!'

Having opened his eyes and looked about him, Messer Torello discovered to his great joy that he was in the very place where he had asked to be left. And whereas he had known of the munificence of Saladin in the past, when he sat up now and surveyed, one by one, the objects with which he was surrounded, he was all the more conscious of it and deemed it greater than ever. But meanwhile he could hear the monks running away, and guessing the reason, he began, without stirring any further, to call to the Abbot by name, begging him not to be frightened as it was only Torello, his nephew.

On hearing this, the Abbot's fears increased, since for many months past he had assumed Torello to be dead. But after a while, drawing strength from the power of reason, and continuing to hear his name being called, he crossed himself devoutly and went cautiously up to Torello, who said to him:

'Oh, my father, of what are you afraid? By the grace of God, I am alive, and I have come back here from across the sea.'

Albeit Torello was thickly bearded and dressed in Arabian clothes, the Abbot soon recognized him; and being wholly reassured, he took him by the hand, saying: 'My son, I bid you a hearty welcome.' Then he continued: 'Our alarm ought not to surprise you, for there isn't a man in the whole of Pavia who is not convinced that you are dead. Indeed I may tell you that your wife, Madonna Adalieta, overcome by the threats and entreaties of her kinsfolk, has been forced to remarry. This very morning she is to go to her new husband, and all is made ready for the nuptials and the banquet.'

Messer Torello stepped forth from his sumptuous bed, and after cordially embracing the Abbot and the monks, he begged them one and all to say nothing to anyone of his return until he had attended to a certain affair. He then saw to it that the precious jewels were left in a safe place, after which he gave an account to the Abbot of all that had so far happened to him. The Abbot, delighted with Messer Torello's good fortune, joined with him in giving thanks to God, after which Messer Torello asked the Abbot the name of his wife's second husband; and the Abbot told him.

Then Messer Torello said:

'Before my return is made public, I mean to find out how my wife comports herself at these nuptials; so although it is not the custom for the religious to attend such a banquet as this, I want you to arrange, for my sake, that we should be present.'

The Abbot readily agreed; and soon after daybreak he sent a message to the bridegroom, saying that he wished to bring a friend to the nuptials, to which the gentleman replied that he would be very glad to see them.

When the hour for the banquet arrived, Messer Torello went with the Abbot, in the clothes in which he was standing, to the bridegroom's house, being stared at in amazement by everyone who saw him, but recognized by none. The Abbot told everyone that Torello was a Saracen whom the Sultan had dispatched to the King of France as his envoy.

Messer Torello was accordingly placed at a table directly facing his lady, whom he gazed upon in rapturous delight, at the same time thinking that she wore a troubled look on account of these nuptials. Every so often, she returned his gaze, not because she had the slightest idea who he was (for his long beard, his strange attire, and her

conviction that he was dead made this impossible), but by virtue of
the extraordinary clothes he was wearing.

But when he felt that the time had come to put her memory of
him to the test, Messer Torello took hold of the ring which the lady
had given him on the day of his departure, and, sending for a young
man who was waiting upon her, he said to him:

'Tell the bride, with my compliments, that in our country, whenever any stranger such as myself attends a bridal feast such as hers, it
is the custom for her to send him the cup from which she is drinking,
filled with wine, to signify her pleasure at his coming. When the
stranger has consumed his fill, he replaces the lid of the wine-cup, and
the bride drinks up the remainder.'

The youth conveyed this message to the lady, who, displaying her
wonted tact and courtesy, supposing him to be some great panjan-
drum, hastened to show him that she held his presence dear. And she
ordered that a large golden cup, which stood on the table before her,
should be rinsed and filled with wine and taken to the gentleman.

Messer Torello, having meanwhile placed her ring in his mouth,
drank in such a way as to let it fall into the cup without anyone
having noticed. Leaving no more than a modicum of wine in the
cup, he replaced the lid and returned it to the lady. Then the lady
took hold of the cup, removed the lid, raised it to her lips to complete
the ritual, and caught sight of the ring, which she inspected closely
for a while without saying a word. Identifying the ring as the one
she had given to Messer Torello at his departure, she picked it up and
fixed her gaze upon the so-called stranger. And now that she could
see who it was, she overturned the table at which she was sitting, as
though she had gone berserk, and cried out:

'This is my lord; this truly is Messer Torello!'

She then ran over to the table where Messer Torello was sitting,
and, heedless of the drapery and the other things lying upon it, she
flung herself bodily forward and clasped him firmly in her embrace;
nor could she be detached from around his neck, no matter what anyone present said or did, until she was told by Messer Torello to curb
her feelings a little as she would have all the time in the world to
embrace him afterwards.

She accordingly stood up straight, and although by now the

wedding-feast was in total disarray, the return of so valiant a knight gave rise to greater rejoicing than ever. But then, at Messer Torello's request, everyone was silent as he narrated the story of all his adventures from the day of his departure, ending up by saying that the gentleman who, believing him to be dead, had married his wife, could hardly take it amiss, since he was really alive, if he claimed her as his own.

The bridegroom, though somewhat embarrassed, freely and amiably replied that Messer Torello was at liberty to dispose in whatever way he pleased of that which was rightfully his own. So the lady restored to the bridegroom the ring and the crown he had given her, and in their place she wore the ring she had taken from the wine-cup, and the crown sent to her by the Sultan. They then went forth from the bridegroom's house, and made their way, with all the pomp of a nuptial procession, to the house of Messer Torello, where there was no end to the rejoicing of his sorrowing friends and relatives and of the townspeople in general, who looked upon his return as nothing short of a miracle.

After giving away some of his precious gems to the gentleman who had borne the expense of the wedding-feast, as well as to the Abbot and to various other people, Messer Torello informed Saladin, through more than a single messenger, of his felicitous return to Pavia, declaring himself to be his friend and servant. And for many years thereafter, he lived with his admirable lady, comporting himself more courteously than ever.

This, then, was how the trials of Messer Torello and his beloved wife were brought to an end, and how they were rewarded for their prompt and cheerful acts of courtesy. Many are those who attempt to perform such deeds, who, though they possess the wherewithal, are so inept in carrying them out that before they are finished they cost the recipient more than they are worth. So that if their deeds do not redound to their credit, neither they nor others should have any reason to marvel.

TENTH STORY

The Marquis of Saluzzo, obliged by the entreaties of his subjects to take a wife, follows his personal whims and marries the daughter of a peasant. She bears him two children, and he gives her the impression that he has put them to death. Later on, pretending that she has incurred his displeasure and that he has remarried, he arranges for his own daughter to return home and passes her off as his bride, having meanwhile turned his wife out of doors in no more than the shift she is wearing. But on finding that she endures it all with patience, he cherishes her all the more deeply, brings her back to his house, shows her their children, who have now grown up, and honours her as the Marchioness, causing others to honour her likewise.

The lengthy tale of the king, which everyone seemed to have greatly enjoyed, being now at an end, Dioneo, laughing gaily, addressed them as follows:

'If the poor fellow, who was looking forward to raising and lowering the werewolf's tail on the very next night, could hear the praises you are heaping on Messer Torello, he wouldn't give you twopence for the lot of them.' Then, knowing that he alone was left to tell his story, he began:

Sweet and gentle ladies, this day has been devoted, so far as I can see, to the doings of kings and sultans and people of that sort; and therefore, so as not to place too great a distance between us, I want to tell you of a marquis, whose actions, even though things turned out well for him in the end, were remarkable not so much for their munificence as for their senseless brutality. Nor do I advise anyone to follow his example, for it was a great pity that the fellow should have drawn any profit from his conduct.

A very long time ago, there succeeded to the marquisate of Saluzzo a young man called Gualtieri, who, having neither wife nor children, spent the whole of his time hunting and hawking, and never even thought about marrying or raising a family, which says a great deal for his intelligence. His followers, however, disapproved of this, and repeatedly begged him to marry so that he should not be left without an heir nor they without a lord. Moreover, they offered to find him a wife whose parentage would be such as to strengthen their expectations and who would make him exceedingly happy.

So Gualtieri answered them as follows:

'My friends, you are pressing me to do something that I had always set my mind firmly against, seeing how difficult it is to find a person who will easily adapt to one's own way of living, how many thousands there are who will do precisely the opposite, and what a miserable life is in store for the man who stumbles upon a woman ill-suited to his own temperament. Moreover it is foolish of you to believe that you can judge the character of daughters from the ways of their fathers and mothers, hence claiming to provide me with a wife who will please me. For I cannot see how you are to know the fathers, or to discover the secrets of the mothers; and even if this were possible, daughters are very often different from either of their parents. Since, however, you are so determined to bind me in chains of this sort, I am ready to do as you ask; but so that I have only myself to blame if it should turn out badly, I must insist on marrying a wife of my own choosing. And I hereby declare that no matter who she may be, if you fail to honour her as your lady you will learn to your great cost how serious a matter it is for you to have urged me to marry against my will.'

To this the gentlemen replied that if only he would bring himself to take a wife, they would be satisfied.

Now, for some little time, Gualtieri had been casting an appreciative eye on the manners of a poor girl from a neighbouring village, and thinking her very beautiful, he considered that a life with her would have much to commend it. So without looking further afield, he resolved to marry the girl; and having summoned her father, who was very poor indeed, he arranged with him that he should take her as his wife.

This done, Gualtieri brought together all his friends from the various parts of his domain, and said to them:

'My friends, since you still persist in wanting me to take a wife, I am prepared to do it, not because I have any desire to marry, but rather in order to gratify your wishes. You will recall the promise you gave me, that no matter whom I should choose, you would rest content and honour her as your lady. The time has now come when I want you to keep that promise, and for me to honour the promise I gave to you. I have found a girl after my own heart, in this very district, and a few days hence I intend to marry her and convey her to my house. See to it, therefore, that the wedding-feast lacks nothing in splendour, and consider how you may honourably receive her, so that all of us may call ourselves contented – I with you for keeping your promise, and you with me for keeping mine.'

As of one voice, the good folk joyously gave him their blessing, and said that whoever she happened to be, they would accept her as their lady and honour her as such in all respects. Then they all prepared to celebrate the wedding in a suitably grand and sumptuous manner, and Gualtieri did the same. A rich and splendid nuptial feast was arranged, to which he invited many of his friends, his kinsfolk, great nobles and other people of the locality; moreover he caused a quantity of fine, rich robes to be tailored to fit a girl whose figure appeared to match that of the young woman he intended to marry; and lastly he laid in a number of rings and ornamental belts, along with a precious and beautiful crown, and everything else that a bride could possibly need.

Early on the morning of the day he had fixed for the nuptials, Gualtieri, his preparations now complete, mounted his horse together with all the people who had come to do him honour, and said:

'Gentlemen, it is time for us to go and fetch the bride.'

He then set forth with the whole of the company in train, and eventually they came to the village and made their way to the house of the girl's father, where they met her as she was returning with water from the fountain, making great haste so that she could go with other women to see Gualtieri's bride arriving. As soon as Gualtieri caught sight of her, he called to her by her name, which was Griselda, and asked her where her father was, to which she blushingly replied:

'My lord, he is at home.'

So Gualtieri dismounted, and having ordered everyone to wait for him outside, he went alone into the humble dwelling, where he found the girl's father, whose name was Giannùcole, and said to him:

'I have come to marry Griselda, but first I want to ask her certain questions in your presence.' He then asked her whether, if he were to marry her, she would always try to please him and never be upset by anything he said or did, whether she would obey him, and many other questions of this sort, to all of which she answered that she would.

Whereupon Gualtieri, having taken her by the hand, led her out of the house, and in the presence of his whole company and of all the other people there he caused her to be stripped naked. Then he called for the clothes and shoes which he had had specially made, and quickly got her to put them on, after which he caused a crown to be placed upon the dishevelled hair of her head. And just as everyone was wondering what this might signify, he said:

'Gentlemen, this is the woman I intend to marry, provided she will have me as her husband.' Then, turning to Griselda, who was so embarrassed that she hardly knew where to look, he said: 'Griselda, will you have me as your wedded husband?'

To which she replied:

'I will, my lord.'

'And I will have you as my wedded wife,' said Gualtieri, and he married her then and there before all the people present. He then helped her mount a palfrey, and led her back, honourably attended, to his house, where the nuptials were as splendid and as sumptuous, and the rejoicing as unrestrained, as if he had married the King of France's daughter.

Along with her new clothes, the young bride appeared to take on a new lease of life, and she seemed a different woman entirely. She was endowed, as we have said, with a fine figure and beautiful features, and lovely as she already was, she now acquired so confident, graceful and decorous a manner that she could have been taken for the daughter, not of the shepherd Giannùcole, but of some great nobleman, and consequently everyone who had known her before her marriage was filled with astonishment. But apart from this, she was so obedient to her husband, and so compliant to his wishes, that he thought himself the happiest and most contented man on earth. At the same time she was so gracious and benign towards her husband's subjects, that each and every one of them was glad to honour her, and accorded her his unselfish devotion, praying for her happiness, prosperity, and greater glory. And whereas they had been wont to say that Gualtieri had shown some lack of discretion in taking this woman as his wife, they now regarded him as the wisest and most discerning man on earth. For no one apart from Gualtieri could ever have perceived the noble qualities that lay concealed beneath her ragged and rustic attire.

In short, she comported herself in such a manner that she quickly earned widespread acclaim for her virtuous deeds and excellent character not only in her husband's domain but also in the world at large; and those who had formerly censured Gualtieri for choosing to marry her were now compelled to reverse their opinion.

Not long after she had gone to live with Gualtieri she conceived a child, and in the fullness of time, to her husband's enormous joy, she bore him a daughter. But shortly thereafter Gualtieri was seized with the strange desire to test Griselda's patience, by subjecting her to constant provocation and making her life unbearable.

At first he lashed her with his tongue, feigning to be angry and claiming that his subjects were thoroughly disgruntled with her on account of her lowly condition, especially now that they saw her bearing children; and he said they were greatly distressed about this infant daughter of theirs, of whom they did nothing but grumble.

The lady betrayed no sign of bitterness on hearing these words, and without changing her expression she said to him:

'My lord, deal with me as you think best for your own good name and peace of mind, for I shall rest content whatever you decide, knowing myself to be their inferior and that I was unworthy of the honour which you so generously bestowed upon me.'

This reply was much to Gualtieri's liking, for it showed him that she had not been puffed with pride by any honour that he or others had paid her.

A little while later, having told his wife in general terms that his subjects could not abide the daughter she had borne him, he gave certain instructions to one of his attendants, whom he sent to Griselda. The man looked very sorrowful, and said:

'My lady, if I do not wish to die, I must do as my lord commands me. He has ordered me to take this daughter of yours, and to ...' And his voice trailed off into silence.

On hearing these words and perceiving the man's expression, Griselda, recalling what she had been told, concluded that he had been instructed to murder her child. So she quickly picked it up from its cradle, kissed it, gave it her blessing, and albeit she felt that her heart was about to break, placed the child in the arms of the servant without any trace of emotion, saying:

'There: do exactly as your lord, who is my lord too, has instructed you. But do not leave her to be devoured by the beasts and the birds, unless that is what he has ordered you to do.'

The servant took away the little girl and reported Griselda's words to Gualtieri, who, marvelling at her constancy, sent him with the child to a kinswoman of his in Bologna, requesting her to rear and educate her carefully, but without ever making it known whose daughter she was.

Then it came about that his wife once more became pregnant, and in due course she gave birth to a son, which pleased Gualtieri enormously. But not being content with the mischief he had done already, he abused her more viciously than ever, and one day he glowered at her angrily and said:

'Woman, from the day you produced this infant son, the people have made my life a complete misery, so bitterly do they resent the thought of a grandson of Giannùcole succeeding me as their lord. So unless I want to be deposed, I'm afraid I shall be forced to do as I did before, and eventually to leave you and marry someone else.'

His wife listened patiently, and all she replied was:

'My lord, look to your own comfort, see that you fulfil your wishes, and spare no thought for me, since nothing brings me pleasure unless it pleases you also.'

Before many days had elapsed, Gualtieri sent for his son in the same way that he had sent for his daughter, and having likewise pretended to have had the child put to death, he sent him, like the little girl, to Bologna. To all of this his wife reacted no differently, either in her speech or in her looks, than she had on the previous occasion, much to the astonishment of Gualtieri, who told himself that no other woman could have remained so impassive. But for the fact that he had observed her doting upon the children for as long as he allowed her to do so, he would have assumed that she was glad to be rid of them, whereas he knew that she was too judicious to behave in any other way.

His subjects, thinking he had caused the children to be murdered, roundly condemned him and judged him a cruel tyrant, whilst his wife became the object of their deepest compassion. But to the women who offered her their sympathy in the loss of her children, all she ever said was that the decision of their father was good enough for her.

Many years after the birth of his daughter, Gualtieri decided that the time had come to put Griselda's patience to the final test. So he told a number of his men that in no circumstances could he put up with Griselda as his wife any longer, having now come to realize that his marriage was an aberration of his youth. He would therefore do everything in his power to obtain a dispensation from the Pope, enabling him to divorce Griselda and marry someone else. For this he was chided severely by many worthy men, but his only reply was that it had to be done.

On learning of her husband's intentions, from which it appeared she would have to return to her father's house, in order perhaps to look after the sheep as she had in the past, meanwhile seeing the man she adored being cherished by some other woman, Griselda was secretly filled with despair. But she prepared herself to endure this final blow as stoically as she had borne Fortune's earlier assaults.

Shortly thereafter, Gualtieri arranged for some counterfeit letters of his to arrive from Rome, and led his subjects to believe that in these, the Pope had granted him permission to abandon Griselda and remarry.

He accordingly sent for Griselda, and before a large number of people he said to her:

'Woman, I have had a dispensation from the Pope, allowing me to leave you and take another wife. Since my ancestors were great noblemen and rulers of these lands, whereas yours have always been peasants, I intend that you shall no longer be my wife, but return to Giannùcole's house with the dowry you brought me, after which I shall bring another lady here. I have already chosen her and she is far better suited to a man of my condition.'

On hearing these words, the lady, with an effort beyond the power of any normal woman's nature, suppressed her tears and replied:

'My lord, I have always known that my lowly condition was totally at odds with your nobility, and that it is to God and to yourself that I owe whatever standing I possess. Nor have I ever regarded this as a gift that I might keep and cherish as my own, but rather as something I have borrowed; and now that you want me to return it, I must give it back to you with good grace. Here is the ring with which you married me: take it. As to your ordering me to take away the dowry that I brought, you will require no accountant, nor will I need a purse or a pack-horse, for this to be done. For it has not escaped my memory that you took me naked as on the day I was born. If you think it proper that the body in which I have borne your children should be seen by all the people, I shall go away naked. But in return for my virginity, which I brought to you and cannot retrieve, I trust you will at least allow me, in addition to my dowry, to take one shift away with me.'

Gualtieri wanted above all else to burst into tears, but maintaining a stern expression he said:

'Very well, you may take a shift.'

All the people present implored Gualtieri to let her have a dress, so that she who had been his wife for thirteen years and more would not have to suffer the indignity of leaving his house in a shift, like a pauper; but their pleas were unavailing. And so Griselda, wearing a shift, barefoot, and with nothing to cover her head, having bidden them farewell, set forth from Gualtieri's house and returned to her father amid the weeping and the wailing of all who set eyes upon her.

Giannùcole, who had never thought it possible that Gualtieri would keep his daughter as his wife, and was daily expecting this to happen, had preserved the clothes she discarded on the morning Gualtieri had married her. So he brought them to her, and Griselda, having put them on, applied herself as before to the menial chores in her father's house, bravely enduring the cruel assault of hostile Fortune.

No sooner did Gualtieri drive Griselda away, than he gave his subjects to understand that he was betrothed to a daughter of one of the Counts of Panago. And having ordered that grandiose preparations were to be made for the nuptials, he sent for Griselda and said to her:

'I am about to fetch home this new bride of mine, and from the moment she sets foot inside the house, I intend to accord her an honourable welcome. As you know, I have no women here who can set the rooms in order for me, or attend to many of the things that a festive occasion of this sort requires. No one knows better than you how to handle these household affairs, so I want you to make all the necessary arrangements. Invite all the ladies you need, and receive them as though you were mistress of the house. And when the nuptials are over, you can go back home to your father.'

Since Griselda was unable to lay aside her love for Gualtieri as readily as she had dispensed with her good fortune, his words pierced her heart like so many knives. But she replied.

'My lord, I am ready to do as you ask.'

And so, in her coarse, thick, woollen garments, Griselda returned to the house she had quitted shortly before in her shift, and started to sweep and tidy the various chambers. On her instructions, the beds were draped with hangings, the benches in the halls were suitably adorned, the kitchen was made ready; and she set her hand, as though she were a petty serving wench, to every conceivable household task, never stopping to draw breath until she had everything prepared and arranged as befitted the occasion.

Having done all this, she caused invitations to be sent, in Gualtieri's name, to all the ladies living in those parts, and began to await the event. And when at last the nuptial day arrived, heedless of her beggarly attire, she bade a cheerful welcome to each of the lady guests, displaying all the warmth and courtesy of a lady of the manor.

Gualtieri's children having meanwhile been carefully reared by his kinswoman in Bologna, who had married into the family of the Counts of Panago, the girl was now twelve years old, the loveliest creature ever seen, whilst the boy had reached the age of six. Gualtieri had sent word to his kinswoman's husband, asking him to do him the kindness of bringing this daughter of his to Saluzzo along with her little brother, to see that she was nobly and honourably escorted, and to tell everyone he met that he was taking her to marry Gualtieri, without revealing who she really was to a living soul.

In accordance with the Marquis's request, the gentleman set forth with the girl and her brother and a noble company, and a few days later, shortly before the hour of breakfast, he arrived at Saluzzo, where he found that all the folk thereabouts, and numerous others from neighbouring parts, were waiting for Gualtieri's latest bride.

After being welcomed by the ladies, she made her way to the hall where the tables were set, and Griselda, just as we have described her, went cordially up to meet her, saying:

'My lady, you are welcome.'

The ladies, who in vain had implored Gualtieri to see that Griselda remained in another room, or to lend her one of the dresses that had once been hers, so that she would not cut such a sorry figure in front of his guests, took their seats at table and addressed themselves to the meal. All eyes were fixed upon the girl, and everyone said that Gualtieri had made a good exchange. But Griselda praised her as warmly as anyone present, speaking no less admiringly of her little brother.

Gualtieri felt that he had now seen all he wished to see of the patience of his lady, for he perceived that no event, however singular, produced the slightest change in her demeanour, and he was certain that this was not because of her obtuseness, as he knew her to be very intelligent. He therefore considered that the time had come for him to free her from the rancour that he judged her to be hiding beneath her tranquil outward expression. And having summoned her to his table, before all the people present he smiled at her and said:

'What do you think of our new bride?'

'My lord,' replied Griselda, 'I think very well of her. And if, as I believe, her wisdom matches her beauty, I have no doubt whatever that your life with her will bring you greater happiness than any gentleman on earth has ever known. But with all my heart I beg you not to inflict those same wounds upon her that you imposed upon her predecessor, for I doubt whether she could withstand them, not only because she is younger, but also because she has had a refined upbringing, whereas the other had to face continual hardship from her infancy.'

On observing that Griselda was firmly convinced that the young lady was to be his wife, and that even so she allowed no hint of resentment to escape her lips, Gualtieri got her to sit down beside him, and said:

'Griselda, the time has come for you to reap the reward of your unfailing patience, and for those who considered me a cruel and bestial tyrant, to know that whatever I have done was done of set purpose, for I wished to show you how to be a wife, to teach these people how to choose and keep a wife, and to guarantee my own peace and quiet for as long as we were living beneath the same roof. When I came to take a wife, I was greatly afraid that this peace would be denied me, and in order to prove otherwise I tormented and provoked you in the ways you have seen. But as I have never known you to oppose my wishes, I now intend, being persuaded that you can offer me all the happiness I desired, to restore to you in a single instant that which I took from you little by little, and delectably assuage the pains I have inflicted upon you. Receive with gladsome heart, then, this girl whom you believe to be my bride, and also her brother. These are our children, whom you and many others have long supposed that I caused to be cruelly murdered; and I am your husband, who loves you above all else, for I think I can boast that there is no other man on earth whose contentment in his wife exceeds my own.'

Having spoken these words, he embraced and kissed Griselda, who by now was weeping with joy; then they both got up from table and made their way to the place where their daughter sat listening in utter amazement to these tidings. And after they had fondly embraced the girl and her brother, the mystery was unravelled to her, as well as to many of the others who were present.

The ladies rose from table in transports of joy, and escorted Griselda to a chamber, where, with greater assurance of her future happiness, they divested her of her tattered garments and clothed her anew in one of her stately robes. And as their lady and their mistress, a rôle which even in her rags had seemed to be hers, they led her back to the hall, where she and Gualtieri rejoiced with the children in a manner marvellous to behold.

Everyone being delighted with the turn that events had taken, the feasting and the merrymaking were redoubled, and continued unabated for the next few days. Gualtieri was acknowledged to be very wise, though the trials to which he had subjected his lady were regarded as harsh and intolerable, whilst Griselda was accounted the wisest of all.

The Count of Panago returned a few days later to Bologna, and Gualtieri, having removed Giannùcole from his drudgery, set him up in a style befitting his father-in-law, so that he lived in great comfort and honour for the rest of his days. As for Gualtieri himself, having married off his daughter to a gentleman of renown, he lived long and contentedly with Griselda, never failing to honour her to the best of his ability.

What more needs to be said, except that celestial spirits may sometimes descend even into the houses of the poor, whilst there are those in royal palaces who would be better employed as swineherds than as rulers of men? Who else but Griselda could have endured so cheerfully the cruel and unheard of trials that Gualtieri imposed upon her without shedding a tear? For perhaps it would have served him right if he had chanced upon a wife, who, being driven from the house in her shift, had found some other man to shake her skin-coat for her, earning herself a fine new dress in the process.

*   *   *

Dioneo's story had ended, and the ladies, some taking one side and some another, some finding fault with one of its details and some commending another, had talked about it at length, when the king, having raised his eyes to observe that the sun had already sunk low in the evening sky, began, without getting up, to address them as follows:

'Graceful ladies, the wisdom of mortals consists, as I think you know, not only in remembering the past and apprehending the present, but in being able, through a knowledge of each, to anticipate the future, which grave men regard as the acme of human intelligence.

'Tomorrow, as you know, a fortnight will have elapsed since the day we departed from Florence to provide for our relaxation, preserve our health and our lives, and escape from the sadness, the suffering and the anguish continuously to be found in our city since this plague first descended upon it. These aims we have achieved, in my judgement, without any loss of decorum. For as far as I have been able to observe, albeit the tales related here have been amusing, perhaps of a sort to stimulate carnal desire, and we have continually partaken of excellent food and drink, played music, and sung many songs, all of which things may encourage unseemly behaviour among those who are feeble of mind, neither in word nor in deed nor in any other respect have I known either you or ourselves to be worthy of censure. On the contrary, from what I have seen and heard, it seems to me that our proceedings have been marked by a constant sense of propriety, an unfailing spirit of harmony, and a continual feeling of brotherly and sisterly amity. All of which pleases me greatly, as it surely redounds to our communal honour and credit.

Accordingly, lest aught conducive to tedium should arise from a custom too long established, and lest, by protracting our stay, we should cause evil tongues to start wagging, I now think it proper, since we have all in turn had our share of the honour still invested in me, that with your consent we should return from whence we came. If, moreover, you consider the matter carefully, our company being known to various others hereabouts, our numbers could increase in such a way as to destroy all our pleasure. And so, if my advice should command your approval, I shall retain the crown that was given me until our departure, which I propose should take effect tomorrow morning. But if you decide otherwise, I already have someone in mind upon whom to bestow the crown for the next day to follow.'

The ladies and the young men, having debated the matter at considerable length, considered the king's advice, in the end, to be sensible and just, and decided to do as he had said. He therefore sent for the steward and conferred with him with regard to the following morning's arrangements, and having dismissed the company till supper-time, he rose to his feet.

The ladies and the other young men followed suit, and turned their attention to various pastimes as usual. When it was time for supper, they disposed of the meal with infinite relish, after which they turned to singing and music and dancing. And while Lauretta was leading a dance, the king called for a song from Fiammetta, who began to sing, most charmingly, as follows:

'If love could come unmixed with jealousy
Then there is not a living woman born
Who could be merrier than I would be.

'If these effects a woman may content:
Deserving virtue and gay youthfulness;
Wisdom; fair conduct; prowess; dauntlessness;
Perfection of address; speech which doth move;
Then I should be that she, whose happiness
Is thus attained in person of my love.

'But other women are as wise as I,
I fear the worst, and tremble with dismay
Seeing those others seek to steal away
Him who has stolen mine own soul, and so
Turning my great bliss into misery
Whereat I sigh aloud and live in woe.

'Felt I his faith as equal to his worth
I would not feel this jealousy and pain.
But such his worth, and such the ways of men
And such the wiles of women who allure,
I fear that each one seeks my love to gain
And, heartsick, I would gladly death endure.

'But, in God's name, let every woman know
Not to attempt such injury on me:
For if there should be one whose flattery
Or words or gestures should entice him hence
Then may I be deformed if bitterly
I do not make her weep for her offence.'

No sooner did Fiammetta end her song, than Dioneo, who was standing beside her, laughed and said to her:

'You would be doing all the others a great kindness, madam, if you were to tell them his name, in case they unwittingly take him away from you, seeing that you are bound to be so angry about it.'

After this song of Fiammetta's, they sang a number of others, and when it was nearly midnight, they all, at the king's behest, retired to bed.

Next morning they arose at the crack of dawn, by which time all their baggage had been sent on ahead by the steward, and with their wise king leading the way they returned to Florence. Having taken their leave of the seven young ladies in Santa Maria Novella, whence they had all set out together, the three young men went off in search of other diversions; and in due course the ladies returned to their homes.

AUTHOR'S EPILOGUE

Noble young ladies, for whose solace I undertook this protracted labour, I believe that with the assistance of divine grace (the bestowal of which I impute to your compassionate prayers rather than to any merit of my own) those objectives which I set forth at the beginning of the present work have now been fully achieved. And so, after giving thanks, firstly to God and then to yourselves, the time has come for me to rest my pen and weary hand. Before conceding this repose, however, since I am fully aware that these tales of mine are no less immune from criticism than any of the other things of this world, and indeed I recall having shown this to be so at the beginning of the Fourth Day, I propose briefly to reply to certain trifling objections which, though remaining unspoken, may possibly have arisen in the minds of my readers, including one or two of yourselves.

There will perhaps be those among you who will say that in writing these stories I have taken too many liberties, in that I have sometimes caused ladies to say, and very often to hear, things which are not very suitable to be heard or said by virtuous women. This I deny, for no story is so unseemly as to prevent anyone from telling it, provided it is told in seemly language; and this I believe I may reasonably claim to have done.

But supposing you are right (for I have no wish to start a dispute with you, knowing I shall finish on the losing side), I still maintain, when you ask me why I did it, that many reasons spring readily to mind. In the first place, if any of the stories is lacking in restraint, this is because of the nature of the story itself, which, as any well-informed and dispassionate observer will readily acknowledge, I could not have related in any other way without distorting it out of all recognition. And even if the stories do, perhaps, contain one or two trifling expressions that are too unbridled for the liking of those prudish ladies who attach more weight to words than to deeds, and are more anxious to seem virtuous than to be virtuous, I assert that it was no more improper for me to have written them than for men and women at large, in their everyday speech, to use such words as *hole*, and *rod*, and *mortar*, and *pestle*, and *crumpet*, and *stuffing*, and any number of others. Besides, no less latitude should be granted to my pen than to the brush of the painter, who without incurring censure, of a justified kind at least, depicts St Michael striking the serpent with his sword or his lance, and St George transfixing the dragon wherever he pleases; but that is not all, for he makes Christ male and Eve female, and fixes to the cross, sometimes with a single nail, sometimes with two, the feet of Him who resolved to die thereon for the salvation of mankind.

Furthermore it is made perfectly clear that these stories were told neither in a church, of whose affairs one must speak with a chaste mind and a pure tongue (albeit you will find that many of her chronicles are far more scandalous than any writings of mine), nor in the schools of philosophers, in which, no less than anywhere else, a sense of decorum is required, nor in any place where either churchmen or philosophers were present. They were told in gardens, in a place designed for pleasure, among people who, though young in years, were nonetheless fully mature and not to be led astray by stories, at a time when even the most respectable people saw nothing unseemly in wearing their breeches over their heads if they thought their lives might thereby be preserved.

Like all other things in this world, stories, whatever their nature, may be harmful or useful, depending upon the listener. Who will deny that wine, as Tosspot and Bibber and a great many others affirm, is an excellent thing for those who are hale and hearty, but harmful to people suffering from a fever? Are we to conclude, because it does harm to the feverish, that therefore it is pernicious? Who will deny that fire is exceedingly useful, not to say vital, to man? Are we to conclude, because it burns down houses and villages and whole cities, that therefore it is pernicious? And in the same way, weapons defend the liberty of those who desire to live peaceably, and very often they kill people, not because they are evil in themselves, but because of the evil intentions of those who make use of them.

No word, however pure, was ever wholesomely construed by a mind that was corrupt. And just as seemly language leaves no mark upon a mind that is corrupt, language that is less than seemly cannot sully a mind that is well ordered, any more than mud will contaminate the rays of the sun, or earthly filth the beauties of the heavens.

What other books, what other words, what other letters, are more sacred, more reputable, more worthy of reverence, than those of the Holy Scriptures? And yet there have been many who, by perversely construing them, have led themselves and others to perdition. All things have their own special purpose, but when they are wrongly used a great deal of harm may result, and the same applies to my stories. If anyone should want to extract evil counsel from these tales, or fashion an evil design, there is nothing to prevent him, provided he twists and distorts them sufficiently to find the thing he is seeking. And if anyone should study them for the usefulness and profit they may bring him, he will not be disappointed. Nor will they ever be thought of or described as anything but useful and seemly, if they are read at the proper time by the people for whom they were written. The lady who is forever saying her prayers, or baking pies and cakes for her father confessor, may leave my stories alone: they will not run after anyone demanding to be read, albeit they are no more improper than some of the trifles that self-righteous ladies recite, or even engage in, if the occasion arises.

There will likewise be those among you who will say that some of the stories included here would far better have been omitted. That is as may be: but I could only transcribe the stories as they were actually told, which means that if the ladies who told them had told them better, I should have written them better. But even if one could assume that I was the inventor as well as the scribe of these stories (which was not the case), I still insist that I would not feel ashamed if some fell short of perfection, for there is no craftsman other than God whose work is whole and faultless in every respect. Even Charlemagne, who first created the Paladins, was unable to produce them in numbers sufficient to form a whole army.

Whenever you have a multitude of things you are bound to find differences of quality. No field was ever so carefully tended that neither nettles nor brambles nor thistles were found in it, along with all the better grass. Besides, in addressing an audience of unaffected young ladies, such as most of you are, it would have been foolish of me to go to the trouble of searching high and low for exquisite tales to relate, and take excessive pains in weighing my words. And the fact remains that anyone perusing these tales is free to ignore the ones that give offence, and read only those that are pleasing. For in order that none of you may be misled, each of the stories bears on its brow the gist of that which it hides in its bosom.

I suppose it will also be said that some of the tales are too long. To which I can only reply that if you have better things to do, it would be foolish to read these tales, even if they were short. Although much time has elapsed from the day I started to write until this moment, in which I am nearing the end of my labours, it has not escaped my memory that I offered these exertions of mine to ladies with time on their hands, not to any others; and for those who read in order to pass the time, nothing can be too long if it serves the purpose for which it is used.

Brevity is all very well for students, who endeavour to use their time profitably rather than while it away, but not for you, ladies, who have as much time to spare as you fail to consume in the pleasures of love. And besides, since none of you goes to study in Athens, or Bologna, or Paris, you have need of a lengthier form of address than those who have sharpened their wits with the aid of their studies.

Doubtless there are also those among you who will say that the matters I have related are overfilled with jests and quips, of a sort that no man of weight and gravity should have committed to paper. Inasmuch as these ladies, prompted by well-intentioned zeal, show a touching concern for my good name, it behoves me to thank them, and I do so.

But I would answer their objection as follows: I confess that I do have weight, and in my time I have been weighed on numerous occasions; but I assure those ladies who have never weighed me that I have little gravity. On the contrary, I am so light that I float on the surface of water. And considering that the sermons preached by friars to chastise the faults of men are nowadays filled, for the most part, with jests and quips and raillery, I concluded that the same sort of thing would be not out of place in my stories, written to dispel the woes of ladies. But if it should cause them to laugh too much, they can easily cure themselves by turning to the Lament of Jeremiah, the Passion of Our Lord, and the Plaint of the Magdalen.

There may also be those among you who will say that I have an evil and venomous tongue, because in certain places I write the truth about the friars. But who cares? I can readily forgive you for saying such things, for doubtless you are prompted by the purest of motives, friars being decent fellows, who forsake a life of discomfort for the love of God, who do their grinding when the millpond's full, and say no more about it. Except for the fact that they all smell a little of the billy-goat, their company would offer the greatest of pleasure.

I will grant you, however, that the things of this world have no stability, but are subject to constant change, and this may well have happened to my tongue. But not long ago, distrusting my own opinion (which in matters concerning myself I trust as little as possible), I was told by a lady, a neighbour of mine, that I had the finest and sweetest tongue in the world; and this, to tell the truth, was at a time when few of these tales remained to be written. So because the aforementioned ladies are saying these things in order to spite me, I intend that what I have said shall suffice for my answer.

And now I shall leave each lady to say and believe whatever she pleases, for the time has come for me to bring all words to an end, and offer my humble thanks to Him who assisted me in my protracted labour and conveyed me to the goal I desired. May His grace and peace, sweet ladies, remain with you always, and if perchance these stories should bring you any profit, remember me.

Here ends the Tenth and last Day of
the book called Decameron,
otherwise known as Prince Galahalt.

MORE ABOUT PENGUINS
AND PELICANS

For further information about books available from Penguins please write to Dept EP, Penguin Books Ltd, Harmondsworth, Middlesex UB7 0DA.

In the U.S.A.: For a complete list of books available from Penguins in the United States write to Dept CS, Penguin Books, 625 Madison Avenue, New York, New York 10022.

In Canada: For a complete list of books available from Penguins in Canada write to Penguin Books Canada Ltd, 2801 John Street, Markham, Ontario L3R 1B4.

In Australia: For a complete list of books available from Penguins in Australia write to the Marketing Department, Penguin Books Australia Ltd, P.O. Box 257, Ringwood, Victoria 3134.

LANGLAND: PIERS THE PLOUGHMAN

Translated by J. F. Goodridge

Piers the Ploughman, the work of an unknown minor cleric of the late fourteenth century, was perhaps the most widely read work of its day and is now recognized as the great representative English poem of the late Middle Ages. While it offers a vivid picture of fourteenth-century life and is placed firmly in the world of every day, its theme is the pilgrimage of man's soul in search of ultimate truth. Alone among English poets, Langland combines satirical comedy with a rare power of prophecy and vision.

CHAUCER: THE CANTERBURY TALES

Translated by Nevill Coghill

The Canterbury Tales stands conspicuous among the great literary achievements of the Middle Ages. Told by a jovial procession of pilgrims – knight, priest, yeoman, miller, or cook – as they ride towards the shrine of Thomas à Becket, they present a picture of a nation taking shape. The tone of this never-resting comedy is, by turns, learned, fantastic, lewd, pious, and ludicrous. 'Here,' as John Dryden said, 'is God's plenty!'

Geoffrey Chaucer began his great task in about 1386. This version in modern English, by Nevill Coghill, preserves the freshness and racy vitality of Chaucer's narrative.

Also published

TROILUS AND CRISEYDE